THE REMORSELESS TRILOGY

BRITISH CRIME THRILLERS

WILL PATCHING

COPYRIGHT 2017 WILL PATCHING

PUBLISHING HISTORY
FIRST PUBLISHED AS A COMPILATION IN 2017

THIS 2021 EDITION OF THE REMORSELESS TRILOGY HAS BEEN UPDATED AND REWRITTEN BASED ON READER AND PROFESSIONAL EDITOR FEEDBACK.
COVER IMAGE © CAN STOCK PHOTO / MCGILL

REMORSELESS
FIRST PUBLISHED IN DIGITAL FORMAT IN 2012.
FIRST PUBLISHED IN PAPERBACK BY
TIMEFRAME BOOKS, ASIA IN 2006.
COVER IMAGE © CAN STOCK PHOTO / GSAGI

MUTILATED
FIRST PUBLISHED IN DIGITAL FORMAT AND PAPERBACK IN 2016.
COVER IMAGE © CAN STOCK PHOTO / CONTRAIL

GASLIGHTING
FIRST PUBLISHED IN DIGITAL FORMAT AND PAPERBACK IN 2017.
COVER IMAGE © CAN STOCK PHOTO / SMIT

EDITED BY JAMES JONES OF PROOF EGB.
ANY REMAINING ERRORS ARE ENTIRELY THE AUTHOR'S.

AUTHOR'S FOREWORD

VIVID IMAGERY, PROFANITY, BRITISHISMS & A DISCLAIMER…

SENSITIVE READERS MAY FEEL SOME SCENES DEPICTED IN THIS TRILOGY CONJURE UP DISTURBING IMAGERY, SO IF YOU NEED A TRIGGER WARNING FOR ANY REASON, MY THRILLERS ARE PROBABLY NOT FOR YOU. I AM TRULY SORRY.

SOME OF MY CHARACTERS USE PROFANITY TOO, OCCASIONALLY WITH ABBREVIATED SPELLINGS TO CONVEY HOW THEY TALK, SOMETIMES WITH A BIT OF COCKNEY THROWN IN FOR GOOD MEASURE.

IT IS TRUE THAT SOME U.S. READERS FIND BRITISH SPELLING A LITTLE OFF-PUTTING AND FOR THAT I ALSO APOLOGISE / APOLOGIZE.

MANY OF US BRITS ARE JUST A BIT ODD, AND DESPITE FEEDBACK SUGGESTING OTHERWISE, THESE ALTERNATE FORMS OF ENGLISH ARE NOT ACTUALLY TYPOS. IF YOU DO FIND A GENUINE ONE OF THOSE, PLEASE LET ME KNOW AND I'LL DO MY BEST TO PUT IT RIGHT. AS USUAL, ANY ERRORS IN THIS PUBLICATION ARE ENTIRELY MY OWN.

MY NOVELS AIM FOR A HIGH DEGREE OF REALISM BUT TWO MEDICAL PROFESSIONALS HAVE SUGGESTED I ADD THIS WARNING REGARDING THE COUGH C.P.R. TECHNIQUE USED BY A FICTIONAL CHARACTER IN A SCENE IN BOOK THREE, GASLIGHTING:

IF YOU EXPERIENCE CHEST PAIN OR FEEL AN IRREGULAR HEARTBEAT, CALL THE EMERGENCY SERVICES. DON'T DELAY AND CERTAINLY DON'T TRY COUGHING AS YOU COULD STOP YOUR HEART.

WILL PATCHING
WWW.WILLPATCHINGAUTHOR.COM
WILL@WILLPATCHINGAUTHOR.COM

REMORSELESS

A BRITISH CRIME THRILLER

DOC POWERS & D.I. CARVER INVESTIGATE

THE REMORSELESS TRILOGY
BOOK ONE

'HAD I READ WILL PATCHING'S NOVELS WHILE STILL A SERVING OFFICER I'M SURE HIS INSIGHTS INTO THE WORKINGS OF THEIR MINDS WOULD HAVE HELPED ME UNDERSTAND THE MOTIVES AND ACTIONS OF THESE PEOPLE...'

RICK ASKER
RETIRED UK DETECTIVE AND
FORMER UNDERCOVER PRISON INTELLIGENCE OFFICER
SPEAKING ABOUT PSYCHOPATHS

PROLOGUE

THE SNAKE

PETER LEECH LEANED on the railing and surveyed his kingdom from his vantage point on the top level. His cell was on this floor, the third, and he often stood here as he had no desire to join the sweaty throng in the common 'association' area below.

The screws are such lazy bastards, he thought, as he watched three of them chatting, huddled, largely ignoring the forty or so inmates socialising around them. The fat slugs, don't like climbing stairs unless forced to. He snorted, disdainful but grateful that they only ever bugged his floor when they had to.

His green eyes roved through the bodies, hunting his prey. Cochran. The man watched the TV, giggling like a little girl at some pathetic cartoon. Leech squeezed the cast iron railing, knuckles threatening to burst the skin from the force of his grip.

Come to me, you lanky faggot. Come and dance with the Snake. If you dare.

Eventually Cochran glanced up and their eyes locked. Cochran spoke to the two men sitting next to him, and they too looked up.

Leech ignored them, his attention on Cochran, all his venom focussed on the big convict. Cochran lifted his hand, swept his fingers across his Adam's apple in a chopping motion, and mouthed, *You're dead*.

The Snake continued to hold its prey with its eyes, challenging until the man rose and swaggered to the stairs. He took the steps two at a time, his gaze breaking from Leech only to confirm his two mates were behind him. The flunkies followed, but less eager. Reluctant even.

Cowards.

Leech realised Cochran was unaware how tardy his cronies were being as he clambered up the iron stairs, his soft trainers barely making a sound.

Leech's peripheral vision was excellent, and though he was fixated on Cochran, he was aware that the guards were still engrossed, oblivious to the burgeoning conflict. Some cons sensed a fight was brewing, but only a few of them dared to gaze up at the protagonists.

Cochran reached the flight below, and grinned as he bounded up the last dozen steps, enthusiastic now, clearly confident that Leech was about to take a beating.

Leech was in a zone beyond fear or elation. He was intent only on his prey. His brain computed, calculated, and he struck.

Cochran had almost reached the top step, his right leg mid-air, searching for purchase, his rear leg stretched two steps below, powering him upwards. Perfectly unbalanced and moving fast.

The Snake was faster.

Leech leapt towards Cochran, a blur of limbs, connecting with his target at a forty-five degree angle. His electric speed, combined with the weight and power of his athlete's body, delivered a pile-driving punch so swift Cochran had no chance of avoiding impact. This fearsome mass of energy was concentrated and delivered in a bone-splintering blow that connected with Cochran's temple.

The force literally sent the big man flying. Leech continued moving past the top of the stairs as his victim flipped over the handrail, bounced off the edge of the suicide netting, and plunged backwards down the stairwell, his body hurtling past his two comrades.

Leech was still in the killing zone, everything around him seemingly in slow motion as he speed-walked away, watching Cochran floating earthward, startled, spread-eagled, face-up, mouthing a garbled scream.

He slammed into the first floor landing head first, tumbled down another flight of metal stairs and smashed onto the concrete floor with a resounding thud.

Silence.

And then the roar and near riot as the prisoners realised what had happened. The screws, one blowing a whistle signalling the alarm, scurried to Cochran's corpse, the blood already pooling round his ruined skull.

Leech, standing several metres beyond the stairway, his back to his own cell, arms folded on the railing, nonchalantly observed the goings on. He was detached. Not a hint of concern anywhere in his consciousness. Intrigued at what would happen now. Nothing more than a curious spectator.

Prison officers were flooding the floor below, rounding the men up to return them to their cells—early lock up was inevitable. Diarmud was with them, seemed to take it all in with a glance, spotted Leech. His voice whiplashed through the pandemonium. 'What the hell happened here, Leech?'

Silence, again. Ten seconds passed as Leech eyed the senior officer. Then he grinned and shrugged.

'I'm not sure, Mister Dire Mud. I think maybe he dived down the stairwell head first. Didn't have him pegged as a suicide but you never can tell, can ya?' He pointed at Cochran's two henchmen, dithering on the stairs, visibly unsure what to do now their leader was gone. 'Ask Headless and Chicken there. They were right behind him. Must've seen it all.'

The two cons glanced between themselves, at Leech and then the warder, neither wanting to be first to speak. Snake eyes held them as they considered how to respond.

Diarmud yelled at them. 'Well? What happened? The truth. Now...'

'He just dived off, Mister Diarmud...'

'Yeah, we was follerin him up and he just jumped when he reached the top, like...'

A wag from the floor below quipped, 'Maybe he thought he could fly, sir. Him doin bird an all.'

Then another, quick to respond added, 'Nah mate. He just forgot to strap on his fucking hang-glider!'

The cons started laughing and joshing, more facetious comments flew.

Diarmud, his authority sapping, screeched, 'Lock up! Now. Move…'

The cons were shepherded away, while Leech continued his vigil, well satisfied with the mayhem he had created.

Diarmud climbed to his level. 'Get in your cell, Leech.' The officer's face was scarlet, his neck pulsating, threatening to burst his collar. 'I'll be talking to you very shortly.'

Leech shrugged. 'I'm looking forward to it, Mister Dire… Mud. You should get your blood pressure checked. Look a bit stressed, if you don't mind me saying.' His smirk firmly in place, he turned and sauntered into his cell.

PART I

CRIME AND PUNISHMENT

'Hɪ Doc. Come on in and take a seat. How are you?' The Judge peered over his half-moon glasses and twitched an eyebrow at him.

Doctor Colin Powers scraped the chair back and plopped his wide rear end onto it. He surveyed the chaos of the Judge's desk, gazed at his boss for a few seconds too long, and said, 'I'm okay. Little steps. You know?' He smiled, the muscles working hard to remember the movements before fading back to their neutral position.

'Sure?' Those beady eyes hooked him like a fish. Doc wriggled, unwilling to share how he truly felt.

'Yup. I'm good, Judge. Ready and willing.' He shifted his focus, tried to change the subject by eyeing the stacks of papers piled on the mahogany desk. 'Looks like you could use some help.'

Judge Potter scrutinised him for a moment longer, then sighed. 'We're reckoning on one thousand oral parole hearings this year, as well as several thousand recalls. I'm swamped, Colin.' He waved his hand over the mounds of documents. 'The Home Secretary expects us to do the job regardless. The team's working flat out and we're still falling behind.'

Doc Powers could see the weight on his boss's shoulders, a sagging that had not been there just a few months before. Once again Doc wondered how his old friend, now sixty-seven, coped with the pace and pressure of a job that would probably outdo most men half his age. Still, he thought, despite the lines and unhealthy pallor of the Judge's skin, the eyes twinkled with intellect. His sardonic smile was an acknowledgement that the job was never really going to get to him. Doc knew the Judge loved it.

The current Chairman of the Parole Board for England and Wales had, until three years before, been an eminent high court judge, recognised as one of the sharpest minds in the legal profession. He was well respected for his measured judgements and there had even been talk of him becoming a Lord, eventually perhaps, Lord Chief Justice.

Yet his boss was also a man with charisma, Doc thought, as he watched the Judge root through some files. Enough to woo him away from the offer of a professorship at Cambridge to become his Vice Chairman.

Doc had taken to the job with enthusiasm. At least, until three months ago… His shoulders shuddered at the thought. Fortunately the Judge did not notice, his head was down and his hands were burrowing in the mounds of documents, hunting an elusive file.

'I'm glad you're back. We've got a mandatory lifer hearing coming up and I want you involved—that is if you're ready to get back in the stirrups?' Again the eyebrow flickered, the sharp blue eyes skewering Doc.

'Definitely.' He thought it sounded convincing. 'What have we got?'

'It's in two weeks. You may remember the case. Both you and I were involved in it.' The Judge proffered a folder.

Doc noticed his own rumpled sleeve as he reached across, wondering how he could have forgotten to iron his shirt before meeting with his immaculately turned out boss. He shunted the thought aside even as he realised the Judge's obvious concern was heightened by his appearance. Christ, he thought, I don't even remember brushing my hair. He thrust his left hand over his scalp, the fingers combing, struggling to control the unruly curls, feeling stale grease there. Jesus. He focussed on the file.

The name on the cover rang vague bells for him. Peter Leech? The Judge, though apparently ignoring his unkempt appearance, clearly wanted a positive response. Eyes like laser lights probed Doc for some sign of recognition.

'Sorry, Judge. Give me a minute?' He dropped his eyes to the folder, concentrating hard on the sparse summary there. After reading for a few moments, realisation hit him. 'I was the consulting psychiatrist. At the trial. One of my first cases.'

Doc looked up, saw the Judge nodding, smiling. Relieved. 'Go on.'

He glanced at the notes, but got little help there. Slowly his brain started to unfreeze. The case should have been memorable enough. The teenager had murdered his parents. And now he was eligible for parole.

Doc subconsciously massaged the livid pink scar on his forehead as he racked his brain for more. Why was he struggling to remember? Was it the fog of time? No, he thought, frustrated as he fumbled around his ravaged memory.

Justice Potter puffed out his cheeks as he contemplated his subordinate, then said, 'If you need more time before returning to work, Doc, I'll understand.'

'No!' Leech. Dammit, I know you, he thought, as the vision of a surly teenager finally surfaced in his mind. 'I remember the case.'

His boss sighed, relaxed back in his seat. 'Go on.'

'The defence claimed temporary insanity and the lad tried to convince everyone he had no memory of the murders. I assessed him.' The facts of the case spilled into his mind as if a clumsy brute had upended a foul concoction, saturating his brain. 'A nasty piece of work. Clinical psychopath. Extreme. I had no doubt he remembered everything. He could lie though, very convincingly, and he displayed no feelings of guilt. But definitely sane. He'd just turned eighteen when he killed his parents. Right?'

The Judge nodded again, then added, 'Sane?' The eyes smiled. 'I thought that was something for a judge and jury to determine.'

Doc's rusty muscles tried to respond, grimacing instead of returning a smile. 'Of course. In my professional opinion, he could tell the difference between right and wrong. Legally I think that makes him bad rather than mad.'

'Yes, which is why I sentenced him accordingly. He's due parole. I want Judy Finch to interview him tomorrow.'

'She's new, I haven't even met her. Is she up to it, boss?'

'I believe she is. I know she lacks experience but she's keen, sharp, resilient and very fair-minded. I've asked her to report on Leech prior to his hearing. Can you meet up with her tomorrow for lunch? Give her some tips. She'll meet Leech in the afternoon.'

'No problem. What do you need me to do?'

'It's her first parolee interview. We need all the information we can get in a case like this. Frankly, if it weren't for the Home Secretary's cuts I would do more of them. But costs rule these days.' Doc saw stress flit across his boss's face for a moment. Then it was gone. Back to business. The Judge patted the files in front of him. 'All these criminals were deemed dangerous, but some more than others. As ever, our first priority is to ensure they are no longer a danger so that—'

'We can release them,' Doc interrupted. 'And save the government around a thousand pounds for every week of sentence unserved.'

'So that we can help them re-integrate with society, Doc.' The Judge flipped off his glasses and hard stared his colleague. 'We don't need cynicism. We need you thinking straight.'

'Sorry, boss.' Doc felt his cheeks flush. 'The girl. Judy Finch?'

Muscles bunched in the Judge's jaw. 'She is not a girl. She's over thirty years old, has a Masters in Sociology, is a Home Office high-flyer, fast-tracked for promotion, and she is a single *mother* too…'

Doc recoiled in shock. Surely the Judge had not meant to stab him in the heart by emphasising the word mother? He shook the thought away, though he knew it would fester and revisit him later when he was alone. He swallowed hard. 'It's just a figure of speech.'

'One I don't like. She has been an absolute godsend, standing in for you while you've been on extended sick leave.'

'Sorry, boss. Again. I'll help her as best I can.' He felt like a schoolboy in the headmaster's study.

'You've over twenty years' experience interviewing violent offenders and murderers. It's her first time. Give her some pointers in how to deal with Leech. But do not prejudice her views. She's there to hear from Leech. An impartial ear. Clear?'

'Sure, Judge.'

'And I want you on the panel for the oral hearing.'

'What? I can't.' Things were moving too fast now and Doc was teetering on the brink.

'Why on earth not?'

Doc scrabbled around in his mind for a reason, though in reality he just wasn't ready. 'Well, I was involved in the case.' He tried another almost smile. 'I'm not exactly impartial am I?'

'Do you stand by your professional opinion of eighteen years ago?'

'Of course—'

'Exactly. There is no conflict of interest.' The Judge smiled. 'Don't worry. Any forensic psychiatrist on the team would take account of your views from the trial, in the same way the panel will take account of mine in my summing up, along with my comments from the sentencing hearing. Then they'll make their decision whether Leech should be freed.' It seemed to Doc that Potter's eyes shone with a hint of zealotry as he added, 'British justice is the best in the world. So let's make sure we're up to it. Call me after you've met Judy.'

The Judge dipped his head to read more papers and Doc realised he was dismissed. He scuffed his chair back and muttered, 'Good night, Judge.'

As Doc pulled the door open the Judge glanced up and called to him.

'Oh, Colin.' Doc paused, listening to the Judge's softly barbed words. 'Can I suggest you put some freshly *ironed* clothes on tomorrow? Goodnight.'

Leech's pulse rate had barely changed throughout the entire Cochran episode, his breathing was calm, not a drop of extra sweat had been shed. Yet he felt the thrill, an endorphin buzz, which really started to kick in as he lay on his bed. He let the video in his head replay the scenes over and over, could feel again the sensation of his fist lifting Cochran off the steps, watching the con in free-fall as he plummeted to his death.

Leech did not even notice his cell door close. Was oblivious to his environment. He experienced a sense of freedom. Control.

Over life and death.

He was pleased with himself. On this occasion his timing was perfect. A fatal blow delivered with incredible speed and power.

Snakebite.

Bye-bye Cochran. You fuckin muppet.

Leech had reckoned Cochran would try to do him in the shower, mates in tow, that being the preferred location for disputes to be settled. Cochran and his two chicken-shit boys would have been planning to drag him to the bathroom at the end of his landing, well away from the screws and the other cons three floors below…

Leech's six-pack rippled and twitched as he laughed at the man's stupidity. Cochran had undoubtedly decided Leech would not dare attack him in the open, would not risk his parole. Probably thought that made Leech a passive victim, easily beaten, pummelled into submission in the showers like some sprog con.

Wanker! That's the difference between me and the losers in here. I'm better than any of them.

And he just knew there would be no more trouble for him. His reputation would guarantee that. Or so he thought.

His door clattered unlocked, and opened.

'Mister Dire Mud, what can I do for you?'

'Stand up, Leech, for a start.'

He did, though oozing reluctance, relishing the moment, not letting the prison officer's apparent power over him unsettle his sense of well-being.

Diarmud continued, 'You think you're such a smart-arse, don't you? You think I don't know what you're up to…'

The warder's breath was foul and right in Leech's nose as they went head to head, Diarmud's peaked cap brushing his brow. He refused to be cowed or provoked, just waited for Diarmud to say his piece, aware that the rage stirring and building inside him could not be directed at this man right now. Especially with two burly officers standing in his doorway, watching. Chaperones.

'Well, I've got news for you, sunshine. At your parole hearing in two weeks time they need a representative from the Prison Service… Someone to put the case against you getting let out to torment the unsuspecting public.' Diarmud's mouth flecked with foamy spittle as he spoke, some of it landing on the convict's face. Hatred and anger knotted inside Leech but he still did nothing as Diarmud taunted him. 'And guess who has volunteered to present the finer points of Her Majesty's Prisoner, number B620061!'

He tried to get back in his zone, to relax, but could not. He wanted nothing more than to smash the old man's face to pulp and toss him down the stairs. He could do it, even with the two ponces in the doorway. He considered it for a split second, but decided he had more pressing matters to contend with—outside.

He really had learnt something in those anger management classes. The thought consoled him, and he tried to replay in his mind's eye the moment Cochran fell. It worked and the pressure dissolved. He threw back his head and laughed in Diarmud's face.

The warder spun, his voice lashing his men as he vented his frustration on them. 'Strip his cell. Strip him. I want his every orifice probed. For contraband.'

Diarmud stepped out the door, shoving his own men aside.

Leech tossed some words at the departing figure, weaving sarcasm into his voice. 'Oh. I almost forgot to mention. Young Johnny Bloom wants to see me.'

Diarmud grunted a reply, 'Don't push your luck, sonny.'

'But Mister Diarmud, I don't think the Governor would want young Johnny doing a Cochran now, would he sir?'

Leech waited as Diarmud turned back, his face a livid scowl.

'What?'

'Sorry sir, but I obviously can't reveal who inside here is suicidal. That's *con*fidential.' He drew out the word, winked, and added, 'But the Governor wouldn't be pleased to hear you were hindering a Listener from helping a disturbed young inmate, would he now?'

A wordless Diarmud retreated to the cackling laughter echoing from within Leech's cell.

Today is a white day, thought Doc as he made his way to Covent Garden for his lunch appointment with Judy Finch. Some days are grey, but most are black.

As a psychiatrist he knew all about depression. He had studied it, opined on it, been involved in the treatment of convicts suffering from it. But now he really understood it.

Today he was feeling neutral, neither glad to be alive nor crawling blindly in the chasm of despair that so often consumed him these days.

A day with a mission, some objectives. Some purpose. At least that was something.

He wondered about Judy, what sort of character she was. What were her motives for joining the Parole Board? Most of all he hoped she was tough enough for the job.

He strolled into the restaurant and spotted her immediately—a petite strawberry blonde waving to him from a table tucked in the corner.

'Hi. Colin Powers,' he said as he reached a hand across the table to her. 'You must be Judy.' His rusty smile cracked into life and then slid away, as if frightened she might notice.

'Of course! I recognised you. I attended one of your lectures at Cambridge several years ago. Criminal profiling.' She shook his hand, a surprising strength in her grip.

'And you remember me from then? I'm flattered.'

Judy laughed, a bubbling cascade of warmth and wit that caressed his fractured senses. Her smile radiant, drawing him in. He liked her.

'Hardly. It was a fascinating lecture. And of course, there were larger than life posters of you everywhere. Even if I hadn't asked you to sign a copy of your book for me I'd have recognised you.'

She beamed at him. She's cute. Dimpled cheeks and piercing violet eyes that could cleave open and search a man's soul.

Doc coughed into his hand, choking at the thought of what she would see in his soul should she choose to look. He glanced up, saw her still smiling, the mood not ruined except inside his own head.

'It's a good spot you've picked—discreet enough so we won't be overhead.'

'Mmm. I'm a regular here and they know I often have secret trysts.' Her lopsided grin made her even more attractive in Doc's eyes. 'And the food's superb. Shall we order?'

The waiter fussed over her, yet barely acknowledged Doc. She seemed to have that effect on men, Doc decided.

Drinks arrived—water for her and red wine for him—as they got down to business.

'Doctor Powers, I hope you don't think I'm being rude, but I'm not sure why the Judge asked you to meet me today. I know I'm pretty new to this job, but I've interviewed plenty of people in my various roles with the Home Office. Social outcasts, misfits, abusers... and that's just my colleagues!' She laughed again, the happy bubbles engulfing Doc, forcing another reluctant smile to his lips.

'Call me Doc, please, Judy. Everyone else does.' He swirled the wine in his glass and took a deep swallow. He was drinking way too much these days. The smile dissolved again at the thought. He forced himself to keep on track. 'The Judge wanted me to talk you through things.' Doc held up a hand as Judy pushed herself forward as if to interrupt. 'I'm something of an old hand when it comes to interviewing felons. Dangerous criminals, Judy. Not just misfits and outcasts, but predators of the worst kind. Believe me, it can be the hardest thing in the world.'

Almost.

Her expression hardened. 'I've been trained for this. I'm ready for it. *I'm* strong.' He noticed the emphasis and wondered whether she was implying he was not. She continued, as he mulled that one over. 'And I'm sure you wouldn't try to intimidate me right before my first parolee interview. Would you?' Her chin jutted at him, her voice bristling with anger.

'Whoa, Judy!' Both Doc's hands were in the air now, palms forward, as if physically pushing her back into her seat. She was a feisty one. And sensitive too. 'Look, I didn't mean anything, kid—'

'What did you say?' Her eyes were fierce now, sparking dangerously. 'Don't you dare call me kid,' she hissed. 'How condescending is that? Now, I'll tell you what I think, Doc. I think the Judge asked you to *help* me,' her fingers crooked into speech marks as she emphasised the word, 'because he wants to help *you* get back in the saddle.' She sat back, her face flushed, as the waiter delicately placed their dishes before them.

'Bon appétit.' The waiter glared at Doc and left.

They ate in silence for a minute as Doc gathered his thoughts. Was she right? Was this about him, his problems, rather than her inexperience? He shook his head. Regardless, he needed to help her. There was no doubting she was a tough one though.

'I am sorry, Judy.' She peered up at him, her eyebrows in a deep vee as she popped some chicken into her mouth, and nodded for him to continue. 'It's true, I haven't been around for a few months,' ninety-eight days actually, 'and this is my first assignment since…'

'It's okay, Doc.' Her frown softened. 'I heard about your wife. I'm sorry. You really don't need to talk to me about that. Okay?'

Her words burst something deep inside him, like a champagne cork popping, liquid spraying, out of control. He shoved his uneaten food away and swirled his drink again. 'I suppose you heard that I killed her.' He threw the wine into his mouth.

'Doc, you don't need to explain anything to me.' Her expression was shocked, but Doc could not stop himself, he ploughed on, his voice brittle.

'I was driving. We'd been out to dinner… We were celebrating.' He banged his glass on the table, the stem exploding, but he barely noticed, continuing his confession, the words unstoppable now. 'I'd been drinking. We crashed on the way home.' His mouth twisted into an ugly grimace.

'Really, Doc—'

'They said it was an accident. I don't know… It happened so fast, I couldn't do anything.' He shrugged, a tear in each eye shining at her as he sucked in a juddering breath. 'She died. I lived.' He squeezed the tears away and held her gaze, wondering why he was finally able to spill it all out, to someone. Anyone. 'I killed her. Although I was technically under the legal limit, maybe she'd be alive today if I hadn't had any drink.' He lifted the glass, realised the bowl in his hand was missing its stem. Stunned, he dropped it on the table, the cloth spattered bloody red with the dregs.

'Is everything alright, Miss?' The waiter hovered, sweeping the remnants of the glass into a silver dustpan, the miniature brush deftly cleaning the tablecloth. He eyed Doc's hand, now a clenched fist. Doc forced himself to relax.

'Everything's fine, Genarro. Please bring a fresh glass. That one must have had a faulty base.' She smiled her charm at him and he tutted away.

It was several moments before Doc broke the embarrassed silence. 'Sorry, Judy… I'm so sorry. I don't know what got into me. I'm never…. God! I'm not exactly the professional today, am I? You must be mortified. Can we start over?'

She reached across the table and squeezed his hand. Electricity sparked into his fingers as she spoke. 'I shouldn't have said what I did. I have a bit of a short fuse I'm afraid, and I can be insensitive at times.' She smiled ruefully as she corrected herself. 'I was insensitive.'

'Maybe you were right.' Come on, Doc. Professional. 'But even so, we really ought to talk about your interview. If I sounded condescending I really didn't mean to. I may not be all there yet,' he tapped his temple and forced a sickly grin, 'but I'm not completely useless.'

Genarro arrived with another glass, scowled again at Doc as if warning him not to break this one, rolled his eyes at Judy and scurried away.

'Well, my understanding of my brief is to meet with Leech and listen to his side of things. I'll prepare a report, he'll sign it—if he agrees it's a fair summary—and it will be presented at the parole hearing. Along with his prison dossier, of course.' Judy swigged some water, thoughtful, her brow rippling. 'I'm supposed to be an impartial ear. That's the bit I'm struggling with. After all he's been found guilty even though he claims he's innocent.'

'We aren't expected to second guess the courts. It's neither here nor there if he's guilty or not.' He watched as her expression deepened. She was obviously very bright. 'Yes, you need to be impartial in the sense that you listen and record what he says. You don't judge him. In a way you're just a facilitator, there to help him put his case across to the parole board in the best light.'

'Mmm. That makes sense. I'm sure I can do that.' She nodded to herself, then asked, 'Do you think he's still dangerous?'

'Sorry, Judy, I really can't answer that.' She seemed confused so he continued. 'You see, I'm part of the team scheduled for the parole hearing.' She still looked perplexed. 'We will decide in two weeks whether Leech represents a danger to the public. First and foremost the Parole Board is here to protect the good citizens of the UK. If we think Leech is a danger he will not be paroled. Full stop.'

'Okay... I know my job is to act as the impartial mouthpiece, but I remember you saying psychopaths are not ill, and therefore can't recover. They don't change. And you called Leech a psychopath at his trial. Doesn't that condemn him for life?' She quizzed him with her violet eyes, clearly frustrated with herself for her lack of understanding.

'A psychopath will always be a psychopath. True. They can, however, modify their behaviour. And that is what we hope to see in Peter Leech's case.'

'What? Some signs that he's normalised after eighteen years in prison?' She paused, then added, 'As if!'

Doc, having re-read the case notes that morning, had his own doubts but went on, explaining, 'Not all psychopaths are killers. It's estimated that around one percent of the population could be classified as sub-clinical or compensated psychopaths. They are often very successful people in their chosen field—chief executives, bankers, doctors, even judges—they're all around us. And by the same token a criminal psychopath can re-enter society and never commit another offence.'

'One percent? That's like, maybe, three quarters of a million people in Britain alone. You're joking, right?'

The waiter arrived, cleared their plates, took their order for coffee and disappeared.

'The way he keeps looking at me, maybe he's one!' Doc had made a feeble joke and surprised himself. It took a moment for him to get his bearings again. 'The term Clinical Psychopath is a label for a personality disorder—an antisocial personality disorder. The most extreme individuals suffer no remorse, they have no conscience. No guilt.' Doc paused, contemplating how his life would be if he felt no guilt. Sliding the thought from his mind, he concentrated on Judy. 'They're ego-centric in the extreme and see other people purely as objects to be used and manipulated. Weak people are especially vulnerable. Hence the success of so many psychopaths—they have qualities that allow them to succeed in our competitive corporate society. In spades.'

'Well, I can see that, but…'

'They're often compulsive liars who are able to switch mid-sentence, contradicting themselves without shame or embarrassment. They don't feel the same as you or I. Their emotions are shallow and hence they cannot empathise with the rest of us. They don't fully understand such things as fear, even.'

'Okay. Okay. Professor! So, Leech is one of these. And a violent killer, to boot. It sounds like I'm going to have a ball.' She sucked at her top lip as she thought about it.

'He may well seem charming.'

She muttered, 'Now that I cannot believe.' She gulped her coffee, checked her watch, then added, 'I've got to dash, Doc. It's been… interesting. Any final words of advice for me for this afternoon?'

'Try to keep the word impartial in your mind. Interview him and don't let him probe you—especially about your personal life.' Doc finished his coffee and added, 'He may well try to manipulate you. Just don't let him sucker you in… And remember, psychopaths love to lie.'

Doc hailed a cab and bundled himself in just as it started to rain. The June sky was overcast and grey.

'Paddington station, please.' The rain drummed on the roof of the black cab as Doc watched the world go by, the images distorted and fractured by rivulets streaming down the window.

Just like my life, he decided. Distorted and fractured. But it had done him some good, finally talking about Natalie and the accident. His stomach swooped as he thought about his wife and for a few minutes he was tormented by memories. Eventually he re-surfaced and remembered to call the Judge. He flipped open his phone and hit the speed dial.

'So how did it go, Doc? She up to it?'

'You know damn well she is.' Doc heard the Judge chuckle. 'Five foot nothing of pure dynamite. Like a tough little lioness. I certainly gave her a few things to think about… Don't know if I helped much.'

'I'm sure you did fine. It's good to have you back, Doc. See you Monday. Have a pleasant weekend.'

Doc cut the connection and decided that yes, it was good to be back. But something nibbled at his mind, fraying the sense of well-being he was experiencing for the first time in months.

Judy.

Some anxiety, some primitive instinct, was eating away at the confidence he felt for her. As he sat gazing at the warped kaleidoscope of London street life through the taxi's rain soaked window, he began to wonder if the Judge had just thrown the convict to the lion—and which one he was actually condemning.

Peter Leech was waiting for Judy inside a room like a goldfish bowl. She had expected to be interviewing him in an office environment, maybe even the Governor's office. Certainly not in this glasshouse, with its three transparent walls, a table plus two seats and not much else. It did give her the chance to observe the prisoner as she was escorted to the door by a surly female officer—a six foot lump of a woman, maybe twenty stone, reeking of cigarettes.

In fact the whole place stank. Judy's nose had started twitching the moment she entered, wondering if stale male sweat was solely responsible. She doubted it—the stench was far worse than just body odour. More like raw sewage was leaking somewhere, tainting numerous unwashed bodies.

Okay, she wondered, what's this Leech like? As she approached, he was sitting motionless at the table bolted centrally in the room. A steel slab, with two metal chairs, also bolted in place, facing each other. Hard chairs, one of which held a hard body.

Leech's blonde hair was tied in a pony tail, possibly to disguise the thinning on his crown. Judy's feet stalled as the head swivelled, the neck of an ox rippling beneath. Green eyes bored into hers.

In that instant, irrationally, she wanted to flee. A mad moment of panic, the primeval reaction of prey to a predator. She pushed herself forward and tried to smile through the glass, her eyes dropping from contact with his, checking out his body, the muscles stretching his lightweight cotton tee shirt, his exposed forearms huge and powerful. The effect was intimidating and Judy sensed danger, felt it exude from the man, a disturbing aura charging the air around him.

His eyes were burning her, devouring her. She trembled and tried to recover her composure.

Relax. She counselled herself inside her head. Focus. He is not going to hurt you.

The officer was speaking as Judy entered, repeating the rules, but she did not hear. She was thinking of Doc. And realised his warning had been well founded. She had never in her life met a man like this. And how the hell was she supposed to be impartial? She shivered as she stepped into the room. The officer remained outside, closing the door, leaving Judy alone with a killer.

He held his hand out to her. A smile that did not quite reach his eyes flickered into place. She could not help but compare Leech with Doc Powers in that moment, how his smile had also seemed stilted, never reflected in his eyes. The emerald chips now inspecting her were different though. They were hard. She decided Leech did not miss much.

She took his outstretched hand, expecting a bone-crushing grip. Instead he surprised her, gently shaking hands, pitching his voice low as he said, 'You must be Ms Finch. I would stand but I have been told to remain seated. Thank you for coming to see me.'

Judy was immediately disarmed, the tension rolling off her shoulders, her neck relaxing. She had not realised how uptight she was until he had spoken. She breathed a sigh of relief. Her imagination had been running riot—after all she had never been inside a prison before. It was, well, she supposed, daunting. The walls, the bars, the razor wire, and heavy steel doors everywhere, clanking shut with a finality that seemed to deny the existence of a world outside. The real world, she reminded herself.

She fondled her prison issued wrist-band—her ticket out of here to a place where you didn't need to be watched through armoured glass while you did your job.

She glanced up and noticed Leech's eyes were fixed on her fingers, watching her fiddling with her pass to freedom. She picked up her attaché case, refusing to be unsettled any further, took out her miniature recorder and pad in as businesslike fashion as she could muster. She concentrated on his nose, avoiding those feral eyes, yet knew she was giving him the impression she was looking directly into them. A little deception to help her get back in control. And a relief from that intense stare.

'You don't mind if I record our conversation, do you?' She fumbled with the machine as she set it down between them.

Get a grip, woman.

Leech yawned, stretching his arms, flexing his biceps. They were huge.

Show off! she thought as she forced her attention back to his nose.

'No problem. I understand you're here to help me. Is that right?' The empty flickering smile was back.

'In a way, yes. I'm tasked with preparing a report based on our interview today. This is your opportunity to put your case to an impartial party.'

He laughed. A stabbing, guttural rasp, devoid of humour.

'Yeah. Right. And who do you work for, Ms Finch?'

'I work for the Parole Board. But,' she added hastily as the laughing increased in pitch, 'I want to record your views regarding your incarceration, how it has affected you and what you feel about the victims, as well as anything else you feel should be considered by the Parole Board.' She cocked an eyebrow at him, more comfortable now she was in work mode. 'You will be able to see the report and make amendments before it's submitted to the panel. This is the extent of my involvement in your case.'

'Sounds good, but you've presumably read all the reports and records about me. You've already made up your mind.' He craned forward, his chunky forearms pushing across the table at her, hands clasped. He reminded her of a praying mantis. Only bigger. Much bigger.

'Not true, Mister Leech—'

'Call me Peter, please… Judy.'

The familiarity ruffled her and she wondered how he knew her first name. 'It's Ms Finch, Peter.' She tried to assert control, her voice stern now. 'I have read the bare minimum, an outline of the crime and sentence, a record of the various institutions you've attended and what courses you've undertaken. That's all. It's up to you to fill me in on the rest.' She dipped her head and picked up her pen, poised to write, her eyes questioning.

He shoved himself back in his chair, folded his arms, the tee shirt protesting, seams threatening to rip at the shoulders.

'Yeah. But you think I'm guilty, don't you?'

'It doesn't matter what I think—'

'It does to me.' He turned away, looking through the glass at the officer strolling freely outside. He spoke in a hushed voice, still turned from her. 'You feel it don't you? Prison? You know…' He jerked his head back to face her, pinning her eyes with his. 'The hopelessness. Oppressiveness. I saw it when you came in. You can't wait to get out of this place. You've been in here five minutes. Now try to imagine how I feel after eighteen years.'

Judy tried to shift her gaze from his, to find the bridge of his nose, but she could not. He's mesmerising! Anger, bottled but palpable, coursed through him and she felt it.

'I was just eighteen when I was first thrown in a cage. You have no idea, do you?' He squinted at her, put his hand to his mouth, spat something into his palm as she watched, horror building inside her.

Her imagination leapt out the starting gate, ready for full flight. What is that? A hidden blade? Alarmed, she almost stood, her legs tensing as she tried to push the chair back, but it was bolted to the floor.

And then he bared his teeth at her. Or what was left of them. His tongue, ugly wet and purple-pink, flicked at her through the gap where his top teeth should have been. He opened his hand, and showed her the denture, then lisped at her, 'A gift from my brother. He knocked my teeth out just after he killed my parents. And thisss?' He nodded at the pink and white plastic trophy. 'Fitted months after I was convicted. Stupidly I chose not to have my teeth fixed before the trial. Refused treatment in the misguided belief the jury would realise I was the victim, and understand what sort of madman my brother was.'

Judy watched the agitation growing in him, the cords of muscle twitching under the material of his shirt, a tic beating at his right eye. Then his shoulders slumped and rounded, as if fearful of something, maybe a memory that made him flinch.

'And the worst thing, Ms Finch, started when I arrived at Belmarsh. The place for high risk inmates—I found myself in great demand.' The purple underside of his tongue snaked out of the gap in his teeth, wiggling suggestively. 'You see, the other lifers, the murderers and rapists, took this,' he opened his mouth wide again and the hideous tongue worked itself slowly in and out, 'as a sign.'

Judy was struggling to understand, though her feeling of horror was intensifying. Her stomach flipped as she blurted, 'A sign of what?'

'Oh, Ms Finch.' He popped the denture back in his mouth, slurping it into place. 'For fellatio, of course. I was face-raped... And buggered stupid. Fresh young meat you see.' He glared at her as she felt the hot red blotches dapple her cheeks, surging embarrassment searing her ego—roasting her for her naivety as much as for the hideous vision he conjured up.

Judy realised her hand was covering her mouth as she muttered, 'Good God!'

'I was just a kid. An innocent kid.' His voice rose and spat the words at her, harsh, defying her to deny him. He leaned back again, puffed out his massive chest, held his arms wide, biceps bulging, palms open. 'I didn't look anything like this then, ma'am. What you see is a product of my time here. I was a harmless, feeble teenage druggie. A school kid, for fuck's sake!' His head snaked forward, his jaw thrust at her. 'And guess what? I tried to escape—'

'Escape?' That was not in the file.

'Oh not physically. No, I used heroin to find oblivion.' He gazed up at the ceiling, as if talking to God, his voice hoarse. 'I was sick of swallowing sperm and my anus was ruptured.' He riveted his eyes back on hers as he added, 'And remember, many of these animals don't wash.'

He was studying her now, and she could not bring herself to speak. He watched her for a minute or so, then sank back, his expression contrite, voice low, an almost whisper. 'I didn't mean to shock you, Ms Finch. It's just I don't get to talk to proper people that much.' He seemed relaxed again as he gave her a feeble smile.

Judy's hand was still covering her mouth. She became conscious of it again, snapped it away. She'd dealt with rape victims and knew the pain, the embarrassment, the guilt and psychological damage it caused. But even the worst of them had not suffered like this. Month after month of brutally enforced oral and anal sex. She could barely imagine the effect on a young man. His words echoed in her head, *just an innocent kid*.

Finally, she found her voice. 'I'm so sorry, Peter. I didn't know such things happened in our prisons.' She was floundering, the words inadequate, dying on her lips.

He seemed to change then, a switch flipped in his mind, his point made, subject dismissed, voice flat again. 'Yeah, well. That's how it is inside. The system brutalises the cons and the guards. But not me. I came through okay. Volunteered for re-hab six months into my sentence. Got cleaned up. Got fit. Kept my nose clean, you know? I'm a survivor. And I'm better than any of them in here, including the bastard screws.'

She did not like that, hearing him brag, as if the sensitive, damaged man of a moment before had left the room. Then she wondered, perhaps it was just a defence mechanism. His strategy for coping. God only knows, he must need one.

She had to take a break, to get away from this man to recover her composure. She said, 'Do you think I can get us some coffee in here?'

'Yeah. Flip a finger at the fat bitch outside. She'll open up and bring some.' The soft tone had gone, replaced by ice as he stared at the guard through the glass wall.

Judy was shocked by the callousness in his voice. She motioned to the guard and the door swung open. It was only then that Judy noticed there was no handle on the inside. She really had been trapped in here with this man.

She lifted her case, popped her pad and recorder inside. Her brain struggled to make sense of things. She stood, feeling relief now, looking down on him. He panicked then, finally giving her the sense of being in control.

'You aren't leaving already, are you? We've only just started.' It sounded to Judy like a pouting teenager was speaking from inside this big man's body.

Maybe he had never really grown up, she thought. 'It's okay, Peter. I just need to freshen up.' She forced a smile.

He grinned back at her, reclining as best he could on the unyielding chair, clasping his hands behind his head, legs wide, his crotch pointing at her.

'You take your time, darlin. I'm not going anywhere.' He dropped his gaze to her breasts, and leered.

She barely stopped herself from sprinting from the room.

Shaun Leech stared at the panorama before him, the stunning view of the Thames, with Tower Bridge dominating the windows of his office. The bridge was opening, a high-masted yacht waiting, causing chaos as the heavy Friday afternoon traffic clogged local roads.

Shaun, normally enamoured of the view, and always fascinated when the bridge opened, had his eyes focussed on nothing. His head was full of dark thoughts. His mind so consumed that he did not hear the knock on his door, or his secretary asking if he would take a call.

'Sorry, Shaun. I know you said no interruptions but it's Walter Topkin calling from the States.' She repeated it louder this time, and edged into the room.

Shaun realised then that she was there and snapped at her, head swivelling to spit out the words before returning to the view. 'Not now, Trish. Get out!'

The door clicked closed as his secretary retreated, but she had ruptured his reverie. He thought about Trish, probably wondering what was eating her boss this evening. Topkin was by far his biggest client, and as such, effectively funded their prestigious office by the river.

Too bad, he thought, as he picked up the letter that had spoilt his day.

He sagged into his executive chair, the smell of leather pleasant in his nostrils, unnoticed as he re-read the words he had long dreaded:

NOTICE OF PAROLE BOARD HEARING: PETER LEECH

Scheduled for less than two weeks time, and as *Victim*, capital vee, he was invited to make a 'Victim Statement' regarding the bastard's potential release.

He twitched a cynical smile to himself as he thought about that. What about Mum and Dad? They were victims but they won't be making a statement, will they?

What a fucking nightmare.

He let his head fall to his hands, tried to decide what to do.

Surely 'life' should mean 'life'. Yet his miserable shit of a brother, the spoilt little brat—literally spoilt—was up for parole after being convicted of butchering their parents.

Unbelievable.

The anger frothed up in him and he decided he had to do something. He grabbed the phone and punched in the number on the letterhead, stabbing the buttons so hard the machine skidded across the desk. He was a strong man, kept himself fit and active, reckoned he was sleek and trim for his thirty-nine years.

His eyes scanned the letter, found the name at the bottom: The Right Honourable Mister Justice Potter, Chairman of the Parole Board. It took a few minutes, but he waited, drumming his fingers as he fumed at the injustice of it all. The very same judge that had convicted his brother was now considering him for parole! It made no sense.

'Good afternoon, Mister Leech. How can I help you?' The Judge's measured tones, rich and reassuring, did nothing to defuse the fury overwhelming Shaun.

He blurted out, 'I can't believe you, of all people, can allow this. My brother,' the words strangled in his throat by anger, 'is an evil monster. He hacked my parents to death, tried to destroy my life, and now you want to release him? It's madness.' Shaun's voice escalated. He expected Trish could hear him, but he didn't care. 'The Americans have the right idea—they'd have stuck a needle in him years ago!'

The soothing voice caressed his ear. 'I know how you feel, Mister Leech, but—'

'You have not the slightest clue how I feel... Victim Statement! What a bloody farce. You take no notice of the victims. You and the rest of the bleeding heart liberal mob just pretend to rehabilitate criminals, then let them loose on society as soon as possible. What bullshit. You don't care what Joe Public thinks. As if my brother will ever be normal. He's a menace.' His voice petered out, his fury subsiding as the diatribe released some of the pressure within.

'I really don't think this is helpful. Perhaps we should talk when you've calmed down…'

'Look. I didn't mean to swear. Forgive me, your Honour.' Is that how I should address him? Shaun thought. Calmer now, forcing himself under control, a well practised manoeuvre. 'I will send a statement to the Parole Board, but I need to understand why he's even being considered for release.' Shaun's free hand was clenching and unclenching, his subconscious miming the movements his conscious self would like to perform on his brother's throat. 'He still claims he's innocent! He still maintains it was me, despite being found guilty and being banged up for eighteen years.' He paused, struggling to understand. 'I thought parole was only ever considered once a convict admitted his guilt and showed remorse… Please tell me he'll automatically be refused.' The anger spiralled up in him again. This just couldn't be right.

'I'm afraid that's something of a myth, Mister Leech.' The Judge was formal, respectful, but firm. 'All convicted persons, regardless of their denial of guilt, are eligible for parole. In fact, it is illegal for the Parole Board to discriminate against those who maintain their innocence. Last year, roughly one in three successful parolees was a denier.'

'A denier? Is that what you call him? And he can be let out?' This was terrible news. 'But Judge, you labelled him a *monster*. He's never shown any remorse. Surely that makes him totally ineligible for release. Ever!' Shaun was sure he'd read somewhere that an expression of remorse was necessary for a convict to get parole.

'The Parole Board does take account of appropriate levels of remorse. Indeed the convict usually needs to show an understanding of his responsibility to, and effect on, the victim. Clearly a denier cannot. However, we can still assess whether he's likely to be a menace to the public and we try not to release dangerous individuals who are likely to re-offend.'

'TRY! Jesus Christ! Just listen to yourself.' Shaun was yelling, his voice quivering. At least the flush of rage felt good. But he knew he was going to lose the Judge's attention if he didn't keep it together. He forced himself to moderate his tone. 'Surely it's better to keep him behind bars, rather than releasing someone who could kill again. Can you honestly say you never get it wrong?'

'Sadly I cannot. Of course, there are rare exceptions. But our records show that parolees are less likely to commit another offence than those released when their sentence has run its full course. The process of parole encourages the offender to rehabilitate.'

It sounded almost sensible when the Judge said it, his persuasive manner smoothing away doubt. Except Shaun would never be convinced. He tried another tack.

'I know my brother. He's sick. He's beyond rehabilitation. Beyond salvation. In his case life should mean life. Don't I have any real say in this?' The letter suggested his views would be taken into consideration. But what did it mean?

'The Victim Statement allows us to better understand the impact of the crime on the victims, and also allows us to take an account of any requests with regard to conditions of parole, such as limiting the parolee from contacting you or living close by.'

'And if he ignores your conditions, Judge? What then? A slap on the wrist? Puh-lease!' Shaun let his frustration worm out. 'He's always broken the rules, ever since he could walk.'

'Let me re-assure you…' The honey voice oozed into his ear, failing to affect Shaun in the slightest. 'He can be recalled if he breaches the terms of his parole.'

'Recalled? What, back to prison?'

'Exactly, although the severity of the breach would be taken into account and a Parole Board hearing would convene to decide—'

'So he doesn't automatically go back inside?'

This was mind-blowing. Shaun was finding it all too much. He regretted never investigating the possibilities regarding his brother getting parole, choosing instead to ignore him completely. *My brother died with my parents.* Move on. That had been the plan. He had been convinced that a dysfunctional idiot like Peter could never get through eighteen years in jail without screwing his prospects for parole.

'As I said,' Shaun recognised the impatience finally breaking through the unruffled persona, the Judge's voice now had an edge to it, 'we convene a hearing and consider the facts. Then decide the appropriate action.' The smile in his voice returned as he tried to reassure. 'I think you need not worry unduly. Firstly, your brother has to meet with the members of the Parole Board for a formal assessment of whether he is suitable for early release. Secondly, if he is released on licence he will be subject to close supervision and any geographical or personal contact restrictions imposed by the Board.' Despite the politeness Shaun sensed the Judge was ready to finish the conversation as he added, 'Please return the Victim Statement as soon as possible so that we can take account of your views. Is there anything else?'

There was plenty, but Shaun thanked the Judge and hung up. He felt numb as he considered his brother. He had honestly thought he would rot in prison, a consequence of his refusal to acknowledge his guilt. Yet the bastard could be out—in what? He checked the letter again, calculating. Christ! Six or seven weeks.

Shaun's eyes tracked across the desk, over the blotter, the empty in-tray, to the picture of Suzie and Billy. His wife, still beautiful despite being a little overweight, smiling as she hugged their son. The boy grinning the toothless smile of a seven-year old waiting for his new front teeth.

Another picture flashed into his mind. His brother, mouth swollen and bruised, the same top teeth missing, but from Shaun's raging blow—the one delivered after their mother and father had been carved to death.

He focussed on the photograph again. The worst of it was that Billy even looked much like Peter had at that age.

Weird.

Shaun grated his teeth at the thought. His brother, still spoiling his life even in the here and now.

I can't even look at my own kid without thinking of that bastard.

And Suzie. He could just imagine how she was going to react when she heard his little brother could be out on the streets in a few weeks. She hated Peter for her own reasons. And Shaun had almost lost her to him once before.

There really is no justice in this country, he thought, clutching the letter before balling it and lobbing it across the room.

He stepped back to the window, resuming his unseeing vigil over the Thames, his fists rhythmic in their clenching and flexing, his handsome features warped with hatred. For a moment his vision cleared and he found himself focusing on the tormented reflection in the glass, barely recognising himself.

God, he thought. Just look at yourself. The bastard is still capable of ruining things after all these years. It was bad enough when the lunatic had been limited to sending a condolences card every year on the anniversary of their parents' death. Peter's birthday. Each time the words had differed, but the gist was always the same: 'I'm looking forward to when we can play happy families again.'

It was a not-too-subtle threat, probably meant more for his wife. After the first one had left Suzie in hysterics, Shaun had his solicitor arrange a restraining order, but each year they still arrived, anonymous, typewritten and sent from different places around the UK. Shaun's solicitor could do no more, even though they guessed Peter's lawyer, a seedy little man with a very dubious reputation, was the conduit for these sick reminders.

Well, maybe it would be no bad thing if his little brother got parole. After all these years Shaun might finally have the chance to make good on the promise he made to himself years before, and kill the sick fuck.

Let him come.

Judy sat in the cubicle in the female officers' restroom, hands supporting her head, her elbows on her knees. She was not using the toilet, just sitting on the lid, trying to gather her thoughts, wondering if she had underestimated the job.

She was good, very good, at just about everything she had ever tried. Her application, determination, I'll-take-no-shit attitude and sheer stubborn pig-headedness, meant there was no glass ceiling for her. She had worked for the Home Office since graduating from university some ten years previously, and she was a rising star. She was on the fast-track to the very top, having been spotted by the mandarins a few years ago. Doors had opened for her and others like her, speeding the brightest, most able, on their way to stellar careers. Part of the deal was that she would spend a year to eighteen months on secondment to different government departments. The Judge had snapped her up a month ago, convincing her and her bosses she needed insights not available within the normal hierarchy.

But nothing had prepared her for this.

She thought back to her lunch with Doc Powers, his slightly flabby, unthreatening maleness and his brown eyes brimming with sorrow. He'd reminded her of Bambi. Such a contrast to the man she had left moments before. Doc had tried to warn her. The Judge had told her he was throwing her in at the deep end. And boy, did he mean it. She would call him tonight. Apologise and explain that she now realised he had not meant to be patronising. Maybe she could arrange to meet him. Talk through her report.

She snorted. She didn't need help with writing a bloody report. In reality she just needed to chat with someone with an insight into the creature in the fishbowl.

Well, so be it, she decided.

She stood and smoothed her pantsuit, glad she had dressed severely, her shoulder length hair pulled tight in a business bun. She was wearing the bare minimum of make-up with just a touch of mascara and some lip salve. She went to the sink and checked her face in the mirror.

God, I still look shocked.

She opened her bag to get her make-up and then remembered she had left all but the essentials—pad, recorder and pen—at the gate. Prison rules. She was glad in a way. Her wallet, with the picture of Josh, was safe outside this hell-hole. She did not want her son's presence inside here, not even a photograph of him.

She splashed warm water on her cheeks, smoothed her hair. She had deliberately ignored Leech's gaze when it lingered on her breasts, he was a man after all, and he had been in prison eighteen years. She found herself thinking of his physical presence. He was in exceptional shape, so macho, yet he also seemed sensitive and damaged too. He had certainly suffered when he'd arrived here.

But... She really could not make him out.

'Come on, Judy! You've barely started. You can do this.' She spoke to the woman in the mirror. 'After all, he won't hurt you. He wants parole in a few weeks and knows you're here to help him. He's not stupid. And he's not a monster.'

Is he?

'Okay Peter, let's crack on.' The recorder was propped up between them, Judy's pen poised. Her eyes were latched onto the bridge of his nose. She was back in business, determined not to let him get to her again. 'Let's talk about the victims—'

'Victims? I'm the victim!' He snapped the words at her, a wet towel cracking against exposed flesh.

'I mean, how do you feel about your parents now?'

'My parents are lucky! At least they're dead! I'm the only victim now.' His arms windmilled in emphasis. 'I'm stuck in here. What about me?'

Judy noticed the creepy sulk in the voice again, the callousness of his dismissal of his parents as 'lucky' like a slap to her face. She focussed on her pad, the raging light in his eyes cowering her.

After several seconds he said, 'Sorry, Ms Finch.' She glanced up and saw he was breathing deep into his lungs, as if oxygen alone was capable of calming him.

'Okay,' she hesitated. 'How do you feel about your brother?' Judy expected another outburst in view of Leech's claim that Shaun had framed him.

Instead his shoulders collapsed again, hunching forward, a target trying to shrink, desperate to make itself too small to hit.

'Shaun is not who you think he is.'

Judy was baffled by that. 'He is your brother?'

'He was. Until the trial. Now I'm just a dead man to him.' He perked up then. 'But I'm not dead, am I?' A self-congratulatory tone seeped into his voice.

'You said in court that he framed you. Do you still believe that, Peter?' She watched as an earnest frown appeared, the eyes gleaming at her, for all intents an honest face, but she could not help but wonder, *What the hell are you really thinking?*

'You may not believe me, but I can't remember what happened that day. You see, I was high on a cocktail of acid and ecstasy. I think I was in my den all day. I took a shower to try and clear my head, stepped out straight into my brother's fist. He was very handy with those fists of his. Karate Kid. Always bullying me.' Self-pity whined out of him. 'When I woke up I couldn't even remember him hitting me.' He turned his head, and his index finger traced a scar behind his ear. 'This cut was from the shower tap cracking open my skull as I fell. A double whammy and I ended up with partial amnesia.'

'So in all honesty you can't say for sure that you're innocent—if you can't remember.'

His fists drove into the unyielding table top, the vibration toppling her recorder. She righted it as his voice ripped through the air.

'I would know if I'd hacked my own parents to death! I was a scrawny harmless pot-head, for fuck's sake. My dad was twenty-odd stone and used to box for his university. It was my brother who killed them, and I swear he framed me. He's even bleedin admitted it to me. Of course, he's never gonna admit it to anyone else, is he? I'm the innocent victim, Ms Finch. Remember that.'

She was glad to see his temper subside as quickly as it arose, and pressed on with her point. 'So, if it really was Shaun who killed them, are you going to seek some sort of revenge, Peter?' She let the thought reach her tongue before she considered the consequences. It was a stupid, provocative question and she was ready to signal to the warder, catching her eye, glad for the solid steel table separating her from this hulk. But his reaction surprised her.

'My brother's already dead.' Totally calm, the tone level, not a hint of emotion now. Certainly no malice. It didn't sound like a threat to her, just a bald statement. 'He said that about me, Ma'am. And that's how I feel about him now.' He gave her a mirthless smile, then surprised her again as he seemed to contradict himself. 'You know why that fucker killed them? Greed. Out and out selfish greed. He was furious that they were giving so much to charity. Said it was his money—his inheritance! Then he stole my inheritance—the lawyers challenged my parents' wills after they died so that I couldn't benefit from the crime. So the greedy bastard got it all. How about that?' The venom of his words made her cringe.

Judy decided to move on, to try and get through this as quickly as she could. 'So, what will you do when you get out?'

'I've got money of my own. My share of the proceeds from the family business. Mum and Dad gave us both some shares when we were born, held in trust so my brother couldn't get his grubby hands on that. Mind you, I had to pay out shedloads in legal fees for my defence, all because that shit refused to open the family coffers to cover my costs…' He scowled. 'But I've been studying in here, y'know? I've taught myself economics and dealt shares through my solicitor for years now. I've got a tidy sum waiting for me. Not like most of the sad sods in here who'll leave with fifty quid in their pockets, courtesy of Her Majesty.'

'So what work will you do? Where will you live?'

'I've already bought a pad. Lovely place. Overlooks the Thames. I've seen it. They let me out, supervised of course, to check it out. Locked me back up after, though. The system stinks. It was torture.'

'And work?' Judy jotted some notes then looked up at him.

'Well, I've studied psychology to degree level. I'd like to help people… Maybe do therapy or something.' He must have seen the doubt in her eyes as he continued, voice rising. 'I've started in here already. I'm a Listener.' He jabbed his thumb to his chest. Proud.

'And what does that involve, exactly?' She was genuinely curious.

'I've been trained by the Samaritans to act as an ear for the poor sods in here who've got no one else to listen to them.'

Judy thought that comment odd in view of his apology and remark earlier: *I don't get to talk to people much.* Ah! She remembered, *proper people.* Not convicts then.

29

He carried on. 'I have to listen to them whingeing on, you know, the ones who can't cope, maybe thinking of suicide, or maybe just getting done over like I was when I was first here. But I get privileges. I can move around during lock up, visit their cells to talk to them.'

Judy smiled at that. 'You mean listen to them.'

'Yeah, whatever.' He looked and sounded peeved at her interruption, as if it was irrelevant. 'Anyway, I've also done other courses, y'know? Anger management, thinking skills, assertiveness and stuff.' He beamed at her now, obviously very pleased with himself. 'I've learnt more inside than I did in thirteen years of private school, though I couldn't exactly play hooky in here!'

She smiled again, remembering a statistic she'd read somewhere claiming that almost a third of all prisoners had been habitual school truants during childhood. 'Good for you, Peter. Tell me more about how you feel you've benefited from your time in here.'

He went on to describe the courses in detail and how he was now a better man, a reformed character. He sounded just like an enthusiastic newly-minted graduate and Judy found herself drawn in to his story. 'I just want to be a solid citizen, you know? Be a part of society again.' He looked piously at Judy, his hands held as if in prayer.

A deadly killer mimicking a priest, she thought.

'A final couple of points, Peter.' She was keen to finish now, to get away, to cleanse the stink of this place that seemed to be permeating her skin. 'You asked to be transferred from open prison after just two weeks. Why would you want to come back here? It's a high security unit?' This had genuinely perplexed her, and the lack of rehabilitation and preparation for release could jeopardise his chances of parole. Why return to a higher category prison with a more rigid system?

'That place was rife with drugs, it was far worse than here. Just about everyone was doped up or on heroin. I didn't want to be around those wasters. When I get out I want to keep my nose clean. Literally, y'know?' He stuck a thumb over one nostril and sniffed hard for her benefit, as if he thought she was that naïve.

'But your rehabilitation and resettlement prog—'

'I don't need re-hab. There's nothing wrong with me. And I've already got a pad sorted. I can do voluntary work. I don't need any more income, I've got plenty of money invested. What re-settlement do I need? Good looking guy like me... I'll be fine.' He winked at her then, his cheeks bunching in a grin. 'I reckon you like big guys, don'cha?'

She thought it best to ignore the comment, and just looked blankly at him.

'Well, Peter, I think that's everything, unless you've got anything to add...' Judy was relieved to be finishing. The last two hours had felt like ten.

'Nah. Not about this place or my parole.' He had a sly look now.

Judy did not know what he meant, but picked up the tape recorder and thumbed the 'off' switch anyway.

'There is one thing... When I get out—'

'If your parole application is a success.'

He flapped his hand at her, dismissing the possibility of parole being denied. 'Whatever. Maybe we could get together, y'know? We've had such a good heart to heart and I feel really good about you. You fancy that?' He was still grinning, his eyes roving, crawling over her breasts again. She could see he was certain she would respond positively.

Judy was flabbergasted. Here he was, a convicted killer, hitting on her at the end of a formal prisoner interview. The man's ego was beyond comprehension.

Unbelievable.

Then she wondered if, perhaps, it was a consequence of his incarceration since his teens. Maybe he was just not aware how inappropriate it was. She busied herself bundling her things away as she thought how best to respond.

'I don't think so, Peter. I have a husband.' She avoided any sort of eye contact for that one. She almost added that she had a son too, but something, maternal instinct perhaps, stopped her from mentioning Josh to this man.

And anyway, it was true. She had been married. Even though her husband had left her. Well, she had kicked him out really. Either way, there was no need for Leech to know.

'So why no ring, Ms Finch?' His words harsh and suspicious.

She felt like prey again as his eyes lingered on her body. She sensed him stripping bare the partial truth inside her head, while undressing her inside his. She shuddered. Her imagination was running amok again. She cleared her throat, tried to sound authoritative.

'I never wear it to work. But I married my childhood sweetheart when I graduated from university. Goodbye, Peter. I doubt we'll meet again.'

She stood and shook his hand in an effort to signal the matter was closed. He held on for a second too long, and dangled some words in front of her, barely audible silky vocal threads, his face devious.

'Whatever, Birdy. We'll see.' His green eyes were drilling into her as he spoke.

She snatched her hand away. Surely she must have misheard him, but preferred not to ask him to repeat it. Did he call her Judy again? And what did he mean?

She scurried from the room and eventually surfaced on the street outside the prison, grateful at last to be able to suck in some fresh air. It tasted sweet.

She gulped it down and hailed a cab, her mind tumbling over his audacious request for a date. His cocky look. His lust for her body. And his parting words.

What did he say?

Whatever, Judy. We'll see?

He must have been mistaken, thinking she was going to attend his hearing.

Of course he was.

Finch, he thought. A good name for her. A shy little bird, frightened but determined to keep on coming. Peck, peck, pecking at him.

Finch.

My little bird.

Leech shoved his arms straight, feeling satisfaction, his muscles working a steady rhythm as he bench-pressed two hundred pounds. His body worked while his mind considered the woman he had spent the last couple of hours with.

Woman. She smelt so good he had wanted to eat her, consume her, make her part of him. Shy little Birdy she may be, but all woman. Not like the fucking dyke warders that stank of fags and sweat. Not for the first time he wondered why the Home Office employed women, if you could call them that, to keep men like him locked up.

Bitches.

But the Finch. She had wanted him. He could see it in her eyes. Those coy, violet gems had tickled their way across his shoulders and chest, checking him out, fearful of showing just how much she wanted him.

Oh yeah, little Birdy. I can read your mind.

Leech stood, smiling to himself as he flicked the sweat from his forehead. The gym was small and crowded with machines and weights, but only a dozen inmates were permitted to use it at any given time. One screw sat, idle, turning pages of a magazine, supposedly supervising the cons.

Lazy bastard.

Leech grabbed the two largest barbells, shouldering a dread-locked Rastafarian aside, scorching him with a look, defying the bigger man to respond. He did not. He just walked away.

Pussy!

Pussy? Mmm, he thought. Ms Finch. Yeah. She came across like a virgin, but he knew better. She was hot.

Virgin? In one way she was—it was obvious this was her first time inside. The way she kept fondling her 'awayday' pass, as if the wrist-band was a talisman to ward off the evil of this place. And her birdy, birdy twitching as she kept glancing outside the glass walls, checking the guards were watching over her.

Yeah, little miss virgin.

But it can only be good for me, he decided. He knew that a hardened Parole Board Officer with experience of many prison visits would not have felt the same sense of shock and hopelessness. Would not respond to the pressure of prison squeezing the fresh air from his lungs.

And her face when he'd shown her his teeth! Ha! And the bullshit. As if he'd put up with being face-fucked and shafted for six months. Six days more like. What had he told her? Oh yeah, he'd squeaked like a little girl when he'd said he was just a harmless feeble druggie. He laughed aloud, oblivious to the glances from the other inmates, though if any one of them caught his eye it would lead to trouble.

He studied his forearms as he curled the dumbbells, not bothering to count, just pushing until fatigue finally made him cease the regular pumping. One thing was true, he had not looked anything like this good when he first arrived. He was lazy back then. But inside here there was not much else to do. And no one messed with him now.

His biceps were burning, but he ignored the pain, concentrating on his refuge, his private inner world. Thinking was free. Thinking was freedom. Well, as close as you could get inside here.

His mind floated back to that first week after his conviction. Yes, a few of the more aggressive cons had forced him to perform, had violated his body, had drawn blood.

Even then, he was better than them. Smaller too. But brighter, quicker. More deadly. Sometimes he imagined he was a snake. A cobra, its strike a punching blow, hard, piercing skin, ruining flesh. Fatal.

It was not difficult to get a weapon in prison. You were only limited by your own imagination. And Leech's imagination had no bounds.

He set the weights down, let his arms recover, and then strolled over to the leg press machine. Another inmate, pneumatic muscles slick and bulging, an advert for the steroids on offer from the dealers inside, was straining as he used the machine

Leech wanted. Leech stared hard into the man's face, screwing into him with his eyes.

The challenge was obvious. Eye contact is considered an aggressive action by inmates and inevitably led to violence.

Or acquiescence.

The other con stepped off the machine, muttering, 'It's all yours, okay man. I'm finished anyway.'

Leech blanked him, increased the setting and settled back to push his legs to exhaustion. His reverie continued, his thoughts ranging back to his first week in prison. And the start of his reputation.

McCauley was his name. He reminded Leech of his father. Six foot three, heavy set with solid muscle. A boxer's build, not a gym junkie's drug bloated frame. Inside for murder and gang rape, Mack was a forty year old lifer with no hope of parole. Or sex. Other than with another male, willing or not.

He had been using Leech for most days of that first week, along with two other inmates who had taken a fancy to Leech's youthful body. Everything changed that last time though.

Leech's face contorted as he squeezed his thighs against the weight, the memory rather than the effort twisting his features. He had been sitting on his bed, reading, when Mack entered his cell, pulling his hard, fat, stinking cock out and, as usual, shoving it at Leech's face.

Leech almost gagged at the recollection, legs straining against the weights, eyes on the ceiling, unseeing. He groaned aloud, the events replaying in his mind.

Mack, cock in hand, voice rasping and urgent as he grabbed the back of Leech's head, pulling the young boy's mouth towards him. 'Suck it, bitch. Suck it hard.'

He was prepared for Mack this time. It had cost him though. He'd paid twenty quid to a trustee who worked in the kitchen. He wanted a knife but the trustee told him that was not possible. The warders were not that stupid. The best he could do was supply a tin lid, discarded from one of the many giant cans of beans they used every day.

To Leech it was a bargain. He sharpened the jagged edge on the concrete wall of the exercise yard, and then bent the metal to fit comfortably in his palm. Now he had a shiv with a viciously serrated blade.

And as he ducked his head forward, as if to take Mack into his mouth, he whipped his hand up between the big man's legs. The weapon sliced through Mack's lust-swollen scrotum in a flash. Leech was euphoric, the adrenalin pumping as he struck again, ripping the blade through the head of Mack's penis. A piece of purple flesh flew off in a gout of blood.

Mack did not even have time to cry out, he was so shocked and stunned by the speed of the attack. Leech pressed home the advantage. He rocketed up off the bed, battering the top of his skull into Mack's face, the satisfaction of the crunch of bones lifting his spirits for the first time since his sentencing hearing.

Mack collapsed at his feet, unconscious. Leech strolled out of his cell to the washrooms. He had been sitting in his underwear, baiting the trap, and all he needed to do now was wash the spattered blood from his chest and face.

He showered, bent the metal weapon into a tight wad and poked it down the drain. He was whistling, towelling himself off when the alarm sounded.

That was the day his life finally changed for the better, he thought, as he got off the machine. He took a breather and a swig of water before leaping onto the jogging machine. No one was using it, very few of them did. He sneered at the posers, grunting and pumping iron for all they were worth while he built his stamina by running. He knew it was a slow way to create muscle, and it made him feel good that none of the others put in the effort. But he knew that muscles built quickly, faded quickly. Fitness was four things to him—strength, suppleness, speed and stamina. He had all four. An athlete.

He cranked the controls, jacking the velocity up, and pounded the rubber mat, all the while repeating his mantra: I'm better than all of them.

Once more his inner world took over as his body pushed itself on autopilot, his legs and lungs stretched to their limit by the miniature conveyor belt.

He had expected trouble from the Governor. An inquiry, some extra days of time or even a criminal court action against him.

McCauley had been carried from his cell squealing like a baby.

Hard man? Like fuck… Not that McCauley was much of a man any more.

Leech chuckled to himself at the thought.

He had been called to the Governor's office an hour later, while his blood-drenched cell was stripped and searched, then hosed clean. They frog-marched him to the boss's office, hands cuffed and chained to a leather belt. Leech felt nothing but elation. No apprehension or fear for the consequences. He never had.

What will be, will be.

But the outcome surprised him.

The Governor rattled off a little speech. 'Okay, Peter. Inside this office you can tell me anything. No one else will know. Not the inmates, not the other prison officers, not even the police. Just you and me. You're a young man with many years ahead of you in here and you need to decide whether you trust me and the system. Okay? Now. What happened?'

Did he think Leech was stupid? He never trusted anyone, was always suspicious of other people's motives, and this was no exception. His answer was a popular catchphrase inside: 'Yeah. Right.'

The Governor flushed, his voice hardening. 'So, you prefer the pathetic prisoners' code of silence.' He shook his head, then sighed. 'I have a good idea what McCauley was up to, but I need you to tell me. Otherwise how can I improve things around here?'

Leech just shrugged. 'I have no clue, Governor. I don't even know what Mack was doing in my cell. Having a wank over my underwear, maybe? Caught his dick in his flies? I was in the shower.'

'Bullshit. I don't believe a word. You'd better keep your nose clean, Leech… You've had your chance. But now I know which side you're on.' The Governor shrugged and dismissed him. And that was that.

No prosecution. No comeback. McCauley was transferred, and even though Leech hated the man, he gave him his due for not grassing him up to the authorities. Never spoke about the incident at all.

Must've known he just got what he deserved. Fuckin pervert.

From that day on, his time had got easier and easier. He had that most elusive and valuable asset inside prison: respect. In fact he became something of a minor celebrity and actively cultivated his iron man image. Even adopted a nickname.

The Snake.

He was patient too. The other two men who had abused him decided he was best left alone after the incident, turning their attention to others more vulnerable. And nobody liked Mack, the big man had no friends inside, so no one was out for revenge.

Far from it. Leech remembered one of the hard-asses back-slapping him and telling him, 'Well done, kiddo. That ugly bastard's days of fudge-nudging are over for good.'

He slowed the machine, satisfied he had worked his body enough for one day. He stepped off and stretched out. He ignored the other inmates. And they ignored him.

It did not bother him. He was a loner. Self-sufficient. Superior.

And he never, ever forgot a slight. Always took his revenge.

It had taken several months, but both the other two abusers died. One 'over-dosed' on heroin, the other 'committed suicide' with a bed sheet. Subsequently Leech's reputation grew to a point where no one messed with him. Men who had nothing, and so respected nothing, except physical strength and ruthless aggression, stepped aside for him. He was a king amongst fools.

He rubbed himself down, considered showering but couldn't be bothered. He headed back to his cell, his subconscious throwing a vision of the Finch twittering at him in the interview. Her tight-fitting suit barely disguising the luscious body beneath. Horny little bitch.

So like his Susan. His childhood love. He'd seen her photograph recently and of course, she'd aged. Finch reminded him of her, but was even better looking.

And she had such lovely tits.

Then he frowned as he remembered the rejection. 'I don't think so. I have a husband.'

What bullshit. Why would she tell him to call her Ms and not Mrs? And where was her wedding ring, eh?

She was just spoofing him. Yeah, that was it. Didn't want to seem too keen. The little prick tease.

He felt better. No, she wouldn't be able to resist him.

After all, she wouldn't want a Snakebite, would she now?

Judy was clinging on to the grab handle in the back of the black cab as the driver, who seemed to think he was in Formula One rather than London rush hour, raced around the back alleys and hidden short cuts to avoid the snarled up traffic.

The meeting had left her dazed and confused. Or rather, the man had. After leaving the prison she walked around for a while, found a park bench and tried to make sense of her first prison experience.

Her first prisoner experience.

Normally, after rising to a challenge, as she had many times in her academic and professional career, usually having exceeded her own expectations, she would be exhilarated, charged with excitement at conquering a new task, a new experience. But this?

She did not know what to think. And would she ever get used to prison?

Did she want to?

She had no ready answer, rousing herself to hail a cab only when the rain started and she realised how much time had ebbed away.

As the vehicle jolted her through the Friday rush hour traffic she glanced at her watch—it was getting on for six. Her mother would be disapproving, as usual, though reliable as ever, baby-sitting Josh and preparing dinner for all three of them.

'Traffic's solid up ahead, love. I'll avoid the south circular if that's okay. Might be no quicker, but worth the risk?' The cabby's eyebrows were raised in question as he watched her in the rear-view mirror, waiting for her reaction.

'I don't mind. Do what you think is best.'

She almost fell off her seat as he swung the cab into a U-turn and they rattled off in the direction they had come.

London. Traffic still bad, despite the congestion charge. She had no car now, unwilling to pay several pounds a day for it to spend most of its life parked outside her Fulham home. Shame though. She just fancied a trip out to the coast or the countryside this weekend. Some clean air. As she considered the idea she concluded—why not? Josh would love that. They could take her mum too. A train ride to Brighton would do them all the power of good. That's that, she decided.

The cab driver had been right. It seemed she was home in no time, pulling up outside her little sanctuary in a leafy London backstreet. She had bought it with the proceeds of the sale of the old family home after the divorce.

The garden flat had cost almost a million pounds, but was worth every penny. It had seemed a lot for a couple of small bedrooms, a galley kitchen that, she thought guiltily, she rarely cooked in, and two large reception rooms—a playroom for Josh and a quiet lounge for her. She loved the place.

She opened the front door and heard Josh squealing, 'Mum's home,' as he bounded out of his playroom, followed at a more sedate pace by his grandmother.

'Hi honey.' She ruffled his head, knelt down and gave her six-year old pride and joy a hug. She pulled a face at her mother while clinging to him. 'Sorry I'm late. It took longer than I expected.'

'Don't worry, love. We've had a great afternoon, haven't we, Josh?' The barb was not lost on Judy. Her mother was dumpy, frumpy, white-haired and wrinkled beyond her years. Laughter lines she called them, with disarming accuracy. She was a godsend for Judy, even if she did still think a woman's place was in the home.

'We've baked cakes, Mum. Little cupcakes with icicles on!' She allowed her son to drag her into the kitchen, his hot hand straining as he tugged her along.

'They look lovely! But I think you mean icing sweetheart.'

'Uh—icing. Whatever.'

Her heart frosted at the word and the way it was uttered.

Whatever.

Her mind wrenched her back to the prison, making her think of Leech, his attitude and his parting words. She clutched at her chest, eyes wide, shocked.

'Are you alright, love? You look all in.' Her mother's tone was not at all comforting, more of a rebuke. Judy heard her mother's oft-repeated words in her head: You're working too hard. Josh needs his mother. Take time off, for yourself and your family.

Judy turned, stared out the window into the beautiful garden, the tiny space full of blooming flowers, reds, yellows and oranges, the rain now stopped and a bee hovering in its never-ending quest for nectar.

Busy bee, just like me.

'I'm fine, Mum, just tired after a long week.' Josh was offering her a cake and she smiled down at him, thinking how like a puppy he was. Every day was a world of wonder to him, to be grabbed and squeezed for all the fun that could be had. She hoped he would never lose that, never grow out of it. 'No thanks, darling. I'll wait until after dinner.' Judy cocked an eye at her mother.

'It'll be ready in fifteen minutes. Enough time for you to shower and perk yourself up. Shepherd's pie.'

'Blaagh!' Josh grabbed his throat and fell to the floor, choking to death at the very thought.

'And fish fingers for you, sunshine. Then you can eat cake, okay?'

'Aw Gran. Can't I just eat cake?' He sat on the kitchen floor, eyes begging, bringing that puppy to Judy's mind again.

'No you cannot! Now go and play, and let your mum drink her tea and get cleaned up.' Gran handed Judy the cup without bothering to ask if she wanted a drink.

Josh scooted from the kitchen and moments later they could hear his Playstation blasting away.

'Thanks, Mum.' She was glad Josh was out of earshot. 'I was thinking, how about we all head off to Brighton tomorrow? A family outing?'

'Oh Judy, I'm sorry, love. John called earlier.' Her mother's lip curled as she uttered Judy's ex-husband's name. 'He's flying off to the US for several weeks and said he wanted Josh for the weekend… If it had been up to me I'd have told him to get lost. But he said he'd pick him up tomorrow morning at ten.'

'Bugger!' Judy took a gulp of tea. It was good, but her mother's scowl was not. 'Sorry, Mum. Josh can't hear with that din going on.'

'That's hardly the point, is it?'

Judy loved her mum dearly, and appreciated everything she did for her and Josh. But she still, like all mothers everywhere, treated her grown-up daughter as if she was a wayward teenager.

'So his highness is going away again and demanded his son's presence before he jets off?'

The sour note was unusual, and Judy realised she was being petulant. She purposely tried to ensure the best possible relationship between Josh and his father, and had always acquiesced when John's work shifted their schedule for sharing their son.

She suspected John took advantage and she wondered if he had today. She was certain he must have known he would be away earlier in the week. He had just not bothered to tell her. Well, she should not be surprised. Once a selfish bastard, always a selfish bastard.

'Josh is looking forward to it. And you'll have him all to yourself for the next few weeks. Let's go to Brighton next weekend, eh, love?' Her mum patted her arm and said, 'Now, how about that shower or the pie'll be spoiled?'

Judy felt revived. She'd had a scalding shower, used a whole tube of gel and washed her hair four times. The stench of prison had eventually rinsed away, the memories of her ordeal fading with the stinging jets of water, her sanctuary having its usual anaesthetic effect on her.

The shepherd's pie settled her even more, comfort food and one of her favourite meals.

Good old Mum. She's worth her weight.

Judy played with Josh, helped him bathe, or rather bombard rubber ducks and flood the bathroom floor, then tucked him up in bed before reading him some more Harry Potter. His eyelids drooped so she kissed him goodnight. His little arms crushed her neck as he squeezed her and whispered, 'I love you, Mummy. I love Daddy too, but I love you more. I'll be back on Sunday.' She felt tears well up, gave him a final hug and left him clutching Bruno Bear.

Gran handed her a gin and tonic the moment she entered the lounge. Mozart wafted from the speakers and some candles threw a cosy yellow light, turning the room into a haven for relaxation.

'Sit down, love. Put your feet up. You look exhausted today. Do you want to talk about it?'

'Not really, Mum.' She sank back into the soft sofa and leaned her head back, absorbing the music and tranquillity.

But she did want to talk about it.

'Well, I'll be off then. I'll pop over in the morning. I'll be here when John comes.'

'You really don't need to, Mum.'

'I want to, love. Family. That's what's important.'

She heard the door click as her mother left for the ten-minute walk to her own tiny flat on a warden controlled estate for the elderly.

Elderly? Judy thought her mother probably did more for the other residents than the wardens ever did for her.

She emptied her mind and tried to relax. To let the music invade her soul and prevent unwanted thoughts...

But then a killer's face floated into her head, it leered at her, the front teeth missing, and a lewd purple-pink tongue waggled at her.

She sat bolt upright. It was no good. She would make the call.

She fumbled in her bag for a moment, found her office diary with his number and dialled it before she could change her mind.

'Doc? It's Judy Finch. I hope I'm not calling too late?'

The Judge had given her Doc Powers' mobile number, just in case.

'Oh. Hi. I erm... How'd it go this afternoon?' He sounded polite, but a little odd, even uninterested.

She hesitated, wondering if this was a mistake, but ploughed on. 'I really don't know... It was, umm, confusing.' She wanted to say intimidating, frightening, uncomfortable, nauseating. Her pride netted the words before her mouth could release them.

'Do you want to talk it through? Only I'm—'

'It's okay. Not right now,' she answered hastily, sensing his reluctance. Was this such a good idea?

There was an awkward silence then he spoke. 'How about tomorrow? Are you busy?'

'Not at all, Doc. That would be perfect. Any time to fit in with you.' Relieved.

'I'll tell you what... I haven't cooked for a while but I can actually do a mean curry. If you fancy, I could knock something up for tomorrow evening and we could chat in private at my home. Take our time.' He sounded eager, almost desperate now.

'I'd love that. I adore curry.' And any man who volunteers to cook. 'That's a date… Well not exactly.' She felt her face flush. Jesus!

She made a note of his address and hung up.

Idiot. Hardly a date!

But she felt better just knowing she had someone to share the burden. Someone who understands…

An understanding man.

She poured herself a nightcap and went to bed, the hideous vision thrust from her mind.

Leech sat alone, chewing curried beans and baked potatoes, barely tasting the food. It was nothing more than fuel to him.

Gourmets and celebrity chefs, on endless crappy TV shows. He couldn't see what all the fuss was about. And so many of the tossers in here complained about the grub. Free board and lodgings, most of them were so fucked up they didn't realise how lucky they were. Better off inside than out.

But Leech wanted out. He could taste it. Not freedom. Oh, no. He had long ago come to terms with prison life, its petty regulations and controls. After that first run-in with the Governor he realised he had a great deal more freedom inside the nick than he had ever had in the supposedly free world outside. That thought had helped him accept the minimum term of eighteen years… Still, he was ready for release now.

Funny though. He had been pushing hard for a regrading to a level D facility, an open prison, yet he realised it was a mistake the moment he got there. Too many tear-aways and no-hopers in for misdemeanours. There was no challenge. Nothing worthy of his time, nothing worth lording it over. Within a couple of weeks he was bored, asked to be transferred back here. That had shocked them.

Idiots.

No, he had achieved all he needed at Ford. He had been out on supervised day release searching for a flat to buy. And he found one in the ideal place.

Overlooking his cunt of a brother's office.

Oh yes. See you soon, big bruv.

Freedom meant something different to Leech. Inside he had plenty. Parole meant something else to him too. Something precious.

Revenge.

His jaw muscles pulsated as he chewed his food, the ill-fitting denture moving inside his mouth, a constant reminder of who put him inside.

He finished his meal, burped, and scanned the other cons, chatting, arguing, laughing in groups at the other tables.

Morons.

He picked up his plastic tray, the surface scoured clean in his quest for calories to replace those burnt in the gym, and dumped it on the counter.

On his way back to his cell he spoke to the senior officer. 'Mister Diarmud'—

Leech exaggerated the syllables, pronouncing the name Dire Mud—'Young Johnny Bloom asked to see me after dinner. Would eight-thirty be okay?'

Diarmud eyeballed him. 'You don't fool me with that Listener shit, Leech. I see right through you, you evil bastard. If I had my way, you'd die in this place. Fucking parole. You jammy git.' There was hatred tinged with resignation in his tone.

'That's as maybe, Mister Dire Mud. And no doubt I too would be twisted, bitter and cynical if I had worked in here for thirty years.' Leech was proud of himself. There was no way he would let this twat provoke him, despite many years of trying. 'But Johnny's having a hard time. You know? I'd say more but I'm sworn to secrecy.' He put his finger to his lips and shushed. 'Surely you wouldn't deny the poor lad access to a sympathetic Listener's ear… I'm sure the Governor—'

'Just piss off back to your cell. Eight-thirty. You'll be escorted.'

Leech licked his lips, letting his tongue linger as he did so, then pouted a kiss for the warder before he spun on his heels and laughed all the way back to his room.

Diarmud watched him go, shaking his head, his face screwed up as if he had just chewed a rotten maggot-ridden apple, and then been forced to swallow.

Leech waited on his bed, his cell door, like all the others, closed as part of 'lock up', the worst time for most prisoners. But not for him. Not for the Snake.

He had managed to wriggle and slither his way through the system, finally achieving the lofty status of Listener. He was one of the select few prison trustees who had been trained by the Samaritans to help other convicts who were finding time hard to do. The suicidal, the despairing, even those who just wanted to talk, to get the guilt off their chests.

The latest Governor, a bleeding-heart liberal, had been keen to promote the scheme when he first arrived some years ago. Leech had volunteered, purely for the enhanced privileges.

But now he loved it.

Not the listening. He had little time for the other cons, their endless whingeing and whining, the self-pity and weakness that lay like pus under a scab, just waiting to burst open.

Oh no. Definitely not.

But some of them did have fantastic tales to tell. Details of crimes, betrayals and evil deeds that most people could never comprehend. Truly a masterclass for him. And far better than the cinema or TV. True crime in the raw and Leech sucked it all in, absorbed it and stored it away for future reference.

The entertainment value alone was worth the effort and his learning curve about the criminal psyche had been ballistic. But more important to him was the freedom the role provided.

He had achieved the highest level of privilege for an inmate. He was allowed to wander the corridors during lock up, while the muppets in here were facing up to sixteen hours a day in cells measuring just six by ten feet. He made the most of it, and almost every day someone 'asked' to see him. And everything they discussed was in total confidence, just like the real Samaritans.

Leech's door clanged open. A ginger-mopped officer gestured to him, not even bothering to address him. Leech didn't care, he just followed, in no hurry now he was out of his cell.

He whistled again, happily mulling over the very best reason for being a Listener. They came to Johnny's cell and Leech stepped in. The boy was like a deer caught in blinding headlights, fear creasing his features at the sight of Leech, dark rings under his eyes, his anguish not registering on the warder as the door slammed shut, leaving the two convicts alone.

'Hello, Johnny boy. Sit down, son...' Leech pushed Bloom back to the bed, the hard mattress against the back of the boy's knees, forcing him to sit. 'And keep your hands open and where I can see them.'

'Please don't... Can't we just—?'

'Shush, boy. Just be good to me and open up. And no talking with your mouth full. Remember your manners!'

Leech caressed the boy's head, then held him, letting his thumbs work lightly on Bloom's eyelids, not enough to hurt, but enough to warn him and to control the movements, the leisurely rocking to and fro, dominating the young man.

Leech felt a rush as he revelled in the warmth, the wet softness, the pleasurable sensations spreading through his belly, his back, his legs.

But his mind was not on the boy.

'Suck it, you bitch... Suck it hard, my horny little Birdy.'

Saturday did not start well for Judy. She had a whispered row with her mother—they were well practised in the art by now—as Josh busied himself packing toys with the clothes his mother had put out for him, ready for the weekend with his father.

The subject matter was the same tired old one, the same as before the divorce, but now concentrated, acid burning Judy's conscience whenever her mother started.

'You don't need to work so hard, so why on earth do you?'

Her mother went at her almost the moment she entered the house. Judy had been thinking the day might be a good one and her heart slid a few inches in her breast as her mother, meaning well as usual, rubbed the raw nerve of her guilt.

'The state of you last night! Like a bloomin zombie.' Gran rarely swore and *bloomin* rated as a powerful curse in her books. 'Poor Josh needs his mother now more than ever. Why can't you just... John should provide but you're just too proud to ask. I don't know. If you insist on working, then stop putting in such ludicrous hours.'

Judy scraped a hand through her hair, felt lousy from a dreadful night's sleep. Leech had invaded her dreams, turning them to nightmares, leaving her drained from wrestling the sheets.

'I don't need this right now, Mum.'

'And Josh doesn't need an absentee mother.'

Judy let the irritation sound in her voice. 'I'm not going to waste my life and be chained to the kitchen sink.' The implication of Judy's comment seemed totally lost on Gran. She was thankful, she didn't really want to hurt her mother with the outburst and knew she would regret it if she did. She sighed. 'Times have changed, Mum.'

'Well, not for the better, if you ask me.'

'I'm not.'

The bing-bong of the front door bell brought Josh cantering out of his room, howling down the hall, the word stretched out as he yelled 'Daddeeeeee!' He scrabbled at the lock, swung the door open and bear-hugged his father's thighs, almost unbalancing the man.

Saved by the bell. Judy was rarely pleased to see John these days, but right now she was glad of the interruption, the chance of a truce with her mother as her ex-husband stood ruffling their son's hair, love plastered on his grinning chops as he gazed down at the little boy.

She stood in the hall as Josh dragged his father in, John pecking her cheek as he passed her.

'Hi, Judy.'

She allowed the familiarity, did not want Josh to feel any animosity between his parents, wanted no fuss in front of him. She detested John for it, but acquiesced for the sake of her son.

Despite how she felt after she found out about the affair. No, she thought, affair was the wrong word for it, far too gentle a euphemism for what he was doing. Shagging his secretary in his office most nights. Working late, he'd said. The lying bastard.

She smiled at him now, the veneer cracked and worn but still there, masking the pain and the strangled love that was gradually morphing into hatred.

'I'll make some tea.'

She went into the kitchen, leaving her mother with Josh and John to finish packing his things. The few moments alone allowed her to unwind, to shed some emotional baggage before her ex-husband reappeared.

Josh was jumping up and down, pogo-ing into the kitchen behind his father as Judy asked, 'Any plans for the weekend?'

She almost dropped the mug of tea she was offering her ex when Josh squeaked his excitement in reply. 'Mummy! We're going on a heckilopter. Up high over London!'

Oh, God! She eyeballed John.

'Sorry, Hon. I should've said…'

Judy fumed inwardly: Don't call me that! I'm not your honey any more. Was he deliberately winding her up today?

'Meant to call you Thursday when I got the word. Have to go to the States Monday, may be there six weeks. Maybe more.' He shrugged, his disarming smile ineffectual, the charm incapable of breaching her armour ever again. 'You know how it is.'

Bastard.

'Yes, John. I know exactly how it is. Are you taking your secretary?'

His smile evaporated at the cheap shot. Judy felt her satisfaction immediately obliterated by concern that Josh had picked up on her hostile tone. He was watching her now, still as a statue, puzzled. She forced some levity into her voice. 'So you're going on a helicopter flight? Don't forget to take—'

'To take his puffer.' John hoisted the boy up so that their eyes were level. 'We won't forget, will we Josh?' He glanced at Judy over his son's shoulder. 'And we will be careful. So don't worry.'

Josh frowned. 'Will I need to use my puffer? On the heckilopter?' Judy could feel the panic rising in him, the prospect of a perfect trip with his father no longer such a source of wonderment.

John threw Josh over his shoulder and patted his backside. 'There's nothing to worry about. You're my big boy, and we won't be going much higher than my office building. Okay?'

Judy decided his reassurance was aimed at her as much as Josh.

John carried on explaining. 'There'll be plenty of air. Not like in a plane.' His eyes probed Judy's face, questioning her as he repeated, 'Okay?'

'Okay.' She gave in before the prospect of some sort of tug of war in their love over Josh manifested itself.

And their son was really excited by the idea.

But...

Josh had been almost three years old when they first took him abroad. A short flight to Paris. And he had almost died.

He had never suffered from asthma before, but like many youngsters these days, had developed the condition at an early age. The thin air in that plane, combined with his hyper-ventilating in excitement, had prompted that first episode. By the time the hostess had popped an oxygen mask over his face Josh was blue. Judy was near hysterical, so shocked at the rapidity of the onset of the attack, the hopelessness she had felt at his distress. When the hostess asked where his inhaler was, Judy had no idea what she meant. The French doctor confirmed it was asthma when they landed. They took the train back to London later that day.

So much for a second honeymoon, she thought. And ever since then she had been 'over-protective', at least according to absentee father John, fount of all knowledge.

Arrogant prick.

Judy's thoughts stalled. Absentee. Isn't that what Mum just said about me? She shook her head, trying to dislodge that unpleasant comparison.

'Okay, let's get your things Josh. And John...' He turned to her, hovering on the threshold, keen to get away. 'Sunday. No later than eight.'

'Of course... Hon.'

She followed them to Josh's room, then the front door. Gran stood in the doorway to the lounge, hands on hips, glaring at John. She had no compunction about letting Josh know how she felt about his father.

After a long, crushing hug farewell for Josh, she closed the front door on the two men in her life, sagged back against the solid wood, and clenched her eyes shut tight.

'You're too soft on him, love. I know you think you're doing the best for your boy, but that man has proved he's irresponsible. A helicopter flight. What is he thinking? Maybe it's time you got things formalised. A court order restricting his parental visits...'

Judy sighed, slumped into a sitting position, opened her eyes and looked up at her mother, pleading, 'Mum. Not now. Please.'

After a soak in the bath, a flannel draped over her face, Judy felt refreshed. The rest of the day passed in a blur of activity. Her mother helped her do the shopping, or rather she helped Gran, as the housekeeping role largely fell to her mother. Judy paid for the shopping of course, but otherwise her contribution was to throw a few favourite treats and luxuries into the trolley as they wheeled the cart through the aisles of Waitrose.

After they'd dropped off the groceries Judy dragged her mother back out for a late lunch, but began to regret it as Gran studied the menu, clucking over the 'ridiculous' prices being charged. She insisted she could have prepared something much better for a quarter the price. Judy kept her mouth shut, nodded her agreement and thought to herself, Mum, you're missing the point.

Then they hit the shops again and Gran really came into her own. Judy loved shopping with her mother.

She may be in her sixties but she has an eye for a bargain and she knows what looks good on me.

They spent the next few hours and a couple of hundred pounds on a new outfit after Judy had tried on most of Oxford Street's stock.

'I'm whacked, love. Mind if I head home?'

They were in the cab surrounded by carrier bags full of goodies.

'Course not, Mum. We'll drop you off first.'

'Thanks, love.' Her mum squeezed Judy's thigh and added, 'So when am I going to meet him?' She then gazed at her daughter, eyes wide. If there'd been a pat of butter on her tongue it would have hardly melted. Innocence personified.

'Who?' Judy felt the unwelcome dappling rouge her cheeks. 'Doc? It's just work. Hardly a date.'

'Of course not, love.' Her mother's hand now patted her thigh. Then she started rummaging in her bag. 'These looked lovely on you.' A cheeky smirk was dimpling her jowls. 'Even if it's not a date...' She held up some diamond earrings that Judy had dismissed as too expensive, even though she had loved them. It had seemed over-indulgent so she had refrained. Gran must have bought them when she was supposedly using the loo. Crafty old dear.

'Oh, Mum. You spoil me.' Judy took the sparkling jewels, and clasped them to her chest. 'You don't miss a thing, do you?'

'Not as far my own daughter is concerned. And don't give me that nonsense about it not being a date. You like him, don't you?'

'Aw, Mother! He's a work colleague.' She was trying to sound earnest, and wondered why she had to try. 'Colin is very depressed. His wife died only a few months ago.' And he sounded lonely on the phone last night... Very lonely.

The old lady turned to stare out the window as Judy replied. When she turned back there was a tear in her eye. Gran was wistful as she spoke. 'I met your dad at work. Gave it up when I fell pregnant with your brother. Never went back, even after you were born...'

Judy did not want to talk about her brother, and was surprised at her mother telling her how she had met her father. She had always thought they met socially. Funny that she had never asked her mother about it.

'Let's not go over that, Mum. I like my job. Okay? I am not giving it up for Josh. Can we let that drop?' Judy spoke gently and put an arm round her mother's shoulders, wondering if the tears now trickling down her cheeks were for her late husband, or for her only son who had died fighting in a war over oil in Iraq.

They arrived at Gran's estate, and her mother dried her cheeks, wiping away her grief, before switching into her more familiar role of caring parent.

'You have a good night. You deserve it. Just let your hair down. And don't let work keep getting in the way of your life.' With that, nimble, if a little creaky, she hopped out the cab and slammed the door before marching off to her home.

Well, that told you, didn't it? Judy thought as the cab pulled out and headed for her home.

Doc Powers was having an equally hectic day, only he was suffering from a crippling hangover. When Judy had phoned the night before he had been sliding from grey to black as depression engulfed him. Having just got back in the saddle at work, he promptly fell off when he arrived home.

Alone. The weekend yawning before him, an abyss of black nothingness. That same abyss he had been in for much of the last three months.

As a psychiatrist he recognised the signs, knew how to handle the symptoms of numbing grief and crushing guilt. But, like many professionals in the health business, he took less care of himself than he would have of the most awkward, non-compliant patient.

So, Friday night had seen him retreat from his empty home to a local pub. He had never been to the place before and immediately started wondering why he was there. It was trendy, too bright and brash, full of well-heeled city types celebrating the end of another busy week in a haze of alcohol tinged with the promise of random sex.

He took his drink outside and watched the Thames eddying past the beer garden, his mind in turmoil, struggling to achieve some inner peace. But it would not come, so instead he supped his pint. Then another. And another. He was on his fourth beer, feeling its effects combining with the red wine from lunch, when his mobile rang.

He considered ignoring it, or cancelling the call, just content to sit and wallow in self-pity, letting the beer deepen his mood. He shrugged off the lethargy and finally answered.

At first he'd struggled to understand why Judy had called. She had made it pretty clear to him that she was up to the job. The lioness surely would not admit to weakness? Yet, what was it she had said that wrenched him out of his fug of booze and blackness? Oh yes, he remembered then: It was confusing. She'd sounded rattled and his heart had responded.

So today here he was, cleaning, tidying, shopping and cooking. The place was a tip and it was only when he woke, his head thumping and banging with every move, that he realised how much he had let things go. Why he had cancelled his cleaner, he had no idea. It was just too bad that she could not come now when he phoned. It really is something when your cleaner's schedule is too full to help you out. Oh well, he thought as he finished tidying the lounge, at least it gave him something to do today.

The only time he had stopped dead and felt the sting of hot tears was when he had dusted off the pictures of Natalie. Long blonde hair, crystal blue eyes, a snub nose, great bone structure and those beautiful bee-stung lips. Gorgeous, and to top it all, easily as bright as him.

God, he missed her. Her laughter, her radiant smile, that quirky sense of humour, always puncturing his pretensions. And, of course, her loving. He had never felt so loved before. And so in love. It had been almost obscene how happy they were.

Half an hour passed with him frozen there, weeping, thinking, remembering, suffering his loss over again, the intensity of his grief crucifying him.

Finally, he had roused himself and focussed on the future.

Tonight. Okay, I know I need to look ahead, not back.

He was under no illusion regarding the reason Judy wanted to see him. Just work, after all. Even so, her call had been something of a lifeline for him, pulling him back from the abyss.

Judy seemed sharp as a knife. And incredibly cute. How could he fail to enjoy her company? Even if their chosen topic for discussion was a prisoner convicted of multiple murder.

He finished the cleaning and stood under the shower, the hot needles stimulating his flesh, massaging his scalp, rinsing away the remnants of his hangover.

As he towelled himself dry he spotted himself in the mirror. Fat, forty-four, pasty and past it. Nothing to be depressed about then! He twitched a smile at the thought, and consoled himself. Oh well, at least I still have my mind. Though some weeks ago he'd started to wonder if he was losing that too. He wagged a finger at his naked torso as he spoke to the image in the mirror.

'You will not let yourself get in that state again.'

As he crossed the landing to his bedroom he sucked in a breath of fragrant spicy curry, the aroma wafting up the stairs, warming him inside. He wondered then, for the first time since Natalie had left him, is it possible that tonight might move him beyond neutral white to a bright sunny yellow, at last?

'Wow! Judy, you look fantastic. Have you popped by just to tell me you've changed your mind and decided to go out clubbing instead?' Doc did not mean to embarrass her as he held the door open, but realised his feeble attempt at humour had rather more than fallen flat when he saw her cheeks redden. 'Sorry. I'm such an arse sometimes. Forgotten how to treat people. Please come on in.'

Doc had ironed his best shirt and chinos but felt decidedly shabby as she brushed past him. She was a knockout.

Well, that'll set the neighbours' tongues wagging, he thought as he pushed the door to.

'I brought some wine.' Judy's voice was strong, no evidence of the fleeting embarrassment of a moment before. 'The food smells fabulous, Doc.'

He ushered her through to the kitchen, sorted out their drinks while he tried to undo the damage of his faux pas. What had he been thinking?

'I've been cleaning and cooking all day. Didn't realise what a slob I'd become since...' He bit his tongue rather than let the words dribble out. What was happening to him tonight? He had lost the art of making conversation.

'It's a beautiful house.' She crinkled her eyes at him, a smile finally emerging from the corners of her mouth. 'You must have robbed a bank to afford this place.'

As ever the subject of house values, or rather house price inflation, was the popular topic of conversation at any London social gathering.

'No. I bought it a few years back before the area became trendy. Fortunately, my book sold rather better than I, or my publishers for that matter, ever expected. It seems I managed to hoodwink a lot of people into buying it. Including you I think. Didn't you say I signed a copy for you at Cambridge?'

'I didn't buy it. I stole it from the library... And I still haven't read it!' She giggled as she teased him.

Touché.

'I doubt most of the people who bought it finished it either. *Insights into the Criminal Mind* isn't exactly bedtime reading, is it?'

'That's as may be, Doctor Powers, but I just wish I had re-read the sections on psychopaths before I went to see Leech... And I'm sorry for snapping your head off yesterday. It's just—'

'You're well used to arrogant men treating you like an inadequate girly. And I'm sorry for calling you kid. It was a particularly stupid figure of speech and certainly no indication of how I view you professionally.' He let his face smile and for the first time in months it felt natural. The sensation was good. 'So now we've got that out of the way, let's eat. I'm starving. Housework is very tiring and builds up an appetite.'

'Really? I wouldn't know.' They both laughed at that as she went on to explain, 'My mum does pretty much everything for me, I'm ashamed to say. I'm no superwoman juggling career and home life. Strange as it may seem, but I'm not genetically conditioned for it. I take after my father in that respect.' Her laughter was a joyous bubble straight from her belly. 'Actually I'm not really ashamed, though I can barely cook and have no clue where anything is in my own kitchen. Three months after we moved in I had to phone my mother to ask how to get the oven to work.'

Doc's kitchen was massive and well kitted out with stainless steel equipment and Shaker style furniture. It was straight from the pages of *House and Home* magazine.

'My mum would love this place.' She peered out the window as Doc put on the patio lights, dispelling the hint of dusk in the garden.

'I'd planned to eat inside, but we can dine on the terrace if you prefer.' The evening was pleasantly cool, and the flowers were in bloom. 'Rather stupidly I sacked my cleaner when I came out of hospital. I don't know why. Maybe I couldn't stand the thought of anyone in the house.' He realised then that Judy was the first person he'd allowed inside his home since Natalie had died. 'At least I didn't sack the gardener. If you could grab the cutlery and plates I'll bring the food.'

'It's a lovely spot, Doc. You could almost believe you were outside of the city, in the countryside. My Josh would have a field day here, literally. Your garden looks the size of a football pitch.'

Doc cast his eye round the garden, noticing it as if for the first time. It was huge, even if Judy was exaggerating somewhat. He would admit the land alone was worth a fortune here in the heart of the city. His gardener, an old boy who popped round for a few hours most days for not much more than the price of a few pints and a packet of cigarettes, had transformed it with shrub borders, flowering blooms, ornamental trees and vines. It was an oasis in a desert of concrete.

'How old is he?'

'Josh? He's six. He's with his father, which is why I am footloose tonight.'

'He's home babysitting? Your husband?' Doc was serving food and paused, mid-spoonful, as he waited for the answer he hoped was coming. He remembered then, the Judge had called her a single mother, and the way she had said *his father* had sounded as if something noxious had slipped onto her tongue. Were they divorced?

'Can I pour another?' Judy tipped some wine into both their glasses as Doc stood waiting. 'My husband is no longer my husband. Not since I surprised him one night at his office.' She swigged her wine, looked off at the lawn, avoiding Doc's eyes. 'You see, he had been working late so often I decided to go to his office to drag him out for supper. A romantic gesture on my part. A surprise.' She twirled the glass, her concentration now on the red liquid swirling, she gulped another mouthful and then her violet eyes glistened at Doc as she added, 'Surprise, huh! It certainly was... I caught him screwing his secretary on his desk. We're divorced now.'

Doc finished serving and sat, letting the moment pass as Judy composed herself. He was used to revelations from his years in psychiatry, and this was fascinating.

'You suspected him, of course?'

'Not really... This food is excellent, Doc. I'm impressed.'

'You think so? I'm a little out of practice. At many things it seems.' He grinned at her as a cool breeze floated a whiff of fragrant perfume from the flowers surrounding them, mixing with the aroma of exotic spices steaming from their bowls of curry. Doc was feeling... what exactly? Better, at least a little, he decided. 'You may not have suspected him on a conscious level, but your subconscious is an entirely different matter. Sometimes we refuse to see the obvious around us, to analyse things honestly and logically. It's a self-protective, and sometimes self-deceptive, mechanism.' Doc realised she was staring at him. Bugger. 'Sorry. Did I say something wrong? I didn't mean to lecture you or offer you therapy. Oh, Lord... I seem to be putting my foot in my mouth every time I open it tonight.'

'No. Far from it. I think you've hit the nail on the head. I should have been shocked, devastated. But I wasn't. At the time I put it down to my incredible self-control.' Her smile was sardonic. 'It was as if I was above having a tantrum, screaming and shouting. I cried a lot later, of course. I don't know. It seems I've always striven to stay in control, not show weakness.' She pursed her lips, pensive now. 'It probably comes with the territory. A woman working in a man's world. And my ex, John, was so competitive.'

'Really? How so?' This time Doc topped up their glasses.

'I didn't take much note of it at first, when we met at university. I just assumed he was pitting himself against all-comers. We married when we graduated. I went on to do my Masters and he was snapped up by a merchant bank I'd never heard of. One of the top five in the country by all accounts.' She cleared the last of her curry, wiping naan bread round the bowl before popping it in her mouth. 'Delicious. When I told him I planned a career in the civil service he actually sneered at me. Told me it was a waste of talent. I should've realised then...'

'And then Josh came along?'

'Yes. Both of us were throwing ourselves into work, desperate to impress our respective bosses. I've always wanted to be better than the rest, you know? I don't know how I got pregnant...'

She almost sprayed her wine as she sipped it, and simultaneously laughed at the apparent naivety of her remark. Doc surprised himself as he found himself laughing aloud with her, spluttering into his glass too as she went on.

'Of course, I know! What I mean is, we weren't exactly trying, and we were like ships in the night. Then Josh arrived. We settled into a routine. I was back at work within three months, much to the disgust of my mother. She wanted me to stay home, you know, and pop out a few more grandkids for her.'

'And she still makes you feel bad about it? Working mum?'

'She can't help it. She's from a different era, but I'm a double failure by those stan-dards. I couldn't even keep my husband.' She grinned and shrugged at him.

Doc's professional side, unprompted, decided she was handling it all rather well. She was a tough girl all right, but not hard. Sensitive but resilient.

'So, not Superwoman. I'm surprised. You gave me that impression yesterday.'

'Not at all. The only super woman in my home is my mum. I'm terrible. I slag her off but I have no idea what I'd do without her. No, she's my rock. She just happens to be helping me build a massive guilt complex though, and I do find that difficult.'

'About Josh, with you working full-time?' Doc lit the two giant candles at the corners of the patio as he explained. 'Keeps away the mosquitoes.'

'Exactly. For dereliction of my maternal duty. For the fact that I was too proud to bleed John dry. He can afford plenty, but I took just half the value of the family home, and Josh… John's paying for Josh's education from now until he graduates. Private of course. He also invests money each month for our little boy, who will be a very wealthy young man eventually.' She sighed, 'I don't know whether that's such a good thing but I could never afford private schooling let alone put money away for him. I'm just trying to provide a happy home for him.'

'I'm sure you're doing brilliantly.'

'Try telling that to my mother. Anyway, thanks for the therapy session, Doc.' She pouted at him. 'I feel much better, though I think it may have something to do with this excellent wine.' She held out her glass and waited while he opened another bottle. 'Oh dear. I'm going to get a little tipsy tonight. I'm a derelict mother, a failure as a wife and something of an alcoholic to boot!' She giggled as he poured another glass for her.

'A failed wife? Come off it, Judy. It was him who was screwing around. He's the guilty party, not you.'

'Ah. Except a good Catholic girl like me, well, lapsed Catholic actually, really knows how to do guilt. And if I'd been a better wife, a mixture of Katie Price and Nigella Lawson, maybe John wouldn't have strayed, would he?'

'Look, I don't know him but I know his type. And he probably would. Some men are just wired that way, the sort that count their conquests. Especially extremely competitive men. It's all to do with testosterone. At least that's one theory. The act of competing raises testosterone levels, which in turn leads to a higher sex drive and the desire to spread one's seed, as it were. It's probably in his genes.' Doc paused, thinking he was in lecture mode rather than conversing, but she was staring at him again, though this time with a warm fuzzy sort of woman look about her. Or was that just the wine? 'Sorry. I'm rabbiting on a bit—'

'No, don't stop. I don't even care if it's bullshit. I'm feeling better. You've no idea… The only other person I've talked to like this is my mother and, well—'

'She just lays yet more guilt on you.'

'Precisely. She was brought up at a time where women knew their place, didn't have career expectations, certainly didn't expect to compete with men. Women were only fit for one thing in her day. Procreation. And I certainly am not a bloody baby factory!'

Doc felt the blow to his heart, his mood burst by her words. Baby factory. Hideous images tumbled into his consciousness and he tried to cover his feelings by clearing the plates. He struggled to speak, just managing to croak out a few words. 'I'll put these in the machine and get some coffee on.' He avoided her eyes as he stumbled into the kitchen, trying to concentrate on the task he had set himself, to steady himself, the wraiths of torment threatening to engulf him.

He had been standing over the coffee machine for several minutes, frozen in time, the sludge of depression oozing through him when she spoke.

'Penny for them, Doc?'

He started, then turned to look at her. She was radiant, framed in the doorway, hair willowing around her face, concern written on her features, her forehead furrowed.

He tried to force a smile, but the muscles seemed to be paralysed. He muttered a response, his voice cracking as he spoke, 'Just give me a minute. I'll be fine.'

She studied him for a second, hesitating, clearly uncomfortable, unsure what to do. After a moment she shrugged and said, 'Okay.' Then she went back outside.

Doc, in slow motion, his movements hindered by his emotions, eventually managed to make the coffee. He tried to breathe deeply and focus his mind back on the vibrant young woman he was finding so fascinating. He prepared a tray and finally shuffled his way out to the garden.

He poured the coffee in silence, then tried to get back on track, though his light mood was lost now.

'So, without plugging into that same nerve your mother keeps prodding, have you considered working fewer hours? There are plenty of part-time opportunities these days.'

'Oh, Doc. You certainly know how to build a girl up and then knock her down again.' She gave him a brilliant smile, taking any sting out of her words.

'No, I'm serious. Ever ask yourself why you push yourself so hard? Why you try to be better than the rest? Those are your words, not mine.'

'Ambition I s'pose. Competitiveness? Wanting to be the best you can be? The usual.' She looked pensive, her chin on her palm, elbow on the table.

'Can I give you a word of advice? It's well meant and not a stab to your conscience. I think you should maybe take some time to consider it.'

'Mmm. Maybe.' He could hear she was not convinced as she diverted the conversation. 'We've hardly mentioned Leech. I'm not exactly a workaholic, am I? Alcoholic tonight, maybe.'

'This should perk you up.' Doc poured her another coffee. 'So, tell me about Leech.'

'To be honest, Doc, I felt really down yesterday after I met him. In fact I had no idea what prison was really like... It was so... oppressive. A soul destroying place. Barbaric.' Her shoulders quivered, almost imperceptibly, but Doc noticed and realised how deeply she had been affected. 'You see it on TV or at the cinema, hear the right-wingers bleating about prisons being more like hotels and so on. Yet, until you've actually been inside. Felt it. Smelt it. And then left it behind. Tried to scrub it away...' She seemed to have run out of words, floundering as she tried to describe the experience.

'Oh, I know, Judy. I've been interviewing and assessing criminals in prisons all over the UK since the year dot. I still haven't got used to it.'

'Don't tell me that, please!' She stared at him, horrified. 'I really want to do this job. Mind you, yesterday, my confidence was wrecked. And that man, Leech... Really freaked me out.' She sipped at her coffee, held the cup and saucer to her chest, relaxed back, eyes closed.

Doc watched her and found himself thinking what a catch she would make for some lucky guy. A lucky young guy. He let her sit in silence, waited for her to continue.

Eventually she put her coffee down and said, 'Frankly, I don't want to talk about Leech tonight. I feel so good, so relaxed that yesterday seems a lifetime away. Let's not spoil it?' Her eyes shone, appealing to him in both senses of the word.

'No problem. If you change your mind you've got my number. Just call me. Any time.' He surprised himself by adding, 'Please.'

She grinned, her light mood returning, then yawned. 'I should get a cab, it's late.'

'Okay, I'll call for one.' He used the kitchen phone then returned and said, 'Sorry, they reckon at least thirty minutes. Could be longer. Fancy a nightcap? Cognac, port, Cointreau—'

'Cointreau! Just a small one, please.'

He found some miniature glasses and poured.

Judy continued, 'I've had a lovely evening, Doc. It has been great to talk to an adult. I mean, someone who understands, but doesn't judge.'

It was Doc's turn to be embarrassed. 'Thanks for coming. I've really appreciated it. I'm still struggling. I tell myself to take baby steps every day. It's hard though.' He felt the tears well and excused himself to the downstairs loo.

When he returned he put on some music and they relaxed in the kitchen as Judy waited for her cab.

'I love this stuff.' Judy popped her little finger in her glass and then sucked at it.

Doc was stunned. It was one of the most erotic things he had witnessed, yet she seemed oblivious, almost childlike in her appreciation of the rich liqueur. She was quite something.

The doorbell rang, and he walked her to the taxi. She surprised him again when she said, 'I've not had food that good at a dinner party for years. Everyone seems to be into pasta and sun-dried tomatoes these days. I'd like to return the favour, but please say so if you'd prefer not, okay? I won't be offended.' She was rushing her words, slurring as the booze tripped her tongue. 'My family, my mum and Josh, well, we are going to Brighton next Saturday or Sunday. Would you like to join us?' She squinted at him in the yellow light of the streetlamps, then backed herself into the cab, eyes on him, searching for a reaction. 'No pressure. I'll understand if you prefer not, after all, it's not most men's idea of a fun day out, but I thought…' She tailed off, her expression questioning him, sounding him out.

For some reason Doc's stomach swooped, a pleasant sensation although unsettling, and he found himself beaming at her.

'I'd be absolutely delighted. I'd love to meet Josh and your mother. Thanks, Judy.' He leaned into the cab, grinning as he answered.

She reached forward, grabbed his neck with her palms and brushed a chaste kiss on his cheek.

'No. Thank you, Doc.' She released him, pulled the door to and disappeared into the night.

Doc stood there for some time, bathed in the golden glow of the street lights, a soppy grin creasing his face.

He looked through the window, watching his brother playing with their new puppy, Sam. Shaun was in his bedroom, peering down as Peter teased the dog into a frenzy of yelping and yapping. Peter was not being gentle, and Shaun was uneasy, jealousy snaking through his insides, coiling into a knot that threatened to rupture his guts.

The labrador bounced around the garden, tail flapping, trying to reach the stick. Peter held it a few inches from the dog's nose, occasionally clouting Sam on the head with it before pulling it just out of reach again.

Then the dog, in its excitement, nipped his brother's hand. But somehow Shaun felt the teeth sinking into his own thumb, felt the surge of madness and anger at the puppy.

The need to punish. To hurt back.

He saw Peter react, furious, and anticipation crushed Shaun's insides. He knew what was going to happen.

Peter screamed at the puppy, grabbed it by the scruff of the neck, shaking it like a baby's rattle. Shaun wanted to run downstairs, but could not. His feet were welded to the floor. His mouth opened to shout at his baby brother, but no noise came.

Peter tossed the squealing pup into the kettle barbeque and slammed the lid on it. He disappeared into the garden shed and Shaun, anticipating the horror to come, started quaking uncontrollably.

Peter reappeared, a bottle of lighter fluid in his hand. He danced a little jig around the barbeque, Sam's muffled barking testament to the puppy's confusion and panic, Peter's voice joining in, wailing with excitement, nothing recognisable as words, nothing human.

But was it Peter? Shaun was confused. He could feel himself dancing wildly yet his feet remained stuck to the ground. He was just an observer. Wasn't he?

Peter poked the nozzle through one of the holes in the kettle lid, squirting liquid over Sam, the yelping and yapping increasing in pitch as the fuel stung the dog's sensitive nose and eyes.

Shaun panted, his head light, not able to do a thing to help, raw emotion locking him in its grip.

He watched as Peter dropped a lighted match through the hole.

'Nooooooo...' Shaun was finally free, his feet whisking him down the stairs, Sam's screaming agony goading him on, telling him he was already too late.

Peter was leaping round the barbeque, manic features contorted into a wicked grin, a sickening display of his true inner nature.

Shaun pulled the lid off and Sam leapt at him, but he fumbled and the dog crashed to the ground. The brown fur was blackened and smoking, Sam's breath was blue vapour, his lungs seared and ruined. The squealing finally ceased as Sam lay broken and scorched on the concrete patio.

'What's up, Shaun? Thought you liked hot dogs!'

Peter's laugh was ugly and tore into Shaun, stirring him to action. He stepped towards his brother, grabbing the lighter fluid with one hand, his brother's throat with the other, not sure whether to choke him or burn the tormenting bastard. But the younger boy's laughter dissolved into tears, driven by horror and shock.

Peter was hysterical now, yelling at him. Accusing him of killing the dog.

Shaun was confused. He hadn't killed Sam.

Peter bellowed, his high-pitched voice boosted by fury and pain, an unearthly sound that deafened Shaun. 'Daddy! Daddy! Shaun burnt Sammy!'

He let his brother go. The boy was pointing at him, accusing, tears streaming down his grubby cheeks.

Then Shaun wondered if Peter was right as he re-lived squirting the fluid over Sam's head. Dropping the match. The sensation of power. Of life and death.

He shook off the memory, tried to visualise his brother doing it, tried to convince himself he was innocent.

He turned as he heard his father roar his name. The flat of a massive hand connected with his face and hurled him to the ground. His father bent down and checked the charred remains of their pet as Peter hopped around, pointing at Shaun, repeating over and over, 'Daddy, he burnt Sammy!'

His father gave Shaun a disgusted glare before he picked up the distressed lad, cooing to him to calm down.

The boy's face scrunched into a grin. But it was no longer Peter staring back at him over his father's shoulder. It was his own son.

Billy!

Mouth contorted, sneering at him.

Shaun screamed.

His father turned—but it wasn't his father. It was Peter, now the eighteen-year old convicted of killing their parents, his face swollen and front teeth missing from Shaun's blow. He hugged Billy to him, one hand on the boy's throat, squeezing. Billy's face was puce and his eyes bulged as Peter said, 'You're the guilty one, Shaun.'

Shaun heard himself screaming again as he sat bolt upright, found himself in his bed, arms outstretched, sweat cascading, eyes wide and unfocussed.

Suzie called to him, her voice soft. 'It's okay, honey. You're here with me.' Her arms wrapped around him, her head nuzzling his face.

Shaun slumped against her, his pyjamas saturated, their duvet tangled round his legs.

'God almighty. I haven't had that nightmare since I was a kid... Sam...' He croaked, his throat crusty and dry.

Suzie just held him, caressed his neck with her lips. 'It's okay.'

'I didn't want to tell you just yet...' He moved his own lips closer to her, whispering into her ear.

'What..?' She continued kissing him, a butterfly brushing his throat, calming him as ever.

'It's Peter.' He felt her go rigid, her soothing actions ceased. A beat passed, then she pulled her head back to peer at him in the half light.

'What about him?' Her tone was flat, no emotion, but he knew how she felt about his little brother.

They never mentioned Peter. To them he really had died eighteen years before. And gradually the nightmare memories had subsided—for them both.

Until that letter arrived.

'They're considering him for parole... I'm sorry, babe. I just hope they refuse him.'

He could see the memories replaying on her face. And fear there too. He thought how weak she was. He wanted to push her away but stopped himself.

Suzie's head collapsed forward onto his shoulder. She was silent, her hot breath erratic on his neck, mingling with the soft, warm trickle of her tears.

Shaun spoke into the night, more to himself than his distressed wife. 'Don't worry. If that sick bastard comes anywhere near us, I will kill him. I swear it.'

The Hemson Banking Corporation helicopter hove into view and Josh bounced with anticipation, the steady whump of the rotor blades thrilling his little body.

John patted his son's shoulder and told him to stand still and wait for the machine to land. Their view was already spectacular, the day had turned out fine and the cobalt sky was flecked with white fluff balls of cloud. John felt his own excitement soar to meet the aircraft as it hovered and sank to the rooftop. The helipad was on the thirty-third level of the Hemson UK head office, and the express lift would whisk you to this level only if you were in possession of an exclusive Managing Director's pass.

Managing Director. John wondered at the stupidity that allowed his firm to have seventy-two MDs when most companies got by with just the one. But the nature of his role demanded a title commensurate with the status of the people he dealt with. The movers and shakers, the deal makers and breakers, individuals who could mobilise hundreds of millions of pounds to further the advance of capitalism.

And right now John was enjoying one of the benefits of his stellar career in the company. The machine's engines wound down, the man-made wind buffeting them subsided and then ceased.

'Can we get in now, Daddy?' He tugged at John's hand.

'Come on then, son. Before the pilot goes without us.'

He watched as the pilot showed Josh around the aircraft, the young tyke jabbering enthusiastically as he went, then John helped him clamber aboard. They were seated in the row behind the pilot who squeezed an arm between the two front seats to pass them headsets and throat microphones so that they could all talk when the machine was thundering through the air. Then he started to give them a safety briefing as he helped them strap in. John tuned out, finding himself thinking about Judy and wondering what she was doing for male company these days. He was sure she missed him, but was too proud to say so.

The pilot turned back to the front and said, 'Don't be alarmed when I start her up. She's supposed to be noisy. And if she didn't vibrate she'd probably break apart and we wouldn't want that, would we?'

Josh pulled a face at that so John wrapped an arm round his shoulders, trying to reassure the boy with a squeeze. 'I think our pilot thinks he's a comedian.'

'That's right, sir. Eavesdropper too. You can hear me and speak back to me, as well as talk to each other. Except when I mute your mics when I talk to air traffic control. Which I am about to do, so here goes...'

The pilot's hands were flicking switches, adjusting dials and checking controls as he sought permission to get airborne and follow his flight plan.

Josh's mouth hung open as he watched, and even John was impressed by the man's professionalism.

The motors whined and the blades took a lazy turn, then another, accelerating into a blurred disc. The noise was deafening as the big machine lifted off, and Josh's fingers were rigid and white as he dug his nails into his dad's thigh. The perspex bubble surrounded them, and John experienced his first taste of vertigo as he watched the office roof disappear below them, the view through the floor unnerving him. He thought he'd left his stomach somewhere between the roof and the helicopter as he exclaimed, 'Oh, my God!'

Josh's fingers delved deeper as if prompted by the fear in his father's voice.

The machine lurched, the nose tilting down, giving John the sickening sensation of hanging just by his straps, London's Docklands spread beneath him. Then they swooped down towards the Thames, the machine rolling and turning, gathering speed.

'We have to go quite low here, gents, otherwise a jumbo heading for Heathrow might give us all a haircut.'

John wanted to puke. He forced his head back, drew in a rancid gasp of air, tasted the tang of kerosene seeping through every pore of the machine. He felt worse and groaned. This was a nightmare.

Then he remembered Josh, whose rigid digits had bruised his flesh. Enough! He would tell the pilot to land immediately.

And that was when the realisation hit him. Oh shit! Josh's puffer was in the car. Worried, he inspected his son's face, fearing the worst, but Josh had a strange expression, a beatific smile that John had never seen before. He groaned. 'I might've known you'd love this, Josh.' But Josh was rapt in the wonder of the flight, the sights he had never experienced in his short life.

John thought back to their first trip to Alton Towers a few months before. His boy wanted to ride on everything and only Josh's diminutive height had prevented them from experiencing the biggest rides, saving John's gall from erupting on the most vicious rollercoasters. He leaned back, closed his eyes and, for the first time in years, actually considered praying.

Josh, face blooming with wonder, turned to his dad for a moment, shouting above the din, the words exploding in John's earpiece. 'Dad, look! It's the Thames Barrier and the ships. This is brilliant!'

'Mmm,' was all he could manage.

'We can take a closer look if you like, young sir.'

'Yaay!'

His son was in ecstasy as the machine dipped and banked, but John's free hand clutched at his harness, the other arm neither giving nor receiving comfort as Josh wriggled against it.

They were low now, skimming the water, Josh whooping with joy as they passed below the mast of a ship, seemingly close enough to reach out and touch it. The pilot, thus encouraged, jinked, climbed and swooped again. Josh clapped his hands, noises and words mingling as his excitement sirened ever louder.

The pilot steadied the machine and levelled off as he spoke to the air traffic controllers. Then he banked sharply, throwing John's full weight against the Plexiglas. John, terrified already, nearly lost control of his bowels at the thought of a mere quarter inch of perspex separating him from a few hundred feet of nothing and the estuary below.

'We're heading north now. I can't go any lower as the birds are breeding and we don't want to scare them too much.'

Scare them? What about me? John's panic was mounting. He'd had enough. He wanted to go home. He kept his eyes closed and tried to pretend he was somewhere else. He stayed like that for several minutes.

And then the world turned upside down. The aircraft jolted and heaved upwards, a rapid drumbeat thumping against the airframe. He opened his eyes in terror, the aircraft was darker now. They were flying through a flock of geese and the canopy was peppered with bodies and smeared with their blood and guts. The pilot had spotted the danger, responded by hauling the nose up, a standard manoeuvre designed to intimidate the birds into thinking the helicopter was a predator, forcing them to fly below, but too late. The drumming and thudding continued for no more than a few seconds but it was enough.

The vibration increased in intensity as the aircraft tried to throw off the birds, like a dog shaking its fur to shed water. The machine shrieked in protest, the rotors damaged by the impact of so many carcasses.

Josh screamed, but the pilot was speaking, his calm clipped tones cutting into John's mind, driving home the seriousness of their predicament. 'MAYDAY! MAYDAY! MAYDAY! Three POB, emergency landing…'

There were more words but John's panic escalated and obliterated them as the helicopter bucked like a stallion on heat. His teeth rattled and his vision jumped so much he could not focus. He heard the pilot yelling 'BRACE! BRACE! BRACE!' and tried to get his brain to function, to respond in this alien environment where the horizon swung by him, the world plunging, rotating and disorienting him. Vomit sprayed from his mouth as he struggled to remember the emergency brief and realised he had no idea what to do.

All he could think about was Josh. He held him tight with his arm, crushing the boy to him, hoping to protect him from the worst. And then he realised, to top it all, Josh was having a full blown asthma attack. Josh had his head between his knees, but his frantic gasps for air were audible through John's headset.

The pilot was good. He wrestled the machine to the ground, delivering them and his aircraft safely through what he would later describe as a 'controlled crash'.

It did not feel very controlled to John. His butt, spine and neck screamed with pain from the mind-numbing impact, and for a moment he wondered if they were really down or whether he still might die. He sucked in a lungful of air and immediately became conscious of the stench of puke, his stomach contents having pebble-dashed the interior. Even the pilot's helmet had not escaped unscathed.

The pilot was unfazed, his hands flashed across the controls, flicking switches, probing, checking. The rotors slowed and stopped. Silence. Then he spoke, his voice showing no tension, as professional and calm as it had been when they were being given the pre-flight brief.

'Okay, sir. We can get out now if you would care to unstrap yourself and your son.'

'Wait!'

The pilot turned at John's voice, immediately checking his precious cargo and finding something there that finally registered alarm on his face. He grabbed the first aid kit and yelled at John as he shoved it at him.

'Get out. Bring this. And follow me.'

He hopped down, wrenched the door open, unstrapped Josh and threw the little lad over his shoulder. He then started jogging some fifty yards across the sucking mudflats, away from the machine, stopping on an elevated patch of grass.

John, his senses still in turmoil from the crash, waded through the marshy ground, lugging the box, feeling as if he was in a nightmare. He could not turn his head, the muscles of his neck flamed with pain as he tried, and his back, arms and legs felt as if they had been beaten with clubs. Then the urgency of the situation hit him as the pilot called out.

'I need that kit. Now!'

John pushed himself forward, and dropped down beside them. He called to Josh, stroked his forehead, tried to soothe him. Josh's eyes bulged, the sinews in his scrawny neck visibly straining as he urged his lungs to suck in air. His chest jerked as he choked, his face turning blue.

The pilot ripped the oxygen mask out of the box, fitted the bottle to it, and, while covering Josh's face asked John, 'What's the matter with the boy? Was he hurt?' The pilot tore Josh's tee shirt at the neck, trying to see what the problem was. John said nothing so the pilot turned his attention to him. 'I need some help here, sir.'

'Er. He's… asthmatic. We forgot his inhaler.' John was overwhelmed with shame and guilt for putting his son's life at risk, but worse was the liquid fear freezing his heart at the thought that Josh might die. The oxygen was having little effect.

The pilot stared hard at John for a second longer then got back to the task at hand. He scrabbled in the first aid box for a hypodermic, cracked an ampoule and drew liquid into the syringe.

'I have nothing for asthma but I do have adrenalin… I think it might help him. Would you rather, sir?' The pilot proffered the syringe to John who could only shake his head, the nightmare now complete.

The pilot slid the needle into Josh's arm and squeezed the fluid home. It seemed to take an eternity to John, but Josh's breathing eased, the frantic gasping subsiding to a rasping wheeze.

'I've done all I can for him, let's hope he'll be okay now. We'll get him to hospital soon. Either the Air Ambulance or Search and Rescue will have a chopper here in no time. We're miles from the nearest road, I'm afraid.'

Oh Christ. Not another bloody helicopter, please!

Doc Powers woke to the familiar drum tattoo of a stinking hangover after a night of welcome oblivion. Last night he had been as close to happy as his fragile mind allowed, and he had continued the celebration after Judy left. The bottle of Cointreau was now empty.

He rolled out of bed and made it to the en suite just in time for the retching heave of brown, stinging sludge that erupted from his throat. He hung onto the porcelain bowl, on his knees, as if enacting some sort of profane penitence.

It was only fair. This punishment, he decided. Natalie was still too large a part of his life, his anguish, to allow an interloper. And he didn't deserve happiness, did he? He was responsible. He should be miserable. What had made him think he could somehow snap out of it?

Judy.

You stupid old man. She must be twelve or fourteen years younger than you!

Interesting. Bright. Articulate. Drop dead gorgeous. Yet self-deprecating. She had everything.

Except her husband.

But Doc could see no future in a relationship with Judy. She was just being kind. Was surely not interested in romance. Just friendship. A colleague to develop as a pal. Nothing more.

He heaved again, scalding his throat. Almost dry now. Slobber, tinged with bile, drooled into the pan.

I'm disgusting. I allowed the booze to kill the love of my life and now... I'm trying to kill myself with it.

Another wrench as his gut spasmed. Nothing. Just pain as his own muscles tried to tear his insides apart.

Maybe I deserve to die. I'm used up.

He staggered to the sink and grasped the taps for support, the sledgehammer in his skull pounding his brain to jelly. He struggled upright, tried to brush his teeth without gagging. He saw himself in the mirror. Eyes red and swollen, his face grey, sagging and creased, advertising his unhealthy inner state.

He stumbled back to his bed, collapsed onto it, and immediately regretted the action as the drumbeat crescendoed inside his cranium. He squeezed his eyes tight shut, sparking stars in the blackness.

Therapy. I need therapy. Or maybe just a friend to share the burden with.

He had wanted to talk to the Judge. In fact, the Judge had called him ten or fifteen times in the weeks after he had been discharged from hospital, bones mended but his life shattered. He could not face talking to anyone, and the Judge's voice sounded more concerned with each message he'd left on the voicemail.

Doc had been drunk. Every day. And although he'd seen the weight fall off in hospital, he had been drinking so much since, he was now fat.

He had been confused. Was still confused.

He knew the theory of talking through his grief and depression, to help him work through it, come to terms with his life. Even so, he could not bring himself to bare his soul to his friend, the Judge. Instead he had lied, had told his boss he was ready to come back to work...

Yet, now there was Judy. Maybe, just maybe, given a little time, he could share the true extent of his pain with her. Tell her everything.

His eyes flickered open, found the photograph of Natalie by the bed.

I'm so sorry, darling.

There were no photos of Natalie in the kitchen and he had deliberately kept Judy away from the lounge, not wanting her to see the pictures of his wife in there, to give her an opportunity to probe, to tug at the tattered edges of his raw wounds.

Or... Or just maybe he did not want Judy to see this other woman, the one whose life was suffused with his.

Sorry. Sorry. Sorry.

And then it started. The clacking inside his mind, as if some psychotic projectionist was tormenting him, flicking through the horror film, full colour, wide screen.

The truck, surging into his car. The nearside door collapsing in. The dashboard airbag exploding into an ineffectual safety cushion for Natalie. Her head, bouncing off the canvas balloon, ricocheting into the distorted door post, her skull shattering, blood spurting, showering him. Her blue eyes, staring at him. Dead. Unseeing.

Now in close up. Closer. Closer still. Her crumpled, lopsided face filling the screen of his inner world, shredding his heart. He howled as the vision faded to black.

He reached over, clutched her photo to his chest, then wept, wondering yet again whether he was losing his mind.

Judy also woke up on Sunday with a pounding brain. She managed to lever herself out of bed and perform her patent hangover cure—she swallowed a fresh raspberry smoothie with some paracetamol and then purged her body with a four mile run.

She almost gave up just a few hundred yards from her home, had to stop and bend double to let the nausea pass, the smoothie close to making an unscheduled reappearance.

I will not be beaten.

She straightened, forced herself to keep moving, the slap of her feet on the pavement jolting her aching brain until, gradually, as she knew it would, the pain eased and she started to feel alive again.

By the time she returned to her flat the last traces of the hangover were gone. She was delighted to hear Gran pottering in the kitchen, and even more so to smell the heavenly aroma of fresh coffee welcoming her as she pushed open the front door. Her mother was busy stuffing a chicken when Judy pecked her on the cheek, grateful that today's lunch was already on its way.

'Hi, Mum, thanks for coming over. I've got stacks to do today…'

'Oh, Judy! Please tell me you aren't working. It's Sunday. I thought we could have lunch together and just relax, maybe have a nice chat.' Gran returned to the task of preparing the bird for the oven, plunging her hand inside the carcass in a way that made her daughter cringe.

'I will never be able to do that. It looks so disgusting.' Her mother tutted as Judy spoke, but said nothing. 'Anyway, what's to chat about?' She was teasing Gran now. 'We talk every day, Mum. Anything in particular? Have you something on your mind? A problem I can help you with. Haven't you been to church this morning? Surely that's the best place for confession.'

The stuffing was almost complete, but Gran turned, hands smothered in sage and onion, and waggled a greasy finger at her.

'Don't be so cheeky, madam. I have nothing to confess…' She grabbed the bird and jammed the last of the mixture into it, none too gently. 'I just wondered if you had something you wanted to tell me.'

'I already told you.' Judy fished a raw carrot from a pan on the stove, crunched it as she said, 'It was work. Just business with a colleague, that's all.' She munched another carrot.

'Humph. Leave those, they're for lunch.' There was a touch of petulance in her tone as she huffed, 'Well, I must say, if it really was just business then why did we spend four hours finding you the perfect outfit?'

Gran slapped butter on the bird's pallid skin and Judy was sure her mother wished it was her wayward daughter's behind she was slapping instead.

'You know me, Mum. Work is sooooo important to me. Isn't that what you always say?' Her mother washed her hands, obviously frustrated now. Judy could not resist a final teaser. 'I'm off for a shower,' she said, and then tossed more words over her shoulder as she headed for the bathroom. 'Oh, I almost forgot to mention. Doc, my work colleague, is joining us for our family trip to Brighton next weekend.' With that she waltzed away, and though she could not see her mother's face, she knew the sweet old dear would be open-mouthed with surprise and delight. And totally beside herself with frustration and curiosity.

Well, let her wait, Judy thought as she stripped. The nosy minx!

As she stood under the powerful spray, alternating hot and cold to invigorate her skin, she allowed her mind to wander back to last night. Yes, she had been a little tipsy, in fact rather more than that. And she knew it was time to leave when she started imagining taking Doc by the hand and leading him to the bedroom…

God! What was she like? She started scrubbing herself with a loofah, the sensation bordering on discomfort as she turned her skin pink. It felt good.

What was it about Doc that she found so attractive? She certainly was not on the rebound. It was well over two years since she had split with John. And she had been with a few men since, though they were more akin to one night stands in terms of the depth of relationships. The longest she had managed to stick with any of them was four weeks, before she gave up on the emotional dead zone that was an estate agent called Robert. A man even more in love with himself than John had been, a muscle-bound buffoon who thought he was a gift from the Almighty sent to be admired and appreciated by the inferior species—women.

Dickhead.

It was after that disaster had run its brief and inevitable course that she gave up on men. They were just such immature, self-absorbed arseholes. Maybe it was because she was targeting men in their thirties, singletons, many of whom had never settled and probably never would.

Which may be the reason why Doc seemed so different to her normal mating fodder. Judy mulled that over as she stepped from the shower and towelled herself down. The full-length mirror displayed her in all her glory. She approved of what she saw. Still petite, but well-rounded where it mattered and with no cellulite or stretch marks. Not too shabby, she thought. Surely a man like Doc would be able to appreciate her. She dressed and analysed her feelings for him, again wondering what it was about him that she found so damned attractive.

Physically he was no specimen. Not gross, but certainly chubby. Cuddly, even.

Yes, cuddly.

He was intelligent too, exceptionally so. That went without saying. And she knew he had a great sense of humour, even if his laughter lines no longer seemed to fit his face…

She could see he was trying his best to amuse her last night, but his few attempts had fallen flat. Yet she knew he could make people laugh. She remembered his lecture at Cambridge. A very dry subject delivered with a sparkling wit that turned education into entertainment, surely the very best way to learn.

He was a truly interesting man. Deep too. She paused as she brushed her hair and then spoke aloud to her mirror twin. 'But it's his eyes, isn't it?'

She carried on thinking, sweeping the brush through her damp tresses, letting the hair air dry in the summer warmth.

Doc's eyes, the liquid sorrow not marring their beauty, if anything, enhancing it, baring the man's sensitivity, his capacity for love and pain.

Bambi!

She had seen it the moment they met for lunch and her heart reached out to him…

Then he'd called her kid!

She had erupted at that, though not purely at the condescension it implied. No, she had realised last night it was an over-reaction based on something deeper, her own desire to be viewed as a woman, not as some girl, too young for him.

Which is, she thought, quite possibly a problem in Doc's mind.

Along with the ghost of his wife.

She knew that would be the biggest challenge, but she decided she was willing to play the long game. Be patient. Play for keeps.

The man was so perceptive, a great listener. Well, she supposed, he is a psychiatrist, which may also explain why she found it so easy to share her secrets with him.

But, best of all, she had seen something in him when she asked him, her words propelled by alcohol, to come out with them next weekend. She had gambled, hoping he would not be put off by the family aspect.

Yes, he was different alright. Nothing like that jerk Robert and the rest of them. Oh, they had wanted her body, but ran a mile at the prospect of being involved with the product of it.

Whereas Doc had reacted with yearning and deep sorrow pooling in his eyes when she had used the term *baby factory*. She knew, in that moment, he wanted kids. So, she wondered, why did he not have any with his wife?

Well, she thought, as she finished dressing, I'll just have to find out. What had he said? *Baby steps.* That was it.

That was exactly what she needed to take. Little steps. Take it slowly. But she had already made her mind up. He was the man for her. So he had better watch out because, when Judy Finch set her mind on something or someone, she would not be denied.

'Coffee, love?' Gran was leaning against the kitchen sink, already sipping a cup.

'Yes please, Mum. I'll grab it and sit in the lounge. Get my work done. How long before lunch is ready?'

Her mother was crestfallen, and Judy could see she was bursting with questions and miffed that her 'coffee' ploy had not had the desired effect.

Gran muttered, voice sour, 'Two hours, if that's okay. I'll pop the chicken in now.'

Judy's resolve, not to discuss Doc until lunch, almost slipped as she said, 'Perfect… A bit like the new man in my life.' Gran almost dropped the chicken as she lifted the tray, her face a picture. Judy relented. 'Don't worry. You'll hear all about it over lunch. Can you wait that long?' She chuckled as she took her coffee to the lounge.

With the door closed she knew there would be no interruptions—the house rule to allow her the freedom to work at home—but when she pulled out her briefcase, a thread of dread wormed through her. Her good mood dissipated. Her plan was to listen to the tape, make notes and then type out her report. It would be a good few hours work. Not a problem for her, she was conscientious, but the thought of listening to Leech's voice in her own home made her shudder.

The man had spooked her badly, yet she was committed to producing an impartial document, just as Doc had ordered. Despite her unease and her own qualms about the man's attitude, she felt obliged to put Leech's case across in the best light possible. She pulled out her notes and, sparse as they were, she determined to write the report from memory with just those as prompts.

She justified it easily, she had done the same thing many times before, and anyway, she knew Leech's words would echo in her mind without her having to suffer the experience over again.

Decision made, she flipped open her laptop and got straight down to it. By the time Gran's golden roast chicken was adorning the kitchen table she was confident the report had covered everything necessary. She was comfortable too with the thought that Leech would have a chance to review and amend it before the hearing, if he felt it necessary. She doubted he would need to.

So, satisfied, she joined her mother and they spent an enjoyable lunch discussing men in general, and one man in particular, as well as gossiping and putting the world to rights.

Then the phone rang and Judy's day was ruined.

'Now don't panic, love.' John's tone quaked as he spoke, rattling her immediately. She did start to panic as he went on, 'The helicopter crashed. It was a nightmare. Don't worry though, we're both okay.'

'Crashed?' She had finally found her voice, and heard its shrill urgency as she spoke. 'Oh my God, where's Josh? How is he? Is he hurt?' Gran appeared at her elbow and tried to listen as John replied.

'He'll be fine. He's in for observation. He had a very bad seizure from the shock. Had to have adrenalin.'

'Seizure? Jesus Christ! Where is he now? I want to see him.' She felt Gran put a steadying arm around her shoulder, visions of Josh having a fit on the flight to Paris blinding her, her legs trembling as she envisaged the worst.

'St Thomas's. They say he'll be kept in overnight. Should be home in the morning.'

'I'm on my way.' She slammed the phone down, steadied herself and said to Gran, 'Can you get some things for Josh. John says their helicopter crashed... The stupid, stupid bastard. I'll call us a cab.' She punched in the numbers, anxiety and fear eating her from the inside.

Thirty minutes later Judy and Gran arrived to find John waiting in reception. His neck was in a brace, the brown cushion forcing his chin up, giving him an even more supercilious air.

Seeing him fuelled Judy's anxiety, already bubbling furiously in the cab, and it boiled over as she hissed at him. 'Tell me what happened. You tell me the truth right now. Is he hurt at all?'

'He's very shaken up and a bit bruised, but calm down. No bones broken. Okay, okay!' He stepped back as Judy shook her fist in his face.

'What happened?' She spoke through gritted teeth.

'The pilot was taking us on a tour round the Thames estuary, flying like a lunatic in my opinion. I'm beginning to think I might sue.' He gazed at her, pathos incarnate. She knew him too well, knew he wanted her to sympathise with him. She was having none of it.

'Are you saying the pilot was dangerous?' Judy did not for one moment believe that. She sensed he was trying to deflect her.

'Well, not exactly. But we crashed, didn't we?' He sniffed, started rubbing his neck brace. 'And I'm more hurt than Josh!'

'Good. You bloody deserve it. Now, for the third and last time, WHAT HAPPENED?' She let go, the words jetting forth, filling the air like a sonic boom. She ignored the nurses gawping at her as if she was a mad woman. Her focus was on the man she was starting to despise and her outburst finally elicited a response.

'We hit a flock of geese. It was awful. I've never been so scared in my life.' He paused, but the sympathy he so transparently desired was not forthcoming. He continued. 'The pilot did his best to avoid them, but they just came out of nowhere. They smashed into the screen, the rotor blades, some even got sucked into the engine.' His hands were palsied as he spoke, face ashen, and Judy felt a momentary twinge of sympathy, but saved it, stored it up for the one person who deserved it. Her son. And, she thought, if this shit had not taken Josh flying in the first place...

Her stomach churned as she wondered how her little boy must have felt. He was just six. If John, a fully grown man, was affected this badly, how was her son coping?

John was floundering, groping for words. 'It was dreadful.' His voice cracked and tears glistened, but Judy could see the outpouring of emotion was focussed on himself. The selfish prick was not thinking about Josh. And he was hiding something. Of that, she was certain.

John went on, Judy's silence goading him. 'We were spinning and bucking. I thought we were dead...' The tears actually flowed now, but she felt nothing for him except anger.

Gran piped up, not letting him fob them off. 'Go on.' Urgent. Demanding. Cold.

'The pilot was fantastic.' Judy made no comment on this contradiction, let it slip by as her suspicions mounted as to what had caused Josh's seizure. 'Cool as ice. He managed to drop the helicopter into some marshland. Saved us from drowning in the estuary. And it was soft ground... A really hard crash landing would have shattered my spine. The man deserves a medal. As it is, the whiplash is killing me.' He smiled ruefully.

Nothing.

Four angry eyes were on him and he squirmed as he finally started to spill the beans. 'The pilot got us out, but by then Josh was...'

He was reluctant to say the words so Judy spurred him on. 'For fuck's sake! Just tell me!' She didn't care what her mother thought right now, though she heard her sharp intake of breath expressing disapproval at the expletive.

'He almost died from the asthma attack. The doctor said it was the pilot's quick thinking that saved him. Fortunately he had adrenalin in the emergency kit. Thank God for that. Even if he'd had his inhaler—'

'What? He didn't have his puffer?' She knew it. The useless bloody idiot!

'No.' Again that pathetic smile. 'Josh forgot it.'

'YOU FORGOT IT!' Judy wanted to punch him right then, but screamed the words at him instead, their force throwing John back a step.

'Even if he'd had it the doctor said he would've probably needed the injection. It's not my fault, for Christ's sake! It was a bloody accident. And I almost died too!'

His voice whined into her brain and Judy, who had never raised a hand to Josh, who believed that violence adds nothing to the sum total of humanity, lost it. She slapped his face with such ferocity the explosive crack stopped two passing nurses in their tracks as they stared at the spectacle she was making. She didn't give a damn. All the hurt, the pain, the agony of guilt and failure that represented her marriage to this fool, surged within her, combining to power a blow that almost knocked her ex-husband to the floor.

Judy heard her mother mutter, 'About time too.'

She was still too furious to speak and watched in satisfaction as John reeled, whimpering, holding his neck, obviously blinded by the pain from the injury already there, now rekindled and accentuated by her ferocious smack.

He then made the mistake of filling the silence. He stammered out, 'You... heartless... bitch!'

The second blow, a roundhouse punch she had learnt in self-defence classes at university, finished the job the first strike had started. He stumbled back, hit the wall and slumped to the floor.

Judy stood over him, seething, refusing to scream at him, just letting forth the words she wished she had said when she caught him rogering his secretary.

'You are a selfish, arrogant, insensitive, thoughtless, feckless bastard. You are an unfit husband, and now I realise you are an unfit father. You'll be hearing from my lawyer on Monday—'

'Oh come off it, Judy. I'll be in America tomorrow—'

'I don't give a damn!' She heard nothing from Gran this time, sensing her mother's approval now. 'If you cared about your son more than your precious career, you'd cancel the flight.' She leaned right down into his face, and he actually flinched, holding his hands out to fend her off. 'You are pathetic. I wish you were dead. You bastard.'

With that Judy marched to the startled receptionist and, in a perfectly modulated voice said, 'I'd like to see my son now, please.'

A nurse led Judy and Gran through to a private room. At least that was *one* thing she could rely on John for. Josh was sitting, propped up in bed, watching an old Shrek movie. Her heart lurched at the sight of him, the green translucent oxygen mask on his face, his eyes dark in their sockets, face deathly pale. But when he saw his mum, he smiled, and relief washed through her.

'The oxygen isn't really necessary, Mrs Finch—'

'Ms Finch. We're not married any more. Thank God.' Judy's words were out before she realised, breaking her vow not to let Josh know what she really felt about his father. Oh well. Maybe for the best after all...

'I'm sorry. I just assumed... Well, anyway, we can pop this off for now. It's just a precaution.' The nurse plucked the mask off Josh's face and let it drop to his chest. 'It's there if you need it Josh, but you can give Mummy a big hug and kiss if you want.' She patted his head. 'And remember young man. No smoking!' She laughed at her own joke, but pointed at the oxygen bottles by his bed and added to Judy and Gran, 'Not a good idea for you either.'

'Okay.' Judy went to embrace her son, wanted to crush him to her, hold him so tight he became part of her again, but she feared his fragile lungs would object. She planted a lingering kiss on the top of his head as Gran moved to the other side of the bed. They each held a hand. Judy was weeping, but had not noticed.

'I'm sorry, Mummy.'

'What? Don't be daft. What on earth is there for you to be sorry about?' Her heart flew to him, she hugged him hard again, not sure what he was thinking.

'I forgot my puffer. I was so scared. I'm sorry. I won't forget it again.'

'It's not your fault sweetheart. Daddy should've remembered.' She'd even made a point of reminding him. 'But it's good that you'll always remember it in future.'

Judy loved her boy, had always thought she could not love him any more than she already did. But right now, right here, hearing her little boy taking more responsibility for himself than his father had, sent her emotions soaring to a dizzy height, to a level she had never experienced. More tears streamed and she smiled weakly at her mother. 'He's my little trooper.'

'Yes, love. Takes after his mother. Fort—'

'Fortunately.' They both said it at the same time, then burst into laughter, tension finding release through the safety valve of humour.

'Snap!' Josh shouted, and they all laughed far more than the pathetic joke deserved.

'So, my little soldier. Tell me. Where does it hurt? They say no broken bones, just some bruises.' She brushed tender fingers over his neck, the imprint of the harness a purple stain there.

'I ache, Mummy. Everywhere! But I listened to the pilot when he told us what to do before we left... He told us if he ever said *Mayday* to bend over, put our heads in our laps and to hug our knees. Daddy didn't. That's why he hurt his neck.' He was proud of himself and added, 'I did better than Daddy, didn't I?'

Judy caught Gran's eye, and they laughed again. Served the bastard right.

'You are a very good boy. And as a special treat we are all going to Brighton on Sunday... And I'm bringing a special friend called Colin. You'll like him.' She was sure.

'BRIGHTON!' Josh tried to bounce but winced instead. 'Oh, Mummy. Thank you.' He snagged his arms round her neck and snuggled to her. She knew Brighton was Josh's favourite place in his, admittedly limited, universe. She felt on top of the world.

Josh whispered to her, and, despite his effort at confidentiality, his voice was clearly audible to Gran.

'I heard the pilot call Daddy a *stupid arse*, Mummy. I think it's rude. What does it mean?'

Judy heard Gran's throaty guffaw, the reaction startling her, and was then even more shocked to hear her prude of a mother blurt out, 'He certainly got that right!'

Judy's giggling fit started as a vibration and soon escalated into a full-blown belly laugh. She wiped away the tears and gave Josh another sloppy kiss before saying, 'He did indeed, Mum. He did indeed.'

The doctors decided Josh needed to stay in hospital overnight for observation and so Judy slept in the armchair next to her son, her hand in his, his arm draped around Bruno Bear. Gran had taken a taxi home and said she would wait at Judy's flat in the morning.

They arrived back at midday. Josh, subdued from his experience and a little groggy from painkillers, Judy in a determined mood, even angrier with John than she had been yesterday.

He had popped in to Josh's room early that morning to say goodbye before his trip, and had tried to talk her out of her threat to speak to her lawyer. She blanked him, ever more convinced the man she had married, the man whose child she had borne, was so obsessed with his own career that he felt nothing for his son. Otherwise he would have stayed to try and convince her to relent.

Well I won't.

She picked up the phone and dialled her solicitor, an old friend from her time at university, and explained what had happened.

'I think we have a solid case for restricting access. He's shown gross negligence and endangerment... Are you certain you want to go that far?' Sarah Vaughn had graduated top of her class in law and had been involved in many high profile divorces. A celebrity lawyer, no less.

'I want to go in as hard and as far as I can. Honestly, Sarah, I really have been such an ass. I let that bastard walk all over me. And the worst of it is, you warned me.'

Judy regretted not listening to her friend. Firstly at uni when Sarah told her the man was no good, and then again during the time when they separated, advising Judy she should get a chunk of John's earnings too. But Judy's pride won out.

Sarah then dropped her own bombshell. 'Yeah, but I'm not so perceptive when it comes to my own feelings. Andy and I are splitting up. Men, huh? How about we catch up over lunch, assassinate their characters together, eh? But first, let's agree what I'm going to do.'

Judy appreciated her friend dropping everything to take her call and help her. 'I hope I can afford you these days, Sarah.' She was genuinely worried, Sarah was much in demand by people with far more cash than she had. These days she was something of a legend.

'Don't you worry about that. I'll just add it to the costs, which he'll have to settle. Okay? We can go for some more cash, an income and also determine visiting rights to suit you.'

Maybe she should take as much as she could from John and wind down her work hours. The thought came unbidden, but, this time, was not unwelcome.

'Brilliant. I want to restrict his visits to specific times when I can be available, or he'll have to be accompanied by an independent chaperone. I don't think he's as well paid as you think, though.'

'You remember Jerry. Thick but posh, scraped an Economics pass?'

'Vaguely.'

'Never mind. What is important is that I saw him recently and discovered he works for John's firm. No high-flyer like your ex, but he tells me that the bastard pulled down between one and a half and two million last year in salary and bonuses, and expects to double that this year.'

'Two million?' Judy was astonished. She thought John earned a few hundred grand at best. But this! It was obscene. 'That's ridiculous. How can anyone deserve that?' Especially John.

'Don't knock it, love. How do you think I got rich?' It was not a gloat, merely a statement of fact. 'Anyway, if he deserves it, so do you. I'll get things moving, but trust me, Josh will be well protected and John-the-bastard won't know what hit him by the time he gets back. Okay. Got to fly, babe. Speak soon.'

Judy was still holding the handset, disbelief on her face, as Gran walked in.

'You okay, love? Looks like you could do with a cuppa.'

Judy started at Gran's voice, finally coming out of her trance. 'Please, Mum.' She was thinking how John had made such a big deal out of investing a thousand pounds a month for Josh in addition to agreeing to pay his school fees. A thousand pounds would be chickenfeed to him… 'The bastard.'

Gran, halfway out the door, heading for the kettle, knew she meant John.

'I never liked him. Never trust a man who carries a comb. I told you that when I first met him.'

'Aw, Mum.'

'I know you think I'm dotty sometimes, but it's a sure sign of an insecure man with a very big ego. You mark my words.' She did not stop to discuss it, just pottered off to the kitchen, case closed.

And Judy could not help thinking, maybe the old dear was not so daft after all.

That morning, Doc had another hangover. This time, because he had barely eaten on Sunday, preferring instead the fugue of alcohol, at least he was not sick.

His own slack features and tortured eyes stared back at him as he stood doubled over the sink, numb in spirit while his body ached in protest at the continual abuse.

'You stupid, useless old man.' The mirror image spoke to him, and he wondered, had he uttered those words? He was startled, certain he had not spoken, or even thought the words. The psychiatrist in him stirred, sent an alarm signal to his brain, a warning to his inner self.

'I've really got to get my act together.'

This time he did speak and the psychiatrist in his head whispered back: Talking to yourself is normal, but hearing the mirror lecture you is something altogether different.

Doc pushed himself upright, swayed and then regained his balance, determined to make it to the shower. He let the water cascade over his scalp, driving the dull throb from his temples, letting the ion-charged water weave its magic, refreshing him.

The psychiatrist started working. Analysing the experiences he had undergone recently. The persistent visions, replays of the crash, Natalie's voice breaking in on his thoughts at random moments, the smell of her perfume in his nostrils sending his senses reeling—even after he had thrown it all out. He knew there were no such things as ghosts, just constructs of a bruised and battered mind.

No, it was not the supernatural that concerned him. Doc was sure there was no life after death. He was more worried for the flesh and blood, the patient, could feel his sanity coming unravelled from his very core, leaving his nerves vulnerable and exposed.

'I hear voices.'

It echoed in the cubicle and again he was not sure. Had he spoken? He sagged against the wall, rivulets streaming, steam swirling round him.

Memories of interviews jostled in his head, audio clips of the words spoken by numerous convicts, justifying their vile acts of perversion and death, all with the same refrain.

I hear voices.

He wept. Groaning, heaving sobs wrenched from deep within his soul.

What the hell was happening to him?

Doc roused when he heard the phone. He had no idea how long he had been sitting on the shower floor, knees to his chest, arms hugging them. The answer machine picked up but he could not make out the words, the voice a low murmur, mixing with the hiss of water.

What time is it?

His brain was rational again, although, inside, he felt disjointed, limbs stiff, the short walk to the answering machine a trek through marshmallow.

The Judge. 'Where are you? Call me please as soon as you get this.'

He glanced at the clock. Eleven-twenty? Doc was shaken. He was certain he had woken up at seven-fifteen and started showering pretty much straight away.

Four hours. Four whole hours of his life had gone missing.

This really was not good.

He dressed, drank some coffee and then called the Judge.

'Sorry, boss. I had a bad night. I'm on my way.'

'Thank heavens you're not going to let me down, Doc,' the pressure none too subtle. 'We have so many recalls and hearings I'd be tearing my hair out if I had any left.' He chuckled, then he was serious again. 'I don't know if you've heard, but poor Judy has experienced something of a personal crisis. Her son was involved in an accident at the weekend. He's due home from hospital today but she needs some time off to look after him… Which is why I really need some help. Right now.'

Judy?

'Of course, Judge. I'll try and pick up the slack.' Throw myself into work again, that'll help. 'Has she completed the report on Leech?'

'It's with me now, emailed a few minutes ago. Not had time to read it yet. Anyway, Leech needs to see it and then it can be added to his dossier for the hearing.' A beat passed. 'How long before you get here? There's a mountain of work.'

'I'm on my way.' Doc hung up, hesitated, then dialled her number.

'I just heard. Is Josh okay?'

'He'll be fine, Doc. He's very resilient. To be honest it's a nice change to have him resting rather than crashing round the place, yelling.' He could tell by her voice that she was putting a brave face on things.

'What happened? Are you okay?'

'I'm okay, thanks. His father took him on the helicopter trip of a lifetime. It was almost the last trip of his lifetime. They crash landed and… I'll tell you all about it later. Are you still on for Brighton? I think we'll go Sunday, if that's okay. Josh should be fully fit by then.'

Brighton? He'd forgotten. His demons had managed to shunt any thoughts of the future from his frazzled mind.

'Of course I am. I'll see you then. I'll call Friday to confirm the arrangements. You take care.' He managed to stop himself adding 'kid'.

68

'Oh, one thing. Do you mind if I introduce you as Colin? To my mother, and Josh. It's just...'

'No problem. We don't want them thinking I'm there to check up on their mental well-being, do we?' He felt better. Something to look forward to.

'Exactly! Thanks for calling, Colin. I really appreciate it.' Her voice was a sunbeam, bathing him in its golden warmth.

Was there a possibility he might get through this after all?

Doc spent the week attempting to subjugate his demons, with some success. He worked from the moment he woke to the moment he reached the oblivion of pharmaceutically induced sleep.

Physically he was wrecked, the punishing schedule and artificial rest a recipe for a full blown breakdown. But he was in denial, ignoring the professional inside himself, scolding, telling him he needed help to recover, demanding the therapy his conscious mind refused to consider.

The Judge was delighted as Doc ploughed through the workload, poring over dossiers, leading parole board discussion groups, organising and attending oral hearings, and scheduling the training that had been deferred since the car accident collided with his life.

At night he took a triple dose of sleeping pills and read case files until his eyes could no longer focus. He set two alarms to drag himself from narcosis, and needed three double espressos to kick his brain into gear first thing each morning. By the time Saturday arrived he was exhausted but he pressed on, immersing himself in work to divert his mind from his personal tragedy. That evening, after a day reviewing files for upcoming parole hearings, he eventually came to Leech's dossier. He re-read it twice and was staring at the police photograph from Leech's arrest when he slumped into a state of unconsciousness, somewhere beyond sleep.

His demons, no longer held at bay by the barricade of sleeping tablets, took their revenge.

Clack. Clack. Clack-clack-clack...

The cruel projectionist tormented his spirit with constant replays of the crash. Natalie's voice screeched at him, crying and wailing for a life lost.

And the evil men, the faces of the hundreds of criminals he had interviewed, all with twisted, vile tales to tell, were judging him, laughing at him, finding him insane.

Then one face floated out of the ether, a toothless man-boy, green eyes alight with hatred, knife arcing, stabbing Doc over and over. But worse, with each painful blow Leech shouted the word that plagued him.

Guilty!

And gradually Doc shrank back, and realised Leech was not stabbing him. He was plunging the knife deep into Natalie's belly. The blade sliding in and out, slippery with blood, Leech's hand inside her, her precious mound torn open, their baby boy exposed. And Leech continued slashing, carving the baby inside her belly as Natalie screamed at Doc, words now coherent and ugly.

'You killed my baby! You killed us both!'

Her scream bored into his very marrow, and he fought against it, straining with all his being. Finally he managed to surface to the sound of his own demented wailing bouncing off the walls.

Oh, God! Please make it stop.

He sobbed.

'Mum, this is Colin.' She glanced at him, a reassuring smile. 'And Colin, this is Betty.'

Doc felt the old lady's eyes beetle over him, checking him out, exposing him, making him wonder if he'd forgotten to shave or brush his hair... It wouldn't be the first time.

'Call me Gran, please.' Her features melted into a cheery smile, welcoming. She shook his hand and then patted it with the other. 'Nice to meet you at last. Judy's told me so much about you...'

Judy's face splotched red. She called to Josh but Doc saw the look, the warning flash at her mother.

The boy was the image of Judy, and polite too.

'Pleased to meet you, Doctor Powers.' Doc shook the tiny hand and smiled at the lad.

'My name is Colin. Only people who consult me professionally call me Doctor.' Josh was quizzical, but Doc just added, 'According to your mum she's the only one here that might need a psychiatrist, because she says you might be driving her crazy!' Judy had made the joke on Friday when she had called to confirm the trip.

The little group stood on the platform at Victoria Station, their train due to leave in ten minutes, allowing Doc some time to daydream.

Judy was stunning. Casual, but like a model who had stepped from some genteel country lifestyle magazine. In fact the three of them were so well turned out that his own outfit—check shirt and faded corduroys—was decidedly scruffy by comparison. Natalie would have had a fit.

Natalie.

He felt his conscience prickle. Here he was, not yet four months since her cremation, playing at happy families with this woman he barely knew. He thrust the thought into a box in his mind, nailed it like a coffin and buried it deep, certain his demons would dig it up and rip it open later.

Oh, well, he thought, right now I am going to try and have a good day. Baby steps.

The train ride that morning breezed laughter into his crushed and crumbling spirit. Judy's family was a delight. Joking, teasing, poking fun, but never with malice, the affection and warmth radiating from them sucking him in. He really started to enjoy himself.

Much of the day was spent on the beach, skimming stones and paddling in the chilly water, Josh squealing as he chased seagulls, splashing and filling the air with his joyous laughter. They picnicked on the pebbles, a sumptuous feast of delicious sandwiches, pies and cakes, all fresh baked by Gran.

Doc lay back, the ground a lumpy bed, the warmth of the sun soporific as it spread a comfortable glow through his body.

Josh, far from having exhausted himself, pestered Judy to take him to the games arcade. All three adults were reclined, in postprandial nap mode, the food and heat relaxing them to the point of sleep.

Gran creaked her way to her feet, joints protesting and audible to everyone, took Josh's hand and said, 'I'll take him. If I doze off now I'll not sleep tonight.' Doc saw her wink at Judy through his half-closed eyes. Gran went on, 'We'll leave you two sleeping beauties alone for an hour or so. Come on tiger, let's go.'

Judy sat up, called after them, 'Nothing too violent, Mum, and don't let him play any of those shoot-em-up video games.'

'I know. I know. Aliens only. No humans.' She trudged off, Josh dragging her, their feet crunching the pebbles.

Judy was looking down at Doc, eyes roaming over his face.

'Are you asleep?'

'No, just… totally relaxed. I haven't felt this good for ages. Thanks for inviting me.'

Judy lay back, propped herself on her elbow facing him. Close enough for him to smell her, her scent wholesome and fresh, yet with the promise of excitement. He felt like grabbing her, kissing her. Instead he said, 'You have a wonderful family. You must be very proud of Josh.'

'They like you too. They must do to be having such a good time. Believe me, you'd soon know if my mother didn't.' She gazed out at the sea, grey-blue waves, topped with froth, breaking with a gentle shush on the shingle. 'She detests John.'

Doc listened as Judy recounted the events of last weekend. He rolled to face her, head on his hand, supported by his elbow, mirroring her posture. Shocked, he blurted, 'You hit him?'

'Twice. I knocked him down! But don't worry. I don't make a habit of hitting men.'

'You really are full of surprises,' although, as he spoke, Doc remembered his first assessment of her—the lioness, now protecting her young. 'So how will John react?'

'He's in the States.' Bitterness seethed in her voice. 'His bloody work is more important to him than our son. Well, sod him! By the time he gets back he'll be restricted to seeing Josh two weekends a month, daytime only. No more overnight stays, and either I'm with them or he pays for a chaperone.'

'And Josh?' He asked gently. 'What does he say? Have you talked to him?'

'I've explained that his father is so important in his company now that he has to share his time more carefully. Josh just nodded, said he hoped his dad would one day own a helicopter.' She laughed, an incredulous gurgle. 'Can you believe my son? He not only wants to fly again. He wants to be a helicopter pilot! For his dad!'

A gust blew hair into her mouth, she ignored it, grew more serious as she carried on. 'He said he wanted to look after his father… Poor boy. I doubt asthmatics make good pilots.'

Doc wriggled, his hip shifting stones, worming into a more comfortable position. He wanted to reach out, brush the hair away for her. He tossed a stone at the sea instead, unsure of what he was doing with this beautiful woman.

Judy went on, 'The whole episode has made me rethink things. After our meal the other night I was still wondering who was to blame for things going wrong between John and me. I've always felt culpable. God knows, I even felt I messed up by choosing the wrong man to father my son. This week has changed that. It helped, talking things through with you… And then the crash.' She stared at the sea again, her physical presence with him, her thoughts far away. He waited a few minutes for her to go on, sure something important was coming. 'I'm seriously thinking about going part-time. Almost losing Josh has made me realise what a hole that would leave in my life.'

She sighed, her violet eyes now on him, searching for... what? Doc kept silent. The demons rattled their cages, crying to be let out. He made a decision. He needed to talk too, to tell someone. So he did.

'Family really is the most important thing, Judy. Procreation is what drives us, at our most primitive level.' He felt the next words try to throttle him as he uttered them. 'Natalie was pregnant.'

She said nothing, her violet eyes just seemed to turn a deeper shade, sympathy and sadness transmitted without a word. Encouraged, he continued.

'We'd been celebrating. That night... We'd been trying for years. We thought it was impossible. Even IVF had failed.' Tears streamed as he spoke, but Doc could not feel them, his body numb. 'She was almost four months with child. Our child. A boy. Daniel.' He stopped, almost clammed up. Pushed himself to continue. 'We decided to celebrate—we'd made it past the worst period. You know, not much chance of a miscarriage after three months. We thought we were home and dry. Even decorated the nursery.' It was the only room in the house he had not entered since the accident.

'Oh, Colin.' She reached out, squeezed his arm. 'I'm so sorry.' She left her hand there, her palm hot, the body heat slicing through his numbness, urging him on.

'The worst of it was that it was all my fault. I killed the woman I loved. And our unborn baby.' He swept his hand over his forehead and down his face, surprised to find his palm slick with tears.

'It was an accident! The other driver jumped the lights.' Judy shook his arm, eyes feverish. 'It wasn't your fault. The police report was clear on that.'

Doc, whose mind was not as sharp as it should be, failed to ask her how she knew what the police had said, though it would occur to him later. He shook his head.

'I'd been drinking—'

'You were under the limit!' Her vehemence startled him. 'How can you blame yourself?'

'Listen. I know you're trying to help, but—'

'Okay. Tell me. I'm listening. I'll be quiet.'

Her grip on his arm relaxed and he was surprised to see white finger marks there, had been unaware of her strength.

'I'm a forensic psychiatrist. I deal with people who commit crimes. Sometimes they claim to have been drunk. Under the influence and therefore not responsible.' He snorted his disgust. 'I assess them. Determine for the court whether they can be fully held to account for their actions.' He could see she wanted to speak, but ploughed on. 'I know the effect of alcohol on an individual. I am an expert on the effects of a given quantity on a specified body mass index.' He dragged the words out. 'How one glass of champagne dulls reactions, how one beer shrinks peripheral vision, how one measure of whisky undermines mental capacity... the ability to judge speed.'

He sat up, tossed a pebble at the water, watched as it clattered on the rocks and bounced with a splash, lost beneath the waves.

'We were travelling at about thirty miles an hour, the lights were green. I was holding her hand. We were laughing about something she'd said… She'd called herself a baby factory, promised me she would pop them out like peas.' Judy gasped at that, but Doc kept on. 'It was a wonderful night. Both of us with successful careers, deliriously happy, so in love and with our lives ahead of us.' He gulped, voice hoarse now. 'I didn't see him. He ran that red light, ramming his truck into our passenger door. Into Natalie… Smashed us up against a traffic light. I was crushed against her. It took nearly two hours to cut me free. And I was conscious the whole time. It was worse than the most terrible nightmare.'

And it keeps on coming back.

Clack. Clack. Clack.

He stopped speaking, concentrating instead on trying to block out the images swamping his mind. Judy prompted him for more, and her words pulled him back. He sensed pity as she spoke.

'So it was the other driver's fault. An accident.'

He would not acknowledge the point. 'She died on impact. Her airbag only served to hold her head up. The truck was travelling so fast she was catapulted into the doorframe, fracturing her skull.' Fracturing. Wrecking. Destroying. 'Three lives were lost that night. The driver,' he could not bring himself to speak the man's name, 'Natalie and Daniel. Of course the police report and the newspapers said two people…'

'You poor man.' She pressed into him, hugged him to her as they sat by the gentle lapping of the Channel.

'We hadn't told anybody. We planned to announce it that weekend. Natalie's parents were coming down. They were desperate for grandkids.' He sighed, a mournful note, then started sobbing quietly.

She held him close, her head to his shoulder, sharing his pain, his misery.

By the time they arrived back at Judy's apartment it was pushing 8pm, and Josh was spent. While Judy tucked up her son, Gran, who had invited Doc back for supper, sipped her tea with him in the kitchen, and asked him about himself.

Doc had the definite impression that he was being interviewed, but he did not mind in the least. He liked Gran, her homely, down to earth approach, and her sparkling eyes that were so similar to her daughter's.

'So, how old are you, Colin?' She asked without a hint of embarrassment. Colin knew that politely spoken rudeness was the domain of the aged.

'I'll be forty-five in September… I won't ask how old you are, you might think me impolite!'

He grinned and then answered a few more questions about his career and book before she finally nodded and smiled back. 'I gather you can cook exotic foods, too. Quite something!'

'Nothing to compare with you, Betty, just curries and the like.'

Judy joined them and they ate, homemade minestrone and fresh baked bread. Doc thought the food divine. He told them so as he started to clear the dishes.

Gran stood, plucked the crockery from his hands and told him, 'I'll clean this up. This is my kitchen, Colin, and I won't have you interfering!' It was actually Judy's kitchen but nobody would dare argue that particular point. 'Why don't you two go and have a nightcap?' She put a hand on the small of his back and gave a gentle push. 'Go on...'

'There's a nice pub at the end of the road, if you fancy?' Judy cocked an eye at him, and he nodded. They strolled in the cool night air, Judy slipping her hand through his arm as they walked, both pensive, silent, wrapped in their own thoughts.

By the time they arrived at the pub, Doc was a confusion of emotions, concerned that he might be reading too much into today. Was she just being a good friend, supporting a colleague in need?

He decided to stick to a safe subject.

'So, what do you think of your new role?'

'Oh, I've hardly got into it yet. But I've never been called Ma'am before!' Her laughter tinkled, breaking the stilted atmosphere that had threatened to engulf them. 'That episode with Leech shook me up... I began to wonder if I could do the job. Don't look so shocked. Even I have doubts sometimes.'

'You're a fast-tracked super-achiever according to my sources.' He grinned cheekily.

'Come off it. Here I am, supposed to be part of a team that ultimately decides whether criminals are fit for release, yet I'm not exactly the best judge of character, am I? I mean—look at who I married!' Her eyes shimmered at him, her sultry look accentuated as she gazed at him over her glass.

Doc pressed on with the work theme, despite her light-hearted response. He did not know what else to say, thinking he might be making a fool of himself.

'Seriously though, would you consider a career with the Parole Board?'

'Career? They're mostly part-timers, legal types with other jobs, aren't they?'

'Mostly. I'm full time, along with a handful of others. I'm officially Vice Chairman. The Judge is grooming me to take over in a couple of years... If he ever retires.'

'Oh, so you think I should be aiming for that too? I'm only seconded temporarily.'

'But if you wanted a part-time career with real prospects, why not aim for it? If you take more time with Josh for the next few years, then switch back to full-time when he's older... Who knows? It's worth thinking about.'

Judy sucked in her lip, gnawed at it, her thoughtful gesture sexy as hell from where Doc sat.

'Is that how it is? You work for the Judge, then get his job. I work for you and then I take over yours. Sounds like nepotism to me!' She was being flippant, but still thoughtful.

'Hardly. The Secretary of State makes the appointments but he has a limited pool of talent to choose from. And you're already a high flyer. Think about it. You could have your cake and eat it.' Doc finished his drink. 'Fancy another?'

She did, so they sat huddled in a corner, thighs pressed together, enveloped in the warmth and buzz of the busy bar.

'What about you. Why did you give up profiling?'

'I didn't give up completely.' Doc sipped his beer as he lied, the cold bite of alcohol settling him. 'I still get called to advise on the odd case.' That was true, but these days he always refused. 'When I first started, it was all jiggery-pokery. Black magic. The police didn't trust it in those days, but the process developed, proved its worth, and now profilers are two a penny. I'm past it!' His laugh didn't quite mask his feelings, but his comment had shifted the conversation and he felt Judy's hand on his thigh.

'Past it? I don't think so.'

'Judy… I'm not sure—'

She placed a finger to his lips.

'It's okay. I know. We have time, Colin.'

His doubts about her intentions swooped away and his spirits soared.

But then the clacking started.

No!

He shut his eyes, pushing his palms into the sockets, trying to force the images away. It worked. The noise quietened, the movie fading. He dropped his hands, and saw the concern written on her beautiful face, eyes aglow with compassion.

He said, 'I thought it was a vino-ego thing the other night—'

'A what?'

'I thought the wine had convinced me that a fat old man could find a beautiful young woman like you. Vino-ego.'

She leaned forward and kissed his lips with a gentle touch, a fleeting promise, no more. She whispered into his face, 'And I didn't expect to find a man like you.'

Then it spilled out of him. 'I'm no great catch, Judy. I think I'm losing my mind. I have such awful nightmares. The crash. Flashbacks too… I'm a psychiatrist. I could certify myself. You really don't know me.' He pulled back, held her face in his hands. 'The truth is, I gave up profiling because I was haunted by the evil of it all. My mind is riven by monsters. I'm burnt out… I'm a mess!'

She covered his hands with hers and said, 'It's not working, Colin. You may not know how to show a girl a good time, I'll give you that, but you should already know an insanity plea rarely has the desired effect!'

Doc threw back his head and guffawed, his laughter a delighted rumble that saw off his demons.

At least for now.

'You're going to have to face it, Peter. You may not get parole.'

The obese man with greasy hair and an oily smile was serious. Leech hated him. He wanted to belt the smug fucker in the teeth.

'I've done my time. I've kept my nose clean. I've done everything you told me to do.' He growled, but blubberball was unfazed.

'The odds aren't good,' his solicitor told him. 'Normally a lifer would transfer to open prison for six to twelve months before being released on license. You haven't done everything I told you. You asked to be transferred back to this place.' Gruber flicked an imperious hand at the room, the walls, the steel door. 'What particular moment of craziness inspired that inane request, pray tell?'

'I prefer it here. What the fuck's the difference? They should be pleased. Low category prisons are overcrowded as it is. And I could've busted out of that shithole, no problem.' Leech paced the interview room, the two of them unobserved, lawyer client privilege intact. He stopped, placed his knuckles on the table, eyeballing his brief. 'Anyway, I had unfinished business here.'

Gruber was unflinching. 'Well, Peter, on your own head and all that.' He shuffled his papers and told him, 'The good news is that I have received details of your parole hearing. We have the names of the triumvirate that hold your future in their hands.'

Leech sat down, eager to know more. 'Can I see?'

'Of course.' Gruber passed some documents across. 'The hearing will take place on Friday in the governor's annexe. A judge will preside. He's the best bit of news.'

'No judge is good news, Gruber.'

Again the little man was unperturbed by the aggression in Leech's voice. 'In this instance, be assured Judge Jeffries is about the best news you could hope for. The full Parole Board consists of some one hundred and twenty members. Around thirty are judges. They always preside over parole hearings. From this limited pool of judicial bias I have managed to secure the best of the bunch.'

Leech very much doubted that his oleaginous lawyer had the clout or the contacts to influence such a choice, but he let it slide. In any event, the man was his solicitor specifically because he was as straight as a lavatory u-bend, but, unfortunately, often as full of shit. Leech nodded, listened.

'Jeffries is always a soft touch on the bench and has only recently been in the news for giving a rapist a four year sentence. Ludicrously soft, but worse, he made a comment about the girl asking for it, or some such nonsense.' Gruber riffled through his notes and added, 'He also has the highest number of parolees given licences as a percentage of hearings undertaken. In other words, we have the best chance of success with him.'

'You mean I have. I'm the one in here.'

'And so am I, right now.' Gruber slipped a finger under his collar and loosened his tie. 'Frankly, I would prefer not to be.'

'You're getting well paid. Stop bleating and get on with it.'

His equanimity apparently inviolable, Gruber stoically carried on. 'You have Judge Jeffries' details there. Rather more than you should have... so I'll be taking the documents with me.'

Leech read them—a biography, some personal notes, and his address—branded the details on his memory, then threw the papers back at Gruber.

'Is that it? What about this one..? Looks like a dyke to me.'

'Unerring as ever, Peter. I gather she is rather fond of tribady. However, although your undoubtedly male charms will be of little use, I believe this may be.' He slid a newspaper clipping across the table to Leech. It was an article from the Guardian, recommending radical prison reform. As Leech started to read it Gruber added, 'You can read that at your leisure. It's yours to keep.'

Leech continued scanning the page and then laughed.

'Sometimes you're almost worth the money, Gruber.'

His lawyer smiled, it could have been a nervous tic, it twitched and disappeared that quickly.

'The bad news, and I'm afraid it is potentially very bad indeed, is the medical professional... Jeffries is soft, but still a judge. The lady whose ridiculous jottings you were just reading is an independent member of the Parole Board—'

'Independent! Bullshit. No such thing, Gruber.'

'In the sense used by the Parole Board, there is. Any hearing is chaired by a judge. A psychiatrist or psychologist is in attendance to advise on the potential parolee's mental well-being. The third member is neither necessarily a judge nor a medical professional. In that admittedly limited sense, she is therefore an independent. There are many of them, some drawn from the police, others are solicitors, probation offi-cers, assorted legal bods. The civil service accounts for most. The best... for our purposes, is this lady and her ilk.' Gruber tapped her photograph with a finger. 'Sophie Pugh is a social worker. Her whole life has revolved around assisting inmates to resettle into society.'

'Yeah? Excellent.'

'Yes, all good news. Except this.' Gruber placed the last set of details in front of his client. 'The psychiatrist, I'm afraid, is none other than your nemesis. One Doctor Colin Powers.'

It took several minutes for Leech to calm down enough for Gruber to continue. His solicitor resumed as if the outburst had not happened. Leech had to admit, his brief was one cool bastard.

'In terms of our strategy, I would suggest that we try to create some friction between Ms Pugh and Powers. I believe he is the weaker party, whereas she is some- what of a firebrand. I've heard he has recently suffered a bereavement and may have a problem with alcohol… Regardless, I believe she is sufficiently persuasive to sway Judge Jeffries.'

Leech was looking sideways at Gruber, chin in his hand, his temple and jaw muscles in spasm as he ground his teeth.

Powers!

'This is all wrong. Get him dismissed from my hearing, Gruber.'

'I'm afraid I cannot.'

'Why the fuck not? I'm paying you plenty. You said you got Jeffries appointed, so get Powers un-appointed.'

Gruber's eyes slid away and he shifted some papers as he spoke. 'Sadly, he is an immutable choice. Personally appointed by the Chairman of the Parole Board himself. This document is for you to keep too.' Gruber held up a green brochure enti- tled Report and Accounts of the Parole Board for England and Wales. 'You'll recog- nise the man, I'm sure.' He tossed the booklet to Leech, folded open at the Chairman's statement, a picture of Justice Potter sneering down at the reader.

Leech's fist hammered down onto the face, the skin of his knuckle rupturing from the uncontrolled power, blood spattering the photograph.

Gruber spoke into the ensuing silence.

'As I said, Peter. We have to accept the possibility that you may not get parole this time round. I'll give you a minute.' He tapped the door and left Leech sitting, brooding over the injustices of his world.

'Coffee, Peter?' Gruber returned holding two plastic cups of what passed for coffee in this place. He sipped his and moved behind Leech, placed a hand on his shoulder, then hastily withdrew it.

'Don't ever fucking touch me.' Leech snarled at the solicitor. 'And sit where I can see you.'

Gruber returned to his side of the desk, sat, leafed through some files and then asked, 'How do you get on with the senior prison officer?'

'Dire Mud.' Leech spat the words out, a foul taste on his tongue. Then he laughed, a mirthless, hollow noise. 'I'm well and truly fucked!' He took his coffee and returned to pacing the room, head down, shoulders rounded.

'Tell me about him.'

'He hates me. Seems to think I'm a bad man.'

'What could possibly give him that impression?' Gruber was sardonic, but Leech took him literally.

'Accidents happen in here. You know?'

'Indeed I do. I get to help clean them up sometimes. But your record is clear, Peter.'

Leech flopped into the chair and explained. 'A few years back one of the cons, guy called Riggs, was bad-mouthing me. I slapped him. Just the once, nothing much, with my open hand.' Leech could see the scepticism in Gruber's face. 'Really... Trouble is, it was at the top of the stairs and he fell backwards. Bounced down them like a ball. Broke his back. Diarmud was there.'

'But I don't see anything?' Gruber leafed through his files again, searching. 'And why wasn't I involved in the inquiry? As your lawyer?' He looked up, confused now.

'Everyone said he slipped and fell. Then some slag grassed me up. My word against his. Fortunately he committed suicide a few days later.'

'Suicide?'

'That's what they said. Found him hanging in his cell, bed sheet tied to the bars. Wrapped it round his neck and jumped off his bed they reckoned.' He grinned, sly humour in his voice. 'Sadly missed. Not.'

'And the inmate with the back injury?'

'He was in a coma for a week but when he woke up he confirmed it was an accident, that he slipped and fell. Sued the prison service for a small fortune. He's in a wheelchair but was released on compassionate grounds and is living it up in Marbella now. Sent me a card. The lucky bastard.'

'Sounds like he wasn't the only lucky one.'

'What are you talking about? I'm still in here.'

'Indeed you are. Is there anything else about this Diarmud I should know?'

'He fuckin hates me.'

'I meant anything more material?'

'That not enough?' Leech stood and paced again. Then sat and said, 'Jesus, I'm gonna be stuck in here.'

'Quite possibly. We need to be realistic, and not build up false hope.' Gruber took a hefty manila file and plopped it in front of Leech. 'However, you have the right to read everything in the dossier that has been presented to the parole board.' He glanced at his watch. 'Take your time. I need to make several phone calls, but I'll be back. I think lunch may be served in here. I requested sandwiches as I knew it would be a long session. Oh, and Peter.'

'What?' Leech was already studying his file.

'Don't do anything stupid. Let's stay positive, assume we still have an evens chance.' His hand hovered above Leech's shoulder, about to pat him, but Gruber left before making the mistake of completing the gesture.

Leech became engrossed in his dossier. He was fascinated by the details of his life inside, pleased that he was, quite rightly, the centre of so much attention.

It went right back to the court case, and that slime-bag Potter's summing up. Apparently Leech was an 'evil monster', the perpetrator of a 'vile deed', the gruesome nature of which made him an 'affront' to families everywhere. He had stabbed his parents to death in a 'frenzied' attack of such ferocity that his mother's neck had been perforated to the point of severing. Blah. Blah.

But it's not all bad, he thought.

Potter had also stated that he hoped a lengthy period of incarceration would allow him to return to society as a useful member.

Well, he had learnt his lesson. Hadn't he?

The Prison Assessment Report was even better. It detailed the courses he had attended, commented on his positive attitude, his intelligence, the progress he had made. He barely recognised himself, wondered who the creep was, checked the front of the file to confirm the name. It was his! He loved it.

The Prison Psychiatrist's report was also positive. He had managed to pull the wool over that idiot's eyes. The courses in psychology had been a godsend. He thought then, maybe Powers wouldn't be the kiss of death after all. He studied the document, stowing it in his memory.

Only the probation officer's report had any significant negatives as far as he could see. The man said he would be concerned about him after release. Called him unemployable. Not well socialised. An unstable loner.

The cunt!

He flung the papers across the room. Started pacing again, wondering, where did the twat get that from? The psychiatrist's report had not said that.

Then it came to him. His last interview with the probation officer in the open prison had not gone well. Leech had been dismissive of the man. A pompous, puffed up moron. Leech had become frustrated, then shouted at the officer. Had told him he could take care of himself, that he did not need assistance from some bloody social worker. That he did not need to work as he was rich.

Rich!

He had yelled the word into the man's face, prompting him to terminate the interview. Leech had taunted the officer as he left, told him he would never have as much money…

Damn.

He would have to think how to handle that.

The last file was marked Interviewing Officer's Report. And above the date, her name, JUDITH FINCH.

Judith. Judy. My Birdy.

He held the papers to his nose, sniffing, hoping to catch her odour, disappointed that he could only smell cigarette smoke.

He read the report twice, certain there were hidden meanings aimed at him, and him alone. He was not sure it reflected everything he had told her—sometimes he confused himself, he had woven so many lies into the faction of his life—but it was punchy, well written, and extremely favourable. She was openly on his side.

Of course.

She wanted him.

And he would not disappoint her.

'I want to read his book.' Leech munched on his beef sandwich, spitting flecks of partially chewed food, his open mouth a cement mixer. 'This grubs good. Best I've had in ages. Can you get me a copy?'

Gruber fished in his briefcase. 'Here.' He spun Doc's book across the table to Leech, *Insights into the Criminal Mind*. 'Don't underestimate him, Peter. He's quite brilliant.'

'Yeah, but so am I.' Leech opened the Prison Psychiatrist's Report, and pointed at it. 'Says so right here. An IQ of 138. I'm right up there with Bill Gates apparently.'

'Indeed. Let's hope you're up to it on the day. Are you absolutely certain you do not require my services? You have the right to professional representation.' Gruber's beady little eyes reminded Leech of a gaming machine with pound signs rolling into view.

'Nah. The barrister screwed things up for me at the trial. I prefer to do this myself.' Besides, Leech was convinced the lawyer was always trying to rook him for a bigger fee.

'Fair enough. Have you checked the Interviewing Officer's report. You need to sign a copy if, that is, you agree it's a fair representation.'

'It's not bad. She's got a bit of a thing for me that bird, Finch.' He licked his top lip suggestively at his solicitor, while Gruber frowned back.

'I doubt that very much. A member of the Parole Board is hardly likely to—'

'What? To fall for a prisoner? A con? A lifer? A murderer?' He flared at Gruber, growling now. 'Plenty of women do y'know.'

It was true, he and others regularly got letters and sometimes visits from admiring women attracted by the extreme violence they had committed. It never failed to amaze Leech, though the nutters did not really appeal to him. But Finch, well she was different. Quality totty.

'She knows I'm innocent. She'll be waiting for me when I get out. Guaranteed.' His posture and expression challenged Gruber to dare say different. He did.

'I don't think so. If you approach her, in the event your parole licence is approved, you will inevitably be in breach of the conditions.'

'Not if she doesn't tell them.'

'Peter, please listen to me. The Parole Board will insist on conditions that you must abide by. Any failure to do so could lead to recall. They can revoke the licence and put you back in here to serve the remainder of your sentence. Life.' He shook his head, as he emphasised the words. 'It is not worth the risk.'

'Life's a game of risk. And I'm a winner.' The irony of his comment, made in these circumstances, in this environment, escaped him.

Gruber gave up. 'Okay. Final matters. Your property purchase was due to exchange, but I have held back, despite your instructions to go ahead.'

'Why?' Gruber was starting to really piss him off. 'I told you I want that apartment.'

'I thought it prudent to await the outcome of the hearing. We'll know within the next few weeks. I've stalled the developers, and we can exchange and complete the same day we know you are successful.'

'No! Do it. Push for completion now. I want to rent it out in the future anyway. I don't plan to live there for long.'

'Parole conditions will require a permanent abode. That was the whole point—'

'Just fucking do it. Are you deaf? You have Power of Attorney. Sort it. And don't you dare overcharge me again.' He would throttle the little turd if he tried that on.

'Very well. I have given my advice, I can do no more. Is there anything else?'

'Yup. I want a passport.'

'A passport?'

'Are you a fucking parrot now? Yes. A passport. So I can piss off abroad.'

'There's no point, Peter. You will be unable to travel abroad… Unless you'd like me to—?'

'Yeah. Not in my own name. You've got a few weeks. Plenty of time, and they'd better make it perfect.'

'That'll be expensive. I'll have to transfer some funds from your offshore trust—'

'Just get it for me.' Leech could see Gruber mentally rubbing his hands at the prospect of ripping him off again. The greedy shite. 'And I want a breakdown of costs, for you managing my affairs since I've been in here. Detailed.'

Gruber was standing, packing files into his case. Leech had finally got to him, broken through the placid, detached, professional air the man perpetually exuded. The solicitor froze at the threat in his client's voice. Leech saw sweat glisten on his forehead and, for a moment, just a second, he wondered if Gruber would prefer his parole denied.

'I can assure you there are no irregularities… I will admit that my time does not come cheap, but then again, you do enjoy, shall we say, additional services others in my profession fail to provide. All in all I think you'll find I have been, and will continue to be, exceptional value for money.' He recovered his composure as he completed his speech, only the tell-tale sheen of moisture on his brow giving away his tension.

'You'd better be. I may be stuck in here now, but soon I'll be able to take control of my own affairs. Manage my investments myself.'

'Peter, my track record speaks for itself. I've turned your trust fund into millions while you've been in here. Around a fivefold increase, net of my charges. I doubt you'll do better elsewhere, or even by investing yourself.'

'We'll see. Make sure I have that cost breakdown.'

Gruber headed to the door, knocked to signal the guard.

Leech said, 'One more thing. I want her address, too.'

Gruber was puzzled. 'Whose?'

'My little Birdy, of course. Judy Finch.'

The door opened and Gruber said nothing more, just nodded and left.

Leech lay on his bed and, despite himself, was fascinated by Powers' book. His own studies in psychology were superficial—he'd exaggerated when he told Judy he had studied to degree level. The truth was that he bored easily and never bothered going further than reading the juicy stuff. He had learnt much more about criminal psychology from studying his fellow inmates.

Yet this forensic psychiatrist, whatever that was, who had assessed him eighteen years before as a psychopath, also had plenty to say about the criminal mind.

By all accounts Powers had been involved in the early research that helped lead to the development of a checklist for measuring psychopathic personalities, pioneering the shift from the label used previously, Antisocial Personality Disorder.

The man was a liar. Leech could see that. The book claimed psychopaths had no depth of emotion. And, according to Powers, he was one. What bollocks. He felt as much as everyone else. He could tell that from their reactions.

Okay, he was different. Stronger. Better. But he had passionate feelings, he suffered rage, his jealousy knew no bounds.

He thought of Shaun. His brother. Oh, how he hated him.

That emotion was real, not imagined.

And he had loved his parents. All kids love their parents. If he had not loved them so much, how come they could make him so angry?

He consumed the pages. Delving into the mind of the man who had tried to peer into his own, questions in his head now, demanding to know—who are you Powers? What drives you?

The chapters detailing Powers' time as a criminal profiler were incredible. It was like a manual for anyone who wanted to confuse the police. The idiot. And did he really believe all this stuff?

He sniggered as he thought about his interviews with the prison psychiatrist. How he had dissembled and lied, pretended to feel things he did not, piling on the bullshit by the ton. Even fooled him by manipulating those pathetic psychometric tests. Supposedly infallible yet he had convinced the so called expert he was not dangerous! These academic types were a piece of piss to fool.

He went back to the book.

The very best was the section on his own case. The details had been altered a little to disguise him, but Leech immediately knew it was himself being described.

A savage attack. Both parents killed. The young man labelled a psychopath. Definitely not psychotic. In other words, sane but capable of evil. The frenzied attack, the dozens of puncture wounds, purportedly his handicraft.

And the brilliant profiler, the man they called Doc, bragging that he knew the killer was a close friend or relative of the victims, the passion of the attack testament to it.

Yet, if I did it then, smart-arse, I do have deep feelings. Passionate feelings. So, Doctor, how does that fit with your assessment that I'm a psychopath, a man with stunted emotions?

Leech had to laugh at that.

According to Powers, a murder occurring as a result of say, a robbery, would result in the victim being stabbed once or twice, just disabling blows, to allow rapid escape.

Leech thought that was interesting. He read on.

The perpetrator turned out to be the son. Yet he claimed to have amnesia, his purported memory loss a result of a blow from his brother that rendered him unconscious at the time of the murder. Doctor Powers concluded he was not amnesiac, but many would consider him bordering on stupid.

'STUPID?' Leech roared the word as he read it, flinging the book at the wall.

'I'll show him who's stupid.'

He calmed himself, and then thought again: See Powers, I do feel extreme emotions, I'm no psychopath. I'm normal.

He picked up the book and found the paragraph. The genius doctor continued to say that his subject, if not stupid, was prone to flights of fantasy, and had the ability to mix fact and fiction to the extent of confusing himself.

Leech read on, at times angered, at times laughing aloud at the man's idiocy, at others absorbed by the uncanny insights.

His cell door opened. Time for some lunch and free association, prisoners' social time. He was gobbling his food when he spotted Diarmud. He felt his hatred well up and he visualised himself killing the bastard. Not for the first time—the fantasy was a regular diversion for him.

Later, Leech was idly standing near some inmates playing pool while he leafed through a magazine, not reading, just observing. The prisoners had dispersed after lunch and Diarmud sat at a table, filling out papers. Two other warders were laughing and joking in the canteen, their line of sight to the senior officer blocked.

Leech sneaked toward Diarmud, the man oblivious to the approaching Snake.

And he wanted to strike. To kill again.

He closed in on his prey. His focus was on Diarmud's neck, his attention riveted on the delicate pulse fluttering beneath the skin, the vulnerable carotid arteries exposed by the very mechanism that gave life.

The Snake wanted to kill the man. Silently. Instantly. Without trace.

Some years before, an old lifer, a martial arts fanatic and one of the few cons Leech had ever admired, explained the move to him. 'You have to get it just right. Just enough pressure on both carotid arteries.' His guru had touched his own neck, demonstrating the exact location to apply pressure, warning Leech, 'Don't try it on yourself. Unless you're suicidal.' Leech listened, wanted so much to try it on someone. 'If you hit the pressure points exactly right, at exactly the same time, the brain reacts by shutting down the heart... You need to deliver a rapid squeeze rather than a blow—if you don't want to leave any bruising.'

Since then Leech had tried it several times—and not once had he succeeded. Each time he had merely provoked a fight, which was no problem as he always won.

He had started to doubt the man's word, decided it was Bruce Lee bullshit, fantasy stuff from Hollywood.

And then he had seen it with his own eyes. The old lag, sixty but as fit as many twenty-year olds, had been insulted by a new inmate. Leech was behind them, queuing for food, as his teacher delivered a blurred jab to each side of the inmate's neck, felling him instantly. The coroner confirmed heart failure, and since that day Leech had hungered for a chance to deliver such a perfect death.

He now stood, fixated on Diarmud's arteries, the warder unaware of the Snake's presence, within striking distance of a swift death.

Baro-receptors. That's what the old man had called them. Ultra-sensitive to changes in pressure, and capable of fooling the brain into killing itself.

The temptation was almost too much. He wanted to make Diarmud his first success. He stepped forward.

Powers' words, read only minutes before, jangled in his head.

'A psychopath is a hostage to magical thinking. He will act on impulse, without fear of the consequences and may give the impression he is stupid as a result.'

Well, Powers was wrong about him. He wanted his parole. He wanted out now. He had things to do. And he had a woman waiting for him. His Birdy.

He bent down and whispered into Diarmud's ear. 'Boo!'

Diarmud jumped up and turned on him, face red, furious that Leech had managed to creep up behind him, yet unable to punish him or charge him with anything.

And Leech knew it—he had been careful not to touch the officer. Diarmud would be laughed out of the Governor's office if he accused Leech of abusive language, or unacceptable behaviour. For what? Saying 'boo' in a quiet voice?

Leech was pleased with himself for his self-control but more so with the result of his prank.

Diarmud was beside himself. 'You evil shit, Leech. You almost gave me a heart attack.'

'If only you knew, sir. If only you knew.' He touched his middle finger to his forehead in a mock salute and sauntered back to his cell.

As Vice Chairman of the Parole Board, Doctor Powers shared much of his boss's enormous workload. Only the 'political interface'—the Judge's term for the interminable meetings he spent with government bureaucrats and the Secretary of State himself—was outside Doc's remit. He helped organise the hundred plus part-time members of the board and ensured the thousands of oral hearings and recalls were distributed evenly and in good time. It was an onerous task, trying to fit in the schedule to suit so many busy professional people. Additionally he was responsible for training.

The workload was massive and only seven of the entire team were full-time, including the Judge, Doc, Judy, a couple of legal executives and secretaries.

It was not difficult for Doc to immerse himself in the job, especially as the Judge had fallen behind while Doc had been away recuperating. Or, at least, mending his broken bones and innards. Complete recovery was something else, something more elusive.

Doc was preparing for three hearings today, the first at lunchtime. Leech. A meeting Doc was not looking forward to.

For each hearing for full parole, or for breach of the terms of the parolee's licence, the three person panel had to study the entire prisoner dossier. That in itself took an hour or more. In addition, there was the hearing itself. Recalls were speedier than full parole hearings as there was no prisoner representation, the parole panel made its decision on the written submissions alone. One team could clear ten to fifteen cases in a day, as long as they had studied the dossiers beforehand.

Today, Doc had just the hearings. But all three were oral hearings with the prisoners present, along with their professional representative. Each hearing would take two hours or more in total. It was gruelling work.

As Doc ate his breakfast and supped his coffee, he leafed through Leech's dossier for the umpteenth time, wondering if he could be impartial in this case. The man's inside my head, he thought.

He re-read Judy's report and it sent his mind reeling back to the weekend. The nightmares and the hallucinations were still featuring in his life, but at least now the sense of hopelessness was diminished.

Judy.

Just talking to her had lifted his spirits. Opening up to her had been therapeutic. But, even so, Doc had thrown himself into work, and here he was, Friday morning, worn out from the punishing schedule, drained by the pills and the booze that had been his refuge.

I'll see Judy tomorrow.

He reluctantly pushed her from his thoughts and focussed on the dossier. Leech.

Last night the man had appeared again, looming ever larger in his nightmare. Doc let out a troubled breath.

Damn, Leech! Why are you in my head?

Was it just because he was dealing with Leech's case right now? His first task from the Judge since the accident? His first discussion with Judy had been regarding this man. Was that it? Had his tormented mind sucked in memories from eighteen years before, to torture him yet more? To twist them like a knife in his own belly?

He tried to analyse it. Could it be a demonised version of his own self-blame, coming to him in the form of this 'monster'?

Doc scowled at the boy-man's photograph, taken at the time of the trial, wondering: Was I wrong about you? Is that why you've invaded my guilty conscience?

Yet he knew, professionally, the most difficult person to psychoanalyse, to help with the problems of mental health, was himself. He shrugged the thought away, determined to discuss his feelings with Judy. Surely between the two of them they could work it through.

For a moment he drifted. Luxuriating in the affection he had felt radiating from her. His own emotions, his own attraction to her, were strengthening. He was allowing himself to fall for her. And why not?

Natalie.

But she's dead. Gone. I must look forward.

But it's only four months.

Clack, clack, clack, clackclackclack…

Oh, God!

The film filled his mind.

No!

He grasped his head with his hands, palms crushing his temples, fingers gouging his scalp.

'Get out!' He yelled and the words ricocheted around his house.

But to no avail. The projectionist inside his head continued the replay of the accident, until Leech loomed into view, his hands outstretched and bloody. And, as the leering image expanded, came into ever sharper focus, Doc realised what Leech was holding.

He screamed.

Leech was offering him his son. Daniel. The ravaged foetus of Natalie's unborn child.

'So before we invite the others to join us, are there any questions or anomalies in the prisoner's dossier? Anything anyone wishes to raise?' Judge Jeffries sat at the head of the table, between Doc Powers and Sophie Pugh. They were in the Governor's annexe, a sombre room adjacent to his own bright office, the mahogany table stretched before them with three empty chairs arranged at the other side facing them. A legal secretary was sitting to the side of the room, ready to take notes.

Doc's nervousness was mounting. The thought that the green-eyed man-boy that haunted his dreams was about to enter his reality unnerved him. He needed another drink. Could taste the vodka he had swigged before attending this morning's hearing. He had also slipped a valium in his mouth as he arrived at the prison. It was having little effect.

He was certain his inner turmoil was visible to his colleagues. Jeffries had asked him how he was when they had shaken hands. Was he being polite, or was Doc's appearance askew? He straightened his tie at the thought, trying to remember if he had brushed his hair.

And the woman. She was something else. Barely concealed disdain as she shook hands. He thought he saw her wipe her palm on her trousers afterwards. She was a severe one. Hair cropped, face devoid of make-up, and strong features, hard set, as if she had seen everything bad the world had to offer.

Sophie Pugh.

Doc had not selected her, the Judge had, along with Jeffries and himself, and notified them prior to Doc's return to work.

He dredged up her details from his memory. Social worker. Re-settlement officer. Prison Welfare Trust Director. Keen on radical reform. She had been working for the Parole Board for several months, but Doc had only met her during her induction training. She was intelligent, opinionated, and not the slightest bit worried whose feathers she ruffled. He had sensed some animosity then. Why? he wondered. Perhaps he would find out today.

It did not take long.

'Yes, Judge. I'd like to talk about *labels* and how we address Mister Leech.' Sophie Pugh's attention was on Doc as she spoke and he felt the heat of her words scald him.

'Well either Mister Leech, Peter or—'

'I'm not talking about his name, Judge. I am talking about labels.' Her gaze was like the sun's rays through a magnifying glass. Burning into Doc. 'I'm a little confused. Doctor Powers seems wedded to the term psychopath. Yet other forensic psychiatrists, including the prison psychiatrist, whose report is in here,' she slapped a hand on her copy of Leech's dossier, 'prefer the terms Extreme Antisocial Personality Disorder and Dangerous Severe Personality Disorder. And he is not convinced Mister Leech is either.' Her face, not unattractive in itself, took on an ugly expression, her eyebrows plunged down, her eyes slitted, her mouth a mean line, lipless. 'It seems to me that if the professionals can't agree on a label then we should disregard them all.'

Judge Jeffries, a master of arbitration turned to Doc and shrugged. 'I have no view on the subject.' His frown quizzed Doc.

'Well, without wishing to lecture—'

'Please don't.' Pugh was adamant.

'I am a consulting forensic psychiatrist. My use of the term psychopath is based on over twenty years experience, empirical data and research. I use the Psychopathy Checklist which is recognised throughout the world as the definitive test for this disorder.' He nodded to Jeffries, preferring not to engage Pugh's powerful glare. 'Leech is a psychopath.'

'That sounds reasonable. Sophie?'

She obviously did not think so.

'My suggestion is that we dispense with all labels, and we treat each potential parolee as an individual. In my experience of these hearings, that approach works well for all involved.' She sat back, arms folded.

'Mmm.' Jeffries appeared bemused, but came up with a solution. 'My own experience is, that during hearings, the best approach is to avoid jargon. The prisoner concerned is, after all, no expert. And, so, discussions with regard to psychological terms,' he checked with Pugh, 'or labels, will be the preserve of our own private discourse, after the parolee has had his say. Agreed?'

Pugh nodded. Satisfied. Jeffries turned to Doc, eyebrow arched.

Doc was outraged. He was here in his professional capacity to act as an expert. Round one to Pugh, he thought. He fumed at what he saw as yet another example of liberal thinking bringing about more dumbing down. But he was not up to fighting. His own grasp on reality was just a shimmer from slipping away. He acquiesced.

'Fair enough. Although I do want to probe this man, this psychopath, very carefully.'

'Then let us continue.' Jeffries motioned to the clerk to bring in the prisoner, his legal counsel and the Home Office representative.

Doc wiped his brow with a tissue, then rubbed his sweaty palms. Pugh stared at him. He tried to ignore her, his heart racing as he anticipated the arrival of the boy-man. Dreading the clack-clack-clack in his mind. Desperate to maintain his professional facade. He glanced down. His hands trembled. He clasped them in his lap.

I'm a basket case, he thought.

He looked up as the secretary re-entered.

A prison officer, probably in his mid-fifties and fairly senior, followed her in. Doc forced himself to check the agenda. Andrew Diarmud. Thirty-seven years service. Unblemished record. Doc watched him introduce himself to Jeffries, then Pugh. Doc felt the hand in his, the determination there. And a steadiness, a firmness, in the eyes. Doc liked him.

Diarmud sat in the right hand seat facing them. Doc felt calmer now, the moment of trauma passed. Another officer appeared, an escort for the prisoner, and motioned someone to enter before him. Leech appeared and paused in the doorway, surveying the room.

Only this was not the man-boy of Doc's nightmares. The toothless, scrawny teenager had been replaced by this great bull of a man. Doc would never have believed it was the same person had it not been for the eyes. Those piercing, hard green eyes.

Leech was inspecting them! He was acting as if he was in control here, and using eye contact to intimidate. The emerald chips glowed at Doc. He could feel the man's hatred. Those eyes made Sophie Pugh's seem as soft as cotton balls.

Any doubts Doc had about his diagnosis evaporated in that moment. His mind super-imposed the boy-man on the specimen before him, recollections of their interview boiling in his mind. How could he have doubted himself? Relief ebbed the tension from him. He could do this.

And he certainly would not be intimidated by Leech.

'Hello, Peter. Please sit down.' Doc sensed Jeffries frown at the breach of protocol —the judge was chairman of the panel—but kept his focus on Leech.

The prisoner had blocked the entrance, his escorting warder shut out, peering round his charge's head, clearly not wanting to push Leech, wrong-footed, unsure.

Doc knew Leech had intended it. A way of subconsciously demonstrating his power, his control. He may be a prisoner here, it said... *But.*

So, Doc punctured the illusion. Told him to sit. Politely, but an instruction all the same.

Control.

Leech's jaw muscles twitched, then he smiled and strolled in.

'I'm representing myself, so we won't be needing this.' He indicated the middle chair as he seated himself in the one opposite Pugh, distancing himself from Doc and Diarmud.

Jeffries gestured for the escorting warder to remove the middle chair, and Doc could see how things were going. The prisoner should sit in the middle, facing the presiding judge. Leech's little play had undermined the system, already declaring to their collective subconscious: I'm different, I'm better.

Very clever. Very manipulative.

Leech shifted his chair diagonally to better view the four people ranged around him. Passive yet confident. His hands on his knees, legs apart, but not so wide as to offend or threaten Pugh, his crotch now aimed squarely at Doc instead.

Jeffries started speaking. Doc tuned out as the judge explained what the process entailed to Leech and Diarmud.

Jeffries finished by saying, 'Our aim is to assess whether you are a risk to the public at large and determine your readiness to re-enter society.'

'I'm ready.' Leech's cheery face flicked between Jeffries and Pugh.

'You'll have your turn to speak, Peter, as I have explained.' Jeffries addressed Diarmud. 'If you would like to lead off with the Home Office view based on the prisoner's behaviour and attitude during his time in prison, and whether you feel he is fit for release on licence.'

'Of course, your Honour.' Diarmud rattled through the record of prisons Leech had attended, and confirmed that he had no ADAs—Additional Days Added—for infringements of prison rules.

Sophie Pugh butted in. 'So, in all the time he has been inside he has been a model prisoner!' She got an appreciative look from Leech for that.

'Hardly a model prisoner, Ms Pugh.'

'But you just said he's never given cause for ADAs, he's a trustee, a Listener, and gets privileges for his contribution to prison society. In fact he is at the highest level of earned privileges a prisoner can achieve, isn't he? Has his own clothes, a single room, a TV, extra time out of his cell and so forth. Sounds like a model prisoner to me.'

Doc was sickened to see Pugh glance at Leech, as if seeking his approval. And she got it as he nodded at her.

Diarmud aimed his response at the judge. 'In my mind a model prisoner is not only one who sticks to the rules, but is a positive force in the prison's population. Someone the other prisoners can look up to in terms of good behaviour. I'm afraid Prisoner Leech does not fit that category.' He turned to Leech, who was openly scowling at Diarmud now, and added, 'His exploits as a Listener don't fool me.'

'Objection! That's just his opinion.' Leech thrust himself forward, angry, his bovine head switching between Diarmud and Jeffries, nostrils flaring.

'Peter, this is not a court of law. Although you have opted to represent yourself please wait until I invite you to speak. You will have your turn to ask Officer Diarmud questions.'

Leech settled back, muttered, 'Sorry.' He had made his point.

Jeffries asked Diarmud, 'On what basis are you doubtful? I gather the Listener programme is a remarkable success and helps numerous prisoners to adapt to prison life. It's even reduced the number of suicides. Surely it is commendable that Mister Leech freely gives of his own time to assist other inmates.'

'Well sir, Leech is not popular—'

'That's just his opinion!'

'Quiet please, Mister Leech. No more outbursts or I will terminate this hearing. I have explained the process. You will have your turn.' There was no arguing, Jeffries meant it, and Doc could see Leech swallow and digest the implication.

Diarmud pressed his point. 'He's not popular. He's a loner. Even eats alone and is rarely involved with other prisoners during association, never partakes in team sports, not even a game of pool or darts.'

Pugh stopped him.

'Mister Diarmud, there are many reasons why a prisoner may not wish to associate with other inmates. He could be shy. Perhaps unwilling to be seen as a member of one particular social group, clique or gang. Could it not just be the rational response of an individual surrounded by threat?'

Leech was doing a good impression of one of those plastic dogs that people used to place on the rear shelf of their cars, his head bobbing furiously in agreement, and Doc could almost believe the two had colluded prior to the meeting. He dismissed the thought.

Diarmud, was calm, if a little condescending. 'In my experience, and I have been working inside prisons, Ma'am, for almost forty years, a loner is usually an inmate who fails to bond with others. It is rarely a matter of choice, but usually the result of the prison population despising or fearing the individual.'

'I see. Yet he is a Listener. Hardly someone to be feared or despised.'

'Yes, Ma'am. And as Judge Jeffries has pointed out, Listeners provide a very useful confidential service for those who are being bullied, are depressed, are potential victims of abuse and so on. Believe me, I am a great fan of the programme. It makes my job easier.'

Doc spoke before Pugh could twist the advantage.

'So why do you feel Peter's involvement is a sham.' Doc's words almost provoked another outburst from Leech, and Doc could see him struggle to keep quiet. He probed the officer further. 'I think you said, *His exploits as a Listener don't fool me.* Please explain.'

Diarmud dipped his head at Doc in acknowledgement, then spoke to Jeffries, a lesson taught by attorneys the world over—always address the judge as he is the man to convince, regardless of who asked the question.

'Normally a prisoner requests a Listener's ear. On occasions a Listener might identify a prisoner who is struggling, a potential suicide for example. The Listener then requests the opportunity to speak with the prisoner. In confidence of course, usually in the man's cell.'

'Are you inferring that Mister Leech is an unpopular man and therefore an unpopular Listener?' Jeffries had understood the point.

Leech was picking at his nails, shaking his head, eyes downcast. Doc noticed that Pugh, though silent, had also shaken her head at the word 'unpopular'.

'Exactly, your Honour. He is never requested through the prison officers. He always imposes himself or tells us he has been requested by the inmate directly. In my view he is using the role purely to impress this board. To influence your decision.'

Pugh went on the offensive. Doc was intrigued and wondered if she had information that he and Jeffries did not.

'You don't like Mister Leech, do you?' Her right hand balled into a fist, slapped into her other palm, then thumped onto the table.

'Ma'am. I have no feelings either way. I treat all prisoners equally.'

'I seriously doubt that. But isn't it true that you once erroneously accused Mister Leech of the attempted murder of another inmate?'

'Really?' Jeffries seemed bemused again, his head swivelling from Diarmud to Pugh and back.

Diarmud coloured. Was it anger or embarrassment? Doc was not sure.

'Indeed I did. A prisoner supposedly fell down the stairs. The stairs are cast iron and not forgiving. He broke his back.' Diarmud took a moment, licked his lips, attention still on Jeffries. 'A prisoner came forward and identified Leech as having pushed the man—ran into him with a rugby-style palm to the forehead, knocking him down the stairs. I investigated and recommended the police were brought in. The victim was unconscious at the time.'

'But Peter was innocent, wasn't he?'

Leech was nodding at Pugh's words again, his face a shining beacon of honesty, an angel. Doc was certain it was an act.

'Well, Ma'am. The police dropped the case when the witness died. Supposedly suicide.'

'Oh, and I suppose you think Mister Leech killed him!'

Leech laughed at that, enjoying himself now.

'I couldn't say, Ma'am.'

Pugh pursued him. 'I think it is clear you feel animosity for Mister Leech. In your mind, he got away with it. Yet he was innocent.' She was pummelling her fist in her palm again, punctuating the last four words.

'Is that right, Mister Diarmud?' The judge's voice was soft, smoothing the waves, oiling the waters.

'The victim came round several days later. Claimed it was an accident and that Leech was not involved. It's the prisoners' code...' Diarmud's voice petered out, his explanation unconvincing.

'His back was broken! Do you seriously believe this man would forgive and forget because of some mythical code of silence between criminals? Mister Leech is innocent.' Pugh collapsed back in her seat, dismissing his assertion. 'I think you have more than demonstrated your bias in this case, Mister Diarmud.'

Diarmud was bright red now. Angry and embarrassed. Doc thought Pugh had tried to destroy the man, and almost succeeded.

'I think bias is a strong word.' It was a mild rebuke from Jeffries. 'Mister Diarmud has experience and is allowed an opinion.'

'Thank you, sir.' Diarmud pointed to Leech. 'I was asked to assist your assessment of this man's fitness for release. My opinion is that he should not be paroled.'

Diarmud was defiant, finally addressing Pugh, the judge forgotten. 'Accidents have a habit of occurring around this man. Release him at your peril.' Diarmud's cheeks faded. He had said his piece.

Then Pugh applied the coup de grace.

'Asked? You were asked to assist? I was under the impression you volunteered for this hearing. Isn't that so?'

Diarmud squirmed, his cheeks darkening again. Rumbled.

'Well, in a way—'

'In the way of volunteering.' She turned away from him and looked intently at Jeffries. 'I'm sure we'll give Mister Diarmud's recommendation the appropriate weight it deserves, Judge.'

'Perhaps we should have some coffee.' Jeffries indicated the legal secretary to fetch some. Doc felt the air discharge, the judge successfully releasing the electricity energising the room. 'Now, are there any other questions from the panel for Mister Diarmud?' Both Doc and Pugh shook their heads. Jeffries addressed Leech. 'Okay Peter, as you are representing yourself, you have your opportunity to question Mister Diarmud.'

'Not so much a question, your Honour, more of a statement if that's acceptable.' He didn't pause for a response, merely aimed his comments at Pugh. 'The Prison Reform Trust recently criticised the parole system. Their actual words were—it's a lottery.' He wagged a finger at Diarmud. 'And this officer is an example of that principle in action. Any other officer would've given a more positive opinion. In fact the one I report to has put a favourable view forward. It's in my dossier.' Then his eyes were on Jeffries. 'I just hope you take that into account, sir.'

Finally he looked at Doc, his lips curling, satisfied he had scored. Doc was sure he had somehow known Pugh had some inside information on Diarmud. And now Leech was quoting the Trust! He still could not believe Pugh had colluded, but wondered how else Leech had turned the Home Office representative's negative recommendation on its head.

'I think the Trust's comment was a little harsh,' Jeffries gave a weak smile to Pugh and then turned back to Leech, 'but I take your point. You can address the panel now, and we will ask you some questions. Ah, coffee.'

The Governor's secretary appeared with a tray. A cup for everyone but Leech, so as they sipped their coffees he asked if he could stand up and stretch his legs. The judge assented.

Leech made a show of yawning and taking a few paces around the room, then stood behind his chair, hands clutching the back rail. He beamed down at them. 'The first thing I would like to say is this. If a person is innocent, there is no risk to the public if he is paroled.' With that, he pulled his chair round to the end of the table, perched on the edge of it, placed his hands on the table before him and clasped them devoutly. 'And I am innocent.'

He looked at them as if he had said the most profound words they had ever been blessed with. Doc's biscuit was freeze-framed, half-way to his mouth, in awe at the man's gall.

Leech continued with the air of a benevolent educator, as if he were conferring some great honour on them, sharing his presence and insights. Diarmud almost spoiled the effect with a sneeze into his hand that sounded to Doc suspiciously like the word 'bullshit'.

Leech ignored the interruption. 'It really is that simple.' He paused for effect, two members of his audience spellbound. 'By releasing me, you will be making a good decision. I've quoted the Trust once already,' he winked at Pugh, 'but they also say the parole system is performing poorly. In my case, I don't doubt you'll make the right decision.'

Doc dropped his biscuit and it shattered into crumbs on his plate. Leech had winked at a Parole Board member! In three years of being involved in these sessions he had never seen anything like it. The man's arrogance was breathtaking.

He's a convicted murderer! Doc wanted to yell it as he saw the judge and the independent hanging on Leech's words.

'Now, you're probably thinking, doesn't he realise he was found guilty in a court of law? Of course I do! That decision had the single most devastating impact on my life. Yet I've come through it. I hold no malice. No thirst for revenge against the system. In fact, the experience has held some positives for me. My education. My work as a Listener.' He smirked at Diarmud, but Doc doubted Pugh or Jeffries noticed. He certainly did.

'Anyway, if you believe I really was guilty, that I was a parent killer, then I'm no danger, am I? I've run out of parents, haven't I? They're dead and buried! Who is there left for me to kill?' The callousness of his tone, the brutal dismissal of his own parents' savage murder, confirmed to Doc his own diagnosis.

Psychopath.

He tried to catch Pugh's eye. Surely even she would recognise the trait, or at least be perturbed by his attitude.

She was nodding at Leech! For chrissake.

As if Leech could read his mind, he funnelled his diatribe at Doc. Doc felt like a target. A bull's-eye.

'Some say I am a psychopath. Others say I have Dangerous Antisocial Personality Disorder... I say they are wrong. I'm none of these things. Even the prison psychiatrist agrees.' His eyes were triumphant as he smiled patronisingly at Doc. 'Despite what some so-called experts might think.' He held Doc's gaze for a moment longer then aimed his comments at Pugh again. 'I admit I was a disturbed teenager. A truant. I took drugs, but I have been clean since my incarceration. I've been educated and improved by prison. I am innocent, but I've made the best of my time here.'

Despite himself, Doc had to admit it was impressive. If he really was innocent.

'Please,' his eyes back on Doc, skewering him, then shifting to Pugh, his expression softening, 'don't apply a label to me. Psychopath, DPSD, ASPD. Convict. Loner. Loser...' He waved a hand over Diarmud's head. Pathos in his delivery as he spoke the last of his set piece. 'Please don't keep me in here. I'm already a victim of a gross injustice. Don't compound it.'

Doc felt like leading an ovation for the performance. For that was what it was. Leech deserved an Oscar. At the end of his speech he had slumped, head bowed before them, hands still clasped in prayer. And somehow he had hit Pugh's hot button—labels.

'Peter,' Pugh was clasping her own hands in a gesture like Leech. 'Thank you for that. I have only one major concern, regardless of your guilt or innocence, as it is clear to us all you are a reformed character—'

Oh my God! Doc held his forehead in frustration. Can the stupid woman not see through it?

She went on, confirming Doc's fears. 'Tell me, why did you transfer from an open facility back here? You see, I help a lot of clients make the transition back to society and it is a necessary step in the process for most inmates.'

'I understand that, Ms Pugh, but in my role as Listener, I felt I could be of more use here. The added freedoms of open prison were no attraction for me... Since I've been here I have realised my vocation is to help people. It would have been selfish of me to stay there—they have a soft ride. They don't need me.'

Doc noticed Diarmud stare at the ceiling and wondered if he too was hoping for a miracle, for the others to understand this charade.

He pulled out Judy's report. He was sure Leech had given her a different reason. 'You told the interviewing officer, Ms Finch, that you transferred back to here because of the prevalence of drugs in the open prison. Is it possible that the tempta-tion was too much for you? There was certainly no mention of your pious vocation at that meeting, was there?' Doc let the sarcasm tinge his voice, deliberately provoking, needling for a response.

For just a flash, a nanosecond, Doc saw fury in Leech's face, and then the mask, the reasonable man, slipped back into place. Doc was not sure anyone else noticed.

'I think Judy... I mean Ms Finch, must've left it out of the report.' Leech switched his attention to the other two members of the panel. 'We got on very well. We chatted for over two hours. Lovely lady, but her brief report left out a number of things.' His tone was supercilious, but forgiving of the oversight.

Judy? Got on very well? Lovely lady? Doc heard a warning blast in those words... and the delivery. Leech surely thought he had made some sort of connection with Judy, yet she was freaked out after meeting him. Doc needed to speak with her. He had thought her report was impressive—concise, impartial and thorough. Now he wondered what she had left out.

Pugh spoke again. 'That's a very noble reason, but you must have known it might disadvantage your parole application this time round. You've had little or no advice or experience in facing the realities of life outside.'

'It's not a problem for me, Ms Pugh. I'm very wealthy and I've learnt how to make money from trading stocks and shares. I won't be in the same position as most of the poor bastards who get out of here. I don't need to work.' He sneered at Diarmud as he added, 'My portfolio makes several times the income a scr... a prison officer earns.'

Doc piped up. 'Some might say that in itself is evidence that you are not socialised, in the sense that you would prefer a solitary life managing money rather than engaging with people.'

Leech was unmoved, blasé in his response. 'I plan to work for the Samaritans. For free. I'm already trained and with my experience in here, I am, they say, ideal. Hardly unsocial, eh?' He made a face at Pugh. *Obviously*, it said.

'I have some other concerns.' Doc waited, dragged Leech's focus back to him. 'You say you were innocent—'

'And the lie detector confirmed it. I took a polygraph for the prison psychiatrist.' Leech had lowered his head and Doc imagined him pawing the ground, a bull ready to charge. He decided once again to try to get him to see red, to show his true nature, to drop the mask.

'Indeed? But polygraphs are inconclusive and unreliable at best.' Doc dismissed it with a wave of his hand. 'You accused your brother of the murder. Of framing you.

As a, what did you call yourself?' Doc made a show of consulting his notes. 'Oh yes, as a parent killer, you point out you have no more targets. I disagree.' Leech glowered at him, and Doc felt that aura of menace, of power. He was disturbed by it, thrown slightly, fearing a relapse into his hallucination, but plunged on. 'I'd suggest your brother Shaun could be in danger... from you, Mister Leech. From the killer of his parents.' Doc was determined to antagonise, to goad Leech into losing his temper. An outburst might just get Pugh and Jeffries to see through the fiction Leech was maintaining. Doc could see the convict rising to it, the green eyes glowing at him.

But Pugh craned forward, hostile, and attacked Doc.

'Is that really a fair question? Shaun Leech and Peter Leech had the same parents.'

Doc was livid. Leech had been rattled and Doc was sure he could make him lose it. She had ruined the moment. Leech was relaxed again, inspecting his fingernails, carefree.

Ignoring Pugh, he concentrated his reply on the man.

'But only one of them has been convicted of killing Mister and Mrs Leech. And he,' Doc stabbed a finger at the prisoner, 'blames his brother for his incarceration. I believe Shaun Leech could be at risk. What do you say to that, Peter?' He deliberately shut the door on Pugh answering.

Leech took his time to reply. His threatening tone chilled Doc when it finally came. 'My brother is dead.' Then Leech looked up from his impromptu manicure, eyes shining wet, for all the world, close to breaking down and crying. 'That's what he said about me. But I forgive him. Sadly, to me Shaun is as good as dead too.' Sorrow oozed from him now, the powerful bull of moments before displaced by this tearful, sensitive soul. 'I know I have to stay away from him when I am paroled.'

Doc was not fooled. He interpreted the words as a threat.

My brother is dead.

Shaun is as good as dead too.

His gut told him Shaun was at grave risk. Peter Leech would kill him.

Leech and Diarmud were dismissed from the meeting, leaving the three parole board members to deliberate. Jeffries and Pugh were using the restrooms, the legal clerk was organising more coffee, leaving Doc alone with his thoughts.

Doc was stunned. Jeffries had summed up and then asked Leech if he had any final comments to add. Of course he had.

Leech had put on a pleading face, speaking to all three of them, but starting with Doc.

'Please don't label me a psychopath. Even you, Doctor Powers, say the word is much abused—in your own book!' The eyes sparked victoriously before he added, for Sophie Pugh's benefit, 'I don't like labels. In here you hear them all the time. Raghead. Nigger. Nonce. Even the warders are screws, the female ones all lumped together as dykes.' Leech spread his hands, palms out, now addressing the judge. 'Such labels are destructive. Another form of prejudice. I'm really just a normal man in abnormal circumstances.'

The coffee arrived and Doc poured himself a strong one. He waited for the others to return, reflecting on what he had heard. Leech had tagged Pugh, quoted her views to them all. How had he done that?

94

Pugh and Jeffries arrived. The three of them spread out around the table, laying papers before them. Jeffries kicked off.

'This is an exceptional case, I think we can all agree. I'd like to hear from Doc first for his expert opinion. Then you, Sophie. I'll then determine how we should agree to proceed.'

Doc needed no encouragement.

'My view is that he is institutionalised. His rationale for returning to high security from open prison beggars belief. Indeed he contradicted himself. The interviewing officer gave a very different reason to the one we heard today.'

'But he explained that. It was an oversight on Ms Finch's part.'

'Sophie.' He faced her, his eyes intense, trying to drill his thoughts into her skull, trying to make her see reason. 'My expert opinion is that Leech is an accomplished liar. I don't doubt that if we were to ask Judy Finch she would confirm the reason given in the report.' He rubbed his palm over his forehead, frustrated, impatient with Pugh's bias. He made his next statement as forcefully as he could. 'My view is that releasing this man represents a risk, at the very least to his brother.' Doc could see Pugh winding up for a fight, but kept on. 'We must assume he is guilty and that he killed his parents. If there is any residual animosity, and it certainly sounded like it to me, then Shaun Leech is in danger.'

Pugh could barely contain herself at that.

'Doctor, please clarify for a layperson, his motivation in this respect as logic seems to indicate he has none.' She was ironic as she explained her point for him, as if he were a child failing to grasp a simple problem. 'His assertion of innocence, if true, would mean he has no history of killing. Ergo, he would be no threat to anyone, not even his brother.' She paused, letting the words sink in, then went on. 'And if he did kill his parents, as we are led to believe, in a fit of rage over money, then he has no reason to harm his brother—obviously he would know he wasn't framed!'

'She's got a point, Doc.'

Doc was exasperated. He could not get them to understand, nor were they giving his opinion the weight it deserved. He knew he wasn't on top form, knew he would normally be able to convince Jeffries. He tried a different tack.

'Leech is a psychopath. When he said, *My brother is dead*, I took that as a threat.'

Pugh let out a loud, disbelieving snort, making Doc more determined to ram home the point.

'We don't know whether Leech had planned to kill his brother along with his parents. Nor do we have any real evidence that he's forgiven him. He was ferocious in his condemnation of Shaun when I met him eighteen years ago.'

'Isn't that the problem? You can't see how much he has changed? He's a reformed character.'

'Psychopaths don't change, Sophie. They merely adapt.'

Jeffries dithered. 'Mmm. What do you think, Sophie?'

'He is independently wealthy. He has his own home. He is therefore in a better position than any other inmate I've ever dealt with. Most of them leave prison with a few pounds in their pockets and head for a hostel. No prospects!' She was getting worked up. Passionate in her mission in life. 'He may have a strange view of the re-settlement process, but I agree that he doesn't really need to go through it.' She sipped her coffee, then added, 'As for that dinosaur, Diarmud, he quite obviously had it in for Leech. Talk about biased! Well, I've made my mind up. We should parole him.'

Jeffries asked Doc, 'Can you say for sure that Shaun Leech would be in danger?'

'Of course not.' Doc wished he could. But one hundred percent certainty was impossible in his field. 'But my experience, my gut feel, his blatantly manipulative behaviour today,' his colleagues looked blank at that comment, 'and my belief he has become institutionalised, all lead me to recommend he spends the next twelve months in an open facility as a minimum. Then he should be reviewed with the possibility of parole. Let's take it slowly.'

Jeffries sat back, steepled his fingers, thumbs on his chin, his lips almost kissing his fingers.

'I hear what you say.' He glanced at the time. 'We have two more to review today.'

Doc was mentally urging Jeffries to see his point, could sense prevarication. Then the bombshell.

Jeffries turned to Doc as he said, 'A prisoner costs the taxpayer over a thousand pounds for each week of incarceration...' Doc's heart pounded his chest as he listened, incensed, not believing the cost argument could outweigh his professional assessment. 'Since you can't be more definite in terms of potential threat,' he checked with Pugh who was openly delighted, already anticipating what was coming, 'I find myself confirming Sophie's view. We will recommend to the Home Secretary that Leech be released on his Parole Eligibility Date in three weeks. He will be restrained from contacting, or otherwise interfering with, his brother, Shaun Leech...' He shuffled his papers and said, 'So, who's next?'

Later that day, as they were packing up, Jeffries asked Pugh, 'As a matter of interest, how did you become aware of Officer Diarmud's history with Leech?'

'You mean the accusation of attempted murder?'

'Indeed. An impressive piece of research.'

For the first time that day Doc heard a genuine gurgle of laughter from Pugh.

'Oh, hardly. I received an anonymous note yesterday. It gave details of the stairway incident.'

'And you verified it?'

'Of course. I telephoned Mister Riggs, the victim. He confirmed it was an accident.'

'I see.'

'He was the one who suggested Diarmud may not be totally impartial with regard to Leech. Which was the case.'

As they filed out, Doc could not help but wonder, who had sent that note? Somehow it had to be from Leech himself, he decided. And had some of Leech's excessive wealth found its way to Riggs' bank account, thereby encouraging the man to support his parole application? Doc could think of no other reason.

Then Pugh spoke, contradicting his thoughts.

'It seems that Mister Leech does have some friends, after all.'

Doc was not so sure.

Doc was glad to finally get out of there. He waited for a cab, waving Pugh and Jeffries into the first ones to arrive, happy to relax alone and take the air. Not that it was particularly fresh, but it still smelt pure and clean after the musky tang of prison. He ignored a few taxis before finally hailing one.

He got in, gave the driver his address and flipped open his mobile. His motives for calling Judy were a tangled mess. He certainly found her attractive in so many ways. He could feel himself being drawn in deeper each time he saw her...

But today, he reasoned, his need to speak to her was purely professional. Not as his therapist or potential lover, although he did look forward to sharing his trauma, his burden, with her sympathetic ear.

Right now, he felt concerned for her, with fear sneaking into his heart and lodging there. It was the way Leech had spoken about her. As if they were close. As if they were friends, or maybe more. Doc did not like it at all.

Am I jealous?

The thought jumped into his head as he punched Judy's number into the phone. He stopped, examining the idea, trying to detach himself for a moment.

No.

It was not an overreaction. He had seen it in Leech's mannerisms, heard it in the prisoner's speech patterns. His experience had sent him a warning and he knew not to ignore it. His professional judgement was that Leech genuinely felt some sort of bond, some connection with Judy.

And yes, she could be in danger.

But how to warn her without freaking her out? Her one encounter with Leech had disturbed her enough already. She had told Doc so, had even wanted to meet him to discuss it.

Or did she? Maybe it was just a ploy... An excuse to see him again! He gave himself a goofy grin at that thought. She had made it quite clear she wanted a relationship with him. Could she have been manipulating him?

Then, his ego under control again, he thought it unlikely. She would not need an excuse. She would have just called him, invited him for a drink.

He redialled, a fuzzy glow spreading through him as he anticipated hearing her voice. The taxi arrived at his home as he heard Judy's phone ringing. He gave the cabbie twenty pounds, not waiting for change. He heard a cheery, 'Good on yer, mate,' as he turned away.

'Hi, Colin. How was your day? And Leech?'

'Oh, he performed like a pro. Fooled at least two of the three of us.'

'But not the amazingly perceptive Doc Powers?' She teased him. He liked it.

'Well, maybe that's a little strong. I merely recommended he serve a year in open prison, before parole is considered.'

'And they ignored your advice? When is he out? Two or three weeks?'

'Assuming the Home Sec rubber stamps things, then three... One thing—he said he told you the reason he requested a transfer back from open prison was so that he could continue his work as a Listener, helping inmates. He felt he was no use at Ford.'

'That's rubbish! He said nothing of the sort.'

'Are you sure?' She certainly sounded it.

'Positive.' Not a smidgeon of doubt there. 'You can listen to the recording if you want.'

'No, no. That won't be necessary. As long as you're sure, that's good enough for me. Just confirms what I suspected. He's a compulsive liar.' What other porkies did you tell us, Leech?

'It's here if you change your mind. I certainly won't be needing it. I couldn't even face listening to it after our interview. He really gave me the creeps...'

Acid squirted, burning his stomach. He rubbed his chest and belly, trying to ease the pain, and it occurred to him that he may have abused his body beyond repair. He ignored the discomfort, keeping his attention on Judy. Her words had not only confirmed his suspicions, but it was worse than he thought.

Christ, she couldn't even listen to the interview again. Had been that disturbed by the man...

Doc tried to be gentle, to probe, not criticise. 'Was it so bad? You had to do the report from your notes?'

'I'm perfectly capable, Colin! I've written more reports from memory than I've had hot dinners.' She flared, about to bite his head off.

'Judy, I am not criticising. Just concerned. He really did get to you, didn't he?'

She sounded mollified. 'Yes... I've interviewed all sorts. No one like him though. He was...' she struggled for words to describe Leech.

'A green-eyed monster?' His own jealousy remembered as he joked about Leech, trying to lighten the mood.

She giggled. 'Yeah. Anyway, I'm over it now, and I've had several oral hearings myself this week. I'm getting to like this job.'

'Good. Now, how about tomorrow night. Can I cook again, or am I likely to offend Betty?'

'I'd love that.' She sounded like she meant it, her smile visible to Doc as he heard her utter the words. Her voice husky. So sexy.

They arranged things and Doc hit the 'end' button.

He had managed not to worry Judy about Leech's release. But he would listen to that recording.

He hoped he was overreacting. Misreading Leech. But deep down, he knew he was right.

What do you want with her, Leech? What?

Judy replaced the receiver. She was in the kitchen and Gran had plopped a cup of tea down for her as she had been speaking, then busied herself washing the dishes. There was no question of the nosy old dear leaving her to it, to talk to her new man in private.

Her new man? Was he?

Not yet, but he will be. Of that, she was certain.

'So, how is Mister Wonderful?' Gran was only mildly sarcastic. Judy knew she liked Colin.

'Busy. Like me.' She picked up a tea towel and started the drying up.

'I take it my services as a Josh-sitter will be required for tomorrow night? Going somewhere nice?'

'Please, Mum.' She pecked the downy cheek. 'You're such a gem. He's cooking again.'

'Great!' Gran was impressed by any man who could cook. 'But you haven't said much about him to me, love.' She sniffed.

Judy burst into laughter. 'Mum! We've done nothing but talk about him…'

'Yes. All work and how bright and supportive he is.' She studied her daughter, the plate in her hand receiving extra attention as she spoke. 'But do you really see him as the man for you, love? Long term?'

'Mum, please give it a rest. I know I've met some misfits and creeps… Colin's just different.'

'Don't get me wrong, dear.' Gran waggled a soapy brush under Judy's nose, finally relinquishing the pristine plate. 'I just don't want to see you hurt again. That's all…'

'I'm a big girl, Mum.'

'You're my daughter, and you know I think the world of you. Now, Colin, although I hardly know him, from what little you've told me, he seems a lovely man…' She thrust the brush in the bowl and attacked another helpless plate.

'Exactly. I don't see him hurting me.' Not like John. 'If anything I think he's more sensitive than me.'

'Bambi!' Gran passed Judy the plate and plucked out the last. Her frenzied motions trying to scrub away the frustration she felt with her daughter. 'That's what you called him. With his brown eyes and long lashes. I can see why.' She stopped, brush poised. 'But there's a lot of sadness there sweetheart… His wife's been dead how long?'

'Four months.' Judy spoke quietly. Her mother unerringly homing in on her own concern regarding her new relationship.

'Your dad died seven years ago. I still miss him, love.' She popped the last of the dishes in the rack, held Judy's hands, soap suds dripping to the floor as she searched her daughter's face. 'I hope it works out for you this time. God knows, you deserve it. But…'

Judy was not sure she wanted to hear. Waited. Then asked, 'But what, Mum?' She thought she knew what was coming, her heart chilling as she wondered—was Colin really ready? But her mother came up with something much worse.

'Men sometimes use us, my love. He's a lovely man, and he may not even know he's doing it. Just take it slowly. Be careful. Don't push him.' She gave Judy one of her *I know you* looks. 'Just be prepared for him to move on… when he's feeling better about himself.'

'What?' She squeezed her mother's slippery hands, not liking what she was hearing, seeing the worry lining the old lady's face. 'Don't you think I'm good enough for him?'

'Of course I don't think that! There's never a man been born who's too good for my Judy… But,' she shook her head, firm in her view, 'right now? There's no woman that can replace the wife he still loves. Just like me with your dad. Take my advice.' She patted Judy's hands, reassuring. 'Take it slowly. Let him fall in love again in his own time. And let's both pray he doesn't hurt you.' She hugged Judy, snatched the tea towel from her and ushered her out the kitchen. 'Go and have a shower. And cheer up. You know I'm just an overprotective old biddy!'

Judy kissed her mum's forehead and headed for the shower. The phone chirped.

'I'll get it... You shower. Then we eat.'

Judy did as she was told. For once.

———

'Oh, it's you.'

John was surprised at the cold voice. He thought Judy would be home by now. It was two o'clock in the afternoon in New York, seven o'clock in London. Damn! The dragon was awkward at the best of times, and this certainly was not one of them.

'I would like to speak to Judy.'

'Well, I'm afraid she doesn't want to speak to you—'

'Just put her on, Betty.' He was in no mood for this. The cantankerous old bag.

'You really don't get it, do you, John? You no longer call the tune in this household, thank goodness.' She was gloating!

He hardened his tone. 'I really don't want to argue with you. I'm very busy, I haven't got time for this. Here I am, working flat out, and I get this ridiculous letter faxed by my solicitor. I need to speak to my ex-wife. Now.' These days John was used to getting his way. People jumped when he spoke.

But not Gran.

'You pompous little prig—' It sounded like *prick* to him over the satellite connection, and he was astounded that she had sworn at him. 'Judy has an injunction preventing you contacting her or Josh. Can't you read? This telephone call is an infringement of that order and will only cause you more trouble, I'm hanging up.'

'Please don't, Betty!'

More trouble, she'd said. As if!

He took a deep breath, the line was still open, though she was not speaking. 'I'm sorry if I was short-tempered. Believe me, I'm exceptionally tired and will be working solidly over this weekend. In fact I'll be slogging away for sixteen hours every day for the next four weeks. I really do need to sort this out...' He tried the one thing he knew she would respond to. 'Please, Betty. For Josh's sake.'

It did not wash with Gran.

'Hah! You are a very selfish man, John. There is only one person you've ever cared about and that's you.'

'That's not true. I care about my son.'

'Oh really? So much so that you almost killed him?' Her sarcasm cut him like a blade. 'You're irresponsible. Not fit to tie his shoes.'

'It was an accident!' He heard himself bleating and hated himself for it. 'I didn't—'

'You didn't take care of him. You forgot his inhaler. You thoughtless, arrogant... bastard!'

He heard her phone clatter and the connection died. And there was no doubting what she had just called him either.

Jesus Christ! They've both gone mad!

John cradled the phone and stood at the desk by the window of his hotel suite, forty floors up, the Big Apple spread before him. The excitement he felt at being here was physical.

But the prospect of a fight over Josh crushed the sensation.

He took a hundred dollar bill and rolled it, his eye drawn to the fax. It was clear—he had to attend court to argue for the right to visit his own son.

It was so unfair. He bent forward, poked the tube in his nostril, placed a finger over the other. His eyes focussed on the phrase: To determine access rights. He inhaled, the line of white powder, transferring a wave of energy and excitement through his nervous system.

Well, fuck them. I've got one of the best barristers money can buy to argue my case. I'll find some dirt on her. I'll get a private investigator if I need to. Yeah.

His confidence soared with the cocaine rush. He was the one with the money. He was the one with the clout. She'd regret the day she did this. Fucked with him.

He blocked his other nostril, sniffed up more of the drug.

He really didn't deserve to be treated like this.

And she wanted to change the financial terms of the divorce agreement.

Well, she can go to hell!

He leaned against the window, placed his forehead against the cool glass.

Some people think it is easy to earn big money. Here he was, thousands of miles from home, working his arse off, to complete a deal worth hundreds of millions of dollars. Not any Tom, Dick or Harriet could do his job. Oh, no.

He rubbed his nose. The buzz diminishing. Should he have another line now? He knew he'd snorted too much this week already, had to slow down.

He returned to his desk, sat. Once again considered doing another line, once again deciding to wait.

Soon.

He picked up the framed photo of his son. He loved the boy. But he had to admit he had been taking the arrangement for granted. He had left calling Judy about this trip and wanting Josh for the weekend until the Friday before. Had other things on his mind... He smirked at the thought. He knew Judy would roll over for him. He had spoken to Betty that time, just told her what he wanted and got his way.

But now, even the old bat had openly turned against him.

In reality he had not been sure he wanted Josh until the last minute... The other things on his mind had revolved around a leggy brunette, a real tiger between the sheets, and he had originally planned to spend the weekend with her. Until the girl's husband had arrived home three days early from his business trip to Germany.

John laughed out loud as he remembered Judy's face when she had caught him fucking his secretary a few years before. No danger of that happening with the cuckolded husband, John's paramour having warned him off in time.

So he had taken Josh instead.

That bloody helicopter. The ride from hell.

He checked his watch, wondering, *Where are they?*

His mind went back to Judy. Until now his tactics with her had been infallible. Think of Josh. Let's be friends. Let's not fight. Let's be flexible, in view of my job. A boy needs his father. Even if it is only a couple of weekends a month.

He loved the lad. Didn't he?

Mind you, after a weekend together he was always pleased to hand the boy back. There was a knock at the door. At last!

He went to open it, heard a giggle, then, 'Room service!' He jerked the door open, grinning in anticipation. Both of them stood there, tittering, sexy as hell.

Yes!

He inspected his latest purchase—two pneumatic blondes, big hair and huge boobs, micro skirts and thigh boots.

He licked his lips at the prospect of the night ahead of him.

Now this, I do deserve.

'She called you steady. Docile!' Judy was sitting in Doc's garden again, chuckling, the warm evening a perfect temperature, their second bottle of red wine almost finished. Earlier, Doc had told her she was getting sexier every time he saw her. Had told her that it felt good to be with her. But she could see he did not take Gran's assessment of him as a compliment.

'Docile?' He made a face. 'Hardly macho though, am I?'

'Macho is not a word I would use to describe you, for sure.'

'It's true, I suppose. I rarely lose my temper. In fact I can't even remember the last time I did. Some people take that as coldness, as if they think I don't feel anger. Of course, I do. I just choose to express it differently. I prefer the word stable rather than docile though!'

'It was her word, not mine. She thinks you're a lovely man.' She let her eyes roam his face. 'Bambi!' Then her laughter erupted, nothing sexy this time. Like a chicken clucking and choking at the same time. His face was a spectacle. 'Oh, Lord! I'm sorry. It's just your eyes, and that cherubic face.' He still looked offended. 'Really, it's a compliment.'

'Then you must thank your mother for me.'

'Sorry, Colin. It's *my* nickname for you. It just popped into my head when we met.' He was frowning now, so she tried to reassure him. 'Listen. Too many men are just puffed up egos, brainless penises obsessed with sex and their wallets. Trust me. Bambi's good.'

'Sure?'

'Oh yes. And my mum says you don't carry a comb. That's apparently a good thing too… You don't, do you?'

'Actually, I only ever brush it, usually first thing in the morning. If I remember. It's curly anyway, doesn't need much attention.' He swiped a hand through his locks as if demonstrating the action for her.

'Ah, you see, Mum's right. Men with combs can't live without mirror time. It's their egos.' She leaned over the table, finger-brushed his hair for him. The curls bounced back into place. 'Not too much grey either. Distinguished.' She wrinkled her nose at him and sipped her wine.

'I take it your ex carried a comb.'

'Three. Car. Office. Jacket pocket. Just in case!' She rolled her eyes. 'Prat!'

'Superego?'

'Believe it.'

She wasn't sure she wanted to talk about John, then thought: *Sod it! This is a part of my life, let him hear it.*

'I've slapped an injunction on him, after what happened with Josh.' She explained that John was away, working, and how she went ahead with legal action regardless of the fact he was disadvantaged by being out of the country. 'What do you think? Am I a bitch?'

He avoided her eyes, poured the dregs of the wine before answering. 'This really isn't any of my business.'

'It is. If you want me in your life.' Gran's words, her comments about being too pushy, skimmed through her mind. She ignored them.

'I do. I do. It's just...' His eyes pleaded, desperate to be understood. 'I told you, you don't really know me. I'm a mess. I mean it.'

'Talk to me. Please.' She reached across, took his hands in hers.

'You're not a bitch, for starters!' They laughed, the uneasy moment now past. 'You want my opinion?' She nodded so he continued. 'If he really cares about Josh, he'll drop everything, fly back. Do whatever it takes for you to relent. And I suspect that's what you really want him to do. Am I right?'

He was. 'You are an extremely perceptive man, Doctor Powers. John won't, though.'

'No. Probably not.' They sat in silence for a while, comfortable in each other's company.

'I thought you were a lioness. When we first met. And again, after you hit John... Protecting your cub!'

'Nah, maybe a pussycat!' She purred. Or tried to, her lips felt loose. Boozy bitch.

'I'm not convinced. And if I'm Bambi and you're a lioness, I could be in trouble.'

'Believe it!' She held up her hands, fingers crooked into claws.

Doc went quiet, gazed up at the stars.

Tick tock, tick tock, what are you thinking, Doc?

She waited.

He seemed to shake himself, coming back to earth, and then went to the kitchen. He returned with a fresh bottle of wine. Finally he spoke, eyes aloft once more. 'I told you I'm fearful that I may be losing my mind?'

'Yes.' When Doc had started to open up to her it had sounded to Judy like his problems were a mixture of mourning and work pressures, liberally seasoned with a sprinkling of guilt. 'Are you telling me you're a candidate for a breakdown?' She wanted to help him. Her mother's comments once again skittered through her brain.

Men sometimes use us.

And she thought: Yes Mum—and sometimes we use them.

'I am exactly that and I've been closer to breaking down than you would think... But it's strange. I feel better when I'm with you.' He let his eyes fall to hers, moist now. 'It's cathartic for me. Talking things through. With you. In some ways I am getting better. I now feel hope... for the future.'

'But?' She could hear it coming, leaned toward him, as if her proximity could comfort him, help suck the words from him. She could see the effort it took for him to speak.

'Oh God... I have this... cinema. In my head. Full glorious technicolour. Gory images, in close up. Natalie, her beautiful face distorted and ruined.'

'From the accident?'

'Yes, but it's more extreme, not just memories. The film changes each time. I get a warning that it's about to start, I hear a projector clacking as it winds the film.' He stopped, stricken, the terror in his face, his agony surfacing for Judy to glimpse.

'I'm sorry, Colin.' What else was there to say? She moved her chair closer, put an arm round him. The poor, sweet man. She felt not a hint of jealousy for Natalie.

'Worse still...'

Worse?

His shoulders jerked as he fought to speak, forcing the words out between sobs. 'I see Daniel.' He leaned his head on her shoulder, his voice barely audible. 'His body. Not yet fully formed.' He shifted his head, still resting there, spoke more strongly now. 'It's a mind movie, you know? Not like a dream, much more realistic.'

She touched her lips to his temple, tasted his sweat. Listened.

'And it's a full blown horror film… Someone is slashing my son with a knife. All the while, killing him, yet telling me I murdered him. It's diabolical.'

She swallowed. Sober now. This was worse than she had imagined.

'Someone? Do you know the person?' She was sure it was Natalie. What he said next sent a lightning bolt through her spine.

'At first it was faces of different men. The evil criminals I've interviewed. But now it's just one of them. You know him.' His voice quavered. 'Leech.'

She was speechless. Green eyes flashed inside her head. She shivered.

'I've analysed it. I can rationalise it. But even then it's still devastating. I can't stop it. Yesterday, I thought, after meeting him again, after all these years, it would help me. It didn't.' Now he sat up, grabbed his glass, slopped more wine in it, then threw it to his mouth, gulping the alcohol down. 'I'm weak. I shouldn't say any more.'

Judy eventually found her voice. 'It's good to talk. You can tell me anything. Okay?' His look of hope, the desperation, stole her heart. She was sure she was starting to fall in love with this broken man, was determined to help him heal.

'It's my nightmare. I know it's only a nightmare. I must surely be able to drive it away.' His features were hopeful, interrogating her, finding something, spurring him on. 'Last night was the worst. The film clacking through my soul.' He put his head in his hands, voice muffled, yet his pain still obvious. 'Then Leech appeared, but no longer the boy-man from my past. He was the bull I met yesterday.'

Bull. That summed Leech to a tee.

'And?'

More wine slopped into his glass. Gulp. Gulp. Gulp.

'Judy… You don't need to hear this. I should see someone. A shrink!' A barked laugh. Mirthless, but devoid of self-pity.

'Please go on.' I can stand it. It's only a bloody nightmare!

'Oh, my love.' He went back to staring at the heavens. It took some time before he let her hear it. 'Leech rips our baby from my wife's belly. Holds it out to me. A blood soaked foetus, my Natalie howling. Then he stabs Daniel. Time after time. Yelling at me that I killed them both. That I'm the murderer, not him.'

It was grotesque. Horrific. How would she sleep tonight? The thought was unworthy. She ignored it, but those emerald lights still lurked somewhere inside her skull.

She held Doc. Trying to smother him with comfort. Her lips to the top of his head, kissing away the pain. His sobs subsided. She spoke, but soon wished she had not.

'Colin, it's just a nightmare. Your mind working things through. The body recovers during sleep. So does your mind. These are just vile dreams.' She felt him shift, try to speak, but she held on, kept on. 'Dreadful, despicable dreams. That's all.'

'I know all that. And I would say if I thought you were right. But you're not.' He sat up now, pulled himself from her, his words ripping her comfort away. 'I am losing my mind, Judy. I know it. You see, I'm not sleeping when these visions visit me. Oh, no… I'm wide awake.'

PART II

RETRIBUTION

PETER LEECH'S first day of freedom was not going as well as he had expected. They released him shortly after seven that morning and, at first, he had revelled in the sense of freedom, walking the few miles to the station, whistling. But gradually he began to feel overwhelmed by the rush hour crowds, the frenetic pace of the unsmiling hordes, the strange sights and smells that bombarded his senses.

He took refuge in a café, ate a greasy breakfast, not tasting it as he munched, and tried to make sense of what he was feeling. He could not.

After four coffees had set his head buzzing, he ventured out again. The pavements were less crowded now, the drones in their office hives until lunchtime. Yet he felt bereft, insecure. Unusual feelings that he could not understand.

He tried to ignore the sensations and continued heading for the station, took a train and then tube to Holborn, and made his way to Gruber's office. It occurred to him that his solicitor was his only real contact outside prison, at least, one who had known him for any length of time. And Leech did not trust him.

Trust? Who could you trust? No one.

Even that bitch Finch had blown him off. He had sent a note to the address Gruber had provided, thanking her for her help, telling her he was being paroled, that he wanted to see her. Asking her to meet him today on his release from prison.

She had not even answered him. He had written again. Still nothing.

At first he was confused. He had been certain she wanted him—she hadn't been able to keep her eyes off him. She had swallowed his story, gulped it down. And the love he could see in her expression when she realised he was the real victim had convinced him she would be there for him.

Who can you trust?

No one.

She had not lied about being married, though... Gruber had dug out some papers on her. Had her down as living in Islington. With her husband, John Finch.

Bitch.

Well, he was going to Islington tonight. To confront her. Fuck her husband!

He cackled then, a sound that turned heads at Holborn station. Maybe he would. Fuck her husband.

A few minutes after leaving the tube station he was at Gruber's office. The reception area was a dingy cell of a place that reminded Leech of prison. He felt better, sitting in an ancient leather chair while the secretary fielded phone calls and shuffled papers.

Gruber kept him waiting twenty minutes, the secretary apologetic and plying him with yet more coffee. He was hyped by the time she waved him into the lawyer's office.

'Welcome, Peter, please sit. I'm sorry to keep you waiting.'

'So you should be,' he snapped. 'I'm a good client. Shouldn't be treated like this.'

The lawyer frowned at the gruffness in his client's voice, but otherwise seemed unflustered.

'We expected you at nine o'clock this morning. I do have other clients, Peter. And they are rather more punctual. However, to business.'

Leech checked out the office. It was like something out of a Dickens novel. He could imagine Gruber using a quill pen in the musty dump. It was cluttered with papers and barely illuminated by dim light from the filthy little windows.

'Not exactly state of the art, is it?' Not even a computer. The prison library was better equipped.

Gruber glanced up as Leech sat across from him, shifted a pile of files from his desk and put them on the floor, then said, 'We manage perfectly well. Now, I have the papers you requested, detailing your investments, a copy of the title deeds to your new home, a set of keys,' he dangled them and then passed them over, 'and this.' He held up a passport and riffled through it. 'You'll see that I have included all costs to date in the statement of your holdings, including a sum for your new identity.' He held the passport open and placed it face up on the desk for Leech to view. 'The photograph has been digitally enhanced.'

Leech peered at the image, recognising himself, though a softer, chubbier version with no hair. And blue eyes.

'You stupid cunt! My eyes are green.'

'Coloured contact lenses.' Gruber pushed over a small box. 'All the rage these days. You can even get animal eyes and others that glow in ultraviolet lights. Popular in nightclubs by all accounts.'

'Yeah?' Animal eyes? He would investigate that later, but now he was checking the details of his new identity. Nigel Grove. 'Never thought of meself as a Nigel.'

'You can make your face appear fatter by stuffing cotton wool pads in your cheeks.' Gruber gave him a hard look. 'Peter, why don't you just accept the terms of your parole? You can live in the UK very comfortably.'

He had other plans, and Gruber, bent as he was, might be a little too squeamish to hear them.

'I want to go somewhere sunny. And I don't like to be controlled.'

He was banned from travelling overseas, for an indefinite period, as a condition of his parole. He would not be able to leave the country on his own passport, even had Gruber obtained it for him. They would nab him the moment he tried to get through passport control. Nigel Grove would be let through with no problem.

But then Leech's naturally suspicious mind kicked in.

'Who is he? Grove? And who picked him? Is this stolen?' Leech jammed a finger on the passport photograph and scowled at Gruber.

'Peter, relax, please. The individual concerned is a, let us say, street person. Of severely limited means, and intellect, I might add. He has no need of a passport and has never applied for one in his life. Until now. For a relatively modest sum we have purchased his identity. No one will ever connect you to him. It is a genuine UK passport and will safely see you anywhere you wish to go.'

Placated now, Leech just grunted.

'You'll be needing these.' Gruber tossed two chequebooks across to him. 'One in each name, although the funds are drawn from the same offshore account in the Turks and Caicos. You have cash accounts to the tune of one hundred thousand pounds, as you directed, and you can get money from an ATM at any time of day with this.' He handed Leech a card and PIN number. 'Your trust fund is held by the same bank, they have the original title deeds to your various investments, and all the details are in the documents I have just given you. As of midnight last night, I no longer have Power of Attorney for you.' He stood, held out his hand. 'Good luck, Peter. Call me if you need me.'

Leech remained seated, ignored the hand.

'You've forgotten something.'

Gruber sat again. He heaved a weary sigh. 'The addresses?'

'I told you. I need my brother's current home address. Judge Potter's home address. Powers' too. Finch I've got but I want Diarmud's address as well. The bastard.'

'Peter, you've been paying me very well for my services. Please take this piece of advice for free. Whatever it is you have in mind, leave it. Take a flight today, if you must. Put it all behind you.'

'I won't hurt them! I just want to write to them. Send them stuff. Like I was doing with my brother before you had to get involved.' He did his best to look innocent.

Gruber hesitated and then, as he handed the details across, he spoke the words that sealed his fate. 'Okay. But if any of these people come to any harm, I would be obliged to speak to the police. Some crimes are outside my comfort zone and I will not be party to encouraging violence. Clear?' He stared hard at Leech as he gave the warning, bringing to mind his trial and that superior bastard judge, Potter.

Leech seethed, but hid it well as he replied, making a scribbling motion with his hand. 'I told you, I just want to write.'

'That's your decision, but it is still a breach of your parole conditions. Think about what I said, Peter. Good luck.' This time Leech did shake his proffered hand.

Leech was smouldering with hatred as he left Gruber. He should have topped the bastard there and then.

After all the money he's ripped off over the years, he threatens me! To snitch to the filth. What's the matter with the man?

He allowed his mind to run riot, thinking of different ways he could terminate his solicitor, calming himself in the process, and made his way to Tottenham Court Road to do some shopping. After an hour or so he was satisfied he had what he needed. He had planned to buy new clothes too, having dumped everything from prison except the outfit he was wearing, but he was not enjoying himself so he took a cab to his new home.

It was a one bedroom, loft style apartment overlooking the Thames. It had been the developer's show home, so he had managed to buy it fully furnished. As he strolled around, inspecting his purchase, he was well pleased. He did not expect to be staying there long, but, as it was held in the name of his offshore trust, he was sure he would be able to rent it out, even after he had finished his business in London…

He unbundled his purchase and set it up on the balcony. The sky was cloudless and the day was one of those rare scorchers that made England seem almost exotic.

He put his face to the eyepiece and focussed his new telescope on an office block on the opposite bank of the river, slightly downstream and just this side of Tower Bridge. The windows jumped into sharp relief and he scanned them, determined to find his target.

Half an hour later, he decided to take a break. But he had learnt patience in prison, and he had all the time he needed. He would keep trying until he caught a glimpse of the person he despised most in the world.

His brother.

He went back into his apartment. He felt good inside here. It had upset him, being on the streets, surrounded by humanity. Inside was good.

He wanted a drink but the fridge was empty and stank of plastic. The tap-water ran brown at first, before clearing. He slurped some, then, while checking things out, he discovered the shower, a pumping monsoon that sprang from the top and sides. He spent twenty minutes in there, unable to soap himself as there was none. When he finished, he had to dry himself on his tee-shirt—there were no towels as he walked around naked, luxuriating in the freedom. It felt good.

Diarmud had hissed in his ear as he was leaving prison. 'You'll be back. Scum like you always come back.' Leech wished he had killed him when he had the chance, but just laughed in Diarmud's face.

Pathetic loser.

Now, in his new home, he held his arms wide, turned through three-hundred and sixty degrees and yelled, 'Just look at this place, Dire Mud. Scum?' He felt the laughter vibrating inside him, then it welled up, exploding out of him like an erupting volcano. 'I'm never coming back!'

The words echoed and bounced off the walls of his sterile home.

He padded over to his telescope and, stark naked, resumed his vigil.

Several hours later, he still had not seen his brother. No longer naked, having pulled on his jeans as the day clouded over and cooled, he felt restricted and pent up on the little balcony.

The frustration and anger blasted out of him as the flimsy rein on his impatience finally snapped. He hefted the telescope, still attached to its tripod, and hurled it from the balcony. It bounced off the roof of a Porsche and shattered on the pavement. The honking and flashing of the car alarm was nothing compared to the bellow he let out at the building opposite.

'Where the fuck are you?'

For eighteen years he had looked forward to this day, anticipating his triumph. Seeing his shit of a brother for the first time since just after the trial.

Nothing was going right. First off, he had felt weird this morning. Then that traitorous turd, Gruber, had threatened him. He had hated the shopping and, at the thought of the crowded streets and stores, he kicked the box containing the mobile phone he had purchased across the floor.

He was starving but there was no food or drink in his apartment. He had been sucking water from the tap all afternoon, there was not even a mug in the kitchen.

Why hadn't Gruber sorted it for him? Useless toe-rag.

And now, after spending all fucking day waiting, it was as if his poxy brother had deliberately not been in his office… As if he knew Peter was watching for him.

Yeah! That's it. He knew I was out today. Probably shit himself and poked off somewhere for a long weekend.

Leech's mood improved at the thought.

He pulled on his damp, creased tee-shirt and stomped from the room. He slammed his front door so hard the new paintwork flaked around the jamb. His neighbour opened his own door as Leech walked past.

'Oh, hi… There's been rather a lot of noise from your place today. I hope that's not going to continue, otherwise I'm afraid I'll—'

'Fuck off!' Leech stopped, but not to pass the time of day. He stared at the man and snarled. 'You useless yuppie twat.' His lip curled, showing bare teeth at his new neighbour, like a dog ready to fight over its territory. He willed the man to respond. Just one cocky word from the lairy bastard's mouth and Leech would knock his teeth down his throat. The man wisely decided it was not worth the hassle, pushed his door to with a gentle click. 'Wanker,' Leech growled at the door, then left.

An hour later, fed and watered, but still feeling exposed on the streets, he arrived at the house in Islington. It was a white stucco-fronted Georgian style terrace. He checked the address on the paper he held, rang the bell and waited.

Come on, my little Birdy. Your man's here.

A grey-haired matron opened the door, peered down at him for a second as he stood on the steps below, then started to push the door closed again.

'Not today, thank you.'

Leech's hand became a solid wall, the door wedged against it, ajar.

'Sorry to disturb you. I was expecting Judy Finch. Is she home, love?' He switched on his most winning smile, his voice gentle.

The woman, initially dismissive, then fearful, now seemed relieved as he spoke the name.

'Oh, I'm afraid the Finches no longer live here. They moved out two years ago. Are you a friend?'

'Very close friend.' He nodded, saw her frown at his answer and hastily added, 'But I've been away. Working abroad and I've just got back. I'm not in London long. Do you have their forwarding address?' The door opened fully, the old lady convinced. Leech kept smiling, refusing to let his temper loose.

'Give me a moment.' She reappeared a few seconds later. 'Here we are. Good luck.' She closed the door successfully this time.

Yet another plan gone wrong today!

Then he perked up. Thinking, that's why Birdy didn't reply to his letters. Of course! He checked the address the old dear had given him. His new destination. He decided he couldn't be bothered tonight. It was getting dark already and the air had cooled.

He needed a jacket. He wandered around until he came across a boutique with a selection of leather clothes, found what he wanted and paid with his new debit card.

Warmer now, he set off to walk the streets, more comfortable in the dark, less vulnerable. A creature of the night.

He walked for miles and eventually lost himself among some seedy streets, ignoring the peep shows and sex bars. He was not interested. Those places were for losers. A vision of his luscious Birdy was in his mind, and he wanted to sit in a bar, drink and think.

He came across a traditional pub and ordered a pint. Before he finished it, he could feel its effect on him. He had not had booze for most of his adult life. Well, tonight he decided, he would get pissed.

The barman made an attempt at conversation but backed away as Leech told him, 'I'm here for a drink. Not to listen to some fat faggot barman.' Leech inspected the other clients. A bunch of no-hopers. Social dregs. He spluttered in his drink as he thought to himself they looked as if they'd be equally at home in the nick.

By his third pint he had concluded that today was not such a disaster after all. Then a toffee-coloured girl, similar age to himself, settled on the stool next to him. She fiddled with her cigarettes and lighter, nodded as the barman held up a glass for her. He filled it and placed it in front of her.

Leech stared at his pint, re-living his interview with Finch. She was such a minx, and his current version of their one and only meeting involved her giving him a blowjob while the dyke guard looked on. He wondered if he had fallen in love with her. She often interrupted his thoughts. And since that precious couple of hours he had spent with her, he had regularly fantasised about how he would fuck her senseless.

Today.

And here he was in this shit-hole. Alone.

Just then he noticed the flash of trim tan legs on the stool beside him, became conscious of heady perfume. And something else. He let his eyes slide up her legs to her crotch, barely covered by the tight white micro-skirt. He already had a hard on from his daydream.

Damn that Birdy.

He shifted his attention to her breasts. She leaned forward to get her drink, tilting them at him, two deliciously rounded lumps, swelling with each breath, inviting him.

She blew smoke at him. 'See something you like?' Her accent was rough, and he felt deflated—he had expected something exotic. Her face was a little too angular to be beautiful. Pretty enough though. She certainly made the best of what she had. Her cherry lips shone at him, pouting, head cocked, her straightened hair stuck to her head and held in a bun.

Prozzie.

'Piss off, love. I don't pay for pussy.' And then he thought—why not? He had not had sex with a woman since his school days. In fact he had never been with a woman, only experimented with a couple of school girls. Yet now, with no immediate prospect of seeing his Birdy, what was holding him back? Only his pride. He swallowed some beer as she swivelled to face him.

'What's up, tiger? Girlfriend meeting you?'

'In this place? You havin a laugh?' He turned on his stool, their knees now touching. She wasn't so bad.

'Too good for here then, is she? Hey, Mike!' She turned her back to Leech, legs still touching, as she twisted her shoulders toward the barman. 'Prince Charming here says your bar's not good enough for his Cinders!'

The barman, a fag perched in the corner of his mouth, scratched his belly and belched. 'Yeah? In his dreams.' He polished a glass, ignoring them again.

She slurped her drink. 'You just got out?' She opened her legs, shifted forward, and trapped his knees with hers.

'What did you say?' How the hell did she know?

'You just got out?' She sniffed, wiped her nose with the back of her hand, eyes squinting as the cigarette, held between her fingers, almost singed her brows. 'Prison.' She pulled hard on the cigarette, opened her mouth allowing him to see her tongue in a grey cloud. She held it for a moment, then the smoke disappeared as she inhaled, leaving her wet tongue, pink on pink, as she touched it to her top lip.

His erection subsided. His paranoia ratcheted up a notch. He checked the faces in the bar, thinking back to his original impression that the customers would be at home inside prison. Not one face he recognised. How could she know?

She must have seen his frantic scanning of the clientele. 'It's alright, babe.' She rested her cigarette hand on his thigh, the drink hand propped up by an elbow on the bar. 'I can always tell.'

'How?' He wanted to know. Did he stand out so much. Was it that obvious?

'Do you want the truth, or a white lie?'

'You daft cunt. What are you on about?'

She ignored the insult, looked him up and down. 'You look like a big boy. Think you can handle the truth?'

What?

'Course I can.'

'I sometimes tell you lot I can see it in your eyes.' She finished her drink. Once again barman Mike filled it without a word. 'That's bollocks of course. All men look at me like that.' She used the end of her cigarette to light a fresh one, crushed the used one, the tips of her red nails digging in the filth of the ashtray. She placed both hands on his thighs, the cigarette dangling from her mouth, leaning in to him as her hands crept upwards. 'Don't take it personal. Okay? But I can smell it. Even with a fag in my face.'

'You cheeky cow—'

'Serious, love. It'll take you two or three weeks to get rid of it. Bet you were wearing those clothes this morning, when you got out.' She drew back from him then, hands busy with drink and fag.

Leech felt sick. This filthy stinking whore had told him he smelt! Christ, he'd showered only a few hours before. He picked up his beer mug, ready to smash it in her face, wanting to rip her flesh open. His arm started the motion, just a fraction, a twitch.

No! I am in control here.

Instead he fought her off with words. 'Piss off, you slag. You're just winding me up.'

'Fair enough. I didn't say it bothered me though, did I? If you fancy a quickie, it's fifty quid.'

He bought another pint as she waited. He did not look at her as he said, 'I told you. I've got a girlfriend.'

'Bullshit! Where is she then? First night out in how long? Years, I bet. You ain't got fifty quid.' She slid back on the seat, pulling her knees from his, swung the stool to face the room, her back propped against the bar. Making a point of looking for other punters.

He pulled out his wallet, paid for his drink and waved the notes, crisp and fresh from an ATM, at her. She turned back, clamping his knees again, placing a hand at the top of his thigh, the tips of her fingers touching his crotch.

'Sorry, darlin. It's just you boys sometimes don't have a pot to piss in. So, finish your drink and let's go. I've got a room two minutes round the back.'

'No thanks.' He quaffed a good half pint in one go, wiped his mouth with his palm, and said, 'I don't want AIDS.' He put a hand on her leg and slid it to her skirt hem, groped her inner thigh and added, 'Anyway. You aren't worth fifty quid.'

'AIDS?' She dropped her fag hand over his, trapping it on her leg. 'I always use a rubber darlin, and I get checked every couple of months. If anyone's got AIDS, it'll be you.' She tugged his hand, slid it further under her skirt, letting him feel the heat of her. 'I don't do Greek, rubber or not. But I bet you took it up the arse in the nick. Without a condom.'

Leech twisted his wrist, grabbing her hand, clutched her fingers hard, feeling them click. For a second he saw fear in her eyes and it started his balls tingling. He let her go. 'I've got a classy woman. Works for the government. My Birdy. I'm seeing her tomorrow.' He could see she didn't believe him, though she nodded, clearly relieved he was no longer crushing her hand. 'So tell me, why would I go with a dirty slapper like you for money?'

She let her hand slide over the inside of his thighs, then she hefted his balls. 'I'm here now, darlin.' She pulled her hand back, fiddled with her lighter. 'For fifty quid you could take your bird out for a meal. Get invited in. For a coffee. Maybe more… With me you get no meal, no coffee, and no complaints.' She went back to eyeing other customers, her pitch made.

Leech needed to wipe her smug face across the bar, could feel himself hammering her head on the solid wood, mashing her nose and shattering her teeth on it, using her bun as a handle.

'Let's go.' He stood.

'Mike. Got an envelope for me?' Mike slipped a plain brown one to her. Leech could see it was empty as she held it out to him. 'Okay, Mister Loverboy, just pop the cash in here. See, Mike looks after it for me. I never carry the readies and there's no dosh in me room either. Some nasty bastards don't like to pay, y'know. And some try to steal a working girl's hard earned cash.' She handed him the envelope.

'Whatever.' He slid a note inside then passed it to Mike.

She was as good as her word. She led him to a scummy bedsit right behind the pub.

'House rules,' she began to say, pulling her top over her head, manoeuvring the cigarette from her lips and back again in a well-practiced motion. No bra. She dropped her skirt and kicked it off, slipped off her knickers and stood before him naked, apart from her heels. It took seconds.

Her body was as good as he imagined, though her skin was pockmarked in some tender places.

'You've got fifteen minutes. Don't just stand there…' She tugged at his shirt. 'It's another fifty if you take longer. Even if you can't get it up.' She pulled the tee shirt over his head, though he stood unyielding, not helping. She continued explaining her rules. 'I only kiss me boyfriend. And you get rubbered up.' She had discarded his belt and was undoing his flies. 'Blowjob's an extra twenty.' She bent as she pulled his jeans down. This time he helped, lifting his feet in turn to let her get them off. He stood in his boxers, shoes and socks, as she finished her spiel. 'If I'm not back in the bar thirty minutes from now, Mike'll call the police and then he'll be straight round here so don't go getting any funny ideas.'

Leech doubted the barman would take that much interest, but let her spin him her line. She dropped his boxers to the floor, her cigarette dangerously close to his dick.

'Not much happening here.' She grabbed his penis, started pulling and squeezing, as if she were milking a cow, now kneeling before him. 'I'll give him a suck, wake him up, but it's an extra twenty. Don't worry love. A floppy dick's a common thing when you first get out. But as I said, I don't get no complaints.'

Leech couldn't believe this tart, trying to rook him out of more money. He watched her tits jiggle, angry that he wasn't getting hard. She let go, turned and grabbed his jeans from the floor, started searching the pockets.

'I'll get your wallet—'

He'd had enough. He grabbed her bun, yanked her back, bellowing at her. 'You fucking thieving bitch!' He hauled her to her feet, almost lifting her off the ground by her hair. She had her hands over his, trying to stop the tension ripping her scalp off, and suddenly, he felt the stinging pain as she stubbed her fag on his thumb. It sent him ballistic and he bellowed his pain.

'Cow!'

'You stupid bastard.' She screamed back. 'I'm not nicking nothing. I was just—'

He spun her round and slapped her, such a vicious blow that she somersaulted backward onto the bed, a tangle of limbs.

Leech's balls were throbbing now, the naked flesh finally doing its job, his lust kick-started by the feel of her jaw breaking against his palm.

'Telling me I stink? That I took it up the arse? Let's see how you like it, you filthy nigger whore.'

When he finally finished with her he pulled his clothes on. Calm again, he considered putting her out of her misery like the mangy bitch she was, but a half remembered conversation with an old con bubbled up in his mind. What had he called prozzies?

Oh yeah, that was it. Disposables. Reckoned the police didn't bother too much with the odd dead one.

But Leech was smarter.

The man was inside for rape and murder, wasn't he? Rape a prostitute and no one will believe her. Kill her and they might just come looking for you.

No. I've got more important things to do.

He crouched over her. She was in a foetal position, moaning and whimpering. He wasn't sure she was fully conscious but he whispered to her anyway.

Then left.

At least the day had ended on a high, he thought, the last few drops of his ninth beer of the night in front of him. He had moved on, found a new pub away from the area, just in case Mike the barman really did give a damn about the whore.

He was confident she wouldn't call the police. In her business a bit of rough sex was just an occupational hazard, and he had paid her, hadn't he? It wasn't even rape.

Anyway, he didn't need to rape anyone. He had prospects. One prospect, at least. He fingered the paper the old lady had given him, Birdy's address scrawled in shaky script in blue ballpoint. The dopey old bint had probably forgotten to forward his letters. Which was why Birdy had not come to meet him today.

Even so, a doubt nibbled at his confidence in her love for him... Birdy worked for the parole board. Surely she must know he was being let out today. He decided it could be difficult for her if her husband was around. That would be it.

He needed to see her, but the place was just too far. And he was too far gone.

He pulled his list from his pocket. It was tempting to see someone... So many to choose from. And he needed to add Gruber's name.

He had difficulty focusing.

Nah, not tonight.

He refolded the paper, slipped it into his pocket, but his elbow caught his beer mug, knocking it from the table to the floor.

The explosion of splintering glass silenced the bar, a number of trendy youths turning to stare at him, to check out the source of the commotion. Leech was swaying, the glass crunching underfoot. He reached the bar, steadied himself against it and heard the barman tell him, 'I think you've had enough, mate. Time for beddie-byes, eh?'

The buzz of drinkers chatting started up again, the incident over, Leech sent to bed. He was slow, figuring out what to say in reply, considering whether to leap over the bar to give the lippy prick a pasting. Then one of the lads in the group next to him commented, voice overloud, 'Tosser can't take his drink.'

Enough!

Leech slammed a hand onto the boy's shoulder, planning to spin him round, when he felt two mammoth arms trap him from behind in a bear hug and lift him off the floor.

'You really don't want to make any trouble, do you, son?' The bouncer murmured in his ear, his arms crushing Leech against his chest, all the while shuffling backwards towards the exit.

Leech could not comprehend what was happening. He was being carried! Like a baby! He may be pissed, but he was ready to kill this man. He controlled himself until they reached the exit, then he lashed back with his head, expecting to burst the man's nose.

Nothing there. Just air.

'Unless you fancy a right kicking I suggest you calm down and run along. Playtime's over.'

This time, Leech could not stem his anger. He kicked out, his feet flailing wildly, again connecting with nothing. He felt the man's arms release him but the unexpected sensation of falling was immediately halted by the bouncer's knee connecting with his coccyx.

The pain was excruciating, the blow paralysing his legs. He went down, the bruised base of his spine thumping the pavement, the jarring agony winding Leech, cutting short his scream.

'I warned you, you scrote.'

The last thing he remembered was the underside of a massive Doc Marten bludgeoning his face.

Light. Bright. Burning his retina, he tried to shut it out, but it still hurt. Then his body started firing messages to his brain, his pain pathways on overload.

He wanted to howl his agony, but his mouth would not work. Something was inside, hard and sharp, cutting his gums. He spat. His bloody fractured denture exploded from his swollen lips.

'I think he's alright.' The light went off and his eyelid could close again. He could still see the white circle, but it no longer burnt. 'Looks like he's taken a beating. Nothing broken though, except his dentures.'

Leech tried to stand, vomited a gush of beer and a little blood. He could see his denture in close up, now coated with sour booze and partially digested food.

'I should take a minute, sir.' A hand pushed his shoulder blade, encouraging him to lie back down. The touch sent a bolt of mind-numbing pain to his brain, dazzling him.

He stayed on all fours for a few minutes, gathering himself. His nose wasn't working properly and he could see lumps on his bruised cheeks below his eye sockets. He heard the voice again, finally realising it must be a paramedic.

'We'll get you to the hospital for an X-ray, check the old cranium, but I reckon you're pretty tough, eh?'

'No ambulance.' His lips were rubber, raw with pain as they flapped. 'No ambulance.' He repeated himself, tried to make it sound more like the words. Another gout of puke jetted from his throat.

'We'll just put you on a stretcher...'

With all his effort he thrust his arms straight, forcing himself halfway to his feet. Another rush of stinking beer cascaded to the gutter, then he hauled himself upright. Lights flashed inside his head, pain bombarded his befuddled brain. But he was standing, if a little dizzy, and steadied himself with a hand on the medic's shoulder.

'I really think—'

'Puck op!' With that, he tottered away. The air was reviving him, every breath clearing his head, but sharpening the claws of pain inside, shredding his senses. He propped himself up against a lamppost, tried to take stock of where he was. He had no idea. The bouncer must have dumped him in this backstreet well away from the bar.

He stumbled on, people avoiding him as he zigzagged along the pavement. Finally he saw a kiosk with a sign advertising minicabs. He fell in through the door.

The faces were Asian. They surrounded him, and none of them appeared friendly.

'Tashi!' He propped himself by a wall map and pointed to where he needed to be.

'Sorry mate. You ain't worth the fare. You stink. And it costs a bundle to clean if you puke in the motor.' The accent was pure cockney, not a hint of Asian roots.

Leech had finally had it. He wished he could just kill every one of them. But his body was not co-operating.

Instead, he took out his wallet, peeled off four fifty-pound notes and put them on the counter. He flopped forward, wanting to lie down, to get some relief. As his forehead touched the cool plastic surface a brown hand scooped up the money.

'If you chuck up in my motor, it's another hundred.'

Leech closed his eyes and let them carry him out.

On Monday morning, three days after Leech was released, Doc arrived at the Parole Board office feeling better than he had in over four months. Just telling Judy about the hallucinations had diminished their power over him.

They had not gone completely. The clacking would start unbidden, and he would still get flashbacks, freeze-frame shots of Natalie's death, vivid and cruel. Even Leech re-appeared, usually with their son's under-developed flesh.

The difference was that he was now able to confront the visions. Instead of dying inside by degrees, screaming and huddling himself, he would push through it. Focus on Judy and a positive future. He could even talk to Leech now, tell the image to leave him alone.

He was moving on, healing. Gradually the frequency had diminished and he no longer sought refuge in pills and alcohol.

Yes, he was doing well.

The weekend had been idyllic. He'd spent both days with his new family. He had delighted in Josh's boisterous good humour, in Judy's obvious and growing affection for him, and Gran's homely warmth. It was his new comfort blanket, something to smother away the nightmares. The hallucinations.

He could get through this.

With Judy.

Their attraction for each other was ever more powerful and, although still chaste, the sexual tension was building a head of steam that had them both fizzing when they were together.

He grinned to himself as he thought of her, his mood soaring. Given time, he would be whole again. Enjoy life, live it to the full.

The Judge was finishing a phone call when Doc walked in, and within moments Doc's bonhomie was destroyed.

His boss's bald dome shone in the sunlight, his dark suit and crisp white shirt an advert for Armani. But his head was shaking, his expression thoughtful as Doc walked in.

The words, 'Morning, Judge,' died on his lips as the Judge pierced him with eyes of ice while dropping the phone back in its cradle.

'I'm afraid we made a mistake with Mister Leech.'

Doc's heart skipped a few beats at the name and the ominous words. He hoped it was nothing serious.

'Has he failed to contact his parole officer? That's minor—'

'Worse. Much worse.' He indicated the telephone. 'That was your old friend DI Carver of the Met. Leech beat and raped a prostitute on his first night of freedom. Threatened to kill her. The police have visited the address he gave, but there is no response, and the neighbours have not seen or heard him since Friday afternoon.' The Judge smoothed his scalp with his palms, let his hands rest there for a moment, his mind elsewhere.

Doc saw him turning his thoughts over and wondered what personal nightmares his boss experienced when things went wrong. He waited.

'I know I don't need to tell you how serious this is, Doc. If the press get hold of it...' He shook his head and added, 'I've offered the police whatever assistance we can give. It is, after all, our mess... and we should help clean it. I've told Carver to expect you at his office this morning.'

Doc knew there was no point arguing. He nodded and left.

In the taxi, heading to Carver's office, Doc was raging at himself internally. He should have resisted Leech's release more forcibly. He could have destroyed Pugh's arguments if he had been on form. And he knew the outcome would've been different had the hearing been scheduled for today—just a few weeks later.

But at the time, his own confidence had been sapped, his professionalism at a low ebb. He knew Leech was a dangerous psychopath. Yet he had allowed them to release the man against his own better judgement.

Doc, though sympathetic for the woman Leech had assaulted, was certain the attack was just the tip of a very destructive iceberg.

Leech had become institutionalised. The killer could be translating the behaviours he had learned inside prison to the free world outside, without modification or amelioration. And now his boundaries were no longer rigidly defined. Doc was acutely aware that, with an unreformed psychopath, this presented a terrifying scenario.

Or, rather, a terrifying experience for those who encountered him.

DI Carver was waiting for him. 'Hi, Doc. Good to see you again... At least it would be if not for this Leech character.'

They shook hands and Carver waved Doc towards his desk. They sat. Doc wondered what Carver had done to be rewarded with such a lowly crime. He had worked with the detective many times in the past on high profile murder cases, so much so that he considered him more of a friend than a colleague, and had always been impressed by his acumen. He decided he would find out the reason, if and when Carver wanted to share it with him. Right now he was more interested in what the detective had to say about Leech's victim.

As Carver described the girl's ordeal, Doc's dread escalated, peaking when the policeman finished the tale with Leech's whispered warning to his victim.

'Told her not to call us. Said he wouldn't just kill her if she did. He threatened to abduct her and keep her alive as his own personal sex toy, warned her that cigarette burns would be nothing compared to what he'd do to her before he put her out of her misery.'

'Cigarette burns?'

'Yeah. Seems the poor kid has had a rough life. Her pimp used to burn her belly, underarms or breasts if she wasn't making enough money for him. Unbelievable. Eh?'

'And what? He thought that would make her more attractive? Enable her to make more money? That's crazy!'

Carver's face was world weary, an *I've-seen-it-all-before* look. 'I think we both know, for some of her punters, that's very likely to be the case.'

'God.' Doc had studied the depths of depravity plumbed by the most evil of men, but the more shallow yet disgusting perversions of so-called normal men still had the capacity to shock him. 'So how is she? Can I see her?'

'She is one tough cookie. Her jaw's wired but she can talk. I'm afraid I can't come with you right now, though.'

'No problem. I'd prefer to see her alone. Thanks, Jack.' He took the address and left his old friend and colleague, his sense of foreboding growing.

He had worked with Carver on many occasions, respected the man's dedication, had become close to him over the years. Carver, in turn, had always treated Doc with immense respect in his role as consulting forensic psychiatrist on the Met's cases. Now Doc was back, slipping into the role he had come to despise.

Hunting a man Doc should never have allowed to be released.

What a bloody mess.

The address Carver had supplied took Doc to a down-market pub. A bulky giant, probably the landlord going by Carver's description, was half-heartedly pushing a broom over the sticky floor. Doc could feel his soles gluing and then ungluing themselves as he walked through the bar.

He handed the man his card and explained. 'Although I'm not a police officer, I am here to help with their enquiries and I need to speak to Sade.' Pronounced Shah-day, like the singer, Carver had told him.

'I'll get her. She's in bed upstairs. I'm Mike.'

Before Mike could leave, Doc said, 'Do you mind if I ask what your relationship is to Sade?'

The man, lugubrious features sagging, jowls dangling like a bulldog, let out a harsh laugh.

'What? You think I'm her fucking pimp?' He towered over Doc, a jellied mountain of blubber, but one exuding menace all the same. 'Didn't protect my whore?' He pressed a finger into Doc's shoulder and dug at the flesh. 'I'm her boyfriend. I wanna marry her. We want our own pub. I don't like her doing the job but she says it's the only way to get decent money quick enough. She's her own woman. You'll see that. Alright?' The finger was withdrawn and Mike disappeared up some stairs behind the bar.

Doc surveyed the pub, taking in the assorted memorabilia tacked to the walls. The only common theme he could identify was grime. Everything was coated in a layer of dust cemented into place with congealed grease and the tar from thousands of cigarettes. He was inspecting an ancient wooden plough, wondering what it had to do with this central London watering hole, when Sade's voice brought him back.

'I've told the police everything. It hurts to talk, y'know.'

She was in a tatty dressing gown, probably naked underneath, Doc thought as she sat, not bothering to cover her thighs, the gown falling aside exposing her almost to the waist. He noted a pock mark on her breast close to her cleavage. A cigarette burn. He forced himself to concentrate on the task.

'I know. Thanks for seeing me, Sade.' He tried not to stare, was not sure where to put his eyes, the naked flesh or the distorted face. One side was badly bruised and swollen…

Clack. Clack. Clack.

He looked away, had an internal monologue for several seconds, determined to dispel the visions.

'Christ! Do I look that bad?'

Doc resumed his stare. Sade had pulled her robe round her, her left hand covering the battered side of her face. She was distraught.

'No. Not at all… I'm sorry. You… You reminded me of someone.' He squeezed out a smile, heart thudding, the visions fading. He wanted a drink, the stale stench of rancid alcohol, distasteful when he first arrived, now made him lick his lips.

Sade, sharp as a stiletto, must have seen his eyes flick away and then linger on the optics displayed behind the bar.

'You need a drink or somethink?' Her voice was muted, the words sounding tight as she spoke through jaws clamped shut with wire.

'No, really, Sade. But thank you.' Get on with it, man. 'Let me explain. I need to understand the mental state of the man who put you through your ordeal. Obviously we don't want him to attack anyone else.'

'Bastard. That's why I went to the police. I knew he was a bad 'un, a con, but they're usually okay when they first get out, y'know?' She sniffed, pulled some cigarettes from her pocket, offered Doc, then lit up. 'He was an odd one though. In the bar. Like he was superior. The tosser.' She blew ash off the end of her cigarette, watched the red glow.

Remembering other times? Other men who liked to hurt women? Doc felt for her, wondered at her story. What life had thrown at her to bring her to this—risking her life and her health every day. For the dream of a pub with Mike.

'Why do you say that? Was it his body language?' Prostitutes were often expert readers of the signals men sent.

'Yeah, a bit. But he also kept on about his bird. Some posh tart he reckons he's got.' She snorted. 'Soon burst his bubble. Told him he stank!' She laughed at the memory, but then winced as the mirth pained her broken jaw. Her muffled sounds became a whimper before she continued. 'Prison. You know, makes them stink.'

Doc knew.

'You insulted him? Deliberately?' That insult alone could be enough to justify this attack in Leech's mind. 'Is that a good way of getting customers?'

'Listen. I used to work the streets. I had to shag the dirtiest bastards you'd never want to meet. I've done things I'm not proud of. And I was hurt real bad by a pimp.' She chain-lit another cigarette. 'Mike rescued me.' She blew smoke, a lungful that billowed round them. She waved a hand at it, making no difference but the action seemed to help her find more words. 'Beat him to pulp and I moved in here. Got a place nearby for punters. It's my business see. Not Mike's.'

'It's okay, Sade, Mike's not in any trouble.'

'Too right he's not! All he does is keep an eye out for me. And it was him what got that sick fucker Leech's fingerprints. Kept his beer glass, just in case. Always does that for me.' He saw her expression soften, thought that maybe she had found something that passed for love in her depressing life. 'Got worried when I hadn't come back after forty minutes. His mate watched the bar while he came round the back and found me. I was in a right state.' Her eyes hardened again. 'He called the police. At first they weren't convinced it was rape.' A tear trickled and she swiped it away as if the display of weakness made her angrier than Leech or the police. She sucked hard on her fag.

'Really? I thought it would be obvious...' Carver had told him there was no question, it was rape.

'He'd paid, hadn't he? But not for this!' She touched her cheek. 'And I told him I don't do Greek... You know? Anal. All my regular punters will tell you that. Even Mike don't go there. A girl's gotta have some things for herself. Well that's mine... But that mean shitbag. He split me open. Hurt me real bad. Then made me clean him with my mouth, busted jaw an' all. Evil bastard.'

Doc gave her a minute as she chained her third cigarette, her fingers trembling. She filled her lungs again and blew out as she spoke.

'S'probably all he knows. The copper I spoke to reckoned he'd been inside since he was a kid. Anyway, when that fucker Leech said he thought I might be diseased I told him he was more likely to have AIDS than me. From taking it up the arse!' She whimper-laughed again as she remembered.

Twice. She had insulted Leech twice.

'What did he say to that?'

'Not much. We went round the back soon after.'

'And he attacked you immediately you arrived in your room?'

'Nah. I got stripped off and he just stood there. No expression. Dead face. Apart from those bloody eyes. I'll never forget them. Having nightmares about them. Glowing green... Like luminous snot. Ugh!'

'Then what happened?'

'I undressed him. Some are passive like that. Didn't think much of it, just wanted to get it over with. Know what I mean?'

He nodded, encouraging her to continue.

'Anyway, he was Mister Floppy, y'know? Told him it was normal after coming out the nick. I'm pretty good with my tongue though. Said I needed extra, reached for his jeans to get him his wallet—he was just stood there still! Next thing I know I'm airborne, he's got me by the hair, thought the top of me head was gonna rip off. Then he yells something about me thievin and whacks me...' She paused for a nicotine break.

Doc's fear for Leech's state of mind was spiralling as her story unfolded.

'I reckon that's what got him hard. I was out of it—that man knows how to slap.' She fingered her face, her limited expression rueful. 'Didn't know whether to puke, faint or piss meself.'

'I know it's difficult—'

'Nah. I've had worse.' Doc didn't want to hear it, was finding it harrowing enough listening to her talk about Leech. 'It fuckin hurt, though, I know that. He was angry. Kept on about his birdy.'

'This girlfriend? The posh one? What did he say?'

'I can't remember exactly, I was too busy surviving. It was as if he was shaggin her though. In his mind like... I wouldn't want to be her for any money... Thought he was bullshitting me at first.'

'And now?'

'Oh she's real alright. Even in the bar those green eyes got all misty when he mentioned her. Must be one of those stupid bitches that write to murderers and offer to marry them. Serve her right if he does!'

Doc would check. Find out if any of the prison groupies had been in regular contact, possibly even visited Leech. He was in no doubt the woman was in danger.

'Did he tell you anything else about her?'

'Said she worked for the government, though I didn't believe that. And it was like a nickname he had for her.'

'What, birdy?'

'Yeah. It was my birdy this, my birdy that. I reckon he's obsessed with her.'

She had not mentioned this to the police. Or if she had then Carver did not realise the significance, the danger this woman was in. He needed to call Carver, have them find this birdy.

'I think you are very brave for coming forward Sade. I know he threatened you.'

'You think so? I just don't want him doing this to some other girl. I'll be alright, I've got Mike, though I'm gonna be off work for a few weeks. Do me a favour, just catch him, will you?'

'We'll do our best. Thanks for your time.' He stood to go, but she reached out, took his hand for a moment.

'You're a nice man. I can read it in your eyes. Dunno what you're doing this job for.'

'Sometimes I wonder.' He was touched.

'One last thing. After what he did to his poor old mum and dad, they put him away for life... Why the fuck did they let him out?'

He had no answer for her.

'We've got a real problem, Jack.' Doc's taxi was heading for Tower Bridge. 'I'm sure he'll kill again if we don't get him back inside.'

Silence.

Then Carver's raised voice echoed down the line. 'Why the fuck did you let him out then?' He calmed almost immediately, business-like in a moment. 'Okay. I know that shouting won't help. Tell me, if you think he's going to kill, why is that prostitute not in the morgue?'

The doubt in Carver's words, hope perhaps in his voice, needed to be quashed.

'He didn't think he needed to kill her. Otherwise she would be dead. He thought threatening her would be enough. And how many girls like Sade get taken seriously when they cry rape? Even your team was sceptical.'

'True... So you think he expects her to keep schtum?'

'Yes. She doesn't realise how lucky she is. She needs protection.'

'Oh come off it, Doc!'

'Needs it, Jack. If he comes back for her and finishes the job you'll be blaming yourself for the rest of your life.' Doc would blame him too, and though unspoken, he knew Carver got the gist.

'We don't have the budget or the manpower. Christ, Doc, you know how it is... And for a hooker?'

'A girl. A vulnerable, abused, beaten, raped girl who has had a far tougher life than you or me. Someone's daughter... How's Sally, by the way?' Jack's daughter. Doc may be a nice man as Sade said, but he would stoop as low as he needed to get what he wanted, especially if someone's life was involved.

The line was quiet as Carver digested that. 'You haven't lost your touch have you, Doc? Okay. I'll put a man in the pub to keep tabs on her from opening to closing, see if Leech returns. Her boyfriend can cuddle her at night.'

'Fair enough. But just make sure you have a team on standby to take him down. He's a powerful guy. And he won't worry about harming or even killing anyone, uniformed or not.'

'Are you sure you're not overreacting?' Again Doc heard the doubt, the hope. Was he?

No. They had made a mistake releasing Leech. A potentially fatal mistake. He knew it.

'I think this could get very bloody. Call it instinct or gut-feel. But just believe me.'

'Fair enough. We'll keep a car in the area, a few of our heavies. We'll give her an emergency alarm, though I think the pub's wired into the rapid alert system already. God knows what the PTBs will say...'

Doc remembered. PTBs. Jack's shorthand for the Powers That Be. The faceless bureaucrats and bosses with the budgets at their command and the power to say yes or no.

'Leech threatened to come back for her. I think we should take him at his word. If I'm right about his current state of mind, anything that upsets him, if someone doesn't do what he wants or insults him, could trigger him off.'

'And other girls are at risk?'

'Not just street girls, Jack.' He told him what Sade had said about Leech's girl-friend, asked him to check prison visitors and any mail. 'He may be obsessing. We need to find her. Quickly.'

'Is this just about sex, Doc?'

'No. Although in his mind he almost certainly equates violence and domination with sexual arousal. Prison conditioning, I'm afraid. And it's not just women... He's probably anally fixated, though he may not realise it, or may be in denial.' The cab pulled up outside a gleaming smoked glass tower. He fumbled for cash, almost dropped the phone as he juggled it and his wallet.

'Anything else, Doc?'

'Yes, I'm at Shaun Leech's office now. I think he may be in danger too.'

'Thanks for seeing me at such short notice, Mister Leech.'

Doc had called the Judge's office before meeting Sade, and had a secretary call to forewarn Shaun that he was on his way.

The man was unsmiling. 'I gather my brother has already broken the terms of his parole. He's broken the rules all his life Doctor Powers, so there is no surprise there.'

Doc took a seat in a white leather sofa tucked in a corner of the plush office. The view was stunning, like an IMAX screen, only better. Shaun sat opposite and poured them both coffee.

'Unfortunately, it's rather more serious than that, Mister Leech. Your brother has assaulted a lady. Beaten her rather badly.'

'Really?' Shaun seemed uninterested. It was as if it had nothing to do with him.

Doc needed to shake him up a little.

'He was released on Friday morning.' Doc knew parolees' victims were not given the exact date or location of release. 'By ten o'clock that evening he had brutally raped a woman. I think anyone he sees as having committed an act against him is in danger.' Doc sipped his coffee—it was good. 'Including you.'

'So, a few weeks ago you were on the panel that released him. Now you're telling me I'm in danger?' His scowl raked Doc's conscience, turning over the guilt, exposing it to unforgiving light. 'Tell me, Mister Expert, why did you release him?'

It was the third time Doc had heard the question this morning, and he still had no viable answer. Prison budget cuts? Expedience? Woolly liberal thinking? His personal problems getting in the way of his professional ability? All of the above?

Instead, he avoided the question. 'I'm trying to help put him back behind bars. I need to understand him... I know it's been a long time.'

'Oh, don't you worry. I can't forget the life I lived with my brother. I could tell you stories all day and still not cover the extent of the malignancy inside that evil sod's head.' .

An attractive brunette appeared at the door, timidly opening it to tell her boss, 'There's an urgent call—'

'For fuck's sake! Not now. I'm not available.' Shaun finally showed some emotion, Doc assuming the anger he felt at his brother was being displaced, redirected at the secretary.

She closed the door without a sound.

'Thank you.' Doc appreciated the time he was being given, even if the man was hostile.

'Right.' Shaun's lips compressed. 'Since I heard about the chance he would be paroled my life has gone to hell. I can't concentrate on my business. I'm losing clients. My credibility and reputation are my business, and I'm in danger of losing everything. I'm a consultant, like you... I thought he was in for life.' His eyes speared Doc, held him as he said, 'He stabbed my father in the back. Literally. Severed his spine. My dad was a big man. It was the only way that cowardly shit could've killed him... Then he went for my mother, hacked her to death as my father lay bleeding. They say he came back and finished my father as he tried to drag himself across the kitchen floor. They could tell by the blood. The pattern.'

Doc could not remember that detail, it was so long ago and Leech's file contained only a summary. He could only wonder how Shaun's life had been since that day, the nightmares, the mind videos... Reliving the horrors in his imagination.

Shaun went to the window, gathered himself. 'He was trying to reach my mother. Or maybe the phone... Who knows? They're dead now. And, until a few weeks ago, as far as I was concerned, so was my brother. You think he'll come after me?' Shaun had his back to Doc as he spoke, any fear in his expression unreadable, but not a trace of it in his voice. Then he spoke more strongly, not waiting for Doc to respond, confident now. 'I hope he does. Then I'll have an excuse to kill him.' He came back and sat as he added, 'It seems the justice system in this country can't protect us from people like him, so I'll just have to take my own chances... And so will Peter.'

Doc did not know what to say. He felt inadequate. But there was something else troubling him. To hear Shaun threaten to kill his own brother, making a bald statement, devoid of any feeling, made Doc wonder, was Shaun more like Peter than anyone realised?

He tried to shake off the thought, but for a sliver of a moment, a microsecond, Peter's claim that Shaun was the killer seemed credible to him.

He probed. 'Can you tell me about that day?'

'Of course, it's as vivid as if it happened yesterday.'

He heard himself whistling as he slid the key into his parents' front door lock. His mind was buzzing. Nothing could spoil his mood. After all, he had just completed his final exams, the sun was warm on his back, the whole lazy summer stretched ahead of him.

And Suzie. She was desperate to see him. She'd been practically panting on the phone, describing in delicious detail what exactly she planned to do to him later. A bitch on heat. Life was fantastic for Shaun, he was rich, brilliant, handsome and great company. He also knew he was a babe magnet. And Suzie. Well, she was the best.

He shoved open the oak slab door. 'Mum! Dad! Surprise!' He dumped his suitcase in the hall and burst into the kitchen. 'I'm back a night early...' The words choked and died in his throat as his eyes registered the scene.

His brain struggled to make sense of what he saw, his world collapsing in on him. He dropped to the floor, gagging, his lunch threatening his tonsils. Some detached part of his mind insisting he mustn't puke on his mother's floor, a ridiculous whisper in his head, while another part of his brain screamed back at him, 'She's dead. Dead. DEAD!'

He felt lead in his arms as he struggled to push himself to his feet, the muscles refusing to take his weight, the ground sponge beneath his hands.

He tasted bile, burped a lump of half-digested lunch into his throat, the clogged food almost suffocating him. He sucked at the air, wheezing, feeling faint, the clot of cheesy bread, tainted with stale Guinness, finally shifting back to his gullet.

He stood in the doorway, unable to think, not aware of the passage of time.

Then his brain stung him to action. Maybe she was still alive.

He went to his mother, rolled her over, his gorge rising at the sight of her disembowelled guts spilling to the floor. He checked her pulse. She was dead. Warm, but dead. Her head flopped and he could see her neck had almost been severed.

Sliding, kneeling in the pooled blood and filth, he crawled to his father, also lying on the tiled floor, checked a carotid artery for signs of life, his brain avoiding cataloguing the numerous puncture wounds he could see. He gulped down air as he sobbed, the smell of faecal matter and lifeblood assaulting his nostrils, threatening to overpower him.

Nothing.

Both dead.

He turned back to the hall, fumbling for his mobile phone. Automatic pilot drove him to make the call, summon assistance. Somebody. Anybody.

His quaking fingers missed the digits before finally jabbing in the three numbers. A steady, placid female voice asked him which service he required.

'Police.' It sounded like a stranger speaking. A composed stranger. Not the hollowed out, devastated child residing in his body right now.

The calm adult voice spoke, using his mouth again, baffling the frightened boy within. 'My mother and father have been hacked to death. Please hurry.'

He turned back to the kitchen, vaguely hearing the woman speaking. She was insistent. What was she saying?

'—need your address.' He gave it, ended the call just as she added, 'Are you sure you are in no danger, sir?'

Danger? It had not occurred to him.

Burglars?

Hardly likely in broad daylight.

Enemies of his parents?

But they had none. Everyone loved them.

Then a light flipped on in his mind.

Not everyone.

It was his brother's eighteenth birthday. And today his parents would have told Peter he was not getting his trust fund money for seven more years.

That little bastard Peter had killed them!

And today, returning early from university, his parents lying dead but still warm on the kitchen floor, Shaun had unwittingly stumbled upon his little brother's crime.

He opened the back-door, his feet sliding in the blood, his ears recognising the thump of angry heavy metal music. It was Peter's favourite band at full volume, the din pumping out from the granny annexe just beyond the pool.

Shaun, his mind in turmoil, was wondering if his pathetic kid brother, little shit that he was, could really be capable of such an act. His feet floated him across to the annexe, through the open door, the screeching vocals spewing hatred, thumping from the speakers, drilling into his skull. He entered the bathroom, ears now focussed on his brother's whining imitation of the lead singer, the noise of the shower like raging snakes hissing inside his head.

The hissing stopped and Peter stepped out of the cubicle, his face registering shock as Shaun's fist, smeared with their parents' blood, shattered his little brother's front teeth.

Shaun left his brother unconscious on the shower floor, made his way to the kitchen, and sat with his parents until the police arrived.

'You had no doubt? That he was responsible? You didn't consider he might have been another victim lying elsewhere in the house?'

Doc was impressed by Shaun's account, his recollection of the details. He wondered how often Shaun had relived the experience since that day.

'No doubt whatsoever.' Shaun covered his mouth with his hand, thumb and fingers squeezing his nose, sniffing as he did so. Then he looked up. 'You see, my brother was sick in the head as a child. I knew it. I saw what he was capable of. But my parents...' Doc could see the wrench of mourning revisited, twisting Shaun's features. 'They thought he was a little angel. For years he convinced them it was me that was sick. That I was the one responsible for the terrible things he did... And he did some evil things.'

'He got away with it? Blaming you for everything?' Doc felt the shadow of doubt, that niggling thought that maybe Shaun was not as innocent as he made out.

Psychopaths, and he was certain Peter was one, are expert dissemblers, but to fool his parents for year after year? Convince them his older brother was the bad egg? That Peter was an angel? Doc was not so sure.

'Only until he was seven or eight, then they started to believe me. Before then, they sent me for therapy. For two bloody years!'

'What prompted that?'

'Peter, of course. I had a pattern developing, misdeeds my brother performed became my track record... Then he burnt our puppy. Of course, I got the blame.' Shaun went on, describing the hot-dog episode.

'They thought you were responsible and decided it was time for therapy, to help you? Then what happened to convince them it was Peter who needed treatment?' Doc could feel something was not adding up, but wanted to hear Shaun's version.

'Fortunately I was around less, with schooling and therapy, so he finally showed his true colours. My dad caught him torturing our neighbour's cat. It had scratched his arm. It was nothing really, but Peter has this temper, and when he loses it...' He gave a rueful shake of his head. 'He crucified that kitten. Nailed it to the neighbour's back door. The row the poor thing was making brought my father to its aid. Caught Peter red-handed, hammer in his hand. Peter still tried to blame me. Can you believe it?' He shook his head, as if mystified at his brother's machinations.

'After that? Did things get better for you? Now they knew you were innocent?'

'Not immediately. They thought we were both evil. Blamed me for being a bad influence on Peter! They cried a lot over us. Wondered where they'd gone wrong.'

Doc still had the twinge of doubt about Shaun, but wanted to focus on Peter. He was the immediate danger.

'I believe that people like your brother are predisposed to these actions from birth. They think differently. And they don't feel guilt.'

'So what? Surely feeling guilty after the event is a bit late.' Shaun sounded smug, once again causing a ripple of doubt to disturb Doc.

Doc explained. 'The guilt mechanism is usually a force for the good. It's our internal policeman. It stops us doing things that harm others. We don't want to feel bad about what we've done to them. The prospect of suffering guilt controls our behaviour.'

'And this mechanism is missing in my brother?' Shaun was fascinated, as if Doc was helping him understand something profound, esoteric even.

'Exactly. He can behave without fear of punishment from within, from his conscience. He is guilt free, no matter what crime he commits.'

Shaun was avid now, concentration furrowing his brow, as if Doc had lifted a curtain and allowed him to get a clear peek at this aspect of his brother's nature for the first time.

'I feel guilt. Every day, I wonder what would have happened if I had arrived home an hour earlier. Would they still be alive?' Shaun's eyes shone at Doc. 'I had a few beers with my lunch that day—celebrating finals being over. If I had been a better son... If I had come straight home, instead...' He shrugged.

'And the police. Did they believe your story, right from the start?'

'No. They thought we were both in on it. When they pitched up I was covered in my parents' blood. But then they found traces in the shower drain in Peter's annexe, his fingerprints were all over the knife, and his bloodstained clothes were smouldering in the barbeque. Even so, it was lucky I'd been speaking to my girlfriend on my cell phone only a couple of minutes before I made the emergency call. It confirmed I couldn't have been in the house long enough to kill them.'

'Yet Peter still insists he's innocent, that you were the killer.'

'I think he's got False Memory Syndrome. I'm pretty sure his therapist—we both ended up seeing the same guy—confirmed that to my parents. Peter had been blaming me for his actions for so long, from very early on, he would replay the events in his mind. Until he believed the false version.'

'I do know what FMS is… I have some experience.' Doc thought back to the many cases where convicted felons had convinced themselves they were innocent, even in the face of unimpeachable evidence. He asked, 'Is that why he accuses you still?'

'Either that or he really did lose his memory when I slugged him.' Shaun's face turned mean as he remembered.

'You knocked his teeth out. In the shower?' Doc remembered Peter had tried to claim amnesia from the blow.

'I should have killed him then.'

The sheer venom in the delivery of that sentence spiked Doc's heart. Could Shaun kill? Had he killed?

As if reading Doc's mind, Shaun explained. 'Not only do I carry the guilt, for both of us it would seem, I suffer nightmares about that day, along with many other awful events from my childhood. I doubt you'd understand. But I also wonder about myself… Peter and I, we share the same genes, you see. That's the thing that gives me the worst nightmares.'

Doc felt he was well qualified to understand nightmares, better placed than most psychiatrists. Was Shaun trying to tell him something? That he too was capable of terrible things? Blaming his genes?

Shaun went to his desk, picked up a framed photograph, brought it back and showed it to Doc.

'This is my son. He reminds me of my brother when he was that age. They are so alike in looks they could be identical twins, just thirty years apart. So far my little boy doesn't seem to be like him in character. But I find myself looking at him, wondering. You know?'

Doc did know, could see this man was in turmoil, and his conscience tweaked him. By allowing Leech to be released he had opened the floodgates for Shaun's memories and negative feelings. He hoped these emotions would be the worst Shaun would suffer as a consequence of the parole panel's decision, but he thought not.

'You should go away. Take the family abroad. Give us some time to find him. At least then we can be sure you are in no danger.'

'I can't. My work is already suffering.'

'If you don't, it may be more than your business you lose.' Doc picked up the photograph and handed it to Shaun. 'Think about it.' He gave him his card. 'Call me if you think of anything that may help… Or if he contacts you.'

'If he comes for me, I'll deal with him in my own way.' That deadly determination was back in his tone.

'He may telephone you. Send you notes or items. He may try to confuse us by using you. Or your family. You really should take them away. But please, let me know if you hear anything from him.'

Doc's hand was already turning the doorknob, but stopped when Shaun spoke again.

'He's raped before, you know.' Shaun was holding the photograph to his chest. 'It was a schoolgirl. She was sixteen, he was fourteen. Came up behind her, knocked her unconscious, then raped her. She didn't know who did it. Didn't see him. I did.'

Doc vaguely remembered reading something on the file.

'The case was dropped. Why? If you saw him?'

'No one would believe me. Peter accused me of course. Then said we were both in on it. Both raped her.'

'And the evidence?'

'Oh, the girl was in shock. Showered and scrubbed herself. There were no traces. Just two boys, with a history of trouble and therapy, arguing over who was responsible. My father, a very wealthy, influential man, squashed it. Had the police drop it. The girl never fully recovered.'

'I'd like to talk to her.'

'I'd rather you didn't.'

Doc was confused, wondering why. Yet Shaun sounded adamant. Could he be hiding something? Again Doc was diverted. He had to remind himself it was Peter he needed to catch.

'And why would that be? After all these years?'

Shaun explained. 'You see, she was my girlfriend at the time. Peter always wanted my possessions. Envied me for everything I had. Hated for me to have something better than he had. She was the school beauty queen.'

Doc remained puzzled. He could not make the connection between a girlfriend from over twenty years before with Shaun's assertion, *I'd rather you didn't*, as if he controlled the woman. He looked askance, wanted to tell Shaun to go to hell. That he would talk to whoever he wanted. But knew it would not help.

'I'm afraid that's not really your concern.'

'Her name's Suzie, Doctor... Suzie Leech.'

Doc's jaw dropped at that.

'She's my wife.'

Doc needed some time alone, to think. He walked along the Embankment reviewing what he had heard.

Shaun was smooth, sophisticated, articulate and intelligent. Doc had spoken briefly to the man's secretary and she'd confirmed her boss, although a cactus at times, was usually charming and well thought of by those he met. However, she admitted she had only been in the job a few months, his only permanent staff position, as he had a history of hiring and firing his secretaries.

Doc pondered the enigma that was Shaun Leech. What if...? What if Peter had not killed his parents? Could it be that Shaun was in no danger at all? He remembered Sophie Pugh's summing up of Leech's lack of motivation for killing anyone...

And if it were the case that Peter was innocent, what did that make Shaun?

No. Peter Leech is a violent psychopath, now out of control. A court found him guilty. Stick with the realities, he told himself.

Given their history of animosity, Peter's accusations levelled at Shaun, the matter-of-fact statement that Shaun was a dead man, everything indicated that Peter would attack his brother.

Doc wondered how Carver would feel about protection for Shaun Leech and his family. He soon found out.

The voice detonated in his ear, and Doc wondered if his mobile phone actually had sufficient volume to burst an eardrum.

'There is absolutely no bloody way I can do that. We have absolutely no reason to think the brother's target. I've got no men available, two of them are tied up babysitting that bloody whore, but at least we know Leech threatened her life.'

'He said his brother is dead.'

'Who did?' Carver, quick to explode was also always quick to recover. His voice was back to normal.

'Well… both of them. But the important thing is, I remember at his parole hearing, thinking Leech was making a threat. You know, *My brother's dead.*' Doc tried to inject the right emphasis to make it sound like a warning, a threat.

'C'mon, Doc. You're reaching. I don't believe he said it like a bad actor from the Sopranos. Otherwise even your mob would have kept him locked up and tossed the key.'

Your mob? The Parole Board. Doc did not like to feel he was on a different side, but the way Jack said it, he could have been.

'Not enough then?' He knew it was not.

'Not nearly enough. Sorry, Doc. And don't try tugging my guilt strings on this one.'

Doc knew when he was beaten.

'Can I see the original files for a rape that occurred twenty-four years ago?' He gave Carver the details.

'I'm not hopeful, if the case was dropped. But… I'll see what I can do. Interesting though, if he has a history of rape. Oh, and I've hit a roadblock on the birdy thing.'

'No one in the frame?'

'Not a single female visitor for several years. The last was from one of those volunteer groups and she stopped after one meeting with our boy. Said he really freaked her out, but I doubt Leech would be interested in her. She was already in her sixties when she visited him.'

Doc did not hear Carver's last words. He had made the connection, knew that his nightmare was now real, that the hallucination had materialised and entered his personal life.

Freaked. Leech had freaked her out.

'You still there, Doc?'

Doc's voice quavered as he answered. 'He did have one female visitor, Jack. Very recently.'

'No, Doc. I've checked it out.'

'The Interviewing Officer for the Parole Board. Judy Finch.'

His birdy…

———

Leech was sick of the noise. The constant hammering, as if someone wanted to get inside his head.

He surfaced from his half-wakeful state, his face throbbing. It was his third day in bed and he had never felt this rough in his life. Until now, there was only one person who had got away with laying a hand on him. His brother. And he had plans to put that right.

Yet here he was, laid up like some animal licking its wounds. He sipped some milk through a straw. He had vague flashbacks to Friday night. He could not remember where it happened. The name of the bar. Nothing. And as for the vicious bastard who mashed his face, he didn't even know what he looked like!

He punched his bed, pummelling harder and harder, rage building, his frustration goaded by the pain. Then he heard the banging again. It was the door. He wanted to bellow, to tell whoever it was to fuck off. Leave him alone. Instead, he sagged back on the bed.

Friday night… At least that cabbie had brought him back. Leech had even managed to ask him to stop at an all night store on the way, to buy him some soap and medical supplies, some food and drink. He didn't get any change from the fifty quid he'd handed the driver, but at that point couldn't care. He had just been glad to get back home. His own home.

The noise stopped. At least that was something. He rolled off his bed and staggered to the bathroom. He could smell himself.

That made him think of the prozzie.

'Fuckin tart.' He said it to himself as he stepped into the shower and soaped his battered body.

He checked his wounds. Not too bad really, some purple, green and blue swelling on his face where the bouncer's boot had stomped him, and numerous bruises over his body. But he was hard, and knew he would be right as rain in a couple of days.

He almost admired the handiwork. The bouncer had given him a pasting, but had been professional enough not to break any bones, not rupture anything, not maim him. Leech reckoned he could never do that. That job was beyond him.

After his shower he felt better, but when he went to put on his clothes, his jeans and tee shirt, they stank of vomit and were streaked with stains. He hammered his fists on the dining table, blows thundering down on the glass top. For a minute it held against the onslaught before disintegrating into thousands of tiny fragments, like a shattered car windscreen.

As it exploded he heard himself wailing.

He was losing it. He knew it. He had to get his act together…

He went back to the shower, dressed while standing under it, allowing the stream of water to cleanse the stench. When he emerged he shrugged the clothes off again, wrung them out, letting the water pool on the lounge floor, and then put them back on.

That's better.

He picked up his jacket—at least that was pretty much unspoilt—and opened his front door.

His neighbour was standing there, as if about to knock. Leech suspected this was the source of the constant hammering he'd suffered for the last few days.

'What?'

'I could hear you were home.' The supercilious twat was complaining about the noise again. The man was scrutinising Leech's face, clearly pleased that someone had the balls to do what he could not. His voice seeped with glee as he said, 'The police have been looking for you. In fact, they were here again this morning. I'm sure they'll be back soon...' He smirked as he added, 'I think you'll find someone has called them to let them know you're here.'

Someone?

'You cunt!'

The words were mushy, Leech's lack of teeth and swollen lips slurring the consonants, but the meaning and rage contained in the outburst were quite clear to his neighbour. The smug expression vanished as he realised he might just have put himself in harm's way.

He was too late.

An iron fist slammed into the man's larynx, bursting the fragile cartilage, bone and tissue at the front of his neck. He was felled by the single blow.

Leech observed, intrigued, as his victim dropped to his knees, suffocating already, clawing at his throat, his windpipe swollen shut in an instant, eyes wide, bulging at death's approach.

Leech left him gasping for air, kneeling in the doorway, and went to his desk. He pocketed his passport, chequebooks, cards and his few papers, returned to the man, now lying face down, grabbed his collar with one hand and heaved him into the apartment.

'Snakebite!' He booted the corpse, said, 'Goodbye, wanker,' slammed the door and left his new home for the last time.

It was Monday lunchtime, another bright sunny day, the streets crowded with office workers, shopping or heading out for a much needed break, maybe some food, a breath of exhaust filled London air.

Leech felt the sun trying to scorch through his skull, hated the crowds barging into him, the noise and grime of the streets. He would move. The Caribbean. He'd been there before with his parents. Loved it when he was a kid. He would settle there... But he had some things he needed to settle here first.

He eventually managed to flag down a black cab, had to give the address three times through his swollen mouth before the driver understood. His face ached, so he took a handful of aspirin and swallowed them dry.

He asked the driver to wait while he completed his task.

'Peter? What on earth happened to you?'

Gruber was tucking into a sandwich at his desk, nonplussed at the sight of this snorting bull standing in his office doorway. His secretary was at lunch and so he had no warning of his client's arrival. Not that this one needed an appointment. 'Sit down. Sit down.'

Leech sat. 'Why are the police after me?' Leech could see Gruber struggling to understand him. 'You heard from them, right?' The confusion in his solicitor's face reminded him of the unfairness of his situation, his self-pity a short fuse inside him, burning, burning, inexorably towards his explosive rage.

'Ah! The police? Yes. I'm afraid that two things have happened. Firstly, and the more minor of the two, you failed to contact your probation officer within the first twenty-four hours of your release. That, I think we could contend with if it were not for the second matter.'

'What you on about?' Leech watched Gruber toy with his sandwich, could see he was hungry, but also keen to rid himself of the problem that had barged into his office.

'Apparently a young lady of the night has accused you of rape. Although she admits receiving money, thereby undermining her case somewhat, she insists she was, er… anally penetrated.'

Leech read disgust in the solicitor's face, just a wisp, a hint, but there all the same. The fuse was running out.

'That could be just a… a slip up, perhaps? A misunderstanding on the part of a, shall we say, over-eager client after some years without female company.'

Leech did not like how that sounded.

'Quite possibly I could get the charges dropped on that basis. However, the broken jaw is something of an immutable fact. Witnesses agree that when she left with you she was in rude health. Some forty minutes later, she was seriously in need of hospital treatment.' Gruber finally succumbed and stuffed the sandwich into his mouth.

Burning. Burning.

She'd told the police, the stinking filthy cunt!

He would find her. Yet another thing to do before he jetted off.

And this useless fart was sitting ramming food into his fat face while he was being hunted by the police!

The fuse was close to the end now. He barely kept control, waiting while his solicitor swallowed and then sucked air through his teeth to clear some edible debris.

Sated, Gruber turned his full attention back to Leech, absently cleaning his fingers on a tissue as he said, 'You have two choices, Peter. You can go to them voluntarily and we can front it out. It is only her word against yours. We could contend it was merely horseplay perhaps? Some over-enthusiastic horseplay, admittedly. And in her particular profession I understand that money is the… how shall we say? Lubricant? We could consider a disbursement to allow her to have a more accurate recollection of events. That might work.'

Gruber waited for a response. Got none.

'Or you can run. Hide. And they will catch up with you, unless you manage to skip the country, and stay away. I think the first option is preferable, although with your passport and altered looks,' Gruber's eyes scurried over Leech's face, 'we could get you on a plane this afternoon. It's your decision.'

'False passport.' Gruber narrowed his eyes as he tried to understand Leech's mangled speech. 'Only you know it's me?'

The fuse was almost there now, so close.

'Of course.' Gruber was relieved, relaxed back in his seat as if a difficult problem had been finally resolved. 'So, you want to fly today?' He checked his watch. 'My secretary will be back from lunch in about forty minutes. I'll have her book for you… Nigel. I had wanted to contact you this morning to warn you, but I still have no number. Did you buy a mobile telephone as I suggested?'

It was on the floor of his apartment, still in its box. But Leech's mind was not there. It was exploding in the here and now.

He launched himself across the desk as the fuse finally ran out.

Twenty minutes later, Leech emerged. The cabbie was tapping his fingers on the wheel, impatient but not anxious. It was not unusual to wait an hour or more with the meter running, and it was a lot less stressful than navigating through London's clogged arteries.

As Leech jumped in the back the cabbie asked, 'Where to now?'

This time Leech just showed him the note. The driver sucked in his cheeks and told Leech it was way outside his area, though he could take him if the price was right. Leech just waved a fistful of notes at him, and settled in the back, his clothes almost dry now.

He could disappear at any time. He had money, he had an identity, and now there was no one to blab about Nigel Grove or his offshore funds.

It was a good feeling. Things had gone wrong for him, but they were looking up now. Gruber was no longer a threat to his well-being.

And there was still Judy Finch. He was on his way now, would soon be seeing his Birdy.

The taxi threaded through London's suburbs then entered green belt country. It took some time to find the property and the gates were shut when they arrived. The road, a typical English country lane, was deserted. No traffic.

'Sorry, mate. If you're visitin, I don't fink anyone's home.' The driver had leaned out and pressed the intercom at the gate, then tried again. 'Unless you've got the code?' There was a keypad below the loudspeaker, ready to swing open the gates for the right combination of digits.

Leech replied, 'Hang on.'

The cabbie had been staring at Leech in the rear-view mirror all the way, and continued to scrutinise his passenger as he got out. Then he poked his head through his window again as Leech came level, still watching him as he stepped up to the intercom.

Instead of jabbing the keypad, Leech pivoted round, the forefingers of his right hand held in a rigid vee, and stabbed them into the driver's eyes. He felt the satisfying squelch of the man's sight being extinguished, let the screech of anguish wash over him as he whispered, 'Thnakebide.'

Did the cabbie understand that? Snakebite. Leech didn't care.

The driver was scrabbling at his eye sockets, a keening noise streaming from his mouth. Leech grasped the man's head with both hands and spun it hard, the sound of the neck vertebrae snapping like the pop of a Christmas cracker.

He opened the door and dragged his latest victim into the back of the cab, leapt into the front seat and drove off. He thumped the wheel with his fist, the car careening as he drove. Although he had learnt to drive in his early teens—his father hoping go-karting, stock car racing and riding trail bikes might keep him out of trouble—and he had passed his test soon after his seventeenth birthday, he'd not been behind a wheel for eighteen years.

He was blinded by rage, frustrated yet again in his quest to find Judy Finch, and he was struggling to control the cumbersome taxi. He was in the middle of the road on a bend, unaware that a lorry was bearing down on him.

The sound of its klaxon brought him back to reality. He swerved, avoiding collision, but the cab left the road and rammed a tree instead.

The impact threw him forward, smashing his face on the wheel. The pain from the bouncer's boot that had delivered him to unconsciousness on Friday, surged through him yet again, a thundering shockwave this time, magnified by the latest impact.

He threw back his head and blasted his agony and frustration at the roof.

'BIRDY! WHERE THE FUCK ARE YOU?'

'Judy! Thank God you answered.'

Doc's voice was frantic.

'Are you okay? You sound as if you're having a bad day. Is it the visions?'

'No, no. Nothing like that, my love.'

Despite herself, Judy felt a thrill at the sound of his voice. My love. It sounded so good when he said it. She let him continue.

'We have a... a situation. I need to see you at a police station.'

Police station?

'I'm busy. I'm about to assist in a parole hearing. You should know. You scheduled it!'

'That doesn't matter. Please listen, sweetheart.' Again, her heart skipped at the term of endearment. He sounded concerned though, taking the shine off the moment. Then he ruined her mood completely. 'It's about Leech.'

It was as if iced water was washing through her veins, flushing her good humour away.

'What about him?'

Doc hesitated. '...It would be better if you come to the station. I'm on my way there. Jack Carver is the man to ask for. Believe me. It's important.'

'Is he up for recall already?' Judy's mind scrambled to understand why it was so important to meet Doc to discuss Leech now.

'It's worse than that. I'll explain everything. I promise.' He was panicky, not at all like Doc, and that broke through any hint of complacency she may have felt.

'Okay, okay.' She took the directions, made a note of Carver's name.

'One other thing. That recording. I never did listen to it. Do you still have it?'

'The interview with Leech?' Now her confusion peaked. What the hell could he need that for? 'I don't have it here... It's at home. I can go there first.'

'NO!' His vehemence startled her. 'Call Betty. Tell her where it is. I'll have a squad car pick it up. Is Josh at school?'

'Yes, of course. What's going on?' Her heart was racing now, his panic contagious. 'You're scaring me, Colin.'

She heard a deep intake of breath and then, 'I'm so sorry, sweetheart. Please don't be alarmed. Just come. Eh?'

'I'll be there as soon as I get a cab. You can explain to the Judge why I'm playing truant, okay?'

'No problem.' Relief now, his panic subsided.

After finishing the call she ordered a cab, and then apologised to her colleagues, leaving them baffled and their hearings cancelled.

What could possibly have spooked Doc so much?

Her mind fumbled at the edges of the possibility that some half-remembered words from the end of her meeting with Leech might just be important. But her consciousness refused to consider it, to acknowledge the connection.

Later, she would regret that.

———

Doc and a police officer she did not know were waiting in an interview room. It was pleasant and light, venetian shutters over the transparent internal walls to allow privacy, one side a picture window overlooking the street.

At least she wasn't about to be grilled.

Doc was pale, his complexion greasy with sweat. She wondered again if he had been visiting his own private purgatory this morning. Was Leech becoming an obsession again? Floating in and out of his vision, disrupting Doc's life? Whatever it was, she knew her man was suffering.

It turned out that the policeman was DI Carver and he started by describing the ordeal Sade had suffered at Leech's hands.

'The poor girl. But I don't see how I can help?' She really did not. 'Or that recording from my interview with him?' She turned from Carver to Doc but neither man would look her in the eye. Doc was leaning against the door, left arm folded across his chest, the hand supporting an elbow, his other fingers fondling his chin. He seemed miles away.

'Colin?' He glanced up, his face haunted. 'Are you okay?' She noticed Carver giving her a strange look, but she didn't give a damn.

'I'm okay. We're worried about you.'

'Me? Why?' She felt her heart icing over as she started to realise this really was about her. 'What is it? You think he wants to do the same to me? Oh come on! Get real. He met me for less than two hours. I doubt he even remembers me. I'm not some street-walker.' Still they avoided her eyes. She did not expect this from Doc and their attitude was starting to piss her off. She slammed her palm on the desk. 'If you've got something more to tell me, then spit it out.' She aimed the comment at Carver but hoped Colin would answer. He did.

'Jack, please give us a minute.' Carver left, promising to return with coffee in five minutes. 'We think... I think, Peter Leech may have developed a dangerous fixation. On you.' Doc sat on the desk and took her hand. 'Sade told me he went on and on about a girlfriend.'

'Don't be ridiculous. He can't think I—'

'He called her his birdy... Birdy. As in Finch.'

There was a roaring in her ears. Was it blood rushing? God knows, she thought. She tried to breathe away the panic rising in her chest.

'That may not be me. It could be his nickname for any girl.' She was clutching at straws and knew it.

Doc was relentless. 'Birdy is intelligent. Beautiful... And she works for the government.' His voice from a distance now, the roaring unabated. The thought of that beast wanting her. Coming for her! Her panic escalated, almost engulfed her, Colin's hand a lifeline.

She panted, desperate, 'There's nobody else?'

'He's seen no other women, except prison officers, for several years. Only one female has visited him recently. Had any meaningful conversation with him. Connected with him... Judy, that's why I need to listen to that interview.'

She wanted to vomit, but forced some words out instead. 'What will that tell you?'

She watched as he kissed her fingers, held on to that hand, trying to be there for her, then focussed on his lips as he explained, though barely grasping the meaning.

'I hope it will prove me wrong. The clues should be there. If he was developing an obsession with you.' He then made a feeble joke and she wished he hadn't. 'Looks like I might not be the only one who has fallen under your spell!'

Comparing himself to Leech was no help. And then her emotions hit fever pitch.

'Josh! And Mum. What about them? Are they in danger?'

Doc patted her hand, puncturing her panic with his reassurance. 'Jack organised cars to collect them. They're on their way. Don't worry. And we'll make sure Josh is entertained when he gets here.' Doc's watery smile appeased her, and then she started to think again.

'But we can't stay here! And how could Leech know where I live? Please, Colin, don't panic my mother and Josh. Don't tell them about this!'

Before Doc could answer, Carver burst in.

'Doc. I think you need to see this. Looks like our man has murdered his brief.'

'Holborn called. They knew we were after Leech, I'd spoken to my opposite number there this morning on an unrelated matter. Otherwise we might have been several hours behind the curve on this one.' Doc and Carver were being driven at speed through London traffic, the siren blasting vehicles aside.

'What happened?'

'The ME reckons he was stabbed to death… and raped. He's not sure yet in which order.'

Doc stared out the window, wondering if he could get into Leech's head, knowing that Leech had been inside his.

He could.

'He was alive.'

'How can you be so sure? This guy's so far off the rails he's in the ticket office!'

'He's not psychotic. He's rational. But also very angry.'

'Not psychotic? Are you kidding me, Doc? He's a loon! He stabbed and fucked a fat old man. Get real.'

'There will be a rational reason for it, in his mind at least.' Doc revisited his interview with Sade, thinking through what had sparked the attack on her. 'It's most likely something Gruber said that prompted the action. Not voices in Leech's head, telling him what to do, Jack. Gruber's words initiated it.'

Not psychotic. But thinking of voices had Doc wondering about himself again.

'Right…' Carver did not sound convinced.

'Trust me. He's bad, not mad.'

The car swerved to the kerb and they jumped out, entered Gruber's office. A middle aged lady was weeping in reception, being attended by a WPC.

Carver whispered to Doc as they passed them, 'The secretary. She found him.' Then he shook hands with another detective, thanked him for letting them in on the investigation.

'We could do with any help you can give us, Jack. I've got an incident suite arriving, we're setting up on the road outside. At this stage we can't be sure it's your man.'

Carver turned to Doc. 'A neighbour saw a cab outside for about half an hour round the time of the murder. Gruber was killed during the fifty minutes his secretary was out of the office. A man was seen leaving. Roughly matches Leech's description.'

The other detective then said, 'If you want to take a look you can. The ME and forensics have released the scene to me. If you'll excuse me, I've got a lot to organise.' He left them to enter Gruber's room alone.

The solicitor was spread-eagled face down on his desk, head resting to one side, a brass letter opener protruding from his upturned temple. There was surprisingly little blood.

'Apparently he was partially throttled, Doc, probably just fingers. The coroner will be able to tell for sure. Buggered and knifed.' The office was littered with papers, the drawers and cabinets wide open. 'Seems like he was looking for something.'

'I agree. It's not a staged burglary.' Doc was pensive, absorbing the scene.

'No. Your common or garden thief doesn't usually stop for sex. Most of the amateur burglars are so nervous they shit themselves. Leave the place smeared with their mess.' His tone was level, no feelings evident. Just a statement of a sad fact of life.

'Our man doesn't suffer from nerves. He has no fear of being caught, at least not in the sense of experiencing anxiety. He may prefer not to suffer the consequences, but then again he may choose not to acknowledge them.' Doc had walked round the desk. Gruber's shirt was pulled up his back, his trousers securing his ankles, his legs and butt were naked.

'No fear, huh?' Carver was peering at the entry wound. 'I think he took his time with this.' There were numerous speckles around the wound as if pricked with the knife before it was forced in.

Doc stooped to see.

'Yes... Throttled his victim to subdue him. Had his way and then held the knife to his temple. Talked to him for a while.'

'Yeah? You can tell all that? So, what'd he say, Doc?'

Carver was not kidding, he knew from past experience Doc would have some ideas.

He carried on with his inspection while Doc pondered.

It took only a few moments before he answered.

'I think he explained.'

'Explained?'

'Yes. I think he explained why Gruber needed to die this way.' Doc was staring at the corpse, but he was seeing Leech crushing the man's throat as he held him, abusing his body. Then, subdued, still being pinned by Leech's weight, the words whispered into the solicitor's ear as the knife twitched against the man's temple. 'I think he wanted his victim to understand. He needs something... What it is, I'm not sure yet.'

'You're convinced it's him?'

'Oh yes. You'll find his prints on the knife, on Gruber's desk, his throat. Even some DNA inside the man, no doubt. If he bothered trying to cover his tracks it will be rudimentary. He thinks he's invulnerable. That we won't catch him.'

'Don't they all, Doc?' Carver was riffling through papers now, not looking for anything specific, just doing the random detective thing that Doc found so fascinating. Many times he had seen Carver stumble on a critical piece of evidence, the needle in a haystack, in this apparently haphazard way.

'Not all. Some want to be caught. I don't think Leech is one of those. Though he may not care either way.'

'Great.' Carver was sarcastic.

Doc reviewed the scene again, the papers littering the floor, the drawers tugged open.

'He was after something here too. Some information. Something on paper. Or in here...' He indicated the top of Gruber's head.

'Yeah?'

'Yes. He gouged Gruber's brain as if to scoop something out... Or maybe destroy something in there. Maybe he knew too much?'

'Dangerous game, playing with fire. Gruber had so many dodgy clients he was bound to get burnt in the end.' Carver's mobile buzzed. A moment later he finished the call and said, 'We've convinced a judge to issue a warrant already. This solicitor may have been a friend to the underworld and as bent as a paperclip, but he was still a member of the legal profession.'

'Leech's apartment?' Doc did not expect them to find much there, after all, Leech had only been living there a few days.

'Oh yes.' Carver's voice was etched with the acid of irony. 'A battered prostitute's word is not reason enough, but Mister Gruber's corpse apparently is.' He took a last look around the room and said, 'Let's go.'

Doc was thinking about Judy, keen to get back to her. 'You want me to come?'

'You betcha.'

He shrugged and followed the detective out.

Carver had three burly uniformed PCs to help him serve the warrant. He told Doc to wait to one side of the door.

The detective knocked. No answer.

Carver stepped aside, joining Doc as one of his constables moved into position, a steel battering ram dangling from his arm. Three blows later and the frame and lock splintered.

As the door swung open Doc pushed himself forward and caught sight of the man's legs.

'It's not him.' He felt it. Then, for a split second, two green eyes hovered, disturbing his vision.

Disturbing him.

Not now!

'No.' Carver and his men were inside already. The constables searched the flat for Leech—it took just seconds—while Carver checked the man. 'Dead... And your parolee's flown the coop. Looks like he's out of control now, Doc.' His anger was not directed at Doc, more likely the system that allowed men like this to walk among the innocent again.

'He's not. He's in control. At least in his mind. Is it a neighbour?'

Carver gave him a strange look. He was still crouched by the body, had taken a wallet from a bulging pocket, had been reading something inside.

'Tom Colvin. He lived next door… That's freaky, Doc. How d'you do that?'

Doc did not answer, just took in the state of the apartment, the shattered table, the litter of food and cartons, the smell of decay already taking hold.

Carver made a call and then said, 'Well, Doc. This crime scene is well and truly compromised. I've got a forensic squad on its way so we'll seal it off. Not much doubt though. Looks like he ruptured the man's throat.'

Colvin's face was contorted with agony, his last moments a desperate struggle for oxygen as his own throat betrayed him, choking him to death.

'Yes. I think we'll find Mister Colvin offended Leech in some way.'

'No shit, Sherlock!'

'Verbally. Insulted him? Complained about noise perhaps?' Doc was staring at the remnants of the table, thinking of Leech's rage. 'He struck at the source of his distress. The man's voice… His throat. Different modus operandi but still strikingly similar to the knife in Gruber's temple. He goes for the thing that upsets him, homes in on it instinctively.'

'This is one sick puppy we have here.'

'Sick? Not in the medical sense. He may not seem it, but he's rational. And he won't return here.'

'So, no point staking it out? You sure?' Carver frowned.

'You've had police here looking for him earlier, knocking, but not authorised to enter.'

'Yeah.'

'He won't be back.'

'So where is he, Doc?'

'Now that… I can't answer.' He paused, reflecting. 'But I think I know where he'll go.'

Josh had been thrilled when he arrived at the police station, jabbering about the ride over. The police driver had blue-lighted and used the siren to satisfy the schoolboy, speeding through town despite having no genuine reason to do so.

Judy had held her son for too long when he arrived, crushing him to her breast, determined to protect him, not let him be harmed. He had squealed, 'Mummy, you're hurting me,' before she had put him down.

Gran arrived soon after and took Josh off to play in an area the station provided to amuse fractious children while their wayward parents were being interviewed.

Judy's head ached. It was now two hours since Gran had whisked Josh away, and she had been listening to the eerie voice, amplified through loudspeakers, forced to re-live her interview with Leech.

Doc had arranged for her to sit with a stenographer who was transcribing for him, and he'd told Judy, 'Make notes. If you remember anything…'

'Like what?'

'The way he was. The words on the recording will tell me some things. But you may be able to tell me more. Just jot down anything that occurs to you. Okay?'

She'd smiled, said, 'Fine,' but doubted she could remember much. She was convinced time had placed a barrier between her and her interview with Leech. It no longer gripped her with dread.

At least, until now.

When she heard that voice, wheedling, probing her, she felt physically sick. She had listened, her horror worse than the actual meeting, this time tinged with half-remembered anticipation of the words to come and the knowledge that he was obsessed with her. Eventually she had settled down, but she knew her nights would be disturbed by refreshed memories of the man.

The stenographer finished and went to organise transcripts, taking Judy's notes with her. Doc arrived shortly after.

She was lost in thought as he entered the cramped room, more a cubicle really, a technical office stuffed with computer screens, DVD players, tape decks, control panels and other items she could not identify.

Doc came to her. They hugged. Judy felt drawn to him, and was sure he felt the same. Holding him, in his arms, she felt some relief and her shoulders relaxed. Despite everything, she had this man. She was grateful for that. So grateful.

He pulled away from her, still holding her, eyes intense. 'He's killed at least twice that we know of.'

She was stunned. Unable to speak.

'One of the bodies was in his apartment. There's not much doubt in Carver's mind, and I'm one hundred percent certain. He's extremely dangerous. Possibly for you too...'

She had been thinking about this. 'Surely he won't hurt me. If, as you say, he thinks he's in love with me. Is obsessed, like you said.' She so desperately wanted to believe it. Especially now. Especially after his voice had invaded her again.

'Sit down, my love.' Doc pulled a chair to face hers. They sat, knee to knee, holding hands. 'If he does feel anything for you... it's not love. At least, not as we know it.'

'Can you really know what's in his head?' She respected his opinion, but wanted to reassure herself, was reluctant to believe she was truly this madman's target.

'I am as certain as I can be about this. To Leech, love is a mixture of sexual desire and an urge for control over his victim.'

'Victim? We are talking love, aren't we?'

'No! Not as you or I feel it.' He was struggling to explain. Judy was patient, determined to understand, as he added, 'He is not looking for a partnership of equals. A trophy... perhaps. A possession, oh, definitely. The good news is that reality may disturb his fantasy. Throw him.'

'What? If I turn out differently to how he imagines?'

'Exactly.' She could see him agonising over what to say next. 'Judy. We will catch him. We'll protect you. I'll protect you. You and Josh can stay at my home until this is over. Jack Carver is arranging personal security for you too. You'll be safe...'

'But?' She knew there was more.

'I need to hear the interview. Check your notes. We could still be wrong. I don't doubt he has some fantasy about you. I need to see how deep it goes...'

'Yes. But?' It was still there, the unspoken something. She had to drag it from him.

'If you don't measure up. To his idealised view. He may well discard you... Or he could kill you.'

'Well that's not going to happen.' She clutched his hands, her life threatened yet she was comforting him. 'I'll stay with you. Josh too. Mum'll want to come over—and take over your kitchen.' She shaped her facial muscles into a smile. 'He won't ever get close enough to harm me. Fair enough?'

He held her then and she realised how Josh must have felt earlier when she had almost smothered him.

John Finch did not sleep much on the transatlantic flight, despite the much-feted 'bed class' seats the airline charged so much for. The takeover he was working on was almost complete, albeit at a critical stage, but his barrister had called to tell him he must return to the UK if he wanted to protect his right to spend time with Josh.

The lawyer had told him, voice booming over the long-distance line, 'The judge will take a very dim view of an absentee father who won't even make the effort to attend a hearing concerning the welfare of his own son.'

He had replied, 'Surely you can argue the case for me. Or postpone it… This deal I'm working on is massive.'

'You're charged with reckless endangerment and this matter is not something the court will defer. Is this deal more important to you than being able to spend time with Josh?'

John had agonised over that. Finally he relented, booked the flight to arrive back for Monday. He had spent the last week, including his weekend, working at fever pitch to set things up for his absence, and was now fretting about all the things that could go wrong without his presence.

He was still worrying about work as he drove from Heathrow to his Berkshire home, a short run on the M4 and then some twisting country lanes to negotiate outside Windsor.

He called his colleagues in the US for the second time since landing and they tried to convince him they were coping just fine without him.

Normally he took pleasure from handling his Jaguar sports saloon, but this afternoon he was pre-occupied with work. And his son.

Damn you, Judy!

What was wrong with the woman? Was it just spite? Did she resent the time he spent with their son?

That made no sense. She had been fine about the arrangements. Until the accident. And that was all it was, an accident. Well he would meet with his barrister tomorrow. Judy's shark of a lawyer had pushed to expedite proceedings this week, scheduling the hearing for Wednesday.

Sarah the shark. He had never liked her. Ever since she knocked him back when he'd tried it on with her at university. Told him to *Piss off!* just because he'd been screwing Judy at the time.

Now she and Judy were apparently convinced he would not turn up. What did Sarah say to his lawyer? Oh, he won't be back. He cares more for money than his kid.

Well, he'd show them. In fact he couldn't wait to see their faces when he arrived in court on Wednesday. Stupid cows, the pair of them.

He turned into his drive, pressed his remote control and waited a few seconds as the wrought iron gates swung open. He drove up to his imposing home, gravel scrunching under the car's fat tyres, allowing himself a moment of self-congratulation. The building was not visible from the road, but as he rounded the sweeping bend, his beautiful Queen Anne mansion came into view. It never ceased to give him a thrill.

The grounds extended for eight acres, and he employed a full-time gardener to keep it well manicured. He also had a cleaner-cum-housekeeper who would cook for him if he desired. Not tonight though, he would be alone, which was fine by him. He would set up a video-conference with New York. No point allowing things to go too long without his input.

With that thought, and convinced of his own indispensability, he left the Jag in his huge garage, disabled the alarm system and entered his home.

———————

It was shortly after five in the evening and John felt refreshed. He had showered earlier, and now held a glass of red wine in one hand and a rolled up twenty pound note in the other. He threw back his head, drew in air through his nostrils so hard the sides were collapsing in on themselves, and felt the rush. Cocaine no longer gave him the thrill it had when he first experienced it, but it still had the power to spread euphoria through his being, boosting his confidence.

Skewing his judgement.

He licked his finger and tapped the few dregs of powder from the table onto the tip, then massaged it on his gum.

Yes… Tomorrow he would see that private investigator his barrister had arranged to dig some dirt on Judy. John had initially resisted the idea, but had been convinced by the brief's argument—better to fight and win even if you have to resort to dirty tricks.

And anyway, she'd started it.

He was about to phone his brief when he was interrupted by someone banging on the front door. The massive chunk of teak had black cast iron furniture, including a giant knocker. It was that knocker he heard now.

'What the hell?' He stood and walked to the hall, his mind racing. No one ever used the knocker—it was purely for show, though Josh occasionally irritated him by playing with it.

But visitors? They announced themselves at the gate and then he or his house-keeper would let them in, and wait for them at the door.

The gate. Damn. He'd not checked whether it closed behind him. Probably jammed open again. He had instructed his gardener to get it sorted out while he was away, an intermittent problem and one the old man must have forgotten.

He went to the door, thinking a concerned neighbour had spotted the problem again, driven up to inform him. He swung the door wide.

John's brain registered the apparition before him—a huge ox of a man, his face bloody, swollen and bruised, the mouth gaping, front teeth missing, yelling something indescribable, demonic eyes alight—a fraction of a second before his world disintegrated.

———————

When Leech finally calmed down after the taxi crash he decided to walk back to Birdy's house and break in. First he hauled the dead cabbie out of the rear and propped him in the driver's seat.

The problem was the man's eyes. Or rather lack of them. Leech wanted to make it look like he had died in the accident, but the sight of his mashed sockets would ensure no one would believe he'd been driving.

He chatted to himself as he decided what to do.

'Blind cabbie. No wonder you had an accident!' He cast around, looking for a broken branch. 'This'll do.' He hoisted a six foot log and smashed it through the windscreen.

'That's better.' The end of the log was lodged in the driver's forehead. 'Won't fool them for long, but it'll do for now.'

He brushed himself down and shouldered his way through the shrubs and bushes back to the road. The taxi was no longer visible.

For a moment he wondered why the truck driver had not stopped. Didn't want to be involved? In a hurry perhaps? Couldn't be bothered? All good enough reasons as far as Leech was concerned.

It didn't matter, he was fine. But what should he do now? The first address Gruber had supplied him was a couple of years out of date. The old lady had given him the Finch's current address, but why no Birdy today?

He realised now, he had been so frustrated earlier that he was not thinking straight. Of course! They were at work! It was Monday. They would be back this evening... Might even be home already.

So he hiked back along the road until he reached the gates. He scaled them and dropped into the garden, impressed at the grandeur. It reminded him of Hampton Court...

And a childhood visit there with his brother. Shaun had taken him into the maze, got him lost, left him there. He was screaming hysterically when his father finally found him. Was he four or five at the time?

Shaun. He would kill him. Soon.

First, he wanted to see his Birdy. Tell her he loved her. Explain how they could live together in the Caribbean. She'd jump at that. And he'd deal with her husband, no problem.

He strolled up the drive and the house came into view. He felt the excitement build. He would see her soon. A vision of Judy filled his mind. It was love! He had never felt this way about anyone before. It must be love.

He took hold of the knocker, gave it a few satisfying thumps.

When the door opened a man was standing, startled, wine glass in one hand, the other on the door handle.

Her fucking old man!

'Thnakebide!' Leech's fist crunched into the man's temple. Judy's husband was unconscious before he hit the ground.

Leech stepped over the body and yelled, 'Hi, honey. I'm home!'

He slammed the door, and waited. There was no answer.

Oh well. She'll be home soon.

He dragged John into the lounge and then went hunting until he found some rolls of gaffer tape. He wanted to kill him, Judy's husband, but some base instinct stopped him, whispered to him that he needed the man alive. For now.

A chunky rustic oak coffee table was ideal for what Leech had in mind. He bound John's hands and feet to the table legs, his body facing up, his head hanging over one end. Leech had to force the arms into position, could hear the joints popping and tearing, his victim stirring, groaning, but still unconscious.

Perfect. Judy's hubby wouldn't be going anywhere. Leech could explore the property at his leisure, until Birdy got home.

He started upstairs, checking out the bedrooms, and became agitated as he realised there were no women's things. No female clothes. Nothing his Birdy would wear.

Had that stupid old bag given him the wrong address?

He flopped onto the massive bed, the master bedroom enormous, a giant sized bathroom suite attached, a walk in wardrobe bigger than his prison cell.

Stuffed full of men's clothes.

Why was everything going wrong for him? It wasn't fair. All he wanted was to see her. Talk to her. Tell her he loved her. Take her with him. Why was it all so difficult?

Then he saw it. The photo on the dresser. Three people. Two adults and a young boy. He snatched it up, excitement building as he tore the back off the frame and tugged the picture out.

'My Birdy!' He had found her.

And the man in the picture. He was downstairs. Leech bunched his fists and held them over his head in triumph.

'Yes!'

But who was the kid? Must be theirs. He wondered if that could be a problem. He knew women got very attached to their kids. And there was no way he wanted someone else's snotty brat in tow.

How would she react if he killed the little bastard? He wasn't sure but he remembered how he had felt when Shaun burnt his puppy.

Evil cunt!

'Where are you, my Birdy? Where?'

Then he heard the man groaning from downstairs.

The husband. He'll know.

John's eyes refused to focus at first and when they finally did he was baffled to see everything was upside down. He could see the door, his lounge furniture, all recognisable, but most definitely the wrong way up. He shook his head to clear his vision —and the pain rampaged through his consciousness. His head felt broken, his shoulders on fire.

What the hell was happening?

He pulled his head up, tried to move his body, his arms, his legs. He panicked and struggled, crying out and groaning as molten pain lanced through his chest and neck. Eventually he calmed down, forced himself to relax, let his head droop, allowing his body to recover from the pain, less intense now he was still.

He tried to fathom out what had happened to him. He remembered the door knocker hammering. Opening the door. The apparition, the mad green eyes. And then nothing. Until now.

Oh God… He had been burgled and left trussed up. And no one was coming to find him. His housekeeper did not expect him back. He had not contacted her and she thought he would be in the States for another couple of weeks. Panic swelled inside him, and then he remembered. The gardener. He would be here in the morning. Thank Christ.

He tried to see how he was bound, but could not. Then he realised, from his location in the room, the view he had, he was bound to his coffee table.

That's it!

He tried to push his feet on the floor, but only his toes had purchase. His hands were useless, the fingertips barely scratching the carpet. The furniture in his house was heavy and solid, and this table was no exception. It was not going to budge.

He was stuck fast, like a bug on flypaper. He would have to wait until morning. Scream for help when he heard his gardener pottering outside. But that would be in twelve hours or more… Twelve hours, stuck like this. He groaned at the thought.

He closed his eyes, emptied his mind, tried to meditate. He had not tried it for years, but he had little else to do now.

Minutes later, he felt something, a disturbance of the air around his head. His eyes blinked open and he screamed.

The mad man was still here! And his eyes were only a few inches from John's, the mangled face grinning at him.

'Wakey wakey! You and I are going to have a little chat.'

The panic, submerged but barely beneath the surface, was rising again. 'Please. If you want money—'

'SHUT UP!' It sounded more like 'Thutub!' but John got his drift.

'I'm very wealthy. I'll—'

The sentence was lost, stillborn as the explosive slap almost dislocated John's jaw. His synapses sparked with pain overload.

'I said, shut up,' the man lisped at him, then crouched, sitting back on his heels. He was holding a photograph to John's nose.

Judy, Josh and himself.

His mind whirled. Had this monster kidnapped them? Is that what it was all about? He opened his mouth to ask. Closed it again, not wishing to invite another manic blow.

Concentrate. Listen.

'This is your wife. Why don't she live here?'

John caught the gist, desperation helping him to decipher the man's speech.

'We're divorced. We split up a couple of years ago.'

The man's face turned even uglier as he vented his anger. 'My useless fuck of a solicitor didn't tell me that. Gave me your old address too.'

Did he say solicitor? Was this some legal problem? Hope flooded through John. He could afford the best legal advice. No problem… Except. Why was this man in his home? And why was John now trussed up?

'Who's the kid? Yours?'

'Of course.' Moron.

Another slap, the other side of his face this time, took him to the edge of consciousness.

'Don't get cocky with me, you fuckin yuppie. *So where are they?* Judy? And the kid?'

Judy? He wants to see Judy?

'At home, I should imagine…'

'And where would that be?' The green eyes lit up with excitement.

Was he hunting her? And Josh? He toyed with the idea of giving a false address. But he was no hero, and justified his cowardice by thinking the man would find out anyway—it was in the address book on the hall table.

If the cretin lets me go, I'll call her. Call the police. I must not give him reason to hurt me.

He weaselled the words out. 'Look, the address is in my personal directory, by the phone in the hall. I don't know what business you have with her, but it's clearly nothing to do with me. I don't even like her any more!'

The man got up, left him alone for a few minutes. He returned with the book.

'Got it. This is up to date, eh?'

'Certainly. I called her home last week.' He did not mention that Betty had screened the call, that he could not even talk to the mother of his child.

'Good.' He walked round the room, picking things up at random, inspecting them, as if he was some fine art collector or expert on antiques. 'Nice gaff you got here. I think I'll stay the night.'

Oh please, no!

'You can take my car. It's a Jaguar. You could see her tonight.' The wheedling tone slithered from his tongue again.

There was no answer. He could hear the intruder fiddling with something, then he came back into view.

'You naughty boy! Didn't you know possession of Class A narcotics is a punishable offence? You've got enough here to deal! Is that how you got the dosh for this place?' He laughed. 'With this lot, you'd go down for years.'

He disappeared from view again and moments later John heard a loud sniff. Then another.

'Nah. I'm all in. Think I'll relax here for the night.' The grotesque head hovered over him, cocked to one side, puzzled. 'Dunno what to do about you though.'

John heard a ripping sound, then felt the gaffer tape being plastered to his mouth.

'That'll keep you quiet. Just while I go take a jacuzzi and think about it.'

———

John attempted to meditate again, but his discomfort and pain would allow him no peace. And sleep would not come. He dreaded the man's return, but wanted to convince him he should be released. He tried to understand what was happening here, to make some sense of his situation.

Why would he keep me here? He doesn't want me—he wants Judy. His hopes lifted.

Perhaps he thinks I'll warn her. Will he leave in the morning? And will he release me, before he leaves?

The glimmer of hope faded. There was no way. And if the lunatic planned to hurt Judy, why not kill him? John had seen his face—would never forget it.

His mouth was parched, his tongue swollen in its search for moisture. There was none. He was dehydrated from the flight, and had only sipped a little wine since he arrived home.

He thought of New York, his inadequate staff and his mega deal, but his concerns were chased away by self-preservation and the instinct for survival. Suddenly he attained a perspective on life he had never achieved before. Money really was not that important.

Unless… He had to talk to this man. Befriend him. Tempt him. But how?

Eventually his mind ceased turning over. He slipped in and out of consciousness, delirious at times. Hours passed, but how many, he could not say.

He awoke with a start. Alert, immediately aware of his predicament.

The intruder was back. He ripped the gag off, none too gently.

John tried to speak, plead for water, unable to, his tongue filling his mouth, stuck to furred teeth, the gummy roof.

'What's that outside?' His head was to one side, listening to the faint sounds of John's tractor mower doing the grounds.

The man's speech was better now, barely impeded by his injuries, but John's attempt at communicating was far worse.

'What?' He moved closer, straining to hear the word.

John tried again, making a massive effort just to squeak, 'Gardener.'

'You cunt! You didn't warn me about him!'

John wanted to say, 'You didn't ask.' The effort was too much, and anyway, he thought better of it, not wishing to receive another ferocious slap. He rotated his tongue, trying to create some saliva, to ease his discomfort. It was impossible, his mouth arid.

'Has he got a key?'

John gestured 'No,' with his head, too feeble to do much more than tremble. 'Water.' He repeated it, hoping his tormentor understood.

The man disappeared again, John thinking he was finally getting him a drink, bringing some relief. Instead he heard the tearing of gaffer tape.

'No—'

'You don't deserve water. You should have warned me. Anyway,' he stuck the tape to John's mouth, 'what d'you think I am? Your fuckin nursemaid?'

John groaned and wondered if his tormentor would just leave him here to die, pinioned to his thousand pound coffee table, surrounded by the wealth that no longer seemed important any more. None of it mattered—the house, his cars, the deal he was brokering, even his job.

He just wanted to live. To see Josh grow up.

Panic took hold again, and he used what little energy he had to fight against his bindings, achieving nothing except re-igniting the grinding agony in his shoulders, neck and chest. Then spurting bile burnt his throat, and the taste of it cut through the panic that was saturating his senses, the clarity of one thought paralysing him.

If I vomit—I'm dead.

149

It was bad enough to think he might die of thirst in a few days. To choke on his own puke would be a nightmarish way to go.

He focussed. Don't panic. Old Fred, the gardener, may be able to see him, could get help. If Fred stood on the patio, he would get a partial view of John's position. Or if he saw movement, the brute roving around the house, he would know something was amiss…

Then John realised it was already Tuesday. His lawyer was expecting him today. Maybe he would raise the alarm when John failed to show for his luncheon appointment.

What would he do? Call John's office and they would confirm he flew home yesterday. Yes, he would definitely raise the alarm—possibly send the police.

No. Maybe he would wait… to hear from John? After all, John had not been definite about when he was coming back, the lunch just pencilled in, waiting for confirmation.

He let out a moan, the tape muffling the noise, but the despair obvious to his own ears.

Surely, the solicitor would do something when he failed to show at the hearing tomorrow. All John had to do was tough it out until then. Wednesday night, at the latest.

He heard a crash from the kitchen and the bellowing of the madman. Moments later he entered John's field of vision.

'Bloody burnt meself on your cooker. But this curry smells great.' He placed the tray on John's belly, picked up a fork and started feeding himself.

He's using me as his dining table!

John, whose pampered existence had insulated him from the more unsavoury realities of life, who had known only luxury, had been surrounded by assistants and servants fawning over his every whim, was nothing more to this man than a convenient place to eat. Any doubt he had that this crazy thug would kill him vanished in that moment.

'Looks like your gardener's pissed off for the day. Hope you aren't paying him too much.'

The sound of the man eating disgusted him, but the spices were teasing a few drops of saliva from his tongue. Even so, it felt rough and stiff, his mouth full of gunge and the tang of bile.

'That was good.' He lifted the tray off, placed the remains under John's nose, and settled back on the sofa. John heard the TV burst into life—his captor had obviously found the remote—when he felt the man's feet resting on his stomach. 'Think I'll watch TV for a while. Got things to do this evening, but not much use going out now —everyone's at work.'

John let his head sag and wondered why this reject from hell had entered his life. It was lunchtime, the news blaring. Although he could not see it, he could hear it, and tried to turn his mind inward—he had enough problems without listening to doom and gloom from around the globe.

'Bollocks!'

John felt the feet shifting off him, and listened to the TV newscaster, intrigued by the man's reaction.

'…very dangerous and should not be approached. Leech is wanted in connection with two suspicious deaths in London yesterday, and for the vicious assault of a female on Friday night. Leech, who was jailed for life eighteen years ago for the savage murder of his parents, was released on parole on Friday morning. The leader of the Opposition lambasted the Home Secretary in the House of Commons today and criticised the government's record on law and order. Victim support groups have unanimously condemned the release of this violent offender...'

John listened as various individuals were interviewed, all spouting the same rhetoric: life should mean life, our prison system is too soft, why was this man paroled?

Right now, he could not agree more.

The upside down face was thrust into his own, filling his universe, mad eyes wide, a lopsided grin on the battered lips, cheeks blue-green and swollen from bruising.

'Looks like you've got a celebrity house guest. I'm famous. Good job I had my face re-shaped. I look nothing like that photo! Still, you don't mind if I borrow some of your hair dye, do ya? You bloody pooftah.'

The celebrity house guest left him, and John allowed himself to wallow in his terror, self-pity and hopelessness.

Why was this happening to him?

'What d'you think, Doc?'

DI Carver and Doc were back at Leech's apartment, both of them on the balcony overlooking the Thames.

'He bought the telescope and the mobile phone for a purpose, Jack.' Doc pointed across the river. 'I've been to that office building, it's where his brother Shaun works.'

'So why did he lob it off here onto his neighbour's car?' Carver leaned out, peering at the road below. 'We know from the receipt he only bought it Friday. The guy reported his car vandalised that evening. Doesn't seem very rational to me...' He straightened and made a face at Doc.

'Mmm.' Doc pondered on that too. 'His brother was out of his office all day Friday.' Doc scooped up the boxed mobile and handed it to Carver. 'Leech wanted to watch his brother. Talk to him with this. Observe how he reacted through the telescope.'

'Whoa, Doc. I know he's not exactly been a model parolee, but the moment he contacted his brother we'd have been here arresting him. Terms of his licence—no contact with his brother or the man's family. To be honest, I'm surprised they let him live so close.'

'London's a big place. We couldn't ban him from the whole city on the off chance he would bump into his brother.' Doc lifted his shoulders, spread his hands, explained. 'Four hundred metres from the office, that's the boundary. We're probably not much more than that here, are we?'

Carver shook his head. 'He's allowed out, sets himself up here to spy on big brother, wants to phone him... Taunt him? But I still don't get it. Shaun would call us and have him back inside in a flash.'

'Would he?' Doc's question was aimed at himself, not the detective, but Carver answered.

'Why not? He objected to the parole, and with good reason. Surely he would be delighted to see his brother behind bars again?'

Doc chose not to answer that question, allowing himself time to chew it over. Instead, he said, 'The telescope must be enough to warrant some protection for Shaun Leech and his family.'

'Sorry. It's out of my hands anyhow. There's a taskforce being set up to hunt Leech down. I've been sidelined, though I'm still on it,' he grumbled. 'They want you to liaise with them directly. And I doubt you'll convince them to put his brother under protective observation.'

'Tell them I will only liaise with you.' Doc's stomach flipped at the thought of being dragged back into the full team on a major operation. He had been there, done that. 'No more politics for me, Jack. I also hate having to educate everyone involved. I'm not going to do it.' He tapped a finger on Carver's arm as he said, 'I'll only act as a consultant to you. Fair enough?' Doc knew it would give Jack some leverage, some elbow to regain his status within the operation.

'Thanks, Doc. They'll go for that. They could get another profiler, sure, but you've got personal experience of our man and a track record second to none... I still doubt they'll give Shaun Leech protection though.'

'He won't want it, anyway.' Doc saw Carver's face scrunch in confusion. He shared his thoughts. 'I said the other day that Peter Leech had threatened his brother and you told me I was reaching.'

'Yeah. What'd he say? My brother's dead?'

'Uh-huh. They both said it. Shaun after the trial and Peter at his parole hearing.'

'Now what? You saying they want to kill each other? That Shaun Leech would refuse protection to draw his brother to him?' Carver pointed at Shaun's office block. 'His parents died at the hands of his lunatic brother. He knows what his brother's capable of. The man's a suit—a business consultant, for chrissake. You think he would go head to head with psycho-sibling? You think he's got a death wish?' Carver turned away, his expression doubtful.

'Phone him. You've got his number. Call him now. Ask him how he would feel about protection.'

'We can't promise him that, Doc.'

'Don't offer it. Tell him the truth. That it's a possibility we would consider if he requested it, if and when we feel the threat is justified. It's his choice whether to accept. We need to know how he'd feel about that.'

Carver said nothing, flipped open his phone and made the call.

Doc thought things through, tuning out Carver's conversation as he was convinced he knew the outcome. He considered the relationship between the Leech boys. Shaun had told him outright he would kill his murderous brother if he came near his family. Certainly, Shaun believed himself capable... Had told Doc how he sometimes wondered if it was in his genes.

'You really spook me with this shit sometimes, Doc.' Carver joined him on the balcony again. 'On the strength of a busted telescope you make the leap to his brother not wanting protection. How the fuck did you do that?'

Doc allowed a little smugness to creep into his voice—he had not lost his touch, despite everything he had been through. 'The telescope was smashed in a fit of rage, as was the table top.' Doc pointed at the broken glass, then to the new mobile. 'He wanted to speak to his brother, let him know he was hunting him. Wanted to see how Shaun responded. Wanted to see his brother scared.'

'And he knew his brother wouldn't call us? How?'

Doc eyed him, his own face quizzical, mirroring Carver's expression.

'Now, that is something we need to find out... There's more between these two than meets the eye. Let's head back to the station. There are some things I'd like to research.'

'The recording. The Judy Finch interview. What did that tell you?' Carver drove through the London traffic, manoeuvring into the bus lane to speed their progress.

'Rather less than I hoped.' Doc had been horrified at the content, the man's blasé attitude, the manipulative nature of his exposés of prison life, obviously scripted to wrench Judy's heart strings. Doc had also checked on some of the things Leech had stated as fact. 'It confirms he's a compulsive liar. I think he may even believe some of his own fictions.'

'Sounds like a screwball to me, Doc. You still pronounce him sane, if he can't tell fact from fiction?'

'False memory syndrome is not insanity. Sane, in the legal sense, is a term used to determine if someone is fit to be punished, or whether treatment is more appropriate.'

'Too right he needs some sort of treatment. An injection, maybe. A lethal injection.' He grinned humourlessly. 'The Yanks have the right idea when it comes to dealing with his type.'

Doc ignored the comment, knew too well Jack's views on capital punishment and would not be drawn into that argument.

'Peter Leech really may not know if he murdered his folks.' Something about the claim from Leech that his brother framed him fluttered into Doc's brain. What? He was not sure. 'He was in therapy as a boy. I don't remember a therapist testifying at the trial.'

'No.' They arrived at the station and Carver opened his door, paused half in, half out. 'They didn't need him. You testified as to Leech's state of mind.'

'Was he interviewed?'

'No. At the time they decided it wasn't necessary, and anyway, the guy had suffered a stroke around the time of the murder, if my memory serves.' Carver eased out of the car and slammed the door.

Doc remained inside, staring out the windscreen, making no move to follow. Carver grew impatient, went to his door, tugged it open.

'You okay?'

'The therapist. What happened to him?' Doc dragged himself out. 'Did he recover?'

'No idea. Why?'

'Oh. It may be nothing... but I'd like to meet him.'

'Is it really that important?' When Doc did not reply Carver stomped off to try to track the therapist while Doc headed to his office, continuing his research into the man they were hunting.

The Judge called as he opened the file. 'I'm having a dreadful day, Doc. This

Leech affair is throwing everything out. Worse, the Home Secretary carpeted me for recommending paroling Leech in the first place.' He sighed. 'I've not had a rollicking like that since school.'

'Aren't we supposed to be independent of the politicians?'

'That's irrelevant. I'm the whipping boy. And if you still want my job in a couple of years then you had better get used to the idea.'

Doc could tell his boss was tired, and crotchety too. Not surprising since he had lost two staff to the Leech affair—initially himself, and now Judy.

'Have you managed to reschedule everything?' He felt guilty, but there was no option. He was obliged to help find Leech, after all, he had paroled him. There was also the issue with Judy... She was in danger, so he had two powerful reasons to focus on the hunt. The self-justification did not help. He felt sorry for the Judge and the extra load he had placed on his boss.

'We'll cope. Although Judy did call.'

'And?' Doc sensed some bad news.

'She said she is available for work. I've scheduled her back in for the hearings she was due to undertake this week. She has her divorce hearing tomorrow too.' The Judge sounded businesslike as he added, 'Sorry, Doc. She told me you wouldn't approve but she was adamant.'

'That's okay. Thanks for the call.' He hung up.

Damn you, Judy.

She was supposed to be at his home, under police protection. He had needed to agree it as part of a decoy plan. He had recommended that a female police officer, with a passing resemblance to Judy, should stay in her apartment in the hope that Leech would appear there. A team of officers would stake out the house.

Not much point if the real Judy was wandering round, showing her face everywhere.

She had spent the night at his house, but objected to being kept prisoner there. He thought he had convinced her when he left that morning. Clearly not.

In a way, he was proud of her. But his overriding concern was for her safety. He called her.

'Look, I'm going mad here, Colin. Josh and I are bored. He wants to go to school tomorrow. And I am going back to work too.'

He imagined how she looked, het-up, the red splotches on her cheeks. Warmth spread through him at the thought. She was a true English rose—beautiful to look at but prickly as hell.

'Okay. I understand. But you be careful.'

'Think about it. I'll be in closed sessions at our office or at prisons... I'm hardly likely to bump into him there, am I?'

'True.' He felt a little better... She would be okay.

'And the police have agreed to escort Josh to and from school. Please don't worry about us. Just catch him. Soon.'

Well, he was doing his best. He returned to his files, searching for enlightenment.

'School tomorrow, sunshine.' Judy ruffled Josh's hair as they snuggled on the sofa in Doc's lounge. They were watching their third video of the day, microwaved popcorn half eaten in bowls in front of them. She kissed her son's head, inhaled his scent.

'Brill! Are we going home, Mummy?'

'Not just yet, sweetheart.' He must be petrified, she reasoned, despite her efforts to reassure him, to keep the full details from him.

She had told him that there was a tiny chance that a bad man from prison might visit their house. So they were moving into Colin's home for a few days while the police caught the man. From those sparse facts Josh had somehow divined that his mummy was in danger and he had cried last night, tearing her soul with his great gut-wrenching sobs of fear.

It must be the divorce too, she decided. Losing his father, in a way, especially if she got her way at the hearing. Poor Josh, first losing his daddy and now facing the prospect of losing his mummy. Oh well, she thought, we'll just have to snuggle again tonight.

Her eyes roved to the picture of Doc with Natalie. He had even asked her if she minded, if she would prefer he put it away where she could not see it. She had pecked him on the lips, told him, of course not, not to be so silly, Natalie had been a big part of his life, that she understood.

And now she wanted to be the biggest part of his life. She smiled at the photo, Doc's boyish face splitting in a smile, the love and affection radiating from them both.

She drew a juddering breath, felt her boy nuzzle closer in response, wondering if her son was trying to comfort her, allay her fears. She gave him a squeeze and then shuffled her thoughts back to Doc and Natalie.

No. It was not jealousy, but a different emotion she felt. Such a shame she had to sleep with Josh tonight... It was the perfect opportunity to move things on with Colin. Her stomach tingled at the thought.

She hugged her son closer, ashamed of herself. There would be plenty of time for that later.

Then she began to wonder, was Doc overreacting, out of his feelings for her? He had listened to the recording last night, checked her notes and quizzed her about the interview. He had then pronounced himself satisfied that Leech thought he'd made some connection with her, that he could be obsessing over her, that Birdy and Finch were too close to ignore. He had justified the move to his home, said he would try to convince them to put a decoy in her apartment.

But still she wondered, just how serious was this threat to her? How can a man, admittedly one with limited experience and zero availability when it came to women, believe, after speaking with her for just two hours, that he could be in love with her?

Despite Colin's explanation she had her doubts. She had pushed him until he had admitted it was not definitive, although he fell short of admitting he could be wrong about the whole thing. No, just that it may not be as serious an obsession as he thought likely.

They both hoped so.

Except in Judy's mind, a maggot of doubt wriggled, munching away at her reassuring logic, gradually exposing a half-remembered comment at the end of the interview. She tried to put herself back in that room, mentally reliving the meeting, Josh now asleep on her lap.

What had he said, after she had stopped the recorder, while she was packing up to go?

Then it came to her. He had asked her out.

Oh, Christ!

That was it. She hadn't told Colin, they had been so focussed on the recording, the transcript, her notes, with her mind blocking the memory anyway. Should she call him, tell him now?

No. It would only worry him more. What was the point?

But she knew, with absolute certainty, Doc was right. A connection had been made. Leech wanted her.

She found herself holding on to her son, his warm body close to her chest, chilled despite his body heat.

The maggot continued wriggling, chewing away, finally forcing her to recall Leech's parting words, uttered after she had refused to meet him outside of prison.

We'll see.

Doc's eyeballs were in meltdown by the time Carver arrived with coffee later in the afternoon.

'Eff Plo!' He said it with a toothy smile as he entered.

Doc assumed he had misheard, but the detective went on, 'F.P.L.O. That's me. The Met's one and only Forensic Psychiatrist's Liaison Officer. It's official. I'm back on the inside track thanks to you, Doc. I'm grateful. I've been in the doghouse lately with the PTBs. Got caught with my pants down. Literally. She was worth it though!'

Doc shrugged and smiled, too preoccupied with Leech to probe Jack for more.

Carver placed a cup in front of Doc, sipped his own and tapped the files with a finger.

'The court transcripts? What are you hoping to find there?'

Doc was not yet ready to share his suspicions with Carver, but what he had found was adding plausibility to an idea he had been loath to give credence.

'Did you find anything out about the therapist?'

Carver appeared to have forgotten his own question—he knew Doc moved in mysterious ways.

'Yeah. Name's Henley. He hasn't practised since his stroke. He says he's reasonably fit but he's nearly seventy now. Will be happy to see you, though he doesn't know what you expect from him.' Carver was curious but if he was expecting enlightenment he would have to wait.

Doc merely asked, 'Can I see him? Today? Now?'

'Yeah.' Carver chuckled. 'That important huh?' Still nothing from Doc. 'It's a drive, just south of Bristol. You can take my car. I warned him you would want to see him. Said he's usually available as he has nothing much to do these days. I'll call and confirm you're on your way.' He fished in his pocket for the car key. 'Probably a couple of hours drive, Doc. If you leave now you should just about miss rush hour.'

'No time to lose then.' Doc gulped his coffee, grimaced as he swallowed the lukewarm gunk, and followed Jack out. 'If I can have the file and the address I'll get going.'

<hr>

While Doc threaded his way through city traffic Carver spoke to Henley, confirming he had a visitor on the way, then called Doc. 'No problem. He's expecting you between five and six.'

That gave Doc a couple of hours alone, time to let his brain sift all the information he had absorbed over the last few days. He disliked driving, found it a chore, and since the accident he had been reluctant to get behind the wheel again.

This was the first time he had driven since Natalie's death, but it was not as bad as he thought it would be. As he joined the M4 motorway the autopilot inside him took over the mechanical function, allowing him the freedom to think. To analyse.

Was it possible that Leech really was innocent of murdering his parents? That was the question uppermost in his mind. It could explain why Shaun Leech had no fear of his brother... If he knew Peter was not responsible for their deaths. If he knew his little brother was not the murderer.

Yet Peter was *a* murderer... Gruber and his neighbour were dead and there was little room for doubt at whose hands. Violent deaths, one a stabbing, the knife in Gruber's temple covered in Leech's prints.

Like the knife he had used to kill his parents.

Doc shifted lanes, glanced at the driver overtaking. The man had been flashing him and Doc moved out of his way as soon as he became aware of the car behind, but not quickly enough. The driver was purple in the face, mouthing at Doc as he passed, his fist pumping a livid middle finger at him. The man was in his forties, was smartly dressed and had a top end Audi.

It saddened Doc, this display of intemperance, the fact that such a small thing could incur disproportionate anger. For a moment he was diverted, the thought of road rage breaking his pattern of thought.

Rage.

The knife wounds from the original Leech murders were indicators of an attack provoked by extreme fury. The motive had been obvious. The delay of trust fund monies enough to push a psychopathic son over the edge, inspiring a furious frenzied attack.

Or...

Could it have been staged to look that way? By Shaun? Wanting to inherit everything, to see his brother jailed?

Yet, the evidence pointed to Peter. The blood in the shower drain from both parents. His bloody clothes aflame in the barbeque.

But could Shaun have killed them and framed Peter?

What evidence was there? Doc pondered.

The phone call had clinched it. The cab driver had confirmed Shaun had been speaking to his girlfriend when they arrived at the house.

Or seemed to be... The driver only heard Shaun speaking. Could he have pretended to be on the phone, killed his parents and then phoned Suzie a few minutes before calling the police?

She had testified that she heard background noises, Shaun slamming the cab door, speaking to the driver as he paid. But that could have been recorded on a miniature device, similar to the one Judy used for her interviews, played back by Shaun for the benefit of his girlfriend during their brief phone conversation. Placing him in the cab, arriving home, supposedly with insufficient time to commit the murders.

A perfect alibi.

The cab driver was unsure, vaguely thought he may have dropped Shaun several minutes earlier… Until the exact time was confirmed by the mobile phone company. That was the critical factor that led the police to drop their investigation into Shaun and to focus on Peter.

Which left the murder weapon and Peter's bloodstained clothes in the barbeque.

Peter's bloody prints were on the knife. That was the most damning piece of evidence. Yet Shaun had knocked him cold before the police arrived. Could he have murdered their parents, found Peter in the shower, thumped him hard enough to send him unconscious, breaking his teeth?

And while Peter was out cold, could Shaun have put the knife in his hand? Showered blood off himself to ensure some 'evidence' was found in the drain? Lit a fire with some of his brother's clothes, having smeared them with parental blood first? Maybe even worn some of them for the attack? Setting his brother up for the fall?

Then called Suzie. Then the police. And sat with his parents, not bothered that he was coated in their blood again.

How many minutes would it take in total? Ten?

Doc pulled in at a service station, his mind reeling. It was all highly speculative. All highly unlikely. But all totally plausible. He sat in the car, staring out at the Wiltshire hills, unseeing.

Could they really have convicted the wrong son?

———

Rose Cottage. It certainly was—the front garden and walls were covered with the thorny plants. It made him think of Judy again. He felt a smile flicker on his face as a vision of his own English Rose appeared. He needed to concentrate. He pressed the bell.

A scrawny old man answered and invited him in.

'Thank you for seeing me at such short notice, Doctor Henley.' They shook hands and Henley led Doc through to his lounge.

'Please sit.' Henley walked with a limp and had an odd expression when he spoke, Doc assumed from the remnants of the stroke. The cadaverous geriatric lowered himself into his ancient leather armchair, the type that would be at home in an old gentleman's club. Doc sat on the sofa opposite and quickly took stock of his surroundings.

The overall impression was dark. And there was a smell, a vague aroma that Doc could not figure, one that seemed out of place in this room. He tried once more to concentrate on the reason for his visit.

'Peter Leech was your patient? For therapy? For how long?'

Carver had explained the reason for this meeting and Doc was not about to waste his time on pleasantries.

'Peter? Several years. His parents brought him to me when he was almost seven. Just before his birthday, I think.'

'So, you knew him well? How often would he come? What sort of regime were you treating him under?'

Henley cackled, wheezed then coughed into his hand. A smoker's cough, but there were no cigarettes to hand.

'Regime? Oh in those days therapy for wayward little rich boys was a relatively new phenomenon in the UK. It was all rather casual. He would come for an hour most weeks.'

'I see, but you did get to know him well. Say forty sessions a year. Several years?' Doc hoped he had not wasted his journey, began to wonder if the old man actually had any professional qualifications.

'Oh yes. It's what caused my stroke, you know. Well, triggered it. I think we can safely say my diet, lack of exercise, drinking and smoking caused it.' A humourless grin made his skinny head seem even more like a skull.

'What do you mean? The murders? They affected you that badly?' This was news to Doc. And made him more hopeful that Henley might be able to give him some insights into Leech.

'Indeed. It happened the night of the murders.' The old man's eyes were dreamy, remembering. 'I was watching TV when the news came on. Of course, I was devastated that a boy I had treated could have done such a thing...' He gazed at the ceiling. Lost to Doc for a moment.

'The shock. Brought on the stroke?' Doc tried to keep Henley on track.

'Yes.' He dropped his gaze to Doc's face. 'A detonation in my head, as it were. Followed by the headache from hell. It was like someone had parked a car on my skull...' The dreamy look had gone, a twinge of fear there instead. 'I collapsed and Mary, my wife, heard me fall from the kitchen.' He waved his fingers vaguely at the doorway. 'I was paralysed down one side.'

It seemed to Doc a massive overreaction to the shock. Okay, Henley knew the Leech family personally, but he could not understand the reason the psychologist had been so badly affected.

'But you had stopped seeing Peter some years before, hadn't you?' Doc vaguely recalled from his involvement in assessing Leech's mental state for the trial.

'Yes. He had started using drugs. Initially just harmless experimentation with marijuana. He was about thirteen then.'

Marijuana. Doc placed that strange smell now.

'And he stopped coming? Just like that?'

'Not exactly. He came. His father drove him, physically handed him over to my care. I had rooms near Reading then. It didn't do much good. At the end he just refused to speak. Wouldn't answer me. It was a waste of time, and his father's money. I told him so. Peter did start visiting me after though, for casual advice. He was much more himself, relaxed when he was no longer compelled to attend.'

Doc wondered about this man, this product of the sixties. Even wondered about how Peter Leech had discovered drugs... There had been a time when some Californian psychologists advocated its use with troubled patients. But on a young boy? Doc tossed the thought aside.

'My wife died.' Henley had drifted off track, the words rending the delicate fabric of Doc's composure.

My wife died too. He wanted to say it. Then he heard the clacking.

Not now. Go. Leave me.

Silence.

Henley continued speaking, unaware of the impact his words had had on Doc.

'She was careworn. I had to give up my practice. Mary looked after me—us both. Initially, they thought I would never walk again. The poor woman. Died five years after my stroke, even though I had started to improve. She just gave up. Seven years older than me.'

Doc felt for the man, but needed to hear about Leech's psychotherapy. 'You were trying to help Peter? To moderate his behaviour? To control his impulses?'

'What?' Henley was confused, then seemed to remember why Doc was sitting in his lounge. 'Of course. That's what the father wanted…' Henley seemed to float away again, searching for his dead wife perhaps. Doc knew how that felt.

'Peter. Did he respond to your treatment?'

'No. Not really. I thought he was in denial. Accused his brother of being responsible for his misdeeds.'

'The pattern started young, then…' Doc could see how the young boy could have entered a parallel universe, his life a mixture of fact and fiction, blurring the realities of life.

'The pattern? Oh, of blaming Shaun? I don't know any more…' Gone again.

'Doctor Henley? What do you mean?' Doc leaned forward, wanted to wring the man dry of his knowledge, frustrated at Henley's inability to concentrate. It was his age, combined with the stroke, of course.

'I believed him about Shaun. Not at first. But gradually it made sense.'

Doc fell back on the couch. Shaun? The hypothesis he was developing took on more shape. Could Peter have suffered at his elder brother's hands since early childhood. Been cynically framed, and ultimately blamed, for everything the older boy did? Exactly the opposite of what Shaun had told him.

'Please explain, Doctor Henley. What brought you to that conclusion?'

Henley stood up, wobbled a little, reached behind his chair and got a walking stick. 'I'm going to make some tea. By all means join me in the kitchen.'

Doc screamed inside, his frustration peaking. Then Henley answered as he disappeared out the door.

'Animals, Doctor Powers. Pets and the like.'

They were in the cramped kitchen, the tea brewing, Henley pottering around, talking to himself, it seemed. He was talking about his dog. Long since dead. How playful it was, how it sometimes nipped but never drew blood. Then he got to the point.

'Peter loved that animal. In all our meetings he never once harmed him, even when the dog gave him a playful bite.'

Doc's mind leapt back to his meeting with Shaun Leech. His story about why he had been forced into therapy. How Peter had blamed him for cremating their puppy. It made no sense if Peter was a dog-lover.

'You think he could have burnt his puppy?'

Henley seemed not to have heard the question. 'At first, I thought it was an act. To convince me, and then, of course, his father. Later I understood. He loved all animals. The devastating thing was that his parents refused to allow him another pet after the episode with the dog. Mind you, he wanted a snake.'

'You couldn't convince them it would have been good for the boy?'

'No. You see, Mister Leech also caught Peter apparently crucifying a cat.'

Doc remembered that from his meeting with Shaun. The boy caught red-handed.

Henley continued, 'Poor Peter was there, hammer in his hand, the cat nailed to the door, screeching.'

Poor Peter? What was Henley thinking? Doc probed. 'His father found him like that… Pretty conclusive don't you think?'

'Not at all.'

Henley poured the tea, infuriating Doc with his procrastination. The man probably had few visitors, made the most of those he had by stringing them along. Doc held himself in check. Waited for Henley to spit it out.

'Peter's story, the one I dismissed at first as fantasy, was that Shaun had taken him in hand, together with the cat, to see, in Shaun's words, something really funny. He nailed the creature to the door while Peter pleaded with him to stop, the younger lad frantically pulling at his much larger brother. Shaun was laughing, but when he realised their father was coming he handed Peter the hammer and told him to put the beast out of its misery. Then he ran off.'

'Leaving Peter to carry the can.'

'Uh-huh. Mister Leech caught Peter as he smashed the animal's head. He was almost seven. Was brought to me almost immediately after the event.'

'My God. If that's true—'

'I don't doubt it. You see I grew to rather like the boy. I told his father that I didn't think he was as bad as they thought… By then Shaun had turned into something of an angel. His behaviour seemed impeccable. The bad apple was the one in therapy, eh? Got blamed for everything rotten that happened.'

'And it was too late to convince them otherwise?'

'Bear in mind, Doctor Powers, it took me a good few years to start believing him and eventually be convinced myself. Things calmed down for a while, although his father did consult me again when Peter was fifteen or so. When his girlfriend was raped… Susan. I think that was her name.'

Henley seemed sharper now, his concentration improving as he got into his stride, but Doc realised the therapist's memory was not up to scratch still.

'You mean Suzie. Shaun's girlfriend. Now his wife.'

'Suzie. That's her. She was Peter's girlfriend, not Shaun's…' He was visibly shocked. 'Did Shaun really marry her?'

Doc had asked Carver to see if there were any of the original files on the rape, but other events had taken over. Instead, he now probed Henley's recollections.

'Peter had not seen me for a year or two, in my professional capacity. He'd occasionally come by, to walk the dog. Chat… I like to think I helped him. I was one of the few people who believed anything he said.'

Doc speculated on the marijuana again. Let it slide. It was not important now and the old man would never practise again. His mind pictured the two of them, a younger, hip Henley and the teenaged Leech, sharing a joint, putting the world to rights. He let Henley talk.

'When he was accused of raping his girlfriend, I was confused. I didn't see it as something he would do... He was obsessed with her. His beautiful classmate. They had been seeing each other for some months. No sex, just some adolescent foreplay. He asked me for advice. I think they were both planning to take it further.'

Doc was certain about the dope now. That Henley and his young friend had a strange relationship that extended beyond the professional boundaries. His distaste must have been apparent.

Henley pierced him with a hard stare, seeing the expression, but misreading it.

'Why would he knock her unconscious and rape her? Sex was likely to occur naturally and he was not unduly impatient. I advised him so. To take it slowly. He was only fifteen or thereabouts. And so was she.'

Doc reached back again, thinking. Didn't Shaun say she was older than Peter by a couple of years? Making her appear to be nearer his own age? No wonder he didn't want Doc to speak to her. 'Shaun told me Peter was jealous of him. That Suzie was his girlfriend.'

'Rubbish. I'd seen Peter with her. They sometimes came by together, to walk my dog... She was Peter's first love. He was infatuated with her.'

Doc's mind boggled. Shaun was a liar. A very accomplished liar. But how deep did it go? He started to wonder about False Memory Syndrome in relation to Shaun's version of events the day his parents died.

'The case was dropped?'

'Yes. Suzie's parents were having financial troubles. Mister Leech assisted...'

'And they dropped it? For money? I thought it was through lack of evidence.'

'Oh, that too. It was Shaun's word against Peter's. The younger boy claimed he'd left Suzie alone in their annex, a teenage den the Leech's had built, somewhere for the boys to get away from their parents. They'd been drinking and smoking weed, and Suzie was feeling the effects. He went to get some coffee from the house for her... When he got back Shaun was in the act, with Suzie unconscious. Peter went for him, of course. But Shaun, always bigger, stronger and trained in karate, beat his young sibling senseless. Dragged him to his father and accused him of the deed. Meanwhile he had roused Suzie and told her to use their shower. She was in shock. She did as he bid.'

'Hence, no evidence.' Doc could see it. How the bad boy would never be believed. How big brother, the angelic Shaun, could convince their parents of his own innocence and Peter's guilt.

'That's right.' The faraway look returned to Henley's eyes. Then he said, 'That night. When I had the stroke. I knew it was him. Just knew it.'

The man's erratic mind had lost Doc for a moment. Was he saying that Peter Leech was innocent of rape, but killed his parents? He pressed for clarification.

'Peter? You knew he killed them?'

Henley laughed, coughed and wheezed again before replying. 'Not Peter! Shaun... I knew *he'd* killed them.'

Henley was back in the kitchen again. Doc, this time, had opted to gather his thoughts and leave the man to make yet more tea.

Everything he had heard confirmed what he now believed was the truth. Shaun had bullied his little brother throughout the whole of his childhood. Doc knew the younger lad had psychopathic tendencies—a fondness for animals rather than humans was sometimes a trait. As, conversely, was torturing them…

It was in their genes. Both of them capable of murderous behaviour. Not just the one convict. Not just the one who went to prison.

Prison. That would have toughened the young boy-man like tempered steel. And now he was killing… He had moulded himself into the thing he was accused of being. The system had created a beast—the raw material was there already, but even with a personality disorder he could have led a near normal existence.

Only he had been convicted of a heinous crime. And Doc had labelled him a dangerous psychopath.

Which is exactly what he had become.

How could this have happened?

Henley returned, rattling the tea tray as he entered. Doc wondered if his drink would arrive safely as Henley teetered in the doorway.

'Did you get to know Shaun well, too?' Doc did not wait for him to sit and pour before asking, but had to wait while Henley did so before answering.

'Know him? Why, of course. He was in therapy too. In fact, I met him first.'

That did not tally with what Shaun had said, but Doc was getting used to that phenomenon.

'Their father consulted you, after Shaun cremated their dog? Mister Leech wanted the older boy to see you, was convinced he had done it.'

'And so was I… He hated animals. I caught him tormenting my dog on two separate occasions. He had a lot of anger in him.'

'He was jealous. Of his brother?'

'Very much so.' Henley relaxed back, cup and saucer rattling in his palsied hands. It appeared to Doc that the man's shakes had worsened during their meeting. Probably needed some herbal relief. Doc suspected the psychologist's tea may have had an additive.

Henley went on, 'Mister Leech first brought Shaun to me as a small child, well before that episode. I think he was about five years old. He had tried to smother his younger brother. Peter was barely walking at that stage. He was a late developer and still spent a lot of time in his cot. Shaun was found sitting on a pillow. On Peter's head.'

Henley shook his head at the memory, slopping his tea in his lap. He glanced down, as if he had forgotten it was there. He took a sip, closing his eyes as he inhaled the aroma.

'The parents saw this?'

'Mister Leech caught him. They put it down to sibling rivalry and a lack of understanding on Shaun's part. Not many people can believe a five-year old is capable of murder. Perhaps he really did not know the consequences of his actions… He tried to drown him too.'

Christ! 'Drown him? In a pool?'

'No. Bath time. Mother left the two of them alone for a few minutes, to fetch a towel or some such. She came back and found Shaun holding Peter's head under the water. Had to revive the poor mite.'

'What age was this?' Doc was now pretty impressed with Henley's recall from some thirty years ago.

'I think they were three and six or so. Shared bath time was supposed to be fun. It was almost murder.' Henley gave Doc a look, one that said Shaun was bad from the off.

'You said he was angry, in therapy.'

'Always, until his brother was made to start. He was a changed boy then. As if his problems had vanished… Thinking back it's obvious why.'

'He'd managed to have his brother labelled as the bad apple.' Doc remembered Peter Leech's little speech, his appeal to the parole board not to label him.

'Yes. Their father, having seen a dramatic improvement, took Shaun out of therapy soon after Peter started. They dismissed the early attempts on Peter's life as aberrations. High jinks. Growing up. Humph!'

'But not you?' Doc was intrigued. After treating him for a couple of years, Henley seemed adamant.

'Definitely not. Shaun was the bad seed. I knew it, even before he told me, but what he said merely confirmed it.'

Had Doc missed something?

'What did he say?'

'The words that eventually ruptured my brain.' He let the ghost of a smile quiver on his lips. 'He actually said, *One day I'm going to kill them all.*'

Doc was at the door, keen to get back to London, to Judy and Josh. He must call her, it was past seven o'clock already.

'You've been very helpful, Doctor Henley. Your memory is remarkable.'

'Hardly. I barely remember most of my clients. Those boys though, they were different… I knew things would go bad. I just thought it would be Shaun. By the time I had recovered sufficiently from my stroke, Peter had been convicted… I sometimes wonder if I could have helped him. At the time.'

Doc wondered too. The stroke had taken Peter's one and only ally out of the frame. But the reality was that 'Doctor' Henley was not actually qualified, and would have had no credibility on the stand, was no 'expert' witness. Henley had been ashamed when he admitted it as Doc stood up, ready to leave, justifying it as part of the culture at the time, the rapid growth of new-fangled therapists unregulated by government. It was all history now and Doc could not find it within himself to condemn the old man. In a way he had helped young Peter for a while, if a little unconventionally.

They shook hands and Doc went to the car, breathing in the evening air, the scent of roses relaxing him. Clearing his mind.

There was no way the police would reopen the investigation into the parents' murder. Peter Leech may not have been guilty, but he was certainly a killer now. Why create problems by pursuing Shaun Leech on the basis of an unqualified old man's opinion? That would be the response from the PTBs. Doc hated to admit it to himself, but Shaun had got away with murder. Case closed.

Then again, was there some way he could get them to listen, to consider the possibility that a double murderer was walking free? That an innocent victim had been jailed and brutalised as a consequence?

He got into Carver's car and turned on his phone. It told him he had missed several calls, so someone was desperate to speak to him.

Carver five times and Judy once.

Damn.

He called her first. Reassured her he was okay, checked she was fine and at home in his house. Then told her he was on his way, almost told her he loved her, but could not.

He finished the call, tried to shake away the vision of her filling his mind, when a vague memory clicked into place.

The photos on Shaun Leech's office desk. The picture of his wife, Suzie. It had struck him at the time, but he had ignored the thought as irrelevant. Now he wondered how important it was…

Suzie was quite similar in looks to Judy. Could that explain Peter Leech's obsession? Doc groaned. The recording had given him false hope, that maybe Leech was less focussed on Judy than he thought. There had been little in the way of flirting, yet Leech certainly felt there was a connection. And this explained it.

It was a disaster. Judy was most definitely in danger… And Suzie? Probably her too. Then his laser brain carved through the mass of data, the muddy thoughts on Shaun and Peter, their history.

She was bait. Suzie. Shaun wanted his brother to come for her. Then Shaun would kill him.

Doc was absolutely certain now, was about to enlighten Carver, had his phone in his hand, when the detective called him.

'Where the hell have you been, Doc? I've called a dozen times—'

'Sorry. I was with Henley. We need to—'

'Doc. I've very bad news. You're not driving, are you?'

'No. I'm about to leave Henley's.' Doc dreaded what Carver had to say. What could be such bad news that Carver was worried about Doc hearing it while driving? And Jack's voice was riddled with stress.

'It's Justice Potter. He's dead, Doc. Sorry to have to tell you like this.'

'Dead?' Doc's mind fizzed and popped. He had not seen this coming. 'Murdered?'

Leech? Was it revenge?

He was sick to his heart. He liked the Judge, had appreciated his friend's support during his time of crisis. Had thought the man indestructible.

'No. Looks like suicide. A ritual or something similar…'

'No way! Impossible.' Doc punched the words at Carver. 'Ritual suicide? Never. Not the Judge.'

'I can't say more… Not on a mobile phone.' Doc then realised there was something very strange here. Why would Jack be worrying about eavesdroppers?

'I'm on my way. Where are you?' Doc started the engine.

'At the Judge's home. The ME's almost done, then they'll take the body—'

'No! I'm coming. I want to see it exactly as it is. Do this for me, Jack. Please.'

'C'mon, Doc! It was suicide. You're two hours away. These guys have got homes to go to.' *And so have I*—Doc got the implied point.

'I'll break the speed limit. I'll be there as soon as I can… Please wait.'

Carver muttered something inaudible and sighed. 'Okay. You'll need some blue lights. You're coming M5 and M4?'

'Yeah.' Doc was easing the car away, desperate to end the call, tuning Carver out. 'Where are the switches for the siren and lights in here?' He was scanning the dashboard, could see nothing obvious.

'It's not a police vehicle. It's my personal chariot, so be careful.' With that, he hung up. He sounded mightily pissed off to Doc.

Too bad.

Doc joined the M5 ten minutes later and wound the engine up until he was touching one hundred miles an hour. Much of the traffic was moving at a similar speed, though generally a little less fast. Doc stuck in the outer lane, flashing slower movers, closing his mind to the possibility of another accident. He felt bad enough as it was.

The Judge.

It was unthinkable the man would take his own life. Okay, he had been stressed out when they last spoke, but the Judge thrived on the challenges of work.

Was he supposed to have committed suicide in response to the political fallout from Leech's parole?

Never!

Doc's heart sank as he focussed on his rear-view mirror. 'Oh, Christ! That's just what I need.' A blue light was flashing, the police car behind him with headlights blazing at him, indicating him to pull over. To stop.

Doc had been doing ninety-five. This would delay things. He just hoped Carver could sort it.

He pulled into the middle lane, slowing, intending to slip across to the hard shoulder. The police car pulled alongside, the officer in the passenger seat gave him a cheery thumbs up and jerked a finger in a *follow me* gesture.

'Jack, you bloody genius!'

Blue lights.

Doc pulled behind the patrol car, realising that another was right behind him. He had a police escort, sirens wailing. Doc saw his speedometer wind all the way up to one-hundred and twenty, and stay there.

Peter Leech had been busy that afternoon. He had left Judy's ex-husband and decided to take the man's Jaguar to Reading. Although he had noted two other cars under canvas covers also parked in the massive garage, he plumped for the big cat.

He had never driven anything with as much power, and he thrilled as he pumped the throttle, filling the garage with the V12 engine's roar.

Fortunately the car was automatic, given his limited experience, so gear changes were one thing less he needed to worry about. As it was, he almost wrote the rear end off as he shot out the garage, clipping the nearside panel as he misjudged the triple doorway.

Wow!

He found the remote for the gate, blipped it and then meandered through the leafy Berkshire lanes. He soon got used to the feel of it, enjoying the surging accelera-tion and the sure-footed handling of the modern sports car.

He opted to join the M4, and was surprised at how much traffic there was—and how fast it was moving.

He was soon travelling at over a hundred, swerving and cutting up other vehi-cles, enjoying himself immensely, laughing manically at the horrified faces as he played his own version of high speed dodgems.

This driving lark is a piece of piss, he decided. He was fearless.

He cut off on the motorway spur and headed for his old stamping ground. Read-ing. He was amazed to see how much had changed since he had been away, new developments had sprung up everywhere, and the town centre was unrecognisable.

He followed signs for parking and wandered round a riverside shopping complex that had not existed when he had last visited. The Tuesday afternoon crowd was bearable… Maybe he was finally getting used to the tempo of life outside prison, no longer feeling insecure around the throngs of shoppers.

He peered into people's faces as they hurried by, checking for signs of recogni-tion, to see if anyone made a connection between his current appearance and the lunchtime news photograph.

His face felt a lot better today, his lips were no longer flaps of rubber, his bruising, though colourful, no longer ached. Sometimes he thought people made too much fuss about pain. It was not so bad.

Those people who did look at him soon glanced away, intimidated, the beaten features a perfect disguise. Even so, he wanted a store that stocked a wide range of contact lenses.

The third optician he tried had what he wanted and he was on his way again.

He was going home. As he drove he was stunned by the lack of recognisable landmarks on this side of town, overwhelmed by the clusters of booming high tech-nology businesses, the smoked glass temples to mammon.

When he arrived at his old village he realised he must have driven past his family home. He turned the car, scuffing the bumper on a low garden wall as he swung onto the pavement, startling a young mother pushing a child in a buggy. She yelled at him, but he was oblivious, wondering how he could have missed his own house.

He followed the road back, slowing at the bend where his home had been. He now knew why he had missed it. A courtyard development of mock Tudor farm-houses stood where he had played as a boy.

What the hell?

So they had knocked down the old house… Was it because of the murders? Perhaps no one would buy it, knowing the history. He thought that must be it. People were so squeamish.

And Shaun. The bastard! He must have made a fortune flogging the old place to the developers. Peter had only a vague idea of current property values, but he knew this was one of the most expensive areas in the UK.

Shaun. Fallen on his feet again. A house he could not sell bulldozed into a fortune.

It made him sick. The golden boy. Always coming out on top. Well not any more. Not today. It was time for the Leech boys to have a reunion.

With his thoughts goading him on, he headed back to his current residence, ramming the beautiful car into the rear wall of the garage as he parked, buckling the sweeping bonnet, reshaping the majestic Jaguar into a bull-nose terrier.

Fuck it!

He got out, slammed the door. Now what? He needed a car. He eyed the canvas clothed vehicles, wondering why they were under wraps. He tore off the first cover, exposing a flawless red Ferrari. He got in, fiddled with the controls. Nice.

Then he unveiled the second car and what he saw made his day. It was the car of his dreams, the vehicle he had hankered after since his father had taken him to a classic car rally at Windsor racecourse when he was eight. He had been happy that day. One of the few days he could say that about when recalling his childhood. Just him and his dad. Shaun was at his martial arts club, practising karate blows. Would test them on his punchbag brother that night...

The car sparkled under the fluorescent lights. It was immaculate and he decided it was quite simply the most beautiful thing he had ever seen. The AC Cobra. The original muscle car. The vehicle responsible for the introduction of a speed limit on the UK's roads during the early sixties, instigated by Parliament after the car had been reported tearing down the M1 at one hundred and sixty miles an hour.

He caressed its metallic blue flank. He would use this car and even try to take care of it. He was in love!

Leech had explored the whole house earlier, and inevitably found the gun locker with the two matching shotguns fitted snugly inside. He now sawed them both down to make them more manageable then strung them together with nylon twine, first threading the string over his shoulders then through the sleeves of the Barbour huntsman's coat he'd found in Finch's wardrobe. With the guns tucked inside, he checked they would stay hidden until he wanted to swing them into view.

Perfect.

He felt great. Ready to meet his bully boy brother.

John wanted to die. He was struggling to breathe now. His position, arms folded back unnaturally, was restricting his chest and, as he weakened from the lack of food and water, with the grinding pain in his dislocated shoulders and ravaged back stripping him of reserves, he could feel himself slipping away.

He was sometimes irrationally exuberant. It was the lack of oxygen, hypoxia, fooling him, tricking him with light-headedness. Then he would have a spell like this, coherent and suffering in the most dreadful way. His neck screamed at him, his throat ached with the strain, mouth ablaze, long ago devoid of moisture. His feet and hands had lost sensation, at first tingling and then shutting down. Lack of blood flow, and therefore lack of oxygen, he reasoned. If he ever did get out of this alive, what sort of state would he be in?

He had heard the madman coming and going all afternoon, and now he re-appeared. John watched him come through the door, his hair different this time, much darker from John's dye. But something else too. Then it came to him. The nutter was wearing his clothes.

It deflated him entirely. He had hoped for some water, some relief maybe, but instead, this. A view of the man, from the feet up, wearing his things.

'What d'ya think?' He did a twirl, as if he were on the catwalk at a Paris fashion show.

Unbelievable.

'Bit tight across the shoulders, had to find your baggiest tee shirt. Levis are almost the right length.' He peered down at the bottoms, a few centimetres above his boots. 'No matter. But I love this coat!' It was John's brown Barbour. The lunatic looked as if he was about to join a shooting party.

In his right hand he held a shotgun.

One of my Purdeys.

John thought it, but could not find the energy to care.

Just go away, you odious man.

Then he realised the gun appeared shorter. Was it just the angle he was seeing it at? No… The cretin had cut the end off!

The bloody heathen.

Then the thought whistled through him. Was the maniac planning to shoot him now? He was sure the man could see the terror in his eyes, John once again wanting to live, not die here, like this.

'You like it? My modification?' He held the gun up for inspection, then aimed it at John's head. The barrels appeared massive this close up. 'Had to saw it off in your garage… You didn't tell me you collected classic cars, did you? I take it they all work.'

John nodded slowly, once, careful not to nudge the weapon with his forehead. This man was barking mad. Hadn't told him! It's not as if they'd been having little fireside chats, was it? His mouth was still taped, for goodness sake!

Yet, John knew he could easily die over the 'omission'. Maybe they had been chatting, but only in the twisted mind inside that mad head. That was probably it.

'I'm afraid your Jag needs a bit of attention!' He held up the Cobra keys. 'This one's a beauty though. Must've cost you a couple of hundred grand. You certainly know how to spend it, don't ya? Anyway, enough chit-chat. I'm going for a spin… And maybe I'll fit in a little hunting.' He giggled and then sucked air through his lips. 'But what do I do about you? Shall I finish you now?'

John shook his head, launching his brain into a whole world of pain. The barrels pressed into his nose, squashing until he could barely breathe. Was he about to die?

The pressure released.

Thank you, God!

'Tell you what. You promise to be a good boy and I'll come back. Might even let you go.' He crouched down, patted John's head.

Then John saw him rip something and drop part of it on the floor. It was the photo, the one of himself, Judy and Josh. A precious drop of moisture dribbled from the corner of his eyes as he saw it, just in his line of vision. The fragment was of him and his son. The man had pocketed the piece with Judy on it.

The lunatic studied him, watching the tears form as John's thoughts turned to better times, memories of his family life. The life he had allowed greed and lust to ruin. And right now, all he wanted was to see his son again. The picture reminding him that he had one very good reason to live.

'You're alright. Not a bad bloke… Got no reason to kill you.' The words were gentle, but then John heard a hideous blast, as if the gates of hell had opened and the devil himself was braying at him. The lunatic was in hysterics, finally spitting out the words he had found so funny. 'But no phone calls while I'm gone, eh? There's a good boy.'

He patted John's head once more and left him transfixed on the torn photo.

Doc's escort slowed then stopped at the start of the Hammersmith flyover. The co-driver in the vehicle in front came to his window.

'Please pop into the squad car, sir. It'll be quicker. I'll take the Saab and follow on.'

The patrol car following them had tucked into a police observation lane, set back from the road, invisible to speeding drivers until it was too late.

Doc was relieved, exhausted from driving for an hour or so at the speed of a racing car. At each county boundary his escort had changed, one pair of cars peeling away as the new patrolmen joined him. He marvelled at what Carver had pulled off. He felt like royalty.

And now his police driver was definitely able to navigate his way through London at a faster pace than Doc could. They arrived at the Barbican apartment complex in just minutes.

Carver, alone now, was waiting in the Judge's flat. He was tired and cranky.

'I used up every favour I have with the provincial boys to get you here. Yet the more I think about it, the less suspicious I get. He killed himself, Doc.'

'Show me... please.'

Carver led him through to the Judge's study. The room was larger than average and included a TV and DVD player, bookshelves lining the walls with legal journals and reference manuals, a sofa, an antique desk and a matching chair.

The chair had been placed in the middle of the room, facing the TV. The Judge, pallid, his waxen skin sagging in grey folds, was semi-naked, sitting on the chair. He was wearing suspenders, stockings and a bra. No other clothes.

His feet were tucked under the chair, tied to a rope that extended up the back and looped in a noose round his neck. Doc crouched down, peering closely at his old friend and mentor, inspecting the rope, noting the bruised skin and indentation where the ligature had cut into the Judge's neck.

The hands were cuffed and folded in his lap, clutching his penis. The Judge's head was bowed, as if ashamed of his terminal sin.

'His daughter found him... She ran out, shocked. Called an ambulance. Refused to come back in. The paramedics called us... But you've got to admit, Doc, it is suicide.' Carver grumbled, 'We're wasting our time.'

'I don't believe the Judge was a pervert, Jack.'

'We found a stack of porno DVDs. Young teens. Probably illegal... One was in the DVD player. His wife's been dead for several years. Plenty of time for an old codger to go off the rails.'

Doc did not like the lack of respect in the detective's voice, but let it slide. He now understood why Carver had been reluctant to discuss the case over the mobile network with so many tabloids and amateur sleuths potentially earwigging in.

Suicide? Only inasmuch as he had killed himself. But by accident... Which is what had thrown Doc. The Judge was no suicide candidate. But, then again, he was no pervert either.

'I'm not convinced. This could have been staged. What did the ME say?'

'Only that he appears to have throttled himself. His feet were positioned to enable him to put tension on the rope round his neck, allowing him to choke off his air supply. Never seen anything like it myself. But the ME has.'

'Yes.' Doc was not sure whether he was allowing his personal view of the Judge's good character to get in the way of his professional opinion. 'AEA. It's more common than you might think.'

'AEA? Is that what you call it?'

'Uh-huh.' Doc swallowed back the emotion. His boss, his good friend, now being labelled an accidental suicide, a pervert.

Labelled.

His synapses sparked a connection, already racing to another conclusion, but he continued his explanation to Carver anyway.

'Auto Erotic Asphyxiation. Practitioners experience enhanced orgasm by restricting the flow of oxygen to the brain. Trouble is, it's very easy to overdo it. Literally masturbating yourself to death...' Doc checked the knots holding the Judge's feet, went on, 'It's possible that as many as one in three of all suicides resulting from hanging are a consequence of AEA.'

'You serious?' Carver had seen many things, but this was news to him, and it showed. 'You know some really weird shit, Doc, I'll give you that. So, case closed. Accidental suicide.' He blew air through his lips, then asked, 'Why the cuffs?'

'Bondage. Part of the sexual fantasy. The transvestism. The video. Who knows what's in someone's mind when they're in the throes of fantasy?' But it still did not feel right to him. He glanced at Carver and said, 'Any poppers?'

'Amyl nitrate? Not here. Why?'

It did not fit.

'They are invariably used to further heighten the sensation. Any other drugs?'

'None. Doc, for chrissake. He wanked himself to death. It's a sorry end for the old man, but he chose it. Let's go. I'll get the coroner's boys in to remove the body. I sent them for a drink. Let's hope they're not too drunk to do their job.'

'Jack.' Doc called to him as Carver headed for the door, the detective's face darkening as he stopped and turned to listen. 'There's one thing we should do... Just to be sure.'

'What now, Doc?' Carver trudged back. 'You're rapidly running out of favours, y'know?' He was reluctant, shaking his head, but continued, 'Okay, I know he was more than just a boss to you. So, tell me.'

'The video cameras. They're on the corners of the building.'

'No fucking way! What? You want us to go through hours of video footage.' His head was jerking spasmodically now, a rapid side to side motion. An emphatic negative. 'Have you any idea what that'll cost? In overtime? For what? It's not going to happen.' He settled down, his eruption over, possibly mollified by the sorrow in Doc's eyes.

'He was a great man, Jack. I don't believe this!' Doc gestured at the corpse. 'I think someone wanted to ruin his reputation. To label him this way, in death. To devastate his good name, to wreck his daughter's image of the good father. Someone out for revenge...'

'Leech? Are you suggesting he came here? Did this?' Carver fingered his chin, head dipped. 'It's too elaborate for him. Why not just stab him or beat him to death? I don't see this as Leech's MO.'

'He wanted to label the man who labelled him. The Judge called Leech a beast at the trial.' Doc acknowledged to himself it was a tenuous connection, and in reality he agreed with Jack's assessment, that this would not be Peter Leech's way of dealing with the man.

Carver was still unconvinced, rubbing his brow, the head shake back again as he listened.

Doc tried one last appeal, for his dead boss's sake. 'Please check the tapes. Only from this evening. He was always late home, probably not much more than an hour's worth of video to check before his daughter found him. And if Leech was here...'

That clinched it.

'Okay. Okay. There's several cameras. I'll see what I can do. We'll check for Leech.' He was on his way out. Again.

'Jack.' He was at the door, his hand on the handle, and he held on to it, just looking at Doc, now visibly pissed off with his friend. 'Both Leech boys. Check the tapes for either one of them. Peter or Shaun.'

Unlike the Jaguar, the Cobra was difficult to drive, it had a manual gearbox and a clutch designed for a gorilla. The bloated tyres spun and smoked as Leech wrestled the machine on the winding roads.

By the time he reached the M4 and joined the London bound carriageway his confidence in the vehicle had soared. It was awesome. Freedom incarnate. And great fun. He used the car to intimidate other drivers, roaring along, revelling in the responsiveness and the power he controlled. It was definitely the best sensation he had ever felt in his entire life.

He gave no quarter, often zipping onto the hard shoulder to overtake on the inside and then veering back across the lanes of traffic, fishtailing in a cloud of burning rubber. Car horns bleated at him, but he was oblivious. The thrill of the race, the danger and possibility of violent death, combined to boost his spirits.

This was nothing like racing go-karts or old bangers. This was a real man's car. He felt alive. The king of the road.

He glimpsed the blue lights way behind him and slowed to seventy, pulled into the middle lane to let them pass. Lucky! It was some sort of escort, two squad cars either side of a big Saab. They were shifting—he wanted to tuck in behind them, but thought better of it. No point tempting fate. The cars disappeared from view and he let his own speed increase again.

Before long, he was almost at the end of the motorway, joining the elevated road section at Hammersmith. He didn't notice the patrol car until it was too late. A siren whooped as the hidden vehicle emerged and accelerated behind him.

Leech had been doing eighty, overtaking on the inside. But now he had to slow for the press of traffic ahead, the bottleneck of the motorway entering the city an effective roadblock. There was no hard shoulder to escape onto, and the patrol car was on his tail.

Shit. That's all I need.

He pulled in to the left and stopped, the police car thirty feet behind him. One officer got out, the other had his head down in the cockpit. Leech guessed he was checking the car registration.

Oh well. Time to go to work.

In a liquid movement he stepped out of his car, opened his coat, levelled both shotguns and blasted them simultaneously. The policeman walking towards him was thrown backwards as he buckled at the waist. The one in the car disappeared from sight in a shower of blood and glass.

Leech switched his attention to the traffic bearing down on him. He turned all four barrels onto the lead cars and let off the two remaining shells. The result was spectacular. The cars slewed and struck each other, one hit the central barrier, the other spun round to face the oncoming vehicles. Everyone was travelling too fast, cars and lorries piling up, smashing into the two stationary vehicles, turning the motorway into a breaker's yard in seconds, replacing the potential bottleneck in front of him with an actual one behind him.

Leech watched, awed at the power he had unleashed.

Then he returned to the Cobra, ignoring the squeals of the policeman squirming on the ground, trying to stuff his guts back into his belly cavity.

He took one last look at the scene of devastation he had created, sucking in the thrill and satisfaction, then uttered just one word.

'Snakebite!'

He parked the Cobra near Hammersmith tube station in a resident's zone, and gave the bonnet one last lingering touch. He vowed he would buy one of these magnificent beasts when he settled abroad. It occurred to him that the roads in the Caribbean might not be as much fun as the motorways of Britain, but he decided it didn't matter. He just wanted to possess a thing of such beauty.

He needed to get to Chelsea and, at the entrance to the underground station, he picked up an A to Z of London and checked the address.

Within fifteen minutes he was walking through the streets of select Georgian townhouses that screamed money. The property he wanted was nothing special, just another fancy townhouse amongst the many. He wanted to blow a hole in the door and kill his brother there and then. But was Shaun even home? No sense going in guns blazing, alerting him and the police if the bastard wasn't there.

Darkness was almost complete now, the air cooler and his long coat no longer out of place. There were few people on the street anyway, a dog walker, a courting couple, an old lady with a Harvey Nichols shopping bag. He didn't think anyone would pay him any attention.

Leech went to the end of the road to see if there was rear access. There was none. The end of terrace property had a three metre wall topped with broken glass protecting its rear garden. Leech reckoned there would be a series of walls like this separating the gardens, a series of hurdles, some sixteen of them between him and his target, each two or three metres high.

No way.

He went back down the street, monitoring the few pedestrians, scanning the vehicles. Still no sign of his brother's car. Or the police.

Leech climbed the steps of the next door neighbour's house, and knocked. A long-haired, middle aged man answered, reefer in one hand, a bottle of beer in the other. Leech double-checked the street, hoisted the guns and stepped inside.

The man stumbled back at the sight of him, jaw jerking silently as Leech followed him inside, guns held at the man's face. He hoofed the door to behind him, and said, 'Evenin. You home alone?'

The man, pale and trembling, nodded. Leech noticed a dark patch appear on his victim's crotch, spreading down the trouser legs as he soiled himself.

'Don't be scared, mate. I won't hurt you.' Leech released one gun, letting it swing back inside the coat, reached out and took the reefer. 'But you really shouldn't open up to strangers.'

The ageing hippie found his voice. 'What do you—?'

Leech smashed the other gun barrel against the man's ear, knocking him unconscious. He caught the beer bottle as the man sagged to the floor.

'I didn't say you could speak though, did I?' He took a drag on the joint. 'Not bad!' Then he sucked down some beer, let go the gun and rummaged in his voluminous pockets.

'Ah! Gaffer tape! Never travel without it.'

Leech was enjoying the moment. He had helped himself to another joint from Shaun's neighbour's stash, having gagged and bound him to the downstairs toilet, then stationed himself at the upstairs window. He had his feet up and was watching, waiting for Shaun. His excitement was mellowed by the dope, but even so, he could visualise himself crushing the life from his brother's throat. The thought had given him an enormous erection.

He pulled out the picture of Judy. Touched her face with his thumb, stroking her image... She was so like her. Suzie. His Suzie. Stolen by his brother. Possessed by Shaun.

But not for long.

Yes. Tonight he would take back what was his due.

He stroked the photograph again and resumed his vigil. Waiting for his brother's car to arrive and take up position in its bay. He did not have to wait long.

The moment Shaun entered his house, Suzie rushed him, held him tight.

'Oh my God! I'm so glad you're home.'

'Hey, it's okay sweetheart.' He kissed her forehead. 'I just got held up.'

She stepped back, flushed. 'Your phone was off. I've been so worried... I kept calling you.'

'Sorry honey, I was in a meeting... Must've forgotten to put it back on.' He pulled it from his pocket and showed her, surprised at her agitation.

'Peter's been on the news this evening. He's wanted for murder...'

'I heard.' He did not tell her he had spoken to the detective on the case, had refused to consider protection. 'Don't worry, darling.'

She wept as she spoke, tucking herself into his arms again. 'He's only been out five days and he's killed two people already. He's a lunatic.' Her snuffles were pathetic.

'They can't be sure, darling. They only have some circumstantial evidence.' Peter was no killer, of that Shaun was certain, and he let the thought slip out. 'He's not capable of killing anyone.'

She pushed him away. 'How can you say that? He murdered your parents...'

'I mean he's never killed anyone else.' She was still looking at him with a strange expression, so he went on, 'Perhaps the police are exaggerating. Automatically assuming he's responsible because of his history.' That would be a familiar theme, he thought, allowing himself some satisfaction.

'They found a man murdered in his flat!' She was staring at him, confusion on her face. 'He's gone mad, Shaun. And I'm petrified he'll come here. Try to harm us!'

Shaun had not taken much note of the news and for the first time in his life he wondered if he had underestimated his brother. Maybe the little pussy had developed a spine in prison?

'Don't worry, sweetheart. They'll catch him soon.' He eased past her into the lounge. She followed him and watched him pour himself a drink, sniffing at her tears. He wanted to shout at her, tell her to pull herself together.

'How can you be so... so bloody calm?' Suzie was verging on hysteria, her voice a shriek, piercing him. 'If he comes here he might try and kill you. Me! Billy! He's fucking mad. Your brother is twisted, sick and bitter... For God's sake!' She collapsed on the sofa, tears streaming again, her panting gasps suggesting she would hyperventilate.

At times like this, Shaun wanted to kill her himself.

'Calm down, Suzie. He won't come here.' He said it with conviction, though he was lying. And until a few moments before he had been convinced his runt of a brother was incapable of killing, but now he wondered. He'd wanted the confrontation. Had planned to rip Peter apart. Doubts fluttered somewhere inside his head— was his brother a killer too?

But Shaun had always been stronger, smarter, more ruthless than his baby brother.

Reassured by that thought, Shaun downed his gin and tonic, poured himself another, all the while willing his wife to get a grip. Reluctantly he went to her, sat on the arm of the sofa and draped an arm round her shoulder, the sobbing quieter now.

'Don't you worry. I'll protect you. And Billy. Trust me.' He stood up and held his hands in a fighting stance. She gazed up at him with wet eyes. Pathetic cow. 'Remember. I'm a lethal weapon!' He grinned his soppiest grin, knowing the effect it would have on her.

She laughed, finally breaking out of her hysteria. Yet the funniest thing was, it was true. He was a martial arts expert, a karate instructor. He knew how to kill with his bare hands. And he had killed before...

But a voice whispered in his head: So has Peter. It's in his genes too.

'That's very reassuring, but... perhaps we should ask the police to park outside. Scare him away if he comes.'

'Suzie, I'm tired, hungry and in need of some supper.' She nodded, went to the kitchen and he followed. At least that was something. He went on, 'If the police did bother, how long do you think they would be happy to sit outside. One night? Two, maybe? And then what? It's pointless.'

'Please, Shaun.' The tears were back again.

He made a show of giving in. 'Listen. If you really want, I'll get some proper protection. A couple of heavyweight security guards.'

It was not such a bad idea and one he had mentioned to that copper who had called him earlier. Some extra muscle, just in case. No need to involve the police. He wanted to deal with Peter in his own special way.

'Then, if he does come, I can make sure he never bothers us again.' He made a pistol with his fingers, blew the tips as if puffing at the smoke from a bullet. 'Now. What's for supper?'

He left his wife in the kitchen tending to his food, and sat in the lounge, the breeze cooling him through the open patio doors, the garden a mass of shadows behind him.

He relaxed in his armchair, drink in hand, leafing through the Yellow Pages, searching for security consultants with a twenty-four hour contact number. He could probably get someone here within an hour or so.

Except his brother had other ideas.

Shaun's world disintegrated into an agonising confusion of dazzling lights, then total blackness.

Peter Leech had spotted his brother's car as Shaun pulled into the bay outside the house. Gruber had got that right at least, a silver Mercedes sports with a personalised number plate. SL 500. Shaun Leech and Suzie Leech. How fortunate they had the same initials as their car. He seethed with envy as Shaun had sauntered up the steps, as if he owned the whole world.

Peter had seen numerous photographs of them both over the years, provided by Gruber, giving him something tangible to focus on, the images stoking his anger, ensuring the furnace of his hatred would never cool.

Even if Peter had failed to recognise the man, his attitude, his swagger would have been enough. As it was, Shaun was familiar, but smaller and softer looking somehow. Peter felt his body vibrate with anticipation. He had waited so long for this moment. Imagined different scenarios every day for eighteen long years.

He slipped into the Barbour and adjusted the twine attached to his shotguns. He was ready. He went to the back door and outside into the night, pulled himself up onto the two metre brick wall separating the gardens, feeling his muscles respond, the sensation good, and sat astride the top, observing Shaun's lounge, the lights inside giving him a clear view whilst he loitered in the shadows.

He felt in great shape despite the beating of a few nights previously, the exertion and anticipation not affecting his heart rate one bit. He almost whistled to himself, he was that relaxed. He heard their conversation, was amused by Suzie's display of fear, delighted that his brother had not felt it necessary to involve the police.

Not that they could do much.

The moment Shaun sat down, Peter leapt off the wall, landed silent as a cat, clutching the guns to prevent any tell-tale noise. He waited a beat, just to see if Shaun was aware of his impending fate.

No.

Peter savoured the moment as he took hold of one of the guns, grasping it by the barrel. Ready! He launched himself through the doors, swung the stock of the shotgun and cracked it at the base of Shaun's skull with a force that was almost erotic in its intensity.

Shaun toppled forward and Peter manhandled him to the floor, cautious at first until certain his brother wasn't playing possum. He used gaffer tape to secure Shaun's hands to his feet and a short strip to cover his mouth. He stood over his nemesis, finally able to confront and control the person who had tormented him all these years.

It felt fantastic.

Suzie was clattering pans in the kitchen and he followed the noise. She must have heard him coming as, although engrossed, her head almost in the oven, she spoke.

'Can you pour me some wine? I'm almost done.' She reversed out of the oven and turned. Peter watched, fascinated as the lasagne she was lifting out slipped from her oven gloves and splattered at her feet, a bubbling mess of red sauce and white pasta.

She skipped back, an automatic response to the scalding sensation on her legs, her mouth wide, ready to scream. But Peter had a finger to his lips, and more effectively, his weird eyes on hers. Vivid red, no white to be seen. If that didn't get her attention, nothing would.

Everything was tinged a vague pink from his new contact lenses. He rather liked the effect, it brought to mind the term rose-tinted spectacles, and he could finally understand what that really meant. More importantly, he'd been startled at the effect when he had seen how he looked in the optician's, and could now see the impact on Suzie. He was well chuffed.

The idea was to mimic the eyes of an albino cobra. Like the one he asked his father to buy him as a boy. The pet he never had because of his brother.

He grinned at her, the shotgun aimed at her midriff, dropped his finger from his mouth and said, 'You always were a clumsy bint. Is that the best you can do to welcome your brother-in-law? Chuck his dinner on the floor? Tut! And after all these years...'

'Please don't hurt us. We've done nothing—'

'Hah!' Peter's laugh was a raucous rough sound, a hasp file grinding steel. 'Right, Suzie. You really believe that?'

She was cowering, had backed up to the kitchen sink, as far from him as possible. He stepped over the mess on the floor and moved in close to her, making a show of breathing in her scent. She flinched as he brushed a hand down her cheek, a tender lover's touch.

'He framed me. You married him. Call that nothing, my little Suzie?'

He pressed himself against her, excited, wanting nothing more than to possess her again.

She spat in his eyes, tried to knee his groin, caught his rigid cock a passing blow. He smothered her resistance with his body as she hissed, 'You're disgusting. You raped me. You killed your parents. They should've hung you!'

His moment of triumph was not as he had wanted. He needed her to understand. He screamed in her face, his breath a gale, a hurricane of torment released in fury.

'It was Shaun! All of it!'

He felt his erection ebb away, the excitement replaced with frustration. Why wouldn't she believe him?

There was a smidgeon of doubt in her eyes, then nothing.

'Liar... You always were a liar. Even when we were together.'

He slapped her then. She fell and crawled away, slipping in the sauce, the grease slicked tiles giving no purchase for her scrabbling claws. Then he kicked her in the side of the head, yelling at her, his foot pumping again and again, at her ribs, her belly, her legs, repeating with every blow, 'It was Shaun. It was Shaun. Always Shaun.'

'Mummy!' A little boy in pyjamas, barefoot, a teddy bear dangling from his hand, ran into the room and started kicking Leech's own shins, howling at him, 'Leave my mummy alone!'

'You must be Billy. I'm your Uncle Peter.'

Leech had the boy pinned to his body as he hauled him back upstairs. Billy was quiet now, his confusion apparent, his burst of aggression quelled by the giant now carrying him to his room.

'I've been away a while and I need to talk with your mummy and daddy. So I want you to wait in your room until I tell you to come out.'

He checked several rooms, eventually found one that was obviously the boy's and placed him on the bed.

'I need to put some of this on you.' The lad cowered, scurrying to the end of the bed, eyes wide, pupils dilated from shock. 'Billy, please don't make me hurt you, because I will. You hear me? I've got no quarrel with you.'

Billy lay still, passive, Leech binding him, leaving the little lad hog-tied, lying face down on his bed.

Leech went back to the kitchen and dragged Suzie to her feet. She was a dead weight and he wondered if he had killed her. He checked her neck for a pulse and, satisfied she was merely unconscious, threw her over his shoulder and took her to the master bedroom.

Their home was beautiful and Peter could not contain his jealousy as he thought of all the years he'd been deprived while they lived in the lap of luxury.

He tossed her on the bed, considered stripping her and fucking her but he was no longer aroused, and anyway, her face was all messed up from his blows. She had put on weight too. He felt let down, his expectations, even of that simple pleasure, ruined by the reality.

He spread-eagled her and taped her wrists and ankles to the bed posts. He did not bother with a gag. Blood dribbled from her mouth, and her ruined features left him regretting his temper tantrum. He should have fucked her first.

He cocked his head, comparing the Suzie of today with the girl he had known. Even allowing for the extra weight, he had not felt the same attraction for her when he had seen her in the kitchen. The reality was just not as appealing as he remembered. Was it because she was his brother's? Had been Shaun's wife? Mothered his son?

He was not sure, just knew he felt nothing for her. His childhood obsession had translated into something else. He took the tattered photo of his Birdy from his pocket—now, she was beautiful. He tucked it back, patted Suzie on the head and said, 'Sorry doll. You're past it.'

He tramped down the stairs wondering why he felt so hollow. He should be happy. Oh well, he thought, it's not over yet.

Shaun groaned as Peter lifted him in his arms like a toddler. He carried his semi-conscious brother up the stairs, all the while chatting to the unresponsive ears.

'Bet you were surprised to see me. Bit different to how I was when they banged me up. I s'pose you expect me to thank you for that—making a man out of me? Well, you can fuck off!'

He dropped his brother to the bedroom floor, eliciting another deep throated moan, and fetched a hard wooden chair, propped his brother in a sitting position and then taped him in place, his feet and hands now bound together, the knees up, feet perched on the seat. He taped his brother's torso to the chair back, trapping his arms too, securing his brother exactly as he wanted. He was on his second roll of tape, but still had plenty for his finale.

'Comfy?' He stood back and viewed his handiwork. Shaun gurgled, gave off a few muffled grunts and gradually came to, finally focusing on the red-eyed apparition before him. Confusion telegraphed through his own eyes, but no fear.

Peter ripped the tape from Shaun's mouth.

'What? Don't you recognise your own brother? Must be my red eyes... These funky contacts?' He swelled his chest with pride, rippling his shoulder muscles for effect. 'Or is it my stunning physique?' He thrust his face up close to his brother's. 'Take a good gander—'

The head butt was fearsome and took him by surprise. Shaun's head whiplashed, his forehead connecting with the bridge of Peter's nose. Peter felt the bones fragment under the impact, the crunching sound audible to both of them, the exquisite pain blinding him, sending him staggering back, his world dimming as his brain rattled in his skull. One of his contact lenses flew out from the force, and many men less well conditioned, less able to withstand pain, would have succumbed and collapsed from the blow.

'FUCK!'

Peter cupped his hands as the blood gushed, some clods of tissue, nasal membrane, dropping onto his fingers. He was dazed. He had forgotten how dangerous Shaun could be. Peter's ears were whistling, but he heard Shaun's words, his brother's voice knifing into him, slashing at his confidence.

'You're still an ugly, useless, pathetic piece of shit. Looks like I'm not the only one who's tried to re-shape your face.' His guttural laugh echoed in the room.

He still has power over me! He cringed inside.

For a minute he stood frozen, the familiar self-pity of his childhood consuming him, nasal blood pooling in his palms, his day ruined yet again.

But surely he was still in control...

The voice continued to needle him.

'You've put on some weight boy, I'll give you that. Why not release me? Do this properly. Let's see if those prison muscles are any good in a real fight. That is, unless you've turned queer after all those years of taking it up the arse! Is that it?'

The tone was hard, sharp as flint, striking, slashing at his brain.

No. I am in control.

'You always were a coward... Tell you what. I'll even let you use a knife, you gutless poof. Just to make it more equal.'

The sneer that had featured so much in his life finally roused him. Peter hefted a shotgun, pointed it at his brother's face, his own features a grotesque mask of hatred, and fingered the trigger.

'Don't tempt me...' But he was seeing double, now not sure if the pink tinge to his sight was blood or the remaining contact. He groped his way to the en suite, took a towel and staunched the flow of blood. The other contact dropped into the sink as he stood over it, massaging his eyes and tenderly testing the bridge of his damaged nose.

He could hear the insidious voice still taunting him. 'I see you've thumped Suzie. She's about your level. Yeah. Or maybe Billy! That would be a fair match for you... bearing in mind he takes after his dad. You're just scared of me. Always have been. Come on, you fucking chicken!'

Peter stared in the mirror at his flattened nose, thinking his brother sounded like he should be in a playground. Peter was not stupid. He refused to let the bastard get to him. He would stick to his plan.

He returned to Suzie, but addressed Shaun. 'I could shoot you now. But you aren't going to get off so lightly. All my life you've bullied and tormented me. Even stole her...'

She was coming to, her face swollen, a reminder of his own a few days before.

Shaun spoke to his back. 'You haven't got it in you. You're a wimp. Always have been. Always will be...'

Suzie moaned as Peter slapped her face, trying to bring her round. He said to Shaun, 'I've killed better men than you. And I've always got away with it... I planned to rape her. Staple your eyelids, make you watch.'

'Try it, fatboy. I'm helpless... How's that nose doing?' Shaun guffawed at his little brother.

'Then I was going to do the same to Billy.' He turned to Shaun, leered at him. 'Thanks to you I'm not so fussy these days.' He turned back to Suzie, patting her back to wakefulness, her eyes still not registering. 'I was then going to skin them alive. Before cremating you like you cremated Sam. It was the worst thing I could think of. I wanted to hear you scream like my puppy.'

'Dream on, little brother. Now, let me go and I'll forgive you. How about that?'

Peter's loathing for his brother sky-rocketed.

'FORGIVE ME!'

He hoisted a shotgun by its barrel, swung it over his shoulder and drove the stock down onto Shaun's right knee.

The animal scream, the rage and pain erupting from his brother's mouth, brought him some satisfaction at last, pulling his temper back to earth.

'That's better. I usually find a busted kneecap a good cure for verbal diarrhoea. Now, you smug bastard, where was I?'

He checked Suzie again, to see if she was alert now. She was still moaning but her eyes were open and he wanted to know if she could hear him.

'Yeah. I was gonna rape Suzie and Billy. Skin them alive—'

'No. Please.' Suzie's voice trembled as she spoke, any fight now beaten out of her.

'Force Shaun to watch, but then I realised there was no point.' He skewered Suzie with his eyes, wiping blood from his face with the towel as he spoke. 'It wouldn't do any good. You see, Suzie... He doesn't care... About you. About Billy. About anyone, except himself.'

Shaun, subdued, but not completely out, made the error of speaking again. 'Don't listen, sweetheart. He's a mad—'

Peter whipped round and jammed the stock of the gun into Shaun's mouth, breaking his front teeth, shutting him up. Shaun spat blood and tooth fragments to the floor.

Peter spoke softly now. 'I'm quicker too. They called me the Snake, in prison, I struck that fast. You should be careful. Snakes can kill.'

Suzie let out a wail, a garbled plea. 'Billy... Not hurt him... Kill me...'

He stroked her head. 'Don't worry. I've had a change of plan. First I want you to know what really happened.'

'Don't listen to his lies, sweetheart...'

The gun was hoisted once more and delivered to Shaun's other kneecap with devastating force. Peter had to let him finish screaming before he could continue his heart to heart with Suzie.

'He raped you that day. I came back, caught him, and he beat me shitless! Then he convinced my father it was me. And you believed him!' He could see her doubt, her loyalty to Shaun too strong. His words unconvincing.

'Not true. You... always... liar!' Her voice strengthened and faded as she gasped the words out.

'Tell her, you bastard.' He went to Shaun, who was no longer the cocky big brother he had feared. He poked the barrel under Shaun's chin, lifting his head with it. 'That's if you don't want me to revisit your knees.' He placed his other hand on Shaun's shattered right kneecap. His brother winced at the touch, his face blanching at the pressure. 'Tell her.'

Shaun hesitated. It was enough. Peter gripped the fractured bone fragments, twisted hard. Shaun screeched and fainted.

'Who's the wimp now, big bruvver?' Peter went to the bathroom, soaked another towel, returned and wrung it over Shaun's head. Shaun roused, but was not fully conscious. Peter slapped him a few times.

Shaun's focus returned from some dreadful distant place, defeated. Humbled, bettered by his brother.

'Now tell her.'

Peter did not need to touch his brother now, the confession dribbled from his lips, a statement of fact. No apology, no emotion.

'Yeah, I fucked you that day, Suzie. I was sick of seeing you with him. I wanted you and I could see you wanted me... Okay? What's the big deal anyway? You were unconscious.'

'Shaun, I know that's not true!' Suzie was appalled, denying it still, her words forceful as she regained full alertness. 'He made you say that.'

'YOU CUNT!' Peter whirled on her, the gun butt raised to crush her face, to stop that stupid mouth speaking, accusing him again.

He stopped himself.

I'm in control.

He panted, rapid breaths, trying to bring himself back, finally gaining the upper hand on his fury and frustration. He let the gun fall to his side. 'No one ever believes me. But it's true. Your hubby killed our parents too, Suzie.'

'Noooooo!' Suzie's face twisted in disbelief and horror at what she was hearing. 'Not possible... Shaun?' She looked from one brother to the other and back.

Peter went back to Shaun, stroked a knee with his hand. 'The truth, Shaun. Tell your little wifey the truth.' He needed little prompting now.

'Oh, fuck you! Both of you... Yes I killed them.' He spat more blood from his mashed mouth. 'Happy now, little brother? And it's not as if you could give a shit about our parents.' He glanced over at Suzie. 'We both hated them.' His brittle laugh cracked in his throat. He glared at Peter now, defiant. 'And you got locked up, you sap.'

Peter tapped a brief tattoo on Shaun's knee with his knuckles, let his brother keen with the pain, then said, 'This is what you married, Suzie. A killer. He'd been planning it for years. Told me he would set it up to look like burglary.' He was back, looming over her, peering down at her. 'He's such a lying cunt. Told me we'd both be rich. I would've been happy with half, but no—'

'I wanted it all. And I got it!' Shaun the braggart resurfaced. 'You were just a junkie. A fucking waster, squandering the money on booze and drugs.'

Peter addressed Suzie, determined she should know the truth, could see she was becoming convinced. Saw how she was looking at Shaun, as if she did not know what to think of him any more, anger and fear mingling behind her eyes.

'Shaun even convinced my parents to defer my trust fund. It was supposed to be my motive. What bullshit! It also meant he got even more money when he killed them. He's a clever fucker. But I'm better.'

Peter was happy now. At last someone, someone he once wanted for himself, believed him. Believed the truth. It was what he came for. He put the gun to Shaun's cheek, his finger tickling the trigger.

Then Suzie spoke, her strength returning with the revelations, but her voice still tremulous. 'I loved you, Shaun... Now I don't think I ever knew you at all.'

'Oh stop whining, you pathetic bitch. I've had it with your endless whingeing. God knows, there have been many times I could have happily topped you myself.'

'You... don't mean that...' She started to weep.

Peter watched, satisfied that despite her initial doubt, she was starting to understand how she had wasted her life by marrying his brother.

Shaun looked at her with disgust, then grinned his bloody lips at Peter and said, 'Do me a favour. Give her a whack and shut her up... That's about your level, isn't it, baby brother? How about you cut me loose? I'm legless. It'd almost be a fair fight. I'll still kill you...' He hawked and spat more muck.

Peter considered it. It was an attractive proposition. But he didn't want to kill his brother... And certainly not like that.

'No. I've got a much better idea.'

He noticed Suzie's weeping had intensified at Shaun's callous words, and thought: Good. You deserve it you heartless slut. He really didn't fancy her any more.

'I thought I'd want to fuck you, Suzie. But I don't. You're past it. You need some surgery too. And I reckon I can help with that.' He mopped his face with the towel again. The bleeding had eased. His forehead, eye sockets and cheeks felt numb, but otherwise his whole head throbbed. No problem, he would have another joint later.

'I was going to share it with you.' Shaun held his head back and was looking down his nose at his brother, despite being seated.

Peter shook his head, a bull dislodging tiresome flies. 'So now you want me to believe you really wanted to cut me in... Bollocks!'

'It's true. I thought we'd concoct a story of how I came back and disturbed a burglar. I was going to have to stab you, wound you, of course.'

'But then you had a better idea?' Peter wanted to hear his reason, waited, hands on hips, amazed at Shaun's neck.

'Fraid so. I went a bit over the top with the knife. And then I saw you in the shower. It struck me that the police might not believe our prepared fiction—a phantom attacker who was never caught… They'd have eventually sussed it. Then we'd both have been inside. I couldn't have that.' It was said without malice.

Suzie, her weeping now subsided, stared at Shaun, her face twisted in horror and abhorrence as she spoke to the man she had loved. 'So you decided to frame Peter?'

'Please,' Shaun, ignoring her question, addressed Peter. 'Just put her out of her misery, will you?'

Peter put his mouth next to Suzie's ear and whispered like a lover. 'I bet you're real proud of yourself now. He's your hubby. The father of your little boy… Little tyke reminds me of me.' He straightened up, eyes on hers as he spoke to Shaun. 'So, I was in the shower, and it came to you. Inspiration. No phantom. A pissed off son instead. A compulsive liar. A druggie. A waste of space. And genius boy Shaun, butter wouldn't melt in his gob, the poor orphan, arrives home early to find the black sheep was actually an evil wolf.' He saw the defeat in Suzie's face, the capitulation, she was totally convinced. He glanced at Shaun. 'It worked. But they weren't meant to release me, were they?'

'That seems to be the current problem. Let me loose. We can sort things out, man to man. For old times' sake.'

Peter was sure he could take his brother, especially now Shaun's legs were ruined. But, he would not allow himself to be diverted.

Keep control. Don't let him wind you up.

Suzie started sobbing again.

Shaun raised an eyebrow at Peter as he said to his wife, 'Oh do shut up, you soppy cow! None of it matters. He's going to kill us all anyway.'

'Well, that's where you're wrong, Bruv.' He flipped the gun in the air, caught the barrel and slammed the stock into the side of his brother's neck, then whispered, 'Goodnight, Shaun. Been nice talking to you again…'

'Thanks, Jack.'

Carver placed the pint in front of Doc. They were both exhausted, trying to unwind over a late beer. Doc had called Judy and told her the Judge was dead. She tried to press him for details but he had fobbed her off, would tell her all about it later. We'll talk, he had said.

He was numb. The Judge. Dead.

He could not accept it was an accidental suicide. 'I think we may find something. At the scene… Pointing to Peter Leech.' He sipped his beer. It tasted too good.

'Jesus, Doc. You never let it rest, do you? Tomorrow, okay? I'll have the tapes checked. As a favour. You hear me?' He clinked his glass with Doc's.

'Yeah. Thanks. Not just for that Jack… The car, everything.' Doc placed a hand on his friend's shoulder, gave a little squeeze. 'I didn't realise it was your vehicle.'

'Thought it was an unmarked patrol car?' The DI laughed. 'Nah, that Saab's my pride and joy.'

'Anyway. Thanks. For trusting me.' Doc let go of Carver's shoulder, sipped his beer as memories of the accident tried to crowd into his mind.

Carver diverted Doc as he spoke. 'You know, you might not trust yourself to drive, but I do. Okay?' He landed a playful punch on Doc's upper arm. 'Anyway, why d'you think I got that escort? It was for my car, not for you!'

Doc couldn't help but laugh. Despite his day, the shocks, the stress, the bereavement, his laughter silenced the demons, the camaraderie he felt soothing his soul. He took a long draught of his beer, thinking Jack was a good friend to have.

'You know, you were lucky. You missed a pile up at the end of the M4 by just a few minutes.' Carver's light-hearted look turned to stone as he spoke.

'Really?' It happens, thought Doc.

'Yeah. Some idiot was weaving in and out of the traffic doing eighty or ninety. A couple of the guys who'd been escorting you pulled him over.' Carver's voice was serious. Back to business. It was not just Doc who could not let it rest. Carver's work was his life.

'The car behind?' Doc vaguely remembered the second police car pulling off the carriageway as he sped away in the patrol car, chauffeured to the Judge's apartment.

'Yup. Anyway, this guy is driving an AC Cobra. A sixties muscle car, all curves, chrome and engine, you know?' Doc did not, but nodded so Carver went on. 'Anyway, they stop him, he gets out and just blows the two poor traffic boys straight to the emergency room—with a sawn-off! Then, get this, he shoots up the traffic. Hence the pile up.' Carver downed his pint. Stood to get more.

'Really?' Doc was not giving it much thought, he was just glad he missed the chaos. He handed his empty glass to Jack.

'Funny thing, though. The car's registered to a guy named Finch. Weird huh?' He was about to move to the bar as Doc's hand gripped his arm.

'Finch? As in Judy?' Doc's brain wound up, a jet engine, starting to whine.

'Yeah, John Finch. Some rich fucker, lives near Windsor. They've got a Tac squad on the way there now.'

'John Finch?' Judy's ex-husband, John, lived near Windsor. And he collected classic cars. This was unreal. Doc's head spun.

'That's right. Are you gonna let go of my arm anytime soon? I need it to get us another pint.' Carver was watching Doc closely now. 'You look like you could do with something stronger... Do you know him, Doc?'

'No. But I think I know his ex-wife.'

'Did I tell you, the cabbie's missing?' Carver had been to the bar, bought more beer and made a quick phone call. They were waiting for the response to his query, the beer a lubricant for their tired brains.

'The one at Gruber's office?' It was the only taxi driver Doc could think of. 'You reckon Leech abducted him?'

'He's certainly missing. The boys in blue, the street soldiers, have interviewed just about every black cab driver in central London. Only one cab is missing. And the driver...' Carver was blunt. 'Do you think he's dead?'

'I don't know… but, in all probability? Yes. He was in the wrong place at the wrong time.'

'This Leech is one weirdo.' Carver's phone rang before he could complete the thought. He went outside, away from the hubbub of the bar. A bell rang for last orders.

Almost eleven. What a day.

Carver slipped back onto his stool, a sombre expression on his face.

'One of the patrolmen just died in hospital. Any reason why Judy's ex would shoot up a couple of police officers, then create a pile up on the motorway?'

'It is him? Judy's husband?'

'We'll find out soon enough. The Tac team are at his home now. Should be inside in the next few minutes. They'll call me if he's there.' He was all business again. 'What's the story, Doc?'

'I don't know him. Only what Judy has told me. This doesn't sound like him… He was in the States on business. Although…' Could he have flipped out? Over Judy and Josh? Jesus, that's all he needed. 'Although he is supposed to be in court tomorrow. She's trying to restrict his access to their son.'

'What, the kid who was at the station? Yesterday?'

'Uh-huh.'

Doc refused to believe it, his analytical mind on overload with this latest piece of the jig-saw. Judy's ex a cop killer, the Judge a pervert, Peter Leech an innocent victim, Shaun Leech a manipulative killer… It was too much. His universe had somersaulted. And Judy. Christ knows what he would tell her.

He downed his pint and went to the bar, just getting there with seconds to spare before the final bell chimed 'time'. He slopped Carver's beer as he put the mug on the table, his thoughts transported back to his interview with Henley. He was about to speak when Carver's phone trilled again. Doc waited as the detective walked outside to better hear the caller.

He tried to stop his mind wandering, tried to clear his head. He was not doing too well and was relieved when Jack came back.

'I need to sleep on this Doc.' He had a strange look on his face. 'John Finch was found in his home, bound and gagged. He's in a coma and they're taking him to hospital now.'

'I don't understand. Was he burgled? And his car stolen?'

And could it really be Judy's husband?

'Looks that way. Anyway, I've asked them to call me if they get more… How did it go with Henley?'

'Huh?' Doc was elsewhere. Then he switched back into gear, refocussed. 'You won't believe this, but he thinks Peter Leech is innocent.'

'Too right, I won't. Innocent? My arse. He's almost certainly killed three people since getting out!'

'And I agree. With Henley.'

Carver slapped his forehead, exasperated. 'Right… Mother Theresa did it. With her knitting needles.' He sank his beer and slammed the glass down. 'Next, you'll be asking me to reopen the case.' His smile slid off his face as Doc answered.

'Yes. I think you should.'

The shotgun was wedged between Shaun's legs, his arms bound either side of his bent knees, hands and ankles conjoined. Peter stepped back to admire his handi-work, then added a few more turns of the tape to his mummified brother. He checked for any movement in the arrangement. Occasionally he bumped his broth-er's knee, but Shaun was still out cold. Peter would have preferred his victim to be awake, would have to make sure he was conscious when his time was up.

Finally he shoved the end of the barrel into his brother's mouth, taping it to his skull, winding the adhesive material round the back of Shaun's head several times to secure it.

Suzie watched the operation in silence, her eyes gaping, her mouth paralysed. Eventually she spoke.

'Peter. Please let me go… I never meant to hurt you.'

He snorted, a sound like a horse. 'Not hurt me? You hurt me more than anyone. We were together. Friends at first, then boyfriend, girlfriend. Then he lied. You thought I raped you!' He shook a fist at her. 'Believe me, you hurt me, Suzie. It doesn't matter that you didn't mean to.'

He found the fishing line he'd taken from Finch's house, deep in one of the pockets of his coat, and started rigging it to the trigger, feeding it to the door handle. He went back to Suzie.

His belly was ice and fire. Placid on the surface, yet still the rage was burning within him. 'He ruined my life. You were part of that.'

She begged him, 'I didn't know… Forgive me. Please. He was so convincing. I married him for chrissake! He fooled me… Everyone!' She tried to appeal to his altruism. 'Let me go… for Billy. He's your nephew. Your own flesh and blood…'

It was a waste of time.

He rounded on her. 'You are such a stupid bint, you know? You mean nothing to me. Billy is nothing to me.' He held her with his green eyes flashing anger. 'And Shaun feels the same! He doesn't give a damn. He only wanted you because you were mine. That's all you were to him, my possession, and he always had to have what was mine.'

'No… You're crazy. He must've loved me—'

'He told me, Suzie! Just after my sentencing hearing, he came to gloat. The only reason he wanted you was to hurt me… He taunted me, wanted me to think about you being with him every day while I rotted in prison.' The anguish was visible in his face as he jutted his chin at her. 'And I did. But not now. Not any more…'

She was crushed, the nightmare decimating her life. Peter could see it, knew the sense of desolation she now felt, had experienced it himself.

'Please,' she sobbed. 'I'll tell the police, explain you're innocent.' Desperate, grov-elling. 'Peter. Please…'

He gripped her chin and held her, his face touching hers, nose to nose, forehead to forehead, his angry words spattering her mouth with foul saliva. 'You think they'll give me back my eighteen years? My youth? Half my fucking life? My innocence? Look at me, Suzie.' He stepped away from her, held his arms apart. 'Am I the boy next door? I don't think so. Not any more.'

'Look… We have money.'

'Fuck you! You have my money! My inheritance. That cunt of a brother of mine,' he shook a fist at Shaun's unconscious form, 'stole everything. He took it all. You, the money, the estate. All I had was my childhood trust fund. What's he worth? Fifteen, twenty million?'

She turned her head away, unable to meet his eyes. He wrenched her face back to his, closed in on her again. 'Tell me.'

'I don't know… Probably more.'

'He sold the house. Had the land developed. I didn't even know!' He was worked up again, the sheer unfairness of it all, his life wrecked by his own brother.

He closed his eyes, thought of Birdy. The one thing his brother could not take from him… The one precious thing Shaun did not even know about. It made him feel better, just thinking of her. It must be love.

His voice was level now. 'Anyway, that's not important any more. What is important is the future… and I've decided how that looks.' He pulled a knife from his pocket, flipped open the blade. 'And for you, darlin… it don't look good.' He placed the knife on the bed beside her, tore a strip of tape to cover her mouth and said, as he fixed it into place, 'Don't want to worry Billy any more than we already have, do we? No noise, eh?'

Only her eyes could scream at him. The anticipation of what was to come, the powerlessness of her position, her dread of a bleak future, all combined to freeze her vocal cords.

'Thing is, I want you to remember tonight. To remember me. What Shaun did to me. What you did. I want you to think about it every time you look in the mirror.' He lifted the blade, let her see her reflection there, her own wild eyes, bugging out of her head in terror. 'And your Billy. I want him to remember this day for the rest of his life too. To have nightmares. To wet his bed when he thinks of Uncle Peter… To know what it feels like to be blamed for the death of a parent.'

Then, the tip of the knife slid into Suzie's eyeball.

Carver was back. Two fresh pints in his hands.

'One of the perks of the job. Afters!' He lifted his pint and said, 'Cheers, Doc.'

For the next fifteen minutes, Doc relayed a summary of everything Henley had told him, giving Carver the benefit of his own interpretation at the same time.

'But this guy, who's not even a real doctor, just a dope fuelled old hippy, thinks Shaun did it? Nah, I think I'll go with the Judge.' Carver was dismissive, the alcohol loosening his tongue. 'Anyway, it was probably the pot that brought on his stroke. The guy sounds full of shit.'

'Okay, the stroke was due to a combination of things. Abuse of drugs, too many cigarettes, the shock, intense feelings of guilt over the murders, the foreknowledge that Shaun would kill, they all combined to wreck his brain that night.'

'Wreck his brain! And you want us to reopen the case on his say-so? A solved case, for fuck's sake.'

'Only if you're concerned that a murderer is still at large.' Doc lifted his pint and tilted it at Carver.

'Yeah, yeah, yeah…' Jack pondered on that. 'Big brother bullies little Peter. Blames him for everything from pet-icide to rape, and, being seen as a little angel, he's believed. Then threatens to kill his parents… so he must have done it! Blah. Blah…'

No. Peter Leech was found guilty. In a court of law. By a jury. Twelve good men and all that. Sorry, Doc, sounds like sympathy for the devil.'

Doc shared his theory, explained how Shaun could have set things up. How the jury could have been misled.

'Okay... I see it. It's possible, I s'pose.'

Doc was losing him, tried harder to convince his friend. 'Who had most to gain? From the deaths?'

'The will was for an equal split.'

'Contested. After Peter was convicted.'

Carver swilled the liquid in his mug, studying it, as if it was a fortune teller's glass capable of divining the truth.

'You've got a point there. Shaun got the lot. But it's... fantastic. The planning, the organisation. You'd need a computer brain to make it work.'

'He's MENSA. His IQ is one-hundred and sixty plus. Computer brain.'

'You're really screwing with my brain, Doc. I'll sleep on it.'

'I think Suzie Leech is bait.'

'Bait?'

'Shaun wants his brother to come. He doesn't think Peter's a killer.' He explained the rape accusation, Peter's infatuation with his girlfriend. 'Shaun lied, told me she was his girlfriend.'

'Maybe he forgot. The details. It's a long time ago.' They both knew that was weak.

'Forgot? The details of your supposed girlfriend's rape?'

'Okay, Doc. I think I'm heading home.' He dangled the car keys. 'Need a lift? Another perk of the job.' He was referring to drinking and driving. If they were stopped he would flash his warrant card. There would be no breathalyser for him.

They made their way to the Saab.

'Why d'you think she's bait?'

'Shaun wants Peter to come. Thinks his brother will be mad at him for marrying her. He wants to put right what the law failed to do...'

'But you said Shaun killed their parents. What's the law got to do with it?'

'Life. Peter needed to be put away for life. For the crime Shaun committed.' And that's why the Judge had to die! Doc's brain sizzled. He stopped dead. Carver continued mooching towards his car, not realising Doc was no longer with him until he heard the voice from behind him. 'Shaun Leech killed Justice Potter. Because Peter was freed.'

'What?' Carver fumbled with the lock. 'I thought you said it was Peter Leech getting revenge, in the unlikely event the Judge didn't accidentally top himself.'

He unlocked the car, held his door open, scowling at Doc who remained immobile.

'You'll find Shaun's face on those tapes. I'm certain. It makes sense, Jack... And they are in serious danger. Shaun Leech. And Suzie. For her sake, we—'

'He doesn't want protection.'

'But she might. Send a car. Now, Jack.'

'Doc! It's almost midnight. You're pissed. It's been a long day. Get in.'

'Send the car. Now. Please... Humour me.'

Peter Leech finished fiddling with the fishing line and took a last look around the bedroom. Shaun was trussed with tape, bound like a dead pharaoh, knees up, the shotgun barrel well inside his mouth. He was struggling, trying to move, but he was bound fast, the chair immobile, taped to the end of the bed. Neither the man nor his seat were going anywhere.

Suzie was still spread-eagled on the bed, her face a mound of bloody meat.

Perfect.

He tied off the end of the fishing line and pulled the door to.

Billy was in his room, lying placidly where Leech had left him, eyes still staring, seemingly too big for his small head.

Leech tore the tape off the lad's mouth. He then showed Billy his one remaining shotgun.

'Do you know what this is, Billy boy?' His nephew nodded, tears pricking his eyes. 'Don't worry. If you do exactly what I say, I promise I won't hurt you… But…' He tapped the muzzle on the boy's skull, making the lad flinch. 'But if you misbehave, if you try to run, try to hit Uncle Peter again, I'll have to use this… And it'll be your fault, not mine.' He raised his eyebrows as he spoke, emphasising that it was up to Billy.

Leech let go of the shotgun, let it fall, dangling at his side, and pulled out the knife. The lad gasped as Leech touched the blood stained blade to his tiny nose.

'I'm going to release you. And then I want you to count to a hundred. Can you do that for your uncle? Count that high?'

Billy nodded, grubby wet streaks on his cheeks.

'You didn't know you had an uncle, did you? Mummy and Daddy didn't tell you, did they?'

Billy shook his head, his face a picture of misery.

'That was very bad of both of them. Don't you think?'

The boy was confused, but nodded.

'If I were you, I'd want to punish them. For lying. Lying's bad, isn't that right boy?'

Again a desperate nod.

'So. As it's not your fault, I'm going to let you go.'

Billy's eyes, already huge, threatened to pop out, either in fear or disbelief.

'R-r-really?' His voice squeaked.

'Really. But you'll have to promise. You'll never forget Uncle Peter. That you'll think of me every day.'

'P-p-promise.' Billy's head jerked up and down. 'Every day, Uncle.'

'You know, boy. Normally I think people tend to lie. But today, I believe you.' He giggled as he cut through the tape holding the lad's hands and feet together. 'You can use a phone? Dial 999? Okay?'

'Yes, Uncle Peter.' He wriggled his feet as if to test the blood was flowing.

'Did you know that I was accused of killing my mum and dad, your granny and granddad? I never did it. No one believed me.' He went to stroke Billy's hair as he added, 'I was just like you.'

Billy bridled at the touch, and Leech's hand hovered.

'Right. When I close your door, I want you to start counting. Slowly. Okay?'

'Yes… Like this? One… two… three.' The boy was eager. Keen to please.

Or keen for Uncle Peter to go.

'That's good. If you come out too soon, my shotgun will go off. And it'll kill you. We don't want that do we?'

'N-n-no, Uncle.'

'Good lad. Now, when you get outside I want you to go to your mummy and daddy's room. They're waiting for you... They might sound strange, but that's because they're tied up, like you were. We've been playing a game. Okay? Just go in and release your mummy. Then you can call an ambulance.'

'Amberlance? Is Mummy hurt?' His pupils expanded, irises almost totally black now.

'A bit. I'm sorry. It was a little accident. But you're a big strong boy. You can help your mum as I can't hang around, I have to go somewhere.'

Leech walked to the door and said, 'Bye bye, Billy. Welcome to my nightmare.' He shut the door behind him and heard the boy start counting.

He whistled as he went down the stairs. Finally, something was working out for him. His nose was mashed, his face still a battered mess, but it was not important. Tonight he was putting things right.

He clambered onto the back wall and waited. His eyes were on the bedroom window and his spirit soared as he saw the flash, registered the boom of the explosion, and then heard the shrill, piercing shriek from Billy.

In his mind's eye he could see the scene. Shaun taped to the chair, his head a raw mush, his brains and skull scattered in a scarlet porridge, sprayed over Suzie as she lay on the bed without a face.

Oh, yes, this is definitely one night young Billy would never, ever forget.

Leech hopped off the wall into the neighbour's garden, went back to his observation post and waited for the police to arrive.

PART III

REDEMPTION

JUDY WAS WORRIED. It was after midnight and Doc was not yet home. She knew he was working too hard on the Leech case and she was fretting that he might not cope, that it could be dangerous to his fragile state of mind.

And now his mentor, the Judge, was dead. She knew how close they had been... Yet more bereavement for him to handle. She was sad for the Judge, but even more so for poor Colin.

Josh stirred as she rolled away from him, watching him sleep in the half-light of their new bedroom. In her man's home.

Her thoughts shifted, to the other man in her life. Tomorrow she would see John, assuming he made the effort to return from New York. Of that, she wasn't sure and Sarah, her solicitor, had said John's barrister was being tight-lipped about it.

Oh well, we'll see tomorrow.

She brushed Josh's hair from his face and thought how innocent boys can look while sleeping.

Was she being too hard on John? The doubts had crept up on her, escalating as the court hearing approached. Was it going to be hard on Josh, limiting his father's time with him, insisting on a chaperone?

Maybe she was overreacting. She told Sarah so that morning, but her solicitor was adamant. 'You must do this. To protect the boy's interests and your own.' Sarah had told her she should drop the name Finch too, go back to her maiden name of Turner. Her hand stroked Josh's neck, an automatic gesture of love and affection, one she was barely aware she was doing.

No, she would keep the name Finch... It was her son's name. Sarah had accepted that as reason enough, but was dismayed to hear Judy and Josh were living somewhere other than their home. That they may be in danger, as a result of Judy's job.

She had been aghast, concerned for their well-being of course, but more than that. She was paranoid that John's barrister would get to hear of it. He would have the judge laugh her out of court for accusing John of endangerment when her own job put both her and her son at risk. From a lunatic killer. Judy had not even considered that.

Anyway, she decided, there was no way John would find out... at least until after the hearing, and then it would be too late.

Her mind drifted to Leech. Was he a threat to her? Would he really harm her if, as Colin said, she somehow failed to live up to his fantasy, his idealised version of her?

He had to find her first.

No, it could never happen. She would never see the man again...

We'll see.

His voice, revisited when she listened to the recording, echoed in her ears. She moved closer to Josh, her arm wrapped round him now, protecting him.

That was what he'd said to her. We'll see. Was he stalking her?

She still had not told Colin about Leech asking to meet her when he got out... Colin had so much on his plate right now.

She had seen a change in him, seen him totally relaxed with her and Josh, becoming absorbed into the family. The hallucinations were fewer and he was controlling them now... But she wondered, how would he react to the blow of the Judge's death? How would he manage?

She would be there for him. That was for sure. She had decided it was time to nail shut the revolving door of her love life once and for all.

Her mobile vibrated, the backlight flashing in the gloom. Colin!

'You must be psychic. I was thinking about you.' She whispered to him as she tiptoed to the hall, determined not to disturb Josh.

'I'm sorry I'm so late... Things have gone pear-shaped today, sweetheart.'

'Are you on your way home now?' She was hopeful, but he sounded preoccupied.

'Not yet. We're on our way to Chelsea. I'll be home in an hour or so... You should sleep.'

'So should you! Why do you need to go to Chelsea now. Can't it wait?'

'No, not really... I don't want you to worry, but it looks like Leech just killed his brother. We're on our way there now.'

'Oh, my God!' Chelsea was just a stone's throw away.

'I'll be with you as soon as I can.' He was distant again, as if there was something else on his mind, something other than her safety. Then he asked, 'Do you have John's current address? It's Windsor isn't it?'

'What the hell do you need that for?' What could Colin possibly want with John?

'It may be a coincidence, but a man named John Finch from the Windsor area has been taken to hospital. He's at the Royal Berks in Reading. He's in a coma, Judy...'

'And you think it's... Josh's father?' She was flummoxed. She was not even sure John was back in the UK.

'It's just a possibility. Maybe one of those odd coincidences.' His voice said he did not believe that. 'If you give me the address I'll check it out.'

She did.

Before they said their goodbyes he added, 'Try not to worry. Get some sleep.'

She was not sure she could, but then examined her feelings. What if it was her John in hospital, in a coma? She felt nothing. That was good.

But what about poor Josh?

And would this delay the court case? She hoped not.

She went back to bed, snuggled up to Josh's hot little body, her fingers crossed, thinking: Let's hope there are two John Finches living near Windsor.

––––––––––

A few minutes before Doc's call to Judy, Carver's phone had rung. The squad car he'd sent had arrived at Shaun Leech's house too late.

Now Doc and the detective were almost at the house, Doc just ending his call to Judy. He gave John Finch's address to Carver who asked, 'You think it might be a different John Finch?' His voice was sceptical.

'Not really. It's too much of a coincidence… and I don't believe in coincidences.'

'Yeah, me neither… We're almost there.'

Carver steered the car into Shaun Leech's street. A gurney was being loaded into an ambulance, two police cars blocked the road, blue lights bouncing off the white terraced homes. Some neighbours stood on their doorsteps or the pavement, gawping.

'I don't suppose they see much crime in this neighbourhood.' Doc noted the preponderance of top end Mercedes, BMWs and Porsches filling the residents' parking bays.

Carver led him through the cordon, then went off to introduce himself to the lead detectives on the site. He chatted with them for a few minutes.

Doc watched as a WPC hugged a young boy not much older than Josh. Shaun Leech's son.

'We've got to wait a while, Doc. They need to finish up inside. Cut and dried this time though. It was our man. Seems the little boy was screaming about Uncle Peter, and his mum managed to confirm it was him. Though she's not in any fit state to talk.'

Doc felt wretched. He had let them down. He wanted to speak to the woman. To apologise. But he knew it would be a futile gesture, more to assuage his guilt than help her. After speaking with Henley he should have insisted on a police presence to protect her. Now she was not even able to talk…

A freezing hand gripped his heart and two green eyes floated before him. What did you do to them, Peter?

'She can't talk?' He dreaded Carver's reply.

'He sliced off half her face. Most of her right cheek and her nose. Cut out one eye… The sick fuck! She almost drowned in her own blood. And the poor kid's a mess. Can you imagine having to see your own mother like that? Saw his old man with his head missing too… So tell me again, Doc. Leech isn't mad?' Carver had seen plenty, but he was angry, could not fathom this crazy man.

Doc shook his head, a vigorous movement more to shift the spectre of Leech's eyes than to answer the question.

Carver took it as a negative. 'Well he sure seems it to me!'

Doc managed to pull himself together. 'No. There's a rational explanation, in his mind.'

'Oh well, that makes it okay, then!' Carver was outraged, but continued, striving to understand. 'What was she—too pretty? He wanted to spoil her… If he couldn't have her, he wanted to be sure no other man would desire her? So he turned her face into fucking dog meat?' Jack's voice spiralled upwards as he spoke and the WPC comforting the child gave him a black look, silencing him.

'Possibly. Though if Henley's memory is as good as I think it is then Leech had been obsessed with her. But Shaun raped her. Spoilt her for him. Then she went to Shaun voluntarily. I think he wants her to suffer, every time she sees her face. He wanted to spoil her for herself.' A wicked action, but perversely logical. 'How's the boy?'

Carver's temper was under control again and he spoke quietly now. 'In shock. Apparently Leech rigged a gun so that the kid would set it off when he opened the door to his parents' bedroom. We'll get inside in a minute. Very messy.'

'Of course! The boy killed his father.' Very callous, very logical.

'In a way, yeah. That's not how a court would see it.' Carver added, his voice tinged with disgust, 'For fuck's sake, Doc. You sound like you admire the sick bastard.'

'No, I just understand him now. The boy will see it that way, Jack. He killed his father, and for the rest of his life he'll carry the guilt of his actions tonight.'

'He isn't to blame, poor little tyke!' Carver was shouting again, pointing at the boy. The WPC scowled and put Billy in a squad car, slamming the door while glaring at the detective.

'That's not what he'll be thinking. He'll need some intensive therapy, if he's ever to put this behind him.'

Carver, the heat finally dissipated by his latest outburst, turned thoughtful, then shrugged. 'Yeah, pretty shitty all round... We can go in now.' The other detective had waved them over, and had a few more words with Carver before they made their way inside.

Carver explained. 'Place wasn't broken into... It seems your theory was correct, Doc. Looks like Shaun just let him in. Peter probably banged on the front door. Then all hell broke loose.'

'Yes.' Doc remembered how matter of fact Shaun had been when he had told him he would kill Peter. 'I think he underestimated his little brother.'

Carver was nosing in the study, both of them still downstairs, taking in the layout. A breeze swept through the house, gusting through the open front door to the gaping patio. Neither of them thought anything of it.

'Looks like he could handle himself,' Carver said, as Doc followed him into Shaun's study. The walls were dotted with certificates for martial arts, one shelf full of trophies, including a gold figurine of a man kicking another in the head.

'Uh-huh. But not much good if you're up against a man with a gun. Any idea where Leech got it?'

'Not yet. Maybe one of his old mates from inside. Let's go up.'

Doc took a look in the kitchen. Saw the spilled food, the tomato sauce mixed with blood, smeared on the tiles and units. He imagined Leech arriving at the front door, forcing his brother inside at gunpoint, Suzie dropping the food in shock. It fitted. He went upstairs.

Carver walked to the open bedroom door, stopped several feet from Shaun Leech's body, and just said, 'Bloody hell!'

The shotgun was still taped to Shaun's jaw and, where the strong binding stretched around his head, he still had part of his cranium. The top half of his skull had been liquefied and splattered on the ceiling, bed and wall.

'Suzie Leech was found strapped to the bed, delirious. That I can understand, after having her face carved off and then being hosed with the contents of her husband's head.'

'Gruesome.' Doc was appalled at what they had let happen here. 'We should've had some men here. Should've given them protection.'

Carver was less convinced. 'Easy to say with hindsight. Leech told me he could handle it. That he would get private security if he thought it necessary.' He shook a finger at the devastated corpse. 'It was his fault. Not ours.'

Doc did not remind Jack that they had not actually offered protection, had only made the call to confirm Shaun wanted Peter to come to him. He let it slide. At least Judy was safe.

He pulled on a rubber glove then picked up a photograph of the family from the bedside table. It was speckled with blood and tissue, but even so he could see the likeness between Suzie and Judy. In this picture it was even more obvious than he remembered.

Leech had cut Suzie's face, disfigured her rather than kill her, so that she would live in torment. Just like he had in prison.

Justice.

Doc knew that in Leech's warped view of the world that's what he had achieved. He almost dropped the picture as an image of Judy crystallised, superimposed over the photo of Suzie. It was a hideous vision, half her face was missing, a bloody mess of gore in its place. He doubled, almost vomited, gagged but recovered.

'Hey, Doc! You're not going all squeamish on me are you?' Carver was bending over the body looking at the gun, then glanced up at Doc. 'Shotgun. I can't see much of it for all the tape. Looks expensive. Engraved. Could be silver on the stock. Not your average criminal's choice.'

'Stolen?' Doc had overcome his moment of weakness. Connections were firing in his brain again. 'Sawn-off, right?'

'You're thinking what I'm thinking.' Jack's lower jaw was thrust out, his teeth pulling his top lip inside his mouth. He sucked on it for a second. 'You're thinking he's John Finch's burglar. He stole the gun, stole a fancy car, blasted our boys in blue, shot up the traffic and then came here.' He pulled the lip back in for another suck, then his phone rang.

Doc inspected Shaun's remains. It was clever. The way he had been bound, the arrangement of the gun, everything designed to keep the weapon in place. He had seen it before, several years ago.

But this time it was Peter Leech. He had come here with this whole scenario planned out. Was that why he had taken so long to get here? Did it take him four or five days to get prepared, to equip himself?

This was not a crime of passion. It was cold, premeditated, and designed to destroy three lives. Carver was right... A part of Doc's mind did admire the man's thinking.

And it was this part of his mind that repelled him. The part of him that had grown as he hunted more killers, profiled more murderers, allowed their perversions into his life, defiling him. It was the side of his personality he had been determined to quash. The real reason why he had opted out of the role.

It had been while he was contemplating a change that the Judge approached him... Now he too was dead, and the ugly part of Doc's brain was reaching out again.

'You sure you're okay, Doc? It's been a long day.' Carver was giving Doc an odd look.

'Mmm. I'm fine. Just thinking, Jack... It's what I do.' He gave his friend a mirthless smile.

'Fair enough... Here's something else to wrap your brain round. It's just been confirmed. It was Judy Finch's ex. The address you gave me is the one where John Finch was found bound and gagged. With gaffer tape.' Carver did not have to point it out.

'The gun?'

'Yup. Two. Purdeys. A matched pair. Worth tens of thousands apparently. Both missing from the gun cabinet according to the housekeeper... Seems we only know where one is.'

Doc's mind was in overdrive. 'Why did he attack John Finch?'

'That's what I was about to ask you. You're the expert and we can't ask Finch, he's still in a coma.' Carver was reluctant to ask the next question and Doc sensed it. 'His heart's a bit dodgy... Did you know he used cocaine?'

'You're joking. I didn't know him at all. Never met the man.'

Doc needed to get back to Judy. How would she take all this? And little Josh?

'He had two hundred grams stashed. Do you think he was dealing?'

'Impossible! He's a city banker. Earns millions.' Doc was more dismissive than he intended, his irritation at Carver's comment unreasonable.

'Okay. Okay. Then he must've had one giant habit... I can't believe his wife wouldn't have known about that.'

The gentle prod was unnecessary. It was already in Doc's mind. Along with the traitorous thought: Just how well did he know Judy?

Leech was still at his observation point, sitting in the upstairs window in Shaun's neighbour's house, his feet on the sill, the lights off. He had been amazed at how quickly the first police car had arrived—even before an ambulance. Young Billy must have had more spunk than he'd given him credit for and called them straight away.

He was ecstatic. His luck had finally changed tonight. He was still revelling in the sensation of release and the sheer joy of sweet revenge.

He had heard Billy screaming as the policewoman brought him out, his shrill voice repeating over and over, 'I killed my daddy!'

It couldn't have been better. The runt would suffer... Guilt. Leech contemplated the word, knew what it meant, but had never really felt it. Guilt was for weaklings and fools. Anyway, Shaun had always said it was not a real emotion, just something parents tried to drum into their kids, to control them. Peter knew he was right, and hoped Shaun had drummed it into Billy. He giggled to himself as he considered that gem. Tonight was just magical.

It had not taken long for the second police car to arrive, then an ambulance and the detectives in an unmarked vehicle. It thrilled him to see so many people involved. All because of him! He was fascinated when the forensic team arrived, and entered the house after donning their white suits and rubber boots to preserve *his* crime scene.

'Not an accidental death, I presume, Watson.' He tittered at his own black humour as he spoke aloud, replying to himself in a falsetto voice, 'Surely we must treat it as murder then, Holmes!'

For several minutes more he watched the to-ing and fro-ing of people until Suzie's body was being hoisted into the ambulance. Then he saw him.

He recognised the tubby bastard from his parole hearing.

Powers. Here!

Leech put his face to the glass to get a clearer view. Powers was hanging back, surveying the scene. The psychiatrist glanced up and down the street then his eyes tracked along the windows, pausing at his. Leech felt an electric surge as he imagined Powers seeing him there despite the darkened room. It wasn't fear that jolted him. It was anticipation.

He's hunting me! They must've wheeled the old fart out of retirement. Got him profiling again... For me!

Maybe they thought Powers knew him.

He whispered to the window, his breath misting the glass. 'Is that right, Powers? Do you think you know me?' He wanted to open the sash, to yell the words at the man. He did not—he was in control.

The fat man's attention had moved on, but Leech was riveted. 'This is personal now. You and me.' He chuckled, watching as one of the detectives waved Powers over and they disappeared inside.

Leech reclined again with his feet back up, a casual observer now. He might stay here for a day or so. There was no reason for them to suspect he would be here and it would give him some time. He knew better than to appear on the street just yet. The woodentops would be doing a house to house, enquiring whether anyone had seen him. Showing that photo he had seen on the telly.

He checked his reflection in the glass. Still misshapen, especially after Shaun crushed his snout with that ferocious head butt. His self-congratulatory mood dissipated for a minute as he remembered the mind-numbing intensity of the pain from that single blow.

Dangerous. Never underestimate your enemy.

He smiled again, his reflection grinning toothlessly at him. 'I didn't though, did I? Didn't underestimate our Shaun!'

No. He had come armed, and very definitely dangerous. Shaun had often beaten him with his fists and feet as a boy, and despite his experiences in prison, and his added bulk, Peter knew the sneaky bastard could still hurt him.

The shotguns had been a real bonus. He reached behind him and grabbed the second weapon. It was a thing of beauty.

He tapped his temple with it, wondering if Powers was underestimating him too.

Probably. After all, he had fooled them all at the parole hearing, hadn't he?

Not important. Maybe he would toy with him. Call him. Taunt him. If he could be bothered.

He tugged the fragment of photograph from his pocket and shrugged any further thought of Powers away as inconsequential. He had a purpose. A destination of his own. He smoothed the picture on his thigh.

'Tomorrow. Then we'll be together. My Birdy and me.'

'Stop beating yourself up, Doc. You're not to blame.' Carver clipped his seat belt into place.

'They should've had protection.'

'I told the PTBs you were worried Leech was a target. They were the ones who decided it wasn't necessary.' Carver sat there, arms folded, making no move to start the engine.

'I should've pushed harder.'

'Take a look around you, Doc. What do you see?'

'What's that got to do with anything?' Doc's mood shifted from morose to exasperated.

'This street. The properties... The cars.' They were surrounded by prestigious vehicles, top of the range models of the best marques in the industry. Carver prodded him verbally. 'That BMW is eighty grand's worth... The average value of the motors on this street must be close to fifty grand. The cars alone are worth more than many a street in some parts of Wales or Liverpool!'

'And your point is?' Doc was tired and bored. He just wanted to see Judy now.

'The people in these million pound homes can all afford private security. But they don't have it. Why?' He paused and Doc stared at him, wondering if he would ever start the engine and drive him home. Carver answered his own question. 'Because the area is safe.'

'Not today.'

'It's safe because the average number of bobbies per household is about three or four times the number in say, the rough end of Brixton, where crime is a problem.'

'Really?' Doc was surprised as he started to see the point Carver was making.

'Yup. And the PTBs decided Leech already had sufficient protection—they just notified the locals to keep an extra eye out. To increase the frequency of patrols in the area. Drive-bys and on foot. Okay?'

Doc felt the load lift a smidgeon, though he still protested. 'But it didn't do the family much good, did it?'

Carver finally started the car and moved off. 'True, but it was out of your hands. Full stop... Let's talk about John Finch.'

'Okay, Jack. I've been thinking about him and why Leech would have attacked him.'

'Me too. Your theory about Leech being obsessed with your Judy... Could he have gone to Finch's place expecting her to be there?'

Doc liked the sound of the term *your Judy*. His friend was astute, but had made no comment on the developing relationship until now. Doc said, 'That's the conclusion I'm coming to... Perhaps he thought they were still married, living together.'

'Probably.' Carver waited at a red light, and while staring ahead made a point that had not yet registered with Doc. 'Could be that anyone close to her is in danger... A target. Leech might be trying to eliminate the competition.'

The light was green, but Carver turned and stared at Doc, his face full of concern. His comment shook Doc, he had only considered himself an observer, an analyst, an adviser. He had been thinking he was outside looking in, whereas, in reality, he was too close to see the obvious. Defence mechanisms kicked in, denying Carver's assessment.

'No. Leech didn't kill John Finch, did he?'

'He had no reason. Once he realised they were divorced. Whereas you...' He tailed off, the words hanging. The lights had cycled back to red and then green again. This time Carver drove on, the streets empty at this time of the morning.

'Ha! So now I need protection! Your PTBs will love that idea. I can hear the debate over budgets already.' Doc's sour face reflected on the screen in the yellow street lights. He did not like what he saw. 'I don't think I'm in danger, Jack. He doesn't know I'm with Judy and I was on the panel that released him... He's probably grateful!'

'I'll draw a weapon anyway... And your decoy idea for Judy. I think I might be able to swing it now. There were some questions before, that, well, put it on hold.'

This was news to Doc.

'Questions? Not over the bloody costs again?'

Carver seemed reluctant to tell him, but finally let it spill out. 'Don't take it personal, Doc. Okay? But there were questions asked... About your involvement.'

'You cannot be serious! They really think that I—?' He was furious, anger sparking from his eyes as he glared at Carver, as if it was his fault.

Carver interrupted him, raising his own voice to match Doc's. 'When I told them she and her kid were staying at your place, it undermined the argument somewhat... Sorry.'

'Oh great! They think my professionalism and integrity are at that low an ebb, do they? For Christ's sake!' He was livid. How dare they?

'Relax. It was a fair consideration... Especially as you refuse to address them directly. There were some doubts about how fit you were, to cope. They were concerned. Maybe I should've told you.' He apologised again. 'Sorry, Doc. Really.'

Doc sat in silence, trying to calm himself. In a way he could see it. He did not like it, but he understood their mentality. This merely confirmed his decision to liaise through Carver as not only justified, but essential for his own peace of mind.

Carver broke into his thoughts. 'Obviously I've been telling them everything you say, even the stuff I'm not so sure about. I think there's no doubt you've proved you're back, fully capable. Okay?'

He stopped the car outside Doc's house. It was almost two in the morning.

'You had doubts too, Jack?' His voice was soft, his expression hopeful that at least this man had faith in him. 'Yet you supported me in the first place?'

'You keep thinking about Natalie. I see it in your eyes. On top of that, you opted out of the profiler role a few years back due to stress... But I never doubted you could do it, that's why I asked for you back on this case. I was just concerned to see how you would handle it. And you're doing good, Doc.' He reached across and opened the passenger door. 'Now piss off out of my car and go and see that young beauty you've got yourself. I'm knackered and I'm up for an eight o'clock meeting with the PTBs.'

Judy heard the front door close and waited a few minutes for Doc to appear. He did not, so she gently disentangled herself from Josh, careful not to disturb her son's slumber. She crept out to the landing and stood, horrified. Colin was sitting on the hall floor, his back against the front door, sobbing and calling out in a hoarse whisper, 'Please leave me… Please leave me!'

He was staring up the stairs and, for a devastating microsecond, she thought he was looking at her, talking to her. Her heart thundered into her throat.

Then Doc dropped his head to his knees, rubbed his eyes so hard she thought he would damage himself. His voice moaned the words, 'Natalie!' and 'No!' over and over.

Judy was relieved. And then angry with herself at the selfish thought. She went to him, sinking to her knees and hugging him in one fluid motion.

He was trembling, his life-force fluttering, but the moans died away as she clasped him, cooing in his ear, 'It's okay, Colin. I'm here. It's Judy. I'm here for you.' She stroked his hair and held him to her breast, the twirling emotions in there driving her heart rate to such a pace she thought it might burst. It was as though his troubled soul was transferring its pain, nullifying it, converting it to love during their tender embrace. She had never felt anything this intense for a man before, it was as powerful as her love for Josh though different—something she thought impossible— and the sensation made her lightheaded.

Doc raised his head and she saw once more the hell of his loss etched on his features, his eyes dull and hollow.

He croaked, 'I'm sorry sweetheart. I've had a really shitty day. It's getting on top of me…'

'Come.' She stood and tugged his hands. 'I'll get us some wine, you go upstairs and I'll join you.'

He nodded, a vague action, but made no effort to stand.

'Colin. Please. It's not very comfy here. Let's go and lie down. Okay?' There was nothing more in her mind than trying to help him relax, to unwind from his day. To expunge the vivid hallucinations.

He hauled himself up, nodded more firmly this time, and traipsed up the stairs.

Judy went to the kitchen and while she organised the wine and some glasses she thought of Josh, and how he had learnt to walk. His determined little face filled with frustration as she held his hands and he tottered, always falling. Sometimes he gave up and cried. Other times he laughed and giggled with her at the inanity of his attempts.

Baby steps. That was what did it in the end. He took his first little steps… and that was what she needed to do with Colin. Support him, be with him when he cried, laugh with him when she could.

She realised she had been standing motionless, the corkscrew in one hand, the wine in the other as visions of her son and her man dominated her thoughts.

But I am not going to be Colin's mother figure!

She stabbed the cork and wrestled with it until it came free with a pop that she found unusually satisfying.

Strange she thought that now, as she had wondered at first whether he might subconsciously be some sort of surrogate father for her.

Far from it.

Glasses and bottle in hand she went up to her would-be lover.

He had dropped his jacket to the floor, kicked off his shoes and loosened his tie. He was on the bed, one arm covering his eyes, his breathing suggesting she was too late.

'Damn.' She placed the bottle and glasses on the bedside table, turned off the light and eased herself onto the bed beside him. In a few moments her eyes adjusted, and she thought the moon, shining through the open curtains, bathed the room in a romantic light. Shame. Tonight was definitely not the night. She moved closer, Doc stirred.

'Hi.' His arm came off his eyes and wrapped itself round her shoulders. She laid her head on his padded breast. It felt so right. She heard his voice echo in his chest as he said, 'Sorry. It has been a long day.'

'Tell me.'

So he did, starting with his meeting with Henley. She listened, rarely interrupting, letting him meander through his day, hoping it would help. When he started explaining his new theory on Leech, the possibility that he was framed, she sat up and said, 'I don't know about you but I need that drink.' She poured as Colin slid up the bed, propping his head and shoulders against the headboard.

In the half-light Judy decided his eyes no longer appeared hollow…but sexy. She felt warmth in her lower belly, amazed that she could feel that way while discussing Leech. She brought herself back to the matter in hand.

'So Shaun Leech thought he wasn't in danger. Because he knew his brother was no killer. But he was wrong, wasn't he?'

'It gets worse I'm afraid.' He told her about the Judge, sparing no details, explaining AEA. 'Oxygen deprivation is very common among S and M practitioners, gays and fetishists of all kinds.'

The Judge! How could he? And here she was, discussing kinky sex on her man's bed. She almost laughed aloud, but Colin's sombre mood and his obvious pain from the loss of his friend strangled it before it could form in her throat.

Instead she said, 'I don't believe it!' He seemed puzzled at her comment. 'No. I mean, I believe the kinky mob get into stuff like this… But I just don't believe it of the Judge. I didn't know him well, but…' She ran out of words.

'I don't either. I've asked Jack Carver to check the surveillance tapes to see if either of the Leech brothers was in the area at the time. I don't know if he'll swing it though. The powers that be may decide to take it at face value.' He slurped some wine, then poured more for them both.

'That's terrible! Budgets again?'

'It's often the way… Anyway, I was expecting to get home around midnight, then we got called to Shaun Leech's home.' He described what he had seen, explained about Suzie Leech and the boy.

'And Peter Leech definitely did this?' It was a rhetorical question. She was visualising the green-eyed beast, feeling his presence again, suffocating from his malevolent magnetism. 'He is evil. How could we all be fooled by him?'

'The Judge would never have admitted it, but it happens far more regularly than the media realise. Only a few instances ever hit the headlines, yet recidivism abounds. It's the system. All we can do is try our best to improve the odds. Make things better… In memory of the Judge, may he rest in peace.' They clinked glasses and sipped their wine.

'He lost his wife to cancer, didn't he?'

'Yes, almost ten years ago. He was stoic. Strode through it. A stiff upper lip concreted on his face!' They chuckled. Then Doc quietened, thoughtful. 'Not like me.'

'Cancer's different, Colin. You usually know what's coming. Can prepare yourself for it... Very different.'

'To my situation? You're right, I suppose. Such a wise head on those young shoulders.'

He finished his wine, poured himself more, her glass still full from last time.

'I'm not that young any more. And I'm not that wise.' Was he worrying about the age gap again? She opened her mouth to ask, but he spoke first, and what he said left her chin frozen where it was.

'It was John who was attacked in his home. He's in hospital. In a coma. Sorry, Judy. I didn't know how to tell you. I needed to unwind a little first.' He was reading her face, searching for something.

She was sure all he could see was shock. No feelings for the man. Confusion certainly.

'What happened?'

'It seems Leech went to his home, assaulted him, bound and gagged him and left him, seemingly not too concerned if he died.'

The compassionate Judy, the loving side of her, was appalled for John, experienced a tinge of horror at his plight, the terror he undoubtedly had felt. Sorrow too for his current comatose state.

The wronged Judy, the spiteful vindictive one, the spurned wife who had socked her ex-husband and knocked him to the ground, whispered to her: He deserves it.

She did not want to inspect the thought any further. And then she heard her comment at the hospital, remembered hissing at him, *I wish you were dead.* Was that the very last thing she had said to him?

She blurted out, 'How bad is it?' Stupid question. A coma. How much worse can it get?

Doc put his arm round her shoulder, touched his head to hers. 'His heart shows some signs of damage. It's touch and go whether he'll survive.'

'Josh! Oh Lord! What will I tell him?' The poor mite. He still loved his father.

'You want my advice?' He gave it anyway. 'Tell him nothing yet. See how things progress.'

'You mean, see if John lives or dies?' Her heart lodged in her throat again.

Colin nodded. 'He thinks his dad is away. Very busy. If John comes through in the next few days, then no problem. Why worry the boy?'

She lay back, stared at the ceiling. She thought how strange it was that colours faded to grey in the half light. Like her love for John. Faded to grey before it disappeared altogether.

'You're right. I'll say nothing. See how John is by the weekend. I'll call the hospital tomorrow, find out how he's doing.'

Colin rolled onto his side, his face looming over hers, and she thought it was an inappropriate moment for a kiss. She was right. She did not get one.

'Did you know he was using cocaine? Large quantities too.'

'Are you serious? My John? Impossible! He detested the drug users in his business.'

'It was in his bloodstream. It's probably why his heart is dodgy... The police found a big stash in his home.'

'No!' An explanation occurred to her. 'You say Leech went to his home?' The full implications would strike her later, but right now she couldn't believe John used drugs. 'Leech took it there! Planted it. Perhaps he wanted to ruin John's reputation too, like the Judge.'

'Firstly, there is no reason for Leech to want to harm John's reputation. I can't see him having any motive for framing John.'

She chewed on that. Had to admit it was true.

'And secondly?'

'Jack Carver said there was physical evidence in his nostrils.'

'It could've still been planted! Leech probably forced him to take it.'

'Judy… The doctors found long term damage to the tissue. Rotting membranes. Erosion of the septum. The nasal cartilage.'

'Good grief… How long?' Was he a junkie when he lived with her? She had been unaware of his infidelity until she caught him with his pants round his ankles, but this?

Was she really so naïve?

'Several years in all probability. Certainly while you were still together.'

'Jesus!' She sat up, glass held out. 'I need another drink.'

He picked up the empty bottle. 'I'll get another.'

He left her to her reminiscences, trying to fit John's behaviours into what little she knew of cocaine addiction. It began to make sense… He had often complained of hay fever. Sniffles. Watering eyes. Nose rubbing. It had come on over the last few years they were together, not long after Josh had been born… He blamed the pollen in the summer, the polluted city air in the winter.

The bastard!

It was another little stab to her heart. He really was an unfit parent. There was no way she was going to put off the court case just because he was in hospital.

Sod him. She hoped he didn't recover until after the court decided Josh needed protection from him. She would call Sarah and tell her about the cocaine, first thing.

Colin returned with the wine, refreshed their glasses and moved close in to her. She rested her head on his chest again. He was so comfortable to lie on. A padded quilt of a man, not unyielding and muscular like John had been when they were first together.

'Why would Leech attack John?' She was puzzled, and though she knew Leech was violent and out of control she could not understand how John had become involved in all this.

Colin's arm folded round her again, the reassuring gesture welcome.

'I think he went to John's home looking for you. Perhaps he thought you were still married.'

She started. Of course! She had told Leech she was married when he had come up with the ludicrous notion of meeting her if he was paroled. Having given Colin a sanitised version of her meeting, preferring to keep that little conversation to herself, she decided not to enlighten him now.

'Although we separated a couple of years ago, John contested things at first, slowed everything down, told me to see sense! I said I had, which was why I was divorcing him.' She giggled. 'The decree nisi only came through in January. We've been officially divorced only six months. Wherever Leech got his information, it was obviously out of date.'

'That would explain it. Did you ever use drugs?'

The question would have knocked her down if she had not already been lying prone. She jerked up, slopping wine on his shirt as she did so.

'Do I strike you as a bloody dope-head, or coke-nose or whatever you want to call it?' She could feel her cheeks radiating heat, the red warning flashes glowing in the dim light.

'No... No! Of course not. It's just that, since you knew him for what, twelve years? It's possible you—'

'Never! I didn't even use weed at uni! Not one drag, not even a puff, let alone inhaling. As for cocaine, I've never seen the stuff except on films.' She had met many junkies in her work though, street people who had shaped her view of what a drug abuser was like, none of them in the slightest bit similar to John. None of them using in her presence either.

'Sorry—time out!' He sipped his wine, brushing at the stain on his shirt. He tutted, sat up, pulled it off, dried his chest with it, and then tossed it to the floor. 'I'll sort that tomorrow.' Then he held her shoulders and gave her a trust-me-I'm-a-doctor look. 'Sorry I asked. It's just, sometimes, because I'm so comfortable with you I forget we've only really known each other six weeks.'

Six weeks! Is that all? She was mollified, her nostrils no longer flaring spasmodically. He was right.

She leaned forward, touched her lips to his nose and said, 'You know, for such an old man, you have a remarkably wise head on those shoulders!' They laughed at her hijacking his remark about her, the tense moment passed. 'I feel like that too... the comfortable thing. It's like we're soulmates.'

'Yes.' His eyes seemed to shutter, like the high speed movement in a camera lens at the moment a photograph was taken. Was he thinking of her? Of Natalie?

She wanted to kiss him, full on. Instead she pushed him back down, laid her head on the pillow of his chest, and said, 'Try to get some sleep. G'night, my love.'

Judy woke soon after dawn, the strong sunlight beaming through the open curtains making her eyelids seem pink before she opened them. She glanced at the clock. Ten past six. Her mouth was wine furred and she felt grubby, rumpled and sweaty from sleeping fully clothed. She gave Doc a soft kiss on the lips, not disturbing him, wrinkling her nose at his booze-breath, convinced her own was worse. She went to Josh's room to check he was well before changing into her running kit. She brushed her teeth and then let herself out into the cool fresh air of pre-rush hour London.

She pounded the streets, found a park and jogged through trees, almost losing herself but getting directions from another early riser to make sure she was heading the right way home.

Home? Not my home really, she thought. Not yet, said a little voice. She ignored it and stretched her legs into a sprint. This afternoon she was due in court and she needed to call Sarah's office to leave a message. Let her know about John's Class A substance abuse to guarantee the verdict. The medical evidence of long term addiction would be the clincher. She wanted to hammer John today. He deserved it.

Her thoughts turned to Leech. She wondered what he had done to John... And why was she still so reluctant to tell Colin about Leech's proposal?

Was she just protecting him? Colin was plenty worried already. Before he had nodded off he mentioned the probability of a decoy being used in her home, if she agreed. She would call DI Carver and leave him a message too. It was a brilliant idea. Let the psycho come to her and be met instead by the UK version of a SWAT team of armed bobbies.

The thought was comforting. Her optimism would not allow her to dwell on the possibility Leech might find her first.

No. It will all be over in a few days. And for Josh's sake she hoped John would pull through. That's another call she should make. The Royal Berks Hospital in Reading. Check his condition.

She felt a tremor of guilt. Her first thoughts this morning had been for herself while John was lying in a coma. And here she was, planning to kick him while he was down. Christ, he could be dead already…

Her optimistic nature hammered that thought away, but she would call the hospital as soon as she got in. Then shower, get Josh up and take him to school. It was end of term week and Josh wanted to see his friends.

I must call Mum. She'll pick him up for me this afternoon.

She had no idea how long the hearing would go on. It was scheduled for two o'clock.

She arrived back at Doc's home, stretched out, feeling reinvigorated. She had only dozed with Josh before she slept those few hours with Colin, but despite everything, she was on good form. She towelled herself and made the first of her three calls.

'Don't tell me I woke you up!' Carver's voice burnt through Doc's skull like a welder's torch, sizzling the grey matter inside. He was not feeling at all refreshed.

He groaned, checked the clock. Midday!

Carver continued soldering his neurones, chirping at him, 'I've been in with the team most of the morning. Thought you'd want to know about the decoy.'

Doc grunted, one hand absently scratching his crotch while he tried to shake the fuzz of a mild hangover. As he sat upright his stomach signalled a liquid rebellion in the offing, his head was a pinball machine, the silver orbs banging and bumping, lighting up his brain, setting bells ringing.

'Sorry, Jack. I'll be okay. Just a little groggy.' He sagged back on the bed, phone to his ear, eyed the empty bottles, evidence of the cocktail of beer and wine that obliterated him for the night. At least he'd had no nightmares. 'Go on.' He concentrated, his memory booting up.

'First the good news. Judy left me a message, so we can go ahead. All approved and being organised as we speak. Our cutest WPC should be on site by now. Judy's mother has a key and is over there helping them get set up.'

'How exactly does this work?'

'A six person team including the decoy. All from the Armed Response Unit. Quality, experienced.'

'Six? Is that enough?' Doc heard Carver's sigh as he asked.

'Six, each shift of eight hours. Eighteen man days every calendar day. Plus overtime payment. If he hadn't already shot those two uniforms, if he wasn't a cop killer, there would be a four man team.' Carver had sounded very pleased with himself when he'd first called, but that had gone now, chased away by Doc's negativity.

'But is it enough? We know how dangerous he is.'

'They're the best. Our very own SAS.' Doc was sure that was an exaggeration but was not about to argue. Carver went on, 'Two inside, four outside. We're setting up in a British Telecom van. Our boys are disguised as workers in overalls, the baggy clothes cover their body armour. And a utility van is less obvious than a parked unmarked surveillance vehicle. Quicker for reaction too. They'll set up so they'll already be outside the van if he appears.'

'Okay. I just hope your boys know what they're doing.'

'I've also checked the videos. It pisses me off to admit it. I was wrong. I thought the staged suicide theory was a flight of fancy. You know, the Judge being your friend and all.'

It was the second time Carver had raised the question of his ability to remain professional, detached enough to do his job. At least Doc had been proved right. Talking it through with Judy, her apparent lack of insight into her own husband's behaviour, had made him doubt his judgement regarding the suicide. After all, how well did he really know the Judge? He was relieved though at Carver's comment.

'Who was it? Shaun?'

'Spot on. Appeared in the area about an hour before the body was discovered. Which explains why the Judge would have just let him in.'

'Why?' Doc's pinball had not sparked everything yet.

'There was a record of a call to the Judge's home from Shaun Leech's mobile. The Judge was expecting him.'

'To discuss the parole. To allow him to vent his anger...' Just like the Judge to invite a distressed victim to come to his home. Dedicated and compassionate to the end.

'That's what we think. And we found John Finch's car at Hammersmith, Peter Leech's prints all over it.'

'You've been busy.' And I should be up. He hauled himself off the bed, rubbed his scalp, yawned. 'Anything else?' He needed a shower.

'Okay, Sleeping Beauty. The bad news is... we found the cabbie.'

'Dead?'

'Very. I've spoken to the provincial mob. The lad who spotted him is bright, will go far. I've commended him. Saw a reflective flash from his headlights as he left Finch's place. He noticed the roadside vegetation had been disturbed and, there it was, tucked away from the main road. He found the missing cab.'

'Close to Finch's home?' The trail was clear now. Their surmises confirmed.

'A few miles down the road. The local PC took one look at the scene and decided it was moody, an amateurish attempt to make it look like an accident. Subtlety is not Leech's strong point, is it?'

'No.' Unlike big brother. The thought prompted him to ask, 'Are you checking the Judge's apartment again. I'd be very surprised if there was nothing there implicating Peter Leech.'

'I was waiting to see if the videos yielded anything first. Unfortunately the cleaner's already been in...'

'Oh well. Is that it?' Doc's mouth tasted of raw sewage and he desperately needed to clean his teeth.

'Not quite. One last bit of bad news. It just confirms what we know. There was a family photo at John Finch's place. It's been torn up, Doc. The woman's head and shoulders were removed...'

'Leech took it. A picture of Judy.' Feeding his obsession. Doc was wide awake now, as if an ice bucket had been tossed over him. 'Let's hope the decoy works.'

'Yeah. You coming down the station?'

'I'm on my way.'

Immediately after Doc hung up, the phone rang again. Had Carver forgotten something?

He answered. And the ice bucket became an avalanche, a whole mountainside of freezing slush.

He could not believe who was calling him.

'Doctor Powers, I presume.' The voice set the nerves in his neck tingling, the hairs on his nape springing to attention.

'Peter? Peter Leech?' He asked, but had no doubt it was the voice from the parole hearing.

'Bravo, Doc.' The familiarity jarred him. 'Don't mind if I call you Doc, do you? I read it on the cover of your book, that's what people call you. Oh, and it was crap, by the way... The book.'

Doc flipped through the possibilities of why the man was calling, simultaneously considering, and then ruling out, trying to call Carver on his cell phone to trace the call. The Nokia was in his jacket pocket across the room, and he was tethered to his home phone.

Dialogue. But what to say?

Doc was an analyst. A profiler. He advised on interrogations, but he was no therapist. Let alone a negotiator.

'Cat gotcha tongue? Bet you're wondering why I'm calling you... I saw you last night.'

Doc's mouth finally kick-started into action. 'Last night?'

'Yeah. I decided to stick around for a bit. Checked out the police reaction to my beloved brother's sad demise... Fancy his own son blowing his fuckin head off!' He guffawed, self-satisfaction riddled with malice. 'Must run in the family. Patricide!' That laugh again, like knives clashing in his throat.

'I know Shaun killed your parents, Peter. I know you were innocent.' Doc was thinking: Get him on your side by letting him think you're on his.

'Yeah?' The confidence evaporated. Doc's unexpected yet genuine declaration puncturing the bravado.

'We were on to him.'

'Well too fuckin late for me!' Doc jerked the phone from his ear, the words rattling his eardrum from the force, the vehemence. 'Eighteen years too fuckin late...' The voice petered out, leaving only an echo in Doc's ear.

What could he say?

'Why not come in and talk to us about it. We can at least put the record straight.'

'Fat load of good that'll do me! Anyway, there was a stiff in my flat. News says they've already found him.'

'We can talk about that too, Peter.' It was the best Doc could do. What else did he have to offer?'

'Piss off! I didn't ring you to turn myself in. It's only because I saw you at Shaun's house. They must be desperate to have wheeled you out of retirement, eh Doc? How's the lovely Suzie, by the way? *Facing* up to the consequences of stabbin me in the back?' He tittered like a schoolboy who had pulled off a classroom prank.

'You didn't rape her, Peter. All those years ago. I know. I spoke to Doctor Henley.'

'Yeah?' Curious now. 'How is the old bastard? Still puffin weed?'

'Shaun manipulated everything, didn't he?' Could Doc convince Leech he was an understanding ear, someone to talk to? To confide in? To surrender to?

'Too fuckin right he did! What about his final gift to me? Potter. I've just seen the news. That's why I called… I want to put you straight. I didn't do him, okay?'

'I know that too. Shaun was in the area. You weren't, Peter. I think he might have been trying to set you up though. Again.'

The line was quiet for a minute, and Doc began to think he should fill the silence, but was unsure what to say. He had been using Leech's first name a lot, trying to cement the relationship. But what now? Fortunately, Leech spoke first.

'You're alright. I'm surprised… You were such a wanker at the parole hearing, trying to wind me up like that. That dyke was putty though. I read her article in the *Guardian*. Labels! Stupid fuckin lesbo hates 'em! Brilliant, eh?'

So that's how…

'Let's get together, Peter. I'd like to talk more. Maybe I can help you.'

'Fuck off! Just wanted to put you straight on Potter… I was gonna do him, mind. And I was thinking of tracking you down… Like you're trying to track me. But I can't be arsed. I feel like a new man now my brother's got what he had coming. Anyway, I've got better things to do.'

There was one thing Doc could offer. He didn't want to, but, desperate now, he did.

'Judy Finch works for me. You could talk to us both.'

God, I hope that wasn't the wrong thing to say.

The silence extended this time.

When Leech did speak, he was conspiratorial, sneaky even. 'Judy… She been asking after me? Told you she fancies me, right? I'm not surprised. Most of these posh tarts love a bit of rough.' His insidious giggle crawled into Doc's ear. 'Not that I was rough until that cunt Potter put me away. Went to private school… Well, when I could be bothered!'

Leech's little speech sickened Doc, his stomach lurching, fragile already from the booze.

'If you come in I can arrange for her to be involved in your interviews.' The lie trickled off his tongue, while his mind screamed, *No way!*

'Don't you worry about my Judy. Tell her to call me on her ex's number. It's a mobile so you can't track me down on it.'

Wrong! Doc was hopeful now. That was something.

'I'll see what I can do.' How would Judy feel about that? Maybe they could use a negotiator to advise her on what to say…

'Just do as I say. Give her my message. I know she wants to see me. Could tell as much when I asked her out. Could see she was desperate for it… Dunno why she lied about her hubby, though. Little minx.'

What did he mean? There was nothing on the tape about John Finch. Doc's brain spun like a washing machine. What else had they discussed that was not on the tape? And why the hell hadn't she told him Leech had asked her out?

'You might want to call in on her ex. He's a bit tied up right now!' The brutal laughter cascaded again. 'He's alright too, not a bad bloke for a yuppie.'

'He's in hospital. He should pull through.' Doc was not sure if his approach was right, but he wanted Leech to know they were not far behind him, that they were aware of everything.

Leech was suspicious now. 'Who found him? The gardener?'

'That's right.' Doc's lies were easy. The man was contemptible. Right now Doc wanted him put away. Permanently.

'Divorced the gorgeous Judy quite recently,' he said. 'Loves his kid, I think… Anyway, gotta go. Things to do. Don't you forget to give my little Birdy the message. Or I will come after you.' Click.

For several seconds Doc stood, numb. His nightmare was real, flesh and blood, a mountain of vicious muscle threatening to hunt him down. The fear of this psychopath, the pure malevolence of the beast, rooted him to the spot.

He replayed the conversation in his mind, fixing it. Then he called Carver. The DI was flabbergasted at first, then his enthusiasm kicked in as Doc recounted the call in detail.

'This is great news. We'll get his mobile number from your Judy. I'll talk to which-ever service provider is responsible for his network. We should be able to locate him, as long as he's in an area with a signal. Should be able to triangulate to within twenty yards of him, maybe even get him on GPS!' Carver was excited now. Then asked, 'Judy'll be comfortable speaking to him?'

Comfortable? Hardly.

'Jack, I think we should speak to an expert, someone who specialises in talking people into surrendering. I'm an amateur at this…'

Carver made a sucking noise as he contemplated. 'Yeah. Okay. Come on in, Doc, I'll see what I can do. I'll try and set up a meeting for, say, half-one?'

An hour. It should be enough time.

'I'll be there.' Doc finished the call and showered.

It was good that Leech had called him… But if John Finch had given him Judy's address, he would surely already have her home number. Why hadn't he called her directly?

Or had he?

Probably.

And he was bound to call her home again.

Doc decided to let Carver know, tell him to put a trace on her phone, have the decoy leave it on voicemail, but get it rigged to keep the connection open even after Leech thought he had hung up. Doc was not sure it was possible, but he hoped so. Then maybe they could locate him, and Judy would not have to talk to him at all.

He cleaned his teeth as he showered. His conversation with Leech had douched away most of his hangover. The shower completed the job.

———

What did Powers take him for—a complete idiot?

Leech finished the call, muttering to himself.

'Half my life spent inside and he thinks I'm going to give myself up to spend the rest of it there! Twat.'

He put John Finch's mobile in his pocket—he'd seen Judy's home number listed there, had tried several times, but got no answer. Just a bloody machine. He left no message. Where was the fun in that?

No, he would visit her this afternoon. She would probably be picking her kid up from school around three o'clock so he'd pop round soon after.

He had some time to kill so made himself some food. He had spoken to his captive late last night, and confirmed the man was expecting no visitors today. Shaun's neighbour was still bound and gagged in his downstairs loo, so Leech had the place to himself.

The police were doing their house to house calls to see if anyone had seen anything suspicious, but he ignored their knocking. They just moved on. Bloody idiots. Mind you, it was raining so the coppers weren't exactly full of enthusiasm for the task.

Leech was bored. He had seen the news and laughed when he heard Potter was dead, especially as the police were now treating the death as suspicious.

He thought back to that one time Shaun had visited him, gloating about getting away with rape first, and then murder. Shaun had told him that if Peter ever got out, he would kill him. And if he couldn't do that he would kill Potter instead, and frame him for the murder. Shaun had said, 'One way or another you're going away for the rest of your life, so get used to it.'

Well, he was wrong, wasn't he? Leech belched, took another swig of beer and tucked into a microwave ready meal that was definitely superior to anything he had eaten inside.

He thought about his conversation with Powers again.

'Fuckin twat!' He tossed the empty plate aside. 'As if I'd go through that again! Give myself up!'

For what? To bare his soul to Powers?

And then the bastard had mentioned his Birdy, as if he knew how they felt for each other.

How would he know? Had she spoken to Powers? About him? Powers said they worked together. But why hadn't she been in touch?

Maybe she'd tried... Well, she had his number now. Ironic too, it being her ex's old phone. He laughed at that.

Later, he rooted round in a cupboard and found what he was looking for, tugging it over his head. There were half a dozen coppers on the street, all with photos of him. Probably knew his face was bruised and lumpy, Suzie or the runt would have told them, for sure.

But what he was wearing now was superb. A full face crash helmet. It was tight, but bearable. He checked the mirror. There was no way anyone could identify him, he could barely tell it was his face and he'd lived with it for thirty odd years.

They would have to be nose to nose to tell it was him. Brilliant.

He slipped it off and then rigged his remaining shotgun to hang off his right shoulder, the length adjusted to ensure the butt would fall into his palm. He then checked the Barbour. Would they recognise it? He had been wearing it when he arrived at the house, and when he blew away those cops on the motorway. He went for another rummage.

The man's clothes were smaller than John Finch's and none of them fitted. It was a dilemma, he would have to risk sticking with the overcoat. At least it was raining so he wouldn't stand out. He put it on, with the helmet, and inspected his image in the mirror.

'Nice. Imposing. She'll be weak at the knees when she sees me. Lucky cow!'

He was almost ready, but needed to prepare a few props first. He went through the man's study, found brown paper, tape and a big black felt marker. He picked a few random books from the shelf and then wrapped them into three parcels. On one he scrawled 'Judy Finch' in bold script above her address. He picked up a clipboard, some papers and a pen, then peered out the window to check the road was clear. There had been a lot of activity earlier in the day when a mobile Serious Crimes Investigation Unit trailer had been parked opposite his brother's home, and he knew there was a risk he could be spotted when he left the neighbour's house.

It looked clear. Not a copper in sight.

Good. And if that prat Powers thought he was stupid then he was going to get a big surprise…

'If the pigs have set a trap for me, now they know I want to see my Birdy, they will regret it!'

He grabbed the key with a Ducati fob from the rack in the kitchen, and left, slamming the door behind him.

The bike was parked right in front of the house, a beautiful piece of machinery that he estimated must have cost twelve grand or more. He wiped rain off the seat, swung a leg over the saddle, tucked the clipboard and parcels in a side pannier and searched for the ignition. It took several precious seconds and he knew he was vulnerable. If the police saw him leave the house or spotted him now, they would be suspicious, wondering why he had not answered when they knocked. And that would mean he would have to use the gun again.

He finally found the ignition, congratulated himself, twisted the key and revved the engine. He roared down the street, wheels skidding in the wet. He was very rusty on bikes too, but he loved the thrill. He really didn't give a shit about the police now, two of whom, house-calling at the end of the road, turned to stare as he zoomed past. He was on his way, confident he would soon be with his Birdy.

The only fly in the ointment, apart from the possibility the police might be watching her place, was her son. He really didn't know what to do about the kid. Maybe the boy's old man would take him in, then he and Birdy could head abroad.

Yeah. That would work…

He got lost. The traffic was heavy in the fine rain, many mums on the school run clogging the roads, and it seemed there were no-entry signs and one-way streets everywhere he wanted to turn. His patience soon ran out so he roared the wrong way down one anyway, weaving through honking cars, tempted to stop and give a few of the idiots screaming at him the benefit of a quick blast from his shotgun.

The short cut worked but he was confused now. He pulled the A to Z from his pocket and checked.

Yes, not far now.

He found the road and scanned the blocks of flats for Judy's. He stopped the bike just past the building, and made a show of pulling out the parcel, inspecting it and the clipboard, as if to check he had the right address. Satisfied, he dismounted.

All the while, his eyes roved, checking the pedestrians—an old man and some kids—the windows overlooking her door, and the cars parked nearby. Nothing remotely suspicious.

Except the BT van with its little workers' tent next to a manhole in the road. Directly outside the path to Judy's ground floor apartment.

One of the engineers was sitting, legs dangling in the hole, another passing tools, yet another had a fancy laptop with wires trailing while a fourth man stood watching. The tent was crowded, covering all but the man in the hole, as if they were sheltering from the rain.

Leech was suspicious. It was too much of a coincidence.

Fuck it! He should never have called Powers. And Birdy should've kept her trap shut and not talked to him either.

He wanted to see her. It wasn't her fault they were watching her home, was it? She wouldn't collude with the filth against him. Would she?

He had come this far, had waited too long to get here. He was not giving up now.

Fuck them! I'm going in.

He strolled toward the path, acting his role, as if uncertain of his 'delivery' address, striding past the van, the tent and the path, then spinning, turning back, apparently comparing the address on the packet with the number on the door. Nodding to himself as he walked down the path.

He put a thumb to the buzzer and held it there until the door opened, alert for any movement from the BT outfit.

He felt the anticipation as the door swung wide, a petite strawberry blonde standing there, then a massive disappointment as he realised it was not his woman.

Several possibilities flooded his mind. Sister, perhaps? Looked vaguely similar. Visitor? Lodger? Baby minder? But she was staring hard at his face, trying to identify him he decided, and he did not like that one little bit.

He took in her bulky sweater, saw sweat beads on her upper lip, then smelt her fear. Simultaneously he heard a man's voice from the hall behind her, a low murmur, almost inaudible through the helmet, and sensed movement from the BT van. It was enough. He made a decision.

He thrust the parcel and board into her stomach, driving her back, slipped his fingers round the shotgun and swept it forward as she fell. She was scrabbling behind her back for something, mouth opening to shout an alarm.

The shotgun blast drowned out everything. He had aimed at her knee, speed essential, convinced her pullover hid body armour. Another old lifer had once told him, *Shoot their heads or limbs if you ever have to deal with armed coppers.*

The WPC collapsed as Leech threw himself forward, kicking the door shut, slamming it in the face of one of the BT team. The man in the hall, similarly dressed in inappropriate clothes for a damp summer's day, was turning, a pistol drawn, the muzzle sweeping towards Leech. The shotgun was almost up, searching out the man's head, but now in line with the policeman's gun.

The sawn-off erupted again, at exactly the same moment the pistol fired. Leech's head snapped back from the impact, the explosion rattling his skull, his legs buckling.

The officer fell backwards into the kitchen, squealing in agony. The pistol flew through the air over his shoulder, along with an emulsion of gore, his hand and forearm now crimson fragments and droplets misting the air.

Leech landed on his knees, rolled to the side, part of his mind detached, wondering if he was dying, trying to understand why he could still control his body if he had been hit in the brain. Meanwhile, some feral part of him was assessing the status of the girl and the position of her weapon. She was busy, struggling to control the arterial blood geysering from her severed leg. Leech was well impressed with the damage his weapon had created at such close range.

He pushed himself up, punched her in the face, rolled her unconscious body in front of the door, like a human doorstop, and grabbed her gun. It would be quicker than reloading his weapon. He leapt to the kitchen and shot the other officer in the head.

It was all over in seconds, but he knew time was not on his side. He yanked the bloody headset and mic off the dead male officer and listened. He imagined the rest of the stake-out team would be outside the front door already, probably about to smash it down to get in.

'...status report?'

He answered that one. 'Don't come near the flat. Just listen.'

'Leech?'

'Don't talk or I'll kill them both. Their status is that the pretty one won't be doing any more marathons and the ugly one won't be playing the guitar again. But they're both still alive. For now.'

The policeman was very dead, but that was no big deal for Leech—he'd killed one yesterday, according to the news.

He heard a gasp and continued with his commentary.

'So, you and your mates are going to get back in your little tent. Right away. No helicopters, or they're dead. If I see anyone who even looks like a cop, if anyone approaches this flat, your buddies are dead. Now you can speak, but only to say, I understand.'

A pause, then, 'I understand, but—'

'No buts. Call your Commissioner. Tell him I'll negotiate with him. No one else. I want him here within half an hour. No flak jacket. Just in his fancy uniform. I'll only talk to him. Tell him if he is not here in thirty minutes, I will start blowin more bits off his boy and girl. Don't call me. I'll call you.'

He then stamped on the headset, searched the two inert bodies for weapons and ammunition, stuffed what he found into his voluminous pockets, then grabbed the other gun off the floor, wiping bloody bits of copper off the handle with a tea towel.

He slipped off his helmet, a clock now ticking inside his head, advice from yet another con flitting through his mind. The man had taken hostages, killed one, and had been banged up because he was too slow getting away. His advice: Don't hang around. Make them think you're still there. But find a way out, and do it quick. Two minutes tops. Or you'll be dead or back inside.

As he dropped the helmet to the ground he saw his own blood on the entry and exit points from the policeman's bullet. Another inch to the left and it would have pierced his eye and come to rest in his brain. Instead it had creased his scalp above his ear. Blood was hot and sticky on his face. He wiped it with the tea towel and it started stinging.

'You cunt!' He kicked the corpse, stamped on the face. 'I got you though. Fuckin SNAKEBITE!'

Control.

He had to get out. Now.

He ran to the backdoor and into the garden.

Fuck!

It was a tiny brick courtyard. He leapt at the wall, hands clutching for the top. He screeched as the broken glass embedded there lacerated both hands. Yet he would not let go, knew it was his only chance. He hauled himself up and over, into the next garden. A three storey block of flats backed onto Birdy's apartment. He ran to the patio window, booted it, expecting it to shatter. It didn't. His foot bounced off and he yelped as pain jetted through his ankle.

He was bleeding from his hands and head, and he hurt. A lot. He was furious. The frustration of missing Birdy again welled up and he yelled at the door to open. After a moment he pulled the shotgun up, slick with blood from his ruined palms, slippery as he tried to reload.

'Get in!' The shell flew to the ground.

In his mind the clock had reached the magic two minutes and he wanted to be away. He lifted the gun and hammered the stock into the door. The glass curtained down, the fragments glittering and crashing as they landed. He was in! He ran through the apartment, the alarm siren almost deafening him, found the front door and tried to open it. Double locked, and a mortise too.

'FUCKFUCKFUCK!'

He barged into the lounge, fumbled for another cartridge, managed to load it, then fired at the window as he leapt through, landing in the front garden in a cascade of glass. Airborne shards had pricked his face and neck but the heavy coat protected his body. He was out. The rain was a fine drizzle, almost stopped now.

He sprinted across the lawn, vaulted the wall into the road as a woman was opening her car door to get out. She started to scream as the gun butt smashed into her throat. He grabbed her by the hair and threw her to the pavement, jumped in the car and started it up. After a quick scan of the street for police activity—there was none—he juddered away, cursing the old crate and its knackered clutch.

Less than five minutes after arriving at Judy Finch's address he was almost half a mile away, safely lost in London's traffic.

'Bitch! Bitch! Bitch! Fuckin bitch!'

Leech thumped the wheel as he drove, aimless now, his brain in turmoil. His wounded hands screamed pain back at him, creating a vicious circle, winding him up all the more.

It isn't fair. None of it!

His brother. The torment of his youth at Shaun's hands. The loss of Suzie. The alienation from his parents who labelled him a bad kid.

Then the big one.

Eighteen fucking years. Half his life in prison for something he did not do.

And now the one woman he wanted to be with was beyond his reach.

Worse.

She was a traitor. She must have let the police in, let them use her home as a trap. Like he was some sort of vermin, a rat to be put in a cage.

Why? She definitely had the hots for him... There's no way he could have misread the signs. She'd been practically drooling over his body at the interview.

So, what now? He could get a flight with his false passport and never come back. Try to live happily ever after.

Or he could exact revenge.

Birdy.

Powers.

And then fuck off abroad. Oh yes. That's a much better idea.

He dumped the old lady's banger near Earl's Court tube station and started walking. He stopped at a pharmacy and asked for bandages for his hands and head. He told the friendly young shop assistant he'd had an accident with a patio window, that it had shattered and cut him. The girl was kind and helped dress his wounds, though she told him he should see a doctor and get some stitches. Fifteen minutes later he was on his way.

To see Powers. At the address Gruber had provided. Let's hope he's not moved, he thought as he opened the A to Z to get his bearings.

Doc was having a rough afternoon. He spent much of it with a police negotiator deciding how best to handle Leech if he phoned again. At one point they decided to call him, but his mobile was off. After two hours going over their approach and trying to absorb all the advice, Doc had had enough. He and Carver went for a late lunch. They strolled to a café near the station, Doc wanting to avoid the canteen in a bid to get some air.

It was drizzling and Carver had objected. 'What's wrong with our canteen?'

'Nothing. I just need to get out.'

'It's pissing down.' Carver grumbled some more but Doc had lured him out with the promise of paying for them both.

Doc's thoughts were with Judy. She would be in court now and he had tried to call her to wish her luck, but to no avail. Her mobile was off too.

It should be pretty cut and dried with the drug abuse on John's part, but she had told him the opposing barrister always had tricks up his sleeve. He might ask for a deferral if he knew of John's medical status, or he may have found out about the threat from Leech and Judy's subsequent displacement from her own home.

They arrived at their destination, a greasy spoon, much frequented by the bulkier policemen who were addicted to lard, and ordered full English breakfasts. It was after three-thirty, but the café served traditional fry ups all day.

They settled down in a corner, mugs of tea in hand, when Carver's phone rang. Doc ignored him, his own obsession on his mind again. Why hadn't Judy told him Leech had propositioned her? It was important. There seemed to be no rational explanation.

Unless... It occurred to him she might have been concerned about how he would react. It was sort of comforting, but also yet another slight on his professionalism.

'Bad news, Doc.' Carver pocketed his phone. 'I don't know how close Judy Finch was with her ex...' His eyes held Doc's, flinty now. 'But he died about half an hour ago. Leech is leaving a trail of corpses. The man's remorseless.'

Doc was silent for a few beats, thinking that Judy was wasting her time in court. Then he thought about Josh. He would try Judy's phone again later, or he could try to call the court from the station. Their food arrived as Doc answered Carver's implied question.

'She doesn't have any time for him. She's in court now, trying to restrict his access to their son. And she has never taken drugs, Jack. She was astonished her ex was such a heavy user.' Carver's head was down, as if his food was the sole focus of his attention. Doc went on, chewing and thinking at the same time. 'Remorseless is a good word to describe Leech. In both senses.'

Carver stopped chewing and glanced up. 'Both?'

'Uh-huh. In the sense you meant—relentless, an unstoppable force. He is a man on a mission. A psychopath doesn't give up. And if he feels harmed or slighted in any way he'll never forget. He'll find his moment for revenge.'

'Yeah?' Carver held some bread, hovering over his egg, ready to dunk. 'And the other sense?'

'Totally lacking remorse. No guilt to trouble his conscience. He acts, and has no empathy or concern for any of his victims. His only focus is his objective. In Leech's case, Judy.'

Carver scooped the last of his yolk into his face, and said through a mouthful of egg, bread and beans, 'I suppose it's best not to piss him off then! At least, not until we've got him nicked.'

Doc tried Judy's phone again. No answer still.

'When we get to the station can we get a message to Judy? Or the court clerk? It's all a bit pointless now, and she'll need to be with her lad.'

'Okay, let's go.' Carver had eyed Doc's uneaten food, but just belched and stood as he swallowed his last mouthful. A candidate for an ulcer, Doc decided.

The rain had eased now, though the traffic was heavier than normal. The rain always did that.

They arrived at the station and were making their way to Carver's office when pandemonium erupted. A breathless PC grabbed Carver's arm and said, 'Leech is holed up inside the Finch place. Got our decoy and her baby-sitter as hostages—'

Carver's face drained of colour. 'You're kidding me! What happened to the rest of the Tac team? Why the hell did they let him in?'

'Sorry sir, I don't know... He's asked to see the Commissioner. The team is meeting to discuss what to do.'

Doc spoke, 'I'll dip out now, Jack. You've got the negotiator here. You don't need me any more. I'll head over to the court and meet Judy if that's okay.'

'Sure. No problem... You were right again though, Doc.' Carver's eyes glistened, and Doc wondered if Jack knew the team personally. Or maybe the girl intimately. Could she be the reason Jack was in the doghouse?

Doc put a comforting hand on his friend's shoulder. 'Right about what?'

'You said six wasn't enough. We should learn to listen to you more... but at least we know where he is. We'll get him now, Doc. Hostage takers never win. Thanks for everything. I'll call you when it's over.' Carver spun away and jogged to the briefing room.

Doc went outside, arm up, signalling to every passing cab he was a willing fare.

Despite the rain drying up he still had to wait ten minutes before an empty taxi stopped for him. In that time his emotions ebbed, relief his overriding sensation.

Judy was safe.

He would do his best to help her and Josh through John's funeral... and after. Perhaps his own demons would die now.

As he sat in the cab, a little niggle started in his mind. And the more he considered it, the more it took root. He stared at the passing street, his eyes not registering.

Why had Leech asked for the Commissioner? It was not like him at all... And why not ask for Judy? Or himself?

There was no connection between Leech and the top policeman in the capital. Was it ego? Leech undoubtedly had a massive one. But it did not feel right to Doc. He mulled it over as his cabbie did battle with the traffic on the way to Fulham Magistrates Court.

———

Judy hugged Sarah, her lawyer and old friend. 'Thank you, thank you. I don't know what I'd have done without you.'

'Yeah, me neither. Now let me go, you soppy cow. I have other clients waiting for me. And they pay me!' With a final hug she said, 'I hope this new man in your life really is all you say. Just look after him, and don't let this one play away!' Sarah disentangled herself, kissed Judy's cheek and headed back to her chambers.

Judy was overjoyed at the result. And suddenly thrilled. Her man was here, climbing the steps to the court. She went to him as he reached the top step, gave him a hug too.

'It's all sorted. I got exactly what I wanted...' The words came out in a rush, then she realised how miserable he looked. 'Colin? What's the matter? Are you okay?' His face was stressed, the lines deep and his skin slate grey in the damp afternoon light. It started drizzling again.

'Listen, my love... John didn't recover... He died this afternoon. I've been trying to call you.'

'Oh, Christ... No!' She did not want this. She'd been celebrating her victory over him just moments before and he was already dead.

Shame swept through her, her last words to John echoing in her head again and again.

I wish you were dead.

It wasn't true. She didn't mean it!

Colin was holding her tight as she sagged against him, the expression on his face deepening as her tears spilled onto her cheeks.

He was downcast. 'It's okay to cry, sweetheart. I'm sure you feel something still, and it's okay.'

She sniffed. 'It's not that... I said some terrible things to him the last time we spoke. I told him I wished he was dead.'

Doc was applying gentle pressure to her shoulders, trying to get her to move inside. He stopped, put his face to hers, his brown eyes peering deep into hers. 'Your wishes had nothing to do with this. And you know it.'

She nodded, wiped the tears, fumbled for a tissue.

Doc went on, 'It was Leech. Only Leech.'

'But why did Leech harm John? Because of me! It's my fault. Leech is obsessed with me. I told him I was married.' Judy could feel depression sit on her shoulders, her guilt pressing down on her, a flower being crushed by heavy weights.

'You told him?' Colin's voice was sharp.

'Yes… He asked me out! Can you believe it?'

'No! That wasn't on the recording!'

'After the interview. He just came out with it. I told him I was married, but he could see there was no ring on my finger.'

'Why the bloody hell didn't you tell me?' His face was flushed now, no longer pallid, his mouth screwed up in anger.

She bristled, her own hurt and guilt over John redirected outward. At Doc.

'It wasn't important. And anyway, what's it to you? We aren't bloody married.' She should have stopped then, but could not. 'And you don't own me.' She felt her cheeks pulse with excess blood.

'Ugh!' Doc raised his voice, something she had never witnessed before, as he said, 'I'm talking about colleagues. Professionals. I'm supposed to analyse all the data. Why the hell did you hold back?'

'I was worried about you!' She closed her eyes, put a hand over them, cleared the moisture there. 'You've been such a basket case—'

'A what? Is that what you think of me? Jesus Christ!' He slapped a hand to his forehead, his expression alternating between disbelief and fury.

She ploughed on, feeling less emotional now, having successfully transferred her anguish to Doc.

'You know what I mean. The nightmares. The images… I've been concerned for you. That's all.' She tried to put a hand to his face, but he pushed it away.

'That's all! I'm a bloody basket case. That's what you said!'

'Oh… please, Colin, I didn't mean it.'

'I know what you meant! You think I can't even be trusted to do my job… And I thought you and I had something special. Pah!' He puffed his lips out as he said it to her. 'Were you just keeping an eye on me for the Judge? Is that all it was?'

His words were a punch to her gut. She hadn't really meant to hurt him. She wanted to rewind the whole conversation, go back and replay the scene.

'No, Colin. Please don't—'

'Don't what? Wonder what else you haven't told me?'

His anger was such a shock, she was at a loss, didn't know how to handle him. He had always been so placid, even under pressure. Why was he so animated now?

'I'm going for a drink.' He left her, forlorn and bedraggled on the court steps, and crossed the road to a pub opposite.

Oh, you stupid cow!

What had she done?

She ran through the conversation in her mind. She had insulted his professionalism. He was right. She should have told him everything. It was stupid of her not to. Could he have worried any more for her? Hardly.

Trust.

He had believed they had it. And she had let him down. It was her fault and he was justifiably pissed off with her, she decided. And had she really called him a basket case?

Well done, Judy! Supportive. Understanding. Subtle and empathetic… Not!

She ranted at herself. Her guilt over John paling, compared to the possibility she had screwed up her chances with Colin. That she might just lose the best man she had met in years.

And his comment about the Judge… Had she honestly given the impression that she was babysitting him for his boss?

What a complete shambles she had made of things.

She ran her hands through her hair, not sure what to do, her insides churning at the thought of losing him.

Then she made her decision. Apologise. Wholeheartedly.

She followed him to the pub.

Doc supped his pint, his blood pressure approaching normal again. What had she said to him? He was such a basket case she had to protect him from the truth. He quaffed half the pint at the thought of that little gem.

Yet… He had to admit. Was it really such a bad description? He thought back to Leech's hearing just a few weeks ago… Hadn't he called himself the very same thing?

But it's one thing thinking it yourself, and quite another to hear it from someone you love.

He finished the beer, slammed the glass down and signalled for another. He had never sunk a pint that fast in his life.

Love?

He examined his feelings. Did he love her? She had certainly got under his skin… In much the same way Natalie had.

Natalie… It was one of the rare occasions he had been able to think of her without the images battering his consciousness. He glanced around the bar, half expecting to see her lovely face, warped and bloody.

She wasn't there.

No clacking. Nothing.

Was he finally through it?

Last night had been awful… When he had arrived home he'd been hallucinating again, and was desperate for more alcohol. But the warmth of Judy, both physical and spiritual, had helped him.

Was he healed?

He tried to bring the images to mind. He could, but they were no longer accompanied by the noise, there was no movie, just memory photographs, and the desolation he'd been experiencing had diluted to grief.

Oh, he missed her. But he certainly felt better.

He picked up his second beer, wondering if it was the high speed pint that had done it. He raised the glass to the barman, said, 'Cheers,' and took a pull just as Judy appeared in the doorway.

She cast around the bar and saw him. Her hair was damp and straggly, her eyes tearful, sorrowful as she came towards him. His heart did a back-flip. She was even more beautiful than he realised.

She stopped in front of him and they said the same thing simultaneously.

'I'm sorry!'

They dissolved into laughter.

Doc spoke next, smiling. 'Would you like to join this old basket case for a drink? Peace offering?' He saw her face light up, her sorrow dissipated, and his heart did more acrobatics.

'Why not? I think Josh can wait a little longer to hear about his father... You know, I really do feel nothing for John. Even now that he's dead. Does that make me a heartless bitch?'

Doc moved his lips to her ear and whispered, 'You have the biggest heart of anyone I know.' He then kissed the nape of her neck, a tender touch that made his head spin as he breathed in her scent. 'Wow. I think I'd better get you that drink.' He wanted to make love. It was the first time he had felt that urge since the accident.

Accident.

What had he told her about her wishing John dead? About Leech? That it wasn't her fault... In the same way the car crash was not his fault. It was exactly that, an accident.

He felt lighter, as if a great load had been shifted from his soul.

He ordered Judy's drink, and then remembered he had not told her the latest on Leech.

'Forgot to mention, Leech is holed up in your apartment... Surrounded by armed police. I don't think we have to worry about him any more.'

'Well, I can't say I'm thrilled that he's in my home, but it's fantastic news if he's trapped. Well done, for yet another brilliant idea. I think we should celebrate. And I don't care if it's inappropriate because of John.' She leaned across the bar, flagged down the barman and changed the order to a bottle of champagne.

'It's not inappropriate. John was never the man you thought he was. And he was no longer part of your life. Will you go to the funeral?'

'I don't think so... I could ask John's parents to take Josh. They'd like that.'

They drank champagne, and chatted, just another couple in a London bar during a wet rush hour.

Doc's phone rang. He considered ignoring it, the cosy sensation of being with the woman he loved shunting everything else into second place.

But it was Carver's name on the display and Doc hoped it was news that Leech was in custody. He hit the button to answer.

'Hi, Jack. Have you got him?'

Doc listened, the colour washing from his features, his insides shrivelling at Carver's news.

It was after five o'clock by the time Leech arrived at Doc's street, the traffic was building and the pavements were busy as people started heading home on this grey, dismal July evening. Leech hated London, there were too many people shoving past. And he was still not comfortable with so many bodies around.

At least I'll not be spotted so easily, he thought. He had seen no policemen since leaving the tube station and was now checking house numbers, looking for the psychiatrist's home. Leech felt better here, this leafy avenue was pretty empty.

Powers was not doing badly for himself either. Leech took in the opulence, the large detached houses, expensive motors everywhere... and security cameras on some of the walls, lenses covering the front doors of the flashiest homes.

So what? There was not much chance anyone here would know him, except Powers. He wondered whether to bang on the door.

With his brother, he had not wanted to risk it. He knew Shaun would be lethal given the chance. But Powers? The fat wanker! No need to dick around. He would go straight to his door. If Powers was in, all well and good. If not he would retreat to the pub at the end of the road and try again after a few beers.

He stepped through the gate. No cameras evident here. Presumably Powers did not see himself or his home as a target in the way some of his neighbours did.

Wrong!

Leech strode to the door, one fist tucked under his coat, the shotgun in its grasp. With his other hand he pressed the bell, the chimes ringing out part of a familiar nursery rhyme. Weird choice for an old fart.

After ten or fifteen seconds he repeated the action. Looks like I'll be getting that pint then. The thought was transmitting itself to action, his feet shifting just as the door opened.

A white-haired old lady was looking him up and down as if he was a beggar or a tramp. He knew he was not appearing at his best with the bandages on his head, the plasters on his face and the blood soaked strapping on his paws all clearly visible to her.

'Are you alright?' Her voice was kindly and he immediately blamed Gruber for screwing up again, thinking he must have given him another wrong address... Unless this old dear was the fat wanker's mother. Too old to be his missus.

He adopted his most charming voice. 'I'm fine. Sorry to disturb you.' His feet were still angled away, the shotgun hidden from view by his coat and body as he stood side on to her. 'I came to see Doctor Powers. Have I got the right address?'

'Oh yes. He's due back tonight, but he's not that kind of doctor.'

The charming persona disappeared, replaced by a shotgun to her throat and a rasp from his. 'In that case I'll come in and wait.' As he shoved the gun at her she fainted, falling at his feet as if her bones had turned to mush and could no longer support her weight.

'Shit!'

He stepped inside, dragged her body into the hall and slammed the door. The stupid old bag! He had not even done anything to her! At least he was inside now. They could wait for Powers together.

The thought of the man made his balls ache, the prospect of revenge now so close he could taste it. Powers made him sick. Pretending to know him, to understand him, when he actually knew nothing. And he had betrayed him. Like that whore Finch. Powers would know where she was, and he would tell.

Leech booted the old lady in the face, her head bouncing with the impact. 'Who the fuck are you? The bastard's mother?' He would have some fun with them both. Then find the prick tease. Deal with her and piss off to the Caribbean.

He wrapped a thick bunch of white hair round his hand then winced at the sharp jolt of pain in his severed palm as he hauled the old woman along the hall and into the lounge. Once again his gaffer tape did its work on hands, feet and mouth. He was running short of it now, but did not think he would need much more. As he worked he wrinkled his nose.

'Jesus wept! You stink of piss!'

He stomped on her face and ribs for the offence to his nose, then went to explore the house.

He was half-way up the stairs when he heard it. Some sort of computer game, like they had in the arcades he had seen while walking round London the night of his release. He followed the sounds to one of the bedrooms.

A young lad was engrossed, his back to Leech, a gun held in both hands, blasting away at aliens on a giant screen. Leech was mesmerised. It looked great fun. But he preferred a real gun. He crept up behind the boy, his own weapon pointed at the screen, the barrel almost resting on the top of the lad's head.

He fired.

The screen imploded with the blast from his gun, a spectacular display of glass, fireworks and smoke.

Bloody brilliant!

The boy was rigid, his toy gun pointing still, as if his own actions had caused the disaster. Leech shouted in his ear, 'Boo!'

The gun was still hovering above the boy's head and connected with his skull as he leapt out of his chair. His voice was like a little girl's, high and shrill as he let go a terrified squeal.

He spun round and Leech recognised him immediately. It was the kid from the photo he had found at Finch's house.

What the hell was their brat doing here?

The lad was quick. In the instant Leech's mind was preoccupied with the question, the boy's foot jack-knifed into the chair, ramming it into Leech's lower body. It was a lucky hit, the corner jabbing Leech's left testicle, the shock of pain flooding his belly, doubling him up. Even so he made a grab for the boy with his left hand. He caught hold of the tee shirt and, though his lacerated fingers were numb, hung on, but the material ripped and the boy was out the door.

'Fuck!' Leech stood and fired the gun at the doorway.

Missed.

He sucked in a breath to calm his lower abdomen, filtered out the pain, and staggered after the runt, the jolting action aggravating his testicle more with each step.

He hollered after the kid, 'I'll kill you for that, you little bastard.' He frantically reloaded as he hobbled to the landing.

He reached the top of the stairs as the boy was scrabbling with the front door lock.

Don't let him get outside!

Leech, eyes watering from the sensations rampaging through his nether regions, aimed the shotgun down at the boy as the door flew open. He blinked to clear the tears and pulled the trigger as the lad bounded outside, shredding the front door with the shot.

Missed again! He would have to get out of the house now. The filth would be here in no time.

'SHIT!'

He leapt down the stairs, ignoring the insistent ache in his groin, the queasiness and fire in his belly.

What now?

Just get out. Away.

He ran into the street in time to see the little boy sprint into the road from between two parked cars. A black SUV was travelling too fast to stop. The car tossed the boy into the air like a matador being flipped by an angry bull.

Leech stopped and watched, fascinated as the limp figure crashed to the tarmac.

Served the little shit right.

Leech considered whether to go back inside now, but the police would definitely be arriving soon and he did not want to chance them linking the boy to Powers, and then knocking on the ruined door.

No. He should walk away.

He did.

Judy could see from Colin's expression that the news was not good. His face was pale as he grunted the odd monosyllable to Carver, his knuckles white as he pressed the phone to his ear. She finished the last of her champagne, convinced the celebration was over.

Colin clicked off his phone.

'He got away... Leech.'

'How?'

All the relief she had felt earlier was gone, replaced by paralysing anxiety. Was there no stopping this man? He was still out there, somewhere, and there was no way she could convince herself he was not coming for her. He had been in her house! Indigestion ripped her gullet, shooting a jet of acid champagne that bubbled up and burnt her throat.

'They think he fooled them from the outset. Made them think he wanted to negotiate. That's why he asked to see the Commissioner.' Judy could see Doc was having a eureka moment as he went on, 'He wanted to confuse the lines of authority, delay normal procedures, involve the big boss... Very clever.'

Judy did not like the sound of that one bit. Very clever? The man hunting her was being described by this incredibly intelligent man as *very clever*. Her spine chilled at that, and she certainly did not appreciate the wonderment Doc was displaying, either. She asked, 'He planned to escape all along?'

'Yes. While the police were trying to get organised he slipped out the back.'

'But my yard has a two metre wall and backs onto other flats.'

'He clambered over it, smashed his way through the apartment backing onto yours, stole a car and disappeared. It didn't take them long to link it all together and realise what had happened... but it was too late. The Tac team were still yapping with their control centre about hostage negotiation and all the while he'd already flown the coop.' She could hear the appreciation in his voice.

'Weren't there six police there? All armed?'

'There were. Not just any six coppers either. They'd all been to Hereford and undergone specialist training for this type of operation. Elite protection and hostage rescue... It didn't do them much good. He killed two of them.'

Judy wanted to be anywhere in the universe other than in the path of this monster. 'Killed them... Two more policemen?' She could not absorb it.

'One policeman. One police woman. Apparently he was executed. She died from blood loss. Leech shot her leg off and left her bleeding to death. Help was delayed for about ten minutes while they thought they had a hostage situation rather than merely an injured colleague inside. She would probably have lived if they had got to her immediately.' Doc's face had a look that suggested the world was full of evil. 'Leech used one of John's shotguns.' He finished his drink and said, 'Let's go. You still need to tell Josh about his father.'

The rain had gone now, the roads still slick, the splashing and hissing of tyres a miserable soundtrack to a depressing day. Judy was not looking forward to seeing Josh, and that was a first. Her thoughts flittered, from Josh to Leech and back. Everything was such a disaster. Her fear of Leech nudged aside by her concern for Josh and his reaction to John's death. Then it resurfaced again.

'Why did they let Leech in my house? Why didn't they stop him on the street? Ambush him? Shoot him?' Her brain clawed, desperate for understanding.

'Unfortunately, our police cannot just shoot a suspect on sight, not even a man as dangerous as Leech.' Doc thought back to the uproar over the shoot to kill policy for terrorists suspected of intending a suicide bombing. Even that seemingly reasonable approach had been slated by the liberal press after an innocent man had been shot. 'Leech was disguised as a motorcycle courier. Brilliant.'

'Brilliant? You sound like you're about to join his fan club.'

Colin gave her a look that bordered on the patronising, and said, 'The helmet covered his features, what little they could see of his hair had been dyed brown, so the team couldn't positively identify him. The four members of the squad stationed outside were waiting for a signal from the decoy. It came too late. And Leech must've immediately twigged it was a set up. He was inside before they could stop him.'

'Why the hell didn't they just grab him when he arrived? Even if they weren't sure?'

'They wouldn't want to blow their cover for the wrong guy. The courier disguise worked perfectly. He was just too quick.'

'I'm really scared Colin... No, I'm bloody petrified. He's coming for me and no one can stop him.' She started crying and he held her. They stood like that on the pavement outside the pub until an empty cab eventually arrived.

They did not speak in the taxi. Judy nestled against Doc's chest, his arm hugging her. She let out the occasional sob, fear and sorrow leaking from her.

She began to wonder who was the basket case now? She was losing it.

She sat up as they entered Colin's road, wiped her eyes and took out her compact to tidy herself up. She did not want Josh to witness her terror, to see her in pieces.

The cabbie spoke. 'I'm gonna have to drop you here, guv. Road's blocked. Looks like an accident up ahead.'

They stopped outside the pub at the end of Colin's street and Judy could see an ambulance double parked not far from his house.

She felt herself tumble into a nightmare now, her sixth sense filling her entire being with a chilling premonition. She flew out of the cab, Colin's words to her lost as she ran to the ambulance. Some bystanders blocked her view and she barged her way through, dodging under a policeman's arm as he tried to stop her. She got to the ambulance as they were loading a small body into the back.

She could hear the siren. But it was not coming from the ambulance. It was a wailing sound of torment and sadness beyond endurance.

It was her own voice.

The tiny body on the stretcher was her son's.

Doc caught up with her, the awful din she was making curdling his blood. He took in the scene. A large SUV with a damaged grill and bonnet, a pool of blood, Josh on the stretcher, his own front door open and a policeman standing beside it.

He knew.

Leech had been here. To his home.

He held Judy until her scream died away. She kept repeating, 'It's my Josh, it's my Josh,' several times, as if unable to accept it, then her words disintegrated, became a babble of unrecognisable sounds.

Doc explained to the paramedics who she was and helped her into the ambulance. She was still not fully coherent when he spoke to her.

'Sweetheart, I need to go to my house and then I'll come to the hospital.' She looked at him, uncomprehending, so he repeated his words, adding, 'I'll be there as soon as I can.'

Tears dripped off her chin as she quietened, then mumbled something that sounded like, 'Sorry.' She was clutching Josh's hand as the paramedic locked his stretcher into place. Doc jumped down and watched as the doors closed and the vehicle moved off.

He was wondering about Betty. If Leech had been here, what had he done to her? He wore concrete boots as he trudged to his house.

'This is my home. What happened?' Doc fumbled in his pocket for his identity card as he spoke to the PC on his doorstep.

'We're still making enquiries, sir. I'm afraid you can't come in just yet. Perhaps you could answer some questions—'

'Call DI Carver on this number.' Doc passed him his mobile phone. 'He's involved in this. He'll answer all your questions. Now answer mine.' He flashed his official ID and the constable blanched.

'Forensic Psychiatrist? Sorry, sir. I didn't know.'

'What happened here?' Doc's impatience was at its limit. He wanted to be with Judy, but needed to assess things first. Assess the threat from Leech. He could see some evidence already, where the shotgun had splintered his front door.

'It's not completely clear, but a neighbour saw the little boy come tearing out of the house before hiding between some cars. A man followed several seconds later. Then the boy ran out into the road and the SUV failed to stop in time in the wet. The neighbour thinks the lad may have been running away from the man.'

'He was. The man is Peter Leech. Recognise the name son?'

The policeman stuttered, 'Y-yes. How can you be so sure?'

'I just know. Radio it in and let Carver know. But first, was anyone else injured?'

'Yes.' The PC keyed his mic as he spoke to Doc. 'We're waiting for the ME and forensics. An elderly lady is bound and gagged inside. I'm afraid she's dead, sir.'

Doc fell against the door jamb. Will this never end?

Then he saw those luminous green eyes. The monster's harsh laugh clattering, like swords duelling. He looked around but it was inside his head.

No! Not that again!

The PC completed his call and said, 'Are you okay, sir? Was she a relative?' He placed his hand on Doc's shoulder.

'No. I'm not really… How did she die? Was she shot?'

'Not shot, sir. We aren't sure yet. We'll have to wait for the ME. We entered the house after speaking with the neighbour... The door was open and there was evidence of a weapon being discharged—'

'It's okay, no need to explain. I'll go to the hospital. Where did they take the little boy?'

'One minute, sir.' He keyed his mic again.

Doc sat on his doorstep, contemplating throwing up a beer and champagne cocktail. A few weeks ago he had not been sure life was worth living. Then he had found someone good, someone to live for.

How would she feel now? Her mother murdered. Her son's father killed by the same man. Josh in hospital with God knows what injuries... How would Judy take it if her boy died?

'Sir?' The PC's voice brought him back to the present. 'He's been taken to Charing Cross hospital. We can get a car to take you, but DI Carver is on his way and asked if you'd wait.'

Leech had retired to the pub at the end of Doc's street and watched the chaos he had created build as the road became blocked, the rubberneckers milling around until the police arrived with the ambulance. He was confident no one had noticed him sneak in here, all eyes having been focussed on the kid and the car driver. Not that they would think of looking in here, right under their noses, less than one hundred yards from the scene of his latest crime.

He was untouchable. They kept underestimating him. Especially that useless bunch of pussies at Judy Finch's house.

He swigged his beer, a self-satisfied smirk on his face. Two more coppers down because of him. And he could have taken out a couple more if he had wanted.

He shrugged off his coat in the warm bar. The place was empty apart from some old codgers playing dominoes. Neither of them looked up from their game as he took the shotgun from the loop around his shoulders and tucked it under his coat on the seat next to him. That's better. He relaxed, and the beer tasted good.

He could run... Catch a flight today. Things were getting dangerous now. Having shot and killed some police he knew they would be pulling out all the stops to find him. They probably had an up to date description too—that neighbour had spotted him leaving the house, had checked him out as she ran past to help the kid.

He inspected his damaged palms, the thumbs and fingertips exposed but smeared with dried blood, the white cloth stained red but not saturated. There was a *Guinness is Good for You* mirror above his seat so he checked out the wounds on his head. At least that bandage was dry.

He looked tough as nails now though, his bruises green and blue, his swollen nose a purple mess from Shaun's head butt, and red pock marks dotted his cheeks alongside the plasters that covered the worst cuts from his leap through that window.

Not bad. Even his bollock had settled down to a mild ache.

The little toe-rag. I hope he dies.

Typical, really. Now he had decided he didn't want Birdy she probably wouldn't be lumbered with a kid...

He still wanted to punish her. For leading him on like that. Then betraying him for no reason—he had done nothing to hurt her! And she had never even called. Not once.

Maybe he would phone Powers again. He rooted around in his pockets, the two police issue handguns clinking against their ammunition clips as he searched for John's mobile.

It was off. He did not understand. He poked at the buttons, trying to remember what the salesman had told him when he bought his a few days ago.

Friday. His first day out. What day was it now? Tuesday? Wednesday? He was not sure, but he was certain he could not turn the phone on.

Dead battery?

Yeah. Probably.

He tossed it aside and gazed out the window.

That Powers was such a bastard. Leech definitely would like to beat the fat wanker to death. Oh yes. The smartarse had tried to trick him too.

But I'm better than you, Powers.

Something occurred to him then, the thought that had flashed through his mind when he'd recognised the kid's face. Finch's brat. What was he doing at Powers' house?

Then he twigged. Of course, she would need somewhere to stay while the pigs had been in her home waiting for him… So her and Powers must be real friendly.

The familiar sensation of envy swirled, a vortex of evil intent inside him, as a taxi stopped outside the pub, two lovers in the back snuggling together, head to head, arms entwined.

It was her! Birdy! And Powers!

He's been shagging my bird!

Even though he had already dismissed her as a traitorous bitch, unworthy of him, the sight of the two of them, all lovey-dovey, especially after what they had tried to do to him with the police ambush, incensed him.

He would kill them. No question about it.

He sank his pint, and considered what to do. He would finish them right now. He grabbed the shotgun, ready to stride outside and blow them to hell.

But he was too late.

Through the window he saw Birdy was already out of the cab, sprinting up the road to her kid. And now the fat wanker was paying the driver.

He had missed his moment to get them both. If he went out with guns blazing now, he would almost certainly get himself caught before he could top both of them. He watched Powers jog after Birdy.

No. He let go of the gun and tucked it under his coat again. Forced himself to go to the bar instead, ordered himself a scotch. The last time he had tried the spirit was from his father's drinks cabinet when he was fifteen. He drank over half the bottle and vomited, and vowed never to drink the stuff again.

He threw back the spirit, the burning sensation a reminder of his youthful binge, the heat inflaming his hatred and anger. He ordered a second and then went back to his observation point.

There must be a better way. The scotch was coursing through him, dulling his aches and pains, helping him think with clarity. The answer was obvious.

The hospital. The brat would be taken to hospital. He would head there. Mummy was bound to show up too.

Yeah. The hospital.

He checked his reflection again in the Guinness mirror and beamed a huge toothless grin at what he saw.

Hospital. I'll fit in perfectly there!

'Hi, Doc… Sorry about this. Give me a minute and I'll run you to the hospital. Why not wait in the car?' Jack's voice pierced through the fug of his brain.

A WPC helped Doc to his feet. He was still on the doorstep when Carver had arrived, his brain shut down, overloaded from all he had experienced in the last few months. He had no idea how much time had elapsed while he had been sitting and he felt like an old man as the young female officer helped him to the car.

Pull yourself together. You're no use to anyone like this.

At least his hallucination had gone now. And there had been nothing about Natalie, no visions, no movies, no screams. Just Leech's eyes burning into him, the manic laugh taunting him, while he sat waiting. His mind had fought to clear the image, deaden the sound, and then closed itself down, like a computer on standby.

He was exhausted. Yet Leech was free… Where would he go now?

Doc waited, trying to fathom what could be motivating the killer. Carver's bulk rocked the car as he got in.

'Got an unmarked patrol car today. My Saab's off the road… How you feeling, Doc? You look like shit.' He fastened his belt and set off.

Doc had not even noticed he was in a different car. He tried to switch on again.

'I feel worse than shit. And Judy… God knows how she's feeling. Any news on Josh?'

'Her boy? He's in surgery. Some broken bones, possibly fractured skull, and some internal organs may be damaged. Doesn't look good.' Carver was matter-of-fact but Doc knew he still felt it inside—even the most hard-bitten coppers hated to see kids harmed.

'In the space of a few days, her life's been turned upside down by Leech. Her ex, her mother, Josh… Even her home's been invaded… And my place too, and that was supposed to be her sanctuary. I thought they would be safe there.'

'Hindsight is a wonderful thing. Bet you wish you'd never let the fruit loop loose.'

Doc did not appreciate the comment, never did like the stating-the-bleeding-obvious approach to problems. He ignored it.

Stay focussed.

'He came to my home… For what reason? To kill me? Possibly. Your competition theory… Or he may even blame me for the police presence at Judy's flat.'

'You? Why? Because you spoke with him about her?'

'Yes. That could be justification enough to him. The alternative is less palatable.'

Carver was negotiating traffic, occasionally using his horn and headlights to hurry things along. He stared at Doc long enough to worry his passenger, the road ahead was congested and they were moving fast.

'Jack!'

Carver returned his attention to the matter in hand, swerved round a taxi, hit the siren to make it seem as if he meant it.

'Sorry. What's less palatable than Leech coming after you? Coming to kill you?'

'Perhaps he knew Judy would be there.' Had he gone there to wait for Judy to return?

'How could he have known that?'

'I don't know... Maybe we should be asking who knew she was there. Who could've told him. Inadvertently. Or otherwise.'

Carver burnt rubber as he swung into the hospital entrance, then screeched to a halt in the ambulance bay.

He gave Doc a hard look. 'Come off it. Conspiracy now? You think someone on our side would help this guy? He's shot four policemen. Three are dead. One is critical, almost certainly blinded.'

Doc had almost forgotten about the policemen at Hammersmith who had escorted him on his trip back from Bristol, it seemed so long ago.

'I didn't mean...' His voice faded. He was not thinking clearly, not sure what to say any more. Befuddled. 'You're right. We should assume he came for me. That I'm a target now.'

'You were a target the moment you and Judy became an item.'

'Not if he didn't know, Jack. And I ask again, how could he know these things? About Judy and me, about her living in my house?'

Carver pursed his lips. 'You've got a point. Whatever, we should get you some protection too. I'll square it with the PTBs.'

'While you're at it can you get an armed guard to watch over Josh? If anything more happens to him...' Doc could not conceive of how Judy would react. He willed Carver to say yes.

Carver spoke gently, but his attitude was sceptical. 'Are you honestly telling me the lad's in danger?'

'Leech could've been trying to abduct him. To draw Judy to him. I really don't know, but please...'

'Okay, I'll get them both an armed guard. The good news is that Leech is hurt.'

'Really? But not badly enough, it would seem.'

'I don't know, Doc. His head and hands are swathed in bloody bandages according to the neighbour who saw him leave your place. Should make it easy for us to catch him now. The update is with every beat bobby and patrol car in London. Fingers crossed, eh, mate?'

'That seems to be what we need to catch Leech.' Doc opened the car door as he spoke. 'Luck. Just about everything else is failing us. He's a regular Houdini.'

'Yeah, and look what happened to him!'

As Carver drove off, Doc was trying to remember what had happened to the magician. He had seen a film about the man when he was a boy.

Oh yes.

He died, trying to escape.

Doc crossed his fingers.

Leech went to the bar and asked the barman, 'Hey, mate. I'm not feeling too great, where's the nearest casualty department?'

'I did wonder when I saw you come in. You don't look too good, pal. The nearest Accident and Emergency is at Charing Cross hospital. You been in a fight with a lawnmower?'

'Nah! Fell through a window. Patched meself up and came for a few jars. But I feel like shit.' He rubbed a hand over his lower belly and added, 'Think I might've ruptured something too.'

The barman pointed at the window, the ambulance visible as it passed the bar, lights flashing. 'Shame you couldn't hitch a lift with that, eh? They'll be from Charing Cross. Sit down, and I'll order a taxi. Don't go fainting on me though, will you?'

Leech returned to his seat, well satisfied. He would sort Finch. And then Powers. After that he would disappear. He poked around in his coat pockets and found the fake passport, thinking how handy the huge poacher's pouches were, so much better than lugging a bag around. He fondled the document, slipped it into his jeans back pocket.

He should lose the Barbour. He had been seen wearing it too many times already. The rain had stopped and he could buy himself another jacket later. He made the decision, went to the bathroom, miming to the barman that he was about to throw up. Once inside the gents he emptied the pockets, stuffed the coat in the rubbish bin, smashed the shotgun butt on the toilet cistern, shattering the wood and removing a chunk of porcelain simultaneously. He rammed the bits under the coat, thinking it was a shame, he had grown rather fond of the weapon.

He untucked his shirt, poked one police pistol in his waistband, discarded the other, jammed a couple of spare clips of ammunition in his pocket along with a can of pepper spray he had salvaged from his would be ambushers, shoved the remaining duct tape in the other, and selected a small round plastic container for his next task.

He opened the box and removed the blue contacts Gruber had given him. He was impressed with the effect. His eyes sparkled a Caribbean turquoise. He looked fantastic!

He chucked the remaining items into the bin, and went back to the bar, clutching his head for effect, avoiding eye contact with the barman who said, 'Taxi's outside, mate.'

He grunted his thanks, went out and sank into the back seat of the cab. The driver pulled away, confirming his destination but saying nothing more, leaving his passenger to suffer in silence.

Ten minutes later he arrived at the hospital.

'Hello. I wonder if you can help me.' Leech was in the Accident and Emergency reception, but there was no sign of Birdy or her kid. He turned up his charisma levels, smiled toothlessly at the nurse, a young girl oozing compassion and sympathy.

'I'll certainly try. You've been in the wars, haven't you?'

'Fraid so. But I'm more worried about my nephew. He was just brought in… Hit by a car. Name's Finch.'

She checked her computer, and moments later said. 'Joshua? He's in theatre. You can wait?'

Damn. He did not want to hang about. He glanced around, worried the police would be here. They were never far from a Casualty Department, many of their 'clients' often finding themselves in need of treatment.

The nurse saw his frown, and smiled at him. 'His mother's here. She's in the relative's room. She could probably do with some company right now.' She gave him directions, probably mistaking his gummy grin as thanks for a job well done.

Perfect. He had her now. At last. Six weeks since he had met her and he would finally be with her. He felt himself harden, aroused at the prospect.

Oh yes, Birdy. We'll play a little. And then I'll finish you off. Make sure lover boy Powers is in mourning again... when he dies.

He let his thoughts dwell on what he would do to them, the anticipation of revenge delicious, a flavour to be savoured and enjoyed. He swaggered through the corridors, bounded up the three flights of stairs and found the relatives' suite. Room three, the nurse had said.

The blinds were down, no one could see into the room. Or out. He placed his hand on the doorknob and, with his penis engorged and throbbing, drank in the moment, groped for something in his pocket, then opened the door.

———

'He's still in surgery.' The nurse on reception looked about twenty years old to Doc, fresh faced and cheery in this place of broken bones and mangled bodies, of gushing wounds and terrible trauma. Misery all around and she appeared for all the world as if she was at a picnic or theme park. She chirped at him, 'You can wait upstairs. Third floor, family room three. His mother and uncle are there.'

'Uncle?' Judy's brother had died years ago and she had told him John was an only child. His mind cranked slowly, still suffering from the shock of his recent experiences. 'That can't be right.'

'Oh yes. He arrived several minutes ago.' She was reacting to the alarm in his eyes, her own transmitting caring concern. 'He was pretty badly injured himself. His head—'

'And hands were bandaged?' She was nodding, expression shifting to bewilderment as Doc backed away, his voice urgent, demanding. 'Call security and the police. His name's Leech. He's armed and extremely dangerous.'

She dithered, gave him a look that told him she thought he was a madman. He pulled out his ID and slung it at her.

'I'm with the police. DO IT NOW!'

He ran to the stairs, not bothering to check whether she was doing as he said. His palms were sweaty as he gripped the rail with one hand, the other clutching his mobile. His foot slipped off a step as he hit the speed-dial number for Carver, the phone spinning from his fingers, tumbling down the stairs and exploding into pieces as it landed.

'SHIT!'

He flew up the steps, three at a time, collided with an old man hobbling down who smacked him on the head with his stick as he ricocheted past.

He did not stop. He ignored the abuse that echoed after him, his own mind full of horrors far worse than the old boy could ever wish on him.

An illusion, a hallucination appeared that almost stopped him in his tracks. It was Leech, raping Judy from behind, his green eyes alight, his face leering at Doc. He managed to fight through it, stopped a nurse and asked her, 'Where's family room three?'

She stared down at his hand. He was gripping her arm, his fingers white from the pressure as they dug deep into her flesh. He forced himself to release her, eyes frantic, jerking round the hall looking for a sign to guide him.

'Do you realise that's assault, sir? You need to calm down. And please don't run in the corridors... Room three is straight on, second on the left.'

If she said anything else he did not hear her. The adrenalin pumped through him, his ears roared, his heart hammered and his lungs swelled. He was out of shape but he sprinted for the room, not sure what he would do when he got there.

He had no weapon. Nothing to handle Leech with. What was he doing? He didn't know, he only knew he had to get to Judy. Now.

He turned into the passageway and crashed into a trolley. The patient was feet first toward him and Doc doubled over as the metal railing slammed into his belly, knocking the air from his lungs. His head swung down from the momentum of the impact and cracked on the man's plastered leg. They both yelped. Doc shoved the trolley away as the orderly made a grab for him, throwing himself at the door marked number three.

He hit it full pelt, blasting it open with his shoulder, bursting in, hardly slowing.

His hallucination was real.

Leech was behind Judy, her small frame bent over the back of the sofa, his hands round her throat, her face puce from lack of oxygen, a strip of grey tape on her mouth and more of the same binding her hands. Her eyes bulged in recognition and terror as Doc burst in.

His emotions congealed into an overwhelming mass of fury at the sight. He registered Leech's eyes as the thug's head jerked toward the door. They were blue in this light and the battered face barely recognisable, but there was no doubt it was Leech. The bandaged hands and head, the sick, smug smile Doc had glimpsed at the parole hearing.

He was still moving as he took it all in, his legs pounding into the room, barely five paces between them. Leech let go of Judy and turned to face him, his manhood angry and red, poking proud of his jeans zipper.

Doc was conscious of it all, his outrage and wrath powering him towards the odious creature. In a moment of total clarity he became aware of the balcony behind Leech. And the open door at the man's back...

Doc had never played rugby. But he had watched it.

He slammed into Leech, ducking his head below the outstretched hand, his skull connecting with the solid midriff, the obscene penis waggling in Doc's face as he connected.

It was like hitting a brick wall headfirst and at that moment Doc knew he was going to die.

But his own flabby bulk, his momentum, and the sheer force of his animal rage, took Leech by surprise. The bigger man stumbled back towards the balcony, his hands scrabbling and groping, then linking under Doc's chest, hugging him under the armpits, trying to regain his balance and get some purchase.

Doc would not have believed he had any reserves, felt Leech's immense power start to crush his ribs, but yet more adrenalin swamped his system as he struggled. He felt his ribs starting to crack just as Leech's tee shirt rode up, exposing a handgun right before Doc's eyes. He let go of Leech with his right hand, and grabbed at the weapon, accidentally pulling the trigger as he tried to wrench it from Leech's waistband.

The detonation so close to his face stunned Doc and he let go of the gun as Leech's inner thigh flowered into a red rose of bloody flesh, the wound giving Doc the edge. Leech grunted with the pain, faltered but held on.

Doc was unrelenting, seizing the advantage, he ploughed forward, arms clamped round Leech's buttocks again, lifting and toppling Leech backwards. They hit the balcony wall like that, in a deadly embrace.

Doc's fingers were crushed on impact, the combined speed and weight of their bodies driving the delicate bones into the concrete, rupturing his joints. He didn't feel it. His feet kept moving, shoving, determined to push Leech over. He could sense Leech was weakening from the wound in his leg, his lifeblood pulsing from a ravaged artery.

Leech pivoted back over the balcony wall, his legs swung up either side of Doc and he howled a hellbound scream as gravity started to take effect.

Doc had him.

But Leech had Doc too.

Their momentum kept them moving, toppling them both over the parapet. Leech's legs flailed then clasped Doc's hips as they swung out above three storeys of nothingness.

Doc tried to stop himself, but it was too late. He had over-committed. He thought he heard Judy call his name as, entwined with Leech in some perverse parody of gay lovers, they went over the balcony together.

EPILOGUE

A LIFE AFTER DEATH

'DYING DIDN'T HURT.' He was talking to Natalie. She was floating with him, her beauty radiating, dazzling.

'You aren't dead, honey.' Her smile dissolved him.

He was confused.

'I must be dead. I'm with you.'

'No, you're not.' It wasn't Natalie. It was Judy. How could he have made that mistake? He heard her calling to him now, her face a halo of sunlight. 'Come back to me, Colin. Can you hear me? Don't you dare leave me…'

He spun away.

He was a light. A fluorescent. A strip light with a faulty starter. He was on the ceiling and, below him, in the strobe effect he was creating, he saw a bed, machines, a man, bandaged, legs under a canopy, wires and tubes leading from his body to the machines. And a woman sitting with him, weeping.

The woman was familiar.

She spoke.

'Colin. Can you hear me?'

His light flickered.

She was gone.

Then nurses came. Cleaning the man. It was him. He looked destroyed. It didn't matter. He felt nothing.

'Hey, Doc? You awake?'

Carver's voice hovered above him. Where was he now? He couldn't see, the lights blinding him.

'Jack? I'm here.' He thought he spoke, but could not hear his voice.

'Nurse!' Carver's voice, moving away from him now. 'His eyes opened. Just for a few seconds…'

Natalie was back. They drifted and chatted. He felt fabulous. Then her voice shifted again.

'Colin. Look at me. I'm here. It's Judy.'

Her face. The halo, again.

'I'm fine, Judy. I feel good.' He still could not hear his voice.

Blackness.

His eyes hurt, refused to focus. Too much light overloaded his optic nerves, blurring his view. Then everything clicked into place with a clarity well beyond his normal vision.

Carver was sitting by the bedside, reading a magazine. His nose was covered with black pores and fine hairs—Doc had never noticed those before. And lying where he was he could see the black bristles, short and stubby, poking from Carver's nostrils.

He laughed.

And this time he heard himself. A bubble and rattle that hurt his throat. There was a tube there.

Carver dropped his magazine, startled. 'Doc! You're back!' He went to the door and called, 'Nurse! He really is awake this time.'

He was not awake for long, but Carver was still with him when he re-surfaced.

He felt alive with pain, all over his body. He did not laugh this time, he groaned as he woke.

'Glad you could join us, Doc. How you doing?'

It hurt to speak, but at least the tube had gone.

'I don't know, but I need something for the pain.'

'You're already on a morphine drip and I don't think they plan on giving you a shedload more of the stuff… You've been under for three days.' Carver's expression was filled with warmth and sympathy, his mouth curving into a smile, his eyes twinkling. 'Some people will do anything to get a few days off!'

'Why am I in here?' He tried to think back. Was it the car crash? It couldn't be that, he remembered coming out of hospital already. 'What happened?'

'You really don't remember?'

Doc was tired, wanted to sleep, the short period of concentration draining him. But he needed to know.

'No.'

'You're a real life super-hero.' He held up his magazine with a picture of Doc on the front page. The headline screamed, 'Flying Doctor to the rescue!'

Flying? Doc had been flying with Natalie in his dream… It must have been a dream because he knew she was dead.

He wanted to know more, but his throat was too sore to speak. He waited for Carver to explain.

'Leech? You must remember Leech! He was assaulting your Judy. He'd arrived here, at this hospital, about five minutes before I dropped you off to see Josh.'

Carver raised his eyebrows, trying to see some sign that Doc remembered.

It started to come back.

'Josh… He was hit by a car. How is he?' His voice was croaky and dry. Carver held a glass of water with a straw to his mouth. It tasted delicious.

'He was smashed up pretty bad. Broke both legs, had some internal injuries and a fractured skull. They took his spleen out… But they reckon he'll make it. Judy's with him now.'

Judy? The thought of her energised him, his voice stronger now. 'She's okay, then?'

'Yeah. She took a load of pepper spray in her eyes. Leech hosed her the moment he walked in the door. Whacked her in the chops, almost knocking her cold, and then nigh on throttled her… Well, then you arrived… She's bearing up. She'll be thrilled to see you awake.'

'Leech?' He could not remember the details but he knew the name tasted vile to his tongue. He decided he would never utter it again.

'Leech? Oh, you pancaked him! After you rugby tackled him, shot him in the leg, and then tried to fly him off the balcony some thirty-odd feet above the ground. You landed on top of him… He died, but saved your life in a funny sort of way. Ironic, huh?'

Doc still could not remember. He was not sure he wanted to.

'Me?' He could not ask the whole question, his eyelids were desperate to close and his throat was refusing to acknowledge his brain as he tried to speak.

'You? What? Apart from being one lucky son-of-a-bitch? Broken back, but no permanent spinal damage. Legs were shattered, you've got enough metal in your shins and ankles to set off the alarms at Heathrow security next time you hobble through, mate. Both your arms were broken, clean fractures at the wrist and elbow. Not that you'll be playing tennis for a while with your busted hands. You dislocated both shoulders. Got some internal bruising, so you'll be pissing blood for a while…'

Doc was asleep.

———

Judy's voice. 'Hey, hero, it's me.'

His eyes opened. His pain was gone thanks to the morphine and he was euphoric at the sight of her, the smell of her.

'Hi… I'm a bit broken.'

'Yes. The doctors say you're amazingly strong.' She was smiling, yet tears were dribbling as she said, 'They nicknamed you Superman. You know, leaps off tall buildings?'

He wanted to laugh, but thought better of it, morphine drip or not.

'My legs, though…'

'Yes. It's going to be a long time before you'll be leaping anywhere.'

She held onto his fingertips—the only part of his arm visible, protruding from the end of the white cast. She leaned over and kissed him on the lips.

In that moment he felt fantastic as he inhaled her essence, his body awash with tingling heat.

She whispered to him, her wet eyes dripping tears onto his cheeks.

'Don't worry, my love. I'll help you walk again… We'll start with baby steps.'

MUTILATED

A BRITISH CRIME THRILLER

DOC POWERS & D.I. CARVER INVESTIGATE

THE REMORSELESS TRILOGY
BOOK TWO

'RIGHT UP THERE WITH JAMES PATTERSON AND STEPHEN KING.'

PROLOGUE

A NIGHTMARE DISCOVERY

THE OLD MAN'S dog bounded in and out of the bushes as it sniffed its way round Clapham Common, searching for odours to savour and maybe some squirrels to worry. His owner, hobbling along behind, using a cane to aid progress hampered by his arthritic hips, heard his terrier as it started yapping and growling with excitement. It was a distinctive noise, one the man recognised. His curious mutt had discovered something out of the ordinary.

The dog was waiting for him, quivering, tail beating a steady rhythm, his head switching between the old man and the focus of his excitement. The yapping quietened to a throaty grumble punctuated by whimpering, as if the dog was asking his owner what it was he had found.

Although his eyesight was no longer good, particularly in the dawn half-light, Gerald Butler could make out the shape as he stepped tentatively through the sodden undergrowth, and at first, thought it looked like the top half of a clothes store mannequin. Alabaster white, with a hairless head perched atop a limbless torso, with ribs and collarbone in sharp relief.

The head was slumped on to the chest, looking down at him.

Or at least it would have been except it had none of the usual features, just two dark orifices where the nostrils should be, with the surface of the rest of the face smoothed over. No eyes, no mouth and no ears. As if the factory had made a cursory attempt at realism with the breathing holes but not bothered to finish the rest of the human facial form.

As the old man approached the figure, he began wondering who had hung it there, upright against the trunk of this towering oak tree, with supporting wires stretching from its rear to the branches above, and why they would do such a thing. It had been positioned close to the footpath but just out of sight, and now, as he began to distinguish more detail, he realised the object he was peering at was stranger still.

Although the body was also smooth, there appeared to be thick, livid pink lines at the truncations where the shoulder and hip joints should be, in distinct contrast to the unearthly luminous paleness of the abdomen. On closer inspection he could see more jagged pink stripes on the head. And the pudendum looked odd too, like the plastic had been badly welded where the crotch should be.

He shrugged and turned to go as he called Smudge to follow, but the terrier just kept growling and whining while standing on his hindquarters, front paws clawing at the tree, snuffling and sniffing at the thing, then appealing to his master, eyes alert, intelligent, trying to communicate something. But what?

Gerald had seen all manner of horrors in his long life, some terrible things still buried in the murky depths of his memory, brought out for inspection only on rare occasions these days. He never discussed his time in Kenya, serving the British Empire as its post-war sphere of influence waned and the locals fought bloody battles for their independence. He had been a good military man, fresh out of school, had followed orders, that was all.

Yes, he had helped intern the dissidents, had 'disciplined' the worst of them, had 're-educated' the Mau Mau thugs, castrating the men with fire and pincers. Had pierced some eardrums with a screwdriver. Had done rather more than merely witness dark-skinned limbs being hacked from screaming adult males…

But he knew he was a decent man at heart, a good soldier, a patriot, a caring grandfather, a kindly old soul—one who had no desire to rekindle those memories right here, right now.

Yet, as he turned back at Smudge's bidding, finally closing in on the hideous object to satisfy his own curiosity at his dog's behest, he felt his heart start to canter wildly and his breath shuddered a hoarse rasp from his throat. At first he doubted his own failing eyesight, but as he placed his hand on the pallid breast he knew he was not mistaken.

It was no mannequin, no tailor's dummy.

His fingers flew away at the touch of cool flesh and he realised he was staring at a dismembered body, desecrated and ruined beyond recognition, but definitely human. Of that, there was no doubt in Gerald's now fevered mind.

But his brain still scrambled to make some sense of what he was seeing, demanding to know who had placed these remains here, just a few metres from the footpath, the route of his and Smudge's regular pre-dawn walk. He immediately concluded that this was no coincidence—the disfigured body had been placed here, for him to find.

As the discovery catapulted him back to his long dormant past, conjuring in his mind's eye a world of screaming madness, of suffering and torment, he cursed the person who had done this to him.

Then, worse, much worse, was the sudden realisation that the thing seemed to be moving. Gerald once again reached out, this time with tentative trembling fingers, their tips sensing the unmistakable texture of human skin while simultaneously registering the evident movement. The chest was rising and falling, almost imperceptibly, but definitely breathing.

While his overwrought mind tumbled and twisted, he tried to process the enormity and implications of Smudge's discovery. Then he backed away, his cane tumbling to the undergrowth as he became unbalanced, the shock slamming his heart against his ribs, his mind spinning like a Catherine wheel.

The old man stumbled, then felt his hip crack against a prominent tree root, pain searing through his body as he collapsed to the ground. He groaned as Smudge bounded to him, nuzzling his face, barking softly, urging him to get up. As Gerald Butler tried to haul himself upright, fumbling with his cane and then putting weight on his legs, he screeched, unable to stifle the agony.

The grinding bone and torn nerves screamed at him, blinding him, ripping through the reawakened memories saturating his mind. Then he collapsed again as the refuge of unconsciousness enfolded him and Smudge's soft pink tongue washed his bristled cheek.

BANK HOLIDAY MONDAY

A BLAST FROM THE PAST

DETECTIVE INSPECTOR JACK CARVER squinted up at the louring sky, wondering if he was going to get soaked if the heavens opened again.

He was not happy. He'd had to hike almost a kilometre from his car to this spot and there was pretty much nothing to see by the time he'd got here. Some blue and white crime scene police tape had been draped around the bushes and undergrowth surrounding the ancient oak tree he was now sheltering under, as four local constables did a fingertip search of the immediate area, looking for gawd knows what, he thought.

After checking in with one of them, he took possession of the tablet with the crime scene photographs they had taken before the body had been unhooked and carted off to hospital. A few swipes of the screen later, Jack finished reviewing the images, then made a cursory inspection of what little evidence they had already bagged. Two items. Stainless steel wires, each with fearsome looking barbless fish hooks attached to the end, both with traces of blood and tissue on them. The hooks had been removed from the flesh in the victim's upper back by the paramedics before they put him in the ambulance, and the wires released from the miniature pulleys securing them to the branches, then tagged and bagged.

Carver considered launching into a tirade about the officers messing with his crime scene before he'd had a chance to inspect things in situ, then took pity on the small team. All four were on their hands and knees, meticulously scouring the immediate surroundings, despite the ground being saturated from overnight storms. Their forensic suits were paper thin and offered little protection from the mud, let alone the thorny undergrowth, and they had found themselves here at the end of a night shift, forced into reluctant overtime by the sergeant at the understaffed local police station on the western side of the common.

Instead, he muttered under his breath before checking the grass either side of the footpath for tyre marks. Nothing visible, even though the ground was soft. So, no joy there, he thought, before stomping his way back to his car, his mood darkening to match the threatening skies. He had been assigned to the Homicide and Major Crimes Command at Scotland Yard for almost two years but had been hoiked off a high-profile serial murder case this morning to take on this rather less sexy instance of grievous bodily harm, and he was not best pleased.

He knew the reassignment made sense, but that did little to ease his grumpiness. He had just about cracked the 'Brentwood Beast' case—the label the press had given his quarry, and a term his colleagues had adopted with some relish. They were almost ready to charge their suspect, a man they already had in custody, just waiting for the Crown Prosecution Service to give the nod, so Jack did not appreciate his boss, Soundbite Sadie Dawson, an over-promoted female with an inflated sense of self-importance combined with a gift for office politics and media showboating, dragging him from his bed at the crack of sparrow fart. It was supposed to be his well-earned day of rest, too...

Oh well, he decided, maybe it would be an even bigger feather in his cap if he managed to solve this latest crime, along with the cold case Soundbite had suggested might be related.

Sometimes he wondered if the witch actually slept. She had a habit of calling in the early hours as if determined to prove she could not only keep up with the best males on the force but outdo them in the number of hours she put in. He begrudgingly gave her her due. She must be another Maggie Thatcher, one of those lucky buggers who could function perfectly well on just four hours sleep a night.

If only, he thought.

He turned up his collar as the wind freshened, gusts now buffeting him as he walked, day-dreaming about what he would do if he could find another few waking hours a day.

A speck of rain fell on his nose, so he picked up the pace, almost breaking into a trot. Only a few hundred metres to go. But luck was not on his side. The skies ripped with an ominous yellow flash, accompanied by a vibrating crash and rumble as lightning struck a solitary birch tree at the edge of his peripheral vision. He sprinted as the deluge saturated much of south London, the late summer storm blasting fat pebbles of water at him, bouncing them off his head, each with an uncomfortable thud, with yet more jumping into newly formed puddles as he splashed along the path to his car. Drenched, he opened the door to his BMW, slid into the now damp seat and cursed his luck for the second time today.

He fastened the seat belt and headed for St George's Hospital, wondering if there would be yet more to sour his mood, as, although he did not consider himself a superstitious man, he knew bad things always came in threes.

Doctor Colin Powers had risen early that morning in the hope of getting on with the research for his upcoming TV series and accompanying book. As usual, his first task, after making himself a large latte, involved checking his email. And, also as usual, he got diverted from the task in hand by the contents of his inbox.

Displacement activity, he thought, a twinge of guilt rippling his brow as he did so. Sometimes it seemed as though anything was better than getting on with his work these days, or at least what passed for work.

He was in his study, looking out over his garden as rain lashed the windows and the heavy skies ripped and crackled with high voltage energy. Although it was almost eight in the morning on this August bank holiday Monday, he had to switch on the desk lamp to dispel the gloom.

Muggy weather was enervating at the best of times, but for Doc it was worse. Humidity compounded the sensations he could feel, the surgical pins and plates in his body reacting, as if under some external pressure, twisting his limbs and joints, accentuating the residual aches and pains he continued to suffer from his supposedly mended bones.

Ignoring the discomfort, he tried to concentrate on the screen of his MacBook. He preferred working here, sitting at his desk, even though the laptop computer could be used pretty much anywhere.

Work mode.

Doc grimaced at the thought. He found it difficult to focus, had felt that way ever since he'd allowed his life to spin off in a direction he'd never planned.

Chasing fame and fortune. Things he had never really desired. Symptoms of a mid-life crisis.

Regrets, I've had a few…

The framed photograph pricked his conscience, the image of Judy Finch and her son Josh, sitting on a beach at Brighton with Doc, all three faces glowing with happiness, unaware of what was to become of them all in the coming months and years. Josh and the person holding the camera, Judy's wonderful mother, had both passed on and, despite Doc's best efforts, his relationship with Judy had died as a result.

With a grunted rebuke at himself for wasting time reminiscing, he focused on his inbox, scanning dozens of email titles before highlighting most and then dumping them in the trash.

Fan mail.

He snorted as he deleted them all, along with one piece of hate mail. Two interview requests from magazines he had never heard of, also binned. A university in the US wanted him to speak to a Forensic Psych class in Milwaukee in their first semester. A polite rejection.

Then he spotted the note from Celene Brooks, an old friend and colleague he had lost touch with, now the chief administrator of Broadmoor, the UK's most secure hospital for the criminally insane. Her email was headed:

A letter arrived for you Doc. Didn't you tell people you'd retired?!!

Celene was a very highly regarded psychotherapist with a wicked sense of humour, so her email immediately piqued his interest, especially as he had not worked at Broadmoor for several years. Doc sipped some coffee as he opened her note and viewed the attachments.

Hi Doc,

It's been a while and I've been meaning to congratulate you on your excellent TV series last year, but this is something altogether more serious.

We received the attached letter and gruesome images through the post this morning, in an envelope addressed to you. I have already informed the local police and my boss at the Home Office, but wanted you to hear directly from me.

As you know, we always open mail for staff and inmates alike, and although you no longer officially work as a consultant here we felt it was best to check the contents, especially as we had already opened an identical envelope addressed to a third party. An inmate.

It turned out that the two envelopes contained the same contents. That is strange enough, but I'm sorry to inform you that the other addressee is Antony Harding. Of course, he is unaware of the letters or the contents, or that you were both targeted recipients.

I hope this is nothing more than a dreadful prank, perhaps perpetrated by a disgruntled former inmate determined to cause some emotional distress, possibly someone you were involved with who is jealous of your celebrity status, maybe prompted by your TV series. I have no idea if the images are even genuine, given the abilities of any competent Photoshop expert, but I found them disturbing and hence, potentially so.

Bearing in mind that your rather distressing history with Harding is hardly a secret, my first thought is that this is probably nothing more than mischief making. I hope so.

However, I know you would prefer the unvarnished facts and will want to consider all possibilities. I apologise for being the bearer of bad news and hope this does not come as too much of a shock to you.

Please call me when you have had a chance to consider the attachments.

With kind regards,

Celene Brooks PhD, MBChB, MD, FRCPsych
Chief Executive Officer

Harding?

That was a name from Doc's past, one he would prefer not to be reminded of, but here it was, in ugly black and white. He scrolled down the page and gasped at some even uglier images. They certainly looked real to him. And one of them, he recognised immediately.

A shaven-headed Caucasian girl had been dismembered. Her torso had raw open wounds where the limbs had been removed, her face a mask of disfigured meat where her lips, nose and eyelids should have been. The eye sockets were empty and her ears and tongue were gone. Her breasts had been carved away leaving gaping wounds that bared the bones of her upper rib cage.

Doc was familiar with a similar image, definitely the same victim, but this photograph was not one from her police file, of that he was certain, as he had selected the girl to feature in one of the episodes for his first TV series on unsolved crimes. The scanned photograph had been shot at a location that differed from the site where the girl had been discovered, and was almost certainly a memento taken by her murderer.

He checked the other two images, both similarly mutilated and posed for maximum effect.

During his career helping the police solve numerous sadistic murders he had seen many victims of psychopathic crime—his area of expertise—often in the flesh. He had become hardened over the years, but each of these images was designed to shock, the impact made worse by their unexpected arrival in his inbox.

He struggled to concentrate on the photographs, forcing himself to inspect the savagely devastated remains as dispassionately as he could. The technique was rusty, but he managed to compartmentalise his mind, part of his brain screaming in outrage while a murky corner of his consciousness became aroused, fascinated.

He shrugged off the disgust he felt at his own callous reaction—another reason he had resigned from his role as forensic consultant for the police several years ago—and concentrated on the attachment, a letter, with no salutation, though the words were clearly aimed at Doc.

Secrets.
Those closeted skeletons, the unwashed linen hidden from prying eyes, the shadowed stains upon the soul.
Everyone tries to smother them, the evil deeds and rancid thoughts they hug to them-selves. Feeble cringing creatures, terrified of the response their revelations would garner, they hide them, buried deep within their anima, festering, denied even to their dearest friends and closest family members.
I derive great joy from such secrets. I harvest them.
But what does it take to pluck confessions of heinous deeds and sinful desires from their bosoms, to drag them into the light, to examine them, to share them?
It is so simple. Just two things are required.
Pain.
And, of course, someone unique.
Me.
My craft is truly fascinating:
I collect the most private treasures from the damaged souls I release while creating fantastic new secrets of my own. Such humble specimens, yet I get closer to my own immortality through my actions, through the enlightenment I gain from my chosen path. My criminal undertakings…
Society's petty laws mean nothing to me. Society means nothing to me.
And I suspect, these things mean little to you too. But we do differ.
I have embraced true evil and relish its ubiquitous nature.
Does that make me insane?
I don't think so. But you, good doctor, may disagree…
You claim to understand people like me. Is that because you are?
Like me?
I believe so, and as I watched your trashy TV series in which you claimed to unravel the knotted threads of unsolved crimes, I wondered why you had faltered when it came to my own. For many years I admired your work from afar, your uncanny insights, but now you seem adrift, as if your mental state has been weakened beyond repair.

You appear to be such a lonely, desolate soul, as if merely going through the motions.
Is it because of a love lost, never to be found again? I fear so…
Well, here I am. Offering a gift. And with it, a challenge to drag you from your intel-
lectual torpor.
The three lost souls in these photographs have one commonality of significance.
Me.
And now, as you read this, another:
You.
So take a careful look at my gift, and perhaps you will finally make a step towards
solving your unsolved mystery.
But a word of caution: be careful, for I know you have many secrets, ones I would will-
ingly hear.
Memories you prefer to repress may well surface too. You see:
The past is never truly passed, but ever present.
Sometimes, it reaches out to destroy the future…
Just ask Harding.

Doc reread the document, scanning the vocabulary and syntax while trying to fathom the mind behind the words. He decided the writer suffered from a god complex and was likely a braggart, prone to exaggerating, detached from society's mores, but not from reality. Definitely well educated and quite likely a high-achiever. Not your typical troll.

Although he was no linguistic expert, the style was formal and somewhat affected. The average person would not write this way. In fact, it was stilted almost to the point of parody.

Sent to confuse? Or just a prank?

An uneasiness settled like sludge in the bottom of his stomach as his subconscious ruled out the latter. It was true that any of the photographs could have been manipulated, digitally altered to show what they purported to, but he was convinced the snapshot of the victim he recognised had been taken by the author of this letter. And that fact led him to conclude the other victims were also real.

The 'love lost' comment was worrying too, as it was either a reference to his deceased wife, or possibly to his missing lover, Judy. Given Doc's celebrity status, it would be easy enough for anyone to find out more about both, but the thought of this anonymous correspondent delving into his personal relationships sent a tremor of fear through him.

Why send this letter now, though?

It was several months since his series had aired on TV, so it seemed unlikely to be the trigger prompting this missive.

What of Harding? What did he have to do with this?

Why was the letter copied to the inmate even though it mentioned 'good doctor' and was clearly speaking to Doc directly? The author must surely have known such a provocative letter and lurid contents would never reach an inmate addressee—it would inevitably be intercepted by the hospital staff.

As Doc pondered this conundrum, his phone vibrated and threw an image of Jack Carver on to his screen. It occurred to him that this was no coincidence. His detective friend would not normally call him on a Monday morning, holiday or not, their relationship these days being purely social and their contact usually limited to a beer on occasional weekends.

Doc guessed that Carver had received a copy of the email too, his brain leaping to the conclusion that someone wanted them to reprise their roles, to entice them to work together on a murder investigation again.

The email was a grisly invitation.

One he would refuse.

Carver came to the conclusion that he was right. Bad things do indeed come in threes. As he dried his hair with a hospital hand towel, provided by a very attractive nurse who had taken pity on him, he eyed the junior doctor while the younger man uttered the words he dreaded.

'You can't talk to him, Detective. Not now. Not ever.'

The stress was etched across the medic's face, deep frown lines in his forehead, his eyes sunken dark hollows beneath, making Jack wonder how many hours the man had been working. Before he could confirm why he would never be able to question the victim, already convinced the dismembered man had succumbed to his grievous injuries and died—and that this was now an active murder inquiry—more words tumbled from the harried tongue.

'Follow me. I'll take you to him and you'll see what I mean.' He marched away and Jack did as he was bid. 'I—I've never seen anything like this before… It's like the most dreadful sort of horror film come to life. I—I just don't know. You're probably used to this sort of thing, but even with the worst cases I've handled in Accident and Emergency, I have never come across such a… a… monstrous thing. God knows how any human being could do this to another. And a doctor, too…'

They had reached a private room and the houseman stopped outside the door, then spun to face him, voice quivering, either with anger or fear, but Jack could not decide which.

'It is the most evil thing. Worse than death itself.'

'Would you please stop talking in riddles and tell me what the hell happened to this guy!' Jack allowed some harshness in his tone as he realised the victim must still be alive, but then saw tears welling in the medic's eyes a moment before he turned away to swing open the door.

'Come in and meet Mister Mutilated. That's what that bloody reporter from *The Crusader* said he would call him. Vile parasite.'

'Cooper? That sick tabloid twat hardly qualifies as a reporter. He was here? Earlier?'

The bastard was always monitoring late night and early morning police radio chatter to get ahead of the pack, and no doubt *The Crusader* headlines would already be screaming the nickname on their website in advance of the print edition due in the shops tomorrow morning.

The doctor ushered him into the room, went to pull the curtain from around the bed, then looked over his shoulder at the policeman as he replied.

'Yes. I caught him in here taking snapshots with his bloody iPhone! Had him escorted off the premises of course, but I could do nothing about the pictures. I have no idea how he found out or how he got in here but I think you should put a copper on the door asap. This man needs protection. Even if it is a bit late.' He swished the green material aside and beckoned Carver to come forward. 'Here he is.' His voice was softer now, tremulous again. He reached a hand out to the bald forehead, but there was no response. 'I have no idea if he can feel anything. We will give him an MRI scan to see what brain activity there is. I hope, for his sake, there's none.'

'What?'

Jack was shocked at the comment but was even more taken aback at the sight of the man's face. Or rather his lack of one. Despite having seen the crime scene photos he had not fully taken on board the state the victim was in. Now he noted the weird marbling, created by lines of pink tissue, scars from the look of them, tracking a pattern over his pale death mask. For that was what it looked like to Jack. Hideous. Barely recognisable as human.

More dead than alive.

'Why would you hope that?' The sharpness had reappeared in his voice and it elicited a scowl from the doctor.

'Well, I guess you have no medical training, Detective, but even so I would think it's pretty obvious this man cannot see, hear or speak. His eyes were removed and fleshy tissue transplanted over the hollow sockets. You can see the scars here.' His fingers traced the marbling as he went on. 'The nose has also been smoothed away in a similar fashion, amputated then skin grafted to leave these breathing holes, enough of an airway to keep the man alive... If you consider the state he's in as being *alive*.'

Carver grunted, his brain finally catching up with the sentiment being expressed.

'You see how the chin appears too close to the nasal cavity.' The medic glanced up as Carver nodded in understanding, then continued. 'The teeth have been removed and the jaw somehow disabled before the lips were amputated and the mouth was sealed with stitched flesh. The poor chap must've been kept alive with nasal or intra-venous feeding—just as we are having to do right now.' He gestured to the bag of nutrients dangling from a hook above the bed, a transparent tube from there leading through a cannula into a vein in the patient's neck.

'Christ!' Carver's head was shaking in disbelief at what he was seeing and hear-ing, the full implications of the man's state finally sinking in. What he had initially thought was a straightforward case of dismemberment and disfigurement, some-thing he had encountered before, was actually much worse. 'You mentioned a doctor did this to him. Are you certain?'

'Absolutely. And he'd have to be a senior surgeon to do this...' His hand hovered over the forehead again, then settled back there, his own face quizzical. 'But I can't believe anyone who trained to do this job could inflict this on another human being...' His words seemed to melt away as his face contorted with confusion, then he added, more determined now, 'I'd imagine that'll make your job easier. The range of suspects can only be a few thousand or so.' His cheeks darkened and his mouth twisted as he added, 'You need to catch this sick fucker before he does this to anyone else.'

Jack pondered on that before asking, 'Does he have any movement, control over his body? He seems as still as a statue.'

The doctor tugged back the bed covers and the man's appearance immediately reminded Carver of museum exhibits. He thought of the figures of Roman gods, similarly created with just head and torso, marbled too, but with faint blue lines rather than these welt-like scars. He shrugged the images from his mind and peered at the dark cavity of the man's right ear-hole.

'Can he hear us? I can see the ear has been lopped off and the skin smoothed like the nose, but what about inside?' He glanced up and was not surprised to see the tears welling again. Perhaps the man's idealism, the humanitarianism that drove him to study hard to help the sick and wounded, had been dealt a deadly blow by the enormity of such a heinous act so clearly performed by one of his Hippocratic brethren.

'No, I'm afraid not. His eardrums are gone, and there's scar tissue inside the aural canal suggestive of burning.'

'What the hell? His eardrums were burnt out? Jesus wept!'

'Probably acid.' A juddering sigh slipped out, then the houseman turned to leave but Jack laid a hand on his elbow, stopping him.

He waited until the man's eyes met his.

'Please wait. This is important.' As the doctor nodded, tears now flowing freely, Jack asked, his excitement mounting, 'Is there any way we can communicate with him? You must know how. Surely you have colleagues who deal with the deaf, dumb and blind. And he wasn't born like this. If his brain is working we have to find a way to reach him. And some way for him to tell us what happened. Who he is... Why this was done to him... Maybe even who did it to him.'

A hopeless expression greeted his flurry of enthusiasm, immediately quashing the thoughts that were cascading onto Jack's tongue.

'From my initial examination I can tell you the man is immobile and appears to have no control over what's left of his body. I guess some nerves have been severed or paralysed—'

'What? Is that why what's left of his face looks like someone overdid the Botox?'

It was true, the smoothed features reminded Jack of the worst examples of over-enthusiastic plastic surgery inflicted on Hollywood celebrities, but his coarse question drew a disapproving glance.

'Rather more than that. Without detailed tests and a thorough examination by a neurologist it's difficult to say, but from the overall state of him I'd suggest the evil person who did this deliberately shut him inside his body. And threw away any keys that could help him escape...'

It made sense.

Finally, the rationale started to form in Jack's mind, his detective's instincts leading him to the conclusion the doctor had reached before him.

'It's punishment. He's been locked in... It's an extreme form of solitary confinement.'

'That's what I meant earlier. He would be better off dead. And since he's not, and by law we have to do all we can to keep him alive, I just hope for his sake that inside that cranium there's nothing more sentient than a garden vegetable... If not, we can be absolutely certain this poor chap is suffering in the most unimaginable way.'

A crash alarm sounded and the houseman made his apologies as he dashed off, leaving Jack alone with his thoughts. It was not long before his optimism resurfaced as he considered the cold case his boss was convinced was related to this one, an investigation he had revisited as a consultant for a TV series on serial killers. Perhaps the host, his old friend Doc Powers, similarly baffled by the unsolved mystery, would be sufficiently intrigued to lend a hand now there was a second victim.

'Doc, I need your help.'

DI Carver's voice rasped in Doc Powers' ear, the telephone echoing the words as if the policeman was calling from a car phone on hands free.

'Jack! It's been a while. I've been planning to call you about appearing in my upcoming TV series. Just haven't got round to it.'

Doc and the detective had both experienced their five minutes of fame, although Doc's celebrity was rather more enduring as he was the star and driving force behind the series Cold Case Killers. Some years prior to their brief foray into the world of media and the small screen, they had worked together on many high-profile murder investigations, but that was before Doc retired from his role as consulting Forensic Psychiatrist with the Metropolitan Police, a role he had come to despise.

He shuddered as he remembered their last investigation, one he had been forced to undertake, and one that had left him physically and mentally scarred.

It seemed likely that Jack was calling about the Broadmoor letters after being notified by his Berkshire colleagues, maybe even hoping Doc would automatically want to pursue the case. Well, the detective was out of luck. Doc was determined not to get dragged into another investigation, despite the emailed teaser, and regardless of Jack's pleas.

'Sorry for calling early like this.' Carver sucked hard on a cigarette, the sound unmistakable to Powers, the detective's stress signalled by the sharp exhale that followed. 'I'm caught up in a really difficult and unusual case—'

'Jack, images of severely mutilated victims sent by a self-professed killer with a poetic bent are not enough to drag me into another investigation. Seriously, I am not interested. Full stop.'

'Hang on a minute. How did you know about the mutilated—?'

'I'm *really* not interested.' Doc's jovial tone turned acid as the urge to hang up wrestled his naturally courteous nature. 'I received Celene's email. I can tell you what I think. It'll take less than a minute. Then I'm out of it. Fair enough? Find yourself another profiler, Jack. I've got the second series to prepare and the accompanying book to finish.'

For a moment, the line was silent, then Carver's voice boomed at him, full of confusion, impatience and not a little ire.

'What the bloody hell are you on about, Doc? What email? And what images? And how did you hear about Mister Mutilated so quickly? Don't tell me it's all over the internet already! Jesus! And Celene who?'

Now Doc was confused.

'*Mister* Mutilated?'

Before he could say more, Carver, calmer now, answered.

'Yeah… I think we need to rewind a bit, Doc. I'm actually calling you about a case I think you might want to help me with. Not a murder. At least, not yet…' Doc sensed Jack was reluctant to expand on what it was he needed help with as he went on. 'But before we talk about that you'd better explain to me what you meant about an email and mutilated victims. I'll tell you what. I'm only ten minutes away from you, I'll drop by and you can make me a piping hot coffee with that fancy machine of yours. I'll grab a couple of bagels on the way.'

As Doc opened his mouth to answer, to try and fend off his friend, the line went dead. He swallowed back his frustration, cursed his bad luck, and wondered if he would ever get his work done.

Detective Sergeant Fiona Fielding, known affectionately to her mates as 'Fifi', made her way through St George's Hospital to the Accident and Emergency Department, though she still thought of it as the 'Casualty Department'. The nurse on Reception had corrected her when she used the old term but Fiona had just smiled and shrugged, admitting, 'I was a big fan of the TV programme. It's not my fault you lot changed the name!'

As she arrived at her destination, she had to admit, real life was pretty similar to the on-screen version, albeit with a few significant differences. That unique hospital odour for a start. And of course, the people in the waiting area were all actually suffering to some degree or other, either as a sick or injured party, or as a friend or relative of the poorly person. Most were sitting, some sleeping, while a dozen or so others, unable to find a spare seat, were leaning against the walls in various states ranging from somnolence to outright distress. Other patients were on gurneys, seemingly abandoned, their temporary beds pushed up against the walls of the passageway to ensure they did not impede access.

Budget cuts. Austerity. The big government lie, Fiona thought, her mood souring as she saw the degree of misery, the result of pampered politicians' misguided actions.

Bastards.

The same had happened with the police budgets, and even the Fire Service had not escaped unscathed. Fifi had first-hand experience of the dreadful results of the latter idiocy…

She shook her head, dislodging the thoughts as she focused back on the task in hand. A quick scan of the crowded room and she spotted her likely target. A pale, gangly youth, still dressed in his running vest and shorts, hugging himself as if chilled by the aircon, perhaps unaware he was standing right under the vent, its cooling effect aggravated by the sweat from his run.

Maybe not the sharpest tool in the box, she thought, then mentally berated herself for allowing such an uncharitable first impression.

No, he's probably suffering mild shock, she decided.

Fiona strolled over to the young man, estimating his age at late teens as she matched his description to the one she had been give earlier. She smiled at him as she asked, 'Are you Piers Reid? I'm DS Fielding. Can we have a word in private?' She flashed her warrant card and watched as he perked up, his eyebrows lifting in surprise as he looked down at the diminutive detective.

'Really? I was expecting someone… else…' His words tailed off as he finished, then he stammered in embarrassment, probably in response to the scowl that had replaced Fifi's smile. 'I'm sorry… I didn't mean… Er…'

'What?' She was pretty immune to people's reactions, but had allowed her face to react, an automatic defensive response, more to put him in his place than anything else, then she relented. A grin appeared and her harsh tone softened. 'Is it 'cos I is black?'

Fiona uttered the words quietly, just for his ears, mimicking the accent of the comedian who had made the phrase famous. Although she wondered if he was too young to get the joke, it was one she often used to break any initial tension with her 'clients'. She chuckled and took his arm, leading him outside to where the air was warmer.

'No! Not at all.' He giggled, a little nervously it seemed to Fiona, as he added, 'They told me to expect someone called Jack, so I wasn't expecting a lady detective. That's all... Honest!'

Although the storm had passed, the air was humid and the tarmac glistened with rain. An ambulance swerved into the unloading area with a splashing of tyres and screeched to a halt, so Fiona and Piers moved further from the entrance, found a quieter spot under an awning.

'Doesn't look like it'll rain again just yet,' she said, then pulled out her notebook. 'I need to ask you a few questions about this morning. Thanks for waiting for me... Well, Jack. He's my boss, so I'll make sure anything you tell me gets to him.'

Piers nodded, clearly warmer now, no longer trying to generate some heat by rubbing and hugging his bare arms, more relaxed than the tense bundle he had appeared to be when she first saw him.

'Yeah, sure. Bloody nightmare. I was just out for a run through the Common... Didn't expect anything like this.' His prominent Adam's apple bobbed, highly visible to Fifi even though it was well above her eye level.

'You found the old man. His name's Gerald Butler. Do you know him?'

'No. Though I have nodded to him on occasion while out running. He's a regular and so am I... Never spoken to him, other than *Good morning!* or *Alright mate!* Stuff like that. Poor old bugger. He was in a right state when I found him.'

Piers shivered, but Fiona guessed it wasn't from the cold.

'So, can you describe what happened?'

She already had a brief verbal description from the first uniformed copper on scene, but wanted a first-hand account, like any good detective. And, she thought, I'm a bloody good detective. She also knew how this repeated questioning irritated a lot of witnesses and suspects, both innocent and guilty, but it was just part of the job. An essential part, as each interview might yield something new, seemingly insignificant, but sometimes very important.

The lad was no trouble though, keen to help. Shocked, but not in shock, she decided.

'His dog. Name's Smudge. Spotted me a couple of hundred metres away, running on the grass. At first I thought he was chasing me, had gone loopy and wanted to bite me. I put on a bit of extra speed but that mutt can run! He just started leaping up and down as he ran beside me, yapping like crazy, then sprinted off the way he came, stopped, looked back and barked at me, and started running for the trees again. I almost carried on jogging away, but thought it odd he was running free like this. Never seen him without the old boy in tow.'

'So you followed him. What time was this?'

'About six ten I reckon. Hang on.' He plucked his iPhone from the pouch on his upper arm and checked the screen. 'I dialled the emergency number at six twelve so, yeah, took a couple of minutes before I called. The old boy was lying there, in absolute agony. I could see he had dragged himself from the bushes almost back to the path. I didn't see that... hideous thing. Not at first.'

Fiona gave him a moment as Piers' right hand massaged his eyes, thumb and forefinger pulling at his closed eyelids, then the palm wiping down his face, his cheeks crumpling as if he was in pain. His other hand was on his hip so she reached out, gave his forearm a reassuring squeeze.

'Go on, Piers. I know it's difficult but it's important you tell me what you saw.'

'Yeah.' His hand shifted to his forehead, thumb on his temple, the four fingers rubbing back and forth, digging into the flesh above his eyebrows. He took a deep breath and added, 'I tried to make him as comfortable as I could, used my sweatshirt to cushion his head. Forgot to grab that before jumping in the ambulance with him. By the time it arrived, he wouldn't let go of my hand. Broke his hip they reckon, made it worse trying to crawl. Internal bleeding apparently. He might die…'

The forehead rubbing became more pronounced as his distress increased, but Fiona wanted to plough on. She'd been too late to interview Gerald, had arrived at the hospital as he was being wheeled into surgery so had to make do with the lad's account of the victim's discovery.

'Let's hope he pulls through Piers. How about we grab a coffee, eh? There's a Costa just around the corner. Come on son.' She tugged his forearm and led him away, thinking he was a good lad, kind and thoughtful. So different to many of the nineteen-year-old scrotes she'd had to deal with. 'My treat. Might even manage a sarnie if you're up for it. Dunno about you, but I'm starvin-Marvin!'

'This coffee's good.' Carver's exaggerated sniff as he inhaled the aroma preceded a yelped moan accompanying his first slurp. 'Bloody hell, that's hot! Burnt me tongue.' He glanced up at Doc, standing impassively by the espresso machine, his back to the detective, waiting for his own brew to dribble through the roasted grounds. 'And scalded me throat too! Are you trying to kill me Doc?' He waited a few beats but Doc was silent. 'Not very welcoming today, are you?'

'Uh?' Doc turned his shoulders to the detective, murmured something indecipherable that sounded like *Hardly*, then returned to making his coffee.

Carver, impatient as he was to get on, had to wait for Doc to finish, so idly asked, 'You heard anything from Judy since we last spoke?' An awkward silence greeted that enquiry.

Jack was about to speak again, to probe some more at the unhealed wound of his friend's love life when Doc, still facing the machine, spoke.

'So, what are you doing here, Jack?'

'Bringing bagels to my old mate! What d'you think?'

Carver had been determined not to bite, but his grouchiness had only worsened as he sat, waiting in Doc's showhome kitchen, wearing a soggy jacket and damp trousers, without even the offer of a towel. His voice had seemed over-loud to his own ears but he couldn't help thinking, *What the hell's up with Doc this morning?*

'Can I have a towel? I'm soaking wet.'

Doc had been preoccupied since Jack had arrived, had not noticed his discomfort.

'Oh, I'm so sorry, my friend. I didn't mean to be rude. Hang on.' He ducked out of the kitchen and a moment later reappeared with a giant fluffy bath towel, a dry shirt and some slacks. 'Here you go. Should fit, now I'm back to my former slender self.'

There was truth in Doc's words, Jack thought. His old friend had been decidedly podgy a few years ago, having hit the bottle after his wife had died. Then came the event that shot him to fame, followed by over a year of recovery, firstly in hospital, then rehabilitation and physiotherapy clinics, at the end of which he was a gaunt, hollow remnant of his former self. Since then, yoga and a relatively healthy diet had helped him recover, so now he looked in excellent shape, despite nearing a major milestone—his first half-century on the planet.

Fitter than me, that's for sure, Jack decided, though he would admit, he had been pretty lucky in the gene department, and didn't need to work out to keep himself in shape. He even had an on-off love affair with nicotine that had done him no harm. He was a good few years younger than Doc, and his job kept him on the go, especially as his role allowed him to fob off most of his admin to his subordinates, along with much of the grunt work.

'Cheers, Doc. I only put these on a couple of hours ago, but I got soaked three times already, just getting to and from my car in the pissing rain...'

He stripped off in the kitchen, down to his damp underwear, and dried himself off before dressing in Doc's clothes, totally unfazed by the fact that his ex-colleague was watching him. He just asked, 'What were you on about, when I rang you? You tell me all about that, and then I'll share with you the details of the case I'm working on. I promise you, you will find it intriguing. Maybe enough to join me working on it.' Stony eyes were the only reply, so Jack added, 'You know, consulting. Never seen anything like it. And I guarantee you haven't either...'

Doc, having finished making his coffee, had settled his rear on one of the designer stools surrounding the kitchen's central island, propping himself there, facing Jack, arms folded.

'I told you, Jack. It's not going to happen. But let me show you what arrived in my email this morning. I honestly thought that was why you called.'

Once again Doc popped out, and by the time he returned Jack was fully dressed and back on one of the stools gulping at his coffee.

'Here you go.' Doc had the MacBook open and swivelled it round for Jack to view Celene's email. 'Just scroll down and by the time you get to the bottom you'll know as much as I do.'

'What the bloody hell..? Harding?' He glanced at Doc's expressionless face before turning back to the email, simultaneously realising what Doc had been muttering about while he'd been making coffee. As Jack scrolled through the photographs he said, 'Jeez! We both know this girl! Well, not personally, but she's that cold case from the show, the victim we dismissed as we had nothing to relate her to the other unsolveds...'

Jack noted Doc's reaction, a reluctance, almost as if he wanted to back out of the room, while simultaneously being drawn into an intriguing case. Like the poles of a magnet, attracted or repelled by another, depending on how it was approached.

'I thought... Well, I hoped this was just a crank trying to wind me up. That the pictures weren't real... But then I realised who she was.'

'This photo's about ten or eleven years old. She did her business at King's Cross. Prostitute called Diana Davies. Apparently, her mum named her after the princess, which was a bit optimistic... Then life did this to her. Poor kid.' Jack was thinking about his boss who had mentioned this unsolved murder while assigning this morning's case to him, and how strange it was that Doc had received the victim's photograph in amongst the others. He began scrolling between the three images on the screen, flicking back and forth, then focused on the letter that accompanied them.

'Nutter. Total bloody nutter. Secrets? What bullshit! These all look like ancient crime scene photos. Probably found them on one of those crappy serial killer websites.'

He did a quick impression of a bullfrog, puffing out his cheeks and exhaling with an exaggerated burp. His verbal outburst had, like many of his instant judgements, reached his tongue before he had properly considered all angles. Although he was correct about internet availability of police documents, illicitly obtained and posted online, he knew the timing and content of this lunatic's message to Doc was unlikely to be pure coincidence.

'Hang on a second, Jack.' Doc fiddled with the MacBook and found the file, extracting the information about Diana Davies from his TV series database, and then pulled up the official images. 'Compare the background!'

'Bloody hell! The photo sent to Broadmoor ain't from the crime scene.' The images were side by side and there was no doubt. He tapped the screen. 'Only the killer or an accomplice could've taken this... The guy who sent you the letter.'

Jack's mind hit overdrive. A mutilated victim on Clapham Common, discovered at roughly the same moment Broadmoor received Doc's letter, sent by someone involved in the Diana Davies murder. But how were they linked? And Harding? What about that piece of human excrement? A sicko with a self-professed history of dismemberment...

Before Jack could share his thoughts, Doc pushed himself upright, an audible click from his stiff joints bringing forth a mild curse before he limped the few steps to his coffee machine again. 'Bloody weather...' The jet of steam, bubbling milk to a foam, filled the room with white noise, leaving Jack straining to hear Doc's words. 'My first thoughts were that it was not serious, though obviously the local bobbies would have to check it out. You know, since we did that TV series I've been getting a crank letter, email or phone call every couple of weeks, but so far they've amounted to nothing more than just that. Cranks.'

The hissing of steam stopped as Doc turned to face Jack, leaning his hip against the worktop, his right hand plucking at his chin, thumb and forefinger squeezing the flesh before letting go, then repeating the action.

'And now?' Carver could sense the excitement starting to emanate from his friend, and hoped he would convince himself to get involved in the case.

Doc's intent stare settled on Jack, his eyes lively, challenging.

'Why send this letter, like this? Obviously in the hope of drawing me back into the investigation, but for what? This is no random stalker, disgruntled at my short-lived moment of fame. Seems way too elaborate for an ex-con's revenge plot... It's some sort of sick game this psychopath wants to play.'

'I think there's more to this, mate...'

For a moment, it seemed to Jack as if Doc had drifted away before snapping back, his brown eyes sparking, his voice stronger, more determined.

'This thing with Harding. That's got me thinking too... Why send a copy of the letter to the man who murdered my father?'

Fiona and Piers had found a discreet corner in the coffee shop, even though it was already humming with customers queuing from the doorway, all desperate for their morning caffeine fix. Both had large bowls of hot latte in front of them, with the lad wolfing down some carrot cake, despite having already scoffed a ham and cheese toastie.

Fiona's plate was empty other than a few crumbs of burnt bread, but she waited patiently, happy to see him unwind, released from the tension he had exhibited earlier. As he finished his breakfast he muttered a mumbled, 'That was awesome, thanks,' through a mouthful of confectionery, then gulped his milky drink.

He looked a lot better, the paleness of his cheeks, something she had noted outside, was now gone. She opened her notebook again.

'Okay. So you found Gerald, made him more comfy and called for an ambulance. Then what happened?'

'I was standing in the bushes while on the phone, and just wandered back the way I could see he'd crawled. I wasn't really thinking. Just an automatic reaction I s'pose. Then I saw it...'

'You were still on the phone? To the emergency services?' She made a note to check the recording when she got back to the Yard.

'Uh-huh. I freaked when I saw it, and suddenly realised what Gerald had been babbling on about... When I put my trackie top under his head, making him comfortable, he was muttering stuff about Kenya, lopped limbs and a dismembered torso, not making any sense... Said it had been put there for him. I think. I hadn't been taking much notice, so you know, I just wanted to get help. He was delirious. Or that's what I thought, before I found it.'

'Can you remember anything else he said?' Fiona was wondering why Gerald had thought the mutilated victim had been placed there for him to find as she underlined her note on the comment.

'Erm... Not really... Only that he kept repeating, *It's alive!* Over and over. And, *Get help! Now!*'

'And what exactly did he say about the torso being placed there? Please try to remember his exact words, if you can.'

'Just, *They put it here for me.*' He hesitated, frowning as he tried to remember. 'No, hang on, he said, *He put it here to torment me.* Yeah, that's what he said.'

'Are you sure?'

This was very strange. Fiona began to wonder if the discovery was mere happenstance as she'd initially been led to believe. The constable who had taken a brief statement from Piers had not mentioned this. Now she needed to check what Gerald had said to the officer before he was whisked away to the hospital. Delirious or not, it might be important. Another note went into her little book.

'Yeah, pretty sure. This is difficult y'know? I'm supposed to be at uni too.' He checked his phone. 'Christ! Is that the time already?'

'I think you might give college a miss today, love.' He nodded reluctantly as she went on, 'So tell me about the other person.' He looked confused. 'The victim. The torso hanging in the tree.'

Fiona had seen the crime scene photos already, emailed to the tablet tucked in the glove compartment of her car. She couldn't help but wonder what effect seeing something like that would have on the young lad's mind.

'I had no idea what I was looking at. But Gerald kept repeating, *It's alive!* At first I didn't think it was human. That's why I freaked. It looked like a ghost, floating there.'

'So, you were on the phone? Calling the ambulance for Gerald?'

'Yeah. When I realised it was human, and Gerald was screaming that it was alive, well, I just told them to bring two ambulances and the police too. I wanted to check it really was a person, and not a dummy or something, but couldn't bring myself to go any closer… And anyway, there didn't seem anything I could do… Poor old Gerald was crying out still, so I went to comfort him. That's when he latched on to my hand, like I was his lifeline. He just wouldn't let go, even when he was semi-conscious. Like a limpet, he was… That's why they brought me with him, here.'

Fiona knew better. The paramedic had taken in the scene and assumed Piers would need treatment for shock. He had told that to the first uniformed officers to arrive when they had insisted Piers remain, so that they could properly interview him.

Overruled.

'Was there anybody else around? Did you see anyone else in the area? Anything or anyone unusual?'

'Nope… Just a couple of other early morning regulars. Familiar faces. Joggers, like me. I try to run a few miles each morning, and if I can, I head out at night too. Run twice, most days. I've done the London Marathon and want to enter again next year… Love it. Running clears my head. Not that I'll ever be able to wipe from my mind the vile images from today. Unbelievable…'

Fiona was not surprised. The perpetrator was almost certainly well away from the area by the time Piers arrived on the scene. It would take very big balls and a total disregard for common sense to hang around, though plenty of criminals have fallen into the trap of loitering to observe the reaction to their handiwork.

Someone would have to check all the surrounding CCTV camera recordings for last night through until dawn. After all, at least one person had managed to lug a dismembered victim hundreds of metres from the nearest road and carefully position him, suspended with wire and hooks from the branches of an old oak tree. That must've taken time, even if there were two people manhandling the body. Maybe someone local had seen something. They'd have to get an appeal out on the radio and TV as soon as she got back to the office.

She sighed, a long mournful note as she corrected herself.

Not *someone* reviewing the CCTV footage. Jack would want her to check the videos personally. She knew it without even asking him, having worked with him before. It had been a while, but she was back as part of his team on this new investigation, assigned at seven-thirty this morning, the moment she arrived at the office, and she had literally spoken to him for no more than a minute before heading to the hospital. He was going to check the site and then the victim, he'd said, while she followed up with the witnesses. An *almost* murder, he'd told her, with possible links to an actual murder. He'd explain later…

Fiona flipped shut her notebook and pocketed it, scraped back her chair and said, 'Come on, sunshine. I'll give you a lift home.' The initial report had confirmed Piers' address, an apartment in a converted house in a suburban street just off Brixton Road about a mile from Clapham Common. 'I'm heading over your way so it's no trouble.'

Like any good detective, Fiona was always suspicious of people who were among the first at a crime scene, but she was pretty sure Piers would check out. A word with his neighbours was in order too, just to be sure, but she was convinced he was a regular on the common and had just stumbled across the old man and the victim. She was much less certain about Gerald though.

'That'll be cool. I was wondering how I'd get home. I haven't got any cash on me for a bus or a cab. Thanks, that's really kind of you.'

It wasn't such a generous gesture on her part. It just meant she could probe him for any other recollections or inconsistencies in his statement as she drove, and check his address when they arrived, given that he had no formal ID on him.

Fiona smiled inwardly as they headed to her car, thinking:

I'm a conscientious copper, not a bloody taxi service.

She'd also call the boss and tell him about the potential connection with Butler. It seemed unlikely, but the possibility that the old man was somehow the target of this atrocity added a new dimension that had to be explored. Her instincts told her it was an important piece of the puzzle, and she'd act accordingly.

The *Hope, Not Fear — Tattoo & Piercing Parlour,* situated on a side street just off Streatham High Road in a narrow Victorian building, was officially closed for the bank holiday, but in the cavernous cellar, with hardcore punk blaring from the wall-mounted speakers, a select team of willing assistants were helping the first volunteer for this morning's session.

Harry Hope, wearing tattered jeans, a black tee shirt with a death metal band's logo, and blue surgical gloves, was using a marker pen to meticulously trace a line on the bare back of his client, just above the shoulder blades. He had already measured the points he needed to pierce, and was careful not to confuse the locations with other markings in the vibrant pattern on the youthful skin—a beautifully crafted three dimensional tattoo of an android's internal mechanism that seemed to burst forth from the upper torso, as if the flesh and skin had opened up to reveal the truth inside the human form.

He sat back for a moment, admiring the handiwork.

His handiwork.

An artistic creation that had taken several extended sessions to complete, and the main reason his client, a young man of roughly half his age who he only knew as Slim —an apt name, he thought, given his skinny frame—was here today. Each time Harry had taken his needles to the young man's skin, he had noted Slim's reaction. Initially tense, a natural reflex caused by the discomfort of the rapid piercing and inking, Slim soon relaxed into a state of euphoria, something Harry recognised. So, during their lengthy sessions together, Harry had introduced Slim to his other, less well known and unadvertised service, something he reserved for the select crowd he felt might benefit.

The five members of this exclusive club who were here this morning all sported tattoos and piercings along with other less common body decorations. Shazza, one of the girls, had circular plugs in her ear piercings, having stretched the holes to the size of curtain rings, almost matching the size of those in Harry's own lobes. To achieve this effect, a body modification based on an ancient African tribal tradition, the size of the plugs had to be increased gradually over time. Each newly inserted plug stretched the fleshy flaps a little more, and, of course, pain accompanied the procedure, just as much as with tattooing and standard piercings.

For Harry and his small crowd of enthusiasts, pain was not to be avoided, but welcomed. Not so much for the pain itself, but for the pleasure that inevitably followed. Pain was the key to a door they willingly stepped through, to a spiritual plane most people would never experience.

'How're you feeling Slim?' Harry was tugging Slim's shoulder flesh between each thumb and forefinger, as if loosening it, while checking that the procedure would not damage the muscle and nerve tissue beneath.

'Not great. Apprehensive, bro… It's stupid, but I keep thinking the hooks will tear out.' Slim was face down on the stainless steel table at the side of the room, with Harry leaning over as he pulled at the flesh.

'Don't worry, Slim, with your weight that's almost impossible. And anyway, that only happens if the procedure's not done properly. Never had a problem, have we guys?' Harry aimed the question at his little team, who were busy preparing the rig, pulleys and wires attached to the metal eye-bolts in the ceiling in the centre of the room.

Comments from the others, rapid fire, shot back at Slim.

'You'll be great!' Tamsin, a punky girl sporting a scarlet Mohican with three dimensional butterfly tatts on the shaved area above each ear, grinned through lips sporting numerous rings and studs, completing the matching set for her ears, nose and eyebrows.

'It's no worse than piercings, honest, bro!' Glen, a hulk of a guy, his face a spider's web of fluorescent inking, his bare arms covered in sleeve tattoos, like a coat of many colours, was inspecting the pulleys and wires. He was considered to be an expert rigger now, by the select bunch of people who were aware of his hobby, having worked alongside Harry for nearly four years, and had personally undertaken dozens of suspensions despite his bulk. 'If I can do it, while humping this around,' he patted and rubbed his beer gut with relish, 'you'll have no probs, you scrawny little git!'

'You'll love it. You won't wanna come down.' Shazza had edged closer to the table, all the while watching Harry who was now swabbing Slim's shoulders with alcohol. She stroked Slim's head and purred, 'We'll help you sweetie. I've done this hundreds of times. You're only a virgin once!' She leaned down and lightly kissed his temple, grinning all the while. 'You won't believe how good it feels.' She straightened and asked Harry, 'Ready?'

Harry nodded, so she rinsed her hands with alcohol, then pulled on her surgical gloves before whispering into Slim's ear. 'Take a few deep breaths and try to relax. I know it isn't easy, but do your best. You'll feel an intense stinging sensation but that doesn't last long. Okay?'

She and Harry each pinched Slim's back exactly where marked, made eye contact for a moment in acknowledgement as Shazza said to Slim, 'Okay babe, deep breath in… and now, out!'

As Slim exhaled, Harry and Shazza simultaneously plunged the stainless steel hooks, not unlike those used by tuna fishermen, through the flesh of Slim's upper back.

Doc stood alone in his kitchen as Carver paced the few metres of path outside the patio doors, sheltering from the wind and rain under the overhang as he tried and failed to light his cigarette. His mobile phone was jammed between his chin and his shoulder as he spoke to one of his subordinates.

The call had interrupted their breakfast meeting just as Jack had started to explain about the poor soul who had been discovered hanging from a tree on Clapham Common a few hours before. He had apologised to Doc as he headed outside, explaining, 'It's my sergeant... Won't be a minute.'

Doc took the opportunity to check online as Carver had mentioned that the news was already on the internet. True to form, the tabloid rag, *The Crusader,* had their homepage plastered with sensational photos of the man they had named *Mister Mutilated* lying unclothed in his hospital bed, with his groin pixelated so as not to offend reader sensibilities. It was a disgraceful breach of the man's rights to privacy, but the idiot journalist speculated that the victim had probably died since the photograph was taken, a result of exposure rather than his grievous injuries.

The journalist, or what passed for one these days, Doc thought, went on to liken the lower part of the victim's face to Lord Voldemort, a fictional figure from the Harry Potter series, which was bad enough. But then the article went on to describe the most salacious element of the story—the lack of genitalia—and then suggested the police should be looking into the man's history as it was possible he was a paedophile.

Doc snorted and slammed shut his MacBook in disgust, wondering when the world had gone mad. It was as if the news these days was nothing more than a guessing game, one in this case designed to titillate the public's most prurient tastes.

Instead, he picked up Jack's tablet, but the screen was locked so he would just have to wait for his friend to return and share the crime scene images he had been about to show Doc before his phone interrupted their discussion.

'Jesus, this weather! One minute you think it's finished pissing down, then the bloody heavens open again.' Jack used the same towel to mop down his freshly saturated trousers. 'The wind was blowing the rain under the awning, coming at me sideways, but it's just the bottoms that are wet... Anyway, that was Fifi, our very own West Indian Miss Marple.' He chuckled, then said, 'She's actually one of the most conscientious detective sergeants I've worked with, and whip smart with it, so that's one silver lining in this cloud of confusion confronting us. Let me fill you in on my case, then we can see how it links with your crank's email.'

Doc, having already pretty much convinced himself there was a link, sat on the stool beside Jack as the detective tapped his password into the tablet before scrolling through the pictures from this morning's discovery. As Doc inspected the images, Jack described the way the victim had been positioned, hanging in the tree, secured with wires and hooks.

'Hooks?'

'Yeah. Like big fish hooks, but with longer, finer points. And with no barb.' Carver swiped the page to bring up a picture of the victim's back, taken before the paramedics had removed them. 'I think they're a specialist item. Not sure what you'd normally expect to catch with these though. Being checked out as we speak.'

'Not *fish* hooks Jack... These are designed for precisely this purpose.'

'You what? For hooking flesh?' He thought about it for a moment, then added, 'You mean like butcher's hooks? They're different... Double ended like an S shape. One hook to stick in the meat and the other to hang on a rack or bar. You see 'em in old-fashioned butcher shops still, but these are different. They have eyes on the end... For fishing line.'

'I don't think so. I'm pretty sure these were designed for human suspension.'

Jack's blank look turned to disbelief as Doc explained about the subculture, about suspension's popularity among those who practised piercing and body modification, and why a small section of society would choose to inflict such wicked looking items upon themselves.

'What? They do it for FUN?' Jack's voice escalated in disbelief. 'Seriously, Doc? Is it some sort of sadomasochistic fetish? Self-harm? What on earth prompts people to do this sort of thing? Voluntarily!'

'It's not self-harm Jack. That's a psychological problem that results from a specific set of character traits, usually the result of early childhood trauma, accompanied by feelings of low self-esteem. And suspension is not sadomasochism either. Practitioners aim to achieve an elevated spiritual experience—'

'You what? No way! It's just madness... Another crazy idea thought up by some demented youth group, just to show how different they are. Outsiders... Cranks.'

'It's not a modern phenomenon, Jack. Indigenous American tribes were doing something similar for hundreds of years, using sharpened bone and twine rather than wire and hooks, but with the same desired result. It's a spiritual experience. Trust me.'

'Mmm.' Jack swivelled on his stool, then tugged at his upper lip, considering Doc's explanation. After a moment or two cogitating, his voice strident, he came to his conclusion. 'Regardless of why they do it, there can't be that many nutters into something this weird. That should help us narrow down the list of suspects. And there's another thing.' He explained the theory mooted by the medic who had been so distraught after admitting this morning's victim, then summarised, his voice dripping with irony. 'So, we're looking for a skilled plastic surgeon with experience of amputating limbs, with a kinky sideline in hanging himself up on hooks. A doctor who thinks he's a side of beef... Well that narrows things down a bit!'

Doc's brain started working overtime, making some tentative connections. Reluctantly, he decided Jack was correct about at least one thing... This whole affair was sucking him in, and there was no way he could deny he was somehow involved.

As they sat in silence, both men mulling over the morning's events and their implications, Doc had to admit, he felt alive, stimulated and challenged in a way that he had not for some years. He had turned down the offer of the chairmanship of the Parole Board when he came out of hospital, instead succumbing to the lure of his own TV programme. Since then, well, he had agreed to a second series with a companion book to coincide with the broadcast, but by now, he had begun to hate himself for his weakness.

Fame was not all it was cracked up to be.

In fact, it was a pain in the arse. Just like the bloody book. What had made him think he would enjoy this Mickey Mouse media nonsense?

Doc took a sideways glance at his friend, who was still mired in his own thoughts, chewing on his lip while staring at the photos on his iPad, and came to the conclusion that he actually missed working with his old pal. The thrill of the chase, the delving into warped minds during an active hunt, and, not least, indulging the dark side of his own psyche, letting it loose, but in a controlled fashion, only ever in pursuit of those who acted on their psychopathic impulses....

He made his decision.

'Okay, Jack, I'll help. Let's talk about Harding.'

'He's just come out of surgery, but I doubt you'll be able to get any sense out of him just yet. And anyway, he's in ITU, so you can't talk to him until the consultant says it's okay.'

DS Fiona Fielding, having satisfied herself that Piers, her only other witness to this morning's crime site, really was who he said he was and did actually live where he said he did, was now back at the hospital, hoping to interview the other person who might help them unravel the mystery of the mutilated man on the common. The nurse was decidedly unhelpful, so Fiona just thanked her and went off to see the victim instead.

She knew the copper sitting outside the private room the hospital had allocated, and he stood and opened the door for her as she approached.

'Got you on door duty, Bill? Jack thinks he's in danger then?'

This was news to Fiona, but just one of the minor oversights she had come to expect from her boss when he had his teeth into less mundane matters.

No biggie.

'Ah, visitor for Mister M. Didn't realise DI Carver had managed to con you into working on this one. It is only GBH after all, not even murder. Bit of a step backwards for you, isn't it, Sarge?'

'I think this bodily harm is a bit more than just grievous, Bill.'

She didn't much like the vic's nickname, but knew it was pointless trying to stop any of her colleagues using it. She also didn't bother enlightening the constable about Soundbite's suspicion that this was linked to a cold case, a murder victim. Nor did she share the news that Jack, initially unconvinced of the connection, but more open-minded now, had just called her to relay his conversation with Doctor Powers, or that the esteemed criminal profiler would be joining their little team. No, she just flashed her bleached white teeth, a radiant contrast to her dark skin, smiling broadly at the uniformed constable as she entered the room.

Although she thought she was already prepared for what she was about to see, having viewed the shocking photographs, she couldn't help but shed a tear for the remnants of the man in the bed. She brushed tender fingers across his right cheek, then the other, and did her best to imagine what it would be like to be in his place.

Fiona's ability to empathise with victims of criminal acts was one of the traits that made her such a good detective, but today, confronted with this deformed body, she struggled to do little more than weep for the tortured soul locked inside.

Her fingertips traced the line of his jaw, wired shut before the mouth had been sealed, according to the doctor. The first signs of stubble scraped against her nails and the sensation surprised her, given his hairless appearance—he had reminded her of a limbless crash test dummy on first seeing him. This developing five o'clock shadow made him seem even more vulnerable, but also signified a defiance on his part. It was as if his body was trying to tell her, *I'm still human, I'm still a man.*

Before her brief conversation with the nurse about Gerald Butler's hip surgery, she had managed to track down the young houseman responsible for admitting the victim. She could see he was completely frazzled, in emotional turmoil, and exhausted. He told her he had been working thirty-eight hours without a break on this holiday weekend, and was now desperate for sleep.

'I went to the staff room and put my head down, but immediately started getting visions, my mind attempting to fathom the unimaginable torture that man must have suffered. And still is... I needed to be sure... Whether there was any brain activity, you know? So I got up, had him put on a gurney and wheeled him to the MRI suite myself. I demanded they test him there and then. At first they refused, but I invited the technicians to take a look at him for themselves... The moment they saw his mangled form their attitude changed, and they managed to squeeze him in for a cursory examination between two other appointments.'

Fiona had waited as the medic choked on the words, then gathered his composure, his voice brittle, ready to crack again.

'He's trapped in there. Inside that... that body. A living, functioning human mind, fully cognisant, aware of his flesh-bound prison, but unable to interact with the environment. Nor communicate with other humans around him. Can you imagine?'

She could not.

Fiona, hoping the victim could at least feel something still, continued caressing his face, then put her lips close to his cheeks, an almost kiss as she murmured, her breath warm on his skin.

'I promise you, I will find the bastard who did this... And I will make him pay.'

Fiona's footsteps pounded her determination into the tiles of the hospital corridors while she wondered if the victim's DNA would lead to a speedy identification.

There was nothing else to go on. No fingers to print. No teeth to match with dental records. No ID of any description. All they had were the twisted spiral strands of acid that made up the unique markers of all life on earth.

The problem, she knew, was that the DNA database was limited in scope. Criminals' tissue samples accounted for the majority of records, with additional samples from police personnel, innocent individuals and so on that were stored for elimination purposes.

The other major group they had records for was the MisPers, and she crossed her fingers in the hope that this poor fellow had been reported missing, and that some of his DNA had been collected as a result. Not good odds, she thought, but the best they had as things stood.

Surely someone somewhere was missing a white male, who, until some demonic psycho had decided to apply unnecessary surgery, was probably just an average guy. The young doctor had estimated his age at late thirties or early forties, but then acknowledged that he was no expert, and given the man's emaciated condition, only a full examination by his senior colleagues would yield more detail.

As she stomped down the stairs and along the corridors, following signs for ITU, her mind swimming with thoughts about the man, it occurred to her that he might not be just a regular guy, a family man, but perhaps he was a criminal himself. It was also possible that, in the moral fog of London's underworld, he was a man who deserved everything that had happened to him.

The thought gave a her a momentary sliver of comfort, but until they had his identity, she would keep an open mind regarding his history.

Maybe they would get lucky with the DNA match, MisPer or criminal.

Well, either way, she wanted to get to the bottom of this, and maybe, just maybe, Gerald Butler would have some answers for her.

'Well, well. Doctor Powers. You've not been here for that long, we were beginning to think you might be too good for us... Now you're famous!' Winston Diamond grinned as he stretched a hand out in welcome. 'I'd have rolled out the red carpet had I known you were coming.'

Doc's fingers and palm disappeared into the grip of Diamond's handshake, the massive black fist of an ex-heavyweight boxer, yet the fingers were gentle, as if the man, who had to duck to get through standard sized doors, was aware he had to control his outsized strength when around normal mortals. Doc could feel his presence, even without the mighty fist, and sensed the dark suit, white shirt and clip-on tie were all straining to keep the man's energy contained. He was always reassured by Winston's powerful aura.

'I think being greeted so warmly by Broadmoor's Head of Security is welcome enough, Winston.'

Doc had already passed through three security gates, including one not dissimilar to the body scanners at Heathrow airport, and now stood in reception, with a dancing smile for the big man.

'Well, you know you're on TV again, Doc.' CCTV cameras covered every aspect of this, the most secure hospital in the UK, so Doc assumed Winston had been alerted to their celebrity's arrival by his staff in the monitoring station. 'Here's your pass.' A plastic card on a lanyard that was designed to break if pulled too hard. 'Pop it round your neck and I will escort you to see the boss. Celene's expecting you... Are you able to share with me why you are here? She said it concerned the letter we intercepted. The one destined for Harding.'

Broadmoor may be a hospital, but its security measures reflected the nature of the inmates. The criminally insane. The sick minds capable of the worst atrocities.

Doc's chosen area of expertise.

Four locked doors were between Doc and Celene's office, and the two men chatted as they made their way through each of them, opened with keys from a bunch of dozens hanging from Diamond's belt.

'The letter is only part of it, Winston. I'll explain when we meet Celene. But I want to see him. Today...'

'Harding?' Winston, who knew about Doc's history with the man, was reluctant. 'I'm not sure we can let you do that, Doc. He's back in a seclusion suite again, though due out tomorrow. He's been there since stabbing an inmate some weeks ago. Managed to sharpen a plastic spoon handle into a three inch shiv. Plunged into the inmate a half a dozen times before he was stopped. Broke it off inside the man's liver.'

'Paedophile?'

Doc asked, but was pretty certain he knew the answer, even though it was years since he had given Harding, or his motivations, a moment's thought.

At least, until this morning, when that bloody letter arrived. Then Jack had appeared on his doorstep like a bedraggled Rottweiler, enticing him back...

'Yeah. He's still in hospital.' Diamond chewed the inside of his cheek a little before adding, 'Harding's made no real progress in all the time he's been here. Bounces back and forth between the units. Happens whenever his meds are reduced. He lasts a few months, then something sets him off and he reverts to being a vicious animal.'

'I think that's his preferred, natural status, Winston. That or being drugged to the eyeballs.'

Despite Doc's professional recommendation, Harding had wangled things so that he was in a hospital rather than a high security prison.

'He's sedated, and on anti-psychotics again.' A pharmaceutical cosh, Doc thought as he listened to the baritone voice rumbling out of Winston's barrel of a chest. 'I doubt you'd get anything out of him. Even if we could allow you to see him.'

They'd arrived at Celene's office and she ushered them both in while also signalling to her assistant to organise coffee. Doc had always liked Celene, had enormous respect for her professional abilities, her status among his contemporaries unhindered by her appearance. She had one of the most challenging and prestigious jobs in the health service, a role she relished.

He recalled asking her, when they were newly qualified psychiatrists, whether her multicoloured hairstyle, tattooed limbs, nose ring, and self-inflicted scars on her wrists—the result of an abused childhood, she'd admitted to him—might affect her career prospects. This was in the days when punk rock was young and women with visible body ink were a rare sight.

Celene had shrugged and said, 'Both of us will be dealing with the criminally insane. Outsiders. You want to catch them by getting inside their heads. Well, I want to understand them too, but help them get better... Both of us need to empathise, but in different ways. My lifestyle choices should help me with that. I'm an outsider, like most of them. Maybe that'll give me an edge... And anyway, I don't give a shit what anyone else thinks. Never have, never will.'

Doc had thought her naive at the time. Then watched as her career went into overdrive. He admired her for sticking it out during the tough times, the snooty looks from colleagues and condescending attitudes from most of her managers, heaped on her in those early years, though her rebellious appearance had moderated somewhat since.

'Good to see you, Celene. It's been too long.'

The three of them settled into the sofas in a corner of the room as the assistant rattled in with a tray of cafetières, cups and saucers, one for each of them. The aroma reached Doc even before she entered, and it smelt good, even to his discerning nose, leading him to reflect on the differences between this place and its prison equivalents. Decent coffee was a rarity there, but many of Broadmoor's inmates had access to proper kitchen facilities—at least, those patients who had graduated from the most secure wards. The majority of inmates progressed in this way, ultimately in preparation for release.

But not Harding...

'So Doc, you must've decided to take the letters very seriously. I certainly didn't expect you to head here this morning. Definitely not a crank then?'

Doc had called Celene from his car as he made the journey from central London to Crowthorne, a village just north and west of Camberley, less than an hour's ride via the M3 motorway.

'Yes. I wanted to talk to you both after I met with DI Carver first thing this morning. There's been a... development. I think it's related.'

Winston, his face questioning, interrupted Doc. 'Jack Carver? He was on the BBC news just before you arrived. A female reporter was asking about a mutilated body discovered in south London earlier this morning. Dismembered, she'd said. He had no comment for her, but you think that investigation's related? To those photos you received?'

Celene's brow scrunched in confusion, her attention on Doc. 'He was the one who arrested Harding, wasn't he? Carver? Your friend?' She then directed a piercing gaze at Diamond. 'A dismembered body, Winston, like in the photos that were sent to Doc? I haven't seen the news yet.' Her eyes tracked back to Doc's, the mind behind them sharp and incisive. 'This is very strange. The three of you, linked like this, today, over twenty years since Harding's arrest. Especially given his history...'

Both pairs of eyes were now on Doc, expectant.

'Okay, let me explain.'

Jack had told Doc not to divulge the details of the Clapham Common victim, his detective's propensity for suspicion kicking in. He'd insisted, 'None of the staff at Broadmoor can be trusted. I know you have friends there Doc, but the letters arriving at the same time as our victim was discovered... Well, it's just too much of a coincidence. There must be some insider connection with Harding. My guess is it's a member of staff. So, as far as anyone at Broadmoor is concerned, the two incidents are totally separate. At least for the time being. I'll get down there tomorrow and make some enquiries. Fair enough?'

Doc had other ideas. He had known Celene since their university days, so Jack's suspicions about her were simply too ridiculous to contemplate.

And Winston could be trusted. Of that there was no doubt in Doc's mind...

He could almost feel the chokehold, the sting of a hypodermic pricking the skin on his lower eyelid, the roar of a deranged inmate's angst searing his eardrum. The bellowed threat to 'Kill the motherfucking psychiatrist' who had poisoned his mind with questions about 'evil crimes' he 'did not commit!'

It was at a time when the hospital's security was less rigorous and Winston had been a new member of staff, not long retired from the ring, a junior guard fresh out of training, assigned to keep an eye on Doc while he interviewed the patient. One moment, Winston was attempting to calm the tense situation with softly spoken words, the next, a panther, springing at his prey, too fast for the inmate to react.

The incident had been over in moments, but Doc still occasionally suffered nightmares, vivid scenes involving a needle spearing his eye before being jammed into his frontal lobe.

That was the day he almost died, here, in Broadmoor... A wake up call early in his career, when he had discovered just how dangerous his job could be.

The day an ex-boxer had saved his life with one blurred jab to a disturbed inmate's temple.

Sorry, Jack.

Doc could trust these two people, so he shared everything he and Carver had discussed earlier that morning.

'Fuck me! That hurt. Felt like you ripped my back open.' A few beats passed and then Slim added, as he sat up, 'Phew… Wow! Actually, it's not so bad already.' Then, eyes wide and startled, 'Jeez, guys, my head's spinning.'

'Drink this.' Tamsin handed a warm cup of sweetened tea to him, followed by a boiled sweet when he'd finished that. 'Your blood sugar will have dropped as the adrenalin kicked in. Don't worry, the flood of endorphins will soon have you feeling great, luv.'

Harry was double-checking the rigging with Glen, but could barely hear the conversation thanks to the music, specially chosen by Slim for this, his first session. He had decided to go for a simple two hook 'Suicide suspension', so Harry was working with just two wires, both connected to what looked like a giant metal coat hanger with holes drilled through for pulley attachments. Satisfied, he gestured to Slim, who was still sitting on the table sucking his sweet. Tamsin and Shazza held his elbows as he took a few unsteady paces towards Harry.

'I'm good now, man. Feeling it!' He laughed, a little manically, his eyes glittering as the high kicked in.

'This will sting a bit too.'

Harry straightened up the hooks, attached them to the wires, and then indicated to Glen to start tightening them. Shazza stood behind Slim using sterile pads to mop away the trickle of blood from each of the fleshy mounds created as the wires pulled at the piercings.

'Woah! *Sting?* That really hurts, Harry. Fucking hell! Stop!'

Slim was shaking his head, snorting and groaning, his confidence, having resurfaced earlier, had fled again. Stress and fear were scrawled across his face and, for a moment, Harry wondered if Slim was really up for it.

'The worst is over, bro. It may seem hard to believe, but trust me. When you get up, it's… it's a total mindfuck! Let's get you up there to see for yourself. Then you'll find out what it's all about, my friend! You're not gonna bottle out on me at this late stage, are you?' Harry again noted hesitation on Slim's part, so added, 'If you're having second thoughts you can wait until these guys have all had a turn, but you did say you wanted to get it over with by being first up…'

For a few seconds Harry could see indecision, a brief internal conversation taking place behind Slim's eyes, but then the lad bit his lip and nodded.

'Okay, I've come this far, bro… But you will stop if I say so?' His eyes flicked to Glen and then Harry, who just winked back at him.

'Deep breaths, sweetie.' Tamsin crooned the words to Slim, taking one hand, then the other as she positioned herself in front of him. 'Just say if you want to go up, down or stop. No pressure. Okay?'

Harry stood back and observed as Glen gradually tightened the wires while Tamsin encouraged Slim to rock forward then back. They were in the middle of the room, directly under the rigging and, as the tension on the hooks embedded in Slim's back started to pull him towards the ceiling, he groaned, then murmured, but always nodded when Tamsin checked he was happy to continue.

Finally, on tiptoe, Slim was almost off the ground.

'Are you ready?' Tamsin, still holding both Slim's hands, checked before nodding to Glen. One final tug on the pulley and Slim was airborne.

As Tamsin let go of his hands to join her friends clapping and laughing, Slim was hoisted higher still. He was suspended, hands by his sides, head flopped forward on his chest, the image he created similar to a suicide by hanging.

Only, he was alive and conscious.

Tamsin and Shazza stood in front and behind him respectively, and pushed him gently to and fro, with Slim now flying across the room like a drugged version of Peter Pan.

'Dude, this is awesome!' His head came up and he beamed a huge grin at Harry. 'This is better than ecstasy! Yo! Swing me faster, girls!'

Harry's face lit up, a brilliant smile aimed at Slim, their new bond unbreakable, signifying the beginning of an enduring friendship—the kind of relationship reserved only for those who have shared a life-affirming spiritual experience.

He turned and pumped up the music, the volume now at max, the metallic roar of hardcore punk rock pounding the walls as Slim floated above their heads, a euphoric expression creasing his face.

Fiona arrived at the Intensive Therapy Unit and strode directly to the nurses' station to confirm where Gerald was located. This time she would not be fobbed off. She would insist on waiting with him until he recovered so that she could interview him the moment he was sufficiently aware. He had been out of surgery for hours already, so surely she would not have to wait long.

'The priest's been called… I'm sorry, Sergeant, but it doesn't look like he'll pull through. There were complications. He lost a lot of blood from internal bleeding, his liver is in terrible condition and his heart was already weak. At his age…'

'Oh shit!'

Fiona had seen a priest loitering when she had been here earlier, so without another word to the nurse, who was clearly about to object, she strode to the door labelled 'G Butler' and let herself in.

She was no medic, but she could see he was in a bad way, and paused as she realised the holy man was still with him, offering comfort. She shuffled into the room, pulled up a chair beside the bed opposite the priest, and let him finish what she assumed were the last rites. As she sat, she took one of the old man's hands in hers, without even realising she was doing it.

Fiona had no idea about religious mumbo-jumbo, despite her parents' Caribbean origins. They were secular, though would, if pushed, claim they were Christians, but had never forced her to worship anyone or anything. For that, she was ever grateful. She had no time for formal religion. It had always been, to her mind, the cause of so much distress and heartache around the world.

'Are you a relative?' The kindly eyes assessed her, and mistook the hand-holding as a sign of familial relationship rather than a natural response from one human being to another in distress.

She puffed a little air through her lips, then pulled out her warrant card as she spoke. 'No. Just here on business. Did he say anything to you? Can he still hear me? Can he speak?'

The priest, probably a little put out by her demeanour, her demanding tone, nodded. 'Gerald can hear and has managed to speak. He said a few things, a little garbled, though I took it as his confession.'

'Can you tell me what he said?' She was hopeful, but then immediately disappointed as the priest stood to leave.

'No, I'm afraid not young lady. That conversation was between Gerald and God alone. Good day to you.'

Well, she thought, that certainly put me in my place.

The moment the door clicked closed behind the clergyman, she took hold of the green oxygen mask covering Gerald's nose and mouth and gently pulled it below his chin.

He can't be that close to death if the priest left him alone. And anyway, it's just for a minute. Won't do him any harm.

With those thoughts justifying her actions, she started to interrogate her witness. She noted the unhealthy yellow hue of his skin and wondered what had caused that discolouration, but then reminded herself why she was there, determined not to be distracted by his medical status. As the mask slipped from his face, Gerald managed to pry his eyelids open, though she was not sure how much he could see through the narrow slits. Despite this limited movement, Fiona could see the yellow had spread, discolouring the whites of his eyes. It was difficult to tell how alert he was, but she would ask him her questions anyway.

'Gerald. Can you hear me? I'm a detective and I need you to answer a few questions, if you can. Is that alright? Just blink once if you can hear me and you understand.'

He did.

Then, his eyes, as if struggling to make the effort, slid sideways, trying to focus on hers.

'Good! Stay with me Gerald.' She gave his hand a squeeze, careful not to crush the fragile bones she could feel under his parchment skin. He looked to her as if he was a hundred years old or more, but the contents of his wallet had confirmed he was just about to turn eighty-two.

Except, he won't live that long.

The thought spurred her on, the words jumping from her tongue, eager.

'You said something to the jogger who found you. I need to ask you, did you really tell him you thought that horribly disfigured man was put there for you to find?'

Gerald tried to speak, but all he managed was a gurgle, splutter and a weak cough, so she said, 'Blink once for yes, twice for no. Okay Gerald?'

One slow, purposeful blink, then his pupils were focused back on hers again.

'Do you think you know who the person is, the person who did this? Just blink for me, sweetheart.'

Again, a single languid movement of the eyelids, this time with a hint of moisture welling from the tear ducts.

Fiona was excited, itching for a breakthrough, but wondered how she could get this old man, given his current state, to tell her the name of the person he thought had committed this deed. She assumed the freshly forming tears were just a reaction to the horror he had seen, or maybe they were just moistening the lenses as he forced his lids to respond.

As she was about to ask another question, the door opened and the Ward Sister confronted her, presumably summoned by the young woman at the nurses' station.

'You were told earlier, you can't be in here. Leave the poor man in peace. We've made him as comfortable as we can. The last thing he needs is some overenthusiastic copper badgering him when he should be coming to terms with his situation.'

Fiona, frustration propelling the words, snapped at the nurse. 'On the floor immediately above us, in this very hospital, there's a man, at least, what's left of him, who's been dismembered and disfigured, probably tortured, then left for dead on Clapham Common. Gerald here,' she added, turning back to her interviewee, 'thinks he knows who did this. Now, just give me a moment longer.' Without waiting for another comment from the nurse, she asked him, 'Please try and whisper the name to me my love. It's really important... If it is the last thing you can do before you leave us, please do this one thing.'

She heard a gasp from the nurse, but ignored it. The old man had already heard the last rites from a priest, and apparently made his peace with his maker, so he would hardly be shocked by her request, even if Florence bloody Nightingale was.

He blinked, once.

Brilliant!

As Fiona turned her head and leaned in, her ear almost touching Gerald's lips, he whispered one word.

'Barry? Is that what you said, Gerald?'

She looked at his eyelids, but this time they closed twice.

Shit!

The machine monitoring his heart then started running erratically, the beeping as urgent as the hand the nurse placed on Fiona's shoulder, insistent, tugging at her conscience, trying to encourage her to leave. The detective could see for herself that the effort the old man was making was weakening him.

Killing him...

'One minute!' She grunted her anger at the sister, shrugged the hand away, focused back on Gerald. His eyelids had started fluttering, then dark brown drool appeared at the corner of his mouth, dribbling down his chin into the oxygen mask. Fiona's voice, sharpened, like a needle, probing, urgent. 'The name! Tell me his name, Gerald.'

He opened his mouth and a flaccid yellow tongue quivered with effort, so she moved her ear in close again, barely in time to hear him squeeze out a single word.

Gerald's very last word, uttered immediately before his throat rattled and his final breath left him.

'Good grief! You are heartless! I can't believe you did that. And for what?' The sister, her face flaring red, unhooked the monitors and then punched the buttons on the beeping machines until the alarms ceased. 'You should be ashamed of yourself. I'll be making a formal complaint to your boss, young madam.'

Fiona, already halfway out the door, knew what her immediate boss's reaction would be, so stopped, turned and channelled her best impression of a Gorgon's face at the old dragon.

'His name is Detective Inspector Carver. He's based at Scotland Yard. You shouldn't have any trouble finding him through the switchboard. My name is DS Fielding. I report to him. Thank you for your help today... Always appreciated when fellow public servants do everything they can to help us in our enquiries.' With that, she slammed the door and power walked past the nurses' station, heading for her car.

She would have liked to ask the old man more questions, and normally, with an interview terminated before she had completed the task, she would have been disappointed. But not today.

No, she was absolutely delighted with the result—and she was certain the DI would be too. Her fingers were trembling with excitement as she hit the speed dial on her mobile phone.

She ignored the signs on the walls indicating that phones were not to be used in the wards and corridors, despite the disapproving glances aimed at her as she barged through the crowded Accident and Emergency Department towards the double doors of the exit.

'Sir, great news! I've got a solid lead from my interview with the old man...' Fiona could hear her own voice, at least an octave higher than normal, her shrill enthusiasm bubbling through the ether into the DI's ear.

So what?

This was *her* moment of glory. She was convinced. She may just have found the key to crack this case wide open.

The single word she had gleaned from Gerald's dying lips.

'I think you should see this, Doc. Before you make up your mind.' Winston's baleful eyes scanned Doc's face for a moment, then he sighed. 'You already have, haven't you? I might've known... You still need to watch this.' Diamond nodded to one of the six security guards, each seated before a bank of screens, their combined gaze monitoring almost one hundred cameras located throughout the hospital complex. 'You have the latest Harding incident for me?'

The guard responded by tapping into his control console. The top right hand screen in front of him turned black, then the three letters REC appeared. He explained to Doc as he worked.

'We track every patient and every member of staff throughout the day, so we know their exact location at any given time. That way, we can be sure not to expose vulnerable inmates to those who are potential aggressors. Among other things... The live pictures you can see are just a fraction of the total being recorded, most for both sight and sound, twenty-four seven. For every screen you can see right now, there's another five cameras observing every corridor, ward, security door, social area, staff room and so on. We also monitor the grounds outside, approach roads, access points, gates, and of course, the footpaths between the nine blocks. This was recorded four weeks ago.'

Doc was silent, just keen to get on with his meeting with Harding. He kept his frustration brewing below the surface, unwilling to show his impatience, respectful of Celene's instructions to Diamond. Instructions her security boss was now fulfilling.

'Your man was being escorted to the Visitors' Centre.'

Winston had taken over the narrative, and Doc, still thinking, *Get on with it!* logged that piece of information for later inspection. He would remain silent, if only to keep things moving. He glanced at his watch, certain that Carver would not wait for him if they kept this up.

As the screen focused, Doc instantly recognised Harding, even though it was many years since he'd had any dealings with the criminal. The recording showed

Harding with his escort, a male nurse, strolling along a footpath between red brick buildings towards the inmate entrance to the Visitor Centre, seemingly passing the time of day. Without warning, Harding spun on his toes and slammed the elbow of his right arm into the side of the nurse's temple, flooring him, but instead of a futile run for the nearest gate or perimeter fence, he sprinted across the grass, vaulted a chest high wall, and disappeared from view.

'One blow and he knocked that nurse out cold. Harding's kept himself in excellent physical condition, despite his age.' Diamond's observation merely confirmed Doc's own conclusion. 'Late fifties but just look at him go.'

The screen flickered and then showed a new camera angle. This time, the path leading from the exit at the back of the visitors' block.

The guard, satisfied he had the correct recording, pointed to the two men on the screen, a different couple, but again, an inmate with a nurse, walking away from the rear of the building.

'This chap has been treated for paedophilia, with a great deal of success. He was due to be released to a less secure facility for three months before being completely discharged into the community... And here comes Harding.'

Doc thought he knew what was coming, and braced himself for the attack that was about to take place. Harding, like a wraith materialising from the shadows, leapt a knee high hedge and pounced on the two men from behind. It looked to Doc as though Harding had flown into them, one knee in each of their backs, felling them instantly, before delivering a swift kick to the nurse's face. Harding was as lethal as ever, he thought, as the murderer's hand arced time and again, plunging his home-made knife into his victim's belly and crotch, then he stood, facing the camera, legs spread, arms wide, hands in the air, making two fingered gestures at the viewers.

Doc felt a frisson of admiration in some dark corner of his mind, then a wave of self-loathing for the lapse. He grunted and Winston seemed to take that as a signal of his disgust at the violent assault.

'Incredible, eh? Less than a minute passed between the moment he whacked that nurse escorting him, to this point.' Winston reached his bulky frame over the guard's head and let his finger trace the numerals on the twenty-four hour clock displayed in the corner of the screen, just as four guards in riot gear appeared from off camera, two pairs covering the path from each direction. They did not hesitate, just tackled the vicious inmate to the ground in a flurry of limbs.

Doc could see Harding laughing, not even trying to resist, and for a moment, despite this video being sound free, he heard that raucous, humourless noise jangling inside his skull. He shook it away, urging himself not to let the bastard get to him.

Again.

Doc was older now. Wiser too.

No, Harding would not get under his skin. Would not goad a response from him. Not this time.

'Sorry, Jack. That's the best I can do.' Acting Detective Superintendent Sadie Dawson, known throughout the Metropolitan Police Force as Soundbite Sadie, shrugged at her *least subordinate* subordinate officer, the white tips of her luxury French manicure tapping the cover of a thick file on the desk in front of her as she spoke. 'The Brentwood Beast case has sucked our resources dry over the last six months—'

'Yeah! But we caught the bastard didn't we?' Jack bounced out of his chair, almost upending it, as he bent forward and added his own angry finger, jabbing at the file. 'He's been charged this morning, thanks to my team's efforts. We worked our nuts off for this arrest, boss. I expected a pat on the back, not to be punished for my success.'

For a moment, Jack could see impatience telegraphed across Sadie's brow, almost imperceptible though it was, the woman's mask so perfectly managed and presented to the world. He realised his outburst, having deflated his own anger, may just have inflamed hers. Her eyes, grey granite pebbles, stared at his. She was impassive on the surface, but he was sure the woman had some emotions, buried somewhere deep within.

She never lets anyone see anything beyond what she wants them to see, he thought, as his own rear slowly descended back on to the hard chair situated across the desk from his boss. As his buttocks hit the seat, Dawson carried on as if Carver's outburst had not happened. In Jack's considered opinion, she always reacted to his temperamental flares like this, hoping it would wind him up even more.

'We sidelined several suspicious deaths, some gang related, and a dozen other serious crimes that now need to be dealt with. Investigations we put on hold while we concentrated our energies on *your* latest collar.'

'Aw, come off it, Boss!' His voice climbed again, then dropped back to normal as he caught himself. 'This is not about me!'

Jack wished he had just half of Soundbite's self-control, but the truth was, he had always engaged his mouth before fully working things through in his head, and although the passage of years had mellowed him and enabled him to rapidly reassert control over his tongue, he still had difficulty resisting letting loose his initial reaction.

'Our clear up rate…' She paused, her gravestone stare holding him, unblinking.

Like a bloody automaton, he decided, waiting to see if the unstable human specimen who had stomped into her office would respond. He held himself in check, so she went on.

'…has been badly affected by the Brentwood Beast case and I have to carefully consider where to focus our efforts. We do not have a limitless budget, Jack. We have targets to hit. The overtime bill for the last quarter has wiped out the budget for the rest of the year. I can't let you have more staff at this time.'

'Seriously? Me and one sergeant? Plus some other back up personnel on a shared basis… For a murder investigation…' The sourness in his tone leaked out despite his best efforts to mimic her lack of emotion.

'It is not a murder, Jack. At least, not yet.' She shuffled some papers from her in-tray and offered them to him. 'If you want, you can take your pick. Dump Mister Mutilated for a proper murder enquiry. You said DS Fielding had a promising lead already. Looks like she can handle this one.'

'But what about the other vic? Diana Davies? The cold case you convinced me was related—when you woke me up this morning.' He almost added, *Don't you ever sleep?* but thought better of it.

'Well, that was slightly premature on my part, as I misinterpreted the initial reports. This latest individual seems to bear little resemblance to the Davies case.

Dismembered and disfigured, yes, but there the similarity ends. Female. Crude hacking of the limbs, no real effort to keep her alive, a likely sexual dimension given the traces of semen inside her. And so on...' She steepled her fingers and pressed herself back into her executive chair. 'On balance, I'm inclined to think they are unrelated.'

'Well, I don't agree.' When Jack had arrived at the office and discovered Sound-bite had cut their team to the bone he had stormed up the stairs to her office determined to get more resources, but now, with the benefit of her calming influence, he realised he had taken the wrong tack. He should have explained about Doc's letter and how it had apparently been timed to arrive this morning, coinciding with their grisly discovery on Clapham Common. He filled her in on his conversation with Doc in the hope he could convince her to give him more men, his enthusiasm for the case building as he explained. 'I don't want to switch. I want to find the evil git that chopped all these people to pieces.' He tossed his copies of Doc's other photographs across the desk, and sat back, arms folded.

'So, Doctor Powers is joining your team? Well, that's good news, Jack, although I had not budgeted for a consultant profiler... Here's the deal.' She smiled, but the Botox smoothed lines of her face eliminated any humanity from the gesture. 'I'll find the money for your pal,' a pause, as if waiting for Jack to interject, then, 'and he can join your team. I'll review your resources *if* the victim dies...'

'That's almost inevitable boss. The hospital houseman I spoke to this morning thinks he was left in the tree for hours. The perp probably expected our vic to be dead by the time the old boy discovered him.' Fifi's report on her interview with Gerald Butler had already reached Dawson, and the sergeant was now downstairs, working on locating her suspect. Carver was yet to be convinced that the victim was posed deliberately for the geriatric to find, but held his scepticism in check for now. 'Apparently, Mister M was dehydrated almost to the point of no return by the time the ambulance arrived. Needs to be fed intravenously, around eighteen hours a day, every day, if he's to live.'

'Parenteral nutrition, Jack.' An almost smug look visited her plastic features before they relaxed back to neutral. 'Very common for people who've had their bowels removed. But rife with complications... Go on.'

Jack wondered how his boss knew the technical details of such an unusual procedure, and almost asked if a friend or family member had suffered the experience, but her businesslike attitude always left him floundering when it came to personal matters. He decided to stay on track.

'Yeah, that's what the medic called it. Anyway, they aren't sure how long they can keep him alive. Days maybe.'

Good thing too. Trapped inside that flesh prison, still suffering horrendously...

And Jack would get the resources he needed if the victim died.

'Keep me posted.' The Acting Super glanced at her Rolex, then added, 'I've got a news conference in fifteen to tell the world we've charged the Beast. I think we're done.'

Jack eased himself upright and muttered, 'Bloody press. Parasites, the lot of 'em.'

'And that, Detective Inspector Carver, is one of the reasons you will never be behind this desk.'

Carver paused, and watched her as she took a compact from her drawer and checked her hazel bangs, smoothed her pencilled brows and twisted some red lipstick from its miniature phallic container before applying it to her lips. He thought she was goading him, aware of their nickname for her, her reputation for a love of the limelight. He kept quiet, made a move for the door, then her voice cut through him.

'I know you think I only got here because of what I have between my legs, Jack. Positive discrimination and all that. Women promoted over their more able male counterparts. That's total bollocks, you know?'

He had reached the door, had a hand on the knob, ready to get out of here and do something useful. Like finding a killer.

'Why would you believe I think that?' She was right, but he would not admit it to her.

'I've been on the job for fifteen years, Jack. I know what a misogynistic bunch you old timers can be. I've suffered first hand… Okay, I'll admit you're a great hands-on detective. Probably better than I was.'

There was not much doubt about that, in Carver's mind.

'My clear up rate is the best in the division, ma'am.'

'Indeed it is, Detective, but that's not enough. Your problem is one of attitude and suitability—or rather, lack of it. You are too impetuous at times, and that makes you something of a liability.'

'That's not fair—'

'You don't know me well, Carver, but in the six months I've had the pleasure of working with you, *observing you*, I can tell you that your obvious disdain for your superiors, your reluctance to engage with the politics of the job, well, these things will continue to hold you back.'

'Meanwhile, you're about to go and take all the credit and glory for *my* team's efforts, preening in front of the cameras, as if you single-handedly nicked the bastard yourself, despite being sat behind a desk all the time. That's not what the job's about! Or bloody budgets!'

'Well there you have it, Jack. I read about your insubordination, though this is one of the rare occasions I've witnessed it first-hand. I'll give you a pass today given the result you have just delivered. But you need to understand, the press can be a useful tool for us. They make better allies than enemies… I saw your performance this morning. Scowling at that BBC reporter, repeating *No comment!* over and over as you brushed her questions off. Learn to throw them a bone or two without compromising what you're doing.'

'Oh, right-oh then! You know there are pictures of our latest victim all over the internet? Mister Mutilated was a term coined earlier this morning by one of those bloody press parasites from *The Crusader*—he breached all sorts of newspaper rules and ethics getting those photos, but we can't even charge him with a crime. No complaint from the victim, and one of the nurses in the hospital stupidly left the bastard alone with him…'

'I sense a bit of kettle and pot calling, Jack. You also seem to have a habit of disregarding the rules. Your, shall we call it, liaison with that rather attractive female PC… Erm, Wendy Turner. That too, showed a blatant lack of respect for the rank you hold and the role you should play as one of the Met's senior officers.'

'That was three years ago. Long before you arrived. I paid my dues for that!' And liaison seemed a rather polite term for what they were caught doing. A blow job in the ladies' loos. His tone quietened, a gruff acknowledgement of his guilt. 'Shouldn't have happened, I know.'

Wendy had been shot by a lunatic on parole shortly after the event, something that should never have happened either. He swallowed back the thought, the sudden uninvited weight of grief over her death surprising him.

'Yes, indeed you did. It was a good job for you that you were both off duty. Otherwise...'

Carver wondered then, why she had brought this up. And why now?

Okay, it was true. He'd been caught with his pants round his ankles, immediately after knocking off for the night... Caught with a junior officer, a uniformed copper he'd been *liaising* with for some time.

'Is this gonna be a problem between us, ma'am?'

He did not want a transfer, but if she had a grudge against him, maybe thinking he was some sort of misogynistic predator, abusing his seniority, well, he'd just have to get out of here.

'No, Jack. I just want you to understand that I'm not some bit of fluff. Not some weak female, over-promoted despite there being supposedly more able male officers. I worked my tits off to get where I am. I've consistently put in more hours than any of my colleagues, and still do. My results may not have been as stellar as yours over the years, but unlike you, I also know how to play the game. Which is why you're in your mid-forties reporting to someone in her mid-thirties. So just deal with it. And get me some results. Now bugger off. I have a TV crew waiting.'

Jack, duly castigated, fumed inwardly at the truth of her words. Then it occurred to him. Was she purposely antagonising him? As he mulled that thought over he wondered whether it was some weird management ploy. Maybe she was trying to get him worked up enough to prove he really was better than her.

Well, if she was, the ploy worked.

Then the realisation hit him. She had done the exact same thing when they first started working together, when he had been tasked with the Brentwood Beast case...

Maybe she was smarter than he gave her credit for. Giving him limited resources while demanding a wide-ranging investigation with a potential link to other serious crimes—three unsolved cases to clear up. Then rubbing his nose in his shitty career prospects...

Was this just a challenge to his ego?

Of course it was.

The manipulative cow.

Well, he would show Soundbite Sadie just how good he really was, and not only crack the Mister Mutilated case, but solve the other cold case murders too.

All four for the price of one.

Fair enough! Now, how's Fifi getting on with her lead?

He took the stairs two at a time, also thinking he had yet to properly fill his sergeant in on the expanded scope of their investigation. He would do that now and also let her know the three of them were pretty much on their own, thanks to Dawson's lack of support.

At least, until their victim died.

DS Fiona Fielding's eyes were itching from screen glare. She tried to rub the sensation away with the back of her fists, pressing her eyeballs into their sockets in a vain search for relief. She had been through all the available CCTV coverage of the nearest road adjacent to the footpath on Clapham Common where Gerald had discovered Mister M. The common was mostly open, with a football pitch, ponds and green space for people to play frisbee or picnic or soak up the sun's rays.

Jack had suggested she concentrate her efforts on the access points in the southeast corner. Here, he had explained, the shrubbery and tree cover was sufficient to prevent passing motorists on the South Circular Road from seeing someone humping a human torso through the undergrowth before hanging it from a tree. It was unlikely the perpetrator would have taken a longer route than necessary, and probably parked nearby before manhandling his victim to his chosen site, close to the footpath several hundred metres from the road.

The uniforms had collected the videos earlier that morning, not that there was much to work with. Two all-night stores and one solicitor's office with security cameras had offered up relevant coverage, overlooking that section of the common. Carver had suggested checking from two until six in the morning, given that the victim would likely be dead if he had been dumped any earlier. Twelve hours of tape to view, and, as she suspected, he insisted she checked it all out, personally.

And for what?

Nothing. Nada. Zilch. A big fat zero.

She checked her watch, thinking she was now seriously hungry, and not a little grumpy.

Jesus! I've spent three fucking hours at this.

Yes, she had increased the playback speed, zipping through most of the recordings and then slowing to check out any activity, suspicious or otherwise, involving passing vehicles or pedestrians, so now, her brain was melting.

Enough!

She would check with the General Register Office to see if they had made any progress in locating the suspect Gerald Butler had identified. As she shut down the monitor, she heard her belly grumble.

Time for a spot of lunch.

But then her boss, puffing from exertion, poked his head into the viewing room. He had other ideas.

She turned at the noise and saw his face, now pink and sweaty, peering round the door, and she wondered what had happened. Was he having a heart attack or something?

'Come on, Fifi. You're not still watching telly, are ya?'

No, not a heart attack then.

She pursed her lips as he winked at her, grinning inanely.

'Don't just sit there, Sarge. Get your arse into gear. We've got work to do!'

'So, tell me why you reckon it's the grandson.'

Carver stuffed the remains of a gourmet bacon, egg and tomato sandwich into his mouth, finally giving Fiona enough time to answer properly. He was definitely in one of his hyper moods, having fired off a dozen questions about the videos and her interview with Piers Reid, cutting off the answers as soon as he was satisfied he had heard enough.

He could be maddening, but he was also a stimulating boss, and she felt totally comfortable with him. He was thoughtful too. Enough to order sandwiches for them both, from Pret a Manger, not the canteen, and he'd even remembered she didn't eat mustard on her ham and Brie baguette. So here they were, in his new BMW 5 series, ploughing through London traffic on their way to Gerald Butler's home, having an impromptu working lunch.

Carver had also filled her in on why he thought they were on to something much bigger than just Mister M, and she was well pleased to hear that Doc Powers was joining them officially as a full-time consultant too. Jack and Doc had a pretty amazing reputation and now she would be working with them both in an *elite unit*, no less, according to her boss. A tight team, with no outsiders. It would mean working long hours, but it would be worth it.

Fiona was convinced.

Her mood had lightened as she followed in the trail of the whirlwind her boss created before leaving the office. Four idle officers had been sitting, yakking about taking down the Brentwood Beast, wallowing in reflected glory, when Carver had descended on them and dumped Fifi's unfinished tasks on them.

'You lot. Stop loafing around. You waiting for some work?' He didn't give them time to answer, though it was obvious they were just finishing their admin for the Beast case, tying up loose ends, while revelling in a rare moment of kudos. 'Right, Gerald Butler found a mutilated body on Clapham Common today. You've all heard, right?' He snatched a file from Fiona's fingers and dumped it on one of their desks. 'He told Fifi here that his grandson put the victim there for him to find. I want that person traced. Details are in here. The Registry have been working on this already so check what they've got, and then find him for me. And yeah, Butler may have fifty male grandkids for all we know, so get on with it.'

Fiona had not been unhappy to have that bit of grunt work passed off to her colleagues and now slurped her coffee before answering Jack's question.

'Well, it was like a confessional boss, he'd already had the last rites. *Grandson* was his very last word when I asked him who had put Mister M there for him to find, and I'm absolutely certain he understood exactly what I was asking.' She was not sure she had convinced her boss, and the few hours that had passed since she had left the hospital, walking on air, elated at the lead she had wheedled out of Butler, had filled her with doubts too, but she still wanted to believe it was true. 'The young lad who found him said the old man was adamant, too. Kept repeating over and over that the victim had been left there for him.'

Carver smacked his lips and made hoovering noises as his tongue sucked the last crumbs from between his teeth and cheeks. 'Mmm.' More oral cleansing took place, then, 'Seems pretty unlikely, don't you think? And Butler gave no explanation why a member of his own family would leave a mutilated victim for him to discover, almost certainly knowing his grandad would finger him for the deed. Hardly the actions of a successful serial killer.'

The thought had occurred to her, and when Carver had explained about Doc receiving that letter this morning, her own line of enquiry seemed much less certain to yield a result. She just frowned, her frustration and disappointment surfacing as her boss continued to shred her confidence in the old man's assertion.

'And why did he tell the paramedics he had no next of kin? Even in the hospital, before surgery, no mention of kids, or grandkids, no spouse, nothing. Just a bleedin dog. That's all he kept on about according to the uniforms on the scene. His mutt… Probably already in Battersea Dogs Home by now.' Carver swerved into a parking spot, his tyres squealing in protest as he scraped the kerb, cursed under his breath and said, 'We're here. Don't look so downhearted, Fi!' He reached into his jacket pocket and pulled out a house key attached to a white rabbit's foot. His toothy grin shone at her as he added, 'Lucky for us, we found these at the scene. Must've fallen out of Butler's pocket.' Another canine grin with a wink. 'Let's see what secrets the old boy may have been hiding, eh?'

'We don't get too many incidents like that these days, Doc. The violence in here is usually aimed at the staff. Most weeks it seems, one or more of our two hundred plus inmates has a pop at a staff member. We've got seven employees on long term sick from serious assaults, with three more due back this month.' Winston's stride had Doc struggling to keep up as they progressed through the maze of corridors on their way to Harding's seclusion suite. The security chief went on, 'We have physical security, including the cameras, walls and these doors of course,' his keys rattling as he unlocked the last of several they had to pass through, 'as well as the procedural. Everyone's movements are tracked, no inmates can move between blocks without an escort, but neither of those things would work half as well without the relational security. The trust we build with the inmates. They usually tell us when things aren't right—both with themselves and with others.'

'And Harding?' Doc was certain his father's murderer was not the sort to confide in anyone. He was also unconvinced that the criminal should be in a hospital, and had raised his concerns with the Broadmoor staff on previous occasions. 'Celene still convinced he's mentally disordered? Not just a very cunning psychopath, manipulating the system? Still adamant he can be rehabilitated here?'

'Not just Celene, Doc. He's had several therapeutic assessments over the years, all with the same result. A varying degree of psychosis with underlying Dangerous Antisocial Personality Disorder. Mind you, an old colleague of yours, Professor Richard Maddox, took over his case earlier this year. He's just submitted a report on Harding. Since the knife attack, he's been seeing the inmate daily…'

'Maddox? I had no idea he was back doing psychiatric consulting.'

'Yes, and enjoying it by all accounts. Popular with the inmates too, though not Harding.'

Doc had thought the man, an egotistical high-achiever with a narcissistic personality—largely justified by his genius—had been diverted by more lucrative medical fields many years before. He would have to square things with Maddox at some stage, aware that Celene acquiescing to his request to see Harding could put the consultant's nose out of joint.

Too bad.

Doc had more important things on his mind than the febrile ego of a self-important colleague.

They finally arrived, with Doc checking his watch for the third time since leaving the security control room, wondering if he would be too late to fulfil his arrangement to meet Jack at the hospital. Thinking of the detective prompted him to raise his suspicions with Winston.

'How did Harding know? About the other inmate being at the Visitor Centre immediately before him?'

'You're thinking one of the staff must've told him? Leaked the information to him? No, Doc. Possible, but highly unlikely. The inmate himself may have been mouthing off about it, and this place has an effective grapevine, despite all the security measures. If anything, given his history of attacks on paedophiles since he's been here, we should've made sure there was zero possibility of the encounter, but we slipped up. The medical staff thought Harding was doing well, ready to graduate on to Occupational Therapy. Though that's about the tenth time he's almost reached OT... This is his room. I'm coming in with you.'

Doc's immediate reaction was to object, as he wanted to see the man alone, but knew that was out of the question after what had happened the last time he had been allowed to visit the inmate. The big man's presence would be a comfort too.

'Okay, Winston. But do me a favour. Don't engage him in any conversation, no matter what he says.'

Winston's head bobbed in acknowledgement before he indicated to the nurse, sitting outside the room, observing her charge through a panel in the door, to step aside and unlock it for them. As she did so he asked her, 'Has he had his meds?'

'No, sir. He's a little overdue already but Celene's office called and asked us to delay them. Professor Maddox has been gradually reducing his medication too and has just approved his transfer back to a room in the secure wing. He's due to be moved tomorrow.'

'Okay... Ready Doc?'

Doc, his knees wobbling, his belly swirling with acid, and with the irritating flutter of butterfly wings brushing his stomach lining, let his eyelids fall closed, counted to four while taking an inward breath to fill his lungs, held it for a count of seven and then slowly exhaled.

He was as ready as he would ever be.

Gerald Butler's home in Wakehurst Road was less than a hundred metres from the eastern edge of Clapham Common in a high-density residential area of bay-fronted terraced houses, most with pebble-dashed walls alongside red tiled bow windows. Many of the larger properties were now luxury homes or converted apartments, despite the houses being barely two paces from the pavement.

The faded red paint was flaking off Butler's front door, and Jack's thumb brushed some to the ground as he rang the bell. He murmured to Fiona, 'Just in case he didn't live alone.'

No sounds came from within so he slotted the key in the lock and, with his sergeant in tow, stepped into the gloom of the old man's home.

'Jesus! Stinks of wet dog in here. And the place is filthy. I think we'll be wiping our feet on the way out, Sarge.'

He pulled at his nose and then wiped it with his wrist as they stood in the narrow corridor. Fiona pushed the door to behind them.

'Well this won't take long, it's not very big. We've got a two-up two-down. You want me to check the bedrooms, Boss?'

'Yeah, you pop upstairs and see what you can find. Anything that might give us a clue as to why he thought he was the target of this maniac, and anything that might help us identify any family links. I'll do the lounge. Not sure we'll find much in the kitchen or bathroom.'

Jack had already stepped into the cramped front room and could hear the thump of Fifi's footsteps on the stairs as he flipped on the light switch.

What a state! he thought, as he took stock of the place.

A sofa that looked like it doubled as the dog's bed was littered with the animal's toys, some half eaten bones and doggie-chews, plus a blanket that needed fumigating. A person's sense of smell deteriorates with age, but Jack decided Butler must have had nothing left of his olfactory equipment. The detective also concluded that the armchair must have been where the sad old man spent most of his life. It was almost threadbare except where the dirty brown material of the arms had been patched, and the seat cushion was sagging on springs that had left the factory many decades before.

Bay windows that had not seen a wash rag or chamois for many years filtered much of the light through a coating of grease and grime, while grey netting, speckled with mould, blocked most of the rays that did struggle through. The curtains, probably purchased at the same time as the lounge furniture, were a similar colour to the carpet. Brown was big, back in the nineteen seventies, so Carver did his own version of carbon dating, based on personal observation rather than an element from the periodic table. The sofa faced a TV in the corner of the room, and he decided the device would not look out of place in the technology wing of the Science Museum.

An ancient mirror, with an ornate gilt frame spanned the width of the open fireplace below. Jack noted that the mantelpiece, an original with intricate coloured tiles and a slab of dark wood that would probably fetch a fortune, had three framed pictures propped there, so he homed in on them.

The first was of a youthful soldier wearing corporal's stripes, dressed in full kit, standing at ease with his rifle held at his waist. The uniform was khaki battledress, with shorts, boots and puttees. Although Jack could not make out where the image was taken just by looking at the background, he decided the photo was probably from the tropics or somewhere equally hot. Gerald Butler's stare, straight to camera, was slightly unnerving, even though the black and white image was faded and yellowed with age. Jack felt uneasy, an unusual reaction that startled him.

'Must be getting old.' He said it aloud, to himself, but glanced over his shoulder to check whether Fifi had heard.

No chance.

She was still upstairs, he realised, her footfall creaking above his head as she searched the front bedroom.

The second picture, similarly faded and discoloured, was of the same young man looking a little older, now in a suit, with a woman of about the same age, probably early twenties. They were on the steps of Lambeth Register Office, according to the brass plaque on the wall beside them. Hairstyles and dress gave Carver the impression he was looking back to the early sixties.

So, Gerald did have a wife. At least back then. Dead? Divorced?

He made a mental note to have her traced.

The third photograph was similar to the first, though this one was in colour, with a fresh-faced soldier in a relaxed pose, again casually holding a weapon, but in this picture the lad was hefting a shoulder-held rocket-launcher. His back was pressed against the bull-grille at the front of a sand coloured armoured car and his cheeks and forehead were ruddy from wind and sun. He too was looking directly at the camera, but his face was cheerful, less full of pride, more adventurous. Not threatening, or unsettling, like the other.

Jack immediately compared the youthful faces of both soldiers, and estimated the photos were taken a good few decades apart. A definite family resemblance, he decided, then took stock of the background in the more recent image.

Probably Afghanistan. Or Iraq. Definitely the Middle East.

He made a quick calculation. If soldier boy Gerald was in uniform around 1960 and the other lad in the early noughties, then this could well be the grandson that Fifi had been so excited about... Just as the thought entered his mind his mobile started chirping, then he heard a thump and a squeal from the room above.

'Boss! I think you'll want to take a look at this!'

DS Fielding could hear Carver muttering in the room below as she started searching old man Butler's bedroom. She had already taken a quick peek in the bathroom, decided not to set foot in there, given the state of the toilet pan, and then checked the other bedroom. It took her just seconds.

A box room, not much wider than she was tall—and she was a short-arse, by her own admission. There was a single metal-framed bed, made up military style, with blankets that felt to her like they were made out of horsehair, smoothed and tucked as if ironed and measured for maximum precision. No headboard, just one pillow that had seen better days. Although the room was relatively clean, it smelt earthy and damp from the dark patch of fungus growing in the corner adjacent to the bathroom.

She got the impression that the room had been unused for years. It contained no photos, no mementoes, no hint of personality. Just the bed with a unit to the side containing three empty drawers, and some equally barren shelves on the wall at the head and foot. Even so, it felt cramped to Fiona, and the bare walls, magnolia paint on plaster, seemed to exude sadness. She crouched to the wooden floorboards and checked the underside of the bed.

Nothing. Just a thick layer of dust.

So now, she was creeping around in the musty dimness of Gerald's bedroom. Like Carver, she had turned on the light despite the open curtains, but the low wattage bulb barely managed to overcome the filth of the cloth lampshade. She sighed and pulled out her iPhone, and used the torchlight to illuminate the contents of Gerald's bedside drawers.

The room was just big enough for his double bed, a wardrobe that looked pre-war and a dressing table with a grimy mirror tucked into the window bay. A tatty oriental rug in faded red and gold covered a patch of bare wooden flooring, but otherwise the room was cold, unwelcoming. A crucifix hung from a nail in the wall above the bedhead. No photographs, no pictures, no decoration, and although lived in, the old man's bedroom had a similar atmosphere to the other.

Decaying and devoid of personality.

The bed had also been made by someone with a military mind, but the odour in this room was of urine, not mould, and her nose twitched as she sat perched on the edge of the mattress, delving into Gerald's life.

Poor, lonely old man…

The drawers yielded very little of interest to her, just some pill bottles, a thumbed paperback, an empty hot-water bottle, a Swiss Army knife and a silver hip flask with what smelt like brandy inside. She was beginning to think she was wasting her time, hoping that the DI might have found more, but she pushed herself off the bed, dropped to her knees and took a quick look underneath.

Nothing. Again.

She was about to get up, her right hand pressing on the floorboard between the bed and the drawers, when she felt the wood move. It was a short section, and she wondered why it had been sawn as it looked as though it had been cut long after the floor was laid.

With excitement mounting, she scrabbled at the wood, but could not get purchase. She was not one for fancy manicures or acrylic extensions, but she did look after her fingernails, kept them neither short nor long, lacquered a near natural colour. Even so, in her enthusiasm she managed to tear one.

Bugger!

She sucked at her index finger, tasting the blood, then remembered the knife in the drawer.

Idiot!

She grabbed it, fumbled with the blade, determined not to rip another precious nail as she eased it open. The knife was old, well worn, sharpened so often that the blade was thin and slightly bent. As she eased it into the crack between the floorboards to prise open the hidey-hole, she wondered how often Gerald had done the very same thing.

The wooden slat flipped up with a clatter and she grabbed her phone light to inspect what lay beneath. Between the joists holding up the floor, with the ceiling fixed to their undersides, was a gap of maybe twenty centimetres, and within that cavity she found nine metal tobacco tins, each of them green, silver and gold with an Old Holborn logo on the lid.

Okay, Gerald. What have we here?

She lifted out the first stack of three tins, sat with her back to the bed, and popped them on the floor between her outstretched legs, eager to see inside.

Fiona used the knife blade to flip off the first lid and almost dropped the tin as she realised what she had discovered.

'Boss! I think you'll want to take a look at this!'

'Well, well, well! If it ain't the Prodigal Son. Doctor Colin Powers. Or is it Professor these days? Oxford University offered you a job telling lies to their students, have they, now you've made your name by appearing on telly?'

Doc was certain that Harding would not have been allowed to watch his unsolved crime series last winter, regardless of how well the inmate had manipulated and wriggled his way through the hospital categories, from most dangerous, unstable patient to one ready for Occupational Therapy and potential rehabilitation. Harding could have heard about the show from any number of sources. Although it had been a long time since he'd had dealings with the killer, Doc knew this would end up as a cat and mouse game.

Who was the cat?

Well, only time would tell.

He gave himself a mental shrug, counted his breath in and out again and said just two words.

'Hello, Antony.'

The inmate, dressed in casual clothes, was sitting at the small table adjacent to the side wall in the rather grandly named Seclusion Suite. His hair was greasy, with lank dark strands intertwined with steel coloured streaks, giving the effect of barbed wire highlights. Although Harding had aged since their last meeting, Doc would have recognised those lopsided eyes, one a lifeless grey the other glacier blue, and that pinched ferret's face as surely as if they had last met just hours before. Despite the passage of years, there was still no softness emanating from the man, just an air of superiority, all-knowingness, and a sense that violence was never far from his thoughts.

Doc always felt a similar aura from Winston, but it was a benevolent power, with violence held in check except where necessary. Harding was at the other end of the scale, and Doc wondered how he could still fool Celene, but hopefully, not Maddox.

Maybe I'm just totally biased, considering what he did to me.

Harding, sensing Doc's discomfort, tilted his head, as if trying to bring his eyes into alignment. The asymmetrical features were the unfortunate result of a childhood incident when Harding's junkie mother had dropped her infant boy on his head at the top of some concrete steps leading to her front door. A neighbour found the boy on the pavement and took him to hospital, but it was too late to save the sight in his left eye, or the hearing in his adjacent ear. His fractured skull had healed but he would be labelled FLK by health and social workers soon after—Funny Looking Kid —thanks to his misshapen head and mismatched irises.

Recent research had confirmed that the amygdala, the part of the brain responsible for processing emotions, was underdeveloped or damaged in most psychopaths —often the result of head trauma in childhood—and Doc wondered whether this unfortunate start to Harding's life had led him down the vicious path he had trodden. Not that it mattered. The man had been dangerously violent for most of his life, and was rightly kept under lock and key.

It was as much as Doc could do to stop himself from turning to check that Winston had followed him in as he sat, but he knew the inmate would pounce on it, would see it for the weakness it was. He stared back into the unmatched eyes and took a seat opposite the man who had butchered his father.

'Don't call me that. Me name's Tony. You know I hate…' A sly twitch at the corner of his mouth would have been a response to humour in a normal person, but Doc knew it was pure cynicism as Harding took the measure of the man he was already jousting with. 'So, I see you've got the big Pooh Bear with ya! Hey Winnie, are you here to make sure I don't hurt him? Or are you here to stop this bastard trying to throttle the life out of me again?'

He broke his gaze from Doc's for a second, his eyes tracking upwards and to the left, unwittingly giving Doc the reassurance that Winston was indeed right behind him. Probably leaning a shoulder against the wall, arms folded, in a typically relaxed pose that belied the power he was ready to unleash if the inmate made a move towards Doc. Winston also kept silent, as requested.

'No one is going to hurt you… Antony.'

A pause, a little verbal stab at the man's self-assurance, his ability to manipulate and control, challenged with just the one word, the given name he despised. Another fraction of a smile tugged at Harding's lips, but again, it was not a sign of humorous appreciation.

Doc was not here as a healing physician, he was here for answers, and if he could get under the inmate's skin—and not let Harding get under his—then maybe he would learn more from the man's riddles than normal. He was calmer now, still controlling his breathing, almost subconsciously, as the fluttering and burning in his stomach subsided.

This is not so bad.

'Well, Colin—'

Doc heard the rustling behind him, and sensed Winston stiffen. Then a response rumbled over his head.

'It's *Doctor Powers* to you Harding. This may be a hospital and not the high security prison where some of us believe you belong, but you need to show respect for all the medical staff, including outside consultants. Have some manners.'

Harding dipped his head, and clasped his hands on the table in front of him, the tattooed words LOVE and HATE on his knuckles intertwined, fingers whitening as he squeezed. Probably daydreaming about strangling the security chief.

Or maybe me?

Doc let the thought evaporate, as Harding spoke again.

'Well, Doctor. I've been expecting you.' His knuckle joints popped in protest as he wrung his frustration out on them. 'Thought you might be keen to come to see me.'

The claim sounded like bravado to Doc, not a genuine prediction, so he ignored it, though would circle back to it later.

'I'm hoping you can shed some light on something I'm currently working on.'

'Fuck off! Why would I help you? If it wasn't for you I wouldn't even be in here.'

'No. You're in here because you're a violent killer with a mental disorder, according to some experts.'

'Yeah. But the pigs only realised…' Then a pause before the ferret's nose and mouth lifted, his buck teeth exposed in what passed for a Harding grin. As if a little thought bubble had appeared by his head, like in a cartoon, Doc could have predicted the words that came out next. 'What's in it for me then, Doctor Powers?'

'I have some images I'd like you to view. Images I'm sure you'll appreciate.'

'Ooh, you've got some photos, have ya? Crime scenes? Victims? Yeah, is that right?' He hunched forward, his clasped hands dancing a jig on the table top, tap, tap, tapping the surface, betraying his excitement. Even his dead eye seemed to glow at the prospect for a fraction of a second.

'Indeed. You will get to see them, but only if I get what I want first. Quid pro quo. Fair enough?'

Another uneasy rustling from Winston suggested that Doc was overstepping the bounds Celene had set. He could always square things with her, as well as Maddox, later, if need be. But right now he wanted answers.

'What makes you think I can help? I've been in here twenty years! You think I've got underworld links still? You're off your head, pal.' Then, the rodent grin reappeared and he added, 'You still don't know what happened with your old man, do ya? Is that it? You want chapter and verse. I can do that for yer. Tell you how he looked as I watched the life drain out of him!' Harding laughed then, a guttural, gurgling noise that shredded Doc's equanimity like a cheese grater.

Doc forced himself to monitor his breathing, mentally checking his emotions, then considered the truth of the statement and began to wonder if that was the real reason he had come.

Harding's laughter had morphed into a coughing fit that gave Doc enough time to get himself back on track. The noise came to an abrupt halt as Harding wheezed in some air and gasped, 'I need some water. Haven't had this much excitement in ages!'

The nurse, who had been on observation duty, brought him a paper cup and he took it without a word of thanks, then sipped at it. He inspected Doc over the edge of the cup as he drank, his brain ticking over, almost certainly considering how best to wind up his special visitor.

It was quite conceivable that Harding actually had nothing to do with Carver's cases, both current and cold, and that whoever sent the letters that morning was just playing a game with Doc, drawing him to Harding like this, knowing their history would guarantee some emotional fireworks.

It seemed unlikely, but Doc needed to be sure. Either way, he could not let the inmate decide how this meeting would go.

'I'm not here to talk to you about my father, Tony. I'm here to ask about your speciality. Dismemberment.' Doc let the teaser hang between them, watched as the slippery tongue slid across Harding's lower lip. 'But before I show you these images,' he patted his jacket pocket, 'I want you to explain about the instances you claimed you were involved in...' As Harding sat back, and started to protest, Doc continued. 'I'm not looking for a formal confession of murder. I know you say you didn't kill those victims, just disposed of the bodies.' The almost grin, the cunning printed on Harding's lips, quivered as Doc went on. 'I'm not interested in details relating to those crimes, just some background on the process involved. You claimed to be something of an expert, if I remember rightly.'

'Yeah. Used to work for the Adkins firm, south of the river. I was a doorman on their clubs, but also did some cleaning work for 'em. None of this is a secret. All in the court records.'

Cleaning for the Adkins family.

Doc translated the euphemism: disposing of competitors or anyone else who crossed the most vicious gang of criminals in the south of England. He was sure there was more to Harding's past than just the handful of brutal murders he had been found guilty of, despite the man's claims to the contrary.

'Yes, I remember, at the trial, you seemed to think admitting to four instances of dismemberment of corpses and disposing of the bodies in the New Forest would be considered in mitigation. That surprised your defence team, but your cunning ploy helped convince the judge to assign you here, rather than high security prison, didn't it?'

The tongue darted into view again, tasted thin lips, then words oozed out of Harding's ugly mouth.

'Well, doing all that gave me a sort of traumatic stress disorder. I had to do it or I'd've ended up joining 'em. What with the abuse I suffered at my mother's hands and then as a boy in care homes… Damaged me. I've never been right since. Hacking up dead bodies didn't help my mental state none, I can tell ya that. And it ain't easy, cutting up corpses, y'know?'

The whining tone, the plea for sympathy implied by his words, did not convince Doc. The man was a psychopath, incapable of feeling for his victims. No compassion, no empathy. Dismembering human corpses would have affected his mental state no more than a slaughterhouse worker chopping up an old nag for dog food. If these criminal acts had any impact on Harding's mental state at all, it would have been the sensations derived by his pleasure receptors from the 'entertainment value', or the feeling of superiority he would inevitably experience undertaking such deeds.

'But you became an expert, Tony. Correct? If I remember rightly, you would cut around the joints, rather like a butcher, or even a surgeon amputating a whole limb. No chainsaws for you. Finesse was your MO.'

Doc tried to sound admiring, but was finding it difficult to dissemble. His current emotions ranged from revulsion to hatred with regard to this particular criminal.

'Correct. Chainsaws make a terrible mess. Throws traces of blood and tissue all over the place too. Not good. Unprofessional… I just used chefs' knives on 'em, did 'em in the bath. Cut round the joints then just popped 'em apart. Disposing of bodies is the toughest part of getting away with murder… Not that I murdered anyone else. Just that fucking paedo priest and the others I was done for… Including your old man!' A smug-ugly smile. 'He was a right cunt, y'know? You still have no idea why he had to die, do ya?' He laughed again, and pointed at Doc's face. 'You look just like him. Nasty fucker. He was a total psycho too… I reckon you take after him. Doing your job, and all!'

Doc swallowed back his hatred, his brain struggling to count as he breathed in, but his ears were roaring and the urge almost overpowered his self-control. He wanted so desperately to let go, and launch himself at the killer, to wring his neck, to choke the life out of him.

Just like the bastard had done to his dad.

'What the bloody hell do you mean, you've been re-assigned already? The job I gave you lads should've been done and dusted by now.'

Fiona could hear Carver's footsteps tramp up the stairs, his voice echoing in the corridor, then he paused for a few seconds, presumably listening to the excuses emanating from one of the four coppers back at the Yard. While she waited for him, she pulled her protective gloves from her pocket, wondering if she had discovered evidence relating to a current crime, or just a historical one.

'Oh! Good. So you did get somewhere then. Leave it on my desk.' The DI appeared in the doorway, grunted an unidentifiable syllable at her, pocketed his phone and then said, 'We've got a name, Sarge! Harry Butler. Just the one grandson. And I think I found a photo of him in the army.' He waggled the framed picture in triumph as he entered. 'No other info on him yet, though.'

'Harry?' *Not Barry, then...* 'That's what Butler said. At the hospital...' Her mood had shifted, and she knew she sounded unenthusiastic. Morose, even.

'So what was all the excitement about, Fi?' She watched as his eyes, accustomed to the gloom already, took in the prised open floorboard, the array of tins she had since placed on the bed, and her hands, pulling on her gloves. 'Well, I take it that ain't a secret stash of roll-up baccy then!'

Fiona lifted one of the tins, the lid already off, and proffered it to him as he strode towards her.

'Not tobacco, boss.' Her voice was dull, in direct contrast to her initial shrill excitement. 'Two ears, dried up and shrivelled, but undoubtedly human...' She held one of them by the lobe between finger and thumb, then pulled it from the tin, the other dangling below it, attached by a short link of leather thong. 'Both pierced through the middle before being strung together. A collector's item.' Her belly was queasy, her ham and Brie baguette not far from resurfacing.

'Bloody hell! Trophies. Must be the old boy's...'

'Yeah, but not taken recently. Here, look.' She gently laid the ears on the lid lying on the bed cover, then tipped three tattered photographs from the bottom of the tin beside them. As she played her light over the faded grey images, she said, 'This is the victim, before his ears were lopped off. A simple mugshot. This one was taken some time after.' In the second photo the man was naked, standing alone, hands and feet bound to a vertical post, his body badly beaten, blood from his severed ears streaking his neck, shoulders and chest. 'And going by how he appears in this third picture, very dead.'

'Firing squad. Shot him from the looks of it... That's Butler, I think. Holding the poor bugger's head up for the camera in that last shot. Why cut his ears off before shooting him?' He did not wait for her to answer, just asked, 'Anything on the back? Date, place?'

She flipped to the rear of each of the pictures but only one had any ink visible on the blank side, and that was difficult to read as the scrawled handwriting was almost illegible from age. Only the date was readable: 1958.

'So what's in the other tins? More of the same?'

'I don't know sir, I haven't opened them. Is this a crime scene now? And do you think this has anything to do with our victim?' Anger was hot on her tongue, her voice climbing as she let rip at Jack. 'D'you think *his* ears might be in one of these tins? Or was it just people of colour that bastard Butler mutilated?'

'Hold your horses, Sarge!' He seemed to realise then, that she had been affected by her discovery, and not in a positive way. 'Are you alright, Fi?'

'Yeah. I'll be fine...'

She wasn't convinced by her own words. And neither was he, from the look of it. He waited, eyeballing her, gave her a few seconds before speaking, his voice softer now.

'First, let's take a gander at what's inside the rest of the tins. What have you got, eight more? Then we'll be better placed to understand what's going on. But if I was a betting man, I'd say we'll only see more photos of dark-skinned fellahs who suffered amputations before joining Butler's gruesome trophy collection... Having said that, at the moment, I can only take a wild guess about how this links with our Mister M. And we're detectives, so let's leave the wild guesses to the muppets, eh?' He pulled his own gloves from his jacket pocket and said, 'I can do this myself, Sarge... Why don't you check out his kitchen diner. Maybe make yourself a cuppa while you're at it. You look all in.'

She was not sure whether to thank him or slap him. Was he being condescending? Treating her like some over-sensitive girly who couldn't cope? Couldn't do her job?

The thought whistled through her mind and exited as quickly as it had arrived.

No, not Jack.

Fiona could see the concern on his face, the genuine expression behind an equally genuine offer for her to take a brief time out. He could be gruff and full of bluster at times, but he had good people radar and had obviously sensed the underlying reason for her distress.

She was torn between staying and confronting the savage nature of the man whose hand she had held to offer comfort in death, or getting out of here, avoiding the truth, even if only for a few minutes longer.

The gruesome discovery had delivered an unexpected and unwanted cultural clash inside her mind, hammered into her psyche like a stake through the heart. She heard her own voice inside her head, repeating the line she had delivered with humour earlier that morning, now carrying a vicious undertone:

Is it 'cos I is black?

Maybe. Maybe not.

'Okay, boss. I won't be long.'

She left him to catalogue the contents of Gerald Butler's vile memento collection and found herself in the kitchen-cum-dining room, barely aware that she had traversed the stairs and corridor.

Snap out of it, Fi!

She checked the fridge for milk, but found nothing in there other than three bottles of cheap vodka, some dill pickles, a half opened tin of dog food, and some left over pizza.

No tea for me then.

She took a moment to root through the drawers and cupboards, listless, barely noting the contents, convinced there was nothing else to find here. They had the grandson's name, a photo of him, and the old man's disgusting trophies. If Butler had taken the trouble to hide his stash of human remains, then, she reasoned, it was unlikely she would find much else down here.

Fiona was about to call Carver to see if he was ready to leave, when she remembered the under stairs cupboard. She grabbed the handle of the triangular door and pulled, but it was much heavier than she imagined. At first, she thought she might need to find the key, but she managed to wrench it open using both hands, fully expecting to be confronted by a vacuum cleaner, brooms and mops, the usual assortment of household items. Instead, she discovered an empty space, dark inside and with no light switch she could find. As she bent to take a closer look she noticed scratch marks on the inside of the door.

At first, she thought they might be from the dog, pawing at it, trying to get out of a makeshift kennel, but as she inspected the ancient paint and ragged exposed wood, she thought she could see a tiny fragment of yellowed fingernail embedded in one of the scratches. Very small hands had made the marks, she decided, many years ago.

So, what had Gerald been up to?

She got down on her knees again, ducked her head inside the doorway and used her phone light to check the cupboard really was full of nothing, the beam sweeping the floor and then the back wall.

Her head came up with a thud, her scalp scraping a sliver of skin on the door frame, as she reacted with shock at what she saw.

Ow! I'm jumpy as hell today. Calm down, Fi. Think!

Her mind started to connect the dots.

The spartan single bedroom. The twisted grandfather who tortured people and collected body parts as trophies. The grandson who might well have been corrupted by the old man. And now this.

The miniature prison cell under the stairs.

Doc replied to Harding's outburst with a fixed stare and the words, 'I told you, that's not why I'm here.'

Not this time… And I will not let you get to me!

'So where's these photos you want me to look at, then?' Harding's voice slithered into Doc's brain, slicing at his self-control. Suspicion loitered on the inmate's face as his spiked eyebrows lifted. 'Or are you absolutely sure you wouldn't prefer to chat about your daddy some more? I could talk about him all day.' A slow smile formed, completely bereft of humour, followed by a farting noise squeezed through wet lips. 'How he squealed like a little girl. Begged me not to kill him. Pissed his pants, he did… I reckon you'd rather hear all about it, from the horse's mouth. None of it's in the police reports. You don't know the half of it!'

Doc could feel his world starting to come unhinged again, sliding perilously into the nightmares that occasionally plagued him, both asleep and awake.

He didn't need this.

Maybe he should have listened to Jack and let the detective follow up on the letter and photographs with this excuse for a human being instead. Doc's stubborn streak would not allow that, and although the memories relating to his father's death were buried very deep, there were questions he had always wanted answered. Not least of all:

Why?

Instead of allowing himself to be sidetracked by his own morbid curiosity, he took the photographs from his pocket, aware of greedy eyes following his hand as he did so, then placed them face down on the table before him.

'Four images. Four victims. Four questions.'

In truth, Doc did not expect to get any relevant information directly from the man, given the length of time he had been incarcerated and the recent nature of the latest crime. He also knew Harding enjoyed playing games, but was sure he could gain some insights into questions he would not ask the inmate outright. And he had no intention of showing the psychopath these images.

'What makes you think I ain't seen 'em already?' Harding sprawled himself on his chair as he tipped it up on its rear legs away from the table, one arm slung over the back, dangling to the side. Like a teenager, presented with a meal he did not want.

'Well, this was taken this morning.' Doc touched the back of one and circled his finger there, pushing the photo forward, as if to tempt Harding. 'So I know you haven't seen that. And the others, well, although they might be on some illicit websites, I can guarantee you haven't had access to them.'

Broadmoor policy did not allow any mobile telephones, smart or otherwise, on the premises, for staff or inmates, and no internet access for the latter, just supervised email sessions. All contact with the outside world was monitored and controlled, determined by the specific care plan tailored for each of the hospital's charges.

'I might have.' He dropped the front chair legs back to the floor with a thud, and reached forward as if to snatch the picture from under Doc's finger, but Doc did not flinch, just sat scrutinising the man's reactions. Harding laughed at his own feint, pulled back his hand and added, 'In fact I'm sure I have!' He locked eyes with Winston, and aimed his words at him. 'I'm guessing you stole them from my letter. The one you censored and decided I shouldn't read... Arrived this morning, did it, Winnie?' His face relaxed back to a supercilious stare, his chin lifted and eyes narrowed as he returned his attention to Doc. 'Security in here's gone downhill since the bloody golliwog took over. Don't believe the Broadmoor bullshit, Powers... I know exactly what you got in the post... But you ain't here for that, are ya?'

Doc scooped up the images and tucked them back in his pocket, placed his palms on the table and pushed himself upright, looking down into Harding's disturbing—and disturbed—gaze.

'Thank you, Antony... You've told me all I need to know today.' He straightened and turned to Winston, whose face seemed a shade darker, his lips curling, as if he wanted to respond to Harding's insult. He nodded as Doc added, 'We're done here.'

Harding, seemingly unfazed, tutted. 'I don't think so... You'll be back!'

Doc turned and thought about how often he had dreamed of throttling the life from this being's larynx, but decided he had no wish to spend another moment in Harding's suffocating presence. No reply was necessary. He had what he came for, and that was enough.

Winston gestured to Doc to step out of the room before him, but as Doc reached the door Harding's voice rattled his sense of well-being, like dirty fingernails being dragged across his brain.

'Oi, Powers! One last thing. You should take a closer look at those photos you got this morning!'

Doc tried to ignore the implications, convinced this was yet more gamesmanship, so he carried on walking, his pace quickening as he tried to get away from his tormentor.

Harding, frustrated at having the meeting cut short, shouted after them, his words echoing with harsh laughter, amplified as it bounced off bare corridor walls before his door slammed shut.

'You really should. Check out the females. You might just see someone you recognise! Hahaha!'

Carver's shoes came clomping down, drumming above her head, his voice slightly muffled to her ears.

'How're you doing, Sarge? I'm done...' His voice became clearer as he stood behind Fiona. 'Found anything in there?'

She shuffled back on her hands and knees, blew some hair out of her eyes, rubbed her sore skull with her fingertips, and said, 'Yeah. It's like a little dungeon in there, Boss. There are shackles hanging on the end wall. It's small inside, but I reckon I could just about stand upright where they're fixed in place. There's a crucifix nailed above the chains... And there's an enormous image of an angel's wings etched into the paint at the back. Nothing else.' She traced a finger over the inside of the door as Carver bent to take a closer look. 'It's like someone tried to claw their way out. A little person.' She pushed the door to, and stood, pointing at the handle. 'This is not a normal cupboard door, sir. Much thicker. And this lock is heavy duty too. My guess? It hadn't been opened for years, it was so stiff. I doubt the old man could've used it recently, given how feeble he was...'

'Mmm.' Carver placed a hand on her shoulder, massaged it for a second, as if trying to comfort her. 'Our Mr Butler was not a very nice man, Fi. I've organised a couple of uniforms to come and collect those tins.' He dropped his arm back to his side, and said, his voice more formal now, 'Well done on finding that little lot, Sergeant. We'll get some photos of this too, but it's all history. Nothing that relates directly to any of the more recent victims on our list... I'll tell you all about the trophies inside the other eight baccy boxes on the way to the hospital.'

'Hospital?'

'Yeah. We're supposed to be meeting Doc Powers there, and I'm hoping Bob Koch can join us too.'

'Prof Koch? The Home Office Pathologist? What's going on, sir? Is there another body? Or has our victim died?'

'Not as far as I know. We're all going to have a little chinwag together. With our Mister Mutilated. See what he can tell us.'

Fiona was baffled by the DI's optimism, given the state of the vic, but she kept her own counsel and followed him to his car.

'Bloody hell, Winston! This place is supposed to be the most secure facility in the UK. And when I say, *Don't speak to the inmate, whatever he says,* that's exactly what I mean. As if I'd care if he's rude. Christ!'

Doc's elevated blood pressure had created a pulsating sensation at his temples that had already developed into a dull thudding headache. He wanted to meditate, to stretch his body into awkward shapes, to feel the burn of yoga returning his equanimity. Instead, he continued to blast his frustration and anger with Harding at Broadmoor's head of security.

'A hospital for the criminally insane is supposed to control *everything* the inmates see and do. Fat lot of good it does, censoring their mail, if they're getting help from someone on the inside!'

'We don't know that's what happened, Doc—'

'Oh, really?' Doc rarely raised his voice, but now he was ranting as he paced Winston's office, burning carpet fibres as he stomped back and forth. Without breaking stride he counted off on his fingers. 'One. How did he know that paedophile he attacked was due to leave the Visitor Centre immediately before his visit was supposed to take place? Two. Who authorised for those two visits to coincide like that, despite his known hatred and violence towards paedophiles? Three. How did he know I received a letter—a letter sent here, remember, years after I last did any work for Broadmoor? Four. Had he already seen those images? Even though you intercepted his mail? Did someone here sneak him copies? And finally, why does he think I'll recognise one of the victims? Who *told him* the person's identity?'

'Woah, Doc! I'll admit we have some questions to answer, but let's not get too hasty, eh? You're upset. Understandably so. The guy's a piece of work. And I will be looking into this—'

'That's not good enough, Winston. Sorry.' He saw the security chief squirm with embarrassment at the failures Doc was listing, felt for the man, but this was a serious breach. And it related to a current criminal investigation. 'I'd suggest you do that today, because tomorrow, I will be back with Detective Inspector Carver who will undoubtedly want to make this an official part of his enquiries. You need to have answers for him. And for me...'

Doc, calmer now, though his brain still thumped, needed to get away from here. He had to talk to Jack about that parting comment from Harding. It had started a cascade of worry tumbling through him, and his stomach now harboured a murder of ravens, beating their wings against his heart, not mere butterflies.

'Yeah... Okay, I'll get a report sorted for you both tomorrow. We have all the records of who has had contact with him, where and when, going back years. I'm on it, Doc. And I'm sorry you had such a crappy meeting.'

Doc stopped pacing the room, saw the crestfallen look and decided he needed to reassure his old friend.

'We'll get to the bottom of this, Winston. One way or another. Okay?'

'You know, there's been only one break out from here in almost twenty years. And although we have had some issues with smuggling, our security is pretty rock solid. But metal detectors and X-ray machines aren't designed to pick up a few photos or typed sheets, Doc... Much of our focus is on weapons, or contraband like drugs or phones. But paper?' He shrugged. 'Short of strip searching all five hundred or so staff and consultants when they arrive each day, well... We have to rely on their moral standards. We vet them all, but occasionally we get a bad one.'

'I know, Winston. And you need to find that bad apple. Fast.'

'We tightened things up after last time, three years ago.' In response to Doc's quizzical look, he added, 'We had a bit of a scandal with a couple of nursing staff feeding confidential info to the press. They were taking backhanders to supply the tabloids with salacious details of our worst offenders, including Sutcliffe and Napper.'

'Celebrity criminals. And the journalists paid for information... What is the world coming to?'

Doc's words were laced with irony, considering his own part in the phenomenon. Sutcliffe, nicknamed the Yorkshire Ripper, brutally killed thirteen women, with ongoing police investigations into the same number of killings, possibly related. James Napper was convicted of double murder, manslaughter and rape. Both cases had featured in Doc's TV series, in which he posited the theory that many unsolved murders were the work of these and other convicted serial killers.

Like Harding...

Doc wiped that thought from his mind as Winston made excuses.

'We've not been immune to the government slashing state funded enterprises either. Many of our security staff are on contract these days. Employed by GCS, and their reputation's not exactly top drawer. We do incredibly well, considering...'

Global Contracting Services.

A highly profitable organisation, but one whose standards were questionable, and their incompetence a matter of public record.

'It amazes me that the government still gives them contracts after they screwed up security for the Olympics. But let's keep an open mind, Winston. It could well be an NHS employee in need of some extra cash, unaware of how serious this is.' Doc joggled his car keys impatiently, then made for the door. 'I'll be back tomorrow morning, with DI Carver. I'll leave you to brief Celene as I'm in a hurry. I'm supposed to be meeting him right now.'

Doc jabbed the unlock button on his remote control and his British racing green Jaguar XK convertible honked a welcome as he approached. The car park, with space for over a hundred vehicles for staff and visitors alike, was almost full, but only one car was moving.

The purr of a Bentley Mulsanne was almost drowned out by the swish of bloated tyres on the damp tarmac, and Doc turned as the luxury saloon, registration plate MD1, pulled up beside him. He got a waft of cigar smoke from the interior as the driver's window descended silently, along with a booming greeting from a voice he had not heard for years.

Today was turning into a real trip down memory lane, but not a pleasant one.

'Well, Colin Powers! Good to see you back at the sharp end. Not everyone's cut out for a career in TV. How are you, old boy?'

'Dickie Maddox. I was hoping to catch up with you but I have to dash... Are you here tomorrow? I'd like a chat about an inmate you're working with.'

'Let me guess. Harding.' Doc must have looked taken aback, as the other psychiatrist explained. 'I only consult for a handful of patients here, Colin. He seems the most likely candidate for your attentions given what happened not long after I graduated. Dreadful business. Your father. Happy to help in any way I can.'

'It's all rather more complicated than that. But I wasn't aware you were back to psychiatry. I thought you still spent most of your time at your plastic surgery clinic in Los Angeles, filming episodes for your TV series. What was that called? *Ask the Dick Doc?* I never saw it. Unfortunately.'

Despite having been involved in a series of his own, Doc was no fan of the small screen and rarely watched any TV programmes, and although he knew the series title he could not resist a little jab at the man's Zeppelin sized ego.

'Not quite, Colin. *Ask Dick, the Doc...* Number one across all major US cable networks for six seasons. The last series was shown over here too, on Channel Five. I also did a series on war medicine, but that's all history now... Are you in a hurry then?' Doc had pulled open his door and already had one boot inside, but the *Dick Doc* was blocking his exit. 'We could catch up this afternoon. Better for me as I have no pressing need to be here tomorrow. Harding's being moved up a level, so I'll no longer need to see him every day.'

'I have to go... Would you mind?'

Doc waved his hand in a *move on* gesture, but Maddox responded by plucking a business card from his breast pocket, then held it out for Doc.

To fetch.

Like a dog.

He sighed and went to the window, took the gold embossed card, and muttered, 'Thanks. But I really must go now.'

'Call me. We can meet at my clinic. In Harley Street. Address is on the card. I'd really love to catch up. Cheerio, Colin!'

Doc rarely disliked anyone to a degree that could be described as hatred, but today he'd had the misfortune to meet up with the two people from his past who had amply qualified for entry into that category. Harding was bad enough, and now this…

Maddox.

A man he had met as a student at Oxford University, three years his senior, undertaking the same degree. Both of them, the youngest medical students in the UK at the time they entered college, precocious and brilliant, with just thirteen weeks separating them in age as freshmen. Maddox was sixteen years three months on arrival, but Doc's sixteenth birthday was on his first day on campus, and so he took over as Oxford's youngest ever medical student, eventually taking the mantle as Britain's youngest qualified doctor. His record would never be beaten either, as the minimum age for entry to medical school had been increased to seventeen years sometime after he graduated.

Maddox, piqued at having his record taken from him, even before either of them had qualified, used his seniority to make life hell for Doc, never missing an opportunity to belittle him, to play practical jokes on him or embarrass him. It was obvious he wanted Doc to fail, or at least have to take an extra year to reach finals, but it only spurred the younger man to greater endeavour, and they ended up as rivals, jockeying for the higher honours.

Doc's car gave a throaty roar as he gunned the throttle, his recollections fuelling a dark mood as he sped through the Berkshire countryside back to the motorway. The rain had stopped and the air tasted clean and fresh, so he flicked a switch and let the roof fold away, and did his best to calm his nerves as he drove.

His brain, firing like the eight pistons in his racing engine, was turning over the unlikely occurrences that had happened since he'd woken that morning. He could not help but wonder who might be behind the unhappy coincidences that had congealed around his visit to Broadmoor today.

But the most pressing issue on his mind, the one that had him on tenterhooks, with his belly being chewed from the inside out, was the last thing Harding had yelled at him.

The photographs were burning his chest through his jacket pocket, and he found himself thinking of the dismembered torso and the ravaged body of what appeared to be a female victim. Her hairless head held no clue to her identity, but he held her image in his mind's eye as he drove, burning rubber while joining the M3.

He had not seen the woman he loved in over eighteen months, had tried not to dwell on her departure, but found himself visualising her, conjuring her in his mind, creating an image as detailed as if she was sitting beside him. As he joined the three lanes of traffic, he used his voice command to make a call. He uttered the name with a croak, but his smartphone responded, recognising who he needed to talk to, and Jack's voice answered immediately.

'Doc, where are you? We've just arrived at the hospital. Got Bob Koch coming over too.'

The two pictures in Doc's mind's eye finally coalesced, and freezing tentacles of panic gripped his throat. He managed to force out the words that were determined to stay lodged at the back of his tongue, only to be replaced by the sourness of bile. He gulped in air as he spoke.

'Jack, we need to find her... I think... Harding said... Christ... I think it's possible... The other woman in the pictures... It could be Judy...'

'Calm down, Doc!' Carver was standing outside St George's Hospital main entrance with the phone pressed to his right ear, a finger poked in the other. 'You knew he was gonna wind you up. Don't let him get to you.' He paused for a moment, then continued, the voice of reason. 'We have nothing, not a shred of evidence even vaguely suggesting any of the victims we're investigating, current or cold is...' Another moment, then, his exasperation steeling his tone. 'Judy Finch isn't even officially missing—'

DS Fielding stood patiently, observing her boss as he held the phone away from his ear, the words from Doc's rant audible but indecipherable from where she stood, then silence for a moment before Jack put the device to his cheek again.

'Listen to me, please. Just try to calm down and get over here asap without writing your motor off. We'll talk about it then. I think you're overreacting, my friend, but we'll see what we can do to track her down.' He snapped his phone shut and marched through the doors. 'Come on Sarge, Koch'll be waiting for us.'

Fiona half-jogged along behind him.

'So who is this Finch woman? And why was Doc so upset, boss?'

Fiona had heard enough to get the gist, but she had no idea about the woman's history or relationship with the psychiatrist. She also could not grasp why this female was suddenly of interest, and wondered who would be on the receiving end of Jack's promise to track her down.

As if we haven't got enough on our plate already...

'Judy? Oh it's a long story, Fi, but let's just say: Doc fell in love with her a few years ago, then her seven year old son died, not long after Judy's mother and ex-hubby were murdered by a psycho who'd been let out on licence... Doc worked for the Parole Board at the time and played a large part in the decision to release the lunatic. Leech was his name.'

'Peter Leech? I remember.' It was a big manhunt, all over the news after he killed some of their colleagues. She sensed Jack starting to close down as she spoke, as if this was all rather personal for him too, but could not stop herself. 'Nasty bit of work... But what's this woman got to do with us, and our current enquiries? You said yourself, Doc's overreacting. I know he's your mate and—'

She tried not to sound peeved but could feel some resentment brewing. It had been a long day already, and her own emotions were shaved raw by everything that had happened. Fiona could not help but wonder, why the bloody hell waste precious resources trying to trace Powers' old flames? She didn't join this team, sold to her by Jack as an elite unit, to end up as a dogsbody, aiding and abetting their consultant profiler's love life.

Carver stopped, whirled to face her. Fiona almost collided with his chest, the tip of her nose brushing his shirt as he halted. She took a pace back and saw a look of thunder in his eyes.

Oh shit…

Good job she had not vocalised that previous thought about old flames.

'Sergeant Fielding. Don't question my ethical approach to this—or any other investigation—ever again. Yes, he is a friend. He is also the best forensic psych I have ever worked with. My clear up rate is unbeaten in our division, and that is partly down to the partnership Doc Powers and I developed. Over the years I've learnt a great deal from the man and I continue to respect his judgement and insights, so please, keep your mind on the job. And just in case you are in any doubt, *the job* is whatever I tell you to do. Got it, Sergeant?'

'Sorry, sir. I didn't mean anything by it—'

'So, we don't have a problem then?'

'No, sir. Not at all.'

'Good. Get your notebook out.' He didn't wait as she fumbled for her pad and pen, just fired more angry words at her. 'Judith Amelia Finch. National Insurance number: YV010134B. Worked for the Parole Board for England and Wales until three years ago. Recent pictures: on file from her Home Office employment. You'll find those and more in the top right hand drawer in my desk. Although not officially missing, she disappeared at the beginning of the year. Seems she couldn't cope after her little boy died from complications after an RTA. That accident only happened because the lad ran into the path of an SUV while he was trying to get away from the same fucking bastard that killed four coppers—one of whom was a very close friend of mine. He also left a string of civilian bodies in his wake. And if it wasn't for *my mate,* Doctor Colin Powers, he might still be out there causing bloody mayhem. Is all that clear, Sergeant?'

'Yes, Boss.'

He seemed slightly mollified as she scribbled the details, though she could still feel his wrath, almost telepathically transferred, his head craning forward, brushing hers, checking her notes, reading them upside down, his breath more rapid than usual.

'Now, the last I heard, she was working as a volunteer in a church soup kitchen near Brixton Market. But she had no permanent address, just hotels. She sold up everything she owned, including her property, and gave most of it to Shelter and kids charities. Now go and find her, and Gerald Butler's grandson, Harry. And see how they're getting on with identifying who might've sold those hooks, pulleys and wires. I'll meet Bob Koch alone and catch up with Doc when he gets here. I'll see you back at base when I'm done.'

Wow!

Fiona was left standing in the corridor, pad in hand, stunned at the DI's response. She had seen him flare up before, but he usually just calmed almost instantly, back to business in the blink of an eye. But this?

It must be personal, surely. For him to be carrying round the Finch woman's NI number in his head, and verbally downloading her details, just like that. A file in his desk drawer…

For a person who was not even officially missing?

She still had doubts about the necessity of locating this woman, but she would do as he said. If Carver had been trying to track Finch down already, it was not going to be a five minute job, that was for sure.

She let out a troubled sergeant's sigh signalling acceptance of her lot, turned and trudged to the exit. Then she remembered.

Jack had been driving.

She didn't have her car here.

Bollocks!

Today is just getting better and better, she thought.

'Thanks for volunteering to give us a hand on this one, Bob. I know you're more used to meeting your clients on a slab downstairs or moribund at a crime scene, but I really could do with your opinion on this guy.'

Carver shook hands with Professor Robert Heinrich Koch, the medical examiner most often consulted by the Major Crimes Command for cases involving suspicious deaths in the south east.

'No problem, Jack. Glad to help.'

'The reason is, we've got a few other victims that may be connected, and I want your input. Unfortunately, we only have photos to go on for two of them. You're familiar with the other one. Diana Davies. Did you bring the file?'

'Yes. I have her post mortem report here, from a little over ten years ago. I've refreshed my memory as best I can but it's rather hazy I'm afraid. There really is nothing I can add. You really think the chap they found today might be linked to this butchered lass?'

Koch handed a beige file to Jack, who could not help but notice the colour coordinated perfectly with the pathologist's houndstooth jacket and waistcoat, and almost had the same hue as the bow tie, though that was a smidgeon darker. The man was invariably immaculately turned out, but always wearing garments more suited to a feature in a nineteen-fifties fashion magazine. A full head of hair settled like a snowdrift on his shoulders, the effect making him even more owl-like than his startling yellow-green eyes, magnified through thick lenses, and his predator's stare. His intense focus was the perfect bedside manner for his uncritical patients, but Jack still found him to be an unnerving companion.

Despite this discomfort, Jack had enormous respect for the man's professional opinion, and hoped that today he would not be disappointed.

'It looks like Doc Powers is going to be late. I'd hoped he could join us.'

'Powers? He's retired from the Met, hasn't he? Busy with his dreadful tabloid TV programmes from what I gathered. I thought he was well past his sell by date, in any case. I heard he'd admitted to mental health problems of his own. Breakdowns, memory loss and so on. You honestly think he can help with something like this?'

Jack sensed the immediate chill and animosity in Koch's tone, wondering what might have spurred that reaction.

Probably no bad thing Doc's late.

He just nodded, then said, 'Shall we go in?'

They had met in the reception area reserved exclusively for the private rooms where their victim was being treated.

Well, kept alive, for now, Jack thought, then said aloud, 'Our victim's in a very bad way and we suspect the person who left him expected him to be dead from exposure by the time he was found. Without round the clock nursing he couldn't survive more than a few hours, even in here… Meet Mister M.'

Koch approached the bed, eager, fascinated already. He turned down the blankets for a closer inspection, exposing the entire remnant of the man, much as he would with a corpse.

Carver was no softie, no bleeding heart, but he had more humanity in his big toe than he'd ever witnessed from the pathologist. He cringed inwardly as he saw the victim being handled like a slab of beef, rolled on to its side with about as much finesse as he'd expect from a butcher, then blurted out, 'He is still alive, Bob! He might not weigh much but he is still in there!'

'Mmm. I'm aware of that, Jack… I assume these small dressings on his back cover a recent injury.' A quick tug at the corner of one and a peek underneath confirmed it.

'We found him suspended, with hooks.' Jack explained and offered to show Koch the crime scene photographs, but the medic's attention had already moved on.

Koch tore away the hospital diaper from the mutilated victim's lower body and rolled him on to his front.

'Most extraordinary thing. His anus has been sealed. Look!' He straightened up, took a square of blue cloth from his pocket and frantically cleaned his lenses, his head swivelling between Jack and the object of his fascination. He perched the glasses back on his beak, and continued his close examination of the man's nether regions. 'And just a small hole created for urination. I wonder why they used a nappy rather than catheterise him… There's no possibility of faecal matter leaking.'

'What d'you mean?'

'Well, he's not eaten solid food for some time, and as a result I would say many of his internal organs will be atrophied. His upper bowel and so on. Looking at the degree of healing, these scars where his anus should be, I'd say he has been like this for some months.'

'Months? Like this?'

'Uh-huh. The doughy, pallid flesh is most unhealthy, with muscle wasting and overall deterioration suggesting he's been maintained in his current status for some time.'

'Really?' Jack had assumed the surgery, the amputations, the overall mutilation, had been inflicted more recently.

Never assume.

'I'm certain of it.'

'So what about his other scars. The face? And limbs? Over what period was this done to the poor chap?'

Carver's stomach was threatening rebellion. He thought he had been prepared for the worst, but this was diabolical. He was literally sick to the stomach, then realised that unpleasant feeling was one the victim would never experience again.

'I prefer not to say until I get him opened up, but based on a cursory examination like this, I'd suggest these wounds,' he indicated the pink tissue lines in the flesh where the shoulder joints should be, 'are older than the others. The degree the scar tissue has faded rather suggests the legs went next.' He rolled the head and torso on to its back again, none too gently, then felt the flesh around the mouth wounds. 'The houseman I met just before you arrived confirmed the teeth have been removed, the jaw immobilised and the mouth sealed, just like the anus. No mucus membranes remain exposed, with skin and flesh grafted where required. Mmm. Probably taken from the thighs before they were disposed of. This is stunning! A work of art, Jack.' He actually grinned, his bulging eyes gleaming with the joy of discovery. 'I have never, in thirty years of tending the dead, been presented with anything like this! The attention to detail, the work that went into it. It's mind-boggling.'

Jack didn't feel much like applauding the sicko's skill and creativity, and had never seen Koch so animated. Maybe it was the thrill of examining a not-quite-dead victim for a change. He wanted to get out of the room. Koch's enthusiasm for the corpse-to-be was nauseating, so he thought it best to keep quiet as the waves of adulation washed over him.

'This will make an intriguing case study for students involved in amputations and plastic surgery. The person who did this has a high level of skill in both. Look!' Jack made a token movement of his head, as if really keen to see. The ME continued, finally offering up something of real value to the detective. 'This demonstrates a great deal of practical experience in both fields. The ears were relatively easy to slice off with less repair work needed after removing the fleshy outer. But see how the eyes and nose have been removed, the wounds carefully sealed, apart from these breathing apertures. The contours of the face smoothed… The stitching, the tissue transplantation, the entire operation. Amazing! A highly skilled individual, with a qualified assistant. Nurses. An anaesthetist too, maybe—'

'Hold on a minute, Bob. This needed a fully trained medical *team* to perform? Not a single surgeon, with all the mod cons, top notch equipment?' The hospital medic who had admitted the victim that morning had been adamant they were looking for a qualified doctor without expanding on the subject. Koch's comment could help narrow the field considerably.

It was beginning to look like the Harry Butler lead was a dead end, though. His grandfather's accusations merely the rantings of a man riddled with guilt, the shock of discovery dredging up memories of his own atrocities in Africa, convincing him his grandson was somehow punishing him, taking revenge for an abused childhood.

Yet, it was an unlikely coincidence, the old man finding a mutilated body, with a history like his. Perhaps Harry Butler was a surgeon. That would make life very easy indeed, Jack concluded.

'Yes, a team, Jack. I'm no expert on modern surgical techniques and equipment used on the living, but my guess would be three specialists as a minimum, plus a nurse or two… Probably. You really need to talk to someone who performs this sort of operation on the living and breathing. I can't really help any more… Fascinating though it is. I'm looking forward to meeting your Mister M again, when he's ready for me. Not long to wait from the look of him.'

The owlish stare was back as Koch rubbed his hands together in anticipation. Jack wanted the man gone, but wondered if there was more relevant information he could provide in his current joyful state.

'Is there anything else, Bob?'

'Well, I don't know. The guy's probably been hungry for months, since they started feeding him like this.'

'Hungry?' That seemed like a minor irritant compared to the state of his body.

'Oh yes. Being fed intravenously merely sustains life but does not satiate. You remain hungry all the time. The brain won't be receiving any signals from the stomach indicating it's full. Quite tormenting for sufferers, I hear. A constant gnawing at your insides. Can you imagine?'

Jack was a snack and go man, generally eating on the hoof, but he did enjoy his food, and loved nothing better than a pukka full English breakfast.

Christ! Starving hungry, day in, day out, month after month…

It was inconceivable to him.

'This is all just so cruel. You really think he's been without solid food for that long?'

'With no anus it would have nowhere to go, and he lost that many moons ago. And anyway, I can see these scars here, here and, most recently, here.' His index finger circled a point between the collarbone and neck that looked like a bruise to Jack, with some scarring around it, and then a faded mark near where the cannula was now positioned. 'The hospital had to access his veins here because the other sites have been compromised. I'd say, though won't be able to confirm until I cut him open, that he had a series of infections around the points of access. Not uncommon with parenteral nutrition, but this chap has a limited number of locations to choose from, being a quad.'

'A quad?'

'Sorry. I do try to avoid jargon when I'm with you Jack, but occasionally revert to type. Quadruple amputee. You're most likely to see quads who've served in Iraq or Afghanistan these days. IEDs usually.'

IEDs. Jack knew what they were. Improvised Explosive Devices. The idea that the man might somehow have incurred these injuries as a serviceman had not occurred to him. The placing of the victim, hung out to die, had really narrowed his focus, and he chastised himself for the lapse.

'So, this might not be a deliberate act, a case of GBH, but the results of prolonged surgery in the aftermath of an explosion? Are you saying an army medical team has put him back together as best they can?'

As he asked, he realised it was an unlikely scenario as it failed to answer many questions, not least, why he had been left to die on Clapham Common.

Or the letters to Doc.

'Not a chance. Too messy. IEDs don't generally remove limbs at the joints. You have ragged bits of flesh and bone to excise and repair. The stitching wouldn't be fastidious like this either, if done by a field hospital. Shrapnel leaves numerous smaller scars too, but none of this chap's wounds suggest a massive trauma like that. And his eardrums, burnt with acid… The anus… No. As I said, I'm no expert, but I am one hundred percent certain these grievous mutilations were not the result of an IED or similar… I'll tell you who you should speak to. My old pal Dickie Maddox. He was a surgeon in the Army. We both served in Northern Ireland during The Troubles. Mind you, he's a war hero and all that. Expert in explosive wound trauma. Also kneecappings, by bullet and Black&Decker, probably undertaken more amputations than any other surgeon in the UK. And he became highly skilled in plastic surgery too… Well he was, before his accident.'

'I don't know him, but if you think he could give a more detailed assessment…' This might be a result. A specialist surgeon could possibly help narrow the field of suspects, identify other medical professionals with the requisite skills. 'Do you have contact details?'

'Not with me, I'm afraid. He's got a clinic in Harley Street though. I'll dig out his number when I get back to my office in the basement. Sadly, Dickie and I lost touch some years ago. No longer bosom buddies, I'm afraid.'

Rather uncharitably Jack wondered if Koch had any close companions, other than chilled cadavers. He had never probed, never met him socially, and found it hard to imagine the pathologist making small talk with anyone exhibiting a pulse. Perhaps this remoteness from the warm blooded was a natural consequence of working with the dead for so many years. However, he was always grateful for Koch's help and today was no exception.

'One other question. Diana Davies. Do you see anything that would link the two victims, ten years apart?'

'Well, they were both similarly mutilated but with very different techniques, and this fellow was clearly kept alive for a long time whereas Davies wasn't. I'll know more when I get this chap opened up… You know I'm taking early retirement, Jack. Let's hope I can get him on the slab before I finish on Friday.'

The throwaway comment confused Jack. Did the ME think he was uniquely capable of assessing Mister M? Or was it just that he would be disappointed if he did not have the opportunity to dissect the poor bastard himself, before heading off into the sunset?

Don't ask. Time to wrap things up.

'Any final thoughts, Bob?'

'It's deliberate… Emasculation. Immobilisation. Emaciation… Left deaf, dumb and blind, suffering total isolation. The most severe punishment you could inflict on a living soul, I'd venture to say. I think you'll find this gentleman upset someone he shouldn't have. I wonder what he did to deserve it…'

With that masterful understatement and unwarranted slur on the character of his first warm-blooded client in years, the owl flitted from the room, leaving Jack alone to ponder the enigma that was Mister M.

The drive back to Tooting in south London gave Doc time to think and recover his composure. He knew he had jumped to an unrealistic conclusion regarding Judy Finch and the likelihood that she had been abducted, mutilated and dumped. Without any visible clues as to the two anonymous victims' identities, it was simply his mind playing tricks on him.

It took him most of the journey to convince himself.

While driving he tried to achieve a semi-meditative state, the wakeful zone of mindfulness his yoga classes had taught him, and that simple exercise dragged him back from the brink of hysteria. Even so, as he turned into the hospital car park he felt an overwhelming sense of dread as he thought of her.

The psychiatrist in him knew this was, in part, propelled by guilt, his own role playing no small part in the disintegration of her life. Judy had almost lost her mind when her son Josh had died, and, although she had told Doc she did not blame him for the tragedy, she had distanced herself from him while grieving for her boy.

At the time, Doc was still recovering from major surgery for bones shattered by a three storey fall, one that disabled him for over a year. It was a difficult period for them both, then she disappeared, sending him a single email consisting of just these few sentences:

I'm truly sorry, Colin. I can't be with anyone right now. I need some space. Please don't try to find me. I'll contact you when I feel ready. With much love, Judy x

It felt like losing an arm when she left, and he missed her badly, but, since then, had heard nothing. Jack had made some enquiries at Doc's insistence, but, as he had pointed out, Judy was an adult who had chosen to go off grid, and, it seemed, deliberately made herself difficult to find. There was little Jack could do, officially.

Oh well, best focus on an actual victim, not an imaginary one.

'Hi, Jack. Sorry I'm late. Did I miss Bob Koch?'

Carver was still at Mister M's bedside, standing over the victim, staring down at the naked form, but glanced up as his friend entered the room. There was no welcoming smile, just a haunted look on Jack's face, a rare sight Doc thought, and a sign that this case had deeply affected the detective.

'Yeah. He left a couple of minutes ago... Are you okay, Doc? I've got someone trying to track Judy but I honestly think you've put two and two together and made five.'

'Thanks for doing that. Finding her, just knowing she was safe, would put my mind at rest.' That was true, though he did not add that locating her was the *only* thing that would quash the ominous dread he had managed to divert for now. 'So, what did Koch say?'

Jack started to fill him in on the pathologist's opinions regarding the victim while Doc took a closer look at the state of the man. Horrifying though it was, he found himself trying to imagine what it would be like to suffer this degree of isolation. He knew of coma victims who had been in a submerged state of consciousness, only aware of what went on inside their own minds, but apparently dead to the world outside. With no way of communicating, with nothing getting in or out of the prison defined by flesh and bone, it had to be the most dreadful form of solitary confinement anyone could endure.

He listened as Jack took him through Koch's comments, but when he recounted the ME's view that a full surgical team would be required, Doc stopped him, his mind trying to fathom the motive for this travesty.

'I don't think he needed an anaesthetist, Jack. I think this was inflicted as an extended form of torture... I agree with Koch that it was carried out over many months though, in fact possibly as much as two or three years.'

'Bloody hell! What sort of sicko are we dealing with? No anaesthetic? Wouldn't he have died, from shock or something? How could anyone survive having bits lopped off 'em like that?'

'The human body's a remarkably resilient organism, and death from shock hardly inevitable... The surgery was done piecemeal, and, judging by the difference in the ageing of the scar tissue, in a specific sequence. It looks like each operation was allowed to heal before further trauma was inflicted. You don't need the anaesthetic. There are drugs that can be used to immobilise a body without bringing on unconsciousness... And the shock? That too can be ameliorated with drugs and by regulating the operating environment.'

Doc was already forming a mental image of how the surgery could have been performed, as Jack asked, 'So how many in a team to do this? Doctors, nurses... Koch thought maybe as many as four or five.'

'No... In a well-equipped surgery, with state of the art facilities, maybe two.' As

Doc spoke he was imagining himself performing the amputations, thinking how he could inflict the maximum pain on the victim. 'This is about punishment and revenge. I would guess the man's eyes and hearing were the last of his faculties to go... The perpetrator would have wanted the victim fully aware of what was happening to him, right up to the end. Tormenting his victim, informing him of what he was about to suffer next, revelling in having total control over a powerless victim. Gloating as he tortured him.' He paused, his mind filled with a vision of the man, immobile, eyes bugging from his head as his limbs were gradually severed. 'Forcing him to watch as the scalpel blade carved into his flesh.'

'Watch? How the hell—?'

'A mirror, perhaps. Or a video screen?' Doc realised his eyes had drooped closed as the vivid images swamped his brain. He tried to force them to withdraw as he turned his attention to Carver, ramming home the nature of the man they were dealing with. 'He'd want to hear the screams, so the tongue and mouth would have been reserved for the final stages too.'

'Bloody Norah! This just gets worse and worse... And I was thinking being hungry all the time, on top of being unable to talk, or hear, or see, was bad enough. It's pure fucking evil, Doc! It's like the Devil's own work.'

'Mmm.' Doc, like Koch just moments before, was admiring the handiwork, the degree of commitment on the part of Jack's devil. 'Not devilish... He thinks of himself as godlike. The giver of life and death, the distance between the two states nothing more to him than a stroke of his scalpel. Not uncommon with very skilled medical professionals, Jack. A narcissism that develops into a god complex.'

'So, what are we looking for? A lunatic surgeon who thinks he's some sort of avenging god?'

Jack's words sparked a whole series of connections in Doc's brain, but he just muttered one word as he tried to get back into the mind of the man who did this.

'Maximón.'

'Eh? Maximum what?'

Doc ignored him as he felt himself drawn back into the vision, his brain recreating the screams of agony, the sensation of delivering devastating pain with precise incisions of the blade. He could feel the scalpel between his own fingers, carving into flesh and sinew. Then a revelation.

'He may not even be a surgeon.'

'What? To do this? Koch reckoned whoever mutilated our guy was very skilful. Surely, only someone with decades of experience could've kept him alive while slicing and dicing him like this.' Jack's voice betrayed his disappointment. 'I thought we would have a really narrow range of suspects. What are you saying? Surely not just anyone could do this. Even with all the best modern gear and a top notch medical centre to do it in.'

'Not just anyone, no... Have you taken a close look at the photos I received this morning?' Once again, Doc dragged himself from the hideous depths of depravity he had been experiencing, mentally shaking himself, like a dog that had fallen into a cesspool, now determined to remove the filthy residue from its fur. He still felt tainted...

But also, not a little exhilarated by the experience.

'Yeah. What about 'em?'

Doc tugged them from his jacket pocket and laid them on the bed beside Mister M, refusing to let visions of Judy interrupt his thought processes as he did so.

'I don't know if they were in any particular order in the envelope when they arrived at Broadmoor this morning. The staff didn't realise how important that could've been when they opened the letter, but look. It's a sequence, Jack.'

'You're convinced he murdered these others too?'

At first, Doc had not realised the significance himself, but now, after examining the live victim, he could see it clearly. 'These three images show an obvious progression, from butchery to a primitive form of surgery. Davies was just hacked, but look, these others have some rudimentary stitching to repair the joints where the limbs were removed.'

'You think he was practising… Developing his skills on these others? He started keeping them alive, after the Davies girl…'

'Looks that way, Jack. But the thing is, even this one,' he selected the third image in his sequence and held it up beside Mister M for Jack to compare, 'is a long way from demonstrating the skills needed to do this to our victim…'

'You think there are more? Other people he's done this to? Perfecting his technique…'

'I'm afraid so, my friend. I can almost guarantee it.'

'Here you go, Fifi. Oh, and check your inbox. Sam said he'd sent you some more info he found on Butler after he spoke to Carver. Said the boss was right pissed off when he phoned him. And you look like Detective Doom and Gloom. You alright? Where's that sunny Caribbean smile gone?'

'Thanks, Tim.' DS Fielding took the slim file from her colleague and shrugged. 'I'm okay. Just been a long day. I'll catch you later.'

She plonked herself down at her desk, ignored the hubbub of the open plan office, booted up her desktop and tried to get some perspective back. She had been so fired up by Jack's outburst that she had started walking from the hospital, thinking she would calm down and then grab a passing cab. Twenty minutes later, her pantsuit clinging to her thanks to the humidity of a burgeoning storm, she had finally managed to dissipate the one threatening to burst inside her head.

In the cab, she examined why she had felt so perturbed by her gruesome discovery in Gerald Butler's house, and realised she had some atavistic hatreds awakened by the man's past. She rarely thought about colonialism, slavery, the critical events that led to her own ancestors having their freedom ripped from them and exchanged for a life of hard labour half a world from their birthplace. Fiona would not shed a tear right here, right now, but later, and only in the sanctuary of her home would she allow herself that luxury.

Then Jack had phoned her, back to his usual chirpy self, and rapidly summarised Koch's assessment of the victim. Then he dumped another pile of work in her lap when he said, 'Surgeons, Fi. We need a list of people who are capable of performing amputations and major tissue grafting. Should help us narrow it down. I'll see you in an hour or two.'

Her own enthusiasm had yet to recover, and his call had not helped. But, she reminded herself, she was bloody good at her job, and would not allow her feelings to let her down.

Come on, get back to work.

She mentally prioritised her tasks, and started with the file Sam had given her. She riffled through the handful of sheets, printouts from UK suppliers selling the unique pieces of equipment they had found embedded in Mister M's back that morning. Specialist pulleys, wire and stainless steel hooks, for the sole purpose of suspending the human form. Although unlikely to lead anywhere, she had to start somewhere.

This was all new to her too, so she spent the next half an hour educating herself online, and became engrossed in the videos of this fascinating, though somewhat peculiar, activity. Although a niche interest, with devotees from what she thought of as fringe members of society, it seemed a harmless enough pursuit.

What possible significance does this have?

She parked that thought and made some calls, and soon discovered that the market for these specific items was limited to fewer than a handful of commercial customers throughout the UK, plus a couple of dozen individuals and clubs. It was still a very large number and, as she had no help right now, she decided to narrow the range down by selecting the ones in south London within reasonable distance of Clapham Common.

There were just two. A tattoo parlour in Streatham, and a Body Modification club located in a previously derelict church in Putney. She would visit both but made a note of one of the addresses in her iPhone, thinking she'd take a short detour on her way home and stop by the *Hope, Not Fear* tattoo place, since it was less than a mile or so from her one-bedroom apartment in an art deco block located in Balham.

Damn.

Bank Holiday Monday.

She had forgotten.

Well, she would drop by anyway, and see if anyone was working this evening, or maybe the staff lived above the premises. She was keen to learn more, and, with such a small community, largely made up of outsiders, she hoped it would not be too difficult to narrow down some suspects.

Specifically, a surgeon who indulged in, or at least was involved in, this weird but intriguing pastime.

'Maximum? What did you mean by that, Doc?'

Jack had observed Doc getting into the minds of numerous weirdoes and psychopaths over the years, yet was still amazed at the ease with which he seemed to slip into the psyche of even the most vicious and heartless criminals. It was unsettling, seeing his old friend and comrade almost change before his eyes, with his body sliding into character, assuming different mannerisms, as if Doc had multiple personalities lurking behind his professional facade.

Seeing this amazing party trick had often left Jack wondering what sort of toll these mind-trips took on Doc's own psyche, and how much they had been responsible for his friend's breakdowns, the most recent after his wife's death a few years ago. Sometimes the strain of it visibly drained the psychiatrist, but Jack thought the technique had rarely appeared as discomfiting as it had today.

He had known what was happening the moment he saw that weirdly ethereal look, the one he recognised as soon as it surfaced on Doc's face, despite not having seen it for some years. And, as usual, some enigmatic observations always popped out of Doc's mouth while channelling the murderer's heinous deeds.

'Not maximum, Jack. *Maximón.* A Mayan patron saint some consider to be a god. Still worshipped in parts of Guatemala. Often by devout Catholics, even though he is spurned by the Church. Devil worship they call it.'

'What's that got to do with our Mister M?'

Doc's thought processes often left Carver confused, and today was no exception. What possible connection could there be between their victim, carefully posed on Clapham Common, and some South American icon?

'Vengeance, Jack. Legend has it, the men from Maximón's village returned from working in the fields to find he had slept with all their wives. They hacked off his arms and legs as punishment—'

'Really? So you reckon there's a sexual element to this, then?'

'No, I don't think so. The removal of genitalia, both sexes involved, our man here, neutered… It's about power and revenge. We are looking for a highly educated, sophisticated, organised killer. Definitely male. Mid-thirties, absolute minimum. In all likelihood, significantly older. Some form of medical experience, almost certainly.' Doc seemed to look inside himself for a fraction of a second, then added, his voice soft, 'Is he a surgeon? Probably not.'

'Why not?'

If Doc was right, this would make the investigation more difficult, but Jack knew better than to ignore his views, regardless of what Bob Koch had said. He let out a plaintive sigh as his original hopes, that the deadly needle they were searching for was to be found in a conveniently compact bale of hay, were dashed.

'Why would a surgeon need to practise on several victims like this, Jack?' Doc shrugged, then shook his head. 'No. I could be wrong, but I think we're looking for a wannabe… A paramedic. A failed physician. Maybe somebody like a General Practitioner, frustrated he couldn't make it as a surgeon. Possibly someone struck off the medical register for misconduct or whatever. Perhaps even a mortician. They have a good knowledge of anatomy… ' He gave himself a little nod before adding, 'A decent veterinarian, one used to operating on large mammals, would probably have much of the equipment needed to do this, too.'

'Come off it, Doc. Surely, all this… The level of skill. You can't teach yourself all that. A DIY surgeon? Not possible!'

'Normally I'd agree. But, if you already had some rudimentary medical knowledge and wanted to teach yourself the necessary skills related to amputation, tissue grafting and so on, you could use an online course. There are plenty of websites with all the details you'd need to get started, with thousands of detailed videos demonstrating the techniques involved. Of course, you'd inevitably fail in your early attempts.' He waggled a finger at the photographs still on the bed. 'You'd end up making so many mistakes, you'd leave a trail of corpses behind you…'

'So, not necessarily a surgeon. Someone with a little formal training… I'm just wondering how many missing persons have ended up as guinea pigs for the sick fuck that's doing this.' He picked up the photos and had a closer look. 'Like these poor buggers.'

'A lot. I'd say a double figure body count. This has been going on since Diana Davies went missing. That's more than ten years, Jack.'

A nurse bustled into the room and gave Doc and Jack a severe talking to when she saw Mister M lying naked on the bed. The woman's strident tones reminded them that he was a patient, not a laboratory specimen and that he needed to be kept warm, so they retired to the coffee shop where Fiona had interviewed Piers several hours earlier.

As they sipped their lattes, Jack asked Doc, 'What sort of equipment would he need, then?'

He was thinking he would have someone investigate historical purchases of the necessary items supplied to private individuals and independent clinics. Specialist gear purchases always helped narrow the field. He also wondered about registrations for online medical courses, what was available and what info he could find on the students. This was rapidly turning into a major operation. He would have to have another word with Soundbite tomorrow.

'Well, at the very least he'd need access to a fully equipped operating theatre, most likely a private facility, sufficiently secluded so that he was in no danger of being discovered.'

'Soundproofed, maybe, given the screams.'

'Or somewhere very isolated. He'd need a bedroom too, somewhere secure, but sufficiently equipped and monitored, giving his prisoner time to recover ready for his next operation. Other than that, I'm not sure I can help. I'm no surgeon, Jack. You need an expert who—'

'Dickie Maddox! Koch recommended him. Forgot to mention that little detail when I was filling you in.'

'Maddox?' Doc's cup rattled in his saucer as he almost dropped it, clearly stunned to hear that name on Jack's lips.

'Yeah… D'you know him?'

'I saw him at Broadmoor, earlier today… He's treating Harding.'

'Harding? What? Is he having surgery? That's a bit of a coincidence, don't you think?'

Another one, Jack thought, his suspicions automatically aroused.

'Not surgery… Maddox is a polymath.'

'A polly what?'

'An expert in many disciplines. Not only is he quite brilliant, but he also has an eidetic memory. It gives him a real edge when it comes to learning.'

'A photographic memory? Lucky bugger. So why's he seeing Harding?'

'He's a well-respected forensic psychiatrist… I first met him at university. He was studying medicine too, but got a little bored, said it wasn't challenging enough. He was always interested in how the mind works, opted to undertake a psychology degree simultaneously, and became fluent in several languages in his spare time too. Went on to specialise in cosmetic surgery. Said he planned to make a fortune. And he did… Foresaw the boom before most medical professionals realised how big the market would grow.'

'Hang on a minute. Are we talking about the same bloke? Bob Koch reckoned Maddox was a military doctor, served in Northern Ireland. Did a lot with trauma victims.'

Jack's brain was starting to make its own connections now, but could it really be the same medical professional?

'Yes, he joined up immediately after he finished his medical training. Became a proper war hero and a highly proficient field surgeon. When he left the military he became a multimillionaire in his mid-thirties, performing facelifts in LA. I think he got bored with that too, so trained to qualify as a forensic psychiatrist. I sometimes wondered if he was motivated by wanting to outdo me, to beat me at my own game. He's a very competitive chap.'

'You don't sound like you like him much, Doc… And what about Harding?'

'Maddox is treating him. He's his consultant… I can see why Koch recommended him to you though. Here.' Doc pulled the card Maddox had given him from his shirt pocket and handed it to Carver.

'Am I missing something? This guy,' he flapped the card under Doc's nose, 'who is now all matey with your old man's murderer—'

'Hardly matey. He's a consultant psychiatrist—'

'Treating a killer who was also on the mailing list for these victim photos…'

'But Harding didn't receive them, Jack.' Doc paused, then after a moment's reflection, said, 'Although, he certainly knew about them. He suggested he'd even seen them.' Doc rapidly updated Jack on his meeting with the killer earlier in the day.

'Well, there you go. Maddox seems to connect rather a lot of dots, don't you think? I know you said the person who did this to our Mister M is *probably* not a surgeon, but this polly-wally doo-dah has the all the requisite skills, masses of experience, and now you tell me he has a relationship with Harding…' He checked the address on the card. 'Plus, he has his own private clinic, too!'

'What about these other victims? The learning process? He'd hardly need to go through that.'

'Yeah. True. But think about it, Doc. We only know that one of the pictures is genuine. Diana Davies. For all we know, the others could be photoshopped. Maybe he just mailed them to confuse us. To send us on a wild goose chase. Drawing you in, using Harding as bait, knowing your history with the man, just as a diversion… To throw us all off his scent.'

'I'm not convinced. There's no love lost between us but I can't see Maddox in that light… We can't just dismiss these other victims either.'

'I'm not dismissing 'em. Just saying, it's quite possible none of them have anything to do with our Mister M. Unrelated crimes.'

'Well, I suppose, if we discounted my involvement entirely, ignored the photos and the email to Harding, then Maddox *could* be a person of interest. It just doesn't feel right to me though, Jack. I think we should keep working on all of these cases as one investigation.'

Doc's words almost swayed Jack, but his own gut feel insisted Maddox had a larger part to play. The letters, Harding, Doc being dragged in thanks to the discovery of a victim bearing similarities to the images he'd received. Then there was Butler and his grandson.

It was all very messy.

'I hear you, Doc. Even so, I think we should keep an open mind.' He remembered then, what Koch had told him about motive and added, 'This poor guy probably just pissed off whoever did this. Big time. So maybe he is the only victim. Think about it. If that's true, Maddox fits all the criteria for a prime suspect.'

Fiona decided to move on to number two on her list of priorities, and opened the email from Sam. The researchers had been beavering away at finding some background information on Harry Butler, with limited success.

Another bloody ghost! Like that Finch woman...

According to Sam, the grandson had also dropped off the grid. She skimmed through the attached documents and mentally thanked him for what he had delivered—a comprehensive compilation of files going back to Butler's teens—and logged everything in her mind as she read.

Harry Butler was forty-three years of age, but his history was only documented until his early thirties, shortly after his release from a secure hospital facility in Berkshire.

She read how he had been referred for psychiatric assessment by a magistrate after being arrested for threatening behaviour, disturbance of the peace, and possession of an offensive weapon. He claimed to have severe post-traumatic stress syndrome and was being prescribed anti-psychotic medication at the time the event took place.

As she absorbed the story of Harry's life, her excitement grew, and she found herself wondering just how damaged Gerald Butler's grandson really was.

He had been dishonourably discharged from the Army over eleven years ago having served in Iraq and Afghanistan. He started his military career as a gunner, but then he had switched to the medical corps for his final years of service, not long before an incident in which he lost several comrades. A blue on blue attack.

What the hell is that?

A moment later, thanks to Google, Fiona had the answer. It transpired that Harry and his seven-man band of erstwhile comrades had been decimated, not by the enemy, but by 'friendly fire' in a drone attack. They had been on a routine night patrol, after being dropped by a helicopter from Camp Bastion, when they came under attack from a jihadist group holed up in a farmstead. Due to some sort of screw up with the coordinates, the US Predator mistook the military team for the insurgents and delivered a Hellfire missile right in their midst.

Harry, despite suffering severe shrapnel wounds to his legs, managed to crawl to his one remaining colleague, applying critical first aid that kept him alive until a Chinook helicopter arrived to whisk them both to the nearest field hospital.

He had been decorated for valour, and she could understand why when she came to this brief account, read out in court by Harry's solicitor after the machete attack in Brixton Market led to his arrest:

After we were hit I fired off several rocket-propelled grenades at the farmhouse until the insurgents stopped shooting, then managed to get to Corporal Rigsby. He was in a bad way. Both his legs were gone, his left arm and right forearm looked like they'd been turned inside out, with shattered bone and tissue hanging off, only held together by his uniform.

I did what I could for him, using the medical kit we had, with tourniquets and field dressings, but I couldn't find any morphine as the bag had been damaged when the Hellfire hit, and I'd already injected my personal supply as I was in agony myself. Rigsby's injector was gone, along with his legs, and the other guys were just bits of charred meat dotted around us. It smelt horrible, like the Devil was roasting humans for a demonic barbecue.

I sat with him like that for forty-five minutes, waiting for that chopper to come. I was in a pretty bad way myself, but he was wailing, screaming his head off, a horrible sound straight from the fires of hell. The Yanks gave their bloody missile the right name, that's for sure.

I see Rigsby every time I close my eyes. Every time I try to sleep. He visits me. I can hear his screams still, all the way from Helmand, echoing inside my brain.

Without my meds, I can't cope. That morning, when they say I was waving a machete about, I'd run out of tablets. I'd been taking more than I'm prescribed. I have to, otherwise I can't sleep. Rigsby won't let me. So, I was on my way to the doctor to beg for some more when I just blacked out. Next thing I knew, I was in Brixton nick, in the cell, wondering why I was there.

The magistrate, not fully convinced but swayed by the defendant's recent military service, had remanded Harry in custody on condition that he was assessed at Broadmoor. Fiona made an intriguing discovery about his treatment there, apparently successful, as three months later he was sent to a secure rehabilitation unit, then, six weeks after that, released to a hostel.

Within days, he was living on the streets, just another vagrant wandering around Brixton, moved along by a local bobby after a kebab shop owner complained about him sleeping in his doorway. And that was where the trail ended. Not a thing after that.

Harry Butler had completely disappeared from the radar.

As Fiona delved further back in the file, she came across an address she recognised.

The one she had visited with Carver earlier in the day…

Gerald Butler's home had been the address Harry had given when he was arrested, a detail that made her wonder why he had been released to a hostel instead of going back there. More questions fired into her brain as she read on, discovering other facts about this man's past and his troubled mental state, her suspicions spiralling.

The cell in the old man's house, with its intricately drawn angel, also began to make some sense. Harry's grandfather, one Gerald Butler, had been his official carer since the lad was just five years old, taking the boy in after his parents died in a car accident. Gerald's own wife died shortly after, so it had been just the two of them in that dismal, depressing house.

The researchers had managed to dig up little else about Harry's childhood, but had located an arresting officer's statement, taken in the early hours of the morning immediately after his eighteenth birthday. It seemed the young man had a history of violence. On that occasion he had been given a formal caution for the brawl he had instigated in a nightclub during an overenthusiastic celebration. He signed up for the military shortly after.

Fiona's head was swirling with ideas, then DI Carver's voice cut through her musings.

'Sarge! I'm starving again. It's already well after seven o'clock, and I bet you've had nothing since that sarnie for lunch, so I'm taking you for a well-deserved Ruby. Come on.'

A Ruby Murray.

An Indian curry, in Cockney parlance. Now that was more like the Jack Carver she knew and loved to work with.

His voice, initially coming from right behind her, was getting more distant as he called from the corridor. 'After my chat with our pathologist, Bob Koch, about Mister M, I got some even more weird and wonderful insights from Doc Powers. Let's eat and I'll fill you in, and you can tell me what you've been up to all evening too.'

She grabbed the Finch file she had taken from his desk drawer earlier, convinced she would look at it at home, thought about her plan to follow up on that Hope and Fear tattoo place, but decided to leave it for tomorrow, and hurried after her boss, who was already thumbing the elevator call button, holding the doors open for her as he beckoned with his other hand.

'Get a move on Fifi! Chicken vindaloo and a pint of lager. The food of the gods is waiting for us!'

'Are you sure you're going to be okay, babe?'

Shazza crouched before Harry Hope, who was sitting cross-legged on the cellar floor as if in meditation. She placed a finger under his chin to raise his head and then checked his pupils. Dilated, just as she expected and his breathing was slow and rhythmic. Although he did not speak, a small twitch of his brow was enough to answer her query.

Satisfied, she stood then stepped behind him and gave a thumbs up to Glen.

Harry's arms were gradually pulled away from his lap until they were spreadeagled, level with his shoulders, each supported by two wires attached to hooks through the flesh of his biceps and the back of his forearms. These wires led to the rigging a few metres above his head and Glen continually adjusted the pulleys, evening out the tension, until Harry's outstretched arms were in line with the row of four hooks that pierced his upper back.

Slowly, as if he was liquid rather than solid form, in an effortless motion, Harry came upright and then floated until he was almost a metre off the ground. Shazza had already dabbed away the little trails of blood leaking from the hooks in his back and arms but remained behind him, taking a moment to view her beautiful man, hanging in cruciform before her.

She loved his tattoo, a symbol of his time in Iraq and Afghanistan. The reluctant warrior who had decided he no longer wanted to kill brown-skinned citizens in foreign lands...

Her eyes lingered on the angel-like wings that appeared to pulsate across his shoulders, the feathered tips reaching to his upper arms. The angle she was at, along with the dimmed lighting, brought the visage to life, the startling effect of the three dimensional tattoo breathtakingly realistic.

The fabulous decoration continued the length of his spine. A wooden staff, with two green and yellow serpents intertwined throughout its length, their heads facing each other just below the wings, their eyes shining from the ruby red crystals implanted in Harry's skin. Their mouths were open, split tongues appearing to flicker, the illusion of motion caused by Harry's back muscles as he breathed.

Shazza's own forked tongue flicked out, and she waggled the two halves independently, sniggering at Glen as she did so.

'I'm Harry's *snake* charmer!' Then, serious again, she added, 'He's fine. Tie him off.'

Glen did as she bid, using a cleat on the wall to secure the wires, as Shazza circled round to the front. Harry's expression was one she had seen many times, and still aspired to, though doubted she could ever attain. She had been suspended in a dozen different positions, including once earlier today with six hooks in her belly to recreate the Resurrection position, but she had yet to reach the same state of bliss Harry could so effortlessly achieve.

She felt not a hint of jealousy, for she knew that Harry's life experiences, his tormented upbringing and his tortured past, had allowed him to experience a spiritual plane only possible for those who had previously suffered in the most dreadful ways.

'Hey babe, we'll be upstairs. I'll check in on you every half hour, but just shout out if you need us. Okay?'

Shazza knew it was risky and not recommended, leaving someone suspended like this, but Harry always insisted. After Shazza and Glen had refused to leave him alone he had just built himself a remote controlled winch which allowed him to dispense with their assistance. He had never had to use it as his lover and his closest friend acceded to his wish to be left hanging in solitude, while they busied themselves upstairs, but always within earshot.

As Glen's heavy footfall made the stairs creak and groan, Shazza lingered for one last admiring glance at her man's near perfect physique. Harry was in superb physical shape for a man in his early forties and, suspended in silence, hanging there in the semi-darkness, his naked body seemed radiant despite the gloom.

An ethereal angel, crucified and earthbound, but part way to heaven.

For Shazza, this very special man was more precious to her than Jesus Christ himself.

'So, you found nothing on those CCTV files.' Carver dipped some naan bread in rich vindaloo sauce and sucked at it before loading a wad on to his tongue. His words were slightly muffled but DS Fielding got the drift as he added, 'Maybe we need to check other access points, Fi. Mister M weighs next to nothing, could've even been loaded into a suitcase or similar, and wheeled along the footpath. A big enough bloke could've wrapped him in a blanket and tucked him under his arm. No need to have a car or van parked close to where he left the body.'

These alternative possibilities had already occurred to Fiona, but the perimeter of Clapham Common was several miles in total, most of it overlooked by private properties, with precious few offering CCTV coverage. The video she had already viewed had been a major waste of time, and she was not keen to focus more effort on that. She wondered how she could shift Carver's focus as she pushed her plate of uneaten biryani to the side. Normally, the exotic spices and fragrant aromas that drifted through her favourite Brick Lane curry house would tease her tongue until she was bloated, but today, after all she had experienced, her appetite had shrivelled. She was ready for bed, even though it was barely nine o'clock.

'Mmm. I s'pose so, Boss. Or maybe he was there an hour or two earlier. Perhaps the vic was not as frail as we thought and could've survived a bit longer. I'll check tomorrow.'

The words came out without enthusiasm. Fiona was preoccupied with how best to share her suspicions, how to approach a very delicate matter with her boss, given his earlier outburst about professionalism when she had questioned his impartiality over his close relationship with Doc Powers.

What was on her mind was far worse.

They had arrived in separate cars and had not had a chance to discuss progress, so, after ordering their meal, Carver had given her a full update on his meetings regarding Mister M, plus a brief outline of Harding's conversation with Doc, finishing with his theory that Maddox might be responsible for their victim.

She had listened as he explained that the letter and photos may be a diversion, wondering why Jack was missing the obvious, and whether he would reach the same conclusion she had drawn from her research into Harry Butler. He had not even asked about the grandson, as if he had forgotten the old man's accusation and what they had found in his house. Of course, Jack was unaware of one vital piece of information, a discovery she had made earlier this evening. A discovery she was still reluctant to share with him, fearing the reaction she might provoke.

'Yeah. Might be worth a look, Fi. You get anything from the lads?' He swilled some beer, banged the empty glass down, burped unceremoniously and then said, 'Handsome! That filled a hole!' before waving to the waiter for a refill.

Fiona put a hand over her glass in response to his enquiring look.

'No thanks, Boss. I'm knackered already... I've got some leads on that specialist gear I need to follow up, and some info on the grandson, but we really could use some more help. I think we have to find this Harry Butler, and it won't be easy. He's gone off radar too.' The subtle implication, the oblique reference to Doc's ex-lover and her increasing workload, elicited a more positive response from him this time.

'I'll talk to Soundbite in the morning about allocating us a few full-time bodies to give you a hand. According to the hospital our Mister M is unlikely to last the week. His insides are in a right state. Atrophied is what they called it. In fact his whole body is weak from lack of use, compounding his health problems. His heart's barely ticking... Immobility's gonna kill him.'

'So it's going to be a murder case.' Well, that would help, she thought, as homicides always grabbed the bulk of resources. Death would be something of a blessing too, as the vic seemed to have very little to live for. As that thought surfaced she began to wonder about his family, whether anyone was missing him still, years after he had been taken for some sicko to experiment on. To practise on. 'Let's hope we get a hit on his ID from the DNA database.'

'Yeah. Speaking of ID, tell me about this Harry bloke. You still think he's in the frame?' His brow rippled, a fleeting frown that disappeared into a wide grin as another pint was placed before him.

'Well, he has a history of violence, severe post-traumatic stress disorder. He has to take powerful medication. He also underwent basic paramedic training in the army, suffers nightmares about a dismembered colleague, and is probably riddled with survivor's guilt after seven of his comrades were blown to bits. He's got to be in the frame, Boss.'

As Jack nodded, she continued fleshing out the details for him, skirting the one very significant fact that was troubling her.

Then he asked, 'Broadmoor? You say he was there before he disappeared. Strange. I wonder if he met Harding while he was there.' Another burp and a few gulps of beer were followed by his cheekiest smile, as if he was proud of his stomach's efforts to join their conversation. 'Tomorrow's another day. I'm gonna have to sleep on this Sarge... Anything else?'

He may have had a few beers, giving the impression he had wound down completely, brain fully relaxed as his belly digested his food, but his eyes scrutinised her face in such a way she was sure he suspected she was withholding something significant from him. She could see the detective in him was fully roused. Fiona had often heard him use the term *bullshit antennae,* and he told all his subordinates they must develop their own, preferably one like his, always working even when his conscious mind was off duty.

She had to tell him, but needed to check something first.

'Have you mentioned Gerald Butler to Doc Powers, Boss?'

'Not by name. Why?'

'What about Harry Butler? Did you mention his name?'

Carver shook his head, clearly frustrated, convinced she was holding back, his face devoid of mirth now.

'Talk to me, Fi. What aren't you telling me? You should know better than to keep anything from me when we're on a case.'

There were dozens of questions on her tongue, all related to Doc Powers. His role as a profiler, his apparently mystical reputation for visiting inside the minds of criminals, the rumours that he'd suffered several near breakdowns, had given up profiling as a consequence. Then he'd killed a man... But Jack was his friend and although she knew her boss was a professional copper, after her rollicking earlier today, she was not sure how far she should push.

Oh, what the hell!

She could be off the case by morning but she decided to just blurt it out.

'About eleven years ago, Harry Butler was assessed, then treated for PTSD after a violent psychotic event that took place shortly after his discharge from the military. By a psychiatrist at Broadmoor. The same psychiatrist who has a personal history involving Harding—'

'Maddox!'

'No, Boss! Not him... The consultant who is *supposed* to be helping us with this investigation. The same guy who received a letter this morning, timed to coincide with the discovery of Mister M...'

She could see the scepticism already as Jack realised what she was suggesting, his lips compressing, nostrils flaring, both hands flat on the table as if he was about to rocket himself out of his seat.

'Now hold on a minute! Broadmoor got that letter—'

But Fiona could not still her tongue, she had to dump it all out there, get it off her chest and on to his shoulders.

'A letter he could have sent to himself.' She could see he was about to speak again, to slap her down, his anger visible, now pulsing blood to his ears, like a traffic light flashing *Stop!* but she would not. 'A letter containing images that effectively *guaranteed* he'd be *invited* into this inquiry, taking a role that allows him to *monitor* our progress. An *expert* capable of influencing the direction we take. A lover, desperate to find the woman he lost. A widower whose bereavement had him on the verge of insanity. A man who has proven himself capable of killing. A genius when it comes to understanding the thoughts and deeds of the worst serial killers in the UK, by imagining himself in their shoes, as if he was *capable of committing their crimes…* Your friend, Doctor Colin Powers.'

TUESDAY

MIND GAMES

By now, good doctor, I am sure you have been to Broadmoor to speak with your nemesis, but I can guarantee he has more to tell. Perhaps, sometime soon, he will visit you. Or has he already?

Do you still suffer vivid, blood-drenched dreams about your father's dying moments, his screams of agony as his hands were hacked off before his last breath was crushed from his trachea? Has Antony shared his secrets from that night with you? The vicious brutality of his actions?

Your father's last words?

I thought not...

And, most pertinent, of course, the reason why Daddy had to die?

Perhaps I can help. Would you like that?

Or do you want to live to your dying breath in ignorance, to continue in the belief that your father was a good man?

I wonder.

Are you a good man?

And where are you now, in your hunt for the killer of Dirty Diana, the HIV riddled railway station whore? Still nowhere, even with the stunning bonus images I sent you to peruse?

How about my special gift to you, the one tied to the old oak tree?

Oh yes, a modern sculpture, my tribute to the art of the possible.

An unidentifiable live body.

There is one more victim I will give you. Someone very close to you...

Unfortunately for your friend—Carver the Incompetent, a passed over detective, well past his prime—you won't find any other physical remains unless I choose to share them. The rest are gone, forever, dust to dust, and like Daddy, ashes to ashes.

Meanwhile, enjoy some additional mementoes of my handiwork, as I know you will.

Try to step inside my mind again, good doctor.

Then you may just connect with your true nature.

The secret buried deep inside your psyche.

'Bloody hell, Doc! What is he on about?' DI Jack Carver, seated on the same kitchen stool less than twenty-four hours after he had last been here, growled as he added, 'I'll give him *Carver the Incompetent...* The twat!' Despite his bluster, Jack felt a prickle as the follicles on the nape of his neck reacted to the three new images on Doc's MacBook.

Three more mutilated victims.

Some forty minutes earlier, Broadmoor had received another letter in the snail mail, subsequently scanned and sent to Doc by email with a covering note from Celene. The staff had been informed to take care with any further correspondence addressed to Doc, so these photographs were in sequence, exactly as they were when taken from the envelope. This time, Jack did not need Doc to point out the obvious.

'You were right. It's a progression. These are much more sophisticated dismemberments than the earlier victims. The faces too... He really has been practising, on human guinea pigs. Jeez!'

A cup of scorching latte appeared at his elbow as Doc peered over his shoulder at the latest collection and muttered, 'I have no idea who these victims are, Jack. You?'

'Nope. Don't recognise any of 'em. Not even from my time working cold cases. Believe me, if we had found this many bodies, all chopped up like Diana Davies, we'd have had a major task force on it long ago.' Carver was due to meet Soundbite this morning, maybe this would swing it with her, convince her to give him the resources he needed.

'Did your team identify any of the others?'

'Not yet. I managed to get our IT chap to do some digging, but he had nothing on them by the time he buggered off home last night. We'll see what we can find out today... Shame we can't communicate with our Mister M, get him to tell us who he is. Maybe finger the perp too.'

'I was thinking about that, Jack. He seems to have no muscle control—'

'Yeah. Had his voice box nerves severed the doc reckoned, and something like permanent botox injected in his facial muscles too. Shame we can't rig him up like that genius astronomer bloke. You know, the one in the wheelchair, the guy that sounds like a Dalek.'

'Stephen Hawking?' Doc chuckled at Jack's description, then continued. 'He communicates by moving a single cheek muscle that's picked up by a facial recognition camera, plus his eye movements are monitored through an infrared device in his specially adapted glasses. These are linked to a computer synthesiser designed by Intel and developed over many years. Not much chance of them being able to help our chap before he passes away, even if they were so inclined.'

'Well that rules that out then. No eyes, no muscles moving. No way of communicating.'

'I am not so sure. It's a bit of an outside chance, but while I was lying in bed, meditating—'

'I didn't know you were into that.'

'Yes, it really helps me relax and overcome the residual pain from my operations. I use a specific technique. Controlled breathing. It didn't work last night, as it set my brain alight, wondering about the possibility that our victim could do the same. You see, the nerves controlling his chest muscles couldn't be paralysed, otherwise he would've suffocated, being unable to breathe.'

'Okay. But how can that help us? It's not as if he can make any sounds through his nose holes, or hear us asking him questions, is it?'

'Do you know Morse code? The old dot dash system for communicating? Used to be taught by the military.'

'Yeah, learnt it in the Scouts as a boy. I doubt I can remember any of it. Why?'

Doc took Jack's hand and placed it on his own chest, and said, 'I don't remember much either, but let's see. Feel my breaths, and try to understand what I'm saying.'

Jack's hand sensed three sharp intakes of breath, then three longer inhalations followed by three short ones again. Doc exhaled, rested for a moment, then repeated the pattern.

Dot-dot-dot dash-dash-dash dot-dot-dot...

'You bloody genius, Doc! SOS. The old distress signal. If Mister M can do what you were doing, we can talk to him!'

'Only if he knows Morse code too, Jack. Long shot or not, can you get someone proficient enough to work with him? A colleague of yours perhaps, or a military signals specialist. It's really old technology so not many people use it these days... I'd suggest they start with that distress message tapped on his chest to see if he responds.'

Jack was up already, pacing the room, his mobile to his ear.

'Too right I will. I'll get someone with him right now. Before he pegs it!'

'Blimey Fifi, didn't you go home last night?' DS Sam Sharpe dumped a cup of vending machine coffee next to her computer monitor and slurped at his own before asking, 'What's so important that you're here this early after working late? Did you get anywhere with that info I sent you yesterday?' He perched his left buttock on the edge of her desk and swung his leg back and forth, his other supporting the rest of his weight. 'You look like shit, darlin!'

'I feel like shit. Couldn't sleep, mate. But thanks for the files. Did we get anything back from Missing Persons on the DNA from our Mister M?'

Fiona liked Sam, he was a good colleague, one ever willing to help, and they often sat like this at the start of the day, catching up on things. When she'd first arrived at the Yard he had attached himself to her, as he was a newbie too. She'd been delighted to discover he was a decent bloke, not sexist, not arrogant, just bloody efficient at his job. He was a wizard with all things computing and could dig out information she had no idea was to be found online or buried in the various database collections available to the UK police force, let alone the wealth of files held by HOLMES—the Home Office Large Major Enquiries System, named in homage to the fictional Sherlock—housed in the basement of this very building. Sam was happily married too, and had never hit on her, which made him even more special to Fiona.

'Nothing on him yet. He's nowhere near the front of the queue as they're dealing with a backlog of rape kits Soundbite wants clearing. She gave them top priority after that Asian girl got gang-banged by a bunch of Britain First morons at the weekend.

Was on the telly again last night, promising to put rape cases at the top of her agenda now *she's* caught the Brentwood Beast.'

'Yeah? She doesn't miss a trick, does she?'

'Nah... Why couldn't you sleep?'

His genuine enquiry, not one intended to put her down or question her ability to do the job, elicited a quiet moan, accompanied by a welling of tears. She hastily turned from his concerned eyes, and punched some keys that brought up an article on the screen for him to view. He pushed himself upright, then crouched beside her to see better.

'The Mau Mau uprising? What's that all about?' He watched as she scrolled down the page to an image, his face disbelieving. 'Is that a native being spit-roasted over an open fire? Those are British soldiers looking on, aren't they? What is this, Fi? Looks like photoshopped bollocks to me.'

'Gerald Butler served in Kenya when things like this really were happening. Took part in it all. Took some souvenirs too. I did some research after I discovered a collection of ears in his house. I just can't get the horror of it all out of my head.'

Sam put a comforting arm round her shoulders, gave her a quick squeeze, then asked, 'What's this got to do with our vic? Torturing black folk in Africa sixty odd years ago? You need to move on to more recent events, I reckon!'

Although his words made sense, Fiona's discovery had sparked a flame that burnt brighter and brighter as she tried to sleep. Finally, the conflagration had been too much to ignore and she had made her way to the office, bleary eyed, emotional and frustrated. Sam might be able to help her make sense of the idea now consuming her.

'Did you know, in parts of Africa there's a trade in body parts, Sam?'

'What, like kidneys and hearts, for transplants? I've heard of it, but it happens in many other third world places, from India to Mexico. What's so special about Kenya?'

Fiona also had doubts about the possible link she'd identified, but just as she did with their list of suspects, which in her mind included Doc—despite Jack's reaction—she would keep an open mind. Her nascent theory was based on gut feel so, in this instance, she would run things past Sam before mentioning anything to the DI.

'Magic. They call it *kamuti* or *muti* depending on the whereabouts, mostly in East African countries.'

'Magic! Mmm... You know, I saw a documentary about albinos in Tanzania. Little kids with their limbs chopped off, and worse. Just for superstition and tradition... Bloody heathens. Still happens, even in this day and age, they said.'

'Not just albinos. A victim is chosen for different reasons—sexual potency, power, money, youthfulness—the usual mix of desirable traits. Some places, they even eat body parts, but most just use them as lucky charms.'

'Ugh! Like rabbit's feet? Is this common?'

'Well, there are plenty of confirmed cases and many more rumoured. But something Jack said got me thinking. You remember that boy they found floating in the Thames? Torso boy they called him at first, then they named him Adam.'

'That was a bit before my time, but I vaguely remember. I think they thought it was a voodoo related killing at the time. What happened?'

'Not voodoo, Sam. Muti magic. This was back in 2001 and the team investigated it for years, even took a couple of trips to Africa. It was never solved, and the whole thing was allowed to die a death… Politics.'

'What d'you mean?'

'It's just a rumour, but race riots were going on at the time. Complaints against the police about discrimination were flooding in. It was all very tense for ages, so the PTBs decided to drop it. No further action. Thought the investigation would just stir up more trouble, heighten tensions between white and ethnic communities, given the barbaric nature of the crime and all that.'

Fiona rather liked Carver's shorthand for the powers that be, the decision makers who often moved in such mysterious ways, as the abbreviation suited the aloof and anonymous nature of the beast.

'So you're thinking Mister M is a muti victim? Seems a bit of a stretch.'

'Not exactly, but I am wondering if there's a connection. Do me a favour, Sam. Can you check what we have on file, anything related to the Adam case? Also, anything HOLMES has on record involving human body parts used for rituals and so on since that case.'

'Cool. I'll have a dig around later.'

Fiona's mobile buzzed and vibrated so she grabbed it from the desktop, grimaced at Sam and said, 'It's the DI. Do me another favour. Don't mention any of this to him just yet, eh?'

Sam nodded and headed off to his own desk as she hit the answer button.

'Morning, Fi! I need someone with Morse code skills to head to the hospital asap.'

'Morse code?'

Carver explained Doc's idea about how they might communicate with Mister M, then said, 'But we need to get a move on. I just spoke to the hospital and the vic's in terminal decline, but there's no one there who knows Morse.'

'Hang on, Boss.' Fiona signalled Sam to come back to her desk, her eyebrows raised in question as she called out to him. 'You're a radio ham, correct? Do you know Morse code?'

'Yeah, I dabble on the airwaves a bit. And of course I know Morse. Why?'

Instead of answering his question, she addressed the DI.

'DS Sharpe's on his way, sir.'

'It's not genius, Jack. I should've thought of it yesterday.' Doc knew his faculties had not been working at one hundred percent when he had met Carver at the victim's bedside, thanks to his prior meeting with Harding and attendant worries over Judy. He'd had a troubled night, and not just as a result of the belated realisation regarding the possibility of communicating with the victim. No, the worst occurred when he did sleep, and suffered nightmares in which he had been dismembering his own father. His breath juddered at the recollection, then he returned his mind to the present. 'Morse has been used with stroke victims and other patients with locked-in syndrome in the past. It's not that common, but I'm surprised the hospital didn't think of it.'

'Well, perhaps the state of the poor bloke had them in shock too. So what about this latest letter from our DIY surgeon. I'll pass a copy of these new photos on to our researchers though I'm not hopeful they'll be able to ID 'em. All are white victims though, no ethnic blend here from the look of it. You can barely tell what sex they are, either. Maybe Bob Koch can help.'

'Definitely difficult to tell.' Hairless, featureless, limbless, no breasts or genitalia. 'Not much for the ME to go on either, without their remains… This latest communication tells us a lot about the guy who sent it though.'

'What d'you mean?'

Jack scrolled through the images again, hunting for something but finding nothing.

'He's dismantling them. Stripping away their personality. Removing anything that identifies them, removing the things that make them human. It's about what he wants to do to the victims, not about avoiding detection by masking their IDs.'

'You really think they were alive while he did this to them?'

'Not all of it, Jack, but definitely some of this was designed to torture them before death.'

'So why is our vic still alive, in his bed in St George's then?'

'Mister M is the ultimate creation, the perfection of his art. This may be his final victim, or he could be moving on to a new phase, a new MO, having achieved his ultimate objective for this part of his criminal career.'

Doc felt that twinge of admiration again, and thrust it back to his subconscious where he knew it would fester.

'Is that why he wrote the letters? Taunting you like that, convinced he'll get away scot free if he stops after Mister M?'

Doc sucked air through his teeth into his cheeks, audibly mulling things over, then said, 'This letter. I think it confirms his motive for contacting me.'

'He's playing a game. That's pretty clear.'

'But why now, Jack? Was it really the TV series that sparked him off, prompted him to contact me? Think about it. He would've already been working on your Mister M when the programme mentioning Diana Davies was broadcast late last year, so what has prompted him to send me the letters? My theory, that serial killers are responsible for many more victims than they've been convicted of, applies to him and he wants us to know. Davies was one of his earliest, your cold case. We dismissed her as a one off, but she wasn't.'

'He's bragging. Letting us know he's outsmarted us, telling us 'cos we couldn't see the connections… To seven vics in total.'

'The seven that we're currently aware of. And with no human remains we wouldn't even know about five of those victims without his *gifts* to me. He's challenging me to find him, though is pretty sure I won't, especially if he makes me suffer along the way… Hence his taunts about Harding.'

'I still can't see how that mad bastard's involved with our Mister M case… My Sarge has a theory. She thinks you're a suspect!'

Jack's chuckle sounded a little forced to Doc.

'What? Your Sergeant Fifi?'

'Yeah. She was well put out when she told me. I started to get angry, but then saw the funny side and pissed meself laughing.' He chuckled at the recollection, a genuine sound this time. 'Last night, over a curry. It seemed absurd… She'd wound herself up real tight about telling me. That girl's got some balls, mind. She'd had a bad day already, but she was right to share her suspicions.'

'Which were?' Despite trying hard, Doc could not dilute the acid in his voice.

'Well, after I told her Maddox was a suspect, and that all this,' he shoved Doc's MacBook at him, 'could've been a diversion to put us off his trail, she said we should consider the same might just as easily apply to you.'

'Seriously?' Doc scoffed, but then realised this was actually serious.

'Yeah… Did you send these letters to yourself, Doc?'

Carver's wolfish grin had Doc wondering.

'Really, Jack? You believe that?'

'No, mate. I have to ask though, now she's officially raised it as an issue.'

'Of course I didn't! And anyway, what about all these other victims. Hardly a diversion.'

'If they're real.'

'I don't doubt it.'

'Funny. She said you'd say that. She also said, you could've tossed in the Davies girl's photo along with some mocked up victim images just to create some credibility in the letter's contents. You didn't though, did you?'

'Enough already! That Davies photo is not from police files, so how could I have got hold of that? Or does your brilliant sergeant think I killed that prostitute all those years ago too, for some unknown reason. That I kept the photo as a memento, then taught myself to operate on Mister M? It's ridiculous!'

'Calm down, Doc. All we know for sure is there're two victims, M and Davies, both hideously mutilated though with varying degrees of sophistication. The other two photos from yesterday have not been matched with any vics in our databases, though we're checking with Europol and the FBI too. We'll do the same with the three that came through today, but I'm not hopeful they'll be identified considering the state they're in, especially with what he says here, about the remains being gone forever.'

'Mmm.' Doc was counting out his breath then said, 'So why leave the one victim, a prostitute, for us to find? Perhaps he left her as a deliberate clue, almost eleven years ago, and has been laughing at us ever since.'

'Possibly… Who's Harry Butler?'

'Who?' Doc vaguely recalled the name, but was not sure where he had heard it. 'Has he got something to do with this?'

'My Sarge thinks he might.'

'Your Sarge seems to have a lot of suspects on her list, Jack.'

'You don't remember him?'

'The name has a familiar ring to it. Who is he?' Doc was genuinely confused, more by Jack's tone than this Harry Butler chap.

'He's the grandson of that bloke who found our victim yesterday morning.'

'Okay. And why should I remember him?'

'You treated him. At Broadmoor. Around the time Davies was found.'

'Well I don't recall. I've met with hundreds of inmates there over the years, some for only one or two meetings. My memory's pretty good, but I don't recollect the details of everyone. What was he there for?'

'Assessment. PTSD sparked a psychotic break. Waving a machete about—'

'Ah! I do remember. Yes, I saw him maybe a dozen times at most.' An image of Harry Butler was now in his mind's eye, helping him drag the details from his memory. 'I assessed him and recommended he was treated instead of convicted. That's all I can tell you about him.' *Another coincidence?* He could read his detective friend's suspicious mind, and fully understood it. Neither of them believed in random coincidence. 'Honest, Jack!'

'No contact since then? You sure?'

'Of course not. I'd have said.' Jack's eyes met his and Doc could see another question lurking behind them, reluctant to be exposed. 'What now, Jack? Why are you are looking at me like I'm a total stranger?'

'I was just wondering… When you stopped working for the Met as a profiler, you'd been having some problems. Psychological problems. You only told me about how bad it all got after the Leech affair, yeah?'

'Yes, you know very well I did. I shared that information with you when I was in hospital, when I told you about my most recent breakdown. Well, almost breakdown. What are you thinking?' He was asking, but he already knew the answer.

'You couldn't cope with the job any more, long before that. Raging demons you called them. The serial killers and the like, they'd got to you, warped your mind, you said, from spending too long inside their heads… It was only in hospital that you came clean about how bad it had got. Remember? You even told me you'd been having blackouts, had been losing days sometimes.'

'My wife died in a car accident and I was the one driving, it screwed with my brain—'

'You told me you'd lost track of time, had blackouts for years before Natalie died, mate.'

'Oh, come off it, Jack. Don't even go there.'

Doc was beginning to regret opening up to his friend during that most vulnerable period, lying flat on his back for months. The confession had been cathartic, and subsequently Doc had even spoken about his reasons for giving up profiling in a magazine interview, had mentioned it during the introduction to his TV series too, though Jack knew rather more than Doc had admitted in public.

'Several hours might go by, without you knowing what you'd been doing or where you'd been… *I'm losing it,* you said. Told me you couldn't do the job any more. That you'd never enter a murderer's head ever again… But I saw you, at Mister M's bedside. You are doing it again… You're right back in the thick of it.'

Doc felt a sudden rush, a surge of adrenalin, as he remembered how many times he had questioned his own sanity while doing the job, and how his world had disintegrated, flirting with madness after his wife had died.

His eyes were drawn to the laptop, the final words from the latest letter, the screen glaring at him, accusing him:

Try to step inside my mind again, good doctor.
Then you may just connect with your true nature.
The secret buried deep inside your psyche.

He could understand Jack's reluctant but evident suspicion, the duality of the meaning now obvious to them both.

He had a flashback to yesterday, his vision at the hospital, the feel of the scalpel in his hand, the man's face, fully featured, a recognisable human, screeching his agony as Doc carved his flesh.

It had all seemed so real, but was not.

It couldn't be…

Could it?

———

'Well, ma'am, we need more bodies helping with this case. I've already managed to cajole DS Sharpe and DS Pearce to give a hand, but I could do with them full time.'

Carver watched the Acting Superintendent as she weighed him up, totally unsure which way this would go. She opened the file he had given her and spread the seven photographs on the desk before him, each of them now numbered in the sequence he and Doc had determined.

'So tell me again, Jack. Have you got any evidence that these six cold cases are linked to the current victim, other than these photographs, received by Doctor Powers, a man supposedly assisting this investigation who you now tell me should be considered a suspect?'

'I didn't say that, ma'am.'

Not exactly.

'Don't fudge this. You should know better than to try that on with me.' The ice maiden, po-faced, added, 'Telling me about DS Fielding's concerns may cover your arse, but if it turns out she's right I'll hang you out to dry. Got it?'

'Yes ma'am. I will bear that in mind, but we have more promising avenues of enquiry, including this genius doctor, Maddox. There's also the grandson, Harry Butler, and—' His phone vibrated in his pocket and he considered ignoring it, knowing how it would annoy Soundbite Sadie if he answered, but he had to check who was calling. It could be the breakthrough they needed. He snatched it from his pocket, checked the screen to see who was calling, then hit the green button as he raised his other index finger in a *just a minute* signal to his boss. 'This might be important, ma'am.' He then spoke into the phone without waiting for her to reply, 'Tell me Sam. Make it brief. I'm with the Acting Super.'

Dawson drummed her fingers on the desk, still wearing that mask Jack could never read, though he knew it would incense her, doing this. She stayed silent, waiting for him to finish, as he just muttered 'Mmm… Mmm… Go on… Great work, Sergeant. Now get your arse back here.'

'DI Carver, you know I don't allow calls when I am in a one to one with my staff—'

'Yes ma'am. Apologies. But that was DS Sharpe calling from the hospital. Our Mister M just died. This is now a murder investigation.'

He could feel the frost thaw as she acknowledged the necessity of his interruption, then her voice steeled as she said, 'My murder investigation. I am still the SIO, a fact you would do well to remember.'

Jack eyed his Senior Investigating Officer, wondering what he had done to deserve being assigned to her, then added, 'How could I forget, ma'am? You'll be delighted to know we now have a name for the victim. Patrick Rawlings. Unfortunately the DS couldn't get anything else out of him before his heart gave out.'

'Really? Good work, Jack. But how? I thought the victim was incommunicado.'

'You might want to scrub Doc Powers' name off your list of suspects, ma'am.' He couldn't help the snark in his tone, though knew it would do him no favours. 'I was just about to explain.' He did so, told her about the Morse code, then added, 'It was his idea. A long shot that came off. Brilliant, eh?'

'You still need to keep an eye on him. I'm not totally convinced.' Jack, a little taken aback, then realised she was now the one covering her rear end as she explained. 'Perhaps this Rawlings chap didn't know who did this to him. Offering this unlikely possibility of unlocking his mute status would present little risk to the killer, if that was the case, would it?'

Well, actually, yes it would.

Jack thought it wise not to give her a lesson on basic detective work so just smiled as he said, 'We have a name and can start working up a list of suspects, people who knew him, maybe had a motive to do this. We really do need some additional full-time help now, ma'am... Incidentally, Doc's waiting downstairs as we speak, as I wanted him involved in the team briefing.'

Jack had hoped she would give the green light for a more substantial investigation based on the latest photos and the ever widening scope of their operation, but the victim's name, along with his deceased status, would clinch the deal.

'Right then!' She clapped her hands together and clasped them on the desktop, her only outward sign of enthusiasm. 'Let's go and rally the troops. I'll allocate some additional officers and then we'll brief the entire team.' She stood, smoothed her immaculate trousers, touched her immaculate hair with her immaculately manicured fingertips and said, 'Let's go, Jack. And don't look at me like that—as if I never address our staff! I may delegate a lot to you but I am still a detective you know. Come on, get your skates on.'

Carver unsuccessfully tried to stop a wry expression forming on his face. He knew exactly why she was suddenly so energised. Another murder enquiry, with possible serial killer connections, a chance to mop up several more cold cases immediately after catching the Brentwood Beast.

Oh yes, she was like a racehorse galloping out of the gates, jockeying for position. The prize was not a silver trophy, but the crowned epaulette of a Metropolitan Police Superintendent. Something far more precious to the ambitious ice maiden—for her acting role to become permanent. Her youth would single her out for rapid progression through the senior ranks soon thereafter.

God, she's obnoxious, he decided, as her svelte, and now very well protected derriere disappeared out the door. He followed.

'Of course, ma'am. I'm right behind you.'

Unfortunately.

After DS Sam Sharpe left for the hospital, Fiona switched her attention back to her research. There was something niggling her, like an insect burrowing in her brain, while she revisited the details she had discovered relating to muti magic and what she now thought of as The African Connection. Discovering Gerald Butler's macabre collection had been a shock to her system, a profound blow to her identity as a multicultural copper in multiracial London. Frustrated, she decided to put these thoughts aside for now and pulled out the file on Judy Finch.

She had skimmed through it last night and realised her boss had gone out on a limb for his friend Doctor Powers when she discovered the details of the woman's bank withdrawals and credit card usage. All tucked into the file she had found in his drawer, but with one glaring omission...

No warrant.

Fiona was a straight cop, rarely bent the rules, which was one of the reasons she liked Carver so much. He had a reputation for being direct, honest and straight to the point. All of his team knew he occasionally took shortcuts, but only when necessary and generally merely minor infringements that would not compromise a case. Yet here he was, risking his career for his pal by obtaining information illegally, and then leaving it on the premises.

It was likely that Sam was the source—he could get pretty much anything, legally or otherwise, if it was held in a computer network. She just hoped he had covered his tracks in case this breach of protocol ever came to Soundbite's attention. If that happened she would ensure an enormous pile of excrement would hit an industrial sized fan directed at Carver and anyone else involved. Including Fiona...

She ripped the offending documents in half, almost binned the pieces, thought better of it, grabbed a small paper bag from her bottom drawer, and made her way to the secure shredder instead. The machine hummed and buzzed in an oddly satisfying way as she watched the offending evidence disintegrate into tiny fragments in the transparent bin.

Having satisfied herself her hands were now clean of Carver's mess, she decided it was time for a decent coffee. The kitchenette was often busy, but she found it empty so took the opportunity to make herself a cafetière with grounds from her private stash. The aroma of her favourite blend helped calm her as she spooned the coffee into the glass jug full of boiling water.

Her mind went back to the Finch woman and the evidence she had just destroyed. It was several months old anyway, so pretty useless, she decided, especially as her boss had scrawled *Card not used since Jan,* a barely legible note she could just make out, dated sometime in April this year.

Other scribbled notes on the file indicated the DI had seen her late on New Year's Eve, working as a homeless outreach program volunteer for St Mary's Church in Brixton. After that, Finch had disappeared completely, and according to the notes, took fifty thousand pounds in cash from her bank two days after Jack met with her, having told him she did not want to be found again. She clearly meant it.

Bollocks. This is not going to be easy. Then, Double Bollocks!

She heard Sam's voice, murmuring in the corridor, then another one she recognised, though she had never met the man.

Suspect, she reminded herself.

'Hi, Fifi! I thought you'd be in here when I smelt fresh coffee when we got out the lift. I hope you've you got enough for three cups.' Sam grinned and asked, 'Have you met Doctor Powers?'

She had seen him from a distance once or twice when he had been at the Yard over the last couple of years. Usually with Jack. She put her hand out, and was about to introduce herself, but he spoke first.

'Well, you must be DS Fielding. And I'm your prime suspect... Delighted to meet you, Detective.'

Triple bollocks!

Of course Jack had told him. She knew he would, last night, in the curry house. The moment he went from angry volcano, threatening to erupt, to bubbling with laughter rather than molten lava.

Fiona took Doc's outstretched hand and was delighted to see real warmth in his smile as he continued, 'Don't worry, Sergeant, I fully understand why you came to that conclusion. I respect an open-minded detective, and Jack thinks very highly of you.'

'Suspect?' Sam was helping himself to cups and saucers—all the mugs were dirty and lying in the sink waiting for a volunteer to clean them—and spoke over his shoulder as he depressed the plunger in the coffee jug. 'You must be joking, Fi. I just got back from the hospital. We've got a victim ID thanks to Doc. Bumped into him downstairs so invited him up. You didn't tell me he should be in handcuffs!' He chuckled then poured three cups.

Fiona finally found her voice. 'That's gonna be piss weak, Sam.' She tutted at him as the insipid liquid dribbled into the cups, then turned back to Doc. 'Well, you do fit the criteria. You're on the list with many other potential medical specialists we must automatically consider as suspects. In fact, now Sam's back from the hospital, we can start narrowing things down, but I'm hoping Jack can get us some additional help. He's with the Acting Super now.'

'I know. That's why I'm here too. And now, thanks to Sam's facility with an archaic binary cipher system we can start working up a victim profile. We can hopefully draw some parallels with Diana Davies too.'

Fiona had her doubts about any potential connection, but instead said, 'Did you get anything else out of him, Sam?'

'Nah, mate. Just a name. Patrick Rawlings. I was just explaining to Doc. I did a quick search on him using my smartphone in the car on the way back here. Interesting bloke. City player. Went missing almost four years ago, along with a load of funds. Made a killing from the financial crash in 2008, then some years later his clients got burned investing in his hedge fund. Was being investigated for fraud when he did a Lord Lucan... Now it seems he was abducted. I need to do some more digging, but this bloke had lots of enemies, including some big names, some of 'em decidedly dodgy. Russian oligarchs and the like.'

'Mmm.' This merely confirmed Fi's suspicions. 'A fifty quid a night King's Cross prozzie, a street walker, and a hedge fund manager? I can't see any likely connection—'

Carver's voice boomed down the hall and echoed in the kitchen. 'Oi, you two. You haven't got time for coffee. The SIO has called a briefing. Get your backsides in here, now. I've got a stack of bacon sarnies for brekkers for everyone. And find Doc Powers for me. We need him in here too.'

Carver seemed to have an uncanny knack of locating his team when he needed them, though Fiona and Sam often decamped to the kitchen like this when working together. Doc looked suitably startled that Jack knew where they were.

'I think the aroma of my unique brand of coffee gave us away, Doc... He's a great detective but he can't see through walls.' She took a slurp, grimaced at Sam as she tasted the brew, then chucked it in the sink. 'Cat's piss! You muppet, Sam. Come on, we'd better go.'

Doc's headcount of Jack's expanded team now stood at sixteen, although the Senior Investigating Officer, Acting Superintendent Sadie Dawson, as she had introduced herself—just in case anybody was not sure what she was doing on their floor—was not included in Doc's calculation. From his detective friend's colourful description, 'She's about as much use as tits on a nun', he supposed their total resources for this serial homicide investigation, including himself, reached a grand total of seventeen.

Why so few?

Jack had told him over forty officers had been involved in the last murder investigation overseen by Dawson, and that seemed a more appropriate figure to Doc. Perhaps she had yet to be convinced whether the other victim photographs were genuine, or if they bore any relation to Rawlings and/or the prostitute Davies. He hoped Jack had not shared his sergeant's suspicions with this woman, but she had largely ignored Doc since he, DS Fiona Fielding and DS Sam Sharpe had joined the little group at the back of the open plan office. Dawson did not make him feel welcome at all, and he guessed she was distancing herself, unwilling to be tainted by him in the event he was a guilty party.

After his minor wobble this morning, he had crushed the doubts he was experiencing as he consoled himself with the result Sam had achieved with the discovery of Rawlings' identity. Doc had been chatting to a former colleague in the reception area downstairs, waiting for Jack to buzz him up, when the nerdy Sergeant recognised him. Doc had never met the officer, but Sam had bounced over, full of enthusiasm, and pumped his hand while blurting out the success he had just achieved, thanks to Doc's Morse code idea.

He then insisted Doc join him in the lift, and as they rode up to the fourth floor, he described his fleeting visit to the hospital. Apparently, Rawlings did not know who had attacked him, and just kept repeating 'Kill me' over and over as Sam tried to establish some facts beyond the victim's name. The exertion, probably combined with the shock of finally being able to communicate, had sent Rawlings' pulse racing and within minutes he went into fibrillation. Despite the alarm sounding, the crash team took several minutes to arrive at his bedside, an unusual response, probably reflecting an unstated *do not resuscitate* status for this particular patient. Meanwhile, Rawlings, aka Mister Mutilated, died with Sam looking on. The sergeant's laconic observation, as they followed the aroma of freshly brewed coffee after exiting the lift, was:

'Probably for the best. All things considered, Doctor Powers.'

Sam seemed unperturbed by what he had witnessed, and was obviously on a high from having achieved the seemingly impossible. Doc warmed to him instantly, and, despite Fifi's suspicious mind, she too was someone he felt comfortable with.

The rest of the team were unknown to him, and as Jack and his boss did a double act, firstly introducing new team members then presenting information, it was clear who was in the driving seat, and who was being chauffeured.

It had been a while since Doc had seen Carver working alongside a senior officer, and their body language told a tale of ascendancy for one and frustration for the other. Dawson's stance was open, she stood upright and regularly spread her hands, feet planted shoulder width apart, as if trying to make herself larger than her slimline frame. In contrast, Jack was hunched beside her, arms folded, ankles crossed, making himself seem smaller, diminished next to the dominant female he now reported to.

Doc would have to have a word with him about that.

He had tuned out much of their presentation to the troops as he was aware of most of it from their earlier meeting at his home, but then Fiona piped up. She was hesitant, unsure of herself as she spoke, her head moving like a spectator at

Wimbledon as she addressed Dawson then Jack and back again, over and over, her words hurried.

'I have a theory, ma'am... I haven't had time to run it past the DI but I think it might be relevant. You remember the headless torso they found floating in the Thames in 2001, ma'am? They called him Adam. He was never formally identified. The Met even asked the FBI for help. Their advice was to drop the case—an unknown foreign child, no fingerprints, no head, so no teeth for dental records. But the lead detective, now retired, was convinced it was a ritual killing—'

Dawson cut her off, her voice harsh.

'The little African boy? Of course I remember. It was a high-profile investigation that went on for years, long before I transferred to the Met. I hardly think it's relevant to this case. I don't know if *you* noticed Sergeant Fielding, but all seven victims are *Caucasian* adults. All with heads... Don't be diverted by your discovery of some ancient shrivelled ears from another continent half a world away. Let's stay focused, people.'

Doc was surprised at the condescension Dawson expressed as she swatted her junior down. It was not just Jack who had a problem with this career obsessed woman. Carver had warned him that she took no hostages.

Fortunately, Doc had an advantage over the others in the group, being an outside consultant, feted by officers far more senior than this self-important 'Acting up' Superintendent. He decided to interject, as he started to make connections himself, thanks to feisty young Fifi. Unlike the sergeant, he refused to use the term *ma'am*, even though he knew it would rile this status driven careerist. He had decided Dawson was bloody rude, but probably only to junior staff, while charming those above her on the greasy promotion pole.

'I think the sergeant's right, Sadie.' Dawson's face was inscrutable, but her arms immediately crossed, not in a defensive gesture like Jack's, but one that broached no disagreement. Doc continued, his own voice forceful. 'There may well be a ritual element.'

The Acting Super's tone hardened. 'The Adam case was sealed. Unsolved. I see no reason to link it with our current investigation.'

Doc wondered if they were entering a politically sensitive minefield, and, if so, he was sure she would not willingly step foot there. She needed to be shoved in the right direction and he would have to be the one to push her.

He was on safe ground though, as he had researched the case for his TV series before moving on to other more interesting cold cases, all with potential links to convicted serial killers. Although he had lost interest, the connection Fiona now postulated should have occurred to him too, but the letters and the nature of the photographs, including the victims' skin colour, had diverted him. Fiona's conclusions brought the details spinning into his mind and rekindled his interest. Too bad if Dawson was obstructive. Even so, he verbally tiptoed.

'Ritual killings still take place in parts of Africa. They harvest body parts, ideally from the living. These human remains are used in a form of black magic called muti—'

'For Christ's sake, Doctor Powers... Are you seriously suggesting all of these victims, including Rawlings, had to suffer for some barbaric tribal beliefs originating in darkest Africa? Do you honestly believe there's some massive market for that sort of thing here in the UK?' Dawson scoffed. 'Well, I don't think so. It's pure conjecture, likely to take us in the wrong direction. We have far more promising leads to pursue as we've already discussed.'

The Acting Super's political antennae were up and Doc—who hated office politics with a passion—realised he could lose the chance to find out the truth about Diana Davies and the other victims purely because he was mooting a culturally negative idea. He eyed Jack who, just out of sight from his boss, responded with a little lift of his shoulders. No immediate help would be forthcoming from that quarter. Even DS Fielding had gone quiet, and then Doc realised the whole team was silent, as if aware he was goading their boss. He tried to reason with her.

'I'm not suggesting *all* the body parts taken from each victim were for muti magic, just some of them. This is a sophisticated killer with other motivations too—'

'I'm sure Jack will be keen to hear what you have to say on this subject, Doctor Powers.' The implication being, she was not. She opened her mouth to continue but Doc spoke over her. Her rank was of no consequence to him.

'I reread the ME's report this morning. Bob Koch's convinced some of the Davies woman's wounds were inflicted while she was alive, just as we know they were for Rawlings. Her arms, legs, lips, nose and eyes were taken. Her tongue—the removal of which killed her—was ripped out during the process and, although Koch was not certain of the exact order of dissection, he is convinced this was not the very first action the killer took. It could be that her agonised wailing boosted the supposed power of the muti, thereby increasing the value of her other body parts. It is grotesque, but its logic makes some perverted sort of sense.' Doc could not help himself from adding, 'It may not suit the politically correct brigade but this is an avenue of enquiry we *have* to pursue.'

The Acting Super had taken to scrutinising the file Jack had presented her earlier, head down, fingering the photographs as if they were printed in Braille. A minute passed without a word as she made her mental calculations. Doc could hear the wall clock ticking. Some of the detectives started to shuffle their feet, uncomfortable with the delay, not sure whether to speak. Even Jack was overshadowed by his highly assertive boss. Doc wanted to push her to make the right decision, but decided to let her come to her own conclusions.

When she finally raised her head she said something Doc had not expected, her voice still full of scepticism.

'Our medical examiner, Bob Koch, was born in Africa. He lived in Kenya before moving to the UK as a boy. I'll have him review the Adam file and then I'll see what conclusions he draws during his autopsy on Rawlings, which is due to take place this morning.'

Harry Hope strolled into the twenty-four hour mini-mart at the petrol filling station to pick up some sugar coated vegan doughnuts and two cups of black coffee. It was his usual morning routine. A brisk walk while Shazza set things up in the tattoo parlour ready for opening. He was still feeling euphoric from his extended suspension the previous evening, and his mind was sharper, his eyes bright as they took in everything around him, seeing with a heightened clarity that he knew would only last a few hours more.

He loved the sensation, craved it, since discovering the relief it provided from his usual mental state. These days, he was usually medicated, in a semi-sedated fashion, thanks to the drugs he was obliged to take to maintain any sense of normality. Last night, instead of chomping on tablets, he'd dangled from the ceiling of his cellar, attaining a peace of mind and a level of tranquillity only experienced by the most advanced practitioners of meditation. This morning he felt alive, almost reborn.

As he waited for his coffee he felt himself drawn to the rack of newspapers for sale in the corner of the store, unsure why, as he never bothered much with world events—in fact, any events beyond his own little bubble of friends and their mutual interests. A headline jumped out at him as he approached and his spine prickled as he read the two words:

MISTER MUTILATED!

Below the headline was a picture, much of it blurred, but with enough hideous detail to determine the degree of harm that had been visited on the victim. As he dragged the newspaper from the rack he scanned the sparse details and then scrabbled at the pages to find the main feature inside. He felt his euphoria dissipate as he read the report of how the victim had been found on Clapham Common by an elderly man while out walking his dog.

One Gerald Butler. Now sadly deceased.

Harry felt the ground lurch beneath his feet, and the room distorted, as if he was lost in a hall of mirrors. He stumbled, put a hand out to support himself, but only found the flimsy rack of newspapers and sent the whole thing crashing to the ground as he tried to remain upright.

His ears were assailed by an angry buzzing, as if a hornet's nest had been smashed over his head. He could see the look of shock and concern on the faces of the staff as he tried to steady himself, to get to the door, to get out, to be away from this place now threatening his sanity.

As he reached the forecourt, the stench of petrol stinging his nostrils, the buzzing in his head turned to screams while his mind conjured visions of Rigsby's body, maimed by the Hellfire missile that decimated Harry's team. He started jogging, a lopsided gait, staggering along, just trying to get away from the dreadful sights and sounds pursuing him, infesting his mind. As he sucked the air into his chest, the acrid tang of gasoline gave way to the gut-wrenching stink of burnt flesh. He stopped by a lamppost and dry heaved into the gutter.

After a final retch, he straightened and started to run again, faster, fleeing the memories trying to engulf him, heading nowhere in particular, just anywhere, as long it was away from the photographs in that newspaper.

'Of course, it's highly unlikely these are ritual killings, so I don't want anyone wasting time on this angle before I have confirmation from our *expert* ME.' Dawson paused for effect as she instructed the team. 'Let's not go chasing up a blind alley.'

The sly dig at Doc, the emphasis on Koch's status versus his own was not lost on him. Time for one last plea to reason.

'There are estimated to be well over a hundred suspected muti killings in Kenya alone, every year. What seems impossibly alien to us may not be to anyone born and raised there, no matter where they currently live... Children all over the world are brought up to understand the dangers posed by strangers. African mothers scare their children with tales of being kidnapped for body parts in much the same way as we might warn our kids not to take lollipops from unknown adults.'

'In which case, I'm sure Professor Koch will have a valid opinion to share on the matter.' Dawson clapped her hands together and added, 'We have seven *adult* victims, with Diana Davies, the first, found long after the discovery of that torso boy. But you're still talking about rituals involving children!'

'Not just children.' Exasperation tinged Doc's tone.

Jack finally spoke up.

'I remember the Adam case too. A specialist from Johannesburg was flown in and he confirmed it was almost certainly a ritual murder based on the contents of the lad's stomach. He'd been fed a mix of African herbs and forced to swallow a toxic bean which paralyses the body. We should keep an open mind, Boss. It did happen here...'

'There were other things too.' Doc's own memory was nudged by Jack's comment. 'Critically Adam's first vertebra had been removed. In Africa it is called the Atlas bone and it's especially prized by muti witch doctors as they believe it to be the centre of the body's life force.' Doc could see Dawson was about to interrupt him, so he went on, ramming the points home. 'Muti victims are often discarded in running water to flush away the evil they're tainted with. Adam was pulled from the Thames. Dressed only in orange shorts—the colour associated with muti magic. Diana Davis was found lying by an orange bandanna in a culvert draining into the River Wandle.'

This last point had not seemed important before this morning, but now Doc made the association. It was still not enough for Dawson who turned to address her DI directly.

'For goodness' sake! Jack... Do not get bogged down with the Adam case. The Met has wasted far too much money and manpower on that ancient crime already. Let's keep this whole muti thing at arm's length for now. I've made my decision and will inform you all once I've heard what Bob Koch has to say. I'll head to the morgue and personally oversee the Rawlings post mortem this morning.'

'Yes ma'am.'

'And DI Carver, don't ignore the other things we discussed this morning.' The formal words accompanied a warning glance, and Doc guessed who was the subject of that pointed look. Dawson then addressed the team again. 'I'll leave Jack to allocate your individual tasks, but my door is always open, so if he's not available, just make sure you come to me with any concerns you have.' Her eyes were on DS Fielding, and Doc felt his ears burn at the unspoken slight on his character. He listened, inwardly fuming as Dawson continued while bundling up her files. 'Let's find this lunatic before we discover any more bodies.'

Although Harry's conscious mind was not aware, his subconscious mind was driving his feet to the one destination he had to be right now. As he arrived at the gate, his body slick with a film of grime-laden sweat, his legs aching from sprinting as if fleeing the devil himself, he looked up at the house.

As he recognised where he was, and began to wonder why his legs had brought him here, a part of his mind noted the lack of police tape, or any other indication that they had been at his grandfather's house. For a moment he pondered on that, then went to the door, flicked the mat up with his toe and saw the spare key in its usual place. He bent, scooped it up and, before giving his actions another moment's thought, slid it into the lock.

The run here had blown away most of the terrible noises and sights he had been experiencing, but as he entered the dingy hall, the unmistakeable smell of dog hit him. Even so, he sensed beneath it the more familiar, distasteful odour of his father's father, now clawing at the back of his throat. He wanted to run again, but as if a giant magnet had been placed there, he felt himself inexorably drawn to Gerald Butler's bedroom. As his eyes accustomed themselves to the gloom he realised someone had been here before him.

As far as he was aware, only two people knew of the hiding place, and one of those, if the newspaper was to be believed, was dead. Yet someone had been here and taken his grandfather's prized possessions—the mementoes of his military service.

The last time Harry had seen them, he had been soundly beaten and locked in the under stairs cupboard for three days without food or water. The standard punishment for serious infringements of old man Butler's rules.

Although he had no desire to view the hideous items again, some inner drive had sent him here to collect the evidence, to destroy it, as if by eliminating its existence he could expunge the record of war crimes from his family tree.

It was not as if his grandfather had any close friends who might want to help the old boy protect his reputation. His only companion, since his grandson had left home, was his ratty little dog. As Gerald aged, he had become more and more of a recluse, and Harry had not visited this place since the old man disowned him after his dishonourable discharge had 'brought shame on the Butler name'.

The bloody hypocrite!

The young man, now calling himself Harry Hope, had repressed so many memories of his youth, but in this room, right now, he started to recall his time here, the torment and pain resurfacing, unwanted, unbidden. The house seemed to settle and close in around him, the air thickening, suffocating him.

He took a last look around the room, then almost tripped at the top of the stairs as his mind tricked him. The feeling of a belt being lashed across his back, so realistic he was sure there would be angry welts on his shoulders when he got home.

By the time he reached the street, he was in a state of panic again. His legs began pumping hard once more as he headed back to his tattoo parlour and the one sanctuary he could rely on.

The one person who understood him.

He would curl up and relax in the warm comfort of Shazza's lover's embrace.

'So, Doc. Is there anything you can tell us about The Surgeon?'

The nickname for their perpetrator was now official.

Soundbite Sadie Dawson had left Jack to finish the briefing, and after he had allocated jobs and confirmed which avenues the team were to pursue, he invited Doc to take the floor.

'Thanks, Jack. First thing, and it may sound like I'm stating the bleedin obvious to you rather clever detectives, but this chap—and it's almost one hundred percent certain to be a man—is very dangerous!' He chuckled, joining in the laughter, a release of tension from the team now that their domineering boss had gone.

He ignored the cheeky comments, including one from Jack. 'Thanks for that, Doc. Any more brilliant insights.'

'In all seriousness,' they hushed at the gravity in his voice, 'I strongly recommend you pair up when visiting any suspects or witnesses, even those you may think are merely peripheral to the investigation.' He heard a collective groan, held up his hand for silence, then went on. 'The profile for this person is one of the most dangerous I have come across in almost three decades of studying the criminal mind.' He let that sink in before explaining. 'The perpetrator is a high functioning psychopath. Undoubtedly a well-accomplished professional, possibly someone considered to be a pillar of the community, to all intents and purposes a charming, sophisticated man at or near the pinnacle of his career. He will be mid-thirties at the very youngest, but could equally be a very fit and active sixty year old. He will have had the best medical care for himself, will be extremely vain, and will put in the necessary effort to keep himself at peak fitness. So let's not underestimate him.'

This time the room was silent and attentive. None of them were shuffling their feet from discomfort or boredom, they were waiting for more sage advice from the master. He obliged.

'Our quarry will have a home that reflects his status in life—his self-perceived status as an apex predator, at the very top of the food chain. Possibly a mansion, a country estate or a city loft with a ten million pound view of the Thames.'

Fiona actually put up her hand to speak, as if he was a learned professor, sharing his wisdom.

'Go ahead, Sergeant.'

'He must have a dedicated facility to operate on his victims. Is that likely to be at his home, Doctor Powers?'

'Everyone, please call me Doc. And in answer to your question, I'm afraid that depends. His overriding concern will be to avoid discovery. If he's in London or another crowded city, then I doubt he would risk using his home, but instead might own or rent a suitable facility in a remote location to work on his victims. Of course, I could be wrong, given the proliferation of massive cellars in town, but bear in mind that this has been going on for eleven years, maybe more. At the very least, since Diana Davies went missing. We can assume he's had use of an appropriate facility since then, probably much longer. Part prison, part hospital.'

Just like Broadmoor, he thought.

'You told me you think Davies is the first victim, Doc. Care to explain?' Jack was pinning enlarged copies of the photographs on the end wall, only recently cleared of items relating to the Brentwood Beast case. He had them in the sequence Doc had identified, culminating with the crime scene shot of Rawlings hanging in the tree.

'Sure. If you look at the degree of care taken with each individual you can see a clear progression from butchery to surgery.' Doc stepped forward and caressed the first photograph, his finger tracing the amputated stumps, the careless slashing and stabbing at the face and genitals, the open wounds. 'Compare this image with the last. We think he was practising his surgical skills while inflicting pain on these unfortunate souls.'

'How can you be certain Davies was the very first victim abducted, Doc?'

'I'm not. We have no way of knowing, but the pattern suggests she was at the very start of a series... Serial killers tend to begin their killing careers in their mid-twenties and their victims usually become more frequent as time passes. In this instance, he's extended the period and degree of torture as he perfected his techniques, keeping the victims alive longer and longer. That may even be the reason he began developing his surgical skills. Normally the delay between each abduction would shorten, but in this case it almost certainly increased. We know Rawlings was held captive for years while our wannabe surgeon worked on him.'

'Rawlings could've absconded to escape the fraud case before he was grabbed by The Surgeon some time after. I'm DC Jewell, sir.'

'Absolutely right, Constable Jewell. And, it's possible the victims overlapped. Our villain may have been working on two or more unfortunate souls simultaneously, each suffering different degrees of distress, assuming he has a sufficiently large, secure facility to hold them.'

In Doc's imagination he could hear terrifying screams, designed to strike fear into the heart of any listener.

Judy's screams...

Once again, he had to compartmentalise, to push the sounds from his consciousness as he tried to keep on track. The team were waiting, watching him as he hesitated, gathered himself, then continued.

'A... A second victim might be witness to the suffering being visited on the first, the anticipation of what's inevitably coming his or her way inflicting an additional level of torment. This psychopath is sadistic, cruel in the extreme.'

'Do you think The Surgeon's based in London? Is it worth checking the city planning office for likely locations?'

'You're DS Tim Pearce, correct?' Doc had only given half his attention to the introductions, but his brain was often like an active sponge while his consciousness roamed the ether. The sergeant nodded. 'Given the size of the team and the scope of the task, I wouldn't bother with searching the plans, but that's Jack's call. London is almost certainly where his home or place of work is located. The capital city fits his self-image, and we know two of his victims were found south of the river—'

Jack interrupted. 'Just a reminder though folks. There is still a very slim chance that these other photographs are fakes... If the killer only took Rawlings, it's possible Doc was sent these other images and these letters,' he pinned the photocopied originals alongside the photographs, 'to throw us off his scent, to confuse things. And before you ask, no, there wasn't any trace evidence, no DNA or fingerprints on the letters. He is forensically aware. Doc?'

'He certainly is, Jack. These items could be a diversion but I think there's only a very small likelihood. Also, if you compare victim number six with Rawlings, you may notice the significant differences.'

Fiona, having seen Rawlings in the flesh, inspected the relevant image and said, 'You think there are more victims, don't you Doc?' She added, as Doc nodded, 'This is still pretty crude work compared to what he did to Rawlings.'

'That's my conclusion, Sergeant... Incidentally, I'd wager that all of these other victims either lived or worked in London too. When we identify them—'

'If we identify them, Doc. We can't rely on that.'

'Indeed, Jack. But if we do ID them, I expect to find another pattern, climbing the social ladder, with our prostitute at the bottom and our hedge fund manager right at the top.'

'What occupations would you think for the other early victims?'

'Life insurance salesmen! They're scum!' A ripple of laughter around the room welcomed the anonymous comment.

'The answer depends on the views our perpetrator has…' Harding's manic attack on another inmate flashed before Doc's eyes, distilling and crystallising a victim hierarchy in his mind. 'The worst sort of criminals… Perverts… Child molesters, especially those abusing positions of power.'

'Priests and the like?'

'Could be.' Doc was reluctant to speculate, and Jack jumped in again.

'None of that helps us much without IDs. We'll see if there's any link between Davies and Rawlings. Maybe we'll get lucky.'

'How do you think he disposed of the bodies, Doc?' Fiona's voice cut through the hubbub muttering about the difficulties they faced with identifying their victims.

'For a highly intelligent, resourceful killer, with plenty of funds? It's not difficult. Burial in a country estate. Added to the feed in a pig farm, perhaps. Incinerated. Dropped from a helicopter or light aircraft over the sea, even. This highly intelligent psychopath's imagination is boundless. It's only the lower orders, especially those with little or no money, for whom such victim disposal is a major issue. I'm sure you're all aware the body is often the most important piece of evidence leading to an arrest. And our perpetrator is equally aware. I doubt we'll ever find the others. After Davies was discovered, our surgeon became more cautious.'

Several more disgruntled murmurs greeted that comment.

'And remember, folks, Rawlings was gifted to us.' Jack again.

'You think he's working alone, Doc?'

'Detective Constable Ahmed?' A nod from the questioner, one of only two other dark faces in the team besides Fiona. 'No. I think he has an assistant, a follower. Someone who has been close to him for much of his life. I can't be certain, but the nature of these crimes suggests the necessity of an accomplice, possibly an acolyte. Could be male or female, possibly husband and wife, though most likely both perpetrators are male. This underling is also highly dangerous, totally loyal and completely under his spell.'

'What about this Harry Butler bloke, Doc? You've met him. Could he be our guy? Doesn't seem to fit your high functioning social climber, but he could be his assistant.'

Feisty Fifi, straight to the point.

'Astute observation, Detective. Indeed he could be the number two to our main man. And no, I don't think Harry Butler is likely to be the leader of this particular enterprise.'

Jack butted in. 'Are you sure, Doc? You don't sound it.'

'Profiling is never about certainty Jack, as you well know. All I can do is read the signs and help you folks focus on the leads with the highest odds of success. But yes, Butler could be behind these deaths. He may be sufficiently disturbed, a psychotic, driven by nightmares, voices, visions et cetera. He's not a psychopath though, and the degree of planning, the ruthlessness, the deliberate torture, the fastidious wounds suffered by Rawlings, and other factors lead me to my conclusion that we're looking for a high functioning, highly organised perpetrator. Someone with genuinely psychopathic traits, for whom other humans are simply objects.'

'Objects?' Jack would know what Doc was talking about but clearly wanted his team to fully understand too. 'Care to expand, Doc?'

'Yes. He's cold and callous, and sees his fellow beings as nothing more than chess pieces in this game he's playing.'

The one he's invited me to join.

'Some bloody game!'

A trainee detective, one of several now on the case, but whose name Doc could not recall, had piped up, disturbing his monologue, giving space for a vivid scenario to crowd into his mind...

He was on an operating table, with Maddox leaning over him, wielding a scalpel in blood drenched hands.

Doc stumbled over the next few words, disoriented by the realism of the fleeting experience, shocked to feel pain in his shoulder immediately before his right arm went numb. He managed a calming breath, clenched his fingers rhythmically to get the feeling back, then continued wrapping up.

'He's, erm, driven by... by ego, a.. a god complex, the exercise of power, of life over death... And revenge. He's not deranged or demented, he's in full control of his faculties, but somewhat deluded. His belief in his own superiority will be his downfall. He's invited us to hunt him, but believes he's smarter than all of us put together, that we're too stupid to find him... He's wrong, of course!'

The team laughed again. Jack's smile reached his ears as he slapped Doc on the back, and winked his thanks.

'Welcome back, my friend.'

It was good to be back.

Even if he was still a suspect.

'So, have you done any of these notifications before, Lanny?'

'Yeah. A couple of times, when I was doing my probation, but that was for RTAs and nothing like this.' Detective Constable Lorraine 'Lanny' Jewell nodded to herself without looking at Fiona, her hands in her lap, fingers twiddling with the key before she jammed it in the ignition.

She's still nervous.

Fiona took a sidelong glance at the DC and reassessed the birdlike twitching her junior colleague was displaying. Perhaps Lanny's trepidation was a response to being paired with her.

'You did well in there. Very sympathetic.'

Fiona knew she had a reputation for being direct, undiplomatic, and on occasion, very demanding, but had originally thought the constable's nervousness was to do with Carver assigning them both to the task of notifying Patrick Rawlings' wife of his death—definitely a rather different kettle of fish compared to informing a spouse of a fatality from a road traffic accident. The poor woman had told them how she had been physically and sexually abused by Rawlings for years, long before he disappeared with hundreds of millions of pounds of his clients' money, leaving his abandoned wife to battle their claims for compensation.

While waiting for the lights to change from red, Fiona got a hint of a smile from her highly attractive blonde colleague, who, even with barely a trace of make-up, could adorn the pages of Cosmopolitan magazine looking exactly as she did right now. Fiona had a momentary twinge of envy, but would not let that get in the way of her professionalism, though she did wonder how Lanny put up with the male attention she attracted whenever she entered their testosterone imbued office.

Not my problem.

'Thanks, Sarge. Domestic's the most difficult thing I've had to deal with as a copper, at least until I became a detective. Glad I'm out of it now though. And her... Blimey! She was bloody petrified of the man. Amazing what goes on behind closed doors, even in the richest households... I doubt she had anything to do with the bastard's murder though. What d'you reckon?'

'Well... She was visibly shocked when I told her about the state he'd been in when we found him. That seemed genuine, for sure. She certainly had motive, but not the means... Mmm, she didn't strike me as the sort to have him abducted by a third party and tortured for years either, despite how he treated her. I'm going to have a quick squint at this lot,' she indicated the box file in her lap, 'so you take it easy driving or I'll puke all over you!'

They had just left the multimillion pound Thames-side apartment complex where the Rawlings widow lived, having spent the last half an hour with her. It had not been a waste of time either as the woman had given Fiona a copy of the documentation identifying all the aggrieved clients Rawlings had ripped off. She flicked open the lid and started shuffling through the papers, a treasure trove of suspects, but only half her mind was on the contents. She was hoping a name would jump out at her, perhaps a doctor or similar from among the hundreds, but an unexpected thought occurred to her as she riffled through the pages.

The African connection.

Again.

She had not asked about the Rawlings widow's ethnicity, had been diverted by the sophisticated presence, the exquisitely rounded vowels of private school English. But the latte skin was in sharp contrast to crystal blue eyes, and her perfectly symmetrical face reminded Fiona of Imam, the model from Somalia. The woman was stunningly beautiful, clearly of mixed race, so where exactly had she been born?

Once again, she cautioned herself not to make assumptions but instead she made a mental note to check out the woman's background when she got back to the office.

Lanny spoke then, clearly thinking along similar lines.

'What about the African magic angle, Sarge? Do you think it really is a part of this case? Or is Soundbite right not to pay too much attention to it... And that stuff about flogging body parts. Bones from kids and the like. It's all well weird.'

Fiona did not answer, but Lanny's words helped her thoughts converge.

Bones.

Doc had said something earlier, something that resonated, but Fiona had been busy and distracted since that meeting. Carver had told her to see the Rawlings widow and then follow up with the leads regarding Harry Butler with a view to locating him, and to continue her research into human suspension to see if that line of enquiry would yield some results. Right now, DC Jewell was driving them to a derelict church in Putney, one of the two relevant locations Fiona had identified last night.

Thankfully, her workload had been reduced. Carver had dumped much of it, including the—unofficial—search for Judy Finch, on to a couple of trainee detectives, earning their spurs. He'd also allocated Fiona an underling, Lanny, partly in response to Doc's warning about the dangers of investigating suspects alone, partly to give her some help.

As she shuffled through the pages in the box file, her eyes unseeing, Fiona started to mull over the African connection again. She thought back to Doc's comments, to his mention of one bone in particular. Then it occurred to her.

She grabbed her mobile and called DS Sharpe.

'Do me a favour, mate.' She paused as Sam grumbled in her ear. He had been given a pile of work to do already thanks to his official inclusion in Carver's team this morning, but she overrode his objection. 'That Atlas bone thing Doc was on about. Just do a search for me. I know you're busy... Listen! It must've been about eight to ten years ago, they had a guy in Brixton nick for B&E.' She waited for Sam to finish another tirade before adding, 'I know what Soundbite said this morning and no, of course I'm not interested in scallywags done for breaking and entering. This bloke was originally from somewhere in Africa. And he had a human bone on a chain around his neck... A vertebrae... Please do this for me. I think we need to find him, Sam.'

'It's not exactly a hot lead, is it Sarge?'

Lanny parked their unmarked Ford outside St Mark's church, situated between London's busy South Circular Road and the rail line, both major arteries feeding the centre of the capital. The street was nondescript, a scruffy backwater away from the leafy avenues of Putney proper, in an up and coming part of town. Just a few hundred metres from where they parked, a new apartment block was being built, homes destined for young professionals who could afford a half a million or more for a tiny flat within striking distance of the City.

Fiona didn't bother to answer, just looked up at the church spire, the ancient building a testament to gothic architecture, with gargoyles peering out, mouths agape, their tongues at gutter height, ready to spew water on to any unsuspecting members of the congregation the moment it rained. She noticed Lanny cross herself as they strolled up the path to the door, passing a large sign on the way. There would be no congregation here ever again, she thought, as she read how this old building was to be renovated, improved and converted into four luxury homes.

In the meantime, the Putney Body Mod club were using the facility, probably at a bargain rental, discounted by the developers to ensure no squatters appeared on the scene before their plans could be put into effect. Strains of rock music assaulted their ears, a harsh metallic roar and booming thud that even at this distance set Fiona's teeth on edge. She was no fan of organ music but that would be far preferable to this godless din.

The rear wall and buttress were covered in wire mesh and a *Danger, Keep Out!* sign suggested that part of the building needed some drastic attention, but the doors to the main hall were unlocked so she went in, with Lanny trailing behind. Fiona noted how her colleague made the sign of the cross again as they entered, but she had no such beliefs to distract her.

The sight that greeted them stopped her in her tracks and Lanny grunted, 'Sorry, Sarge' as she bumped into the now stationary detective. Then, as she too took in the view, she uttered a most un-Christian oath, her voice piercing the barrage of sound echoing in the nave. 'Jesus Christ! You're fucking kidding me!'

The church interior was largely empty, the pews all long gone, many adorning the homes of the wealthy as overpriced antiques with a religious provenance. The only pieces of furniture were the three tables butting up against the transept, with two enormous speakers on stands either side. About a dozen people, engrossed in what they were doing, were oblivious to the two policewomen at the door. They looked like rejects from a motorcycle gang, dressed in tatty leather and denims, black gowns and tee shirts, with all of them sporting tattoos, piercings and weird hairdos.

Otherwise, it was pretty unexceptional, apart from the three semi-naked bodies dangling from the roof. That was impressive enough, but their patterned skins glowed like an aerial kaleidoscope, illuminated by the eerie rainbow of light created by the sun's rays beaming through the decorative glass in several giant arched windows along each side of the hall.

Two men and a woman. Each with hooks in their flesh. All of them as if in a trance.

The two men were being pushed to and fro by others reaching up to their hips, but the woman was higher, beyond their outstretched fingertips. Fiona could not take her eyes off the spectacle, her mouth open in awe at what she was witnessing.

The girl had six hooks in two sets of three, embedded either side of her abdomen in vertical rows between hip and chest, the highest positioned just below the sports bra covering tiny breasts. The wires had hoisted her almost to the rafters and she looked incredible from below. Her hands and legs dangled, her head back, as if her eyes were on heaven and she was ascending there by sheer force of willpower alone. Her hair cascaded down her back, a rainbow tangle of tresses that reached her buttocks. Almost all her bare flesh was covered in tattoos, far too intricate to decipher from this distance.

'The Resurrection pose...' The music had been turned down by one of the other males as a strange looking guy sidled up to her and explained in a lilting Welsh accent. 'That's how people will look when they're wafted to the Almighty's side during the End Times... If you believe that crap. I'm Elvis, by the way. You two don't look like you want to hang, though... How can we help? Officers.'

Fiona finally wrenched her eyes from the incredible sight, having barely taken in the poses of the two men, also dangling, but cross-legged, with hooks in their backs and thighs, facing each other as their friends helped them swing back and forth. Like two flying yogis, drifting together, then apart. Repeated over and over. It was mesmerising, but she had work to do. She inspected the freaky fellow now facing her.

He had assessed their profession correctly, but seemed harmless enough, despite the budding horns that appeared to be about to burst through his forehead.

His scarlet forehead.

Why any rational human would pay to have implants under their skin and crimson inked across their faces was beyond Fiona, completely unfathomable. As was the idea of someone sticking giant fish hooks through her flesh and yanking her skyward on wires. As if some disturbed and vengeful god was playing with human puppets. She had never seen an eyeball tattoo either, although her research the night before had prepared her. Elvis had black where his whites should be and yellow irises.

Extreme body modifications.

She wondered what he did for a living, was about to ask, but decided to get back to the matter in hand first.

She introduced herself and Lanny with a wave of her warrant card, then asked, 'Do you have any members from the medical profession? Or similar? You know. Vets and the like?'

Elvis laughed, showing off a tongue that bifurcated at the tip, with gold studs embedded on each half.

What a bloody mess, mate!

She just thought it, waited for an articulate response as his giggling subsided. She wondered what drugs he was using, considered mentioning it, in the hope the implied threat would loosen his split tongue, but he answered, seemingly honest as he did so.

'Sweet-cheeks! You can check our member list. There's fewer than thirty of us and believe me, no one would be coming to any of us for medical care.' He spread his arms wide, and called out to his friends as he turned to them, 'These two lovely lady-pigs want to know who here is qualified in brain surgery! Hahaha!' He turned back to Fiona and said, 'I can give you our membership list. No problem. No warrant necessary. We may look like outlaws but we ain't. Just outsiders, and happy that way. Keep ourselves to ourselves, as most straights think we're a threat because we're different.'

Straights.

Normal people.

'Well, I think that's understandable if you go round looking like Beelzebub.'

'Yeah... Sad innit? Anyway, some of our members are NFA so I don't fancy your chances of tracking them down. Give me a minute.'

No fixed abode.

Oh well, she would take what he offered, and maybe a bit of digging would locate someone with an appropriate history, or some information they could use. Elvis went to the back of the room and the death metal music was cranked back up. Fiona shook her head at Lanny and went outside to wait.

She felt deflated, thinking this was a dead end, but would ask about the equipment they used, or more accurately, the equipment found attached to Rawlings' torso.

'This is like devil worship, Sarge. In a church! It's blasphemy! Elvis the demon—'

'I'm harmless, darlin. I'm a vegan. I don't even eat bacon so you two are safe. Hahaha! Here you go.' He handed Fiona a scrappy piece of paper with a couple of dozen names scrawled on it. 'Sorry, no printer here, but I'm sure you can make out the members from that list... Is there anything else? Happy to help, even if I do look a bit demonic to your mate, here...' He aimed a wicked grin at Lanny. 'I could explain, but you'd never understand. Very few people do.'

'Yeah, strange that people can't empathise with someone who chooses to look like their worst nightmare.' Lanny shrugged, huffed and took a few steps towards the car, keen to see this desecration disappearing in her rear view mirror.

'Don't worry about my colleague's views, sunshine. Just answer a few more questions and we'll both be on our way.' Elvis was bending over backwards to help, and Fiona's cop instinct knew why. 'I'm guessing we'd find nothing stronger than some weed or hash on the premises if we were to take a look. Right?'

He nodded his relief as he said, 'We don't harm anyone, we just want to be left alone, man. Nothing wrong with that.'

'Not at all. So, take a look at these.' Fiona beckoned to Lanny who took a couple of reluctant steps back towards Elvis, then held the iPad out for him to scrutinise the images of the hooks and wires removed from Rawlings' back. As she did so, visibly flustered, she accidentally swiped the screen, unwittingly exposing the crime scene photograph showing the victim dangling in the tree.

Elvis squealed in recognition.

'Fuck me! Is that the bloke they found on the common, over at Clapham? That's why you're here. You think we did this... No fucking way, man!' He backed away from them both, shaking his head. 'Don't go putting that on us. I had no idea he'd been suspended until you showed me that photo. That wasn't in the papers.' He was back-pedalling as if the church would give him, Elvis Beelzebub, sanctuary.

'Stop, you muppet. We're not here to nick anyone.' Fiona was exasperated, and let it show. 'Take another look.' She scowled at Lanny as she added, 'Now my colleague has divulged the details, I'd like you to inspect the pictures and tell me—was this suspension done by an expert? Someone who knew what they were doing?'

'Oh, man. You had me going then.' He wiped his bumpy brow and checked his palm for sweat. 'We get picked on all the time, you know. Neighbourhood Watch, local vigilantes. So-called Christian fanatics who think we're the devil's spawn despoiling sacred ground.' His blackened orbs shifted from Fiona and homed in on Lanny for a moment, then he went on. 'Muslims, claiming we'd be flogged or worse under Sharia law. They're all far crazier than we are. Anyway, let me see those.'

He took the tablet and started inspecting the rigging, the photos taken before and after Rawlings was unhooked. Then he used his fingers to enlarge the image as he took a closer look at the hooks and wires, his head bobbing as he did so. 'You'll want a second opinion of course, but this is amateur hour. The rigging's all wrong. The person who did this got the pulleys the wrong way round, and there's no ink on this guy.'

'Tattoos?'

What the bloody hell had that to do with it?

'No, not tats. Felt tip marker. Any pro, any experienced technician always measures the site for the hooks very carefully, and always marks the skin before piercing. It's a failsafe, to make sure we don't get it wrong and have the hooks rip out. Look!' He pointed to the piercings in Rawlings' back. 'See this one is lower than the other, closer to the spine, and there's less flesh been hooked. Shoddy, man. No, this is someone trying to put this on us. To frame us.'

It occurred to Fiona that he might be lying, but she thought not. And she would get a second opinion soon enough.

'Have you had any thefts of gear lately? Is this the sort of item you keep on the premises?'

'Nope. We've had no break-ins, nothing stolen. It's not like many other people have a use for our gear, though we do keep plenty to hand. We always check all our stuff before and after every session, sterilise it, inspect it for reuse etc. Nah. I'd know if there was anything missing. It's bog standard stuff though. You can get it online easily enough. Why bother stealing it?'

'Maybe the purchaser didn't want us to trace him.'

'Good luck with that, Porky. Anyone with PayPal or Bitcoin can get these items sent over from dozens of countries around the world. There's hundreds of online retailers, some of them on the dark web selling other shit you would not believe. Forget it, love.'

'Yeah. Much as I thought. Now, just add the name of the person who did your horns for you... They are *surgical* implants aren't they Elvis? Unless you really are a reject from hell.'

'Sure. No probs. I use an outfit on Harley Street.' He scribbled the name and address below the list of members and handed it back to Fiona.

'Harley Street?' She knew her expression had given her away, could hear her doubt at his claim woven through the two short words. She could not help but look him up and down, trying hard not to be supercilious, but not succeeding.

'You pigs really are all the same aren't ya? You think you can assess people by what they wear, how they look. How they conform to your idea of society. How well they disappear among the majority, who try to fit in and be good little citizens while their governments make wars on brown-skinned people, like you, but far away. And encourage their elite banksters to play at casino junkies with taxpayers' money. Turn a blind eye to the criminal funds being laundered through million pound properties a few miles from here, while shitting on the little people, forced to work forty plus hours a week to pay off their student loans, their car loans, their mortgages. To eat and sleep and work, day after day, again and again and again... Soul destroying shit that they call normal. Well they can fuck right off!'

He was the most animated Fiona had seen him, but she had heard enough of his anti-establishment rant.

'Yeah, tough life, eh? But how can you afford a top clinic in London? Inherited some dosh did we?'

She mentally bit her tongue, hating herself for the envy in her voice. She'd had a bellyful over the last couple of days though, and the jibe just popped out.

Another assumption, about to be proved wrong.

'Fucking typical. You just can't get it through your porcine head can you? Not all of us want to be like you... When I was sixteen, half a lifetime ago, I came up with a computer game. I created it in my bedroom, in a pokey flat on a Swansea council estate. I licensed it to Sony and I still get a royalty cheque in five figures. Every month... Now I own this church, the development company that will turn it into luxury homes, along with a few other central London properties. I don't work. Unlike you, I don't need to, Officer.'

'Okay, thanks for your help. Do me a favour, Elvis... Actually two favours.'

He shrugged. 'Sure. What now?'

She handed him her card and said, 'Call me if anything occurs to you, or you hear about any medical personnel enjoying your hobby.'

'Will do.' He turned to go back inside, the wall of noise from within blasting at them as he pulled the heavy wooden door ajar.

'And the second thing.'

He let the door almost close as he asked, 'Yeah, what else?'

'Tell your friends to remember this, Elvis. Call me or my colleagues by some variant of pig, pork, bacon or other insult again and I will have this place raided. I'll be having a word with the local bobbies to keep an eye on you lot. Got it, you scrote?'

His miniature horns did a little salute as his forehead creased in response, then he disappeared inside.

'Come on Lanny. That was far from a waste of time—I need to call Jack while you drive. We need to head to Streatham now, and we'll hopefully get confirmation from the *Hope, Not Fear* tattoo place about the amateur hooking skills of the perp.'

Her phone trilled just as she reached for the car door handle.

'Hi, Sam.' She listened.

A sunshine grin surfaced, as she gave Lanny a thumbs up across the roof of the car.

The African connection.

Sam had just shared the name of the burglar wearing the Atlas bone pendant. And Fiona had a pretty good idea where she might find that particular reprobate.

'It's my DS, Fifi. She's just found a link between your mate Maddox and the crowd who are into suspension.'

Doc was busy driving them both to visit the clinic in central London, and Jack was in the middle of taking a call from his sergeant. Even though his mobile phone was not on hands free, Doc could hear the excited, if somewhat muffled female voice on the other end. Jack had his hand over the mic as he made his comment to Doc, then turned his attention back to his subordinate.

Harley Street has very little parking, even for the select few cars with the appropriate disc displayed in their windscreens, but Doc pulled up outside the clinic, thinking Jack would square away any tickets from over enthusiastic wardens.

'Brilliant, Fi! Well done.' He finished the call and turned to Doc. 'This clinic not only does boob jobs and liposuction for the very wealthy, but apparently they'll put weird implants inside your body if the price is right. Unbelievable what people do to themselves these days. Fifi just met a rich kid who's not only into suspension, but he's had little horn buds implanted under the flesh of his forehead. The procedure was done at this clinic. Why would anyone pay serious money to look like a devil?'

'Mmm. It's the times we live in, Jack. People want to demonstrate their individuality, to stand out from the crowd, to be different.'

'I can understand that. But mutilating yourself? That's fucking braindead, if you ask me!'

Doc hesitated, wondering whether to bother explaining how various cultures have traditions of modifying their appearance going back centuries, from Maori facial tattoos to the stretched necks of Thailand's Karen 'giraffe women', the nose plugs of India's Apatari to the stretched lips and ears found among the tribes of Africa and South America. He decided Jack was just venting rather than genuinely interested in understanding the history of body modification, so he put it in terms his friend and colleague would appreciate.

'Well. Think of it like people who modify their cars or motorbikes. They're in part, striving to be different from society at large, while at the same time they want to belong to a group of others who are similar to themselves. Custom car clubs, Harley

Davison chopper gangs and so on. An expression of individuality while simultaneously belonging to a greater whole—a tribe.'

'Right. So they want to be different, but also be the same as others who want to be
different… They sound very confused to me. And making yourself look ugly like
that? I can understand if someone wants bigger boobs or a facelift, but that's just
plain stupid.'

'Standards of beauty vary from culture to culture, as well as shift over time. What
we think of as attractive is considered by some to be *un*-attractive. You only have to
contrast the tanning products in the west with the skin lightening creams and
potions that dominate the shelves of pharmacies in Asia and Africa.'

'Yeah. I s'pose you're right.' Carver had reached his fairly low threshold of philo-
sophical thought, and was all business again. 'Now, this bloke, Maddox. He's
expecting us, but he won't know we have a link, tenuous though it is, to the hooks
and wire brigade. Incidentally, Rawlings' widow gave Fifi a list of people who lost
money investing in his hedge fund before it went tits up. Some of 'em are millions of
quid out of pocket… I was hoping our Harley Street doc might be on the list.'

'He's not?'

'Nah. She's only had a quick look, and said we need to do some research on the
company names on the list, but at first glance, Maddox is not one of the personal
clients so I don't have a motive. Yet. Shame. I could do with a really quick arrest on
this one. Come on, Doc. Let's see the man himself.'

As Carver went to open the car door, Doc stopped him with a hand on his
bicep.

'Am I still a suspect, Jack? Do you honestly think I could do these things? And
then somehow blank them out. It's ridiculous.'

'You were never *really* a suspect as far as I was concerned, and that now goes for
Fifi too. She and I had a little chat after the briefing, and she was pretty impressed
with your contribution. She reckons you aren't trying to throw us off the scent, Doc,
or if you are, you're doing a crap job!' He patted Doc's hand, still gripping his upper
arm. Doc let go as Carver explained. 'Soundbite only wants to keep you in the frame
to cover her arse mate.' Doc's relief at his friend's declaration of trust immediately
deflated as the detective added, 'Anyway, I did some digging of my own this morning. I managed to get Bob Koch to give me a quick verbal summary of this morning's
autopsy over the phone. It's good news for you. According to him, the operation that
removed Rawlings' arms took place between two and three years ago, going by his
estimate of the age of the scar tissue and similar pathologist's magic. All that time,
you were laid up in hospital, recovering from your leap off that that third floor
balcony.'

'Of course, if it was me, I could have had an accomplice continue while I was
incapacitated…' Doc had taken to heart Jack and his sergeant's suspicions,
prompting questions of his own, and his visions had not helped. He knew it was
highly improbable that he could do such things and keep them hidden deep in his
subconscious, unaware that he had even been involved, but it was entirely possible.
Dissociative amnesia. 'An accomplice who could be manipulated. A damaged veteran
with medical training and a history of mental illness… Treated by yours truly eleven
years ago.'

'Harry Butler?' Jack's face closed down for a moment, as if a cloud had thrown a
shadow across it, then brightened as it passed. 'We need to find him fast. Anyway,

let's not hang about out here. Let's talk to Maddox and then we'll shoot off down to Broadmoor.'

Carver took one last admiring glance at Doc's Jaguar before heading into the clinic. The Victorian building was magnificent, beautifully preserved and maintained. He pressed the buzzer and the door swung open allowing them both inside.

Jack had been expecting a hospital odour to greet them, but instead he could smell perfume moments before he saw the orchids and other exotic plants decorating the waiting area. It was like a florist's shop, and nothing like any doctor's waiting room he'd ever been in.

To the rear of the reception desk, stretching from floor to ceiling, was a magnificent wooden carving that Jack recognised, thanks to Doc having explained the significance of the emblem printed on the business card Maddox had given him. The symbol, now used the world over to signify the medical profession, had been embellished for the clinic's logo, featuring two wings and two serpents intertwined round a staff. The Cadaceus Clinic had taken its name from the motif and now proudly presented this three metre high and three metre wide tribute to their craft.

Below it sat the receptionist, all fake tan and white teeth, her chestnut hair immaculately trimmed to frame an oval face, one that shone a smile that could have been radiating from the pages of Playboy magazine. Carver felt his eyes drawn to her rather splendid breasts, and he immediately wondered how much of her appearance was down to nature and how much down to her employer's skills with a scalpel.

'Detective Carver?' She looked from Jack to Doc and back, the perfect smile still in place. Jack nodded and held out his warrant card for her, but she did not even glance at it. 'Professor Maddox is expecting you. I'll buzz you through. Is this your assistant?' She raised a tattooed eyebrow at Doc and asked, 'May I have your name too, Detective?'

'Actually, I am an old friend of Richard's from our Oxford days. Colin Powers. I'm also helping Detective Carver with some related enquiries.'

Jack could hear tension in Doc's voice as he spoke, and he wondered why. His friend was here to observe, to assess Maddox and his potential as a suspect, while Jack did most of the talking. It was most unusual for Doc to display any nerves before an interview like this. In fact, Doc's behaviour had been off since they'd met yesterday morning, shortly after Rawlings had been discovered, and their conversation in the car had not helped. Jack had been wondering about Doc's mental state, and before the boss's briefing he had made a call to the force psychiatrist to discuss memory lapses, the phenomenon of split personality and what symptoms one could expect.

The replies had not been reassuring.

'You okay, Doc?'

'Yeah. Let's go through.'

An oak-panelled door opened and another silicon-augmented nurse ushered them through.

Jack asked, 'Have you worked here long? For Doctor Maddox?'

'Professor Maddox is not often here these days,' she smiled over her shoulder as she led them down a narrow corridor with two doors either side and a staircase at the end. 'I've been here almost twelve years now, not long after the clinic opened. It's a great place to work. We're just a small team of fifteen permanent staff and everyone's so professional. Here we are. Please make yourselves comfortable. He'll be with you shortly.'

She opened a door labelled *Professor Maddox* followed by a string of letters after the name that stretched almost to the door handle, and waved them in.

The room was a shrine to the man's ego. The walls were almost entirely covered with plaques and photographs, with framed certificates and awards bearing testament to an overachieving multitalented professional.

'Jesus, Doc. Looks like he has some very powerful mates.' Jack leaned in for a closer look at the photograph of Maddox shaking hands with the Prime Minister outside 10 Downing Street, prominently positioned in a front page article from *The Times* newspaper, suitably presented here in a gold frame. 'Started a charity outfit helping African kids with cleft palates according to this.'

'Yes, he's done some amazing things, Jack. Crammed a lot into his life, though he did have some natural advantages. The chumocracy being just one.' Doc's tone sounded a little cynical to Jack.

'Chumocracy? What? The old boy's network? Eton and all that? Is that how he knows the PM?'

'They were at school together... You might want to tread a little carefully with your questions, my friend. I still think you're jumping to a hasty conclusion with Maddox. I'm not convinced—'

The door opened and the man himself appeared, his face quizzical, his plummy tones rich with rolled vowels as he asked, 'Not convinced of what, Colin?' Despite his query he went straight to Doc and pumped his hand, his teeth sparkling as he grinned in apparent pleasure at seeing his fellow professional, his question forgotten in an instant. 'Great to see you at last. If I didn't know better I'd think you've been avoiding me all these years.' He turned to Jack and shook his hand, explaining, 'I did torment this young man rather badly when he was my junior at Oxford, though I do hope he's forgiven me now.' He winked at Doc and invited them both to sit with him on some lounge furniture to one side of the office. 'Coffees, gentlemen?'

'No, we're fine thanks. It's very good of you to see us at such short notice, Professor Maddox.'

Jack took stock of the man. He exuded the sleek good health and supreme confidence of the wealthy, the elite who were used to people mentally doffing their caps, servile while acknowledging his innate superiority. Despite this, and the bubbling resentment Jack usually felt when confronted with members of the species, he was drawn in by the man's warmth, the atmosphere of well-being he carried with him. His blue eyes reminded him of Doc's brown ones, lively and engaged as he looked from one guest to the other, intelligence and inquisitiveness transmitted wordlessly with a glance or two.

'Delighted to help. Is this about Harding? I can share whatever you need to know, given that his incarceration in a secure hospital negates normal doctor patient confidentiality requirements.'

The man's eyes lingered on Doc's, inviting a response, and Jack took a moment to consider how much these two doctors' professional lives and attitudes overlapped. They were similar physically too, though Doc's unruly curls contrasted to the immaculate dyed and trimmed head of hair Maddox sported.

'Actually there are a few things you may be able to help the police with, Dickie. They may or may not be related to Harding. Jack?'

Carver laid his tablet on the tabletop and opened up the images of Rawlings.

'Professor Koch recommended we talk to you about a current case.'

'Bob? I haven't seen or heard from him in years. We met when we were younger, had a lot in common then. Funny how life changes. We drifted apart after Northern Ireland.'

'Really?' Jack was not that interested, wanted to get on with the reason for their visit, but Doc, frowning now, asked an unexpected question.

'Northern Ireland? Is that where you met Koch? Rumour has it, he was a spook back then.'

'No, and yes, he was. We first met as boys in Kenya. Both our parents were expats and in that small community, the Nairobi Brits stuck together. We weren't exactly close friends as there was a six year age difference. He got sent to the UK for his senior schooling. I followed when I was eleven. I realise now how much damage it does to little boys when sent away by their parents to institutions like Eton. It's a form of child abuse. Warps your mind… I think that's why I was so foul to you at Oxford, Colin.'

A genuine look of regret accompanied the words, but Jack was impatient to get on as the professor's confession dribbled to a halt. Before he could ask a question to get back on topic, Doc spoke up again.

'And Northern Ireland?'

'We only bumped into each other years later while serving in Belfast. He did some work for the military intelligence boys, all hush hush. Disappearing bodies and all that. Rumours of torture and so on. Funny old world.' Maddox sent a blazing smile at Jack. 'We lost touch after I left the military and struck out to make some money in the US. Plastic surgery was my forte, as no doubt Bob already explained, Detective… So, how can I help?'

Jack and Doc exchanged glances, both noting the significance of this latest information. It had been volunteered in such an offhand manner, Jack thought it was either an innocent throwaway, or possibly designed to muddy the waters. His team would have discovered more about Maddox's history soon enough, though Jack would now put the Met's senior ME under the microscope too. But that was for later.

Jack began by explaining their theory that this final victim was one of a series of similar, though originally much cruder mutilations as he pulled up the images of Rawlings on his tablet. Doc interjected with his postulation that an amateur budding surgeon was honing his skills on live subjects leading to this final 'creation'. All the while both men scrutinised the reaction, alert to any indications that Maddox was familiar with the photographs he was viewing.

'Shocking, but strangely fascinating. There's a high degree of skill evident here though I agree with Colin's assessment that, given sufficient practice, any medic with basic training could achieve a similar result, though would need some very specialist equipment. Of course, we have these facilities at this clinic so I'll have my assistant show you round, and provide the relevant information to help with your detective work, tracking similar purchases et cetera.'

'We think he's been working his way towards this final victim for at least ten years based on his earlier guinea pigs.' Yet again Carver watched for any reaction, a flicker of guilt, a momentary hesitation, an indication that Maddox was uncomfortable being presented with the images, but saw nothing. 'Is it possible he could do this alone? Doc thinks he'd need an assistant, but probably no more than one...'

'Frankly? If I wanted to do this,' he tapped the image of Rawlings, 'I'm sure I could. And, though it would be difficult, I would not need assistance. I'd also have no need to practise on these other poor souls... So that's why you're here, Detective. I'm a suspect! Oh dear!'

He really did find it amusing and Jack found himself doubting Maddox was in the frame at all.

'Well, we are looking at all medical professionals...'

'I don't doubt it. Even Colin has some experience of dismembering a human, just like all other students of medicine. We learn basic anatomy on cadavers donated to medical science while at university, and dissecting them is a major building block of our training. Live bodies are rather different as they bleed, of course. I can see why you came up with your theory of a wannabe surgeon though.'

Maddox then spent a few minutes looking in detail at the wounds on the earlier victims and comparing them with the masterpiece.

Rawlings.

Jack took the opportunity to exchange a silent shrug with Doc who offered a barely perceptible nod in response. They waited in silence until Maddox had made his assessment.

'Difficult to say for sure that the sheer butchery of the earlier attempts was by the same person who did this latest operation.' He swiped back from the image of Rawlings to two others. 'But I'm pretty sure this one and this one were the handiwork of the same man. The stitching is non-standard, and it's exactly the same in both.'

Doc and Jack crowded forward as Maddox enlarged the relevant sections on screen for them to compare. Rough stitches were still in place in the wounds, the thread and knots obviously similar.

'Damn. We missed that, Doc. Thank you, Professor. Anything else?' There was not, so Jack went on, 'We're not sure, but we think Harding may have some peripheral involvement in this.' He explained about the letters, the source of the photographs, without divulging any of the written content, when Doc interrupted.

'I think whoever did this has deliberately involved me by using Harding as bait. Is there anything you can tell us as to why else he might be relevant? Of course, we know he has a history of dismembering victims.'

'Bait? Wow!' Maddox sat back and his quizzical look returned. 'But why would anyone in their right mind invite you into an investigation? That's asking for trouble.' He glanced at Jack and added, 'He's quite brilliant you know.' Then he looked over at Doc, his expression one of genuine admiration as far as Jack could tell. 'I've been watching your progress from afar and I have to say, you are an impressive fellow, Colin. I also think your assessment of Harding is correct.' He laughed, a full-throated guffaw, at the look on Doc's face. Jack could see a mixture of surprised delight there as Maddox continued. 'I've studied all your papers, your books, your impressive history and learnt a great deal from you. You're my inspiration for getting into psychiatry, though I'm a healer... You are something altogether different, Colin.'

Mild embarrassment with a dismissive shrug were Doc's response, along with a few words.

'That's an unexpected compliment, Dickie.'

'Double edged I'm afraid. Your ability to empathise and understand serial killers is frankly beyond me. We all have the ability to kill. The military teaches us that, by othering the enemy, dehumanising them. But your insights are truly remarkable, how you can almost *transform* yourself into a criminal psychopath. I've tried to emulate you but I cannot. I'd love to chat more with you about this unique facility you have, maybe over drinks sometime, but I can see Detective Carver is itching to get on.'

'Speaking of criminal psychopaths, have you any thoughts about Harding that might help shed some light on this current case?'

Jack was torn between watching Doc, whose discomfiture at the professor's words was apparent, and studying Maddox. Was he deliberately unnerving Doc? Was he suggesting Doc was a killer? Or was it genuine curiosity, a need to understand how a fellow forensic psychiatrist's mind worked?

'Harding's not psychotic, never has been. I'm recommending he's reassigned to a high security prison after this last escapade of his. But back to your question about his involvement or otherwise in an active case. I agree, he's being used to throw you off balance, though I doubt you will succumb, Colin… Seems to me that you need to find the link between him and someone on the outside.'

Jack pondered on that, thinking he'd know more after visiting Broadmoor this afternoon. He'd already spoken to Winston Diamond, the security chief, earlier today by phone and planned to determine the extent—or otherwise—of Harding's involvement then. Doc, now visibly warmer towards Maddox than when they arrived, began comparing notes on the villain before Maddox's phone buzzed three times then went quiet when he ignored it.

'My assistant. Our prearranged signal to allow me the excuse to oust unwanted visitors. Harding's definitely got a hard on for you, Colin. I hypnotised him. He agreed because he thought he could outfox me, convince me he was under while faking it. But he's not very bright, rather overestimates himself. If I had known we were going to have this conversation I could've asked him, but sadly, I had no idea he may be involved in a current investigation. I can share some insights with Colin about his father's death though… Sorry. I didn't mean to make you uncomfortable.'

Jack could see Doc's face, grey as if cast in cement. He changed the subject.

'You mentioned the equipment list.'

'Actually, if we're about done, I'll have my assistant show you round.' Maddox rubbed his thighs and stood, taking his guests' acquiescence as a given. They were being politely dismissed.

Jack had one other piece of the puzzle he needed to ask about, thanks to the call from Fiona.

'One thing, Professor. Is it just cosmetic surgery, boob jobs and the like, that you perform here?'

'We do rather more than that, Detective. Why do you ask?'

'Well, one of my colleagues had an interesting conversation with a chap who had some unusual surgery he claims was done here—'

The guffaw again as he opened the door, leading them back to reception.

'Let me guess! One of our sexual reassignments? Or was it one of our body modification patients?'

'Transsexuals?' Doc had found his voice again, the tone betraying his surprise.

'Exactly. Our clinic has more experience than any other in the UK. We're not just a nip and tuck outfit, pandering to the vain wealthy. Hence the soubriquet Dick-Doc. I assumed you knew, Colin! Although I no longer perform operations myself since a rather nasty skiing accident ruptured the ulnar collateral ligament in my right hand, among other things.' Maddox held up his fingers and thumb for them to see, though Carver could discern no obvious injury. 'Unfortunately, I no longer have the fine motor control required for such surgery... It's why I chose to focus my energies on psychiatry. Anyway, my employees and the consultants who assist here are more than capable.'

'So you also undertake wacky implants? My sergeant tells me a gentleman with horns claimed to have been a patient here.'

'Yes, sounds like Elvis.' Jack wasn't sure about any musical connections, was unaware of the name of Fiona's lead, but let Maddox continue. 'We provide a range of rather strange surgical stainless steel and silicon dermal implants for our more individualistic clients. Don't look so shocked, Detective. I'm very relaxed about these things. We regularly undertake operations to split tongues, and rather more rarely, penises, if that's what one desires.'

'Do what? You split penises? Why on earth..?'

'According to those who have braved this extremely painful procedure, having a split end, as it were, doubles sexual pleasure. Adjacent orifices and so on... Ah, here we are.' They arrived at the reception. 'I'll leave you with the lovely Tracy and she'll sort you out with a tour and anything else you need... It's magnificent isn't it?'

Jack was admiring the sculpture again, had reached out and caressed a wooden wing without thinking.

'It really is an impressive work of art.'

Even Doc seemed curious.

'You chose the US symbol, the Cadaceus, not the Rod of Asclepius, the single-winged emblem of the UK medical profession. Why, Dickie?'

'Well, I always preferred the look of it and planned to work in the States too. I commissioned this from a talented young man, a Combat Medical Technician not long before I left the RAMC.' Maddox saw Jack's confusion and added, 'Army medical corps... He was a field medic.'

'Talented bloke.' It struck Jack that the man was wasting those talents in the Army.

'Yes, but it's a sad story. He wanted to train as an Operating Department Practitioner, to assist with surgeries, had high hopes of progressing beyond that, but apparently he really wasn't up to it. His skills with a scalpel didn't match his artistic abilities, unfortunately. Suffered minor hand tremors when confronted with a live body in an operating theatre. Working with wood is rather different.'

Jack felt a tingle of anticipation as he asked, 'A medic? A frustrated surgeon? What was his name?'

'Oh, I doubt this chap would be of interest to you, Detective. I heard he was released from active service after stealing morphine for his personal use. Claimed he was suffering severe PTSD by all accounts, but he was still cashiered out of the service. Made this for me long before any of that sadness occurred. His name? Staff Sergeant Harry Butler.'

Shazza was worried. She tried to concentrate on the customer she was inking, a simple dolphin design favoured by many of the local council house denizens, almost as popular as the butterflies and feathers that most young girls opted for these days. The two aquatic mammals appeared to leap to the small of the girl's lardy back from the pink crease between her wobbling pale buttocks, as if desperate to escape the confines of her ample flesh.

The task was no challenge for Shazza, and these bread and butter tats paid the rent, allowing her, Harry and Glen to live, work and play on the premises. Glen, deep in concentration, was busy with another punter, a rather more complex full sleeve design he had been working on for over an hour, but Shazza was almost finished in half the time.

She sighed as she bent back to work, her mind drifting again to her man, her fingers on autopilot as she wielded the electronic needle to decorate the girl's lumbar region. Harry had arrived back a couple of hours earlier, in a right state. The sort of state she had not seen him in for several years. He had been doing so well, too.

'There you go, my love. You can check it out over there.' She explained how to look after the new skin embellishment as her customer popped her bubblegum then sniffed approval at the sight that greeted her in the full-length mirror.

'Cool!'

The girl paid and strolled out, phone already at her ear as she enthused to her boyfriend about the sight that would greet him tonight when they had 'anal'.

Shazza mumbled a few words to Glen, excusing herself as she made her way up the stairs to the private rooms above the shop.

Harry was in bed, having dosed himself with double his usual medication. She thought he was asleep, but he groaned as she opened the door, and called her name, so she crept into bed beside him, fully clothed against his naked warmth. It was little comfort, she knew, but it was all she could offer her tormented soulmate.

'Are you feeling better, babe? Want to tell me what happened?'

Harry murmured some words into her ear, his breath hot and moist on her skin. She shuddered as he told her his grandfather had died yesterday, shocked by the jagged words tearing at her when he explained why they both deserved to burn in hell for the things they had done.

He seemed to unlock his inner self, exposing things to her she had not heard in all the years they'd been together, at first as friends, then business partners, then lovers. Yet more torture he had endured at the hands of his own flesh and blood, even before the military screwed up his life and almost destroyed him. She hugged him to her, letting his tears flow on to her chest, soaking her shirt, the anguish draining out of him until, finally, his hoarse whispers ceased and his breathing became deep and regular.

When she was sure he was sleeping, she gently disentangled herself from him and went back to the shop, hopeful that he would feel better after a decent rest. Her mind was in turmoil, trying to process the things he had told her, a world of cruelty and abuse that was alien to her. Shazza had the appearance of an outsider, a deliberate reaction to her upper middle class childhood and the restrictions that stain on her early life had created. Yet, when she compared her own past to that of many of her friends, similarly styled as outsiders, she knew she had been lucky in life's genetic lottery. Her safe, secure upbringing in a stable if unhappy home environment was in distinct contrast to the dark experiences of the others, and now she knew the depth of Harry's own suffering.

It made him yet more precious to her.

As she stepped into the shop she saw the two women enter and told Glen, who had just finished with his customer, that he should grab a coffee while she took over.

'Hi ladies. Are you lost? You don't look like you want tattoos or piercings.' Shazza's people radar was pretty good, and she had these two sussed immediately.

Feds!

'No, we need some information. I'm DS Fielding and this is DC Jewell. You work here?'

A warrant card was presented and then disappeared again before Shazza could inspect it, a cursory action that seemed habitual rather than designed to inform. The dark-skinned one was short and stocky, though her tight-fitting trousers indicated well-muscled thighs, and she carried herself with an air that suggested she could handle herself if it came to it. She exuded authority and a physical presence the pretty blonde who strolled in behind her lacked. Shazza would have known who was in charge even without the introductions.

'Sure. What can I do to help?'

'I don't see any photos of your suspension club. You do that here, don't you?'

'Yeah, we do, but we don't advertise. Invitation only. Why?'

The senior plod did not bother answering, just began inspecting the numerous photos of customers' tattoos and various designs pinned to the walls, feigning interest it seemed. The other one shoved a tablet at Shazza with a picture of some basic items of suspension gear for her to peruse.

'Take a look at this lot, love.' The copper tapped the screen. 'What can you tell me about these items?'

'You don't know?' Shazza let the sarcasm seep into her voice. 'We use them on willing volunteers. You look like you'd enjoy a go with these. Might help you relax. What's this all about?'

The Afro piped up then, her face to the wall, nose still rooting round the photos.

'You do the suspension on these premises with like-minded folk who enjoy that sort of thing?' Her gaze shifted to Shazza, who felt herself stripped bare by the detective's stare.

It was unsettling.

Probably a technique she learnt at police academy.

'Yeah. We have a small club, only fifteen members. We get together once or twice a month. There's a massive cellar below that's perfect for what we do. Why? We ain't committing any crime. We don't do no harm—'

'I'd like the member list. Any medical personnel in the group?'

That stare again, boring into her, as if the policewoman could see the dark patch below her shirt collar, could somehow divine that it was freshly damp from Harry's confessional tears. Shazza's hand brushed at it reflexively as she lied.

'Not that I know of...' She took a few paces to the rear of the room and began shuffling through some papers in a filing cabinet drawer as she framed her answer. 'Don't you need a warrant to come round asking for this sort of information?' Shazza had no idea about the law, her question was really just to divert them from the falsehood she'd uttered. She found the list and made a copy, though she could have rattled off all the names from memory. 'They're more like personal mates than strangers, though they all make a small contribution for club funds. I'll just add my name too. I do the admin so I don't have to pay subs. Why do you need this?'

The black detective had followed her, was literally breathing down her neck now. Shazza fumbled with the pen as she amended the document, could feel the woman's breath on her nape.

'Sharon Tait... I'll take that. Thank you.' The detective took the paper from Shazza's fingers without even bothering to answer her questions, her tone sceptical as she asked, 'Is this everyone?'

Those eyes again, carving into hers, as if convinced every word being uttered was an untruth or half-truth. Shazza felt transparent, as if this woman could see into her very core.

'That's all our paid up members. Glad to be of help.'

'Are you missing any gear? Wires, hooks, pulleys and the like? Had any break-ins that you failed to report to the police?'

Failed to report?

Spoken as if Shazza was guilty of hiding something.

I am. But not that.

'Nothing worth reporting to your lot. We think some kids must've forced an upstairs window to try and gain access at the weekend, but we checked, and we're pretty sure there's nothing missing. Are you going to tell me what this is all about?'

'Lanny. Show her.' The senior plod wandered back to the wall to continue her inspection of the customer photos, as if she had lost interest, though she pulled out her phone and took shots of some images while telling her colleague, 'I'm sure the jungle drums in their strange little world will deliver news of what happened soon enough. That's if she hasn't heard already.'

'Take a look at this, miss. I need to know whether the person who inserted these hooks was an experienced practitioner or not.'

The screen showed a close up of a person's back with misaligned suspension hooks unevenly inserted through the flesh. Shazza pointed this out, relieved to be dealing with the less intimidating officer, hoping her deception had gone unnoticed. Satisfied, the copper scrolled on to another photograph, a shocking image that looked unreal, like a deformed mannequin somebody had strung up in a tree. As she took a closer look she could see the suspension wires stretching from behind to the branches above.

'Ugh, Jesus! Is this the front view of the picture you just showed me?' She felt a little faint and nauseous as she realised. 'The hooks are in this poor person's back?'

Her mind was tumbling again. Things she had heard whispered by her agonised lover just minutes before were now whirling through her head. The senior detective must have seen her anxiety and moved in, firing words at her like bullets, blasting through the fog that was engulfing her brain.

'What can you tell us about this? The victim was found on Clapham Common, not that far from here. Left there by one of your fellow freaks.'

'I can't tell you anything. Why would you think I could?' Shazza heard her voice, verging on hysteria, the words almost a shriek.

'What the bloody hell's going on? You okay, Shazza?'

Glen reappeared and his reassuring presence gave her the strength to recover, although the senior detective's stare was stripping her bare again.

'We're about to leave. Can I just take your name, and are you on this list of club members?'

Glen went to snatch the paper from the detective's fingers, but Shazza stopped him.

'It's okay, Glen, they're coppers.' His face reddened but he stayed quiet as she continued, addressing the detectives. 'This is Glen Jackson. He's a member, though he works here too. Has done for the last four years. He's a top tattoo artist.'

The detective scanned the paper and asked, 'Harry Hope? He's the owner, correct? He's not on this list of your suspension club members.'

It was Shazza's turn to redden.

Shit!

Glen answered.

'Not that it's any business of yours, but yes, it's Harry's *and* Shazza's shop. Partners. He does sometimes join in the suspension fun. He's not really a member as such —he lets the rest of us use the premises for peanuts. Now, if there's nothing else—'

'Where is he? I'd like to meet him. I have a few questions for him too.'

The senior copper addressed Shazza, homing in on her weakness, could probably tell she was relieved when Glen answered. Shazza was badly rattled and needed to speak to Harry herself.

'He's not here, but if you give me your number I'll get him to call you when I see him.'

'Does he live here? Above the shop?'

'We all do—' Shazza blurted, her voice trembling, before she was silenced by a look from Glen.

'The three of you? Anyone else?'

'Just us. Why?' Glen threw a questioning glance as he spoke, but the copper butted in with a question of her own before Shazza had a chance to explain.

'Mind if we have a look around while we're here? Upstairs? Downstairs?'

Glen snorted as he said, 'Yeah, you can look all you want. When you come back with a fucking search warrant.'

For several seconds Glen stared down at the diminutive detective, a seemingly immovable object deflecting her from her objective. Then, grudgingly, she plucked a card from her pocket, ignored the man who towered over her and handed it to Shazza.

'Tell Harry Hope to call me.'

Then they were gone.

Shazza felt the air discharge and her shoulders relax at the sight of the two detectives leaving the premises, but their departure gave her barely a moment of false hope. Glen's words burst that bubble.

'What the fuck was that all about, Shazza?'

She blurted out her fears.

'It's about that bloke they found on the common yesterday.'

'What? The one who was dismembered?'

'Yeah. He was strung up in a tree and left for dead.'

'So why would the filth come here? I don't see what that's got to do with our club.'

'The poor guy had hooks in his back, was hung there using suspension gear... I dunno Glen, but Harry said some stuff to me about it just before the Feds arrived...

I'm really worried about him. I think he might've got himself into some seriously deep shit. Again.'

———

'That was Winston Diamond, Jack. Head of security.'

Doc flicked the indicator and guided the Jaguar to the nearside lane, steering with one hand as he finished the call. The blue M3 motorway exit was signposted Crowthorne and they were just minutes from Broadmoor High Security Hospital.

'Don't you have hands free in this motor? Wireless or something? You know it's illegal to use a mobile like that while you're driving.'

'So arrest me then… Listen. Winston reckons he's got something for us. Apparently there's another inmate Harding's been manipulating, and a staff member causing some suspicion. You might be able to get something out of them both.'

'Well, that's possible. I'm still not sure how Harding fits into this, if at all. What did you make of Maddox? He ticks a lot of boxes for our killer.'

'Well, he's certainly mellowed since I knew him, though that's not surprising after so many years. He seemed genuine enough. I'm not convinced he's involved, Jack. He's narcissistic at worst, has the requisite skills, but he's no psychopath.'

'Unlike Harding. Who Maddox is treating. And what about the prior relationship with Harry Butler and that amazing sculpture. A forces trained medic with a history of violence and mental health issues, a frustrated surgeon who fits your profile. It's almost too good to be true.'

Doc had been thinking about the web of connections too, and he did not like the conclusion he was coming to.

'You know I said this is just a game to the perpetrator, our psychopathic surgeon wannabe? He's been planning this for years.'

'Yeah, and then your TV series sparked him off. Your failure, as he sees it, to link his other mutilated murder victims to Diana Davies, the hooker. You offended his sense of pride, failed to give him full credit for his crimes, so he's now trying to prove he's better than we are, even after giving us a load of clues.'

'That's what I thought, Jack, but now I'm not so sure what triggered all of this. It's so complex, with so many moving parts, so many threads… I don't think we have even half the information we need to find the real villain. Or, more likely, villains.'

'Well it's early days, yet. We only found Rawlings yesterday morning. Didn't even know his name until a few hours ago. You sound even more impatient than me! Give it time.'

'I don't think we have much to spare. If he's half as clever as I think, we need to catch him quickly or he'll disappear. This is his endgame. And right now he's controlling the moves.'

'You sure he doesn't want to be caught, Doc?'

'Definitely not. He'll have an escape route and he'll bolt as soon as he feels threatened.'

Jack's phone chirruped as they arrived at the hospital car park.

'Soundbite. I'd better take this.'

Doc stepped out of the car and left Jack sitting talking to his boss, giving him a quiet moment alone to think. His mind was roiling, like muddy water eddying, concealing all that lay below. He had already asked Jack twice today whether the team had made any progress in finding Judy Finch and was not reassured by the answers. She had vanished, although Jack had promised to have all airport and ferry terminals checked, going all the way back to the beginning of January. The detective's reluctance to spare the resources was understandable. They had so many lines of enquiry to pursue already and only a small team but Doc had been insistent, convinced Harding's words were meaningful rather than merely mean.

'Let's see what Winston has for us, eh?' Jack's voice penetrated Doc's thoughts, bringing some relief from the worry eating his soul. They made their way to the entrance gate while Jack explained why his boss had called. 'Bob Koch has given the Acting Super the full report on his autopsy on Rawlings this morning. He was indifferent about the African thing, the muti. That's the word she used.'

'Really? So she's still unconvinced?'

'Yeah. Interesting too, given his background, being born there. Mind you, Koch agreed with your other conclusion—about the practising and so on.'

'Was it your idea for him to come to the hospital yesterday, to examine Rawlings?'

'Er, yes and no. I phoned him and asked him for a copy of the Davies medical file and when I mentioned our new victim, he offered to meet me and give me his opinion on Rawlings while there.'

'He invited himself into the investigation…' Both Jack and Doc knew what that might mean. Many criminals like to involve themselves in police enquiries related to their own misdeeds. It was partly the thrill and partly to keep abreast. 'Perhaps you should take a closer look at him, too.'

'I plan to, Doc. Another one to add to list. He's always been a bit odd, but yesterday, he seemed excited at the prospect of getting his hands on Rawlings. On the mortuary table.'

'Does he have any links to Harry Butler?'

'Now there's a thought. We'll have to look into that, but first, let's focus on Harding and the Broadmoor links, see if we can get to the bottom of why he's been dragged into this.'

They passed through the security scanners and entered reception, gave up their mobile phones and any items that could be used as weapons, took their passes and lanyards and waited for Winston to appear.

It was not long before the security chief arrived, looking haggard, a little unkempt, and Doc had the impression Winston had slept in his clothes as he seemed to be wearing the same items he had on during their meeting yesterday. After hasty introductions he led them through to his office, giving a quick update on what he had found out from his enquiries.

Jack spent several minutes quizzing Winston, demanding answers about what he had been doing since Doc's visit had indicated Harding was being fed information by someone with contacts beyond Broadmoor's walls.

Doc was impressed with Winston, who was thoroughly professional, agreeing when Jack pointed out the failings that had led to the current situation. The entire security team had been working overtime to narrow down the suspects, with their chief beavering away through most of the night, though he'd dozed for a few hours in his office, then started again before dawn this morning in preparation for their meeting.

Finally satisfied, Jack asked Winston for the background on the two individuals suspected of aiding Harding. The security chief presented three files to them, including Harding's, and gave a quick summary of how they had identified the inmate and guard.

'We did a full analysis of all Harding's contacts for the last three months, then in depth background checks of all involved. From that lot, I came up with a shortlist, personally interrogated each of them and narrowed it down to this guard. Meanwhile, all the relevant inmates' rooms were searched, and we found these just before you arrived.' Winston opened a file, and spread some photographs across the desk. 'You'll recognise most of these, although there are four more victims.'

Rawlings was included in this batch, a photograph Doc assumed had been taken not long before the man had been left on Clapham Common.

'No letters, just these pictures? Odd…' Doc could see Jack agreeing, both of them coming to the same conclusion.

The detective's next comment confirmed it. 'It's almost as if Harding expected us to find them, so destroyed any correspondence that came with them.'

'Correspondence that would help us identify who's helping him, Jack, and possibly who took these victim photos as mementos.'

Both visitors took a closer look at the additional photographs to the ones they had seen already, before Jack made an observation.

'These will probably be in the post to you tomorrow morning, Doc. Looks like we're a step ahead of The Surgeon. Finally.'

Doc was not so sure. It was all too contrived. He wanted to know more about Winston's assessment of Harding's Broadmoor assistant.

'Unfortunately the inmate is not likely to be of much help. He's one of our less compos mentis guests. A paranoid schizophrenic who has been manipulated by Harding since his arrival in January this year. I think his room was just somewhere convenient to hide these. Harding knew his own room would be taken apart the moment we received the letters to Doc implicating him. I'm pretty sure the other inmate was blissfully ignorant of these items' existence, just as he claims, but you can make up your own mind, Inspector.'

'And the guard?'

'He refused to speak to me without a union representative and his senior officer present. He's not employed by us directly, just contracted to us by GCS, so he thinks he's off the hook for now, expecting to be reassigned with no serious consequences. I'm sure a detective questioning him will loosen his tongue.' Winston finished his explanations with an invitation. 'You can use this office, Detective. I will need to be present throughout, though. Hospital policy, I'm afraid.'

'Fair enough, but this is my gig, okay? We'll start with the inmate, then the staff member. That'll give us a chance to assess the extent of their involvement before we see Harding. Okay?'

'You want me just observing too, Jack?'

'I'll lead but you can jump in as necessary, Doc, especially with this schizo nutter. That's rather more your territory than mine.' Jack was perusing the inmate's file as he spoke. 'Okay, Winston. Can you get—I'm not sure how to pronounce this—Sudhakar Sakthi in for us now, please?'

'Okay Lanny, let's send these photos to DS Sharpe and I'll ask him to do a comparison with the mugshot we have of Harry Butler.'

The two detectives were sitting in the car outside the *Hope, Not Fear* tattoo parlour, with Fiona buzzing, convinced she had found their missing medic.

'You really think it's the same guy? It's difficult to tell from these shots, especially with those bloody great ear lobe plugs covering half his face.'

Fiona was impatient, but could understand DC Jewell's hesitation as she wirelessly transferred the images from her phone on to the bigger screen of their iPad. Moments later, after scrutinising the three enlarged photos, she was satisfied.

'Yeah, I think it's him but send them now. I'll call Sam.'

Fiona had taken the photographs from those displayed among the 'customer' tattoos on the wall. The design of one had jumped out at her as she absently scanned the display as it reminded her of the angel's wings she had seen scratched into the paint of Gerald Butler's under stairs cell. The tattoo on the person's back was far more intricate as it included a rod with two green snakes slithering up its length, and the artist had created a stunning optical illusion with a three dimensional effect.

The wings were enough to draw her attention, but the man's face was partially visible too. Despite the head being in profile, Fiona had a eureka moment as her mind screamed out: it was Harry Butler she was looking at. Two other photos she'd copied to her phone showed the same guy tattooing customers, but again, his face was not properly visible.

'Drive, Lanny. Brixton Market.' Fiona thumbed her phone contact list then heard Sam's voice almost the moment she dialled.

'Hi, Fifi. Your photos just came through. I haven't had a chance to even open the files yet. I'm working up a list of suspects for the boss, including medical, vets—'

'Sorry Sam, this is more important. I think it's Harry Butler, and I'm pretty sure he's changed his name, unofficially, to Harry Hope. Can you expedite this for me, mate? I need to be certain before I talk to Jack. Check out the ownership and other related documents for the *Hope, Not Fear* tattoo place and see if we can get a signature or other handwriting match for the proprietor with Butler's file.'

A long sigh, followed by Sharpe's resigned tone. 'I have a ton of stuff to do, Fi. All of it has priority... I'll get to it later today when I have a spare moment. Fair enough?'

Bugger it.

'Yeah, thanks mate.' Fiona ended the call, her enthusiasm undimmed, voice bubbling as she asked Lanny, 'What did you think of that girl, Shazza?'

'They're both a right state, Sarge. The bloke with his Spidey face and her with those ear stretching things. So bloody ugly. And her forked tongue! Like an evil snake. She seemed a bit wet to me, though.'

'She was lying through her teeth. *Wet herself* almost the moment she realised who we were. You could see her sweating, her hands in perpetual motion, her shifty glances during questioning. Didn't you see any of that, Lanny?'

Fiona was thinking of Carver's bullshit antennae and hers had been on high alert the moment the freak had opened her mouth. Lanny needed to develop her own.

'Well, a bit. She's totally weird, and definitely shady when it came to your questions about Harry Hope. Lovers, probably.'

Her constable had a lot of learning to do, that was for sure, though she had excelled during their more sensitive meeting with the Rawlings widow earlier.

Sharon Tait's possible involvement with the man Fiona now thought of as Harry Butler-Hope was something Fiona should have picked up on too, rather than automatically linking the girl with Spiderman Glen when he came to her defence.

Good cop, bad cop?

Maybe they would make a good team, given time. A smile crept on to Fiona's lips at the thought before Lanny switched tack.

'What's at Brixton Market, Sarge?'

'It's a hunch I've got about the African connection.'

'The bone guy? The one you were asking Sam about?'

'Yep. William Mutuku. Last name means born at night, apparently. Very apt as this scrote has a habit of breaking and entering during the dark.'

'You know him?'

'Not personally.' It was only a white lie. 'Local character, always in trouble when I was growing up, the sort of bloke your mum warns you off. Not that I needed warning.'

'So what's his deal?'

'He used to nick things to order on my estate. You wanted a computer, TV, microwave, car radio, you'd let him know how much you'd pay and he'd find one to suit your budget. A bit like Del Trotter only a proper crook. To be honest, I assumed he'd been locked up long ago.'

'And you think he can help with the Rawlings investigation?'

Fiona was not so sure now, having once again just convinced herself Harry Butler-Hope was their missing link, their number one suspect. Sam would get on to that soon enough, so now she would confront William Mutuku herself, and reel him in. Hopefully, he would shed some light on the practice of muti magic in London. Perhaps even the murder of Adam, the little African boy whose torso had been found floating in the Thames so many years ago.

'I'm not sure, Lanny. Mutuku had a reputation for being connected to some sort of voodoo outfit, into black magic and so on, used to revel in the notoriety it gave him.'

'Magic? You're thinking he has some links to the ritual killings Doc was on about in the briefing?'

'Yeah. Turns out, he wears a pendant with an Atlas bone, the one Doc said is taken from the neck. It's not voodoo, it's muti. Proper African magic. When I was a nipper the locals all claimed he had a magic charm, and that was why he was never caught.'

'But you said he'd been nicked.'

'Yeah, many years after I joined the force, though he did lead a charmed life for decades before he was collared.'

'We're almost at Brixton Market. Where to now, Sarge?'

They were approaching a new Waitrose, the upmarket store a sure sign of Brixton's ongoing gentrification, gradually sloughing off its previous reputation for riots, Yardie gangs and drug wars.

'Park in there, it's near enough.'

Lanny swung the car into the supermarket car park as Fiona unbuckled and said, 'You grab yourself a cuppa in the coffee shop. It's best I see him alone.'

'The boss said we should stick together—'

'DC Jewell, just do as I say. I know his type, and if I'm to get anything out of him we cannot go in mob handed. Clear?'

'If you're sure…'

'Positive. One look at your pretty white face will shut him down like a clam. I won't be long. And don't fret. If it's a dead end, I'll drop it. Now grab yourself a drink. I'll call you if I need you.'

'Well that was a bloody waste of time, Doc!'

The paranoid schizophrenic inmate, Sudhakar Sakthi, had been true to form, despite the heavy dose of anti-psychotics the nursing staff had injected into his bloodstream. He had ranted about the atrocities committed by the Tamil Tigers in his home country of Sri Lanka, before demanding more protection, here, in a secure facility in the heart of leafy Berkshire. He pleaded with the Detective Inspector to investigate his 'formal complaints' about the lack of security he suffered during his time here, as he moaned about Winston's 'useless' staff, explaining how no one took him seriously while his life hung in the balance each minute of every day.

Only Harding could ensure his safety inside Broadmoor's walls.

Doc had tiptoed through some questions, skilfully calming the highly agitated inmate, and, by the time he had finished, Jack was convinced the schizo knew nothing about the photographs, or that Harding had secreted them in a hollowed out recess under the man's wardrobe.

'Well, it confirms what we suspected, Jack. Harding is a manipulative psychopath, able to latch on to other, less stable inmates, and use them to his advantage. Poor Sudhakar's convinced he's found his saviour. Harding's more dangerous here than he would be in a high security prison.'

'Yeah, well, I was never a fan of putting murderous bastards in hospital rather than where they really belong. Let's get this other bloke in. Another bloody name I can barely pronounce. Daniel Ngwene. What is that, African? There's nothing in the file to indicate the man's ethnic origins, other than the dark skin in this photograph.'

'Understood, Detective.' Winston shrugged. 'I'm not too happy about the sparse amount of the information we receive from Global Contracting Services either, but the government's keen to outsource as many public jobs to private companies as feasible, so my hands are tied. We've been migrating our security personnel head-count from permanent civil servants as they retire or move on. All part of the great capitalist experiment. Daniel's been with us six months, and he's the only recently appointed staff member with access to Harding who also has editing privileges for the visitors' logs. There are a couple of others, but they're long term employees, people I hired personally, and I trust them one hundred percent, having worked with them for years. I'll get him in.'

Winston left to find the guard.

'What do you think, Doc? You trust Winston's judgement?'

'Sure, Jack. And the African link… I think that's the angle we should explore. You can do your bad cop thing, and I'll try to ease some information out of him.'

A commotion in the corridor outside disturbed their ruminations. Daniel Ngwene appeared in the doorway, with Winston guiding him, a massive hand clasped on the security guard's shoulder.

'Get your hands off me Diamond! You want me to talk to this policeman, you get me a lawyer! I have rights. I'll report you to my bosses at GCS. You'll be in big trouble.'

'Sit down Daniel. I'm Detective Inspector Carver and this is Doctor Powers, a forensic psychiatrist assisting the Metropolitan Police with a major investigation.'

'No. I'm leaving now. This is wrong—'

'You have a choice. Either sit down, or I will arrest you for obstructing a police officer in the lawful execution of his duties, haul you down the nearest nick, and make your life a misery for the next twenty-four hours. And that's just for starters. I will also make it my business to ruin your reputation, and ensure you never find another job working in security. So how about we just have a chat here instead, eh?'

The man hesitated. Winston, having released Daniel, leaned against the wall by the door. Doc and Jack were both seated at one side of Winston's small conference table with one vacant chair facing them.

'Please sit, Daniel.' Doc's measured tones did the trick, and Jack watched as the man shuffled further into the room then perched on the edge of the seat with his hands on his knees, as if ready to leave even before they had started. 'I need you to be totally honest, with me. Now, I wonder, can you tell us about your surname? Where your family originated? Ngwene is an African tribal name, correct?'

Jack relaxed back in his chair as Doc took over, gently coaxing information about the origins of the name, probing the man's history, discovering how he had arrived in the UK some fifteen years ago at the age of nine. Daniel began to unwind, as if talking about his childhood on the shores of Lake Victoria was a happy diversion from the real reason for this interview.

Jack could read the word *Guilty* as clearly as if it was tattooed across Daniel's forehead. Doc must have picked up the man's nervous signals, his body language too.

'Well, Daniel, let's discuss the reason Detective Carver and I need to speak with you today. We know you have been helping an inmate with information. Antony Harding—'

'That's a lie, Doctor! I never—'

'Please listen carefully, Daniel. If you refuse to co-operate, I cannot help you, and DI Carver will arrest you. You see, we know you gave information to Harding, but I don't think you knew this would lead to the attempted murder of another inmate...'

'I never gave any information to no one—'

Jack could see the telltale eye movement, up and to the side, that confirmed the lie. Doc continued as if the guard had not spoken.

'Which means you could be charged as an accessory.' A pause to let that sink in. 'Now, I can only help you if you're totally honest with us. I think I understand why you would do something like this and put your job at risk, or worse. You would have to be very frightened.'

'I'm not frightened of no one!'

Another unconvincing lie. Jack wondered how Doc was going to unlock the truth, and was rather surprised at what came next.

'Tell me about the shaman. When did he approach you?'

This was news to Jack. How Doc had made a leap from Harding attacking an inmate to a magic man putting the frighteners on the security guard was, as usual, inspired, if a little mystical itself. Jack would have bullied the man into submission, focused on the photographs. They made a good team. And right now, Daniel was also suitably stunned by Doc's insight.

'How do you know about him?'

We didn't, but we do now. Nice one Doc.

'He threatened you, didn't he? Your family too?'

A nod.

'You had to help him, even though you knew it would put your job, your career at risk. I understand, Daniel. When did he first approach you?'

'I can't talk about him, sir. If I do—'

'His muti magic is not as powerful as you believe, Daniel, especially in this country. If you tell us everything, I can personally guarantee you will come to no harm from this individual, regardless of his magic spells.'

Jack could see hope in the man's eyes, and suddenly realised just how badly affected Daniel had been by the threat from an African witchdoctor. The very idea of it was abhorrent, incredible, to him as a committed atheist, but the shaman was wielding real power over this superstitious young man, right here, in England's Home Counties. Magic or not, the effect was the same.

'How can you guarantee he won't kill me or my mother? He's a really bad man.'

'You see, his power relies on his freedom, his ability to do as he pleases, to create his magic charms and potions. We're very close to arresting him, putting him somewhere where he cannot harm you.' Doc spoke with such conviction that Jack almost believed the lie. 'But if you don't help us, he will find out about this meeting, and then you'll be in more danger. Is that what you want?'

Jack could see the indecision on the man's face. He considered butting in, but Doc placed a warning hand on his arm as he leaned forward to speak. Patience had never been Jack's forte, but he waited.

'Daniel? This is your only chance to escape his power. Talk to us.'

Another few moments passed, with Jack wondering if he would need to prod the man into confessing.

Daniel seemed to pray, his eyes clamped shut, his chin lifting, lips moving silently. Finally, a nod, then the dam burst.

Clearly relieved to be telling someone, someone who understood, Daniel Ngwene spilled everything he knew.

'Remember me, Willie?'

The string hammock stretched from one side of the cramped storage room to the other, probably three metres or so in length. The air was thick with smoke from an aromatic herb, one Fiona had not tried for fifteen years or so, since her rebellious teen years. Despite the fragrant blue haze filtering the streaks of sunlight beaming through the ventilation bricks in the tops of the walls, the stacks of illicit goods surrounding her were easily discernible. Dozens of laptops, tablets and phones of various description filled boxes near her feet, and flat screen TVs and monitors dominated one entire wall, with desktop computers stacked ceiling high against the other.

William Mutuku, the source of the blue haze, shifted his weight in the hammock and craned his neck to see who had interrupted his siesta.

'Whaddafuck? Who's youse?'

Fiona hit the light switch as she stood in the doorway, and laughed as she said, 'Having trouble seeing, sunshine? Here, take a good look. See if that jogs your memory.'

Willie squinted, sat upright then swung his feet to the floor, took a pull on his joint, blew some ash off the end, yawned with an exaggerated stretch, then focused on the rude woman who had interrupted his dreams.

'No idea, darlin. What'ya doin here disturbin me in me man cave? No one comes in here and ev'ybody knows I work nights.'

'Work?' Fiona hoofed a box across the floor at him. 'Is that what you call it?'

'Hey, careful! Them's mine! You break, you pay! Whoddafuck are you? Comin in here like dis? You want trouble, missy?'

'Oh, I think the trouble's all yours, Willie.' Fiona did her magician's trick with the warrant card, making it appear and disappear in an instant. 'Detective Sergeant Fielding. You may remember me as *Fingers Fifi*. The nickname you created for me the day you brought me here and tried to corrupt me when I was just eight years old! A regular bloody Fagin in those days, weren't you? Do you still use little kids to thieve for—?'

He was quick. Like a rugby player sprinting head down for a goal.

Fiona realised too late that his movements since her arrival—the shifting upright, the planting of his feet in an open stance and the feigned yawn—were pure misdirection, carefully choreographed to disguise his preparations to flee.

Unfortunately for them both, she had positioned herself between him and his escape route, the only door in or out of the room. Willie's bony shoulder rammed into her lower chest and she felt the air whoosh from her lungs as her solar plexus sent a surge of pain to her brain, winding her. She should have expected it, knew he was a slippery bastard, but she had been complacent, overconfident, lulled into a false sense of superiority by the scent in the room and the knowledge of his marijuana habit.

Fiona flew backwards and felt her spine slam against the door jamb. Another surge of agony slashed at her senses, but the pain brought her fully alert, with multiple thoughts crowding into her mind, the least useful being her regret at having told Lanny to take a break rather than accompany her.

Willie was almost out the door, but Fiona was quick too, her muscles hardened from regular Thai boxing sessions, her body conditioned to accept physical punishment. She twisted towards him and simultaneously brought her knee in a spinning roundhouse before feeling the satisfying crunch of his thigh muscles as she landed a perfect blow just below his hip.

He yelped and then squealed even louder as she followed up her first attack with a fist hooked to the side of his jaw just as his damaged leg collapsed under him and he started to go down. He hit the floor face first and was sprawled in the corridor, still, as if unconscious.

Fiona, having been outwitted once, was taking no chances. Almost instinctively she aimed her knees either side of his spine and dropped her full weight on to his back. It was his turn to have air forced from his lungs, and he screamed this time. Then, as they both sucked in great lungfuls to recover, she hauled his wrists together and used her speedcuffs to secure them behind his back while he showered her with barely recognisable curses, some in English, others in a foreign tongue, along with threats about suing her for police brutality.

Having secured the thieving git, she plucked her phone from her jacket pocket and called her colleague.

'Lanny, are you still in the coffee shop? Get your arse in here now. The old storage units. Opposite the car park. Number fifteen. Bring the tablet with you.'

'So, what have we got, Doc? Some African witchdoctor called Akachi puts the frighteners on an immigrant security guard, hands him several sealed letters to deliver to Harding who then has his replies smuggled out of Broadmoor. All taking place under Winston Diamond's nose. Daniel Ngwene, suitably terrified, also agrees to rearrange the visiting times to allow Harding to attack another inmate as some sort of bonus benefit thrown in for free. Bloody idiot!'

'Let's not judge too harshly, Jack.'

'Too harshly? For fuck's sake, Doc, we're talking about a corrupt guard aiding a deranged criminal to put a paedophile in a coma. I'm not sure who's the worst out of the three of them!'

'Harding. Without a doubt. He'll have homed in on Ngwene, assessed the man's weaknesses the moment the first illicit letter changed hands. After that he knew he could force the guard to break more rules or suffer the consequences.'

'Blackmail?'

'Yes. Harding was given two gifts thanks to this Akachi's intervention. The content of the envelopes and a guard he could bully into helping him.'

Winston had frogmarched Ngwene out of the office a few minutes before, leaving the detective and psychiatrist to assess the guard's confession. The man's career was over, and it was now down to Celene Brooks, the Broadmoor CEO, to decide whether to press charges too.

'He almost got that paedo killed… Not that that'd be much of a loss to the world.' Jack stood, yawned, stretched his arms over his head and interlaced his fingers, palms upwards, then cracked his knuckles before letting his hands fall to his side. 'I'm getting old… Right, let me call HQ to see if they can track down this Akachi bloke.' He patted his pockets, remembered his mobile phone had been confiscated on arrival, and grabbed the handset on Winston's desk, muttering as he did so. 'Now, how do I get a line out of here?'

While Jack made his call, Doc reviewed the information they had gleaned. Despite pressing Daniel for more details about the shaman, all he could give them was a single name along with confirmation that there was now a powerful muti curse on him and his mother—his only other living family member—convincing the poor soul that both lives would be forfeit unless he did exactly as he was bid.

Daniel's eyes had bulged as he reluctantly shared the information with Doc and Jack, almost choking as he did so, his body giving off a rank odour of fear and sweat as he spoke. Doc felt sorry for him but not surprised. The power of superstition and its more acceptable cousin, religion, still held sway with most of the planet's population. Both men were born in East Africa, both from the same tribe though separated by a border arbitrarily drawn between two countries created by the Europeans during the colonial era, so although they were theoretically foreigners, they had ties that bound them from centuries of genetic intermingling.

Like distant cousins.

Their common roots, language, customs and tribal beliefs transcended the veneer of western civilisation they both maintained here in the UK, but their beliefs went much deeper, imbued in their characters, an essential aspect of their individual identities. Daniel claimed to be a Catholic too, but his attendance at church was no barrier to an equally fervent belief in the dark magic of his home continent.

Jack finished his call and flopped back in his chair beside Doc.

'Akachi's an unusual monicker, so even though we aren't sure if it's a first or last name, hopefully we can find this bloody magician. The muti thing… You still think it's part of the bigger picture? Rawlings, Davies and the others? Feels more peripheral to me, Doc.'

'Mmm. I think the whole thing is like an intricate jigsaw puzzle, and we're just seeing pieces. The pieces the person behind all this wants us to see.'

'These clever fuckers are never as smart as they think. We'll get him, Doc… How about our old friend Harding? Shall we get him in now? You sure you're up for this?'

'Yes, I'm sure.' He wasn't, and could hear the doubt in his own voice despite trying to mask it.

Jack stared at him for a moment.

'I'll take the lead on this one. You can observe, Doc. Okay?'

Doc, struggling to quell the greasy sludge swirling in his guts, grimaced. He tried to be upbeat as he said, 'The good news is that Celene and Maddox agreed. We can tell him, Jack.'

'Excellent. That should send some sparks flying!' Jack chuckled at the prospect and, as Diamond reappeared at the door, asked him, 'Are we all set for number three on your list then, Winston?'

'I brought you a coffee too, Sarge… Bloody hell! I thought you were joking about the Trotters. It really is like something out of *Only Fools and Horses* in here!'

'Dem tings is nuttin to do wid me! Dis stuff ain't mine. I was sleepin here, is all.'

Willie was sitting on the floor by the doorway, hands still cuffed behind his back, his feet bound together with plastic ties. Fiona was taking no chances on him doing a runner again, though she was now sitting in the hammock using her toes to push herself back and forth. Her chest and back ached from Willie's unexpected tussle so she was not in a forgiving mood.

'Yeah, right. Except, when we get forensics to check your little treasure trove, I'm pretty damn sure we'll find your prints on a load of moody goods. Thanks Lanny.' Fiona took the coffee and necked a large gulpful. 'Meanwhile, my colleague is going to take some video evidence of this haul, and once we've checked the reports of thefts in the area, I reckon these items are going tell a sorry tale, Willie. What do you think?'

'I tink I need another toke of dat doobie.' He looked longingly at the half-finished joint lying on the floor where he had dropped it during his bid for freedom.

'Yeah. Drugs. That's another problem.' Fiona, having pulled on her gloves, hoisted the bag of weed in one hand and the slab of hash in the other. The total weight was about half a kilo and she'd found both items tucked in a box beneath the hammock. Willie-the-idiot obviously had no idea the location of his secret Aladdin's Cave had been residing in the depths of her memory for so many years, and he had got sloppy with the passage of time, leaving the door unlocked while he puffed his joint. She'd surprised herself with the recollection. Willie's existence had not featured in her thoughts for almost two decades. He used to live here when she first met him, but he'd presumably moved up in the world based on the address Sam had given her, and now used this space as a stock room. 'Dealing too. You're in some really deep shit this time, my friend. If you answer some questions for me, I might be able to make some of your legal problems go away.'

Lanny started, her mouth open in shock, and almost dropped the tablet on hearing her sergeant's words. Fiona winked at her as Willie inspected his feet, obviously considering her offer of a deal.

'What you want den?' A sly note in his voice warned her he would lie without hesitation if he thought he could get away with it. 'I know loads of young 'uns who do nicking stuff.'

Yeah, kids with fuck all, just like I was, but who don't have parents who know better.

'I'm not interested in kids. Tell me where you got the Atlas bone pendant.'

'Why you care? Dat's legal. Possessing yooman remains ain't no crime in da UK.'

That depends, sunshine.

'Just answer me. I know you didn't get it in Africa, so don't give me that bullshit. You may have fooled my colleagues but it won't wash with me. Just assume I'm already aware of a lot more than you think, and I'll know if you're lying... If I hear one wrong word from you, DC Jewell here will be calling out a forensic team. Now, tell me, where did you get the bone?'

It was only a hunch, but she spoke with more conviction than she felt.

'I bought it. In da market.'

'Bullshit. I'll give you one more chance. You help me, and I'll help you. So, let's try again.'

'You gonna fuck me, innit? How I know you help me like you say?'

'Okay, forget it. Lanny. Call the—'

'Wait, wait, wait! Just dis one ting, huh? I give you dis, you let me go?'

Fiona smiled, then said, 'I'll personally drop charges, but I want the full story. Deal?'

'Okay. I get from a guy for some gear he wuz wantin. He work in a dead man's place. Ya know?'

Dead man's place?

'A mortuary? Funeral parlour?'

Stealing bones?

'Like dat, but where dey burn da bodies.'

'Crematorium?'

'Yeah. Dat's all I know.'

'He does have a name though, Willie.'

'Yeah. Da Hand o' God.'

'The Hand of God? Seriously?'

'I swear, dat's his name.'

'And where can I find this Hand of God?'

'I dunno.'

'You're lying again. Lanny, I've had enough of this scrote—'

'Woah! I know where he wuz workin den, but not now. It's a long-long time ago. Twenny-two years, I fink.'

'Tell me where he was working when he gave you the bone.'

He hung his head, switching it from side to side, his indecision visible, as if he was having an inner debate to decide whether the demon copper was a better bet than relying on the lucky charm that had failed to protect him today. The one that had failed the night he was nicked all those years ago too…

Fiona was losing patience and scowled as she rubbed her ribcage where his shoulder had rammed her, thinking he'd better make up his mind pretty damned smartish.

He did.

'Streatham, where dey burn da dead.'

'Lanny, outside for a minute.'

They left Willie alone in the storeroom and once out of earshot Fiona spoke. The stress on Lanny's face dissolved as she digested her sergeant's words.

'Make the call to the CSI team, then nick him for possession of stolen goods for now. I wouldn't be surprised if we find some class A narcotics in there too.'

'Brilliant! I couldn't believe it when you said you were going to let him off, Sarge.'

'No chance. See if you can find the bone pendant in there. He's not wearing it, I checked, and he says he doesn't have it any more. I don't believe him. He's a pathological liar, a fucking piece of excrement who deserves to be banged up.'

'You think it's from that little boy, Adam? The lad in the Thames?'

'Not if he really has had it as long as he says.' Although Fiona was dismissive, she still had a tantalising suspicion that there might be some link between Willie's Atlas bone, young Adam and Patrick Rawlings. But what?

'Is it true what he said though? Possessing human remains isn't illegal?'

'The Human Tissue Act of 2004 is silent on the subject, Lanny.' Fiona had checked immediately after the morning's briefing, so was fully cognisant of the legal aspects and keen to share her newfound knowledge with her assistant. 'Medics use human skeletons for their studies. Others, collectors and the like, buy human remains on the internet. People were selling skulls, skeletons and bones on eBay until a few years ago, before some tabloid newspaper complained and brought the trade to a halt.'

'I had no idea it was even legal.'

'The law doesn't allow the sale of organs for transplant, but ownership of that Atlas bone doesn't automatically mean Willie's committed an offence, which was why he was only charged with breaking and entering last time he was nicked. That was despite having been caught in the act with a human vertebra dangling from a gold chain round his scrawny neck. Not much of a lucky charm though, was it? Mind you, if it transpires the bone was taken from a dead body without permission, well that's an entirely different matter. We need to find it to check the DNA for a match with any previous murder victims or Mispers too. You never know. It might not have come from the crematorium at all.'

'Yeah. I suppose.' Lanny was not convinced but Fiona felt upbeat about her day.

'You crack on—he's your collar, okay? Then he can't complain about some deal his arresting officer promised him before he was cautioned. Tell him he's lucky I'm not charging him with assaulting a police officer, and that's the best result he can expect.'

'Sounds fair enough, Sarge.'

'I'm going to finish my coffee while I call Sam, see if he can track down a home address for this bloke who sold body parts while working at Streatham Crematorium, and I'll also find out if he's confirmed the Butler ID from the photos we sent him.'

'Well, fuck me! If it ain't the bastard copper wot nicked me all those years ago.' Harding received a shove from Winston as he pulled up short at the office doorway, stopped in his tracks by the sight of the detective. Then his feral eyes swivelled and found Doc, no longer seated by Carver, instead perched on Winston's desk off to the side. 'Whassup Powers? Having Winnie the Pooh as your muscle not good enough for yer? You brought some police protection wiv yer this time too! Hahaha!'

Another shove from Winston and Harding stumbled, then recovered, throwing a threatening glance back at the big man, as if he could somehow harm him, here, inside this place.

'Alright, alright Winnie. No need to get all violent on me.'

'Sit down, Harding.'

It had been a long time since Jack had seen the criminal, and he noted to himself how little the ugly bastard had changed. Aged, for sure, but still the same sly, ratty look about him and that persistent air of superiority despite his circumstances.

Harding sat in the one chair placed opposite, clearly sizing up the detective, as if he could read his mind.

As if he knew why Carver was here.

'So, still a lowly Detective Inspector then? Pretty crap at this stage in your career, Carver. Not quite as sharp as you thought you were, are ya?' He giggled to himself, threw a look at Doc that screamed *Fuck you both!* then said, 'Maybe you think I can give you a leg up the career ladder. Is that why you're here?'

Jack contemplated that one, noting how Harding had some insights that he shouldn't have after so many years locked up in here. Either that or it was just a lucky swipe by the inmate, the usual cocky banter, but Jack would play the game, hoping to lull him into exposing something unwittingly.

'Your pals in here have been helping us with our enquiries, Harding. You're in deep shit.'

'Piss off. I ain't got no pals in here and I can't get in much deeper shit than this, can I? Take a look around you, *Detective*. In case you hadn't noticed, this is Broadmoor!'

'Some of us would say you got off lightly, that this place is a soft option. That you should be in a cell, not a hospital room. In fact, Doctor Powers has something to tell you regarding your status here.'

'Really? I'm all ears, Powers.'

'Your psychiatric evaluation has been updated. As a result, you're being transferred. To Belmarsh, where you belong.'

'Bullshit! Maddox said I'm staying right here until he approves me for release.' Harding's confidence crumbled as he tried to assess the faces of the two men, searching for the lie, then turned in his seat to eye Winston. 'I ain't going nowhere. Tell 'em.'

Winston shrugged, his voice steel as he said, 'Professor Maddox has already approved the transfer, and Ms Brooks has asked the Home office to expedite the move for next week. You're deemed untreatable thanks to your latest escapade.'

Harding, initially shocked and confused, then seemed to recover as he said, 'Next week?' He turned back to Jack, carelessly, as if he was being fed a line. 'You're just full of shit!'

Doc shifted from his perch and slid into the seat beside Jack as he confirmed the news. 'I can show you the written authorisation. You're not suffering from PTSD or anything else, just like I always said. And Dickie Maddox agrees with me. You're just a nasty little psychopath with delusions of grandeur.'

'Maddox! That fucking two-faced shite! He promised...'

It was just a spark, a fraction of hesitation in Harding's assertion, but Jack noted it and wondered, *Is he lying?* He had to ask.

'Promised what?'

'Nuffin.'

The denial did not feel right to Jack, as if Harding was toying with them both, having fun despite the outward show of umbrage.

'Tell me.'

'He said he'd help me, get me released if I helped him!' Harding's apparent reluctance to tell them did not last long. 'The fucker lied to me!'

'And why would Professor Maddox say that? What possible help could you give him?'

'He said he's an old mate of yours, Powers.' He chuckled at Doc, who just stayed silent. 'Some mate. Haha! He fuckin hates you!'

'What did he want?'

'He gave me some photos. Told me who they were, an' all. Said I could use 'em to have some fun with Powers. Told me he'd arrange for him to see me, that I'd have something that would fuck him up.'

Jack knew this was a lie. Harding was unaware that his little charade was already blown, that his real accomplice had been rumbled.

'Maddox gave you photos of what exactly?'

'Crime scenes... Victims. Ten of 'em. Gave 'em to me weeks ago, during my therapy sessions. Said Powers would be here, sniffing around. He was right, weren't he?'

'These?' Jack reached into his pocket and brought out the images Winston's team had found in Sakthi's room and spread them on the desk like a magician with a pack of cards.

'You found them then? That fucking idiot Sakthi. Shoulda known better than to trust a schizo.'

Jack was being played, and knew it. This was an elaborate ruse to frame the professor, and could have worked, especially given the links they had discovered between Maddox and Butler...

If there was a mastermind, manipulating everyone behind the scenes as Doc believed, the evil genius had not foreseen Harding's spontaneous actions in blackmailing Daniel Ngwene and his subsequent attack on the paedophile inmate. Underestimating the psychopath may well lead to The Surgeon's undoing.

Jack decided to play the game, preferring not to disabuse the convict.

'So, did Maddox give you any details on these victims?'

'What are you gonna do for me if I tell ya?'

'If you help us now I might be able to help you.'

'You've got fuck all to offer. They reckoned I was never getting out of here. Now you're telling me I'm going to a Cat A prison. Or can you reverse that?'

Despite the words, Harding seemed indifferent to his fate, as if he didn't give a damn. Jack tried to shake him up.

'No. You're going to Belmarsh, come what may. But the Governor's a personal friend. I can recommend a lengthy period in solitary confinement on arrival... Or not. It's up to you.'

'You cunt!' It sounded playful, rather than aggressive to Jack's ears.

Doc kept quiet, just taking it all in, still sitting beside Jack.

'He gave you names? Let's hear them.'

Jack's bullshit antennae, now on high alert, screamed at him as Harding made a show of considering the offer.

He drawled, reluctantly, 'Yeah. I can't remember 'em all... This one, his name's Patrick Rawlings.'

'Not good enough. That was all over the lunchtime news, you could've heard about him from anyone.'

It was Jack's turn for another misdirection, an untruth. Harding almost certainly wouldn't have heard about Rawlings through the grapevine this quickly, nor would he have known which one of the corpses it was, just from the description on the news. Both he and the inmate knew the information had come in the form of letters, long since destroyed, but Jack pretended he was unaware of the truth.

'This one. Selena Scott. Planning officer, bent as fuck. And this one's Joseph Mitchell, fucking paedo.'

Jack felt the scruff of his neck tighten.

Result!

They would have the names checked against missing persons, though it seemed certain Harding was offering the names as proof that the photos were genuine, that he had unique information, purportedly from Maddox, evidence that the professor was involved in serial killings.

Jack, thoroughly delighted with the outcome, misunderstood the look of triumph on Harding's angular face, the gleaming eyes, the tongue slithering over grinning lips. He assumed the inmate was congratulating himself on effectively framing the professor, the consultant who had just downgraded his status, but he was wrong.

Jack pressed for more information, and immediately wished he had not.

'Who else?'

'Ain't that enuff? I can't remember all the others...' Harding's eyes said differently. A few beats passed. 'Hang on!' He stabbed a thumb on a photo. 'Her name's *Amelia*... Ooh. Last name escapes me... What is it? Canary. Nah, erm, Eagle? Sorry, that's not right.'

Jack started to see where this was going, but he was too late to stop it.

'Okay, that's enough—'

'Wait a minute, Carver! Amelia's her middle name. Silly me. I remember, now!' He shifted his attention to Doc, teeth bared in an evil grin, and with a full-throated cackle he spilled the words that Jack had dreaded were coming. 'It's your girlfriend, Powers. Judith Amelia Finch!'

Jack already had a restraining hand on Doc's arm, but his old friend was lithe and fit from yoga. Doc launched himself, his hands reaching for Harding's neck, clamping round his tormentor's throat, his torso slamming on the table top.

Jack pulled at Doc's shoulders as Winston leapt forward, his huge brown fingers prying at Doc's death grip. After a moment's struggle the reluctant rescuers finally released the puce-faced and visibly shaken inmate.

The fracas was over in a matter of seconds. Harding was dragged from the room by Winston before being entrusted to the guards who had been waiting outside to escort him back to his block.

Jack still had hold of Doc's shoulders, could feel them quivering. Doc's rage, frustration and fear vibrated though his body as if a high voltage had been applied to his tenderest parts.

Despite the bruising attack on Harding's neck, the inmate still managed to bellow threats at them both as Jack restrained the incensed psychiatrist.

'You cunt, Powers! I'll fucking kill you for that! Just like I did your fucking thieving daddy! And you, Carver. You'll be well CARVED by the time I'm finished with you!'

WEDNESDAY

ARMED RESPONSE

DETECTIVE INSPECTOR JACK CARVER already felt decidedly overdressed in his Kevlar vest with the bulky sidearm strapped to his belt, so refused to be encumbered by the helmet proffered by the SCO 19 sergeant leading the six-man team of weapons trained officers. The bright red BMW estate car was the workhorse for the Armed Response Unit, specially equipped with armaments and protective gear required for this sort of operation, but the sergeant's team already had everything they needed so he tossed the unwanted helmet into the back before slamming the tailgate shut.

The dawn sky was overcast and grey, though getting light at five-thirty on this late summer's day. The air was still, though humid, and the streets fairly quiet. Streatham High Road was yet to experience the beginning of rush hour with its accompanying hordes of commuters teeming into their city centre offices.

Jack left the armed specialists making their final preparations and went to check in with the three detectives in his team waiting by his car. Although they had all been briefed back at HQ less than an hour before, he wanted to assess their state of mind before he gave the order.

DS Fiona Fielding was visibly excited to be taking part, despite being unarmed herself. Her hands and feet were in constant motion while she waited with the small team some thirty metres from the *Hope, Not Fear* tattoo parlour located in a nearby side road. They were well out of sight of the premises and just waiting for their boss to give them the nod.

The two junior officers, DCs Ahmed and Jewell, had been markedly quieter than usual as Jack had driven them here, and he was a little concerned that their nerves may lead to a misstep during the raid. He tried to reassure them, with a final reminder along with his version of a pep talk.

'Now listen up. The ARU boys will enter first, with me immediately behind them. According to the schematics there's no back access to the shop, no way out other than the door or windows overlooking the street, so you guys follow in behind me once we've secured the building. DS Fielding is in charge, just follow her lead. I'll be with the firearms team on the upper floors where the living quarters are, and we will detain anyone on the premises. You all have non-lethal weapons and you can use them as you deem fit in the unlikely event you find anyone we missed. We'll assume any civilian inside is a potential threat, and remember, Harry Butler is ex-military, has a history of violence, and may be armed and extremely dangerous. Any questions?'

He knew he wasn't being overly reassuring, but this was a serious operation and the last thing he needed was a couple of jumpy constables getting themselves hurt, or worse, through carelessness.

'Not a question, sir, just an observation.' Carver listened as Fiona tried to boost the confidence of her nervous colleagues. 'Chances are, there are just the three of them inside still, probably upstairs in bed. Even so, we'll wait for the ARU to give the all clear before we enter the basement—we had no eyes on that yesterday so I'm looking forward to taking a gander down there... Look lively! It's gonna be fun!'

'Right, let's go.'

Carver signalled to the ARU sergeant to lead the way and the team of ten coppers, with the specialists wearing full paramilitary gear, marched up the main road before turning into the side street. A passing motorist slowed to gawk, but there were no pedestrians nearby so Carver ignored the spectator as they arrived at the premises.

The solid wooden door shattered under the impact of the first blow from the steel Enforcer battering ram wielded by the sergeant, and they were inside, streaming to the staircase at the back of the deserted shop, now bellowing 'Armed police!' They disappeared from view and more shouts of 'Stay down!' reached Carver as he made one last check to see where Fiona and the others were. Satisfied, he bolted up the stairs two at a time.

As he reached the landing he could a hear a commotion in one of the two bedrooms, and more shouts from the other. It was over in seconds.

'Clear!'

Carver entered the main bedroom where his target was already face down on the floor, hands cuffed behind his back, his arms partially covering the magnificent tattoo Fiona had described to him the night before. He could see the resemblance to the sculpture in Maddox's clinic, then had a moment of doubt. No one could tattoo their own back with a design as elaborate as this, it would be physically impossible.

Perhaps he designed it and had his mate do it for him.

The girl sharing Harry's bed was trying to cover her multicoloured boobs and steel nipple rings with a sheet. Carver noted the stretched ear lobes and the marks on her body that looked like she had been branded, including white welts on her belly in the shape of a peace symbol.

'Go on. Have a good look you fucking pervert!' She dropped the sheet and flaunted her nakedness at Jack while two armed officers struggled to pull her arms into position to cuff her—an angry vixen who then started screaming abuse at the ARU sergeant as he cautioned Harry Butler. Jack closed his ears to her rant and went to the other bedroom.

'What the hell is going on man? You've no right to do this. Stop pointing that fucking gun at me! I've done nothing wrong.'

Jack assumed this was Glen Jackson, based on Fiona's description of him. A flabby mountain of patterned flesh with a spider's web tattooed across his ugly mug, struggling to pull on some shorts with cuffed hands. In those few seconds Jack decided he sounded genuinely stunned at the presence of armed officers in his bedroom.

Not that that meant much.

More significant was the information they had found out about him after Fiona's visit yesterday, especially the fact he had been living in the US until four years ago. Jack was taking him in anyway, though would probably release him soon after—not that Jackson needed to know that.

'Actually, we have every right to be here, Mr Jackson.' Jack chuckled as he added, 'In fact, according to my colleague, DS Fielding, it was you who invited us.'

'Piss off! I never did!'

Jack unfolded a sheet of paper and held it out for Jackson to see.

'You told her to come back with a search warrant if she wanted a look around. So here we are, sunshine.'

Jack left the ARU team to hustle the three residents into the waiting police van, then made his way to the basement, noting that DC Ahmed was standing by the shop entrance, looking a little lost.

'Any problems, Constable?'

'None, sir. The DS is still in the cellar but it's all clear.'

'Okay. Give the CSI team the nod to get in here. I'm going to have a sniff around downstairs. I take it you checked the back room and bog for any strays?'

'DC Jewell's out there now, sir. The rooms at the back are tiny though, and there's not a lot there to see, just some old clothes and stuff. I'll call forensics now.'

The stairway was cramped, narrower than normal, and the low ceiling brushed Jack's head as he clambered down, but he knew this was deceptive. The floor plan indicated the cellar was wider than the rest of the property, and it also extended under the premises built on the back. Positioned in the middle of a row of back to back terraced houses, the basement area had been about a third of its current size, but some previous owners had arranged to take over the whole space during the conversion to commercial premises, and knocked through the adjoining walls to make an oversized storage area.

A doorway at the bottom of the steps opened on to this unusual cellar, a vast room with a ceiling height Jack estimated at over four metres. Even with some tables and other equipment, including a pretty sizeable music system, there was a lot of unused floor space.

'This is where they do the suspensions, Boss. You can see the fixings in the ceiling. It's like a miniature church hall in here. Reminds me of the place in Putney me and Lanny visited yesterday.'

The room seemed less well lit than he expected, so Jack, being a man, had to double check that all the switches were flicked in the correct positions himself. They were, so he nodded at Fiona, then said, 'We'll have the Scene of Crimes lads here shortly, but did you find anything out of the ordinary? You know, a small detail, like a fully equipped clinic for major surgical operations?' A few shakes of Jack's head betrayed his disappointment as he surveyed the empty room. 'Because if you did, I can't see it down here!'

'Sorry, Boss, nothing like that, though there is this.' Fiona used a gloved hand to open a bin and Jack took a few paces to join her, then peered inside. 'Lots of bloody gauze and bandages in here. Thing is, by its very nature, suspension equals blood loss.'

'Yeah, sticking fucking great hooks through your fleshy bits tends to have that effect, Fi! Anything else?'

'There's a small storage area partitioned off at the back, behind that curtain, but there's just some shelves and drawers for their suspension gear and a chest freezer in the corner, probably because there's no room in their tiny kitchen upstairs. I had a quick look inside it, but all I can see are microwave meals and the like.'

'Okay Fi. I'm gonna get back to HQ. I want to give our man Butler-Hope and his two mates a proper grilling. Don't look so crestfallen! I need you here.'

'But, Boss. I found him. I want to be in on the interrogations, not kicking my heels here!'

'You'll get full credit for your part in finding him, identifying him and arresting him, but right now I want someone I trust one hundred percent to oversee the CSIs while they take this place apart. That's your job this morning.'

'Oh come on, please… They don't need babysitting and I can help with the interviews. I've met that girl Shazza already.'

'From what I gathered from your oppo, DC Jewell, you didn't exactly hit it off with that freak, so no, you will be staying here. It's not babysitting. I want you here because I know I can rely on you to relay any relevant findings to me while I'm in with the suspect.' With a frustrated swipe of his brow and then arms spread wide, Jack grumbled, 'Just look at this place! It's not what we expected, is it? Unless they moved the bleeding clinic overnight, we've struck out, Fi.'

'Yeah, not great, sir… I'm good at interviewing—'

'Doc Powers will be doing the interviews with me. I need you here, Sarge.'

After firing off a few more instructions, Jack went to leave the premises, but his mobile phone vibrated in his pocket. He'd put it on silent, just as he always did when on an armed raid, ever cautious, even if there was only a minuscule chance of someone shooting at him thanks to an inopportune call inviting unwanted attention. He glanced at the screen, saw it was DS Tim Pierce calling from HQ and assumed the sergeant was checking up for Soundbite. She'd been in her office already when Jack arrived this morning, and had told him she wanted an update as soon as they were inside. He grinned as he jogged up the stairs and answered.

'All under control here, Sergeant. All three toe-rags are on their way but unfort—'

Pierce was not calling to see how their operation was going. He had some disturbing news of his own to relay, and interrupted his boss with a rapid-fire update.

Jack listened, his face draining of colour.

'Jesus wept! Please tell me you're kidding, Sarge.'

This had to be a mistake, or maybe someone was yanking his chain, but DS Pierce's tone was deadly serious. Jack went rigid as the sergeant gave more details, then he snapped his orders, startling Fiona as his voice filled the tattoo shop.

'Send a car to Doc Powers address right away, and have them bring him to HQ. I'll call him and let him know they're on their way. DO IT NOW, Sarge!'

The sirens, reminiscent of the ones that signified Hitler had sent his Luftwaffe planes or rocket-propelled V series flying bombs to devastate homes and factories in the southeast of England, split the pre-dawn stillness of the patchwork quilt of green, yellow and brown fields and woods surrounding Broadmoor Secure Psychiatric Hospital. The distinctive howling was plenty loud enough to serve as an early wake up call for the residents in the nearby villages of Crowthorne, Sandhurst, Bracknell, Bagshot, Camberley and Wokingham.

These thirteen satellite sirens were tested every Monday morning at ten o'clock, along with the one in the hospital grounds, so the locals were familiar with the warning signal, despite Hitler having faded into the history books decades before Broadmoor's klaxons wrenched them from their slumbers early this morning. Protocols were in place for local schools and other vulnerable institutions in the event of an inmate escape, and each of the relevant police establishments in the area automatically went to high alert the moment the sirens sounded.

The last time Broadmoor's alarm system had been used, other than for the regular weekly test, was in 1993 and that fugitive inmate was captured soon after, not far from the perimeter wall.

Today would be different.

Some thirty minutes before the sirens began their wailing, a state of the art Whisper-Lift drone, designed and built by the Chinese military for clandestine operations, and hence equipped with four rotors that were barely audible unless the listener was within ten metres or less, had flown over the Broadmoor fences under cover of darkness, dropped to the ground and deposited its three and a half kilogram payload adjacent to the wall of the accommodation block housing the most dangerous patients.

A skeleton staff of just two security guards idly chatted while sitting swilling coffee in front of a bank of screens showing random video feeds from the hundreds of CCTV cameras monitoring the hospital complex, and so failed to spot the flight. The stealth drone lifted off vertically until it was once again sufficiently high to be above the cameras and out of earshot of the few guards stationed along the perimeter fence, and returned to the SUV parked almost a kilometre from the hospital where the pilot was sitting guiding the device.

A few minutes later, once again laden, the drone repeated its flight, only this time it deposited a much smaller payload some thirty metres further along the wall of the same block. Similarly unobserved and unheard, it returned to the pilot, another packet was attached, and the machine made its third brief flight. This time it dropped between the perimeter walls directly opposite the block it had just visited. The inner wall, a solid red brick structure, some four metres in height and almost a half metre thick, was the inner line of defence, positioned behind a metal barricade that also extended around the hospital grounds, with a land moat of some three metres between the two walls.

After jettisoning its third cargo right at the base of the brick wall, the Whisper-Lift obediently flew back to its master, still unnoticed by any Broadmoor staff, and began its final journey, eventually dropping to the ground by a hedge beside the footpath between the accommodation block it had visited earlier and the perimeter wall. Then its rotors shut down.

The black SUV, equipped with a steel reinforced battering ram disguised as a giant bull bar at the front end, was harbouring a stage two engine conversion beneath the modified bonnet. The air intakes that sprouted from the top of the engine bay fed a specialist supercharger, now whistling gently as the Ford began meandering down the lane towards the hospital entrance.

The driver kept the headlights off as he crept along the unlit tarmac, dark coniferous woods on either side shielding his approach until he was less than three hundred metres from the hospital, just at the edge of the cleared area around his target. He stopped the car, left the engine purring softly, checked his watch then flicked a switch on his remote control panel to 'ARM'. All three of the devices he had deposited in the hospital grounds were now active, on a sequenced timer, so nothing happened immediately, but he did not have to wait long to feel the effects.

The flash of the first explosion lit up the side of the accommodation block, clearly visible to the driver, his car creaking a little on its springs from the change in air pressure from the shock of the blast. The state of the art plastic explosive, a compound of HMX and CL20 designed by the US military for maximum effect, demolished a large section of the exterior wall of the accommodation block and destroyed several of the inmate rooms inside. Although the IED had been placed at the base of its target rather than attached to it, the effective blast radius extended some ten metres. Immediately after the detonation the building resembled something from a war zone.

The flash from the first blast faded and a fire alarm started ringing, then, several seconds later, a smaller detonation rumbled through the air. The second explosive parcel had been designed with far less power, enough to smash through the wall of the accommodation block without creating the degree of devastation to the interior of the building that accompanied the first.

The driver was unable to directly view the effects of his actions until the third blast lit up the perimeter wall some fifty metres from the main gate, almost directly at the end of the lane where he waited. Two metal panels of the external barrier had been blown outwards, though were still standing, uprooted and now at a precarious angle, leaning inwards, still partially attached to the adjacent sections. They were also held in place by the six rows of razor wire atop them, like freshly laundered sheets pegged to a washing line.

This section of wall would only need one final powerful thrust to flatten it.

The driver checked the feed from the Whisper-Lift video camera, and manipulated the lens to view where the second explosion had punched through the inmates' block. This was the critical moment, and he leaned forward, eyes squinting, trying to determine if his objective had been achieved, or whether this was a wasted journey.

The floodlights suddenly blazed and the entire hospital was illuminated with stark phosphorescent light. In the harsh glare, a figure appeared, clambering over the remnants of wall scattered outside his room. He stumbled and swayed, his gait unsteady, as if dazed, then scrambled across the lawns, making his way to the drone that was silently waiting with the fourth package.

The driver continued watching as a face filled his monitor. The drone's on-board camera presented a close up view as the man inside the hospital compound gathered his special delivery. The driver recognised his quarry's ferret-like grin, still distinctive enough despite the dusting of grey powder and streaks of blood masking the man's lopsided features.

Satisfied, he floored the accelerator and aimed his five-hundred horsepower, two-ton battering ram at the weakened section of outer wall.

Harding had not slept. Excitement at his imminent departure left him awash with adrenalin, the anticipation of what was to come keeping every cell in his frame energised, on high alert.

The nursing staff kept to their usual routine as they patrolled the corridors, checking on his room through the night, and immediately after their seventh and most recent visit to his door he got dressed in his casual clothes, including his prized leather jacket. With his senses working at peak capacity, even without a watch or a clock, he knew the time for his departure was imminent and pressed his ear to the reinforced glass window of his room.

It took a while, but then he heard it, the almost imperceptible buzzing of the drone as it deposited its load directly beneath the window. He reckoned he had about five minutes before the chaos would begin, so stripped the mattress, blankets and pillows from his bed, squeezed into his tiny bathroom, then sat in the corner furthest from the external wall. After tucking this makeshift protective padding all around his body, finally tugging the blankets over his head, he was confident he would survive the upcoming demolition.

In his heightened state of awareness, time stretched with an agonising sluggishness, as if the world had slowed its rotation, time and space had expanded, and everything was happening at a fraction of its normal pace. After what felt like ten minutes had passed, he began to wonder if something was wrong, but did not dare get out of his protective nest, even though he desperately wanted to put his ear to the window again.

To compromise, he pulled back the cover to listen, and was immediately rewarded by a percussive blast battering his eardrums.

The detonation sent lumps of plaster from the wall and ceiling cascading on to his head and he was shocked at the power of the device, had a moment of panic, thinking they had mistakenly positioned the wrong package outside his room. Despite having foreknowledge of the upcoming events, the experience was mind-numbing, and his brain reeled as he coughed and spluttered in the dusty atmosphere now engulfing him.

Rubbing his scalp and shaking powdery lumps of wall from his hair diverted him for several seconds and a thought flashed through his mind at the precise moment a second blast rocked him backwards, taking him to the edge of consciousness as the back of his skull whacked the tiled wall.

The thought:

The second bomb...

But he was too slow.

Despite being battered in the face and chest by sharp pieces of brick and glass when his room's external wall imploded, Harding knew he needed to move—and fast. He got to his feet, steadied himself and tried to take stock of his surroundings. It was dark, the air full of dust, choking him, blinding him, and he almost collapsed as he tried to head where he assumed there would be a gaping hole leading to the hospital grounds. As his body responded reluctantly, listless and apathetic, a reaction to the shock of the blasts and the disorienting nature of his newly modified surroundings, the staff at Broadmoor came to his aid.

The floodlights lit up the entire compound and he stumbled towards the light, through the opening, now clearly visible despite his grit-filled eyes and the tears streaming down dust-caked cheeks. He squeezed his eyelids shut, the sharp bite of sand tearing at his corneas, but he was able to half-focus when he reopened them.

With his one good eye he could just see the drone where they had said it would be, its shadowy black outline partially tucked under a bush almost halfway to the perimeter fence. He started jogging towards it, the ringing in his ears matching the fire alarm bell, almost drowning out the shouts of the nursing staff and guards, their panic evident from their high-pitched yelling, the chaos complete.

Harding reached the drone and fumbled with its payload, then heard the squeal of tyres and the roar of a powerful engine being gunned. He checked the Glock nine millimetre lightweight pistol, and, satisfied it was loaded, grabbed the other small items he'd been sent, then jogged across the lawn to the destroyed section of perimeter wall. It looked as though a giant had taken a bite out of the brickwork then spat out the indigestible meal, so Harding headed for the breach just in time to see the front of a black SUV smash the external metal barrier almost flat. The top of the fence came to rest on the pile of broken bricks, creating a ramp bridging the land moat and inviting Harding to freedom.

Then things started to go wrong.

The engine roared again but the vehicle was stuck. Its front wheels had become entangled in razor wire during the assault, and now dangled over the top of the flattened metal panels, unable to regain purchase as the SUV tried to reverse back on to the street. Harding watched as the tyres spun and smoked, rubber squealing against metal, then the engine died.

'Shit! Now what?'

He cursed aloud, hoping his getaway vehicle was not disabled—that would be a disaster. He turned in time to see two staff running towards him, both in riot gear, ready to take him down with Mace and truncheons.

With no military training, no experience of the Russian F1 anti-personnel grenades delivered to him by drone—along with his gun—Harding pulled the pin on one of the weapons and immediately lobbed it at the oncoming threat. It was a bungled throw and fell well short, not even halfway between him and his objective.

The guards seemed oblivious, perhaps thinking he had chucked a piece of brick at them and continued charging towards him.

Harding was disappointed when nothing happened. It seemed to him that several seconds had passed so he assumed the ancient grenade had failed. He spun round and made a dash for the hole in the wall, started scrambling over the razor wire to the metal ramp, when he heard the driver of the SUV scream at him.

'TAKE COVER YOU IDIOT!'

His potential saviour was cowering behind his vehicle, and Harding, finally realising he too was exposed to the device he had somehow managed to position almost perfectly at the oncoming guards' feet, threw himself to the base of the mound of rubble as the final explosion of the morning hammered his tympanic membranes.

It took him a moment to reorientate himself, but his brain was still fuggy. He scrambled on to the ramp, ignoring the recognisable remnants of human flesh littering the area, then grabbed the SUV passenger door, ready to enter the cockpit.

The driver yelled at him for a second time.

'Leave it. The car's stuck. Let's go!'

The stranger sprinted off in the direction his vehicle had come and Harding, ever loath to follow orders and keen to cause yet more havoc in this place that had tormented him for so long, turned back, about to lob the second grenade as he'd been instructed, to create yet more confusion, but something in his head whispered to him.

Nah! Keep it...

Instead, he took aim at another guard closing in on him and fired four shots. It was enough.

Although he was out of practice and his good eye was still sore and fuzzy, he had been an excellent shot in his heyday, working as an enforcer for the Adkins crime family, so felt immense satisfaction as his last bullet hit home. Harding watched as his victim tumbled to the ground and nosedived into the crater that marked where two other Broadmoor staff members had just been blown away.

It felt fabulous, his brain fully functioning again, hyped up by the surge of adrenalin that accompanied the thrill of the kill. He took one last look at the scene, savouring his superiority over normal mortals, then began legging it after his rescuer.

He was in pretty good shape but the other guy was still sprinting, and well ahead by now. Harding's vision was recovering too, the grit cleared by streaming tears, but he could barely make out the man's silhouette in the pre-dawn twilight. One minute he was just visible, the next he was gone, absorbed into the darkness of the surrounding woodland.

'Bollocks!'

He panted as he ran, trying to put as much space between himself and Broadmoor as possible. With a parting glance back, he grinned, certain none of the guards had the balls to follow him after he'd topped three of the bastards. It also occurred to him that a number of unsuspecting inmates had died or been injured in the first blast —the staff would have their hands full with the nightmare scenario in the accommodation block.

'Fuckin brilliant!'

But now he had a problem too. Where should he run to?

His joy was short-lived as he realised he was on his own and the Thames Valley Police would be on the hunt within minutes, probably had a chopper getting airborne right now. He had no car, and there was no other source of transport within miles, no houses in sight, nowhere he could nick a vehicle. The escape had disgorged him onto the barely populated south eastern quadrant surrounding the hospital complex, so he would have to double back to Crowthorne to be sure of finding a car, and that was not at all appealing.

Insults crowded into his head as he started mentally cursing the coward who had abandoned him at the fence and then fucked off down this deserted road. Then he yelled at the darkness:

'You stupid prat! Where are ya?'

No reply.

The idiot should have known the perimeter of a secure hospital would have barriers designed to prevent exactly this scenario.

More malevolent thoughts circulated in his skull before he heard the raucous roar of a motorcycle engine bursting to life somewhere in the woods to his left. Harding was about to follow the noise when a powerful headlight dazzled him and the bike rocketed out of the trees then slid to a halt beside him.

'Here, put this on and jump on the back. Hold on tight, this'll get very bumpy.

We're going cross-country. When I lean into a corner you lean with me or we'll come off. The pigs'll be swarming all over the local towns and they'll have road blocks on these access routes in minutes, but it'll be rush hour soon enough and that'll fuck 'em up... So get a bleedin move on!'

Harding grabbed the full-face helmet and yanked it over his head, simultaneously straddling the rear of the motorcycle, noting the fluorescent green logo informing him it was a KTM Super Adventure. He had no idea about these machines, was unaware that the 1300cc engine was one found on many superbikes, or that this model was dual purpose, built for both tarmac roads and dirt tracks. It was just a dull-looking bike, and other than the logo's tiny splash of colour on the top of the fuel tank, their getaway vehicle was suitably painted in grey camouflage livery.

The rider was impatient to be away, almost unseating his passenger as he opened the throttle and revved the machine's overpowered engine before slamming the bike into gear.

'Jesus fuckin wept!'

Harding scrabbled for a handhold, grabbing the rider's waist to maintain his balance. He had never felt acceleration like it. The screaming engine drowned out his blasphemous oath as the bike reached sixty miles an hour in less time than it took for him to utter the words.

Just a few minutes had elapsed since the four explosions had ruptured the rural peace of local residents, and now the crackling roar and whine of a high-powered motorcycle once again shattered the silence of the surrounding Berkshire countryside, just as all fourteen Broadmoor sirens wound up to full volume, the antique wailing wrenching even the deepest of sleepers from their dreams.

You seem tired, Doctor Powers.
Is that another coffee in your hand, I see? Are you hoping the caffeine will shake the lethargy, deliver you from the ennui of another day in your hopeless, lonely existence?
How badly was your night disturbed?
Was Antony Harding in your bed with you again?
Or something worse?
Did you twist and turn as visions of your former lover invaded your senses? Could you feel the blade carving her spirit free, the bliss of permanent release?
For you both?
And what of the others?
Ten photographs of my exquisite creations are now in your possession.
So many clues to work with, yet you remain clue-less.
By now, I imagine my dear Antony has shared some names with you, but how about the individuals who remain anonymous?
What if Rawlings and the others deserved their fate?
Do you care about them too? Or is it just the one you truly cared for?
Poor, broken Judith. So close to you, in more ways than one...
Oh how she screamed as she spilled her sweet secrets.
And with your name on her lips, uttered with such contempt, such venom, for the man who stole the most precious things from her.

Would you like to hear? I may send the video to your friend Carver.
Or maybe I will send you something to remember her by.
Look inside yourself and you will realise how badly you desire that…

For a fraction of a second, almost too fast for Doc's brain to register, it seemed to him that a photograph of Judy had appeared on the screen, just long enough for him to question whether he really had seen it or merely imagined it. As he tried to dislodge the vision and concentrate on the words that really were there, his imagination kept thrusting the picture of her into his mind—spreadeagled on a bed, bound and gagged.

Doc understood how the brain can play tricks, had often suffered from hallucinatory events, especially when delving into the depths of the worst criminal minds, so attempted his usual trick of compartmentalising, and concentrated instead on the words he knew were there.

Do you now understand how it feels to know your life is barren, that all is lost, that
you are alone in this world, that everyone you once cared about has gone?
That the release of death is a welcome gift?
Perhaps it is time for you to depart from earthly torment too…
I'm sure Antony would be willing to help you with that.
In fact, I've invited him to assist you in any way he can.
And now you are reading this email with bleary eyes, with tears barely suppressed,
and a desire for revenge.
Good.
I know you, Powers, I know many of your secrets. I am the black mirror for your soul.
I see you.
Are you ready to see me?

The photograph flashed again, and this time Doc was sure it was real, even though it disappeared as quickly as before, but this time the message also vanished, and the black screen reflected his own stunned face staring back at him. He slammed the MacBook shut, his brain refusing to accept Judy's death, refusing to believe this demonic message that blossomed on the screen the moment he opened it.

With shaking hands and his heart pummelling his ribcage, he tried to breathe and stay centred, balanced, yet knew he was teetering on the brink. Moments passed with Doc staring into space, emptying his mind, letting the discipline of yoga calm him. As his trembling eased, then ceased, he once again rationalised what he had seen— no longer concerned that it was a figment of his imagination, but instead decided it was a photoshop montage, otherwise why only flash it on screen rather than send it to him? And if The Surgeon really had Judy, why not torment Doc with the audio and video as he had mentioned?

Then his analytical mind went to work on how the perpetrator had thrown both the letter and these images on to his MacBook while he was reading.

He's hacked into my personal computer!

It seemed unreal, this crazy game being played with people's lives. Precious lives. Possibly even Judy's life…

A careless elbow struck his coffee cup, and sent it crashing to the ground, the hot liquid splashing over Doc's pyjama bottoms as the china disintegrated.

For several seconds, he stared at the mess, thinking it summed up the chaos The Surgeon was wreaking, trying to shatter his world too. Then it dawned on him.

He could see me drinking coffee!

The study curtains were closed, there was no way anyone could be looking in through the windows. Another mental leap and Doc came to a very worrying conclusion.

The MacBook camera... He's spying on me!

More implications trickled into his brain.

He could've heard everything Jack and I discussed these last two mornings, sitting in this kitchen. If he can work the camera he can make the mic live, too...

Doc was not prone to irrational actions but in that moment he wanted to drown the computer, like an unwanted cat, to wrap it in a sack and dump it in the Thames. Or better still, do it right now in the kitchen sink.

Fortunately, common sense took hold before either course of action took place. The rational thing to do was to hand the item over to Jack's team in the hope they could use it to locate The Surgeon. So, still calming himself with regular counted breaths, he took the offending item to his bedroom and layered his quilt and pillows over it.

His own assessment of his current mental state was not pretty, but paranoia was not high on the list of problems he had identified. However, he would have Jack's boys check his mobile phone in case that too was being tapped, and whether the mic could be controlled remotely to enable a third party to listen to any conversation within range.

That would be a disaster.

If the eavesdropper could listen in to his meetings with Jack, had been aware of all their musings, could hear everything they discussed at any time Doc had his mobile within earshot, well that would have put them at a serious disadvantage.

Although Doc was no expert, he was aware that hacking a computer was relatively easy compared to a mobile phone, but any device connected to the internet was vulnerable. There was no immediate problem though, as his was still in the car, left there after he returned home the night before, his mind consumed by worry over Judy. He would use the landline to call Jack, as he knew that was far less likely to be compromised, but even then, he would be circumspect in his choice of words until the Met technicians had checked all his electronic devices.

He organised his thoughts before calling the detective, and replayed the latest message in his mind. Their adversary was not as omniscient as he believed, and was wrong about one thing, at least.

Doc's bed had not been slept in last night, the quilt undisturbed until he bundled the MacBook under the covers just now. Worry had kept his brain firing, an all encompassing dread that Harding was telling the truth about Judy. Doc, aware there was no possibility of restful sleep, was determined not to use drugs or alcohol to achieve a state of unconsciousness. Instead, he had spent most of the night in various yoga poses, eventually reaching a state of peace that had surprised him. For some hours, he had remained in a lotus position, and towards the end of his meditation he had felt connected.

To Judy.

In his blissful state he imagined she was still with him, sitting right beside him, her vibrant spirit reaching out to him. She was not dead—she was alive and well.

He could feel it.

Doc snorted at the memory.

What a ridiculous self-serving notion!

He would not succumb to delusional thinking. It was sheer idiocy and he knew it.

The sensation was not spiritual, it was glandular. A chemical reaction, nothing more.

His proficiency at yoga was responsible for the happy hormones flooding his system, natural drugs released by his endocrine glands. Endorphins, dopamine and oxytocin were each capable of lifting his mood, and mixing all three would certainly allow some overly optimistic thoughts and exuberant feelings to enter his normally logical mind.

The yoga had the desired effect though. This morning he felt refreshed, fully recharged, despite having no sleep in the traditional sense. Doc had no idea how long the effects would last, but he would channel this energy into finding the mastermind responsible for this week's events, no matter what it took.

As he reached for the phone on his study desk, another thought took hold. At least their meetings at Broadmoor were secure. Doc's mobile had been left at reception along with Jack's, as required by hospital policy. That was something, and the implications quite important.

In this latest letter there was no mention of Maddox, no indication that the sender was aware of their discussions on the subject. Could it be that The Surgeon was overestimating his ability to control so many moving parts, was unaware that the plan to frame the professor had already fallen apart?

Could they really be one step ahead?

The phone rang just as Doc's fingers curled round the handset.

'Doc! What the bloody hell is up with your mobile? I've tried it several times already.'

'Sorry, Jack. I left it in the car but I can't use it anyway—'

'Listen! There's a squad car on its way to collect you, should be there in less than ten minutes. Be ready when it arrives. Sorry my friend. I've got some terrible news for you—'

'Noooooo! Not Judy... Please, Jack—'

Doc felt his world crumble, the study walls closing in, his ribcage contracting, a steel vice squeezing the breath from his lungs, his heart about to burst. The image of her, restrained on the bed, reappeared at the front of his consciousness and almost blotted out Jack's words of reassurance.

'No! Listen, Doc. There's absolutely nothing to suggest she's a victim, other than Harding's bullshit. We know he's a compulsive liar, mate.'

Doc panted, his throat still constricted as he sought reassurance, his legs unsteady, his mind trying to regain control over the momentary panic assaulting his senses.

'Not just Harding's lies, Jack. There's been another message... Dammit, I can't talk now. I think my laptop and phones are being monitored—'

'You think you've been hacked? Bugged? For fuck's sake, Doc!' A beat passed as Jack's volatile outburst receded, his voice then back to its normal gruff mode again. 'Listen to me. Harding's escaped. He's armed with a pistol. Used that and a hand grenade to blow away three GCS employees.'

'Escaped?' This was unheard of. Broadmoor was as secure as Britain's toughest prisons. Doc's brain scrambled to make sense of it all as he tried to recover his composure. A guard smuggling some photographs and papers into the hospital was one thing, but this? 'How did he get a grenade?'

'He had outside help. They used a sophisticated stealth drone. Left it behind too. Forensics are on it, but I don't expect it'll tell them much. Apparently designed by the Chinese military but anyone can buy one on the dark web for several grand. This was a pro job, though. They wouldn't have left it for us if it was gonna lead anywhere.'

'Did you say he *killed* three guards?'

'Yeah, but that's not even half of it. They broke him out using high explosives. Destroyed half an accommodation block as a diversion. Full of sleeping inmates. Two of them died and there's about a dozen others injured including three nurses. It's bedlam at Broadmoor this morning, Doc.'

Bedlam…

Doc was unsure whether Jack meant to refer to the original UK asylum where the term originated, but his own mind was sharp now. Analysing.

'When was this?'

'Just before dawn, while I was busy arresting our prime suspect. Harry Butler.'

And at almost the exact moment Doc opened his MacBook.

'This has taken a lot of planning. Months of preparation, Jack.' That sneaking admiration crept into Doc's tone again, his mind compartmentalising, separating his thoughts about the evil nature of his opponent from the torment he was suffering, his fears for Judy. 'Everything that's happened this week is all part of his devilish game.'

'Yeah. And Harding may be on his way to see you right now.'

'You think he'll come for me? Really? After all these years I'd think he would want to disappear…' Doc knew the doubt in his voice was misplaced as he spoke the words.

'Of course I bloody do! He knew he was getting out when we saw him yesterday morning. Those weren't idle threats he was yelling at us as Winston dragged him away!' Now Jack was yelling too, his anger almost certainly not aimed at Doc, but a knee-jerk response to the inmate's audacious escape and his overt hostility to them both. His voice was more subdued as he added, 'He'll probably have a go at me too, but he'll want to do you first. You're a soft target by comparison, and he hated your guts even before you tried to strangle him yesterday. For the second time.'

'Okay, Jack, I'll be ready when the car arrives.'

'Good. I'll see you back at HQ. I'll fill you in on last night's team briefing with Soundbite as soon as I get there. I'd like you in on the interviews with Butler and his oppos. Oh, and bring your computer and mobile for my analyst to check over, but make sure they're both turned off, not on standby.'

Doc slammed the phone down and trotted to his bedroom, stripping off his night clothes as he went. Carver's words had shaken him and he needed to be ready when the police car arrived. Normally, Doc would shower, but not today. After throwing on some clothes, he grabbed the MacBook from under the bedclothes and stuffed it into the pillowcase, thinking it would muffle any conversation until Jack's technician's had their hands on it.

He bounded down the stairs, thoughts of Judy swamping his mind. Was it really possible The Surgeon had found her, even though Jack's team had been unable to? That the photographs—the ones now scorched into Doc's memory—were genuine?

With a shake of his head, he cleared his mind again, and thought instead of the threat included in this latest note. Harding was coming for him.

I've invited him to assist you in any way he can.

As Doc forced himself to confront the reality, he reached the kitchen utility room and pushed at the door to his garage, thinking he would grab the phone and stuff it in the pillowcase with the MacBook. Although the door was never locked, it seemed to be jammed, and, despite putting his shoulder to it, refused to budge. Perhaps something had fallen and blocked it after he had parked last night.

Without further thought for why, Doc grabbed his car keys, trotted to the front door, and let himself out just as a patrol car arrived in his driveway. One of the two officers appeared at his side as he hit the remote control for the garage door to open.

'Doctor Powers, you won't need your car—'

Doc faced the policeman as he interrupted. 'I'm just getting my phone, Sergeant. Here, take this. It's my laptop. Needs to go to the technicians.' Doc thrust the pillow at the officer's midriff and thought the stunned gasp that resulted was an over-reaction.

Then he turned to see what the officer was staring at, eyes transfixed, mouth drooping open.

At the back of the garage, illuminated by the harsh fluorescent tubes that automatically came on when the door was activated, and clearly visible above the roof of his Jaguar, was a sight that drew a wretched howl of anguish from Doc's throat.

A freshly mutilated victim was hanging from wires that extended to the garage ceiling, the bloody stumps where arms and legs had been severed were still glistening, the face and chest like raw minced beef, ruined beyond recognition, though this was clearly a blonde female.

As the words 'No, Judy!' stretched and disintegrated into demented wailing, Doc sank to his knees.

He was certain it was her, the hair alone enough to convince him. Even so, as if the horror of what he was seeing was not enough to rip away the last shred of doubt, any hope for her, one line from the latest missive from The Surgeon repeatedly screeched inside his skull:

Poor, broken Judith. So close to you, in more ways than one...

'Thanks for getting here so quickly, Bob.' Jack had been on his way to Scotland Yard when the call came through, alerting him to The Surgeon's latest victim. The CSI team had just finished pitching a tented canopy around the garage entrance, occasionally illuminated by the flash of the photographer's camera as he recorded the scene. Jack was watching as he conferred with the Met's senior pathologist. 'Poor Doc Powers—being confronted with this first thing this morning. I can't imagine what he's going through.'

Professor Bob Koch just smiled and shrugged as he finished dressing in his forensic gear. 'I was just leaving for work when your boss called, so I was in the neighbourhood. Any idea who she is? At least it's obvious it's a female this time.'

'We're not sure yet. Can you take a DNA sample for me straight away? I'll have it expedited… We think it might be Doc's ex.'

Koch cocked his head to one side as he pulled on his gloves, his tongue sliding over thick lips as if he wanted to taste Jack's words.

'Really? Well, well. What a strange mess he's got himself into. Any thoughts on the perpetrator?'

'Seems likely it's The Surgeon again. Er, I'm in a bit of a hurry, Bob.'

'I must say, this doesn't look much like The Surgeon's handiwork at first glance.'

Jack felt his own doubts surface as he replied. 'Hung on wires, like Rawlings. Reminds me of Diana Davies. She was hacked about like this.'

'Mmm. I can see similarities, but the hair, the genitalia were missing on the Davies woman, whereas this one… Powers' ex, you say?' Koch's eyes, greatly magnified through thick lenses even when he was not bemused, seemed to expand, ready to pop. Then he blinked slowly before his head swivelled, bringing to Jack's mind that owl again, now inspecting its prey. Red meat. 'He's a suspect, then?'

'Uh-huh.' Jack was pretty sure Doc had not had time to abduct and butcher this victim, but had no desire to explain. 'First, we need to identify her. That's why I need that sample.'

'I gather you arrested some other suspects this morning. You've been busy! Is it true that the Butler lad is an ex-military colleague of my pal, Dickie Maddox? This really is a most intriguing case.'

'Yeah. I want to get back to do the interviews. Just take a DNA swab for me, then I'll dash.'

'That's rather irregular, Jack. I know Doc Powers is your friend, but he most surely is a suspect and I doubt Sadie Dawson will—'

'I'm not asking, Bob. I want to see the official sample taken from that body,' Jack's finger stabbed the air in the direction of the mutilated corpse, 'with my own eyes. When I tell my *friend* who she is, I want to be certain there's no cock up with the sample, no possibility of confusion at the lab.'

Koch reddened, opened his mouth as if about to protest again, but Jack was in no mood for this, and was not about to enter into an argument over procedure. He interrupted the ME even before the words had formed.

'There have been two DNA cock-ups this year already. This will not be another. I need to be certain if that victim is Judy Finch—or not… The sample. Please.'

Koch stared at him for a moment, blinked, then nodded.

'As you wish. But I will have to inform the Superintendent.'

'Do that. And take a sample to check for yourself. That way you can be sure I'm not a crooked copper interfering with evidence.' Jack let the anger loose in his voice, even though he knew Koch had a point. The ME had made no move towards the body. 'Get on with it, Bob. I haven't got all day.'

Another shrug, then Koch went to work.

The Crime Scene Investigators arrived fifteen minutes after Jack left Fiona fuming over the injustices her boss had heaped on her in the last few days.

Now this latest indignity, after last night when Jack had been most dismissive of her findings in Brixton, her arrest of Willie Mutuku while following up on the source of an old Atlas bone. By the time Soundbite had called the team meeting, Fiona had convinced herself she had single-handedly identified and then found their prime suspect in his Streatham shop too, and deserved more recognition for her contribution to the investigation.

Of course, she knew that locating Harry Butler was a team effort, that Sam and others back at HQ were equally responsible for tracking him down, feeding her the information in the first place. But she was the detective who spotted the photo of the winged tattoo, who'd seen the likeness in the man's profile, who'd then suggested checking for a handwriting match in any of the official business documents held on file. In fact, she was the one who got the old man to finger his grandson in the first place—while on his deathbed!

If it wasn't for me there would've been no dawn raid and no arrest. And now the boss wants me to hang around here, wet nursing the CSIs.

Well, she would not loiter here any longer than she had to, but would follow up on the Hand of God lead as soon as she could get away.

And Jack Carver can piss off if he doesn't like it.

Anyway, he always told her to trust her gut instinct, so she would. Later today she'd confront this crematorium employee who had been stealing bones from uncomplaining corpses all those years ago.

If Sam can find an address for the bastard…

Mmm… Teamwork, Fi.

She sighed. Sometimes she just wanted to be like James Bond and do her own thing regardless of what the boss said. Well, today she would have a minor rebellion. Following up on the Atlas bone was important to her, even though Soundbite had insisted it was irrelevant to their current investigation. The Acting Super was probably right too—Willie had been wearing his Atlas bone for over twenty years, long before Rawlings' killer arrived on the scene.

Too bad.

This was just something she had to do.

Her thoughts were interrupted as the four CSIs arrived, introduced themselves and asked her where they should start and what they should focus on.

'Blood. We're looking for evidence there's been a murder-dismemberment anywhere on the premises. We were hoping to find a fully equipped clinic in the giant cellar, but didn't, so if you turn up anything suggesting something like that was once here, that would be a great help.'

The odds did not seem good, but some luminol in the bathroom and in the basement might just turn up some gory evidence. They'd also need to check any suspicious items, surgical implements and the like, as well as the bloody bandages in the trash. They would bag that lot up, plus all the suspension gear and so on, then document the entire haul before taking it back to HQ.

After directing them to the task in hand Fiona went for a root around in the office filing cabinet, still wearing her blue gloves, though not bothering to don the white forensic coveralls her colleagues were pulling on. Her boots had already traipsed all through the place so she did not feel the need, she would just have a nosy round the shop while they did their thing on the other two floors.

There was little of interest in the filing cabinet. Some letters from suppliers, fancy tattoo designs, bills and receipts, and plenty more of the usual small business admin.

Butler's partner, Sharon Tait, aka Shazza, had been rifling through these cabinets for the list of members, but was there anything else of significance?

Nothing.

Then she came to the lowest drawer. Her mood had dictated that she slam each of the others shut, so she was not being at all gentle as she yanked the last one open. It felt odd as it flew out and hit the stops, as if something had shifted inside, so she pulled the files apart, and squeezed her hand through. Almost out of sight, tucked underneath the green hanging folders, she could make out a shiny metallic glint and felt her excitement surge as she retrieved the hidden device.

A notebook computer.

Brilliant!

Jack, after his phone call to Doc, had bundled up the desktop computer at the back of the shop and taken it with him as potential evidence. This was something altogether more interesting.

The device booted up on command, but was password protected, so Fiona, with nothing better to do, started putting in various combinations of phrases that Shazza or Harry Butler—or Harry Hope—might choose. Sam Sharpe would probably access the machine in no time, but he was not here and anyway, his full attention was on the shop's computer or Doc's laptop right now, if her boss's comments in his final flurry of instructions were anything to go by. So, Fiona plopped herself down in a tattooist's swivel chair, propped the computer on her lap, and idled away thirty minutes while listening to her two crime scene colleagues clomping around upstairs. The other two were down in the basement, no doubt spraying luminol over walls and floors. They would be some time so she was in no hurry either.

Having exhausted every combination of Harry Butler/Hope and Sharon/Shazza's names and their dates of birth—information she had gleaned from the files in the cabinet—Fiona had just about had enough. As she went to bag the computer ready to take to HQ, a final thought occurred to her.

Maybe Harry used something related to his life with his grandad. The old man's dog's name was unusual. She wracked her brains to try and remember what the uniforms had called the terrier when she had read their report. Then it came to her.

Smudge.

Fifteen minutes later, having tried that name, and every likely combination she could think of, she was about to give up for the second time when inspiration hit her again.

Angel wings...

The picture under the stairs in the old man's house, the image tattooed on their suspect's back... And Carver had told them in their briefing last night, Maddox used the same symbol for his clinic's logo, and had a sculpture in his reception created by Harry Butler.

She tried some variations around that theme, but nothing worked. Then she remembered, the clinic was named for the symbol. Now, how to spell the word, she wondered. A quick Google search turned up the result she needed so she typed the letters in upper and lower case:

Cadaceus

She was immediately rewarded with a view of the desktop, empty except for a file marked 'Private'.

It bloody well is!

Frustrated by another layer of security, she tried as many of her previous combinations of password as she could think of, but got absolutely nowhere. Finally, she gave up, and grabbed an evidence bag for the offending item just as a voice reached her from the basement stairs.

'Sarge! You will not believe what we've found down here.'

'Hi, Doc. How're you doing?'

Jack, having just arrived back at HQ well over an hour after leaving a visibly disgruntled Fiona at the tattoo parlour—the delay thanks to his detour to Doc's home to confer with his colleagues at the latest crime scene—was concerned at the sight of his old friend. Doc's clothes were rumpled, a shirt button undone allowing a peek of greying belly hair, and the tail was poking out of his trousers, as if he had dressed without care, hurrying to get away from his house even before the gruesome discovery in his garage. Brown eyes, rimmed with worry, clouded with sadness, told a sorry tale.

Jack didn't really need to ask. He could see that Doc was barely holding it together, probably hadn't slept after yesterday's little performance by Harding. Then being confronted by a mutilated body in his garage... And his old man's murderer was on the loose, too.

The Thames Valley Police had already launched a full-scale hunt for the absconded criminal, and national media ensured the whole nation was on the alert for an 'armed and extremely dangerous' escapee, but there were no valid reports of sightings, not even a sniff of him at the roadblocks that ringed the area. Hundreds of square miles of the south east of England were being disrupted as a result of the breakout, with lengthy tailbacks on southern access routes to London already, as the police tried in vain to catch Harding while the morning rush hour got under way.

Jack was not hopeful. The people who executed the escape had the hallmarks of ex-military, professional mercenaries, willing to sell their deadly expertise to the highest bidder, with any notions of patriotism long forgotten. Harding was probably well away by now, hiding out somewhere secure, waiting for the dust to settle before making his move against Doc.

And me...

As an Authorised Firearms Officer, Jack could draw a weapon as required, as long as his senior commander authorised it, and Soundbite had already done so for this morning's arrests. Jack was determined to keep his pistol with him at all times until Harding was safely behind bars. He would square it with his boss later, but right now he wanted to quiz the three freaks they had in custody.

Is Doc up to it?

As if reading Jack's mind, Doc spoke, his voice quavering but determined.

'Your man, Sam Sharpe, has my MacBook and phone.' Doc went on to describe the latest letter that had appeared on his screen this morning, and his theory that The Surgeon had knowledge of some of their discussions.

'Fuck it! That's all we need.' Jack wrestled with himself to regain control as his temper flared. 'Let's hope it was only the laptop and not your bleedin mobile too.'

'The body in my garage. Am I a suspect, Jack?'

'Not as far as I'm concerned, Doc.' It was true, though Soundbite was still unconvinced. Jack, having dropped off the DNA sample, had arrived at his office to receive an earful from his boss about the irregularities of this case, but he had insisted Doc continue in his role as consultant. Her words echoed in his head as he reassured his friend:

'Well, this is formally against my recommendation, Carver. You'd better keep a close eye on Powers. Treat him like you're joined at the hip. And I don't need to tell you the consequences if you are wrong about him.'

'Thanks, Jack.' Doc sighed a mournful note, then asked, 'Is it... Judy?'

The pleading look, the desperation, like a dog begging not to be whipped by a cruel owner, cut through Jack's cynical outer shell. He wanted to put Doc's mind at rest, but had little to give him.

'I've asked for a DNA comparison to be expedited. We can't be sure it's her, and if it's not, we'll track her down, mate.' He put a hand on Doc's shoulder, massaged the taught muscles there for a few seconds, could feel his friend's anguish through his fingertips. 'We're checking all points of departure, in case she left the UK, but it's a big job. We should know if she used her passport by close of play tomorrow at the latest. Let's stay positive unless we hear otherwise, eh?'

'DNA. How long?'

'Later this morning if we're lucky. We know the victim's a female, but that's all for now. The ME's team have Judy's photos on file, hospital records and other details to compare as well as the hair sample you provided for lab analysis. The experts are working on it all as we speak. If Koch finds any distinguishing marks, we'll soon know. Sorry, Doc, that's not a quick job either.'

Doc's fingers, white with tension, burrowed through his curly hair, visibly digging into the scalp. Jack guessed there were terrible images buried beneath, visions Doc was trying to expel. He changed the subject.

'I wonder why he contacted you directly this time, rather than via snail mail like the two previous times. Risky, if my technicians are half as good as they reckon they are.'

'It's another taunt. A signal of his superiority. I doubt your team will be able to trace him... He also wants us to know he's been listening in... How he manipulated us both into meeting with Harding. Congratulating himself by blasting the evil sod out of Broadmoor while watching me sip coffee in my pyjamas. And leaving that awful *gift* for me.'

'Yeah. But we do have Butler in custody. If there are two perps, and Butler's one, then I'm sure we'll get the other one, too.'

'The point is, you were arresting Butler when that message appeared on my screen. He can't have sent it, Jack. And think about it... We were led to him. Thanks to the old boy who discovered Rawlings.'

'Yeah. Right in a spot where the grandfather was guaranteed to find the mutilated victim. Suspended.' Fiona had informed the team last night that the hooks were probably placed by someone with little experience in the strange hobby, but Jack had pointed out that it may have been a hurried job, done in darkness at an unfamiliar location, so that simple fact did not rule out an experienced suspension practitioner as the killer. He ploughed on with his theory that they had arrested the guilty party. 'Harry Butler left Rawlings strung up in a tree on the old man's regular dog walking route as a reminder of his war crimes, a form of psychological revenge undertaken by an abused grandson. A disturbed individual who did not expect us to trace him, didn't imagine his own flesh and blood would finger him as a prime suspect while lying on his deathbed. Doc, he's the best lead we've got.'

Doubt wrinkled Doc's forehead, the mind behind it working furiously. Jack could sense the frustration as his friend continued down a different path.

'The more I think about the Butler-Maddox link, the more I think this is all an elaborate set up. Butler may be innocent, just a patsy, being used to point the finger at Maddox. I think they were both being framed.'

'Well, let's not get ahead of ourselves, eh? I'm going to interview him and I want you in the observation room. I'll have an earpiece so you can talk to me. And although he won't be able to hear you or see you, I can. You might want to finish dressing, mate.'

A wink took the edge off the comment, and Doc, startled, checked where Jack's finger brushed the offending button.

'Damn!' Doc's eyes shifted back to Jack's, determination signalled with a firm nod, a tightening of the lips. 'I'm fine, Jack. Let's do this.'

Fiona left the evidence bag containing the computer on the desk, double checked that the shop door was sufficiently secure to prevent entry despite the shattered lock, then headed down to the basement. She expected the room to be in darkness with special lamps casting a blue light, illuminating traces of blood splattered everywhere, but the view she encountered on entering was much brighter than when she had been here with Carver, with three forensic floodlights all ablaze.

The two crime scene officers were at the back of the room, partially obscured behind the curtain, but the flash of a camera bulb told her where they had found something of interest. She felt a surge of excitement again, a tingling in her belly, anticipation that Harry was their perp. As she reached the curtain she wondered what they had discovered that she had missed earlier.

The bulb went off again just as she stepped through, the sudden flare of white light burning the image into her retina, scorching it into her memory, never to be forgotten.

The two white suited technicians had laid a blue plastic sheet on the floor and placed the contents of the freezer on to it. Boxes of burgers, ready meals and bags of vegetables were strewn at their feet, but the officer with the camera was standing over one bag as he pointed the lens at the piece of evidence Fiona was sure would put Harry behind bars for a very long time.

She took a step forward, careful not to tread on the sheet, not to disturb anything as she stared at the white object, clearly visible through the transparent freezer bag.

'Is that real?'

There was no doubt in her mind, but the nod from her colleague confirmed it even before he replied.

'It'll go to the lab, but I'm ninety-nine percent certain. It's a woman's hand.'

'No comment. Thirty times. No bloody comment! His brief's told him it'll go against him, if it gets to court, but Butler's sealed his gob shut like a clam.'

Jack had joined Doc in the observation room and was now staring morosely through the one way glass at Butler junior, venting his anger at the recalcitrant suspect in the full knowledge he could not be heard through the soundproofed walls.

Doc had expected as much. Harry had almost curled into a ball when Jack started with his questions. Had barely looked at the images, was visibly disturbed by the sights Jack thrust under his nose. Not surprising, Doc thought, given the man's experiences in the army and the resultant PTSD. Even with Doc's words, delivered through Jack's earpiece before being repeated aloud, Butler remained uncooperative.

'Perhaps I can get him to talk if I speak to him in person, Jack'

'Be my guest. You want me in there too?'

'No. We'll switch places. I'll keep DS Pierce in with me.'

The sergeant was waiting in the room, as was the station lawyer and Harry Butler —at least their unwilling suspect had confirmed that was his real name. Not a big win as his fingerprints were on file from his machete attack in any case.

'Go for it. I want to let his two mates sweat a bit before I interrogate them, though we haven't got anything concrete on either of them yet.'

'Do we have any of Butler's DNA on file?'

'Not yet. Why?'

'Diana Davies, the hooker. She had semen in her body the day she was found. It was degraded and at the time they weren't sure it would be definitive—'

'Yeah, you're right. LCN testing was banned when her body was found!'

Doc was thinking the same thing. Low Copy Number testing for DNA samples had been controversial, and banned by the High Court at the time the prostitute's body had turned up in a drainage ditch in south London. Reopening the case and using the technique to compare with other serial killers was an idea Doc had promoted in his series on unsolved crimes. However, the DNA from the semen had yielded no results when compared with the database, so they had no likely suspect.

Until today.

Jack was having a hurried conversation with a fellow officer as Doc squeezed past and eased himself into the interview room. He fiddled with the earpiece now lodged snugly in his aural canal and took a seat opposite the purported serial killer.

'Hello, Harry. How are you doing?'

Harry's head bobbed up, his vacant stare slipped across Doc's face, then his gaze dropped again, as if the floor was an object of fascination. It took a moment, then Harry's head came up with a jolt, his eyes alert with recognition.

'I know you. You're not a copper.'

It was the longest statement Harry had made since being hauled out of bed by armed policemen at dawn this morning, and Doc was encouraged by the reaction.

At least he remembers me.

DS Pierce spoke for the benefit of the tape, informing any future listener of Doc's entry into the room, ensuring Harry's words would be admissible as evidence.

'No, I'm a psychiatrist, Harry. We met at Broadmoor after your last run-in with the law.'

Harry had perked up, his body language more open as he spread his hands on the table top, leaning forward, eager now.

'Yeah! You were the only one who listened to me. You got me released. What are you doing here, Doctor?'

'Call me Doc, everyone else does.' It was a line he used a lot, but he hoped the more casual approach would help loosen Harry's tongue. Even so, Doc wanted to be clear about their relationship. 'You are still under caution Harry, and you're here on suspicion of murder. You need to realise how serious this is.'

'I've done nothing! I'd never seen those hideous photos before that bastard copper started shoving them in my face.'

'I understand why those photographs would make you uncomfortable, Harry. Are you still taking your medication? Did the Duty Sergeant allow you to take anything before they brought you here, for interview?'

'The station medic sorted me out with something when I got here. I asked them to bring my meds when they nicked me, but they wouldn't let me have them...'

'Do you still get memory lapses, even while taking the drugs?'

'No... They sort me out. Totally.'

'But you used to get lapses even while you were on the meds. Like the day you were caught with the machete.'

'That was after I ran out. I was on my way to the GP to get a repeat prescription.'

'Refresh my memory for me. Tell me about the other occasions, Harry. Lapses that occurred around that time.'

'Often I'd wake up in the morning parked outside the graveyard where my parents are buried.' Harry peered at him, earnest as he asked, 'What does that mean, Doc?'

'Maybe nothing.' Which was the opposite of what Doc was thinking but he sensed Harry was holding back from him. 'Anywhere else?'

Harry's cheeks reddened as he confessed to something Doc had suspected, something half remembered from their brief meetings at Broadmoor eleven years before.

'Sometimes I woke up in bed with a hooker...'

'Your subconscious was just looking for comfort, Harry. No need to be embarrassed.'

'I'm not! She was a friend, really... A fuck buddy.'

'Good. I have a photograph I'd like you to look at for me.' Doc could see Harry's more open demeanour start to retreat again, so hastily added, 'Don't worry, this is nothing untoward. Just a woman who I think you may be able to help us identify.' Doc riffled through some pages in one of the files Jack had left with the sergeant, then pulled out a photograph of Diana Davies before she had been tortured and left as a mutilated torso. The photo was taken before her career as a sex worker too, and she was quite attractive, not yet ravaged by STDs. Doc ignored the other images of her as a street walker, when her experiences had jaded her, taken its toll on her body and soul. 'She used to work near King's Cross.'

Doc slid the picture across to Harry who took it in his hand, fondled it for a few seconds, his features softening as he nodded.

'That's her. She was an old school buddy of mine. We had a bit of a thing until I found out she'd contracted HIV and hadn't told me. Haven't seen her since. Diana Davies. Why?'

Jack's voice echoed uncomfortably in Doc's ear as the detective swore aloud, clearly forgetting his full-throated curse was amplified until it was too late. Doc's fingers plucked out the offending ear bud and he pocketed it without missing a beat while Harry's eyes were still scrutinising the photograph.

'I'm afraid she was a victim of whoever has been butchering the people you saw in those photographs the detective showed you. She disappeared over ten years ago, not long after you turned up in Brixton swinging a machete. We think someone abducted her and held her for some time, torturing her and mutilating her before dumping her body in a ditch... What can you tell me about any of that, Harry?'

'N-n-nothing. I lost touch with her. I didn't even know she was missing. I swear, Doc! You know I was a mess myself after leaving the forces. I could never do something like that, though.'

Doc felt sure Harry was telling the truth. At least the Harry that was sitting here, in this interview room, right now.

In all his years in psychiatry Doc had only ever witnessed a handful of genuine cases of Dissociative Identity Disorder, but Harry's behaviour might be explained by a second personality existing inside him, unknown to the conscious individual arrested today. A psychopathic alter ego capable of butchering Diana Davies while his law abiding self was unaware it had happened.

The parallels with Doc's own experience of similar fugue states, where he had periods he could not account for, were not lost on him, and no doubt Carver too.

Maybe Harry was the killer, the demonic murderer they were hunting. His traumatic experiences in Afghanistan could have triggered the creation of a second identity feeding off the terrors residing inside the memory of the original personality. Although Doc had seen no evidence of multiple personalities when he first met the tormented veteran, another character may have lurked, hidden within. They had only spent a dozen hours together at most, for the court mandated assessment, so it was unlikely that *any* competent psychiatrist would have diagnosed the disorder from that brief interaction. Doc probed him further.

'Tell me more about the headaches and the memory lapses. You still suffer from them, don't you? You don't always take your medications as prescribed, do you?' Harry's medical files from his time at Broadmoor were also on the table, and Doc thumbed through them as he asked. 'How long do the lapses last? How much time goes missing when they occur, Harry?'

Doc felt discomfited by the questions, ones he had often asked himself, but kept his focus on Harry, watching as the man's attitude shifted again—angry now, his voice raised, fist banging the table as he yelled.

'There's no way I could do any of this! You think I could carve up my friend and not even know about it? You're mad if you think that's even possible.'

'Did she infect you Harry? Are you HIV positive?'

'No! What? Is that supposed to be my motive for chopping up a girl I used to love? Jesus! I've had enough of this. Now fuck off and leave me alone. I'm not saying another word.'

Harry's neck and face were flushed, his fists both bunched, quivering, the joints pale and prominent as his hands vibrated against the tabletop.

Doc was about to try another tack, but the door opened and Jack entered . He announced himself for the recording, pulled a chair up beside Doc and said, 'I'll take over now, Doctor Powers.' Jack's eyes bored into Harry, who was glaring back defiantly. 'You see, we've made an important discovery in your shop, Mr Butler. Something that will see you banged up for life if I have anything to do with it. I'm sure you know exactly what I'm talking about.'

Harry's anger flared again, his head snaking forward, the muscles of his face in spasm, wrenching his lips away from his teeth, creating a disturbing rictus grin as he tried to outstare the detective. This time, his voice was quiet, controlled as he said, 'I have no comment. End of!'

'Oh, I think you might want a word with your brief.' Jack ignored Harry's glare and addressed the lawyer. 'We found a human hand in a bag in his freezer. My team are dusting it for fingermarks as we speak, though I'm pretty sure we're going to find your client's hands have been all over it. You might like to advise Mr Butler to confess everything before we have all the evidence we need to charge him with murder.'

'YOU FUCKING LIAR!'

Harry leapt to his feet, as if about to stomp from the room but was trapped behind the table between the wall and his solicitor who looked him up and down, shaking his head as he addressed Jack.

'I'd appreciate some time alone with my client, Detective, if I may.'

'We're just about done here, Sarge. I've secured the door and added some crime scene tape. You need a lift?'

A couple of hours earlier, a squad car had picked up the frozen hand, carefully packed into a special cool box designed for organ transplant deliveries, and blue-lighted it back to base, along with the notebook computer Fiona had discovered. Both items had been dusted for fingermarks by the team on site and the results relayed, but Jack wanted the hand with the lab technicians as soon as possible, and would also have DS Sam Sharpe working on the computer without delay.

No additional evidence had been discovered, but things were definitely shaping up, Fiona thought. All in all, a good morning's work.

'Thanks guys. I'll hang on here for a bit.'

'You're not coming back with us, then?'

'No. I'm going to grab some lunch and head to HQ later. My car's just round the corner.'

Although Fiona was planning to eat, her stomach having been grumbling at her for the last hour while she waited for the forensic team to finish their work at Harry Butler's place, she had other plans for this afternoon. The DI was convinced he had their killer and was tied up with interviews. Apparently, Carver had no need of her assistance, convinced he could sweat out the names of any accomplices from Butler.

The Rawlings investigation was coming to a conclusion, and normally Fiona would have felt a thrill at having played such a major role in the team's success, especially given the speed with which they had arrested their man. Instead, a dark cloud infested her mind, along with an uneasy suspicion that the evil undertones of the case were still unresolved. The feelings she had experienced from her discovery at Gerald Butler's house were still fresh and raw, an open wound that would fester until she closed the case to her own satisfaction.

Willie's Atlas bone may be old, quite possibly legally imported, but she wanted to meet this Hand of God character, just in case the bastard had been pilfering bones from Streatham Crematorium, hacking the body parts from the deceased before burning the evidence.

During Fiona's conversation with her boss to inform him of the CSI's discovery, Carver had told her to stay with the team until they had finished. This did not help her mood, so she had spoken with DS Sam Sharpe to press him for the list of names of the crematorium staff working at the time Willie had received the Atlas bone. Although Sam had baulked at first, claiming he was far too busy with work for the DI, Fiona had convinced him it would take him just minutes and she would buy him a slap up meal if he could just do this one thing for her.

About ten minutes before the crime scene boys had finished, her phone beeped and a file arrived with a couple of dozen names and addresses. There was no accompanying message other than a handful of emojis of food and beer and a smiley face.

Sam, you gem!

It took her a moment to identify the most likely contenders from the list, based on some rudimentary racial profiling. Just two names jumped out as having potential, so she sent a note straight back asking for confirmation of current address for home and workplace for each of them, along with a website link to the photo gallery for the curry house in Brixton where she and Carver had eaten just two nights before.

While Fiona waited for Sam to respond, the CSI boss rounded up his men and ushered them all outside, then sealed the premises before offering her a lift. Fiona stood alone on the pavement as they drove off, thinking she would pop into the nearest corner shop and pick up a pie or a sandwich just as Sam replied with another sparse message.

Excellent!

Thanks to her colleague she now had the details she needed. Only one of her two suspects was still alive, and his home address and his business address were the same, roughly fifteen minutes' drive from Butler's shop. Maybe half an hour if she stopped for a decent coffee and a sarnie on the way.

'Arthur Abimbola.'

Fiona spoke the name aloud, rolling the vowels and consonants on her tongue, wondering:

Are you Willie's Atlas bone supplier? Dealer in stolen body parts?

Are you the Hand of God?

Antony Harding was having a terrific morning, the best he'd had in twenty years. After the euphoric sensations caused by hormones racing through his nervous system during the breakout, then the crazy cross-country bike ride through Berkshire farmland, across golf courses, along the Kennet and Avon Canal and then the Thames towpath, he felt elated and ready for anything.

Well, almost anything.

'This van stinks of horse shit, mate!'

The rider ignored the comment as he dismounted the bike then pulled up the ramp at the back of the motorised horsebox before drawing down the shutter from within. Harding watched as the light inside the vehicle dimmed but could still see both the bike and the rider clearly. The other man's fist banged a signal on the back of the driver's cab and they started moving down the country lane several miles to the west of Windsor.

'Stop whingeing. We'll be in here for a while, pal. We have to stick to minor roads until things die down, then you're on your own. Here, the boss sent this for you.'

The rider handed a holdall to Harding then checked the bike was secured with elasticated packaging straps before settling on a ledge at the front of the horsebox.

Harding joined him and perused the contents, glad to be back in the game.

'Who are we working for?' His naturally suspicious mind kicked in as his colleague started to rattle off his instructions. The feeling he was being set up only began to dissipate as he riffled through the cash pile he'd found in an envelope at the bottom of the bag. 'Ten grand, eh? And another ninety if I do what he wants.'

'Yup.'

'Why me?'

'Don't ask me, pal. But if it was up to me, I'd be the one on the receiving end of that wedge of cash. For some reason, the boss thinks you're the right candidate for the job.'

'And who is the boss?' Harding asked again, but the man's reply was not enlightening.

'No idea. I'm a contractor. I get my instructions, I fulfil them, I get paid. You should be fucking chuffed I broke you out of that lunatic asylum, especially now you're standing here with that pile of dosh in your hand. The bike's yours too, if you can ride it. It's clean—not nicked. If not, there's a London taxi you can use. Black cabs are great for getting round London—no one notices cabbies. You'll want to ditch that tonight, when you've done the job. The driver's missing...' He smirked. 'But his disappearance won't be reported until he doesn't turn up for his dinner tonight. I assume you can drive.'

'Course I fuckin can. And I have to do both targets in the next nine or ten hours, max, or I don't get paid?'

'S'right.'

'And what if I don't want to do the job?'

'You can piss off now if you like. Keep that money and run. I'm happy to do it if you're too chickenshit.'

'I'll take the cab then.'

Harding rarely felt gratitude for anything from anyone, and today was no exception. The man would regret his insult too, but for now, Harding listened to more instructions about the tasks he had been assigned, inspected the other items in the holdall, and wondered why this anonymous boss wanted these two individuals assassinated today.

———

Doc Powers watched through the observation window as Jack introduced himself at the start of his interview with Sharon Tait.

Shazza had waived her right to legal representation, although Doc suspected that would change once Jack divulged their latest discovery. Even so, Doc's assessment of her body language and general attitude did not point to her as an accomplice to the crimes Harry Butler was now presumed to have committed. The girl had no previous form, no medical training, and according to Glen, the third person arrested in the tattoo parlour, a love of animals and all things living. Including humans.

The sneaking suspicion that Doc had felt since the outset of their investigations, that the whole scenario was being manipulated, had taken more solid form during this morning's events. Jack was not convinced, and given the latest evidence, was becoming more and more certain they had their man.

And his accomplice.

Doc only half listened as Jack completed his preliminaries with the woman, confirming Glen's statement regarding her relationship with Harry, the circumstances of their first encounter, the time they had known each other, how long they had worked the tattoo parlour together, and what her role was in the business. Everything tallied and Doc only fully tuned in properly as Jack finally moved on to Harry's dual identity and his history.

'You knew his name was not Harry Hope, Sharon. Did that not strike you as suspicious?'

'Nah. He wanted to forget his past life. The military and what went before. His parents died when he was a kid and his grandad treated him like shit. Used to beat him and lock him up for the smallest infringements of his strict house rules. He was a right bastard. His mum and dad weren't much better when they were alive either. Harry wanted nothing to do with the Butler name.'

Sharon's attitude was helpful, open, as if trying to explain, to help her man with her honesty, clearly convinced he was innocent of any wrongdoing. Her hand gestures were firm, positive, her stance open, confident. Unless she was a very accomplished liar, Doc was convinced she knew nothing about any darker side to her man.

But then again, she did speak with a forked tongue...

'So, you suspected nothing, even when he asked you to run the admin, to open the bank account in your name. Did you ever ask why he didn't change his name officially?'

'No. That shit's not important to us. He needed to change his name so he did. Simples.'

'No National Insurance number, no bank account, nothing in his name other than a lease made out to Harry Hope from a landlord who was happy as long as the rent was paid. In cash. You didn't think that was odd? That the rent you paid was double the official amount on the lease?'

'Listen. If our landlord wants to dodge some tax, that's his problem. Why is any of this important? Harry was a broken man thanks to the UK government sending him and others like him off to fight an unnecessary war. I helped put him back together. We never harmed anyone. That poor bloke on the common had nothing to do with us. The only reason we're here is 'cos we do suspension and stuff!'

'Well, that's not strictly true, Sharon. I'd like you to take a look at something.'

Jack fiddled with his tablet and selected a photograph of the hand in its transparent bag and spun the device for her to view.

'What the fuck is that?'

Shazza's genuine look of horror—eyes wide, eyebrows arched, mouth open— once again gave Doc pause for thought, and he whispered into the mic, remembering how the earpiece had amplified Jack's outburst earlier.

'Unless she's a great actor, she's shocked to see that Jack, and not shocked you found it. I'd say she's never seen it before.'

If Jack heard the comment, he made no sign, his tone dead flat as he went on. 'It's a human hand Sharon, but I think you knew that.' With a swipe on his tablet Jack pulled up a picture of the freezer, its contents spread on a blue plastic sheet, the hand clearly visible among the food items stored there. 'We found it in your freezer. Care to explain?'

The reaction was unexpected, and Doc, only able to see Jack's back from the observation window, would have given good money to see his expression.

Sharon Tait threw back her head and cackled, a piercing shriek of genuine mirth at the stupidity of the Metropolitan Police. Jack sat back and waited for her spirited response to die down.

'You really think, planting shit like that is going to work, Detective Carver? This is bollocks and you know it! What is this, some sort of weird game you're playing, thinking you can con me into saying something other than the truth? Harry's innocent! INNOCENT!'

'This is no game Sharon. Tests have confirmed the hand is human and we're searching for a DNA match with known victims and missing persons. You need to tell me what you know about this—'

'Oh fuck right off, you idiot.' Again, Doc sensed the truth as Shazza dismissed the damning evidence. 'We're vegans! We don't believe in harming any living creatures! Why the hell would we have a human hand in our freezer? Take a good look, *Detective*.' The irony she invested in that one word, the sheer disbelief at what he was suggesting, the idiocy he was demonstrating, all clear to Doc and, almost certainly, to Jack too. She tapped the screen and added, 'There's not one animal product, not even dairy foods in this freezer. You planted that hand there. Admit it. Wanker!'

Shazza sat back with her arms tightly folded against her chest, her breathing fast and angry, her neck and face tinged with blood. Doc could almost feel Jack rising to the taunt, as if the earpiece was sending furious signals back to the mic in the observation room. He waited for the inevitable explosion, but Jack's shoulders, having tensed at the insults, visibly relaxed as his words, deadly calm and controlled, hit home.

'Is that the best you can come up with? Perhaps you'd care to explain how Harry's fingerprints came to be all over this item.' Once again, that genuine look of shock passed over Shazza's face, but the worst was yet to come. It was Jack's turn to tap the screen, the crime scene photograph of the bagged hand expanding as he spread his fingers. 'Along with yours, Sharon…'

'Tell me the truth, Harry. You aren't on medications provided by a GP, are you? How are you getting the drugs? A false name won't fly with the NHS, so you must be getting them from a private source.'

Doc was trying to interview Harry again after Jack had been summarily dismissed by Shazza demanding a phone call before she would say another word. Harry was also back in clam mode after Jack had informed him of the latest damning evidence, the couple's fingermarks all over the bag containing the hand found in their freezer. Doc had yet more bad news to share with the suspect.

'They're gonna lock me up forever aren't they, Doctor Powers?' Tears were moistening the corner of Harry's eyes as he spoke, voice soft. 'I honestly have no idea how that hand got in my freezer… And yes, I get the drugs I need online.'

The 'medications' Harry had insisted the police bring with them during the raid at his house this morning had been analysed, and they told Doc a sorry tale.

'Self-medicating with MDMA bought online is not the best way to treat your PTSD, Harry. LSD won't help either.'

'Ecstasy really works, Doc! It's better than the shit the GP gave me. And I haven't had any major psychotic episodes for years.'

Many veterans were claiming the same result and research into the drug's beneficial effect had confirmed the potential of this rave favourite for treating PTSD.

'It only works when administered under supervision and accompanied by some psychiatric counselling, Harry. You could be giving yourself the wrong dosage, storing up more psychological problems, possibly even experiencing fugue states you aren't aware you're having... Why did you change your name?'

'I wanted a new me. A Harry that was full of hope. Harry Hope! I changed my name. Why is that so hard to get your brain round?'

'Officially, you're still Harry Butler—'

'Yeah, I know that. Doesn't matter. I just wanted to cut myself off from my old life completely. No trace for anyone from my past. With Shazza, I was doing great!' He swiped the tears from either side of his nose, and then used the hand to rub at this forehead. 'I don't believe I could have done any of this. And if Shazza's prints are on that bag, well, I can only say this is all bullshit! Even if I somehow did stuff, bad things like that detective says, cutting people up like that... Well Shazza would have nothing to do with it! She couldn't hurt a fly.'

'It's not just the hand, Harry. The police found your notebook computer.'

Sad eyes lifted to Doc's, confusion scrunching Harry's face, a genuine look of puzzlement.

'What notebook?'

'The one you kept at the bottom of your filing cabinet.' Another baffled look. 'Sorry Harry, the technicians have opened the files and found the photographs.'

'What are you on about now? I don't own a notebook.'

'The file containing the first two letters you sent to me.'

'I never sent you anything!'

'No? The documents are in a file on a computer discovered on your premises... And what about the message that appeared on my MacBook this morning? Who sent that?'

'What the fuck are you on about?'

'Why did you send the victim photographs to me, Harry?'

This time, Harry shrugged, his head frantically moving from side to side, as if in spasm, then he clapped his hands over his ears with his elbows on the table. The lawyer looked concerned at the state of his client, was about to object, but Doc kept on, his voice louder, demanding.

'And Harding. Tell me about him. Why did you involve him?'

There was no spark of recognition, so Doc repeated the question, wondering if Harry could hear, this time emphasising the name.

The head shaking stopped and Harry's head came up, his chin resting on his palms, elbows still propped on the table top.

'Please stop... I have no idea what you're talking about, Doctor. Honestly.'

Despite the overwhelming weight of evidence, Doc believed him. But how to convince Jack?

The horsebox swayed as it braked and came to rest on a deserted track, the driver pulling up behind the only other vehicle in the vicinity—a black taxi parked outside the entrance to a disused sewage treatment plant just south of Mitcham Common.

During the journey, Antony Harding had tried to find out more about his employer from the mercenary who had helped him escape, but to no avail. The other man had just grunted and repeated his comment that he would take over the assassinations if Harding was 'too cowardly' to do the job. He was, he bragged, ex-special forces and well versed in assassinations, not some 'broken down old ex-con' who had 'gone so soft' he couldn't even escape without assistance.

Harding ground his boot heel from side to side, feeling the 'special forces' nasal bone and cartilage crack and crumble under the pressure. Having already slammed an elbow into the younger man's temple and felled him with that one unexpected blow, he now mashed the nose into a bloody pulp as his semi-conscious victim gurgled and groaned. There was no way he was going to leave this individual—or the driver—alive to tell tales about the plans his benefactor had for further mayhem. The possibility that Harding was disposable too, once he had completed his tasks, was also at the front of his mind.

No.

Much better to finish them both, here and now.

Harding stamped on the supposed ex-SAS hero's jaw, searched the inert body for any documents or a mobile phone with some clues as to who was paying him, found nothing, so attached the silencer from the bag he had been given, touched the end of it to the man's fractured temple and pulled the trigger just as the horsebox lurched to a standstill.

Harding waited for the driver to open the rear compartment doors, then grinned as the man's jaw flopped open at the sight of his comrade lying in a pool of blood by the motorcycle, then the flinch as he focused on the gun now pointing at his forehead.

'Your mate's a bit rude. Now, tell me, who else knows about our little escapades this morning?'

'N-n-n-no one… Just… Just the client.'

'And who exactly is that?'

'I don't know. None of us—'

The bullet ripping through the man's brain curtailed his explanation, and he sagged to the ground, his head splashing in a puddle as he landed.

'Well then, you're no fuckin use either, are ya?'

Harding jumped down, scanned his surroundings to be certain there was no one else in the vicinity, hoisted the body into the back of the vehicle, did a cursory check of the driver's pockets, found nothing again, and then slammed the rear doors. He found the key in the ignition, so locked the horsebox and left the two corpses entombed within, to be discovered some days later when their odour would alert a passing dog-walker.

He strolled to the black cab parked nearby, his lungs filling with the sweet clean air of the woods and grassland around him, thinking how good it tasted after the rank stench of horse shit he'd been made to suffer for the last couple of hours.

After chucking the canvas holdall inside the cab, Harding checked the satnav his rescuer had shown him how to operate, and realised he was less than two miles from his first destination.

For five or ten seconds he scrutinised the photograph of his first target, storing it in his memory, certain he would recognise the man instantly, then considered the warnings his rescuer had relayed with his instructions.

'Dangerous! Fuck off! I just topped a bleedin SAS boy!'

He chuckled at the thought as he turned the key in the ignition. It had been so simple, the devastatingly accurate surprise blow delivered mid-conversation as the two men stood side by side.

Today he would earn enough from two more dead bodies to fuck off abroad, though he would have to sort out Powers and that cunt of a detective before he left. His employer had suggested he might like to do Powers for free, as a bonus, which seemed reasonable enough, but had to complete his paid tasks first.

Time to go to work.

He hit the throttle and bumped his way back to the main road, then turned on to the tarmac towards The Art of Africa Import Company showroom.

'Any word on Judy?'

'Great news, Doc. The body in your garage was not her. DNA does not match the hair sample you gave us. So as long as you're sure—'

'That's fantastic! And I'm absolutely certain the sample's Judy's.' The photograph of her that had appeared on his laptop made a momentary appearance in his head, but Doc managed to shunt it away as he continued reassuring himself and Jack. 'I took the hair strands from a brush she had left at my house, when she was staying with me before Josh died.'

Judy's son had lost his spleen after a car accident, then the poor lad's immune system had failed and a lung infection terminated his short life. Despite the unpleasant memory, Doc felt light-headed with joy that Judy was alive.

'So, she's still out there. I've got my team hunting for her and her face has been on the TV news too. We'll find her. Now, here's your phone. Sam says it's clean, but you were right to bring it in.' Doc could feel Jack making another mental assessment of his professional state as he asked. 'Are you okay, mate? You seemed to be giving Butler a bit of an easy ride in there.'

'I'm not convinced he's the killer, Jack.'

'Fuck me, Doc! That hand in his freezer came from one of the victims in his photo collection. A collection that included Rawlings!' The outburst made Doc pull back, as if Jack had physically struck him, and his friend's voice calmed as he realised. 'He's got medical training. And both his and his bird's fingerprints are all over that hand.'

'No, they're not, Jack. Their prints are all over the *bag*… Were there any latents on the actual hand itself?'

'Well, no—'

'So anyone could've placed that hand in a used food bag they'd both handled, then hidden it in the bottom of that freezer—for us to find.'

'Yeah, right…' Jack's ironic tone said it all. 'Sorry, I'm not convinced, Doc. The photos, the letters he sent to you in the encrypted file on his notebook. How do you explain that?'

'The break in.'

'No way! Don't even go there—'

'The girl, Sharon Tait, told your officers they had a break in at their premises over the weekend. A break in, Jack, where nothing was taken.'

'So, you're saying some devious criminal mastermind—who remains anonymous —has set up the two of them?'

'Possibly.'

'His grandad fingered him. After finding the body his grandson left for him, hanging in a bloody tree on Clapham Common!'

'Someone else must've known about Butler senior's history and hung the body there...'

'Who? Who the fuck is this mystery man behind your massive conspiracy theory? Are you thinking straight—?'

'Listen! What about the Harding link? What reason would Butler have for breaking him out of Broadmoor? He has no reason to harm me, to set my father's killer on to me. And what about this Akachi? What has this shaman got to do with Harry Butler? And why send me and Harding those photos, and the letters taunting me?'

'Well we don't know yet, but I'll have another go at Butler and Tait, see what I can sweat out of them. You said yourself, Butler won't remember everything he's done if he has a split personality.'

'Jack... It's inconceivable that Butler could undertake dozens of operations on Rawlings with sufficient proficiency to keep him alive while some other personality controlled his actions. Dissociative Personality Disorder does not work like that.'

'Look, I respect your opinion but on this I've already made enquiries, and other experts think it is possible.'

'Who?' Doc bristled, wondering if Jack's enquiries had been aimed at his own mental state rather than Butler's. Soundbite distrusting him was one thing, but Jack was his oldest friend. 'When did you ask these experts?'

'Yesterday—'

'When you suspected I was the one doing this!'

'Don't get your knickers in a knot! I have to follow up on all leads, no matter how ridiculous. You know that, so get off your high horse. And anyway, my team's working on those loose ends, and we have Butler and Tait so I'm pretty sure we'll soon have all the answers. If you still want to help, that is.'

'Of course I do!'

'Right, let's get on with nailing down our prime suspects then.'

'Boss! The Acting Super's waiting.' DC Ahmed dropped her phone to its cradle as she called to Carver across the room.

'Dammit. Doc, you have another go with Sharon Tait. Tell her the bad news about her boyfriend's drug abuse and his split personality. Get her to think he's already spilling his guts about what they've been up to, and see if you can get her to talk. I don't buy this vegan bullshit. It's a cover... Now, I need to update Soundbite, but I'll join you as soon as I can.'

The *Art of Africa Import Company* premises seemed strangely out of place situated in an old mill house on the southern edge of Mitcham Common, just a stone's throw from the golf course. The old windmill had long gone, but the two storey granary that remained was imposing, with a gravel drive and manicured gardens that reminded Fiona of the stately homes she had occasionally visited as a kid. The idea that an African importer was now doing business from a place like this seemed incongruous to her as she drove up to the building.

There's obviously a lot of money to made in African art, she decided, as she estimated that the property would be worth several million in this peaceful semi-rural setting within easy commuting distance of London.

The brass plaque at the gate had informed her she was in the right place, as did her satnav, so she hoped the lack of a vehicle parked at the front of the house was not an ominous sign. She had her fingers crossed that her suspect was here, working from his home office. She was not disappointed.

The gloss black door swung open in response to her thumb squashing the doorbell for several seconds, and a handsome gentleman she estimated to be in his mid-forties smiled down at her, welcoming, his dark chocolate eyes crinkling at the sight of her.

If Fiona was expecting someone dressed in traditional African garb, she would have been disappointed. His beautifully tailored suit and white shirt gave him an image more suited to a banker or a lawyer, as did his accent. In truth, she had no idea what to expect—the only information from Sam had been the name and address—so the man's appearance and attitude threw her. He seemed almost regal, and unsurprised at her appearance at his door, as if he'd been expecting her. Tall and broad, in great shape, with a handsome face. His voice was low, sexy, rich and seductive.

Bloody hell, woman. Get a grip!

'Good afternoon, sir.' Fiona's warrant card made a swift appearance, then slid back into her jacket pocket as she spoke. 'Detective Sergeant Fielding. I'm hoping you can help me. Would you be Arthur Abimbola?'

'Detective? Well, that's a surprise. Please come on in. I was in the middle of a phone call when the doorbell interrupted me. We don't get many visitors except by appointment. Please give me a moment to finish the call. Make yourself at home in the showroom to the left.'

Before she could speak again, the man turned and disappeared out of sight into a room to the right, and resumed his conversation in a language she did not recognise, the words muffled through the closed door. Having been invited in, Fiona wandered through to the showroom, though it reminded her of a museum rather than a business run from someone's home.

The room extended the full length of the building, maybe twelve metres, and was about half that wide, the entire space packed with African artefacts. The walls were decorated with various weapons from the dark continent, including spears, blowpipes, wicked looking wooden clubs, and shields made from zebra hide. There were mounted animal heads and numerous traditional hardwood carvings too and dozens of glass cases were dotted around the place. Some were on pedestals containing ornate jewellery, others with intricately designed masks, both beautiful and disturbing. One long display case held decorative bone necklaces, lip and ear plates she guessed were made from clay before being painted with vivid colours.

One illuminated display cabinet in the corner seemed out of place to Fiona. A strange skull, lit up with an eerie yellow-green tint, seemed to grin at her, the contrast of light and shadow giving the illusion of movement as she walked around it. The hairs on her forearms were at attention, the sight disturbing her in a similar fashion to her discovery of the ears secreted beneath Gerald Butler's bedroom floor-boards, although this seemed barely human, the weird conical shape perhaps the result of a disease.

Fiona, despite being fascinated by the vast collection, began to wonder if she was wasting her time as she bent at the waist to get a better view of the distorted head.

'Sorry about that, Detective. All done. I see you like my elongated head display. A most unusual artefact.'

'Is it real?' Fiona had never seen anything like it.

'Of course.'

'What caused it? Encephalitis?'

'No, not disease. It's traditional in certain cultures. The baby's head is kept bound during the first six months or so, with wooden braces held in place to create the desired shape. Young skulls are soft and pliable, relatively easy to mould as they grow. This technique has been practised for millennia and examples can be found across the continents. The one you find so fascinating is from Egypt and is over two thousand years old.'

'But why do this? Surely the baby must suffer.'

'Ideas of beauty change over time, and with location too. Humans have always had the desire to modify themselves, to make their appearance special. You pluck your eyebrows, no doubt shave your legs, armpits and so on. Modern society dictates you do this, an aesthetic imperative. Your ancestors and mine would probably have decorated their skin with carefully carved, patterned scarring. Pain in the pursuit of beauty is nothing new. Had we been born in Chad a century ago, our heads might look like this too.'

Fiona straightened, mildly disgusted by her own morbid curiosity as she considered the provenance of this collector's item, once a warm-blooded person's head, now reduced to a conversation piece for a buyer with more money than sense.

'I guess a client would pay a lot for something like this, Mr Abimbola… You are Arthur Abimbola, correct?'

'So sorry, Detective. Yes, I thought I'd made that clear when I invited you in. This item is not for sale. It's priceless and very precious to me personally. Let's sit, and you can tell me why you are here.' He waved an imperial hand towards the room he had just appeared from and she followed him as he led the way.

A grey leather suite with enormous cushions almost absorbed Fiona entirely as she sat, then she pulled herself forward to better view the man. His eyes twinkled at her, amused, not at all threatened by her presence. In this light she could see his tight curled hair was greying well beyond the temples, so perhaps her earlier estimate of his age might be wide of the mark.

Maybe mid-fifties?

Like a well matured Idris Elba…

'You used to work at Streatham Crematorium. Correct?'

'Well, yes, but that's ancient history, Detective. I left there about seventeen or eighteen years ago. I doubt I can help you with anything relating to their current operations.'

Abimbola's air of amusement started to rankle, although Fiona knew she was on something of a fishing expedition so shouldn't have been surprised. A more direct approach might shake him, she decided.

'You also sold human remains at the time.' Still no reaction, just that confident smile, a man secure in the knowledge he had done nothing illegal. 'An Atlas bone.'

'Ah! In all my years in this business I have sold just three. While working at Streatham my import business was in its infancy, a part time hobby that later grew into what you now see here. I did indeed sell one such item all those years ago. The Atlas vertebrae is a rare artefact, so I remember that sale well despite the intervening years.' Then he chuckled, his head thrown back as he realised what was on her mind. 'You think I stole the bone from a body prior to cremation. Oh dear, do forgive me for finding that rather amusing! It was imported, Detective.' He continued laughing at her, prompting a stony faced request in response.

'You can prove that, can you, Mr Abimbola?'

'Of course.' The outburst of humour had subsided at her serious tone, but his mouth twitched with amusement as he spoke. 'I'm sure I still have the paperwork relating to its provenance. Somewhere.'

If Abimbola had records confirming the purchase and import of the bone then she'd definitely had a wasted journey. Fiona sighed inwardly at the prospect.

'May I see? I know it's a long time ago, but even so—'

'No problem. In my business, record keeping is essential. I like to ensure each item I purchase and then sell is within moral and legal bounds. I have documentation for every sale I have ever made. Please give me a moment, my archives are in the back room.' He stood with a lithe athlete's grace, as he added, 'I shouldn't be long, Detective.'

'One more thing.' Abimbola turned at the door as Fiona threw a question that should've occurred to her sooner. 'Are you a shaman?'

'A shaman? Hahaha!' He spread his arms, palms open and laughed at her question as he answered. 'Do I look like a witchdoctor to you?'

It certainly seemed a ridiculous accusation for this clearly wealthy, urbane gentleman, living in a magnificent country house, running a legitimate business importing items from Africa and beyond.

'My informant tells me you called yourself *the Hand of God*. Is that true?'

Another sprinkling of laughter peppered his words as he replied. 'I'm a businessman. Of course, I have, on occasion, suggested to some of my more feeble-minded clients that the items I sell possess mystical powers. In my early years in this business many of my sales were to, how shall we say, rather backward tribespeople, making their homes here in an unfamiliar country. Some called me *God's Hand*, others *the Hand of God*, and of course, I allowed the myths to spread. Think of it as theatre if you must, but no, I am not invested with magical powers.'

With that, he disappeared, leaving Fiona alone in the study. Despite her conclusion that this was a wasted journey, she decided to have a sniff around anyway. A large desk dominated the room, though its surface was clear of any papers, just a blotter, some ornaments and a telephone. The drawers were locked, so Fiona focused instead on the wall behind the chair.

Dozens of framed documents were displayed, and even at first glance, Fiona realised they were all from satisfied clients, suppliers and dealers who had sent letters of commendation to the company. It was impressive, but as she turned away to find something more interesting, one word jumped out at her just as her eyes finished scanning the pages.

In that moment, Fiona felt a surge of panic, finally realising she may have unwittingly put herself in harm's way. Doc's warning from just two nights before, not to tackle any suspects alone, but always with a colleague, had seemed irrelevant to her enquiries into the Atlas bone, especially with Harry Butler in custody. Now, she fumbled with her mobile phone, wanted to call for back up and get herself out of here without Abimbola suspecting she had made the connection.

She was too late.

'Where the hell's Fifi, Sam? I thought she'd be back by now.'

Jack had returned from briefing Soundbite Dawson on the day's results, including the latest damning evidence, and was on a high as a result. They had spoken after Doc's latest interview with Sharon Tait, but his old friend had been unable to work his magic on the suspect and get her to confess. That would've been the final nail in their coffin, Jack thought, but Doc was increasingly adamant the whole gamut of evidence they were compiling was some elaborate frame up.

Harry Butler was now their major suspect for the Diana Davies murder too. Traces of his DNA were found in the semen taken from her mutilated corpse, discovered in a ditch over ten years before, and although not conclusive, the human hand hidden in the freezer was plenty damning enough. The hand belonged to the female victim identified by Harding, Selena Scott, the planning officer who had gone missing seven years ago.

Doc was in the kitchen making himself a coffee, having given up with Sharon Tait. Apparently, the freaky girl had no further comment since Doc had shared with her their most recent discovery… Her failed career as a nurse, a fact she had chosen not to divulge.

It all fitted. They just had to get a confession, or find more evidence relating to the other crimes.

Jack wondered if Doc's mental state had led him to ignore what was obvious, the evidence right in front of them. Perhaps his concerns over Judy were warping his professional viewpoint, and his theory about Butler being framed was a result.

But Jack knew better than to ignore Doc's suspicions, so was now focused on another lead—a folder that had been left on his desk this morning, one that contained a newly compiled computer generated photo-montage of Akachi. The man who Daniel Ngwene, the corrupt Broadmoor guard, claimed had used muti magic and threats of imminent death to coerce him into smuggling sealed envelopes to and from Harding. Although Jack had not admitted it to Doc, this was the piece of the puzzle the detective found most baffling, but he knew it was only a matter of time before Harry Butler's links to the shaman were revealed.

In fact, Jack was mightily pleased with himself, and with Fiona who also deserved a pat on the back.

But where is she?

He aimed the question at Sam Sharpe, the DS who always seemed to know what she was up to.

'She was following up on that Atlas bone lead she got from that bloke she nicked with Lanny yesterday. Fi's been a bit obsessed since finding those ears in Butler's gaff. It must've been over an hour ago when I texted her the address she wanted. She said she'd head to his place in Mitcham this afternoon.'

'What the bloody hell for? Get her here now, Sam.'

'I can't, sir. Her phone's dead and her car radio's not responding.'

Sulking?

But Jack knew DS Fiona Fielding better than that. No matter how pissed off she was with him for being left to babysit the CSI team, he knew she would never knowingly put herself out of comms reach while on duty.

'Mobile battery's dead, maybe...' That was wrong, and Jack realised as he said it. She had charged it overnight, and Jack had seen her unplug the device earlier, not long after they arrived in preparation for the dawn raid on the tattoo parlour. 'So she went off to meet this bloke? Where is this place, then?'

Despite Jack's good humour at their results today, his gut was telling him there was something badly amiss. He listened as Sam explained, his unease spiralling. Jack's fingers, working independently of his conscious mind, opened the folder, his eyes drawn to the image of the alleged shaman. Every molecule in his body was telling him there was something desperately wrong, that this Akachi was somehow a threat, that the man had some link to what Fiona was doing right now.

It wasn't magic that was making him feel this way, but years of experience.

'She went alone? For fuck's sake, Sarge!'

'Sorry, Boss. She said it was no big deal, that the Hand of God was unrelated to this case. Just something she had to do. A hunch—'

'Get me everything you have on this Hand of God bloke. Now, Sam!'

It was like an itch in his brain, one he had to scratch.

And who the fuck is this guy, Akachi?

He stared at Daniel Ngwene's photo-montage of the shaman, the composite image shaking as his hands trembled.

Finding Fifi was now at the top of DI Jack Carver's agenda.

Fiona, mobile phone in hand, turned as Abimbola re-entered the room, and saw his eyes registering the shock on her face, her fear, just for a moment. He stiffened, then recovered, back to his jovial, superior self.

'Oh dear, Detective. Your mobile phone won't work in here. I'm afraid this old building is rather like a Faraday cage, and signals neither enter nor leave. By all means, feel free to use my desk telephone. Or perhaps you would prefer to use your car radio.' He held out an envelope for her, his feet stationary, waiting by the doorway. 'I have the paperwork you requested.'

The desk was between them, and Fiona was not sure what to do. She could bluff, pretend she had not made her most recent discovery and head for the car, then call the cavalry. Or she could front it with him now, use the landline to call for help, and fend him off with her martial arts skills while waiting for backup to arrive. Maybe she could do enough damage to him, disable him, before he had a chance to overpower her, but he was a towering presence, and she had no idea if he too had some fighting skills.

With Doc's warning ringing in her brain, discretion seemed the least risky course of action.

'Thank you, Mr Abimbola. If I may take that receipt, I'll be getting on my way. I hadn't realised the time.'

'Of course.'

The door was open, all she had to do was walk through it, remain calm and collected, just get to her car and make that call. The envelope felt hot to her touch as she took it from him, then she slipped past into the hall, holding her breath subconsciously, her eyes on him at all times, her body tense and ready to repel an attack.

The smile was back in place, but it seemed supercilious to her now, not in the least charming. Abimbola was calm, unhurried, unperturbed. Fiona let out her breath as she reached for the front door latch.

Almost outside now.

Her fingers, slick with nervous sweat, slipped against the metal lock as she scrabbled to open the door, her attention still on the man she now considered a major threat.

Finally, the door swung open and a rush of air gave her a taste of freedom, the safety of the car just a dozen steps away. Without relaxing her guard she scrunched her way across the gravel, the keys in her hand, the lights flashing as she pressed the remote.

Nearly there.

Abimbola let the front door close behind him as he stood just outside, fiddling with an oversized cigar. Or, at least, that's what Fiona thought it was. He waved a friendly hand at her, started to stroll towards her car, as if seeing her off, then placed the cigar in his mouth.

The pinprick in her breast almost went unnoticed as she tugged the car door open, her relief palpable. The man's entire presence no longer felt benign, but sinister as he closed in on her.

Fiona tried to enter the cockpit, to slide herself into the relative safety it offered, desperate to reach her pepper spray, the small canister lying in the coin tray, almost within her grasp. But she could not move, as if her limbs were suddenly cast in concrete, yet she felt the ground turn to sponge beneath her feet and the world seemed to sway, then tilt wildly before she fell to the gravel, still conscious, fully aware of her predicament.

'Blow dart, Detective. Simple, but effective. Sorry, I had to. You clearly don't play poker... From the look on your face you made a significant discovery in my study, and I can only conclude that your enquiries into my nickname might, let us say, embarrass me, or worse.' The car door slammed and he grabbed the remote from her fingers a moment before she heard the familiar clunk of the locks engaging. Abimbola's face loomed as he scooped her into his arms, then tossed her over his shoulder and hauled her round to the side of the house, chatting to her as he did so. 'You see, Arthur is my official name. My slave name.' The words were full of disgust as he added, 'My *Christian* name.'

Fiona tried to speak, but her mouth was frozen, her tongue swollen and her throat constricted, as if a great wedge of meat had lodged there. Side effects from the drug administered by his dart, no doubt, combined with the terror she now felt at her helpless situation. Not that anything she could say would make any difference anyway.

Half her brain was desperately wondering what was going to happen to her, the other half analysing what Carver had told them during the team briefing last night about the shaman who had manipulated Daniel Ngwene, the Broadmoor guard.

How the witchdoctor had threatened to kill both him and his mother to convince Daniel to risk his job by smuggling illicit mail to Harding.

A shaman named Akachi...

'My mother, a Kamba from the land you would call Kenya, chose to name me after my father. I was born two weeks after the British murdered him in one of their concentration camps.'

Fiona's mind was whirling, the man's involvement now beyond doubt.

But how is he involved?

Was he The Surgeon? The mastermind behind the Rawlings mutilation? Working with Harry Butler, his accomplice? Had she unwittingly bumbled into a fearsome spider's web thanks to her determination to follow up on the Atlas bone?

Her stomach churned and she felt the urge to vomit down the back of his jacket and on to his legs as Abimbola started down some steps to a cellar, carrying her like a fireman rescuing her from a flaming building, but her mouth remained frozen.

With Fiona over his shoulder, he had both hands free to unlock the heavy door before taking her inside. The cool air below ground chilled her, her clothes now saturated with sweat, and she felt the sensation despite the paralysis. In fact, her body seemed hypersensitive with the hard muscle and bone of his shoulder digging into her belly, bruising her. Even the slight friction from her blouse was uncomfortable, rasping at the tender skin battered by Willie Mutuku's rugby tackle. Abimbola's voice rumbled and vibrated into her as he spoke.

'You see, my true given name, my tribal name, is Akachi, an Igbo word from my father's ancestors meaning God's Hand. A few of my closest African friends and clients prefer to use that rather than Arthur. Others use the western version or a variation of it—including the one you mentioned. Personally? I think it's a very fitting name for the work I do.'

Akachi was the forename Fiona had recognised, spotted among the salutations on the letters displayed behind his desk.

Christ, he's going to chop me up and kill me!

Fear of a kind she had never felt, a burning embrace that consumed her, flaring in her soul, blinded her, scrambling any further rational thought. Warm urine soaked her pants, and her shame at her body's feeble reaction dragged her back from the brink. The panic subsided as she tried to focus on her surroundings again, to see if she could identify some possible means of escape, however remote a prospect it seemed in her powerless state.

The cellar was brightly lit and kitted out like a hospital or surgical clinic. Abimbola dumped Fiona on the steel operating table in the centre of the room and began fiddling with some medical implements on a trolley to the side. Panic surged again, smothering her, strangling the thoughts of escape, her imagination thrusting hideous images of the man's mutilated victims into her consciousness, ratcheting up her terror ever more.

Her own voice erupted inside her head, chiding, as if some highly disciplined alter ego within her consciousness was trying to regain control of her faculties.

I'm a policeman. He will not hurt me... He cannot!

Surely he knew that other coppers would be banging on his door if she failed to return. These thoughts broke through, finally calming her as she tried to console herself, thinking he would probably leave her, tied up here, as he made his escape.

It was a forlorn hope and she knew it.

Abimbola turned to her, a syringe in his hand and a grin on his face that brought to Fiona's mind the hideous death mask collection in the showroom above.

'Now, I have some questions for you that you must answer. After I inject you with this cocktail of drugs you'll be able to speak, but your limbs will remain immobile. Unfortunately for you, Detective, I find the judicious administration of pain a necessary adjunct to receiving an honest response. The dart I applied contains a drug designed to elevate such sensations, heightening the signals from your nerves while paralysing your major muscle groups. Now this concoction,' he squeezed a jet of fluid from the syringe to expel any air, 'will also diminish the chances of you dying from shock.'

Oh God! Oh God! Oh God! Nooooo!

He plunged the needle into her neck and murmured, 'Let us begin.'

'What's up, Jack? You look really pale? Here, drink this.'

Doc had emerged from the kitchen and now carried two mugs as he arrived at Jack's desk. The aroma of freshly brewed coffee was already perking him up, although he felt a twinge of guilt for having raided Fiona's secret stash before making the cafetière for them both.

Jack ignored the outstretched hand so Doc placed the cup on the desk and craned his neck to see what the detective was staring at. A composite photograph of the man Daniel had called Akachi.

'I have a bad feeling about this, Doc. DS Fielding has gone AWOL, and your outburst earlier set me thinking about this shaman bloke. What is his involvement? And who else is there?'

'Fiona's missing?'

'Sort of. She's off on a lone wolf hunt for some bloke called *the Hand of God*.'

'Seriously, Jack? I meant to tell you, but with all the things that have happened this morning, it slipped my mind. Akachi. I Googled it. It's an African name meaning *God's Hand*—'

'Oh Christ, Doc! Why the fuck didn't you tell me?'

'I had no idea it was so important until now.'

Jack was already moving fast. He pulled open his desk drawer and grabbed his gun, then yelled across the room as he headed for the door. 'Sam! Give me that bloody address you sent Fifi. And Ahmed!' The DC looked up from her screen, her mouth open ready to respond, but Jack cut her off as he headed for the lift. 'I'm gonna jump in my motor but see if there's a chopper available to take me to Mitcham, and get the local nick to send a car to the location. Right now!'

Jack's face was as dark as a storm cloud as he punched the lift call button, then stared at the level indicator as if willing the thing to hurry down to him.

'I'm coming with you.'

'Sod off, Doc!' This was a first, and Doc would have taken offence in other circumstances, but Jack just carried on with his stream of rapid-fire words. 'You wait here. I can't be looking out for you too. With Harding on the loose, you're better off in this building than anywhere else.'

The doors pinged open and Doc followed Jack inside, ignoring the scowl, and hit the button for the basement car park. Although Fiona's safety was of immediate concern, Doc had other considerations too.

Like Judy Finch.

'Listen, Jack. We need to know the extent of this Akachi's involvement. I want to interrogate him as soon as possible. I'm coming.'

Doc's words were spoken defiantly, his tone broaching no disagreement. Jack glared at him for a second then nodded.

'If he's harmed Fifi…'

'We need him alive, Jack.'

Doc had seen his friend like this on only a few occasions, and knew he had to keep Jack from overreacting. Interrogating the suspect was now only of secondary concern to the detective.

'Just don't get in the way if I need to put him down, Doc.'

Antony Harding parked the cab, grabbed the twenty-five litre petrol can from the luggage compartment with one hand, his holdall with the other, and walked unseen through the woods and heathland until he reached the waist-high perimeter wall enclosing the old mill house near the centre of Mitcham Common. He used the binoculars he had found in his holdall thinking he would scope out the building before he made his approach, and started to skirt the whole site to decide how best to achieve his aim.

The instructions he had been given confirmed the man would be alone but a car arrived almost at the same moment as the escaped convict. A diminutive dark-skinned girl in a trouser suit strode up to the main entrance to the building as Harding was starting his recce.

'Bugger!'

He would wait and see if she left, but if not, he might have to kill them both, and remove her body from the scene of the supposed suicide he was about arrange. Confronting a twosome was a complication he could do without, and her presence would make the whole scenario more difficult, his task more dangerous.

After about fifteen minutes his patience deserted him and he decided to head inside. The thought was about to be converted into action just as the woman emerged from the building, so he resumed his concealed position in the undergrowth behind the wall, his binoculars focused on the man in the doorway.

He was big, maybe six foot six or more, and his stature and skin colour reminded Harding of Winston Diamond, the head of security back at Broadmoor. That thought dragged a quiet chuckle from Harding's throat as he recalled the state of the place after this morning's events.

Maybe Winston'll lose his job. Serves the bastard right!

His reverie was punctured by what happened next.

The woman slumped to the ground immediately after opening her car door, and Harding was not sure what had caused her to faint. He continued to observe, fascinated as the man went to the car and slammed the door before locking it rather than aiding the stricken woman.

Well ,this is interesting…

Harding got a better look at him, recognising the face from the photograph in his holdall, confirming his target. The man was strong, demonstrably so as he lifted the woman like a giant soft toy, a raggedy doll, tossed her over his shoulder in an effortless sweeping motion, then carried her round to the back of the building. Harding took great care not to expose his presence as he followed the pair, crouching while keeping watch.

The man went down to a cellar, accessed through steps and a door at the rear of the property, opposite a double garage with shutters drawn. The careless way he carried the woman suggested to Harding that his intentions were not good.

Well, well. So she didn't just faint. She was drugged! What have we here then? Rape?

Harding was old school, with the warped moral compass of a London gangster who had no problem with torture and deadly violence, but was unforgiving of rapists and paedophiles. Nonces, he called them, but after so long inside, well, he would have willingly reassessed his standards. She wasn't unattractive, if a bit short and dumpy...

He lifted the binoculars for a better look and saw the woman's eyes were wide, terror readily apparent as she drooled over the back of the man's trouser legs, her arms flopping, her cheek bouncing against his back as he walked.

Harding fiddled with his gun, feeling potent with lethal intent as he handled the weapon, while simultaneously disappointingly impotent. He could kill without a moment's thought, but the medications he had been subjected to and his years of incarceration had softened the one thing he would need to partake in sex, forced or otherwise.

If I can't shag the dirty bitch, then why the hell should he?

The sickening knowledge that he could not join in the fun created a bubble of fury that expanded through his chest, brought him to his feet and had him marching across the gravel towards the cellar steps just as he heard a vehicle swing into the forecourt.

Damn! So much for the target being alone.

He sprinted back to the perimeter and leapt over the wall just in time to hear the car scrunch to a halt.

Jack drove furiously, swearing at the many drivers who failed to respond with sufficient haste to his blue lights, wailing siren and flashing headlamps. The nearside wheels mounted London pavements several times as he weaved his precious BMW through city traffic.

Doc's left hand threatened to pull the grab handle off the roof as they swerved around another corner before finally hitting the A23 and blasting their way along Brixton Hill.

'Jack! Watch out!' A cyclist made the mistake of ignoring a red light just as Jack carved his way through the nearside, using the bus lane to pass the other vehicles. 'If we're to help Fiona we need to get there in one piece.'

Jack ignored the slight, the criticism of his driving as the bicycle struck the nearside wing with a glancing blow, shock and then fear on the rider's face as he scraped the paintwork before slithering into the gutter, his helmet bouncing as he came to rest. With one eye on the rear view mirror and only one on the traffic in front, Jack managed to manoeuvre round another idiot pedalling with no thought for other road users. He noted, with some relief, the first idiot was getting to his feet while shaking his fist at the disappearing police vehicle.

'Stupid bastards.' His phone chirped and he pressed the *answer call* button on his steering wheel. 'Tell me some good news, Sam.'

'Sorry, sir. No choppers are available… And I think we might be overreacting, anyway.' Jack could hear the doubt in the sergeant's tone, waited for him to explain. 'I've been on to the Mitcham mob about this Abimbola bloke. He's a real friend of the local bobbies, big in charitable works, raised loads for the Police Benevolent Society, organises fund-raisers and the like.'

'A real pillar of the community then. Didn't Doc say we were looking for one of them?' Jack's tone was sharper than he intended, but he got a nod from Doc, so carried on with his high speed drive while asking Sam, 'Have they sent a patrol car or not?'

'Uh. Yes, there was one nearby when I called. They've been to the Abimbola place and left already.'

'What?'

'They reckon the building was deserted, locked up with no sign of his car. Only Fiona's, sir. They were pretty dismissive… Apparently this Abimbola's a real ladies man, and they reckon he must've taken her to lunch. No sign of his motor. No sign of him or her. And his mobile phone's off. That's not unusual either they said, especially when he's out with some bird.'

Some bird?

'DS Fielding is not some bird! She's a bloody excellent detective, she's on duty and there is no effin way she would bugger off for lunch with someone she suspects may be involved in a crime.'

'She wasn't too sure about that either, sir. She was working on a hunch she thought wasn't connected to our main investigation.'

Jack would have some choice words for his team about solo operations when he got back, but this was not the time for bollocking anyone, least of all Sam.

'You must have a driving licence photo of this Abimbola bloke in the system. Get Ngwene in asap to confirm whether he's the same guy, the one he knows as Akachi.'

'We're on it, sir, but he was suspended so he isn't at work today and he left here after doing the photomontage this morn—'

'Just find him!'

Jack cut Sam off with a thump on the *end call* button, then changed gear rapidly, spinning the wheels as he turned off the trunk road to follow a signpost indicating two miles to Mitcham Common.

The patrol car stopped at the front of the building and the two occupants, uniformed bobbies, clambered out, then sauntered to the door. Harding could see there was no urgency, no sense that there was danger in the vicinity, so relaxed as he monitored their movements.

They got no answer from ringing the bell so circled round to the back of the building, checked the garage was locked, but could do no more to determine whether the cars housed inside were there as the building was windowless. They tried the main house, first the back patio, then the cellar door.

All locked.

So matey boy's playing possum while the pigs snuffle round his gaff.

Generally incurious unless things impacted upon him personally, Harding now wondered what this character had done to deserve being on a professional hit list and why the police were interested in him too.

Maybe the nonce raped the wrong bird?

It didn't much matter, the target would be dead as soon as the pigs were done with their nosing. Harding focused his attention back on them.

One of the two officers used his radio to inform his colleagues that they had checked out the building, that nothing was out of the ordinary and that 'the dirty dog' was probably 'off somewhere, hoping to get his leg over' before ending the call.

The sound of their receding footsteps was followed by the patrol car firing up then creeping out of the drive.

Seconds later, Harding sprinted across the gravel, bounded down the steps and inspected the door to determine how best to enter. Having observed the man carry the woman to the back of the property he guessed there was no internal access to the cellar, so he would have to use this entrance, but the metal door confronting him was solid, probably reinforced.

Fortunately, his holdall contained the very thing required for a rapid forced entry.

The needle pierced Fiona's carotid artery and she felt her world tumble and spin as these latest drugs flooded her brain. Abimbola's face hovered over hers, in focus then blurred, rotating and then leaping back to where it started, again and again.

Her belly was wrenching in spasms and she felt her bowels squirting into her pants, fouling her clothes, the nauseating stink assaulting her nostrils, her throat automatically gagging in response.

'Not an unusual side effect, Sergeant.' The man's head disappeared for a couple of seconds, then returned with a surgical mask covering the lower half of his face. 'That's better. Camphor and eucalyptus helps with the smell.' After neatly folding his suit jacket, he rolled his sleeves to the elbow, slipped off his tie, undid his collar button and pulled on some surgical gloves.

Fiona began to focus again, the world no longer topsy-turvy, her mind crystallising, though she was already in severe pain. She tried to take an audit of how her body was responding to the chemicals in her bloodstream, determined to keep the panic from blotting out her thought processes again. This new found clarity, she thought, was possibly assisted by the concoction Abimbola had just administered.

She could feel her ribs against the steel table, as if a great weight was crushing her, driving her into the unyielding metal slab, squashing soft tissue, bruising bone. The backs of her legs and buttocks were similarly distressed and she sensed all her millions of nerve endings, as if her consciousness had only just become aware of the multitude of sensors now feeding her fears. She had little control over her muscles, could barely twitch her toes or fingers, could not rotate her head, but her nostrils flared and her eyes were moving. Even her mouth felt better, her tongue had shrunk back to normal size and was moist as she swallowed. Her heart had been racing before the syringe had emptied its contents into her, but now it pounded steadily, though faster than normal.

Should she speak? Perhaps if she pretended not to be able to, it might delay his plans to hurt her. Why would he torture her for information if she could not respond? Could she fake a reaction to the chemicals, winning some precious minutes of life in the hope someone would come to her aid?

It was a distant prospect, but her natural optimism kept her buoyed. Even in these appalling circumstances Fiona Fielding would not give up.

Decision made, she rolled her eyes back into her head and managed to dribble some spittle from her lips as Abimbola leaned in, scalpel in hand.

'Nice try, Detective. But I'm afraid your acting skills fall rather short of Oscar standards.'

Oh shit!

Just then, an alarm sounded, a beeping that warned her tormentor of an intruder. Abimbola disappeared from view and she heard him cursing, then he wheeled a video screen into her field of vision.

'It seems your uniformed friends are looking for you. Their car triggered a sensor at the entrance to my driveway. Let's watch what happens. Perhaps you'll give up your pretence of being allergic to the drugs.'

Fiona stared at the screen, her mind trying to send psychic signals to the two coppers strolling round the exterior of the house. Hidden CCTV cameras on each corner of the building were transmitting the images now displayed on the four quadrants of the large LED screen Abimbola had swivelled into view.

He laughed playfully as he asked her, 'Are you able to scream, Detective? Or are you still planning to convince me you are mute or that you have a vow of silence? Like a nun. We'll soon break that.'

Fiona gagged and pretended to try to shout, but nothing coherent left her lips as she waited until one of the uniforms descended to the cellar door. Then she let rip.

'HE-ELP! HELP ME! I'M IN HERE!'

The bobby at the door's grinning face and chatty attitude remained undisturbed by her shouts, the reality on the screen denying her the relief of a suitable response. As she yelled again and again, her words blurring into a mess of screams, pleas and whimpers, Fiona's optimism and self-discipline finally abandoned her.

Abimbola was back, his eyes triumphant, peering down at hers, his head partially blocking the view on the screen as the policemen got back in their car and left her to her fate.

'We are totally soundproofed so that little exercise did nothing more than demonstrate your perfectly adequate powers of speech. Now, where were we?'

Harding moulded the plastic explosive into a conical shape round the door lock. While he did so, he tried to remember the short briefing SAS boy had given him about how to use the stuff, warning him that it was more powerful than anything he would have used a few decades before.

Unfortunately, Harding could not recall exactly what he had said… How much it would take to blow a door open, how much to blow it right off its hinges. All he knew was that the full batch was enough to knock down an entire house if positioned correctly.

The plan had been to demolish his second target's home, with the bastard inside, but Harding had other ideas of his own about that little job. Meanwhile, the obstacle he needed to overcome right now was like a prison cell door, possibly even heavier, so, to be sure it would be blasted open he used a third of the amount he had been given.

That should sort it.

It wasn't that important, as long as he could get inside, so he armed the electronic fuse by rotating the end exactly as he had been shown, plugged the cigarette-sized charge into the rubbery compound, scampered up the steps and jogged to the side of the house, taking shelter there in case he had miscalculated.

If he had been a religious man, he would have said a few words to his maker, but he was not, so, instead, took a deep breath and pressed the red button on the remote control.

———

The scalding touch of a scalpel lacerating the back of her wrist left Fiona breathless, as if the surgical instrument had been attached to electric terminals before being applied to her body. Agonised beyond words, her breath panting, sweat trickling from every pore as the blade seared her flesh, she lay there, powerless to resist.

The alien object invading her body, slicing into her, finally ripped away her last remaining shred of resistance. The animal howl of anguish, a sound like a demented foghorn, shattered any coherent thought she had at the precise moment the figure of a man appeared on the screen behind her tormentor's head, unnoticed by either of them.

'Yes. The sensations you feel are rather enhanced, so I'll do a deal with you. Tell me everything you know and I'll spare you a prolonged death.' Abimbola held the bloody scalpel for her to view, the blade weaving in the air before her eyes, like a snake about to strike. 'But if I think you are holding back, keeping secrets from me, I will dance the pain through your nerve pathways until you cry out for the release of death. And then I will dance some more.'

Fiona had to use all her willpower to focus on his words, and tried to nod her head to show she understood, but her neck was still paralysed. Her rapid, shallow breaths were making her light-headed, so she tried to control her chest muscles as she grunted a reply.

'Any-anything. Tell… You…'

The words trickled out just as she saw it.

The CCTV cameras had to be playing tricks on her. The man who had escaped from Broadmoor early this morning, a convict whose image she had become familiar with over the last few days, was now standing at the cellar door where a policeman had been just a few moments before.

It can't be true. I'm imagining things… The drugs!

She let her eyelids droop then reopened them.

Harding was still there.

'Look at me!' She did as he bid. 'A word of warning, Detective. The drugs you have swimming through your veins encourage a degree of honesty, so why resist? Do we have an understanding? Complete disclosure on your part is essential.'

'Uh-huh.' She let her eyes wander, left and right so as not to alert Abimbola to what was happening on the screen behind his head. The pain had receded somewhat, though the after effects were still brutally alive, grinding into her senses. By channelling these sensations she tried to remain fully aware of everything around her.

What is Harding doing? Why is he here?

Abimbola was oblivious as Harding ran up the steps and loitered round the corner of the house, still in full view of the cameras.

Nooo! Come back! Don't leave me!

Even a crazed killer like Harding was welcome in her current desperate state.

'Sensible decision, Detective. Now that I have your attention, I need to know why you came here, to determine how urgent my departure will have to be. I was planning to leave the country for good next month anyway, but now I'm wondering if my departure will have to be sooner. Was it really because of an artefact I sold, the Atlas bone from so many years ago? Or is there something more?'

'Only… bone.' The words stuck in her throat but she managed to squeeze the lie out through her terror.

'Oh dear. I thought we had an understanding. Let me remove your left hand and then we'll talk again.'

'No! No—puh-lease…' Fiona could feel a plastic tie, similar to the cuffs she used, being tightened around her arm above her wrist joint. It was excruciating, just the unearthly pressure, but the reason he had applied it came to her just as he informed her.

'Unfortunately my surgical guru is at work today so I'll have to operate on you by myself. He's taught me a great deal over the years, so don't worry, you're in capable hands.' A deep chuckle followed as his eyes crinkled with dark humour. 'Even so, I'll have to use this makeshift but effective tourniquet. It'll prevent the arteries in your lower arm from bleeding out before we finish our little chat.'

'Stop! I—'

The scalpel carved into her wrist, deeper this time to separate sinew from the joint, eliciting another demented bellow. The noise filled the chamber and vibrated into her own ears, magnified as it echoed off the walls, then a massive blast further overwhelmed her senses.

Fiona's last conscious memory was the sight of Abimbola being launched across the room in a shower of debris a fraction of a second before her world blossomed with bright light and then smothered her, suffocating her in darkness.

'Fuck me!'

Harding chuckled as he reappeared at the rear of the building and observed the devastated doorway, then hesitated, wondering whether to enter. Perhaps he had damaged the structure and would be risking his life by heading into the cellar. The target was probably dead anyway.

Nah, it'll be alright.

The remaining funds would only be paid to him if he confirmed the kill by sending a photograph using the smartphone he'd been given. SAS boy had warned Harding he must also follow all the instructions if he wanted to be paid, though making this look like suicide might be a bit of a problem. And he still had to access the computer his employer had indicated was in the man's office. Although the building was pretty remote, that explosion might bring unwanted attention, especially after those coppers had been lurking only minutes before.

The petrol canister was behind the perimeter wall where Harding had left it, so having retrieved it and another fuse from his holdall, he trotted back to the cellar and stepped inside, his gun leading the way.

The blast had shattered the door, the frame and much of the surrounding brick and stonework, and sent a shower of steel and rubble into a room. The place reminded Harding of a war torn hospital, but there was no time to loiter, he had to get the job done and be away. He ignored the woman spreadeagled on the steel table, covered in debris with a screen above her hanging on its cables, though he did note the video feed and the view of the property's exterior.

Much more important was the big man, sprawled on the concrete floor, propped in a sitting position against the wall, blood dribbling from a gash on his scalp—a direct hit from a chunk of brick, from the look of it.

Dead already?

Not that it mattered, though Harding checked and felt evidence of life throbbing into his fingers as he probed the man's neck.

Strong as a bleedin ox. Glad I knocked him cold already.

A Colt revolver, its silver handle engraved with the initials AA, was one of the items in the holdall, so, using a rubber glove from the same treasure trove, Harding tugged the medical mask from the unconscious man's face, placed the weapon in his unresisting fingers, the barrel to his throat, leaned back at arm's length and pulled the trigger.

The handgun was not particularly powerful but, at this range, the bullet was devastating. A gout of grey matter and blood erupted like a giant red rose on the wall behind, accompanied by a fine mist of human DNA that landed on Harding's sleeve.

Bollocks!

His leather jacket was ruined.

Too bad.

Satisfied with his handiwork, Harding let the gun fall to his victim's lap, index finger still entwined round the trigger, giving the appearance of suicide. With a photograph on his smartphone for proof, he had almost completed his first task, though things had not gone quite to plan.

I ain't lugging him upstairs to his office. He's too bloody heavy. And two bodies...

The petrol had been supplied to burn the place down once the suicide had been staged. It didn't matter why to Harding, though he realised it would confuse the investigators once it had done its work. Hopefully he'd get paid on the basis of the photo before the anonymous boss discovered the screw up.

Without a thought for the woman lying inert on the steel table, Harding placed the canister between the man's outstretched legs, twisted the second fuse to arm it then placed it inside the plastic neck immediately above the petrol and screwed the lid back on.

The smell and the excitement made him giddy. He took a deep breath, savouring the chemical tang, and with a last glance round the room, he hefted the holdall, and headed for the steps in time to hear a siren approaching.

Damn! How do I get the other stuff done if they're coming here?

The thumb drive was still in his palm, the job not finished.

Maybe the client won't know about that, either, until it's too late, especially with the building in flames.

If I finish the other target quick enuff, I'll get paid anyway...

These thoughts came and went almost instantly. He turned to leg it then heard a beeping noise, so glanced over his shoulder at the screen dangling over the woman. The video showed a BMW with blue lights flashing under the grill swerve into the front of the drive and slide to a halt in a shower of gravel.

Time to go!

Harding leapt up the steps, ran past the side of the garages, and dived over the wall. He was on a high from the adrenalin, the anticipation, the acrid fumes from the petrol still clinging to his hands. He desperately wanted to detonate his improvised explosive device but controlled himself.

Barely.

The reason for his delay? The delicious thought flashing like a brilliant neon sign in his mind.

Maybe I can incinerate a couple of pigs before I finish my work here...

He fished his remote control from his holdall and waited with his finger twitching, itching to press the red button again.

'Her car's still here.'

Jack stated the obvious for his passenger's benefit as they swung on to the gravel forecourt and skidded to a halt next to Fiona's Ford. Before Doc could answer, his colleague was out of the car, the door flung shut with a force that shook the whole vehicle. Doc followed at a more sedate pace as Jack hammered on the door.

'Can you smell that, Jack?' There was an odour in the air that was out of place, here in this little slice of rural suburbia. Doc tried to place it, but could not. A burnt chemical smell, something he had not experienced for some years.

'I can't smell a thing. I guess it's the fags.'

'Smoking can do that to you. It's... It's like Guy Fawkes night.' Doc took a deep breath, his nostrils flaring. 'No, that's not it. Like the smell at a firework display but much stronger, sharper.'

'Really?'

Dammit! What?

'I know! It's like cordite. On a firing range.'

Jack shook his head, discontinued banging on the unresponsive door and cursed. Doc started following his nose, making his way round the side of the building and heard Jack's feet scrunching, jogging to catch up. They rounded the rear of the main house together.

'Yeah, I can smell it now.'

They surveyed the garages, locked and blindly silent, then came to the cellar steps.

'Someone's used explosives to get in here, Jack.'

'Oh shit! Explosives… That's all I need. We'll have the anti-terrorist boys all over this place. Let's have a look before I call it in. Maybe Fifi's in there.'

'Jack!' Doc shouted as his friend started for the steps. 'Don't be daft. The ceiling might fall in! We should call the fire brigade for assistance—'

It was no use, Jack was already inside. Doc dithered for a moment, then punched three digits into his mobile and got an immediate response. He told the operator that explosives had been detonated on site, asked for all three emergency services to respond at once. When she started to ask for more details he gave her Jack's call sign and told her the detective may be in danger, mentioned that the Mitcham police had been here earlier and finished the call just as Jack's panicky yell for assistance reached his ears.

He calmed himself with a few breaths and followed the detective into the cellar.

Harding was marvelling at how today was turning out, how much his life had changed for the better, and all in such a short space of time.

The escape, the ruination of Broadmoor, the dead guards, the satisfaction of topping an ex-SAS man, the successful hit he had just performed here, the money he'd been given already, the prospect of much more to come, and now, this!

He drove his thumbnail into the back of his left hand, pinching himself. Someone looking like Powers had appeared at the side of the building, making Harding wonder if the petrol fumes, the excitement, elation and his lack of sleep had created this illusion, like a thirsty desert traveller espying an oasis only to find it was a mirage. As the man came closer, Harding was convinced.

It is him! Powers!

Then Carver had trotted up behind the bastard!

The two men had been on Harding's personal hit list for over twenty years, though he had resigned himself to his life inside, unable to get to them. That had changed a couple of months ago when that pathetic guard had handed him the first envelope. Several more had changed hands, including notes from Harding to his nameless benefactor in the world outside, and promises made by both parties. Not that he really believed any of it would happen. That was until Powers had come visiting on Monday, as promised, even before that drone buzzed by his window this morning, right on time.

No. Life had finished throwing shit at him, he decided. Seeing Carver and Powers here together was like a gift from some perverse god. For the second time, Harding would have prayed if he had been religious, this time in thanks rather than hope.

The gun!

As the thought skimmed through Harding's brain and his hands reached for the holdall to extract the Glock, Carver ran down the cellar steps. Powers stood at the top, bouncing from foot to foot, as if unsure what to do, then pulled his phone out and spoke into it for several seconds before a voice yelled from inside.

He too ran into the building.

Unbelievable.

Harding was buzzing with energy, all thoughts of his other assignment now banished from his mind.

Powers and Carver.

He wanted to look into their eyes as he gut-shot them and watch them writhe in agony before finishing the job. It was tricky though. Two men in an enclosed space, especially one as chaotic as the cellar, now in disarray thanks to his overenthusiastic entry. It would be better to ambush them as they climbed out.

I need to get nearer the top of the steps to be certain of getting them both, though.

Only a minute or two elapsed as he considered his options, sight lines, where he could be concealed enough while guaranteeing he could shoot them both. He began to doubt his plan as the faint sounds of yet more sirens wafted across the common.

Nah. Shame... Time for Plan B.

Harding didn't need the gun. He dropped it back into the holdall and fondled the detonator again.

Death by immolation was a pretty good second best, he decided.

He giggled with anticipation as he plunged the red button.

'Are you okay, Jack?'

'Over here, Doc! I need some help.'

Jack gently patted Fiona's cheeks, relieved to see her breathing, though unconscious. 'Fifi! Can you hear me?'

The sight of her, laid out on the steel slab, her hand a bloody mess and her skin slick with sweat, clothes fouled and stinking, had wrenched his heart, dislodging it in his chest, as if it was about to emerge from his throat. There was some blood pooling on the floor below where her arm had flopped, but the injury to her wrist did not look like a result of the explosion.

Doc arrived at his side and made a comment that confirmed Jack's own thoughts.

'This was where Rawlings and the others were mutilated... How is she?'

'Her hand's hanging half off. Take a look for me, Doc.'

The man Jack was now convinced was Akachi was clearly dead. It didn't take a detective to work that one out since the man's brains were splattered up the wall. He'd immediately wondered about the petrol canister between the apparent suicide's outstretched legs but turned his attention to his injured sergeant as soon as he saw her. She seemed so fragile and vulnerable here, laid out on an operating table, still fully clothed but with her left sleeve sliced off and her hand almost the same.

Doc started tending to her arm, then wrapped a bandage round Fiona's wrist while asking, 'Are you sure her airway's clear, Jack?'

'Yeah. Breathing but unconscious. I'll carry her out. The ceiling has a fucking great crack in it from right above the doorway. The building's very solid but it could fall in so we'd best get outside.'

'I've called for an ambulance and the fire brigade. Everyone's on the way, including the bomb squad.'

Jack was shocked by Doc's voice. The quivering tone, his shaking hands. He wondered if Doc was imagining Judy, here, on this slab, in this place, being tortured to death.

'Doc, stay with me, mate.' Jack hoisted Fiona into his arms and headed for the wrecked doorway. Doc's footsteps even sounded despondent, depressed. 'I know what you're thinking. We'll go through this place with a fine-tooth comb and if there's any trace of Judy we'll find it. But stop thinking the worst. There is nothing to suggest she was a victim.'

'Nothing? Come off it, Jack! Nothing except that last letter. The contents pretty much confirmed Harding's comments—'

'Yeah, but we know they're fucking with your brain. That body at your house was meant to make you lose your mind, thinking it was Judy. If they had taken her, it would've been her. Why use a lookalike to hang in your garage if they already had her?'

'I hope you're right.' Doc's voice was still distant, not fully convinced.

'I can hear sirens. It's a squad car from the sound of it.' Jack climbed the steps and carefully laid his colleague on the gravel, still trying to reassure Doc. 'Fiona seems stable enough and we've had a real result here, mate. Let's not worry about Harding right now.'

He took off his jacket and put it under her head as a pillow, then straightened up again just as his world ignited with a lightning bolt of pain.

The bullet spun him round and his body collided with Doc's at the top of the steps, tumbling them both back down to the cellar as a flurry of shots ricocheted around them, chips of brickwork sparking and showering them both as they hit the floor in a mess of limbs and spurting blood.

———

In his elevated emotional state, with the world seemingly brighter, in sharper relief than at any time during his pharmaceutically depressed years at Broadmoor, Harding was effervescent with energy. Increasingly impatient too.

What the fuck is wrong with it?

He could not comprehend why the detonator had failed. He pressed the button on the remote for a second time. Then again, and then again, his thumbnail white with the pressure, the plastic housing cracking from the force of his grip.

Perhaps he was too far from the electronically triggered fuse, although the squaddie had told him the remote was good for up to a half a kilometre in the open, and maybe around a fifth of that if there were buildings blocking the signal. He was well within range.

'Fuckin hell! Work you bastard!'

Harding leapt on to the wall and held the device at arm's length, aiming down at the cellar entrance.

Still no response, and the sirens were getting louder. He hurled the thing to the ground in fury, the pieces flying apart.

What to do?

The choice was simple. He could jog off, fire up the cab and disappear into London, find his second target and earn his final instalment for a job well done.

Or he could stay here and finish off Powers and Carver.

The two cunts responsible for putting him away and ruining his life.

Powers, like a dog with a fucking bone, never letting go, insisting the police reopen the investigation into his old man's death over three years after the event...

And Carver, an ambitious newly minted detective, a lowly constable, working with Powers junior, the grieving son, even in his spare time, long after the Met had given up on their enquiries.

Powers, the sneaky bastard, had somehow managed to nick a sample of his DNA without consent and passed it to his detective friend. Of course, the pigs matched it to the murder scene, despite an earlier, official sample, having cleared him—a sample swabbed from his mate's mouth with a cotton bud during a mass DNA collection arranged during the original murder investigation. The chaotic event had been easy to manipulate, the harried staff easily fooled with a false ID…

What was then a fairly new forensic technique became the nail hammered into his coffin after Carver identified Harding as the killer using the sample Powers had stolen. So he went down for doing Powers' old man. Along with a few other murders he thought he'd got away with…

The scum responsible for buggering up his life, the bastards who put him away for the last twenty odd years, with no chance of ever getting parole, were right here, right now.

Nah! I ain't leaving.

Harding jumped down, fished the Glock from the bag, replaced the empty ammunition clip, checked the mechanism and the silencer, then settled into a crouched shooting stance with the butt on the wall and the barrel aimed at the top of the cellar steps. It was not an easy shot, well over twenty metres, but he had done it before.

If the sirens heralded the arrival of too many cops, he'd leg it back to the cab. No one would suspect he was here and there was plenty of cover from the trees and undergrowth on this part of the common.

Having convinced himself he had made the right decision, his first target appeared and it was as much as he could do to stop himself blowing Carver to hell right then, but he wanted them both in his sights before he squeezed off the first lethal round. He controlled his breathing, became aware of his heart beating a steady thumping rhythm, sighted the gun, ready to let off an aimed shot at the detective as soon as Powers was also visible.

Carver crouched and tended the woman he had rescued, then straightened as Powers appeared just behind him, a little to the detective's left.

Perfect…

Harding took aim at the centre of Carver's torso, fired the gun, timed perfectly between the beats of his own heart, then swivelled the extended barrel to Powers as Carver twisted, flung backwards and to the side, almost airborne from the force of the bullet. A second shot may or may not have hit his other target as the men tumbled back down the steps together. Harding unloaded the rest of the clip at the flailing tangle of limbs as they disappeared from view.

The hammer clicked on an empty chamber just as a vehicle swept on to the forecourt, sirens blaring. The police seemed to come out of nowhere, with Harding unaware of their arrival, having shut out all else while concentrating on his objectives.

What were the chances the car contained armed coppers?

Pretty much somewhere between zero and fuck all.

Reassured by the knowledge that British bobbies rarely carried lethal weapons, Harding fished out the final clip of ammunition, replaced the empty one, grabbed his spare grenade from the bottom of the holdall, and, keeping low, jogged to the far side of the garage, hopped over the perimeter wall and landed on the gravel just as the patrol car arrived at the back of the main building. The two uniformed policemen had obviously spotted the girl lying unconscious near the cellar steps as their car navigated its way round her before coming to a halt immediately in front of the garage.

Harding did not wait for them to get out. He sprang from his concealed position and snapped off two shots through the windscreen from less than five metres. Already certain he had put two more bullets into two more brains, he made his way to the cellar, gun held ready in case the detective and his idiot psychiatrist friend were lying wounded at the bottom of the steps.

Disappointment tugged at the corners of his mouth as he realised they were gone, had managed to take cover by crawling inside.

Not dead then…

Another distant siren suggested he only had a few precious minutes before more coppers arrived. He made some quick calculations.

Four bullets left in this gun, but no more loaded clips, though he did have most of the plastic explosive in the bag, plus the one grenade now in his pocket. Enough weaponry to go into the cellar to finish the pair of them off, and get away if more coppers arrived while he was down there.

The crack of a pistol being fired startled him and he immediately felt a punch to his left bicep. He automatically responded with a glance at the limb, blood already oozing from the wound, the entire arm now unresponsive. It seemed unreal to him as he felt no pain, the adrenalin in his system blocking the signals to his brain.

Shit! I've been hit! They've got a fucking gun! Where the hell..?

Harding swore out loud as he remembered.

Of course they have…

He had forgotten about the weapon he'd left in the victim's hand—his 'suicide' victim's hand.

Another shot skimmed past his ear, so he dived to the right, self-preservation demanding he stay out of the line of fire. He pressed his back to the wall and took stock again. The revolver was an unexpected and unwelcome consideration, and he had no idea how badly hurt either of the men were.

Won't be long before more filth arrives. Bugger!

There was only one thing for it.

With his good hand Harding slipped the gun into his belt before he snatched the grenade from his jacket pocket, then held the device between his legs as he pulled the pin. He thought about holding on to it for a count of five as instructed, but bottled out of it, not convinced the adjustable timer was all that accurate, and just lobbed it down the steps.

Having seen the effects of his attempt at removing the door, and the current state of the wall around the cellar entrance, he decided it would be prudent to move, so staggered back to the garage building to take shelter. He swore as the movement joggled his injured arm, the grinding, tearing sensations deep within his muscle finally breaking through the chemicals flooding his system, making him light-headed with pain. The bullet must have slammed into the bone and sheared it. The limb dangled, useless.

It occurred to him that his other job would be impossible now. He was in no fit state to assassinate anyone, probably couldn't even drive the cab. It was barely worth going on the run with just the ten grand in his holdall. It was not enough cash, especially as he was badly injured.

No big payday for me then… You fucking pair of cunts!

They would be history soon enough. Maybe with Powers gone he could convince his benefactor to cough up some cash and help him out, even though he couldn't complete the other tasks he'd been set. He had a number to call between six and nine o'clock tonight to arrange where to pick up his dosh, so would see about it later.

That bloody grenade should have gone off by now…

Maybe time was stretching again because of his hyped up state of mind and the anticipation of what was to come. After what he had seen the first one do at Broadmoor, he was pretty sure the two men inside would be dead around ten seconds after he had tossed the anti-personnel explosive through the door.

And burnt alive if not, thanks to the petrol canister.

Haha! The fuse didn't work but that grenade should detonate the fucker…

The last second ticked by as the thought scurried through his head, a grim smile on his face as he simultaneously winced with pain.

As the brickwork above his head was being peppered with bullets, Doc dragged Carver into the cellar, ignoring his friend's curses and groans as he did so. The stomach wound looked nasty and Doc wanted to find some dressings to tend to it, but Jack had other ideas, his voice loud and strong, though tight sounding, uttered through gritted teeth.

'Take this and shoot the bastard!'

Jack was offering his sidearm, but Doc, who had only ever fired a gun once in anger, and only then at a distance of zero centimetres, shook his head, horrified at Jack's suggestion and almost witless with fear. His concerns over Judy's fate had been superseded by this latest assault on his well-being, and no amount of yogic breathing was going to settle him. This was Doc's first time under fire, and his entire being was swamped, overloaded with an accumulation of worries, dread, stress and now a desire for self-preservation.

'No! You know I couldn't hit a barn door at the best of times, Jack.' He held out his hand, the fingers splayed, clearly palsied. 'I'm shaking like a leaf in a gale! What the hell's happening? I didn't even hear that gun going off.'

'Then help me.' Jack pulled himself along the floor in a sitting position, smearing a trail of blood like a giant snail as he struggled the few feet to the doorway. Doc assisted as best he could. 'He was using a silencer.' Jack hawked and spat a mouthful of blood and then bowed his head, as if about to faint from the pain. He coughed and spluttered, then sat up, his eyes gleaming as he grinned with rouged lips at Doc, like some mad male prostitute on the pull, then focused on the man who had been hunting them. Jack poked his head round the doorway, startled by what he saw. 'It's Harding! Here!'

Doc's mind could not process the information.

Harding?

This was like a bad dream.

A shoot out with an escaped convict—one with a massive personal grudge against Doc—trapped in the cellar of a serial murderer's house, while the perpetrator they were hunting, a villain with a penchant for medically mutilating his victims, lay dead, an apparent suicide. And the only assistance Doc could call on right now was two wounded detectives, one of whom was lying outside with her hand half severed, unconscious…

As Jack fired off a couple of rounds, the situation became even more surreal to Doc.

'I hit him!' Jack laughed, but blood sprayed from his mouth. Doc grabbed a thick wad of dressings from a nearby shelf, dusted them off and jammed them against the wound. Faint sounds of sirens encouraged them both, although, for some reason, there had been no assistance from the first emergency vehicle they had heard arriving a few moments earlier. 'Jesus, Doc! Lay off a bit mate, I'm gonna… Ugh.'

Jack fainted and slumped forward.

Doc knew he would die from loss of blood without a transfusion, and he had no idea what equipment was in this cellar. He just hoped the ambulance would arrive soon, along with some coppers.

Armed ones, preferably.

Surely things could not get any worse.

They did.

A miniature pineapple bounced past him with a metallic clunk, then rolled across the floor. Doc watched with horror as he realised what it was as it came to rest right next to a petrol container situated between the dead man's legs.

If anyone had asked Doc how he would react to being trapped by a gunman in a cellar with an unconscious friend, a grenade rolling across the floor, his brain barely functioning, he would have said: his life would flash in front of his eyes and he would cease to exist shortly thereafter.

His feet decided differently.

Doc found himself standing by the dead man, scooping the grenade into his still shaking fingers without any conscious recollection of having decided to move, let alone *actually* move several paces to his current location.

It was as if he was observing himself from outside his body, and a serene sensation flooded through him as he saw his other hand grab the petrol canister and slide it across the room. The stranger that was Doc then pulled the lifeless man from his sitting position, easing him to the floor.

In his surreal state, Doc felt no fear, had no concept of time. No clue as to how many seconds had elapsed, how many ticks of a clock remained before the grenade would disintegrate and strip the earthly flesh from his ethereal spirit.

Again, without conscious thought, he placed the weapon on the floor, rolled the dead man on to it, satisfied the explosive would detonate under the heavy corpse's chest, then lay face down on top of the body to further smother the blast.

The muted crump made by the exploding grenade surprised Harding—he had anticipated a much more audible and visible result. Maybe the distance and the underground location were responsible, but the flaming secondary blast he'd expected to accompany the initial explosion failed to materialise.

Was it a dud?

The sirens were almost upon him now, but he could not leave without first checking the bastards were dead. A quick fumble through his holdall using his one working hand found the plastic explosive and the fuse, but as he pulled the items out he realised.

The remote detonator's fucked!

It was lying on the gravel in pieces where he had hurled it in disgust earlier. He threw the explosive back into the bag and tossed the lot behind the perimeter wall, furious that he'd been given such substandard tools.

Four bullets would just have to be enough even if he had to use a couple to finish Powers and Carver. There should still be a few in the revolver too, so he could shoot his way out of the cellar, if need be.

Taking careful steps so as not to aggravate the graunching agony in his arm, he descended into the cellar with the gun held out in front of him.

Carver lay collapsed by the doorway, his pale face in sharp contrast to the crimson pool surrounding him. He looked dead enough to Harding who would have liked to make certain but had no bullets to waste.

Then he spotted Powers, sitting on the floor next to the 'suicide' corpse, a dazed expression on his face as he stared at the now mangled body. He did not seem to notice Harding's approach, or the barrel of the gun pointing at his head.

'Look at me, you fuckin piece of shit.' Harding's anger swelled, his throat tightening as he saw the revolver lying by Powers' fingers.

So this was who had shot him.

'YOU CUNT!'

More pain. More torment from the same bastard. After all these years locked up with a bunch of lunatics, druggies and paedos…

As if awakening from a dream, still apparently dazed, eyes unfocused, a hand rubbing his scalp, Powers stared through Harding, giving the distinct impression there was nothing in his line of sight, no one there. Not even giving Harding the satisfaction of an acknowledgement.

No fear at death's approach. No response at all.

Harding jammed the tip of the silencer against Powers' skull and screwed it round as if trying to bore into the man's brain, determined to make an impression.

'Wakey wakey, dopey.'

Nothing, still.

The sirens arrived outside before they were silenced, and although he knew he had to get moving, Harding wanted Powers to know he was about to die. This zombie act was not going to stop the inevitable bullet.

'I told you to look at me.'

He stepped back, the gun still aimed at Powers' face.

Finally, a response. Powers' head jerked back as his eyes focused on Harding's, then his expression changed to one of confusion, his brow contorting as he spoke, voice unsteady.

'Harding… Why are you here?'

'Haha! Why am I here? To kill you, you twat.'

Unbelievably, Powers' hand began creeping towards the revolver, then, fingers trembling, the idiot gripped the handle.

As if!

'Oh, just fuck off and die, Powers!'

Harding took aim between his victim's eyes and the explosive crack of a bullet echoed through the cellar.

Jack was spinning wildly, the sensation similar to an extreme funfair ride, his belly on fire, his throat wet with coppery tasting blood. This vertiginous state of consciousness hauled him from the darkness, suddenly alive to the agony burning through his guts, the searing heat of a glowing red poker gouging and boiling his insides.

At least, that was how it felt. And to feel it, he thought, he must still be alive.

He tried to remember where he was, his eyes gradually focussing on the cement floor, his nose also registering the sticky blood under his cheek, pooled around him.

Someone was talking, but it was not Doc's voice. He tried to focus on the sound. The words. Then the yelled insult lanced through the fog of pain.

'YOU CUNT!'

Harding's voice.

We're in the cellar...

Jack tried to raise his head, but it was too heavy. Instead he felt the skin of his cheek being sandpapered off by the abrasive floor as he rotated himself, struggling to find a position from which to view Harding. The movement set off more waves of pain in his insides, almost unbearable, taking him to the brink of consciousness and back.

He tried to roll to the side, managed to force his body off his arm, his right hand released, the gun still clutched in his fingers.

I can hardly feel it. My hands are numb.

Harding jumped into focus, his back to Jack as he jammed his pistol into Doc's skull.

God! It's too heavy.

The gun weighed about fifty kilos in his current state, but Jack forced himself to lever his torso, to get better purchase on the weapon while still lying on the floor. His brain processed the sound of ambulance sirens coming from outside, now louder, almost drowning out the conversation. The noise stopped as Harding took a few steps back, another two metres closer to Jack's gun, but with his own still pointing at Doc's head.

Could he do it? Raise the barrel in time to shoot before Harding finished his friend? Could he hit a target—even one this close—with numb fingers?

He tried again to aim the pistol as Harding laughed and grunted more indecipherable words. The distance had closed and maybe Jack could hit his target if he could just turn the gun upright. With hands slick with blood, he forced the butt into position by swivelling his forearm and wrist, his finger curling round the trigger.

It was not going to do the job, aimed at the man's legs, especially with Doc sitting right behind them. A bullet from Jack's gun was as likely to kill his friend as it was to disable Harding, but the situation was urgent.

Jack knew Doc's final moments had arrived as Harding shouted, 'Oh, just fuck off and die, Powers!'

With one final mammoth effort Jack forced the barrel up, thinking a bullet hitting home anywhere in the torso would do, though he had a specific target in mind, and in normal circumstances it would have been an easy shot for him.

The movement sent more blood rushing to his mouth but he hoped the bullet would hit home, would sever the spinal cord between Harding's shoulder blades to paralyse his gun hand. He squinted, aimed and squeezed the trigger immediately before unconsciousness engulfed him again.

Doc was convinced he was about to die.

Lying on top of the corpse felt surprisingly peaceful. A warm, contented embrace from his burgeoning fate.

Then his world went crazy.

The blast lifted him off the ground and tossed him to the side, smacking his head on the wall. Stunned, his mind refusing to cope with anything happening around him, Doc was relieved to find himself alive. He tried to get up to check his friend's status, but could not.

Was he wounded?

There was a woolly silence engulfing him too, his vision was blurred, and the cellar seemed darker now.

The shadow of a man appeared before him, but he could not make out the words vaguely reaching him through his deafened ears.

Doc knew then. He was suffering concussion and a wave of nausea swept through him, gurgling some bile into his throat, the sharp taste rousing him from his torpor.

The muddy words continued, the tone belligerent, yelled by a voice he recognised.

Harding.

The shadow man.

Then he felt pain in his skull, his eyes managing to focus on the weapon just inches above, gouging his scalp.

More words came, still too muffled to understand, but he could see the silver glint of the revolver near his hand, and wondered if he could reach it, aim it at Harding and shoot him before he was on the receiving end of a bullet himself.

Despite the air pressing into him, heavy like syrup, he managed to reach a hand for the revolver, felt his fingers wrap around the handle. It took all his effort to overcome this unexpected resistance from the thickened atmosphere, finally managing to raise the gun from the floor in slow motion. He started to bring it to bear on Harding's belly.

Before he could aim and squeeze the trigger, he was stunned by a hammer blow to his temple just as Harding disappeared from view, spinning off to the side in a shower of blood.

As the shot reverberated around him, Harding was confused.

His gun was silenced, so why was the noise so deafening?

The few nanoseconds it took to process this thought, along with the knowledge that his one remaining functioning hand was no longer under his control, also saw the world twist and warp, his mind flying in a vicious spiral as he started a slow motion tumble to the floor.

His entire head felt like it had exploded, and nothing was under his control any more. He couldn't even breathe.

What's happening to me?

Powers' gun hand had hardly been raised, he was still sitting there, like Buddha, as if in a trance, blood pouring from his head.

How could he have shot me?

With that final lucid question screaming in his brain, Harding's miserable life flashed before his one good eye, then his head slammed to the ground, the light dimmed in a blur of pain and then extinguished for the very last time.

'Are you feeling better, sir?'

Doc was still in a daze, now sitting on the back step of an ambulance with a bandage wrapped round his head, watching Jack being loaded into the rear of another. His friend, the man who had just saved his life, was alive, but unconscious from blood loss. The paramedics had attached fluids to his arm and were feeding him oxygen through a mask as they slotted the gurney into their vehicle.

'I'm a bit concussed but I'll be fine.' A bit concussed was an understatement. Doc's brain felt like a hundred migraines had been crammed into his cranium. 'How's Jack doing?'

The paramedic glanced in the direction Doc was staring before turning back to shine his miniature torch into Doc's left pupil.

'The male detective? He'll be in surgery soon enough, but we won't know until then.' The light flicked into Doc's other eye as the paramedic continued. 'The lady we found, well she'll survive. Her hand's a mess, but they reckon the surgeons will sort it.'

'And the other man?'

'Well, there was a rather messy corpse beside a very poorly individual with a bullet through his neck. He would have drowned in his own blood had he been breathing, but his chest muscles were paralysed. They got to him in time though. He was resuscitated before they carted him off.'

Doc must have been totally out of it when that had happened. More lost time, memories vanishing even as they were made.

'Harding. He's alive?'

'Yeah, for now. He'll be lucky to survive, if you can call life as a quadriplegic lucky. Who is he?'

'Nobody. Are we done?'

'Well, we'll get you to the hospital too, for a check-up. I've stitched the flap of skin back into place, but we should get some fluids into you too.' The paramedic tried to push him back down, pressing a hand to Doc's shoulder as he started to get up. 'Steady on! Why the hurry? That bullet grazed your skull, and we need an X-ray to check for fractures. Concussion is serious enough—'

'I know, I'm a doctor. Now, if you'll excuse me, I need to talk to that detective.'

The paramedic sucked at his lower lip for a moment, then shrugged. 'I can't force you to come with us, but you really should… If you feel sick, or sleepy, then get yourself to hospital. Don't drive.'

Doc nodded, instantly regretted it as the flare of pain smacked his frontal lobe, but managed to get to his feet and join the nearby huddle of detectives. Several plain-clothes officers had arrived on the scene shortly after the uniformed police, who had already taken a brief statement from Doc. An ambulance had been first on the scene, followed by the fire brigade, another ambulance and about a dozen local coppers. The grounds around the house were now crowded with vehicles and people, voices babbling. The initially sombre atmosphere that pervaded when they found their dead and injured colleagues now had an undertone of excitement threaded through it.

Some of the detectives were members of Jack's team, and DS Sam Sharpe had the skills Doc needed right now.

'Hi, Doc! How're you after your shoot-out at the Mitcham Corral?'

The black humour masked the underlying worry for Jack and Fiona, no doubt, but Doc replied by tossing the holdall at the sergeant's feet.

'It was Harding's. Take a look inside.'

Doc had spotted the bag, tucked behind him in the bushes, while he was sitting on the perimeter wall, huddled in a foil blanket holding a dressing against his head wound, waiting for the paramedics to finish giving aid to the two injured coppers and, as it turned out, reviving the man who had just tried to kill him.

Perhaps Doc should have felt some joy at this final turn of events. Death was too easy for a man like Harding. His body incarcerated in prison, his brain similarly constrained in a paralysed body. Well, that somehow seemed a more fitting punishment, but Doc wasn't inclined to gloat.

Until this week, Harding's existence had been consigned to some isolated neurons in Doc's brain, locked in a memory compartment as secure as Broadmoor. The key tossed many years ago, after the first occasion Harding had wound him up so much that Doc had lost his temper and tried to throttle the inmate...

Sam pulled on his gloves, unzipped the holdall and started describing the contents.

'There's a satnav, a photograph of Abimbola with a diagram on the back—this house from the look of it—two thumb drives marked #1 and #2, some rubber gloves, two empty ammunition clips and a mobile phone. So Harding came here to top Abimbola. Hence the photo—the target wasn't familiar to him. Hang on!' Sam's hand fished out a lump of plasticine-like material. 'What the hell? Plastic explosive. Where did he get all this stuff?'

'Whoever broke him out of Broadmoor had more in mind than just setting him free. I found this card in there too.' Doc had been fingering the object subconsciously while waiting for the paramedic to finish, but now handed it to Sam. 'The numbers... They're security codes.'

'Three six digit numbers? They could be anything, Doc.'

'This one,' Doc's finger traced the last number on the list as the sergeant held the card, squinting at the digits, 'is my home alarm code.'

'Jesus, Doc! Harding was coming for you too... You think these ones are entry codes for other targets?'

'I guess so. You need to check if there are any locations saved in the satnav memory. That can wait as Harding's no longer a threat. More importantly, I want to know what's on those thumb drives Sam, and we need to take a look at what's on the man's personal computer inside this place.'

'The boss is on her way. We should wait as it's her crime scene, with Jack—'

'Sam. I'm not asking.' Doc turned on his heel, and, ignoring the desire to retch and the hammers using his brain as an anvil, did his best not to stagger on his way round to the front door, now hanging off its hinges after the local bobbies had forced entry some twenty minutes earlier. Once inside he found the room he identified as the study, based on the written directions he had discovered on the back of the photograph in Harding's bag.

Sam followed him in without a word.

'Fire this up for me, and let's see what's so important.'

A flash of lightning lit up the room, startling Doc before he realised it was actually inside his head. Queasiness and light-headedness almost pole-axed him, but he forced himself to remain upright, regulated his breathing and placed his palms on the desk for support.

'So this is the computer marked on the back of the photo, Doc. Harding was told by some mysterious third party to use the USB sticks... To do what, exactly?'

'We won't know until you've accessed the contents, but my guess? They contain some incriminating evidence pointing to the man we already have in custody. Maybe another person too.'

'Who?'

'Maddox?' Almost sure, but not certain. 'I think these,' Doc slid a finger over one of the thumb drives, 'were intended to misdirect us. The one marked #1 probably contains whatever information the person behind the murders wanted planted here.'

'What? I'm confused Doc. Why plant incriminating evidence here? The operating theatre downstairs is enough to confirm what was going on. That doesn't make sense.'

'Mmm.' Doc had another theory developing, but just said, 'I'm guessing there's a suicide note on there. But why use a USB drive, rather than the internet... Surely they could've hacked into this computer like they did with mine?'

'Could be one of several reasons, but most likely an effective firewall, or just a cautious, tech savvy user. Either would prevent someone gaining access like that.'

If it was a dig at Doc's inability to protect his MacBook, he didn't notice.

'Well, Sam. Your colleague Fiona wandered in here, poking her nose around at the wrong time. Abimbola was obviously not expecting her or Harding.'

'You know, just before I left the office Daniel Ngwene, the security guard at Broadmoor, identified the photo of Abimbola as the guy he knew as Akachi, the bloke who was coercing him to pass letters to Harding...'

'Just as we suspected. Looks like Fiona made the same discovery.' Doc tapped one of the letters on the study wall. 'Look.'

'Addressed to Akachi... Well I was just talking to the others and we've all pretty much agreed the case is sewn up. We've found the two men who were responsible for Rawlings and the other murders. Abimbola and Butler. Working as a team. Shouldn't be long before we find the link between them. Dawson, the Acting Super, is convinced—'

'Well, I'm not so sure, Sam. Think about it. Why would Abimbola feed information to Harding, possibly even arrange for his release, and then instruct Harding to come here to kill him in a way that suggests suicide?'

'Maybe he couldn't do it himself, was too scared, so—'

'The person who wrote the codes on that card was neither Abimbola nor Butler. It was someone else, Sam. The puppeteer pulling everyone's strings.'

Including mine.

'Really? Is that what you think? Abimbola's corpse didn't look like any suicide I've ever seen. What was he supposed have done? Blown his brains out after sticking a hand grenade in his shirt pocket, just to be sure?'

Doc sighed, too weary to explain, his mind recycling his uppermost concern now that Jack was in safe hands.

'Come on, Sam. Let's boot up this computer and see what we can find.'

'What are we looking for, Doc?'

'Anything on the victims. Any links to any of them. Photographs, letters to me, anything relating to the case. Anything at all… More specifically, I need to know if Judy Finch was ever held here.'

'You should be in hospital, Doctor Powers.'

Acting Superintendent Sadie Dawson bustled into the room, her voice cutting through Doc's head like a chainsaw. The dizziness had returned and his aching brain was threatening to burst through his skull.

Just concentrating for the few minutes Sam had been trying to work some magic on Abimbola's computer had left him drained, and it was all he could do not to puke on the keyboard. Everything was still a little muffled and distant to him, but he had to know.

'I'd rather stay. I can help.'

'No. I'll arrange a car to take you. You have no business being here, interfering with my crime scene.'

'Sadie, please listen to me. The investigation isn't over. Butler and Abimbola… I think we only have a part of the story and—'

'I'm not listening, Doc. You're not thinking straight and, according to the para-medics, in no fit state to help anyone. I'll see you in the morning. I've been apprised of your initial comments about what took place here, the brief summary you gave the first officers on the scene, but we'll take a full statement tomorrow. You're all lucky to be alive. You, DS Fielding and DI Carver. Meanwhile, you need a formal check-up and some bed rest.'

'No, I can't. There's a lot of info—'

'Yes, you can! You are not indispensable. However, you are under contract to the Met and have been injured while involved in an active operation with my team. Your well-being is therefore, technically, my responsibility. I won't have you collapsing on my watch.'

'Please, I have to know—'

'Constable.' A uniformed copper appeared at Dawson's elbow. 'Escort Doctor Powers from these premises. Immediately. Take him to St George's Hospital. They're expecting him.'

There was no arguing. Doc acquiesced.

'Hospital it is, then.'

Doc steadied himself with a hand on the constable's arm as he was led away.

'Well, if it isn't Colin Powers!'

Five hours after Soundbite Sadie had thrown Doc out of the *Art of Africa* office, he felt much better, more alert and in less pain, though had been resting his eyes as he lay on the hospital bed when his visitor arrived. Even his ears were back to normal, though Bob Koch's booming greeting might have benefited from some muffling.

'Bob! What are you doing here?'

'I heard you'd been shot so had to come and see for myself.' A wicked grin split the man's features, his yellow-green eyes magnified through his horn-rimmed glasses as he leaned over Doc's prone form. 'I thought you were going to end up on my slab in the morgue downstairs, but apparently it was just a flesh wound.'

'You sound disappointed.'

He did. But like Jack, Doc was aware of the man's strange manner, though had always assumed the pathologist had Asperger's Syndrome.

'Nothing personal, Doc.'

The freakish way Koch was staring at him made Doc distinctly uncomfortable. Like all medical professionals, the pathologist was one of their original suspects, and although Soundbite had convinced herself the investigation was over, Doc was certain it was not, and he was now wondering about the oddball ME, his detachment, his lack of affect. Koch certainly had some of the character traits associated with psychopathy, but Doc had never formally assessed him, or even interviewed him with surreptitious assessment in mind.

And what is he doing here?

'How's Jack?'

'Oh, he's out of surgery and they think he'll make a full recovery. Lucky man. The bullet missed his liver by a hair's width. If that had been punctured, well… You know, you're a doctor. I hear it was your old pal Harding that shot him. And you. What's that all about then?'

Again, the looming head, the oversized eyes, the predatory gaze that Jack said reminded him of an owl. Doc could see it now. It was more than unsettling.

Threatening.

'I guess he bears a grudge, Bob.'

'Oh, that, I can understand, Colin. But after all these years. You'd think he had something better to do.'

'I'm tired and really need to rest. Is there anything else?'

'Actually, two things. I thought you might like to know Harding's in the recovery room. He'll pull through. Shame. I'd love to take a look at what's inside his head.' Koch's mouth curved into an unhealthy smile. 'I've been researching the physical differences between killers' brains and normal people. I've almost finished a paper on my theories regarding early cranial structural damage and its effects on what we call good and evil. I'd really hoped to have Harding on the slab today. Shame.'

This paper Koch claimed to be writing had been mentioned many times over the years, but Doc had often wondered how serious the medic was about publishing his results. Other thoughts crowded his mind as he considered whether Koch might be the one who arranged for Harding's escape, maybe even had plans to murder the killer.

For his brain?

Surely not.

'Sounds fascinating.' Doc meant what he said. 'I'd like to read it when you finish, Bob.'

'Almost had your brain too. That would be quite something to study...' Koch's manner was seriously disturbing

'What?'

Doc's nausea returned and, despite the drugs he had been given, his head began throbbing. Koch's words were burrowing into his sense of well-being, the stress of this unwelcome visit reprising the effects of the concussion.

'As a psychiatrist you must realise you are a strange beast, Colin. Your abilities are truly unique and highly intriguing. Not only do you understand serial killers on an intellectual level, you feel them viscerally. It's uncanny. As if you have a violent psychopath dwelling inside your mind, sharing your brain with the supposedly normal you. Loitering within, just waiting to be let off the leash.' The owl's head peered through the observation window at the adjacent nurses' station, as if he was more interested in what they were doing. It was the fourth or fifth time and, at first, Doc thought it was a nervous twitch, but the feeling of menace emanating from Koch made him uneasy. 'Surely you must wonder about yourself. You could so easily be a serial killer too!'

Of course Doc wondered, but had no desire to discuss his concerns about his mental state with this man.

Koch's attention was once again on the nursing staff, both of whom appeared engrossed in some paperwork. Was the ME waiting for an opportunity to harm him?

What's he got in his pocket?

The pathologist's right hand was hidden under the pocket flap of his beige jacket, and Doc felt a surge of panic, his own hand sliding under the covers, reaching for the patient alarm dangling to the side of the bed. The touch of the cable reassured him.

Stay calm. Breathe.

Was he being paranoid? Or was it just disordered thinking, a consequence of the concussion? Irrational fears colliding with reality? His thumb depressed the emergency call button just as Koch's hand started to emerge from his pocket.

The alarm sounded immediately, and the piercing noise outside the room brought both nurses' heads up, two pair of eyes now staring through the window at the two pairs staring back.

The Ward Sister popped her head round the door and asked if Doc was okay.

Koch's hand had disappeared into the safety of his pocket again, and his mouth curled into a sickly grin. 'Everything's fine, Sis—'

'Sorry, Bob. I'm feeling really nauseous. Nurse, please help me sit up.'

'Perhaps you should leave Professor. Doctor Powers needs his rest.'

Koch's neck reddened and his jaw clenched, but he just nodded and strolled to the door as the nurse helped Doc to a sitting position then shoved a bowl onto his lap in case he vomited.

'Oh, the other thing, Colin.' Koch stood in the doorway, his parting words spoken with a tint of black humour in his voice. 'I came to invite you to my retirement do. This Friday after work. An informal affair, a select few of us will be heading to the local, but since you're here rather than avoiding me, I thought I'd pop up and ask you personally.' Then he was gone.

Avoiding him?

Now, who was being paranoid?

'I'm not surprised you're feeling sick, Doctor Powers. You should be resting. Why did you ask him up?'

'Ask him? I didn't!'

'Well, that's what he told us. He's a strange one. If you ask me, he should stay in his subterranean empire with the dead instead of disturbing the living.' The nurse shuddered. 'He's ghoulish! We'll be glad when he's gone, he gives the staff the creeps.'

Me too.

Doc wanted to get home, to his own bed, away from this place.

Away from Koch.

If he stayed here, he would get no sleep at all, worrying if the pathologist wanted to get his brain on the dissecting table along with Harding's.

'I need to get up.'

'You really shouldn't, Doctor.'

'I've had a CAT scan, there's no subdural bleeding, my skull's intact, if a little bruised. I'm just… Oh, let me have some anti-emetic tablets. And where's my phone?'

THURSDAY

INNOCENT UNTIL PROVEN OTHERWISE

'MORNING, DOC. YOU'RE LOOKING BETTER.'

DS Sam Sharpe was visibly pleased to see Doc up and about, though looked haggard himself, with dark semicircles under his eyes, his shirt and trousers rumpled.

'I feel better, Sergeant. You're the one who looks like you could do with a break.'

After arriving home and changing his security code, Doc had collapsed on the sofa and slept a full twelve hours in dreamless oblivion, with no thoughts of Judy disturbing him. It was the sleep of exhaustion and a release from the tension caused by the week's events. The thump of a mild hangover and the throbbing of the stitches in his lacerated scalp were the only physical reminders of yesterday's adventures, his brain fully functional. He'd arrived at Scotland Yard determined to unravel the truth about Rawlings, the other victims, Harding, Butler and Abimbola.

And, of course, Judy…

'It's been a long night. I couldn't sleep knowing Fiona was in surgery. Took them eight hours to stitch her hand back in place, reconnect the nerves and all that. I just called the hospital, and the docs are pretty optimistic, though. Reckon she'll get most of the use back, though only time'll tell. Glad you came in this morning, Doc, we need to take your—'

'I've emailed you my statement already, Sam. Here's a hard copy.' He thrust the print-out at the startled detective. 'Now that's out the way, I want to know what you found on Abimbola's PC.'

'Hold your horses, Doc!' Sam quickly read the document, nodded, then said, 'I'll get this into the system. Soundbite wanted to see you personally, but she's buggered off for a press briefing and apparently she's having a brunch meeting with the brass afterwards. The CPS have decided to charge Butler with Selena Scott, the planning officer's murder for starters. It was her hand in his freezer… And I unlocked a hidden file on his tablet this morning.'

'And?'

461

'More victim photos.'

'In addition to the ones he sent me?'

Supposedly sent me.

'Yeah. Looks like Butler spent a fair bit of time stalking each target before abducting them, then the evil git took more pictures for his diabolical scrapbook as he mutilated them. Kept a record of his work in progress.' Disgust riddled Sam's voice as he spoke, his face like a spaniel chewing a wasp. 'The team's still reading through all the stuff we found, reams of it including some sort of diary. Anyway, he said he won't talk to anyone, except you…'

'Really?' It was not said with enthusiasm. Doc had other concerns on his mind. 'Did you find any photos of Judy Finch?'

'No, Doc… I've spent hours on that tablet and there's nothing else on there. Our technicians have also analysed all the other images from the device and she's not one of the mutilated victims.'

'Really, Sam. Are you sure?'

'One hundred percent. All of them have been identified as the people Butler was stalking beforehand. There's absolutely nothing to suggest she was ever grabbed by Butler and Abimbola.'

That was a relief. But still not enough.

'So where is she? Any news from Border Control? Did she leave the country?'

'We know she didn't fly overseas or use the Eurotunnel. We're still waiting on some of the ferry crossing records from around New Year. It was super busy and there was a problem getting all the info. I'll let you know as soon as we hear anything.'

'Thanks, Sam. What about Abimbola's computer? Anything on there?'

'I was here all night going through it and also cross checking Harry Butler's tablet, looking for duplicates between the two, any links at all. Didn't find anything, except Abimbola had a whole file on Gerald Butler.'

'Harry's grandfather.'

This latest revelation sent Doc's mind spinning in a different direction as Sam continued.

'Apparently, the old boy did a stint as a guard at a British run camp in Kenya around the time Abimbola was born. This was back in the late fifties. Thousands of innocent families were interned during the Mau Mau uprising and Abimbola's father died while being detained. Looks like Abimbola blamed Butler senior for the death, for some reason. There's no specific detail in the files linking the father's death to the old man, though it does have some related military records plus some atrocity photos, including a couple like the ones Fiona found at Butler's house.'

'Along with the severed ears… Trophies, taken from Kenyan dissidents—terrorists, if you believe the UK government propaganda of the day.'

'Seems Abimbola and Harry Butler set things up for the old boy to discover Rawlings hanging from that tree. They would've known he had a dickey heart, though surely didn't expect him to point the finger at his own grandson before he pegged it.'

'Jack's revenge theory…'

Again, Doc was unsure. It was like a jigsaw where the pieces appeared to be correct, but needed too much effort to squeeze into position.

'Rawlings' widow's records threw a bit of light on things too. It seems Abimbola lost a shedload of money when her hubby buggered off with clients' funds.'

'Motive. For torturing and killing the hedge fund manager.' The thread of doubt regarding Harry's involvement still felt unbound, though Abimbola's was beyond question.

'Yeah, and incidentally, your mate Professor Maddox lost millions too. Or, rather, his company did. Cadaceus Holdings.'

'You said you'd identified the other victims?'

'Yep. We've been going through all the details from the surveillance files we found on Butler's tablet, matching them with Misper records.'

'But you found nothing on Abimbola's computer, just Harry Butler's? Strange…'

'Yeah. Though Soundbite has sent a forensics team to his place. They're tearing it apart as we speak. They found a hidden room, tucked away at the back of the cellar.'

'A recovery room. For the victims, after each operation…'

'Looks like it. Two beds, inside separate cages. There were loads of CCTV feeds around the place too, but we haven't found the recordings yet, though there was a camera situated right above the operating table.'

'The victims were forced to watch their own torture.'

'You reckon?'

'Almost certainly. I'm sure Abimbola and his partner will have kept the files too, recordings of the operations. We need to find them.'

'Well, we're still looking, Doc. Forensics are digging up the gardens today, looking for any bodies or sign of other human remains.'

'They're wasting their time. They went up in smoke.'

Doc recalled the note he had received stating that the other victim's bodies were gone forever, then his mind made the leap, confirming to him his suspicions about who was responsible for the deaths.

And it was not Harry Butler.

'You reckon, Doc? They burnt the bodies?'

'Double-deckers, Sam…'

'What have buses got to do with it?'

'Not buses… Abimbola worked in a crematorium for years. I suspect he still has contacts, possibly some access. You would be better off focussing on that angle.'

'Why?' Sam's puzzled expression once again reminded Doc of a dog, a puppy confused by a simple ball throwing trick. 'Sorry, you've lost me—'

'On occasion, the security services need to dispose of an unwanted body. Unofficially. They have arrangements with certain crematoria… Two bodies are sent through the furnace together, both in the same coffin. A disappearing trick which leaves unsuspecting families with caskets of loved ones' remains intermingled with the spooks' victims.'

'Oh, jeez! That's terrible, Doc! Double-deckers… Never heard of that before.'

'It's not common knowledge, but I suspect that's why we won't find any human remains buried in Mitcham or anywhere else for that matter.'

'What about the muti angle? The body parts. Selena Scott's hand was kept for some reason. Abimbola definitely sold that Atlas bone. He had paperwork from Africa confirming its provenance.'

'I'm not sure that that means much. People have bought their own death certificates in Nairobi and tried to claim on their life insurance. Anyway, I'm sure we'll find more evidence if we keep looking. Did Abimbola have a cloud server? Storing files remotely?'

'I didn't find anything on the computer indicating that, but he was a cautious man. The property was wired to prevent any electronic intrusion. No Wi-Fi or mobile signals in or out of the place, only landline links to the outside world. I've requested his browsing history from his internet service provider, so maybe that'll throw up something.'

'Let's keep looking.' Doc wanted to talk through his ideas about who was behind the crimes with Jack, but his old pal was only recently out of surgery. Perhaps Doc could get the sergeant onside with his theory. A gentle nudge in the right direction might help. 'Do me a favour, Sam. Check out who Abimbola's references were when he got the job at Streatham Crematorium. And see if he was recommended by anyone.'

'That's a bit of a stretch, Doc. He started there well over twenty years ago, and they may not have kept the records.' The determined look on Doc's face must have convinced the detective. 'Okay… Anyone in particular?'

'Well. I suspect a police pathologist working in the local hospitals at the time might have pulled some strings—'

'Professor Koch! You really think the Met's senior ME knew our killer?'

'I do… But more than that. I think Harry Butler is innocent too.'

'So, Harry. They tell me you wanted to speak to me. Well, here I am.'

DS Tim Pierce had accompanied Doc to the interview room and now both of them sat across the desk from Harry Butler and his lawyer. Before they entered, Doc had made it very clear to the sergeant that his role during this interview was to stay silent, assist as required and ensure the formalities were observed.

'They've charged me with murder! You know me. I couldn't… I wouldn't… Help me Doctor Powers, please.'

'I'm doing my best to understand everything about this case, Harry. I need you to take a look at this.' At a signal from Doc, Pierce plucked a photograph from the file in front of him then slid it across the desk for their suspect to peruse. 'Do you know this man?'

'Arthur!' A ripple of confusion and then horror slipped across Harry's face, his eyes wide, a hand to his mouth. 'Please tell me he's not dead! What is he—another victim? Someone else I'm supposed to have murdered..? I *liked* him!'

If Doc was surprised by Harry's reaction, he made no show of it, keen to press on with his line of questioning, but was taken aback when the sergeant sighed a barely audible, yet clearly triumphant *Yes!* under his breath. Doc glanced at him, instructing him to *Shut up!* with an impatient eyebrow lift before turning back to Harry.

'Okay, Harry. You knew him. He was also known by an English nickname and had an African forename too. Did he ever share those with you?'

'No… I knew him only as Arthur. Arthur Abimbola, a trader in African fine arts.'

'How did you meet?'

'Is he dead?'

'I'm afraid so. Suicide, apparently.' Doc chose the words to reassure Harry he was not implicated in the man's death.

'Suicide? Poor Arthur.'

So, tell me, how did you meet and what was your relationship with this man?'

'He came to the shop—the tattoo parlour—not long after we opened. Had been recommended, by a mutual friend.'

'A friend?'

'Arthur never admitted it, but I think he was one of Diana's clients. She was one of only a few friends who knew I was involved in the shop, but I hadn't seen her in a couple of months. That was when we lost touch. I'd also met Shazza by then.'

'So, Arthur came to the shop, as a customer?'

'We became friends... I can't believe he's dead. I... I...'

The words stopped coming, and Harry started to close down, but Doc did not want to lose him, so reached a hand across the desk and laid it on his forearm—a reassuring gesture that drew a glare from the lawyer and an uncomfortable buttock shuffle from Pierce. Physical contact in this situation can be construed by the defence as assault or coercion, but Doc didn't care, saw Harry's tear rimmed eyes peer up at him from his lowered head, a tiny nod of thanks for the compassion.

'Did he come to you for a tattoo?' Despite his doubts about Abimbola's motives, Doc kept his voice level, encouraging Harry to answer.

'He was looking for something special. He had an interest in tribal markings, not just tattoos, but scarification.'

'Scarification? Do you mean patterned cuts to the skin, to leave decorative scarring?'

'Yeah. It used to be common in Africa, though plenty of westerners like the effect, often have it as well as tattoos these days. Shazza was keen. She's got several.'

'And Arthur talked to you about the techniques?'

'More than that. When he realised we weren't able to help him—he wanted one on his back—he taught us how to do it properly, helped out in the shop when we first started, gave me loads of designs to use, patterns from different parts of Africa. We're now well known for it... He was a lovely man... I can't believe he's dead! What's Arthur got to do with all this?'

There was plenty, but Doc was not about to share the details, just offered a sympathetic smile.

'How often did you see him?'

'I haven't seen him for years. Arthur was always too busy in the end. Seems his business really took off, though we did spend a lot of time together before that... He was a regular at the shop. We were friendly and would meet for a drink sometimes.'

'What did you talk about?'

'Why do you need to know all this stuff?'

'Please just answer, Harry. I wouldn't be asking if it wasn't important. Did he ever mention his childhood, his time in Kenya?'

'Sure, he did. We compared notes about all sorts of things, that included.'

'What did he say about that period?'

'He was well angry. There'd been a big case in the news about the Mau Mau uprising, survivors of torture and all that, suing the British government. Told me his old man died in one of our concentration camps. That's what he called them.'

'This was in Kenya. In the fifties.'

'Yeah. Our empire days. We did some terrible things, Doctor. They don't teach this stuff in schools, but our government abused people, treated Johnny Foreigner like shit!'

'You talked about this with Arthur Abimbola? About the abuse of power? The maltreatment of colonial subjects?'

'Yeah. It really wound him up. Me too. The current government isn't much better, when you see what's happening in Iraq, Afghanistan and so on. The way they treat ex-servicemen is pretty shitty, too. We're nothing—civilians, soldiers. All of us disposable to the people in power. It's a crappy world, Doctor.'

'And Abimbola talked about these concentration camps? What did he say?'

'Said he was born in one.'

'Did he ever ask you about your grandfather?'

'Well, of course, we talked about him. My grandad brought me up. I dunno if Arthur ever asked about the old man specifically, but yeah, we talked.'

As Harry sat back and folded his arms, his head to one side as if trying to fathom where these questions were leading, Doc could tell this aspect of the interview was making him very uncomfortable.

'We know about your grandfather's hidden collection of memorabilia, Harry. Diana knew too, didn't she? Your childhood friend, you confided in her when you found them.'

The startled look on Harry's face, the head shake in denial, the open mouth ready to refute Doc's suggestion that he would've betrayed his grandfather's secret, told Doc all he needed to know. Before Harry could deny it, Doc drove the point home.

'It was a terrible family secret. One you still feel guilty about divulging. It's okay, Harry. I understand.'

Harry had not responded, his gaze directed downwards, his shoulders slumped as Doc continued probing.

'And she told Arthur, didn't she?'

'No!'

Despite the vehement denial, Doc was convinced this little 'secret' had been dragged from Diana during her abduction and torture, that Abimbola befriended Harry as a result.

'Perhaps Arthur asked about it over a few beers, you became loose lipped, shared the truth with your African friend when he told you how he'd also suffered as a child... In a concentration camp in Kenya, at the hands of soldiers. Military men. Men like your grandfather.' As Doc probed, his mind was working on other questions, likely links and motivations.

Was it possible that Gerald Butler had been a guard at the very same camp where Arthur 'Akachi' Abimbola had been born? A boy, named by his mother as God's Hand in the hope he might one day act accordingly... A powerful shaman, who on discovering the Butler family secret, befriended the guard's grandson, determined to wreak revenge for the injustices visited on his flesh and blood?

'You empathised with Arthur, a fellow sufferer. You told him about your supposed carer, your grandfather. The man who tortured you as a boy, locked you in a cupboard, beat you and disciplined you in an abusive fashion.'

Doc's hand reached across again as Harry, head still bowed, elbows on the table, slowly nodded, the tears now dripping on to Abimbola's photograph. Another squeeze of his arm encouraged Harry to whisper, his voice regretful as he replied.

'Yes.'

'You told him how you discovered your grandfather's collection of images. How it made you feel.' Another nod from Harry, head down, his shame palpable. 'And the ears? You told him about those.'

Nod.

'I didn't mean to tell him. I've never told anyone else—even Diana only knew about his dreadful photos. I was pretty drunk that night, though. Beer doesn't mix well with my medication.'

Medication?

Drugs, certainly.

'When was this?'

'It was maybe four years ago. I didn't see Arthur after that. I think it offended him. I think I sort of over shared...'

Or else Abimbola had everything he needed from Harry, had squeezed all the information he needed from the damaged soul, after years of draining the young man of everything he knew. Doc asked the question, but was certain he knew how Harry would respond.

'Did Arthur ever suggest hurting your grandfather?'

'No!'

'Not at any time? Not that night, when you were drunk? When he was offended, disgusted by your confession about your grandfather's hoard?'

'Never! Why?' Horror spread across Harry's face as he began to understand where Doc was going with this. 'You think he... You think Arthur had something to do with the body on the common. The one my grandad found suspended in a tree?'

Once again, Doc ignored the question, but Harry was clearly agitated, his fingers twirling as he clasped his hands on the desk, his head frantically shaking in disbelief.

'Did Arthur ever participate in suspension? Or just observe the process when you had clients?' Harry was silent, his head wobbling frantically as Doc pressed him. 'Tell me, Harry! Did he know you undertook suspensions in your cellar—yes or no?'

'Of course he did. You really think he's involved in these horrible murders?'

'We've found evidence that does rather more than suggest that. Much of it ties in with the evidence against you, Harry.'

'What? No... This is so wrong! I don't want to talk any more... Sorry, Doctor. No comment!' He turned to his lawyer, voice raised. 'Tell them to stop. I've had enough. I need my meds. I'm overdue and I'm not feeling well!' The back of Harry's chair hit the wall as he jumped up with a fierce gaze aimed firmly at DS Pierce. 'Take me to my cell! Now, please...'

'Well you just missed some fireworks, Doc!'

DS Sam Sharpe was in gossip mode, but Doc had little time for that.

'Have we heard from the hospital about how Jack's doing? And Fiona?'

'Er, yeah. They're both awake apparently, though dosed up with painkillers.'

'Well, that's great news. I'll head over to see Jack now. Did you get anywhere with the two USB sticks we found in Harding's bag?'

'Not yet. I'll try to get to 'em this afternoon. But two things. The Super wants to see you. And she's on the warpath!'

'Why? I would've thought she'd be crowing to the press about this latest success, with Harding back in custody and Abimbola—'

'Yeah, she did her Soundbite bit earlier, but she's well pissed off about the girl, Sharon Tait.'

'Harry's girlfriend, Shazza?'

'That's right, her. Turns out her old man's some bigshot barrister. Very wealthy and very well connected. Appearances can be deceptive, eh? Makes you wonder why a girl from a nice family would make herself look such a mess. Anyway, we've had to release both her and her mate with the Spiderman tattoo plastered all over his chops.'

Doc did not feel inclined to argue with Sam's assessment of Shazza, was sure she had her reasons, that maybe her family home life was not as *nice* as the detective assumed. He did want an explanation about her release though.

'Really? Weren't the girl's prints on the bag—the one with the planning officer's hand in it?'

'Yeah, but the CPS have said we don't have enough to charge her, just Harry. Her high priced brief argued that the fingerprint—there was just the one of hers—could've accidentally got on the bag while was grabbing other items out of the freezer. You know, getting her lunch out, digging around, touched it without noticing the contents.'

'Hang on. Surely Harry could argue the same.'

'Not really. There were loads of his dabs on it, and anyway, when you take into account the notebook we found, the evidence on it, he's our guy.'

'That device could equally belong to the girl though, surely?'

'No, Doc. I've just been reading a sort of diary with Butler's thoughts, clearly written by him. Apparently he was documenting the victim's innermost secrets, and some of it makes amazing reading. It's really shocking what some people get up to. All the vics were right dodgy bastards... But Butler's the real sicko. Tortured the poor buggers to compile his Book of Secrets. So bleeding proud of it he even created a title page with his name on it. Not that anyone would ever publish it.'

'Secrets. Of course!'

Doc remembered the comment from the very first letter he received, though he found it impossible to believe Harry had written any of those missives to him, and was now wondering if Akachi was the author.

'There's loads of other stuff with commentary and other identifiers on there that point to Harry. Just him, nothing on the girl, Sharon Tait. Soundbite was well miffed that we didn't have enough to hold her without a confession from Harry implicating her... I think that's why Dawson wants to see you. She's already watched the tape of your interview, and was disappointed you didn't get him to hold his hands up to it all this morning, given your reputation for wheedling confessions, and also the fact that Butler would only speak to you... She's really not happy, though she should be. They confirmed her new rank today.'

Doc was getting the message about Sadie's current mood—Sam had alluded to it often enough.

'I'll pop up to her office before I head to the hospital.' Doc turned to go, but then remembered. 'Harding's satnav. Did you get anything off that?'

'We found two other locations programmed into it besides Abimbola's gaff. One of them was your home address, the other was a mansion in St George's Hill. It's where Maddox lives.'

'And the other entry codes? His too?'

'Yeah. One for his main gate and one for the house alarm system.'

The hypothesis Doc had been forming now made complete sense, but he was a little late. The former Acting Superintendent had already announced that the Met's investigation into Patrick Rawlings' murder was being wrapped up in record time, along with nine cold case killings, as well as the body they had discovered in Doc's garage the day before, claims which no doubt secured her promotion.

Without Jack onside, Doc was not sure he could convince Soundbite Dawson she had been a little premature…

It wasn't long before he had her response.

'Harry Butler had Selena Scott's hand in his freezer! And kept records on the notebook computer taken from his premises—photographs of her and the other victims, being stalked and then at different stages of mutilation! And there's his bloody Book of Secrets!'

'I know, but these things could've been planted. Someone broke into their premises at the weekend and nothing was stolen. Were Harry's prints on the notebook?'

'No, but he obviously wiped it down after using it.'

'Well—'

The question as to why Harry Butler would be forensically aware enough to do that while leaving conspicuous fingermarks on the freezer bag was stillborn on Doc's lips as the tirade continued to wash over him. No longer *acting* Superintendent Dawson, frustrated by the overlords at the prosecution service who had forced her to release Sharon Tait, continued to aim her anger at Doc.

'In your interview with Butler, less than an hour ago, he told you he was a long-standing pal of this Arthur Akachi Abimbola. The man whose home business turned out to be a cross between a surgical clinic and a prison. They were working together. Butler honing his medical skills, and Abimbola selling supposedly magical body parts under the cover of a legitimate business. Why is that so hard for you to take in, Doctor Powers?'

'My professional assessment is that Butler is telling the truth. He's genuinely baffled by all that's happened.'

'For chrissakes! You said yourself the man was damaged goods. His PTSD, drug addiction, his history of childhood abuse, all pointed to a fractured personality. The reason he's baffled is because he *genuinely* can't remember his crimes. Fugue states. Split personality. *Your* words, explaining how he can do these things while under stress, terrible things that his memory refuses to acknowledge… I can dig out your briefing notes, the ones you gave Jack Carver if you've forgotten.'

This meeting was rapidly deteriorating, and Doc couldn't wait to be away. Even so, he bristled at her tone, her disparaging dismissal of his current concerns and her overly simplistic regurgitation of his earlier comments.

'As I said… My professional assessment, after meeting Butler again today, all things considered, is that he's been framed. We need to look into Harding's involvement too. What was his role, and why was he at Abimbola's place, apparently faking a suicide?'

'It's obvious isn't it?' Sadie Dawson stood and picked at some errant fluff that had despoiled her immaculate pantsuit trousers, indicating their meeting was over. 'I think you are too close to Butler, you can't see the wood for the trees.'

'Now hang on a minute! How dare—?' Doc stood too, his fists on the table top, his stance like an angry gorilla guarding its territory from an unwelcome invader, but Dawson's voice rode over his words.

'In *my* professional opinion, your joint history is warping your judgement. Harry Butler wanted you drawn into this enquiry for personal reasons, probably related to some residual animosity from his consultations with you over a decade ago, but both he and his accomplice overestimated their control over the psychopath they released from Broadmoor. Harding killed Abimbola because they fell out. Or some other reason. Violent psychopaths, as you well know, don't need much of an excuse to kill, especially those with a lower than average IQ. What's Harding's? Eighty-five? Ninety?'

'About that, but please listen, Sadie.'

'No. I think you should go home, Doctor Powers, but first, visit the nurses' station downstairs. The stitches in your head wound are bleeding into that bandage round your temple. I had high hopes of you gaining a full confession from our one living detainee, but you are clearly agitated, physically distressed and mentally exhausted from the week's events. Thank you for your service. Your contract as a consultant on this case is now formally terminated. We'll send a cheque with an early termination bonus included. Now if you'll excuse me, I have a lot of work to do.'

The Jaguar's wheels squealed as Doc left Scotland Yard's basement car park and joined the traffic on Victoria Embankment. Despite several attempts at controlling his breathing, Doc was furious with the response his assessment received from the newly promoted Superintendent. Any slight on his professionalism always cut him to the core, and she had driven the blade home without a thought.

With a fraction of a second to spare, Doc stamped on the brake in time to miss a motorcycle courier who had swerved across the traffic in front of him. The close encounter forced him to calm down, to drive more carefully. Again, he breathed in, held it, then exhaled through his mouth as he had been taught. Several repetitions later, he was thinking straight again.

Rather than seeking help from the Met's nursing staff, Doc had popped in to see DS Sharpe before leaving, but his only hope for more insights into the case were dashed when Sam said Soundbite had phoned him immediately after their meeting. The sergeant and the rest of Jack's team had been directed not to discuss the case, and instead escort Doc from the premises if he appeared on their floor.

It was this final indignity that had seen Doc accelerate out of the car park in a cloud of burnt rubber.

Oh well, I'll talk to Jack. Maybe he can help.

Doc wasn't sure exactly what his injured friend could do while laid up in a hospital bed, but he mentally crossed his fingers and headed for St George's.

'I'm afraid DI Carver's asleep, Doctor Powers. The lady, Miss Fielding is awake though. She was in surgery most of the night but she's like a human dynamo!'

'It's Detective Sergeant Fielding.' Doc laughed at the description as he corrected the nurse, delighted that Fiona was holding up so well, his good humour restored by the one brief comment. 'If you can point me to her room, I'd like to speak to her.'

The nurse led Doc to a private room and left him with Fiona who was sitting in her bed, surrounded by flowers and cards. She looked fragile but well enough, with her left arm swathed in bandages, and she was just finishing a call on the hospital telephone as Doc entered.

'You're a popular patient, Fiona. Friends and family? Boyfriend, perhaps?'

'Doctor Powers! Just colleagues. My job's my life. And Mum's been living in Jamaica since my dad passed away eight years ago. I don't dare tell her what happened. She worries enough as it is. Anyway, I gather I need to thank you and Jack for saving me from the clutches of that madman.'

That wasn't strictly true since the madman was dead when Doc and Jack arrived, unless she meant Harding. It didn't matter, she was recovering and seemed mentally strong and resilient to Doc.

'How're you feeling, Fiona?'

'Amazingly well, considering. It could be the morphine patch they stuck on my shoulder, though I think it's my reaction to finding myself alive.' She giggled, a little nervously. 'I really thought I was going to die yesterday. Now, my main worry is how much use I'll have of my hand.' She hoisted her injured arm in its sling and dropped it back again. 'It's going to be months before they're sure… I just hope I can still work as a detective.'

'From what I've heard, you'll be fine. The operation was a success and with some rehabilitation you should get most, if not full functionality back. And you can be damned sure Jack won't let them pension you off.'

'Let's hope so. I love the job. Can't even stop while I'm lying here! That was Sam on the phone. He's updated me on everything that's been happening. They've taken my statement already this morning too. Some of it's still a bit hazy, but I'm pretty sure I covered the important stuff.'

'You really should not have gone to that place alone.'

'Mmm. I know. Abimbola was so charming at first. Then he changed, like a chameleon.'

'Psychopaths are often superficially charming, Fiona. They have an uncanny ability to press our buttons, to delude us into believing they're wonderful while manipulating our emotions for their personal enjoyment.'

'I s'pose. I find it hard to understand what motivates these people to do what they do.'

'That's a problem we all have. They operate in an entirely different way, they see normal people as inferior beings, nothing more than playthings to do with as they please.'

'I sort of understand that, but two of them? Working together like this…'

'They also have an innate ability to recognise others like themselves, an affinity in some cases, though psychopaths can't relate in any meaningful way that you or I would understand. They will as easily kill a partner in crime as any other potential victim.'

'Abimbola said something odd in that cellar.'

Her outward confidence and bonhomie disappeared for a shimmer of a second, her face betraying the fear still lurking in her subconscious before her professionalism brushed it back under her mental rug. With some counselling, Doc was sure she would be fine.

'Something important?'

'It may be… I'm not entirely sure, but he mentioned Harry Butler.'

'Really?'

'Well not by name. Abimbola was on about his partner being at work, which is strange as I would've thought he would know Butler was in custody.'

'That is strange. You're sure he said that?'

'I think so, though it's not very clear. I was a bit panicky and freaking out by then.' Fiona's cheeks turned a darker shade, a barely perceptible blush, but Doc noticed, her shame visible, her voice riddled with disgust at her failings. 'I wasn't much of a detective by that stage. Even with my training.'

'Anyone in those circumstances, police or civilian, would have reacted the same way, Fiona.'

'Mmm, maybe… At first I was sure he wouldn't hurt me—me being a copper an'all. Sam said something interesting just now though. Abimbola had already sold his import business, along with the stock and premises. The sale was due to complete at the end of next month and he had booked a one way flight to Kenya for immediately after. No wonder he wasn't worried about my colleagues following up if I disappeared after meeting him. He was mates with the local bobbies too, so he would've been able to blag it for a day or two before poking off overseas a bit earlier than planned.'

'You know, if you hadn't prompted us to make the connection between Akachi the shaman and Abimbola, we might never have done so.'

'I hadn't thought of it that way. With his partner in custody, claiming amnesia, I suppose we'd have just wrapped up the investigation.'

'Uh-huh.' The grunted reply was non-committal, with Doc's mind momentarily elsewhere, thinking about Harding and how the man's overconfidence had revealed the plan to frame Maddox. It could so easily have worked, especially considering the relationship between Maddox and Harry, their military service together, the millions Rawlings cost the professor. 'You did well, Sergeant.'

'Thanks, Doc. I suppose I did alright in the end. It was just so…' Again, the shadow of fear passed across Fiona's face as her voice petered out.

'Do you want to talk about what happened?'

Thus encouraged, Fiona became more animated as she described her ordeal in vivid detail, and Doc let her words tumble out, gently nudging her to recall everything, more as therapy for her than any curiosity on his part. As she continued her explanation she mentioned that Sam had divulged another sliver of information, a detail that Doc had missed out on after being unceremoniously dismissed by Dawson, so he stopped Fiona mid-sentence to probe for more details.

'Sam told you Abimbola kept records, of the sales?'

'Forensics found some handwritten ledgers at the Art of Africa place this morning. You were right about the muti angle. Abimbola was making a load of money on the side, selling his magic body parts. Thousands of pounds for each of them… Dozens and dozens of items—hands, breasts, even a heart… All taken from the victims and sold to buyers, going back years. It's incredible.'

Fiona spent more time unloading her views on muti barbarity, the nature of evil, and how the discovery of Gerald Butler's collection had shocked and upset her on a fundamental level. Doc could tell she was deeply affected and let her get everything off her chest for another twenty minutes before he left her and went to see if Jack had roused.

He was finally awake, but unlike Fiona, he did not look perky and healthy, but wan and haggard, though he managed a washed out grin as Doc entered his room.

'Hi, Doc! Did you bring some grapes?'

'No, but your boss certainly had some sour ones for me this morning. Apparently, I'm a useless failure as I couldn't get Harry Butler to confess to crimes he can't remember ever committing, but she doesn't need his confession anyway as she's convinced he's guilty as charged.'

'Yeah, I heard you're off the case.'

'Wow! The Met's jungle drums must've been banging away for you to hear so swiftly, given you were in the land of nod less than an hour ago.'

'I've got loyal staff, keeping me in the loop. Handy too, now I've been suspended, pending an investigation.'

'For the shooting?'

'Yup. Discharging a weapon. Even a bullet into a scrote like Harding is reason enough these days. He's not even dead, and he shot you, but the PTBs have sidelined me while Soundbite's soaking up all the glory. As usual.'

'How's your belly? Aching?'

Jack tried to sit further upright and groaned as Doc assisted and plumped the pillows behind his back. It was not clear whether Doc's pun or Harding's bullet caused the accompanying grunts of pain.

'Not great.' He chuckled then. 'The doctor who operated joked that my compacted faeces stopped the bullet getting any further. Seems to think my cast iron gut is the result of a diet that's a bit less healthy than it ought to be!'

'Joking aside, are you up for discussing the case?'

'What, your theory that Butler's been framed? Go on then, tell me what's going on in that devious mind of yours. It's not as if I've got anything better to do right now.'

For the next fifty minutes Jack and Doc discussed every aspect of the case, including the scenarios that Doc felt justified further investigation. Initially sceptical, Jack finally caved in.

'Okay, okay. I'll call Sam and tell him to take a look at those thumb drives you found in Harding's bag and also see if we can find any other links to Abimbola that might support your theory. I'm not saying I agree entirely, but it is worth following up, regardless of what Soundbite says.'

'And Judy—'

'Of course, mate. I'll make sure Sam keeps you up to speed on everything, all on the quiet of course. Chuck me that phone.' Doc passed it over and listened as Jack fired off instructions at the detective sergeant. When done, he dropped the handset into the cradle and said to Doc, 'Now let me get some shuteye. I was in so much pain last night I barely slept a wink. I'm absolutely bolloxed! Sally's coming down tonight, so I need to look me best.'

Jack's daughter. A second year student at Durham University, who he had hardly seen since a messy divorce some twelve years earlier.

'Well that's a silver lining, Jack.'

'Yeah. Maybe I should get meself shot more often, might get to see a bit more of her!' Although Jack used dark humour in an effort to mask his true feelings, Doc knew better. As he reached the door, Jack, eyes already closed, his voice back to normal, added, 'And get that bloody bandage sorted. You look like your brains are leaking out, mate!'

FRIDAY

THE STING

'SORRY TO DISTURB you so late, Doc. I hope I didn't wake you.'

'Sam?' Doc fumbled with the phone as he answered, then squinted at the LED display of the bedside clock. Almost one in the morning... 'What on earth are you doing calling me at this time?' Doc came awake with a start as fear clutched its frigid fingers round his heart. 'It's Judy, isn't it? What's happened to her? What have you found?'

'I've got great news, Doc! That's why I'm calling you. I knew you'd want to hear immediately.'

'Absolutely. Go on!'

'Well, the records came through for Dover-Calais. Judith Amelia Finch left for France by foot on the last crossing on the night of the second of January.'

'Thank God! And thank you for letting me know, Sam.'

'There's something else. She was arrested last week.'

'What? Where?'

'Paris. She was at a refugee and illegals' camp. Apparently, she was there working with other volunteers when the police tried to clear the place and a riot broke out. Got caught up in it.'

'But she was released?'

'I've spoken to the Froggy gendarmes and they reckon they just kept her in overnight. There's no record of her coming back to the UK since, so that should put your mind at rest.' Sam hesitated, as if reluctant to ask, then said, 'Er, Jack told me to keep you up to speed with everything... May I come in?'

'What?' Doc hopped out of bed and pulled the curtain aside. Sam was standing under a lamppost leaning against his car, mobile phone to one ear and a laptop bag tucked under his elbow. 'Of course. Is that my MacBook?'

'Yup. All cleaned. And I've got the thumb drives Harding had on him. Can you open the door? It's starting to rain.'

'I'm on my way down.'

———————

'Thanks, Doc.' A freshly brewed Americano arrived on the kitchen worktop next to Doc's MacBook. Sam, sitting where Jack had been a couple of days earlier, plugged an ADSL cable directly into the laptop—the other end was already in the wall socket —and logged on to Doc's ISP. 'Someone has been inside your system since last Christmas. I'm just checking whether your Wi-Fi set up has been compromised too. I'll change the passwords just in case and sort it out so that you can use it again.'

Christmas? Shortly after the TV series broadcast…

It was unthinkable, and Doc decided not to even try to ascertain what the uninvited spy had seen and heard in the nine months since.

'My Wi-Fi? Is that really necessary?'

'Your MacBook was hacked through the internet and if we don't make sure every stage of the connection is clear of malware you could end up in the same situation again.' A few more taps on the keyboard and he added, 'Anyway, it's sorted now. Incidentally, I stored all the files you had on this laptop in the cloud before I cleaned it. We can reinstall everything, but I need to ask a favour first.'

'Go on.'

'It's a long story—'

'Just the highlights will do, Sam.'

'When I was at college studying computer sciences I had a pal who was shit-hot at programming, but he went off the rails a bit, even before he graduated.'

'And?'

'He can help us find out who got into your system, maybe backtrack, possibly even find a way for us to enter the bastard's own files. I've tried, but it's beyond my skill levels.'

'You want to hack into the person who broke into my laptop? Seriously? Let's do it!'

'The problem is… He's on the FBI and Interpol most wanted lists for cybercrime. Nothing bad.'

'Nothing bad? But he's on the world's most wanted lists…'

'Not for fraud or theft or kiddie porn or anything like that. He's a cross between a Snowden and a McKinnon, with a bit of Kim Dotcom thrown in. Last I heard, he's in hiding in Ukraine. He owes me. Big time.'

Although curious to know what exactly this apparently upstanding copper had done for his wayward mate, Doc was more intrigued by the prospect of unlocking the secret collector's own secrets.

'I'm not entirely sure what that combination of names signifies, so just spit it out, Sam. What do you need from me to get your talented cyberfriend to help us? Money?'

'No, nothing like that. He's a mega millionaire. I just need your laptop in its current blank state. Your connection. And plausible deniability. I was never here, and if anyone asks, you were the one contacting him. I'll lose my job, maybe worse if I get found out. You won't.'

'No problem. Just do what you need to do, but make sure my laptop is back to normal when you finish. And what about the USB drives?'

'I'll open those up as soon as I've contacted Rupert.'

'Rupert?'

'Yeah. He hates that name, prefers his online handle.' Sam's fingers were flying across the keyboard as he spoke, his eyes fixated on the screen. 'The Skorpian, spelt with a *k*. It's 'cos he's always stinging people.'

'Well let's hope he can sting whoever's been inside my life.'

———

'Rupe's working on it. Hopefully he'll get back to us shortly. Could I grab another coffee, Doc? I've hardly slept in the last two days. Managed forty winks at the office this afternoon, but that's all.'

'Sure. And what about the thumb drives?'

Doc stood beside his coffee machine, making a second brew for them both. He had a feeling this was going to be a very long night.

'I planned to have a peek earlier but was reassigned by the boss. She thinks Harding's role and whatever he was tasked to do are largely irrelevant now. Here we go.'

Sam plugged the first memory stick into the USB slot as his weary host placed both coffees on the counter then stood beside him. Doc was mildly confused as there was a thumb drive already in place.

'Are you opening both of them at the same time?'

Even with his limited technical expertise, Doc assumed this was a risky approach.

'Nope. This one,' Sam tapped a finger on it, 'is my own special creation. I'm guessing there's some sort of nasty program on Harding's memory sticks designed to wipe files or replace them, or both. This contains a program that'll neutralise the contents on them, then enable us to see exactly what they were designed to do.'

'Will we be able to see the contents of any files on them too? I'm pretty sure Harding was supposed to plant evidence with them.'

'Should be able to.' A whole load of gobbledygook flowed down the screen, too fast for Doc to follow, but Sam kept nodding sagely and grunting approval as the code scrolled past his eyes. 'Brilliant. Let's see what was on this one.'

A few taps on the keyboard and a single folder appeared on the screen, named with a string of characters that also made no sense to Doc. He had an uneasy feeling that Sam may have corrupted the memory stick contents, but the moment the sergeant clicked on the folder Doc's worried frown dissolved into a happy smile.

'A suicide note... Supposedly written by Abimbola.' In his enthusiasm Doc pumped his fist on Sam's shoulder, none too gently. 'You genius, Sam!'

'Steady on, Doc.'

As Doc read then reread the few sentences he could see the truth behind the words:

To my friends and colleagues.
I am so sorry for what I have done. For many decades I have been fighting an evil I
could not contain, and I allowed my inner beast to reign.
I know it is only a matter of time before they will come for me too.
I pray to God that you and He will forgive me.
Akachi

'It's just as you thought, Doc.'

There was a hint of admiration in Sam's tone, thoroughly undeserved in Doc's opinion. It was obvious why Harding had been sent there. Tying up loose ends by murdering The Surgeon's partner, burning the crime scene to the ground to destroy any physical evidence, thereby severing any potential link to the Rawlings investigation. The fire would confuse the authorities, although an autopsy would find evidence of suicide, and this letter on the scorched hard drive would confirm it, if the investigators were suspicious and bothered to salvage it. The evil mentioned in the note could be anything.

It was clever. And totally ruthless. But Fiona had ruined everything for the mastermind Doc was convinced was still at large.

He just grunted as Sam continued.

'Sort of fingers Harry Butler, though it's a bit ambiguous. The *they will come for me too* comment.'

Another non-committal grunt from Doc, then, 'Is that everything?' A nod from Sam confirmed it. 'Let's have a look at this one.' Doc picked up the other USB stick, the one marked number two. 'My guess is that Harding had instructions to plant this on Maddox's home computer.'

'No problem.' Sam swapped the thumb drives and, after a much longer indecipherable screed rolled down the screen, a similar sight greeted them, only this time there were more folders—three in total. With another click, the first folder's contents were exposed. 'These sub folders look familiar. Let's see what we've got.'

The folders contained documents mirroring the contents of the notebook found at Harry Butler's shop, including a Book of Secrets, this time supposedly authored by Maddox.

'This is fantastic, Sam. It almost proves Harry was being set up too.'

'Not really, Doc. Soundbite will say Harry and Abimbola planned to use Harding to plant this to frame Maddox for all the murders, then kill him to shut down any further investigation into the crimes. With all this evidence at the professor's home, well, case solved. But we got them both instead.'

'And what, Abimbola wanted to die once he found out his partner Harry was caught, thinking he'd be arrested too, so arranged for Harding to create his suicide scenario?' That made no sense. He groaned as Sam responded by postulating another possible scenario.

'Harry might have been behind that too. Wanted his partner dead—an unrelated suicide—but didn't expect to get caught, or have us discover his records, his original Book of Secrets and so on.'

Another long sigh from Doc and a weary shrug as he made his way to the coffee machine for yet another refill, then he said, 'Any joy from Rupert?'

'Funny you should ask. He's just invited me to his secure chat-room. Let's see what he's uncovered. And yes, I'd love another espresso, Doc.'

Rupert delivered both good and—potentially—very bad news. Although the web wizard had managed to locate the account on the remote server used by the computer that had hacked into Doc's system, he was confronted with a password that prevented him unlocking the contents.

Access would normally pose little problem for The Skorpian, but he warned Sam that it could take anything from a few minutes to days and even months or years, depending on how effective the account was at fending off the bespoke program now being used to try to crack it.

'It depends on the nature of the password.' Sam explained in response to Doc's impatient muttering as he read Rupert's chat-room messages. 'Most people use names, words they can remember, sometimes in combination.'

'Like me, you mean.' A sheepish look from Doc received a nod from Sam.

'Yup! Using something like *Judith*, as you did, Rupert would gain entry in no time, but for a security conscious user with, say, a fifteen character password mixing numbers, symbols and upper and lower case letters... Well that could take years. Sorry, Doc. We just have to wait and hope for the best. You'd be surprised how many sophisticated users choose passwords that are easy to remember rather than a string of random characters.'

For the next hour they went through everything on the second thumb drive hoping to find something to confirm The Surgeon's true identity, but without success. Nothing they found conclusively exonerated Butler either, merely suggested some ambiguity about his involvement, leaving Doc frustrated. Then the screen vibrated and Rupert's chat-room came to life.

'He's done it!'

Sam let go a little whoop of joy and held up his hand for a high five, but Doc was already busy reading the latest message from the Ukraine.

'We're getting all the files held in the cloud? This is fantastic, Sam!'

Moments later the MacBook started to receive dozens of folders, with one estimating two hours to download as the contents contained such large files.

'Are you thinking what I'm thinking, Doc?' Sam rolled the cursor over the folder and a pop up confirmed it was populating with lengthy video files. 'These.'

'Uh-huh. The CCTV footage of his victims. As soon as the first has completed downloading let's open it. Meanwhile we should check the rest of this treasure trove. There looks to be a lot more than just ten names though.'

There were twenty-two files but only eleven with names they both recognised, including one marked 'Judith Finch'. Doc's heart did a momentary backflip at the sight of it, but the contents merely confirmed Sam's reassurance—there was just a handful of surveillance photos and a couple of pages of notes. It seemed to Doc that Judy had made a lucky escape by choosing to head overseas at the beginning of the year.

Thankfully.

Doc glanced at the kitchen clock. Already three-thirty in the morning, but he felt thoroughly refreshed at the prospect of finally unmasking the evil mind behind the crimes.

'Although we can't visually identify him from the video, I'm pretty sure I recognise his voice, Sam.'

The Surgeon had not said much before eerie chanting and clicking noises dominated the audio, sounding thin and tinny through the MacBook speakers as Doc and Sam observed Rawlings on the operating table. A man dressed in green surgical scrubs, face mask and hat, was leaning over him, scalpel in hand. The camera angle was from overhead and to the side, its focus on the victim, though they could tell

Abimbola was present too. The big man danced in and out of view during the 'opera-tion' dressed in traditional costume while waving a staff decorated with bones, shells and feathers. Doc assumed the performance was for a muti customer, unseen by the camera, as Abimbola was clearly the source of the strange noises they could now hear.

'If only I could get this stuff to the office for proper analysis, but...'

'It's inadmissible evidence, obtained illegally. I know... Can Rupert post it to you at the Met, anonymously?'

'No way, Doc! As far as he's concerned this stuff's for my eyes only, and he wouldn't send this to anyone else in case it ever gets compromised, backtracked. If Rupe knew someone else was with me right now, he would be gone and I'd lose him forever. He's taking a huge risk just accessing this account, sending the files like this... He trusts me, and I've got to respect that.'

'I was wondering how we'd get round this ever since you said your Skorpian pal was on the most wanted lists, Sam.'

'Well, even though we can't use this material in any official way, at least we now know who The Surgeon is. That's something.

'Something, but it's not enough, Sam.'

'True, but I do have the password from Rupe. If we could get a search warrant using some legitimate reason, then I could access the killer's computers, connect to his cloud server to gather this evidence officially. I could claim I cracked his security using my own tools. No one would be any the wiser. But I can't do any of that without a warrant...'

'That's all we need?'

'Yup. But we'll never get one. Soundbite won't listen to us, especially as she's already told the world she's got the killer locked up and his partner's dead. She'd go ballistic if she knew I was doing this, contacting a known felon, commissioning a criminal act from him. And I'm not even supposed to be talking to you... We're stuck with a load of incriminating files we can't use, Doc.'

'There has to be a way...' After another cup of coffee and several laps pacing his kitchen, Doc said, 'Got it! I have an idea.'

After explaining what he planned, initially with much scepticism and resistance from Sam, they agreed to discuss the idea with Jack and only go ahead with his bless-ing. Sam sent a message thanking Rupert before signing off, and for the next hour they worked on Doc's plan.

'He's coming, Doc!'

The detective's gruff voice echoed in the miniature transceiver ear bud as Doc booted up the computer in the office at the back of the morgue situated in the base-ment of St George's Hospital. Jack, though capable of a painful upright shuffle while clutching the wheeled pole supporting the hanging bag of saline attached to his fore-arm, was sitting in a wheelchair, positioned where Doc had left him some ten minutes earlier, keeping watch on the staff entrance. The pathologist was usually in his office at eight o'clock, rarely a moment before or after, so they knew how much time they had before he would arrive, on this, his final day at work.

Doc's plan had not taken into account the geriatric health service computer now confronting him. Frustrated, he muttered his impatience at the screen.

'Come on! Come on!'

It seemed to be taking forever to come to life.

'Stay calm, mate. He's about a minute away still.'

The reassuring voice reminded Doc that Jack could hear every word he uttered—the device Sam had fitted was doing exactly as advertised—but his heart still tripped and stuttered with anticipation and fear. He just hoped his plan was foolproof rather than foolhardy. At least Jack was onside despite both his and Sam's initial doubts.

The welcome screen eventually materialised, but it was not at all welcom*ing*—it demanded a password that Doc did not have. Sam had assured him it would not matter, so Doc went ahead and plugged the thumb drive into the machine, just as Professor Robert Heinrich Koch buzzed himself through the security doors to his place of work.

'Bob!'

Caught red-handed, Doc remained seated behind the pathologist's desk, a guilt ridden look on his face as his voice echoed through the deserted morgue.

Their eyes locked.

Several emotions made a brief appearance on Koch's face at the sight of the tableau visible through his office windows and its open door. Initially consternation, followed by confusion, then, as he took in the empty morgue, determination and finally, triumph. The ME locked the door from the inside, still staring at Doc who appeared frozen, as if a video had been paused, then laughed at the intruder in his domain.

'Well, well! Colin… It's so nice to see you. You're a little early for my retirement party, though.' Instead of making his way directly to his office, Koch took a short detour to a trolley with a gleaming display of surgical implements laid out on it. With a theatrical flourish he selected a scalpel, held it up to the light, squinting, as if checking it was sharp enough for what he had in mind. 'I was wondering whether you would ever connect the dots. Fortunately, we have complete privacy in here this morning. I told my assistant not to bother coming in, to take a long weekend while I pack my things.'

Koch stepped into his office as he completed his little speech, and remained standing, peering down at Doc through his horn rimmed glasses, like a headmaster about to deliver a caning to an errant pupil.

'I—I—I erm…'

'Goodness! It's not like you to be speechless. Your verbal diarrhoea on that trashy TV programme you presented was endless. Talk to me, Colin.' Koch placed the scalpel on the desk, well within his grasp, just centimetres from the fingers of his right hand, but a long stretch for Doc. 'What are you doing in my office?' With his left hand, Koch opened the lid of a glossy wooden box situated just behind the computer screen and made a point of selecting an item out of Doc's line of vision. 'Is that a USB stick you've plugged into my machine? What on earth for?'

Doc snatched the thumb drive from the slot in the computer and palmed it into his pocket, his face red, his voice flustered. 'It's nothing… I just… I needed to check on some case files, some post mortem records. It was urgent and you weren't here so I—'

'Oh, really? Let me see that.'

The cigar Koch lifted to his nose before taking an exaggerated sniff looked to be about ten inches in length to Doc, something that would take hours to smoke. Not that he expected Koch to light it. And it was not the hospital's anti-smoking policy that would prevent him doing so, had he felt inclined.

As if debating whether to bluff or just accept the reality that Koch had caught him in the act, Doc hesitated, then said, 'Celebrating, Bob? That might be a little premature.' He drew his hand from his pocket, and opened his palm with the device lying flat, the markings clear for them both to see.

'A USB stick, labelled number two. Mmm. Intriguing.'

With the cigar in his left hand and the scalpel back in his right, Koch appeared to slice off the end in preparation for lighting up.

'You know exactly what it is, Bob.' Doc's voice was defiant in defeat. 'And so do I. It's the device you wanted Harding to use to frame Dickie Maddox, the thumb drive I found in his possession yesterday. But I made a few minor changes before loading the contents on to your computer.'

'You've stooped that low, Powers? You came here to plant manufactured evidence on me. Wow! You thought that would work? How desperate must you be?' A harsh chuckle, then, 'I'd heard Sadie Dawson had thrown you off the Rawlings case for incompetence... Oh dear! How that must have hurt your enormous ego... This really is an unexpected delight after yesterday's disappointment, missing out on the two brains I'd hoped to have here in time for my very last day as senior Medical Examiner.' Koch licked his lips and placed the cigar in his mouth. Doc felt a moment's panic as the end pointed at him. 'Harding's still clinging to life, but you, on the other hand, well, let's see.'

A pinprick in Doc's neck cut off his next words.

'You planned to kill Hard—' He lost control of his mouth.

This shouldn't be happening.

Yesterday, Doc had listened as Fiona recounted her experiences at the hands of Abimbola, her description of the disguised blowpipe, the dart, the effect it had on her. How she had been immobilised, but able to scream when the police had come to the cellar door.

The moment he'd arrived in Koch's office, Doc had spotted the humidor on the desk, had taken a look inside and realised it probably contained the same weapon, though had not told Jack, fearing he'd call the whole thing off. Having seen the giant cigars, Doc fully expected an attack, to be rendered helpless

But not this.

With his heart skipping, he felt his tongue swell and his mouth seemed to be paralysed too.

This is not right... Is it a different drug?

Poison?

Jack's voice bounced against his eardrum, no longer reassuring, full of urgency and concern.

'Doc! Are you alright? What's happening in there? Say the word and we'll be in.'

The word, the signal they had agreed Doc should use if he felt endangered at any point.

Mutilated.

No amount of effort would force any sound from Doc's throat as he felt Koch's hand on his bandaged forehead, pushing his head back from where it had flopped, the owlish face up close, the flat of the scalpel tapping the tip of Doc's nose.

'Let's have a little fun, shall we.'

Oh Christ, Jack! Help me!

As the drugs took hold, all the plates and pins and screws the surgeons had used to put his shattered body back together again, three years ago, now seemed to tighten, sending bolts of pain lancing into his brain. The bullet wound to his scalp felt as if it had been torn open again, and an angle grinder was being used on his skull. Already in agony, he wished for the relief of unconsciousness, but knew from Fiona's description that it would not be forthcoming.

Doc was utterly—and literally—petrified.

Koch held Doc in place with a hand on his shoulder while he dragged the executive chair from his office into the morgue, the wheels squealing against the tiled floor, then manhandled Doc on to one of the steel post mortem tables.

'Now, let's continue our discussion. This will make you more voluble again. I'm sure we can drag a few secrets from you in the next hour or so before I lock you in one of the cold room drawers. I doubt anyone will miss you until it's way too late.'

With his tongue still frozen, and having feared the worst, the burning syringe needle in Doc's neck came as something of a relief, his panic receding with the knowledge Koch was administering a drug that would allow him to call for assistance. Jack spoke into his ear again.

'Are you okay, Doc? What's going on in there? If I don't hear your voice in the next twenty seconds, I'll set Sam and his boys loose.'

Jack's words calmed him further, along with the knowledge that Koch was in no hurry to finish him off. With the chemicals surging into his brain, every cell in his body sensitised, he tried to isolate the physical pain—though his mind was still hyper aware. Doc needed Koch to properly incriminate himself, and the gloating pathologist soon obliged.

'My former associate came up with that rather ingenious disguised blowpipe design, based on a traditional African weapon, much favoured by the Pygmies. Wonderful continent. I planned to return to Kenya to take over the family's agricultural estates next month, but will leave a little earlier than originally planned thanks to this unexpected development. Extradition treaties are such a bore, too. I'll just have to disappear, which is rather disappointing.' Koch pantomimed the emotion before perking up for Doc's benefit. 'Fortunately, a crooked hedge fund manager left a rather handsome sum in a Cayman Island bank account, one I now control, so I'll get over it!'

It was a struggle to ignore the pain firing along every one of Doc's nerve bundles, but he forced himself to compartmentalise as best he could, to use this well practised technique along with his skills at meditation and yogic breathing to ameliorate the effects of the drugs.

'A few seconds more, then you'll be able to talk. Mmm. Wouldn't it be fun to open up your skull and take a look inside, spend a little time exploring your brain? Ooh, so much better than a leaving party. First, let's have a look at what Harding did to prepare you.'

The bandage round Doc's scalp was ripped off unceremoniously, an excruciating sensation that dimmed his vision as Koch crowed about his African roots.

'It's such a shame, though… My ancestral home near Nairobi is beautiful, and it's where Akachi and I met as young lads. His mother worked for mine, a live-in house-maid, but Akachi was treated in many ways like the brother I never had. We boys grew up together, and became mutually attracted when we discovered how much we had in common.' A smile warped Koch's slug-like lips, as if some exotic pink species was slithering across his face. 'We were separated in our early teens when my mother discovered my sexual proclivities not only favoured the male of the species, but more disgracefully to her colonial mind, a beautiful black boy. I was sent away to the UK to a private school, and it was not until some fifteen years later we were reunited. We spent many years as lovers, partners, fellow pioneers in the search for truth, joined in our quest to expose the innermost secrets of outwardly normal people.'

A look of lust and regret for lost youth momentarily darkened Koch's face, and Doc, his mouth starting to work, grunted a few words, more to reassure Jack than in any great hope of enlightenment.

'W-why... k-kill... th-then?'

Jack muttered in relief at hearing Doc's voice. 'Thank fuck you're still able to talk! I wish we had eyes on you. Just say the word and we'll have him. Admitting his links with Akachi may be enough to convince the Super to arrest him and justify a warrant to search his office and his home.'

May be enough?

Doc heard the uncertainty in Jack's voice, would have to goad Koch to continue his confession, just to be sure.

'Kill who?' A genuine look of bafflement accompanied Koch's question—there were so many victims.

'Ak-a-chi.'

'Oh, he was a greedy man, in every possible way. His fleshy appetites stretched beyond mine, to both sexes. I was never enough for him and, as I aged, well, the attraction he once felt for my youthful body gradually turned to disgust. He thought I'd forgiven him for dumping me, he thought we would fly to Kenya to start a new life there together. That was never going to happen.'

'Su-i-cide?'

'Well, after he abducted that Finch woman lookalike and left her as a gift for you, it seemed best that he should join his victim rather than *hang around* any longer.' Koch chuckled at his own black humour. 'He was very sloppy when he worked alone, and I was a little concerned that the police might link him to Harding too.'

'Har-ding?'

'Yes, that low life criminal was a huge disappointment, only fulfilled part of his contract, but not my plans to bury my former friend Maddox under a mound of incriminating evidence, along with the rubble from his preposterous mansion. Another self-important narcissist who turned my advances down. Akachi didn't realise he too was due for the scrapheap. He thought we were both setting up Maddox and Butler, that we'd be off to Africa together. Such a blind fool.'

This was plenty for a warrant, enough for Soundbite to swallow her pride and accept she'd got it all wrong.

'Rawlings... Mut-i-lated... Framed... Butler... Brilliant!'

The scalpel now hovered dangerously close to Doc's stitches but he hoped the praise might delay his tormentor's blade for a few vital seconds—until the cavalry arrived.

Where are they?

486

On using the trigger word, Doc had expected an acknowledgement. Could Jack have missed it? Doc's earpiece remained ominously silent. Had something gone wrong with the plan? Perhaps the signal had been lost just as Doc had found his voice.

That didn't bear thinking about…

'Brilliant, indeed. When I found out about Harry Butler's history with Maddox, well, I thought we'd play a game by framing them both for our crimes. Akachi was initially impatient when he learned the whole truth about the chap's grandfather, had some plans of his own to punish the family, but he was enjoying our joint venture, learning how to operate, became quite skilled over the years. He planned to set up an unlicensed surgery once he was back in Africa. There's a very lucrative black market for transplant organs, one he thought he could exploit.'

Koch was in full flow, glorying in his smug recollections. Doc was keen to keep him talking, preening himself rather than torturing him.

'Crem-a-torium? Clever… too.'

'I sponsored him, got him his first job in the UK when he arrived. It's very useful having someone with access to such a facility, being able to dispose of unwanted bodies without a trace. I was rather disturbed to discover he was stealing bones from my earliest victims before they were roasted, for his pathetic muti customers. Then I had a better idea. Working together on live specimens.'

'Diana Davies. Was she the first?'

Doc's mouth was almost back to normal now, so he asked, even though he knew she was not, having seen the files from Rupert the Skorpian. On hearing nothing from Jack, he had to keep playing for time.

'Haha! Of course not. The only reason she was dumped where she could be found was because Akachi's idiot client insisted she be cleansed in running water after we'd finished with her. Part of the ritual. That was no problem, we always planned to blame her death on her friend and ex-lover, Harry Butler. Not much of a challenge considering I'm the one who did the post mortem. The police lost interest, though. She was only a hooker, after all. Who would've thought it? Over a decade later and he's finally being charged with her murder!'

'You've been at this for a long time, haven't you, Bob? You did well to get away with it for so long.'

The words, designed to massage Koch's ego, almost choked Doc as he uttered them, while his brain screamed:

Send them in NOW, Jack!

'I've been experimenting with the human form for over thirty years. Northern Ireland was, well, something of a training ground. I had a great deal of fun there working for Her Majesty, extracting secrets from terrorists…'

'Why me?'

'Oh, I watched you over the years and often wondered whether you'd be a match for me. Of course, you weren't. So much for your reputation, your supposed genius!' After a beat, Koch gave a grudging look of admiration as he added, 'Mind you, when Dawson asked about a muti link during the Rawlings post mortem on Tuesday, I will admit, I was rather confounded. An inspired bit of thinking, Powers, along with your idea to use Morse to identify him. I was rather stunned when I heard the police had discovered his name, having thought he'd remain anonymous, but these things still got you nowhere.'

Not quite...

Doc went to speak but the tip of the scalpel suddenly appeared close to his left eyeball, freezing his vocal cords as effectively as Koch's dart.

'At first, I admired you for such insights. Gradually, I became more fascinated by your failures, the mental illness that you tried to hide while working for the Met... Your breakdowns. Your dalliance with that woman, the elusive Finch, after you killed your wife. Your undeserved fame, thanks to the Leech brothers fiasco. But you don't realise, do you?'

A crackle in Doc's ear, then Jack's voice.

Finally!

'We're coming in, Doc!'

For chrissakes, hurry, man!

Doc managed to motivate his reluctant vocal cords, and croaked, 'I don't realise what, Bob?'

'I see inside your mind, Powers. You're like me. Admit it! Be honest, expose the real you, for once. The psychopath residing in your brain...' The predatory stare returned to bore into Doc's eyes, the scalpel still paused. 'I'd always planned to challenge you like this, to play a game with you before I retired, even before your final insult last year.'

The blade flashed before slicing the stitched gunshot wound, intense concentration on Koch's face as he worked.

Oh God, no!

Despite the blinding pain, Doc was determined not to give Koch the satisfaction of hearing him scream, and tried to speak as calmly as he could.

'Insult? Last year? What do you mean? Arghhh!'

In Doc's mind's eye, he imagined the surgical steel delving, slicing into the thin layer of tissue, as Koch tried to uncover the crown of his skull, ready to tear back the flesh in preparation for the Stryker autopsy saw. The blade, spinning at seventeen thousand RPM would take just seconds to rip through the bone to expose the precious grey matter beneath. The images and overwhelming sensations almost blotted out all rational thought, but Doc managed to bring his panting breaths back under control in an effort to remain centred, present. Lucid.

Where the hell is Sam and his team?

Jack answered, as if Doc had spoken aloud. 'Just hang in there, pal. We had a slight technical hitch.'

What?

Doc's mind could not fathom what sort of technical problem would leave him helpless, alone at the mercy of this sadistic killer. Koch's voice needled into him, whingeing about something ridiculous.

'The TV programme. I wasted a whole morning of my life being filmed for your benefit, at your request, and you used none of it... I watched the entire dreadful series and my contribution is lying around in some director's cutting room somewhere, unseen!'

'The producer decided, not me.'

'Bullshit, Powers! It was the best part of the show and you cut it as you couldn't stand to be shown up for the fool you are.' The bloody scalpel flashed again as Koch waved it in Doc's face, his own contorted with rage. 'You've always been arrogant, looking down your nose at others. You and Maddox are peas in a pod. Strutting around as if you both possess unique skill sets, some superior talent that others like me could never aspire to. But you were wrong. Both of you. I've proved it. And you came here, stupidly thinking you could frame me for my own crimes! You egotistical fool...'

Ego?

Is that what this was all about?

The shattering of the morgue door, an unexpected but very welcome explosion as far as Doc was concerned, startled Koch, still holding his scalpel hand in mid air. Doc could not turn his head, was unable to see Sam and the other policemen enter, yelling at Koch to *Drop the weapon!* but he heard the zap of the high voltage discharge of the taser's metal hooks as they latched on to Koch's chest. The evil pathologist's shocked face disappeared from view to be replaced by Sam's beaming visage.

'I told you this was a shitty idea, Doc! We couldn't open the door. When I wheedled the access code from the hospital staff they didn't think to tell us the ME could override it from the inside and lock everyone out.'

'So that's what took you so long...'

'Yeah. And it's high security material, heavyweight stuff to stop anyone coming in here and tampering with the stiffs. The lads had to use Hatton rounds on the hinges to be sure to get in here quick enough.'

Specially adapted shotgun ammunition designed for door breaching. Doc had heard of Hatton rounds, but never before been present when they were used, had no idea Jack's impromptu rescue team had them available. Implementing this hastily formulated plan could so easily have been a disaster.

'That's why you didn't come immediately I used the trigger word.' Despite some residual pain from the drugs, Doc's overwhelming relief at being rescued was making him euphoric.

'Yeah, this was such a half-arsed operation... Off the books with Jack suspended, and you playing at bloody hero. You could've died in here.' Sam was genuinely upset at the prospect, then brightened. 'At least your ruse worked. Koch really thought you came here alone. Twat! Well, we've got more than enough for a warrant with his taped confession. We know what we'll find when we search his computers.' Sam winked. 'Job done, Doc.'

Jack's wheelchair arrived beside Doc's steel bed, his head appearing on the opposite side to Sam's. Doc remained immobile. The two detectives inspected him, apparently amused by his helplessness.

'I can't move, Jack. Just get me out of here!'

'He gave you that stuff, didn't he. Same as Fifi. Haha! It'll wear off in an hour or two, mate.' The grin on Jack's face was borderline manic as he spoke. It occurred to Doc that his friend had been pretty stressed himself during the last ten minutes or so. 'That wasn't supposed to happen. Christ, if I'd known he was gonna fire that stuff into you, I wouldn't have given you the go ahead to come in here alone like this...'

'We got him though, Jack. It was worth the risk.'

Only minutes before, even Doc had doubted his own plan—had almost cancelled the whole operation when he saw the oversized humidor on Koch's desk.

'So much for you being sacked, mate. Hah! Let's see how Soundbite Sadie tries to wangle the credit for this.' The sour note accompanied his chuckle, then a frown as Jack inspected the cut in Doc's scalp, poked at the edge of the wound with a finger, eliciting a yelp of pain. 'Don't be such a wimp. He's cut one stitch. That's nothing compared with what Harding did to my belly. Anyway, looks like we were in the *nick* of time!'

Even Doc had to smirk as both coppers chortled at Jack's pathetic pun before they disappeared from sight, leaving him staring at the ceiling, relieved that his brain was still inside his skull where it should be. He listened as a very dazed Koch was cautioned and bundled away.

EPILOGUE

JUSTICE

THE HOOKS in Harry Butler's back and arms tightened and pulled the flesh with a stinging sensation that began to throb before settling to a steady burn as Glen slowly hoisted him towards the cellar ceiling below his Streatham shop.

Shazza appeared from behind him, her face shining with joy as she raised a pierced eyebrow at him, a silent question to ask if he was okay as his spreadeagled form rose above her, his arms outstretched in the Crucifixion pose. Harry answered with a smile of his own as hormones started to flood his system, a euphoric sensation engulfing him, releasing him from the grasp of the tormented memories littering his traumatic past.

Earlier that morning, Shazza had come to Scotland Yard to meet him, to celebrate his release from custody. All charges had been dropped and although no explanation was given, the newspapers were already full of stories relating to the case. When Shazza had offered copies for Harry to read in the car as they travelled the short distance to Streatham, he had merely shuddered and said he had no further interest in the affair.

The Metropolitan Police had given no apology for his arrest, the interrogations, the accusations and charges made against him, had merely told him he could leave.

It was of no consequence. Harry was just glad to be free, though desperate to meditate in his cellar sanctuary.

Footsteps echoed in the room as Glen tramped up the stairs and Shazza, face still radiant, her love for Harry unquestionable, blew a kiss at her man before dimming the lights, then left him hanging in blissful peace.

'He's in here, Doctor Powers.'

Doc thanked the nurse as she closed the door behind him and he sat down beside the bed.

'Hello, Antony.'

The gentle words elicited no reaction from the patient whose head and neck were swathed in bandages, his body motionless, arms and legs useless, his breathing controlled by a machine.

Doc tried to find some pity in his heart, some flicker of emotion, some empathy for the man who had killed his father so many years before. He searched inside himself, but found nothing.

After a moment's reflection, he stood and bent from the waist, his lips almost kissing Harding's right ear, his voice raised as he spoke.

'You may be hoping to recover your sight when they remove that dressing, but your cheek bone was shattered by the same bullet that entered your spine. The one that destroyed your tongue, pierced the roof of your mouth and exited through the side of your face. When your head hit the ground, a bone sliver from your upper jaw was driven into your one good eye, and ruined it. You'll never see the sun rise again, no matter how long you live.'

Harding's head made a minuscule movement against the padded neck brace, as if he was trying to turn towards the sound. Or perhaps, Doc decided, he had felt the warmth of breath on his earlobe, yet was totally unaware of the coldness of the words.

Even though Doc knew he might be wasting his time speaking to Harding, he needed to talk, to get the years of angst out of his system. He sat and for the next twenty minutes he talked about his father and all the regrets he had, the arguments that seemed so important during that early part of his life, the fights that had left father and son estranged before Doc left for university. His plans to apologise and try to revive things, to start over on graduation...

All this, before the relationship came to a violent and permanent end at Harding's hands.

Being here, just vocalising the feelings, the thoughts, was cathartic, though little more than that, and Doc knew it. He explained to the man, once again pressing his lips close, voice raised.

'They tell me you can't hear me, Antony, but it doesn't matter. The doctors say you're almost certainly permanently deaf as your one good ear also disintegrated that day. They plan to scan your brain to see if you are likely to recover any hearing at all, though they doubt it.'

Again, Harding's head seemed to move a fraction, as if he was aware, listening to Doc's voice.

Or was that just wishful thinking on Doc's part?

'Whether you hear or not, they also tell me you'll be tormented by tinnitus for the rest of your life. Incessant noises inside your head, filling your mind. All day, all night. Every day, every night.'

In many ways, Harding was now suffering something similar to the terrible trauma inflicted on Patrick Rawlings, and the symmetry of it gave Doc a shred of satisfaction.

Justice.

For a few seconds, Doc was silent as he reflected on the reason why his father had died. A phone conversation with Dickie Maddox the previous evening had finally enlightened him, and after ending the call, Doc had been in a murderous rage himself, but now his voice was calm as he continued.

'Your larynx, your voice box was ruptured too, and they've had to remove most of your tongue. You won't be talking to anyone again, tormenting people for fun, like you did with me. You'll never enjoy another meal or a drink. Your life is over, but you will continue to exist—for as long as they choose to keep you breathing while feeding nutrients into your bloodstream. Conscious, but incapable... It's nothing more than you deserve.'

While driving to the hospital this morning, Doc had been sure he would feel an irresistible urge to unplug the device that pumped life into Harding's lungs, especially after Dickie Maddox had explained the reason why Doc's father had been murdered. But now he was just glad he had come to see the convict for himself, finally convinced he could put aside any further thoughts about the man.

'Goodbye, Antony. I have better things to do than waste any more time with you.'

Doc took one last look at the man who had murdered his father, the vicious thug who had almost killed him and his friend Jack Carver, then pulled a ferry ticket from his pocket, his thumb caressing the destination as he thought to himself:

Far better things to do.

If it took him forever, he would track her down and tell her how much he needed her, how much he wanted to be with her.

He was going to Paris.

To find Judy.

GASLIGHTING

A BRITISH CRIME THRILLER

DOC POWERS & D.I. CARVER INVESTIGATE

THE REMORSELESS TRILOGY
BOOK THREE

'SUSPENSE GLUEING ME TO THE PAGES, HEART BEATING FASTER THAN NORMAL, EMPATHISING WITH THE CHARACTERS, FEARING FOR THEM — I KNEW THERE WOULDN'T BE AN EASY HAPPY ENDING...'

READING EXPERIENCE REVIEW

DEFINITION

1). GASLIGHTING (VERB)

A FORM OF MANIPULATION AND EMOTIONAL ABUSE. THE PERPETRATOR AIMS TO CREATE DOUBT IN THE MIND OF A TARGETED INDIVIDUAL, OR MEMBERS OF A GROUP. TARGETS BEGIN TO QUESTION THEIR OWN MEMORY, PERCEPTION, AND SANITY.

THE TERM WAS FIRST USED IN GAS LIGHT, A 1938 PLAY THAT INSPIRED THE 1944 FILM.

2). GASLIGHTING (VERB, COLLOQUIAL)

ARSONISTS' SLANG FOR THE TECHNIQUE OF USING A FUEL-FILLED MOLOTOV COCKTAIL, LAUNCHED FROM A DISTANCE, TO IGNITE A FLAMMABLE OR EXPLOSIVE COMPOUND, THEREBY CREATING A MUCH LARGER INFERNO.

PROLOGUE

SEVERAL YEARS BEFORE…

KINDLING

WHEN BILLY MET UNCLE PETER

'You didn't know you had an uncle, did you? Mummy and Daddy didn't tell you, did they?'

Billy shook his head, his face a picture of misery.

'That was very bad of both of them. Don't you think?'

The boy was confused, but nodded.

'If I were you, I'd want to punish them. For lying. Lying's bad, isn't that right boy?'

Again, a desperate nod.

'So. As it's not your fault, I'm going to let you go.'

Billy's eyes, already huge, threatened to pop out, either in fear or disbelief.

'R-r-really?' His voice squeaked.

'Really. But you'll have to promise. You'll never forget Uncle Peter. That you'll think of me every day.'

'P-p-promise.' Billy's head jerked up and down. 'Every day, Uncle.'

'You know, boy. Normally I think people tend to lie. But today, I believe you…'

SATURDAY

PRE-IGNITION

BILLY LEECH WOKE seconds before his alarm clock had a chance to rouse him. As the usual staccato burst of music from his favourite punk band started playing, his palm slammed down on the *off* button while his eyes focused on the digital display. His ears, alert for any unusual sounds, twitched as he strained to hear if either of the other house occupants were up and about.

Nothing from downstairs.

Just the wind rattling a branch against his skylight window and a few groans from the roof rafters in his attic bedroom, creaking above his head.

Satisfied that he was the only one conscious at 3am, his designated witching hour, he grinned into the darkness, slipped on his shorts and tee shirt, and padded across the bare floorboards to the door. He had no need to be stealthy, but it was a habit ingrained in his psyche, and he seemed to drift down the stairs like a wraith, his feet avoiding the steps with loose planking, so that he arrived outside his mother's room with only the air disturbed by his movements.

In any normal household, the light spilling from the gap at the bottom of a bedroom door would suggest the resident was awake.

But this was no normal household.

Billy's hand twisted the doorknob and he craned his head into the room to check on his mother. A flicker of disgust warped his features for just a moment, before they relaxed back to form his habitual surly teenage scowl.

Suzie Leech was snoring. A snuffling, grunting wheeze that reminded Billy of happier times—their regular family trips to Bucklebury Farm Park when his younger self had been able to pet the animals. Despite the park being just a few miles from his current home, he had not visited for several years. That last time had been a few weeks before he had been forced to come to this place, to live in this dump, all the while thinking it would be a temporary arrangement. Soon after, his mother had followed, insisting they stay in a vain attempt to leave behind the horrors of their house in London. As if their dreadful memories could be expunged by some country air.

'Pah! You stupid, snorting sow.' He muttered under his breath as he pulled the door to, thinking how much he had grown up since his uncle had come to visit them, that one fatal night when events had wrenched Billy from the innocent grasp of childhood.

The image of his mother lying on a different bed floated through his brain for a few distressing seconds, then he squeezed his eyes shut to clear his mind. His feet, as if driven by another soul, a malevolent presence that had visited his family that same night in Chelsea, carried him to his Nana's room.

Billy tingled with anticipation, the thrill of the predator, as he tugged open her door. No light on in here.

Nana was dead to the world.

Well, not quite. Soon, maybe…

The delicious thought murmured in his head as he switched on the light. The old dear did not stir, her breathing was regular and deep—hardly surprising, given the cocktail of drugs Billy had added to the small glass of warm milk he had brought her some five hours before. Empty now, other than some opaque residue, long since dried, clinging to the inside.

Good.

The sickly-sweet smell of Nana's preferred potpourri irritated his nostrils, but it amused him to know why she felt it necessary to have several jars dotted around the room, flooding the place with cloying odours. Lavender with a hint of mothballs.

He gazed down at her for a few moments, wondering if she experienced vivid dreams as she lay there, her wrinkled mouth open and quivering as she breathed, her head nestled, snug in the down pillow with her thinning chestnut hair draped around her. Maybe he would ask her in the morning, though he knew she was probably too far gone from the various medications he had fed her to remember much at all.

'No sweet dreams for you then, Nana… Just another nightmare.'

Billy chuckled, pulled back her duvet and inspected her.

Unlike the dyed hair, the thin yellow silk of her nightgown could not disguise the ageing truth, the frail seventy-four-year-old body, with its bony hips and parchment skin, veined, wrinkled and liver-spotted.

Disgust once again tugged ugly at Billy's lips, and his shoulders shuddered at the sight of her. He knelt on the edge of the bed, unbuttoned the front of his shorts, reached inside and prepared himself.

The stream of warm urine was aimed at Nana's crotch and it stained the silk as it spread down the insides of her emaciated thighs to the sheet below. The sight sent a wave of euphoria through Billy's frame, electrifying him.

Once finished, he eased himself off the bed, checked his handiwork, and, satisfied with the effect he had created, rearranged the duvet to cover his mother's mother again.

Time to up the stakes, he thought.

Tomorrow, he would give an enhanced performance.

With one last glance at her, still almost comatose, he lifted the glass from her bedside table and picked up her slippers, then glided from the room.

Two hours later, he was climbing back into bed, well pleased with himself, convinced his Uncle Peter would approve. As his head dropped on to the pillow, his teeth gleamed in the dark at the thought of what they had planned for the coming days, the special events that would mark the conclusion of his childhood, in celebration of his mere sixteen years on the planet.

With that final thought, he drifted into blissful sleep.

———

Doctor Colin Powers heard Judy's scream but thought he was still dreaming about her at first. Then he came awake with a start. The high-pitched screeching flushed the residue of sleep from his brain as he bounded across the bedroom while yelling a reply down the stairs.

'I'm coming, my love!'

A sickening lurch in his chest warned him that he had leapt into action too fast, and he forced himself to slow down as he dragged the dressing gown from its hook on the back of the door. He was still getting used to his medication, and at moments like this, tachycardia and dizzy spells still caused him some distress. The last thing he needed right now was to have a heart attack or black out and tumble down the stairs to where Judy was waiting, staring up at him.

Even dressed in her running kit, she looked stunning to Doc, and his heart did a little jig at the sight of her, bathed in yellow dawn sunlight as she stood in the hall. Her lovely face, pale and distorted from shock, was still enough to send happy hormones cascading through him, boosting his mood immediately. Despite the accompanying surge in energy levels, he was cautious and used the bannister to aid his progress down to her.

'What's wrong, sweetheart?'

'The neighbours' cat!' She raised a trembling hand and pointed at the front door, her violet eyes still on his.

Although the door was ajar, Doc could not see outside and wondered whether Judy's hyper alertness was caused by something real or imagined.

'I'm sure the cat'll be fine. Why don't you just go for your—'

'It's not going to be bloody fine, Colin!' She took a pace towards the oak-timbered door, hauled it back on its hinges and stepped away as the object of her horror swung into view.

Doc arrived at the foot of the stairs at the precise moment the accuracy of her comment hit him. A brick between the eyes might have had less impact than the sight suddenly confronting him. He staggered back, his ankles tripping on the bottom step, throwing him off balance and on to his butt with an agonising crunch of the coccyx.

The yelp at the back of his throat failed to reach his lips. He was struck mute, though his mind immediately went to work and conjured up a number of explanations for the travesty adorning their front door. None of which would he share with Judy.

'Who'd do such a thing, Colin?' Judy's face started to crumple and Doc knew the tears would be flowing again this morning. Internally, he raged at the idiot who had sparked her grief, but was still winded and unable to reply, so she filled the silence. 'And why? She's just a harmless animal…'

Doc finally managed to speak as he raised himself up, although he had no answer he was willing to mention to her. Instead, he gave her a reassuring hug, all the while inspecting the feline corpse.

Stapled, spread-eagled to the woodwork.

Crucified.

'It's okay. It's just a stupid prank. Probably the Dooley boys and their gang of thugs again.' The lie felt uncomfortable on his tongue, but the local farm lads were the go to suspects for any such acts of mindless vandalism or senseless cruelty. He felt her nod as he went on. 'I'll take Flossy down. Poor Mrs Bunting will be devastated… Are you still up for your run?'

As he held his wife, Doc couldn't help but think back to the sparrow with a broken wing he had found after it had thudded against his study window a week earlier. Its hollow bones, its apparent fragility, almost weightless, as it squawked in outrage at being lifted from the ground, pecking at his thumb as he rescued it. Judy's quivering body vibrated against him in much the same way, the tears soaking into his dressing gown before she grabbed a handful of his lapel to dry her eyes. The very same cat now affixed to Doc's door had made short work of the wounded bird soon after the rescue, having sneaked in through the kitchen window.

Karma?

Hardly.

Nature was often cruel, but humans had easily exceeded the worst she could offer, as Doc knew only too well.

'I'm okay. I just get so tearful sometimes.' Judy shrugged herself out from his hug and nodded to herself, her face rearranged into an expression Doc recognised as one of determination to get on with her life, as best she could. 'Please take her down before I'm back.'

After one last glance at the offending body, and a wan smile offered in an attempt to reassure Doc, she jogged away without a backward glance.

On closer inspection, Doc began to assess the differences between today's unexpected arrival and the only other similar instance he was personally aware of, and he did not like the conclusions crowding into his mind.

As ever, there were many people who had read his books detailing the misdeeds of the criminals he had assessed and helped catch over the years he had worked as the senior Forensic Psychiatrist for London's Metropolitan Police. Many more had watched his TV series, now on its fifth season, in which he tried to relate unsolved murders to serial killers already serving time. Any one of those readers or viewers could have taken the simple details he had relayed and done this for some nefarious purpose.

Over the years, he had been the target of many cranks and pranksters, but nothing so serious that he had ever lost a night's sleep. But today *felt* different.

And the attack on this animal *was* different, he realised, as he compared the circumstances with that other occasion.

No nails this time, just staples. Mrs Bunting's cat was obviously dead long before being pinioned to the door—the stench of decomposition was enough to confirm that —unlike the similar case he had heard about, rather than witnessed, during an investigation several years before. Just someone trying to mess with him, without properly mimicking the event. Probably found the cat already dead, and only thought of the prank after discovering it somewhere, road kill from a careless driver perhaps.

Another bloody 'anti-fan'…

Without further thought he went to the cupboard under the kitchen sink, found a bin liner and a screwdriver, pulled on his gardening gloves and returned to the offending object.

With the tip of the screwdriver he levered the first staple from the cat's paws while breathing through his mouth to avoid choking from the smell. Flossy must have been dead for days, and as he prised another fastening loose, a sense of unease crept over him. Doc tried to ignore it, but could not shrug off the feeling as another part of his brain flickered into life. It gave him a mental shake as he re-assessed the situation.

This was done at night. A lightweight staple gun had been used. On Flossy's rotting corpse.

Not a hammer and nails, used to torture an agonised cat before beating it to death.

Doc had hoped this difference was enough to dismiss the event, but now he knew better. The dark compartment in his mind, one that he'd tried to keep sealed since retiring from his role as a criminal profiler, ripped itself wide open, already drumming the words into his consciousness:

Silent. Stealthy. That's the difference.

Not a prank, then. More like a message.

Doc sighed as he resigned himself to his dark side's discomfiting conclusion.

It's a warning.

A warning of worse to come.

'Oh, for chrissakes, Mother! Not again.'

Despite her diminished olfactory senses, Suzie Leech could smell the tang of stale urine as she lifted the duvet to check, and even her mother's ubiquitous potpourri could not mask the odour.

'I—I'm sorry, sweetie. I don't remember… I was so tired again.' Rosemary Connor cringed with embarrassment as her daughter castigated her. 'Let me get up and I'll change the bedding.' She slid to the edge of the mattress and eased herself upright, wobbled for a few seconds, then placed a steadying hand on the bedside table, her face a mask of confusion.

'Don't be bloody stupid, Mum. You can hardly get down the stairs without help, and look what happened the last time you used the washing machine. Anyway, you'd only forget—'

'Where are my slippers? My feet are cold.'

With the duvet in one hand and the stripped sheet in the other, Suzie wrinkled her nose at her mother, and shook her head. Life here was supposed to have been an improvement, a chance to recover, to gain support from her mother, and it had been perfect at first. Now, well, it was just a constant mind-numbing battle to keep herself sane.

'You must've left them downstairs. And it's August. How can you be cold?' Suzie couldn't help the strident tone sharpening her voice—she had exhausted her reserves of emotional goodwill on her own recovery, and the tank was now running on empty. A gin, vodka and opiate hangover didn't help either. 'Get in the shower, and make sure you keep hold of the rail. Pull the alarm cord if you need me. I'll be downstairs, busy cleaning up your mess...'

'All I had was a small glass of milk at bedtime. Look.' Suzie could see nothing where her mother pointed other than the bedside lamp and alarm clock. Baffled eyes appealed to her, as her mother realised. 'I was sure Billy brought me a glass... Maybe that was the other night. I promise I had nothing else to drink since my dinner. Though I don't remember eating that either.'

'That's a dozen times in as many weeks. Well, you've had your warning, and I won't listen to your pathetic moaning any more. I don't care if it's uncomfortable, I'm putting a rubber undersheet on your mattress after I've disinfected it. *Again*. Or maybe I should just burn the bloody thing. It's starting to stink. We'll be buying you nappies next. What the hell has happened to you?'

The look of sheer misery on her mother's face was almost enough to melt the ice facade Suzie perpetually hid behind, but not quite. Watching the frail old woman turn and limp to the en suite bathroom prompted a rare moment of piercing introspection.

Maybe she's sick. Alzheimer's or something... I'm such a complete bitch!

She opened her mouth to utter something. An apology perhaps, for the woman who had borne her, breastfed her, brought her up, and more recently helped her through the most traumatic period of her life. Before any utterance could break through her self-imposed emotional barricade, the bathroom door clicked closed behind her weeping mother. As the sobs reached her ears, Suzie took a pace towards the source of the sound, thinking she might be able to say something to soften the stinging blows she had just delivered to her mother's pride.

Oh, sod it! It's just not worth the hassle.

It was already after nine o'clock, and her son's tutor was due at ten.

Suzie yelled up the stairs from the landing, her neck arched, her head throbbing as she projected her anger at his attic room door. 'Billy! Get up you lazy blighter!'

'I'm down here. Cooking breakfast. Want some?'

How the hell did he do that? Always sneaking around. She never knew where he was, or what he was doing. It had been happening more and more over the last couple of years. He seemed to materialise in different places, like some sort of magician.

She shrugged and plodded down the stairs, her own heavy footfall telegraphing *her* movements as the smell of bacon wafted up to meet her. It was not at all appetising, it just stirred the queasy sludge in her belly, and made her feel even worse.

'I'll just have coffee for now, love. I'll make us all a nice lunch later.'

'You want me to chuck some vodka in it for you?' Suzie could hear Billy titter as she arrived in the room, even though his back was turned to her as he tended his sputtering rashers. He spun round, and took in the situation immediately. 'Oh God, please tell me she's not pissed the bed again?' Billy hoisted the frying pan and dumped several rashers of bacon on to two thick slices of toast, then ladled ketchup on them before making a doorstep sandwich. He took a hefty bite and watched his mother loading the washing machine as he chewed with his mouth open. 'I'm not surprised. She was down here last night, guzzling milk again. We're almost out thanks to her. I keep telling you—she needs to go into that care home. I found her stinking old slippers under the grill this morning. I think she was warming them up but must've forgotten. We're lucky she didn't burn the place down. Fucking disgusting. Almost put me off my appetite.'

Suzie slammed the round glass door on her mother's stained laundry, twisted the machine's dial with an exaggerated flick of the wrist to kick-start the unwelcome wash load, and turned on her son. 'Enough of the language, young man. And this *is* her home. You know full well she'd rather die than leave this place!'

'Maybe she should top herself, then. Useless old bat.'

'Jeez, Billy! Don't be so...'

Whatever had happened to her innocent little boy?

That train of thought shunted into, and then immediately whistled straight out of Suzie's mind.

She knew exactly what had happened to her son.

But that was over seven years ago.

A whole lifetime ago...

Now he was turning into a handsome man before her eyes. His androgynous good looks would have been equally appealing on a girl, especially when he was just a cherubic child, though he had filled out with puberty, and already sported the same masculine air of impatient superiority his father had possessed.

A twinge of jealousy passed through her as she contemplated his fine features—his long lashes, the two stunning turquoise eyes, sculpted lips and perfect brows. Much of his beauty had come from her genes, though his father had been handsome too. She often wondered what other paternal traits might have been passed down to her son.

Don't think about that!

Suzie didn't notice her fingers climbing to her face, a subconscious reaction whenever thoughts of Billy's father—or the events surrounding his death—entered her head. Better to just think about her son in the here and now.

With his long sideburns, his broad shoulders and imposing height, he could already pass for an eighteen or twenty-year old, and Suzie had little doubt he had been visiting pubs and even nightclubs despite being just fifteen. She hated to admit it, but he was devious by nature, and she was sure he had managed to obtain a false ID, despite his denials—one that would guarantee him illegal access to the local adult haunts.

He probably had a girlfriend too, but refused to share anything personal with his mother since the day he had been struck mute, an affliction that lasted more than three years after that dreadful night...

When he eventually started talking again, there was no hint or possibility of closeness between them. He preferred to confide in his psychotherapists and largely ignored her for most of the time.

The pain of recollection scorched Suzie's psyche whenever her maternal instincts resurfaced like this, which is why she rarely thought back to how their lives had changed so irrevocably, and why they had drifted apart.

Drifted?

No that's not right...

We were driven apart.

'Bloody hell, Mother. Stop doing that. It's gross! Ew.'

Startled, Suzie plucked her right hand away from her face, and saw the blood and tissue under her nails, the tiny slivers of skin she had just torn from her cheek.

'Oh, my God!'

She rushed to the downstairs bathroom, slammed the door behind her, leaned against it with her eyelids squeezed shut, mentally preparing herself to look in the mirror.

Billy had obviously followed her down the hall, though she had not heard him, and he was now banging his fists on the door so hard she could feel the blows as if they were being hammered into her spine. His angry bellow was harsh and raw as it lanced into her skull.

'Why do you keep wasting Dad's money on useless plastic surgery and expensive bloody tissue grafts if you're just going to keep ripping it all off your ugly fucking face? Dad always said you were a stupid cow! You're hideous... You *always* will be... Get used to it!'

The banging ceased the moment his outburst ended.

Silence.

He had magicked himself away again.

She eventually managed to open and focus her one good eye, and, as always, the sight in the mirror devastated her.

Suzie fell to her knees and puked in the toilet pan, and like her mother, only minutes before, wept for the woman she used to be.

The clean sheet and duvet now covered the source of her mother's indignity—the moisture-proof membrane Suzie had bought after the first bed-wetting episode—and now the old lady was ignoring her daughter, staring out of the window at the Berkshire countryside while sitting in her favourite armchair, bundled in damp white towels.

The atmosphere was thick with disapproval, and had weighed heavily on Suzie when she had first entered, carrying the offending item. The half bottle of codeine linctus she had imbibed, immediately after her confrontation with the hideous image in the bathroom mirror, had soon bubble-wrapped her in its familiar warm embrace. Although she no longer experienced the highs the drug used to deliver, she did achieve a sense of remoteness, drifting above day-to-day worries, oblivious to painful recollections of her family's warped history.

She patted the pillows, smoothed the duvet, and then offered an olive branch to her mother, her voice mellow and forgiving. 'Your roots are showing, Mum. I'll dye your hair for you again if you want... No need to get dressed, I can do it now.'

No response.

At times like this, Suzie reflected on the difference she had seen in her mother since her father had died. In the few years since he had taken his life, the formerly energetic matriarch had physically and mentally shrunk into the diminished husk now silently occupying this room.

It was not supposed to have turned out like this.

Suzie and her son had arrived here from their abandoned home in London in desperate need of the type of unconditional love only close family can provide, and in those first weeks, months and years, the support from her mum and dad had been nothing short of incredible.

Suzie had been hospitalised, and only managed to join Billy several weeks after that frightful night had left her a deformed and devastated widow. She could still hear her little boy's screams as she was being lifted into the ambulance, a row that her mother said had continued for three days, almost non-stop, before he finally exhausted himself and fell into a twenty-four-hour sleep. When he woke, he did not speak to his Nana or Gramps, and was still mute by the time Suzie arrived, her lacerated face in bandages, and her mind equally shredded.

That was the first time she'd witnessed the coldness in her child's eyes. Reserved exclusively for her, it seemed. She sighed, her mind returning to the bedroom and her mother's frosty demeanour.

Be a better daughter. A better person. Try again.

'Would you like some breakfast? I'll bring some boiled eggs and some of that soft white bread you like, cut into soldiers, just like you used to do for me… Mum?'

Still nothing.

With the bubble-wrap in danger of popping, Suzie decided to beat a retreat just as the doorbell chimed its jaunty tune.

Billy's tutor.

'I'll get that, then sort some food out for you.'

The short journey down the stairs allowed a few more moments of reflection, with thoughts about her little boy now at the forefront of her blunted mind.

The local school had been a disaster for him. Tormented and bullied for his perceived weakness, his inability or unwillingness to speak, his unsmiling presence, his lethargy, and his reluctance to get involved with any group activity. The teaching staff had initially suggested a special needs establishment might be more appropriate, but her mother had insisted the lad would be better off staying where he was, and for a while it seemed she was right.

Then came the events that finally led to him being expelled.

Suzie let the air from her lungs rattle her lips as she exhaled, as if the act might somehow cure her frustration and impotence. She reached for the door latch, just as her son beat her to it.

'I'll get it, Mummy dearest. Let's not scare poor Smiffy away, eh? Even with that plaster on your cheek you look hideous. And you might want to pull a brush through that haystack of hair before you let members of the unsuspecting public see what's become of you.'

Her hands automatically flew to her scalp, and she pressed her fingertips through the tangle she found there. The sight of her face during her brief foray into the guest bathroom had tossed any thoughts of her overall appearance from her mind, and she hated to admit it, but her son was probably speaking the truth.

Cruel, callous truth, designed to cut deep into her soul.

But the truth, just the same.

And there was more. Delivered with a contemptuous twist of the knife.

'You could do with a shower too. You were wearing those clothes last night before you collapsed. Drunk, as usual. You're disgusting… I had to help you to bed. Yet again.'

Had he? Probably.

She couldn't remember. She clawed at her memory for some hint of what had happened.

Blank.

Since shortly after dinner.

How much vodka and gin had she drunk?

Tears pricked at her eyes as she looked up at Billy's sneering face, so reminiscent of his father, desperate for something to say, to appease him. Would she ever be able to bridge the yawning chasm now separating them?

Irrationally, she wanted to hug him, to tell him it would all be fine, but she knew it wouldn't—and she knew only too well how he would respond to the tiniest hint of affection on her part.

The doorbell chimed again.

'Go on. Run along and sort yourself out. He's getting impatient. And so am I.'

Suzie just turned and plodded up the stairs to her room, already craving the effects of the other half bottle of her pharmaceutical crutch.

'We're supposed to be getting things ready to celebrate my well-deserved and much belated promotion, and here you are, asking your mate, a newly minted Detective Chief Inspector, to investigate the death of your neighbour's cat!' Jack Carver poked a playful finger at Doc's belly as he added, chuckling to himself, 'Marriage is certainly agreeing with you. Not much yoga going on, from the look of it.'

Doc tutted as he bent to open the plastic sack at his feet and show Jack the offending corpse. 'I'm not asking you to investigate. I just want to know what you think, that's all.'

'Whoa, Doc! Wrap it up. It bleedin stinks, mate. I'm no expert on feline homicide but it chucks up like it's been dead for months. Why don't you dump it in the bin, and give me a hand with the gazebo thingy? I've got loads of food and booze too. It's in the car. Come on.'

'This is serious, Jack.'

Doc's frown and funereal tone stopped Jack in his tracks, startled by this seeming overreaction.

'You said it was a prank. Why the worried face?'

'I said, *at first* I thought it was a prank.'

'Yeah, well. There have been a few. It's only to be expected after so many TV appearances.'

'I've got a very bad feeling about this one. You know the reason.'

'Really?' Doc was looking at him expectantly, as if Jack should have immediately made the connection he so clearly had. The moment Jack had arrived, a few minutes before ten, Doc had started on about the neighbours' bloody pet. Jack gave his head a theatrical scratch as he tried to remember some other case involving dead cats, but nothing occurred to him. 'I give in. What am I supposed to be remembering? And can we please get the stuff out the car? We've got forty mouths to feed and they'll start arriving in a couple of hours. If I don't get cracking they'll be going hungry.' The last time Doc had offered Jack the use of his magnificent country home for entertaining his police colleagues, things had been completely chaotic. Judy had almost had a nervous breakdown and Doc had been about as useless as a chocolate teapot.

Which was why Jack was itching to get his celebratory brunch barbie set up right away. 'It won't look good if the new DCI can't even organise a piss up in your back garden, will it?'

Jack hoped his infectious, jocular tone might shift Doc's feet towards the car, but his friend remained rigid. Worse still, his face was a stone mask, all expression gone, and his eyes seemed to be peering inwards.

Seeing Doc like this sent an irrational and unexpected tremor of fear through Jack. The hairs on his forearm jumped to attention, as if static electricity was emanating from the psychiatrist's brain, affecting Jack's follicles, dragging the fine filaments upright. He went to speak, but before he could, a name croaked forth from Doc's lips —one he had not heard his pal utter for several years.

'Leech.'

That unexpected word discharged the strange aura surrounding Doc, and Jack wondered if he had imagined its presence. Perhaps age was finally catching up with them both. An over-active imagination was not one of the many failings Jack would admit to, yet, right now, he had an ominous feeling that Doc was channelling something weird.

Evil.

'Peter Leech? Or his brother, Shaun?' Jack was on firmer ground now, but he still hadn't made a connection with the dead cat, pinned to Doc's door. 'What've they got to do with the thing in that bin bag—other than the fact they're all dead, though the Leech boys'll be even more decomposed than that rotting moggy?'

'Peter was blamed for doing the same thing, when he was a small boy. Shaun was the guilty party, but the younger lad was caught red-handed, hammer in hand, the cat wailing in agony… Don't you remember?'

A vague recollection blossomed into a fully-fledged memory as Doc spoke, and Jack immediately rattled off the reasons why today's little escapade was different, but Doc interrupted him, impatient now.

'Of course, I know all that! Think about it—the cat was *posed* here, at night, and fixed to the door with a staple gun. Easily muffled, no banging, no animal squealing in agony, otherwise I'd have woken up and caught the perpetrator in the act. This is not about torture. Or mimicking the *exact* details from all those years ago. It's a message, a crude and effective one at that.'

'You're doing it again, mate. Reaching.' Jack was automatically sceptical, but simultaneously couldn't shake the sensation that things had changed fundamentally, that their conversation had opened a door—one he was inexplicably reluctant to step through. They had worked together, on and off, for almost three decades, and during that time, Doc's frequent mental leaps had regularly taken him by surprise.

And Doc's accompanying insights were rarely wrong.

As that last thought occurred to Jack, a lone gust of wind caught the bin bag. The sudden movement and rustling noise made him step back. Fearful.

Christ! I'm bloody jumpy today!

He tried to make a joke of his reaction, though he was still unsettled by it.

'Blimey. You sure that cat's dead, mate? Maybe it just needs a bath!'

Doc's impassive face did not crack a smile, or anything else to suggest he had heard, though when he spoke, his voice was firm, determined. Certain.

'Leech. You know the family lives less than six miles from here?'

'What? The wife and the kid? They moved out here too? Where, exactly?'

Doc had relocated from his multi-million-pound home in central London soon after his arrival back from France, having found Judy there after months of searching for her. She could not face returning to his old home—it held too many painful memories—so Doc had sold up and moved to this magnificent country pile near Pangbourne. An idyllic location, with a stunning brick and timber Tudor home, beautiful ornamental gardens that extended down to the River Thames at the rear, with its own wooden jetty where Doc's forty-foot motor cruiser was moored along-side. It would be easy to feel jealous, but that was definitely not one of Jack's char-acter traits. And Doc was generous too—Jack was just starting two weeks' holiday, the first proper break he'd had for years, and would be taking the boat tomorrow for ten nights of leisurely river cruising.

'Suzie Leech's parents have lived on Bucklebury Common since she was a teenager.'

'What? Where that Middleton lass comes from? The one who married prince what's-his-face?'

'They have a house on the very same road, Jack... More importantly, Suzie Leech has been seeing Dickie for treatment and—'

'Prof Maddox? Is he coming today? Did you invite him?'

'Yes, but—'

'He's a psychiatrist... What treatment? Did she go loopy? I wouldn't be surprised after what happened to her. Having her eye gouged out and half her face turned into mincemeat. And her poor little kid, he'd have been a basket case too, after all he went through that night.'

'No, she wasn't being treated for mental illness or PTSD. She was seeing him in his clinic, in Harley Street. She's had dozens of operations since that horrendous night. Facial reconstruction and extensive plastic surgery.'

'I thought the Prof gave up wielding a scalpel.'

'He did but he still personally oversees the team performing the most complex, difficult or interesting cases. And Mrs Leech certainly falls into all three of those categories.'

'So, what has she got to do with this?' Jack used the tip of his foot to delicately nudge the bag at their feet, in an effort to overcome his earlier superstition. 'Your putrid pussy cat.'

'I'm not even sure *her* presence has any bearing on what happened here last night.' Jack sensed Doc was not sharing the whole truth, that he was indeed sure there was some sort of connection, and his next words sort of confirmed it. 'The lad, Billy. He knows all about his family history. Details, Jack. Way more than he should.'

'And you think he did this? How old is he? Fifteen? Sixteen? Why on earth would he? I doubt he even knows who you are, or that you're living round here...' Then another question occurred to Jack. 'And how do you know what he's found out about the Leech brothers' escapades?'

Doc's eyes had that introspective look again, his brow furrowing this time, as if he was firing questions into his own mind, searching for answers himself. Several seconds passed with the only movement coming from another gust of wind rattling the leaves in the trees, once again animating the bag on the ground between them.

'I wanted to help him... But I'm beginning to think I may have made a very big mistake.'

His mother might have been ugly, but Mr Smith, his most recent home tutor, wasn't much better looking than the dopey bitch. Like a deformed bulldog. The pug-faced features. Slobber foaming on his jowls. A vile specimen of humanity, but he was serving his purpose. Well, had been…

'You want me to make a kilo? You're off your head, kiddo. It's bloody dangerous, mixing and cooking such highly volatile chemicals. Do it yourself. Brilliant student like you, should be no problem. Or are you worried you'll blow yourself up?'

'I don't have all the facilities—you do. And I need the enhanced ANFO, made to those specs, and much more of the oxy powder than the tiny amount you mixed for me the last few times.'

'It's not going to happen!'

Billy snatched the single sheet of paper from Smith's hands, crumpled it and tossed it in the bin by his desk, then sank into an armchair opposite the man who was supposed to be teaching him advanced chemistry and physics for the next three hours.

Now *that* was not going to happen. Billy had other plans.

He had selected this individual himself, having dismissed the previous teachers his mother and Nana had foisted on him. And it was not so much for his specific skill sets, although his multi-disciplinary educational credentials were most impressive. Much more important to Billy was the man's personal history.

His criminal past.

'Sometimes, Smiffy, I think you forget yourself. And why you're here.'

'And you're taking the piss, Billy. I know you like to pretend you're some sort of Machiavellian adult masquerading as a young teenager, but the truth is, that's all you are.' Smith's face flushed almost purple as he crouched forward, perched on the edge of the sofa, glaring, barking at Billy. Not that anyone was likely to hear—the study was in a separate brick-built outbuilding that used to be the neighbours' stable. 'Just a spoilt little rich kid who thinks he's in control.'

'Perhaps you need a little reminder of why you're here. *Roland.*' Billy twitched a finger on his remote control and the high-definition screen covering the top half of the end wall illuminated, then a video started playing. A young boy's moans, mixed with Smith's panting grunts, immediately filled the room, blasting through the Bose sound system.

'Oh, shut it off, for chrissakes!' The deformed bulldog's head shook furiously and a few gobs of spittle sprayed from his lips as he yelled. 'Enough, already!'

The child's naked body and the disturbing images showing precisely what Smith had been doing to him were seamlessly replaced with a video documentary explaining the physics of flight, paused on a frame with a lecturer scrawling on a whiteboard.

Billy sucked a little air through his teeth and across his tongue, aware that his mouth would be curling in apparent disgust, as if those few seconds of film had affected him. They had not, other than to reassure him that Smith would do exactly what he was told. The tutor shrank back into his sofa, giving the impression he wanted to melt into the cushions, to be invisible. Or anywhere but here.

Perfect.

'So, you'll do it, then?'

'Sometimes, I think I'd rather take my chances with the police...' Smith tried to sound menacing, threw himself forward again, grabbed a cushion, and wrung it with a vicious twist. 'Or just throttle you right now.'

'You like threatening kids, don't you? Hurting little boys too.' Billy was a big, strapping lad, but Smith was an inch or so taller, and probably twenty kilos heavier. Much of that extra weight was flab—not that it mattered. Billy didn't feel the slightest bit threatened by the big man's bluster. 'You could try it. At best, you'll be arrested for molesting me—like you were for that *other poor innocent child* we were just listening to.' He couldn't stop the snigger accompanying the words he'd empha-sised. 'At worst, I might have to explain to the police why my paedophile tutor was found lying unconscious on the study floor.'

'Jesus Christ, kid! You are so full of shit. You talk like you've stepped out of a gangster movie. How old are you—really?' Smith rubbed at his forehead with the heel of both hands as he spoke, not expecting an answer. 'Yeah. I'll sort it out. When do you want it?'

'I need it tonight.'

'It'll take me all day to source the chemicals and then do what I need. You can't rush a job like this.'

'You'd better poke off and get on with it then. Class is cancelled today. If anyone asks, we were here, together until lunchtime. Just make sure my mother and grand-mother don't see you leave... Sir.'

Smiffy shot upright and towered over him. For a nanosecond, Billy thought the man was going to attack him, that the threat had not been an idle one. His body auto-matically tensed for the assault that didn't come. A sliver of satisfaction gleamed in Smith's eyes as he mistook the reaction for a flinch.

'Be careful, kiddo. You might just've bitten off more than you can chew.'

'Tick, tock, tick, tock. You're wasting time. You should get moving.'

The gleam flickered as Smith hesitated, then extinguished as he nodded to himself before leaving without another word.

Doc watched as Jack put the finishing touches to his temporary gazebo while muttering about the weather.

'No rain forecast but you never can tell. We'll set up the grub and booze on a table under this canopy...' Jack paused from his efforts for a moment, glanced at Doc and then asked, 'So, how's Judy? I assume you can still talk to me about *her* problems.'

They were on safe ground now. After helping Jack haul a couple of cases of booze, several carrier bags full of meat and pre-prepared salad into the house, his friend had finally stopped huffing about doctor-patient confidentiality and Hippo-cratic oaths getting in the way of their *professional* relationship. Doc was relieved at the change of subject.

'Still mixed. She has good days and bad days. She was doing so well, but just recently... I don't know.' Doc did not need to explain more as Jack was well aware that Judy's mother's death had hit her hard, then losing her son less than a year later almost destroyed her. She lost the will to live. 'Getting back to normal's not an easy task for anyone recovering from the depths of suicidal depression.'

'She still blame you for that? Josh and her mum dying?' Jack finished hammering a peg into the ground, tightened a guy line and, satisfied with his handiwork, eyeballed Doc. 'Or does she blame me?'

Maybe this was not such safe ground, Doc thought. Jack, ever the detective, had clearly sensed some animosity from Judy, something that had been building within her over the last year or two. With a twinge of guilt, Doc realised he had been subconsciously encouraging the shift in her attitude, directing her negativity away from himself, and on to his friend. He tried to justify his complicity as he answered.

'It's not so much that she *blames* you, Jack. More that she won't allow me to get involved in your active cases again. She's fine with us working together on the TV series, but she gets pretty irate whenever you try to drag me back into consulting for the Met again.'

'So… what? I can't even ask for your advice now? Is that why you've been so offhand with me lately, when I've called about my investigations?' Jack's voice took on a petulant note as he tossed the rubber mallet to the floor in disgust, then pursed his lips and turned away. His voice was almost back to normal as he added, 'Did you clean the barbie, or have I got to do that too?'

'Jack. Wait.' Jack had started striding towards the Aga-sized contraption that Doc had cleaned and prepared the night before, currently concealed under its vinyl weather protector, standing in its permanent location on the patio.

'What?' Jack stopped and turned to face Doc. 'Did you? Clean it?'

'Of course, I did. Listen. Judy has no problem with us being pals. It's the profiling she has an issue with.' Jack's face was doubtful. Unconvinced. 'Her exact words were: *You can have a beer with him, invite him for a barbecue, consult with him for your TV series and books. But that's it! You almost died twice doing that job, working with Jack and I can't lose another person I love…*'

'So, she does blame me.' Jack had his hands on his hips, his head shaking at the injustice of it all.

'Well, she has sort of shifted her thinking.' Doc didn't add that he had encouraged the shift. 'It's a form of transference. She'd been blaming me for all the bad things that've happened over recent years, but she's largely replaced me with you in that role… Sorry, Jack.'

'Oh, great. Well that explains why she's a bit frosty on occasion.' He shrugged, a resigned smile on his face accompanying his words. 'I'm just glad you two are getting on so well now. You had a tough couple of years when you first got back together. I promise I won't bring up any current cases this time. Okay?' He chortled and slapped a hand on Doc's shoulder. 'Well, not within her earshot. Fair enough?'

Doc was relieved to hear his pal making a joke of it, but Judy really had been upset and distressed at the thought of him being sucked into helping Jack hunt the worst sort of killers again. Her emotions had taken them both on a vicious roller-coaster since he had found her, lying in a coma in a Parisian hospital bed several weeks after she had thrown herself from a bridge into the Seine river. Doc had thought he had lost her, and spent many days by her side, willing her to wake up, clutching her hand as if he could somehow transmit his own life force into her. A lung infection had seen the life drain out of her, and her body, wasted away from months of neglect, had almost succumbed.

'It's been a tough time for her, but we're through the worst. And I'm retired. Officially and forever. No more active cases for me. So, let's get on with preparing for your guests—we've got an hour or so. Judy should be back soon, too.'

They strolled together to the patio and Doc hoiked the cover off the gleaming Weber Genesis gas powered grill, then folded it as Jack stood admiring the device in its full glory.

'I love this thing, but I reckon it cost almost as much as Sally's car!' It was an exaggeration, but Jack's consulting income from Doc's TV series had allowed him to treat his daughter to a second-hand Peugeot cabriolet as a gift when she graduated from university—and buy a brand-new Jaguar XK for himself. 'This barbie's a beaut. Four burners under that grill, a side burner for veggies, a Dutch oven, spit roaster, pizza stone and waffle iron. I'll bet you've not used half that stuff, mate!'

That was true, but more importantly, Jack's good humour was back. Doc grinned, pleased that their brief spat over his reluctance to share confidential details on the Leech boy, and the confirmation that Judy had redirected her animosity towards Jack, had not spoilt his celebratory mood. That was about to change.

As Doc tucked the folded vinyl cover into the stainless-steel cupboard under the grill, Jack hoisted the hood and immediately dropped it back in place with a clang that made Doc's ears ring.

'Jesus fucking wept! I thought you said you'd cleaned this last night!'

'I did.' Doc stood, wondering what had got into Jack, having seen him jump back after slamming the grill hood, as if electrocuted by it, his face chalk white. 'What is it?'

Doc grabbed the handle and opened the grill, stunned by what he saw inside, his mind jumping to conclusions even as Jack murmured behind him, his breath now hot on Doc's neck.

'The Leech brothers again? What the bloody hell's going on, Doc?'

After Smiffy left, Billy sat, meditating for a few minutes, emptying his mind. Then he took some time to assess his plans, trying to decide whether he could control the man long enough to achieve all the things he had set out to do this week. Tonight, he would ask his guru for advice.

Energised by that thought, he jabbed the remote control again to play the documentary, jumped up, stripped off his jeans, socks and tee shirt, and padded across the room to the door at the opposite end of the study. He left the film playing even though he could already recite it in its entirety should he ever need to, then he entered the other half of the building before shutting the door on the droning presenter.

It was unlikely his mother would come near the study, and even if she did she would know better than to enter while he was 'having tuition', but just in case the soppy cow decided to stroll around the garden, she would hear the sound and think he and Smiffy were engrossed in a lecture on aerodynamics.

Billy shrugged into his *karategi*, thrust all thoughts of her and his tutor from his mind, stretched his joints and jogged on the spot for a few minutes to warm up, then started his *katas*, his regular karate exercises, the choreographed martial arts movements, clearing his mind of any external thoughts as he honed his skills. For the next thirty minutes he grunted, pirouetted and kicked through every gruelling move that his body knew by heart, all delivered instinctively, perfectly controlled, yet swift and powerful.

As he towelled the sweat from his body, he thought about how his father's obsession with the ancient fighting skill had come between them during his formative years. Billy had struggled to do anything right despite his best efforts to learn. He was clumsy and forgetful, weak and pathetic, incompetent, even at the most basic techniques, according to his karate instructor.

His father.

The criticism had been unrelenting, not a word of encouragement ever passed his old man's lips, so much so, that it had turned him against both—he gave up even trying to learn karate much to the disgust of his expert father, a man who surrounded himself with trophies won in martial arts tournaments.

By Billy's seventh birthday their relationship was almost non-existent. His dad's cold shoulder offered no comfort, no love, just disdain for his inadequate offspring. Only Billy's mother spent time with him, but that relationship also abruptly soured the night his uncle visited their home in Chelsea…

Billy tossed the towel to the floor and strode to the corner of the dojo where a circular wooden post stood, about the same diameter as a dinner plate, with a punch-ball of inflated vinyl fixed atop, the underside of it roughly in line with Billy's eyes. He bowed before his father's photograph—a frontal headshot, laser printed on to the ball—and started working with the three long pegs protruding from the post, two at chest height and one at the level of his belly button. White rope binding covered the entire section between the upper and lower pegs.

His father's abdomen.

While controlling his breathing, he mentally recited *ulnar high, radial low*, over and over, as he slammed the respective bones of each forearm against the unyielding wood.

When he had first started learning *wing chun*, the Chinese martial art he was currently performing, he had been going through what he considered his transition phase—the three-year period when he had refused to talk. It was his purdah, his secret time of suffering. He had convinced himself he was a victim. The incessant nightmares, the bed-wetting, the bullying, the constant fear and sense of impending doom had all gnawed at his self-confidence, had chewed away his insides.

In truth, he had merely been asleep, hibernating.

Growing.

He thought of himself as a pupa during that painful, but thankfully brief, transformational phase of his life. A crawling, helpless, immature caterpillar beforehand, had bloomed into the powerful creature of beauty he now admired in the dojo mirror.

Thud, thud, thud, thud.

The steady rhythm of his conditioning exercise, strengthening his bones, developing a tolerance for pain, and building his power, echoed around the room. Over the next ten minutes, he would strike the wooden pegs one thousand times, each blow delivered with a thrust of his chest and hips to supplement the power of his biceps.

He grinned to himself, revelling in his mastery of his body and his skill in the fighting arts. Such a difference from his early childhood. And the pathetic pupa.

Yes, he only really began to stretch himself when he had been introduced to Mr Mu Ren Zhuang. The formal name of the device he was now attacking.

Everything had changed so much after Uncle Peter's visit…

Thinking about the man who had sent his life on this exciting new trajectory, forcing him to grow up, tearing away the comfort blanket of childhood even before he'd reached his ninth birthday, filled him with love.

Or what he thought of as love.

A warm, fuzzy glow that emanated from within his chest, his heart a furnace, generating an emotional heat that fired up his soul.

Billy had felt nothing like it for his mother, even before his uncle snuffed her beauty and crushed her will to live, turning her into the drug-addled harridan they both now detested. And by the time his father had met his maker, well, hatred was the only emotion Billy could muster for the pompous, arrogant, bullying bastard.

On that fateful night, when his uncle ripped away the curtain of lies that had obscured his life, delivering Billy from his parents' clutches, unshackling his future—his destiny—he had been confused, terrified, racked with guilt, and facing an uncertain future…

Alone.

A final blow from his inner arm, the one thousandth strike, saw no respite for Billy. He automatically switched to working on his hand strength, slamming his palms up to the underside of the paired pegs, then back down on the top of them, his mental chant shifting to *up, down-hook, up, down-hook* as he did so, this time using his legs to augment the power of his arms.

After a thousand of these strikes, he set about his third exercise with Mr Mu, his wooden victim, this time conditioning both ulnar and radial bones together, just above the wrist. He brought his arms up inside the twin pegs, palms together, and then punched his fists outwards, thinking of Smiffy's ineffectual threat.

For a good half minute, Billy's laughter drowned out the thudding beat of his bones on wood as he imagined Mr Mu was his tutor, trying to throttle him. The simple exercise he was performing right now, part of a manoeuvre he repeated a couple of thousand times every week, was designed to break a choke-hold by delivering a powerful strike to the inner arms of the aggressor. The second part of this technique brought Billy's inner forearms against the pegs with a resounding smack—Smiffy's throat being pummelled—then he repeated the short sequence, each time with the subconscious chant of *up in, out down, up in, out down.*

His last set of hand exercises involved all three moves together, and as he reached nine hundred and fifty repetitions, he sped up until his final flurry of strikes became an indistinguishable blur.

Then he started on his legs, using the lower beam—a four-inch square section of wood that sloped down and out from the post at knee height before dropping vertically to the floor, as if Mr Mu had an out-thrust leg.

Twenty minutes later Billy rounded off his session with a thousand more of each of the upper and lower limb exercises he had practised, but now delivered in a rapid sequence. Finally, he executed a perfect leaping, spinning, hook kick, smashing his heel into the killing zone of his father's temple while in mid-air. He landed with the grace of a ballerina, and, satisfied with his progress, rinsed off in the shower cubicle in the opposite corner of the dojo before changing back into his jeans and tee shirt.

As he strolled back to the house, hoping his mother had been sufficiently functional to prepare a decent lunch, he basked in the knowledge that his Uncle Peter would approve.

They had so much in common, and Billy often wished the man who had changed his life for the better had been his father. Instead, his uncle now filled the role of mentor, was his inspiration, his icon.

His confidant.

The only person he would ever take advice from.

Billy felt that familiar warmth radiating through his frame… Soon enough, he'd have another inspiring chat with his Uncle Peter.

Tonight, in fact.

———

After wrapping herself in a morphine induced cocoon for two hours, Suzie roused from her stupor and showered under cold, stinging needles of water to bring herself fully awake. Her son would be finishing his studies in less than an hour and she was determined to get lunch ready for them all, just as she had promised this morning.

Every day she struggled through her routine, often wondering why she bothered. As she soaped her ample belly and flabby boobs, self-loathing washed through her. When she first came out of hospital and saw the hatred in her son's eyes, she had hoped they could both recover, but things had just spiralled out of control into the mess her life had become.

Billy had been a mummy's boy. At age eight, going on nine, he still had his teddy bear, and craved hugs with his mother, more so in response to his father's increasingly cold, uncaring demeanour. She had done her best to protect her son from Shaun's constant criticism and disapproval but he had become introverted and fragile, a sensitive soul, easily brought to tears.

He had been a small boy too, and Suzie had worried that he would forever be a victim in life, that he might never toughen up. She could not have imagined how he'd eventually turn out…

She stepped from the shower and dried herself, then brushed her hair while staring out of the window, lost in thought. There were no mirrors in her room—none in the house except in the other three bathrooms, and certainly not in her en suite. For a second, her eyes focused on the glass and she turned away, shuddering at the indistinct image of the bloated gurning gargoyle she had become.

Instead of replacing the dressing on the fresh wounds on her cheek she smeared some ointment on them—a mixture of antibiotics, local anaesthetic and antiseptic cream supplied by the Caduceus Clinic in Harley Street to aid healing after her latest round of plastic surgery. She had lost count of the operations she had endured over the years, ongoing still despite her treatment plan predicting she would be near normal by now.

The problem was in her head, not with the surgeons.

Infections had ravaged the new flesh of her cheek, her carefully sculpted lips, her reconstructed nose. Bacteria regularly attacked the flaps of skin that had been nurtured, stretched and then transplanted from her forehead, upper chest and neck, leaving her with suppurating sores that led to yet more medical intervention—a vicious cycle that she caused by constantly scratching at the new tissue. Her latest round of surgery had been successful, but here she was, yet again, with the newly formed skin of her face raked by her own filthy, tattered fingernails.

Suzie had even tried wearing gloves, day and night, to prevent her self-inflicted torment, initially with some success, but would often wake in the morning with ungloved hands and blood on her pillow. The recollection made her fingers tremble as she buttoned her blouse.

What is wrong with me?

It had taken her almost two years to gather enough mental strength to have the first reconstructive surgery, long after the NHS doctors had recommended it. The thought of allowing a man with a scalpel, a blade, near her face again had been too much to bear. It was only Billy's silent stare, his unspoken horror whenever he looked at her, that had driven her to seek out the best surgery money could buy. And even that had failed her.

Or, more accurately, she had failed the surgeons.

Before heading down the stairs, Suzie considered looking in on her mother, but her own state of mind was precarious enough and she could not bring herself to knock on the door. She stood immobile, her hand raised, ready to tap a request to enter, but instead, she turned and plodded her way down to the kitchen.

At least, she could still cook. It was the one thing that allowed her to escape the reality of life, and she became engrossed in creating a deep dish of lasagne—her speciality. The meat sauce had been prepared the day before, and now she layered it with pasta and creamy béchamel before popping the dish in the oven, then created a Waldorf salad—her son's favourite.

'Is Mr Smith staying for lunch, Billy?'

She tossed the question over her shoulder as she heard the back door open. Her son appeared at her elbow, seemingly simultaneously.

'Course not. He never does. Why do you always ask the same stupid questions?' Billy was red-faced as he fished a walnut from the salad bowl she was preparing.

'Leave that, and go and wash your hands. Food is almost ready.'

'I've just had a shower. I keep myself clean, unlike some people.' His sulking voice grated her nerves as he sniffed at her, his nose close to her ruined cheek before adding, 'At least you finally cleaned yourself up. Mind you, that latest botch job on your face looks like it's gonna fall off soon. I bet that bloody Maddox bloke's rubbing his hands with glee. He's ripping you off, you know? Bastard.'

'Enough, son, and I keep telling you to mind your language. My treatment is my business and you really don't know what you're talking about. Now sit down and I'll serve.'

'Alright then, I'm starving. But he's been taking you for an idiot.' He scoffed. 'He ain't wrong though, is he?'

Suzie felt the tears welling again. Why was he so mean to her?

When he had first begun talking after his years of muteness, he had verbally attacked her, his first words to her yelled in her face:

'I hate you! You liar!'

The hatred had never abated, the virulent attacks on her had been constant ever since. Even with numerous sessions of psychotherapy, he had resisted every attempt to smooth things between them, or to shed any light on the underlying problem.

For a while he had been close to his grandparents. Until her father's suicide.

That had just made him worse.

Poor lad.

Suzie had no idea what to do to help him, and was having a hard enough time keeping her own head above water. She watched as he gobbled his food, a fork in his right fist shovelling lasagne into his mouth, his other hand flying over the screen of his smartphone, as if absorbing the contents, downloading the pages directly into his brain.

Billy had always been a bright lad, although shy and deferential around his father. Then his three mute years had interrupted his education, and it had been increasingly difficult to gauge how he was doing. His teachers were frustrated too, and despite their best efforts, concluded that he was falling behind the others in his class, and suggested he might drop back a year. That became a moot point when he was expelled, and as a consequence, became almost impossible to place with any other school.

'How's it going with Mr Smith? You seem to be getting on really well.' Which was a relief—Billy had gone through tutors at a rate of knots, she thought, then asked, 'Do you not miss school? I'm sure we could get you a placement now, having passed your GCSEs a year earlier than most children, and with such good grades. Or how about sixth form college? Bradfield has some great facilities and they're just down the road, and they'll help you decide which is the best university for you.'

She wasn't sure Billy had heard her, as he carried on chomping on his food and swiping his screen, so she sat at the table opposite him, with a plate of food for herself. The rolls of fat on her thighs, boobs and belly were not a consequence of overeating—she merely picked at her small portion of pasta and salad, thinking she would much prefer a freshly shaken Martini right now, could almost feel the silky burn of gin, vodka and vermouth on her throat.

'Bradfield's for thickos.'

'What about Reading College, then? It would do you good to mix with more people of your own age.'

Her son gave the impression of being older and wiser than his tender years. Suzie put his advanced maturity down to his four years of home-schooling, with one to one tuition from some exceptional teachers. Most of the time, he talked like a young adult, and sneered at the local lads with their teenage expressions and mannerisms.

'Yeah, right oh, send me to Reading to mix with those peasants. Sod that. I like being at home and it's done me no harm—I've learnt far more across a wider range of subjects than a school would ever teach me.' The last of his food disappeared into his mouth, and then he glared at her, disdain and condescension lacing his words. 'Why would I want to travel into town every day? You just want me out the house so you can get pissed.'

Suzie dropped her head so that he couldn't read the truth of his statement in her eyes, and forked some lettuce into her mouth instead of firing an angry response back at him. She sat in silence for a few minutes before he stood and started preparing a tray for her mother.

There was obviously still some good in the lad.

Billy often raged about his Nana, but Suzie had never heard him utter a bad thought about her in her mother's presence. He too had seen her fall from a healthy head of household to the frail old dear she had become, and showed a modicum of compassion despite his youthful impatience. He always took his grandmother her meals, milk and snacks, and generally looked out for her. She'd hear him in Nana's room at times, their voices low and indistinct through the door, but her mother never complained about anything he said and was always pleased to see the lad.

At least *their* relationship hasn't been ruined.

Her son's thoughtfulness took a load off her shoulders too, so Suzie was happy about that small mercy.

'Any further thoughts about your birthday celebration? If you want to invite some friends round, that would be fine, and I can cook a nice meal for everyone too.'

It was a forlorn hope. Billy had no friends, at least, not of his own age. She'd seen him with older lads, some of the local farm boys in their late teens or early twenties, and often wondered what they got up to. Once or twice, she'd spotted them together during one of their frequent shopping trips in Reading. Suzie's role was to chauffeur Billy to the mall and then they'd separate for several hours, before meeting at the car to return home. Her son always clammed up when she asked what he'd been doing, as if his private life should remain just that.

He was ashamed of her too. She was certain of it. Even though she wore her 'disguise' when mixing with the public—a headscarf and dark glasses covering her disfigurement—Billy had never willingly introduced her to *anyone*, let alone his mates, or any potential girlfriends.

'Yeah. Me and Smiffy are making fireworks again.' He sniggered and continued explaining, no doubt responding to the worried frown she could feel forming on her lopsided face. 'It's perfectly safe! He's a wiz when it comes to chemistry, and I have to research volatile chemicals for my A level. Don't worry, Mum. I'm not planning to blow up my annex.' He picked up the tray and before disappearing with his grandmother's food, grinned at her, his eyes glinting like rock pools in the sun, disguising hidden depths. 'Or maybe I'll demolish this crappy old house... Though there's plenty of other shit to blow up first. Hahaha!'

Billy's wild giggling faded, and then there was silence—not even the creak of floorboards as he mounted the stairs and made his way to his grandmother's room.

Doc pulled the vinyl cover back over the Weber grill, while Jack stood stock still, staring at him, speechless.

'We'll deal with this later, okay?'

'Deal with it later?' Jack finally found his voice—it erupted out of him. He could see his celebration rapidly turning into a nightmare. 'Seriously? I've got guests about to arrive and you want to leave that crispy fried dog under wraps on your barbie? What the fuck is going on, Doc?'

Doc placed both hands on Jack's shoulders in an attempt to reassure him. 'Let's not spoil things, eh? We'll have to use my old kettle barbecue and I'll fire up the kitchen grill so we can get everything cooked in time. We'll get the party out of the way, then we can talk about it. You're staying over, so we'll have all night to chat things through, if we need it.'

Jack was not sure what he could read in his friend's eyes, the usually sparkling brown was almost opaque, like there was a veil obscuring Doc's thoughts, a reluctance to share what was going on in that oversized brain of his.

'Talk to me, Doc! What aren't you telling me?' Jack shrugged Doc's hands off and shook a finger in his face. 'No more of this doctor-patient confidentiality crap, either. You tell me. Now. Or I will redirect all my guests to the Pangbourne Arms for the afternoon, and get the local bobbies out here to get to the bottom of what's happening.'

'No, Jack. Calm down. Please.'

Jack was not feeling at all calm. The premonition he had felt this morning, with that cat in a bin bag rustling in the wind, had affected him badly, and irrational though it was, he was seriously worried for Doc. An uneasy, swirling mass of fear roiled his insides, and the hairs on his neck and arms were rippling again. Although not superstitious or religious, Jack had great respect for gut feel, the mysterious subconscious workings of his mind.

And today, for the first time he could recall, he felt an ominous and irrepressible sense that something terrible was going to happen to Doc—a sensation that was almost overwhelming.

'Nah. This is all wrong. You aren't taking it seriously enough. I was a bit hazy over the details of the crucified cat but I do remember another one of the Leech brothers' childhood escapades. And that,' his hand flew out, finger jabbing at the offending barbecue, 'roasted canine corpse is not just someone messing with your mind. I want to call it in. Now.'

'Stop.'

Jack's mobile phone was already in his hand, but Doc's fingers were wrapped around his wrist, digging deep. Urgent. Jack twisted his hand down and away, breaking Doc's grip, his tone fierce as he replied. 'I've got mates in the Berkshire force who'll be happy to—'

'What's going on? Jack? I could hear you shouting as I parked in the drive.' Judy was framed by the patio doors, staring down at them, her face glowing red, either from anger or exertion. Probably anger, Jack decided, given what Doc had told him earlier. 'Colin? Why are you two arguing? It's not like you.'

With Judy's eyes shifting back and forth between them, Jack went to reply, but Doc's fingers were once again on his arm, squeezing a subtle warning to keep quiet.

'It's nothing, sweetheart. The barbecue gas pipe's leaking, so we'll have to use the old one, that's all. Jack's worried it'll ruin the day, but it'll be fine.'

Judy squinted at her husband, and Jack wondered if she had picked up on Doc's unconvincing response.

He sounds just like a guilty schoolboy, caught in the act…

This was unusual for Doc. Jack concluded that his pal had been badly affected by today's discoveries too. He jumped in, finally realising Doc's concern was for Judy's peace of mind rather than his own safety.

'Sorry. It's my fault. I'm a bit tense. That's all.'

'I heard you say you were going to call it in? Why? For a gas leak?'

'Yeah, I'm really on edge. It's a big day and I was upset that the grill was out of service. I don't know what came over me, but I was thinking it had been tampered with. I dunno, like someone wants to sabotage my big day… As if!' He chuckled and then said to Doc, 'I'll get the kettle barbie. It's in the shed?'

Doc sent an appreciative glance at him, nodded, then spoke to his wife.

'How was Reading? Your hair looks fantastic. They do a good job in that salon.' He rubbed his fingers through his own curly mop, adding, 'Maybe I should've joined you. Anyway, we'll get the barbecue lit—would you sort out the salads? They're in the kitchen.'

Several seconds ticked by as Judy scrutinised them both, sucking in her cheek, having a little chew on the flesh inside, mulling over the two liars who were loitering on her lawn. Her eyes narrowed, then she tossed her head, muttered something neither of them could hear, spun on her heels and vanished inside.

'Well that went well.' Jack let the irony colour his words as he pulled a face at Doc.

'Mmm.' Doc stared at the patio doors, lost in thought, then slapped his palm on Jack's back. 'Thanks for that. We'll discuss everything tonight. I promise. No more secrets. Meanwhile, let's try to forget about all this. Come on. We need to get the charcoal lit or your guests'll be hungry. They'll be arriving any minute now.'

'Are you okay, Nana?'

Billy placed the tray on the coffee table by his grandmother's favourite armchair, positioned in the bay by the window overlooking the countryside to the front of the property. She was wrapped in a towelling robe and sat motionless, even as Billy approached with the food.

Is she dead already?

Her eyes were open, seemingly fixed on something, but Billy could not see anything outside other than trees, shrubs and green fields, with the track to his study room and dojo disappearing out of sight round the side. He leaned in to get a better look at her face, then waved a hand in front of her nose to see if she blinked.

'I do miss him, you know.'

Not dead. Just gaga.

'Of course you do, Nana. I miss Gramps too, but you need to eat. Mum said you didn't want any breakfast again today.'

'Hmm?' Nana was back in the room with Billy, her eyes tracking across his features as he crouched beside her. She stroked his cheek with the back of a frigid hand, and smiled at him, her thin lips almost disappearing. 'You're an angel... I don't know what I'd do without you.'

'Here. Eat.' Billy shifted the tray to her lap and then sat cross-legged on the floor beside her. Although he could see the residue of powder on the food sparkling in the sunlight, he knew her long-sightedness would prevent her noticing the chemicals he had sprinkled atop his mother's famous recipe. The first forkful made its brief but shaky journey to her mouth, and she mumbled in appreciation as she ate her first solid food for twenty-four hours. Billy encouraged her as he watched. 'It's nice and soft, Nana. Won't hurt your teeth, and it's easy to chew. How're you feeling?'

'Hungry.'

Her voice was distant, and although Billy heard what she said, he chose to twist his reply for her benefit.

'I'm not surprised you're angry. She's really horrible to you.'

'What do you mean?' Another forkful crept into her mouth, and a little red sauce smeared her lips, then dribbled down her chin as she chewed.

Billy wanted to smack her, to knock her head off. Old people were so useless. A waste of space. Oxygen thieves.

'Mum was on about it again. This morning.' Billy waited as Nana's ancient brain whirred, doing battle with the drugs in her system, but could see she was unable to understand what he was implying. He enlightened her. 'She wants to put you in Lakeside.'

'Lakeside?' Several fragments of chewed mince and pasta exploded from her mouth with the word. Nana became agitated, appalled at what Billy was telling her. 'That geriatric home?'

'Yup. Don't tell her I told you, but she went and got all the information from them several weeks ago, not long after your first night-time accident.'

Her whole body was quivering and the tray started to slide off her lap, but Billy grabbed it and placed it on the table before it crashed to the floor. He calculated that she'd had enough anyway.

Enough LSD.

Nana would go hungry for the rest of the day, but that was nothing new. Tears trickled from her eyes and she pushed them aside with an unsteady finger, her breath ragged.

Was she panicking?

'She wouldn't dare. This is *my* house!'

'Yeah, but *she* doesn't think so. She told me all about how you and Gramps managed to afford this place.'

Billy took her palm in his as she gazed down at him, and she stroked his hair with her other hand. It was their little ritual, developed over the years since Nana had started her decline, even before she chose to remain in her room, day in, day out.

'Told you what, son? What do you mean?'

'About the house. How you and Gramps got the money to buy it.'

Nana's shaking became more pronounced, her head wobbling like a jelly trifle, her mouth sagging open, her jaw jerking in spasms as her distress amplified the movements prompted by the chemical additive Billy had used to 'enhance' her lunchtime experience.

'I don't know what you mean.'

Despite her drugged state, Billy could tell she was lying to him—she knew exactly what he meant. As he thought it, a familiar epithet echoed in his head...

His uncle Peter's voice, growling at him:

Everybody lies, my son.

'When Mum was my age, she was raped, wasn't she? At least, that's what she said.'

'She told you that? Why would she do that?'

'She was drunk. She's *always* drunk. She tells me all sorts of stuff when she's had a few.'

'I don't know what's got into her. It's as if she absorbed some evil from the terrible things that were done to her that night.' Nana's hand was no longer caressing Billy's hair, but was now clutching her robe beneath her neck, scrunching the material. The fingers of her other hand were holding the gold crucifix at her neck, as if it would somehow ward off the malevolent presence she could sense in the room with them.

No chance of that, Billy decided.

'Is it true then?' He knew it was, but wanted to play her a little longer, enjoying the sensation of power over her as she vibrated with fear at the prospect of being dumped in a care home. In another ten minutes or so, she would start having visions, hallucinations, and Billy would leave her to those, but would enjoy planting a few thoughts in her mind before he did so. 'Was she raped? By my dad? Before they hooked up together?'

'We don't really know, son.'

'And he blamed his brother, my uncle for it—that's right, isn't it?'

'Oh, Billy, it was so long ago, I don't recall precisely...'

Everybody lies.

'Let me tell you what else she told me, Nana. She insisted I shouldn't, so don't let on that I said anything about it. Okay?' Billy raised himself on to his knees, put his lips to her ear and injected another dose of poison into her increasingly fevered, fragile mind.

Judy had a good view of Colin and Jack undertaking their man-bonding ritual involving fire, charcoal and raw slabs of meat, and let her mind roam over what she had heard as she arrived back from her trip into town. There was no doubt they were hiding something from her.

Again.

Judy cursed under her breath as she ripped open another bag of pre-packaged salad and arranged the leaves in a bowl before adding her own magic touch—a handful of pumpkin seeds. One day, she would learn to cook properly, but not until she had good reason.

I may just have one now, though.

She let the thought linger as she looked up at her husband again, wondering what he and his pal were talking about. Another one of Jack Carver's bloody cases, she assumed, their heads together, faces overly serious as they poked and prodded at the grilling meat.

Doc had been her saviour, had dragged her back from the precipice when she was ready to give it all up. Losing her son, Josh, and her mother, not so many years after her only brother and father had died, left her desolate, depressed.

Suicidal.

For a while, surrounding herself with those less fortunate had seemed to be the best way to deal with her overwhelming loss, but now she knew that approach to dealing with her trauma had only made it worse. In the beginning, she had helped the homeless in London, having sold the home she'd loved as she could no longer stand being inside the place. It had been so full of love and the joys of life—her son's life, her mother's life, both snuffed out so easily.

So wickedly.

The tethers that bound her to a normal existence had been severed and cast adrift, along with her soul.

Her vision blurred as the film of tears slipped across her eyes yet again, but she was determined not to indulge in weeping for her loss today. Her hormones were the problem, of that she was certain. She would never allow herself to get so low again.

Running away from Colin had been a mistake too. While wallowing in misery, giving most of her money to those who had nothing—the homeless, the destitute poor—she had cut herself off from her past, hoping to forget by distancing herself from anything that reminded her of Josh or Mum. Including Colin.

When Carver had tracked her down and approached her while she was working in a homeless outreach centre, serving soup during one freezing mid-winter's night, she freaked out. Instead of welcoming his words, his reassurance that Colin was there for her, that she had a man who loved her, who would help her recover, she had run away to France.

Did she love Colin?

Sometimes she felt sure she did. Even before fleeing from him. But losing Josh left such a hole in her heart she could not believe she would ever feel anything but numbness there again.

The squalor and filth, the sense of hopelessness in the refugee camps around Calais and Paris, had driven her depression to even greater depths. Until she could stand it no more.

When she finally woke in that Parisian hospital, the very first thing she saw was Colin's relieved smile, beaming down at her. At first, she thought she was dead, in some weird place between heaven and hell, their spirits meeting before she was condemned to the latter. Her Catholic upbringing had instilled in her the belief that suicide meant she would spend eternity being punished by the devil, but before jumping from that bridge into the murky depths of the River Seine, she was convinced it could be no worse than the torment she was enduring on earth.

Yet, while lying there, believing she was dead, looking up at his lovely face, backlit by a white glow, almost giving his head a halo, she had finally realised how much she wanted to be with him.

Over the next ten months, they stayed in France and he nursed her back to sanity, and she agreed to marry him and live in England again.

Happily ever after.

Only she was not.

Beneath the veneer she presented to the world, she still harboured suicidal thoughts. Had come close to overdosing several times, but on each occasion, that vision of Colin, wearing a halo like he was her guardian angel, had returned and pulled her back from the brink. She tried to maintain an air of normality, but it was hard, and he did his best to protect her from anything that might upset her.

Like today.

What he didn't realise was how much *that* upset her. She wanted to be Judy again. To be the confident, resilient professional woman she had been before her life disintegrated—all thanks to a criminal she had a hand in letting out of prison on parole…

As did Colin.

He came up behind her and she felt his arms wrap around her as he kissed her neck, audibly breathing in her scent.

'Are you okay, sweetheart? You seem so lost in thought. I need to get the grill going, as that old kettle barbecue's too small, we'll never feed everyone with that.'

The doorbell rang as he spoke. The first guests had arrived.

Judy turned to him and pecked his cheek, said, 'I'll get that,' then slipped out of his arms before he could read what was in her eyes.

The short walk to the door had her wondering whether she should tell him today. Although part of her wanted to be a mother again, to feel a new life growing inside her, another aspect of her damaged psyche viewed the prospect with horror.

How could she bring another beautiful baby into this world, one so infested with evil and rife with unspeakable deeds?

And how would she cope if she were to lose another child? Could she even bear to see a little one battling an illness, to nurse the child back to health, all the time thinking of her son's suffering before he died? It all seemed too difficult. Impossible, in fact. Yet Colin had been adamant that they should start a family.

Although she had agreed, just to keep him happy, she had continued taking contraceptive pills without his knowledge.

That deception had been her guilty secret, but now she had a far more significant one. Thinking about her options made her vision smear with the hint of tears again as she stood at the door, her hand clutching the latch while the bell chimed a second time.

Before letting the first guests in, she mentally prepared herself for the role she would play this afternoon.

The perfect wife.

Judy blinked away the tears, well aware that she was very far from being that.

After leaving Nana with tears streaming down her cheeks, her pupils dilated and her mind unravelling, Billy took the tray to her en suite bathroom, scraped the bulk of her lunch into the toilet pan and threw her untouched glass of apple juice after it. His portion of lasagne was now putting pressure on his bowels, and although much earlier than planned, he decided he would risk it. It took a moment of poking around in the cupboard under the sink until he found the empty coffee jar he had placed there last night, when he delivered her narcotic-laden glass of milk.

He put the wooden seat lid down, placed the opened container atop the lavatory, dropped his jeans and kicked them off, then sprang from the floor, landing with his feet either side of the jar. As he squatted, he allowed his bowels to open, then squeezed out a few inches of filth into it, holding onto his erect penis at the same time, so as not to waste any precious liquor. Once satisfied he had enough brown matter for his needs, he lifted the jar, stood upright, forced his penis to point into it and allowed urine to flow until it was full, then voided the rest of his bladder on to the bathroom mats.

With the jar lid screwed into place, he shook it vigorously until the mixture was the consistency of a lumpy, muddy puddle, then squatted again, this time taking the excrement into his hand as it slipped from his anus, before daubing it on the tiles and mirror above the sink, fingers shaking with excitement. Breathing through his mouth helped, but the smell caught at his throat as he worked. He didn't care.

This was just such great fun.

As he washed his hands under scalding water, soaping them several times then scrubbing under the nails until there was no hint of shit on his fingers, he cracked a triumphant smile in the mirror, his image hazy and disrupted by the smeared brown words he had scrawled there.

Then Billy's uncle's face appeared, superimposed over his own. Also beaming a smile—a toothless one, but glorious all the same. A raucous cackle, like the one that used to terrify him in his dreams, filled the bathroom, and Billy could hear his own voice join with it before silencing himself in case his mother heard the noise and came to investigate.

The thought made his uncle vanish, so Billy secreted the jar back in its hiding place alongside the two others with similar contents, dressed, then closed the bathroom door behind him as he went to see how Nana was doing.

One hand was covering her mouth, and a low-pitched moan seeped between her fingers. Her eyelids had retracted and the orbs bulged out of her face. Her right fist was wrapped in her hair, tugging at the incongruous chestnut locks with grey roots. Billy supposed his mother enjoyed making the old dear look ludicrous, deliberately chose this ridiculous colour, maybe in response to her own horrific countenance. Not that anyone ever saw Nana—she had not been out of the house for over a year, had hardly been out of this room for much of that time either. Most of her days were spent gazing at the woods and hedgerows outside.

Or suffering lysergic acid hallucinations.

'Having a nice trip, Nana?' A snicker. 'I don't think so.'

Billy lifted her from the chair like a child who was too tired to get herself to bed. It took no effort, thanks to the starvation diet he'd imposed on her, and a few strides later he dropped her on the mattress, arranged the quilt to cover her, picked up her tray and left her to her nightmares.

'She ate the lot, Mum.' The tray clattered on the kitchen counter top before Billy loaded the plate, cutlery and glass in the dishwasher.

'That's good news. She still eats well, but I have no idea why she's lost so much weight.'

'She's pining for Gramps. Depressed and all that.' Billy sat at the table next to his mother, inspecting her half-eaten lunch, and brushed a kiss on her good cheek. 'What did the doctor say, last week, when he came to see her?'

Although the question sounded genuine, Billy had no real interest, and relished the look on his mother's face for his unexpected show of affection. He hadn't done that for years. Unsettling people was the easiest thing in the world.

'Er… Not much. He gave a repeat prescription for her various meds, and just said she was getting old, that she seemed to have given up after my dad died. He thinks she's showing signs of early stage dementia too, but she won't go to the hospital for tests.' She took Billy's hand in his. 'I know you get upset about it, and you say things you don't mean, like this morning. But we have to look after her. Okay?'

'I do.' He sniffed. 'She's having a kip now, so we can leave her in peace for a few hours. Would you take me to the river? I'd like to canoe while the sun's shining.' Billy was waiting for her to make some excuse. He could smell the gin on her breath, had placed his lips on her ugly face purely to put his own nose in close proximity to hers, to confirm his suspicion. 'Unless you're pissed already. It's only two o'clock! You lush.'

He thrust himself to his feet, putting on a show of anger, but her response surprised him.

'Okay. I'll take you. Give me half an hour or so. I'll sort out the laundry and then get ready.'

'Yeah. Guzzle some coffee, more like. Maybe stick your fingers down your throat too, trying to get yourself below the limit again. I can drive us.'

'You cannot! You're not old enough so don't be so silly. It's illegal.'

'So's drink driving.'

'I am *not* drunk!'

'Not yet.'

'Enough. I'll be ready by the time you've fixed the canoe on the roof rack. Go on. Clear off out before I get really angry with you and change my mind.'

Billy slammed the back door as he left his mother stewing in the kitchen, convinced she would be craving another drink, but would have to refrain, having committed herself to driving her son to Pangbourne.

Hahaha!

Loading the canoe gear would take him no more than five minutes, and she'd be late anyway, so he unlocked Gramps' workshop situated in a converted garage to the side of the house, and went to work on his most audacious project to date.

Powers' house backed on to the Thames, and Billy had canoed past the property on numerous occasions—had hauled himself aboard the cabin cruiser moored there several times in the preceding months. The modified object he was now admiring appeared to be identical to the one on the psychiatrist's boat, and he was satisfied it was almost ready.

Gramps' man cave was one of Billy's favourite places to hang out, and as he put the finishing touches to his creation, he thought back to how much he had learned at his grandfather's side. Gramps had been an engineer, starting his career as an apprentice with British Rail and then, later, after privatisation, worked for Virgin in the local train repair yards. This workshop had been his sanctuary, and had accumulated all manner of tools, machinery, spares and items collected over decades.

The acrid fumes curling up from the soldering iron mingled with the other odours that lingered in the air, a manly scent that always brought Gramps to Billy's mind—the smell of grease, oil and flux, mingling with a metallic tang, along with a hint of rust too.

During Billy's silent phase, Gramps had taken him under his wing, taught him how to use a lathe, how to shape and bend iron and steel to any desired shape or size, how to tap a screw thread and many other engineering techniques. It had been a revelation to the boy, and Gramps eventually let him loose on his pride and joy. The steam powered locomotive, a one fiftieth scale model, a fully functioning miniature replica, accurate in every detail—a source of magic and mystery to the young lad from the very first moment he saw it puffing along the circle of track specially created for it. Thanks to much patient instruction from Gramps, Billy could, if necessary, take the complex machine to pieces, recondition almost any worn or unserviceable parts—even create new components from scratch—then rebuild it in its entirety.

The pleasure of creation had helped Billy through his pupa phase, and his few fond memories from his years living in Bucklebury had been shaped in this workshop. It was a shame it all went sour in the end, and Gramps had to go and die like that.

Oh well, this is looking good.

With one last dab of the soldering iron, he finished connecting the end of a length of high tension cable to the item he had welded the previous afternoon. A couple of minutes later he finished fixing a short tail of copper wire to the main body, certain this would ensure a good earth for the contraption. Billy hummed to himself as he packed his tools away, wrapped his precious creation in an oily rag, then hid it in a drawer.

Unusually for him, alongside the delicious sense of anticipation he felt, there was a shimmer of concern about his plan. He was convinced he had sufficient cable to connect the device, but he had not yet tested it. And there was a chance the extra cabling could be discovered before the ignition was fired up…

It should work, in theory. Only one way to find out.

'Are you ready, Mum?' With the canoe secured to the roof rack, Billy poked his head round the back door to see if his mother was there. On hearing heavy footfalls from upstairs, he flew into the house, bounded up the stairs like a panther, and managed to reach Nana's room as his mother's bedroom door opened. She was wearing her idiotic disguise. A yashmak or burka would suit her better, he thought. He logged that insult to hurl at her on another occasion, put his finger to his lips and whispered, 'Shhh. She's asleep.'

'Are you sure? I thought I heard her calling out a moment ago when I popped up here to get ready. I was about to check on her before we leave.'

'No need. I've spent the last five minutes in there. She's sparko. Dreaming and mumbling about Gramps like she always does. Come on. You're late. I've been waiting ages. Let's go.'

Billy brushed past her and bobbed down the stairs three at a time. His mother's thumping feet confirmed her lardy arse was wobbling along right behind him.

Jack's guests had started thinning out from five o'clock onwards, largely thanks to his boss throwing a giant spanner in the works.

'Sadie-bloody-Soundbite Dawson. She'll be the death of me, the cantankerous witch. Fancy telling all my oppos not to drink alcohol at my party if they were driving. That was bad enough, but the grapevine tells me she had a quiet word with the Thames Valley traffic boys. Suggested they set up breathalyser stops on the roads around your home this evening. Told them she had no time for coppers boozing then driving, zero tolerance and all that. Reckoned she'd have our badges if any of us were caught.'

'You should've invited her.'

Doc could tell Jack was well beyond driving, or controlling anything more complicated than a pair of tongs and some oven mitts—not that he planned to leave tonight anyway.

Jack snorted, then gurgled a beer-soaked laugh. 'Yeah, I wasn't at my most diplomatic when I told her she wasn't welcome. I'd had a few by the time she pitched up. We were down the pub last Thursday, the afternoon I heard the news confirming I'd got it, when she poked her horrible mug in the bar. Upset me when she told me I'd be reporting to her again as soon as I get back from leave. Took the edge off, especially when she admitted she'd recommended I remain as a DI.' He affected a high-pitched nasal whine, mimicking her as he added, 'You just aren't ready for this, Jack. Fortunately, I can keep a close eye on you and make sure you don't screw up again.' The bottom half of his beer glass emptied into his drainpipe of a throat, before an impatient wrist wiped a dribble of the amber liquid from his lips. 'Bitch.'

'Oh well, it was a good afternoon. Despite everything. You should be pleased.'

Judy had been on good form, bubbling with laughter and enchanting Jack's colleagues, though had excused herself ten minutes ago, saying she needed to lie down. Doc would check on her shortly, but was not too concerned. When there were a lot of people around, Judy was easily overwhelmed, and though she was much better now, and did her best to welcome guests whenever Doc invited them to their home, she would bow out as soon as things got too much for her. She was far stronger, physically and mentally these days, much to Doc's relief.

The last of Jack's buddies said reluctant goodbyes and headed off, leaving just one guest in the garden. Professor Dickie Maddox strolled over to Doc and Jack, pocketing his mobile phone with one hand, a large glass of whisky clamped in the other. He wouldn't be driving tonight, but he wasn't staying over, either.

'Don't worry, Doc. I'll be buggering off shortly, too. Didn't expect things to end so soon, though. The last time you two had a do here, it went on until after midnight. I gather you aren't flavour of the month with your boss, Jack.'

'Don't even go there, Dickie... Right. I'm busting for a leak. Anyone need another drink?'

Doc sipped the last of his wine as he watched his best friend meander into the house, and then chuckled as Dickie muttered, 'Steady as she goes... You think he'll make it back with my whisky in one piece?'

'Don't worry about him. He'll be fine. You know he can drink like a fish. How's things?'

Doc had met Dickie at medical school over three decades before, though they had been rivals there and many unpleasant events had passed between them during their years of learning. For a long while, Doc had harboured a deep-seated grudge against the man, a genius level polymath, a brilliant surgeon turned forensic psychiatrist, and a celebrity with a hugely successful internationally renowned TV series—a track record that made Doc's achievements seem minor by comparison.

Both Doc and Jack had come to enjoy the man's company ever since meeting him on a case involving all three of them some four years before. He was a very generous person, a great host and bon vivant, always ready with a smile and an offer of help. Much of his wealth had found its way into genuinely worthy causes, not the usual artificial charities that so many of the ultra-rich set up just to avoid paying their taxes.

'I'm good, but you two seemed on edge this afternoon. Jack normally holds his drink rather better than this too.' An arched eyebrow questioned Doc as Dickie added, 'It seemed more like a wake at times, not a celebration. Anything you want to share with me before I go? My chauffeur's already here, but he'll wait, so we have time to chat if it would help.'

In some respects, Dickie Maddox had become a closer confidant than Jack, as Doc was able to share his innermost secrets with his fellow psychiatrist and intellectual equivalent. Jack's more down to earth, though incredibly insightful approach was different, and although Doc considered the detective his best friend, Dickie's professional training helped him in other ways.

Doc was about to share his thoughts about this morning's events, when they heard a loud metallic hammering and then the shattering of glass from the front of the house, followed by a querulous racket as two male voices were raised in anger, immediately followed by a woman yelling as well.

'That's Jonesy, my driver. Sounds like he's having a bit of a barney.'

Doc nodded and followed as Maddox started towards the side gate.

Jack was on his way through the kitchen door as the racket escalated, so he dumped the three drinks he'd been hugging to his chest on the patio table and joined Doc and Dickie as they semi-jogged along the path at the side of the house to the source of the noise.

'What on earth is going on?'

Doc took in the sight and stopped dead as he recognised two of the three people on his driveway. Dickie's uniformed driver was sitting on the floor beside his boss's

Bentley, clearly dazed, nursing an eye, while a woman in a headscarf and dark glasses was pulling a young man towards a compact SUV, parked askew across the drive entrance with both front doors wide open, screeching and cursing at him all the while. A canoe paddle, broken into two pieces, was lying on the ground in front of the luxury limousine, surrounded by glass. Headlight fragments, from the look of it.

It took a couple of seconds before Doc got a good view of the lad's face, and the moment he did, his breath whistled from his mouth as if he had been gut punched.

Billy Leech? Here? Today, of all days?

Jack sprang into action, apparently sober again.

'Okay, Madam. You can stop right there. I'm a police officer and I want to talk to you and that young man. Right now.'

Jack's warrant card was already out, and he looked about ready to charge in and arrest the teenager. The woman froze on hearing his voice but her son just ignored the command, jumped into the car and slammed his door.

Before Jack could approach the vehicle, Dickie grabbed his elbow, stopping him dead.

'It's alright, Jack. I'll handle this.' Doc could see Jack was about to explode, his face flaming red, furious. He spun back, no doubt ready to tear Maddox off a strip for interfering in a clear case of assault and criminal damage, but the moment he heard Dickie utter the woman's name, his anger dissipated, replaced by a baffled frown crinkling his forehead, his lower jaw flapping open. 'Mrs Leech. We can talk about this later in the week. I'll call you. Please don't worry. Just take the boy home.'

Dickie helped his chauffeur to his feet and asked how he was feeling. Doc sensed embarrassment on the driver's part, at having been floored by a teenager. The same teenager now beaming a malevolent stare through the car windscreen, aimed at the foursome—his venom now including Doc, Jack and Dickie—as his mother slid in beside him.

Her car had a canoe on its roof, water still dripping from it, and Doc assumed they must have been passing, on their way home from the yacht club at the end of his road. The boy was dressed in a shorty wetsuit, the top half dangling from his waist, and his upper body was bare, exposing a well-muscled torso. More like an Olympic athlete's frame than an adolescent's build.

Doc returned the boy's stare, thinking how much he had changed—almost beyond recognition in the two and a half years since they had last met. A massive growth spurt had added significant height and bulk, and although his face was still refined and vaguely feminine, the look he was giving Doc brought to mind the boy's father.

And his uncle.

As the car drove away, the feral part of Doc's brain once again stirred into life, and the ominous sense he'd had on finding the cat pinned to his front door, then the remains of the dog in his barbecue, delivered a surge of adrenalin and a sickening lurch in the pit of his belly.

'Was that Billy Leech? The little boy, from all those years ago?' Jack glanced from Doc to Dickie, his head alternating between the two of them, shaking in disbelief. 'What's his problem with your motor, Dickie? And your chauffeur? Are you alright, mate?'

'I'm okay, sir.' The chauffeur's dazed look told a different story. He tried to laugh it off. 'That kid, he's a regular Bruce Lee. Kicked me in the head, he did!'

'What happened, Huw?' Dickie's rich voice rumbled reassuringly. 'We'll get you to the hospital for a check-up.' As his driver started to baulk, Dickie became insistent. Employee or not, Doc could tell there was no arguing with him. 'We'll order a cab now.' At that, Doc pulled out his phone and made the call. Dickie added, 'Meanwhile, let's get you inside. You can tell us all about it.'

They made their way into the lounge, Jack found their drinks for them, and offered the chauffeur a 'stiff one', but Dickie stopped him.

'Not a good idea, Jack. Water would be best. How long before the cab gets here, Doc?'

'Ten minutes, maybe. What about your car?'

'My PA will sort it tomorrow. If it's okay with you, I'll just leave it outside for the night. First I want to ensure Huw's been taken care of.' While the chauffeur sat on the sofa Dickie checked his eyes and inspected the bruising on his temple.

'I'm really alright, sir. It's nothing… Their car just swerved to a halt. I was having forty winks, sitting in the driver's seat, and although I heard it, I didn't think anything of it. I had my hat over my eyes, resting, waiting for you, Professor.' Despite his bravado, the chauffeur's hands were palsied, the ice in his glass rattling an accompaniment to his explanation. Doc could see he was in shock, and thought the blow to his head had been more powerful than the man would admit. 'Then I heard an almighty clattering as the lad went loopy. He was smashing his oar on the grill and bonnet, denting it, scratching the paint. I hopped out a bit smartish, but it happened so quick.' He offered his boss an apologetic smile.

'Go on, Huw. It's only a bloody car. Tell us about the boy.'

'Well, I was shouting at him to stop, but he was in such a rage, swearing, ranting about you, sir. I went to grab the oar off him, but he just seemed to… levitate. He flew into the air, spinning and kicking. Next thing I knew, I was flat on me arse. Then he smashed the oar to pieces battering the headlights. His mother had hold of him by then, trying to haul him to their car. Then you arrived. That's it, sir.'

Rage.

Doc had seen it too. There was uncontrolled fury driving the boy. So, what had Dickie Maddox done to upset him? He was about to ask, when Jack intervened.

'What was he yelling?'

The chauffeur seemed unsure whether to say, but Dickie placed a reassuring hand on his arm and nodded for him to continue.

'He was swearing about you, Professor. Claiming you were ripping his mother off. Milking her, he said, charging her for unnecessary surgery… He said you'd failed her, but wouldn't admit it, that you deliberately kept her coming back for more. That's all I can remember.'

Doc and Jack exchanged a glance as a cab pulled up outside, but Dickie was unfazed by the entire episode.

'I'll take him to the BUPA hospital in Reading, make sure things are fine, then pop back before heading into town. We can catch up on our conversation then, if that's alright with you fellows?'

Doc nodded and walked them to the cab, all the while processing the implications of the things he had seen and heard today. As the vehicle disappeared, an unwelcome image crystallised before his eyes.

The look Billy had given them from the passenger seat of his mother's car.

More than just rage.

Doc's stomach churned again as he relived the moment.

An overwhelming sense of hatred had been emanating from the boy.

But why?

'Sometimes I despair of you, Billy.' Suzie Leech mopped tears from her eyes with her sleeve as she drove away from the site of her son's latest indiscretion. 'I encouraged you to learn martial arts to instil some discipline and control into you. You could've *killed* that man.'

'Don't exaggerate. I used just enough power to disable him, that's all. He attacked me!' Billy sent a sulking stare in her direction with his comment, then scoffed at her. 'Anyway, if I'd wanted to kill the idiot, I could've.'

'For chrissakes. That's the second time you've damaged the Professor's car. I hope for your sake neither he nor his driver press charges this time.'

'They won't.'

'Oh, really? You're so bloody sure of that, are you? Did you forget that the audience for today's little tantrum included a police officer?'

'So what? Maddox won't do anything to spoil a good thing. To him you're just a cash cow.' Billy sneered as he added, 'Mooooooo!'

Suzie pulled the car to the side of the road, stopped the engine and rounded on her son. 'Don't you dare be so bloody rude. I've had enough of your attitude, young man. I'm still your mother. Just remember that.'

'Pah! What are you going to do about it? Ground me again?' He snorted. 'That worked well last time, didn't it? You ended up so pissed and off your head with morphine I could've been anywhere. Doing anything... Maybe I was. Hahaha!'

'God! You can be so... nasty. You were never like this when you were younger.'

Suzie swallowed and tried to calm herself, but could not stop her lower lip from trembling. More tears dribbled to her cheeks. It was all so unfair, how her life had plunged out of control, from middle class bliss to this. And how could she blame her son, given the terrible trauma he had endured too?

A jerky sigh shuddered from her and she decided she should get home as quickly as possible. She needed a drink. In her haste to get under way again she stalled the engine as the clutch slipped from beneath her shoe.

'You really are useless, aren't you? I can drive better than you, but I can't even take my test for another year. Anyone should be allowed to drive at any age, as long as they can prove they're capable... And you obviously aren't.'

Suzie eased the clutch up this time, a smooth take off that had them safely on their way. She'd been holding her breath during the manoeuvre without realising, and let it out as soon as she did.

'You'd better hope that policeman doesn't make trouble for you, though I'm beginning to think it might be better if he did. That poor driver really didn't deserve to be kicked in the head like that.'

'Oh, shut up. Just chuck some money at the pleb. That'll sort it.'

'You sound just like your father. As if no one else matters. Only you and what you want. Thinking money will solve any problem, no matter what you do.'

'Haha! Well it will, won't it? You should know that after what happened before.'

What was he on about, now? Was he referring to the previous occasion when he had smashed the Bentley's windscreen, and she had reimbursed Professor Maddox for the damage? She had been about to leave the Caduceus Clinic when Billy had arrived to meet her after his shopping trip to some of the nearby boutiques. When he saw the total on the bill she had just paid he went wild.

Earlier that day, when they had arrived at the Harley Street clinic, Billy had admired the Professor's car parked on the street outside, replete with its personalised number plate—MD1. When he realised that each of her numerous operations were costing tens of thousands of pounds he leapt on the bonnet before slamming his boot through the glass. Maddox had been magnanimous, as he was aware of their family history, and had graciously accepted a cheque without demanding any compensation for the inconvenience Billy had caused.

'I'm keeping tally, you know?' Suzie pulled in to her mother's driveway, and stopped in front of the garage and workshop attached to the side of the house. 'You will repay everything you've cost me over the years. Every last penny you've wasted through your misbehaviour, young man. With interest.'

Billy was almost out of the door as she finished delivering her threat, but paused and turned his head back towards her, snarling at her. 'Cost you? Don't give me that bullshit. It's *dad's* money. He earned it, not you. And it's as much mine as yours. It's you that's squandering it, not me.'

With that, he slammed the door on her startled face, and disappeared round the back of the house, heading for his study room. Suzie considered calling after him, to assert herself in some small way, to make him come and unload the canoe, but she was just too weary, too disheartened to bother.

He exhausted her, physically and mentally, she realised now. Each time they spoke, another slice of her soul was carved away and lost forever.

She let her forehead drop to the steering wheel and sat there, weeping for her lost little boy—and his tormented mother.

———

Doc re-entered his lounge and Jack piped up immediately, clearly wondering if he had missed out on something.

'What was Dickie on about? What conversation?'

Drunk or sober, Jack's detective radar didn't miss much. Doc couldn't help but grin at him. His current look was like a determined terrier, a dog with a bone—one he wouldn't let go.

'I was about to tell him what happened this morning before all that commotion erupted.'

'Repairing that Bentley's gonna cost him an arm and a leg—more than I earn in half a year I should think.' Jack pulled a face, sucked at his lower lip for a few seconds, pensive, then went on. 'And I don't care what he says. I want to talk to his driver. Alone. He can press charges, even if Dickie won't. I can understand him not wanting to upset a patient over some damage to his motor, but that kid… He's a nutter. Dangerous. Just like his uncle—and his old man. Needs sorting.'

Doc, weary now, dropped into his armchair and Jack sat opposite, both lost in thought, sipping at their drinks. Then Doc decided to drop his bombshell, ready for Jack to explode too once he'd heard what had happened.

'He came to see me not long after we moved in here.' Jack's head cocked in question as Doc continued. 'I didn't know who he was, he just turned up on the doorstep one weekend. I'd only seen him briefly, that one time, some four or five years before that afternoon. I didn't recognise him.'

'So, what did he want, then?'

'He said he wanted my advice. Asked me how much I charged for counselling.'

'Counselling. You don't do that. And how did he find you? And why on earth would he choose you?'

'He'd seen my TV series. Read all my books. Knew I'd been at their house, the night his father died. Said he wanted to talk about genetics and psychopathy.'

'Oh... He thinks he's a psycho too? Worried it runs in his blood? I wouldn't be surprised. We see a lot of that—bad families with crime in their DNA.'

'That's what I assumed he wanted. When I told him I don't do counselling, that I could effect an introduction to a specialist, someone who helped young people like him, he said I *owed* him, that he wanted to talk to me and no one else.'

'Owed him? Owed him what? You should've told him to piss off!'

'It was weird, but he was insistent, and he had an air about him. A confidence, a maturity that I'd never seen in a pubescent lad before. Precocious, and intelligent. Conversed like an adult. And I'll admit, I was intrigued... Fascinated, in fact.'

'You said yes.' Jack tutted. 'You can be such a soft touch sometimes.' He swirled whisky round his glass and sniffed at it appreciatively, took a mouthful, then said, 'And what did he mean—you owed him?'

'He blames me for his father's death.'

'You? Blimey. That's a turn up for the books. How did he come to that conclusion?'

'He said that I should never have allowed his uncle to be released, that everything bad that happened to his family since then was therefore all down to me. And all he wanted was a few individual sessions to talk things through, to help him and his mother recover.'

'Mmm. I suppose he has a point...' A final sip of the whisky had Jack smacking his lips for more, then he took his lower one between his teeth for a second before asking, 'So what aren't you telling me, Doc? I can read it in your eyes. Stop holding back. Tell me, and then I'll get us another drink.'

Doc let go a sigh, and then lifted his shoulders a fraction, acknowledging his own stupidity.

'I let him into my house. I let him into my life. I should've known better, but I thought *I* was studying *him*.' Doc swirled the last of his drink around the glass, then threw the wine to the back of his throat.

'I thought you wanted to help him? Not treat him like a bleedin lab specimen.' Jack stood and took both empty glasses to the drinks cabinet, poured more and returned to his seat.

'That too. Of course.' Doc took his glass and stared at the red liquid for a moment, pondering his stupidity. 'At the time, it sparked an idea for a new book, maybe even a TV series. On children who kill.'

'What. The old nature versus nurture thing. You thought little boy Leech might help you with that... So, what happened?'

'Over the next two months I saw him once a fortnight. Four sixty-minute sessions in all. Our final meeting was, well, difficult, to say the least.'

'Okay. I think you need to tell me about it. And don't give me that old nonsense about confidentiality.'

'I will get to that, but it wasn't until this morning that I began to suspect why he'd really come to see me.'

'Eh? So, he wasn't worried about his psycho genes, then?' Like a puzzled mutt, Jack leaned his head to one side, aware he was missing something important, keen to understand. 'I'm getting a bit confused now. Come on, spit it out, mate.'

'Some time later, I started having problems with my MacBook, so I took it to the Apple store.' It may have sounded to Jack like Doc was changing the subject, but he wasn't. He ignored Jack's exasperated look and continued filling in the background. 'After what happened to me before, being hacked through the internet, I've been paranoid and have armour-plated security preventing anyone breaking into my system since then.'

The drink had not affected Jack's detective skills. 'Ah! You reckon Billy Leech managed to hack your MacBook, did he? How?'

'I can't be sure about any of this, Jack. The problem arose more than a year after our sessions together. According to the technician, someone had loaded a keylogger onto my Mac.'

'Keylogger? Is that like a virus? Malware?'

'Yes, but I think they call it spyware… It doesn't affect your system, it just lurks in the background, recording all the keys you type during each and every session you use the infected computer.' With an eyebrow lift and spread hands, Doc explained. 'I had no idea but, apparently, it had been there so long it was eating the memory, storing so much information, and that's what caused the system to keep freezing and locking the screen.'

'Okay, so it was jammed up with too much info.'

'Precisely. The technician cleaned it off for me and I honestly thought there was no harm done.' *So stupid. Complacent.* 'My firewall, and other security would never allow someone to get into my system remotely, or send information from my laptop over the internet without my authority. I soon forgot about it.'

'So how did this keylogging thing get on to your computer in the first place?'

'According to the technician, whoever did this must have had *physical access* to my computer.' It was so obvious, with hindsight. 'Apparently, a USB stick with the spy program on it could've been plugged in while my MacBook was unattended. It would take maybe a minute at most to infect my device before being removed. No sign of any tampering whatsoever.'

'The little bastard loaded something on to your laptop, while he was here, in the house?'

'That's what I've surmised.'

'I'll collar the bloody scrote.' A gulp of scotch, then Jack bounced out of his chair for more, outraged. 'After his little escapade today, and now this…'

'Jack, please don't overreact.' He hadn't heard the worst yet. 'I have no proof it was him, though at the time, I did wonder who it could be. My cleaner? My gardener? Any workmen in the home? A friend or acquaintance I've invited in? Maybe someone at the TV studios when the MacBook was on my desk, left unattended while I was out of the room. But now… After today's events, well, I'm certain it was him. Billy Leech.'

'You think the cat and the dog business this morning was down to him?' Jack squinted at Doc as he sat down again, thinking it through. 'He found your records from the Leech brothers' affair, and decided to mess with you, imitating some of the things they did as kids! What the hell for? And after all this time?' Doc could see Jack's detective mind working through the implications. 'And what else did he get from your computer? Anything important?'

'The question is not: *What did he get?* Jack…. It's: *What didn't he get?*'

'Hang on…' The full import of Doc's security lapse finally sank in, and Jack sprang to his feet as he realised. 'He accessed your confidential files? The records of *all* the stuff we've worked on? For each of your TV series? The official documents? The crime scene photos, court records, interviews with witnesses, interrogations, all the work we did on those unsolved cases? That too? You are fucking kidding me!'

'Worse than that, my friend… The keylogger could've recorded any passwords I've been using. All of them, in fact… All changed since the technician cleaned the spyware from my device, of course. And because nothing bad had happened, either before or since the discovery, I assumed the person who loaded the spyware had failed to achieve his objective. With only half his task completed—compromising my MacBook—I thought my online security system had prevented the spyware from accessing the internet and transmitting whatever it recorded.'

'And now?' Jack was up again, drink forgotten, unable to remain coiled in his seat.

'If it really was Billy Leech, well, he may have taken a copy of all my keystrokes on the Mac between our first and last sessions, using the same USB stick to steal the information. I'm beginning to think that young man may have accessed *everything* I'd stored digitally, here or in the cloud, at the time of our last meeting together.'

'Everything?' Thunderstruck. Stock still, staring down at Doc.

'Uh-huh. Everything. My private and personal emails. My old client files. Records of every criminal enquiry I've ever been involved in. Including the Leech affair—which was probably his reason for coming here in the first place.'

Doc had never seen Jack's chin literally hang open before, with such a dumbfounded look of shock and horror. There was little else to add and he braced himself for the torrent of verbal abuse he was sure he was about to receive.

'Sorry, Jack. I probably should've told you at the time…'

———

'Are you okay, my love?' Doc's head appeared round the bedroom door, a quizzical expression furrowing his forehead.

'Mmm. I'm fine. I didn't sleep so well last night. Sorry I left the party early.' Judy was sitting up in bed, sure there was more to her husband's question than his superficial concern for her wellbeing. 'What was all the shouting about? Outside? Earlier? It woke me up. And what was Jack shouting about just now?'

She had managed to doze, though in truth, she had retreated to her bedroom not through tiredness—entertaining Jack's colleagues had been sucking the life out of her. She always seemed to be playing a role in life these days. The real Judy had departed the planet long ago, leaving just an actress performing all the parts she was expected to play.

'Oh, it was nothing. A car swerved into the drive and Dickie's Bentley came off a bit the worse for wear. No harm done really, though he's taking his chauffeur to the hospital for a check-up. Jonesy banged his head and was a bit shaken up... Do you need anything? I'll be downstairs, chatting with Jack for a while.'

'No, I'm going to read, and just relax here. I feel a little washed out.' She forced a grin and added a half-truth. Why not? Doc was lying to her again, she was sure of that. 'Entertaining takes it out of me. You know.'

'Well, I'll be downstairs if you need me. Sorry if we've been a bit raucous. We're still celebrating.' He gave her a cheeky grin and added, 'I may be a little drunk already!'

Judy had guessed as much. She almost blurted out her secret, but he blew her a kiss and pushed the door to before she could say another word.

Although it was early, she wanted to sleep again. To dream of happier times. For an hour or so she tossed and turned, unable to relax, knowing she had a decision to make. She heard low voices from downstairs as she switched on her light and saw the time. Eleven o'clock. It sounded like the Professor must be back from taking his driver, Mr Jones, to the hospital.

Maybe the Royal Berks, too?

The place where her first husband had died. Not that she cared that much for him at the time. It was also the very same hospital she had visited three hours before her hairdressing appointment this morning.

At the abortion clinic.

Judy had never been particularly religious, though her family was Catholic and so she had the usual range of taboos drummed into her at an early age.

Suicide was bad enough.

But abortion?

Murdering an unborn child.

A mercy killing, in her mind.

The thought that Colin might discover her secret, would somehow find out about her pregnancy, had been worrying her for weeks. He would never agree to an abortion, so she had not told him when she'd first realised, recognising the symptoms from when Josh had made his presence known to her. The sickness and tiredness she was now experiencing for the second time in her life...

It was partly her own carelessness that had led to the dilemma. Forgetting a few of her contraceptive pills had not seemed such a big deal at the time. She regretted those foolish memory lapses now, though.

Well. What to do?

She had to tell him. To let him know. Judy finally made up her mind—for better or for worse.

She opened her bedside drawer and pulled out the envelope stamped with the logo of the Royal Berkshire Hospital in Reading, took a long look at the contents, then sealed it, scrawled *Colin* across the front of it, and left it on the pillow beside her.

With her conscience clear over a decision irrevocably taken, Judy lay her head on her own pillow. For the first time in the five weeks since discovering she was pregnant, she drifted off into the embrace of untroubled sleep.

'How's your man, Jonesy?'

Jack felt wrung out and stressed after all Doc had told him earlier, and he was now determined to see the Leech boy punished for assault, no matter what Dickie had to say about it. First thing in the morning he would get to work on finding out everything he could about the psycho kid. Sunday or not, he knew some of the local coppers and would reach out to them before he took Doc's boat for his vacation. His daughter and her fiancé weren't due to arrive until the late afternoon, so Jack reckoned he would have plenty of time to do some digging before they all departed on their river cruise.

'He's going to be fit as a flea in a day or two. No fracture, though I was concerned for a while. Just mild concussion. No harm done, really, other than a rather devastating blow to his pride.' Dickie chortled as Doc followed him into the lounge. 'Jones served in the Welsh Guards, though that was over two decades ago. Still, I can just imagine how he feels.'

Doc also had a little laugh about it, though Jack could see no humour in the situation at all. His mood had gone from exultant when he'd first arrived, looking forward to celebrating with all his colleagues and friends today, to apprehensive and disturbed with the discovery of the animal remains in the barbie, then mildly inebriated as the party got under way. He was pissed off about his boss putting a dampener on things, and then Doc had shared his thoughts about the Leech brat. Furious barely covered it.

After coming clean, Doc had wisely excused himself to check on Judy, retreating in the face of Jack's invective, blasted at him before he departed. By the time Doc returned, Jack was no longer on the ceiling, but his fuse was about as short as it had ever been. Even chucking a few more glasses of whisky down his neck had done nothing to lighten his mood. If anything, it had sharpened his sense that bad things were in motion, he could feel the evil swirling in the ether around them as they talked. Jack's premonition from this morning, when Doc showed him the dead cat, was now firmly lodged in his brain, an unshakeable presence demanding his attention.

And his gut told him the Leech boy was at the centre of it all.

'Would you like to stay the night, Dickie? We've plenty of room and Jack's not going anywhere until tomorrow evening. No need to grab another cab tonight. Let's just relax and talk through today's events. Jack and I have some things to share with you. Unless you have to be away?'

'That's so kind of you, Colin. I'll take you up on that. I found another bottle of this excellent scotch in my car too.' He handed a Harrods carrier bag containing a fancy box to Doc, grinning. 'I also keep an overnight bag in the boot—carry it at all times. You never know when your luck might change.' Professor Maddox, suave and sophisticated ladies' man and confirmed bachelor, winked as he added, 'So how about another drink for your guest, then?'

Jack and Dickie settled into the lounge suite while Doc filled their glasses, still within earshot as Jack asked, 'What can you tell us about that little performance by the Leech boy tonight, Dickie? He's a wild one.'

'It's a sad story, and I know Doc's familiar with it all. The family history.'

'We're both aware of all that. I'm more interested in why Billy Leech holds a grudge against you. Is it really about money, and you overcharging his mother?' Dickie looked taken aback at Jack's tone and blunt question. Interrogation. Jack softened his voice. 'Well, according to the boy, of course.'

'There's rather more to it, as you rightly suspect, Jack. Thanks, Colin.' Dickie took the glass from Doc, who then flopped into his armchair, saying nothing, just waiting to hear some explanation for the attack on the Bentley and its driver. 'The boy's written to me, a few times over the last couple of years.'

'Wrote what?' Jack leaned forward and in his eagerness to hear more, almost dropped his glass on the coffee table in front of him, slopping whisky as it clattered on the surface. A glance between his two friends suggested he might not be fully compos mentis. 'I'm not pissed, you two. I'm pissed off! What did he say in these letters?'

'Emails. The first one told me his mother was abusing painkillers, and that it was down to me, that she had become addicted after my staff started treating her. In truth, Susan Leech was already showing signs of substance abuse when the clinic first took her on to rebuild her face.'

'So why treat her then? Loads of operations, loads of pain medication? Sounds well dodgy to me.'

Jack couldn't help the edge in his voice, and could see Dickie bristling, but Doc interrupted, smoothing things between them.

'I assume Dickie thought that addressing the root cause of her drug abuse would help the woman. Correct?'

Dickie nodded, continued. 'Of course. We also monitored her progress, and were very careful with the medication we prescribed, both in terms of the opiate content and the levels. I can't divulge more, but let me assure you, Jack, we're not in the business of creating junkies.'

'You said that was the first email?'

'Uh-huh. The second was more ominous in tone, though I dismissed it out of hand.' Dickie let a disdainful snort loose. 'He threatened to sue me. Said he would take legal advice unless the clinic desisted from treating his mother. Told me I was killing the poor woman... A boy of what, fourteen, fifteen, threatening *me* with a law suit. Hah!'

'Did you reply?' Doc had his eyes closed as he asked. Jack had suspected he was nodding off. No chance.

'I ignored the first one, though did inform his mother in the hope she might undertake some effective parental action and stop him. She clearly failed. The second email, I gave to my solicitor to deal with. I thought a formal letter from him would shut the boy up. It didn't.'

'The third email? What did that say?'

'Not much. Just a few words in all.' Dickie took a sip of his whisky, speaking matter-of-factly, unperturbed as he shared Billy's final emailed threat. '*You POS. You'll be sorry.*'

'Piece of shit? Charming little bleeder. When was all this?'

'That latest was maybe four months ago. Or three. I'm not sure. I hadn't given it much thought. Until tonight. It was around that time he first had a go at my car.'

'What? He smashed it up before tonight, then?'

'Yes... The windscreen last time. And a few scuffs on the top of the bonnet.'

'Did you report any of this to the police?'

'Oh, come off it, Jack. He's just a disturbed lad with a very damaged mother. For the sake of a few quid and some silly emails, I was hardly likely to bother the Met's finest, was I?'

'You could've had a word with me about it. Why didn't you?'

'I assumed it was nothing serious. I didn't think it worth bothering with. Mrs Leech paid for the damage, and no doubt will do so for tonight's fiasco too. It's not as if the boy's any sort of serious threat. He's just an angry young man.' Dickie's puzzled frown dissolved into one of concern as he searched their faces. 'What on earth is going on? And why are you both looking at me like that?'

Billy Leech could hear his mother moving around in her bedroom beneath his. Her thumping footfall echoing on the bare floorboards as she hauled her fat arse around the room, doing God knows what.

She should be unconscious by now.

It was after ten o'clock, and by this time of night his mother had usually quaffed several gin and vodka cocktails, usually supplemented by drugs, including that linctus she liked to guzzle down, too. Stupid bitch thought the stuff was harmless, but codeine is converted to morphine in the gut. The over-the-counter medicine she was consuming in mega quantities was highly addictive.

Billy sniggered as he thought about it. He was the one who had ordered her most recent supplies using her credit card and an internet connection. The local pharmacy had refused to serve her after she became a regular for what was supposed to be a medicament to help people with a persistent dry cough—something she clearly lacked. Billy had been doing the 'chivalrous' thing ever since, on several occasions ordering enough to last a normal person a year. She'd get through the latest batch in a month or less.

What she didn't realise was that she was also being dosed up on Temazepam, as was Nana. Billy had ordered a supply of that drug too, using the same online pharmacies—ones that weren't too fussy about the legal requirements demanding a doctor's prescription. The capsules were easy to open, and the powder dissolved in vodka and gin almost as quickly as it did in Nana's milk.

Perhaps his mother was becoming resistant to the sleeping tablets. He might have to find a new drug to knock her out. He'd have a little chat with Smiffy about that, too.

And why hadn't the bastard called?

Billy poked around in his bedside drawer and pulled out his pay-as-you-go mobile phone. A cheap throwaway he had bought specifically for communicating with his tutor. He jabbed the speed-dial for the only contact in the memory, and spoke as soon as he heard the ringtone cease.

'Where are you? Have you sorted out what I need, or not?'

The echo on the line was all he heard for some seconds, then a heavy sigh from Smith.

'I've not been able to get all the chemicals I need. You should've told me what you needed sooner.'

'Don't mess me about, Smiffy. I need that compound and—'

'Tomorrow. I will have what you asked for ready for you by this time tomorrow. Now leave me be.'

Billy was about to speak but the line went dead.

The bastard would pay for that.

He'd been very useful so far, but he was reaching his expiry date.

'Best before—Wednesday this week!' Billy let a secret smile twitch his lips at the thought. He had so many things coming together in the next few days, it sent a thrill through his belly just thinking about it all.

The planning had started in earnest over two years ago, all with his sixteenth birthday as the end date for putting his world to rights. One of Billy's proudest wins had been conning that fool Powers into letting him into his study, then stupidly leaving him alone on numerous occasions to make them both drinks during their 'therapy' sessions.

Therapy?

What a joke that was. Billy had been keen to meet the man who he felt was responsible for the death of his father and uncle. Had read all his books, watched his entire TV series, even checked out the man's scientific papers harking back to his PhD. A treatise on identifying criminal psychopaths.

On first arriving at his grandparents' home, Billy had been kept in the dark about his family's murky past, but over the subsequent years he had gradually learnt more and more about what had happened. An uncle who Billy had been led to believe did not exist had entered his life one night, and, initially, the young boy had seen the man as an ogre, even had nightmares involving him.

Bad enough, but his worst dreams were about his father, who would regularly appear, the top half of his head missing, blasted off by a shotgun cartridge fired up through the roof of his mouth, yet still able to shout and rant, to bully his 'pathetic' son.

Billy sat up on the edge of the bed, his bare feet on the sheepskin rug, wiggling his toes in the fur. He concentrated on the sensations he could feel in his soles, the undersides of his toes, the tickling of the woollen strands on sensitive skin.

'I am not dreaming. I'm awake. When I sleep, I will dream. When I dream, I will know I'm dreaming. When I wake, I will remember my dreams.'

Every day, Billy repeated these words, either aloud or mentally, and had been doing so ever since he had first discovered the possibility of controlling his subconscious while he slept. He dropped the phone back in the drawer on top of his dream diary, the record he kept of each night's adventures—another part of the ritual he had used to train himself.

At first, it had been purely to tame the nightmares involving his father, to be able to push the hideous images away, to replace them with happy thoughts. As time went by and he became more proficient, he began to experience a wondrous new universe.

One that included his dead uncle.

Billy had a scientific bent, and some years ago would have pooh-poohed the idea of communicating with a dead relative, but now, he was less sceptical.

Uncle Peter had taken on a new life of his own, in Billy's dreamscapes.

Reality no longer had such sharp edges, such a definite boundary between the physical world and the spiritual. Billy had studied some recent theories from respected physicists, suggesting our universe is merely a hologram, a projection, one our combined consciousness creates. To him, the idea had more merit than an all-powerful god, and a devil burning the unworthy in the fires of hell.

No, much more likely that we create our own reality.

Billy was certainly creating his.

Finding Smith had been a real bonus. And that was down to the idiot, Powers.

Billy had only been interested in his family history, but was amazed by the treasure trove he had obtained from the psychiatrist's laptop. Among the numerous files and correspondence were some interesting emails. One correspondent immediately caught Billy's eye.

Maddox.

The two were real chummy, if their emails were anything to go by—which also explained why that Bentley, with its distinctive number plate, was parked outside Powers' home this evening.

Regrets rarely troubled Billy, but today's unplanned and unprovoked attack on the man's chauffeur might cause him some problems. His mother was right—it had been stupid to allow his rage at Maddox to overcome him. The red mist had descended—an infrequent experience these days, but one that still occasionally managed to take him by surprise.

On seeing Maddox's car, he had yanked the steering wheel to the side and jammed his foot on the brake, kicking his mother's foot aside simultaneously. The next thing he recalled was smashing the paintwork with the oar before that old git had appeared from inside the car.

Billy had reacted to the man's threatening stance, the tone of his voice, but at least he had maintained control over the power delivered by his kick. No serious injury. He hoped.

The possible unpleasant consequences were shoved from his mind as he went back to his thoughts about Powers and Maddox.

Both trained as forensic psychiatrists. Both had worked at Broadmoor, the hospital for the criminally insane, though Powers had retired from there. Maddox had been referring some patients' details to Powers, and buried in amongst their emails was one that included a rather nasty paedophile who was up for assessment.

A former schoolmaster. A rather brilliant one at that.

A video had surfaced, and the school, a very posh one, had contacted the police. Mr Smith had been arrested, charged and imprisoned. Maddox was treating him and wanted Powers' opinion before recommending release.

Billy had been delighted when he read that Smith had been let loose while being treated with a form of chemical castration that limited his perverted desires.

None of that mattered.

Billy had discovered the video the police had confiscated—the one he had played a brief clip from for Smiffy earlier today to ensure he had the man's full attention. That short film had also been the inspiration for the creation of some other incriminating evidence. And that guaranteed the tutor's total compliance.

It helped that Billy was adept at lying, too.

His unsuspecting tutor had no idea the trouble it would cause him when a certain Mrs Leech contacted him and offered him a highly-paid position working with her precocious son, who had to be home schooled for some unexplained reason. No references were required as her son had personally requested Smith—his services had been 'recommended' to Billy by previous tutors who had struggled to keep up with him.

'If it seems too good to be true, it surely is.' The gurgle of Billy's laughter echoed around the wooden rafters of his attic.

He pulled a thin file from his drawer and flicked through the images he had set up during one of his earliest sessions with Smith—photographs involving the two of them, snapped in Billy's study room.

Both naked.

Posed in a variety of suggestive, almost pornographic scenarios. A convicted paedophile, hired as a trusted tutor for a disturbed young man, clearly taking advantage of his position of power.

Although identifiable as Smith, the adult male's head was always turned away from the camera lens, just enough so that his closed eyes were not visible to the viewer…

'Thank you, Temazepam. Hahaha!' As his giggling died away, Billy listened again for his mother's footfall.

Nothing.

All quiet in the Leech household.

Billy was ready for bed too. Well, almost. One more ritual to ensure his dreams would be as vivid as possible. He tucked the file back in the bedside drawer, took a twist of paper from a box inside, and measured out a tiny dose of the powder he had liberally sprinkled on his Nana's meal at lunchtime.

Lysergic acid diethylamide.

Strange, he thought, as he licked the powder from his palm. It occurred to him that a more accurate acronym should reflect the first letters of the three words in English—LAD seemed far more appropriate than LSD, the abbreviation in common use thanks to the German who first created the drug.

And just like Billy, this other 'LAD' could be dangerous, if not treated with respect.

With the covers pulled up to his chin, Billy drifted off, all the while imagining exactly how much Smiffy would regret dissing him tonight.

Doc had listened to Dickie and Jack discussing the Leech boy's threats with only half his mind on their conversation. Far from being sleepy, he was hyper alert.

When Judy's scream had woken him this morning, he had not been prepared to slip back into his old life, convinced he had left it behind when she agreed to marry him. His own dark side had been dormant since then. Jack had once described it as Doc's pet psychopath, one that resided in a remote part of his brain, lurking there, always ready to spring into action when needed.

Like today.

He was always reluctant to indulge this unwanted and unwelcome side to his character, one that could empathise and understand criminals capable of the worst sorts of deeds. Serial killers, torturers, child molesters, and rapists who then murdered their victims. Even necrophiliacs—who did the same, but in reverse order. He'd met them all, treated some of them, helped convict others. From the crazed and demented through the highly disturbed and deranged, to the worst of all. The stone-cold killers.

The psychopaths.

Peter Leech. His brother Shaun Leech.

And now, young Billy Leech?

Was he merely an angry young man, as Dickie had just asserted?

Or was psychopathy imprinted in his DNA?

When he had first met Billy and they had shared a few hours together, many moons ago, Doc had thought the lad well adjusted, all things considered. He'd not even suspected the possibility that Billy might be developing similar traits until their last session together, and even then had dismissed it as unlikely after he heard nothing more from the boy. Right now, every fibre of his being was electrified, with his dark side screaming in his head that he was being naive. He had not realised he had been staring at Dickie until he heard him ask:

'...And why are you both looking at me like that?'

Jack too had a serious, troubled face. His teeth were slightly bared, and a semi-frown twisted his eyebrows. Even his nostrils were flared—an atavistic reaction of prey to a potential threat, expanding the nasal passages to test the air for a predator's scent.

Doc wondered if his own expression was similar as he answered. 'Let me tell you what happened sometime last night, Dickie, and what else we discovered this morning.'

After Doc brought Dickie up to speed on the details of the dead pets, and the significance of their appearance, he then explained their newly created theory.

'Jack and I think Billy Leech is behind these events. He managed to insinuate himself into my life, with a plea for help, but after what's transpired today, I'm now certain it was just a ruse to allow him to obtain confidential files on his father and his uncle.'

'Allow the little bastard to *steal* confidential information.' Jack was about ready to explode again. 'And not just on his old man and uncle, either. That brat nicked a whole mountain of stuff.'

Dickie's reaction was initially sceptical, though as they recounted the events, he became more open to the idea that one of his patient's offspring might pose a real threat to his wellbeing. His next question did not surprise Doc.

'Children are never formally designated as psychopaths, Colin, as you well know… But I can see why you might think he has the necessary makings of one. Cold, callous, unempathetic. I don't know him well enough to make a proper judgement, but those characteristics certainly tally with his mother's description of his behaviour towards her.'

'What did she tell you about the kid then?'

'I really can't say, but you might find out more by speaking with her yourself, Jack. I'm keen to hear what Colin heard from the horse's mouth. Are you able to share anything with us? Or will you be breaching patient confidentiality?'

Although Doc had told Jack he felt under obligation to Billy not to divulge the content of their meetings—in fact, he had not even told Judy who the lad was at the time, in case that caused her some unnecessary distress—his meetings with the boy had been on an informal basis, with no payment, and not even a commitment from Doc that he was offering a professional service. He had told Billy he was not a counsellor, and had only agreed to chat on that basis. Just a friendly ear, a sounding board, though admittedly an expert on psychopaths.

'Morally and ethically, I should say nothing at all. But these are exceptional circumstances. And Billy Leech is an exceptional young man.' Doc dredged up the details from their early meetings, where the boy had been polite and respectful. He had probed Doc about psychopathy, asking about genetic links, taking away various research papers Doc had recommended he should read. 'He's incredibly bright. He was only thirteen or so, but he studied everything I gave him on the subject. It's like his brain's blotting paper, absorbing anything that interests him.'

'Does he have total recall. Is he eidetic too?' Dickie was blessed with a photographic memory, an advantage in life he had fully exploited. He sounded disgusted as he added, 'What a waste of talent.'

'I don't think so. A highly-trained memory for sure, but not like yours.'

'Tell us what happened during your last meeting with him. You suggested earlier that you began to suspect he wasn't all he seemed after that final session.'

'He started to talk about his uncle—' Doc's explanation was interrupted by Jack's angry voice.

'Peter Leech. That murdering bastard killed friends of mine. On the force. Along with a load of civvies.'

'Yes. I thought Billy would still be traumatised by the night his uncle visited, the night his father died. The night his mother was tortured and left with her life-changing facial disfigurement.'

'He wasn't suffering from post-traumatic stress? Really?' Dickie was familiar with most of the details of the events from that time, shared with him almost exclusively by Jack. Doc was always reluctant to discuss the Peter Leech case and for years, he had even refused to utter the man's name. Even so, Dickie knew enough to be put out by Doc's assessment. 'I find that hard to believe.'

'He was at first. Didn't speak for three years. But the lad's resourceful. He was experiencing vivid nightmares, wetting the bed, reliving that horrific night every time he slept. Screaming his uncle's name and yelling about his father's murder while he slept. Yet he refused to talk during his waking hours. His mother sent him for counselling but he just sat and listened. Did nothing, said nothing.'

'So, what changed, Colin? What prompted him to start speaking again?'

'Something sparked in his mind when his psychotherapist told him about lucid dreaming—'

Dickie nodded, connecting the dots already, but Jack interrupted, grunting at Doc as he said, 'Lucid dreaming? What the fuck is that and what's that got to do with anything?'

'Well, this is probably more Dickie's domain than mine.' Doc let the other genius in the room explain.

'When we dream, our subconscious is making sense of our experiences in its own inimitable fashion. Repetitive nightmares are an unfortunate form of short circuit, if you will. A loop occurs inside the brain when it's unable to come to terms with an event in real life, so the subconscious keeps replaying variations of it over and over. Quite recently, psychotherapists have been using a new technique to help veterans and others suffering traumatic stress induced nightmares. Training them to break out of that cycle.'

'Lucid dreaming?' Despite the late hour and the scotch, Jack was still on the ball. Doc could see he was eager to understand everything, no matter how esoteric. 'What does it mean then?'

'Some people can naturally cross over between the subconscious and the conscious mind while sleeping. While experiencing a dream, such an individual is aware that he or she is asleep, that what they are doing and seeing is not real. Most of us wake up when that happens, as our conscious mind interrupts our sleep state.'

'Blimey. Never heard of that. So, what good does it do? Surely the nightmare would just seem more real, if you know you aren't dreaming.' Jack thought about it for a moment longer. 'Ah, I see... You just wake yourself up if you're having a nightmare?'

'That's the first step these specialist psychotherapists use to help a trauma victim who's suffering nightmares. With some further training, a lucid dreamer can actually *control* the events going on in their subconscious mind during sleep.'

'Control your dreams?' Jack threw Doc a look that said Dickie was completely crazy.

'It's true, Jack. Lucid dreamers can do things that are impossible in real life. Only your imagination limits what you can achieve while sleeping. Flying, levitating, passing through walls, viewing things you could never hope to see in the physical world.'

'Is this an actual thing? People do this? In their sleep? Sounds totally barking mad to me.'

Dickie poked a tongue around the inside of his cheek and made a sucking noise, as if he too thought it was weird. Then he explained more craziness to Jack.

'Have you ever heard of astral projection, Detective? Or maybe, remote viewing, perchance?'

'Nope. Just hearing those names sounds like a load of mumbo jumbo to me.'

Doc was intrigued by Dickie's train of thought, even if Jack sounded dismissive. Doc had never looked into lucid dreaming beyond a superficial interest, just enough to understand how Billy Leech had overcome his nightmares. Now, he suspected there was much more to this than he had first thought. He listened as Dickie educated them both.

'It may seem like it, though the Americans and the Russians take these things rather more seriously than we do. The CIA created a department dedicated to remote viewing... The rather strange belief that practitioners could send their spirits to observe any desired event, anywhere in the world—the universe in fact. Astral projection. There was a book about it, inspired a film starring George Clooney.'

'A book and a film.' Jack nodded to himself. 'It's fiction, then?'

'Hollywood thoroughly sensationalised the story, of course, but the program was real. The CIA and the people they employed in pursuit of their psychic spying plans thought it real enough too. My opinion, for what it's worth, is that these so called psychic individuals were merely experiencing a form of wakeful lucid dreaming.'

'Oh, right. That makes sense—but what about the Leech brat? He thinks he's psychic, does he? Let me guess. He's communicating with his dead relatives. His murderous dad and uncle. Phahaha. The twat...' Doc and Dickie watched scotch spray from Jack's nostrils, as he tried to drink through his mirth. He grabbed a tissue and blew his nose, his face scrunching with pain. 'Cor blimey. That burns a bit.' He sniffed and mopped the tears from his eyes. 'Bugger. That was a waste of good whisky... Ignore me. Yeah, I am a bit pissed.' As he recovered he quizzed Doc with his eyes, looking for some confirmation. 'The boy's deluded then, ain't he? No such thing as ghosts. And as for this astral bollocks. It's just plain silly.'

Doc had another interpretation, one that didn't involve spirits.

'He told me, that final time we were together...' Doc could visualise the boy, standing in his study, hands on hips as he stared Doc down. 'It was then that his whole attitude shifted. He transformed before my eyes, from the passive patient he had been into a scowling, snarling, spiteful adolescent. Full of pent up aggression.' For those few minutes at the end of that session, Doc had felt malevolence emanating from the boy, but had dismissed it, had not given Billy Leech another thought since.

Until today.

Doc was back in that meeting, reliving the sensations. This time, the devious part of his mind reached out and assessed what he had seen and felt. The conclusions were disturbing.

'Go on, Doc. Don't keep us in suspense. What did he say?'

'He said his uncle, Peter, had been visiting him. Had told him all about me. And said I would die a painful death. Then he said those around me would suffer too.'

Jack was dumbstruck. Dickie was fascinated.

'Lucid dreaming... The boy recreated his uncle in his sleep. After turning the nightmares around he must've started communicating with the man in his dreams. About you... In his subconscious, you really were to blame for the bad things that happened to his family, just as he said. But...'

'I'm afraid so, Dickie.' Doc and the Professor had reached the same conclusion, though Jack was still struggling to come to terms with this psychobabble, as he would describe it. It was time for Doc to sum up the problem for his down to earth detective pal. 'Billy Leech is projecting on to me the hatred his uncle harboured for me. There was plenty of evidence of Peter Leech's animosity towards me in the files he stole. The ones detailing my involvement with his family.'

Jack was finally on board, eyes wide as he spluttered out his own conclusion. 'Oh Christ, Doc. You think he's internalised all that stuff. And as a result, he's got it in for you... The cat and the dog... You were right. They're a warning of worse to come.'

'I believe so.'

'And you think he wants to take revenge? On you... Not for letting his uncle out on parole. But for *killing* the bleedin psycho.'

'Hello Billy boy. How you doin, my son?'

Warmth saturated Billy's senses as his uncle's voice reached him.

He glanced down, could see the sheepskin rug below his crossed legs as he floated a metre or so above. He looked up and the sloping roof of his attic became transparent then dissolved, opening up to the clear night sky, full of coruscating stars flickering a welcome to him.

He rotated in mid-air as the walls of his home also evaporated and the rug too disappeared, leaving him alone, suspended in space.

'I feel fantastic, Uncle Peter.'

Speaking that name conjured an image of the man before him. The battered facial features, the massive bull-like body, the green eyes that glowed in the dark. Compelling, mesmerising in their intensity.

'So you should, sunshine. I've been watching you.' Billy's uncle's hand reached out and ruffled his hair. 'You remind me of me... You little tyke.'

The touch of fingers on Billy's scalp sent waves of energy pulsing through his body. Suddenly, they were in his dojo, standing, facing each other. Uncle Peter in his huntsman's overcoat, a sawn-off shotgun dangling on some string hanging from his right shoulder, just visible beneath the material.

'I'm ready, Uncle.'

'I think you might be, Billy boy. You've done everything I asked of you. Now let me in.'

Without speaking again, their minds melded, and then separated almost immediately. Euphoria had threatened to burst Billy's brain as he felt his guru's presence inside him, the wise elder's approbation for all he had planned.

Just one small glitch.

'Sorry, Uncle. I couldn't stop myself.'

'Don't you worry your pretty little head about that copper, my son. He's a fuckwit.'

Billy was relieved. His uncle was so different from his father.

Allowing that thought was a mistake. It brought Mr Mu to life. The vinyl ball that was his head exploded in a mush of gore, as his father's body materialised in the corner of the dojo.

'Just ignore him, Billy. He's nuffin. A dead man.'

But the dead man was stepping towards them both, the top half of his head missing, eyes still shining despite having been blown away.

'I'm dreaming. You're not real. Leave us!'

Normally, the command would work, banishing his father for the duration. But tonight, something was wrong.

'That damn pig, he got to you, didn't he, Billy boy?'

Billy felt his uncle behind him, while his father lurched towards him, arms outstretched like a zombie. Fear swelled inside him, an unfamiliar and disturbing sensation in his dreams these days. Somehow, it seemed right.

His destiny.

'Here you go, Billy boy. Face your fears, my lad. Let's see if you really are ready. To *deliberately* take another man's life.'

'I want to… I really want to…'

He had an irresistible urge to kill his old man with his bare hands.

'Nah, Billy. What have I told you about that? He's dangerous. Always use overwhelming force whenever possible. Don't be a fuckin hero. Try this.' The shotgun was cold and hard beneath Billy's fingers, the touch of the trigger reassuring him as his father went to grab his neck.

'Killing's easy.' A whispered rasp filled his ears. 'Just trust your Uncle Peter.'

Fingers, as strong and cold as the steel barrel of the gun suddenly wrapped around Billy's throat, crushing the life from him. His father's eyes bored into him, and then that voice, the supercilious tones he had always loathed to hear.

'You're pathetic. Just like him, your idiot uncle. Haha!'

As Billy's dream started to fade to grey, he panicked, thinking this wasn't right, that *he* controlled events, but he was convinced he would die tonight if he didn't pull the trigger.

Only one problem—his hands were paralysed by sheer terror. The sight, sounds and smell of his father, so familiar, ripped away his confidence, throwing him back in time, reverting him to the scared little child he had been. He psychically shrank in the man's presence, felt himself deflate like a balloon having the air squeezed from it. He couldn't breathe.

'Just do it.' His uncle's voice sent a final surge of electricity sparking through his central nervous system. Jolting him back from the brink, swelling him back to his full size. He could do this. 'Come on. It's witching hour, Billy boy. Lots to do tonight. Wakey-wakey.'

The deafening explosion of the shotgun transformed his father's body into a crimson blur, and launched Billy back into his bedroom, his hand reaching out to the alarm clock at the exact moment the digits clicked over from 2:59am.

SUNDAY

IGNITION

THE STENCH of excrement punched Suzie in the back of her throat as she opened Nana's bedroom door. Her sense of smell was only half as efficient as it had been before Peter carved off her nose, but it was still plenty sensitive enough to make her retch—and that was before she saw the state of her mother's bed and the wall behind it.

'Ugh...'

She held her hand over her nose and mouth in a vain attempt to smother the worst of it, and managed to get a window open before she vomited. She hauled deep lungfuls of fresh dawn air into her chest, the scent of freshly mown hay a welcome relief from the stink of ordure, smeared on the headboard and paintwork in the room she had just unwittingly entered.

Her mother was still out cold, her wheezing breath testament to the life still pumping through her veins. Suzie wondered whether her mother passing away might be a blessing for them all. The dreadful thought shocked her.

'I'm such a terrible daughter... And a crappy mother.'

She stared out of the open window, guilt at her callous reaction sliding into her heart like a surgeon's blade. Perhaps it would be better if she just threw herself head first to the concrete paving slabs below, though there was no guaranteeing she'd die from the fall. And she just couldn't bring herself to end her own life—God knows, she'd thought about it often enough. Instead, she had been slowly drinking and drugging herself in a painful and tantalising dance with death, often wondering if she would wake up in the morning after imbibing such huge quantities of drugs and alcohol.

This morning she had woken early, and without a hangover for a change. Last night, after her run in with her son and his insults about her failings as a mother, something had snapped inside her brain, and she had spurned the lure of a freshly mixed Martini. Even the dulling comfort of codeine linctus had failed to tempt her, and she had fallen into bed, sobbing into her pillow with the sober realisation of how low she had sunk. A withdrawal headache had pounded at her skull, and she found herself praying to Mary, Mother of God and her divine son, Jesus, in her desperation —something she had rarely done since her teenage years.

Today, she was determined to have a fresh start, and had planned to get her mother up and drag her out of this claustrophobic room, take her downstairs, and set her up in the garden with a bed chair. Then she had opened the door to be confronted by this—the equivalent of a Belfast political prisoner's dirty protest in the front bedroom of her parent's Berkshire home.

Her mother's fingers were stained brown, tangled with her hair on her filthy pillow, drool mixing with excrement at the corner of her mouth. The headboard had claw marks, smeared filth, as if she had unsuccessfully tried to climb the walls in a bid to escape the foulness surrounding her.

Perhaps it was a test. God wanted to know if her prayers and pledges were genuine. Or was her vow of abstinence an empty promise, just like all the times before?

Suzie turned away from the window, went to her mother's side and took her hand in hers, while forcing herself to breathe in the terrible odour. After several panted breaths the smell of sewage seemed to diminish, and the room became bearable again.

'Mum?' Suzie gave the old woman a gentle shake, tugging at her shoulder to wake her. 'Let's get you in the shower, eh?'

Her mother came half awake, her pupils wildly dilated, and Suzie began to suspect the old dear may have taken too many of the pills the doctor had prescribed. Pills that had no doubt constipated her, paralysing her gut, until the pressure inside forced it to vent while she slept in her bed. Perhaps the enormous bowl of lasagne Billy had brought her had finally unplugged her insides.

'You poor, dear woman. Come on, Mum.'

Sympathy for her mother had been in short supply, but today Suzie genuinely felt for her, and decided right then she would nurse her back to health if it was possible, and look after her if it wasn't. As she staggered towards the en suite bathroom, dragging the dead weight of her mum, Suzie had something of an epiphany.

Her son no longer needed her, was beyond mothering, was maturing into a strong, confident young man. It made perfect sense to transfer her caring to her own mother, now that Billy was becoming increasingly independent. It would give her something to live for, something greater than herself.

She swung open the bathroom door, and once more the concentrated faecal odour, this time intensified in the enclosed space, almost felled her.

'Oh, Mother!'

Suzie propped Nana in her favourite chair by the open window and forced herself to enter, clicking on the light and extractor fan as she did so. Then she saw it and felt reality tilt as her universe came untethered. The taste of codeine linctus blossomed on her tongue, and her brain almost collapsed under the pressure of her craving. She stood rooted to the spot, her own image reflected through the words...

The accusation, scrawled in shaky stinking script. A message for Suzie, finger-painted on the mirror, daubed with the contents of her mother's bowels.

YOU KILLED MY GRANDCHILD. YOU ARE EVIL!

'Morning! How's yer head? Sleeping Beauty!' Jack slopped tea in the saucer as he placed the cup on the coffee table in front of Doc, taking in his dishevelled appearance and red-rimmed eyes. 'You were snoring, so me and the prof left you there to sleep it off, and retired to the guest rooms.'

Doc reached for the cup, and groaned as he leaned forward from his armchair. 'Oh, my head. I never drink whisky. And that's tea. You know I only drink coffee in the mornings.'

'Yeah, well, I can't get that monster espresso machine of yours to work.'

'Didn't you ask Judy?'

'Nah. She went for a run just as I surfaced. Dickie jumped in a cab at the crack of sparrow fart. Said he had to get into London before the rush hour. And a low-loader came and took his Bentley away first thing, too.'

'What time is it?' Doc pushed himself from the chair, then dropped back into it. 'Damn. Blood pressure and angina tablets really don't mix well with alcohol.'

'Dickie's to blame. Appearing with that second bottle of thirty-five-year-old Dalmore whisky. It was lovely, but most of it's gone, and I've got a hangover too, thanks to him. I should stick to beer.' Jack peered at Doc's face, noting the deathly pale with a hint of grey in his cheeks. 'Are you alright, mate? You should take a few minutes.'

Doc eased himself into a standing position, swayed, took some deep breaths and said, 'I think I'll just go and lie down. Help yourself to whatever you want in the kitchen. I'm really not up to making breakfast. Or even coffee.'

'Go on then, bugger off and leave your guest, hungry and thirsty.' Jack grinned and punched Doc's arm playfully. 'You want me to help you up the stairs, old man?'

Doc huffed in reply and grimaced as he took halting steps towards the stairs. 'The instructions are on the side of the machine. You can bring me a latte, if you can manage to follow them. See you in a bit.'

Jack had plenty to do, and his head felt tight, not painful, which was about as hungover as he ever got. And he couldn't be bothered reading the instructions on the coffee machine. Judy would be back soon enough.

Time to get on with some work.

He unplugged his mobile phone from the charging unit, and dialled the number from memory. A female Inspector he had met on a recent weekend training course— a colleague he'd had a brief but enthusiastic liaison with.

'Charlie, it's Jack.' No time for pleasantries. He had a lot to do before cruising downriver later today. 'I have a favour to ask. I hope I'm not disturbing your Sunday morning.' He didn't let the dirty snigger loose, the one he could hear in his head as he added, 'Again.'

The line almost sizzled with contempt as she answered. 'Jack... You said you'd call me. It's only been four months...'

Oh shit.

'Really? That long? I've been a bit busy. Promoted too. DCI Carver they call me now.'

'I can think of a few other names for you, Jack. So, what do you want? I'm actually working, but I gather this isn't a social call, since you seem *too busy* for one of those.'

Ouch.

'Sorry. I meant to call...' He had, too, but as the days turned into weeks, he became increasingly reluctant to do so. Stupid, really. He'd never been good at developing personal relationships, blamed his job. 'I'm down your way today and need some info on a young man. A local teenager. I think he's been making a bit of trouble for some friends of mine.'

A sigh, then, 'Does he have a history with us then?'

'I dunno. He may have.' Jack described what had happened to Dickie's chauffeur and car the night before. 'I'll be meeting the driver later, to see if he wants to press charges, but wondered if you could do some digging for me on the boy in the meantime.'

That sizzling was back, then he heard her muttering to a colleague in the background, cursing 'some cocky bastard' she'd met at Sulhamstead House, the Thames Valley Police Training Centre, on a recent course. It was a shame, because he really did like her.

'Alright then, Jack-the-lad. What's his name, this tearaway you're so interested in?'

'Billy Leech. Probably William, officially. Lives on Bucklebury Common. That's in your patch, if I remember rightly.'

'Okay. It'll cost you... A phone call. And a dinner.'

'Haha! Sure. That's a bargain.'

'If we have anything, I'll get back to you in the week.'

'Sorry, Charlie. I'm on vacation and won't be around after tonight. Any chance I could buy you lunch? Today? I'm in the area. You can fill me in then.'

Sizzle.

Jack held his breath, knowing he was pushing his luck with Charlotte Kealey, a very classy brunette with a laser sharp brain. Theirs had been a meeting of minds. And bodies. They had spent a sleepless, sweaty, and highly energetic night together.

'You are such a cheeky bastard...' Jack let out his breath as she added, 'Midday. The Bladebone Inn. A superb gastropub in Chapel Row, very close to your toe-rag's address. Don't be late or I'll be gone.'

Click.

Well, that went rather better than he'd expected. A smug smile grew on his lips just as he heard Doc bellowing at him as he thundered down the stairs.

'Jack! You've got to see this! I can't believe it!'

Doc's head was spinning as he made his way up the stairs, and he hoped Jack would be willing to do battle with the espresso machine for him. It had been a while since he'd been drunk enough to generate a hangover, and mixing wine with whisky had been asking for trouble. By the time he reached the bedroom, his heart was dancing a tango on his diaphragm, and not a particularly rhythmic one at that.

Instead of lying down, he decided to shower, hoping a blast of hot water would refresh him. It did, so he took a glass of water from the bathroom to his bedside table and pulled out a bottle of paracetamol. As he swallowed down two tablets he noticed the envelope on his pillow.

That's odd.

His name was on it, along with a hospital logo. Judy had made the bed before jogging off, so must have placed it there for him. Strange. Why had she left it for him like this?

Was it bad news?

Was she sick?

Why not stay and talk it through rather than go running? Or was it news so terrible that she couldn't bear to tell him to his face?

Perhaps she was angry with him, for not coming to bed last night, but that wasn't like her. Doc had spent several nights asleep in his armchair after yapping with Jack over a bellyful of booze.

No. Only one thing for it.

He ripped open the envelope and pulled out the single sheet inside—then he thought his heart would stop as he took in what he was seeing.

Doc remained frozen for maybe half a minute, his emotions sending hormones raging through his bloodstream, his heart now pumping for all it was worth. He was giddy and light-headed, but still forced himself to jog down the stairs two at a time, yelling at Jack as he descended.

The two men met in the hallway, and Doc couldn't stop himself from blurting out the wonderful news.

'Judy left this for me.' He waved the printout in Jack's face, then stabbed the ultrasound image with his finger. 'Look! She's pregnant, mate! Almost two months already. It's bloody fantastic! I'm going to be a father... Can you imagine? After all this time.'

Suzie had cleaned the entire bathroom before stripping the bed and scrubbing the headboard and walls. The room smelt of bleach now, a refreshing change from the stink that had greeted her first thing this morning.

The mirror was pristine again too. Suzie had avoided looking at her reflection while cleaning it, but as she stepped in the en suite, ready to run a bath for her mother, she caught a glimpse of herself before looking away.

Why not look? Don't be such a coward.

If she really wanted to change, to remake herself, to drag herself back to some sort of normality, she had to confront the worst of it.

Her grotesque face.

A brief prayer, a plea for strength, bolstered her courage as she stood in front of the mirror, eyes closed.

'Three, two, one. Open.'

The involuntary gasp from her lips echoed off the tiles, as she forced herself to properly inspect the state of her face for the first time in years. One half was still perfect, though a little older and more wrinkled, a reminder of the beauty she had carried so carelessly. A precious gift that she had not fully valued, until her brother-in-law had peeled the other half from her skull. Her false eye was a brilliant prosthetic, comfortable and mobile, the colour and shape perfectly matching the other.

Except the pupil never changed in size.

And there was the disconcerting lag, the sluggish movement that never quite caught up with her good eye as it tracked from left to right, or up and down. Over time, the muscles within her orbital socket had strengthened but the surgeon had warned her that her lazy eye would probably always be a visible flaw, something that she would just have to accept.

She had not. Had shied away from viewing herself, partly because of that defect, its permanency a constant reminder that her beauty had gone forever. Hence, dark glasses had become habitual.

The loss of muscle tissue was the other reason why mirrors had become her enemy. The inevitable asymmetrical nature of almost every facial expression was something she could never come to terms with. Professor Maddox had encouraged her to undertake daily exercises, practising in front of a mirror to rebuild and strengthen the fibrous tissues, but the first time she tried, the mangled visage facing her in the silvered glass had sent her diving straight back into the bottom of a bottle —and she had stayed there ever since.

I'm still ugly, but I do look a whole lot better now…

On close inspection, she decided her nose was excellent, almost as good as the original. The cartilage, scraped from between her ribs, had been moulded and transplanted, and now replaced the septum Peter had excised. Flesh from her brow had been expanded and stretched, then skilfully sculpted to create the new nose. Dozens of operations had been necessary to perfect it, and her lips had been artistically repaired, though still mismatched and frankly, to her mind, ugly.

More rib tissue had recreated her severed ear, and she now tucked her hair back behind it to get a proper look. That too was almost indistinguishable from the other —hardly surprising given the expertise of the Caduceus Clinic surgeons who had modelled the new ear on the other one.

It was strange that her cheek had been the most difficult surgical transplant. Every time new tissue had been carefully stitched into place, the flesh became torn, swollen, and infected. Suzy looked at her nails, bitten and tattered, miniature weapons fighting a constant battle with the alien tissue on her face.

It had to stop.

'I can do this. I can be whole again.'

And no more disguising myself. Why should I care what other people think?

A groan from Nana alerted her that her mother was coming around. She felt a twinge of guilt that she had spent the last hour cleaning the rooms, then indulging herself, while her mother was sitting in her own filth, with stinking hair, and stains on her hands, butt and legs.

Suzie started the bath running, the steaming water rapidly misting up the mirror, bubbles foaming, filling the tub.

'Come on then. A quick shower first, then we'll get you into the bath. Warm you up. You're freezing again.'

With renewed vigour, she helped her mother disrobe, but sheer shock at the sight of her nakedness took Suzie's breath away.

She looks like she's been in Auschwitz.

Skin and bone. Barely any flesh on her.

'Christ above. How did I let you get into this state, Mum?'

The question was moot—she knew full well how. Self-indulgence and clinical depression. Alcoholism and drug abuse. Being absent while physically present.

Nana's rheumy eyes blinked open, and Suzie noticed a vague tinge of yellow, colouring the whites.

Jaundice?

How? Are the medications she's taking affecting her liver?

And why was she stick-thin? The amount of food Billy had been bringing her, she should be a healthy weight for her age.

Perhaps she had some problem with her insides.

With a mental promise to call the family doctor, Sunday or not, she stepped into the shower cubicle, propping her mother on the special seat they'd had fitted when her father became infirm. With the shower-head in hand, Suzie aimed the powerful jets of steaming water, soaping her mother from head to foot, gradually reviving her as the brown filth swirled down the drain.

'Now let's get you into this lovely warm bath. Can you hear me?'

'Mmm. I'm hungry. Thirsty.'

'I'll get you some food and drink while you have a nice long soak. What tablets did you take last night?'

'Erm… I don't know. I can't remember going to bed. I… I… don't feel well. So tired. Forgetful.'

Suzie had not helped her mother bathe for over a year, and that was only after the poor woman had tumbled down the stairs. She had retreated to this room after that, rarely venturing beyond the door, though at least she'd been managing to keep herself clean, occasionally with some help from Billy.

'Will you be okay here while I make you something to eat?'

'Mmm. It feels so nice.'

As she stepped from the bathroom, Suzie's brain started firing, reinvigorated as her battered liver gradually cleared the residue of toxic chemicals from her bloodstream. She reached an unpleasant conclusion, but inevitable after what she had seen this morning.

Her son had been lying to her.

Nana had not been eating all the food Suzie prepared for her. So, what had he been doing with it?

And more pertinent was the other question now burning brightly in her mind.

Has Billy been deliberately starving his grandmother?

On any average Sunday morning in this far from average country home, Billy Leech would luxuriate in a well-deserved lie in, catching up on the loss of sleep from his nocturnal adventures, and have a generally lazy day.

Today was different.

He surfaced from his slumbers, thoroughly excited, buzzing with energy, and thrilled as he thought about all the things he was putting into action in advance of his upcoming birthday.

His coming of age.

A true test of his manhood. The rite of passage he and his guru had agreed would signify his transition from adolescence to adulthood.

Earlier, he had been listening to his mother, clomping around below, surprised that the screeching and yelling he'd expected—when she entered her mother's room —had not been the first sound he'd heard on waking. Instead, all had been quiet for the last twenty minutes or so.

He pulled on his jeans and couldn't help the wicked smirk curling his lips. Maybe his mum had collapsed. Fainted on being confronted by the shit storm Billy had created for her. He could hardly wait to get down the stairs to check on them both, though found time to gel his hair and admire his appearance in his bathroom mirror before bounding down to the landing below.

Strange. Nana was not in her bed, and his mother wasn't lying unconscious on the floor in the doorway either. He wandered in while breathing through his mouth —despite the thin film of Vick's vapour rub he had applied to his upper lip before venturing forth from his room—and was surprised to taste the tang of chlorine on his tongue. And the mess in the bed had been cleared up already.

Had his mother really done all this? And why wasn't she screaming blue murder?

For the first time in years, he had a sense that he was not fully in control of events, and it unsettled him. He was better than this—better than anyone, especially these two, who only shared the weak, pathetic half of his unique genetic makeup.

His mask slipped and his surprise at his plan coming unravelled was revealed in his face as he turned to see his mother in the bathroom doorway, staring at him.

Suspicious.

What was she thinking?

'You're up early for a Sunday, son. Did you wet the bed? Again?'

This was all wrong.

Billy felt disoriented, so glanced down at his feet, wriggled his toes on the carpet, and verbalised in his mind:

I am not dreaming. I'm awake. When I sleep, I will dream. When I dream, I will know I am dreaming. When I wake, I will remember my dreams.

Oh, he was awake alright, standing in this room, but his mother was behaving totally out of character. It didn't strike him immediately, but gradually he realised what was different about her—she was sober, and straight, neither pissed nor drug-addled. All he could think of at that moment, was how confident she appeared.

Enlightened even…

He shrugged, and went on the attack. Her jibe about him wetting his bed had shaken him, but the insinuation had not hit home as it was almost five years since the last occurrence, so he just ignored the remark.

'What happened in here then? You two been having a party? You're both full of shit, so I can see how it happened.' He smirked at her. 'The state of your liver, I'd think the pair of you could pebble dash the walls without much effort.'

'Who said anything about shit?'

A beat passed with them eyeballing each other, neither willing to break contact, then Billy waved his hand at the bed, and sniffed hard for her benefit.

'I can smell it. Even through the bleach you've sprayed everywhere.' Billy had slipped up, thanks to being wrong-footed, but was satisfied with his recovery. *Always attack first, my son.* His guru seemed to whisper encouragement in his ear. 'You'd be able to smell it too, if you had a proper nose instead of that mangled lump of meat they stitched in the middle of your deformed face. Anyway, what's going on? Where's Nana? Is she okay?'

'Get out.' His mother's tone was steel, and Billy knew the accompanying glare would intimidate any normal son.

'Does she need help getting in and out of the shower? She won't want you in there, that's for sure. I'm the one who helps her, not you.'

The hideous bitch had her arms folded, and she stood in the bathroom doorway, her bulk blocking him. He stepped towards her, planning to read aloud what he had written, to twist the knife he was sure he had planted in her guts when she first saw the message, but she was immovable, determined not to let him see inside.

'I said, get out! *I'm* looking after her. Now just go!'

He decided to retreat, and regroup. Think through what had gone wrong this morning. A minor setback, nothing more.

Billy slipped from the room and swept down the stairs, his brain processing the brief encounter.

Nothing to worry about. A temporary aberration on his mother's part. That's all.

With a little nudge or two from him later today, she'd be knocking back the cocktails and cough linctus like her life depended on it.

It did.

Hahaha!

Perhaps an acid trip might help the ugly old bag unwind, and plunge her back into the bottom of a bottle where she belonged. Regardless, he would sneak into her bedroom tonight. Thanks to the overpriced Caduceus Clinic, she was sporting another slab of expensive new flesh, a slice of her upper breast masquerading as her right cheek.

A confident grin lifted Billy's spirits as he remembered the last few occasions. In the past, his minor modifications to that most visible part of her anatomy had always had the desired effect…

On finding out he was going to be a parent, Doc had been walking on air, his head light, his mood even lighter. There was no trace of a hangover in his system now, partly flushed away by the two lattes he had made for himself after telling Jack his wonderful news.

On finishing his espresso and immediately before leaving to do some 'errands', Jack had clapped Doc on the back and promised to bring back some champagne to toast their good fortune, a double celebration, to be held that afternoon when Sally, his daughter, and her fiancé arrived.

Doc could not settle to anything—he wanted to hug his wife, but Judy was still out. She had taken her car too, so was probably out with the Caversham running club this morning, so could be back at any time, sooner or later.

What to do?

A third latte was at his lips as he gazed out of the patio windows, his mind on all the amazing things he would have to do as a new father in his early fifties. As his own reflection came into focus, he vowed to lose the little bit of flab he had accumulated since his year in France. He'd let the yoga lapse while there, and had promised himself he would take it up again on his return to the UK. A promise he had broken for nigh on three years…

I'll be almost seventy when my boy—he was convinced his offspring would be male—comes of age.

Eighteen years of parenting, at this time of his life, was a rather daunting prospect, but he would not let that impair his euphoric mood.

I'll get fit and healthy again.

High blood pressure and occasional heart pain were warnings he could not ignore. The dizzy spells had caught him by surprise, as had the diagnosis. Overlooking his own wellbeing, while caring for Judy, nursing her back to health, was no excuse. Doc would have to take much better care of himself from now on.

I'm going to be a daddy!

Despite his elevated mood, that dark and twisted character living inside his brain, the tame psychopath that had enabled his stellar career in forensic psychiatry, crept out of its box and instilled in his mind ugly ideas as it did so.

Will he be like me? And if he is, will he be able to control his urges?

A vision of Billy Leech presented itself before his inner eye—the snarling adolescent from their last session together. His threatening manner, truly forbidding, despite being just thirteen.

More images appeared. Billy's uncle, as a scrawny eighteen-year-old, with similar facial features, though much coarser, standing in the dock at the Old Bailey before being sent down by the judge—an old colleague of Doc's. A good friend who had been murdered by a member of the Leech clan.

Doc's mood soured as another vision took hold. Shaun Leech, the boy's father, standing behind his son, with Peter, older now, after his release from prison, built like a heavyweight boxer, his features battered as if he'd just stepped from a brutal bout of fourteen rounds, green eyes burning with hatred.

All three then converged, morphing into Billy Leech, also older now—the teenager who had been dragged to his mother's car, by then almost fully grown. His athletic body, that of a powerful adult... And his eyes glaring through the car windscreen.

With a jolt, Doc felt the same degree of malignant hatred he had experienced radiating from Peter Leech during their final confrontation.

A sickening swirl of acid in his belly scalded his heart, and he clutched at his chest wondering if he was about to go into cardiac arrest. Panic took hold as he felt a tingling in his left arm.

No... I cannot!

Doc panted and tried to relax. He brought his breathing under control, and then applied the yoga techniques he had learned many years before. Although out of practice, the counted breaths and delayed exhalations worked, his panic receding as he felt the tingling subside.

Not good.

Doc was due at the heart clinic again on Wednesday so would have himself fully checked out then. He glanced down at his third coffee and dumped the cup on the table in disgust at his lack of willpower. One a day was supposed to be his limit. And he hadn't taken his tablets this morning.

Idiot.

A quick trip to the kitchen sorted that out, but as he returned to the patio he found himself staring at the Weber barbecue, still under its vinyl cloak.

Damn.

The dead dog was lying inside the grill. He sighed.

I need to sort that before Judy gets back.

While experiencing a vague sense of deja vu, he took his gardening gloves from the cupboard under the kitchen sink, along with another plastic sack, but this time grabbed a bottle of grill cleaning spray instead of a screwdriver. He was not looking forward to the task, one that extinguished all happy thoughts at Judy's news.

Doc busied himself with cleaning up the mess from the offending corpse. Fortunately, the dog was charred and desiccated, rather than rancid and decomposing like the cat had been, so the contamination inside the grill was easily removed with the caustic solution he liberally sprayed on the metal, then scrubbed and rinsed clean.

With the dog lying on the lawn, he did a cursory post mortem inspection on the poor creature. It was difficult to tell what breed it was—a mid-sized dog, and not particularly well built. Doc would have a word with Jack to see if he could discover any locals who were missing a pet.

Meanwhile, he reached a highly disturbing conclusion as he checked out the charred remains. Going by the curled position of the dog's limbs, the way the snout was stretched in a rictus grin, the bared teeth and lolling blackened tongue, Doc was convinced the animal had been alive before being set alight.

He tucked the corpse into the bag, tied a knot in the plastic to seal it and turned to haul the remains to his wheelie bin at the side of the house.

'What on earth is that?'

Judy had arrived back, and Doc, engrossed in his gruesome task, had not heard the car pull up, or her approaching footsteps.

Several thoughts rattled through his mind, including wondering what she had seen, but the overriding consideration was the amazing flood of endorphins at the sight of her, his wife, carrying his seed inside her.

'Sweetheart!' He dropped the bag, threw off his gloves and rushed at her, swept her into his arms and planted a sloppy kiss on her smiling lips. 'We're pregnant!'

He twirled her round, her feet dangling above the ground, in a pure dance of joy.

'Put me down, you fool! You'll give yourself a heart attack.' She giggled at him. 'I'm sweaty and ready for a shower, but I see you found my note.' She waggled the proof of their good news under his nose.

'I'm thrilled, my love. Absolutely overjoyed.' He was, again. All thoughts of animal corpses and psychopathic offspring banished from his mind. For now. 'You should've told me! How long have you known?'

'I only had it confirmed yesterday, at the hospital.' Judy glanced away from him as she spoke, her voice betraying something, though Doc could not detect what. She held his hands and focused back on his eyes, her voice firmer. 'I planned to tell you last night, after the party, but you didn't come to bed. And you were unconscious when I came down this morning.'

Doc wanted to crush her to him again, but held himself in check. What had he sensed beneath her outward bonhomie?

Some hesitancy? A reluctance to share something?

No. She's just tired from her run.

'Why didn't you say anything when you got back from the hospital, before the party? We could've shared the news with everyone then.'

Her eyes shied away from his again, her answer ambiguous. 'I wasn't sure... I mean, wasn't sure I wanted anyone else to know—just you and me for now.'

'Oops, sorry. I told Jack and he's out buying champagne!'

'What were you doing cleaning the barbecue again?' The abrupt change of subject and tone startled Doc, and he felt his face flush. Guilt glowing red. 'You cleaned it on Friday evening. And what's in that bag?'

'Oh, erm… I came out to remove the leaking gas pipe and take it to the garden centre, but found a dead dog under the vinyl.' It was a half-truth. 'I wrapped it up and decided to spray the grill with cleaning fluid in case it contaminated anything. The animal was in a bit of a state. Diseased I think.'

Judy pursed her lips and viewed him with suspicion for a few beats. Doc could almost hear her thinking, *What aren't you telling me?* He kept quiet.

She nodded to herself, blew him a kiss and said, 'I'm going for a shower. You smell of dead dog… You should come up and join me.' A wink. 'Celebrate properly.' She turned, waggled her butt at him while grinning over her shoulder and then jogged inside.

Doc, his face splitting in a toothy grin, and with all unpleasant thoughts tossed from his mind, chucked the bag in the bin and trotted after her.

'I believe you have a gentleman here by the name of Huw Jones.' Jack thrust his warrant card at the receptionist at the BUPA hospital on the outskirts of Reading. 'I'd like to speak to him, or have you discharged him already?'

'Er, no, he's still here, though will be leaving shortly.' She punched a few buttons on her computer and then said, 'Second floor, room eight. The lift is that way.'

Jack strolled along the corridor, feeling underdressed. When on police business he usually wore a jacket and a clip-on tie, but his holiday attire didn't include formal wear. Summer shirts, with short sleeves, designed to be worn open at the neck, were all he had in his suitcase at Doc's home. As he punched the call button, the lift doors opened and he saw his outfit in the mirror on the back wall.

Hawaii Five-Oh.

He chuckled at the thought and was still grinning when he knocked and entered room eight. Jonesy was half dressed, buttoning his shirt, and he smiled back as Jack greeted him.

'So, how're you doing, matey? We've been a bit worried about you. How's your bonce?'

'I'm all good. Just some bruising, a sore neck from whiplash, but nothing to worry about. A bit of mild concussion they reckoned last night but the doc checked me over this morning and I'm good to go.'

Jack leaned against the door, taking in the black eye that had sprouted from Billy's kick to the man's temple. 'That's quite a shiner you've got there, Huw. Do you want to press charges?'

Jonesy pulled on his jacket, tightened his tie, grabbed his carrier bag of belongings and grimaced as he shook his head.

'Ow. My neck!' He held the bag up for Jack's benefit and said, 'The boss bought me some toiletries and stuff. He's a lovely man. And he asked me not to. So, no. I don't want to press charges.'

'How are you getting home?'

'Taxi. Why?'

'Nah. I'll take you. We can chat in the car. As long as you don't live in Cornwall or somewhere similar!'

'That's kind. Slough, so not too far. But you won't change my mind, Detective. Professor Maddox has given me the week off, and a bonus for my discomfort. He didn't insist, but did ask me to respect his wishes. Left it up to me… And I've made up my mind. Fair enough?'

'Sure.' Jack hid his disappointment at the man's decisive tone. 'Come on then.' He wasn't about to give in that easily, though.

The car nosed out of the car park and Jack headed the few miles to the M4 motorway, cruising through light Sunday traffic, relieved that the journey would not take long. He didn't want to be late for his lunch date with Charlie—she'd be gone if he was, of that he was certain.

'Why's the prof so adamant he doesn't want you pressing charges? I can't believe it's just about money and his precious client—the boy's mum.'

'You should ask him, Detective. He's your pal.'

'I'm asking you. What do you think?'

Jonesy stared out of the passenger window, wordlessly. Jack waited. The power of silence. Uncomfortable seconds ticked by and then Jonesy muttered, 'I s'pose it'll do no harm.' Then more strongly. 'Between you and me—okay?'

'Sure. Mum's the word, Huw.'

'I drove Mrs Leech home one time. From the clinic.'

'From Harley Street? That's a bit unusual, isn't it? Or do you often chauffeur patients around in his Bentley?'

'Highly unusual.' Jonesy remained silent again, and Jack could almost hear the cogs turning in the man's brain, waited for him to continue as they sped east on the motorway. 'Her son was supposed to pick her up at lunch time, had booked a cab to take them both home, but there were complications with her surgery that morning. She was late, but he wouldn't wait for her. Just stormed out of reception when they told him it'd be at least another hour before she'd be discharged.'

'Okay. And Dickie told you to take her home? That was very chivalrous of him.'

'He's very generous, and thoughtful. She needed to be accompanied, but a private ambulance wasn't necessary. I was doing nothing anyway, just waiting, so I drove the hundred-mile round trip, there and back. Mrs Leech was really grateful.'

'I still don't get it.' Jack turned off the motorway and followed signs for Slough. 'Tell me where I need to turn to get you home, mate. And explain why this has anything to do with why you aren't pressing charges. That kid's a menace…'

'He's just had a tough life, Detective. It's not surprising he's gone off the rails a little.' Jonesy huffed, then added, 'When I got to their house, I helped Mrs Leech from the car. I was at her door when I heard the Bentley wheels spin as it shot out of her drive. I'd left the engine running.'

'What happened? Are you saying the little brat nicked your boss's motor?'

'It was just a joyride.'

'When was this—how long ago?'

'Almost two years. I ran after the vehicle, but it does nought to sixty in five seconds, so I had no chance. He roared off down the lane, burning rubber. Turns out he's done it before.'

'Nicking cars?'

'Joyriding… His mother was having hysterics, babbling on about him driving off in her car. Boy's done it quite a few times over the years. I was fuming, wanted to call the police. The car was barely a week old… Cost two hundred grand plus change. Professor Maddox gets a new one every couple of years, and that trip to their home was the furthest it had been since delivery.'

'But you didn't? Call the police.'

'No... Turn here, and then next left. Number thirty-two.'

'Why not? And what happened to the car?'

'He brought it back, ten minutes later. Said he always fancied owning a Mulsanne and thanked me for letting him take it for a test drive. Cheeky bugger... In the time he'd been gone, I managed to calm his mother and she begged me not to tell anyone. She ripped the bandages off her face, showed me... Told me what had happened to them both... I was shocked, still worried about the car, then he pulled up outside. No harm done. It's not the lad's fault he's a bit wild, and it was just a prank.'

'The idiot could've killed someone.'

'Maybe, though he had been taught to drive as a young kid. His grandfather took him go-karting, and later gave the boy lessons on some local farmland. Nothing illegal in that.'

'You feel sorry for him?'

'Both of them. That poor woman doesn't need me making her life even more of a misery than it already is. If the professor hadn't asked, I still wouldn't be pressing charges, Detective. Mrs Leech doesn't deserve any more aggro in her life than she already has. Thanks for the lift.'

'You're welcome, mate.'

Jack pulled in to the kerb, and Jonesy hopped out of the car and left him thinking about the woman's fate. Was he being unfair on her? And was his suspicion about young Billy a hangover from his previous investigations involving the boy's uncle?

And the sins of his father...

Jack's fingers tapped the steering wheel as he sat outside Jonesy's house, deep in thought, reviewing all he'd heard and seen since arriving at Doc's the previous morning. He had been determined to pursue the boy, to punish him, but now he was not so sure. All their 'evidence' was entirely circumstantial, though the pets at Doc's place certainly pointed to some link with the Leech family.

Well, let's see what Charlie has to say. If there's nothing else, I'll forget about Billy Leech, bugger off on me holidays and try to make the best of it.

With his mind now made up, Jack found some rock music on his radio, cranked up the volume and sang along to *Sympathy for the Devil*—an old Rolling Stones track and one of his all-time favourites. By the time the Jag reached the M4, he'd found himself thinking about Charlie, hoping she'd have nothing for him, that he could just relax and enjoy her company over a leisurely lunch.

But as the car began heading west, an ominous feeling crept up his spine, a reminder of his premonition from the day before. Just beyond Reading he spotted the signpost for Chapel Row and Bucklebury Common, by which time the sense of fore-boding, the discomfiting conviction that something terrible was about to happen, had gripped his soul again. By the time he parked outside the Bladebone pub, he was convinced Charlie would have some very bad news for him.

She did.

'How are you feeling now, Mum? I'll cook us both some proper breakfast when you get out. We'll get you dressed and out in the sun. How does that sound?'

Nana held a giant smoothie, a banana based fruit concoction, and sucked at it greedily through a straw as she soaked in the bath. Suzie could see her perk up as the sugar hit her bloodstream. The warm water had added colour to her cheeks, and she began to talk less haltingly as her brain absorbed the nutrients.

'I'd like that. I feel so much better… But everything is such a blur, lately.'

'Did you enjoy the lasagne I made yesterday?'

'I think so. I don't remember eating much… Why didn't you tell me?'

Suzie felt her neck redden, certain her mother was referring to what she'd seen written on the mirror.

'What do you mean?'

'About the baby.' Bony fingers intertwined with Suzie's right hand, and her mother looked at her with pity in her eyes. She certainly wasn't angry. 'You should've told me.'

'Is that why you wrote on the mirror?'

'What? I didn't… Did I?'

'Yes, Mum. You don't remember?'

'No. When? What did I write? And why would I write on a mirror?'

Thankfully her mother must have blotted out the events of last night, although that was worrying. Dementia could well be taking hold.

'You must've been upset, Mum. How did you find out?'

'About your abortion? You did have one, didn't you?'

'I did. When I was in hospital, while they were… After what Shaun's brother did to my face.'

'It was Shaun's baby?'

'Uh-huh.' The familiar prick of tears left Suzie speechless for a second, this time for a life she had destroyed. 'Y-yes… I couldn't bear the thought of his flesh and blood growing inside me again. Not after all the dreadful things I discovered about him—and his lunatic brother.'

'I can understand that, sweetie. You should've let me know. I was here for you, you know that.'

That was the truth, but Suzie had been ashamed, and in a fragile state of mind when she first arrived at her parents' home, only recently discharged from hospital, her face a complete mess still. It required more strength than she possessed at the time, to come clean about everything that had transpired.

'And I can understand why you were so incensed, enough to write that message on the mirror, Mum.'

'I wasn't angry. I was sad when I found out.' Her mother's fingers tightened on hers. 'Sad for your loss and even more so that you didn't feel able to tell me.'

A niggling suspicion was now worming its way into Suzie's mind as she repeated her earlier question.

'How did you find out? It's been seven years…'

'I don't remember. I'm confused… It felt like I was in a dream. Shaun was whispering to me. It sounded like Billy, but surely, he doesn't know. Does he? Did you tell your son and not your mother?'

'Why on earth would I?' The suspicion was taking on more solid form now, and Suzie could feel another idea growing inside her. The unpalatable thought that Billy was turning into his father.

Or worse.

'I don't know. He's such a lovely boy. Always so keen to help me.'

'Mmm.'

Suzie was racking her brains, thinking back through the haze of recent years, wondering how Billy might have discovered her secret. She still had some papers from back then, bundled in boxes in the cellar, untouched by her since being delivered from their London home. All the memories from that time and the years before were sealed, and stored away, forgotten.

Had her devious boy been digging around in there? Had he found some documents from the hospital, tucked in one of the files? Her release notes perhaps, with some indication about the termination? She would go and look through the boxes herself later. And if he had...

Anger clamped down on her scalp, as if a metal band had been strapped round her skull and tightened.

Billy had been foul to her for years, but was he capable of trying to turn his grandmother against her?

Given the range of crimes her husband had committed while pretending to be a normal family man, and considering how she had been fooled for two decades by his superficial charm, it seemed fair to assume that his son may well be similarly duplicitous.

The boy's grandmother was convinced he was an angel, but when he spoke to Suzie about her, he was dismissive, harsh and unsympathetic. And over recent months, he had been getting even more impatient with her. What had he said yesterday? That she was a useless old bat who should kill herself.

Christ. I've been so blind! Again...

'I'd like to get out now. I'd love to feel some sunshine on these old bones, and spend a day in the garden. It's been so long that I've been stuck in this room. Help me out, love?'

Suzie took a bath towel from the shelf and held it as her mother stood, then wrapped her in it.

'Let's get you dressed and I'll help you downstairs.'

Five minutes later, they walked through the kitchen, arm in arm, Nana leaning on Suzie for support, and then stepped out into the back garden. After she had settled her mother on to a lounge chair, and tucked her up with a blanket despite the mid-morning sun, Suzie went to make them all some brunch. Not that she knew whether Billy would reappear, but she would cook enough for him anyway, just as she did every Sunday morning.

It was strange for her to be cooking without any stimulants or depressants in her system, and as she prepared their mid-morning feast, almost on autopilot, it became clear to her that she had been going through the motions for years now. Surviving, just doing as little as she needed to, to get through each day. The result? The increasing distance between her and her mother just as widowhood drained the life from the ageing matriarch.

And Billy had willingly filled the gap.

Until today, it had not occurred to her that this had been happening, let alone the possibility that he might be manipulating them both.

Was he really that bad?

Maybe it was an overreaction. But now that her suspicions had been roused, another uncomfortable conclusion about him started to form.

'Is that my breakfast? I hope so, I'm starving.' Her son was behind her and she flinched as she heard his voice, murmured just behind her ear. 'You smell like a swimming pool. Chlorine. I hope you haven't ruined my grub with your stinky mitts.'

She plated up his food—bacon, eggs, mushrooms, grilled tomatoes and waffles—and shoved it at his hard belly, feeling the edge of the china meet solid muscle.

'Just sit down and eat.'

It was an effort not to shout at him, to throw her suspicions into his smug face. Thankfully, he took the plate and plopped himself onto a chair at the kitchen table and started wolfing his food without another word. The noisy chomping, the smacking of lips, the slurping at his milk, made her want to slap him. He knew how much it annoyed her—another unsavoury habit he'd developed in the last few years.

Better to ignore him, so she busied herself serving two plates more, and arranged them on a large tray with some orange juice in two small glasses.

'Leave that. I'll take it up to her. I'm almost done. She's probably seen enough of your repulsive moosh today. I'll sit with her for a while too.'

Suzie turned and held the tray ready to take outside, and felt an uninvited sense of satisfaction as his eyes widened at sight of the two meals.

'Don't you worry your pretty little head. We'll be eating together, in the garden. And we'll be talking, so I don't want you interrupting us. My mum and I, well, we have a bit of catching up to do. Wouldn't you agree, son?'

His open mouth, wordless for a change, gave her an immense kick. Then she realised how pathetic she was being, jousting with her teenage boy. Kinder words were heading to her lips, when he verbally stabbed her again.

'She *hates* you. You really upset her the night before last. Yelling about all that stuff.'

'What are you talking about? I haven't been yelling.'

Have I?

'Before I helped you to bed. You started ranting on about how you hated your life. That my dad had ruined it. You kept on about how you'd lost his baby—my little brother or sister—while you were in hospital. Then you laughed—cackled about it, just as I tucked you up in bed.'

'No... You're lying.' She couldn't be sure. She remembered *nothing* of that night. A total blank from soon after serving dinner.

'Why would I lie? You shocked me though, and Nana could hear you shouting and laughing about it too. You're really callous and cruel, aren't you? Huh. You admitted it.'

Suzie could hear a rushing noise in her ears, a throbbing inside her brain, as her heart went into overdrive. That bloody smirk again. He was waiting for her to ask. She wanted to run out of the kitchen, but could not. Her feet, nailed to the floor.

'Admitted what?' The words tumbled out, caustic on her tongue, and she knew with certainty and horror what he was going to say next.

'You had an abortion. You chose to *murder* my unborn sibling. Couldn't stand the thought of having another little Leech inside you.' His eyes were gleaming, triumphant and confident. 'Nana went out of her mind about it. Told me not to mention anything to you. You were well pissed. Off your head. I'm not surprised you don't remember.' He snorted and stood up to leave. 'Why don't you go and have that nice confidential chat with her about it, eh? As if I care. I'm going out on my bike, anyway.'

He pushed past her and went to his room as she remained stock still, eyes closed, trying to calm herself with little success.

Come on. Get moving.

With the tray rattling, she plodded across the lawn to her mother, sat beside her on a second sun lounger, and placed their cold breakfast on the low table between them.

There was no point asking her mother to confirm his story, though that niggling doubt about it all persisted. Along with another unlikely explanation.

The thoughts began to coalesce into something almost tangible, but her mind wasn't quite ready to process all the ramifications just yet. She and Nana chewed in silence, both comfortable in each other's company, Suzie noting that there was nothing wrong with her mother's appetite, going by the speed at which she ploughed through her plate of food.

Billy, now resplendent in tight-fitting fluorescent lycra, his muscles bulging, wheeled his powder blue Bianchi Specialissima Limited Edition bike across the lawn —six kilos of high tech machinery, a top of the range model that cost Suzie just shy of ten thousand pounds. He hadn't even said 'Thank you' when she bought it for his birthday.

Paid for it.

He'd actually ordered it, three months early, too.

'I'm off. See you later, Nana.' He simply ignored his mother, just as he had with her instruction not to disturb them.

'Where's your helmet, Billy?'

'Only idiots need them, Nana. I won't fall off, and cars give cyclists more room when driving past if the rider isn't wearing one.'

Whether it was true or not was irrelevant to Suzie. His supercilious attitude made her want to slap some sense into him, but his grandmother just chirped back, 'Bye love. Have fun.'

He turned on a winning smile for his grandmother's benefit, then mounted his bike.

'Billy.'

'What?' He locked the clips on the underside of his cycling shoes into the pedals as he spoke, then balanced on them, standing upright instead of sitting on the saddle, holding the machine with the brakes. A surly scowl aimed at his mother, telegraphing his impatience to be away.

'You and I need to talk. Tonight. You said I couldn't smell what you could this morning. Maybe you were right. I realise why now… My nose was overcome by the smell of your bullshit.'

The bike wobbled, and she thought he had lost balance, but he recovered and scorched her with eyes burning bright. For the first time in her life, she felt real menace in the air around him before he regained control of both his bike and face, then cycled away, whistling cheerfully.

The Thames towpath was busy near Pangbourne. A sunny Sunday afternoon brought out the weekend crowds but Billy, confident in his proficiency, continued cycling fast, weaving through the pedestrians and their dogs before swerving round a young couple pushing a buggy.

'Oi! Slow down you idiot! This is a public footpath, not the Tour de France!'

With his fluorescent yellow outfit, Billy could easily have been competing, but it wasn't a trophy driving his thighs and calves, it was the anticipation of what he was about to witness, mingled with fury at his mother's parting comments.

Her whole attitude had changed, literally overnight, and he could see no reason why. Perhaps his little altercation involving the Bentley had finally shaken her up, and she was trying to be a proper mother again.

No chance!

She had been like this before. Several times, he'd seen her, flushing her 'medication' down the toilet while crying her eyes out, praying, promising God she'd be a better mother and take care of him and Nana.

As if.

It never lasted a whole day, or even a whole night. He always kept a store of drugs for her, and on those occasions she had thrown hers down the loo, he had left some by her bed after visiting her while she slept. He would sort her out again tonight, but avoid her in the meantime. He had more important things on his mind.

Thankfully, the crowds had thinned out to a few random hikers by the time he reached his destination. Once they were out of sight Billy jumped off the bike and swung it on to his shoulder before jogging into the undergrowth for a few hundred metres, certain he was not visible from his target's home.

A lightweight DPM poncho, tucked in a pouch under the saddle, was one of just two specialist items he carried today, and now, he pulled the camouflaged garment over his neon attire, locked the bike to the base of a nearby birch tree, then leapt up to grasp the lowest branch of an ancient oak towering above him. Using his momentum, he swung his body up and over, with his knees arresting the motion as he landed on the top of the branch. A similar manoeuvre hoisted him another couple of metres further into the canopy. Then, with sinuous movements he almost slithered up the tree until he was at roof height of the luxury property on the opposite side of the river.

From the pouch in the back of his cycling shirt he plucked the military grade compact binoculars and unclipped the lens covers while sitting in his regular spot, a natural platform created by the main trunk trifurcating. Billy's legs dangled either side of one near horizontal branch while his back rested comfortably against the two that continued skywards.

From his vantage point, he could see beyond the cruiser into the manicured gardens, and all the way to the picture windows and patio doors of the Powers residence. Despite the bright sunshine, reflections from the glass on this, the south facing side of the property, rarely impaired his view inside the house, and today was no exception.

It was almost lunchtime, and soon enough, Powers began making his way to the boat. Billy felt a thrill as the bastard responsible for killing two of his relatives stepped aboard the cruiser. There was a slim chance Powers would spot it—the lead trailing along the side of the boat furthest from the dock, terminating half way up the transom, just above the bathing platform at the stern. It was a risk Billy was prepared to take.

Not much choice, really.

During last night's witching hour, he had borrowed his mother's car, with the canoe still in place, and driven to a deserted spot on the river bank, then paddled for fifteen minutes to pull alongside the boat he was now viewing through his binoculars. His tutor had bought two duplicate filler caps—at Billy's insistence—despite being completely in the dark regarding what they were to be used for... Just two of the many things Billy had made Smith purchase or manufacture for him since the teacher had become his pet some two years prior.

Haha. You idiot, Smiffy.

The spare had been used to test how difficult it would be to remove the lock barrel, and Billy had been relieved when his tungsten drill bit had made short work of the insides, releasing the mechanism. That same rechargeable Black & Decker tool, muffled with some padded material, had achieved a similar result when Billy had duplicated the process aboard the boat during this morning's witching hour.

He whistled with relief as Powers bumbled past the newly installed items and went to the cabin. The short length of cable that Billy had soldered to the filler cap was covered with white tape, matching the hull, and then disappeared through a hole into the engine compartment. Billy had drilled out that hatch door lock too, and knew this was the other potential flaw in his plan. Having watched Powers prepare for his regular Sunday lunch trips on numerous occasions, Billy was comfortable that the odds were in his favour, confident that the various minor modifications he'd made were unlikely to be discovered until it was too late.

Go on, Powers. Turn the ignition key for me.

The foliage rustled around him, moved by a breeze blowing from the river, but he had not noticed until now. Suddenly, Billy felt his uncle's presence, as if his guru had decided to join him at the last minute, sitting behind him, breathing down his acolyte's neck, he was that close. There were no words of encouragement though—just an overwhelming sense of excitement and impatience, waiting for the show to begin. Then the man's wife appeared on the patio, calling to her husband. Her words were indistinct but Billy saw Powers jump off the boat and head inside.

Bollocks.

Billy scanned the windows and saw they had a guest in Powers' study—the same room where he and the psychiatrist had spent their few sessions together—fiddling with the computer. The binoculars tracked across to the kitchen where Mrs Powers was putting out plates and bowls of food on the table.

No... Of all the summer Sundays for them to decide to eat at home, and they go and choose this one!

Billy's plan for today was ruined. His mother's attitude, Nana recovering her senses while being fed untainted food, and now this. He could barely contain himself as he swung through the branches to the ground, then ripped off his poncho, shredding the thin material in his rage. He thrust his key into the bike lock, and in response to a violent twist of his wrist, the metal sheared before the mechanism opened. Billy was left standing in the undergrowth, with half a key and a bike he couldn't use.

He bellowed in frustrated disbelief.

'FUCK!'

Billy had been anticipating this day for months. And now there was a very good chance someone would discover the booby trap he had spent so many hours creating.

Quaking with rage, he stomped through the undergrowth, and pulled his flick-knife from his pouch. The blade shot out and he swiped a thumb across the edge. The sight of his blood only further incensed him. He swore to himself, then vowed he would stick the blade into the first living creature to cross his path.

Judy felt great. Doc was an attentive lover, and his joy at discovering he would be a father had given him extra stamina this morning. There was no doubt he was besotted with her, though she knew it was undeserved.

When he'd tracked her down in Paris, found her at death's door, then helped her get well again, their relationship was still unconsummated, had remained that way until almost four years after they first started seeing each other. He had waited patiently for her to feel passionate enough, human enough, to make love to him. In France, he had been like a faithful hound at her side, guiding her back from her depression to a life worth living.

He was desperate to start a family before it was 'too late' for him. His first wife died in a car accident, along with his unborn son. Unlike Judy, the experience left him hankering for a child—preferably more than one. She had acquiesced, for his sake.

Well, not really.

She had pretended to acquiesce. While he assumed they were trying for a baby, she was still taking her contraceptives, but didn't have the heart to tell him. Or explain why.

Then forgetfulness and fate had sparked a life in her belly. A life she had not wanted in there. One she was not mentally prepared for.

Judy caressed her midriff as she thought how close she had come to destroying that precious being within her. Lying on the hospital bed, yesterday morning, staring at the ceiling through the tears, waiting for the nurse to inject her before the doctor came and sucked the contents of her womb into the contraption beside her.

Doc's face had loomed above her, her imagination painting on it something akin to the joy she had seen on his soppy chops this morning. She couldn't let them do it, couldn't go through with it.

When the nurse arrived, syringe in hand, Judy was already getting dressed, her frenzied fingers fumbling with her buttons in her haste to escape. Then she spent two hours wandering round Reading's riverside mall, unseeing, wondering if she had made the right decision.

This morning, she knew. She had. She would be a good mother, again.

A glance in the bedroom mirror confirmed she was still bearing that after sex glow, and she grinned at her reflection. With a determined stride, she made her way downstairs, and thought she heard Colin pottering in his study, so poked her head round the door to see if he wanted some lunch—her stomach was rumbling. A man she didn't recognise was sitting at Colin's desk, fiddling with his computer.

'What are you doing here? Who are you?'

'Oh, hi! I'm Sam. I'm a… a friend of Jack's. You must be Mrs Powers.' He smiled and gestured to the screen. 'I'm a computer specialist, and your husband's been having some issues, so they asked me to pop by and take a look.'

'Hmm. Okay. You can call me Judy. If you need anything I'll be making lunch.'

Judy backed out of the doorway and went to the kitchen, her good mood slipping away with this latest unexplained occurrence. She pulled a bowl of salad from the fridge, along with some left-over sausages and ribs from the day before, then slammed the door with her foot and banged the crockery on the worktop in disgust.

I'm not bloody stupid.

She'd planned to quiz Colin about the charred dog she had seen him bundle into that plastic sack. And why he thought it necessary to sterilise the entire barbecue while she was out for her run. It was obvious the dog had been *inside* the grill, not underneath it, and she could see her husband's guilt writ large when he first spotted her.

Rumbled.

Then he lied about it. It had become a habit, not that she was a shining beacon of honesty in their marriage. Today though, Judy had more than an inkling that Colin was trying to protect her from whatever was going on.

A cat, on the door. A dead dog—obviously named Houdini, as it had managed to crawl inside a grill with a heavy steel lid that she could barely lift. And now a 'computer technician' working on a Sunday. One who might as well have had policeman tattooed on his forehead.

No. She wasn't stupid, and she would have it out with Colin later, when their guests had gone.

And where is he?

She went to the patio, called to him, and saw his head come up in the boat's cockpit as he heard her shout, a cheery grin greeting her.

'Lunch is ready. Are you coming?'

'I'm on my way. Tiger!'

'Humpf.' Judy turned her back on him, but his comment brought forth a sly smile and tickled her into a good mood again. She went back to the study and said to Sam, 'We're about to eat—nothing fancy, some cold meat and salad but you're welcome to join us... Officer.'

Another one, with the same look Colin was wearing earlier. The same look Jack had yesterday morning when the pair of them lied about a leaking barbecue.

Rumbled.

Sometimes, Judy thought she would make a better detective than Jack...

'Why do you tell him so much? He's only a child still, no matter how old he looks, or how much he behaves like an adult.'

'I'm sure I didn't say anything to him about the abortion, Mum.' The degree of conviction in Suzie's voice said otherwise. 'He said I was shouting about it. I don't believe it.'

'You have been drunk a lot, lately. It's been getting worse ever since you came here. I can understand why, but you're still young. Forty-five is no age. Don't give up so easily.'

The two of them were reclining, soaking up the sun's rays, holding hands as they relaxed.

'I'm trying, Mum.' Suzie craved the taste of codeine linctus, though she had not touched any today. Or booze. Her body was reacting, and that metal band around her temple, the one she had blamed on Billy, was still tightening. It felt like her head might fracture and then split open under the pressure. 'It's really difficult sometimes.'

All the time.

'It's been so long since we've had a good natter. Years… I missed you, love.'

Suzie squeezed her mother's hand in response. She would not give in to the urge, would fight through whatever withdrawal symptoms she suffered. Penance for allowing herself to get in such a state.

'Me too, Mum.'

'I know I haven't been myself lately, either… You won't ever put me in that place, though, will you?' Nana rolled on to her side and propped herself on an elbow to better view her daughter's face, her own desperate, pleading. 'Promise me, Susan.'

'You know I wouldn't.' Suzie mirrored her mother's posture so that they faced each other.

'Billy told me. You went to Lakeside, spoke to them about me, got the brochures. Please don't lie to me.'

A trickle of cold fear rippled down Suzie's spine. Admittedly, she'd been off her head for years, suffering frequent memory lapses, but on this occasion, she was one hundred percent certain. Forgetting a trip to the geriatric home, driving there and back by car, talking to the staff, checking out the facilities?

No way.

Suzie only ever forgot events in the evenings, between serving dinner and bedtime, when she consumed way too much alcohol in her nightly quest for oblivion —usually successfully. And listening to Nana's trembling voice, she knew this supposed trip to Lakeside geriatric care home was a fabrication conjured into existence by her son.

Billy Liar…

It was the title of a book she had read decades before. A comedy about a teenage fantasist. But there was nothing funny about *her* Billy liar, or this dreadful story he had invented. Nana was devastated by the very thought of it.

I can't tell her… She thinks the world of the boy.

'I think Billy might sometimes imagine things, Mum. He definitely imagined that. I promise you, I've never set foot in the place. And I also promise you, right now, I will never put you in a home. This *is* your home!'

Nana's face crumpled, and she sobbed again, giving the impression she was crying with relief. But she wasn't.

'Please stop lying to me… I can't stand it.'

'I'm not!' Suzie sat up on the edge of the lounger and took both her mother's hands in hers, leaning forward, urging her to believe what she was saying, peering into her eyes, hoping to communicate her total honesty through her own. 'I have *never* been to Lakeside, or any other place like it. Honestly, Mum. Billy's obviously confused—and I'm not.'

'You mean it?' Watery eyes held hers. 'Swear on your father's grave.'

'I swear.' Suzie gave her mother a hug, held her until the juddering sobs stopped. She picked up the tray and said, 'Let me get some tea and some tissues.'

For years, Suzie Leech had been an emotional wreck, buffeted and battered by unwanted and often overwhelming feelings of worthlessness, fear, desperation and depression. As she strode to the kitchen, her face rigid, her muscles tense, her head thumping a painful beat, she felt an unfamiliar emotion welling up inside her.

Fury.

The few minutes it took her to make a pot of tea and arrange some cups on the tray allowed Suzie to calm herself. The rage had not disappeared. No. She had stored it, would let it loose again, later.

The moment she was ready to confront her bastard son.

With a purposeful stride, she carried the tray back to her mother, certain she had heard the worst. Then her mother started on a new tack.

'I know you think this house should be yours by rights. And it will be. When I'm dead and buried... And not before.'

'Mum!' *What is she on about?* 'I don't think that! I have plenty of money of my own. I could buy a dozen houses like this one, and still have enough left over never to work again.' Suzie had not talked to her mother about any of this—her father had helped her sort all her finances when she had sold up and first moved here. 'Didn't Dad tell you?' The plan had been to buy her own place nearby, but Suzie had never felt up to it, and then inertia set in. They had settled here, buying up some land and stables from a neighbour to convert to study rooms for Billy. It had been the ideal solution for a while. Before her father committed suicide.

'It's not the same. This house is special...'

'I don't think you realise, Mum. We're rich. Shaun may have been an evil bastard, but he provided well for us, with millions invested. Our London home fetched five million when I sold it! He left everything to me.' Nothing to Billy, though the boy was also well provided for. Another massive pile of undeserved Leech lucre that her father had ended up managing for the lad.

'Your dad worked hard to buy this place, to make it such a lovely home. I did too. You mustn't think...'

'Think what?'

'It's true... Mr and Mrs Leech did give us some money. But please... That wasn't really how we managed to buy this place. It helped, but—'

'Enough, Mum! I have no clue what you're talking about.'

'I know you do, Susan—even though we've never discussed it. I hate to even mention it... When Peter assaulted you. When you were Billy's age.'

Peter? She still doesn't realise it was Shaun.

Of course, her mother had never discovered the truth, and Suzie only found out twenty years after the event that she had unwittingly married her rapist. She'd been drugged, was unconscious at the time. Everyone had blamed Shaun's brother—the black sheep of the family. The whole terrible event had been swept under the carpet, for lack of evidence—she'd been woken by Shaun and had showered, still groggy and confused, before discovering what had happened to her. It had all seemed unreal at the time, hearing about it and being unable to remember anything.

That was a blessing, in many ways.

But why was her mother bringing it up now?

'So what, Mum? It's ancient history and I put it behind me.'

Twice.

'The money. Mr Leech paid us fifty thousand pounds... It was, well, sort of compensation for all the trouble his lad caused us. I was devastated, and your dad was furious. He involved the police, but there was little they could do, and we didn't want to distress you any further. So, we told them to drop the charges... We had to move away from that boy's house though, couldn't stand to live in the same neighbourhood any more, so we used the money towards this property.'

Hush money?

'Now you think... I think... that was *my* money! And that you *owe* me this house!' Suzie started laughing. Of all the things she had learned today, this was the most outrageous. It took all her effort to speak again. 'Ridiculous! Of course, I don't. I love this place. It's *our* family home. And I guarantee you will never leave here, other than feet first.'

Suzie's laughter dissipated all the tension that had been building inside her today, the steel strip springing from her head, all pressure released. It was a relief to hear such unfounded nonsense was at the root of her mother's concern.

Nana's next words, spoken in utter confusion, choked off the laughter bubbling from Suzie's throat.

'So, are you saying Billy lied to me, then?'

'I'm thinking I might have to cut my vacation short. Well, probably defer joining Sally for a couple of nights. I had a very interesting chat over lunch with an old friend of mine about some of the goings on around here. What d'you know about the Dooley boys and the Richardsons?'

'Not much.' Doc had finished cleaning up the aftermath of their lunch. Judy had been offhand with him while they ate, and he couldn't understand why after she seemed so happy earlier. Hormones, perhaps. He handed Jack a cup of tea and they both settled on to the sofas in his lounge as he added, 'Sam didn't find a trace of anyone accessing my computers. Checked out the whole system. Thanks for arranging for him to come today, Jack—that's a load off my mind.'

'Yeah. Mine too.'

'As for the Dooleys. I can't tell you much, other than they have a gang of mates, late teens I believe, and they cause a bit of trouble. There's no farm work for them, but they make some cash trading in scrap metal. Mostly lead stripped from church roofs and office buildings from what I've heard. There was a load of overhead wires cut down near Thatcham a few months back, and that went missing too. Dangerous business, stealing high tension cables. Why?'

'Billy Leech used to hang out with 'em. Until late last year. Apparently, they think he's a nutter. And I'm inclined to agree after all I heard this morning.' Jack brought Doc up to speed with what Jonesy had said, then continued with his latest findings. 'My contact said he was expelled from school, but everything was covered up. Rumour has it, he was involved in some violence against three older kids who'd been bullying him.'

'Well, I knew he'd suffered for the few years he wasn't talking. They may well have deserved it.'

'Serious violence from what I heard. Three kids from his school arrived in hospital the same day he was suspended, then expelled shortly after. That's all I know. I'd like to go to the school and do some digging, but it's Sunday.'

'Come off it, Jack. You're on holiday. Sally'll be here soon.' Doc tried to dismiss his pal's concerns, though his own suspicions were multiplying. 'How old was he? Eleven? Twelve? It was probably just boys being boys.'

Or a Leech being a Leech?

'Mmm, about that I think. He's not been back to school since. No one would have him, not even the private academies, according to Charlie.'

'What else did he have to say.'

Jack leered as he answered. 'She... Charlotte. Uniformed Inspector, out Newbury way. She said they had looked long and hard at the Dooley gang, but never managed to catch 'em red-handed. Flashing the cash, but no sniff of where it came from. The local nick's too busy to bother with a bit of petty theft, though when that electric cable went missing five local villages had no power for days, so that got some attention. No collars, though.' Jack slurped his tea, his face thoughtful. 'What I found interesting is that there's been a lot of other unexplained vandalism and some serious animal cruelty hereabouts.'

'That's not a good sign, Jack. As you well know.' Doc felt stirrings in the dark part of his mind, unbidden but coming alert with this disturbing news.

'That's what I thought, and when I asked her how long this had been going on for, she said—'

'Seven years?'

'Uh-huh. Almost seven.'

'Shortly after Billy Leech moved into the area.' Doc gulped down his own tea, determined not to touch another coffee today, and cut down from tomorrow. Even so, he felt increasingly tense as they talked.

'Yup. And when I asked her to pinpoint all these happenings she said they started around Bucklebury Common and had spread out over the years to cover a wider area.'

Of course...

'What sort of things? How serious?'

'Serious enough. Charlie said there was no proof, but when they were interviewing the Dooleys about the cables, they laid into 'em about the arson and the animals too.'

'Arson?'

'Hay bales at first, then a couple of barns—the first the farmer put down to spontaneous combustion. Happens, apparently. Then another one occurred a couple of months later just down the road. Fire department reckoned petrol had been splashed around, but by then the first site had been cleared ready to rebuild, so there's no evidence that one was deliberate.'

'Is that it?' Doc doubted that would be all, his mind alive with the possibilities of what was behind these incidents.

'No. A scout hut, a village hall, several private garages—with the owners' cars inside—and the icing on the cake. A school gym went up in smoke last summer.'

Doc's stomach flip-flopped as he heard this, then he asked, 'Billy's old school?'

'You got it in one, Doc.' Jack finished his tea and let the cup and saucer clatter on the coffee table before he spoke again, his tone serious, firm. 'That's why I'm thinking I may hang around. I'm really worried about this kid.'

'So why haven't the local bobbies arrested him? Did the Dooleys say he was responsible?'

'Nah. Just dropped hints. Smug bastards were laughing at the coppers doing the interviews as they knew they were innocent—of the arson. When asked about Billy, they denied they knew him, at first. Then the interviewer told them he'd been seen with them in Reading, hanging around with 'em. That's when the Dooleys said they'd told him to piss off. Too much of a weirdo even for those scrotes.' Jack planted his elbows on his knees, hands clasped, eyes fierce. 'I'd like a little chat with them too…'

'And the animals?'

'Really 'orrible stuff, mate. Horses having their tails sliced off in the middle of the night. Sheep being gutted and left bleating while bleedin to death. Pigs with their ears cut off and eyes gouged. Cows having their udders slashed. An ostrich farm lost two birds one night… Found 'em in a ditch the next morning. Their necks had been tied in a knot.' Jack's mouth twisted in disgust, his head shaking as he eyed Doc. 'Who'd do something like that?'

A budding psychopath…

'Jesus, Jack… And the local police did nothing?'

'Did what they could. But we're in the middle of the countryside. There ain't security cameras on every corner like there is in London. It's a huge area with hardly any people and loads of livestock. This all happened under the cover of darkness too, so there was no one around to witness what was happening.' Jack sighed and sat back again. Shrugged. 'For a sadistic lunatic with a desire to harm animals, it's bleedin Paradise round here.'

'They suspect Billy Leech did all this?'

'Charlie's oppo does. A sergeant in the Thatcham nick. She knows the Leech family from twenty-five years ago—was a trainee on the force when Billy's grandparents were murdered in their home near where she was stationed. She's convinced it's him, though she got short shrift from her boss. She had a gut feeling about it, after quizzing the Dooleys. Even spent some nights on obbo. Outside his gaff.'

Observing Billy's home overnight to see if he went walkabout in the early hours…

'Nothing then?'

'Nah. She gave up after a couple of weeks—was still working a full shift during the day, as a lowly sergeant. Let me show you what clinched it for her though. Charlie's pretty convinced after seeing this too. She put the word out for me after I called her this morning, and this sarge came up with gold for us.' Jack handed Doc a USB stick. 'Don't worry—there's no spyware on it!'

Doc slipped the thumb drive into his MacBook and opened the file marked 'Unsolved Incidents—BL Files'. A map of the local area appeared and Doc could see irregular zig-zag rings spreading out from a location some miles to the south of his home. He expanded the view.

'Bucklebury Common. This is Billy's house?'

'Yup.'

'And the rings? Distance by road from his home?'

'I thought that when she showed me, but she's a clever one, our Charlie. She added them for me after the PC emailed the basics to her. It's the years the events happened. And the little red crosses are fires, the little yellow crosses are the attacks on farm animals, the green ones are domestic pets, either missing or mutilated. The numbers next to them are the month and year they happened. Clicking on the date will bring up details of the relevant incident.'

'Good grief!' Doc estimated he could see over a hundred crosses, almost all within the seven jagged circles, with the most recent events largely confined to the outer rings, the furthest being several miles beyond his Pangbourne home. 'It's a huge area, fifteen-mile radius or more... He went further from home as he got older, as he grew more confident.'

Jack clicked on a yellow cross just outside of Doc's village. 'Pig farm, Doc. Just up the road from here.'

Doc was familiar with the farm, and could hear a sow squealing, screaming in agony as Jack spoke. He thought it was real, it was so vivid, but Jack was still staring at the screen, so Doc closed his eyes and focused.

The sound continued and sent a repugnant thrill through him. He could feel cool wind on his face as a field appeared off to one side in a mind-movie, his attention drawn to the arches of corrugated iron there, the pig shelters, as he sped forward. The sensation of movement was familiar, but it had been a long time since Doc had felt it. He whispered his conclusion, still with his eyes closed.

'A bicycle... As his stamina improved, he went further afield.'

'Are you doing that thing again... You'd better not let your missus find out.' Jack sniffed, scrunched up his nose and muttered his disgust at himself. 'Why didn't I think of that? It's bleedin obvious. A kid with a bike!'

'A young lad, out in the middle of the night? Where was his mother? Why would she let him?' *Psychopaths are devious and deceptive creatures.* The thought whispered itself to him. 'Unless she doesn't know?'

'I'd like a word with her, an' all.' Jack puffed out his lips, frustrated. 'Charlie did say it's not a completely accurate correlation, but there's a definite concentration in the local area, many more incidents than the national average. Several times more, in fact—I checked... Oh yeah, and all the bigger properties were burned down more recently, no matter where they are. Look.' Jack clicked on a fire located in the third ring to the east of Billy's home. 'His old school.'

'That's only two months ago... He's becoming more daring with experience.' Billy had mentioned he had a tutor during their handful of sessions together, but Doc had been unaware of the full story. 'What do they do about schooling? You said he couldn't find a place after being expelled.'

'It's news to me, but loads of kids are taught outside of the system. Special needs usually, but there's others whose parents don't want them *indoctrinated* by the state.' Jack made air quote signs with hooked fingers as he said the word. 'Twats. Probably feed the poor buggers on muesli and wheatgrass smoothies, too. Then there's the hard cases and trouble makers, like Billy Leech, the sort of lout no self-respecting school wants coming through their doors.'

'So, he has no scheduled classes to attend? No need to be up for the school run.'

'Of course!' Jack bounced forward again, his legs and feet jerking as if he wanted to sprint after the lad right now, to arrest him on suspicion for these horrendous crimes. 'He can have a lie in after cycling half the night, maiming animals and burning buildings. It's got to be him!'

'We have nothing more than wafer thin circumstantial evidence still.' Doc pondered for a moment, wondering how they might encourage the locals to investigate Billy more thoroughly. 'Do you think Charlie might run with this? Did you tell her about the dead pets posed on my property?'

'I did. Problem is, her station's snowed under. And there's been loads of gyppos camping out too—regularly get moved on by the local bobbies, then they find another field and squat on that.'

'Travellers?'

'Yeah. Isn't that what I said? Sorry, not very PC of me. Charlie's bosses are convinced the two things are related.' Jack grimaced at the stupidity of the top brass. 'Aren't interested in a Thatcham copper's *vendetta* against the Leech family, apparently. I'm thinking I'll do some interviews and digging around before shooting off on me hols. I'll stay here for a night or two, if that's alright with you.'

'Listen my friend. You should go away with your daughter and do some bonding with her fiancé as planned.' Jack went to interrupt, but Doc insisted, certain he could force Jack to take the holiday he had been promising himself for years. 'It's a simple choice. I'm lending *you* my boat. Not Sally. I'm not about to let her and a guy I've never met take almost half a million pounds' worth of precious nautical machinery without you on board, am I?' Jack started to protest, but Doc was adamant. 'Either you take them tonight or you cancel their holiday too. Just go, Jack. You deserve it. Investigating Billy Leech will wait until you get back.'

Doc was lying again. He planned to visit the young man first thing in the morning, without Jack in tow, to confront the boy about his suspected nocturnal habits, to assess his reaction. And that of Mrs Leech. He was confident he could get to the bottom of this without Jack's help, but he would soon discover just how wrong he could be.

Suzie slotted the giant umbrella into its concrete stand and positioned it to ensure the afternoon sun didn't burn her mother's skin as she snored softly on her lounger, lured into her slumbers by the soporific warmth and a full belly. With her mother in the shade, Suzie scooped up the remains of their early tea and headed into the house.

Billy was still out and about, but, as usual, she had no idea where he was, what he was doing or who he was with.

Is it too late to change that?

Probably.

Reasserting herself would most likely make him even more resentful. *Hateful.* But she had to do something to discipline him.

Starving her mother was pure evil—she struggled to understand why he would do something so despicable. And the Chinese whispers he had sown between them were simply mind blowing. The most hurtful lies. And he had been so cruel to Suzie —his own mother—constantly belittling her, sniping at her, driving her to wrap herself in a morphine comfort blanket. So why was she so shocked that he would lie about Nana's food intake?

Her son had been Suzie's pusher too. Her drug supplier.

Buying sedatives for her at first, when their local doctor had limited her prescriptions. She had embarrassed herself by pleading for more, then demanding more, shouting at all the patients and staff in the waiting area as she was led out. Billy had offered to help her, by buying the drugs she needed on the internet…

It seemed reasonable enough. It's not like she was on heroin or anything like that, buying illegal substances from dodgy dealers on street corners. These were proper medications, the same as her GP had prescribed. Supplied by respectable pharmaceutical companies, so they were okay.

Surely?

Then Billy suggested she might prefer codeine linctus, which sounded harmless enough. Cough syrup, he'd said. It was only later, after it had become a regular part of her routine, that he explained how her liver was converting it into an opiate.

'You're on morphine. Just like a worthless junkie!' he'd said, laughing and sneering at her.

She had merely shrugged off his insult, drank more of the medicine. It felt so good.

Helpful Billy. Always there with the drugs. Her next fix.

Suzie clattered in the kitchen as she scraped the plates and loaded everything into the dishwasher, her mind racing, running through all the different ways she had allowed their lives to nosedive out of control. She was fuming by the time she slammed the door shut.

Time to look in the cellar.

What else have you found out, young man?

The concrete steps were situated at the side of the property, accessed through a door from the garden, and led down into a musty, damp space with a low ceiling. One bare lightbulb dangled from a wire in the middle of the room, and dust laden spider webs spanned from there in every direction. The cool, foetid air sent a shiver through her, and the idea of rooting around down here for any length of time suddenly lost its appeal.

Come on—you must do this.

She rubbed her bare arms, thought about retreating to her room to find a cardigan, knowing full well she would not come back if she did, then gave herself a mild dressing down for being such a wimp.

The cellar was the original boiler room for the property, and still contained an ancient cast iron affair that her father had left in place, convinced the solid antique fitting was far too heavy and way too much trouble to remove. In fact, the place was full of old junk, some of it familiar, like the rocking horse with chipped, faded paint, almost hidden under a pile of other toys and books from her childhood, all coated in dust. There were plenty of items in here to prompt memories of happier times, but her focus was on some rusty shelving that sagged to one side like a drunk leaning against the wall for support. The four boxes of papers from her London home were there, alongside others, stowed by her father, a man who'd thrown nothing of importance away.

And all her boxes had been opened, recently from the look of the dust patterns.

Billy?

Or was it her father when he was sorting her affairs over the last seven years? No. He would have resealed them before bringing them back down here, taped in that precise, careful way he applied to everything he did.

She took a closer look at the contents of her boxes and squinted at some of the papers in the poor light, checking to see what had been stored within them. Mostly correspondence relating to investments, bank statements, household bills, insurance policies, Shaun's company accounts and so on. Then she came across the large beige envelope from the hospital—the one she had been taken to by ambulance, sirens wailing, the night she'd been mutilated by Peter. It had been ripped open, carelessly.

Not Dad, then.

A cursory inspection suggested most of the papers were still in their boxes, as best she could remember. Including the notes about her termination in that envelope, previously sealed and marked 'Confidential' and for her eyes only. When she'd arrived at the hospital she had no idea she was with child. Peter had kicked her stomach repeatedly that night too, so it was a miracle she hadn't had a miscarriage already.

She had blotted out most of the memories from that time, but as she clutched the nurse's report it all came flooding back to her. Screaming at the medical staff when they told her she was pregnant, demanding that they 'Get that monster out of me— right now!'

There was more, but she just dropped the papers to the floor and let the fury fizz inside her again.

Billy had read these notes about the abortion. And then lied to her mother about how he had found out. No doubt he had discovered other records too. Her father's. Had he discovered some documents or letters relating to the time she was raped? And how the resultant cash from the Leech family had allowed her parents to move them all away from the area and buy this house?

You evil brat. And what other lies have you been telling, Billy?

'That was Charlie.' Jack pocketed his smartphone, aware that his gruff manner and tone were due, in part, to Doc's insistence that he should take the boat this evening as planned. The news from Charlie made him more convinced he should stay, but it was pointless arguing. 'A Labrador went missing from Caversham a week ago. Two hundred quid reward being offered for anyone who can bring it back. It was in the owner's backyard, but they assumed it had managed to get out, somehow.'

'A Labrador.' Doc tugged an earlobe, clearly not liking what he was hearing. Jack wondered if they were both thinking the same thing. They were. 'Another little detail, matching the Leech brother's history.'

Jack nodded his agreement, then said, 'There's been a bit of a spate of dog-knapping lately. Seems there's a demand for stolen domestic pets for dog fights, and the local bobbies assumed it was another one of those. Normally they disappear without trace. I've got the owner's number.'

'I should leave it, Jack. There's no way we can be sure it's their pet—it was burnt beyond recognition. Probably best to let them think it's been stolen by a loving new owner.'

'Mmm. Let 'em delude themselves.' The doorbell alerted them to the arrival of Jack's guests. 'I'll get that. It'll be my Sally and her bloke.'

Jack greeted them at the door, and introduced his future son-in-law to Doc who had followed him into the hall.

'Doctor Colin Powers, this is Felix. I haven't nicked him for it yet, but he's the lucky blighter who's stolen my Sally's heart.' Jack forced a laugh, though he would've happily arrested Felix if he could. As far as Jack was concerned, it was absolutely normal for a father to think no man was good enough for his daughter. He tried to keep his animosity to himself, for her sake.

It was difficult.

Jack watched as they shook hands, then Doc gave Sally a hug, all smiles and happy chat. No hint from Doc that he knew of Jack's concerns regarding her choice of partner.

Felix wasn't a criminal. Jack had checked the first time Sally had mentioned the bloke's name, not long after she'd met him in her final year at Durham University. Jack had begrudgingly accepted it when the two lovebirds moved in together eighteen months ago, though he had hoped they might realise they were incompatible.

Fat chance.

Fat chancer...

Felix was a bit of a short-arse too, a round lump of flab, like a soft beach ball with stubby arms and legs. And lazy with it. His career aspirations extended no further than a part-time job in a computer games store, and he seemed to spend a great deal of his leisure time testing out their stock. Sally waited on the guy hand and foot— cooking, cleaning, shopping—everything, while he sat like a barrel of lard in his La-Z-Boy chair playing video games, with his feet propped on a pouffe. God knows why she put up with it, but she did.

After she had announced they were to be married, dropping that gem while visiting London a few weeks ago, Jack had phoned his ex-wife, Sally's mother, a woman he rarely spoke to, but wanted her opinion on their daughter's choice. To commiserate... Moira had given him a bollocking—told Jack to do his best to get to know the lad, had insisted that Felix was a 'lovely fellah', that he had a 'great sense of humour' and made Sally 'laugh but never cry', and as a father he should be delighted his daughter had found someone who 'made her happy'.

The upcoming excursion, just the three of them, crowded together on Doc's boat, was supposed to be a bonding exercise. Sally's idea. Jack had tried his best not to let on about his feelings for her man, but she wasn't daft.

Investigating Billy Leech could have provided a perfect excuse to dip out, but Doc knew the importance of the trip to Sally, and Jack was sure that was the real reason he wouldn't let him wriggle out of it.

'So, is this everything?' Jack pointed to the small suitcase Sally had wheeled in. 'Or do you need a hand getting more clobber from the car?'

'Thanks, Dad.'

Jack went to Sally's Peugeot, the one he had bought and paid for, and hauled out a much larger suitcase, this one without wheels, wondering why Felix had waddled in without it.

'Cheers, Jack. My back's been playing up again. Maybe you could pop it on the boat for us?'

Jack dropped it in the hall with the other one. 'No hurry. We won't be heading off until Judy gets back. She's making a raspberry pavlova for us all before we go. And there's a drop of champagne to go with it as we're all celebrating. Eh, Doc?'

Jack had popped two bottles in the fridge, happy with the prospect of delaying departure for another couple of hours.

Why had he agreed to this bloody trip?

'Can we check out the boat? I've only seen it in photos.' Felix was far more eager to get aboard than make conversation with his hosts, and although Sally had been on a couple of Sunday lunch cruises with Jack, Doc and Judy, she followed him through the lounge as he took his first look at the boat through the patio doors.

'Cheer up, Jack. You're on holiday!' In response to a black look, Doc compressed his lips, visibly suppressing his mirth before calling after Sally. 'The lower cabin's locked, the key's hanging—'

'I know. It's in your study. Thanks, Doc. I'll get it.'

Sally's sunny smile warmed Jack's heart as he watched her go. Felix was already halfway across the lawn.

'What does she see in him, mate?'

Jack felt Doc's arm curl around his shoulder as they stood in the hall gazing through the lounge at Sally bounding after her lover.

'He must have hidden charms. And that's my lovely wife's car just pulling up outside. Let's get this celebration under way. Promotion, pregnancy and an engagement—time to crack open that champagne, I think.' Doc's hand massaged Jack's shoulder as he added, 'Come on, you miserable bugger. Some bubbly will help you unwind before you go.'

'Listen to me. Please don't argue with me.' Suzie tucked her mother into bed and gave her forehead a gentle peck. She had woken from her snooze not long after the cellar discovery had made Suzie's blood boil, and asked if she could go to her room as it was more comfortable. 'Billy's been living in a world of fantasy.' The lie was necessary. Telling Nana the whole truth would break her heart. 'And from now on, I'll look after you. If he tries to talk to you about anything more serious than the weather, you tell me. Okay?'

'Are you sure you're not overreacting, love?'

She still thinks he's an angel. Lucifer maybe.

That was unworthy. She was still his mother.

He's a disturbed young man who needed her help. Her support. Her love.

Along with some parental discipline…

'Just you tell me. Promise?'

'Of course.'

'I'll bring your milk and biscuits later. You're okay with your book? Or would you like the TV on?'

'My book. I haven't felt like reading for months. I feel so much better tonight. Thank you for today, dear.'

It's amazing what a full belly and a bit of fresh air and sunshine can do.

I really could wring his bloody neck. And where is the little sod?

Suzie checked the lounge clock as she arrived downstairs. She assumed it would be a few hours before he would appear as he was usually back by ten. He liked to get to sleep early. Though she was usually comatose by the time he made his way to bed.

Her eyes were drawn to the drinks cabinet in the far corner of the room. She stood in the doorway, her tongue parched, staring at the glinting bottles. A magnet, drawing her in. Suzie could not resist.

She found herself standing with a cocktail shaker in one hand, a vodka bottle in the other, as if her subconscious had decided for her that a drink was now desperately needed.

No. I will not!

She took all six bottles of spirit from the cabinet, loaded them precariously into her arms, and half trotted to the kitchen. The bottles clinked dangerously as she dropped a few on the stainless steel draining board, and two others rolled into the sink, landing with a sound that reminded her of church bells.

Suzie unscrewed the cap of the first bottle and watched with grim determination as the delicious liquid poured down the plughole, wafting the scent of temptation into her nostrils, as if the gin was determined to change her mind. It didn't. She'd even do the same with the bottles of Vermouth after she had got rid of the worst offenders—mere fortified wine with its sickly sweet herbal aroma held no appeal on its own, anyway.

Three more full bottles went the same way as the first, glugging into the drain with a satisfying gurgle before the empties went in the recycle bin, leaving just one of each of her preferred spirits—vodka and gin—that were already open. She upended the first and immediately noticed something odd.

No...

It was difficult to tell for sure, while the contents swirled out of the neck, but as she held the empty bottle up to the light, she could see it clearly enough. Something that should never be in a bottle of distilled spirit.

Sediment.

Like she had occasionally seen in bottles of real ale and scrumpy. A tiny trace in this instance, barely visible, but it was there. A smear of white granules, clinging to the bottom and side of the glass.

She went to the bin, checked the other empty bottles. Nothing.

Suzie's heart climbed to her throat as she tipped out the contents from the last one —the half full bottle of gin.

Again. There.

Not sediment.

Powder residue.

With jelly in her legs, she took both tainted bottles to the kitchen table, and sat heavily as the implications struck home. The frequent bouts of unconsciousness and memory loss, usually early in the evenings... Or whenever she drank her preferred cocktails. She thought about the speed with which she could blot out reality, swilling her home-made Martinis, had put it down to mixing codeine linctus with strong alcoholic beverages—a welcome side effect, knocking her out in no time at all.

Now, she knew the real reason, her mind screaming the answer, but still she tried to deny the inevitable truth...

He wouldn't. Would he?

Poison his own mother?

Was her son trying to kill her? By accumulating toxins in her system?

Impossible. Not my Billy...

Even as she desperately denied the possibility, the rational part of her brain overruled her maternal instincts, shaking her to the core as she finally admitted to herself:

Her husband's son?

Oh, he could, alright.

He is a Leech boy, after all...

Murder runs in his blood.

'You've got all this to look forward to, Doc. Your nipper growing up and turning into an adult. I don't envy you that, not at this stage of your life, but at least you don't have money worries, so that's something.'

Doc placed an ice bucket containing a champagne bottle on the patio table while Jack added glasses and plates. Judy had just thrown him out of the kitchen for picking at the pavlova while she was putting it together. Meringues were one of the few recipes she had mastered, and the delicious sweet fluffy ones she had made after lunch were being smothered with double cream and the fresh raspberries and strawberries she had fetched from their local Waitrose. Doc had developed a sweet tooth—along with a bit of a paunch.

'I'm happier than I've ever been. And kids are worth all the hassle, no matter what you think, Mr Grumpy.' Doc patted his belly as he sat with Jack looking out at the river. 'I'll have to get fit again, though. I shouldn't have stopped my yoga, but you know how it is.'

'Look at her.' Doc followed Jack's gaze and saw Sally prancing on the bow of the boat while Felix was pottering in the cabin. 'I love her to bits, but it's frustrating. You have no say over who they end up with.'

'You sound like you'd prefer an arranged marriage. Taliban Jack! Haha! Your face!' Doc laughed at his pal, who snorted in disgust at the joke.

'Listen. That guy's a bloody parasite. I had to bail them out recently, maxed out their credit cards. I did it for Sally, of course, but I told him to get a full-time job. Mind you, I don't hold out much hope… Stop laughing at me!' Doc didn't. 'You'll understand if you end up with a daughter.'

'The stereo doesn't work.' Felix held up a CD as he called out. 'She wants me to put this on so we can get a selfie video of us doing our own special Titanic on your boat, Doc.'

'Turn the ignition on. It'll work then.' Doc shouted back at him. 'I'm just opening the champagne, so don't be long if you want some.'

Jack scoffed, then pointed a finger at his throat through his open mouth, pretending to gag. Doc didn't know if he meant their Titanic foolishness or Felix being an idiot for not having thought of turning the boat key to switch the power on —until he added, 'Muppet! See what I mean about him?'

'Give him a chance… Right. Judy's coming, I'll pop the cork.'

Doc pulled the bottle from the bucket and started to undo the foil, thinking how wonderful today had been, and how much he loved his wife and his friend, thankful he was so blessed.

The feeling was short-lived.

The explosion ripped through the air, and an orange and green fireball erupted from the stern of the boat. Almost immediately, the sound Doc had heard during his vision earlier today—a pig being tortured with a knife—assailed his ears again, only this time it was not in his imagination. The fireball engulfed his boat from behind the cabin, but Sally, who had been standing on the bow with her arms outstretched, had disappeared behind the curtain of flames. Doc knew the noise he could hear was Felix being roasted alive.

Jack was racing across the lawn before Doc had properly registered what had happened, then he too made a dash to see what they could do for the two young lovers. Jack dived into the water just in front of the boat, and Doc made a grab for the lifesaving ring from the post on his private dock and flung it out to Jack who was just diving under, looking for Sally who was still nowhere to be seen.

The fire extinguishers were inside the boat's cockpit and cabin, but the flames were roaring and Doc couldn't get aboard. Felix's screams gradually subsided to muffled squealing and groaning from the bottom of the cockpit, then nothing.

Doc turned to run back to the house, and saw Judy was on her way with the two small fire extinguishers they kept in the kitchen, horror on her face, but no sign of panic. He ran past her and said, 'You use those, my love. I'll fetch the big one from the garage.'

With his heart racing and stuttering, Doc slowed and paced himself, noting the sharp stitch-like pain, only it was in the centre of his chest.

Surely, it was too late for Felix anyway. But why had the boat exploded like that? And what had happened to the fire suppression system in the engine room—it should have activated immediately on sensing a flame down there. It was just one of the safety features that came as standard, features that had convinced him a petrol engine on a boat was safe enough, even with the danger of a leak causing heavier than air explosive fumes to settle in the bottom of the hull, just waiting for a spark to appear.

Doc clutched at his chest again and leaned on the garage wall as angina repeatedly stabbed at his heart, but after a few breaths he managed to hoist the extinguisher to his shoulder and stagger back to the burning wreck.

Judy and Jack were kneeling on the dock next to Sally's saturated body, with Jack frantically giving chest compression as Judy tried to kiss the life back into his daughter. Doc, struggling to breathe himself, and overcome by grief, shock, guilt and despair, tumbled to the ground as everything turned a murky grey before fading to suffocating black.

Billy jogged along the towpath, the pedal inserts in his shoes clip-clopping a steady rhythm as he worked off the rest of his rage on his way into Pangbourne. The knife was back in its pouch and most of the blood on his hands had been rinsed off in the river, though there were some splash marks, vivid crimson against the neon yellow of his shirt and shorts.

He slowed to a walk, pleased to see the cab, emblazoned with the number he had called thirty minutes earlier, waiting in the car park of the public house overlooking the weir, exactly as arranged.

His iPhone, strapped to his upper arm, was pumping drum and bass through tiny ear pods, the driving rhythm matching his mood and obliterating all external noise—including the distant blast of his improvised explosive device detonating at the end of Doc Powers' garden. Just as the reverberations died away, he turned down the volume, tugged open the car door and flopped on to the rear seat before confirming his name and destination for the driver's benefit.

'You've been in the wars, son. Is that blood? What happened to your bike?'

'I fell off. I don't feel like talking, so can you just drive?'

'Pah. Whatever you say, pal. It's your money.'

Billy tried to relax, but even with his forehead pressed to the window, eyes on the passing countryside, he felt despondent that his plan had been defeated. He would have a rethink tonight. Uncle Peter would help him. He would be sure to have some ideas of what to do next.

'Pull over here, would you? I'm going to be about ten minutes. If you wait, you can take me back to Pangbourne. I need to get some tools to repair the bike. Here's a tenner, and there'll be twenty more if you wait and take me back.'

'Fair enough, kiddo. Ten minutes.'

It was worth double the normal fare to Billy and he trotted through the neighbour's garden, out of sight of his house, and sneaked into his garage. He really was not up to meeting his mother right now. Later tonight, he'd get her back where she belonged.

Under my thumb…

With the bolt cutters tucked beneath his elbow, he jogged back to the waiting car, and saw the look on the cabbie's face at the sight of the giant tool.

'Blimey—what'cha gonna do? Cut your bike to pieces? For scrap?'

'Something like that. Can we go? I'm in a bit of a hurry.'

'Talkative young chap, aren't yer?'

Grunt.

Fifteen minutes later, Billy began jogging back along the towpath, his music throbbing in his ears, his mind empty as he went to recover his stranded bike, but as he got closer to the oak tree, he could see black smoke rising from somewhere downstream.

The possibility that he had managed to achieve his aim catapulted his mood from misery to elation.

It's Powers' boat!

Billy sprinted the last half mile, dived into the undergrowth as he made the final dash to his lookout tree, dropped the bolt cutters by the bike and executed acrobatics worthy of the Olympics as he flew up the branches. Without a thought for his tattered camouflage poncho, lying by his bike, or the fact that his current garb stood out like the proverbial dog's balls—despite the foliage around him—Billy raised the binoculars and almost cheered out loud.

A quick survey of the damage to the boat confirmed that no one could have survived. The hull, still afloat, was covered in foam, and a gaggle of firemen were on the dock, with two more clambering on board the smoking remnants, poking around in the exposed engine room. The cockpit had gone completely, with just a mess of melted fibreglass and twisted metal where the steering compartment had been. The two cabins below decks may have survived, partially intact, but anyone down there would have been overcome by the heat and fumes, either roasted alive or gassed to death.

No survivors, then.

It had worked!

I've killed Powers! I'm a real man!

Billy hugged himself with sheer joy and laughed out loud as he viewed the devastation before him.

The ambulance, with sirens wailing, swerved into the hospital entrance and screeched to a halt. Doc was feeling a whole lot better than he had when he first came to, some ten minutes before. The paramedics had revived him with oxygen and he felt such a fraud for all the fuss he had caused. He plucked the oxygen mask from his face as the rear doors opened, and then tried to sit up on the stretcher bed as Judy placed a gentle hand on his chest to encourage him to lie back down.

'I'm fine, sweetheart. I just blacked out. Stress, that's all. I'm more concerned for Sally.'

Judy did not answer, had been silent for most of the journey. Doc could see she was shocked to her soul by what had happened, her cheeks pale and drained. Her hair, usually vibrant and lustrous, was lank and damp from exertion, stress and fear. Streaks of soot on her brow, neck and chin marked where her fingers had tried to massage the tension away.

The first ambulance to arrive at Doc's house had whisked him to hospital with Sally and Jack's ambulance right behind. Judy had been clutching his hand as the vehicles sped through the country lanes, sirens blaring. She only now let go as the paramedics hoisted Doc's gurney out, unfolding the legs with a clatter before wheeling him in to the Accident and Emergency department. Doc gave silent thanks for his medical insurance as the paramedics whisked him past the mass of waiting wounded, sick and injured, then an orderly and nurse soon had him comfortably tucked up in bed in a private room.

'Please check for me. My friend... Sally Carver. We were with her when she drowned, but she was being resuscitated. I need to know how she is.'

'I'll check but I'm sure she'll be fine, so just relax for me.' The nurse mouthed the platitude on autopilot, more concerned with Doc than anyone else, concentrating on the gel and rubber suckers she was placing on his chest to connect him to the heart monitor. 'You've had an ECG quite recently, haven't you?' She tugged at a few curly grey chest hairs and smiled. 'I don't need to shave any more of your fur—you already have perfectly positioned bald patches.'

'Could you not mention any of my results to my wife, please?' Thankfully, Judy was at Reception, sorting out the necessary paperwork for the insurance company, to be certain they picked up the tab. The nurse's head cocked in question so Doc explained. 'She's not been very well herself, so I don't want to worry her.'

'Mmm. Just relax for me, and don't talk for the next few minutes.' The machine whirred and clicked, then the nurse finished by tugging the suckers off his chest and wiping the gel with a handful of tissue. 'All done. You'll live. The cardiac consultant's been delayed, but should be here soon. Just you rest, okay? I'll be back with him as soon he arrives.'

Doc rearranged his hospital gown to cover his chest, staring at the fluorescent strip on the ceiling as he lay there, and tried to empty his mind, to meditate. De-stress.

It was impossible. How could he relax? Sally could be dead, along with Felix.

Was it my fault? Was there something I should've done to make the boat safer? Or something I missed?

Doc closed his eyes, revisiting the entire scenario. The boat, viewed from his patio, moments before the blast. Sally on the bow laughing and jigging about. Felix in the cockpit, about to turn on the ignition...

This really shouldn't have happened.

The boat's Fireboy detector was designed to sense petrol fumes, and automatically set off the bilge blower to evacuate any potentially explosive gas trapped in the bottom of the hull. The system would also illuminate the red light on the console, labelled 'Gas warning', alerting the owner…

Felix.

It was his first time on board the leisure craft. When he had turned the key, Doc assumed an electrical fault must have sparked and ignited the fumes. Doc, Judy or Jack would have known better—even Sally would have known not to turn that key with the warning light on.

Could the Fireboy system have failed? At the same time as a random petrol leak occurred? And a spark from some faulty electrical wiring had then somehow conveniently appeared at the precise moment needed to ignite the fuel air mixture?

No.

The flash and boom of the explosion replayed in Doc's mind's eye, then freeze-framed a fraction of a second after the blast.

Green?

The fireball, tinged with an unearthly hue…

Petrol burned with an orange glow, not green.

Doc's dark side was whispering the conclusion to him already:

This was no accident. This was sabotage.

He sat up and swung his legs over the edge of the bed, no longer willing to lie there, passively waiting for a consultant to fuss over him.

A myriad of thoughts collided in his brain while he dressed, then he heard a voice from years before. A teenage boy snarling a threat at him. Repeating something he said his dead uncle had prophesied during his dreams:

'You're going to experience a painful death. And the people you love are going to suffer too…'

The voice in his head was that of a highly disturbed young man.

Billy Leech.

Jack stomped along the corridor in a murderous frame of mind, searching for Doc's private room. Judy was at reception, having some hassle over documentation, and Jack had left her there, grunting at her when she warned him not to upset Doc, insisting that her husband needed peace and quiet.

A run in with his ex-wife had not helped either. Sally had called her mother on the way to the hospital, inconsolable at the loss of Felix. The paramedic lent her his phone, she was that distressed, as hers was at the bottom of the river. The two bedraggled, reluctant swimmers had been wrapped in foil blankets, their clothes soggy from their unexpected dip in the Thames. Even now, Jack was thoroughly damp, his shoes squelching wet farts as he marched to Doc's room.

The smell of burnt cloth and singed hair lingered in his nostrils as he strode past the nurses' station in the private wing, thinking of how Sally had wailed and wept at her mother, almost ignoring him. He had saved her life, pulling her unconscious body from the river, then applying first aid to get her breathing again. Surprisingly little water had entered her lungs, and although she had been coughing and choking when first revived, when he told her about the loss of her chosen life partner it sparked a hysterical reaction. Moira had arrived and finally managed to calm her, but had told him to make himself scarce, and said she would look after *her* daughter, as he patently could not…

So now he was on his way to see Doc. Ready to kill someone himself.

Felix may have been a waster, but no one deserved to die like that. At least Sally had not heard her partner's agonised, high-pitched screaming as he was incinerated —a minor blessing in the scheme of things. It was probably best that Sally's mother looked after her now. She was much better at that sort of thing.

And I'll do what I'm best at.

There would be no holiday for him. He burst in to Doc's room, surprised to see his friend getting dressed.

'Blimey. They given you the all clear already? You went down like a sack of spuds, mate. I thought you'd gone and died on us, too. What a bloody day.'

'Jack, I don't know what to say… I'm so sorry. This is such a nightmare. How's Sally?'

'She's in bits about her bloke, of course, but she's gonna be fine they reckon. Wanted to keep her in after chucking some antibiotics at her. Prophylactic dose, they called it.'

'Preventive medicine. For her lungs.'

'Her mum's told me she'll be taking her to her place. I think she blames me! Always was an unreasonable woman. Suits me, though. I want to find out who did this. This was no bloody accident.'

'I just reached the same conclusion. What makes you think that?'

'What? Apart from the dead pets littering your house, and that psycho brat living a few miles away?'

'Uh-huh.'

'The moment I saw my daughter disappear off the front of your boat in that cloud of smoke and flames, I *knew* it wasn't an accident.' Doc may have an unwelcome dark side helping him understand serial killers, but Jack had a detective's gut feel, developed over decades hunting criminals. 'Are you sure you're okay?' Doc seemed to be struggling with tying his laces, the act of bending down clearly causing him discomfort.

'Yeah. Just a bit giddy.'

'Can I borrow your phone? Mine's in the Thames somewhere.' Jack didn't wait for an answer, just grabbed it from the bedside. 'Charlie. I phoned her about ten minutes ago from Reception and she said she'd check to see if there was any news.' He dialled, spoke a few terse words, then listened for thirty seconds, grunted a reply and ended the call. 'The first indications from the fire officers. They reckon the fuel tank exploded, though we'll have to wait for the full report to be sure.

'The fuel tank? How?'

'Mmm. That's what I want to know. I going to go and speak to them. Charlie's sending a car. Are you coming?'

'Definitely.'

The door opened and Judy walked in, looking dreadful. She was normally immaculate, and gorgeous too, but not today. Like a vampire had sucked all the blood from her body. Jack wondered if he looked the same.

Judy took in the scene with one glance, her lips compressed at the sight of Doc, fully dressed.

'Jack. Would you give us a minute? I'd like to talk to my husband. Alone, please.'

'Sweetheart—'

She cut off Doc's words with a searing glance and a wave of her hand, pulled open the door, her voice tight as she said just one word. 'Jack.'

'Okay. I'll be waiting at Reception.'

The door closed behind him with a thump as Judy's scolding started, riding over Doc's objections. Jack strode away, certain Doc wouldn't be coming with him, after all.

'Are you sure he's okay to come home, Doctor?'

'I'd prefer him to stay in overnight for observation as a cautionary measure, but in all honesty, Mrs Powers, if your husband is uncomfortable here then it's probably best for him to go home with you. The less stress, the better.'

'Huh.' Judy could tell the consultant was losing interest in his patient, now that Colin had insisted on leaving the hospital. The consultant's attitude told her he had better things to do than convince a recalcitrant patient to stay in overnight, especially one with medical training, even though he was too polite to say so. Immediately after Jack had left the room, the consultant had burst in just as she had begun berating her husband. She had plenty more to say but the consultant had asked her to wait outside, and Judy had been pacing the corridor for twenty minutes, then she glimpsed Colin dressing for the second time when the door opened so she collared the doctor on his way out. 'You don't know my husband. He needs to rest and he won't if you let him leave.'

'Sorry. It really is out of my hands.' He gave her a supercilious smile, insinuating she might be to blame for his ailments. 'You can take it up with him, but as I say, he needs less stress, not more. Don't nag the poor man.'

He strolled away, unaware that Judy's eyes were planting stilettos in his back.

Bastard!

She opened the door and got a sheepish grin from her husband.

'He said I'm okay, my love, although you'll have to push me to the exit in that thing.' Doc nodded towards a wheelchair in the corner of the room, but before she could protest he said, 'Hospital policy. That's all. No need to worry. I'm fine.'

'Why didn't you tell me? About all the tests you've been having?'

'I didn't want to worry you.'

'Worry me? I thought you'd died earlier! And then—while trying to get the insurance company to pay for this room—I discover you've been having heart problems and had not told me!'

'Well, they were just tests and—'

'You said you had mildly elevated blood pressure. Now I discover you've been having angina too and that you were being checked out for bypass surgery!'

'No—they were talking about a stent but they said it's not—'

'A stent? To expand your coronary arteries because they think you're a candidate for a heart attack.'

'Please listen to me, sweetheart—'

'You treat me like I'm made of bone china. I'm not. Yes, I do still have occasional down periods.' Worse than that—suicidal thoughts had visited her on many occasions since he had rescued her in France. 'But you have to stop lying to me. I can't stand it!'

'The tests have confirmed—'

'Colin. Promise me. You will tell me everything from now on.'

'I'm trying to! The tests results from my visit here last week. I don't need an operation. I've been given some medication for cholesterol and new blood pressure tablets too. The consultant told me off, said I should get fit to keep my heart healthy, that I should avoid getting overstressed—and to have regular check-ups. That's it. It's great news. If I'd told you before, you'd have worried unnecessarily.'

'You have to promise me.'

'I promise.'

'Good. Now tell me what you know about the cat, the dog and why our boat blew up today. You and Jack have been thick as thieves, and I'm not having it any more. What the hell is going on?'

Billy focused his binoculars on the house, the windows and patio doors again, but there was no movement inside. Two hours passed with him sitting, gloating, occasionally filming with his smartphone as the firemen finished exploring the burnt-out wreck, piling the contents on the dock before inspecting, photographing and bagging some items. The two officers aboard the boat called a colleague to inspect what was left of the fuel tank, and a lot of pointing and nodding ensued. The third officer then got on his radio, gesticulating urgently as he spoke. Billy assumed this was the boss.

Thirty minutes later, he was not at all surprised to see a police car arrive. Two uniformed coppers, and one plain clothes detective. Not that his shirt could be described as plain. The garish multicoloured pattern would look more at home on a beach. Billy raised the binoculars for a closer look.

Him?

The detective who had flashed his warrant card and threatened Billy after the car incident last night. Obviously a mate of Powers, then…

The detective had a long chat with the senior fire officer as his colleagues surrounded the boat and dock with crime scene tape. They also took numerous photographs before leaving, though the detective remained in the garden, crouching over the items strewn on the dock. Then he looked up, eyes scanning the river.

The bank opposite.

Shit!

Billy, sat astride his branch, the binoculars to his eyes, could see the man looking directly at him. The distance was the length of a football pitch, so there was no chance he'd be recognised.

But he had no poncho… And he was wearing his neon riding kit.

Time to go.

A grumble from Billy's insides reminded him he'd not eaten since brunch either, so he dropped to the ground, and released his bike from the nearby birch tree with one stroke from his bolt cutters. He would leave the tool here and pick it up another time, he decided.

As he mounted his bike, he felt deflated, had thought he'd still be overjoyed, was surprised that his euphoria had been so short-lived.

You did well today, Billy boy.

I wanted to watch. To witness the explosion.

His uncle's voice didn't have its normal effect on his mood. Today was such a let-down, even though he'd achieved his desired outcome.

Or had he?

Billy's disappointment stemmed from a niggling concern that Powers might not have been on board when the boat exploded. Without seeing the bastard burn before his own eyes, the possibility had been screwing itself ever further into his brain since he'd first confirmed the smoke was pouring from the man's boat.

Was he still a virgin?

Did I really murder a man for the first time today?

There was no reassuring voice in answer to that question.

With anger and frustration powering him along, Billy sped into Pangbourne village for a fish and chip supper to load up on carbs and fat. He took the paper wrapped delicacy to the river bank and sat contemplating his plans for the coming days, tossing the occasional chip for the swans as dusk settled around him.

The food revived his flagging spirits. It wasn't so bad. He had plenty more mayhem in mind to celebrate his birthday week.

Starting with that thieving git, Maddox.

Jack peered across the Thames at the charred remains of Doc's boat, more comfortable now having changed out of his damp clothes. The house was still unlocked when he'd returned, thanks to their hasty departure to hospital. His conversations with the fire officers merely confirmed his suspicions that this was no accident. Right now, the burnt-out hulk across the river fuelled the rage welling up inside him.

With one last glance to check he was following the line of sight from the garden to the trees behind him, he set off to find the oak where the yellow man had been watching him. Jack had seen the fluorescent shirt a few seconds before the person wearing it bounced down the branches then disappeared into the undergrowth, so he didn't expect to find anyone or anything still in the area, but was drawn to the spot. He had driven from Doc's house to the footbridge near the weir and then jogged along the towpath opposite, almost deserted now as dusk settled around him.

The ground vegetation was shaded by the canopy above, and in the half light, Jack stumbled a few times as the brambles and shrubs clawed at his legs. He should have brought a torch, but that was in the car. He normally used the light from his phone—the one that was underwater thanks to his dive into the river to save his daughter.

There were several oak trees which could have been yellow shirt's lookout post, but as Jack circled around the third possibility he had identified, he spotted a dull metallic object on the ground nearby.

Bolt cutters?

And a severed cable with a lock attached.

Jack had no gloves with him, no evidence bags, had not been prepared to find these items, had come here out of curiosity, for something to do, to keep busy, not expecting to discover anything significant. With a sigh, he turned and jogged through the undergrowth, ignoring the thorns tearing at his shins, managing to keep upright despite tripping over roots and fallen branches as he made clumsy progress trying to find the towpath. Once back at his car, he opened the boot, grabbed what he needed and returned to the site using his torch to light the way as darkness descended.

After bagging the tool and the cable lock, he shone the torch at the branches above, stepping back to view the spot where he thought he had seen the man in yellow. It had been his plan to climb up and sit there himself, but that was not going to happen.

Only a monkey could get up there without a ladder.

Or an ultra-fit young man. One who seemed to levitate before kicking a chauffeur in the head…

With the two items in his left hand, the torch in his right, Jack started for the towpath, but noticed something odd about the undergrowth nearby. As he peered at the object he realised it was a military style camouflage poncho, torn and discarded as useless. A third evidence bag joined the others and Jack carried his three prizes back to the river bank.

Tomorrow, he would ask Charlie to arrange for some officers to do a thorough inspection. Jack sensed the yellow man had something to do with Felix's death—surely a deliberate homicide. He and Doc could hopefully convince Charlie to follow up straight away, rather than waiting on the full report from the fire officers.

Across the water, he saw headlights as a car arrived at Doc's house, and assumed it was Judy returning alone after insisting her husband stayed in hospital. It was a shame, but their conversation with Charlie would have to wait until morning.

Forty minutes later, he too pulled up outside the house, but this time had to ring the bell to gain entry. To his surprise, Doc opened the door and waved him inside without a word. Jack could see curiosity in Doc's eyes at the sight of the evidence bags in his arms.

'I think you've got a stalker, mate… Surprised to see you home. Where's the missus?'

They entered the lounge with Doc still silent until he sat in his armchair, pensive as he watched Jack dump the bags on the coffee table.

'She's having a shower then going to bed. And I'm wiped out so I'll be joining her shortly. I had to tell her, Jack.'

'Tell her what?' Jack dropped into the armchair opposite Doc, and ran his hand through his hair, trying hard not to sound as pissed off as he felt.

'Everything.' Doc explained that he had been impelled to come clean, had told Judy about their increasing level of suspicion since the cat had appeared. A difficult conversation during their ride home by taxi. He pointed at the items Jack had brought with him. 'Where did that lot come from? And what do you mean? A stalker?'

'Someone was watching the house, after the explosion. From a tree opposite. Have you ever noticed anyone watching you from there before?'

'No… Never. Are you sure?'

'Yeah. He was dressed like a lemon, bright yellow. Seemed a bit odd, so I assumed it was just someone passing, let curiosity get the better of them. Then I found this lot.'

'What is that?'

'Camouflage. Whoever was up in that tree had planned to wear this, but it's ruined. Found it ripped, caught up in the brambles. Along with these bolt cutters and this cable lock.' Jack tossed the bag with the lock into Doc's lap. 'I thought it was well weird, until I had a closer look.'

'This is for a bike.'

'Uh-huh.' No further words were needed.

'There's a broken key jammed in it.' Doc dropped the bag on the table, and pointed to another. 'Hence the bolt cutters.'

'Yeah. Looked to me like the bike had been padlocked to a nearby tree, in a clear patch, well away from the thorns. Then lemon boy climbed into a big oak over-looking this place.'

'My stalker...'

'Yup. But I couldn't understand the bolt cutters at first, just assumed someone nicked the bike while he was up in the branches. Then I saw that key stuck inside the lock.' Jack leaned forward, scowling as he prodded at the bag with his index finger. 'The bike's *owner* cut the cable...'

'And no one takes bolt cutters on their bike rides just in case the lock jams.'

'Exactly. To release his bike, I reckon he had to go and buy these, or fetch 'em from somewhere. While dressed in yellow cycling kit. Tomorrow, I'll have the local bobbies on his arse so fast he won't know what hit him.' He paused, thinking he had to ask Doc, was sure he knew the answer, but dreaded hearing the wrong one. The chief fire officer had raised the issue when Jack had arrived earlier. He tried not to sound accusatory as he said, 'One thing though. The fire officers need to know.'

'What?'

'The boat. Did you make any modifications to it?'

'No.' Doc shook his head, emphatic in his denial. Jack sighed with relief as his friend asked, 'Why would I?'

'No extra cabling or anything like that?' Jack could see Doc was being truthful, his head still vigorously denying any modifications. He had to press for more confir-mation, to be sure, though kept his tone lighter now that the worst possible explana-tion for Felix's death seemed unlikely. 'No wiring for some new electrical device you fitted yourself? Radio, TV, clock, electrical fan? Nothing?'

'Nothing. Why?'

'The stainless steel fuel tank blew up—'

'Definitely not the bilge?'

'Nope. They said they recovered most of the tank, but the upper part's still in the water. They reckon they're one hundred percent sure that's where it started.'

'So, do they know how?'

'Nah. But they said it looked like some *idiot* had blocked the vent too.' Jack saw Doc bridle at the implied insult, tried to smile to relieve the sting, but was in no mood for this, and could feel his lips warp in a way that was hardly reassuring. *Too bad.* 'Maybe unknowingly, doing some work on the boat.' He paused, then asked, 'You didn't, did you?'

'Of course not. You know me, Jack! I do very little other than fill it up with petrol and clean it occasionally. I always take it to the boat yard for any maintenance or if I need something fitted.'

'In that case, I'll get on to Charlie first thing. Hopefully, by then the fire officers will have a full report for her too. This is a murder scene, my friend. There's no doubt about it as far as I'm concerned.'

'No. And not much doubt in my mind about who's responsible.' Doc shuddered. 'Poor Felix... But *I* was the target. It was me he was after.'

'Oh, yes indeed. And I'd bet my life's wages that lemon boy is Billy bloody Leech.'

When Billy arrived home a few minutes before midnight, the house was in darkness, so his mother must have sunk several Martinis as usual while waiting for him. All night, she had been badgering him with numerous messages to his phone, each using different words, but all repeating the same demand with varying degrees of forceful-ness and anger:

Come home right now. I need to talk to you.

No chance. Much better to let the ugly sow stew in some alcohol—with benefits—collapse unconscious in a drunken heap, and forget whatever it was that was bugging her. Situation normal.

Only it wasn't.

Where is she?

This was most peculiar. The pattern for the last couple of years had been the same. His mother would be snoring on the sofa, with the TV blaring, and Billy would help her to bed. Or carry her, depending on how much she had drunk.

No sign of her in the kitchen, either. Billy opened the fridge and drank milk from a carton, then popped it back inside just as he spotted the empty vodka and gin bottles—one of each on the kitchen worktop.

He sniggered at the sight. So, she must be pissed out of her mind again, and suit-ably drugged. Somehow, she had managed to get herself to bed—an unusual achievement since he had upped her dosage over the last few months. She could be halfway up the stairs again, collapsed there, like the last time she made the effort. That was entirely possible, too.

With his bike shoes in his hand he climbed to her room without a sound. She had even managed to turn off the light herself. After placing his shoes on the carpet, he pushed open the door and crept inside, but some animal instinct within him stayed his hand as he went to switch it back on.

No need.

The light from his phone would provide sufficient illumination for the brief task he had in mind. Then he realised what was different tonight.

She's not snoring...

Again, his acute feral senses thrust a warning at him, but his confidence was such that he ignored it. Having spotted the two empty bottles, both of which had been half full when he left the house, and with the amount of Temazepam he had dropped in them, he was certain she would be nigh on comatose.

Using the backlight from his phone to view her face he pulled her right hand from under the pillow and went to scrub the nails across her cheek.

'Billy?' His mother clutched at his hand, her grip firm, and her other reached for the bedside lamp, the brightness startling him even more than her unexpected wakefulness. 'What the hell are you doing in my room? What time is it? And where were you tonight?'

A flick of his wrist released her grip as she sat up, and he stepped back a pace from the bed. He curled his lip at her, trying to recover from the shock, determined not to let her see his moment of weakness while his mind raced for a viable explanation.

'I was just checking on you.'

His mother, her face twisted in anger and agitation, frowned at him, her lips tight as she replied.

'Really? I seriously doubt that. Now—tell me the truth. What are you doing in here?'

Go on the attack, Billy boy…

That always worked.

'I just told you. I always come in here to see how you are.'

'I am so sick of your bullshit—'

'Sick? Yeah, you're sick alright.' Billy lobbed the insult at her, stepped right up to the bedside and leaned over her. She cowered from him. 'Every fucking night, I come in here and check you aren't puking in your sleep after all the booze you've swilled. I always put you in the recovery position, just in case. Because I *worry* about you. All the time.'

On seeing her reaction, her anger deflated and her guilt resurfacing, Billy was sure he had convinced her. He stood upright again, looking down his nose at the wreck of a woman who had somehow acted as a maternal host to his superior genes. Then she hit back.

'Don't give me that, you bloody liar. I know what you've been doing—'

'Really? Doing what—other than being the sole caregiver to my drunken mother? And *her* demented mother? For years I've been putting up with it—with no word of thanks. Nothing. Pah! I'm going to bed.'

Billy turned to go, but she fired another salvo, hurling herself out of the bed at him.

'You've been tampering with my gin and vodka. I know you have, so don't deny it. What have you been putting in the bottles?' He turned back, startled again, finally realising she was stone cold sober. *But how?* Her voice was shrill and jarring as she levelled accusations at him. 'Rat poison? Is that it? You want to kill me, Billy? Your own mother?'

'Poison? Haha! You think I'm trying to do away with you, like a filthy rodent?' He giggled at the inanity of it all. 'You *are* a bloody pest, but you've been doing such a bang-up job of killing yourself, why would I need to bother?' He shook his head, as if disgusted by her stupidity, at thinking he would do anything to harm her.

'Okay, not rat poison, then. What *have* you been doctoring my drink with? And stop with the smug smirk or I will slap it off your face, young man.'

Just you try it, you witch.

She was in front of him glaring up at his eyes, livid. He put his hands on her shoulders as if to reassure, and she flinched as he grabbed her.

Good.

'Listen to me. I put some sedative in your drink to *help* you. Okay. I admit it.' Her mouth opened, ready to scold him again, but he could see she was having doubts. He pressed home his advantage. 'You've been drinking so much I thought your liver would pack up. I just wanted to knock you out, so you couldn't drink yourself to death.'

All certainty at her discovery dribbled away, and he could feel her shoulders slump as he spoke. He had her again, quite literally in the palm of his hands. Had done for years.

'You drugged me? You thought that would *help* me?'

'Yes, I did. It helped me too.' The snarl in his voice was back, and he shoved her on to the bed so hard she fell, sprawled across it. 'If you weren't so fucking selfish you'd realise how hard it's been for me. But no, all you think of is yourself. Drowning in booze and downing painkillers like the junkie you are.' He shook a furious fist at her as she tried to sit up. 'If Social Services knew half of what I've had to put up with, they would've taken me into care years ago. My dad was right about you. You really are a useless, self-centred bitch.'

His mother's anger dissipated as her face folded in on itself. She clamped a hand over her mouth trying to stop the sobs.

Satisfied with the outcome of their unexpected confrontation, Billy left her wallowing in misery, guilt and a flood of tears.

MONDAY

COMBUSTION

JUDY PUT the finishing touches to her make-up while Colin showered. She wanted today to be as normal as possible, despite the charred wreck at the end of their garden—and the police officers Colin had warned her would be crawling all over the place today. Judy was going to go to work.

A normal Monday morning.

Well, not really, but she would do her best. Her regular run hadn't happened. When the alarm went off at six she had tottered to the bathroom and spent her waking moments retching, thanks to Colin's alien DNA, now growing inside her, sending her immune system into overdrive.

Just get back to work.

Judy's weekdays were spent helping various charities raise money. Today, she was meeting with a local team of Cancer Research organisers and would be participating in several of their events in the coming months. Her time was given freely as she had no need to earn more money, and no desire to get back on the career treadmill either, despite having once been a high-flying civil servant.

Been there, done that.

Tragedy had diverted her from her careerist life, and now she helped others less fortunate. Then tragedy had hit home again, yesterday, with Judy initially convinced it was just an awful and unfortunate accident. Until her ride home with Colin.

His explanation had been evasive at first, and she had pressed him to tell her everything. She understood his reluctance when he finally blurted the name of the boy they suspected may have been responsible.

On hearing it, Judy could not comprehend how this young man had somehow inveigled his way into their lives. Then her husband had admitted it… He'd invited the nephew of the man Judy blamed for the death of her mother, her son, and ex-husband, into their home.

Into their lives.

She had been unable to speak to him since.

Just the name 'Leech' made her tremble, sliding icicles of fear through her veins. That was bad enough, but as Colin's explanation continued, relentlessly driving home his concerns, she just knew the Leech boy had evil in his genes.

With a start, she realised she was staring at her image, lipstick in her hand, poised at her mouth, frozen there.

I look bloody terrified. Come on, Judy! Snap out of it.

Colin wandered in from the shower, towelling himself, trying hard to be cheerful as he greeted her.

'Good morning, my love. No run today?'

Be normal. Try harder.

'No. I was a little sick when I woke.' He stood behind her, a tentative grin on his face, then stooped and kissed the top of her head as she said, 'I'll get over it. Just a little morning sickness. It didn't last long with Josh.'

'That's good to know, sweetheart. I'm heading out with Jack shortly, so I'll see you tonight. And thank you. For understanding.'

Judy nodded. Tried to smile, but could not.

Bloody Jack.

'Just take care of yourself, Colin.'

'I will. I promise. They've adjusted my medication. My blood pressure ended up way too low and that caused me to faint.'

'I know all that.' She turned and stood, kissed him on the lips. He grinned and wiped at the lipstick with the back of his hand. 'I mean, be careful of the Leech boy. That family…' She sighed, went to the door, looked back at him and completed the thought. 'That family has done enough damage to us already. Felix died yesterday, too. At our *home*. And there are three of us now.' She laid a protective hand on her belly as she spoke. 'Remember that, while you're out with your detective friend. Take no risks, Colin.'

'I won't.'

'Promise me.'

'I promise.'

Judy nodded, and left him, standing in his towel, red smeared across his lips, his expression uncertain. Not for the first time, a worrying thought came unbidden:

He looks so vulnerable.

With a final glance back at him from the doorway, she had the urge to hug him, and not let go.

Bloody hormones.

She clambered down the stairs, thinking, *Is the Leech boy really so dangerous?* Judy hoped not, and as she got into her car, she tried to convince herself everything would be alright.

A police car passed her in the driveway and parked outside their front door, and despite her best efforts to feel otherwise, seeing it merely confirmed the feeling she'd had since the boat went up in flames.

The conviction that nothing would ever be the same again.

'It's not surprising she shit herself the night before last.' Billy held up an empty carton for Suzie's benefit as she entered the kitchen. His nose crinkled and his lips folded back in disgust as he tossed it in the bin. 'She guzzled all that prune juice you bought her last week, to help loosen her bowels. Must've been during another one of her regular midnight trips to the kitchen.' He snorted and stared at her. 'And you look even more dreadful than usual. Guilty conscience stop you sleeping last night, did it? After falsely accusing your own son of poisoning you?'

The accuracy of his words made her want to melt into the tiles and disappear. Just like a character she had seen in a movie during happier times, before life had dealt her its devastating and debilitating blows. Suzie's night had been spent tossing and turning, thinking and sobbing, regretting her outburst while still harbouring suspicions about her son. Her mind was not as sharp as it might otherwise have been, but this morning she had been determined to have it out with him over breakfast. Of course, he was already up and about—she had not heard him sneak past her bedroom, even without any booze or drugs dulling her senses.

'We still need to talk, Billy.' She pulled up a chair as he slurped cereal and milk into his mouth while standing, leaning his back against the fridge, his ankles crossed, his eyes disdainful. 'Sit down, son.'

'Talk about what? Why my mother's a drunk, perhaps? Or how I have to look out for her and *her* mother? Every day, every night? Pfah!' His spoon clattered in his bowl as he dumped both on the worktop. 'I'm going for a shower. I need to be out early today. Or did you forget?'

Despite racking her brains, she had no idea what he was talking about. He probably told her while she was pissed. Another spike of guilt, hammered into her heart.

'Forget what?'

'Haha! Yeah, you did. Useless…'

He was at the kitchen door already, and clearly had no intention of joining Suzie for 'a talk'. She saw his shoulders tense as she told him:

'I'm going to have the residue in those bottles tested. You'd better be telling me the truth.'

He spun, leapt at the table in one fluid movement, and slammed both fists down as he landed. She felt the pine slab shudder and crack under the impact and flinched at the raw power unleashed by her boy. That aura of menace, one she had noticed only recently, was back, and his face was wild.

Good God!

'You listen to me. I've had enough of your whingeing. I checked online last night after your little outburst. You've been guilty of criminal negligence as the *supposedly* responsible adult in charge of *this* child. They've imprisoned junkies like you for less. So enough of the sanctimonious crap, eh, Mother?'

He tried to stare her down, and she felt herself wither under his gaze. There was nothing she wanted more right now than to sip a bottle of linctus or down a few cocktails. Preferably both. Instead, she answered him, though her fluttering voice betrayed her lack of confidence as she made her accusations.

'You told my mother lies. That I think she owes me this house, for the money they received after I was raped. You found out about that by rooting through the boxes in the basement. I didn't shout about that, or the abortion, or anything else, did I? I didn't go to Lakeside either—have never been there. But you told her I had. You're a liar, Billy Leech. Just like your father and your uncle.'

She thought she saw a shimmer of doubt swim behind his eyes for a fraction of a second, but it was gone so swiftly she was unsure. Then he laid into her again.

'Oh, brilliant. *Detective*. Not!' He tapped her temple using an index finger with the texture of granite, bruising thin flesh as he emphasised each word with an agonising tap. 'Yes, I did dig around down there…'

She pulled her head away from his finger, and slammed her own palms on the table. 'I knew it!'

'Only to confirm some of the stuff you've been ranting about when pissed. Why? So I could put Nana's mind at rest.'

'Don't lie to me—you've been deliberately telling her things to upset—'

'SHUT UP!' The murderous scowl on his face brought Suzie's husband to mind again, and how he had looked when he admitted to his crimes to her the night he died. 'You can't remember anything. You and your big ugly mouth, screaming stuff no one wants to hear. Poor Nana, she was in bits about it all, so I had to be sure. Yet more of your bullshit that *I've* had to clear up. Fuck you. I'm going out with Smiffy today. We have some fieldwork to do. I'll be back tonight. Or maybe I won't.'

Then he was gone. An angry tornado thumping up the stairs. For once, she could hear him, but wished she could not.

What have I done?

After her discoveries the previous day, she was certain her boy had been playing some evil game with her and her mother, but now, all confidence had evaporated and she wondered if she was suffering some post-alcoholic delusions of her own.

And the worst of it was, much of what he said was true. She had let him down, had not been a good mother. Not been any sort of mother, and for so long. A boy suffering his own trauma, a lonely bullied boy who was not even allowed to attend school.

It's my fault. I've screwed up everything…

Suzie would have cried, except her tears were all used up, soaked into the pillow and sheets on her bed. She was wrung out, dehydrated, and suffering from a lack of sleep. Her reserves were depleted from the abuse she'd heaped on her body, and now crushing guilt was threatening to push her back into the old cycle.

It hadn't been so bad, being wrapped in the embrace of morphine and alcohol. She licked her lips, then opened the empty gin bottle. Sniffed at it. Felt a tremor tickle her belly. A craving.

The doorbell snapped her out of it. Angry with herself for her weakness, she screwed the cap on so tight that the thread broke. She heard Billy's voice, muffled, greeting Mr Smith, before the door slammed behind them.

Suzie forced herself to make some boiled eggs, toast and coffee for herself and her mother, and took them to Nana's room.

Thankfully, there was no smell of urine or faecal matter to greet Suzie today, just lavender and cool morning air gusting in through an open window. Her mother was sitting in her chair, wearing a summer dress. Her hair was neatly brushed too. She looked very pleased with herself as she greeted her daughter, a twinkle in her eye.

As Suzie placed the tray on the low table and sat in the chair opposite, she smiled, thinking how her mother seemed more like her old self.

Before Dad died.

'Brrr. It's a bit chilly in here. Here's your breakfast.' She sipped some coffee but the sight of the eggs made her feel queasy. 'I'm just having a bit of toast.'

'Thank you, love. I was just thinking I'd come down and eat with you both, but I ended up enjoying the view and the morning air. I feel so much better today. I took no medication at all yesterday, and I think it's done me the power of good.'

Sedatives and antidepressants.

Thinking back on it, her mother had become *more* depressed as time went by. Less able, less *alive*, despite the drugs her doctor had prescribed. Yet another thing drunk Suzie had failed to see. At least they both seemed to be coming out of it now.

'You should be careful with the stairs, Mum. I can always help you down. I'm horrified you've been wandering down them in the middle of the night, alone.'

'Have I?' Nana shrugged as she tucked into her eggs, and added, 'I don't remember. I think I'm going to stop taking any pills for a while. See how I feel.'

'We'll get you a proper check-up. Today. I'm taking you to a special clinic to have some tests. Just to be sure.' She could see her mother was about to argue, but Suzie had not told her that her bedroom had been covered with filth just twenty-four hours earlier, and nor would she. No matter how well Nana felt, she was having a check-up. 'I've already booked it.' She chewed on some dry toast as her mother bit her lip, then nodded and spooned some egg yolk into her mouth. Good thing one of them had an appetite today. 'We're going this morning, and afterwards, I'll take you for lunch somewhere nice.'

'Sounds lovely, dear. And so are these eggs.' She was about to start her second already, but her knife hovered instead of decapitating it as she gave Suzie a confused look, her eyes squinting a little as she spoke. 'I know my memory lapses have been getting worse. And after that time I fell down the stairs, well, it took the wind out of my sails. But I won't take any more of those sedative things. They make me feel so woozy.' Her eyes dropped to her plate again and her knife sliced the top of the egg off as she murmured, almost too low for Suzie to hear. 'And I was hallucinating, it seemed, at times.' Louder now. 'I think that's why I fell.'

'The drugs?' Suzie wondered too, but she wasn't thinking about prescriptions. She forced some more toast into her mouth, chewed it for several seconds with insufficient saliva and nearly gagged as she swallowed it, her thoughts almost choking her too as the lump of bread lodged in her throat before slipping down to her gut. 'Mmm. Maybe... What do you mean? About hallucinating?'

'It was like a dream. Well, nightmare.' Her mother was obviously still terrified by the memory, probably reliving it as she talked, Suzie thought, as she watched the quivering hands tackle another mouthful of egg. 'One minute I was in here, the next, I was at the top of the stairs.'

'What were you doing? Going to find more food?'

'I've no idea, love.' Her nose wrinkled and her face, still fearful, wore lines of confusion too. 'Strange, though. Whenever I think about it since, I get a feeling of dread. It was as if someone was whispering into my ear at the top of the stairs. I thought it was your father's voice, to begin with.'

'Whispering?'

'Mmm. It's like he wanted me to join him.'

'What?' For Suzie, this was all startling news... It should not have been. She felt another tremor of guilt at being derelict in both her filial and her maternal duties. Could her mother have been suicidal too? She couldn't stop the shock tinting her voice as she said, 'You think you threw yourself down the stairs because you miss him so much? To be with him? Oh, Mum. That's awful. I'm so sorry.'

I should have been here for you.

'Oh, no. I wouldn't do that!' Having finished her breakfast, Nana sat back, wrapped her arms around herself, rubbing her biceps, as if the morning chill had finally got to her. She gazed out of the window, thinking. Several seconds passed before she spoke again, her voice haunted. 'But the whispering was insistent. It felt like a demon was urging me to do it. I turned to go back to bed, I think. Then I tripped, and fell...' She turned back to Suzie, bafflement and terror on her features, for a few beats. Then she tried to compose herself again. 'Though...' The word tailed off to nothing.

'Though what?' Suzie needed to know. Sat forward, as if urging her mother to speak, to spit out whatever it was that had caused her so much fear. 'Please tell me. What happened?'

'It's so strange, and all so hazy.' A shudder of her shoulders, and her eyes watering. The old dear was close to tears, and Suzie's heart slipped in her chest at the look on her face. 'I thought it was all a dream until I woke up, lying there in pain the next morning.'

'It was no dream, Mum. Billy found you at the bottom of the stairs. You got off lightly with a broken wrist.'

'You know I still can't face the stairs without you or Billy helping. That's why I can't understand why I would go to the kitchen, alone, at night...'

That was puzzling Suzie too. Even with the medications, it seemed weird. 'I'm not surprised you feel that way about the stairs. It was a bad fall. It could've killed you.'

'I know. And I try not to think about it.' The silver crucifix at her neck received a few lingering strokes from her fingers. 'You know I don't really believe in ghosts and demons or anything like that. And your father would never harm me. But last night, in bed, I was reliving that night like I have done so many times since, but this time without my meds...'

'And?'

'Well, honestly sweetheart, take no notice of me. I'm just imagining things.'

'Go on. Tell me.'

'It sounds stupid, I know. But it really felt like I was pushed.'

Charlotte Kealey shook Doc's hand with a firm grip and he immediately thought her an impressive uniformed Inspector. Sharp eyes assessed Doc as she introduced herself when he answered the door, and he invited her in with barely a glance at the ageing female sergeant beside her.

'The famous Doctor Colin Powers. Jack enjoys crowing about his celebrity friend. Nice to finally meet you in person. Sorry the circumstances aren't more amenable.' She dazzled Doc with a smile. 'Jack forgot to invite me to your barbecue this weekend. Apparently'

Doc was surprised to see his friend's ears turn pink at Charlie's jibes as they entered the lounge together. Without a word of greeting to Jack, she instructed her sergeant to inspect the boat. The three of them then sat by the coffee table, still bearing the bagged items Jack had discovered the night before. He launched into an explanation, but Charlie cut him off.

'First, let me explain why I'm here. I know you invited me, Jack. I got your message first thing this morning, but I was already planning on visiting Doctor Powers. I was waiting for the fire officer's interim report.'

'And?' Jack leaned forward, tapping his palms on his knees, rat-a-tat-tat, impatient to hear more.

'You have it?' Doc could see no file, and Charlie had no smartphone to hand. 'And please call me Doc. Everyone else does.'

'My sergeant has it. Before you speak with her, I'd like to confirm what Jack stated in his message to me, Doc. You didn't make any kind of modification to the boat? Nothing at all. Please think carefully.'

'Hang on Charlie. Doc's already—'

'It's okay, my friend.' Doc placed a hand on Jack's arm to quieten him. Charlie was only doing her job, just as he would have done. Friend of a friend or not. 'Nothing, Inspector. The boat's been regularly serviced by professionals at the marina. I can provide all the receipts, and the last time was only four or five weeks ago.'

'And who else has access to the vessel?'

'It sits on the river, day and night. But it's always locked and I have the keys.' Doc shrugged. 'My wife. Jack. A few friends... There were a couple of dozen police officers here on Saturday, and many of them had a look around the boat that afternoon. I'm pretty sure no one I know would dream of tampering with it.'

'Of course. I just wanted to be sure.' She threw him another brilliant smile while ignoring Jack. 'The fire officer's report recommended we get our divers out to recover the missing parts of the fuel tank. I didn't want to do that if you could tell me something that would explain why it exploded.' She paused, the smile switched off like a light. 'Have you been putting additives in the fuel?'

'What?' Jack gave them both a baffled frown, but Doc had been thinking about the explosion and was not surprised at the question.

'No additives, Inspector. Are you suggesting they found traces of unusual chemicals in what was left of the fuel tank?'

Charlie nodded. 'Some pretty exotic chemicals, Doc. A mixture that reacted with the petrol.'

Jack interjected. Excited now. 'Is that what caused the explosion, Charlie?' Her eyes remained on Doc, so Jack demanded to know, voice fierce. 'Chemicals in the fuel?'

'The fuel tank vent had been sealed. Deliberately from the look of it, gummed up with filler. According to the fire chief, the traces of chemical compound they found would've become effervescent in petrol, producing bubbles of gas, creating high pressure inside the tank. Water sprinklers or even foam would've been unable to extinguish the resultant fire. The analysts reckon it had its own supply of oxygen, thanks to the ongoing chemical reaction.'

Doc scratched his head, visualising the green flames in the fireball. 'So it exploded from the pressure?' That wasn't right. 'I thought it was Felix turning the ignition key that triggered it.'

'The fire officer said it still needed a spark. The pressure inside the tank was insufficient to cause an explosion. He likened it to the compression that occurs in a piston engine combustion chamber, but can't understand how a spark could be introduced inside a sealed tank. Airtight, pressurised like that.' With a twitch of her shoulders, she added, 'I had hoped you'd be able to give us an explanation, but now

I think I need to call in the divers and officially make this a suspicious homicide investigation.'

'I'm on holiday, but I'd like to help.'

She finally addressed him, her voice formal. Frosty. 'Wasn't the chap who died your daughter's fiancé, Jack?'

'Yeah. And Doc's my mate. So what?'

The smile flickered on, uncertainly, but her voice was firm. 'I'll keep you in the loop but neither of you can be involved in the official investigation.'

'Come off it, Charlie!' Jack was half out of his seat, his face red, and Doc realised how close to exploding his friend was again.

'Jack, calm down, please.' With his backside still hovering over the armchair, Jack visibly bit his tongue, then sat back down on the cushion with a defeated thump. She continued, words silken and soft now. 'You of all people should know how precious detectives can be, and this case will be out of my hands well before lunchtime. Meanwhile, we'll need written statements from you both.' She smoothed the thighs of her uniform trousers with her palms, then stood. 'Now, excuse me. I have to make some calls. Sorry, Doc. You'll be answering many more questions when my plain clothes colleagues get here.'

Charlie joined her sergeant, leaving Doc in the lounge with Jack fuming.

'Dammit! I hoped we could be involved, that Charlie could get us in. Not shut us out.'

'Mmm. There's nothing stopping us doing our own investigation, Jack. I want to speak to Billy Leech. And his mother.'

'Me too… Charlie didn't seem too interested in this stuff, either.' Jack gesticulated at the bags on the table with a sullen look on his face. 'And she was very offhand with me.'

The sergeant appeared at the patio doors before closing them behind her. Charlie was still outside, standing by the salvaged boat parts with a phone pressed to her ear.

'The Inspector asked me to have a chat with you, Detective Carver. And you, Doctor Powers, if you don't mind.' She gave them several looks each, her head switching from side to side, a robin hunting worms. Then smiled at them. 'Off the record.'

'Really? Sit down, please.' Doc realised then. 'You work at Thatcham, don't you, Sergeant? You compiled a list of attacks on animals and property in the local area. And you suspect Billy Leech was involved. Correct?'

Jack murmured under his breath. 'Ah! Charlie, I get it now.'

'That's right, Doctor. I knew his father and uncle when they were teenagers. They're a bad lot, the Leeches. Believe me. I could tell you some tales about that family that would make your toes curl…'

On the way to the clinic, Suzie, feeling naked without her usual disguise, tried not to think about her son and all the dreadful things she once again suspected he was responsible for. Her mother's latest tale had set her mind spinning, though she had tried to consider everything as dispassionately as she could.

The problem was one of her own making. The months and years that had passed by, with her oblivious to all that was going on around her. She did her chores in the morning, kept the house clean, cooked for her family, did whatever shopping they needed, but always with her mind dulled by chemicals. That morning Billy had roused her, shouting about finding her mother at the bottom of the stairs, should have been a wakeup call for her in more ways than one.

They had driven to the hospital, and returned home with Nana's plastered arm in a sling, but all the while Suzie had been selfishly thinking about the hassle the incident had caused. The inconvenience of it all. Had berated her mother for her stupidity. Shown zero sympathy. Scolded her and told her to ask for help the next time she wanted to get up or down the stairs. And the poor old dear had pretty much confined herself to her room ever since.

I've been so horrible. No wonder Billy calls me selfish.

Nana contradicted the thought. 'You know, I'm so glad you and Billy are living with me. Since your dad died, I would've been all alone in that big house full of memories.' Her fingers stroked the back of Suzie's hand as it rested on the gear stick. 'Thank you, love.'

'For what?'

'For not moving out as you originally planned.'

'Don't be so daft—we should be thanking you for making us so welcome. I don't know what I would've done without you. After everything that happened to Billy and me.'

Billy. I want to know what lies you've been telling.

The terrible prospect that he might have been responsible for shoving her mother down the stairs was one she could barely face, especially after accusing him of trying to poison her.

Falsely accusing him.

Maybe…

Right now, his justification for drugging her seemed less likely than it had last night. Regular doses of sedatives mixed with alcohol were probably just as damaging as drinking more alcohol with no additives. Given Billy's comprehensive knowledge of chemistry and biology, he would be fully aware of the consequences of mixing them, and what that would mean for her liver over the months he had been dosing her.

Years?

As they pulled into the clinic car park, the other ugly suspicion reared up in her mind. She was sure her son had been starving her mother, though had yet to hear his explanation for that, and wanted to find out if he had been drugging Nana too.

With every passing hour, her mother had become sprightlier, more cogent, more aware.

Just like I have…

There was a simple way to find out. This clinic, just south of Oxford, specialised in blood screening for a range of ailments, but also had a lucrative sideline in forensics. Specifically, the identification of illicit drugs, testing blood samples for substance abuse, and checking for chemical contamination of food and drink. Nana gave Suzie a black look when she hoiked the carrier bag from the passenger footwell and the bottles clinked inside.

'You can't drink and drive, my love. I know you find it difficult to face people without your dark glasses and—'

'They're empties, Mum. I want the lab to test them for something.'

'Oh!' Relieved. 'Let's get inside then. I want to get this over and done with. Can they really tell if I've got dementia from my blood?'

That was the excuse for today's outing, although Suzie was uncertain if the analysts could, as she had forgotten to ask when she called to arrange the appointment—her mind being preoccupied with other more immediate concerns. She would find out today, but her mother would remain in ignorance as Suzie had warned the staff not to discuss any of the tests with 'the old dear' as she was 'easily confused'.

'I've heard they can analyse your genes here, check to see if you're at risk. And they do all sorts of other tests too. You don't have to worry. They only take a little blood, and I'm having mine checked too. I want to get healthy again.'

'Really?' A delighted smile accompanied the word as Nana pushed her way into the revolving doors of the clinic. Suzie followed.

'Really. I'm off the booze. And like you, I want to cut out medication if I can. We'll do a deal. We'll look after each other, and do it together, eh Mum?'

They went arm in arm to the reception desk and completed registration details. They were then escorted to two adjacent treatment rooms where a nurse took blood from each of them. Once out of her mother's earshot, Suzie took the opportunity to confirm what additional tests were to be undertaken on both blood samples, and agreed to pay extra to expedite the results. The nurse didn't bat an eyelid when Suzie handed her the empty bottles for analysis too.

Thirty minutes after arriving, they were back on the road.

'Let's go to Wallingford and have lunch by the Thames.' Nana delved into her handbag for a compact, and powdered her face as she continued. 'There's a nice pub near the bridge, and I haven't been there since before your dad died.'

'Sounds nice, Mum.' Suzie had her smartphone in her handbag, and reckoned she would receive the results soon enough. The clinic had promised that a hard copy would be in the post tonight, but she'd asked them to email her as soon as the information was ready and hoped it would be in her inbox by the time they had eaten. Maybe then she would get to the truth regarding her son's machinations.

Please God. Don't let my son take after his father and uncle. Please let him be innocent...

Innocent?

No. Not likely.

After his display of sheer malice at breakfast?

Suzie swerved as his face loomed before her, as if reflected on the inside of the windscreen.

Billy. Snarling, angry, bitter.

Malevolent.

Like the demon that had pushed her mother down the stairs.

'Bloody politics. Makes me sick.' Jack grumbled as he drove Doc into Pangbourne village, his morose mood further soured by Charlie's visit. 'At least she's on our side.'

'Yes... It's not surprising we've been given the official cold shoulder. In many ways, we're both suspects.'

'Suspects?' Jack had been so focussed on Billy Leech he had not really considered himself in that light. It made sense though, and any decent detective would have him pegged as a likely contender for blowing up the boat. The questions Charlie had asked earlier had suggested the fire officers thought Doc might be liable, but given Jack's animosity for his future son-in-law, he was certain to be on the investigators' radar. He snorted in disgust. 'I s'pose so. Especially as we're the only witnesses to the dead pets.'

'You're the only one who saw lemon boy too, Jack. And you went alone to inspect the site. They only have your word for it you found those bolt cutters and so on... I think your lady love has been very helpful in the circumstances.'

'Lady love! I wish.' Jack had missed a trick with her. Why on earth hadn't he thought to invite her to his celebration do on Saturday? Crazy. 'Charlie's a doll. I do like her. When this is all over I'm going ask her on a proper date. Not sure I can remember how to do all that romantic bollocks, though. Maybe you can give me some tips. Here we go.' Jack swerved into the parking bay opposite the station, with the minicab office adjacent, but was in no hurry to get out of the car.

'I'm no expert. Unless you're planning to sit by a hospital bed and then help your paramour through rehab and recovery for several months after.'

'Mmm.' Jack changed the subject, his fingers tapping a tattoo on the steering wheel. 'What did you think of that sergeant? She's really got it in for the Leech clan, hasn't she?'

'I can understand why, though. It was good of Charlie to bring her along. And she could've insisted we stay and wait for her colleagues instead of letting us gallivant off this morning.'

'I wasn't planning on hanging around, waiting for some bumpkin detectives to get their arses into gear. I can't believe Reading nick hasn't sent a team out already. Dithering like that.'

'They need to be absolutely sure it wasn't just carelessness on my part before allocating resources—'

'It's bleedin obvious this was deliberate.' Despite his objections, Jack was well aware of the reasons why the local force was not on the case already. 'We'll just have to do our own investigation for now. Bit like old times.' He threw Doc a mirthless grin, but Doc was deep in thought and continued staring out of the windscreen.

'Let's hope Charlie's divers find enough to confirm our suspicions.' The police underwater search team had arrived as Jack and Doc departed. 'Do you want me to come in with you?'

'Nah. I'll only be a few minutes. You can wait here and flex that giant brain muscle of yours while I'm doing my first interview as a DCI. Unofficially, of course. At least I look the part this morning.' The jacket, shirt and tie Jack had selected from Doc's wardrobe made him feel more business-like too.

Jack entered the cab office and took in his surroundings—it didn't take long. The business premises were about the size of an average bathroom, though the smell was more reminiscent of a public lavatory. A plate glass window with a phone number and the word Taxi stencilled on it faced onto the street, overlooking their car, and Jack could see Doc, now slightly reclined with his eyes closed, no doubt reviewing everything related to their budding investigation. Jack could just about walk between the few brown plastic chairs lined up against the back wall, also mud coloured, and a desk, only just big enough for the computer screen and telephone console crowded on to it. Everything in here seemed to be designed to fit into the limited space, including the dwarf sitting behind the mini desk, shouting into a telephone headset.

Not dwarf. Small person.

Jack mentally corrected himself, wondering if he would ever get the hang of the politically correct language he was expected to use, especially now he'd been promoted.

When the shouting finished, the small person looked him up and down, and said, 'You don't need a cab. What can I do for you, officer?'

'Something very simple.' He flashed his brand-new warrant card—thankfully still dry thanks to being stashed with his wallet in Doc's guest room when he went for his impromptu swim—and introduced himself. 'Detective *Chief* Inspector Jack Carver. I'm hoping you can help me. Yesterday afternoon or early evening, did any of your cabs pick up a cyclist in this area? Without his bike?'

'Cyclist?'

'Yeah. Dressed for the Tour de France. All in yellow I think. Definitely wearing a canary coloured top.'

'Hang on.'

The small person made a call to all his active cabs, relaying Jack's query, and immediately had a response from one. He tapped a button on his console and Jack could hear the cabbie's voice crackling with static through the miniature speaker.

'Took him to a house on Bucklebury Common and then back to the bridge over the river. Young lad. Said he'd had a bike accident. There was quite a bit of blood on his clothes and legs, but he didn't want to go to hospital.'

Jack took a few more details, thanked the small person and bounced into the car beside Doc.

'It was him?' Doc pulled his seat back upright, and clicked his safety belt into place. 'Your lemon boy?'

'It was indeed, my friend. I think it's time we had a little chat with Billy Leech, don't you?'

'What are you planning to do with all this, Billy?'

'I told you. It's for my birthday celebration on Wednesday.' The wooden slats of Smith's gigantic garden shed exuded a chemical odour, absorbed over the years from the gases produced by numerous experiments, and Billy always associated the scent with exciting possibilities. Like this latest creation. 'Fireworks, with an added kick.'

'This much ANFO is not a firework!' Smith struggled as he dragged the plastic sack containing the mixture he had prepared to Billy's specifications towards his pupil's feet. 'With the added ingredients you asked for, it's a high-powered incendiary bomb. If you aren't careful, you could blow yourself up.'

'I'm always careful.' He booted the bag and chuckled. 'It's just fertiliser, diesel oil, some aluminium powder and a few other bits and bobs that'll make it pretty.'

'Pretty? Are you insane? There's enough here to turn this place into a giant fireball. You're not making fireworks, are you?' Smith's grotesque lips, slimy and wet, pouted at Billy as he demanded to know, 'What are you planning to blow up?'

'Nothing. I'm going to make lots of small packages and create a display for my mum and gran. Like last year. Anyway, ANFO's harmless enough, without a detonator.' Billy had already created one of those, using powder from several of Gramps' old shotgun cartridges, and had much bigger pyrotechnics in mind than a firework display to celebrate his sixteen years on the planet. Fortunately, his tutor remained ignorant of his plans. 'You can come and watch if you like.' Smiffy would have a front seat view, whether he wanted one or not.

'Just be careful. I don't want your mother suing me. As you well know, I've had enough trouble with the law as it is.' Smith's ears waggled and his cheeks joggled as he shook his head. A hint of saliva leaked at the corners of his mouth. 'And this is the last time I make anything for you. I know you've been burning things, Billy. I'm not stupid. Your old school gym, for a start.'

Smiffy had finally worked it out.

Too late.

'That place was a fire hazard. Hahaha! Nothing to do with me.' Billy's ironic tone said otherwise. He didn't care what his tutor thought. Smiffy couldn't do anything about it. 'Where's the oxidising powder I asked for? You'd better have cooked it for me?'

Smith closed his eyes and put his head back as if praying to heaven above, then muttered, 'What am I doing?' He let out a mournful sigh, shuffled over to a bench in the corner of the shed and picked up a package about the size and shape of a bag of sugar. He flipped it in the air a few times, as if thinking about what to do with it, but finally chucked it at Billy who caught it with one hand. 'Here you go. And now I'm out. This is the end of it, kiddo.'

'It ends when I say so—'

'No, it doesn't, Billy. I'll take my chances, even with those photographs you created while I was unconscious. And believe me, if I get collared for those bloody fakes, I'll be giving chapter and verse on everything I've done for you. Every bit of powder I've mixed, the *fireworks* I taught you to make, your unhealthy fascination with the properties of gasoline and other accelerants. I'll tell them about your experiments making restricted substances—'

'*Our* experiments!' Billy had not expected this. The bastard was threatening him. He'd finally grown some balls. 'You're the one who encouraged me, allowed me to do all that. My brilliant chemistry teacher, poisoning my innocent young mind.' He snickered as Smiffy gritted his teeth, the noise audible as his molars ground.

'I'll hold my hands up to it all—just not the abuse you fabricated. I'll even confess to the LSD and meth you forced me to make for you—everything. I have all the dates, too. You can stand there grinning at me like you don't give a fuck, but you won't be so smug when the police arrest you for all the previously unexplained conflagrations in your local area, will you?'

'You don't need to threaten me.' This'll be the last time, he thought, trying to keep his voice light. 'You won't have to see me again after this week. I promise.' Billy knew he sounded genuine enough. After all, he wasn't lying. He kept his voice level, despite how he felt inside. 'I'll find a new tutor. No worries.'

'Really?'

'Yup. One last thing to do.' Smiffy was about to object, but Billy held up his hand for silence, got it, and continued. 'Just drive us back to my place, we'll pop this lot in the cellar where it'll be safely out of the way. While we're there I'll destroy the incriminating photos. And we'll both forget everything about each other.' Billy thrust his right arm at his tutor, palm open. 'Deal, Smiffy?'

'Deal!' Smith shook the outstretched hand, his ugly jowls wobbling with relief.

'You can leave a note for my mother too—she's out with my gran for the day. I'll tell her you were called away at short notice. We'll say you had an emergency to deal with. A dying relative up north needs you urgently, and you don't know if or when you'll be back.' Billy grabbed a corner of the plastic sack with one hand, still holding the pack of powder in his other, and said, 'Let's chuck this lot in your car, and we'll get going.'

'This'll be the last time I need to come to your home?' Billy expected to hear suspicion in Smith's voice after all that had passed between them, but instead heard only gratitude at finally being let off the leash. Billy nodded his agreement, and Smith grabbed the other corner of the bag with enthusiasm. 'Great. Let's go.'

Billy detested being threatened. Had been through enough of that during his silent pupa phase, being abused, bullied and made to eat shit. He had managed to hold his anger in check during Smith's outburst, the threat to talk to the police, but it was still smouldering in his belly as they made their way to the car.

Thanks to their conversation, Billy had rapidly revised his plans for his tutor. And that was the one thing keeping his fury in check.

It wasn't just the bag of ANFO that would be residing in his cellar tonight.

'The cabbie brought him here, watched him disappear down the side of that house. Then he reappeared a few minutes later, with bolt cutters under his arm.'

Doc had not been to Bucklebury Common before, a pleasant slice of rural England with some beautiful country homes surrounded by heathland, paddocks and genteel farms.

'Doesn't he live several houses down, going by the address Charlie's sergeant gave us?'

'Devious little toe-rag. Maybe he nicked the bolt cutters from the neighbour's tool shed.'

'Hmm…' Doc was thinking differently, but just said, 'Let's go and ask him.'

Jack pulled the car forward and then into the driveway of Billy Leech's home. They waited on the doorstep for a couple of minutes, with Jack pressing the bell intermittently at first, frustrated, before jamming his finger on the button, ringing it continuously for a good thirty seconds. Then he gave up.

'Bugger. Let's go around the back, have a proper squint at his gaff.'

They did, but there was little to see. The back door and patio entrance were locked, as was the stable block. Doc spotted a neighbour at a bedroom window off to the left, and nudged Jack who was peering into the annex, nose pressed up against the glass, cursing under his breath at the lack of occupants.

'I think we should go, and come back when they're in. The local Neighbourhood Watch will be calling your colleagues if we aren't careful.'

Jack glanced up at where Doc was looking before turning his attention back to the annex, peering through another window after stomping to the far end of the block. 'Interesting place. Big lounge area, and a gym with bugger all in it.' He waved at the nosey neighbour and smiled as he gave her a thumbs up. She disappeared behind her curtain. 'Maybe we should have a word with her. She might know something about the lad's nocturnal habits.'

'Come on, Jack. Let's not waste any more time here. Billy's the one we need to speak to. Meanwhile, let's go and see the Dooley lads.'

Doc was itching to see the boy, but the place was deserted, and just being here filled him with a sense of impending doom. He couldn't wait to get back in the car. Jack traipsed after him, then scribbled on his pad, ripped out a page and poked it through the letterbox.

'Alright… *Boss*.' Jack's bad temper had not been improved by the wasted visit, but Doc let it ride. He sensed that his friend was suffering terribly over his daughter's grief, and probably blamed himself for Felix's death in some way, too. Jack blipped the car remote to unlock the doors and they slid inside simultaneously. 'I've left his mother a note to call me when she gets home. So, let's see the Dooleys instead, then.'

He crunched the gears as he jerked the stick into reverse then swerved out of the drive before heading for Newbury.

'That sergeant.' Doc had been mulling over all the woman had told them, much of it new to him and Jack. Much of it rumour, too. 'She really has a bee in her bonnet about the Leech family. I can see why her bosses have reined her in.'

'Well, she was around when Billy's dad and uncle were teenagers. Hardly surprising she recognised the pattern. Animal cruelty obviously runs in the family. Bloody psychos shouldn't be allowed to breed.'

The vicious night-time incidents sparked a thought in Doc's mind, related to something Jack had complained about the day before.

'Billy Leech's home is on the Middleton lass's road. Her parents' property is further to the north, I believe. Correct?'

Jack accelerated as he joined the A4 following the signpost to Newbury, and nodded, throwing Doc a questioning glance. 'Yeah. What of it?'

'Cameras, Jack.' Doc had noticed that some of the more prestigious properties had them, overlooking their main gates, but as Jack had pointed out before, this was the countryside so they were few and far between. At best, there was a chance of them picking up a fleeting glimpse of Billy Leech riding by in the early hours. Even if they could convince the local constabulary to agree to spend their budget on collecting and scrutinising all the video records from such a vast area, it would still provide nothing more than circumstantial evidence. Doc knew the chance of that happening was non-existent, but there was one other possibility. 'The parents of a princess, even one by marriage, would qualify for the Royal Protection Detail, wouldn't they?'

'Yeah, SO14 will be keeping an eye on 'em. Low profile, but they'll be watching. Why?'

'The area around the house, the approach roads. Won't they have hidden cameras? I'd have thought the immediate area would be bristling with them.'

'Probably. I see where you're going with this, but I'm not sure it helps us.'

'Surely they'll have already checked and logged all movements around that house, twenty-four hours a day, going back years, since the girl became involved with royalty.'

'Ah, right. You're thinking we could ask SO14 to see if they have records of a boy on a bike, on the local roads, in the middle of the night.'

'Yes. The nights that coincide with the recorded instances of animal torture and arson.'

'Mmm.' He sounded not at all enthusiastic. 'It's a long shot, but I'll see what I can do. Here we are. The Plough.'

Jack pulled into the car park at the back of a rundown pub fronting onto the busy main road, proudly advertising *All day opening* and *Full English breakfasts*. Doc didn't need to use his imagination to work out the clientele. The numerous pennants decorating the place with hundreds of triangular flags, each printed with a red cross on a white background, fluttered around them as they approached the entrance. As if the Saint George's theme decorating the exterior was not enough of a clue, the chalkboard by the entrance proclaimed the writer's illiteracy, ignorance and racism:

We don't speek Polish or Muslim here!
And we don't serve no kosher or hallal meat—just propper English grub!

Doc followed Jack into the gloomy interior, his nose wrinkling at the smell. Stale beer and sweaty socks came to mind as he glanced around. The ceiling was covered with full-sized flags, each pinned at the edges, the white and red emblems bellying down above his head, like enormous beer guts. The place was empty of customers, but still made him uncomfortable. Jack seemed unaffected, was already having a quiet word with the barman.

Doc was beginning to think it was another wasted trip, but then Jack turned, gave him a grim nod and jerked his thumb over his shoulder.

'Beer garden.'

Garden was a rather optimistic term for what confronted them at the rear of the building. A concreted area, fenced off from the car park and lined with a few wooden beer kegs, each sawn in half and filled with dirt. Growing weeds. More patriotic bunting was strung above the six round cast iron tables, previously white but now dappled rust brown, each with a handful of matching chairs, all squashed into the area.

Only two of the seats were taken and Jack sat down opposite the shaven-headed lads tucking into their giant plates of 'propper' English grub. Both looked to be in their early twenties, and the scrawny one, wearing tattered jeans and a black tee shirt with a cartoon British bulldog emblazoned on it, had half a sausage paused on its way to his mouth, his eyes slitted as he watched Jack sit and lean back without a word.

Doc had him pegged as the follower, and the other as the alpha male. Or what might be considered one in this seedy dump. They didn't look like they might be brothers, so Doc assumed one was a Richardson, the other a Dooley. From what Charlie's sergeant had told them, Desmond 'Dezzy' Dooley was the gang leader, and the monster ignoring the two new arrivals fitted the description. A fierce redhead, with more freckles on his rotund face than pale skin, sported a thick pink scar running from above his left eye to his chin. Unlike the bony youth beside him, he had the build of a heavyweight boxer, with a thick neck and well-defined muscles bulging under his thin Union Jack tee shirt.

Jack slid his warrant card across the table to the edge of Dooley's plate, while Doc stood to one side, and leaned against the fence with his shoulder, observing.

'I need a word with you, Dezzy.'

'Piss off. I'm eatin.' Dooley tossed his head at his mate, full of bravado, still not looking at Jack or Doc. 'Can't even eat in peace without some piggy snufflin round.'

Jack slipped the warrant card back into his jacket pocket, leaned over and dragged the plate from under Dooley's nose. 'I said we need to talk. And I haven't got all day.'

Maybe Dooley was used to giving the locals the run around, but Jack's manner pulled him up short. Any certainty he had displayed for his mate's benefit dissolved, and Doc had to grin at the look of astonishment on Dooley's face as he sat with his knife and fork in his fists either side of where his plate should have been, unsure what to do.

'For fuck's sake. Give me that back.' Bluster wouldn't work, and Jack had the plate firmly in his grip, not that Dooley had tried to repossess it. 'You can't do that!'

'You can have it back, Dezzy. After we've had a little chat about Billy Leech.'

'Fuck off! I don't talk to no pigs.' The cutlery rattled to the table top, tossed there in disgust by Dooley as he sat back, and made a show of crossing his arms. 'Why don't you piss off back to London where you belong?'

'Listen to me, sonny boy. I will… But not before you've told me everything you know about young Billy. And I really haven't got all day. You see, I'm a homicide detective. Now, in case you inbred illiterates don't know, that means I'm investigating a suspicious death.' Jack picked a piece of bacon off the plate with his fingers, sniffed it, turned up his nose and replaced it, then stirred the baked beans with a finger before using Dooley's napkin to wipe his hands. 'I'm not interested in your petty theft, your dog-fighting, joy-riding, vandalism or anything else.' He slid the plate back in front of Dooley who, with eyes wide, looked at both the food and the detective with disgust. 'Apparently, you do speak to the police, Dezzy. My colleague, a female sergeant from Thatcham nick, tells me you think Billy Leech *is a nutter*. Your words. Why did you say that?'

'You can buy me another bleedin breakfast. I ain't eating that.' Dooley tried to sound menacing, puffing out his chest and thrusting his head at Jack. 'And I don't know no Billy Leech.'

Jack pulled out his phone and waggled it at Dooley. 'One call on this, and you'll both be escorted to Thatcham and detained by my colleagues there at my pleasure. I hope you and Tweedledum here don't have much planned for today. Or tomorrow. So, talk to me. Billy's no pal of yours, is he?'

Doc knew it was a bluff, but it sounded genuine enough, and clearly had the desired effect on the lad.

'We hardly know the cunt.' Dooley spread his hands wide, palms upwards as he lifted his shoulders. 'He's mental. Has he killed someone? I wouldn't be surprised. He latched on to us, but we told him to fuck off.'

'Why? What did he do?'

'You'll leave us be, if I tell ya?' Dooley did a drum roll on the table top with his fingers as he offered to do a deal. 'Off the record, right? And you'll buy me another breakfast?'

Jack pulled a ten pound note from his wallet, and placed it beside his phone. 'Good decision, Dezzy. So, what makes you say he's a nutter?'

Dooley propped his elbows on the table and used a finger to trace the line of his scar. 'This.'

Doc, having been silent throughout, couldn't help himself from probing, disbelief in his voice. 'He did that to you? Did he attack you with a knife?'

Dooley looked Doc up and down, then addressed Jack, obviously having decided who was the one with authority here. 'He didn't cut me deliberately. Wouldn't dare, the little shit.' More bravado. Doc thought Dooley's tone said otherwise, as did the sly look on his mate's face as he continued eating his plate of food in silence. 'It was an accident.'

'What sort of accident?'

'Well, it was an explosion, really.' Dooley's finger stroked his wound again. 'A car's windscreen blew out and some flying glass almost blinded me.'

'A stolen car?'

'Might've been. I can't remember.' He crossed his arms and rested them on his ample belly. 'I think we must've found it… Car's nuffin to do with me, anyway.'

'I don't care who stole it. Why did it blow up?'

'Maybe someone wanted to destroy the thing, stop you pigs finding any evidence of who'd nicked it.' He gave his mate a roguish grin, deluding himself he was full of artifice and cunning. 'Billy had been on about some special powder that would 'blit-erate the thing. That's what he said. Didn't tell us he'd chucked a load of it in the fuel tank though.'

'And when you guys lit it, it blew up instead of burning.'

'I didn't say we lit it.'

'But the car blew up unexpectedly, and almost cut your head off.' With an exas-perated tone, Jack fiddled with the ten-pound note, and waggled it at Dooley. 'Correct?'

'That's about the size of it. Motors normally burn a bit before the tank catches, so some people stuff a petrol soaked rag in the filler pipe to help it along. Even then, only a few go off like they do in the movies… *Allegedly*.' He sniggered, nudged his buddy who had almost finished gobbling down his food. 'Not that we're experts or nuffin, are we, Ritchie?'

Jack tapped the table top, impatient with Dooley's evasion. 'I'm not that inter-ested in what you and your bored mates get up to, Dezzy. Who lit it? You?'

'Billy lobbed a molly at it—'

'A what?'

'A Molotov. Petrol in a bottle with a rag to light it. He'd put a load of his magic powder in that too. Didn't warn us the bloody thing would go off like a grenade lobbed into a load of dynamite. Told the little bastard I'd fucking kill him if I saw him again. Ain't seen him since.'

Ritchie's eyebrows lifted on hearing that, but Doc was sure Dooley hadn't noticed his mute subordinate's non-verbal comment. He was too busy trying to impress everyone with his rapier wit.

'So, Billy's the one who turned you into Scarface… When was this?'

'Last year.' Another nudge and wink at his partner in crime as he chanted, 'Remember, remember… The fifth of November…'

'Bonfire Night. Let me guess. The burnt-out car's long gone.'

'Yeah. It was on the Kennet canal towpath. No idea how it got there. Honest, Guv.' A giggle and elbow dig in his mate's rib. 'The police put an *Abandoned Vehicle* sticker on it, then a few weeks later took it away and scrapped it.'

'Anything else? About Billy.'

'Ain't that enough?'

'What about that rabbit, Dezzy?' The skinny lad, having finished his breakfast, decided to join the conversation. Doc mentally tagged him as Richard 'Ritchie' Richardson, described by the sergeant as the lieutenant in their feeble gang.

'Ritchie's right, Detective. It was weird. I ain't never seen a bloke catch a wild rabbit with his bare hands before. That Billy, he's quick as a snake. Must be all that kung fu shit he does. Saw a flash of grey fur bobbing in the long grass, flew at it, rolled on the ground and stood up with it in his hand, holding the thing by its ears. Like a fuckin magician. Never seen nuffin like it.'

Doc closed his eyes, could see and feel a rabbit in his own hand, dangling, squealing with panic, trying to get away. Excitement swelled inside his chest, an overwhelming sense of having the power over life and death. Then he shook himself, disgusted at what he knew had come next. Part of his subconscious was thrilled by the creature's pain, while his conscious 'civilised' mind was appalled. He didn't need Dooley to tell him what happened, but Jack was probing for more.

'And what did he do with it?'

'He took out his knife and skinned it.'

'What? To eat it?'

'No. I knew he was a wrong 'un, but what he did to that rabbit was pure evil. The thing was wriggling, making an 'orrible noise. I ain't squeamish, but that turned my stomach. I told him to stop but he wouldn't. Said he was enjoying himself. Tortured it to death, he did. I ain't been able to eat rabbit since. That was right before he blew that car to kingdom come.'

Jack had heard enough, was already up, his phone to his ear as he turned to go back inside. Doc could see the anger on his face, his determination to nail Billy sparking in his eyes as he glanced at Doc, his head shaking in disbelief, but Doc had questions of his own for Dooley and his sidekick.

'The powder. Where did Billy get it?'

Dooley stood, Jack's money in his hand, clearly ready to order a fresh plate of food. The muscles of his neck and shoulders twitched in a vague shrug, one that said he couldn't care less. He followed Jack and forced Doc to step aside, pushing past while grunting, 'I have no fuckin clue.'

Ritchie Richardson apparently did. As his leader disappeared inside, he semi-whispered to Doc. 'He made it. Or said he did. Just like that batch of ice he sold Dezzy. Bullshit, I reckon.'

'Ice?' *Methamphetamine.* 'Crystal meth?'

'Yeah. Reckons he's a regular Walter White. You know. From the telly. The prat!'

Doc caught the reference to the *Breaking Bad* character—a fictional schoolteacher who cooked the illicit drug to pay off his medical bills for cancer treatment. Supplying ice to Dezzy explained how Billy had been able to get in with the gang of much older lads, if only for a few months. But was he really able to cook the chemicals himself? And where would he do it, given the poisonous gases and risk of massive explosions during manufacture? Like Ritchie, Doc was sceptical, but parked the thought.

'Dangerous stuff. I'm not surprised you didn't believe him.' Doc sat in Jack's seat, joining Richardson, who was rolling a cigarette between bony fingers, ratty eyes everywhere but on Doc. 'So why didn't your mate Dezzy punish Billy for doing that to his face? Or did he?'

Ritchie belched and Doc thought that might be the only answer he would get.

Perhaps he had misjudged Dooley's reluctant number two, but then Richardson said, 'Better out than in. And Dezzy won't admit it, but he's scared of Billy-the-kid.'

'Scared of him? He's just fifteen and Dezzy's a big fellah with a gang of mates. Why do you say that?'

'After the explosion, Billy was leaping about the place, like a lunatic. The nutter was so focused on the burning wreck he hadn't seen Dezzy go down, but the rest of us had. The twins went for him.'

'The twins?'

'Dezzy's younger bruvvers. We hang out together, his family and mine. Known each other since our dads did time together.'

That figured. Petty criminals, no doubt, breeding more petty criminals. It was the way of the world, a cycle Doc knew was difficult to break.

'These twins punished Billy? For Dezzy?'

'Nah!' Ritchie flicked his lighter several times, his other hand cupped around his skinny roll-up, showering sparks without a flame. He gave the thing a vigorous shake and kept Doc waiting while he went through the motions again, this time with success. He sucked in a lungful of smoke and blew it at Doc, eyes narrowed again. 'They're both big lads too, and Tommy grabbed Billy from behind in a bear hug, while Jimmy went to punch the mad bastard's face. Oh, fuck it!' The glowing red tip of his roll up dropped onto the table top, so he went through his lighting routine again.

Doc took the time to visualise the scenario, and wondered how Billy had escaped, though was sure it involved extreme violence. He could imagine how the lad felt to be held like that, and threatened with a blow from another assailant. Not fearful, but experiencing much the same thrill as he had when he caught the rabbit.

'Billy hurt them too, didn't he?'

Richardson dipped his head, finally made eye contact as he replied. 'All three Dooleys ended up in hospital that day. The twins had several broken ribs, a broken arm and a dislocated knee between the two of 'em. I ain't ever seen that Billy do his kung fu shit before, but he was like one of those MMA fighters—fuckin crazy too.'

'MMA? Mixed Martial Arts?' That received a nod from Ritchie whose eyes had shifted again. 'You and your brothers did nothing to help them?'

'Not on your life, pal.' Beady eyes squinted at Doc through another puff of smoke, then Ritchie paused as he pinched a few stray strands of tobacco from the tip of his tongue, deposited there by the soggy end of his DIY cigarette. 'Billy just stood there, waiting for us to have a go. I told him to fuck off, but he wanted to watch the fire burn, so stood there staring at it for a few minutes, ignoring the Dooleys moaning and groaning on the ground nearby. A couple of us went to help the poor bastards, but he just glared at us, so we backed off. Once the flames had died down a bit, he threatened all of us just before he left. Me, my three brothers and the Dooleys.'

'Threatened you with what?'

'He said it real quiet, like. Not aggressive. Menacing...' Doc noticed the remnants of the cigarette quivering in Ritchie's fingers as he paused, thinking back to that day. 'Said to keep well out of his way if we saw him again... Told us he would kill the next one of us to a lay a finger on him.'

'And you believed him?'

'Too bleedin right, I did. I'd heard about his old man and uncle. Both of 'em murderers. Even topped members of their own family, they did... Billy reckoned they'd told him killing was in his genes too, and he was looking forward to his coming of age. Asked if any of us wanted to volunteer to be his first. None of us said nuffin. He just laughed like a lunatic then jogged off. We've seen him around a few times since, but steer well clear. We're no angels, but he weren't kidding about his family… The Leeches. They're all fucking mental, mate.'

'One last thing, Ritchie. The flames from that explosion. Anything odd about them?'

'Funny you should mention that. I thought that car went up like a truckload of giant fireworks, but my brother reckoned there was dead people's spirits trapped inside, released by the flames. Looked real ghostly… Burning with a weird green glow.'

'Doc!' Jack poked his head round the pub's rear door. 'We've got to go. Charlie reckons they've found something.'

While Smith drove, Billy checked his iPhone for the umpteenth time today. There had been no mention of the exploding boat on the national news last night or this morning, so he had been monitoring the Reading Chronicle website, but had been disappointed to read nothing there either.

Someone must have been on the boat when it went up, triggering the device with the ignition key. But if that person had died, why was there no mention of it anywhere? Surely such a violent death was plenty newsworthy enough.

Billy expected to see the incident described as an accident too, though knew the fire service would investigate and almost certainly find the cause of the explosion.

Another problem for Smiffy…

'What are you giggling about?' Smith glanced down but Billy angled the screen away from him as he scrolled through the local news site. 'You're a weird one, lad.'

'That's a bit rich, coming from a fucking paedo.'

Billy was still furious at being threatened again, and let the anger bristle in his tone, but then he was almost overcome with joy as he spotted a headline about yesterday's event:

ONE DEAD IN PANGBOURNE BOAT BLAST

I've done it! I've killed Powers!

His first victim.

Smith was muttering something in reply, but Billy couldn't hear him. Another voice, his guru, was praising him for his achievement.

Well done, Billy boy. I knew you could do it!

But as he read the article, slivers of doubt became gaping holes in his conviction that Powers had died. There was no one named in the article, although there was a hint that it wasn't the old bastard himself who Billy had turned into a crispy critter. The journalist described the deceased as a 'young man'.

Bollocks!

Maybe it was an error, but Billy thought back to yesterday, to who else had been around at Powers' home at lunch time. Some bloke had been in his study, messing with his computer... He was much younger than Powers. His guru's voice murmured in his head:

Don't you disappoint me, Billy... You need to make sure he's dead, my son.

There was no longer any joy to be had, no gloating to be done. The warm glow from his uncle's adulation had lasted just seconds. He had to stop himself from grinding his teeth, the pressure of his clamped jaws surely enough to crack the enamel. Murderous rage pumped through Billy's heart as Smith parked on Nana's driveway. At least he wouldn't have to deal with his mother right now—there was no sign of her car.

Billy jumped out, and shoved his key into the front door lock, looking back at Smiffy as he went inside. 'You should take the car round the side, and we'll put the bag in the cellar. The door's open. It's that side.' He pointed. 'I'll get the photos for you.' He slammed the door, cutting off Smith's reply.

'Well you could've told me before I parked and—'

Moaning old git.

Billy had been too preoccupied to bother making life easy for Smiffy. In his haste, he also failed to spot the scrap of paper and the card on the hall floor. He bounced up the stairs to his room, unlocked the bedside drawer and took the items he needed. By the time he reached the cellar door, Smith had parked alongside and had the boot open, ready for them to heave the sack of ANFO down the stone steps.

'Before we do that, how about writing that note to my mum?' Billy waved a brown envelope at Smith. 'And you can have these too.'

Smith followed him to the kitchen, snatched the package from Billy's fingers and took out the contents. 'Okay. Are they all here?' Smith inspected them, replaced them in the envelope, folded and pocketed it. 'And how do I know you don't have copies?'

'Why would I bother? They're no use to me now, are they?' Billy tried to look honest as he spoke, despite what was in his mind. 'If you talk to the police about all that other stuff, like you said earlier, I'm screwed too.'

'Mmm.' Smiffy so obviously wanted to be convinced, but also had a suspicious mind. 'You double cross me, and I swear—'

'No more threats. Just write the note. There's a pad and pen by the fridge. Keep it short and sweet. *I have to go away. I'm sorry.* That'll do it'

'Okay. You can explain it to her. Tell her what you like.' It took Smith seconds to scribble the lines. Billy took the note, hustled him outside to grab the bag and help him down the steps with it. Not that he needed help. He could have handled the sack of damp chemicals by himself, but it would make things much easier with Smiffy in the cellar.

'Aaargh!' On the bottom step, Billy yelped with pain and let go of his corner of the bag. 'My back. Oh, bloody hell, I pulled a muscle during karate training and it's just ripped again.' Smiffy peered up at him in the poor light, and Billy made a show of clutching the offending body part, grimacing with pain. 'Ow, that really hurt. Can you just put the sack in that corner by the shelves?'

'Yeah, then I'm out of here, kid.'

Smith turned away, dragging the bag the few paces to the corner, unhurried.

Billy moved fast.

The small bottle in his pocket—the one that had been in his bedside drawer until a few minutes before—contained a powerful homemade concoction. An enhanced mixture based on bleach and alcohol, a recipe he had learnt during another chemistry experiment he and his tutor had worked on many months before. *Time to test it, ready for the big day.* As he poured half the contents onto a cotton face flannel, also taken from his bedroom, he held his breath to avoid inhaling any of the chloroform.

Smith stood upright again, having stooped to place the bag where Billy had indicated, but he still had his back to his precocious pupil—now right behind him. Billy's left arm snaked around Smiffy's neck and his right hand simultaneously clamped the saturated cloth over Smiffy's nose. A brief struggle ensued, with Smith's fingers clawing at Billy's arms, but within seconds the feeble motion ceased. Billy was thrilled to feel his victim wriggling, electric with fear, then sagging, unconscious. He dropped Smiffy to the floor, and heard the thud as his tutor's head slammed against the concrete.

Careful, son. Don't mess him up more than you need to…

A karate blow or stranglehold could have easily knocked Smiffy cold, but both techniques held the possibility of unintended death rather than unconsciousness. The idea was not to harm him any more than necessary, nor leave any clues that he had been held against his will. For what Billy had in mind, Smiffy needed to be alive.

No worries, Uncle. Smiffy'll be messed up far worse by the time I'm finished with him.

With almost a tender touch, Billy pulled off Smith's jacket, took the envelope from the pocket, then stripped his victim until he was just in underpants and socks. He folded the jacket and bagged it with the other clothes for later use, sniggering at the thought of how he would secure his victim—also for later use…

Gramps favoured reinforced packaging tape to seal the stored boxes—the ones Billy had ripped open earlier in the year—and had plenty of it stored in a bag on the shelf. Now he used a roll to bind Smiffy's arms and legs, hog-tying him before pulling him into a sitting position. More tape was wound around Smiffy's neck, securing him to an old cast iron boiler pipe affixed to the wall next to the sack of ANFO, then Billy taped the man's eyes and mouth, leaving his nose free to continue breathing. Smith was still out cold.

Many things had not worked out as planned, and the lingering prospect that Powers had not been the one to die on the boat was still bugging Billy. His mother had seen fit to get sober just in time to totally screw his plans for Nana too. She was probably no longer off her head either as he hadn't been able to administer any drugs since Saturday. He had been certain the shit smeared bedroom and bathroom would have been the final straw, enough to convince his mother that the old dear would be better looked after in that care home. He had prepared everything, had all the papers filled out ready for her to sign—had been badgering her for months to commit to dumping the dopey old bat. It was too late for that now.

How did it all go so wrong?

He leaned down as he heard Smith groaning, gradually coming to, and grabbed the envelope, thinking he would put it back in his room before heading out this evening. As for all the things that had conspired to screw up his day, well, he decided, none of it mattered. He would revise his plans and Nana would just have to take her chances, it was as simple as that. And now, he had an ace up his sleeve.

Well, in his cellar.

'You'll live, Smiffy…' Billy patted his unconscious victim on his head, tittering as he added, 'But not for long!'

Suzie drove south from Wallingford while her mother prattled on about the views of the Thames and the picturesque countryside on their way home. Although she nodded and gave the occasional grunt in acknowledgement, her mind was elsewhere. The damning email from the laboratory had arrived as she had been about to tuck into her lunch.

The best piece of news had been at the top of her mother's report—tests had confirmed there were no signs of dementia and Suzie had been delighted to share that information. Nana had ordered a sherry to celebrate while Suzie sipped her sparkling water, trying to blot out the other details she had scanned in her mother's report. She desperately wanted to read both sets of results, to absorb the details properly, but decided to wait until she was home.

The email contained one other reassuring bit of news that jumped out at her during her brief scan of the documents. The test results from the bottles. At least Billy had not been lying about that, and had 'only' been feeding her Temazepam, not rat poison as she had originally assumed.

That was the extent of any positive news from today's outing. Suzie's appetite shrivelled in the few moments she spent flicking through the rest of their results— had to put her smartphone away, otherwise she would have exploded with rage. Her mother was having such a great time, thoroughly enjoying her food, and was borderline radiant as she reminisced about previous visits to the pub with Suzie's father. It seemed to help her mother finally come to terms with her loss, and Suzie didn't want to dispel her good mood.

By the time they arrived home, Nana had piped down, tired from her day's adventures. She said she was heading to bed for a doze, which suited Suzie just fine.

Time to think.

As they stepped over the threshold, Suzie spotted the note lying on the edge of the doormat alongside a business card, as if brushed there by the door being opened. Her mother hadn't noticed and was already clambering up the stairs, but Suzie recognised the printed emblem on the card even before stooping to pick up the items.

The Metropolitan Police?

She had dealt with them before, in the aftermath of that last night in her Chelsea home, but this was unexpected. The card was from a Detective Chief Inspector Jack Carver. As was the note. It was scribbled on a scrap from a pocket book, and the words set her nerves jangling.

Please call me immediately you read this, Mrs Leech. I need to speak to you urgently about your son, Billy. Thank you. DCI Carver

Was this about the attack on Professor Maddox's car and driver? Surely a senior detective from London would not be involved in such a trivial matter.

What else has Billy been up to?

Suzie went to the kitchen and sat at the table, then laid out the card with the note and placed her phone beside them. She was tempted to call the detective right away, but decided to review the contents of the lab reports before doing so.

With a sickening dread squirming through her bowels, she opened the email and took her time reading through the results. The implications were even worse than she had imagined on first skimming through the contents. The covering letter had been a shock too. The clinic suggested both Suzie and her mother would benefit from attending a rehabilitation centre, and provided links to several local establishments offering facilities designed to help 'alcoholics, drug addicts and other individuals with problems related to substance abuse'.

Suzie was prepared to hold her hands up to being guilty, but her mother? No. However, the clinic could only go by the results they had found, and their analyses suggested otherwise.

Traces of LSD had been found in her mother's blood, along with a range of anti-depressants, opiates and the sleeping pill, Temazepam. Suzie's results were similar, but without the LSD. Where had that come from? And how did it get into her mother's blood—along with the opiates? Maybe the latter could be explained. Perhaps some of Nana's anti-depressants contained them, but Suzie knew in her heart that it was her linctus that had somehow made its way into her mother's body.

And the LSD?

Had Billy been doctoring Nana's food or drink with that hallucinogenic? And why?

He had admitted feeding his mother Temazepam, so the idea was no longer as outrageous as it would have seemed just a couple of days before.

Hallucinations. Poor Mother.

Suzie picked up Jack Carver's card and fondled her phone. She needed help to understand what was happening, but would the detective be sympathetic? Doubtful, given the terse note. Just for some smashed headlights.

And a grown man felled by a single karate kick to the head.

Billy's face that night, swooped at her again, contorted in fury. She had been shocked by the degree of violence, delivered so casually.

Just like his father.

Oh, God help me!

She fingered the phone, wondering what to do, then decided. Before she saw this policeman, she would talk to Billy. Confront him again, tonight, with hard evidence of what he had been doing to them both.

What else have you been up to, son?

Suzie had not been inside his bedroom for over two years. He had insisted he could keep it tidy and clean, that she didn't need to bother—just as she hadn't with so many other maternal duties. And anyway, he didn't want her poking around in his things, he'd said. In her drugged state, that had seemed like a decent enough bargain.

Not any more.

Suzie swept the three items off the table into her handbag before dumping it in a drawer in her bedroom, then continued up the top flight of stairs to the attic. The skull and cross bones logo, outlined in black on a vivid yellow background, was stuck to Billy's bedroom door above a warning, stencilled in red, decorated with blood coloured droplets:

KEEP OUT!

ON PAIN OF DEATH

The warning had not been there the last time Suzie had ventured this far up the stairs, and most mothers would think little of it—such exaggeration was only to be expected from any normal adolescent boy.

But Billy's anything but normal.

For Suzie, the message resonated in a disturbing way, and she hesitated as she went to grasp the door handle. Perhaps Billy was inside. Could he be back from his outing with Mr Smith already? She knocked, just in case, with a gentle tap on the door, and half whispered to him.

'Billy? Are you in there?'

He occasionally slept in the afternoons, blaming his growth spurts for the need to rest, so she tried to make as little sound as she could while turning the knob, telling herself it was for his benefit, rather than to appease her own timidity. The latch disengaged but the door would not budge.

Locked?

Since when had Billy taken to locking his door?

This time her fist hammered on the wooden panelling, her voice angry and no longer a whisper.

'Billy! You open this door, right now!'

With no answer forthcoming, she turned and jogged down the stairs to the kitchen to search for the key. Billy may not have realised, but her father had kept a skeleton key that would unlock all internal doors—a safety measure she remembered he'd insisted on from when she was a small child. It took her a few minutes of frenetic scrabbling in the drawers to locate it, then she stormed back up to the attic room, fitted the key into the lock and burst in.

The evil that greeted her almost bowled her straight back down the stairs again, and she had to hold on to the door handle to steady herself. An involuntary gasp at the sight burst from her throat, then her legs gave way. She collapsed to her hands and knees, her back arching as caustic projectile vomit streamed from her belly and bounced across the floorboards beneath her.

Doc was beginning to wonder if Jack would burn a hole in his lounge carpet, pacing back and forth as he was, propelled by anger and frustration.

'Sit down, Jack. We'll just have to wait.'

'I can't.' Jack stopped pacing, turned his back on Doc and peered out of the patio windows at the two detectives at the end of the garden. 'We've been waiting over an hour for the Keystone Cops to get their arses back in here... I can't believe they're still treating us like suspects.'

Doc patted the sofa cushion next to him. 'Come on, just sit. Try to relax—'

'RELAX?' The detectives must have heard Jack's roar, their attention momentarily on the house before shifting back to the police tug hoisting the remains of the burnt-out boat onto a barge. Jack clasped his hands over his head and rubbed at his scalp, took a few paces towards the sofa and tried to smile at Doc as he apologised. 'Sorry, mate. I'm just... I dunno. My daughter almost died yesterday. And she hates *me* for what happened to Felix.'

Doc had not been listening to the phone call Jack had made while driving them back from Newbury, but had heard Jack cursing when he'd been cut off by his wife immediately after he asked—then demanded—to speak to Sally. That was shortly before they arrived back here, only to be told that Charlie was off the case and the two detectives now engrossed in the recovery of the boat were investigating the crime.

According to Charlie, the divers had recovered an item that confirmed this was a deliberate act of arson, but the detectives had stonewalled them, and told Jack and Doc to wait in the lounge until they were ready to interview them. Jack's allies, Charlie and her sergeant, had been called back to their office, leaving just the police divers and detectives at the scene. The tug and barge had arrived shortly after Doc and Jack pulled into the driveway, and they had been forced to wait in the house, and do no more than watch, ever since.

Doc had been trying to calm Jack from the moment he first blew up at the other detectives, yelling his suspicions about Billy Leech in response to their instructions to remain on the premises. It didn't help when the lead detective, DI Hammond, a gentleman with all the charm of a flatulent horse's rear end, had said, 'Your boss, Chief Superintendent Dawson, warned us about you, Carver. She said you'd want to dominate things, take over, even though this is outside your patch *and* you're supposed to be on holiday. She told me to tell you that if you interfere with our investigation in any way, she'll have your badge.'

Doc had grabbed Jack's right arm, saw his fist balling, ready to swing at the other policeman's head. It had been just enough to prevent the assault, but Jack's anger had been brewing like a volcano ever since.

'We'll just have to do things their way, Jack. And I doubt Billy will be going anywhere. Probably assumed we'd think it was an accident.' Doc didn't really believe that. He too was convinced the boy was at the heart of these terrible events, especially after their chat with Dooley and Richardson. The dead pets were a warning, a threat, so Doc felt sure that Billy meant for him to connect the dots. Eventually. 'I doubt he has any inkling that he's on *your* radar for this already.'

Jack finally let go of his head as he dropped to the sofa beside Doc, breathing a weary sigh.

'I s'pose you're right.'

'We'll get him. Just play along with these two, and if they won't listen, we'll continue making our own enquiries. Sound fair?'

'Yeah. Thanks, Doc.'

Just then, Hammond strolled into the lounge, carrying an evidence bag with what looked to Doc like the boat's petrol filler cap attached to part of the pipe. He chucked it on to the coffee table in front of his 'suspects' with a theatrical flourish, and waited for a response.

'What the fuck?' Jack grabbed the bag to inspect the contents through the clear plastic. 'Someone's welded a spark plug inside it.'

Doc could see the lock barrel had been drilled out, and the electrical component poked through from the underside of the cap. It was not a very subtle modification, the tip of the plug was visible, poking proud of the chrome domed upper part of the cap, but creating the thing was not a five-minute operation. Surely no one could have modified it on board the boat—using a welding torch by the open filler pipe. He was about to say so, but the detective had rather more pressing questions of his own.

'According to the fire officers, this was connected by a high-tension lead rigged through to the ignition. Now, can either of you clever fellows tell me why the boat owner didn't notice a bloody great wire hanging off the filler cap of his petrol tank?

Especially with the *brilliant* Detective Jack Carver wandering around the place all week-end?' Doc and Jack exchanged glances, but neither of them had a viable explanation. The cocky detective continued. 'Or why a bloke with no boating experience, no skip-per's licence, was *sent* aboard this potential fire bomb, with the key in his hand. And—'

'Now, hang on a minute—'

Doc could feel Vesuvius rumbling beside him, and his hand was on Jack's arm again, silently urging his friend to maintain his self-control.

'And the bloke in question happens to be the same young man the so-called bril-liant detective was mouthing off about just last week. The newly promoted Detective Chief Inspector was at the pub, celebrating the news of his elevated status...' The policeman, trying hard to look threatening but failing badly, took a pace forward, bent slightly from the waist and put his face close to Jack's as he spelt out the accusa-tion, waggling his finger under Jack's nose. 'Telling any of his colleagues who could be bothered to listen to his drunken ranting, how much he despised his daughter's fiancé, and how he was dreading spending several days on his mate's boat getting to know the lad.'

'I don't think this is helpful, Detective.' Doc glanced at Jack, could see him trying to contain the pressure building inside, could see the blood surging into his neck and face. Doc gave his right forearm a reassuring squeeze while trying to smooth things. 'You can't seriously think Jack—'

The detective ignored Doc, and spoke over him, still with his accusatory finger in Jack's face. '*I could wring his bloody neck.* Isn't that what you said, Carver?'

'Jack...' Doc held on to his friend's arm, the muscles beneath his fingers tense and rigid.

'And, this.' He straightened, took his notebook from his jacket pocket, and made a show of checking what was written there before he added, '*I'd happily murder the bastard... If I thought I could get away with it.* So, DCI Carver. Did you? Murder your future son-in-law?' He stared at Jack, contempt rippling his mouth. 'With your own daughter aboard—?'

Jack rocketed off the sofa, the large muscles of his thighs powering his upper body at his unprepared colleague. He almost dislocated Doc's shoulder as his arm arced forward and up, still with Doc's restraining hand attached, barely diminishing the power from Jack's fist as it connected with the tip of Hammond's chin.

The detective sailed backwards across the coffee table, shattering it as he landed.

After retching so hard she thought her guts would turn inside out, Suzie backed away from Billy's bedroom, still on all fours, then managed to haul herself upright using the bannister rail. Her entire being was aquiver, and she just wanted to get away from the hideous images, to quaff a bottle of linctus and then stew in an alco-holic haze until the horrific memories subsided again.

She took two tentative steps in the direction of her remaining stash of codeine syrup, but stopped herself before weakness drove her any further down the stairs.

Dear God. Please give me strength to see what else is in there.

Minutes ticked by with her standing motionless, a statue at the head of the stairs, her back to the dreadful place she knew she must re-enter. Her mouth was parched and her tongue tasted foul, the back of her throat raw from the scalding acid ejected from her stomach, along with her semi-digested lunch. She was giddy and light-headed, too.

A few more moments of prayer gave her the courage to turn back and face up to the shrine in Billy's room.

She closed her eyes as she entered, her bare toes slipping in the sludge she had unexpectedly deposited on the bare floorboards. After another brief one-sided conversation with her god, she forced her eyelids open and took in the full horror of his room.

The sloping eaves and gable ends had been painted black, giving the room an ominous feel, but it was the photographs that had sent her mind back to a place and time she had tried to blot from her memory. The biggest image, about half the size of the bedroom door, was pinned to the wall opposite the foot of Billy's bed. Several black candles were positioned on a ledge beneath the oversized picture of a grinning face.

Suzie could barely stop the panic rising in her chest, her breath ragged and panting as she made herself confront the larger than life photograph of her brother-in-law, Peter. Her mind was spinning as she tried to understand why her son apparently worshipped the man who had stolen half her face—and almost taken her desire to live along with it.

More thoughts tumbled into her brain about that night, about how Billy had met his uncle for the first and only time, and how he had been used by Peter as an unwitting accomplice in the murder of her husband, Shaun.

Why has Billy got this on his wall? And where did he get it?

Peter had been in prison for years before the night he entered their London home. He had only stayed for an hour or two, but the mayhem he had wreaked in that brief visit had ruined their lives forever.

From the look of it, the headshot had been taken not long before then. Suzie couldn't scrutinise it, could barely look into the mad green eyes of her assailant, even knowing he had been dead for seven years. She ran at the wall, ripped the poster down, shredded it and threw the scrunched-up pieces to the floor.

There were precious few other items on the end wall, just a few esoteric notes from Billy to himself and someone he called his 'Guru', but the eaves displayed many other portrait photographs, too, some with names she recognised.

John Wayne Gacy... The Night Stalker... Dr Harold Shipman...

Her little boy, the fragile sensitive lad she'd birthed and nurtured, had clearly developed an unhealthy fascination with serial killers. Perhaps, given his genetic make-up and life experiences, Suzie ought not be surprised. Thinking back, he was always a slightly odd child, different from the other kids, far brighter and less emotional—unless hurt by his father's cruel jibes and insults, and then he would come crying to her for a cuddle to make things better. That was before the vicious bastard in that poster had come calling.

Poor Billy... I wasn't there for him when he needed me most.

Suzie bowed her head and closed her eyes in another silent prayer. She begged forgiveness for herself, and asked for help for her son. Again, the simple act gave her the strength to continue.

What else has he got in here?

A shelf below his TV contained hundreds of DVDs. Mostly TV documentaries about serial killers, criminal psychopaths and unsolved crimes. Interviews with real life killers, FBI profilers and forensic psychologists. He even had a video lecture series from a criminology course filmed at Birmingham University.

Suzie found none of the teenage dross she would've expected, and his games console had been lying unused for years—he had told her, they were a waste of time, that they were 'for morons'. She had been thankful for that, thinking the violence they engendered would be a bad thing for him, but surely this obsession with actual criminals—as that's what it seemed to be—was far worse.

An obsession with serial killers, but most worryingly, one in particular.

Billy's bookcase extended from beside his bed to the doorway, but only reached hip height where the walls began sloping to the apex of the roof. She ran a finger along the spines, reading random titles. The shelves were stuffed full of texts with a similar theme to the DVDs, but as she reached his bedside drawers, she picked up the hardback book lying there. She flipped it over without thinking and the picture on the cover startled her, burning her fingers before it flew to the ground.

The same image she had torn from Billy's wall…

She kicked the offending book away, and it skidded across the rug and under the bed.

Best place for it.

She tugged at the handle of the top bedside drawer.

Locked.

Two more drawers. Also locked. And this time, she had no idea where a spare key might be.

Suzie would not be beaten by her son's desire for privacy. She went back downstairs and out to her father's workshop, found a crowbar and returned. With the thin end wedged in the gap between the drawer and the frame, she levered the tool and the splintering wood gave her a moment's satisfaction. She sat on the bed, popped open the top drawer, and picked up the first thing she saw.

A twist of paper?

There were two more, and although she had never bought illicit drugs in her life, Suzie instinctively knew that's what these little baggies contained. She popped them on the bed, thinking she could have the contents tested at the clinic she had been to the previous day. But was that wise? If they were class A drugs—and Suzie had no idea what that really meant—she might end up being arrested. If she tried to explain, Billy would surely lie about them, would tell the police they were hers—or that he had bought them for her.

Better to just flush them down the lavatory.

After putting that at the top of her to do list, she turned her attention back to the broken drawer.

The folded brown A4 envelope was unsealed, and had nothing written on it to give a clue to its contents, but she could feel documents inside as she lifted it out.

More photographs of Peter? God, help me…

She wanted to toss it aside, but something told her, a whisper in her brain, that it was important and she needed to see it, making her wonder if God had replied to her pleas for help.

With her eyes closed, she upended the contents into her lap, and tried to stop her body from shaking by holding the air in her lungs and balling her fists. That didn't help much, so she did her best to prepare herself, then blinked her eyes open again for a quick glance at the jumble of photographs spread across her thighs.

Initial relief, that she was not being faced with more mugshots of the man who had tortured her, turned to horror and disgust.

Bare flesh. Lots of it…

Two males in pornographic positions. She made herself look at them, properly this time, while wondering why Billy had them in his bedside drawer. The possibility that her son might be gay had not really registered, but started to form in her mind a nanosecond before she recognised the participants.

Suzie fainted.

———

Judy pulled into her driveway and saw the burnt-out boat being towed away on a barge just leaving the dock at the end of the garden. There were no police vehicles present, but Sally's Peugeot was still where Felix had parked it and Jack's Jag was in front of one of their garage doors. The other door was shut too, so she assumed Doc's new car, a swanky Aston Martin, was tucked up safely inside.

The trouble-making detective must be in the house with Colin. After turning off the ignition she sat with her hands on the wheel, and rolled her shoulders several times to ease the tension in her neck and upper back.

It had been a long and productive day, diverting her from the previous day's tragedy, but now she just wanted to relax, and Jack's presence was not wholly conducive to that aim. Colin had insisted on working with him, to find out why the boat exploded and whether Billy Leech was responsible, and she knew there was little point trying to convince him otherwise.

With a final shrug she prepared herself to talk to them both without getting upset, and let herself into the house. The scent of exotic spices welcomed her home. Colin heard her come in, and greeted her from the kitchen.

'I'm in here, my love.'

She immediately knew there was something amiss. His tone just sounded wrong, and it was not his usual cheerful greeting. He appeared at the kitchen door as she dropped her bag on the hall table, and she could see his cheeks had a sickly pallor to them.

'Are you alright? What's happened?'

He came to her and gave her a hug, then whispered in her ear. 'I'm fine. It's Jack…'

Bloody Jack, again.

'What's happened?' She pulled away from him and peered up at his face.

'We had another explosion here a little earlier—Jack blew his top and assaulted a local detective. Knocked the man cold.'

'What? Why?'

Doc explained, then said, 'They took him into Reading, to the police station. I followed them but they refused to let me see him. I got back here almost two hours ago but haven't heard from him.'

'They arrested him?'

'No… They detained him. No handcuffs, just demanded he accompany them, or they would arrest him for assaulting a fellow police officer. He was pretty sheepish by then.'

'They can't honestly believe he would kill Felix. That's just… It's ridiculous!' Judy knew enough about the man to know he would never kill anyone, unless in the line of duty. He had saved Colin's life on at least one occasion she knew of, doing exactly that.

'It's just a bit of muscle flexing by the locals. Turf battle. But they wouldn't listen to anything we had to say about Billy Leech. And today, we found out more about that young man and the things he's been up to.'

Judy placed her index finger on his lips and shushed him. 'I don't want to hear his name again. I don't want to know what you've discovered... But if he did kill Felix, I *do* want him caught and punished. I'm sure the local police will listen once they've finished putting Jack in his place.'

'Well, let's hope so.' Doc twitched a smile, the first she had seen since arriving, and then said, 'I've made us some curry. I had to keep busy while waiting for Jack.'

'I knew I could smell something marvellous. I'm starving too. Let me get changed and we'll eat.'

Doc nodded and then his mobile phone chirped. 'That could be Jack.' He disappeared into the kitchen so she went up to their bedroom, tossed her blouse and trousers into the laundry bin, pulled on yoga pants and a tee shirt.

By the time she got down the stairs, Doc was in the hallway, his jacket over his shoulder and his car key in his hand.

'You're not going out now, we're about to eat—'

'Sorry, I have to go sweetheart. I'm not really hungry and I'll be back soon enough. Your food's ready and I've left a plate in the kitchen.' He went to peck her cheek but she turned away from him.

'You aren't looking after yourself, Colin. You should eat too.'

'I will. Later. I really do need to go and—'

'I don't want to know. Just you take care.'

She left him dithering in the hallway, clearly wondering whether to follow her into the kitchen to try to explain. He didn't.

Judy heard the front door close as she sat at the kitchen table, a steaming plate of vegetable korma waiting for her. She picked up a fork, then a feeling of dread folded itself around her, like an ominous fog warning of terrible things afoot.

Why didn't I let him kiss me?

She knew why.

She had not forgiven him for inviting the Leech boy into their lives.

With the fork still clutched in her hand, she raced down the hall, wrenched the front door open, only to see Doc's Aston Martin disappear round the bend in their lane.

'Let me know if you need anything else, Mum. I'll be downstairs.' Suzie carried the tray with the remains of their supper to the door, her own food barely touched, but Nana had wiped her plate clean.

'I'll just read my book and watch some TV later. Thank you for today, my dear. I hope we can do it more often. I feel stronger already.'

Her mother's rosy cheeks were testament to that, and Suzie forced another smile before leaving her to her book.

When she'd regained consciousness, she had no idea how much time had elapsed with her spark out on Billy's bed, but she needed to get out of there, and had taken the envelope and photographs to the kitchen. They remained piled on the table as she made food for them all. Billy was still out, but she assumed he would be back soon, unless he was still angry with her. He wasn't in his annex—she had checked.

While waiting for the kettle to boil, Suzie picked up her phone again, and tried the detective's number. It was still diverted to voicemail and she had already left a message for him to call her, but had heard nothing from him, and that had been hours ago.

Her plan had been to confront her son over his heinous actions. What child would even think of drugging his mother and grandmother? She would also tackle his fixation on his murderous uncle. All of this, before talking to the police, but the photographs changed everything.

Suzie had made herself properly scrutinise the images, and had concluded they had been taken soon after the tutor had begun teaching her son a couple of years before. Billy's face was still almost cherubic, feminine, his body smaller, and his jaw lacked the profusion of whiskers that had sprouted since.

Her conclusion was horrifyingly simple. Smith had been molesting her boy from the moment he'd arrived here. And that had driven Suzie to call DCI Carver.

With no immediate reply, she had considered dialling 999 or calling the local police station, but this other detective had already expressed an interest in her son. Okay, he was probably concerned about Billy's violent display on Saturday, but Suzie was sure her young lad, abused by a trusted adult, had good reason to go off the rails, and she wanted this London detective to understand that, too.

A vulnerable young boy, coerced into homosexual acts by his teacher.

This, on top of what had transpired at their home when Billy was an eight-year-old. And the traumatic years he had been bullied at school. Well, it was no surprise he was as disturbed as she now knew him to be.

But how to help him?

A senior detective might know, and would certainly be in a position to arrest Smith. The odious man must have seen Billy as a soft target, a damaged young boy, and manipulated him into complying.

Why else would Billy have said nothing to her?

Alcoholism…

Drug addiction…

Derelict mother…

There were plenty of reasons, and most of them stemmed from her inability to deal with anything much beyond her own deformed face.

Poor Billy.

At least she was drinking tea tonight instead of Martinis. She plopped a teabag in her cup and was about to pour boiling water on it, when Billy's voice ripped into her brain, throwing her arm into a spasm, spilling the scalding liquid down her leg. She screeched and jumped back, upending the kettle contents on to the counter top, and spun round to face him.

'YOU FUCKING BITCH!'

Framed in the back doorway, wearing a garish green cycling top and black lycra shorts, she could barely look at his face, warped as it was in a demented scowl. His eyes weren't on her, but on the table top, staring at the photographs.

'Billy—'

'You've been in my room, rooting through my private things!' He started towards her, and she cringed away, trying to keep the table between them until the murderous light in his eyes faded. 'What else have you found?'

Billy stopped circling, so she did too, glad for the solid wood separating them, though her mind replayed how his fists had effortlessly caused the top to crack.

'What else? Isn't that enough? Smith has been abusing you!' She jabbed a finger on the pile of photographs and spread them for him. 'And there's the proof of it. I want him arrested.'

With his fists still bunched, resting on the top of a chair back, she could see him take stock of this unexpected situation. The fury abated, and for a fleeting moment he seemed to be calculating, like a machine, his eyes scuttling across her face, then back to the photographs. He pulled the chair out from under the table, the legs squealing on the tiles in protest. Then he sat, and did the one thing she least expected.

He dropped his head to the table top with a thump. Then his hands cradled his forehead and she could see his back shuddering.

He's crying!

It was the first time she'd seen him shed any tears in years. So long that she couldn't recall the last time he had shown any weakness—certainly not since he had started speaking again. She went to him, dropped to her knees and held him as he sobbed.

The sound almost ruptured her heart, and she felt her own tears start to flow.

'Billy. It's alright. It's not your fault. But we must talk to the police.'

All thoughts of his misdemeanours had been chased away and she felt only sympathy for his plight, but he lifted his head from his arms and focussed his ire on her.

'Don't you dare talk to the pigs! I'll be sixteen on Wednesday. What we've been doing will be totally legal then.'

Suzie leaned back, away from his snapping voice, but kept her hands on his back and arm. She would not—could not—let her son allow Smith to get away with what he had done.

'I've called them already—'

Billy leapt from his chair, sending it spinning backwards so hard that it dented the fridge door. His arm flailed, causing Suzie to fall. She ended up sprawled on her back, staring up at his livid, crimson face. He seemed possessed. Even his eyes had changed colour—demonic, glowing, almost emerald green now, rather than a beautiful turquoise. It was a trick of the light—at least, that was what she would tell herself later.

'What did you say to them?'

'Nothing... I just asked a detective to call me back. I thought—'

'Just shut your ugly, stupid mouth... Now, you listen to me.' Billy dropped to his knees, beside her, a fist raised above her face, malicious intent emanating from his. His other hand grabbed the front of her blouse and yanked it, lifting her head clear of the ground, then he leaned in to whisper in her ear. 'I... Love... Smiffy.'

Suzie was beyond words. There was not much worse that he could say or do to her. The term Stockholm Syndrome came into her head. Smith had indoctrinated her son.

He doesn't mean it.

'Please, Billy. He's been using you—'

'You know nothing! He's been more of a father to me than my old man ever was. More of a parent to me than you've ever been. I love him more than I ever loved you.' A blade flashed, sprouting from his fist.

A flick-knife?

She tried to utter something, but fear froze her tongue.

'I should take your other fucking eye out. How dare you look at my private photo collection?'

'Nooooo! Please…' Suzie managed to push back the terror engulfing her. She had to put her own fears aside, had to help him. This wasn't her son speaking. 'We must talk about this.'

'Talk? I've got nothing to say to you except this.' He dropped her head to the tiles, and lightning flashed inside her skull. 'I swear, I will fucking kill you if you come between us.'

'Billy. Stop.' She pushed herself into a sitting position as he went to open the back door. 'I won't tell the police. Not yet… Let's discuss this.' Her voice desperate, pleading. 'And the drugs… The LSD. I know what you've been doing to us—'

'You really have no fucking clue. You're such a moron.' He shook his head, as if weary at having to explain things to inferior beings, like his mother. 'My dad hated you. And just like him, I can't stand being in the same room as you.' He turned to leave, then shocked her even more with his parting comment, yelled at her with sheer vitriol in his voice. 'Poor old Gramps, he hated being stuck in this place with you whingeing females. Told me he'd had enough, that he'd rather fucking kill himself than be with you and that senile old bat upstairs. If it had been me, I wouldn't have committed suicide… I'd have killed the pair of you instead.'

The door slammed behind him, splitting the glass pane with a crack like a shotgun blast.

Suzie's fingers rubbed at her scalp and she managed to get herself upright, though swayed from side to side, had to steady herself before lowering her buttocks on to a chair.

'Susan? What on earth's going on?'

Oh, God, no. Please tell me she didn't hear what he just said.

Her mother, pale and ghostly in her satin nightgown, stood in the kitchen doorway, fingers clutching her crucifix, staring at the back door.

Thankfully, Suzie managed to bundle all the photos into the envelope while her mother stood transfixed. She went to help her back to bed, hoping beyond hope that the poor woman had not been witness to all that had just occurred. The doorbell saved her from having to explain.

'You go back to bed, and I'll get that. I'll bring you some warm milk later, and we can talk about it then.

Nana, dazed and silent, nodded. Suzie was torn between spending some time with her mother, to help her get over the shock, and opening the front door. At least the latter would allow her time to regroup, to think things through.

Mum will have to wait.

Suzie reached for the latch, wondering who might be calling this evening. She hoped it might be Smith, as she would dearly like to tear him a new arsehole.

She swung open the door and was surprised to see a man she immediately recognised. He had been beside Professor Maddox when that policeman shouted at her, after Billy attacked the Bentley on Saturday. Perhaps he was a policeman too, could even be the one who had left his card.

'Mrs Leech... I hope you don't mind me calling on you, but DCI Carver sent me. He said you left him a message but he's been unavoidably detained.'

'Oh, yes... I... erm.' Suzie wasn't ready for a visit from a policeman, but maybe talking over at least some of her concerns would be for the best. She opened the door a little wider, and said, 'Are you a colleague? From the police?'

'Well, yes and no. My name's Doctor Colin Powers.' The curly headed man with boyish looks, despite being clearly middle aged, held out his hand and gave her a firm handshake. A genuine smile creased his face, and warmth shone from his chocolate brown eyes. 'I'm a Forensic Psychiatrist. That hopefully means I have a deep understanding of criminal minds. I met your husband seven years ago. And his brother.'

Suzie's fingers went to her cheek. She was not wearing her disguise, had no scarf, no dark glasses to cower behind. This lovely man had not given the slightest indication he had seen her ugliness, had not averted his eyes from her deformities like most other people.

'Please come in, Doctor.'

'I'd prefer it if you call me Doc. Everybody else does.' Even his tone was reassuring, calm and professional. Relief washed through her. She was sure she could trust this person, she thought, as he said, 'I'd like to speak with you about your son, Billy.'

Billy wheeled his bike around the side of the house, his temper now fully under control, congratulating himself on how well he had handled the nasty surprise waiting for him in the kitchen. He had seen Nana arrive in the hallway from the corner of his eye, so had added the falsehood about Gramps' suicide for her benefit. Short of sticking his actual knife into both of them—something he had often dreamed of doing—he would have to make do with verbal daggers instead.

As he reached the corner of the house, he spotted the Aston Martin in the driveway. There was only one man he knew with a car like that.

Her greedy bastard lawyer.

Billy had seen it and admired it, parked outside the man's flashy Reading offices earlier in the year. He paused, just in time to hear a deep voice murmur before his mother let the man into their home.

What's she doing with her lawyer?

Maybe she had come up with some plan to undermine his wealth, his independent funds, his investments. She was still trustee, would be for two more years, so he was sure the man's arrival had something to do with him. That could cause some problems...

Billy wondered if he should just set the fuse on the bomb in the cellar and blow the lot of them up right this minute.

His bloody mother, breaking into his room like that. Just like Smiffy, she too had grown a proper man-sized pair of balls in the last few days, though it had been gratifying to see sheer terror on her face when he waggled the knife under her nose.

That must've brought back memories.

And the look of shock when he told her he loved Smiffy—that was just too funny for words.

Silly cow!

Would she tell anyone? Her lawyer? The police? Would they start looking for Smiffy tonight?

That could bugger things right up…

But Billy was doubtful she would say anything to anyone until he had spoken to her again—he had certainly put the frighteners on her. In some ways, it was a good thing she had discovered the photos. Her concerns for her abused boy might help, especially with her lawyer's unexpected visit.

What else could it be about? The Bentley and that old fart of a driver?

Probably.

Better to stick to the plan, and worry about his mother later, when he had sorted out tonight's mayhem.

Billy swung a leg over his saddle and pedalled the short distance to where he had parked Smiffy's car earlier this evening, in a clearing, well out of sight of the roads that cut across Bucklebury Common. He had planned to arrive after dark, but it was not yet dusk, with the late summer evening throwing long shadows from the trees. No problem, he could wait here and then drive into town to complete tonight's mission right on schedule.

After removing the front wheel from his bike and popping the dismantled vehicle in the rear of the Volvo, he stripped out of his cycling outfit. Next, he dressed in the clothes he had taken from his tutor, adding some padding around his waist to ensure he matched the bigger man's stature. As he stuffed the bike gear into the bag and hid it in the base of a hollow tree, he wondered about the jacket, thinking it was totally unsuitable for his needs. Unfortunately, Smiffy was not a fan of hoodies—at least, Billy had never seen him wear one. The tutor did own a parka with a fur-trimmed hood, but that was at his home and was not suitable for a summer night's outing.

What to do?

Billy had Smith's house key as it was attached to the car keys. He would head there shortly after dark, collect what he needed and then drive into London.

With his mind now set, he settled into the driver's seat of the Volvo and spent the next forty minutes texting his throwaway phone using Smiffy's mobile, and replying from his own. Once satisfied he had created the narrative he needed, he tugged both batteries from the devices to disable them completely, started the engine, turned on the sidelights and drove off into the gathering dusk.

The call from Jack had come just as Doc had been serving dinner and he had seen Judy's disappointment and anger when he told her he had to leave. Well, she wanted the boy caught too, so should not be complaining about it.

Jack was still at Reading Police Station. His boss was on her way, and there was a distinct possibility he would be suspended the moment she arrived. Doc had taken Hammond, the injured detective, for a check-up at the hospital while the other one took Jack into informal custody. It had taken all Doc's persuasive powers to calm everyone down after Jack had erupted, and convince the other officers not to arrest his friend, given the circumstances.

So, when Jack had called to say Mrs Leech had left a frantic message for him, Doc had not wanted to wait, but had volunteered to see the woman immediately.

When she opened the door, Doc thought she looked ill. It was not the puffy cheek with the inflamed scratch marks that gave that impression, more the shock he could see in her face, something more appropriate for the aftermath of bereavement. He hoped she hadn't just had some bad news about a relative or similar, and was glad that she invited him in and offered him a drink as they reached the lounge.

'No, I'm good thank you.' He was hungry, having teased his stomach with the aroma of curry, but put all thought of food and drink aside. He sat in the armchair opposite hers.

'The detective from London left a note for me to call. Was it about the car and that poor man Billy assaulted on Saturday?'

'Not really, Mrs Leech. Er… I don't know if Billy told you but he came to see me about two and a half years ago.'

'No. Why? Was it to do with his father?'

'Yes.' Doc explained how Billy had approached him and why.

'You're saying he's worried he may be a psychopath too?' Her hand started stroking her cheek as she spoke, and Doc could read in her expression and mannerisms her subconscious worries about the very same possibility.

'That was what we discussed, but I assured him that his future was down to him, the decisions he makes, the actions he takes.' Doc smiled, trying to reassure her, despite his own concerns about her son. 'Genetic influences do not control how we turn out, or how our personalities evolve.' He couldn't tell her that her son had declared his own genes superior in their last session together, nor his remarks about hers being inferior…

'But why did that detective call round? I don't understand.'

'Well, we think your son may have made some poor choices and I'd like to talk with you about his behaviour. Firstly, I'd like to understand what happened at school. Why he was expelled, as there are no records of that and he didn't mention it when I met with him.'

'You know he didn't speak for three years?'

'I do. And I'm aware of the trauma he experienced that prompted his muteness.'

'At school, they thought he was a freak.'

'He was bullied?'

'Yes. Almost up until the time he started talking again. About a year or so before then, his grandfather encouraged him to learn kung fu. For self-defence. Even set up a dojo for him in our annex.'

'Billy's father was a karate instructor, if I remember correctly.'

'That's right…' She shrugged, glanced away, as if some awful memory had surfaced. Then she focused back on Doc. 'But they didn't get on at all, so Billy never learned as a little boy. His grandfather arranged private lessons, and I think my son was motivated to learn, thanks to the treatment he'd been receiving at school. He was also growing, developing greater physical strength.' She shook her head as she added, 'I thought the discipline would be a good thing.'

'It wasn't?'

'Well, he was expelled after attacking the three pupils who had made his life hell.'

'What happened?'

'They'd been doing dreadful things to him…' She rubbed the back of her neck

648

and scalp with her hand, as if she was tender there. When she noticed Doc watching, she pulled her hand away, guiltily. When she spoke again, there was an apology in her voice. 'We didn't know how bad it had got. Billy wasn't speaking, would only communicate with a pad and pen, and even then, told us very little.'

'I heard that three boys ended up in hospital.'

'Really? You know about that? The school said they would keep it all hush hush.'

Protecting their reputation...

'I don't know the details. I'd like to.'

'Billy attacked two of them, individually, one afternoon. The first in the showers after a football match. He shattered his knee with a vicious kick. The second, in the music practice room. He crushed the boy's fingers using a baseball bat. Billy went straight there after crippling the first lad.'

'Sending them both to the hospital emergency room... And the third boy you mentioned?'

'The other lad, well, he was badly burnt, though that could've been an accident. He was doing chemistry experiments that afternoon, when something blew up in his face.' The woman's eyes seemed to swivel independently of each other, with a disconcerting lag as they searched Doc's face for reassurance. She went on, her voice low, mildly embarrassed by the things she was saying. 'Billy was suspected of tampering with the chemicals, but nothing was proven, and he didn't admit to doing anything. He just laughed when he was questioned.'

Laughed...

Yet more evidence that the boy was showing psychopathic tendencies, even at such a young age.

'This was the day he started talking again?'

'Yes.'

'He was expelled, but there was no legal action. Why not?'

'All four of them were expelled...'

'For Billy to get away with such grievous injuries to fellow pupils, there must have been some compelling evidence that the boys had done something as bad to him. Correct?'

'Yes.' Mrs Leech hesitated for a beat, then went to a drawer and pulled out a USB stick. She returned with her tablet computer, plugged the device in for Doc to view the contents. 'I'll be in the kitchen, making us some tea. I can't bear to watch that again.'

She left Doc to view the single movie file alone, and he tapped the screen to set it running.

The person holding the video camera was following Billy across some common land, and Doc heard the excited, shrill voices of pubescent lads, laughing and jeering at him as he made his way through the woods. Billy started to jog away from them, his face full of fear as he glanced back at the source of the noise.

He was slower than the pursuing boys, and the one with the video was at the rear as two others, maybe a couple of years older than Billy, sprinted to catch him. One of them rugby tackled him to the floor, then both started pummelling him as he lay there, his hands over his head, curled in a foetal position trying to protect himself.

When the lad with the video camera arrived—presumably using his mobile phone—the others stood up and sent a few kicks at Billy's head just for good measure. The video lurched, then refocussed as a plastic bag was tossed to the ground beside Billy and the 'director's' disembodied voice commanded him to eat the contents.

Billy sobbed, but said nothing, just sat up and opened the bag as the boys started chanting, their excitement mounting:

'Dogshit! Dogshit! Dogshit! Eat it! Eat it! Eat it!'

Billy, clearly accustomed to this treatment, did as he was bid, gagging as he forced the filth into his mouth, tears streaming down his face.

Even before he finished, he puked, and the boys laughed and left him. The movie faded to black then another appeared. This time none of the boys were in uniform, but all four of them were on the common again. Billy was already on the ground, cowering, crying, his face a picture of misery. The same two boys from the first video had hold of him and, one was undoing Billy's jeans while the other pinioned his arms. Doc watched with horror as they pulled his pants to his ankles and rolled him over.

Jesus Christ!

The video compilation contained more clips of vile abuse—another thirty minutes —but Doc soon stopped viewing. He had seen enough. He turned off the device and Mrs Leech appeared a moment later, carrying a tray with a teapot, two mugs and a plate of biscuits. It seemed surreal to Doc after what he had just seen. To be sitting here, like this.

'They raped him with a Coke bottle...' Kids, maybe twelve to fourteen years of age, taking bullying to an extreme. 'And filmed themselves doing it! Where did you get this, Mrs Leech?'

'Billy gave it to us... My father and I were called to the school after the attack in the gym and music room.' She sat and poured them each a cup of tea, her hands shaking. 'Those vile kids had shown him the video clips many times since. Billy managed to get hold of the boy's phone with it on... Copied it to prove what had happened to him.'

'But he told no one?'

'No. They'd been threatening him with all sorts, and assumed he had no proof anyway. It was their word against his.'

'And when he had the proof, stolen from that boy's phone, he opted to deliver his own form of punishment?'

Of course he did...

'Yes. The lad whose knee he ruined.' She was clearly angry with the boy as she spoke, but Doc also detected concern for the degree of violence her own child had delivered. 'He was being scouted by a professional football team. The lad with the shattered fingers... He was in the school band, a talented guitarist. Neither boy recovered from their injuries well enough to continue either pursuit, at least, not to the same level.'

'And the chemistry student?'

'His face was burnt, and I doubt he plays with chemicals much these days.'

'And the school covered it all up.' This was just incredible to Doc. Was it about money—the potential lost revenue for a private school if word got out? He didn't doubt it.

'Yes. As you can imagine, the other boys' parents initially wanted to involve the police. Until they saw the video. For everyone's sake, the whole nasty mess was swept under the carpet... They got what they deserved.'

Doc was more concerned with what it told him about Billy's character. The fact that he had taken the evidence of the other lads' crimes and chosen to administer his own form of punishment, despite their seniority in years, and clear advantage in size. It must have taken a major mindset shift for him to go from cowering bullied boy to avenging thug.

'How long was it, after the events in these videos, that Billy exacted his revenge?'

'Billy never speaks to me about it, but my father eventually found out from him. Roughly a year passed, and in that time Billy became obsessed with learning kung fu. It gave him confidence, and not long after he started taking lessons he began fighting back. So, the bully boys started picking on someone less able to defend themselves.'

'And when he was ready, he attacked them at school, with extreme violence. Then used the proof he'd obtained to make sure he wasn't punished. He started speaking again that day, to explain his deeds... He's a very clever lad.'

Manipulative, scheming.

Psychopathic.

'I do worry about him. I've not been a good mother. I've not been there for him...' She told Doc about her own troubles, admitting to an alcohol problem too, then about a discovery she had made earlier that day. Billy's shrine to his uncle.

'May I see? His bedroom?'

'If you wish. I'm afraid I ripped the poster of his uncle off the wall. I couldn't bear to look at it.' Doc was glad of that. A larger than life photograph of Peter Leech was not something he would relish seeing—he too had bad memories involving that particular psychopath. 'I'll take my mother some supper and leave you to it. Just go to the attic at the top of the stairs and you'll find Billy's bedroom there.'

'It's getting dark. When will he be back?'

'I'm not sure. We had a bit of an argument immediately before you arrived.' So, it wasn't bereavement, Doc realised. It was her own son that had made her look so shocked and drained when he arrived. She seemed better for their chat, and added with a resigned shrug, 'He may stay with a friend. He does that sometimes...'

Doc was sure Billy had no friends close enough for a sleepover, could hear the lie in her voice too, but chose not to pursue it right now. He left her, and made his way to Billy's bedroom, intrigued by what he might discover there.

———

Suzie waited for the microwave to do its job on the glass of milk she had poured for her mother, and let her mind return to the events from earlier this evening. She could still barely comprehend what had happened, how Billy had threatened her. Or his declaration of love for a paedophile teacher. And all this, on top of his dreadful misdeeds, the drugs he had fed them, the lies, the Chinese whispers sown between Nana and herself.

She also had a suspicion that her mother's tumble down the stairs was not an accident either. Her conversation with Doctor Powers had merely reinforced her concerns about her son's potential for harming others, and their discussion about the events surrounding his expulsion from school had crystallised the worst fears in her mind. Billy had demonstrated a viciousness in that premeditated attack on his fellow pupils, always justified in her mind by the terrible way they had treated him.

Now, it occurred to her that he was possibly even more damaged than she could ever have imagined. More like his father and uncle than she wanted to acknowledge.

Those thoughts had almost reached the tip of her tongue while sitting with that nice man in the lounge. Doctor Powers seemed so personable, so interested in her and her son. A skilled listener, who probably perceived far more than he let on. That was the impression he gave, and if it was false, it was an effective one. She'd wanted to tell him everything, the full extent of her concerns, to share with him her findings after her trip to the clinic this morning, but had curbed her tongue, still thinking she must speak with her boy first. To be fair to him. To let him tell her his side of the story.

The microwave pinged its readiness, so she put the glass of milk on the tray and went to her mother's room. Nana seemed to be in a trance, sitting in bed, staring into space. The glow she had carried all day, her joy of life, so recently re-established, was gone, replaced by sunken cheeks and pale skin.

'Mum? Are you okay?' Suzie placed the tray on the bedside table and perched on the edge of the bed. 'I brought your milk and some biscuits... Mum?'

'Could he really say those things, Susan...?' Her mother's eyes snapped into focus, drilling into Suzie's face as she asked. Pleaded. 'My wonderful Gerald? I thought we were so happy together.'

Billy Liar.

The thought sparked others, including doubts about so many things he had said over the months and years since his grandfather died.

'Billy was just upset, Mum. I'm sorry to say, I think he's been telling us both a lot of tall tales lately.' She took her mother's hands in hers and added, 'He lied about Lakeside. I think he's been saying things designed to make us fight.'

'Why? He's such a good boy.' Nana had never fully comprehended the degree of evil that Suzie had witnessed in the boy's father and uncle, so had no benchmark to compare what was happening to them at Billy's hands. 'I think you're confused, my love.'

Suzie gave up. The man clomping around in Billy's room might be able to convince her mother otherwise, but Suzie had no desire to introduce the two of them.

'We'll talk some more tomorrow. I've got a house guest. You get some sleep and we'll have another lunch outing tomorrow, if you feel up to it.' A gentle kiss on the cheek, then, 'Goodnight, Mum.'

With the door pulled to behind her, Suzie remained in the hallway for a few minutes, thinking through many of the events that had occurred under this roof in the years since her father had died, wondering what effect his death had on her boy.

His suicide.

And Billy had been sitting with his grandfather's body...

As if he hadn't seen enough death and misery.

Since then, the family home had become less and less of a refuge, and more like a prison, where Suzie had been tortured and tormented, day after day.

At Billy's hands.

She didn't want to think about it, just wanted to get today over with, and would talk with her boy in the morning. Meanwhile, she would ask Doctor Powers to leave, and went up the last flight of stairs to tell him she needed to sleep.

He was sitting on Billy's bed, reading something that looked like a journal, and beside him he had another book he must have found in Billy's bedside drawers—the bottom one was still open. He looked up as she entered the room, a deep frown on his features, one of concern and puzzlement.

'I see someone broke open his drawers.'

'Guilty as charged.' She joined him on the bed and looked at what he had laid there. An ancient dog-eared copy of a book with a title that made her shudder—*The Anarchist Cookbook*—the pages covered in tiny script, Billy's neat handwriting.

'From the tatty remnants glued to the wall, I assume that's where you tore the poster down.' She nodded, wondering why this might be important. 'The black candles on the shelf? Is he into the occult?'

'To be honest, I don't think I have the slightest clue what goes on in his head.' *I haven't for years.* She gave him a helpless shrug, too drained of reserves to think straight. 'I can tell you this, though. My son's a scientist, an opinionated atheist who sneers at me and my mother for praying.'

'Well, I'm thinking about something my friend Dickie Maddox suggested the other night—'

'The Professor's hardly met my boy, never spoken to him other than polite greetings and so on.'

'It's a theory. That's all. It's quite possible that Billy's experiencing visions of his uncle, with auditory hallucinations. It happens when our subconscious and conscious minds overlap, blurring reality.' His kindly eyes seemed to turn inwards, fearful of something, then the moment passed. She probably imagined it. He went on, 'I've some personal experience of this myself.'

'He thinks his uncle's alive?' The very thought was idiotic.

'I doubt that, at least not in the sense that you're thinking. But his uncle may well *seem* alive to Billy. Some people would call these visions spirits or ghosts, as they can appear to be as real as you and I, sitting here in this room. A trick of the mind. His lucid—'

'I'm sorry, Doctor. I'm too exhausted to even begin to think about that. I need to get some sleep. Perhaps I can call you tomorrow. I'd like you to meet my son too.'

'Of course. And I'd certainly like to speak with Billy. Please forgive me, it's late, and I should be long gone. May I take these items?'

Suzie knew her son would go ballistic if he found out, as he was sure to, but after tonight's performance, she was determined to re-establish her authority over him.

Please God, if it's not too late already…

'By all means. Is that a diary?'

'Of sorts. Billy records his dreams, but he uses some sort of rudimentary code to disguise the truth from any random reader, from what I can gather.' He bundled the books together, stood ready to go, but dithered, as if he had something important to say. Something he was reluctant to tell her. She stayed seated on the bed, waiting for him to speak. 'I'm… I'm sorry. I'm very concerned about Billy, Mrs Leech. His obsession with serial killers is unhealthy in such a young person, to say the least. With your family history, with Billy's experiences, I'm worried he might harm himself… Or others.'

Suzie swallowed hard, trying not to show her own fears. Didn't want to acknowledge the truth of what he said. She stood and went to the door, expecting him to follow.

'Well let's hope not.'

'Mrs Leech.' He had not moved. She turned back to him, and the light behind his head seemed to shine around him like a halo against the matt black background of the sloping walls. The sight made her heart shift gears, and she put hand to her chest, wondering if he was an angel, sent to help her. 'Please tell me the truth. Has he ever hurt you? Tried to hurt you?'

'No. Of course not!' Suzie heard the crack in her voice as it lifted an octave with the lie. She wanted to tell him, but her maternal instincts demanded that she speak with her son again before sharing her fears with strangers—no matter how much this one might seem like a gift from God.

'Threatened you?'

'No more than any teenage boy.' *One holding a knife to your face...* 'When grounded or whatever. Now, I really need to sleep.'

He stood there unmoving, his brown eyes assessing her, stripping bare the untruths, she was sure, but then he nodded, and followed her down the stairs. As she held open the front door for him to pass, he stopped and put a gentle hand on her shoulder. An angel's feather, landing on bare skin.

'Goodnight, Mrs Leech. Please take care. I promise you, I will do my best to help Billy. But I meant what I said. He may be a danger to the people around him. And that includes you.'

By the time Billy reached his tutor's home, he was totally at ease driving the old Volvo. It was a sedate vehicle with an automatic gearbox, and nothing like the cars he had taken joyriding on numerous other occasions. His preference was for something sportier, stolen for the thrill of roaring down country lanes before destroying the vehicle in an explosive burst of flame. But for tonight's expedition, Billy had a different conflagration in mind.

Smiffy's road on a residential estate in a seedy part of Reading was not particularly well lit, so Billy was confident he could pass for the older man if a neighbour spotted him. There was no one on the street as he took the few paces from the car to the front door and let himself in, and he kept his head down just in case someone was nosing at him through their net curtains.

The parka was hanging in the hallway, but Billy decided to check out the man's bedroom to see if he could find something more suitable for tonight. The place was dingy and cramped, a two-bedroom semi-detached that smelt damp. Its only redeeming feature was the long rear garden with the workshop-cum-laboratory at the end of it, but the house was a mess.

A cursory inspection of the contents of the wardrobe revealed nothing suitable for Billy's purpose—he would have to make do with the parka and a scarf he found in a drawer. He flopped himself on to the bed, thinking he might doze for a couple of hours before heading into London, but he was too excited by the prospect of tonight's adventure. He spent an hour trying to meditate, inviting his guru in, failing badly, and so hopped off the bed to get on with his final preparations.

Smiffy owned two large metal jerrycans, stored in a corner of his lab, and Billy hoped at least one of them contained petrol. He was disappointed to find only diesel in them, though both were almost empty. The rest of the fuel had probably been used during the preparation of the sack of ANFO, the explosive compound sitting in

Billy's cellar, alongside his tutor—ammonium nitrate fertiliser moistened with fuel oil, plus several bespoke ingredients to add a bit of oomph...

Billy chuckled as he pulled on some surgical gloves, taken from Smiffy's locker containing a stock of protective clothing, before tipping the remaining diesel down the drain. Petrol was what he needed tonight, along with a few screw lid glass containers. He took the jerrycans into the house and had a look in the kitchen for a decent sized bottle.

Perfect.

Three large green bottles of Perrier water, with one half empty, were in the rack inside the fridge door.

Covered in Smiffy's fingerprints...

Billy had studied a lot of crime reports and unlike most arsonists, knew that Her Majesty's Fingerprint Officers were able to lift fingermarks from the charred remains of almost any items left at the scene.

He grabbed the Perrier bottles, emptied their contents into the sink, selected a cotton tea towel from a rack, tucked the items under his arm and headed to the hallway with the jerrycans in his hands. Time to go.

A quick check from the front room window to see if anyone was out and about confirmed the street was deserted. With the grandfather clock in the lounge striking midnight, Billy decided to make his move, and expected to arrive at his destination sometime around two o'clock in the morning. Earlier than his usual witching hour, but close enough—he could not wait any longer or he would burst from the anticipation.

Once again, his phone had a dozen messages from his mother, demanding he return home immediately, telling him she was not angry with him, that she loved him, but that Smith 'must be reported' for his criminal actions.

'Must be reported!'

With some satisfaction, Billy noted the future tense, and let himself out of Smith's house.

TUESDAY

IMMOLATION

'FINALLY!' Doc rattled his car keys at Jack, ignoring the uniformed sergeant escorting the errant detective to the waiting area in the foyer of Reading Police Station. 'It's after midnight. What have they been doing with you for all this time? Let's get you home, eh?'

Jack looked worse than Doc felt—more rumpled, frazzled and frustrated, with dark patches beneath his eyes from lack of sleep, stress and tension.

'Yeah. I'm cream crackered, mate.' Jack shrugged off the sergeant's guiding hand as he was silently passed into Doc's care. 'Let's get out of here.'

Once through the revolving doors and in the relatively fresh air outside, Jack paused, closed his eyes and breathed deeply, shaking his head at what had been happening to him. Doc was impatient, just to get them both back home.

'Come on, Jack. Let's get out of here. The car's around the back.'

Jack opened his eyes, gave Doc a sardonic grin, then said, 'I think I've now got the record for the shortest promotion to, and demotion from, Detective Chief Inspector. I'm plain old DI Carver again. Oh, well. Such is life.'

The Aston Martin flashed its lights and beeped a welcome to the two humans, both weary, both groaning as they folded themselves into their seats. The distinctive new car smell gave Doc a minor thrill—the vehicle had only been his for a fortnight and he was still enjoying the flush of new ownership. Jack, usually a sports car enthusiast, didn't even seem to notice, even though he had only been for a brief spin in it the day Doc had taken delivery.

Too much else on his mind.

'What happened? They kept you there for almost eight hours.'

'Yeah… They didn't charge me with assaulting a fellow officer, thank gawd, but I am up for a misconduct review. And I've been suspended pending the enquiry.'

During his trip to the hospital with the wounded detective Jack had knocked cold, Doc had tried to convince the man not to press charges, had explained how Jack had rescued his daughter from drowning, and then had to resuscitate her—two facts that had been missing from the brief statements Jack and Doc had written in such a hurry at Charlie's behest that morning. In Doc's assessment, the blow to the detective's chin had done more damage to his ego than cause any real physical harm. Fortunately, the hospital gave him the all clear after the staff rushed him through to a treatment room past the mass of waiting wounded in reception. Although he had been non-committal when Doc took him back to the station, at least Jack didn't have criminal charges hanging over him.

'Suspended, eh? And demoted already?' It seemed a little hasty to Doc, though he could guess why. 'Soundbite?'

'She fucking hates me. What did I do to deserve such a vindictive boss?' Jack used the heel of his palms to rub at his forehead as Doc navigated the car through Reading towards Pangbourne. 'They kept me waiting in an interview room, gave me some water, then some coffee and a burger when I complained. Treated me like a bloody criminal. And that sodding Soundbite told them to keep me there until she arrived.'

'You've seen her?'

'Yeah. Just before I called you to come and pick me up. Tore me off a strip. Told me to go home, and that she didn't want to see me or hear from me—or about me—until after my holiday. The review will take place on Monday week, my first day back.'

'And did you tell her about Billy Leech, and all the things we've discovered?'

'No one's listening, mate.' Jack blew a gust of frustration across his lips. 'I tried, but the detectives think you and I have a hair up our arses about the lad. Tuh! All thanks to what happened with his old man and uncle seven years ago, and the fact we've been on TV, yakking about that case, and others too. *Celebrity copper.* That's what I am.' He huffed a disgusted puff of air this time. 'Huh! Your sidekick, by all accounts. Mind you, Reading nick don't think too highly of either of us, from what I heard. We hog the limelight, making off with loads of dough, while *proper coppers* like them do the hard graft. As if.'

'Mmm.' This was not the news Doc had expected, or wanted. 'And Charlie? Can she help us?'

'She's uniform. It's out of her hands, mate.'

'So, we're on our own, thanks to your boxing prowess and your flagrant disrespect for authority...' Doc grinned at his pal. 'Just like old times, then!'

Jack's mood finally shifted and they started laughing, like a pair of demented hyena. Doc had to wipe his eyes as he drove, thinking how the stress of the last few days had got to them both, and that a good night's sleep would give them better perspective. They reached his home in silence, with Doc assuming they were both thinking about how to proceed. Neither of them would trust the locals to solve the crimes committed against them both.

'Did you get to see Mrs Leech?' Jack pushed his door open, still sitting, the courtesy light illuminating the inside of the car, his expression thoughtful. 'She sounded proper freaked out on the phone when she left me that message.'

'Let's go inside. I'll tell you all about it over a nightcap, then we'll hit the hay. But if you want my opinion... There's no doubt Billy Leech is involved in all that's been happening. He's obsessed with serial killers, and I remembered something he said to me during one of our sessions, and I think it's important.'

'What?'

'He asked whether I thought psychopaths were superior beings. Their ability to take actions the rest of us shy away from—'

'Superior? You're kidding me. Most of 'em are fucking mental.'

Doc let that oversimplification slip by, as he was in no mood to try educating Jack to change his views. Not tonight, anyway. He just wanted to slip into bed beside Judy.

'His argument has some merit, Jack.' Doc slid out of the car and used his remote to lock the garage door behind it as soon as Jack joined him on the steps to the front door. 'Some of our greatest war leaders displayed psychopathic traits, and Billy had been researching famous historical figures he felt fitted the bill.'

'Like who? Hitler?'

'He was on the list, but our very own Winston Churchill was, too.'

'Winnie? No way!'

'As I said, his argument is valid, given some of the war crimes committed by that famous hero of World War Two, but more to the point, I now suspect Billy hero worships psychopaths in general. His bedroom is like a shrine to them, with one man elevated above all others.'

'His uncle. Peter Leech.'

'Uh-huh. And now I suspect Billy thinks *he* is genetically superior to the normal population. Including his mother and grandmother. Especially them.'

Doc poked his key in the front door latch as Jack asked, 'Are they in danger? Is that why his mum was so freaked out?'

'She was in a bit of a state, clearly trying to hold it all together. And I could see she was keeping something back. I got the impression she wasn't telling me half of what's been going on. We need to talk to them both, together, and that way we'll get the full story. She said she'd call me, but I think we should go there first thing in the morning.'

'Not give the little bastard time to poke off out?'

'Yes. If Billy is as manipulative as I think, we should catch him unawares.'

'Sounds like a good idea to me, Doc. Now, how about that nightcap and you can fill me in on the details?'

Doc closed the front door on the world outside, unaware that Billy Leech was implementing plans of his own—and would soon wreak such havoc in central London that it would reverberate all the way to Pangbourne, and leave them both devastated.

Harley Street is a quiet Marylebone backwater during the day, with minimal traffic compared to many of the surrounding roads. At two o'clock in the morning, it is deserted, with only the occasional passing car or taxi using it to cut through to, or from, other more exciting London venues.

The old Volvo arrived outside the Caduceus Clinic and parked alongside the luxury vehicles that cost many times the average national income. Ferraris, Lamborghinis, Porsches and Rolls Royces were hogging the limited number of parking spots available, but the Bentley that often sat in the designated bay outside Professor Maddox's clinic was missing tonight so the Volvo driver eased his car into its place.

A heavy-set man, overdressed for the cool summer night in a parka with the hood up and a scarf wrapped beneath his nose, obscuring his features from the CCTV cameras bristling from every wall, front entrance and corner along the street, exited the vehicle and opened the boot. A lone taxi passed him, but he kept his head down and once the cab had disappeared, he hoisted a large grey jerrycan from the rear of his car, then lugged it to the clinic's front door.

While hunched over the step, he opened the steel canister and poured some powder into it, roughly a third of the bag he held—one that looked like it contained a kilo of sugar. He then resealed the jerrycan, gave it a shake and left it standing on the step. A second container that matched the first was also hauled from the rear of the car and treated with powder, but this time the man splashed some of the contents over the door, and allowed much of the liquid to flow below it to the hallway floor inside.

A McLaren's headlights passed over the man as he returned to his ancient Volvo, still with his neck bent and his face obscured from view, but the supercar's driver was oblivious to whatever was going on in Harley Street tonight, and did not even spare a glance at the incongruous vehicle or the overdressed pedestrian.

The man in the parka stood by the boot and opened a green bottle, half full of fluid, and added some powder to that, then screwed the cap back on before placing it on the pavement. After repeating the exercise, he shredded a cotton cloth into three strips and sloshed some of the contents of the third bottle onto them before tying each around the bottlenecks. Then he slammed the boot closed, got in the car, drove it around the corner, and left it with the engine running and the driver's door wide as he sprinted back to the waiting Molotov cocktails.

With no motorists or other pedestrians in sight, he took the three bottles to the middle of the road and lit each of the rags tied around their necks, hefted the first, then lobbed it at an upstairs window. The glass exploded in a burst of orange, yellow and green flames, but already a second bottle was arcing through the air, and that too detonated as it disintegrated a first-floor window. An alarm was pealing and some neighbouring security lights flashed on, illuminating the man in a harsh white glare as he tossed the third bottle at the front door, then sprinted back around the corner to his car.

The final blast was many times more powerful than the first two, and set off car alarms along the street as the front facade and entrance to the clinic turned into an almighty fireball engulfing the hallway before rolling up the stairs, green and yellow tongues licking their way to the upper floors, to join their junior partners there.

The Volvo sped away, and the driver, grinning wildly behind the scarf still covering his mouth, was unable to hear the panic-stricken screams coming from the residential apartment on the upper level.

Despite the numerous alarms sounding across this elite sector of London, the emergency services took several minutes to arrive, with a police patrol car first on the scene. By the time the two uniformed policemen had taken stock, and before they had even had a chance to speak to the few residents who had come on to the street to view the inferno, the Volvo was well on its way to the M4, having joined light traffic in Mayfair before passing Hyde Park Corner and then cruising along Knightsbridge to the Cromwell Road.

None of the residents had seen what had happened, and the Volvo registration and the driver's actions were only identified by the police after they had secured the area and obtained video evidence from the residences opposite and adjacent. Even then, it turned out that the license plate had been altered, probably with black insulating tape. The crude technique, often used by criminals on getaway vehicles, had turned an F to an E, and an E to a B on the Volvo's plates Fortunately, the artifice was not able to fool the Automatic Number Plate Recognition computers that checked every car of that make on London's roads that night. The Met soon located the owner's records through the national database.

It was shortly after four o'clock in the morning when a terrorist alert was broadcast to all UK police forces, notifying them of the attack, along with details of the perpetrator's vehicle, his name and home address.

As the alert surfed the airwaves, the Volvo's engine was still cooling while parked on the owner's tiny driveway in a downmarket suburb of Reading. An unmarked patrol car, with lights dimmed, engine purring gently, took a slow pass by the house. A swift radio call confirmed the presence of the Volvo at the owner's home, now with its number plate unadulterated, before the police car departed using the same degree of stealth as it had when it arrived.

Minutes later, in the pre-dawn half-light, a team of fourteen paramilitary Metropolitan Police officers, dressed in plain grey fatigues, each carrying Sig 516 semi-automatic rifles and holstered Glock 9mm pistols, arrived in pairs at the end of the road astride seven BMW F800 motorcycles. The elite Counter Terrorist Specialist Firearms Officers had been dispatched from central London some thirty minutes prior, and sped at one hundred and twenty miles an hour along the M4 motorway before arriving at their target location in south Reading.

They dismounted and filed along the pavement, crouching below the level of the broken fences and scrubby hedgerows bordering the cramped front gardens, their rubber soled boots muffling any sound as they crept towards the house. Once on scene, they split into two groups, with six men ducking through the side gate to the rear of the premises. The remaining officers took up positions at the front.

Two of the men at the rear had a cautious look inside the wooden shed at the end of the garden, shining their torches through the grimy windows before returning to their colleagues.

One of the men at the front of the building placed a strip of explosive charge around the edges of the door, then scuttled back to join his waiting comrades, some behind the car and others behind the low concrete garden-wall facing on to the street. On a silent signal from the leader, the device detonated and the door flew inwards, just as four flash bang grenades were propelled through the front windows, with four more fired through the ones at the rear of the property.

The crump of explosions rocked the street a second or so before the officers swarmed into the house, front and rear, yelling, 'Armed Police!' but they found no one inside.

After securing the premises the senior officer radioed his headquarters, where their Commander was waiting, watching the live feed via the team's body cameras. Moments later, he relayed the Commander's message to his men:

'Boss says we've got to wait for the Bomb Squad to check out the workshop in the garden. Unbelievable… They send us all the way out here, instruct us to storm the suspect's home, giving us zero intel, and only now do they tell us to wait in case the place is bleedin booby trapped!'

Thirty minutes before the police arrived, Billy recovered his bicycle from the hallway of Smiffy's house. He had taken it from the car boot when he'd loaded his jerrycans and petrol bombs, and had left his prized machine securely stored and well away from prying eyes. With the parka hood and scarf still covering his head, he pedalled along the deserted streets to join the Kennet and Avon canal a few minutes ride to the south. He decided on a circuitous route back to Bucklebury Common, looping away from his destination before heading north, all the while avoiding the main roads. It was important to do so, as he was sure the police would soon be descending on the address linked to the car's registration.

Once on the canal towpath, he was beyond the few CCTV cameras that dotted some of the commercial premises in south Reading, but ever cunning, he kept the parka hood up. In the unlikely event he was spotted by anyone out and about this early, he was confident they would not connect him with the criminal actions undertaken in London during the last few hours—and with his features disguised, it did not matter much anyway.

In the weak early dawn light, Billy's face shone with sweat and malicious glee, his eyes triumphant as he pedalled at speed. Although he had not slept, his entire being buzzed with energy, his brain sizzling with excitement at the things he had achieved since the weekend began.

And tomorrow, it's my birthday!

Sixteen.

Yet so mature, so wise. Thanks to Uncle Peter.

When he reached the clearing where he'd parked the car the evening before, he changed out of Smiffy's clothes, removed the translucent latex gloves he had been wearing most of the night, and pulled on his cycling kit. With the parka and other garments stuffed in the cloth carrier bag dangling from the handlebars, Billy sped along the road to his Nana's house, dismounted at a jog as he reached the driveway, and then stowed the bike in the garage.

Before heading into the house, he filled his sports water bottle from the garden tap, went to the cellar entrance and unlocked the door, then descended to the gloomy interior. The stench of urine made him pause before he went to his victim, who was now struggling with his bindings, trying to speak through the tape covering his mouth, croaking urgent wordless pleas for help at his visitor.

'Sorry, Smiffy. No one's come to rescue you.' Billy ripped the tape from his tutor's eyes. 'See. It's just little old me.' He slipped his knife into his hand and the blade flicked at the terrified man's face. Smiffy groaned, his eyes swivelling, head jerking away from the blade as he tried to put some distance between himself and the weapon, unsuccessfully.

'You're shit scared, aren't you? Pathetic old man.'

Billy stabbed the blade through the centre of the tape covering Smiffy's mouth, and then fed the straw from his water bottle through the small slit he had made.

'Drink it all. We don't want you dying of dehydration, do we, Smiffy? I've got a use for you...'

Smiffy relaxed, drank the contents without a break, eyes now grateful, less fearful.

Probably thinks I'm not going to kill him...

'You're an impressive man, Smiffy.'

Confused now, forehead wrinkling, eyes questioning.

'Like a magician!' Billy giggled, then his laughter echoed around the cellar. 'You being in two places at once, like you did last night! Hahaha!'

Billy ripped some tape from the roll, and Smiffy struggled, trying to avoid the strip being plastered across his eyes, but to no avail. Another strip covered the one already over his mouth, closing off the drinking hole.

'There we go. I'll see you later. Keep quiet.' Billy ruffled Smiffy's hair. 'If anyone discovers you, I will have to kill you. And you aren't the first, so don't think I won't. So, keep quiet. Do as I say, and you'll get out of this alive. I'll even bring you a bit of food later, if you're good…'

A whimper was the only response, so Billy left his victim, locked the cellar door and let himself into the house. All quiet still. There had been a slight possibility his mother would still be up, waiting for him, although her urgent SMS demands for his return had ceased some hours before.

He crept past her bedroom door, ears alert for any sounds from within, then climbed to the attic. He thought nothing could spoil his mood this morning, he was still on a high from the adrenalin, but seeing how his room had been violated, his things carelessly tossed around, his drawers broken into, he felt hatred and rage well up inside him.

Then he saw the end wall. The poster of Uncle Peter had gone.

She'll pay for this…

Billy peered into his bedside drawer, taking in the extent of his mother's trespass against him, the assault on his privacy. His dream diary had gone too, not that it would make much sense to anyone else. His fingers scrabbled around the interior, searching for the LSD and Temazepam.

Gone.

'Argh!' He rubbed frustrated fingers backwards and forwards through his hair. 'I needed those today…'

It would be impossible to sleep, he was so wired this morning. And even if he could manage to doze off, with no LSD, he would have difficulty meeting with his guru in his dreams.

I'll fucking kill her.

The knife was in his hand again, cold steel glinting, tempting him.

No… Stay calm. Stick to the plan.

He folded the blade away, then stripped from his cycling clothes, sniffed an armpit, wrinkled his nose in disgust, but did not feel like a shower, so slipped under the covers and rested his head on the pillow, staring at the bare wall where the picture of his uncle should be.

With gritted teeth, Billy reached out for his smartphone, plugged in his earphones, and went straight to the local news site. There was still no confirmation of the name of his deceased victim from Sunday's floating bonfire.

Had he killed Powers? Surely it would have made the news by now if he had—the man was something of a celebrity.

Billy's mood soured more, and he felt an almost irresistible urge to hurt someone. Anyone… Instead, he switched to the BBC news site and what he found there sent waves of euphoria washing through him again.

Jack spent most of the night drifting in and out of sleep, his mind recycling the events from Sunday afternoon, each time with a different outcome, and each featuring a manic Billy Leech, laughing and pointing at the distressed group in Doc's garden from his vantage point in the tree opposite. When Jack heard his borrowed phone bleep with the distinctive tone of a national alert, he ignored it.

Fuck that. I'm suspended.

The device was an old Nokia 5110 'dumb' phone—a miniature brick. Doc had dug out the antique earlier for Jack to use as a temporary measure until he could find the time to shop for a proper replacement for the one at the bottom of the Thames. It was a solid lump of Bakelite with rubber buttons and a small screen, just about big enough for a message of a few lines of text to show against the yellow background light. It even had a miniature aerial poking out of the top on the right-hand side, as thick and round as a pencil, about the length of the top half of Jack's thumb.

Looks more like a walkie-talkie than a bleedin phone!

He'd arranged for all his work, personal calls and messages to be diverted to the Nokia's SIM card, but instead of answering tonight's alert, he tried to relax every muscle group in his body, focusing on each in turn, to lure his mind to the peace of deep sleep. By five o'clock, he gave up and decided to get going, to make more inquiries regarding his prime suspect.

He sat on the edge of the bed wearing shorts and tee shirt, ruffled his hair and yawned, wondering if he could magic up some decent coffee from Doc's NASA-level espresso machine.

With his phone in hand he started down the stairs, then stopped midway as he finally read the brief SMS alert from the Metropolitan Police. He jumped down the last few steps, jogged to the giant TV screen in the corner of Doc's lounge, and jabbed the remote-control buttons until he found a twenty-four-hour news outlet covering the explosions in the centre of London earlier that morning.

'Jesus wept…'

A female reporter was mouthing into a microphone in front of a burnt out terraced property, and it took Jack several seconds to realise it was a place he was familiar with, a clinic he had visited, the first time on duty, and, subsequently, for several social occasions. He turned up the volume to listen to what the woman had to say:

…police have confirmed the suspect is still at large but have not yet released full details. However, the man is considered extremely dangerous, and may well be armed.

She was replaced on screen by a still photo of the perpetrator, standing in the middle of the road holding a flaming bottle in his right hand ready to launch at the building. A parka hood covered his eyes and a scarf was wrapped across his mouth, so even this enhanced close-up CCTV image was not sufficiently detailed to identify him.

Commissioner Davies has confirmed this was a sophisticated arson attack, and not a terrorist fire-bombing incident as first thought. They consider it was most likely a lone wolf with a grudge against the clinic…

Jack, dazed by what he was hearing, slumped on to the sofa, interpreting the Commissioner's words based on the image of the suspect.

A Caucasian. Therefore, not a jihadi.

How times change, he thought. In the eighties, the IRA were the terrorists of the day, and Caucasians with an Irish accent were automatically considered suspects the moment a bomb went off.

Not any more…

But Jack had already concluded who the Caucasian was, and could feel his rage stirring, the muscles of his neck cramping, his shoulders and back rigid with tension. Then the reporter threw out some more details in perfectly modulated BBC English.

The badly burnt body of a man was found at the scene, in the residential apartment above the clinic. No further details are available although the police believe they have identified the victim and will release his name after contacting the next of kin…

Jack put his elbows on his knees, and rested his head in his hands, a surge of acid searing his larynx as he took in this latest piece of news.

Dickie?

Professor Maddox sometimes stayed overnight in his luxury apartment above the clinic instead of commuting to his mansion on an exclusive estate near Weybridge in the cocktail belt to the south of London. With his Bentley off the road and his chauffeur on sick leave, Jack just knew the charred body was that of their friend, the kindly, generous soul he and Doc had been drinking with on Saturday night, in this very room.

I'll kill the little fucker.

Jack leapt up, not sure what he was going to do, just knew he had to get moving. He reached the door at the same time as Doc, still in his pyjamas, arrived from the opposite direction.

'What's going on Jack? I couldn't sleep, so I was going to make a coffee, then I heard the TV. Are you feeling okay?'

Jack stood aside, waved Doc into the lounge, and pointed at the screen.

'Bad news, mate. It's the clinic. Arson attack in the early hours… I think it's…'

'The Caduceus Clinic?' Doc had moved to face the TV, close enough to touch it as he read the headlines scrolling across the bottom of the screen. His face paled and his voice faltered as he said, 'One person dead?'

'Yes, mate. I think it must be Dickie, though they've not confirmed it yet.' Jack did his utmost to keep his voice level, to stop himself letting rip and spewing his temper over his shocked friend. 'I'll get on the blower to my mates at the Yard. See what else I can find out. Maybe you should make us both some coffee… I need a smoke too. I've got an emergency pack in the car. I'll be back in a mo.'

Jack reached the door as Doc replied, his voice razor edged. 'Another arson attack. On a friend of mine… By someone with a grudge against us both.'

'Yeah. A young man with a fondness for Molotov cocktails and a taste for burning things down. We'll get him, Doc. I promise you that. If it's the last thing I do…'

Suzie did not think sleep would ever come, lying there half the night, texting her son to come home. Telling him she loved him in some, furious at him in others, alternately wheedling, then demanding his presence to discuss things.

By one o'clock in the morning, she was about ready to visit Smith's home, to confront them both, convinced Billy had gone there after their fight in the kitchen that evening. It was only after that idea had first blossomed that she realised she had no clue where the man lived, or where to find his address. They had his CV somewhere, but Billy had dealt with all the paperwork, she'd happily handed the responsibility to him, and just signed the few documents he'd presented to her to get Smith on board as his tutor.

God knows where they are.

The cellar?

Suzie thought about going down there to search for the papers, but it had been such an unpleasant experience that last time, she opted to remain in bed instead. If her boy stayed out all night, she would call the police in the morning. They must have the dirty old pervert's address.

I'll be calling them anyway. Or that nice Doctor Powers...

With those thoughts drifting through her mind, she finally nodded off, falling into a dream-free sleep before being woken by birdsong from the garden, wafting through an open window shortly after six o'clock. She pulled on some clothes, brushed her hair and went to her son's room.

The door was shut, and as she climbed the stairs to it, she remembered Doctor Powers had left it open when he had been leaving, and Nana would not have ventured up there—she had been sparko when Suzie had looked in on her at around midnight.

He's home.

She tapped her knuckles on the door and tried the handle.

Locked.

'Billy! Open this door. I want to talk to you.'

A muttered groan reached her ears through the wood.

'I said—OPEN THIS DOOR. NOW!'

'Piss off. I'm sleeping.'

'No, you are not!' She rattled the handle while thumping on the door, frustration screaming from every pore. 'You're awake and talking to me. I want to see your face, young man. So, come on out, right this minute.'

'I'm too tired. Go away! We can talk later...' After a few beats with them both silent, his voice was softer, and she heard a muffled sob, then, 'You really upset me last night. Just let me rest.' Another sob. 'Please, Mum.'

Suzie hesitated, her anger draining away at his conciliatory tone and clear distress. She could get the key and force herself on him, make him talk, but why the hurry? Better to speak with him when he was ready.

'Alright then. When you get up, I'll make you some breakfast and we'll talk then.'

Just a grunt greeted her compromise.

Suzie plodded back down the stairs, thinking it was too early to wake her mother, so went to the kitchen and put the kettle on, planning to drink her tea while sitting in the garden in the cool dawn air, but the idea brought something else to mind.

The annex...

It had been many months since she had been in there. Probably a year or more.

The arrangement was the same as Billy's bedroom—he had guaranteed to keep it spick and span, and always kept to his bargain, as she had confirmed on the few occasions she'd been compos mentis enough to bother inspecting the place. They did have a row in the very first week of the arrangement after he said he would use some of his allowance to pay a cleaner. Her mother would never allow that, so he had learnt how to clean his living areas—which was no bad thing.

What secrets do you keep in there, Billy?

The discoveries she had made thanks to invading his bedroom had left her dazed and confused. She had opted to share just a fraction of her concerns with that friendly psychiatrist, but had not even considered whether there was anything else she might find in Billy's tuition room or dojo. With her son sleeping upstairs, now was a good time to have a snoop around the place.

She took a cup, dropped a teabag into it, sloshed boiling water over it, and thought to herself:

Right then. Where do we keep the spare key?

'I'm going into the city, my love. With Jack…' Judy sat up as Colin placed a cup of coffee by the bed for her, and yawned as he explained. 'Something terrible has happened at Dickie's clinic and we're going to head there now. I'll call you later.'

'So, they let Jack go? And you need to go into London?' Colin nodded, unsmiling. In the half-light through their curtains she could see he was in a determined mood. Sombre, and formally dressed in a dark suit. 'Is he okay? Dickie?'

'We're not sure… That's why we want to get there as soon as we can. We'll beat the worst of rush hour by leaving now.'

'Okay, I've got a busy day at work. I'll see you tonight?' She took his hand in hers, gave him a pleading look. 'Don't overdo it, Colin. Please.'

'I'll be back in time for dinner—I'm sorry about last night. I'll tell you all about what I was up to this evening, if you want to hear it.' Colin bent to her, planted a soft kiss on her lips, then left.

Judy did not feel much like running this morning, so decided to have a leisurely shower and make herself a proper breakfast, as it was only just six o'clock. She had eaten hardly any dinner last night, sitting alone in the kitchen, worrying about Colin before deciding she was being irrational. Hormonal. Hopefully she could stave off any morning sickness today, if she cooked herself some proper breakfast. Bacon, eggs and toast were foods she actually craved this morning.

She hopped out of bed, lifted the duvet cover, planning to smooth the sheets and make the bed, but stopped dead.

Blood?

Three red-brown stains, half way down the bed, each the size of a two-pound coin. Judy's stomach cramped in response, as if trying to protect the life in her belly from this unwelcome sight. Having agonised for weeks before deciding she would keep their baby, the prospect of a miscarriage sent her scuttling to the bathroom fearing the worst. She ripped off her silk nightgown and inspected herself, her ears whistling with stress.

Nothing much…

A hint of leakage, now dried. Judy stepped into the shower and washed herself, thinking she would call her doctor as soon as the clinic opened at eight.

Maybe it's nothing… Just a bit of harmless spotting.

Judy knew it could happen, but had no personal experience, had not leaked blood while pregnant with Josh. She would have talked it through with Colin but he'd already left. She glanced at her phone on the bedside table, but decided it was best not to call him—he had enough on his mind as it was.

I'll call the doctor first, then we'll see.

Having reassured herself, she thrust the worries from her mind and got dressed ready for another day at work, this time raising money for the homeless. Unfortunately, her appetite had left her by the time she arrived in the kitchen, and the thought of a greasy fry up almost made her retch. Even a fruit smoothie would be too acidic, so she made herself a fresh coffee, chewed on some dry toast and switched on the TV to watch the news.

Some grainy footage of a smart London property in flames dominated the screen, and a short clip was on a loop as the presenter spoke over it, driving the name of the clinic into Judy's skull as she watched, her toast forgotten, her mouth agape. As the loop replayed, she could see the man lobbing flaming bottles at Dickie's clinic, and the ensuing conflagration, destroying his property.

Doc's words from moments earlier came to her: *Something terrible has happened…*

Even without any sound from the video recording, the resulting explosions sent her mind reeling back to Sunday and the boat, blazing, her fire extinguishers totally ineffective at dampening the flames.

Again, her stomach went into spasm, and she doubled over, dropping her toast to the floor. Was it the baby? Judy did not think so…

It was stress and worry.

That overwhelming sense of foreboding had returned, and this time she couldn't shake it off. This was personal. Someone was intent on harming her husband and his friends. Judy could not stop thinking the worst as her instincts told her this would not end well.

It took Suzie twenty minutes to find the spare key she thought might open the annex. She slotted it into the mortice lock and was rewarded with the satisfying click as the latch released and allowed her entry into Billy's private domain. The air smelt of sweat and testosterone, a male scent she automatically associated with her husband, and it made her falter as she stepped across the threshold, her fingers to her cheek in subconscious response.

Be strong…

She had to do this, to find out the extent of her son's secret life, to understand just how warped he had become. There were no pictures of killers, no shrine to his uncle, and she was thankful for that small mercy.

The study area was unremarkable, being about the size of Nana's living room, with a sofa, an armchair and a large screen TV. The main difference was the whiteboard fixed to a wall between the windows, the bookcase full of textbooks, and a desk with Billy's personal computer situated on it.

Suzie tried to access the computer first, but without the password there was nothing to see right now.

I'll make him open it for me and then have a look inside.

The two-drawer filing cabinet next to the desk was locked, but her boy was not as security conscious as she thought. She found the key in her father's old pewter beer mug, situated by the computer screen, after tipping out the contents—paper clips, pens, a stapler and a few other items of stationery.

As she rooted around, Suzie thought how little character the room had—almost sterile in its lack of personality. Devoid of photographs and posters, no handwritten notes like she had seen in his bedroom.

Business-like.

What am I doing?

She began to doubt there was much to find in here, but then crouched down to open the filing cabinet, her knees clicking in protest. The first drawer contained a dozen folders, hanging in a green cardboard concertina, just a she expected. All were meticulously labelled with Billy's neat handwriting, all in alphabetical order. What she had not expected were the descriptions of the contents:

Banking T&C
Banking UK
Driving Licence
Journal
Lakeside
London Property
Offshore Portfolio
Passport & Tickets
Recipes
Smith
Uncle Peter Bio
XXX

Several thoughts crossed her mind as she took in the titles of the filing tabs, though it was immediately clear to her that Billy had somehow discovered the full extent and nature of his investments. His bank account in the Turks and Caicos Islands, the London property and the Jersey portfolio were all supposedly confidential, and as the principal trustee, she knew that none of this was supposed to be divulged to him until his coming of age—his eighteenth birthday. It was her stipulation and one her father had reluctantly agreed to.

The boxes in the cellar? Or did Dad tell him before he died? Worried that I was not fit to manage his affairs?

There had been several occasions when her father had scolded her for her drinking, told her to snap out of it, to be a proper mother to her boy. But she had not. Could not. Like many people who have never suffered the depths of depression, he was unable to empathise with her, to understand the sense of desolation and emptiness, the hopelessness, she had to contend with each and every day…

So, what now?

Suzie could not face that last file, though suspected it was important. More photographs of perverted acts between a grown man and a young boy? She decided to start at the beginning, so sat on the floor and began to work her way through the contents of each, flicking through the sheaves of documents, incredulous at what she was reading. The false driving license was as good as the real thing, showing his age as nineteen, and she began to wonder if he also had a car secreted somewhere.

The devious bugger.

Her son's journal made little sense, and read more like a horror story, but the other items were easy to understand. Billy had become complacent, and must have assumed no one would poke around in his secrets, locked away here, in his private annex.

Mind-blowing as it was, she began to build a picture in her mind of what he was planning, and how he could achieve it. By the time she had reached the passport file, she knew his threat to run away with his tutor had not been so much hot air, created spontaneously during their argument last night. He meant it, alright.

Good grief... I've lost him.

Possibly not.

She went to his dojo locker by the shower cubicle and found his old gym holdall. It was empty, so she took it to the drawer and scooped out everything she had discovered there, and dropped the entire concertina filing system into the bag. She would finish perusing the contents later, she was too stunned to do so right now.

One last thing to check. The bottom drawer.

Having discovered so much, it seemed unlikely there would be more files with anything worth reading, and as she opened it, the contents seemed jumbled, with no hanging folders, just a lot of seemingly random items, mostly in ziplock transparent plastic bags, casually dropped into the bottom of the deep drawer, with ostrich feathers tossed on top.

Strange, as Billy was always such a fastidious person.

Suzie reached in, pushed the feathers aside and pulled out a bag with what looked like a decorative horse hair ornament. Then she saw the cut end, the flash of white bone, and dropped it to the floor in disgust.

What in God's name...?

With the feathers and tail out of the way, she could see the rest of the contents more clearly. A single pig's ear in another resealable plastic bag, dark brown but identifiable from the metal clip embedded in it, just as she had seen on the local farms on many occasions. Plus dozens more similar clips also in a clear plastic container, but without pig's flesh attached. She pulled out a pouch containing a bundle of furry ears, from various sized dogs from the look of it, some cat's ears and the tip of a cat's tail. Below that, there was a pack of rabbit's feet, another with feet from what Suzie assumed were sheep, and then a bushy red fur tail, from a fluffy dog or maybe a squirrel, that appeared to be much fresher than anything else, going by the colour of the crusted blood on the end of it.

In a daze, Suzie scooped all the items out, and dumped them in the gym bag, struggling not to vomit. As she zipped the thing, she put the back of her hand to her mouth, then heaved as her insides revolted in protest. A thin stream of tea, bile and drool trickled over her slippers as she stood up, the room spinning around her.

She slammed the empty drawer closed with her foot, and squeezed her brow between her fingers and thumb, her world spinning as she tried to recover from the shock of this latest revelation about her delinquent son.

With her head bowed, she whispered the Lord's Prayer, but her mind still worried at the things she'd discovered. The black candles had taken on new significance, along with the kindly Doctor's words about Billy channelling his evil uncle, conjuring that foul specimen back into their lives. Thoughts of demonic possession entered her mind, but the simple words of the prayer helped push them out.

By the time she reached *Amen*, the room stopped rotating around her. With a silent thanks to her maker, she picked up the bag and went to the house, unable to think any further, her mind refusing to co-operate. On autopilot, she made herself more tea, dumping in extra spoonfuls of sugar to help her recover. She sat at the table, sipping slowly, gradually coming out of her trance, still staring at the holdall, placed on the worktop where she had left it.

The kitchen clock ticked at her, the noise loud, urging her to do something. Anything.

The Business Pages.

With that single thought, Suzie grabbed her smartphone and searched for a list of local emergency locksmiths open for business twenty-four hours a day. It was only a quarter past seven, but she called the first five numbers in turn, finally satisfied when she found one who agreed to come immediately, equipped for the jobs she had in mind. By the time Billy hauled himself out of bed, his annex would be secure. With his important documents, including his passport in her possession, Suzie finally felt she was regaining some control over his life.

While waiting for the locksmith to arrive, she made one other call. To that lovely psychiatrist. Doctor Powers. The man who had promised to help her and her son.

———

'This is about as close as we can get, Doc.'

Jack parked on a yellow line at the junction of Harley Street and Devonshire Street, unable to turn the corner to the Caduceus Clinic as access was blocked by the police who had cordoned off the area. Doc could see the rear end of a fire engine parked in the middle of the narrow one-way street just beyond the blue and white tape, and was glad Jack had managed to get them both here before the traffic started to build up.

Doc let go of the grab handle above his door—his left hand had been glued there since they left Pangbourne. Jack had driven them both in his Jaguar to the centre of London, and Doc had stopped looking at the speedometer the first time the needle hit one hundred and forty miles an hour. Jack had seen Doc's face and given him a grim smile, claiming, 'Don't worry, mate. I'm a trained professional. I've passed all the Met's advanced driving courses with flying colours, and I'm current.'

The reassurance had not done much for Doc's stress levels and his heart had objected to this abuse, banging on his sternum such that he thought Jack might hear the noise, and maybe slow down. No chance of that.

Doc sighed and followed him from the car, under the tape and past the uniformed officer who clearly knew Jack by sight, as he merely nodded them both through. The smell of smoke and petrol, mixed with a hint of burnt chemicals, hung in the air. An oppressive reminder of the heinous murder of their friend. And Felix.

Although the body had not been formally identified, Doc had called both Dickie's home and mobile phones and left several messages for him. All with no response. The man was an early riser, and there was no way he would ignore Doc's urgent requests for him to call back as soon as he woke.

Doc had been hoping they were wrong, but they had both been silent for much of the journey, quietly mourning their friend, trying to come to terms with their grief. He plodded after Jack, then followed him into the mobile incident suite parked in the road outside the clinic.

Where Dickie's Bentley should be.

Doc squeezed into the narrow unit, peering over Jack's shoulder. They shook hands with one of the four plain-clothes policemen already inside, all seated at work stations, each with a PC screen, two on each side of the trailer. The man Jack spoke to swivelled his chair to face them, and slurped at a paper cup full of Costa coffee. It smelt good to Doc, especially after the acrid stink from outside.

'It's not official yet, but we are pretty certain it's Professor Maddox... I've already had a call from the Commissioner. Maddox was very well connected, went to school with our last Prime Minister, she reckoned, so the pressure's on for us to wrap this up as rapidly as we can. Any help you can give us, Jack, would be most welcome.'

Doc wondered just how welcome it would be when Soundbite heard that Jack and he had been here this morning, poking around. Especially as Jack had told his boss he didn't have his warrant card with him when she demanded it last night while suspending him. He was on holiday, he'd said, so claimed he didn't have it with him. In fact, it had been in Doc's lounge—he had poked it down the side of the sofa cushion moments before Hammond regained consciousness, and had recovered it last night.

Jack bent forward, eyes on the other detective's screen as some CCTV footage rolled. Doc stretched his neck to see the images, then one of the other officers pushed past him and let himself out of the cramped unit. With more room, Doc got a better look at the video, and listened as the detective gave them a full briefing on the Met's activities since the first emergency call from a neighbour, including what had happened during the dawn raid in south Reading.

'This doesn't make sense to me.' Jack squashed a finger on the screen as the detective froze the view of the Volvo's registration plate, with the man in the parka stepping from the car to the kerb immediately adjacent to where they were right now. Doc agreed with the point he made. 'Why disguise your face but not bother to nick a car? That parka. It wasn't exactly brass monkey weather last night, either, was it?'

Freeze the balls off a brass monkey.

No, not that cold, Doc thought.

'Yeah, well, the bloke wasn't home when our CT boys knocked on his door this morning. The car is registered to a Mr Smith, can you believe? First name's John.'

'Seriously?' Jack tutted his disbelief. 'John Smith?'

A name that common, the man might as well have been anonymous, but the other detective added, 'Middle name's Roland. He's got previous.' He punched at some buttons on his keyboard and the man's criminal records appeared on screen, with a mugshot at the top of the page.

Doc gasped. The name John Smith had not set any alarm bells ringing in his mind, until the mention of the middle name.

Doc knew a paedophile called Smith, who went by the name Roland, as he preferred it to his formal Christian name of John. They had met two decades before today, although the face on the screen immediately confirmed to Doc it was the same man. As a forensic psychiatrist, he had assessed Smith at a judge's request when the offender was first incarcerated at a secure psychiatric hospital while awaiting formal sentencing for molesting a young boy—one of his pupils at a very exclusive private school.

And more recently, Dickie had called Doc about the same man, long since released for that first transgression, but in trouble again, this time for storing obscene videos of young boys on his laptop. Dickie had been treating Smith, also at Broadmoor hospital, had emailed Doc the man's file for his advice, and they had discussed the possibility of repeat offences if he recommended Smith was released.

'What?' Jack's voice penetrated Doc's mind at the exact same time as the man's history. 'A bleedin paedo. With no history of arson? Fire-bombs a London Clinic for no apparent reason? I'm not convinced.'

'He *knew* Dickie.' All four faces turned from the screens, attention on Doc, as he announced his conclusions. 'Roland Smith was being held at Broadmoor, and Professor Maddox eventually recommended releasing him, but only after he agreed to take an experimental drug. One being tested on paedophiles who have reoffended… A form of chemical castration that dampens their libido. Smothers their criminal sexual desires.'

'Motive.' The seated detective nodded to himself, delighted to hear this unexpected news, a welcome piece of the jigsaw puzzle. 'Well you just saved us some time, Doctor Powers. We'd have found that information eventually, but it's good to know we're on the right track with this bastard.'

Jack was shaking his head, his crumpled brow quizzing Doc for more, desperate for this unexpected insight to be wrong. Jack had already made up his mind about the identity of the perpetrator.

'Possibly…' Doc was thinking about Billy, too. And the correspondence the boy had probably stolen during their sessions together. 'Is there any chance you can get the technicians to enhance the facial features from the CCTV video, and then use recognition software to confirm it's Smith?'

'Not likely from the local tapes, Doctor. Though we are checking everywhere along the route back to his home, gathering any video available.'

'You're checking motorway service stations too? On the M4?' Jack was animated as he made the suggestion. Keen to be proven right, Doc thought. 'He had to fill those jerrycans somewhere. We might get a better headshot from one of their security cameras.'

'We're already on it, Jack. There's one other interesting thing, though.' The detective searched through several video clips on fast forward. All were shot from different angles and locations, none of them directly overlooking the clinic entrance. 'Unfortunately, the security cameras on the premises were destroyed, so we don't have a view from within looking out at him. But we do have this.' He set the film rolling. 'Look.'

Although the video was grainy, they could see the man pouring something into the jerrycan and then giving it a shake to mix the contents.

'Some form of chemical accelerant?' Jack's voice was sharp. 'Mixed with the petrol?'

'That's what the fire officer reckoned—they haven't identified it yet, but hopefully they'll let us know what it is later today.'

Jack explained about Doc's boat, the potential similarities between the crimes, and then left the detective following up with the Reading fire officers to get more information. He did not mention Billy Leech, much to Doc's surprise, especially after what they had read last night. Some of Billy's neat annotations in his copy of *The Anarchist Cookbook* indicated he had more than a passing knowledge of bomb-making and Molotov cocktails. As they walked back to the car, Doc asked him why.

'They think they have the right guy, with this Smith pervert. You've just confirmed the man's motive—Dickie turned his balls to jelly. They won't seriously consider Billy as a suspect—'

'What about the Molotovs? And the powder? His history of arson, blowing up that car with the Dooley gang?' It was unlike Jack to hold back from his colleagues like this, though Doc could have mentioned their suspicions just as easily. He wasn't even sure why he did not.

Jack opened the car door, voice impatient, clearly desperate to get going as he answered. 'If I did manage to convince them, they would only get in the way of my investigation. If they're right, and this was done by Smith, then fair enough. If I'm right, and that little turd has been doing more than blowing up nicked cars and burning down school buildings, well, I want to deal with him. Personally.'

'For Dickie and Felix?'

'For Sally, mate... Get in. I want to get back and talk to the brat, and his mother.'

'Speaking of which...' Doc held up his phone, softly buzzing and vibrating, and held it out for Jack to read the caller ID. 'Looks like Mrs Leech is also keen to talk to us.'

Billy woke with a start, eyes wide. A glance at the bedside clock told him he had slept for less than four hours since his mother had come knocking on his door. A dreamless period of unconsciousness, enough to refresh him for the day ahead.

For a few minutes, he reflected on his achievements, checking the news on his smartphone, luxuriating in the pleasant afterglow of his murderous actions. Powers may not yet have been confirmed dead, but the night's efforts had yielded an unexpected bonus.

Maddox.

Another crispy critter...

He giggled and reached for his erection, then masturbated furiously until he came, all the while thinking about his victims.

I hope the pair of them suffered.

It was a shame he had been unable to witness their agony, but so be it. His birthday would put things right, as he would make sure he had a prime spectator's seat for his grand finale.

He jumped out of bed and went to the bathroom for a shower. On the way, he stopped outside Nana's door and heard his mother talking to her. She was becoming even more of a pain in the arse than usual, and he wondered what the two of them were yakking about.

Probably me...

With them both unsullied by his usual medication, there was a slim chance that they could upset his plans. Unlikely as it was, the idea set his jaw muscles pulsing.

Inferior beings, the pair of them.

No. They wouldn't—*couldn't* stop him. He was superior in so many ways.

Billy showered in a perfunctory manner, then darted back to his room to put on a tee shirt and jeans. He spent a few minutes sculpting his appearance with a hair dryer and some gel, thought about shaving the stubble on his chin and jaw, but thought he looked more rugged with it, then went to the kitchen in search of sustenance.

His mother was still with Nana, but she had left some pancakes for him, so he smeared Nutella on four of them, piled them high and began stuffing the food in his mouth as he went out to the annex. He choked up a clod of semi-masticated chocolate flavoured dough, and spat it to the grass as he took in the new additions to the building.

What the actual fuck...?

Steel security grills were now affixed to the walls, like prison bars preventing access in or out of the windows. This was not good, but worse was the realisation that the person who had done this—and it certainly wasn't his mother as she could barely operate a screwdriver without supervision—had been inside the building, and secured the steel frames from within.

The remaining pancakes slid from his fingers and dropped to the floor unnoticed, as he took in the new additions. He screwed up his toes inside his trainers, checked to see if he was dreaming. He was not.

With a burst of energy, Billy ran at the nearest grill, leapt into the air and grabbed the crossbar at the top with both hands, and landed with his feet planted on the brickwork either side of the window and hauled, with every sinew in his body straining, threatening to pop from the effort. The metal wouldn't budge.

He was grudgingly impressed with the workmanship, and dropped to the ground, wondering why his mother would have paid for this. Was she worried about theft? That made no sense to him—the main house was unprotected by comparison, and it's not as if there was anything of serious value inside the annex. The bars would have cost more to install than his TV and computer would to replace.

Billy went to the door, his key in hand, but there was no longer a single mortice latch to unlock. A new escutcheon had appeared, emblazoned with the Yale logo. He was sure he could have smashed his way through both locks, if it wasn't for the newly installed outer gate. With eight horizontal steel bars on a sturdy frame, hinged then padlocked closed across the entire doorway. Again, bolted to the wall from the inside.

The fucking bitch has locked me out of my own bloody rooms!

Fury at his mother's gall was building within him, a pressure cooker of seething emotions, bubbling away with no immediate prospect of release. He tried to look through the windows to see whether she had been nosing around his things in there too, but it all looked much as he'd left it.

Punishment? Is that it?

Had she locked him out in response to his refusal to talk to her?

That seemed likely, but the thought didn't help make him feel any calmer.

Maybe he could find some tools to force his way back into the place. It was a shame he had been too busy and preoccupied with adjusting his plans to collect his bolt cutters, having left them under that tree with the ruined cable lock on Sunday afternoon. Maybe he could cycle over and retrieve them now.

He went to the garage and Gramps' workshop—only to be confronted by newly installed high tensile padlocks dangling from huge steel hasps. Out of unreasoning frustration, he went on the attack. The raw pain from the thuds of his forehead and fists repeatedly denting the metal of the up-and-over door—a heavyweight steel panel his security conscious engineer grandfather had installed—only further incensed him.

My bloody bike's in there!

The thought that he was without wheels built an even greater head of steam, raging inside him, just as another possibility occurred to him.

The cellar? Noooooo…

He ran to the side entrance, dreading what he would find, and stopped at the cellar door, grateful for this one small victory over his mother. No padlocks, no steel bars, no new security of any description—the door was still locked, and he had the key in his pocket.

Billy leaned his forehead against the wood and tried to meditate, to control the savage urge to kill, now welling up inside him. He could go down the steps and finish Smith right this minute. Or even set up his firework display to detonate the house a day early.

With his mother and grandmother still inside the building…

It was tempting, but with some heavy breathing, and using the martial arts discipline he had spent thousands of hours developing, he brought himself back under control and went to confront his mother.

***

'Sit down, son. I know you're angry—'

Suzie would not have been at all surprised to see steam curling off him. Her boy's face, scarlet, his bright pink ears twitching as he thrust his lower jaw back and forth. His bottom lip, curling over his front teeth, fists bunching and unbunching as he stood with the light behind him from the open back door. Suzie was having trouble trying to stay calm herself, but fear, not rage, was her problem.

'You have no idea how pissed off I am.' Billy moved into the kitchen, placed his bunched knuckles on the table top and stared down at her. Suzie had seen him in the garden and deliberately positioned herself here, seated opposite the back door, waiting for him, with the table a flimsy barrier between them. It was the best she could do, and she was ready to run if he lashed out, or pulled his knife on her again. 'What the hell are you thinking, Mother? First, going through my things upstairs, and now locking me out of *my* annex.'

'It's not your annex any more.'

'WHAT?'

'And you're grounded. You'll be staying home until further notice. No more bike rides, no more canoeing, no more outings anywhere, until I say so.' Suzie tried to put some steel in her tone, attempting to sound like she was in control. His withering stare made it difficult and she heard the fear in her voice as she spoke. 'And if you take my car without permission like before, I'll report you to the police this time, and make sure they lock you up. Now, sit!'

Suzie sensed him coiling himself, getting ready to attack. His journal was on her lap, under the table, along with some other documents she had selected from his files. With one hand keeping hold of the latter, she lifted the book for him to see, and then threw it at his hands, still planted on the table top.

The colour of Billy's face changed almost instantly, from crimson to pale pink, then gradually faded to white. In those moments, he seemed to shrink into himself. Became younger, less threatening, more vulnerable again. He whispered a few hoarse words as he pulled out the chair and sat, wearily.

'You've been through my files.'

'I certainly have. There are some terrible things recorded in that bloody book. All written in your handwriting.' Suzie became more confident. Her son was silent, his head down, staring at the journal, his thumb rubbing at the corner of the front cover. 'Is it a diary? Have you been doing all those terrible things you've written about in there, Billy?'

'No.' Barely audible.

'What is it, then? Because it sure looks like a diary to me!'

'It's not… I'm a bit ashamed of it all, Mum. I often have bad thoughts—'

'Bad thoughts! That barely begins to describe the goings on you've recorded in that journal.'

He fired back at that. 'It's a story—that's all.' Suzie noted the spark, the reappearance of his usual arrogant self before the conciliatory tone returned. 'I make shit up. I'm planning on writing a novel. Okay…? None of it's real.'

A *novel?*

It certainly read like some deranged lunatic's idea of entertainment, if harming defenceless animals and burning things down was on their list of fun things to do. Suzie found that hard to swallow, but would give him the benefit of the doubt. For now.

'And these?' She flung the handful of papers at him, and they fluttered in his face, bouncing off his shocked countenance before floating to the table and floor. 'I counted twenty pages with my signature on them. Only, it's not really my signature, is it, son?'

'What are you on about? 'Course, it is!'

'I know my signature, so don't even—'

'Bullshit! You think you know what you're like, even when you're pissed up? Or high as a fucking kite?'

'Don't you dare…' Suzie grabbed the journal and flicked through it until she found a section headed, *Gaslighting*. She spun the opened book back for him to read. 'Do you really want to play the innocent, Billy? Your *novel* makes interesting reading… I wasn't familiar with the term, but I am *intimately* familiar with the techniques, having been subjected to endless lies and manipulation by my own flesh and—'

'It's just a story! And I didn't forge your—'

'STOP! Just stop it, Billy.' Suzie wanted to pummel his face, to wipe the sly smile that had been twitching at his mouth since she mentioned the word *gaslighting*, as if he was still able to lie and confuse anyone around him, even when they'd found out what he had been doing to them. 'Believe me, son. That's not my signature, drunk or sober.' Suzie grabbed a handful of sheets and waved them at him, furious now, no longer afraid of him. 'I will happily pay a handwriting expert to confirm it, if you continue to deny you did this.'

Billy probed at the inside of his mouth with his tongue. Even with his lips clamped tight, Suzie could see it working its way from one side to the other, first over his upper teeth and then the lower ones. Thinking.

Scheming?

Considering how he could turn this around? How to manipulate her?

He would not succeed. Suzie had read his book of tricks, and would not let him control her ever again. She stood, and now looked down her nose at him, certain she had re-established her rightful parental role, her authority over her wayward offspring.

'You've even been scratching my face, haven't you? At night... Deliberately infecting my transplants... How could you, Billy?' She had to know. 'Do you believe you're communicating with your uncle? I saw the shrine. The black candles.' Her voice, fevered, shrill, almost out of control. 'It's all in your head, son. Peter Leech is no hero. No guru! He's a murderer. He did this to me, for God's sake!' Her hand covered the offending cheek, but Billy smiled up at her, openly sneering now. She bellowed, 'HE WAS FUCKING EVIL... And he is dead. Dead! You stupid, stupid child.'

'You know nothing about him. You know nothing about me.' He slowly got to his feet and said, 'Believe what you like, you dopey cunt.' Suzie's shocked gasp at the uncouth insult, tossed at his own mother in such a casual fashion, merely broadened his grin. 'I'm going to my room. Now that I'm *grounded*... At least, until you hit the bottle again.' He snorted and went to leave.

Suzie lost it.

She flew at him, slapping his head, scratching at his eyes, her mind no longer in control of her limbs, her feet kicking at his shins.

All to no effect.

He shrugged off her feeble blows, grasped her forearms with fingers of steel, probing for her nerves, sending pain jetting through her neck and shoulders, paralysing her. He then pulled her up, until she was on tiptoe, his hands just above his own head, their eyes level.

His, malignant and green-blue, telegraphing his rage at her.

She suddenly realised how powerless she was—how *powerful* he was—and all the fight flushed away as rapidly as it had arrived.

'Pathetic. Cow.'

He seemed to do no more than open his hands but she was flung backwards and felt her lower back slam into the corner of the table, the pain knocking the breath from her lungs, igniting sparklers in her brain, dazzling her.

She blinked through her agony, and tried to stand as she looked up at his cruel face. The same harsh, callous, uncaring face, worn by his father on the worst night of Suzie's life.

She fingered her cheek and muttered, her voice a whimper. 'It wasn't my fault. It was you, all along.'

'Haha! You believe that if you want. You should be blaming that greedy bastard, Maddox... I despise you for squandering our money on endless, pointless operations at his overpriced clinic. But you won't be doing that any more.'

Suzie staggered upright, kidneys bruised and aching, and tried to follow him to the stairs, not understanding his comment. 'Don't you believe it, Billy. I will get myself back to normal. With his help!'

He turned on her, his face a vile mask of demonic intent, as if some creature from hell had taken over his mind and body. His hand shot out and gripped her lower jaw. She thought he was going to break it, tear it off her face, his fingers were that strong. He pulled her to him and she felt hot breath on her ear as she wriggled, trying to free herself by burying her tatty nails in his arm.

'The clinic's gone, Mummy dearest… Someone had the good sense to burn the place to the ground.'

'No! Stop lying—'

'I'm not… You should try watching the news occasionally. You might learn something about the real world.'

He shoved her away, this time without so much force, and left her standing, shivering in the hall, suddenly ashamed that she had wet herself with fear without even realising it.

Billy was gone, as soundlessly as ever.

What did he mean about the Professor's clinic?

And was her son the *someone* who had burned the property to the ground?

Suzie turned on the TV, found a news channel and watched, not sure what to believe any more.

Billy Liar…

When the newscaster finally described the details of this morning's horrific incident in Harley Street, she clapped both hands over her mouth, her knees buckling. Then, yet more shocking news filled her tormented ears. Professor Maddox had been inside his apartment at the time. Suzie bowed her head, tears falling to the carpet as she whispered a prayer for him, the poor soul who had been so cruelly murdered…

Immolated.

By her own flesh and blood.

Chief Superintendent Sadie 'Soundbite' Dawson's voice echoed through the speakers in Jack's car as she berated her most insubordinate senior officer from the comfort of her plush office at Scotland Yard.

'You've been suspended, Carver. What is it about that term you find so difficult to understand?'

Jack grimaced at Doc as he parked his Jag at the service station on the M4 westbound, just short of Windsor, all the while regretting his decision to borrow his friend's spare phone. It hadn't taken Soundbite long to find out they had been to London, although Jack had been hopeful she might not hear about their expedition at all.

Fat chance.

The phrase resonated in his memory, taking him back to Sunday afternoon and Felix-the-fat-chancer. A guilty conscience was a rare commodity in Jack's list of character traits, but he felt it then, though the moment passed as he tried appealing to his boss's better nature.

'I wasn't working, Ma'am. Dickie Maddox is… was a mate, and I just—'

'A mate! And that's exactly why you and your pal Powers should be nowhere near this investigation. Or the one into the explosion that murdered your son-in-law.'

'Felix was not my—'

'Don't argue with me…'

The silence that followed was ominous, and Jack should have stayed quiet and let her continue. He didn't.

'I'm just trying to help—'

'The detectives handling *both* cases do not need your assistance. We already have a suspect, and plenty of incriminating video from this morning. As for the boat, well —just leave the Reading detectives to it. They don't need help from a Neanderthal thug like you. You can't even control your emotions, thumping a colleague like that.'

'That's not fair.'

'Enough! You have an upcoming misconduct review to think about, and I might just convince my colleagues in Reading to press charges against you for assault on a fellow officer if you continue to disobey my direct commands. So, go and finish your holiday, Carver. That's an order. Don't make yet more trouble for yourself by ignoring it.'

'Come on, Sadie—'

'It's Chief Superintendent Dawson to you, Carver. And if I hear any more about you poking your nose in where it's not wanted, I will have you arrested for interfering with an ongoing police investigation. Do I make myself clear?'

'Absolutely, Boss.'

'And I hope Powers is still with you, and earwigging in on this conversation.' Jack and Doc exchanged glances at that, with Jack wondering if the bloody witch had eyes everywhere. 'Because I will have him arrested too, if you two carry on with your unofficial investigations. Christ Almighty—you're both way too close to these events to be involved in any way, shape or form. Now piss off on vacation, Jack, and don't let me hear another whisper that you've been disobeying my orders again. Or I promise you, your career will be over.'

Click.

'Wow.' Doc stared out of the windscreen, then turned to Jack and asked, 'So, what do we do now?'

'We get some bleedin brekkers—that's why we stopped here. They do a great fry up and there's a decent Costa Coffee outlet too.' Jack knew that was not what Doc meant, was aware that he was in denial and that Soundbite meant exactly what she said. He shoved open his door and swivelled his legs out, unfolded himself from the car and yawned. 'That's better. Come on. I'm starving.'

Doc traipsed after him and they ordered their food and drinks without any further conversation, but Doc had plenty to say when they sat down with their loaded trays.

'She's serious. You could lose your job if you carry on with this, Jack. It's not worth it. Let me see the Leeches. Alone. I can get away with it. Think about it. Billy came to me for help in the first place, and Mrs Leech has just invited me to visit them this afternoon, to talk to them both...' Doc ignored his food and coffee, his entire focus on Jack. 'You, on the other hand...' He let the words tail off.

Jack tucked into his plate of eggs and bacon, then took a gulp of scalding coffee before replying. 'Are you gonna eat? We haven't got all day. And stop staring at me like that. I'm coming with you. End of.'

Doc took a few more seconds to eyeball him, then shrugged and started eating. Through a mouthful of omelette, he asked about something that had not entered Jack's mind since Doc first mentioned it. 'Did you get anywhere with the video records from the royal protection squad? Regarding Billy, and any nocturnal activities in the immediate area?'

'It slipped my mind, to be honest. They're very tight-lipped about any goings on around the royal premises they're tasked to watch. They can't risk leaks to the newspapers. Or tip-offs to the paparazzi. Why?'

'Dickie was very well connected…'

'Yeah, I know, may he rest in peace.' The London detective at Harley Street had called to confirm the body was that of Professor Maddox immediately before Sound-bite had given Jack an earful. 'Old Etonian and friend to the former Prime Minister. Regularly invited to lunch at the Houses of Parliament by his Establishment buddies… You think dropping his name with the Royal Protection Detail would help?'

'It's worth a try.'

Jack wiped some egg from his chin with a tissue, then scraped his plate clean with the last of his toast. Doc had not eaten much of his omelette, and now bit into an apple instead.

Maybe he's watching his diet. Heart problems and all that…

Jack took his cigarettes outside and waited for Doc as he smoked. He pulled his phone from his pocket, thinking Charlie might be able to help him.

'I heard you were suspended, Jack. And I'm not supposed to be talking to you.'

He turned on the charm as best he could, given his mood, and promised to take her out to the venue of her choice if she agreed to assist, desperately trying to convince her to help. Then, 'Please, Charlie. I just need you to make the call, that's all. If they respond positively, I'll go and see 'em and keep you out of it. No risk to you. Fair enough?'

'Okay. I'll see what I can do.' She didn't even say goodbye.

Doc joined him and they strolled to the car as Jack finished his cigarette. Jack's phone buzzed as a message arrived.

'Good news?'

Jack looked up from the screen at Doc's question, smiling—and for the first time it felt genuine. Ever since the boat blew up on Sunday.

'Yeah. Charlie's got us in with her mate with the royal protection mob. We'll head over there now…' His grin broadened and he chuckled as he added, 'I might just marry that woman. She's a right gem.'

Billy could hear the TV burst into life as he searched his mother's room. She was such an idiot. Thinking he would just meekly go to his bedroom when sent. And he knew exactly where to look for the things she had stolen from him.

As predictable as ever.

The drawer wasn't even locked. Her old wardrobe had three such drawers, and this bottom one was where she kept her secrets.

Well, my secrets, today.

Only, they weren't there. Nor were the new keys he expected to find…

Shit!

He did discover some papers there, though. Very interesting ones. He pocketed them, then stepped back and looked around the room. It took no time before he spotted the edge of his gym holdall, tucked at the top of the wardrobe, with just a fraction of the logo showing between his mother's empty suitcases, also stowed there.

Billy jumped up, grabbed the handle and hauled the bag down, then checked the contents.

It looked like everything important was in there—his concertina file and the various trophies he had kept. He slipped the passport and bank details into his pocket—finding those was a major relief—but it was good to have the rest of his possessions back too. Not least, the two small ziplock bags containing powder, tucked in the file marked XXX.

He paused, wondering what she did with his cookbook and dream diary, and where they might be, along with the twists of paper she had stolen from his bedside drawer…

It was intriguing, especially the diary, but he was not too worried as it had been written in his own secret code and no one else would be able to make much sense of it.

Having recovered his supply of LSD, maybe he could lie on his bed and visit with his guru—if he could control his temper.

He was still seething.

Even with the psychedelic drug mixed with some Temazepam he may not be able to relax sufficiently.

If he could get some of the drugs into his mother's system, that would be more of a help to him. Then he might be able to blag things…

Except, she still had his journal.

His *novel*.

He was in no mood to laugh, but had to cackle at that cunning comeback. When she had chucked it across the table at him, he'd thought his entire plan would unravel, that she would hand him over to the police. Many of his exploits were laid bare for anyone to read, but she gave the impression she didn't want to believe it was true. He could see her hesitation when he told her it was all just make believe.

It was a good job it wasn't up to date… He'd outgrown scribbling in that thing several months ago.

He pulled her door to behind him and stood on the landing listening. His mother was moaning and sobbing. The sound made him smile so he stayed there, listening to her misery for a full minute, then went to his room.

Time to hide the evidence.

He emptied the DVD rack situated below the bracket supporting his TV screen and pulled it away from the wall to expose the hidden fireplace. The one Gramps had blocked off a couple of decades before, soon after he had installed central heating. The panel wasn't designed to be removed, but then again, this was not a particularly robust piece of workmanship. A few careful strokes from his knife blade unsealed the fibreboard panel—painted the same colour as the rest of the wall. After replacing it with the bag secured behind, Billy was confident no one would find his things in there. He slid the DVD rack back home, and replaced his collection, making sure everything was in alphabetical order, meticulously lined up, just like normal.

Calmer now, and sitting cross-legged at the head of his bed, his back propped against the wall, Billy took a pinch of LSD, dropped it on his tongue, swallowed and then closed his eyes. He controlled his breathing and meditated until the roof opened up, the sky above him blossomed, and his Uncle Peter entered his life once more…

Doc had thought the observation post would be close to the Middleton's home on Pease Hill, but it was nowhere near, located in a grotty terraced house in Woolhampton overlooking the A4. The village was about halfway along the trunk road connecting Reading and Newbury, a good twenty minutes' drive from the princess's parents' home. Jack explained why.

'They can't afford to rent a house out there, mate. Those properties are all worth millions, and rentals are as rare as hens' teeth. Even if there was a place available nearby, the cost would be exorbitant. Hence this dump.'

Dump was an apt description. There was no garden at the front, just some tarmac with tufts of weed growing through it. The entire property was no wider than the Jaguar was long, and the front door looked rotten, threatening to disintegrate if anyone was unwise enough to use the rusty knocker, half hanging off it. They didn't need to—the door opened the moment they approached.

'Jack Carver and Doctor Powers. Well, I'll be damned. Nice to meet you Doctor. Come on in.'

Jack pumped the man's hand as they stepped into the hall. Doc noted the steep stairs to their right, and a tiny lounge off to the left. He could just about see into the kitchen at the back, and it looked to be no larger than his walk-in wardrobe.

Jack made the introductions and then explained to Doc, 'Terry's an old mate from donkeys' years ago.' He beamed at his colleague. 'I had no idea you were working on the royals, matey. I'd have called you myself had I known. Charlie—'

'Yeah, I know. You're not here now, never have been... She said you were suspended for whacking that gobshite, Hammond, from Reading nick. Haha! I'd heard you clocked him one. Good on yer!' Terry motioned for them to join him upstairs and described the operation as he went. Doc was not surprised to see the holster hanging from the back of his belt, the gun bouncing on the officer's bum as he clambered up the steps. 'We just keep an eye on all the cameras and other surveillance kit stationed around the royal residence. We've got about thirty CCTVs in the vicinity, and we can also tap in to any of the traffic cams on the main roads around here, an' all.'

'Thirty cameras?' Doc was amazed. They had driven past the place on the way to the Leech home on Monday, but he had not spotted any. 'And aren't you a bit far away to respond to an emergency?'

'We have a team on location. Armed and extremely dangerous. We take it in turns to sit in here, keeping an eye on the recordings, noting anything out of the ordinary. So, what can I do for you good folks?'

The upper floor was a revelation—like a high-tech cruise ship's control room. The internal walls were gone, opening out the space for the handful of giant screens Doc could now see. These surrounded an impressive comms console with a luxury swivel chair for the operator.

'It's just like Star Trek in here. Are you on your own?'

'Yeah—until seven tonight, then I get relieved. We used to have a duty team of four doing this, round the clock, but much of the job's automated now. Computers with cunning algorithms assess all the movements in the area covered by our monitors, combine that with feeds from regional traffic cams and then alert the operator about anything odd. That info's then sent to the boys on site to check out. Got facial recognition for the drivers and passengers, automatic number plate recognition, and automatic alerts if there's unidentified cars from outside the local area cruising by...

Anything suspicious, like odd deliveries and so on. We scoop it all up, and this,' he patted the console the way he might pet his dog, 'does all the analysis for us. Pretty boring really. Protecting the royals sounds glamorous but it ain't.'

'Bloody hell.' Jack looked suitably impressed. 'So, I'm looking for a kid on a bike, late at night, or in the early hours.' He passed a scrap of paper to Terry. 'Or a car with this registration, also moving at odd times during the night.'

Doc guessed it was the Leech woman's car. Jack would have memorised the number plate during Saturday's attack on the Bentley.

Terry sat at his console, and put a query into the machine, almost in plain English, giving them a running commentary as he typed.

'It's an intelligent system. Bit like a super Google search, and it should throw up anything that meets your criteria. This is state of the art surveillance. Regular GCHQ gear.' Terry was clearly proud of his machine's capabilities. 'Over what time period are we talking?'

Jack laughed and said, 'Seven years would be good, but from last Friday would do us for now.'

Less than an hour after arriving, Doc and Jack were in the hall, ready to leave. Terry shook their hands again and asked Jack, 'Were you really mates with Professor Maddox?'

'Yeah. Both of us knew him.'

'You know they've already confirmed it was his body at the scene?'

Jack just grunted.

'There's been loads of chatter about it on the airwaves, lots of pressure from the top brass to get a result... Mind you, I'd have helped you anyway, Jack, even without Charlie calling me about Maddox. Do you really think that kid on a bike had anything to do with the fire in London?'

'That's what Doc and I are going to find out. Thanks for this Terry.' Jack held up a USB stick between his index finger and thumb. The one Terry had loaded the search results on to for them. 'I owe you one, mate.'

It was not like Judy to skive off work, and although most of her time was given freely, she felt guilty as she arrived home shortly after lunchtime. She wasn't panicking, but was definitely not feeling one hundred percent.

She had called her GP clinic that morning, though the nurse had sounded unruffled when Judy explained about the few blood spots on her sheet. The woman's advice had been to keep a careful eye on things, to check herself regularly and go straight to hospital if there was an actual flow of red blood rather than just a few drips of ruddy-brown gunk.

'Don't hesitate if there's enough red stuff to fill your panty liners, just get yourself to A&E.'

That was her professional advice, although Judy had not mentioned the stomach cramps. And they were the reason she was now home. She had a mild case of diarrhoea, thanks to Colin's curry. That was most unusual, but her hormones had played plenty of tricks on her in the last few weeks, so she would lie down and rest. Listen to her body for once.

On the way home, she'd heard the radio news and the confirmation that their charming friend Dickie had died in that fire in London, and she shed a few tears for him. The newscaster had given scant details of the event, though had issued the name of someone the police wanted to interview.

John Roland Smith.

At least this terrible tragedy had nothing to do with the Leech boy. Perhaps Colin and Jack were wrong about the lad, although two fires in the space of a few days involving them and their friends seemed too much of a coincidence.

Was someone really intent on harming them?

I just hope Colin will look after himself…

That thought prompted her to send him a quick text message, just to let him know she was home and not to worry about her, even made a joke about his cooking too.

Yet she couldn't eat a thing in her present state, even though she was weak from lack of food. She made herself a cup of green tea, spooned in two dessert spoons of honey, and sipped it before mounting the stairs and flopping on the bed. She closed her eyes and was drifting in and out of sleep when she heard voices from the hallway downstairs. Colin appeared at the door a few seconds later, a worried expression on his face.

'Are you okay, my love?' He sat on the bed and ran gentle fingers through her hair, touched the back of his hand to her forehead. 'You look really washed out.'

'I just want to sleep. I didn't have a good night, and had some morning sickness to start the day. I got to work but felt so tired I decided to come home early.' Why tell him more? He had enough on his plate already, and she would be back to normal tomorrow, for sure. 'Nothing to worry about. Just my body coming to terms with the changes. And you? You didn't sleep much either. Any news?'

'Dickie's dead, sweetheart.' Colin massaged the back of his neck, his features pinched with stress. She squeezed his other hand, a feeble effort at comforting him over the loss of a good friend. 'They've identified a suspect, and expect an early arrest.'

'Well, at least that's good news. Did the fire at the clinic have anything to do with what happened here, on Sunday?' Judy could not fathom how the two events were linked, but was worried all the same. 'And the Leech boy? Do you still think he's involved?'

'We're not sure.' Colin's fingers stopped their circular motion on his neck, then stroked her face as he tried to smile, without much success. 'Jack and I are going to see him and his mother this evening. We thought we'd pop back here for a few hours before our appointment. I'm making some food.' His weight shifted from the bed as he yawned and stretched into an upright position, looking down at her. 'Do you need anything?'

'No. I just want to sleep a little. You take care, my love.'

Judy watched him slip away, the door closing silently behind him.

'I can understand why Smith had it in for Dickie, but did he have a grudge against you too, mate?'

'Why?'

Doc arrived in the kitchen at the same time as Jack, who had just finished speaking to Charlie and was tucking his phone back into his pocket. Jack's few minutes on the patio had not been to sample the country air but to chain smoke two cigarettes in the hope of perking himself up—the lack of sleep was catching up with him. Doc looked none too hot, either.

'Petrol filler caps. Nautical ones… Matching the one on your boat.' Jack thought a strong coffee might help them both too, and the smell of it brewing in Doc's machine made his mouth water. He swallowed, then explained. 'Smith ordered *two* of them online, a few months ago, using his Visa card. But he doesn't own a boat.'

'Two?'

'Yeah. Forensics found a couple of them in his workshop—the locks drilled out. They think one was a test run. One was a bit older, showed signs of wear and tear. Looks like it came off your boat. And the other new one—'

'He used it to replace mine. The one he'd welded a spark plug to…'

'Which is why I asked the question. You said you met him ages ago at Broadmoor.'

'I did… But he was released a year or so after, and if he did have a grudge against me, surely he would've attacked me long ago.'

'And Dickie… You said you two spoke about Smith. More recently.'

'Yes, he often asked my advice on Broadmoor inmates, and I had some history regarding this particular individual, but there's no way Smith could be aware of our conversations and correspondence.'

'Mmm.' Jack had wondered about that. Along with another intriguing titbit of information Charlie had just shared. 'There's a load of other interesting stuff in his workshop too, Doc. Actually, it's a laboratory, a right treasure trove from what she said, well kitted out with plenty of pukka gear for experiments and cooking up all sorts of chemical compounds. The Bomb Squad went in there and they found traces of ANFO, among other things they're having analysed.'

'Smith was making fertiliser bombs?'

'Uh-huh. No sign of where any of that stuff went to, though. No reports of any unexplained explosions involving ANFO during the last eighteen months either. They discovered some powder in there too, though it took them a while to identify it. A home-made mixture of peroxides and other chemicals they reckon would give a real boost to petrol if it's added before ignition.' He clicked his tongue, and saw Doc frown. 'As dangerous to make as nitro-glycerine, they said. Highly unstable until it's crystallised into powder form. Similar to solid rocket fuel.'

'Burns without oxygen…'

'Yup. They've sent the sample to the Reading fire department to confirm it matches the stuff in your boat's fuel tank.' They exchanged a knowing look—it was a foregone conclusion.

'Sounds like Smith's something of an expert on bomb-making.'

'Seems that way—more like a rocket scientist than your average paedo chemistry teacher, that's for sure.'

'So, you think we're wrong about Billy?' Doc's voice suggested he thought that unlikely.

'Nah. He's involved. Somehow… I'd bet my pension on it.' Jack waited as the espresso machine hissed steam into milk for their coffees, his mind on his irritating boss. A scowl pinched his features. 'If I ever get one. I bloody well won't if Soundbite chucks me out on me ear'ole!'

'And there's no trace of Smith?'

'Nope. He's gone to ground. Neighbours reckon he keeps himself to himself. Situation normal for a bloke with his history. Records don't help much either. No living relatives. No registered mobile phone to track him with. No easy way to locate him.'

'Damn.' Doc handed Jack a mug of coffee, then leaned his hip against the counter top as he sipped his latte. 'This is all very baffling... Maybe things will become clearer with the application of some caffeine.'

'There is one other thing.' Jack paused as he blew on his drink to cool it, then tentatively placed his lips on the foam, sensing the coffee beneath was still too hot to sip, even for his asbestos tongue. 'Charlie said they've enhanced their best still image taken from a CCTV camera at the back of a warehouse in south Reading overlooking the Kennet, and she's gonna send a copy to my mobile phone as soon as she gets a chance.'

'Smith?'

'Even with computer magic, the image is still grainy, so there's not enough detail to confirm it's him... Especially as the rider's wearing a parka... With the hood up.'

'Rider?'

'Yup. Pedalling along the towpath... On a fancy looking pushbike.'

'How are you feeling, now, Mum?' After the shock of hearing about the Caduceus Clinic, Suzie had recovered her composure sufficiently to make lunch for her mother, but had not felt like eating, and had decided her son could make his own food today. The evil sod was still in his room, so at least she didn't have to tolerate more of his lies. And her mother was looking decidedly peaky today, too. 'You haven't eaten much.'

Nana continued staring out of her bedroom window, wrapped in her dressing gown, exactly as she had been when Suzie came in first thing this morning. Had she slept at all?

Probably not, Suzie decided. Nana was still distressed, thanks to Billy's outburst the night before. Was it just another lie, his claim that her father had said such dreadful things about living with them, before he killed himself?

She went to lift the tray with Nana's untouched lunch, a bowl of congealed spaghetti carbonara, when a cold, bony hand clutched her wrist.

'I want to visit him. Today.' Like an owl on a perch, her mother's body remained motionless as she swivelled her head to face Suzie. Sad eyes, dribbling tears, tugged at Suzie's heart, and she cursed her son for doing this. Her mother had been so much better over the last two days, more like her old self, but had regressed overnight. All thanks to him. 'Take me to the cemetery. Please.'

'I will. Tomorrow, Mum. We'll make a day of it, if you promise to eat something before we leave.'

Her mother was crestfallen. 'Can't we go now, love?'

'Sorry... I have someone coming to visit this afternoon. A psychiatrist.'

'No!' Nana's vigorous head shaking made her voice joggle. 'I don't need one!'

'No, Mum. I want to discuss Billy with him. I'm very worried about my son.'

'Really?'

'Honestly, he's been saying things just to upset us, telling us both a lot of lies... And I'm sure those things he said about Dad weren't true.'

'You really think so?' Her mother's expression became hopeful, and Suzie wondered if the poor woman had been brooding on Billy's comments all night.

'Yes. I'm positive. Now, can I have my arm back?' Her mum released her fingers, clearly surprised that she had been holding on for so long. 'Now you just relax, get some rest. I'll bring you more food later. Something light, like scrambled eggs. And I promise we'll visit Dad's grave. Okay?'

Her mother's watery smile appeared, then faded, before she turned back to her view from the window without another word.

Suzie went to the kitchen and pottered in there to keep busy. Having barely recovered from the shock of the news from this morning, she could not bring herself to read more of Billy's journal. The awful book was with the forged papers, stuffed into a kitchen drawer with the envelope of photographs she had found. Sickening images of Smith molesting her boy.

And where is he today?

The tutor had not arrived at ten this morning. Unusual, as he never normally missed a scheduled day—only Sunday was completely devoid of lessons. Suzie assumed Billy had tipped him off that she was on the warpath after finding out about their—what? Affair was the wrong term for an abusive relationship. Even if her son was infatuated with the man.

The thought of that monster pawing her lad made her blood curdle. She would raise it all with Doctor Powers and that policeman when they arrived, no matter what Billy threatened. He wouldn't be running off anywhere with anyone, and Smith would be behind bars, where he belonged.

The doorbell rang and Suzie glanced at the clock. Right on time. She snapped off her rubber gloves, dumped them on the draining board, took a few seconds to centre herself, ready for the upcoming meeting, then opened the door.

Both men were smartly dressed, in dark jacket and trousers, white shirts and black ties. The impression was more intimidating than she expected, although she immediately recognised them. Doctor Powers spoke, his voice reassuring.

'This is my friend, Jack Carver, Mrs Leech. Although he's a policeman, he's off duty. This is an informal visit, so please don't be alarmed.'

Had she looked alarmed? Suzie guessed so—just one of many unwelcome emotions flooding through her today.

She invited them in, trying hard to stay composed. They followed her to the lounge, the two men taking seats either end of the sofa, while she sat in one of the two armchairs by the fireplace.

Her father's seat.

'My dad died in this chair.' Both men looked taken aback by the comment, appar- ently irrelevant, but Suzie wanted to explain and directed her attention to Doctor Powers. 'That morning, my mother was screaming his name. The noise woke me, and I came down to find the three of them in here. Billy was sitting there.' She pointed to the armchair opposite. 'He was so... calm. Serene. My mother was in a right state. She found them both sitting like that.'

'Billy was just sitting in here? With your father, already dead in the seat opposite.'

'Yes... He claimed he'd been sitting with him all night. Had watched him die.'

'Bloody hell.' The detective sat back as he cursed, astounded, while the psychiatrist leaned forward, hands clasped between his legs, his elbows on his thighs, face questioning as he spoke.

'And how did your father die, Mrs Leech?'

'Insulin. He was a diabetic. He overdosed.'

'Deliberately?'

'Yes… He told Billy he couldn't face life as an invalid. There was a note from the hospital beside him, on that coffee table. It confirmed his appointment…'

Even when my dad was suffering, I was too busy thinking about *myself*. My medical problems.

She would weep for him again, pray for his forgiveness, later. She continued explaining. 'The consultant had called him in to discuss a possible treatment plan. His feet were ulcerated, necrotic. He thought they would have to amputate.' It was only after the event that she discovered the extent of his ailments. She should have been there for her dad, but it was her son who had sat with him, barely thirteen years old.

'No suicide note?'

'Billy was his suicide note.' She would not share what he had told her last night, and hoped the two men could not tell she was holding back. Then she realised her hand was over her mouth, and pulled it away as she added, 'My father's final confession. That's what he told him. My son sat up with him. Watched him inject himself, then drink a glass of scotch… Chatted together until my father went unconscious, then died. They'd become very close since we came to live here.'

'When was this? The suicide?'

'Almost three years ago.' About the same time everything started to go desperately wrong in this household. She thought it, but chose not to tell them. Was this yet another factor explaining why her son was so disturbed? His latest revelation about what her father had said had made her wonder—had that night somehow poisoned her son's mind against her and her mother? 'Please understand, gentlemen… My boy has been through a great deal of trauma.'

'I think we both appreciate that, Mrs Leech. Don't we, Jack?' The doctor glanced at the policeman, then smiled at her, a genuine warmth in his face. 'That's why we're here. To help.'

Suzie was not at all sure about the detective, but she still felt certain she could trust this man.

'I think you might be too late.' Tears began to well, so Suzie eased herself off the armchair and stood. 'There's something I need to show you.'

Some *things*.

She went to the kitchen and pulled open the drawer, hesitating as she lifted out the contents. It felt like a betrayal, but she needed to share the burden with someone, and who better than the two men who seemed to understand her son's problems? She thought about Billy's gym bag, but decided to show them these items first.

With the small bundle placed on the coffee table between them, Suzie explained. 'My son has been in an abusive relationship. I discovered the truth only yesterday.' She slipped the photographs from the envelope and tried not to look at the graphic images as she passed them across to the detective's outstretched hand. 'His tutor. The man I trusted to educate my son.'

Suzie expected them to be shocked, but their reaction confounded her.

'Jesus Christ, look Doc! It's him.' Both men studied the photographs, heads shaking in amazement. 'Smith. The paedophile teacher...'

With Jack outside, lighting a cigarette while trying to get hold of Charlie by phone, Doc gently probed Mrs Leech for more information on the tutor. She had little to add, only that the man had not shown up since she had confronted her son with the evidence, so they had to assume Smith was in hiding for this, too—not just the attack on the clinic.

Before Jack had excused himself to feed this latest piece of information to his colleagues—via Charlie to ensure his disapproving boss was kept in the dark about his involvement in their inquiries—Mrs Leech had explained how Billy had been brainwashed and planned to run away with the man. She had told them:

'He was deadly serious. I found tickets for them both, dated tomorrow night. Billy's sixteenth birthday. They were going to fly to Thailand together...'

No wonder she looked so devastated when they arrived. Doc had thought she was looking grief-stricken the night before, but now, she seemed almost zombie-like. He could see her experiences had all become too much to bear, and he still had the impression that she had many more secrets to share about her son.

Doc could hear her clattering about in the kitchen, making tea, while he read through the journal she had given him to peruse. Billy's explanation for the contents was beyond fantastic. There were many instances logged that matched the unexplained events recorded by Charlie's sergeant—animal mutilations and burnt properties in the vicinity.

When Mrs Leech passed over the book to Doc, she had opened it at a page that she said described how her son had been manipulating her and her mother. She offered to explain more after she had made them tea.

That was just her excuse to leave the room. And the clattering was probably to disguise the sound of her crying.

Poor woman.

Doc had read enough of the book to understand what Billy had been doing, but the most troubling aspect was the boy's underlying objective. Doc needed to think this through—especially with the bombshell of Smith's illegal seduction of the lad. For whatever reason, Doc was struggling to square the circle.

The manipulative student, being manipulated by his tutor...

He parked the thought, would tackle Billy himself, once Jack and Mrs Leech returned. Doc fingered the sheets of paper she had left on the coffee table—legal documents and letters to their lawyers. It seemed she was a trustee responsible for investments held in Billy's name.

'He inherited millions from his uncle...' Mrs Leech placed a tray between them as Doc bundled the papers aside. 'That odious creature died intestate.'

'Billy was his only blood relative?'

'Yes... My father dealt with everything, then when he died, I became the trustee for the small fortune my son inherited. Dad handled it, said I needed to do nothing until Billy reached his eighteenth birthday. Asset management was all set up through our lawyers.'

'And these?' Doc riffled through the letters, then queried her with a look as she hesitated to answer.

Blood flushed her throat pink as she replied. 'My son has been forging my signature.'

'Really?' Doc inflected the word with some disbelief, although he was sure it was true.

'Yes… Billy decided to access his funds without bothering to ask me. That's how he bought two first class tickets to Thailand. Among other things. I only found all of this out this morning…'

No surprise that she looked so deathly grey, then. Doc took her hand the moment she finished pouring his tea, and held it until she looked down at him.

'I'd like to help you too, Mrs Leech. You can call me any time. To talk about anything.' He gave her his most empathetic smile to reassure her. He genuinely wanted to help. 'Really.'

She brushed a tremulous finger at her damp lower eyelashes, nodded, biting her bottom lip as she sat.

'Thank you. I will.'

Jack returned, and Doc could smell the odour of cigarette smoke on his clothes.

My clothes.

Jack had not yet bothered to fetch any suitable work wear from his London apartment, borrowing things from Doc's wardrobe to save time, instead.

'A nice cuppa.' Jack dropped to the sofa beside Doc. 'Thank you Mrs Leech. There's an alert out for Smith. We'll get him, soon enough.'

Doc passed him the journal with a brief explanation of what Billy had claimed it was, and Jack flipped through the pages while Doc turned his attention back to Mrs Leech.

'I'd like to speak to Billy, if he's here.'

'Yes, of course.' Doc could see her having an internal monologue, debating with herself what to tell them. Then, 'But there's more, I'm afraid, Doctor Powers.'

Doc and Jack listened for fully five minutes as she described the things she had discovered about her son in the last few days, relating some of it to how she had been duped. Drugged.

Gaslit.

Everything she described made the supposed love story between the paedophile tutor and the manipulative boy seem less and less plausible in Doc's mind. A paedophile tutor who had been chemically castrated…

Jack remained quiet—largely thanks to Doc telling him beforehand that he would handle the woman, as that would be best, given that she'd already started to open up to him the night before. Then, when she described the contents of the drawer in the annex, he could sit in silence no longer.

'You've got them? Trophies he's taken? From the dead animals?'

'Yes…' Doc thought she would start crying again, from the look in her eyes and her trembling lips, but she stood and said, 'I'll get them. And Billy. You can deal with him, Detective.'

Mrs Leech left them, her footsteps heavy as she climbed the stairs.

'Blimey, Doc. I can't get me head round it all.'

'Me too… Let's see what the boy has to say for himself.'

Billy already had plenty to say from the sound of it. His voice boomed down the stairs, drowning out the querulous tone of his mother, her words indecipherable.

'You're a fucking mad woman… What gym bag? I don't know what you're on about… I'll happily talk to the police. I'll tell them exactly what's been going on. Now get out of my way.'

Billy, face clouded with anger, stormed into the room, but stopped in his tracks, hitting an invisible brick wall the moment he saw Doc sitting in his lounge.

Doc knew then. Billy looked like he had seen a ghost.

Or rather, seen a living, breathing human—one he clearly believed was already dead.

His mother had barged into his room, her hideous twisted mug gurning more than usual. Billy had laughed inside at the sight of her as she ranted at him about the missing gym bag. Then told him the police were downstairs and wanted to talk to him.

He'd enjoy that.

That's what he thought, until he walked into the lounge and saw that bloody psychiatrist staring at him. Billy, distressed beyond words, still managed to assess the man's reaction and tried to recover his own composure as best he could.

It took a mammoth effort.

The bastard should be dead. But here he was, in their home. Sitting beside that copper from the other night. This had not been in the script, and Billy experienced a disorienting sensation, that made him question whether he was still dreaming.

Sadly, he was not.

This was a situation outside of his control, but he reminded himself of his innate superiority, his significant genetic advantage over these two plebs. He announced his terms as his mother entered the room behind him.

'Doctor Powers. I'll talk to you and the detective, but I want her out of here. She's crazy. Always lying about me.'

'Shut up, Billy! Just you shut your mouth.'

Powers went to her, spoke to her in a low murmur, then guided her from the room by her elbow. Much to Billy's satisfaction.

He sat in Gramps' chair, glared at the detective and said, 'I saw you. At Powers' place the other night. Is that why you're here? To arrest me for kicking that Bentley driver?'

The detective slid his warrant card across the coffee table for Billy to read. 'No, son. I'm here about two murders. Along with multiple other offences.'

'Woo-hoo. A homicide detective. How impressive.' Billy smiled, more comfortable with the witch out of the room. He could do this. 'Sounds exciting.'

Powers returned and sat again. 'Your mother has agreed to allow us to talk to you without her presence.'

'So, you're *the responsible adult* then, Doctor? Looking out for my interests? Fair enough.'

'Not at all. You don't need one, unless you want to invite your mother back in… This is not an official police investigation. Just a chat.'

'This detective says you're here about a couple of murders.'

'In part.' Powers smiled, but Billy sensed animosity from the man. Hostility, hidden beneath the false veneer of charm. As a master of the art himself, Billy always found it easy to spot the trait in others.

Be careful, Billy boy…

His uncle's voice, both reassuring and cautioning him.

'And the other part?'

'Your mother has told me—us—'

'She's an alcoholic junkie. You can't seriously believe a word she says. Here. Look.' Billy pulled from his pocket the papers he had found in her wardrobe drawer. 'This letter came in the post this morning, from a clinic she went to yesterday. Had blood tests done.' He slid the documents across the table. 'Go on. Read it all. She's hooked on morphine, drinks herself stupid, and swallows sleeping pills like Smarties. She's demented. They said she should go into rehab. It's all there in black and white.'

Powers glanced at the contents and passed the paper to the copper, his face inscrutable. 'Your mother told us you've been drugging her, Billy.'

'Ha!' Billy said nothing more. Waited.

'She said you admitted it.'

'I never did. She talks such bullshit.' He tapped his temple with his index finger, then twirled his wrist in a circular motion. 'She's barking mad. She also claims she found a load of stuff in my annex—but I have no clue what she's yapping on about. She's off her head most of the time. I'm sick of it.'

Powers sat back, silently passing the baton to the detective. Billy had heard of the technique—good cop, bad cop. He sniggered.

These two are just so transparent.

'I saw you.' The detective placed the letter back on the table as if the content was of no account. It was pure theatre, and Billy's confidence grew. He could outwit these two fools. Then the detective said, 'Watching Doctor Powers' home on Sunday. When his boat went up in flames.'

That was unexpected.

There's no way this pig can be sure it was me.

Okay, the copper had been in the garden in his ridiculous Hawaiian shirt, looking directly at the lookout post.

No one has eyes that good.

'I dunno what you're on about.'

'You killed a red setter, too. Some poor family's pet, stabbed to death while they were out for a nice Sunday lunchtime walk.'

'Me? I've no idea—'

'On your way to meet the taxi. Before coming home to get the bolt-cutters. The ones I found under that tree you were sitting in.'

Shit!

Billy did some quick mental gyrations, considering whether to lie or admit to being there at all. On balance, sticking to a partial truth seemed best.

'Yeah, I was in the tree. Watching the firemen. So, what of it? And I didn't kill a dog.'

'Watching the firemen?'

'Yeah—it was exciting. Nice boat, by the way, Doctor Powers. At least, it was…' Another snigger.

'But you were there before the explosion, weren't you, son?'

More mental calculations, to decide if the detective knew this for a fact, or was bluffing. Again, Billy decided to tell a version of the truth—one that fitted his narrative.

'Yeah. But I didn't see it. I was there for a bit, then planned to go home, but my bike lock busted. That's why I came back for the bolt-cutters you found. I want them back, by the way.'

'So, you admit you were there to watch the boat being blown up.' The detective was getting visibly agitated, and Billy saw the psychiatrist put a calming hand on his knee for just a second.

This is personal.

Billy wondered then—who the bloke was who'd died in Powers' place that day, and what he meant to this angry copper.

Careful, Billy boy. Killing's easy... But getting away with it... Well that takes a special sort of skill...

His uncle again. Whispering inside his head. Guiding him.

Calming him.

'I admit I was there to see something. Something spectacular.' Billy let the sly smile slither into place as the detective bristled again. The psychiatrist pushed himself forward, motioning with his hand, gesturing to his colleague to relax. Time to throw the dog a bone. 'Smiffy actually used that word. *Spectacular...* Roland Smith. My tutor. He told me to be there at lunchtime. He said there'd be a firework display. One he'd arranged, just for me...'

'Do you expect us to believe you knew nothing about this spectacular firework display your *lover* had arranged?' Jack wanted to throttle the little shit. He was on a very short fuse, and this kid, just sixteen years old, who looked and sounded like he was twenty or so, was confident to the point of cockiness. His sneering grin was another invitation to a bunched fist, just like Hammond, so it was tough to stay calm thinking about how Sally had almost died... And Doc had just excused himself to go and chat with the mother so there was no calming influence to steady him. Jack was on his own with the psycho-brat. 'You're saying you had no idea what he was planning for Sunday?'

'Of course not. I would've tried to stop him if I had.'

'Yet you didn't report Smith after the event. Why not?'

'He's like a father to me.' He shrugged. 'And he didn't actually admit that he did it. If you have proof, why don't you arrest him?'

'What I do have, is this.' Jack held up Billy's copy of *The Anarchist Cookbook*, flicked it open at a page on turning a fuel tank into a fire-bomb. 'These days, people get arrested for even thinking about making bombs—'

'It's for my studies—volatile chemicals. Smiffy encouraged me to read that book to show how common household products and other easily obtained chemicals can be dangerous in the wrong hands. In fact, I made most of those notes in class, with him.' A sneer. 'I doubt you study much of anything, do you, Officer? Some of us are academics and aren't interested in politics and terrorism.'

'If I find out you knew about Smith's plans in advance, I'll have you for conspiracy, at the very least...' Jack changed tack, expecting to wrong foot the lad. 'Your mother said she found a load of trophies. From the animals you tortured.'

'That's bizarre... The woman's clearly certifiable.' Billy leaned forward, a giggle dribbling from his lips. 'She read that,' he tapped his finger on his journal, 'and obviously created another fantasy based on the fiction I wrote in there. If she found any of these things—other than inside her demented drug-infested cranium—where are they then?'

Jack wanted to believe the mother, but the lack of evidence—evidence an admitted addict claimed to have found, that had suddenly gone missing—was a major issue. Even the notes in the journal were inconclusive, though Jack flipped it open and said, 'So this is all fiction, you say?' He grunted. 'Funny. It tallies with a lot of what's been going on around these parts.'

'I heard about some awful things, jotted about them as if my fictional narrator had been doing them. That's all part of the art of storytelling—taking actual events and fictionalising them. It's called using your imagination, Detective. You know, like what your lot do when fitting up a suspect.' Another self-satisfied grin. 'Anyway, perhaps you should ask the Dooleys and the Richardsons about these incidents. They're the ones who told me about them.'

'Where were you last night?'

'Here. Sleeping. Why?'

'Take a look at this, Billy.' Jack picked up Doc's tablet computer from the cushion beside him and selected the images they had prepared while drinking coffee before heading to the Leech household. 'Is this you?'

Billy looked appropriately shaken by the photograph of him on his bike. It was clearly him, pedalling along, wearing his green kit. The image was time stamped and Jack slid his finger under the digits as he asked, 'Is this you? Today, at dawn. This was taken not far up the road. Looks like you were on your way home.'

'I'm an early riser—'

'How about this one then? Going in the opposite direction. Last night. Shortly before dark.' The cocksure kid was beginning to melt down. Billy's Adam's apple bobbed as he tried to recover, but Jack was relentless, gravel in his voice. 'You were out all night, son. Don't lie to me. Where were you?'

Billy sat back, massaging his closed eyelids with his knuckles, and Jack wondered what little story he was fabricating now. The boy's voice had lost its confidence as he asked, 'Where did you get those pictures from? There are no CCTV cameras around here.'

'Oh, but there are, sunshine. We've got lots of snaps of you, coming and going in the early hours. So where were you, last night?'

'I met up with Smiffy... In the woods. We often meet at night. To make love under the stars.'

A sickly, perverted grin accompanied that. The bastard was obviously on firmer ground, but Jack could not fathom why.

'Made love, you say? Does he rape you?'

'It's not rape It's consensual. I'm very mature and advanced for my years, as you can probably tell, you being a detective an' all.' He winked, gave Jack a lascivious grin. 'But yes, we do enjoy oral sex. And anal.' That smirk again. 'You should try it sometime.'

'Strange that. He gets an erection, does he?'

'You're a bit of a perv, Detective. But yes, he does. He has a very big—'

'You're bullshitting me.' Jack had him now, and waited a moment, scrutinising the boy's reaction. 'Smith has to have regular, court ordered injections, attends a clinic once a month. Part of his release plan. It's impossible for him to get hard, and his libido's down in his boots... Tell me the truth, Billy. You aren't lovers, are you? What's really been going on between you two?'

The boy's eyes narrowed, thinking that through. Surprisingly, his composure was unruffled despite being caught in a lie. Was quiet for a moment. Then he threw Jack a curved ball with his answer.

'Are you really that stupid? Smiffy got a double first at Cambridge. I take it you know what that means?'

'Yeah, he's a smart fellah. So, what of it?'

'Chemistry and biochemistry. His forte. He created an antidote for the drugs. Injects it the day after his clinic appointments and then he's good to go.' A leer. 'Rock hard every time.'

Was it true? Jack was not sure, though sensed it was another fabrication. He was having trouble reading Billy's expression and body language, would have liked Doc's opinion. Grudgingly, he acknowledged to himself that the boy was good, better than a lot of the scrotes he interviewed.

'Sex. Is that all it is?'

'It's not just about that. He cares about me. *He* loves me. Last night, I told him my mum had found out about us, that she'd threatened to call the police. He flew into a rage, said he would have to disappear. Told me he'd let me know when it was safe for me to meet him, and where. She totally fucked up our plans.'

'What time was this? And what did you do when he left you?'

There was a moment's pause before Billy answered, his eyes flicking up and to the side, and Jack knew there was yet another lie on its way, even before he heard it.

'We were together until just before dark. I was devastated, so waited, then dozed under the trees after he left. I do that a lot. I hate living here.' Were those tears in his eyes? The boy glared at Jack. Trying to convince him he was both angry and distressed? 'It's torment, having a lunatic for a mother. You can't imagine how it's been for me.'

'He left you there. In the woods. While he did what—drive off? In his motor?'

'Yes. His Volvo. He never did come back, so I cycled home when I woke this morning.'

'You know what I think, Billy? I think those are crocodile tears, and you're full of shit...' Jack had had enough of this lying tosser, but they had no concrete proof of anything. It was all circumstantial and totally frustrating. He did have another surprise for the boy, though. The enhanced image Charlie had sent him. With a flick of the wrist, he slid the tablet across the table to Billy. 'This was taken by the Kennet, also this morning. Not long before you were seen coming home on your bike. Take a good look at this one, Billy. It's important.'

Billy lifted the tablet and said, relief in his expression, 'What of it? Who is it?'

'I think it's you. Wearing a parka, with the hood up, to disguise yourself.'

'You really are desperate, Detective.' Billy dropped the device on to the table, none too gently. 'That could be anyone!'

'Maybe... But this person is riding a very distinctive bicycle. Limited edition. I'm sure you recognise it. After all. It is your bike... Isn't it, Billy?'

The instant Billy saw the first picture the detective had shown him, his gullet twisted and somersaulted, his whole plan now in jeopardy thanks to his carelessness. He had scouted the area around his home, scouring the streets for signs of CCTV cameras, and had made a note of all the locations he should avoid. Yet here he was, on a crystal-clear image taken just up the road—where there was no sign of a camera.

Covert surveillance.

He recognised the location from the background, and knew then he was in trouble. The royal in-laws must have hidden cameras all around their place.

Bollocks.

Billy was good at making shit up, but this had thrown him. How many more images did they have of him? And over what timescale?

Then the bastard detective had grinned at him as he unveiled that last picture. Billy had missed that camera too, though it was a long way off, going by the grainy photograph. He had tried to dismiss it as irrelevant, but the copper had a very valid point. He would have to bluff his way out of it.

'That's not my bike. Mine was with me. All night.'

'You know how many of these ten grand bikes were sold in the UK in the last twelve months, since this particular model was launched, Billy? Not many…'

'So?' Billy pointed at the tablet. 'This person must have bought one, too.'

'Yeah. We thought of that. That's why we're contacting all the owners, to check with them whether they were riding along the Kennet this morning. Most of 'em live in the south—after all, this bike costs a fortune, and that's where the money is. Won't take us long to narrow it down.'

Billy shrugged it off. Even if they did conclude it was definitely his bike, he would claim it must have been stolen and returned while he slept… Better to say no more about it right now. It was time to divert the copper's attention.

'I have no idea who that is, or why you're asking me about him, but I do want to talk about Smiffy. I think he did something terrible last night.'

'Really? What did he do?'

'He was angry when he left me. He said there were people he wanted to hurt. I assumed he meant Doctor Powers. That he must've known he missed him when he blew up that boat.' Sceptical eyes interrogated him, but the detective sat completely still, so Billy dropped his own little bombshell. 'But last night, he told me he was going to destroy a property in London…'

That got a reaction.

'He told you that? And again, you didn't think to inform the police?'

'What was there to tell? He could've been bullshitting. And he didn't say which property—it could've been a building he owned himself, for all I knew. Anyway, by the time I heard the news about the Maddox place, well, Smiffy was already named as the main suspect.'

'You expect me to believe all this? Billy Liar… That's what your mum called you. I think she's right, too. Admit it. You and Smith were in on all this together.'

Billy sighed, as if no one in the world had a high enough IQ to properly understand him. 'Let me show you something, Detective.' He pulled out his throwaway phone, punched in the password, then, as if unwilling to do so, handed it over. 'Messages. He's been texting me. You can read exactly what he had to say, and my replies.

I've done nothing wrong. I have nothing to hide. And unless you have something else, something to arrest me for, I'd like to go back to bed. I've had a crappy day, and the man I love is on the run.'

The detective was suitably put out, frantically flicking through dozens of texts Billy had been sending himself from Smiffy's phone, and the responses he had carefully crafted. He wanted to laugh at the idiot copper, but he kept his face sombre as he stood, ready to leave.

'How do I know this is really his phone number?' Carver peered up from the device and then punched the call button and held the phone to his ear. 'If it really is his, and he replies, you just tell him to give himself up.'

'Okay, glad to be of help... I had no idea he was capable of killing. Then again, I suppose we all are, Detective.'

'Unobtainable.' The copper, frustrated, went back to looking at the texts. 'Must be turned off.' Then he glanced up at Billy with suspicion. 'Why no texts from before yesterday lunch time?'

'I delete them every day or two in case my drunken mother pokes her nose where it's not wanted. Now, can I have that back?'

A calculating look, then feigned reluctance as Carver handed it over. 'Yeah, alright then, kid.'

Billy could read his thoughts and would whip the battery out as soon as he got to his room.

'Good luck, Detective. And goodnight.'

Billy managed to get out of the door before cracking a brilliant smile as he reflected on his animal cunning.

Uncle Peter would be proud of him.

Doc left Jack with Billy and went in search of Mrs Leech—he had heard her weeping after he'd led her from the room—and was still trying to fathom the boy, especially the nonchalance he displayed as he answered all their questions. Doc was certain he was weaving a pattern of deceit, and had heard enough by the time Billy mentioned the spectacular fireworks his 'lover' had supposedly arranged for him.

Like a swimmer, coming up for air, he was glad to be out of the room. He climbed the stairs, ears alert for the sounds of crying, and homed in on a tearful Mrs Leech in the attic. Billy's room was a mess, and Doc guessed she had been frantically searching for the bag of evidence she had claimed to have found in his annex. Unsuccessfully, going by the racking sobs escaping through her fingers while she sat on her son's bed, head in hands.

Doc sat beside her, put an arm around her shoulders and spoke as gently as he could.

'I believe you, Mrs Leech.'

She leaned against him, her tearful face turning to look at his, to assess *his* honesty. Her sobs subsided. 'You do?'

'Yes. I think Billy has some serious problems, but I'm also worried about you.'

'I'll be alright. You'll find Smith, though, won't you? After what he's done to my boy.'

'I'm sure the police will catch him soon enough. There's a countrywide alert out for him—he can't stay hidden forever.' Doc had an inkling that all was not as it seemed between the paedophile and the lad, but that was something to discuss with Jack later. His current concerns really were for this broken woman. 'Yesterday, when I asked if Billy had ever threatened you, you fobbed me off. I need to hear the whole truth.' She stiffened and pulled away from him, her body language confirming his suspicion. 'Please talk to me.'

She did. Describing in horrendous detail, not just last night's attack on her in the kitchen, but all her suspicions about her boy, describing his hateful behaviour, his lies and insults. Everything flooded out of her, along with more tears, before she ended her brief rant with the words, 'But he has an excuse for everything. Every time I tackle him on something, he has such a reasonable defence. And I've been remiss too —using alcohol and so on, just to cope... I'm so sorry, Doctor Powers.' She snuffled, and wiped her eyes with her sleeve.

Her tale of woe wrenched at Doc's sympathies, especially as he too had suffered depression, and had flirted with alcoholism in a vain attempt to cope. To discover that the woman's own son, a budding psychopath, had been tormenting her daily like this, was beyond imagining.

Yet there was little they could do to help her. Not without some concrete evidence of actual criminal wrongdoing on his part. There was one thing that could allow them to arrest him today, though for a relatively minor offence, and only then if she pressed charges against her own son. He thought it unlikely, but would offer her the option.

'On Saturday night, after Billy attacked the chauffeur, did you give him permission to take your car, and drive it to the river?'

'What? Of course not.' She sniffed, dragged the damp sleeve across her upper lip to dry her nose. 'Why do you ask?'

'We have CCTV footage of Billy driving your car in the early hours of Sunday morning. With the canoe on the roof. He arrived back here a couple of hours later.'

'No! Are you sure?'

'I'm afraid so. If you don't feel safe, with Billy in your house, we could arrange for him to be arrested for forging your signature on legal documents. Or stealing your car. I gather he's done it before, so a custodial term in a young offenders' establishment—'

'Prison? You want *me* to send him to prison?'

'Well, it might be good for him.' Doc was not a big fan of incarcerating young criminals, but in Billy's case, it seemed the ideal place for him. 'A short, sharp shock, as they say.'

'No. He's been so badly abused, Doctor... I can't.'

It was the response he'd expected. He just hoped Jack had uncovered something substantive while challenging the boy over the images Terry and Charlie had provided.

'Come on, Mrs Leech. Let's go and make some more tea. We'll leave you in peace after that.' *Peace.* Not the best choice of word. 'But you do need to lock your bedroom door when you go to bed. And please call me any time, day or night, if you feel threatened or have concerns you need to share. Okay?'

She nodded, trying not to look miserable, but failing, and followed him down the stairs. At the top of the final flight, Doc could see the door to the lounge as it opened. Billy appeared in the hallway. His face gloating. Victorious.

Billy glanced up on hearing Doc's footsteps, and his expression switched to furtive, then neutral.

A consummate actor.

A mendacious manipulator.

And after listening to Mrs Leech, Doc couldn't help but think her son might already be a proficient killer, too.

Judy heard the phone vibrating on her bedside table and read the message Doc had just sent her. He and Jack were heading to Thatcham to meet a policewoman there, and planned to have a few beers too, but he would come home immediately if she was still not feeling well.

Judy replied to say he should try and relax over a pint or two, and that she was fine, even though she was not. Her brain was woolly, and she was still tired despite dozing for hours. She stood to use the bathroom, but immediately noticed there were more red-brown stains on the sheet.

A whole lot more…

Oh no, please. Not the baby.

After a quick trip to the loo to confirm the bleeding had stopped, she pulled on her clothes and debated what to do. She could call Colin, but he was miles away, and it would be quicker to jump in a cab and head to the hospital by herself. Their local taxi firm answered her phone call immediately, and said a car would be with her in five minutes.

Perfect.

Judy headed to the stairs, wondering what to say in a text to Colin. She was a little worried, but at least the blood wasn't bright red, though there was plenty of it.

Better safe than sorry.

She started down the stairs, phone in her hand, tapping out a message to let Colin know she was going for a check-up.

That was a mistake.

Her coordination was not all it should be, and she twisted a foot under her ankle. She yelped as she pitched forward, head first down the remaining dozen stairs. The carpet cushioned her fall as she hit the lower steps, side on, having swivelled in mid-air, hands on her belly to protect her baby.

Her phone went flying too, and bounced off the wall in a shower of pieces. Judy cursed her stupidity a fraction of a second before her head also slammed into the exposed brickwork, knocking her cold.

With a deep gash on her forehead, she rolled off the last step and came to rest at the foot of the stairs in a bloody, crumpled heap.

Billy saw the knowing look Powers gave him, but he pushed past the man and his mother without a word, and bounded up the stairs, silent as a cat. When he reached his bedroom, he let his anger scream out of him.

'KEEP OUT OF MY FUCKING ROOM!' He slammed the door, then thought better of it, pulled it open and yelled down the stairs again, for everyone's benefit.

'I'm going to bed. And I'm locking my door. Don't disturb me until breakfast is ready —I'm exhausted.'

His bloody mother.

Obviously, she'd been searching his room, had left it in a right state. She had even pulled out all his DVDs, but hadn't found his hidey-hole. Given that copper's suspicions and the look Powers had given him, it might be best to conceal the bag somewhere else.

Billy recovered it, then opened the Velux window, eased the bag through, and let it slide to the gutter before releasing the handle. With his usual feline grace, he followed, careful not to dislodge the concrete tiles as he shuffled down the roof on his backside. With his feet on the cast iron gutter, he tossed the bag to the garden below, then leapt into the tree outside his bedroom window.

He caught a flimsy upper branch with both hands, and heard an ominous crack as it bent under the strain, but he swung his lower body towards the trunk, and landed with his feet on a sturdy parallel branch below. Without pausing, he hauled himself to the lowest branches, dropped to the ground and recovered his bag. He heard Powers' voice from the front garden and then an engine start. Headlights swept across the side wall before the car purred away.

Billy jogged to the cellar entrance, let himself in and changed into his tutor's clothes. Smiffy was groaning, but Billy had nothing for him. No water. No food. Just more misery.

Tough. He deserves to suffer.

But what should he do with the bag?

He'd outgrown the trophies—he'd killed two people this week already. His mother had found the flight tickets a little earlier than planned, but that was no problem. The other papers were largely duplicates from the lawyers, and he had his passport. Why bother keeping anything else? He would destroy it all, tonight.

The bag of ANFO contained far more than he needed for his upcoming sixteenth birthday celebration, so he scooped about ten kilos into the gym bag, dumping the mixture on top of the trophies and papers, and then re-zipped it. With the holdall in one hand and the parka under his other arm, he ran up the steps, locked the door and headed across the common towards Pangbourne.

Billy set a good pace, trotting through the woods, using the light of the moon to guide him. Thanks to that detective, he now knew there were cameras along his road, and would not be caught out again. It took him twenty minutes to reach the picturesque village of Stanford Dingley, and he knew exactly what he would find here. Some scruffy farm buildings had been converted into workshops and his grandfather's car—an ancient MG—had been serviced by one of the local engineers who specialised in looking after older vehicles. When Gramps had become too sick to maintain the classic car himself, he had come here instead, bringing Billy with him on several occasions.

Hence, Billy knew the security was lax. Gramps sometimes left the vehicle the night before it was due for attention, with the key 'hidden' beneath the wheel arch, placed on top of the front nearside tyre. There were three cars outside the workshop, either awaiting attention or their satisfied owners, and Billy chuckled to himself as he pulled on his latex gloves then felt for the key for the vehicle he selected—a battered petrol-driven Land Rover. It was ideal—it even had a large jerrycan strapped to the rear, one not dissimilar to the two he had used in Harley Street, and a rap with his knuckles confirmed it was full.

With the parka hood up, covering his face, he motored from the village to Powers' home, cutting through back routes, and bumping along tracks and common land to avoid any cameras.

The house was mostly in darkness with just the hall and landing lights blazing when he arrived. Even so, he parked a few car lengths further up the road, in front of their neighbour's home—one surrounded by leylandii, an impenetrable hedge twice as high as Billy was tall. The plants were an effective barrier to nosey passers-by, but would also prevent the neighbour from noticing the Land Rover waiting in the dark right outside his property should he be awake.

The road was on a slight gradient, with Powers' home positioned on a bend. The plot sloped down to the river with the drive forming a tarmac semi-circle extending across the entire frontage of the house. Tonight, there were only two cars parked there—a Peugeot and a Mini Cooper situated near the front porch.

A few mental calculations set the adrenalin pumping through Billy's veins, his body tingling in anticipation of what he was about to do.

Still wearing Smiffy's parka, he placed the gym bag in the passenger footwell, then hopped out. It was dangerous, but Billy was a player—and had to be certain his bomb would explode—so he splashed most of the jerrycan contents over the rear seats. The smell of the fuel gave him an instant erection.

With no time for masturbation, Billy merely stripped off the parka, and tipped the remaining petrol on to it, making sure just the arms and the hood were sufficiently saturated before twisting the entire garment into a length of fuse. With the tailgate open, he fed a third of his fire-starter inside the vehicle, then gently closed the door, leaving the rest dangling on to the road.

As an experienced vehicle arsonist, he was pretty sure it would do the job, having used a similar technique on many occasions. Tonight, he just needed to be certain there was enough of a gap for the flames to breach the tailgate—but not too soon. Having inspected the rusty metal and the ancient rubber seal, he was prepared to risk it.

The road was deserted and poorly lit, so Billy took his time, quietly humming to himself as he set about creating his improvised explosive device. The idea had occurred to him after Powers had unexpectedly pitched up at his house.

A dead man walking.

Although Billy could not be sure Powers was home, it was almost midnight, so he assumed the old bastard would be snoring in his bed by now.

Just one last thing to do before he illuminated the night sky with the beautiful colours of combustion—every arsonist's favourite.

Billy tugged Smiffy's phone from his pocket, placed it on the bonnet, and fitted the battery. He pondered what to say while doing the same with his own mobile—the one he had shown the idiot detective a couple of hours earlier—and sent a few brief messages from each before dismantling them both.

Laughter erupted from his lips as he contemplated his stunning genius, then he hushed himself and looked around to check he was still alone. With his lighter in hand, he released the parking brake and turned the steering wheel to line the vehicle up with his target's driveway, then leaned his shoulder against the front pillar to set the bomb in motion.

The Land Rover was heavy, and moved at a slow walking pace on the shallow gradient. Billy strolled beside it, making minor adjustments of the steering wheel through the driver's door window. The stench of petrol fumes wafting out merely increased his excitement, despite stinging the tears to his eyes.

After a dozen paces he stopped walking and flicked the lighter into life as the vehicle rolled away. Thankfully, this most dangerous of moments had passed without blowing him directly to hell, so he touched the flame to the end of the trailing parka, saw it blossom with eager tongues of fire, then started back-pedalling away, his eyes riveted on his handiwork.

The car continued rolling towards Powers' front door, propelled by gravity and malice, with the flaming parka being dragged along the road behind it. The front wheel hit a stone, sending the car on a new trajectory, giving Billy a heart-stopping moment, but the Land Rover continued rolling towards the front door until it thumped a glancing blow against the front wing of the Mini.

Bugger it!

The impact set off the smaller car's alarm. Billy knew the honking and flashing would bring the occupants out of their home, and the improvised fuse could burn for many more seconds before the vehicle exploded, giving them time to douse the flames. His erection died and shrivelled as the sound assaulted his ears, worrying him that his plan had failed.

Desperate now, he waited a moment longer to at least confirm the Land Rover kept moving. It did, at an agonising crawl, but he was relieved to see it crunch into the wall underneath the front room window with flames now licking at the tailgate.

Come on! Explode, you bastard!

It did not.

This was a severe disappointment—he wanted to watch the fireworks just as his sixteenth birthday ticked into existence. He may have been a 'player', but Billy was also a survivor. He turned away and jogged along the road for fifty paces, then on to the public footpath adjacent to a neighbour's home, disappearing into the night as the percussive whump and roar of multiple explosions energised the air around him.

'Like all good coppers, I'm never really off-duty, but I'd love to join you for a beer.' Charlie's laugh, amplified by the car's speakers, put a huge grin on Jack's face as he drove Doc to the pub in Thatcham. 'I'll be there in twenty minutes or so. Mine's a pint of Stella, in case you've forgotten.'

Jack didn't have a chance to reply—she had hung up already. He and Doc had just left the Leech home and the first thing he did was call Charlie with Smith's phone number, to see if they could trace it. She was at home, having finished her shift hours before, but she was his unofficial liaison now, ever since Soundbite had suspended him.

The boy's mother had agreed that they could put a trace on his phone too—the one he had been using to contact Smith for their illegal assignations. Both mobile devices were on pay as you go contracts, and were used purely for the two 'lovers' to communicate, though most of the messages on Billy's phone had been deleted. There was still enough on it to confirm his story—lovey-dovey texts from the paedophile that had turned Jack's stomach.

'You tried Smith's number from Billy's phone?' Doc squinted at him from the passenger seat, tired eyes avoiding the glare from oncoming headlights. 'That was a bit risky, wasn't it?'

'Maybe. It was unobtainable, so Smith must've taken the battery out. Smart fellah. Most people think turning off a mobile phone drops it off the radar, but we can still track 'em. As soon as he gets on the blower again, we'll have him.'

'If he's on long enough.'

'Yeah, but with the fuss over Dickie's death, they'll probably get GCHQ on it.' Jack had little time for spooks, but sometimes the UK's premier spy agency had its uses. 'They'll pick up his location in seconds and get it to our boys immediately. So, what did Mrs Leech have to say?'

Jack listened without interrupting as Doc verbally sketched out the misdeeds Billy's mother had accused him of. As a homicide detective, he had experience of many seriously nasty teens, some already murderers and rapists before reaching the age of consent, so was not totally surprised to hear Doc say, 'And I believe every word of it. He's probably been up to far more than she knows about. It's such a shame she didn't have that evidence she'd found in his annex.'

'Yup. We wouldn't need her go ahead to arrest him, then. It wouldn't take much to tie the dates of the animal attacks together with sightings of him on the road from Terry's surveillance cameras. Still only circumstantial without the trophies, though.'

'Mmm.' An unusually non-committal comment from Doc.

Jack spotted the pub Charlie had suggested, so pulled into the car park and killed the engine and lights. Neither man was in a hurry to go inside, and they sat in the gloom in thoughtful silence for a minute or so before Jack spoke again.

'I still don't understand why she won't press charges against him… After nicking her car. Knocking her to the ground. Threatening her with a knife. Drugging her drink. That little scrote's a proper bloody nightmare, mate.'

'Lucky too… Come on, Jack. Let's try and wind down over a beer.'

Jack noticed Doc limping as they crossed the car park to the pub entrance. His friend was exhausted, and if he overdid things, the various plates and pins holding his limbs together gave him gyp. He patted Doc's back between the shoulders as they entered the bar, and chuckled, putting his own good humour down to the prospect of seeing Charlie. It was the best he'd felt since Sunday's fireball. 'I'll get 'em in, you sit down, mate. You look like you've been through a meat grinder.'

Doc nodded and wearily sat at an unoccupied table in the corner while Jack went to the bar to order drinks. The place was a proper pub, not too busy, and not a gastro-dump or wine bar-wannabe. Jack felt at home, listening to the hubbub of happy customers. He carried three pints to the table as Charlie arrived—wearing a head-turning outfit, a short red dress that showed off her ample curves—and Jack relaxed properly for the first time in days.

Over their drinks, Doc and Jack shared all they had discovered with Charlie, and by the time they'd finished she was also itching to arrest the boy, but for now, all three of them were winding down for the night. With work out of the way, they sat and laughed, chatted and drank, until the publican threw them out shortly before midnight.

Jack kissed Charlie goodnight, wishing he could go home with her rather than Doc, but he couldn't tell his pal to take a taxi. Not tonight. He drove out of the pub car park far more cheerful than when he had arrived, but now his mind was back on the Leech boy and something Doc had suggested while they talked things through with Charlie.

'Do you really think he was in cahoots with Smith, and they both planned to blow up the boat? Even though the phone messages verified what he told me?' Jack had been both furious and disheartened when he had read the texts from Smith yakking on about how disappointed he was that Billy had missed the *spectacular display* he had arranged for him on Sunday.

'Maybe… To be honest, I think he might well be the mastermind, pulling Smith's strings. Everything Mrs Leech claimed—if true, and I believe it is—suggests Billy is no one's victim.'

'Yeah?' Jack mulled that over for a minute then asked, 'So he seduced a paedophile? Aged, what? Fourteen, thirteen? Nah… I can't see it.'

'We only have Billy's word for it that Smith and he are in an unhealthy relation-ship. And I got the impression he's congratulating himself, for pulling the wool over everyone's eyes.'

'Little runt—smirking, and that sly grin of his. I see what you mean.'

'There was other body language too, and not just from our interviews tonight. I saw the way he looked at Judy, when he came to our house… Thirteen years of age, and a raging mess of hormones. He's not gay, Jack. I'd bet my life on it.'

'So, what about the photos then? They look pretty loved up to me. Not that I'm an expert on gay porn. Or paedo porn for that matter.'

'Mmm.'

'Okay mate.' Jack turned off the A4 for Pangbourne, a few minutes out from Doc's home. 'Enough of the enigmatic grunting at me. What's going on in that super-computer you keep between your ear'oles?'

Doc sucked air through his teeth, and said, 'Did you notice, in those photographs…? Smith had his head turned away, and his eyes were never on the camera. That seemed unusual for a start.'

'Well, maybe… And?'

'Billy's been drugging his mother with Temazepam. Spiking her vodka.'

'Bloody hell… You think the little toe-rag set up the paedo. Drugged him and took those photos while he was out of it!'

'That's why I am very keen to meet this Smith character again, Jack. Anyway, I'm shattered. It's midnight already, and I need to sleep.'

Jack wanted to hit the hay, too, even without Charlie beside him. The thought made him grin at the precise moment the inside of his car was lit up by an explosive flash.

He'd pulled into Doc's lane, arriving just in time to see the Land Rover burst into flames, the conflagration rapidly followed by a more violent explosion that blew the car apart. Jack's view through the windscreen brought to mind a training film he had recently seen on terrorism.

A car bomb!

The thought was still entering his mind as a third blast joined the first two—the Mini's fuel tank detonating. It took just a fraction of a second for the combined explo-sive power to erupt, blossoming into a massive fireball, obliterating the entire frontage of Doc's house.

BIRTHDAY

CONFLAGRATION

Jack hit the brakes, but Doc was already out of the car before it stopped moving, his croaked cry of distress choking him as he called her name.

'Ju-u-dy!'

He stumbled on the tarmac drive, his brain in free-fall, saturated with panic, unable to comprehend the extent of the devastation. Or the danger he was heading towards.

The front facade of his home had been breached, with part of the roof sagging above a gaping hole where the windows and wall used to be. Flames lapped at the edges of the jagged brickwork, fuelled by the furniture inside. Shattered glass, shrapnel and larger chunks of car littered the garden, and Doc tripped over a blazing tyre without even noticing the molten rubber scorching his lower leg.

In fact, Doc could not register anything, not even the blast of heat pressing him back, or the crackling and spitting of lethal orange flames. He was fixated on the sight of their bed. The metal frame was askew, dangling by a leg from the wrecked upper floor, hanging into what was once his front room. The mattress, upended, propped beneath the bedstead, surrounded by flaming bedclothes, was already charred and half consumed by fire.

As Doc threw himself forward, ignoring the scorching heat searing his nostrils, desperate to find his wife, his world gave way. He pitched forward, wondering if his heart had given out as his legs locked and the ground smacked him in the face.

'Doc! Stop. You can't go in there. It's collapsing, mate.' Jack's voice, urgent but not panicked, cut through the fog in Doc's head and he looked round and saw him hugging his legs, having rugby tackled him to the ground. 'If you want to go in, we'll use the rear patio doors. We'll see if she's okay, mate. Come on.'

An insane urge to launch himself at the inferno took hold for an irrational moment and he tensed himself, pulling his legs under him the moment Jack let go, ready to spring forward. Then his brain played a trick on him. Judy's voice penetrated his panic, only it wasn't coming from the house—it was inside his head.

'Colin—stop!'

It had to be in his head—the sound came from the back of his skull.

Then:

'I'm here! I'm fine!'

Doc heard it more clearly this time, despite the crackle and roar from the fire—it wasn't his imagination—it was Judy's voice and he turned to see her, stepping from a taxi onto the road by Jack's car, her shocked face dancing yellow from the flames, a bandage round her forehead. Jack grabbed his arm and physically hauled him away from the burning house, and for the first few paces, Doc's stumbling feet dragged as he used his friend's strength for support.

'Thank God!' Doc let go of Jack, and flung himself into Judy's arms, smothering her with kisses. 'I was sure I'd lost you—I couldn't bear the thought of being without you!'

They hugged as Jack spoke with a neighbour who had appeared from the house opposite, and Doc heard him confirm the emergency services were already on their way. The taxi driver was unfazed, and asked, deadpan, 'Sorry to have to mention this, but who's paying for the cab ride? It's fifty quid. It's a fair old drive to the hospital, and I had to wait half an hour for the lady before bringing her back.'

Jack pulled out his wallet while Doc inspected the dressing on Judy's head. 'What happened? you've been to hospital?'

'It's okay. Just a gash that needed a stitch. I fell and whacked my head, but I'm alright. Your legs, though—your trousers are burnt. And you're shaking like a leaf. Sit down, Colin.'

He sank onto the low brick wall at the front of their garden, and breathed deeply, counting the seconds repeatedly—four in, seven hold, eight out—until he relaxed as best he could. Judy put her hands on his shoulders, her forehead to his. He gradually calmed, watching Jack pace up and down the road, phone to his ear, gesticulating at whoever was on the receiving end of his agitation.

'The baby? You said you fell? Please tell me—'

'The baby's fine. I had a scan while I was there. There's nothing to worry about. All three of us are safe, thank God.' She brushed her hair from her face and looked at the wreckage of their home behind him. Resolute. Watching her in the light thrown by the blazing house, it occurred to him that she was much stronger than he gave her credit for. She nodded to herself, as if to say *I'm back, I can cope with this*, a firmness in her voice as she told him, 'Although I think we'll need a new nursery... And a house to go with it.' Smiling at him. Uncertain. 'It looks like a bomb went off.'

'It does indeed, my love.'

The neighbour stepped forward, and Doc went to stand, an automatic gesture of politeness, but the man placed a hand on his shoulder to stop him.

'Colin. I have no idea what's happened here tonight, but you and Judy are most welcome to use our spare room for as long as you need. I have some trousers that might fit you too.'

'Thanks, Phil.' Grateful, though he had other things on his mind than his scorched legs. The wail of distant sirens reached him, gradually getting louder, but Jack, having finished his call, appeared in front of him before any emergency vehicles arrived, his face pulsating with fury.

'Charlie just told me some interesting news, Doc. I'm going over to the Leech place now as I have some more questions for that brat. I'll see you later. You take it easy, mate.'

'Woah.' The word left Doc's lips as he saw Judy's look, a warning not to go rushing off. Not with his house still burning. 'I'm coming, Jack.'

'No, Colin—'

'No, Doc—'

His friend and his wife spoke simultaneously, but Doc was adamant. While sitting morosely, his heart leaden in his chest, watching the flames destroy what was left of his home, Doc's mind had not been idle. He'd been ruminating on young Billy Leech and his supposed lover, and now aimed his conclusion at Jack.

'GCHQ got a hit on both phones, simultaneously. In this vicinity. Correct?'

'Jeez, Doc. How the hell did you know?'

Doc waved the question away as he stood and hugged Judy, whispered in her ear. 'We will get the person who did this, my love. You stay with Phil, and I promise I'll be back in no time.' Her body stiffened and he let go. She stared at him, silently, anger and sadness mingling in the violet of her eyes. 'I have to do this. I love you, sweetheart.'

Her mouth opened to say something, to tell him she loved him, or maybe object, he wasn't sure. He didn't want to argue with her so spun around, jogged to Jack's car, and eased himself in before his reluctant pal could drive off without him. Jack threw him a sour look, shrugged and squealed away, swerving past a fire engine racing down the lane in the opposite direction. When he managed to get the car on an even keel, Doc heard him mutter under his breath and sigh to himself.

'Okay, mate. You knew about the phones. Tell me how.'

'It was Billy at my house. He's been sending messages to and from both phones to back up his narrative, to create an alibi, to throw us off the scent. He's a very devious young psychopath. I'm guessing his tutor's either dead or being held somewhere.'

'Yeah... My thoughts were similar when Charlie told me. I dunno how you worked that out.'

Doc was too tired to explain, too emotionally drained. All he could think of was Suzie Leech. 'She's in danger, Jack. Mrs Leech... Again... And remember what happened the last time we tried to help her—driving late at night to her home in Chelsea.'

Jack glanced at him, then booted the accelerator and sent the car fishtailing along the road to Bucklebury Common. Doc had hold of the grab handle above his door, as was customary during Jack's high speed driving, but at least the roads were quiet now.

Doc dialled her number, his fingers crossed, wondering if she would pick up.

Please let us get there in time... This time.

Billy sprinted across the farmers' fields and paddocks, elated. Effortless feet flew along the dirt and grass tracks, as he revelled in sensations normally only experienced in his dreams. The sheer buzz and thrill of what he had achieved—and what he was still to achieve tonight, on this, his coming of age.

For some cultures, adulthood begins with the onset of puberty. For others, the critical year was the eighteenth, or even the twenty-first. But Uncle Peter had set his target for tonight, and already Billy had qualified as a man. A real man.

A killer of other men.

With his leg muscles propelling him, the burn of lactic acid unnoticed, Billy accelerated, making his final dash through the woods of Bucklebury Common to his home. Breathless on arrival but awash with endorphins, he bent from the waist to recover before striding to the cellar entrance. Once inside, he shed his tutor's sweaty clothes, donned his own, and set Smiffy free.

'Get dressed.' Billy ripped the tape from Smiffy's eyes, but left the strip covering his mouth. He tapped it with his knife blade and said, 'Leave this on. Now get up. We haven't got all night.' He had no desire to listen to the wimp's inevitable bleating, he was feeling blissful and didn't want the moment spoiled.

Billy had to help him to his feet, and Smith groaned with pain as he tried to stand and dress himself. Meanwhile, Billy packed the remaining ANFO into three containers Gramps had stored in the cellar years ago—an old pressure cooker with a busted seal, a bulbous glass flagon that reached Billy's knee height, and a giant metal paint can with dried up dregs in the bottom.

The bottle neck was a shade too big for the detonator, so Billy stuffed the tube of black powder into the mixture, wrapped the attached length of home-made fuse around the bottle, taping the end to the glass to keep it in place, then popped the roll of tape over the neck to make it easier to carry.

Smiffy was watching as he struggled to dress, swaying as he pulled the damp shirt over his head. He was weak from lack of food and drink, which suited Billy just fine.

'Grab the pressure cooker, Smiffy. We're going upstairs to see my mum.' He giggled, then guffawed, verging on hysteria as he tried to stem the laughter, but could not. This was simply the most amazing night of his short life. 'I'm sure she wants to wish me happy birthday. Hahaha! And I've reserved her a front row seat, for the fireworks.'

And one for you too, Smiffy!

Smith struggled to lift the container, although it was lighter than either of the two Billy carried, but with some verbal prodding, his tutor managed to wobble his way up the steps. They continued round to the rear of the house and Billy slotted his key into the back door as Smiffy leaned against the wall, breathing heavily, hugging the steel container to his chest.

The kitchen light was still on, though that was situation normal. A far less usual sight, though one he was getting used to, was his mother, sitting behind the table once again, her asymmetrical facial features contorted with rage.

Suzie had tied herself in knots thinking about her son after Doctor Powers left. She had looked in on her mother, tried to calm her down after Billy had bellowed down the stairs, once again promised her they would visit her father's grave tomorrow, and then spent hours moping in the lounge. Desperate for a Martini.

The fortified wine, the sickly, sweet vermouth, was the only alcohol she could find, but even that had severely tested her resolve not to drink, so she'd prayed to the Virgin Mary, thereby drawing the strength to deny her base desires.

At half past eleven, she went to her room, wondering if she could sleep, knowing all the misdeeds her son had been perpetrating on her and her mother. Doctor Powers had been more than sympathetic and Suzie had almost crumbled, and told him to have the police arrest her son.

Maternal ties are strong though, especially when forged by traumatic circumstances, and she couldn't bear to think of her son behind bars. More prayers had convinced her that all humans have good in them and Billy could be saved. If she could just stay on a righteous path, she could help her boy back from the verge of evil, the temptations the devil had strewn before him.

With visions of hellfire, damnation and demons rampaging through her consciousness, Suzie dozed until a phone call woke her forty minutes after midnight.

'Doctor Powers?'

'Sorry to disturb you so late, Mrs Leech.' His kindly voice had grit beneath it, and she sat up, worried by his tone more than the lateness of the call. 'I need you to check on Billy for me. Would you do that, please?'

'Check on him?' Suzie was groggy from her nightmarish half sleep. 'What do you mean?'

'Can you tell me whether he's in his room? No need to disturb him if he's sleeping, but I do need to know. Right now.'

'Okay…'

Suzie had the master key, and used it to unlock her door before climbing to Billy's room. She still had the phone to her ear as she slotted the same key into Billy's door lock, trying not to make a sound as she twisted it. A soft click, then she eased the door open, the light from the landing sending a shaft across his bed.

Empty.

The Velux window's wide open.

Suzie let a gasp slip from her throat, and Doctor Powers must have heard as he asked, 'Are you alright? Is he there?'

'No.' She flipped on the light and took a quick look around, but the room was much as she had left it, still in a mess. Then she noticed the old fireplace with the covering panel thrown aside. 'He must've climbed out, onto the roof!' She went and checked that her son wasn't sitting perched outside, stargazing. It was a desperate thought and she knew it. 'He's not here, Doctor. But I think I've found his hiding place.'

'Okay. I'm on my way with DI Carver. We'll be with you shortly.'

Then he was gone, with no further explanation as to how he knew her boy was not here.

Suzie stomped down the stairs, her anger at her son at an all-time high—and after the events of the last few days, that was no mean feat. She went to the kitchen, muttering to herself, 'I'll kill him. No, I won't… I'll let the police deal with him.'

She was now ready to do it. Having made that difficult decision, she put the kettle on, sat in the same seat she had occupied the night before, and waited for Doctor Powers to arrive.

The kettle boiled and she heard it click as it switched itself off, but did not move to make a drink. The backdoor was also clicking as the lock turned.

Billy!

He opened the door clutching a large bottle and an old paint can, his face concentrating on his heavy burden before switching to a startled look at the sight of her. The rage swelled in her chest and she prepared to hurl furious words at him, threatening him with the wrath of God, but her tongue had no time to fulfil the urging from her brain to verbally lash him. It was stilled by the sight of the man stumbling into the kitchen as Billy shoved him through the door.

Smith?

With a piece of packaging tape over his mouth. And why was her son wearing latex gloves?

Billy placed his bottle on the table, put the paint can next to it and gave her the wickedest grin she had ever laid eyes on.

'Hello, Mummy dearest. Aren't you going to wish me happy birthday, then?'

'That's right Smiffy, just dump that pan on the table. And why don't you get yourself a glass of water and sit down? I might ask my mum to make you some supper if you're good.'

His tutor needed no further encouragement. He tore off the tape, wincing as the adhesive ripped tender dry skin from his lips, and was at the sink before Billy had finished speaking, a mug of water raised to his mouth. He guzzled it down and poured another, his hands shaking violently as he carried it to the table.

'I'm starving. Please—'

'All in good time, Smiffy. Don't drink too fast or you'll puke it all up again.' Billy moved behind the man, now sipping at his mug, and patted his shoulders in encouragement. Then fished the bottle of chloroform from his pocket. 'I think my mother has lost the power of speech. Better give her a minute or two and then she'll feed you.'

'Billy? What's going on? Why is that pervert here—and why does he smell so bad? Has he been sleeping rough because he's on the run?' While his mother spoke, the words tumbling out in a rapid stream now that the dam had burst, Billy ignored her questions, grabbed a tea towel, tipped some liquid on it and clasped it over Smiffy's mouth and nose. 'Billy!' Her voice shrill, her mouth still flapping after the word left her lips. She went to stand, but remained half upright, hands on the table, unsure what to do. Completely baffled by his actions.

It took a few seconds of struggling, but Smiffy was weak and soon relaxed. Unconscious.

'There we go, Mother. Now you and I can chat without being interrupted.' Billy shoved her into her seat, the chair legs clattering on the tiles as she skidded back, took the roll of tape and waved it at her. 'Is Nana asleep?'

'Yes...' It looked to Billy like her brain was trying to compute what he was doing, what he was planning to do. Perhaps she thought he would use the tape on his grandmother. She certainly looked totally confused, but not yet panicking as she said, 'What's going on?'

Instead of bothering to reply, Billy pounced on her, used the chloroform soaked rag to subdue her, taking care not to overdo it, then bound her to the chair and table leg with the tape.

With both his victims out cold, he replaced the batteries in the phones and took his time crafting and then sending another series of texts:

Smith: I'm so sorry, sweet Billy. I've been stupid. I wanted to punish Maddox and kill *Powers* as a gift to you, my love, before we flew away together. But the police already know two people are dead because of me. We'll never get away now.
Billy: Maybe you should surrender. Do your time. You know I'll wait.
Smith: I can't go to prison. I don't want to live another day without you.
Billy: Don't say that. Let's talk about it. Face to face. We'll find a way.
Smith: I can't eat or drink, I'm so worried about you. I'm crying now—for us both. I so much wanted to release you from your wicked mother's clutches—but cannot. She's a crazy drunken junkie. She's hurt you so badly. And now our plans are ruined. Because of me.
Billy: I need to see you.
He waited a minute or so before sending another message:
Billy: Please, Roland. I must see you tonight.
Smith: Meet me at our secret place. Come now, my love. This will be our sad final farewell. And forgive me for what I'm about to do.
Billy: Don't do anything stupid! I'm already on my way.
Smith: Always remember this—I love you.

It wasn't exactly Romeo and Juliet, but would do the job. Once the fuse was lit, Billy would jog off to the location of their supposed tryst in Bucklebury woods. He would tell the police that his devastated and deranged lover, Smiffy, having tempted him away from his home to spare his life, blew himself—and his 'wicked mother'—to hell.

Billy unplugged the battery from Smith's phone and put the pieces on the table, then pocketed his own device, confident it was sufficient proof of his innocence.

His mother gasped as she woke. Then squealed at her predicament, ineffectually struggling with her bindings.

'Billy! Why are you doing this? You let me go! Right now!' Her screeching grated his nerves, and he pulled a strip of tape from the roll ready to close her grotesque gob for the last time. But she turned her head away as he approached, sputtering at him. 'I've just spoken to Doctor Powers and the poli—'

'WHAT?' He paused, the tape still in his fingers, suddenly wondering if his plan was about to go horribly wrong. 'You spoke to Powers? When?'

Could Billy have missed him again? She definitely sounded convincing.

Jesus, that fucker's got more lives than a cat.

Then, Uncle Peter's voice, purring to him: *Don't you worry, Billy boy. We'll get him another day.*

'Just before you arrived. The police are coming for you, Billy.'

'The police? Coming here? Now?' He could see the cogs, whirring in her mind, working out what to say, and he went to clamp her mouth closed. 'Fuck off! You think I'm stupid.'

'Doctor Powers is on his way here. With that detective.'

'Bullshit!'

Then a moment of doubt. Was she telling the truth? If she was, he should get a move on. Using Smiffy's phone would have alerted them anyway, though he'd assumed he had plenty of time before they arrived. If Powers really had spoken to her earlier, he could be here any minute, probably accompanied by that detective. He could handle them, but the delay could screw up his plan, especially as the Thames Valley Police would soon be on their way.

'Bollocks!' He slapped the tape across her mouth, the terror in her eyes sending waves of pleasure through his groin. 'I hate you… This is all your doing. Your fault.'

She tried to speak, but only unintelligible grunts and groans escaped the tape. Now that he had her undivided attention, Billy started to explain why she was the one to blame.

'You promised me we'd move back to London. When we first came here. We'll find our own place, you said. Everything would be back to normal, you said. When you were well enough, you said… But YOU LIED… You never got any better, did you? You didn't really want to—you absolutely adore playing the victim. So, you kept me here. Even though you knew I loved my old school. Moving to this scum-hole—I lost every single one of my friends. You wouldn't even take me to see them—because you didn't want *your* friends to see *you*. Ashamed of what happened to you —because you were so stupid you married a madman, the one who fucking raped you! BUT WHAT ABOUT ME?' She flinched away from the blast of his breath on her cheek, his mouth roaring at her. 'YOU KNEW I was being bullied at that shitty school. Every fucking day for the first two years we lived here, I suffered while you wallowed in self-pity. You selfish cunt…'

Calm yourself, lad.

It was not easy, so much pent up emotion had finally been released. Billy was that angry he could not speak, so busied himself, moving the bombs to the underside of the table. After unwinding the fuse from around the glass flagon, he placed the end in Smiffy's lap, draped over the palm of his left hand.

Looking good, Billy boy… But think, my son.

After standing, staring at his scenario for several beats, Billy took the chloroform bottle, spilt all but a few dregs on Smiffy's right palm and sleeve, rolled his victim's fingertips on the glass, then shoved it in the man's shirt pocket. There was not much chance Smiffy would wake in the coming critical minutes, given his dire state, but he was breathing, would be alive when the blast happened—and that was important. There would be little left of their bodies, but forensic pathologists were cunning bastards, highly trained in getting the dead to tell tales. If they found traces of chloroform in his blood, the bottle would explain it—he'd probably inhaled some while knocking the witch unconscious.

Stepping back, Billy surveyed the scene, and, content that the forensic evidence was consistent with the story he would tell, went to his mother again, leaned in close, keeping his voice controlled this time.

'Only Gramps ever did anything for me. Since he topped himself, the pair of you miserable bitches have been making my life un-bloody-bearable. I even tried to get you to put Nana into a home. That's why I pushed her down the stairs. I thought that'd finally convince you to park her in Lakeview. Then move us back to London— away from this dump. But no, you kept her here. If she dies tonight, that'll be down to you too.'

For some reason, she was no longer looking at his face as he bent over her, had gone completely still, her eyes bulging as she focused on something in his hand.

The flick-knife, the blade gleaming.

He wondered, how did that get there?

It had been in his pocket and he had no idea that he had pulled it out and flicked it open.

I really want to stick it in the bitch.

No. You stick to the plan, Billy boy. Time to get moving, my son.

'Look at me! I'm up here…'

He folded the knife, popped it away. Stabbing her would ruin his chances of blaming Smiffy, especially if he got her blood on himself. Better to stick a verbal knife in her than an actual one.

'The state of you… Uncle Peter should've killed you when he had the chance. But he knew you would do this to yourself—knew you were a vain, weak, self-absorbed bag of pus… You should thank me for ending your suffering. You'll be better off dead. You've only yourself to blame for being in this position—and for Nana being upstairs instead of in Lakeview. Maybe *she'll* survive—her room's at the front of the house. But you… No chance. Bye bye, Mummy dearest.'

Billy took the lighter from his pocket, touched it to Smiffy's fingertips to make sure his marks were on it, then flicked it alight ready to ignite the fuse, just as the doorbell rang.

Jack's car hurtled down Pease Hill towards the Leech residence before swerving into the driveway. Doc's calves and shins were blistered and peeling, his trousers charred from the fire. He tried to ignore the pain, but it was difficult. The raw wounds needed treatment, but would have to wait, though every movement set off flares of agony in his brain. As he hobbled to the front door, he heard Jack's phone buzzing.

'It's Charlie. I'll take this, you check Mrs Leech is alright.' Jack had his phone tucked between his shoulder and his ear already, a cigarette to his lips and his lighter sparking. 'That's odd. There's a door open down the side of the house and light coming from inside. I'll take a look while I talk to her, and have a quick smoke.'

Jack began talking to Charlie as he disappeared down the garden path in a trail of smoke. Doc rang the bell.

He was about to ring it again, but then saw Mrs Leech was on her way as her shadow moved behind the narrow pane of crazed glass in the top half of the front door. Then it opened.

Only it wasn't Mrs Leech holding it wide for him to enter. It was her son.

Billy looked around to check if Doc was alone, his face panicking.

'Doctor Powers. Quick—come in. Maybe you can talk some sense into him!' Billy waved an arm, beckoning Doc to follow him down the hall to the kitchen. 'It's Smiffy. He's threatening to kill her. Come on!'

Billy's urgent tone was excited, not panicked by a stressful life-or-death situation. A classic psychopathic trait, subconsciously registered by Doc. As he approached the room, a man came into view, sitting at the end of the table with his back to the hall. Totally still.

Smith? Is he dead?

The hairs on the back of Doc's neck sprang upright, his scalp crawling. This was surely not just about a threat to Mrs Leech. The strange mixture of containers, tucked under the table, with a cord from the flagon trailing across the tiles, the end obscured by the chair and the man's leg, all told a different story.

A bomb? With Smith's supposed lover still in the house?

Billy moved further inside and out of sight so Doc entered the kitchen. Took in the situation instantly.

Mrs Leech at the far end of the table, gagged, bound to her seat, eyes wide, her head shaking. She screamed indecipherable words as she tried to warn him.

It's a trap.

Too late.

He turned to see Billy's foot, the edge of his Nike trainer, flying at his face, smashing into his nose, sending him reeling, head bouncing off the wall. A second blow to his chest, a cannonball fist, cracked his sternum and the ribs protecting his heart. The world turned grey as Doc gasped with shock and pain, sliding down the wall to the floor, unable to control his body.

The boy's gloating face hovered above his, though Doc could only make out the shadow, his vision refusing to clear. Head faint. Heart quivering spasmodically instead of pumping.

Arrhythmia? Soon to be followed by cardiac arrest?

Doc coughed deeply, ignoring the searing pain in his shattered chest, concentrating on trying to kickstart his failing heart, desperately hoping it would regain its rhythm.

It did not.

Billy's voice. Cold. Determined.

'I'm so glad you could join us, Doctor. You don't look too well. And that's a nasty cough you've got there.'

Then a guffaw.

Doc placed a hand to his chest, could feel his heart still struggling to work. His vision was narrowing, and he was dizzy and weak, lying on the floor, trying to raise himself on to an elbow, but failing. He had a close-up view of the three containers under the table, could see the home-made fuse leading from the bottle neck to Smith's lap.

'Billy... Stop! The police—' The words coughed out of him

'Fuck the police.' Billy showed Doc the lighter in his gloved hand, the flint sparking as he thumbed the roller while leaning over Smith's unconscious form. 'And fuck you, Powers. You killed my uncle. And now I'm going to kill you.'

The lighter flared and Billy lit the fuse.

'We're already here, Charlie.'

Jack took a tentative step down the cellar stairs, illuminated by a dim dust-coated bulb that threw shadows around the room. The place stank of urine and Jack had a sense of deja vu as the smell hit him. Thoughts of an investigation from the year before, involving a serial killer who kidnapped, raped and tortured his victims for days before killing them. He had rescued the man's final victim from a cellar just like this. One that smelt *exactly* like this.

The thought was forming in his mind as he descended a few more steps, bringing the whole room into view. Charlie was speaking to him, but he didn't register what she was saying—his entire focus was on the tape remnants, still hanging from the steel boiler pipe, more of the same lying on the floor, discarded there. Whoever had been held here had been released. And Jack was certain he knew who the victim was —and who had kidnapped him.

'Jack! Are you listening to me? They're on their way. You and Doc must stand down!'

'What? Why?' He was already jogging back up the steps and flicked his half-smoked cigarette to the lawn as he reached the doorway. 'Listen to me, Charlie. Smith's been held here. I'm sure of it.'

'That's what I just said! We know he's been there—his phone came on—and the Leech boy's mobile was used at the same time, at the same location. Less than ten minutes ago! They were *both* at that house, together, and the boy's phone is still there. There's an armed unit on the way, and so am I—'

Jack was no longer listening to Charlie. Unless his ears were playing tricks on him, he could hear Billy's laughter coming from the rear of the house, so darted the few paces to the corner and on to the open back door.

The scenario was clear to him the split-second he stepped in the room.

Billy, engrossed, unaware of Jack's presence, dropping a lighter into Smith's lap, the tutor unconscious, oblivious to the fizzing fuse burning across his palm. Mrs Leech, unable to move or speak, her chair rattling furiously on the tiles as she struggled to free herself. Doc, gasping for air like a beached cod, sprawled on the floor, one hand on his chest, nose bleeding, face white.

Jack's brain whirled, goading him, flashing a vision of Sally disappearing in a fireball as she was thrown off the boat, Felix being burnt alive. Agonised wailing suddenly loud in Jack's ears. Fury and hatred filled him, but he had no weapon, no taser or gun, just the phone in his hand. Resourceful to the end, he flipped it upside down, clutching it in a sweating palm, thinking he would drive the thing into the base of Billy's skull. He would disable the kung fu kid before the evil shit spotted him.

It's down to me... Charlie's cavalry won't arrive until it's too late.

There was no other option. He plunged headlong into the fray, wondering if this would be the last thing he ever did.

Doc hauled in a deep breath through his broken nose and coughed blood through his mouth. It seemed to help. The world came into focus in stark colours, vivid.

Cough CPR?

As his vision began to grey-out again from the lack of oxygen, Doc decided to employ the potentially lethal technique. From his own medical training, he was acutely aware that this form of cardiac self-resuscitation was not recommended except in a few highly specific circumstances, and only then under strict medical supervision in a properly equipped hospital.

Coughing like this could easily kill him.

Cardiac arrest or being blown to hell...?

What choice did he have, in the state he was in? He would be dead in seconds anyway if he couldn't stop that fuse burning.

With his heart fluttering and stuttering rather than beating and pumping, coughing hard would raise the pressure in his abdomen, forcing blood to his brain, just long enough for him to reach the bomb. Despite the almost unbearable white-heat searing his ribs, throat and lungs, he coughed again.

It worked.

His head cleared, though he still had tunnel vision. Although vaguely aware of the noise from Jack and Billy fighting near the back door, he had to act—just knew he was the only one who could stop the bomb from killing them all.

Could he remain conscious long enough to defuse it?

He had to try so pushed himself to his hands and knees, his head, stuffed full of cotton wool, the floor swaying beneath him like a yacht in a storm.

The weight of his body on his arms almost overcame him. It would be so easy to lie down and roll onto his back. To check whether his bones really were poking through the front of his shirt—as that's what it felt like.

Another cough. The forced breath, bouncing his diaphragm, punching at his heart, sent an agonising blast rampaging through his ribcage, scalding every nerve cell in his tormented frame. Almost overcome, brain fading again, something inside him screamed.

Move!

He could do no more than drop his head to the tiles, beaten.

A dazzling flash to one side suddenly burnt through the darkness closing in on him.

The fuse, sparking along the floor between Smith's feet, heading inexorably for the bottle under the table.

Cough.

Blood forced into his ravaged heart and round his arteries. The burst of oxygen hit his brain. His muscles. Doc willed himself to act. In no fit state to calculate how many seconds he had left to live, struggling to remain on all fours, he knew he had to reach the bottle before the spitting, fizzing flame. He concentrated on creeping across the swaying tiles. Dragging himself, first one hand, then a knee, then the other hand, then the other knee.

The flaming fuse was moving faster than the human tortoise.

Cough.

Another creeping, crawling pace. It was useless.

Lie down. Relax.

What about Judy? The baby?

They seemed so far away, and Doc was sinking, the floor coming up at him as his arms gave out.

Jack? Maybe he can stop the bomb…

But there's no sign of him.

Cough!

He had ceased forcing his heart to pump, had almost lost consciousness, but again his mind cleared. The cough had brought forth a drawn out moaning sound too—but it wasn't coming from his own mouth…

Mrs Leech!

Staring down at him, eyes petrified. He had forgotten about her. Could see her chair, shaking and bumping as she tried to release her bonds. Her son had taped one of the front legs to the table. She was stuck in here with Doc.

With the bomb.

The thought galvanised him. He coughed harder, tasted more blood in the back of his throat, but the surge of oxygen helped him focus. He looked up to see the burning fuse nearing the top of the bottle.

Death was mere moments away.

Doc reached out a feeble hand, his fingers almost touching the glass.

Billy spun round on hearing Jack's feet scuffing the tiles, eyes glittering with malice. Jack had lost the advantage, but kept moving. Committed. At the very least, he would try to delay the boy's departure, keep him here to experience the bloody bomb himself.

Then Billy took to the air, levitating in the way Jonesy had described, flying across the room at Jack. Airborne, one foot straight out, the other bent behind him, shoulders swivelling, driving his fist forward, a knuckle prominent. A lethal weapon designed to shatter the nasal bone in the kill-zone between Jack's eyes—a death-blow if delivered accurately.

It was an uneven match. The young athlete, with honed fighting skills, versus the middle-aged copper with a slight paunch and an intermittent nicotine habit. But Jack was quick, his own training and reflexes snapping into action, his head twisting, side on to the blow as his upper body leant back and away from both leg and fist.

The manoeuvre almost worked.

The bridge of Jack's nose burst, sending a flash of neon blue through his skull and crimson tears to his eyes. The force behind Billy's punch was incredible, even diminished as it was by the sideways deflection, and in that split-second Jack knew he would have died if the fist had hit him head on. He staggered back towards the doorway from the impact and blinding pain, but Billy was relentless, snarling, his lips stretched over bared fangs.

A feral animal fighting to the death.

The boy's other arm became a blur aimed at Jack's chin—a curling roundhouse powering Billy's left hand, palm open to break his opponent's jaw.

Adrenalin flooded Jack's brain, flushing away the pain, slowing everything down for the few seconds they engaged in mortal combat.

Billy had fully committed to his follow-up move—the first blow having failed to do its job. The boy was intent on his victim, clearly frustrated by the miss but sensing an easy victory. His overwhelming superiority became a source of complacency.

Weakness.

He left himself open.

Brawler Jack, a teen street-fighter made good, didn't do the expected. Didn't use his right arm in a blocking manoeuvre to protect his wounded face, but instead arced his arm up and across his body in a looping backfist, aiming at Billy's exposed right temple. With his fingers still bunched around his chunky, ancient mobile phone, thumb hooked over the base of it, the stubby aerial proud of the underside of his palm, he slammed the hardened Bakelite protrusion into the thinnest bone of Billy's skull—one of the few the boy had been unable to strengthen.

The satisfying thud of his fist connecting never reached Jack's brain. His head rocketed sideways, his jaw and neck vertebrae crunching with pain, flinging him into a black void of nothingness.

Cough!

With a final effort, every cell of his body screaming at him to give up and submit to the inevitable, Doc threw himself forward, both hands out to grab the flaming cord, to strangle it as it reached the bottle neck. He clapped his palms together as his chest hit the floor, sending another shockwave through his bruised lungs and battered aorta, blinding him in a roaring flash of white light.

Doc rolled on to his back, spluttering with pain. In that moment, he thought he had died—bomb or no bomb. The world was fading as he looked up at his hands, palms welded together, as if he was being forced to pray to the god he didn't believe in, before being cast down to the fires of hell for his atheist arrogance.

He prized them apart, screaming, coughing and wheezing as the excruciating sensations pounded his brain. Both his palms were black and red, the flesh charred and blistered. The fuse was embedded in the ball of his right thumb, with less than a palm-width in length dangling free to the detonator he had somehow plucked from the bottle.

Sirens sounded in the distance and Doc wanted to cheer as the bliss of pain-free unconsciousness folded round him. As his eyelids drooped closed he noticed movement at the edge of his limited vision.

Cough!

Is that Jack? Or Billy?

A shadow off to his right.

With his world fading then brightening, as if a mischievous child was playing with a dimmer switch inside his head, Doc recognised him. Jack, lying on his back, his jaw at a strange angle. Doc panicked, started pushing himself across the tiles, still almost overwhelmed by the fireworks exploding within him, burning every nerve in his wrecked body. Then he saw his friend's chest moving up and down.

He's alive! But where's Billy?

With another cough to help him see better, he wriggled towards the other shadow on the kitchen floor. The boy, legs wide, sitting against the wall, a body-length from Jack, feet twitching. Defeated turquoise eyes stared at Doc, unblinking. There was no longer any malice or evil intent. The expression on Billy's face was almost angelic.

Innocent again, at the sight of death's approach.

What is that? Something glued to the side of his head?

Doc continued his sinuous movements, snake-like, as he slithered across the tiled floor until he was beside the boy. He felt the limp wrist, checked for a pulse.

My old phone?

It is!

He recognised the object, embedded in Billy's temple, with dark, shiny blood and other matter oozing over it.

Had Jack used it to fell an expert martial artist with a single devastating blow to his head? To one of the most susceptible points on the human body? Was it mere luck, or reflexes learnt from years of police training?

It was unimportant, he concluded, as Billy's ankles stopped twitching. Doc released his forearm, relieved to hear the sirens as the emergency vehicles arrived, wondering if the front door was still open from when he'd followed the young killer inside. It was—several armed officers jogged into view as their warning shouts echoed through the house.

Charlie, still in her red dress and heels, trotting behind them, went straight to Jack, calling to him, as another officer knelt by Doc and asked, 'Is this the Leech boy? Is he dead?'

'No… pulse.' Cough. 'De-fib…' Doc patted his chest with his wrist, trying not to accentuate the pain from his charred palms or busted ribs.

'You'd better lie down, sir. Try to relax. There's an ambulance out front. I'll get the paramedics.'

EPILOGUE

AFTERGLOW

'JACK. Come on in and meet Jack!' Doc waved his friend into the private maternity suite at the BUPA Hospital in Reading, his face shining with pleasure. Then he saw Jack's partner behind him, hesitating, though she carried a giant bouquet of flowers. 'And you, Charlie. Don't be shy. Come on in.'

Doc went to the bed and sat on the edge of the mattress beside Judy, his heart swollen with pride. He put his arm around his wife's shoulders and beamed a smile at Jack Junior—the tiny bundle of humanity lying snug in a blanket in his mother's arms.

'Really?' Jack had hold of Charlie's hand and almost dragged her to the side of the bed opposite Doc. 'You named the little tyke after me?'

Doc glanced up in time to see his pal redden with embarrassment and pleasure at the compliment.

Charlie hugged her man, pecked his cheek, placed the flowers on Judy's bedcovers and said to her, 'He's such an arse. He really does think you don't like him.'

Judy, tired but radiant, and as beautiful as always in Doc's eyes, smiled up at them both and shrugged. 'It's not that I don't like you, you fool. I just don't like you dragging my husband off on dangerous escapades. Especially now, with his dodgy heart.'

'I'm fine! Almost as good as new.' Doc was miffed at her tone, but she grasped his hand and squeezed, then melted him with a smile. He turned his attention back to Jack. 'I think what she's trying to say, is that naming our boy after you is our way of saying thanks, old friend.'

'Thanks for what?'

'For saving my life, before. More than once. And always being there for me.'

'Pah. If that bloody bomb had gone off, I'd have been a goner too. You saved my life, mate. And those other times, I was just doing me job. Wouldn't bother other-wise.' They all laughed at that, and Jack leaned over Judy for a closer look at his

729

namesake. 'Ugly little blighter… All squashed up like that. And his eyes. He's looking at me like that kid in them Omen films… Should've called him Damien. Haha!'

Judy and Charlie slapped his arms, one bicep each, both at the same time, but Doc just chuckled. Jack was obviously thrilled at having the youngster named after him.

'Go on you two.' Judy pushed Doc off the edge of the bed. 'Clear off and have that drink. You can leave Charlie with us both for an hour or so.'

'I'm definitely up for wetting the baby's head, Doc.' Jack planted a soft kiss on Charlie's lips and added, his voice mock serious, 'And don't you go getting any ideas. I'm knocking on a bit now and another sprog is not high on my list of retirement objectives. Sally's enough of a handful for me. Come on, Doc. There's a couple of cold pints of lager with our names on 'em in the pub across the road.'

Doc donned his overcoat and followed Jack from the room. As they strolled down the corridor he asked, 'So, you're thinking of leaving the Yard, then?'

'Yup.'

'Seriously?'

'Uh-huh… These days, the Met's got too many paper-pushing jobsworths like Soundbite. She's still doing my nut in, even though she's not my boss any more.'

'I couldn't believe she tried to get you dismissed. After all, we stopped that Leech boy without any help from her.'

'Yeah, well.' Jack stroked his chin and massaged the muscles of his jaw with his finger and thumb. 'After I came out of hospital and she presented me with all that disciplinary stuff, I told her to shove it, so she added gross insubordination to the list of my misdemeanours.'

'Mmm.' Doc had heard all this before, but let Jack vent as they crossed the road to the pub to join the lunchtime crowd of drinkers in the snug interior.

'I'm just glad the Commissioner saw through it all. She's a decent old bird, told Soundbite to drop the nonsense.'

'Did Soundbite convince the CPS to prosecute Smith in the end?'

'Yeah, though he's been recalled to Broadmoor for reassessment, and to see if he's fit to stand trial. I think we may have to testify for him.' Jack shook his head in amazement, ordered their drinks from the barman and then turned back to Doc with their beers. 'Never thought I'd feel sorry for a fucking paedophile, but with so much evidence against him…' He gave a hollow laugh. 'That Leech boy did a right number on him. Of course, bloody Soundbite was desperate for a collar for the murders.' He lifted his glass and said, 'Here's to Dickie and Felix. May they rest in peace.'

Doc took a gulp of beer in memory of his dead friend and Sally's fiancé, thinking about Jack's old boss and her many TV appearances since they had rescued the tutor. Soundbite had milked it for all it was worth, crowing about how 'her team' had been instrumental in the arrest of a lone-wolf bomber, a deranged killer who also manufactured and supplied drugs, a 'vile creature' who had molested an underage boy in his charge, corrupting the lad. According to the ambitious Chief Superintendent, the full extent of the man's crimes only came to light when the abused boy tried to kill his tutor—a brilliant and manipulative mastermind—together with his mother. Smith had turned young Billy against the woman during an abusive relationship lasting two years, convincing his 'naive young victim' she was evil, that they should murder her and fly to Thailand to start a new life together on the boy's sixteenth birthday. Instead, the 'damaged child' had arranged to use the paedophile's own IED to escape his abuser's dastardly clutches while killing his mother in the same explosion. Only the rapid action of the police had foiled the plot, but Billy had 'sadly died' during an attempt to apprehend him. The policeman responsible for killing the teenager, one of two people badly injured during Smith's arrest, had been suspended from active duty at the time... An internal inquiry into all aspects of the investigation had taken several weeks to conclude. Eventually, the Detective Inspector, recently demoted for assaulting a fellow officer, was cleared of 'any further wrongdoing'.

The tabloids had fun with that lot for months.

Jack and Doc had tried to convince Soundbite of their version of events, pointing out the discarded bindings in the cellar with Smith's DNA on the adhesive, but she said it was inconclusive—probably from a bondage game the pervert had coerced the boy into playing. Even Billy's final texts—sent to and from the same location to create an alibi—got short shrift thanks to her blatant cognitive dissonance. She brushed off their appeals to reason with a dismissive, 'GCHQ said the phones could have been twenty to thirty metres apart at the time those messages were sent. That's hardly unusual. Some families text each other from different rooms in the same house. Proves nothing.'

Before throwing them out of her office, Soundbite had given her verdict. 'Even if you are right about Smith being some sort of victim, and I seriously doubt it, the man's a danger to society. Broadmoor's where he belongs.'

Doc's sense of justice had been offended by that. 'Maybe I'll make some calls, see if I can do anything for him. So, how's the new boss?'

'Pretty decent. Though I'm still a lowly DI.' He chuckled. 'Commissioner told me not to push my luck when I asked her to reinstate my promotion. Probably won't ever get bumped up the ranks again, mate. Not that I care... I'm seriously thinking of moving out to this neck of the woods to rent a place with Charlie. Transferring out of the Met, too. Or maybe retiring and going private. Hooking up with her was the best decision I've made in years.'

'I think so, too, Jack. My round.'

'I'll have a ciggy while you get 'em in.'

With fresh drinks in hand, Doc joined Jack in the beer garden, watching as he chain-lit a second cigarette. Still smoking, still stressed by the whole affair, but mostly incensed at the way the force had treated him. Doc felt for his friend and hoped he would find a less stressful life, and settle down with a woman he loved. Doc also had plans for a major change.

'We're definitely going to live in France for a while... That place we saw. We're buying it. We're going to renovate it. A joint project. Parental nesting, and all that good stuff.'

'Brilliant! That old watermill? The one you put an offer on last month?' Doc nodded and Jack tapped his glass to Doc's. 'Double congratulations then, mate! Cheers. When are you off?'

After all that had happened, Judy wanted to get away from England again, and Doc had agreed. Rather than rebuild their house after it had been wrecked by Billy Leech, they had sold the land to a developer and rented a penthouse apartment in the centre of Reading overlooking the Thames. It was a temporary arrangement, only until baby Jack appeared.

'In a month or so. No hurry. Judy just...' Doc struggled to find the words.

'I understand, mate. You've had to deal with so many nutters, I wouldn't blame either of you for wanting to get away from here.' Jack quaffed his beer, wiped a foam moustache away with the back of his hand to smother a belch. 'If it makes her feel better, safer, less worried, then why not?'

'I'm still doing the TV series. We'll be here at least a few months a year for that.'

'I should bloody hope so, too. I'm your expert consultant, mate, and I need the dough!' With an empty beer glass in his hand, Jack grinned, as if about to ask Doc if he would like a third, but suddenly shifted the conversation from light-hearted to serious. 'Have you spoken to Mrs Leech about it, yet?'

'A little… Calls herself Susan Connor now. Decided to change back to her maiden name not long after burying her son. I saw her again a couple of weeks ago.' When she had first called him, shortly after they'd almost died in her kitchen, she'd asked him if he would help her come to terms with what had happened to her at her son's hands. Much as Doc had with Billy, he agreed to see her on an informal basis for no fee. 'She's a whole lot better now. Taking her mother on a world cruise, and won't be back for several months.'

'So, do you think she'll do it? When she gets back?'

'We'll see, Jack.' Therapy had helped, and Doc's more casual approach had supplemented the regular professional counselling sessions he had organised for her. There was a chance she would agree to being interviewed for his upcoming series too —talking about her experiences with the Leech clan. The therapist had recommended it, convinced it would be cathartic, and help her recover, but Doc was reluctant to press her for a decision.

'Kids who kill… Hard to believe there's so many of 'em.'

Their research for the series had boggled Jack's mind, and he turned thoughtful, quiet, making Doc wonder what it was he was so reluctant to ask as they went back inside. Doc waited while Jack ordered their third and final beer, certain something important was bugging his closest friend.

As Jack handed Doc a pint, he asked, voice pitched low, 'Do you worry about your boy?'

'Of course!'

'Not the normal stuff, mate. The other thing.'

Doc couldn't be sure what the other thing was, though could guess, given what they had just been discussing. 'What do you mean?'

Jack was a detective, and a bloody good one. He had sniffed out the one concern that had kept Doc awake for many nights since Judy had let him know she was pregnant with Jack Junior.

'That brain glitch of yours. The thing you have. Like a bleedin pet psychopath lurking in the shadows at the back of your mind.' Jack cocked an eye at Doc over the edge of his glass as he swilled some beer. 'Your own family history? I know you don't like to talk about it, especially your crazy old grandad, but… Well. Genetics and all that. Are you worried, about Jack Junior? That he might turn out like the Leech brat?'

'I bloody hope not!' Doc tried to laugh it off.

Unsuccessfully.

He had spent a lot of time thinking about his grandfather, a man he rarely acknowledged had even existed. He often thought about his father's death too, and how his own life had evolved in response to that brutal event. In truth, he had already come to some disturbing conclusions about his family's genetic make-up. His own potential to contemplate vicious murder, with his darkest urges chained in his subconscious, restrained there but always ready and willing to be exploited for the benefit of his career.

What of little Jack? How would he turn out?

Well, in the years to come, Doc knew he would have more sleepless nights, and not just from filled nappies and a hungry mouth. With luck, he and Judy would keep their boy on the straight and narrow, despite the worst of the Powers' genes.

Big Jack tried to lighten the mood again, laughing as he said, 'Haha! Well, Doctor Psycho—you didn't turn out so badly yourself, did you?'

Sometimes, Doc worried about that, too. But for now, the happily married husband and proud new father was on cloud nine, and planned to stay there for as long as he could.

'Cheers, Jack. You're a real lifesaver...' He winked, clinked glasses with his old pal and grinned. 'Here's to the future!'

ALSO BY WILL PATCHING

KILLER INSPIRATION:

THE AUTHOR'S GUIDE TO 'THE REMORSELESS TRILOGY'

FEATURING DELETED SCENES, BACKSTORY, PLUS COMMENTARY ON SOME OF THE REAL-LIFE CRIMINAL
PSYCHOPATHS WHOSE EVIL WORDS AND DEEDS SPARKED THE 'REMORSELESS' VILLAINS INTO LIFE.

———

THE WIDOW

A BRITISH POLICE THRILLER

DEADLY INSPIRATIONS — BOOK ONE

FEATURING D.S. FIONA 'FIFI' FIELDING WHO FIRST APPEARED IN MUTILATED

———

THE HACK TRILOGY

INTERNATIONAL CRIME THRILLERS

THE HACK

THE HUNTER

THE HANGMAN

———

WILL PATCHING'S SHORT SHOTS:

BLOOD ON THEIR HANDS

THREE KILLER THRILLER QUICK READS

———

ALL THE AUTHOR'S NOVELS AND SHORT STORIES ARE AVAILABLE IN AUDIOBOOK EDITIONS, NARRATED BY
GARY FURLONG, A TALENTED AWARD-WINNING VOICE ARTIST.

———

FOR MORE INFORMATION VISIT:

WWW.WILLPATCHINGAUTHOR.COM

———

Milton Keynes UK
Ingram Content Group UK Ltd.
UKHW040758010823
426141UK00001B/109